(Continued on the inside back cover)

The Story
and Its Writer

An Introduction to Short Fiction

Ann Charters (Ph.D. Columbia) is a professor of English at the University of Connecticut, where she has taught courses on the short story for many years. In addition to articles on contemporary American poetry and feminism, she has published full-length biographies of the black entertainer Bert Williams, the Beat writer Jack Kerouac, and (with her husband) the Russian poet Vladimir Mayakovsky. She also is a photographer of considerable accomplishment whose portraits of well-known writers and musicians are often exhibited and reprinted.

The Story and Its Writer

An Introduction to Short Fiction

Second Edition

EDITED BY

Ann Charters
University of Connecticut

A BEDFORD BOOK

ST. MARTIN'S PRESS · NEW YORK

Library of Congress Catalog Card Number: 86–60664
Copyright © 1987 by St. Martin's Press, Inc.
All rights reserved.
Manufactured in the United States of America
9 8
f e d
For information, write St. Martin's Press, Inc.,
175 Fifth Avenue, New York, NY 10010
Editorial Offices: Bedford Books of St. Martin's Press,
29 Commonwealth Avenue, Boston, MA 02116

ISBN: 0–312–76254–2

Cover typography and design: Volney Croswell
Cover illustration: Guy Gladwell, as appeared in *The Atlantic Monthly*

Acknowledgments

Alice Adams. "The Swastika on Our Door." Copyright © 1971 by Alice Adams. Reprinted from *Beautiful Girl*, by Alice Adams, by permission of Alfred A. Knopf, Inc. "Why I Write" from *First Person Singular: Writers on Their Craft*, compiled by Joyce Carol Oates. Reprinted by permission of Ontario Review Press.

Woody Allen. "The Kugelmass Episode." copyright © 1977 by Woody Allen. Reprinted from *Side Effects*, by Woody Allen, by permission of Random House, Inc.

Sherwood Anderson. "Hands" from *Winesburg, Ohio*, by Sherwood Anderson. Copyright 1919 by B. W. Huebsch, Inc. Copyright renewed 1947 by Eleanor Copenhaver Anderson. Reprinted by permission of Viking Penguin Inc. "Death in the Woods" copyright 1926 by The American Mercury, Inc. Copyright renewed 1953 by Eleanor Copenhaver Anderson. "Form, Not Plot, in the Short Story" copyright 1924 by B. W. Huebsch, Inc. Copyright renewed 1952 by Eleanor Copenhaver Anderson. Both reprinted by permission of Harold Ober Associates Incorporated.

Margaret Atwood. "When It Happens" from *Dancing Girls and Other Stories* by Margaret Atwood. Copyright © 1977, 1982 by O. W. Toad, Ltd. Reprinted by permission of Simon & Schuster, Inc. and The Canadian Publishers, McClelland and Stewart Limited, Toronto.

Isaac Babel. "My First Goose," from *The Collected Stories of Isaac Babel*. Copyright © 1955 by S. G. Phillips, Inc. Reprinted by permission of S. G. Phillips, Inc.

Toni Cade Bambara. "The Hammer Man'" from *Gorilla, My Love* by Toni Cade Bambara. Copyright © 1972 by Toni Cade Bambara. Reprinted by permission of Random House, Inc. Interview with Toni Cade Bambara from *Black Women Writers at Work*, edited by Claudia Tate. Copyright © 1983 by Claudia Tate. Reprinted by permission of the Continuum Publishing Company.

John Barth. "Lost in the Funhouse" from the book *Lost in the Funhouse*. Copyright © 1967 by the Atlantic Monthly Company. Reprinted by permission of Doubleday & Company, Inc.

Donald Barthelme. "The President" from *Unspeakable Practices, Unnatural Acts* by Donald Barthelme. Copyright © 1964, 1968 by Donald Barthelme. Reprinted by permission of Farrar, Straus and Giroux, Inc.

Ann Beattie. "Waiting" copyright © 1979 by Ann Beattie. Reprinted from *The Burning House: Short Stories*, by Ann Beattie, by permission of Random House, Inc.

Heinrich Böll. "Like a Bad Dream" from *18 Stories*, translated by Leila Vennewitz. Copyright © 1966 by Heinrich Böll. Reprinted by permission of McGraw-Hill, Inc. and Joan Daves.

Acknowledgments and copyrights continue at the back of the book on pages 1411–1414, which constitute an extension of the copyright page.

Preface

The Book's Origin

The Story and Its Writer came into existence because I wanted my students to learn about the short story as much as possible from the writers themselves. In my years of teaching classes in the short story, most of the anthologies I used were either textbooks with a limited number of stories and a great deal of editorial discussion — categorizing the stories by plot, character, theme, and so forth, often restricting the students' interpretations and my classroom presentations — or anthologies collecting many stories with almost no editorial apparatus except brief biographies of the writers that did not suggest their significance as *story* writers.

Purpose

The Story and Its Writer is something different. At the heart of this anthology are 107 short stories, assembled so that students can trace the evolution of this literary form and the lively interaction between short story writers over its 150-year history. I have tried to provide abundant yet unobtrusive editorial apparatus. The stories are neither embedded within the editorial discussions of the elements of fiction nor followed by questions for discussion. In my view, each of these features restricts the ways in which a story might be taught or read. In contrast, my purpose was to provide editorial apparatus that enhances the teaching and interpretive possibilities for each story. Thus, I have moved the necessary discussion of the elements of fiction and the history of the short story to the back of the book, so that they can be assigned at the most appropriate point in a class. In the headnotes introducing the writers and in the commentary section that follows the short stories, I have tried to let the writers speak for themselves about their backgrounds and their methods as storytellers.

Stories and Authors Added

For this second edition, *The Story and Its Writer* is expanded from sixty to eighty-four writers. I have added important American writers like Mary E. Wilkins Freeman, Hamlin Garland, Charlotte Perkins Gilman, Zora Neale Hurston, Bernard Malamud, John Steinbeck, and William Carlos Williams. There are so many fine contemporary American short

story writers practicing their craft that I have also put more of them in this
edition, including Alice Adams, Woody Allen, Toni Cade Bambara, Donald Barthelme, Paul Bowles, Ray Bradbury, Raymond Carver, Louise
Erdrich, Gail Godwin, Mark Helprin, Jamaica Kincaid, David Leavitt, Ursula Le Guin, Bobbie Ann Mason, Cynthia Ozick, Jayne Anne Phillips,
Peter Taylor, and Alice Walker. I have also added several international authors who were not in the earlier edition, including Margaret Atwood,
Heinrich Böll, Elizabeth Bowen, E. M. Forster, Yukio Mishima, Alice
Munro, and R. K. Narayan. The stories include dual and triple selections
from the work of several major writers, so that students have the opportunity to sample the range and variety of these authors' short fiction.

The Commentaries

In the second part of the anthology, thirty-five of the writers — as well
as several other literary figures — comment on the form of the short story
and on specific stories included in the first part. I know from my own experience that commentaries by the short story writers themselves can spark
good class discussion and furnish stimulating ideas for student papers. I was
delighted to have my impression so enthusiastically confirmed by instructors who used the first edition. Accordingly, this feature has been strengthened. I have added considerable variety to the material here. For example, I
have included the first draft of a James Joyce story, as well as longer commentaries by contemporary authors, including a discussion by Isaac Bashevis Singer and an interview with Grace Paley commissioned especially
for this volume.

Organization

For easy reference, readers will find an alphabetical table of contents
on the endpapers of *The Story and Its Writer*. The chronological organization (by author's date of birth) was chosen to reflect important stages in the
evolution of this literary genre. Short fiction can, of course, be taught any
number of ways. Instructors may ignore the chronological order and assign
the stories according to their own thematic or aesthetic context, and students may browse further in the stories on their own, guided in their reading by the headnotes.

The Editorial Appartus

The Story and Its Writer opens with a brief general introduction to
prepare students for the approach taken in the anthology. It closes with four
sections designed to help students become better readers of short stories.
First is a history of the genre, a more extensive survey than ever attempted
in an anthology. This historical presentation refers to works in *The Story*

and Its Writer and integrates the observations made in the headnotes for the individual authors. Second is a section introducing the elements of short fiction. While referring to many stories in the anthology, I have concentrated my analysis on two early stories, Hawthorne's "Young Goodman Brown" and Poe's "The Cask of Amontillado," because students understandably grow restive if literary criticism refers too often to material they have not read yet. A chapter on writing about short fiction, also drawing primarily on "Young Goodman Brown" so it can be assigned early in the course, and a glossary of literary terms for handy reference conclude the anthology.

Instructor's Manual

The instructor's manual for *The Story and Its Writer* has a discussion of each story, questions and writing assignments for students, and short bibliographies.

Acknowledgments

I wish to acknowledge the help of many people in the preparation and revision of the anthology and the instructor's manual. My colleagues in the English Department at the University of Connecticut — William Sheidley (who wrote the manual with me and my graduate assistant, Martha Ramsey), Lee Jacobus, Barbara Rosen, William Curtin, Milton Stern, Jack Davis, Jack Manning, Michael Meyer, David Benson, and Feenie Ziner — generously contributed suggestions and advice at every stage of the preparation. The staff of the reference section of the Homer Babbidge Library, especially Leanne Pander, Pamela Skinner, David McChesney, and Carol Abramson, gave unflagging assistance. Students in my short story classes diligently drafted the sample essays illustrating the various ways to write about stories. Reviewers of the first edition who suggested changes and improvements include Anita Moss and David Nicklin.

In preparing the second edition of *The Story and Its Writer*, I am especially grateful to my intelligent and sympathetic editor, Karen Henry, whose assistance was invaluable. My publisher, Charles Christensen, was an untiring source of suggestions and practical advice. Others at Bedford Books who helped with this edition include Joan Feinberg, Elizabeth Schaaf, Chris Rutigliano, Nancy Lyman, and Susan M. S. Brown, copyeditor. Professor John Repp researched information for some of the new headnotes. Professors John Covolo and Daniel L. Zins wrote me about typographical errors and suggested ways to widen the selection of the stories to include important post-Hiroshima contemporary issues. Other professors who used the first edition of the anthology and generously took time to share their ideas about it include Diana Abu-Jaber, M. Jane Adelsberger, Pamela Barnes, Robert J. Barton, Lee Bedell, Bonnie C. Bedford, Les Bennett, Linda Benson, Michael Berry, Ellen Blais, W. A. Blais, James Blake, Rebekah Bloyd, William O. Boggs, Sheldon Brivic, Carl W. Brucker, Michael K. Bryant, Edmund Cardoni, Michael Castro, Sister Consuela Chase, Sumita M. Chaudhery, Miriam Cheikin, Bell Chevigny, Gwen Cleghorn, Stan Coberly, Stephen Cooper, Doug Crowell, D. Dean Dunham, Jr., S. A. Eisenstein, Sister Mary Ely, O. B. Emerson, Barbara C. Ewell, Miriam Fankhauser, Moira Ferguson, Crystal M. Field, Sheila Fields, Frederick Fischer, Stephan P. Flores, Jean Gandesbery, Joan Gilson, Benjamin M. Glassner, Drewey Wayne Gunn, Don Haines, Vanessa Haley, G. Hayes, Thomas Hayes, Matthew Hearn, Donald Heidt, Edward A. Hungerford, Bruce W. Jorgensen, Gwynne Kennedy, William Keough, Joy L. King, Raymond Klejmont, Sarah Klinefelter, Linda A. Korbel, Dennis Leavens, Rebecca Lee, Nancy Lewis, Robert Lewis, Alexander S. Liddie, Stephen McCabe, David R. MacDonald, Anthony McGurrin, Robert McIlvaine, Gary McLouth, Lawrence W. Manglitz, Lois Marchino, Michael Steven Marx, Hilary Masters, Dan Masterson, Louise Meriwether, Oscar Miller, Jerry L. Mills, John S. Morris, Gabriel Motola, M. Motto, Paul Murphy, Kirsten Nelson, David Nicklin, Michael O'Rourke, P. M. Pallas, Susan Park, Michael P. Parker, Mildred B. Parker, Angela Peckenpaugh, Celeste Pernicone, Beryl Pittman, Richard E. Quaintance, Jr., Phyllis C. Ralph, T. J. Ray, Michael W. Raymond, R. J. Reilly, Carol F. Richer, Timothy E. Rook, Parama Roy, Elizabeth Guiney Sandvick, G. E. Schebendach, Harriet Polt Schmitt, Jeffrey Schwartz, James Shepard, Julia A. Smith, Marilyn B. Smith, Ellen Sprechman, Max Steele, H. Peter Stowell, James F. Sullivan, Stephen Terney, Wendolyn, E. Tetlow, R. B. Thomas, Joyce Thompson, Richard J. Thompson, Arthur Tishman, H. K. Tjossam, Alice Tracy, Shirley Uber, Bernard Verwiel, Cheryl Walker, Howard Wamsley, Sharon Warner, Elliot Wasserman, Deborah Weiner, Luke Whisnant, Chick White, Lana White, Larry Woiwode, Pauline Woodward, and Joseph J. Wydeven. I thank them for their help and encouragement, which made the task of revising *The Story and Its Writer* much easier.

Ann Charters
Storrs, Connecticut

Contents

Part Two
THE COMMENTARIES 1219

INTRODUCTION

THE STORY AND ITS WRITER

Read literature for the pleasure of reading it, Ernest Hemingway once told an interviewer, adding, "Whatever else you find will be the measure of what you brought to the reading." The stories in this anthology have been chosen because — if you bring an alert intelligence and a lively imagination to them — you will find they are usually a pleasure to read. We all have different personalities and read for different reasons, but we all look forward to being entertained when we turn to a story.

Reading short fiction attentively and imaginatively promises further pleasure — the enjoyment of how the storyteller uses language to create a work of art. This way of reading brings us closer to understanding the achievement of the story and its writer. Literature is invention, and storytellers are inventors, whether they appear in the guise of entertainers, teachers, or enchanters. The authors whose stories are collected here are experts in the art of invention. They delight us most completely when we apprehend the genius of their art by studying how they select the details and shape the patterns of their fiction.

What Is a Short Story?

The literary form *short story* is usually defined as a brief fictional prose narrative, often involving one connected episode. Early in the nineteenth century the American writer Edgar Allan Poe was one of the first to attempt an analysis of the short story's aesthetic properties. He stressed *unity* of effect as the story's most characteristic feature. Since the flood of events we experience in life is rarely unified by a single impression, in a sense all fiction — whether short story, long story, or novel — is "lies." Paradoxically, however, the measure of success for all fiction is how *true* it is to our emotions, how accurately it reflects the life that is lived by all of us.

The short story is a concentrated form, dependent for its success on feeling and suggestion. When readers are responsive to both the story and its writer and understand the ways an author uses language to create a fictional world, the unity of the story has an even greater impact. Then every detail of the narrative adds to our enjoyment of the story's final impression. Writers of short stories must forgo the comprehensiveness of the novel, but they often gain a striking compression by using language with the force of poetry. Like poets, short story writers can impress upon us the unity of their vision of life by focusing on a single effect.

Although storytelling is one of the oldest arts, not every story or short narrative is necessarily an example of what has come to be known as the short story. The modern short story is comparatively new in literature, even younger than the novel. It originated in the early years of the nineteenth century, and its vitality may have sprung from the spirit of its age, which nurtured the Romantic movement in literature and valued imagination above all other qualities in writing.

This anthology begins with stories from the period when professional writers began experimenting with forms of short fictional narrative in both Europe and America. Nathaniel Hawthorne and Edgar Allan Poe were among the earliest American authors to achieve success in the genre. In the nineteenth and twentieth centuries, most of the great writers of fiction throughout the world explored the short story. This anthology is organized chronologically to suggest the historical evolution of the form, presenting examples by some of its most notable practitioners. The headnotes for the authors suggest their personal and intellectual backgrounds and their intentions as writers of short fiction.

Fifty years after its earliest appearance, the short story reached maturity in the work of Guy de Maupassant and Anton Chekhov. It flowered into perhaps its most intense expression in the stories of the great modernist writers of the early twentieth century — James Joyce, Franz Kafka, D. H. Lawrence, Katherine Mansfield, Isaac Babel, and Ernest Hemingway, to name only a few of the great innovators who experimented with the structure and texture of literature and challenged its conventions. The short story continues to flourish in the work of many gifted contemporary writers, attracting more attention than ever before. Appendix I at the back of the anthology gives a more detailed history of the genre.

The range and quality of the writer's mind are the only limitations on the shape taken by a story. In the process of creation, authors invent narratives using the different elements of fiction. Among their most important resources are *plot*, the sequence of related events composing the narrative, and *characters*, the persons who play their parts in the narrative. The author's choice of *setting*, the place and time in which the story's action occurs, helps to give the story verisimilitude. The *point of view* establishes a consistent perspective on the characters and their actions as the narrative unfolds. The author's literary *style*, the way he or she uses the multifarious resources of language, also shapes the expression of a story. Finally, the author is guided by his or her perception of *theme*, the unifying idea that brings to life all the other elements of fiction. A discussion of these elements appears at the back of the anthology in Appendix II.

Without human understanding, experience is "the worst kind of emptiness," wrote the short story author Eudora Welty in her essay "Words into Fiction."All stories embody a personal vision, when the elements of plot, character, setting, point of view, style, and theme are set in motion by the writer's perception of the mystery and magic of everyday life. Creating fiction, authors are free to invent and shape experience to the fullest extent of their imagination. The section of commentaries following the stories in the anthology includes many statements by writers about the meaning and form of their fiction.

Human understanding is not the exclusive privilege of the writer, of course. It functions in the reader too. Fiction created by the imagination of the writer for the imagination of the reader is an illusion come full circle. If the story is well told, our imagination will be involved. If the story is a success, our imagination will be ignited.

Reading Short Stories

For most readers, the basic appeal of all storytelling is its narrative pattern, revealing connections and coherence in experience. When writers go beyond this appeal and ignite our imagination, they do so by touching us intellectually and emotionally through language. Using the elements of fiction, they enchant us by evoking our thoughts and feelings about the mysterious nature of human experience. Then we catch a glimpse of what life is like from its reflection in the story.

What is the best way to read a short story? The writer Vladimir Nabokov once suggested that the ideal reader should develop "a combination of the artistic and the scientific [temperament]. The enthusiastic artist alone is apt to be too subjective in his attitude towards a book, and so a scientific coolness of judgment will temper the intuitive heat." Read a story the first time for pleasure; bring out your "scientific coolness" when you study it the second time, preferably with a dictionary at your side.

The first time you read a story, you may find yourself concerned primarily with *arriving* at the end of the narrative, seeing how the author resolves the plot. The second time, however, you can focus on *getting there*, seeing how the author invents and shapes the narrative by using the elements of fiction. Ideally, you should keep a little aloof, a little detached when reading the second time. Cherish the details of the story's pattern. Enjoy the pleasure of beginning to understand its magic.

The meaning of the story (its truth, vision, or reflection of the world) is, in part, a result of the reader's response. As Hemingway said, read literature for the pleasure it brings. Anything else *you* must bring to the reading. A story becomes more meaningful when you read actively, relating the personal vision of the author embodied in the form and content of the narrative to your own experience of life and to the questions you ask of it.

Since the great majority of people need to be reminded more often than instructed, you should remember to read each story at least once in its entirety. The best way to give short stories a chance to enchant you is to sit down and grant them your full attention. Then read them carefully straight through from beginning to end.

The Story and Its Writer is organized in six sections. In the first, the stories themselves appear. Each is introduced by a headnote giving biographical information about the writer and a short description of his or her contribution to the short story form. The date following each story is the year it was published. The next section of commentaries gathers statements by different authors about their practice and theory of writing short fiction, including discussion of the meanings of some individual stories. The remaining four sections present a brief history of the short story as a literary genre, an analysis of the elements of short fiction, an explanation of various ways to write papers about short stories, and a glossary of important literary terms.

Part One

ﬤﬤ

The Stories

NATHANIEL HAWTHORNE (1804–1864), *the novelist and short story writer, was born into a distinguished family in Salem, Massachusetts. His Puritan great-grandfather had been a judge who persecuted the Quakers; his grandfather had been one of the judges who presided over the infamous Salem witch trials; and his father was a sea captain who died in the East Indies when Hawthorne was four years old. After his graduation from Bowdoin College in Brunswick, Maine, in 1825, Hawthorne, who had already decided to become a writer, returned to Salem. He lived frugally at home, undergoing a self-imposed literary apprenticeship, studying literature and the legends and history of his native New England. He also wrote works of short fiction, which he called "tales" or "articles," and tried to sell them to periodicals. American magazines of the time were mostly interested in publishing ghost stories, Indian legends, and "village tales" based on historical anecdotes. Hawthorne (like his contemporary Edgar Allan Poe) brought his powers of genius to the young literary form of the popular magazine story and raised it above the conventional level that most readers had come to expect.*

Hawthorne's first collection of stories, Twice-Told Tales, *was published in 1837, and he published another collection,* Mosses from an Old Manse, *in 1846. That year he stopped writing and took more lucrative employment as surveyor of customs for the port of Salem. This was a political appointment, and after the Whigs won the presidency, Hawthorne — a Democrat — found himself out of a job in 1849. He returned to writing fiction and sketched his "official life" at the Custom House in introducing his novel* The Scarlet Letter *in 1850. He also wrote three other novels —* The House of the Seven Gables (1851), The Blithedale Romance (1852), *and* The Marble Faun (1860) — *several books for children, and another collection of tales.*

In "The Custom House," Hawthorne suggested that his chosen life as a writer would not have impressed his Puritan ancestors:

> *"What is he?" murmurs one grey shadow of my forefathers to the other. "A writer of story-books! What kind of business in life, what manner of glorifying God, or being serviceable to mankind in his day and generation, may that be? Why, the degenerate fellow might as well have been a fiddler!" Such are the compliments bandied between my great-grandsires and myself across the gulf of time! And yet, let them scorn me as they will, strong traits of their nature have intertwined themselves with mine.*

Despite Hawthorne's portrait of himself as an object of misunderstanding, he was recognized by contemporaries like Poe as a "genius of a very lofty order." Hawthorne wrote about one hundred twenty short tales and sketches in addition to his novels. His notebooks are filled with ideas for stories. They show that his imagination was fired more by a curious pas-

9

sage in his reading or by an abstract idea from one of his speculative reveries than by detailed observation of "real" individuals. In his writing Hawthorne demonstrated what he himself called "an inveterate love of allegory," as in the tale "Young Goodman Brown," where he explored the Puritan conscience. He also frequently dramatized his own sense of the precarious nature of our common humanity, as in "Wakefield." "The Wives of the Dead," an early work with a hauntingly ambiguous ending, was not reprinted until Hawthorne's third collection, The Snow Image and Other Twice-Told Tales, *was published in 1851. (See Hawthorne's Commentary on page 1221, Melville's Commentary about Hawthorne on page 1223, and Poe's review of Hawthorne's tales on page 1225.)*

Nathaniel Hawthorne

࿔

Young Goodman Brown

Young Goodman Brown came forth at sunset into the street at Salem village; but put his head back, after crossing the threshold, to exchange a parting kiss with his young wife. And Faith, as the wife was aptly named, thrust her own pretty head into the street, letting the wind play with the pink ribbons of her cap while she called to Goodman Brown.

"Dearest heart," whispered she, softly and rather sadly, when her lips were close to his ear, "prithee put off your journey until sunrise and sleep in your own bed to-night. A lone woman is troubled with such dreams and such thoughts that she's afeared of herself sometimes. Pray tarry with me this night, dear husband, of all nights in the year."

"My love and my Faith," replied young Goodman Brown, "of all nights in the year, this one night must I tarry away from thee. My journey, as thou callest it, forth and back again, must needs be done 'twixt now and sunrise. What, my sweet, pretty wife, dost thou doubt me already, and we but three months married?"

"Then God bless you!" said Faith, with the pink ribbons; "and may you find all well when you come back."

"Amen!" cried Goodman Brown. "Say thy prayers, dear Faith, and go to bed at dusk, and no harm will come to thee."

So they parted; and the young man pursued his way until, being about to turn the corner by the meeting-house, he looked back and saw the head of Faith still peeping after him with a melancholy air, in spite of her pink ribbons.

"Poor little Faith!" thought he, for his heart smote him. "What a wretch am I to leave her on such an errand! She talks of dreams, too.

Methought as she spoke there was trouble in her face, as if a dream had warned her what work is to be done to-night. But no, no; 't would kill her to think it. Well, she's a blessed angel on earth; and after this one night I'll cling to her skirts and follow her to heaven."

With this excellent resolve for the future, Goodman Brown felt himself justified in making more haste on his present evil purpose. He had taken a dreary road, darkened by all the gloomiest trees of the forest, which barely stood aside to let the narrow path creep through, and closed immediately behind. It was all as lonely as could be; and there is this peculiarity in such a solitude, that the traveller knows not who may be concealed by the innumerable trunks and the thick boughs overhead; so that with lonely footsteps he may yet be passing through an unseen multitude.

"There may be a devilish Indian behind every tree," said Goodman Brown to himself; and he glanced fearfully behind him as he added, "What if the devil himself should be at my very elbow!"

His head being turned back, he passed a crook of the road, and, looking forward again, beheld the figure of a man, in grave and decent attire, seated at the foot of an old tree. He arose at Goodman Brown's approach and walked onward side by side with him.

"You are late, Goodman Brown," said he. "The clock of the Old South was striking as I came through Boston, and that is full fifteen minutes agone."

"Faith kept me back a while," replied the young man, with a tremor in his voice, caused by the sudden appearance of his companion, though not wholly unexpected.

It was now deep dusk in the forest, and deepest in that part of it where these two were journeying. As nearly as could be discerned, the second traveller was about fifty years old, apparently in the same rank of life as Goodman Brown, and bearing a considerable resemblance to him, though perhaps more in expression than features. Still they might have been taken for father and son. And yet, though the elder person was as simply clad as the younger, and as simple in manner too, he had an indescribable air of one who knew the world, and who would not have felt abashed at the governor's dinner table or in King William's court, were it possible that his affairs should call him thither. But the only thing about him that could be fixed upon as remarkable was his staff, which bore the likeness of a great black snake, so curiously wrought that it might almost be seen to twist and wriggle itself like a living serpent. This, of course, must have been an ocular deception, assisted by the uncertain light.

"Come, Goodman Brown," cried his fellow-traveller, "this is a dull pace for the beginning of a journey. Take my staff, if you are so soon weary."

"Friend," said the other, exchanging his slow pace for a full stop, "having kept covenant by meeting thee here, it is my purpose now to return whence I came. I have scruples touching the matter thou wot'st of."

"Sayest thou so?" replied he of the serpent, smiling apart. "Let us walk on, nevertheless, reasoning as we go; and if I convince thee not thou shalt turn back. We are but a little way in the forest yet."

"Too far! too far!" exclaimed the goodman, unconsciously resuming his walk. "My father never went into the woods on such an errand, nor his father before him. We have been a race of honest men and good Christians since the days of the martyrs; and shall I be the first of the name of Brown that ever took this path and kept" —

"Such company, thou wouldst say," observed the elder person, interpreting his pause. "Well said, Goodman Brown! I have been as well acquainted with your family as with ever a one among the Puritans; and that's no trifle to say. I helped your grandfather, the constable, when he lashed the Quaker woman so smartly through the streets of Salem; and it was I that brought your father a pitch-pine knot, kindled at my own hearth, to set fire to an Indian village, in King Philip's war. They were my good friends, both; and many a pleasant walk have we had along this path, and returned merrily after midnight. I would fain be friends with you for their sake."

"If it be as thou sayest," replied Goodman Brown, "I marvel they never spoke of these matters; or, verily, I marvel not, seeing that the least rumor of the sort would have driven them from New England. We are a people of prayer, and good works to boot, and abide no such wickedness."

"Wickedness or not," said the traveller with the twisted staff, "I have a very general acquaintance here in New England. The deacons of many a church have drunk the communion wine with me; the selectmen of divers towns make me their chairman; and a majority of the Great and General Court are firm supporters of my interest. The governor and I, too — But these are state secrets."

"Can this be so?" cried Goodman Brown, with a stare of amazement at his undisturbed companion. "Howbeit, I have nothing to do with the governor and council; they have their own ways, and are no rule for a simple husbandman like me. But, were I to go on with thee, how should I meet the eye of that good old man, our minister, at Salem village? Oh, his voice would make me tremble both Sabbath day and lecture day."

Thus far the elder traveller had listened with due gravity; but now burst into a fit of irrepressible mirth, shaking himself so violently that his snake-like staff actually seemed to wriggle in sympathy.

"Ha! ha! ha!" shouted he again and again; then composing himself, "Well, go on, Goodman Brown, go on; but, prithee, don't kill me with laughing."

"Well, then, to end the matter at once," said Goodman Brown, considerably nettled, "there is my wife, Faith. It would break her dear little heart; and I'd rather break my own."

"Nay, if that be the case," answered the other, "e'en go thy ways, Goodman Brown. I would not for twenty old women like the one hobbling before us that Faith should come to any harm."

As he spoke he pointed his staff at a female figure on the path, in whom Goodman Brown recognized a very pious and exemplary dame, who had taught him his catechism in youth, and was still his moral and spiritual adviser, jointly with the minister and Deacon Gookin.

"A marvel, truly that Goody Cloyse should be so far in the wilderness at nightfall," said he. "But with your leave, friend, I shall take a cut through the woods until we have left this Christian woman behind. Being a stranger to you, she might ask whom I was consorting with and whither I was going."

"Be it so," said his fellow-traveller. "Betake you to the woods, and let me keep the path."

Accordingly the young man turned aside, but took care to watch his companion, who advanced softly along the road until he had come within a staff's length of the old dame. She, meanwhile, was making the best of her way, with singular speed for so aged a woman, and mumbling some indistinct words — a prayer, doubtless — as she went. The traveller put forth his staff and touched her withered neck with what seemed the serpent's tail.

"The devil!" screamed the pious old lady.

"Then Goody Cloyse knows her old friend?" observed the traveller, confronting her and leaning on his writhing stick.

"Ah, forsooth, and is it your worship indeed?" cried the good dame. "Yea, truly is it, and in the very image of my old gossip, Goodman Brown, the grandfather of the silly fellow that now is. But — would your worship believe it? — my broomstick hath strangely disappeared, stolen, as I suspect, by that unhanged witch, Goody Cory, and that, too, when I was all anointed with the juice of smallage, and cinquefoil, and wolf's bane" —

"Mingled with fine wheat and the fat of a new-born babe," said the shape of old Goodman Brown.

"Ah, your worship knows the recipe," cried the old lady, cackling aloud. "So, as I was saying, being all ready for the meeting, and no horse to ride on, I made up my mind to foot it; for they tell me there is a nice young man to be taken into communion to-night. But now your good worship will lend me your arm, and we shall be there in a twinkling."

"That can hardly be," answered her friend. "I may not spare you my arm, Goody Cloyse; but here is my staff, if you will."

So saying, he threw it down at her feet, where, perhaps, it assumed life, being one of the rods which its owner had formerly lent to the Egyptian magi. Of this fact, however, Goodman Brown could not take cognizance. He had cast up his eyes in astonishment, and, looking down again, beheld neither Goody Cloyse nor the serpentine staff, but his fellow-traveller alone, who waited for him as calmly as if nothing had happened.

"That old woman taught me my catechism," said the young man; and there was a world of meaning in this simple comment.

They continued to walk onward, while the elder traveller exhorted his companion to make good speed and persevere in the path, discoursing so aptly that his arguments seemed rather to spring up in the bosom of his auditor than to be suggested by himself. As they went, he plucked a branch of maple to serve for a walking stick, and began to strip it of the twigs and little boughs, which were wet with evening dew. The moment his fingers touched them they became strangely withered and dried up as with a week's sunshine. Thus the pair proceeded, at a good free pace, until suddenly, in a gloomy hollow of the road, Goodman Brown sat himself down on the stump of a tree and refused to go any farther.

"Friend," he said, stubbornly, "my mind is made up. Not another step will I budge on this errand. What if a wretched old woman do choose to go to the devil when I thought she was going to heaven: is that any reason why I should quit my dear Faith and go after her?"

"You will think better of this by and by," said his acquaintance, composedly. "Sit here and rest yourself a while; and when you feel like moving again, there is my staff to help you along."

Without more words, he threw his companion the maple stick, and was as speedily out of sight as if he had vanished into the deepening gloom. The young man sat a few moments by the roadside, applauding himself greatly, and thinking with how clear a conscience he should meet the minister in his morning walk, nor shrink from the eye of good old Deacon Gookin. And what calm sleep would be his that very night, which was to have been spent so wickedly, but so purely and sweetly now, in the arms of Faith! Amidst these pleasant and praiseworthy meditations, Goodman Brown heard the tramp of horses along the road, and deemed it advisable to conceal himself within the verge of the forest, conscious of the guilty purpose that had brought him thither, though now so happily turned from it.

On came the hoof tramps and the voices of the riders, two grave old voices, conversing soberly as they drew near. These mingled sounds appeared to pass along the road, within a few yards of the young man's hiding-place; but, owing doubtless to the depth of the gloom at that particular spot, neither the travellers nor their steeds were visible. Though their figures brushed the small boughs by the wayside, it could not be seen that they intercepted, even for a moment, the faint gleam from the strip of bright sky athwart which they must have passed. Goodman Brown alternately crouched and stood on tiptoe, pulling aside the branches and thrusting forth his head as far as he durst without discerning so much as a shadow. It vexed him the more, because he could have sworn, were such a thing possible, that he recognized the voices of the minister and Deacon Gookin, jogging along quietly, as they were wont to do, when bound to some ordination or ecclesiastical council. While yet within hearing, one of the riders stopped to pluck a switch.

"Of the two, reverend sir," said the voice like the deacon's, "I had rather miss an ordination dinner than to-night's meeting. They tell me that some of our community are to be here from Falmouth and beyond, and others from Connecticut and Rhode Island, besides several of the Indian powwows, who, after their fashion, know almost as much deviltry as the best of us. Moreover, there is a goodly young woman to be taken into communion."

"Mighty well, Deacon Gookin!" replied the solemn old tones of the minister. "Spur up, or we shall be late. Nothing can be done, you know, until I get on the ground."

The hoofs clattered again; and the voices, talking so strangely in the empty air, passed on through the forest, where no church had ever been gathered or solitary Christian prayed. Whither, then, could these holy men be journeying so deep into the heathen wilderness? Young Goodman Brown caught hold of a tree for support, being ready to sink down on the ground, faint and overburdened with the heavy sickness of his heart. He looked up to the sky, doubting whether there really was a heaven above him. Yet there was the blue arch, and the stars brightening in it.

"With heaven above and Faith below, I will yet stand firm against the devil!" cried Goodman Brown.

While he still gazed upward into the deep arch of the firmament and had lifted his hands to pray, a cloud, though no wind was stirring, hurried across the zenith and hid the brightening stars. The blue sky was still visible, except directly overhead, where this black mass of cloud was sweeping swiftly northward. Aloft in the air, as if from the depths of the cloud, came a confused and doubtful sound of voices. Once the listener fancied that he could distinguish the accents of towns-people of his own, men and women, both pious and ungodly, many of whom he had met at the communion table, and had seen others rioting at the tavern. The next moment, so indistinct were the sounds, he doubted whether he had heard aught but the murmur of the old forest, whispering without a wind. Then came a stronger swell of those familiar tones, heard daily in the sunshine at Salem village, but never until now from a cloud of night. There was one voice, of a young woman, uttering lamentations, yet with an uncertain sorrow, and entreating for some favor, which, perhaps, it would grieve her to obtain; and all the unseen multitude, both saints and sinners, seemed to encourage her onward.

"Faith!" shouted Goodman Brown, in a voice of agony and desperation; and the echoes of the forest mocked him, crying, "Faith! Faith!" as if bewildered wretches were seeking her all through the wilderness.

The cry of grief, rage, and terror was yet piercing the night, when the unhappy husband held his breath for a response. There was a scream, drowned immediately in a louder murmur of voices, fading into far-off laughter, as the dark cloud swept away, leaving the clear and silent sky above Goodman Brown. But something fluttered lightly down through the air and caught on the branch of a tree. The young man seized it, and beheld a pink ribbon.

"My Faith is gone!" cried he after one stupefied moment. "There is no good on earth; and sin is but a name. Come, devil; for to thee is this world given."

And, maddened with despair, so that he laughed loud and long, did Goodman Brown grasp his staff and set forth again, at such a rate that he seemed to fly along the forest path rather than to walk or run. The road grew wilder and drearier and more faintly traced, and vanished at length, leaving him in the heart of the dark wilderness, still rushing onward with the instinct that guides mortal man to evil. The whole forest was peopled with frightful sounds — the creaking of the trees, the howling of wild beasts, and the yell of Indians; while sometimes the wind tolled like a distant church bell, and sometimes gave a broad roar around the traveller, as if all Nature were laughing him to scorn. But he was himself the chief horror of the scene, and shrank not from its other horrors.

"Ha! Ha! ha!" roared Goodman Brown when the wind laughed at him. "Let us hear which will laugh loudest. Think not to frighten me with your deviltry. Come witch, come wizard, come Indian powwow, come devil himself, and here comes Goodman Brown. You may as well fear him as he fear you."

In truth, all through the haunted forest there could be nothing more frightful than the figure of Goodman Brown. On he flew among the black pines, brandishing his staff with frenzied gestures, now giving vent to an inspiration of horrid blasphemy, and now shouting forth such laughter as set all the echoes of the forest laughing like demons around him. The fiend in his own shape is less hideous than when he rages in the breast of man. Thus sped the demoniac on his course, until, quivering among the trees, he saw a red light before him, as when the felled trunks and branches of a clearing have been set on fire, and throw up their lurid blaze against the sky, at the hour of midnight. He paused, in a lull of the tempest that had driven him onward, and heard the swell of what seemed a hymn, rolling solemnly from a distance with the weight of many voices. He knew the tune; it was a familiar one in the choir of the village meeting-house. The verse died heavily away, and was lengthened by a chorus, not of human voices, but of all the sounds of the benighted wilderness pealing in awful harmony together. Goodman Brown cried out, and his cry was lost to his own ear by its unison with the cry of the desert.

In the interval of silence he stole forward until the light glared full upon his eyes. At one extremity of an open space, hemmed in by the dark wall of the forest, arose a rock, bearing some rude, natural resemblance either to an altar or a pulpit, and surrounded by four blazing pines, their tops aflame, their stems untouched, like candles at an evening meeting. The mass of foliage that had overgrown the summit of the rock was all on fire, blazing high into the night and fitfully illuminating the whole field. Each pendent twig and leafy festoon was in a blaze. As the red light arose and fell, a numerous congregation alternately shone forth, then disappeared in shadow, and again grew, as it were, out of the darkness, peopling the heart of the solitary woods at once.

"A grave and dark-clad company," quoth Goodman Brown.

In truth they were such. Among them, quivering to and fro between gloom and splendor, appeared faces that would be seen next day at the council board of the province, and others which, Sabbath after Sabbath, looked devoutly heavenward, and benignantly over the crowded pews, from the holiest pulpits in the land. Some affirm that the lady of the governor was there. At least there were high dames well known to her, and wives of honored husbands, and widows, a great multitude, and ancient maidens, all of excellent repute, and fair young girls, who trembled lest their mothers should espy them. Either the sudden gleams of light flashing over the obscure field bedazzled Goodman Brown, or he recognized a score of the church members of Salem village famous for their especial sanctity. Good old Deacon Gookin had arrived, and waited at the skirts of that venerable saint, his revered pastor. But, irreverently consorting with these grave, reputable, and pious people, these elders of the church, these chaste dames and dewy virgins, there were men of dissolute lives and women of spotted fame, wretches given over to all mean and filthy vice, and suspected even of horrid crimes. It was strange to see that the good shrank not from the wicked, nor were the sinners abashed by the saints. Scattered also among their pale-faced enemies were the Indian priests, or powwows, who had often scared their native forest with more hideous incantations than any known to English witchcraft.

"But where is Faith?" thought Goodman Brown; and, as hope came into his heart, he trembled.

Another verse of the hymn arose, a slow and mournful strain, such as the pious love, but joined to words which expressed all that our nature can conceive of sin, and darkly hinted at far more. Unfathomable to mere mortals is the lore of fiends. Verse after verse was sung; and still the chorus of the desert swelled between like the deepest tone of a mighty organ; and with the final peal of that dreadful anthem there came a sound, as if the roaring wind, the rushing streams, the howling beasts, and every other voice of the unconcerted wilderness were mingling and according with the voice of guilty man in homage to the prince of all. The four blazing pines threw up a loftier flame, and obscurely discovered shapes and visages of horror on the smoke wreaths above the impious assembly. At the same moment the fire on the rock shot redly forth and formed a glowing arch above its base, where now appeared a figure. With reverence be it spoken, the figure bore no slight similitude, both in garb and manner, to some grave divine of the New England churches.

"Bring forth the converts!" cried a voice that echoed through the field and rolled into the forest.

At the word, Goodman Brown stepped forth from the shadow of the trees and approached the congregation, with whom he felt a loathful brotherhood by the sympathy of all that was wicked in his heart. He could have well-nigh sworn that the shape of his own dead father beckoned him to advance, looking downward from a smoke wreath, while a woman, with dim features of despair, threw out her hand to warn him back. Was it his mother? But he had no power to retreat one step, nor to resist, even in thought, when the minister and good old Deacon Gookin seized his arms and led him to the blazing rock. Thither came also the slender form of a veiled female, led between Goody Cloyse, that pious teacher of the catechism, and Martha Carrier, who had received the devil's promise to be queen of hell. A rampant hag was she. And there stood the proselytes beneath the canopy of fire.

"Welcome, my children," said the dark figure, "to the communion of your race. Ye have found thus young your nature and your destiny. My children, look behind you!"

They turned; and flashing forth, as it were, in a sheet of flame, the fiend worshippers were seen; the smile of welcome gleamed darkly on every visage.

"There," resumed the sable form, "are all whom ye have reverenced from youth. Ye deemed them holier than yourselves and shrank from your own sin, contrasting it with their lives of righteousness and prayerful aspirations heavenward. Yet here are they all in my worshipping assembly. This night it shall be granted you to know their secret deeds: how hoary-bearded elders of the church have whispered wanton words to the young maids of their households; how many a woman, eager for widows' weeds, has given her husband a drink at bedtime and let him sleep his last sleep in her bosom; how beardless youths have made haste to inherit their fathers' wealth; and how fair damsels — blush not, sweet ones — have dug little graves in the garden, and bidden me, the sole guest, to an infant's funeral. By the sympathy of your human hearts for sin ye shall scent out all the places — whether in church, bedchamber, street, field, or forest — where crime has been committed, and shall exult to behold the whole earth one stain of guilt, one mighty blood spot. Far more than this. It shall be yours to penetrate, in every bosom, the deep mystery of sin, the fountain of all wicked arts, and which inexhaustibly supplies more evil impulses than human power — than my power at its utmost — can make manifest in deeds. And now, my children, look upon each other."

They did so; and, by the blaze of the hell-kindled torches, the wretched man beheld his Faith, and the wife her husband, trembling before that unhallowed altar.

"Lo, there ye stand, my children," said the figure, in a deep and solemn tone, almost sad with its despairing awfulness, as if his once angelic nature could yet mourn for our miserable race. "Depending upon one another's hearts, ye had still hoped that virtue were not all a dream. Now are ye undeceived. Evil is the nature of mankind. Evil must be your only happiness. Welcome again, my children, to the communion of your race."

"Welcome," repeated the fiend worshippers, in one cry of despair and triumph.

And there they stood, the only pair, as it seemed, who were yet hesitating on the verge of wickedness in this dark world. A basin was hollowed, naturally, in the rock. Did it contain water, reddened by the lurid light? or was it blood? or, perchance, a liquid flame? Herein did the shape of evil dip his hand and prepare to lay the mark of baptism upon their foreheads, that they might be partakers of the mystery of sin, more conscious of the secret guilt of others, both in deed and thought, than they could now be of their own. The husband cast one look at his pale wife, and Faith at him. What polluted wretches would the next glance show them to each other, shuddering alike at what they disclosed and what they saw!

"Faith! Faith!" cried the husband, "look up to heaven, and resist the wicked one."

Whether Faith obeyed he knew not. Hardly had he spoken when he found himself amid calm night and solitude, listening to a roar of the wind which died heavily away through the forest. He staggered against the rock, and felt it chill and damp; while a hanging twig, that had been all on fire, besprinkled his cheek with the coldest dew.

The next morning young Goodman Brown came slowly into the street of Salem village, staring around him like a bewildered man. The good old minister was taking a walk along the graveyard to get an appetite for breakfast and meditate his sermon, and bestowed a blessing, as he passed, on Goodman Brown. He shrank from the venerable saint as if to avoid an anathema. Old Deacon Gookin was at domestic worship, and the holy words of his prayer were heard through the open window. "What God doth the wizard pray to?" quoth Goodman Brown. Goody Cloyse, that excellent old Christian, stood in the early sunshine at her own lattice, catechizing a little girl who had brought her a pint of morning's milk. Goodman Brown snatched away the child as from the grasp of the fiend himself. Turning the corner by the meeting-house, he spied the head of Faith, with the pink ribbons, gazing anxiously forth, and bursting into such joy at sight of him that she skipped along the street and almost kissed her husband before the whole village. But Goodman Brown looked sternly and sadly into her face, and passed on without a greeting.

Had Goodman Brown fallen asleep in the forest and only dreamed a wild dream of a witch-meeting?

Be it so if you will; but, alas! it was a dream of evil omen for young Goodman Brown. A stern, a sad, a darkly meditative, a distrustful, if not a desperate man did he become from the night of that fearful dream. On the Sabbath day, when the congregation were singing a holy psalm, he could not listen because an anthem of sin rushed loudly upon his ear and drowned all the blessed strain. When the minister spoke from the pulpit with power and fervid eloquence, and, with his hand on the open Bible, of the sacred truths of our religion, and of saint-like lives and triumphant deaths, and of future bliss or misery unutterable, then did Goodman Brown turn pale, dreading lest the roof should thunder down upon the gray blasphemer and his hearers. Often, awaking suddenly at midnight, he shrank from the bosom of Faith; and at morning or eventide, when the family knelt down at prayer, he scowled and muttered to himself, and gazed sternly at his wife, and turned away. And when he had lived long, and was borne to his grave a hoary corpse, followed by Faith, an aged woman, and children and grandchildren, a goodly procession, besides neighbors not a few, they carved no hopeful verse upon his tombstone, for his dying hour was gloom.

[1835]

Nathaniel Hawthorne

∾

WAKEFIELD

In some old magazine or newspaper, I recollect a story, told as truth, of a man — let us call him Wakefield — who absented himself for a long time, from his wife. The fact, thus abstractedly stated, is not very uncommon, nor — without a proper distinction of circumstances — to be condemned either as naughty or nonsensical. Howbeit, this, though far from the most aggravated, is perhaps the strangest instance, on record, of marital delinquency; and, moreover, as remarkable a freak as may be found in the whole list of human oddities. The wedded couple lived in London. The man, under pretence of going a journey, took lodgings in the next street to his own house, and there, unheard of by his wife or friends, and without the shadow of a reason for such self-banishment, dwelt upwards of twenty years. During that period, he beheld his home every day, and frequently the forlorn Mrs. Wakefield. And after so great a gap in his matrimonial felicity — when his death was reckoned certain, his estate settled, his name dismissed from memory, and his wife, long, long ago, resigned to her autumnal widowhood — he entered the door one evening, quietly, as from a day's absence, and became a loving spouse till death.

This outline is all that I remember. But the incident, though of the purest originality, unexampled, and probably never to be repeated, is one, I think, which appeals to the general sympathies of mankind. We know, each for himself, that none of us would perpetrate such a folly, yet feel as if some other might. To my own contemplations, at least, it has often recurred, always exciting wonder, but with a sense that the story must be true, and a conception of its hero's character. Whenever any subject so forcibly affects the mind, time is well spent in thinking of it. If the reader choose, let him do his own meditation; or if he prefer to ramble with me through the twenty years of Wakefield's vagary, I bid him welcome, trusting that there will be a pervading spirit and a moral, even should we fail to find them, done up neatly, and condensed into the final sentence. Thought has always its efficacy, and every striking incident its moral.

What sort of a man was Wakefield? We are free to shape out our own idea, and call it by his name. He was now in the meridian of life; his matrimonial affections, never violent, were sobered into a calm, habitual sentiment; of all husbands, he was likely to be the most constant, because a certain sluggishness would keep his heart at rest wherever it might be placed. He was intellectual, but not actively so; his mind occupied itself in long and lazy musings, that tended to no purpose, or had not vigor to attain it; his thoughts were seldom so energetic as to seize hold of words. Imagination, in the proper meaning of the term, made no part of Wakefield's gifts. With a cold, but not depraved nor wandering heart, and a mind never feverish with riotous thoughts, nor perplexed with originality, who could have anticipated, that our friend would entitle himself to a foremost place among the doers of eccentric deeds? Had his acquaintances been asked who was the man in London, the surest to perform nothing to-day which should be remembered on the morrow, they would have thought of Wakefield. Only the wife of his bosom might have hesitated. She, without having analyzed his character, was partly aware of a quiet selfishness, that had rusted into his inactive mind — of a peculiar sort of vanity, the most uneasy attribute about him — of a disposition to craft, which had seldom produced more positive effects than the keeping of petty secrets, hardly worth revealing — and, lastly, of what she called a little strangeness, sometimes, in the good man. This latter quality is indefinable, and perhaps non-existent.

Let us now imagine Wakefield bidding adieu to his wife. It is the dusk of an October evening. His equipment is a drab great-coat, a hat covered with an oil-cloth, top-boots, an umbrella in one hand and a small portmanteau in the other. He has informed Mrs. Wakefield that he is to take the night-coach into the country. She would fain inquire the length of his journey, its object, and the probable time of his return; but, indulgent to his harmless love of mystery, interrogates him only by a look. He tells her not to expect him positively by the return coach, nor to be alarmed should he tarry three or four days; but, at all events, to look for him at supper on Friday evening. Wakefield himself, be it considered, has no suspicion of what is before him. He holds out his hand; she gives her own, and meets his parting kiss, in the matter-of-course way of a ten years' matrimony; and forth goes the middle-aged Mr. Wakefield, almost resolved to perplex his good lady by a whole week's absence. After the door has closed behind him, she perceives it thrust partly open, and a vision of her husband's face, through the aperture, smiling on her, and gone in a moment. For the time, this little incident is dismissed without a thought. But, long afterwards, when she has been more years a widow than a wife, that smile recurs, and flickers across all her reminiscences of Wakefield's visage. In her many musings, she surrounds the original smile with a multitude of fantasies, which make it strange and awful; as, for instance, if she imagines him in a coffin, that parting look is frozen on his pale features; or, if she dreams of him in Heaven, still his blessed spirit wears a quiet and crafty smile. Yet, for its sake, when all others have given him up for dead, she sometimes doubts whether she is a widow.

But, our business is with the husband. We must hurry after him, along the street, ere he lose his individuality, and melt into the great mass of London life. It would be vain searching for him there. Let us follow close at his heels, therefore, until, after several superfluous turns and doublings, we find him comfortably established by the fireside of a small apartment, previously bespoken. He is in the next street to his own, and at his journey's end. He can scarcely trust his good fortune, in having got thither unperceived — recollecting that, at one time, he was delayed by the throng, in the very focus of a lighted lantern; and, again, there were footsteps, that seemed to tread behind his own, distinct from the multitudinous tramp around him; and, anon, he heard a voice shouting afar, and fancied that it called his name. Doubtless, a dozen busy-bodies had been watching him, and told his wife the whole affair. Poor Wakefield! Little knowest thou thine own insignificance in this great world! No mortal eye but mine has traced thee. Go quietly to thy bed, foolish man; and, on the morrow, if thou wilt be wise, get thee home to good Mrs. Wakefield, and tell her the truth. Remove not thyself, even for a little week, from thy place in her chaste bosom. Were she, for a single moment, to deem thee dead, or lost, or lastingly divided from her, thou wouldst be woefully conscious of a change in thy true wife, forever after. It is perilous to make a chasm in human affections; not that they gape so long and wide — but so quickly close again!

Almost repenting of his frolic, or whatever it may be termed, Wakefield lies down betimes, and starting from his first nap, spreads forth his arms into the wide and solitary waste of the unaccustomed bed. "No" — thinks he, gathering the bed-clothes about him — "I will not sleep alone another night."

In the morning, he rises earlier than usual, and sets himself to consider what he really means to do. Such are his loose and rambling modes of thought, that he has taken this very singular step, with the consciousness of a purpose, indeed, but without being able to define it sufficiently for his own contemplation. The vagueness of the project, and the convulsive effort with which he plunges into the execution of it, are equally characteristic of a feeble-minded man. Wakefield sifts his ideas, however, as minutely as he may, and finds himself curious to know the progress of matters at home — how his exemplary wife will endure her widowhood, of a week; and, briefly, how the little sphere of creatures and circumstances, in which he was a central object, will be affected by his removal. A morbid vanity, therefore, lies nearest the bottom of the affair. But, how is he to attain his ends? Not, certainly, by keeping close in this comfortable lodging, where, though he slept and awoke in the next street to his home, he is as effectually abroad, as if the stage-coach had been whirling him away all night. Yet, should he reappear, the whole project is knocked in the head. His poor brains being hopelessly puzzled with this dilemma, he at length ventures out, partly resolving to cross the head of the street, and send one hasty glance towards his forsaken domicile. Habit — for he is a man of habits — takes him by the hand, and guides him, wholly unaware, to his own door, where, just at the critical moment, he is aroused by the scraping of his foot upon the step. Wakefield! whither are you going?

At that instant, his fate was turning on the pivot. Little dreaming of the doom to which his first backward step devotes him, he hurries away, breathless with agitation hitherto unfelt, and hardly dares turn his head, at the distant corner. Can it be, that nobody caught sight of him? Will not the whole household — the decent Mrs. Wakefield, the smart maid-servant, and the dirty little foot-boy — raise a hue-and-cry, through London streets, in pursuit of their fugitive lord and master? Wonderful escape! He gathers courage to pause and look homeward, but is perplexed with a sense of change about the familiar edifice, such as affects us all, when, after a separation of months or years, we again see some hill or lake, or work of art, with which we were friends, of old. In ordinary cases, this indescribable impression is caused by the comparison and contrast between our imperfect reminiscences and the reality. In Wakefield, the magic of a single night has wrought a similar transformation, because, in that brief period, a great moral change has been effected. But this is a secret from himself. Before leaving the spot, he catches a far and momentary glimpse of his wife, passing athwart the front window, with her face turned towards the head of the street. The crafty nincompoop takes to his heels, scared with the idea, that, among a thousand such atoms of mortality, her eye must have detected him. Right glad is his heart, though his brain be somewhat dizzy, when he finds himself by the coal-fire of his lodging.

So much for the commencement of this long whim-wham. After the initial conception, and the stirring up of the man's sluggish temperament to put it in practice, the whole matter evolves itself in a natural train. We may suppose him, as the result of deep deliberation, buying a new wig, of reddish hair, and selecting sundry garments, in a fashion unlike his customary suit of brown, from a Jew's old-clothes bag. It is accomplished. Wakefield is another man. The new system being now established, a retrograde movement to the old would be almost as difficult as the step that placed him in his unparalleled position. Furthermore, he is rendered obstinate by a sulkiness, occasionally incident to his temper, and brought on, at present, by the inadequate sensation which he conceives to have been produced in the bosom of Mrs. Wakefield. He will not go back until she be frightened half to death. Well, twice or thrice has she passed before his sight, each time with a heavier step, a paler check, and more anxious brow; and in the third week of his non-appearance, he detects a portent of evil entering the house, in the guise of an apothecary. Next day, the knocker is muffled. Towards night-fall, comes the chariot of a physician, and deposits its big-wigged and solemn burthen at Wakefield's door, whence, after a quarter of an hour's visit, he emerges, perchance the herald of a funeral. Dear woman! Will she die? By this time Wakefield is excited to something like energy of feeling, but still lingers away from his wife's bedside, pleading with his conscience, that she must not be disturbed at such a juncture. If aught else restrains him, he does not know it. In the course of a few weeks, she gradually recovers; the crisis is over; her heart is sad, perhaps, but quiet; and, let him return soon or late, it will never be feverish for him again. Such ideas glimmer through the mist of Wakefield's mind, and render him indistinctly conscious, that an almost impassable gulf divides his hired apartment from his former home. "It is but in the next street!" he sometimes says. Fool! it is in another world. Hitherto, he has put off his return from one particular day to another; henceforward, he leaves the precise time undetermined. Not to-morrow — probably next week — pretty soon. Poor man! The dead have nearly as much chance of re-visiting their earthly homes, as the self-banished Wakefield.

Would that I had a folio to write, instead of an article of a dozen pages! Then might I exemplify how an influence, beyond our control, lays its strong hand on every deed which we do, and weaves its consequences into an iron tissue of necessity. Wakefield is spell-bound. We must leave him, for ten years or so, to haunt around his house, without once crossing the threshold, and to be faithful to his wife, with all the affection of which his heart is capable, while he is slowly fading out of hers. Long since, it must be remarked, he has lost the perception of singularity in his conduct.

Now for a scene! Amid the throng of a London street, we distinguish a man, now waxing elderly, with few characteristics to attract careless observers, yet bearing, in his whole aspect, the hand-writing of no common fate, for such as have the skill to read it. He is meagre; his low and narrow forehead is deeply wrinkled; his eyes, small and lustreless, sometimes wander apprehensively about him, but oftener seem to look inward. He bends his head, but moves with an indescribable obliquity of gait, as if unwilling to display his full front to the world. Watch him, long enough to see what we have described, and you will allow, that circumstances — which often produce remarkable men from nature's ordinary handiwork — have produced one such here. Next, leaving him to sidle along the foot-walk, cast your eyes in the opposite direction, where a portly female, considerably in the wane of life, with a prayer-book in her hand, is proceeding to yonder church. She has the placid mien of settled widowhood. Her regrets have either died away, or have become so essential to her heart, that they would be poorly exchanged for joy. Just as the lean man and well conditioned woman are passing, a slight obstruction occurs, and brings these two figures directly in contact. Their hands touch; the pressure of the crowd forces her bosom against his shoulder; they stand, face to face, staring into each other's eyes. After a ten years' separation, thus Wakefield meets his wife!

The throng eddies away, and carries them asunder. The sober widow, resuming her former pace, proceeds to church, but pauses in the portal, and throws a perplexed glance along the street. She passes in, however, opening her prayer-book as she goes. And the man? With so wild a face, that busy and selfish London stands to gaze after him, he hurries to his lodgings, bolts the door, and throws himself upon the bed. The latent feelings of years break out; his feeble mind acquires a brief energy from their strength, all the miserable strangeness of his life is revealed to him at a glance; and he cries out, passionately — "Wakefield! Wakefield! You are mad!"

Perhaps he was so. The singularity of his situation must have so moulded him to itself, that, considered in regard to his fellow-creatures and the business of life, he could not be said to possess his right mind. He had contrived, or rather he had happened, to dissever himself from the world — to vanish — to give up his place and privileges with living men, without being admitted among the dead. The life of a hermit is nowise parallel to his. He was in the bustle of the city, as of old; but the crowd swept by, and saw him not; he was, we may figuratively say, always beside his wife, and at his hearth, yet must never feel the warmth of the one, nor the affection of the other. It was Wakefield's unprecedented fate, to retain his original share of human sympathies, and to be still involved in human interests, while he had lost his reciprocal influence on them. It would be a most curious speculation, to trace out the effect of such circumstances on his heart and intellect, separately, and in unison. Yet, changed as he was, he would seldom be conscious of it, but deem himself the same man as ever; glimpses of the truth, indeed, would come, but only for the moment; and still he would keep saying — "I shall soon go back!" — nor reflect, that he had been saying so for twenty years.

I conceive, also, that these twenty years would appear, in the retrospect, scarcely longer than the week to which Wakefield had at first limited his absence. He would look on the affair as no more than an interlude in the main business of his life. When, after a little while more, he should deem it time to re-enter his parlor, his wife would clap her hands for joy, on beholding the middle-aged Mr. Wakefield. Alas, what a mistake! Would Time but await the close of our favorite follies, we should be young men, all of us, and till Doom's Day.

One evening, in the twentieth year since he vanished, Wakefield is taking his customary walk towards the dwelling which he still calls his own. It is a gusty night of autumn, with frequent showers, that patter down upon the pavement, and are gone, before a man can put up his umbrella. Pausing near the house, Wakefield discerns, through the parlor-windows of the second floor, the red glow, and the glimmer and fitful flash, of a comfortable fire. On the ceiling, appears a grotesque shadow of good Mrs. Wakefield. The cap, the nose and chin, and the broad waist, form an admirable caricature, which dances, moreover, with the up-flickering and down-sinking blaze, almost too merrily for the shade of an elderly widow. At this instant, a shower chances to fall, and is driven, by the unmannerly gust, full into Wakefield's face and bosom. He is quite penetrated with its autumnal chill. Shall he stand, wet and shivering here, when his own hearth has a good fire to warm him, and his own wife will run to fetch the gray coat and small-clothes, which, doubtless, she has kept carefully in the closet of their bed-chamber? No! Wakefield is no such fool. He ascends the steps — heavily! — for twenty years have stiffened his legs, since he came down — but he knows it not. Stay, Wakefield! Would you go to the sole home that is left you? Then step into your grave! The door opens. As he passes in, we have a parting glimpse of his visage, and recognize the crafty smile, which was the precursor of the little joke, that he has ever since been playing off at his wife's expense. How unmercifully has he quizzed the poor woman! Well; a good night's rest to Wakefield!

This happy event — supposing it to be such — could only have occurred at an unpremeditated moment. We will not follow our friend across the threshold. He has left us much food for thought, a portion of which shall lend its wisdom to a moral; and be shaped into a figure. Amid the seeming confusion of our mysterious world, individuals are so nicely adjusted to a system, and systems to one another, and to a whole, that, by stepping aside for a moment, a man exposes himself to a fearful risk of losing his place forever. Like Wakefield, he may become, as it were, the Outcast of the Universe.

[1835]

Nathaniel Hawthorne

ဢ

THE WIVES OF THE DEAD

The following story, the simple and domestic incidents of which may be deemed scarcely worth relating, after such a lapse of time, awakened some degree of interest, a hundred years ago, in a principal seaport of the Bay Province. The rainy twilight of an autumn day; a parlor on the second floor of a small house, plainly furnished, as beseemed the middling circumstances of its inhabitants, yet decorated with little curiosities from beyond the sea, and a few delicate specimens of Indian Manufacture, — these are the only particulars to be premised in regard to scene and season. Two young and comely women sat together by the fireside, nursing their mutual and peculiar sorrows. They were the recent brides of two brothers, a sailor and a landsman, and two successive days had brought tidings of the death of each, by the chances of Canadian warfare, and the tempestuous Atlantic. The universal sympathy excited by this bereavement, drew numerous condoling guests to the habitation of the widowed sisters. Several, among whom was the minister, had remained till the verge of evening; when one by one, whispering many comfortable passages of Scripture, that were answered by more abundant tears, they took their leave and departed to their own happier homes. The mourners, though not insensible to the kindness of their friends, had yearned to be left alone. United, as they had been, by the relationship of the living and now more closely so by that of the dead, each felt as if whatever consolation her grief admitted, were to be found in the bosom of the other. They joined their hearts, and wept together silently. But after an hour of such indulgence, one of the sisters, all of whose emotions were influenced by her mild, quiet, yet not feeble character, began to recollect the precepts of resignation and endurance, which piety had taught her, when she did not think to need them. Her misfortune, besides, as earliest known, should earliest cease to interfere with her regular course of duties; accordingly, having placed the table before the fire, and arranged a frugal meal, she took the hand of her companion.

"Come, dearest sister; you have eaten not a morsel to-day," she said. "Arise, I pray you, and let us ask a blessing on that which is provided for us."

Her sister-in-law was of a lively and irritable temperament, and the first pangs of her sorrow had been expressed by shrieks and passionate lamentation. She now shrunk from Mary's words, like a wounded sufferer from a hand that revives the throb.

"There is no blessing left for me, neither will I ask it," cried Margaret, with a fresh burst of tears. "Would it were His will that I might never taste food more."

Yet she trembled at these rebellious expressions, almost as soon as they were uttered, and, by degrees, Mary succeeded in bringing her sister's mind nearer to the situation of her own. Time went on, and their usual hour of repose arrived. The brothers and their brides, entering the married state with no more than the slender means which then sanctioned such a step, had confederated themselves in one household, with equal rights to the parlor, and claiming exclusive privileges in two sleeping rooms contiguous to it. Thither the widowed ones retired, after heaping ashes upon the dying embers of their fire, and placing a lighted lamp upon the hearth. The doors of both chambers were left open, so that a part of the interior of each, and the beds with their unclosed curtains, were reciprocally visible. Sleep did not steal upon the sisters at one and the same time. Mary experienced the effect often consequent upon grief quietly borne, and soon sunk into temporary forgetfulness, while Margaret became more disturbed and feverish, in proportion as the night advanced with its deepest and stillest hours. She lay listening to the drops of rain, that came down in monotonous succession, unswayed by a breath of wind; and a nervous impulse continually caused her to lift her head from the pillow, and gaze into Mary's chamber and the intermediate apartment. The cold light of the lamp threw the shadows of the furniture up against the wall, stamping them immoveably there, except when they were shaken by a sudden flicker of the flame. Two vacant arm-chairs were in their old positions on opposite sides of the hearth, where the brothers had been wont to sit in young and laughing dignity, as heads of families; two humbler seats were near them, the true thrones of that little empire, where Mary and herself had exercised in love, a power that love had won. The cheerful radiance of the fire had shone upon the happy circle, and the dead glimmer of the lamp might have befitted their reunion now. While Margaret groaned in bitterness, she heard a knock at the street-door.

"How would my heart have leapt at that sound but yesterday!" thought she, remembering the anxiety with which she had long awaited tidings from her husband. "I care not for it now; let them begone, for I will not arise."

But even while a sort of childish fretfulness made her thus resolve, she was breathing hurriedly, and straining her ears to catch a repetition of the summons. It is difficult to be convinced of the death of one whom we have deemed another self. The knocking was now renewed in slow and regular strokes, apparently given with the soft end of a doubled fist, and was accompanied by words, faintly heard through several thicknesses of wall. Margaret looked to her sister's chamber, and beheld her still lying in the depths of sleep. She arose, placed her foot upon the floor, and slightly arrayed herself, trembling between fear and eagerness as she did so.

"Heaven help me!" sighed she. "I have nothing left to fear, and methinks I am ten times more a coward than ever."

Seizing the lamp from the hearth, she hastened to the window that overlooked the street-door. It was a lattice, turning upon hinges; and having thrown it back, she stretched her head a little way into the moist atmosphere. A lantern was reddening the front of the house, and melting its light in the neighboring puddles, while a deluge of darkness overwhelmed every other object. As the window grated on its hinges, a man in a broad brimmed hat and blanket-coat, stepped from under the shelter of the projecting story, and looked upward to discover whom his application had aroused. Margaret knew him as a friendly innkeeper of the town.

"What would you have, Goodman Parker?" cried the widow.

"Lack-a-day, is it you, Mistress Margaret?" replied the innkeeper. "I was afraid it might be your sister Mary; for I hate to see a young woman in trouble, when I haven't a word of comfort to whisper her."

"For Heaven's sake, what news do you bring?" screamed Margaret.

"Why, there has been an express through the town within this half hour," said Goodman Parker, "travelling from the eastern jurisdiction with letters from the governor and council. He tarried at my house to refresh himself with a drop and a morsel, and I asked him what tidings on the frontiers. He tells me we had the better in the skirmish you wot of, and that thirteen men reported slain are well and sound, and your husband among them. Besides, he is appointed of the escort to bring the captivated Frenchers and Indians home to the province jail. I judged you wouldn't mind being broke of your rest, and so I stepped over to tell you. Good night."

So saying, the honest man departed; and his lantern gleamed along the street, bringing to view indistinct shapes of things, and the fragments of a world, like order glimmering through the chaos, or memory roaming over the past. But Margaret stayed not to watch these picturesque effects. Joy flashed into her heart, and lighted it up at once, and breathless, and with winged steps, she flew to the bedside of her sister. She paused, however, at the door of the chamber, while a thought of pain broke in upon her.

"Poor Mary!" said she to herself. "Shall I waken her, to feel her sorrow sharpened by my happiness? No; I will keep it within my own bosom till the morrow."

She approached the bed to discover if Mary's sleep were peaceful. Her face was turned partly inward to the pillow, and had been hidden there to weep; but a look of motionless contentment was now visible upon it, as if her heart, like a deep lake, had grown calm because its dead had sunk down so far within. Happy is it, and strange, that the lighter sorrows are those from which dreams are chiefly fabricated. Margaret shrunk from disturbing her sister-in-law, and felt as if her own better fortune, had rendered her involuntarily unfaithful, and as if altered and diminished affection must be the consequence of the disclosure she had to make. With a sudden step, she turned away. But joy could not long be repressed, even by circumstances that would have excited heavy grief at another moment. Her mind was thronged with delightful thoughts, till sleep stole on and transformed them to visions, more delightful and more wild, like the breath of winter, (but what a cold comparison!) working fantastic tracery upon a window.

When the night was far advanced, Mary awoke with a sudden start. A vivid dream had latterly involved her in its unreal life, of which, however, she could only remember that it had been broken in upon at the most interesting point. For a little time, slumber hung about her like a morning mist, hindering her from perceiving the distinct outline of her situation. She listened with imperfect consciousness to two or three volleys of a rapid and eager knocking; and first she deemed the noise a matter of course, like the breath she drew; next, it appeared a thing in which she had no concern; and lastly, she became aware that it was a summons necessary to be obeyed. At the same moment, the pang of recollection darted into her mind; the pall of sleep was thrown back from the face of grief; the dim light of the chamber, and the objects therein revealed, had retained all her suspended ideas, and restored them as soon as she unclosed her eyes. Again, there was a quick peal upon the street-door. Fearing that her sister would also be disturbed, Mary wrapped herself in a cloak and hood, took the lamp from the hearth, and hastened to the window. By some accident, it had been left unhasped, and yielded easily to her hand.

"Who's there?" asked Mary, trembling as she looked forth.

The storm was over, and the moon was up; it shone upon broken clouds above, and below upon houses black with moisture, and upon little lakes of the fallen rain, curling into silver beneath the quick enchantment of a breeze. A young man in a sailor's dress, wet as if he had come out of the depths of the sea, stood alone under the window. Mary recognized him as one whose livelihood was gained by short voyages along the coast; nor did she forget, that, previous to her marriage, he had been an unsuccessful wooer of her own.

"What do you seek here, Stephen?" said she.

"Cheer up, Mary, for I seek to comfort you," answered the rejected lover. "You must know I got home not ten minutes ago, and the first thing my good mother told me was the news about your husband. So, without saying a word to the old woman, I clapped on my hat, and ran out of the house. I couldn't have slept a wink before speaking to you, Mary, for the sake of old times."

"Stephen, I thought better of you!" exclaimed the widow, with gushing tears, and preparing to close the lattice; for she was no whit inclined to imitate the first wife of Zadig.

"But stop, and hear my story out," cried the young sailor. "I tell you we spoke a brig yesterday afternoon, bound in from Old England. And who do you think I saw standing on deck well and hearty, only a bit thinner than he was five months ago?"

Mary leaned from the window, but could not speak.

"Why, it was your husband himself," continued the generous seaman. "He and three others saved themselves on a spar, when the *Blessing* turned bottom upwards. The brig will beat into the bay by daylight, with this wind, and you'll see him here tomorrow. There's the comfort I bring you, Mary, and so good night."

He hurried away, while Mary watched him with a doubt of waking reality, that seemed stronger or weaker as he alternately entered the shade of the houses, or emerged into the broad streaks of moonlight. Gradually, however, a blessed flood of conviction swelled into her heart, in strength enough to overwhelm her, had its increase been more abrupt. Her first impulse was to rouse her sister-in-law, and communicate the new-born gladness. She opened the chamber-door, which had been closed in the course of the night, though not latched, advanced to the bedside, and was about to lay her hand upon the slumberer's shoulder. But then she remembered that Margaret would awake to thoughts of death and woe, rendered not the less bitter by their contrast with her own felicity. She suffered the rays of the lamp to fall upon the unconscious form of the bereaved one. Margaret lay in unquiet sleep, and the drapery was displaced around her; her young cheek was rosy-tinted, and her lips half opened in a vivid smile; an expression of joy, debarred its passage by her sealed eyelids, struggled forth like incense from the whole countenance.

"My poor sister! you will waken too soon from that happy dream," thought Mary.

Before retiring, she set down the lamp and endeavored to arrange the bed-clothes, so that the chill air might not do harm to the feverish slumberer. But her hand trembled against Margaret's neck, a tear also fell upon her cheek, and she suddenly awoke.

[1832]

EDGAR ALLAN POE (1809–1849), *the son of poor traveling actors, was adopted by the merchant John Allan of Richmond, Virginia, after Poe's mother's death. Poe took his adoptive father's surname for his middle name. He was educated in Virginia and England, served two years in the army as an enlisted man, and then entered the military academy at West Point. He was expelled after a year. When John Allan disowned him because of his dissolute living habits, Poe had to earn his own living. He turned to writing as a profession. In 1833 his story "Ms. Found in a Bottle" won a fifty-dollar prize for the best story in a popular Baltimore periodical, and he obtained an editorial position with the* Southern Literary Messenger. *He became its editor in 1835. The following year he married his cousin Virginia Clemm, who was thirteen years old; she died of tuberculosis in 1847. Poe's reviews, poems, and stories attracted wide attention, but he was fired by the* Southern Literary Messenger *in 1837 because of his unstable temperament. His remaining years were a struggle with poverty, depression, poor health aggravated by indulgence in drugs and alcohol, and grief over the death of his wife. The writer Jorge Luis Borges has observed that Poe's life "was short and unhappy, if unhappiness can be short."*

Although in his personal life Poe was torn by the most contradictory passions, as a writer he professed a belief in reason and championed lucidity. He claimed that rhymed poetry is the highest literary form, but conceded that the prose tale "affords unquestionably the fairest field for the exercise of the loftiest talent which can be afforded by the wide domains of mere prose." Most of his stories can be divided into two categories: tales of terror, like "The Tell-Tale Heart" and "The Cask of Amontillado," where unity of effect or a single impression is of the greatest importance; and stories of intellect or ratiocination, analytic tales that are precursors of the modern detective story. When Poe was accused of imitating German romantic writers in his monologues of solitude and madness, he answered, "Terror is not of Germany, but of the soul."

Poe was a romantic writer who wrote poetry, fiction, and essays containing serious ideas about life and art. "The Oval Portrait" is a tale illustrating his theory that in order to give life artistic form the artist must feed on the spirit of life itself. As the critic Arthur Ransome realized, in this sketch Poe "is using the subtle, half-thought things that an earlier writer would scarcely have felt, or, if he had, would have brushed, like cobwebs, secretly aside." Poe's most extensive comments on the short story form are contained in his reviews of Hawthorne's tales (1842 and 1847), in which he also described his own practices as a writer. (See Poe's Commentary on page 1225 and Lawrence's Commentary about Poe on page 1228.)

Edgar Allan Poe

ఐఐ

THE TELL-TALE HEART

True! — nervous — very, very dreadfully nervous I had been and am; but why *will* you say that I am mad? The disease had sharpened my senses — not destroyed — not dulled them. Above all was the sense of hearing acute. I heard all things in the heaven and in the earth. I heard many things in hell. How, then, am I mad? Hearken! and observe how healthily — how calmly I can tell you the whole story.

It is impossible to say how first the idea entered my brain; but once conceived, it haunted me day and night. Object there was none. Passion there was none. I loved the old man. He had never wronged me. He had never given me insult. For his gold I had no desire. I think it was his eye! yes, it was this! One of his eyes resembled that of a vulture — a pale blue eye, with a film over it. Whenever it fell upon me, my blood ran cold; and so by degrees — very gradually — I made up my mind to take the life of the old man, and thus rid myself of the eye for ever.

Now this is the point. You fancy me mad. Madmen know nothing. But you should have seen *me*. You should have seen how wisely I proceeded — with what caution — with what foresight — with what dissimulation I went to work! I was never kinder to the old man than during the whole week before I killed him. And every night, about midnight, I turned the latch of his door and opened it — oh, so gently! And then, when I had made an opening sufficient for my head, I put in a dark lantern, all closed, closed, so that no light shone out, and then I thrust in my head. Oh, you would have laughed to see how cunningly I thrust it in! I moved it slowly — very, very slowly, so that I might not disturb the old man's sleep. It took me an hour to place my whole head within the opening so far that I could see him as he lay upon his bed. Ha! — would a madman have been so wise as this? And then, when my head was well in the room, I undid the lantern cautiously — oh, so cautiously — cautiously (for the hinges creaked) — I undid it just so much that a single thin ray fell upon the vulture eye. And this I did for seven long nights — every night just after midnight — but I found the eye always closed; and so it was impossible to do the work; for it was not the old man who vexed me, but his Evil Eye. And every morning, when the day broke, I went boldly into the chamber, and spoke courageously to him, calling him by name in a hearty tone, and inquiring how he had passed the night. So you see he would have been a very profound old man, indeed, to suspect that every night, just at twelve, I looked in upon him while he slept.

Upon the eighth night I was more than usually cautious in opening the door. A watch's minute hand moves more quickly than did mine. Never before that night had I *felt* the extent of my own powers — of my sagacity. I could scarcely contain my feelings of triumph. To think that there I was, opening the door, little by little, and he not even to dream of my secret deeds or thoughts. I fairly chuckled at the idea; and perhaps he heard me; for he moved on the bed suddenly, as if startled. Now you may think that I drew back — but no. His room was as black as pitch with the thick darkness (for the shutters were close fastened, through fear of robbers), and so I knew that he could not see the opening of the door, and I kept pushing it on steadily, steadily.

I had my head in, and was about to open the lantern, when my thumb slipped upon the tin fastening, and the old man sprang up in the bed, crying out — "Who's there?"

I kept quite still and said nothing. For a whole hour I did not move a muscle, and in the meantime I did not hear him lie down. He was still sitting up in the bed listening; — just as I have done, night after night, hearkening to the death watches in the wall.

Presently I heard a slight groan, and I knew it was the groan of mortal terror. It was not a groan of pain or of grief — oh, no! — it was the low stifled sound that arises from the bottom of the soul when overcharged with awe. I knew the sound well. Many a night, just at midnight, when all the world slept, it has welled up from my own bosom, deepening, with its dreadful echo, the terrors that distracted me. I say I knew it well. I knew what the old man felt, and pitied him, although I chuckled at heart. I knew that he had been lying awake ever since the first slight noise, when he had turned in the bed. His fears had been ever since growing upon him. He had been trying to fancy them causeless, but could not. He had been saying to himself — "It is nothing but the wind in the chimney — it is only a mouse crossing the floor," or "it is merely a cricket which has made a single chirp." Yes, he has been trying to comfort himself with these suppositions; but he had found all in vain. *All in vain;* because Death, in approaching him, had stalked with his black shadow before him, and enveloped the victim. And it was the mournful influence of the unperceived shadow that caused him to feel — although he neither saw nor heard — to *feel* the presence of my head within the room.

When I had waited a long time, very patiently, without hearing him lie down, I resolved to open a little — a very, very little crevice in the lantern. So I opened it — you cannot imagine how stealthily, stealthily — until, at length, a single dim ray, like the thread of the spider, shot from out the crevice and full upon the vulture eye.

It was open — wide, wide open — and I grew furious as I gazed upon it. I saw it with perfect distinctness — all a dull blue, with a hideous veil over it that chilled the very marrow in my bones; but I could see nothing else of the old man's face or person: for I had directed the ray as if by instinct, precisely upon the damned spot.

And now have I not told you that what you mistake for madness is but over-acuteness of the senses? — now, I say, there came to my ears a low, dull, quick sound, such as a watch makes when enveloped in cotton. I knew *that* sound well too. It was the beating of the old man's heart. It increased my fury, as the beating of a drum stimulates the soldier into courage.

But even yet I refrained and kept still. I scarcely breathed. I held the lantern motionless. I tried how steadily I could maintain the ray upon the eye. Meantime the hellish tattoo of the heart increased. It grew quicker and quicker, and louder and louder every instant. The old man's terror *must* have been extreme! It grew louder, I say, louder every moment! — do you mark me well? I have told you that I am nervous: so I am. And now at the dead hour of the night, amid the dreadful silence of that old house, so strange a noise as this excited me to uncontrollable terror. Yet, for some minutes longer I refrained and stood still. But the beating grew louder, louder! I thought the heart must burst. And now a new anxiety seized me — the sound would be heard by a neighbor! The old man's hour had come! With a loud yell, I threw open the lantern and leaped into the room. He shrieked once — once only. In an instant I dragged him to the floor, and pulled the heavy bed over him. I then smiled gaily, to find the deed so far done. But, for many minutes, the heart beat on with a muffled sound. This, however, did not vex me; it would not be heard through the wall. At length it ceased. The old man was dead. I removed the bed and examined the corpse. Yes, he was stone, stone dead. I placed my hand upon the heart and held it there many minutes. There was no pulsation. He was stone dead. His eye would trouble me no more.

If still you think me mad, you will think so no longer when I describe the wise precautions I took for the concealment of the body. The night waned, and I worked hastily, but in silence. First of all I dismembered the corpse. I cut off the head and the arms and the legs.

I then took up three planks from the flooring of the chamber, and deposited all between the scantlings. I then replaced the boards so cleverly, so cunningly, that no human eye — not even *his* — could have detected anything wrong. There was nothing to wash out — no stain of any kind — no blood-spot whatever. I had been too wary for that. A tub had caught all — ha! ha!

When I had made an end of these labors, it was four o'clock — still dark as midnight. As the bell sounded the hour, there came a knocking at the street door. I went down to open it with a light heart — for what had I *now* to fear? There entered three men, who introduced themslves, with perfect suavity, as officers of the police. A shriek had been heard by a neighbor during the night; suspicion of foul play had been aroused; information had been lodged at the police office, and they (the officers) had been deputed to search the premises.

I smiled, — for *what* had I to fear? I bade the gentlemen welcome.

The shriek, I said, was my own in a dream. The old man, I mentioned, was absent in the country. I took my visitors all over the house. I bade them search — search *well*. I led them, at length, to *his* chamber. I showed them his treasures, secure, undisturbed. In the enthusiasm of my confidence, I brought chairs into the room, and desired them *here* to rest from their fatigues, while I myself, in the wild audacity of my perfect triumph, placed my own seat upon the very spot beneath which reposed the corpse of the victim.

The officers were satisfied. My *manner* had convinced them. I was singularly at ease. They sat, and while I answered cheerily, they chatted familiar things. But, ere long, I felt myself getting pale and wished them gone. My head ached, and I fancied a ringing in my ears: but still they sat and still chatted. The ringing became more distinct: — it continued and became more distinct: I talked more freely to get rid of the feeling: but it continued and gained definitiveness — until, at length, I found that the noise was *not* within my ears.

No doubt I now grew *very* pale; — but I talked more fluently, and with a heightened voice. Yet the sound increased — and what could I do? It was *a low, dull, quick sound — much such a sound as a watch makes when enveloped in cotton.* I gasped for breath — and yet the officers heard it not. I talked more quickly — more vehemently; but the noise steadily increased. I arose and argued about trifles, in a high key and with violent gesticulations, but the noise steadily increased. Why *would* they not be gone? I paced the floor to and fro with heavy strides, as if excited to fury by the observation of the men — but the noise steadily increased. Oh God! what *could* I do? I foamed — I raved — I swore! I swung the chair upon which I had been sitting, and grated it upon the boards, but the noise arose over all and continually increased. It grew louder — louder — *louder!* And still the men chatted pleasantly, and smiled. Was it possible they heard not? Almighty God! — no, no! They heard! — they suspected! — they *knew!* — they were making a mockery of my horror! — this I thought, and this I think. But any thing was better than this agony! Any thing was more tolerable than this derision! I could bear those hypocritical smiles no longer! I felt that I must scream or die! — and now — again! — hark! louder! louder! louder! *louder!* —

"Villains!" I shrieked, "dissemble no more! I admit the deed! — tear up the planks! — here, here! — it is the beating of his hideous heart!"

[1843]

Edgar Allan Poe

⋙

THE CASK OF AMONTILLADO

The thousand injuries of Fortunato I had borne as I best could; but when he ventured upon insult, I vowed revenge. You, who so well know the nature of my soul, will not suppose, however, that I gave utterance to a threat. *At length* I would be avenged; this was a point definitely settled — but the very definitiveness with which it was resolved precluded the idea of risk. I must not only punish, but punish with impunity. A wrong is unredressed when retribution overtakes its redresser. It is equally unredressed when the avenger fails to make himself felt as such to him who has done the wrong.

It must be understood, that neither by word nor deed had I given Fortunato cause to doubt my good-will. I continued, as was my wont, to smile in his face, and he did not perceive that my smile *now* was at the thought of his immolation.

He had a weak point — this Fortunato — although in other regards he was a man to be respected and even feared. He prided himself on his connoisseurship in wine. Few Italians have the true virtuoso spirit. For the most part their enthusiasm is adopted to suit the time and opportunity — to practise imposture upon the British and Austrian *millionnaires.* In painting and gemmary Fortunato, like his countrymen, was a quack — but in the matter of old wines he was sincere. In this respect I did not differ from him materially: I was skilful in the Italian vintages myself, and bought largely whenever I could.

It was about dusk, one evening during the supreme madness of the carnival season, that I encountered my friend. He accosted me with excessive warmth, for he had been drinking much. The man wore motley. He had on a tight-fitting parti-striped dress, and his head was surmounted by the conical cap and bells. I was so pleased to see him, that I thought I should never have done wringing his hand.

I said to him: "My dear Fortunato, you are luckily met. How remarkably well you are looking to-day! But I have received a pipe[1] of what passes for Amontillado, and I have my doubts."

[1] a large cask or keg.

"How?" said he. "Amontillado? A pipe? Impossible! And in the middle of the carnival!"

"I have my doubts," I replied; "and I was silly enough to pay the full Amontillado price without consulting you in the matter. You were not to be found, and I was fearful of losing a bargain."

"Amontillado!"

"I have my doubts."

"Amontillado!"

"And I must satisfy them."

"Amontillado!"

"As you are engaged, I am on my way to Luchesi. If any one has a critical turn, it is he. He will tell me ——— "

"Luchesi cannot tell Amontillado from Sherry."

"And yet some fools will have it that his taste is a match for your own."

"Come, let us go."

"Whither?"

"To your vaults."

"My friend, no; I will not impose upon your good nature. I perceive you have an engagement. Luchesi ——— "

"I have no engagement; — come."

"My friend, no. It is not the engagement, but the severe cold with which I perceive you are afflicted. The vaults are insufferably damp. They are encrusted with nitre."

"Let us go, nevertheless. The cold is merely nothing. Amontillado! You have been imposed upon. And as for Luchesi, he cannot distinguish Sherry from Amontillado."

Thus speaking, Fortunato possessed himself of my arm. Putting on a mask of black silk, and drawing a *roquelaire*[2] closely about my person, I suffered him to hurry me to my palazzo.

There were no attendants at home; they had absconded to make merry in honor of the time. I had told them that I should not return until the morning, and had given them explicit orders not to stir from the house. These orders were sufficient, I well knew, to insure their immediate disappearance, one and all, as soon as my back was turned.

I took from their sconces two flambeaux, and giving one to Fortunato, bowed him through several suites of rooms to the archway that led into the vaults. I passed down a long and winding staircase, requesting him to be cautious as he followed. We came at length to the foot of the descent, and stood together on the damp ground of the catacombs of the Montresors.

The gait of my friend was unsteady, and the bells upon his cap jingled as he strode.

"The pipe?" said he.

"It is farther on," said I; "but observe the white web-work which gleams from these cavern walls."

[2] a short cloak.

He turned toward me, and looked into my eyes with two filmy orbs that distilled the rheum of intoxication.

"Nitre?" he asked, at length.

"Nitre," I replied. "How long have you had that cough?"

"Ugh! ugh! ugh! — ugh! ugh! ugh! — ugh! ugh! ugh! — ugh! ugh! ugh! — ugh! ugh! ugh!"

My poor friend found it impossible to reply for many minutes.

"It is nothing," he said, at last.

"Come," I said, with decision, "we will go back; your health is precious. You are rich, respected, admired, beloved; you are happy, as once I was. You are a man to be missed. For me it is no matter. We will go back; you will be ill, and I cannot be responsible. Besides, there is Luchesi —— "

"Enough," he said; "the cough is a mere nothing; it will not kill me. I shall not die of a cough."

"True — true," I replied; "and, indeed, I had no intention of alarming you unnecessarily; but you should use all proper caution. A draught of this Medoc will defend us from the damps."

Here I knocked off the neck of a bottle which I drew from a long row of its fellows that lay upon the mould.

"Drink," I said, presenting him the wine.

He raised it to his lips with a leer. He paused and nodded to me familiarly, while his bells jingled.

"I drink," he said, "to the buried that repose around us."

"And I to your long life."

He again took my arm, and we proceeded.

"These vaults," he said, "are extensive."

"The Montresors," I replied. "were a great and numerous family."

"I forget your arms."

"A huge human foot d'or,[3] in a field azure; the foot crushes a serpent rampant whose fangs are imbedded in the heel."

"And the motto?"

"*Nemo me impune lacessit.*"[4]

"Good!" he said.

The wine sparkled in his eyes and the bells jingled. My own fancy grew warm with the Medoc. We had passed through walls of piled bones, with casks and puncheons intermingling, into the inmost recesses of the catacombs. I paused again, and this time I made bold to seize Fortunato by an arm above the elbow.

"The nitre!" I said; "see, it increases. It hangs like moss upon the vaults. We are below the river's bed. The drops of moisture trickle among the bones. Come, we will go back ere it is too late. Your cough —— "

"It is nothing," he said; "let us go on. But first, another draught of the Medoc."

[3] of gold.
[4] "No one wounds me with impunity"; the motto of the royal arms of Scotland.

I broke and reached him a flagon of De Grâve. He emptied it at a breath. His eyes flashed with a fierce light. He laughed and threw the bottle upward with a gesticulation I did not understand.

I looked at him in surprise. He repeated the movement — a grotesque one.

"You do not comprehend?" he said.

"Not I," I replied.

"Then you are not of the brotherhood."

"How?"

"You are not of the masons."

"Yes, yes," I said; "yes, yes."

"You? Impossible! A mason?"

"A mason," I replied.

"A sign," he said.

"It is this," I answered, producing a trowel from beneath the folds of my *roquelaire.*

"You jest," he exclaimed, recoiling a few paces. "But let us proceed to the Amontillado."

"Be it so," I said, replacing the tool beneath the cloak, and again offering him my arm. He leaned upon it heavily. We continued our route in search of the Amontillado. We passed through a range of low arches, descended, passed on, and descending again, arrived at a deep crypt, in which the foulness of the air caused our flambeaux rather to glow than flame.

At the most remote end of the crypt there appeared another less spacious. Its walls had been lined with human remains, piled to the vault overhead, in the fashion of the great catacombs of Paris. Three sides of this interior crypt were still ornamented in this manner. From the fourth the bones had been thrown down, and lay promiscuously upon the earth, forming at one point a mound of some size. Within the wall thus exposed by the displacing of the bones, we perceived a still interior recess, in depth about four feet, in width three, in height six or seven. It seemed to have been constructed for no especial use within itself, but formed merely the interval between two of the colossal supports of the roof of the catacombs, and was backed by one of their circumscribing walls of solid granite.

It was in vain that Fortunato, uplifting his dull torch, endeavored to pry into the depth of the recess. Its termination the feeble light did not enable us to see.

"Proceed," I said; "herein is the Amontillado. As for Luchesi ——"

"He is an ignoramus," interrupted my friend, as he stepped unsteadily forward, while I followed immediately at his heels. In an instant he had reached the extremity of the niche, and finding his progress arrested by the rock, stood stupidly bewildered. A moment more and I had fettered him to the granite. In its surface were two iron staples, distant from each other about two feet, horizontally. From one of these depended a short chain, from the other a padlock. Throwing the links about his waist, it was but the work of a few seconds to secure it. He was too much astounded to resist. Withdrawing the key I stepped back from the recess.

"Pass your hand," I said, "over the wall; you cannot help feeling the nitre. Indeed it is *very* damp. Once more let me *implore* you to return. No? Then I must positively leave you. But I must first render you all the little attentions in my power."

"The Amontillado!" ejaculated my friend, not yet recovered from his astonishment.

"True," I replied; "the Amontillado."

As I said these words I busied myself among the pile of bones of which I have before spoken. Throwing them aside, I soon uncovered a quantity of building stone and mortar. With these materials and with the aid of my trowel, I began vigorously to wall up the entrance of the niche.

I had scarcely laid the first tier of the masonry when I discovered that the intoxication of Fortunato had in a great measure worn off. The earliest indication I had of this was a low moaning cry from the depth of the recess. It was *not* the cry of a drunken man. There was then a long and obstinate silence. I laid the second tier, and the third, and the fourth; and then I heard the furious vibrations of the chain. The noise lasted for several minutes, during which, that I might hearken to it with the more satisfaction, I ceased my labors and sat down upon the bones. When at last the clanking subsided, I resumed the trowel, and finished without interruption the fifth, the sixth, and the seventh tier. The wall was now nearly upon a level with my breast. I again paused, and holding the flambeaux over the masonwork, threw a few feeble rays upon the figure within.

A succession of loud and shrill screams, bursting suddenly from the throat of the chained form, seemed to thrust me violently back. For a brief moment I hesitated — I trembled. Unsheathing my rapier, I began to grope with it about the recess; but the thought of an instant reassured me. I placed my hand upon the solid fabric of the catacombs, and felt satisfied. I reapproached the wall. I replied to the yells of him who clamored. I re-echoed — I aided — I surpassed them in volume and in strength. I did this, and the clamorer grew still.

It was now midnight, and my task was drawing to a close. I had completed the eighth, the ninth, and the tenth tier. I had finished a portion of the last and the eleventh; there remained but a single stone to be fitted and plastered in. I struggled with its weight; I placed it partially in its destined position. But now there came from out the niche a low laugh that erected the hairs upon my head. It was succeeded by a sad voice, which I had difficulty in recognizing as that of the noble Fortunato. The voice said —

"Ha! ha! ha! — he! he! — a very good joke indeed — an excellent jest. We will have many a rich laugh about it at the palazzo — he! he! he! — over our wine — he! he! he!"

"The Amontillado!" I said.

"He! he! he! — he! he! he! — yes, the Amontillado. But is it not getting late? Will not they be awaiting us at the palazzo, the Lady Fortunato and the rest? Let us be gone."

"Yes," I said, "let us be gone."

"*For the love of God, Montresor!*"

"Yes," I said, "for the love of God!"

But to these words I hearkened in vain for a reply. I grew impatient. I called aloud:

"Fortunato!"

No answer. I called again:

"Fortunato!"

No answer still. I thrust a torch through the remaining aperture and let it fall within. There came forth in return only a jingling of the bells. My heart grew sick — on account of the dampness of the catacombs. I hastened to make an end of my labor. I forced the last stone into its position; I plastered it up. Against the new masonry I re-erected the old rampart of bones. For the half of a century no mortal has disturbed them. *In pace requiescat!*

[1846]

Edgar Allan Poe

∾

THE OVAL PORTRAIT

The chateau in which my valet had ventured to make forcible entrance, rather than permit me, in my desperately wounded condition, to pass a night in the open air, was one of those piles of commingled gloom and grandeur which have so long frowned among the Apennines, not less in fact than in fancy of Mrs. Radcliffe. To all appearance it had been temporarily and very lately abandoned. We established ourselves in one of the smallest and least sumptuously furnished apartments. It lay in a remote turret of the building. Its decorations were rich, yet tattered and antique. Its walls were hung with tapestry and bedecked with manifold and multiform armorial trophies, together with an unusually great number of very spirited modern paintings in frames of rich golden arabesque. In these paintings, which depended from the walls not only in their main surfaces, but in very many nooks which the bizarre architecture of the chateau rendered necessary — in these paintings my incipient delirium, perhaps, had caused me to take deep interest; so that I bade Pedro to close the heavy shutters of the room — since it was already night — to light the tongues of a tall candelabrum which stood by the head of my bed — and to throw open far and wide the fringed curtains of black velvet which enveloped the bed itself. I wished all this done that I might resign myself, if not to sleep, at least alternately to the contemplation of these pictures, and the perusal of a small volume which had been found upon the pillow, and which purported to criticise and describe them.

Long — long I read — and devoutly, devotedly I gazed. Rapidly and gloriously the hours flew by, and the deep midnight came. The position of the candelabrum displeased me, and outstretching my hand with difficulty, rather than disturb my slumbering valet, I placed it so as to throw its rays more fully upon the book.

But the action produced an effect altogether unanticipated. The rays of the numerous candles (for there were many) now fell within a niche of the room which had hitherto been thrown into deep shade by one of the bed-posts. I thus saw in vivid light a picture all unnoticed before. It was the portrait of a young girl just ripening into womanhood. I glanced at the painting hurriedly, and then closed my eyes. Why I did this was not at first apparent even to my own perception. But while my lids remained thus shut, I ran over in mind my reason for so shutting them. It was an impulsive movement to gain time for thought — to make sure that my vision had not deceived me — to calm and subdue my fancy for a more sober and more certain gaze. In a very few moments I again looked fixedly at the painting.

That I now saw aright I could not and would not doubt; for the first flashing of the candles upon that canvas had seemed to dissipate the dreamy stupor which was stealing over my senses, and to startle me at once into waking life.

The portrait, I have already said, was that of a young girl. It was a mere head and shoulders, done in what is technically termed a *vignette* manner; much in the style of the favorite heads of Sully.[1] The arms, the bosom and even the ends of the radiant hair, melted imperceptibly into the vague yet deep shadow which formed the background of the whole. The frame was oval, richly gilded and filagreed in *Moresque*.[2] As a thing of art nothing could be more admirable than the painting itself. But it could have been neither the execution of the work, nor the immortal beauty of the countenance, which had so suddenly and so vehemently moved me. Least of all, could it have been that my fancy, shaken from its half slumber, had mistaken the head for that of a living person. I saw at once that the peculiarities of the design, of the *vignetting*, and of the frame, must have instantly dispelled such idea — must have prevented even its momentary entertainment. Thinking earnestly upon these points, I remained, for an hour perhaps, half sitting, half reclining, with my vision riveted upon the portrait. At length, satisfied with the true secret of its effect, I fell back within the bed. I had found the spell of the picture in an absolute *life-likeliness* of expression, which at first startling, finally confounded, subdued and appalled me. With deep and reverent awe I replaced the candelabrum in its former position. The cause of my deep agitation being thus shut from view,

---

[1] Thomas Sully (1783–1872), one of the best-known American portrait painters of the nineteenth century.

[2] in the Moorish style.

I sought eagerly the volume which discussed the paintings and their histories. Turning to the number which designated the oval portrait, I there read the vague and quaint words which follow:

"She was a maiden of rarest beauty, and not more lovely than full of glee. And evil was the hour when she saw, and loved, and wedded the painter. He, passionate, studious, austere, and having already a bride in his Art; she a maiden of rarest beauty, and not more lovely than full of glee; all light and smiles, and frolicksome as the young fawn: loving and cherishing all things: hating only the Art which was her rival: dreading only the palette and brushes and other untoward instruments which deprived her of the countenance of her lover. It was thus a terrible thing for this lady to hear the painter speak of his desire to portray even his young bride. But she was humble and obedient, and sat meekly for many weeks in the dark high turret-chamber where the light dripped upon the pale canvas only from overhead. But he, the painter, took glory in his work, which went on from hour to hour and from day to day. And he was a passionate, and wild and moody man, who became lost in reveries; so that he *would* not see that the light which fell so ghastly in that lone turret withered the health and the spirits of his bride, who pined visibly to all but him. Yet she smiled on and still on, uncomplainingly, because she saw that the painter, (who had high renown,) took a fervid and burning pleasure in his task, and wrought day and night to depict her who so loved him, yet who grew daily more dispirited and weak. And in sooth some who beheld the portrait spoke of its resemblance in low words, as of a mighty marvel, and a proof not less of the power of the painter than of his deep love for her whom he depicted so surpassingly well. But at length, as the labor drew nearer to its conclusion, there were admitted none into the turret; for the painter had grown wild with the ardor of his work, and turned his eyes from the canvas rarely, even to regard the countenance of his wife. And he *would* not see that the tints which he spread upon the canvas were drawn from the cheeks of her who sate beside him. And when many weeks had passed, and but little remained to do, save one brush upon the mouth and one tint upon the eye, the spirit of the lady again flickered up as the flame within the socket of the lamp. And then the brush was given, and then the tint was placed; and, for one moment, the painter stood entranced before the work which he had wrought; but in the next, while he yet gazed, he grew tremulous and very pallid, and aghast, and crying with a loud voice, 'This is indeed *Life* itself!' turned suddenly to regard his beloved: — *She was dead!*"

[1842]

NIKOLAI GOGOL (1809–1852) *broke through the eighteenth-century literary conventions that prevailed in his time. He is considered the father of Russian realism — "We all came out from under Gogol's 'Overcoat'" is a remark variously attributed to Ivan Turgenev, Leo Tolstoy, and Fyodor Dostoevsky, and that literary critics feel any of these writers might have said it indicates the story's importance. But Gogol brilliantly used techniques of romanticism and fantasy in his fiction as well.*

Born in the town of Sorochintsky in the Russian Ukraine, the son of a deeply religious mother and a father who owned a small amount of land, Gogol attended a provincial grammar school. At the age of twelve he was sent away to a boarding school; he was so sickly and unattractive that the other students gave him the name "the mysterious dwarf." In 1828, after he left school, Gogol's health improved. He moved to St. Petersburg (then the capital of Russia), passed the civil service examinations, and held various government jobs, but he also entered the literary life of the city, becoming a friend of Alexander Pushkin, the great Russian poet. In 1831 and 1832 Gogol published a two-volume collection of stories, Evenings on a Farm near Dikanka, *and in 1835 a historical novel about the Ukrainian Cossacks,* Taras Bulba. *In 1836 his play* The Inspector General, *a satire ridiculing Russian officials, was considered so dangerously critical of the government that Gogol was forced into a more or less permanent exile in Rome. There he worked on what he considered his most important book, the novel* Dead Souls, *which was published in 1842. In his long years abroad Gogol made several hectic visits to Russia, despite his worsening physical and mental health. He died, insane, at the age of forty-three.*

In The Lonely Voice, *his study of the short story, Frank O'Connor maintains that the expression "We all came out from under Gogol's 'Overcoat'" has a validity beyond its relevance for Russian writers. Written in 1840, "The Overcoat" is neither satiric nor heroic, but ultimately transcends both modes. O'Connor identifies it as "the first appearance in fiction of the Little Man." He goes on to define the special impact of the short story as the literary form that offers the reader an intense awareness of human loneliness. To O'Connor, the short story (unlike the novel) never has a true hero. Instead it features "a submerged population group," which changes its character from writer to writer and generation to generation. "It may be Gogol's officials . . . Maupassant's prostitutes, Chekhov's doctors and teachers, Sherwood Anderson's provincials, always dreaming of escape." Everything about Akaky Akakievich in "The Overcoat" — his absurd name, his absurd family, his absurd job — is on the same level of mediocrity, and yet something about the little clerk moves us to pity and sympathy. When others torment him, we seem to hear him say, "Leave me alone! Why do you insult me? I am your brother." (See Nabokov's Commentary on Gogol on page 1229.)*

Nikolai Gogol

ဢ

THE OVERCOAT

–translated by Constance Garnett

In the department of . . . but I had better not mention which department. There is nothing in the world more touchy than a department, a regiment, a government office, and, in fact, any sort of official body. Nowadays every private individual considers all society insulted in his person. I have been told that very lately a complaint was lodged by a police inspector of which town I don't remember, and that in this complaint he set forth clearly that the institutions of the State were in danger and that his sacred name was being taken in vain; and, in proof thereof, he appended to his complaint an enormously long volume of some romantic work in which a police inspector appeared on every tenth page, occasionally, indeed, in an intoxicated condition. And so, to avoid any unpleasantness, we had better call the department of which we are speaking "a certain department."

And so, in a *certain department* there was a *certain clerk*; a clerk of whom it cannot be said that he was very remarkable; he was short, somewhat pockmarked, with rather reddish hair and rather dim, bleary eyes, with a small bald patch on the top of his head, with wrinkles on both sides of his cheeks and the sort of complexion which is usually described as hemorrhoidal . . . nothing can be done about that, it is the Petersburg climate. As for his grade in the civil service (for among us a man's rank is what must be established first) he was what is called a perpetual titular councilor, a class at which, as we all know, various writers who indulge in the praiseworthy habit of attacking those who cannot defend themselves jeer and jibe to their hearts' content. This clerk's surname was Bashmachkin. From the very name it is clear that it must have been derived from a shoe (*bashmak*); but when and under what circumstances it was derived from a shoe, it is impossible to say. Both his father and his grandfather and even his brother-in-law, and all the Bashmachkins without exception wore boots, which they simply resoled two or three times a year. His name was Akaky Akakievich. Perhaps it may strike the reader as a rather strange and contrived name, but I can assure him that it was not contrived at all, that the circumstances were such that it was quite out of the question to give him any other name. Akaky Akakievich was born toward nightfall, if my memory does not deceive me, on the twenty-third of March. His mother, the wife of a government clerk, a very good woman, made arrangements in due course to christen the child. She was still lying in bed, facing the door, while on her right hand stood the godfather, an excellent man called Ivan Ivanovich Yeroshkin, one of the head clerks in the Senate, and the godmother, the wife of a police official and a woman of rare qualities, Arina Semeonovna Belobriushkova. Three names were offered to the happy mother for selection — Mokky, Sossy, or the name of the martyr Khozdazat. "No," thought the poor lady, "they are all such names!" To satisfy her, they opened the calendar at another page, and the names which turned up were: Trifily, Dula, Varakhasy. "What an infliction!" said the mother. "What names they all are! I really never heard such names. Varadat or Varukh would be bad enough, but Trifily and Varakhasy!" They turned over another page and the names were: Pavsikakhy and Vakhisy. "Well, I see," said the mother, "it is clear that it is his fate. Since that is how it is, he had better be named after his father; his father is Akaky; let the son be Akaky, too." This was how he came to be Akaky Akakievich. The baby was christened and cried and made sour faces during the ceremony, as though he foresaw that he would be a titular councilor. So that was how it all came to pass. We have reported it here so that the reader may see for himself that it happened quite inevitably and that to give him any other name was out of the question.

No one has been able to remember when and how long ago he entered the department, nor who gave him the job. Regardless of how many directors and higher officials of all sorts came and went, he was always seen in the same place, in the same position, at the very same duty, precisely the same copying clerk, so that they used to declare that he must have been born a copying clerk, uniform, bald patch, and all. No respect at all was shown him in the department. The porters, far from getting up from their seats when he came in, took no more notice of him than if a simple fly had flown across the reception room. His superiors treated him with a sort of despotic aloofness. The head clerk's assistant used to throw papers under his nose without even saying "Copy this" or "Here is an interesting, nice little case" or some agreeable remark of the sort, as is usually done in wellbred offices. And he would take it, gazing only at the paper without looking to see who had put it there and whether he had the right to do so; he would take it and at once begin copying it. The young clerks jeered and made jokes at him to the best of their clerkly wit, and told before his face all sorts of stories of their own invention about him; they would say of his landlady, an old woman of seventy, that she beat him, would ask when the wedding was to take place, and would scatter bits of paper on his head, calling them snow. Akaky Akakievich never answered a word, however, but behaved as though there were no one there. It had no influence on his work; in the midst of all this teasing, he never made a single mistake in his copying. It was only when the jokes became too unbearable, when they jolted his arm, and prevented him from going on with his work, that he would say: "Leave me alone! Why do you insult me?" and there was something touching in the words and in the voice in which they were uttered. There was a note in it of something that aroused compassion, so that one young man, new to the office, who, following the example of the rest, had allowed himself to tease him, suddenly stopped as though cut to the heart, and from that time on, everything was, as it were, changed and appeared in a different light to him. Some unseen force seemed to repel him from the companions with whom he had become acquainted because he thought they were well-bred and decent men. And long afterward, during moments of the greatest gaiety, the figure of the humble little clerk with a bald patch on his head appeared before him with his heart-rending words: "Leave me alone! Why do you insult me?" and within those moving words he heard others: "I am your brother." And the poor young man hid his face in his hands, and many times afterward in his life he shuddered, seeing how much inhumanity there is in man, how much savage brutality lies hidden under refined, cultured politeness, and, my God! even in a man whom the world accepts as a gentleman and a man of honor. . . .

It would be hard to find a man who lived for his work as did Akaky Akakievich. To say that he was zealous in his work is not enough; no, he loved his work. In it, in that copying, he found an interesting and pleasant world of his own. There was a look of enjoyment on his face; certain letters were favorites with him, and when he came to them he was delighted; he chuckled to himself and winked and moved his lips, so that it seemed as though every letter his pen was forming could be read in his face. If rewards had been given according to the measure of zeal in the service, he might to his amazement have even found himself a civil councilor; but all he gained in the service, as the wits, his fellow clerks, expressed it, was a button in his buttonhole[1] and hemorrhoids where he sat. It cannot be said, however, that no notice had ever been taken of him. One director, being a good-natured man and anxious to reward him for his long service, sent him something a little more important than his ordinary copying; he was instructed to make some sort of report from a finished document for another office; the work consisted only of altering the headings and in places changing the first person into the third. This cost him so much effort that he was covered with perspiration: he mopped his brow and said at last, "No, I'd rather copy something."

From that time on they left him to his copying forever. It seemed as though nothing in the world existed for him except his copying. He gave no thought at all to his clothes; his uniform was — well, not green but some sort of rusty, muddy color. His collar was very low and narrow, so that, although his neck was not particularly long, yet, standing out of the collar, it looked as immensely long as those of the dozens of plaster kittens with nodding heads which foreigners carry about on their heads and peddle in Russia. And there were always things sticking to his uniform, either bits of hay or threads; moreover, he had a special knack of passing under a window

[1] whereas most clerks of long service wore a medal of achievement. (Leonard J. Kent, ed., *The Complete Tales of Nicolai Gogol*, vol 2 [Chicago: University of Chicago Press, 1985].)

at the very moment when various garbage was being flung out into the
street, and so was continually carrying off bits of melon rind and similar litter on his hat. He had never once in his life noticed what was being done
and what was going on in the street, all those things at which, as we all
know, his colleagues, the young clerks, always stare, utilizing their keen
sight so well that they notice anyone on the other side of the street with a
strap hanging loose — an observation which always calls forth a sly grin.
Whatever Akaky Akakievich looked at, he saw nothing but his clear, evenly
written lines, and it was only perhaps when a horse suddenly appeared from
nowhere and placed its head on his shoulder, and with its nostrils blew a
real gale upon his cheek, that he would notice that he was not in the middle
of his writing, but rather in the middle of the street.

On reaching home, he would sit down at once at the table, hurriedly
eat his soup and a piece of beef with an onion; he did not notice the taste at
all but ate it all with the flies and anything else that Providence happened
to send him. When he felt that his stomach was beginning to be full, he
would get up from the table, take out a bottle of ink, and begin copying the
papers he had brought home with him. When he had none to do, he would
make a copy especially for his own pleasure, particularly if the document
were remarkable not for the beauty of its style but because it was addressed
to some new or distinguished person.

Even at those hours when the gray Petersburg sky is completely overcast and the whole population of clerks have dined and eaten their fill, each
as best he can, according to the salary he receives and his personal tastes;
when they are all resting after the scratching of pens and bustle of the office, their own necessary work and other people's, and all the tasks that an
overzealous man voluntarily sets himself even beyond what is necessary;
when the clerks are hastening to devote what is left of their time to pleasure; some more enterprising are flying to the theater, others to the street to
spend their leisure staring at women's hats, some to spend the evening paying compliments to some attractive girl, the star of a little official circle,
while some — and this is the most frequent of all — go simply to a fellow
clerk's apartment on the third or fourth story, two little rooms with a hall or
a kitchen, with some pretensions to style, with a lamp or some such article
that has cost many sacrifices of dinners and excursions — at the time when
all the clerks are scattered about the apartments of their friends, playing a
stormy game of whist, sipping tea out of glasses, eating cheap biscuits,
sucking in smoke from long pipes, telling, as the cards are dealt, some scandal that has floated down from higher circles, a pleasure which the Russian
can never by any possibility deny himself, or, when there is nothing better
to talk about, repeating the everlasting anecdote of the commanding officer
who was told that the tail had been cut off the horse on the Falconet monument[2] — in short, even when everyone was eagerly seeking entertainment,

---

[2] famous statue of Peter the First. (Kent, ed.)

Akaky Akakievich did not indulge in any amusement. No one could say that they had ever seen him at an evening party. After working to his heart's content, he would go to bed, smiling at the thought of the next day and wondering what God would send him to copy. So flowed on the peaceful life of a man who knew how to be content with his fate on a salary of four hundred rubles, and so perhaps it would have flowed on to extreme old age, had it not been for the various disasters strewn along the road of life, not only of titular, but even of privy, actual court, and all other councilors, even those who neither give counsel to others nor accept it themselves.

There is in Petersburg a mighty foe of all who receive a salary of about four hundred rubles. That foe is none other than our northern frost, although it is said to be very good for the health. Between eight and nine in the morning, precisely at the hour when the streets are filled with clerks going to their departments, the frost begins indiscriminately giving such sharp and stinging nips at all their noses that the poor fellows don't know what to do with them. At that time, when even those in the higher grade have a pain in their brows and tears in their eyes from the frost, the poor titular councilors are sometimes almost defenseless. Their only protection lies in running as fast as they can through five or six streets in a wretched, thin little overcoat and then warming their feet thoroughly in the porter's room, till all their faculties and talents for their various duties thaw out again after having been frozen on the way. Akaky Akakievich had for some time been feeling that his back and shoulders were particularly nipped by the cold, although he did try to run the regular distance as fast as he could. He wondered at last whether there were any defects in his overcoat. After examining it thoroughly in the privacy of his home, he discovered that in two or three places, on the back and the shoulders, it had become a regular sieve; the cloth was so worn that you could see through it and the lining was coming out. I must note that Akaky Akakievich's overcoat had also served as a butt for the jokes of the clerks. It had even been deprived of the honorable name of overcoat and had been referred to as the "dressing gown."[3] It was indeed of rather a peculiar make. Its collar had been growing smaller year by year as it served to patch the other parts. The patches were not good specimens of the tailor's art, and they certainly looked clumsy and ugly. On seeing what was wrong, Akaky Akakievich decided that he would have to take the overcoat to Petrovich, a tailor who lived on the fourth floor up a back staircase, and, in spite of having only one eye and being pockmarked all over his face, was rather successful in repairing the trousers and coats of clerks and others — that is, when he was sober, be it understood, and had no other enterprise on his mind. Of this tailor I ought not, of course, say much, but since it is now the rule that the character of every person in a novel must be completely described, well, there's nothing I can do but describe Petrovich too. At first he was called simply Grigory, and was a serf

[3] *kapot*, usually a woman's garment. (Kent, ed.)

belonging to some gentleman or other. He began to be called Petrovich[4] from the time that he got his freedom and began to drink rather heavily on every holiday, at first only on the main holidays, but afterward, on all church holidays indiscriminately, wherever there was a cross in the calendar. In this he was true to the customs of his forefathers, and when he quarreled with his wife he used to call her a worldly woman and a German. Since we have now mentioned the wife, it will be necessary to say a few words about her, too, but unfortunately not much is known about her, except indeed that Petrovich had a wife and that she wore a cap and not a kerchief, but apparently she could not boast of beauty; anyway, none but soldiers of the guard peered under her cap when they met her, and they twitched their mustaches and gave vent to a rather peculiar sound.

As he climbed the stairs leading to Petrovich's — which, to do them justice, were all soaked with water and slops and saturated through and through with that smell of ammonia which makes the eyes smart, and is, as we all know, inseparable from the backstairs of Petersburg houses — Akaky Akakievich was already wondering how much Petrovich would ask for the job, and inwardly resolving not to give more than two rubles. The door was open, because Petrovich's wife was frying some fish and had so filled the kitchen with smoke that you could not even see the cockroaches. Akaky Akakievich crossed the kitchen unnoticed by the good woman, and walked at last into a room where he saw Petrovich sitting on a big, wooden, unpainted table with his legs tucked under him like a Turkish pasha. The feet, as is usual with tailors when they sit at work, were bare; and the first object that caught Akaky Akakievich's eye was the big toe, with which he was already familiar, with a misshapen nail as thick and strong as the shell of a tortoise. Around Petrovich's neck hung a skein of silk and another of thread and on his knees was a rag of some sort. He had for the last three minutes been trying to thread his needle, but could not get the thread into the eye and so was very angry with the darkness and indeed with the thread itself, muttering in an undertone: "She won't go in, the savage! You wear me out, you bitch." Akaky Akakievich was unhappy that he had come just at the minute when Petrovich was in a bad humor; he liked to give him an order when he was a little "elevated," or, as his wife expressed it, "had fortified himself with vodka, the one-eyed devil." In such circumstances Petrovich was as a rule very ready to give way and agree, and invariably bowed and thanked him. Afterward, it is true, his wife would come wailing that her husband had been drunk and so had asked too little, but adding a single ten-kopek piece would settle that. But on this occasion Petrovich was apparently sober and consequently curt, unwilling to bargain, and the devil knows what price he would be ready to demand. Akaky Akakievich realized this, and was, as the saying is, beating a retreat, but things had gone too far,

---

[4] customarily, serfs were addressed by first name only, while free men were addressed either by first name and patronymic or just the patronymic. (Kent, ed.)

for Petrovich was screwing up his solitary eye very attentively at him and Akaky Akakievich involuntarily said: "Good day, Petrovich!"

"I wish you a good day, sir," said Petrovich, and squinted at Akaky Akakievich's hands, trying to discover what sort of goods he had brought.

"Here I have come to you, Petrovich, do you see . . . !"

It must be noticed that Akaky Akakievich for the most part explained himself by apologies, vague phrases, and meaningless parts of speech which have absolutely no significance whatever. If the subject were a very difficult one, it was his habit indeed to leave his sentences quite unfinished, so that very often after a sentence had begun with the words, "It really is, don't you know . . ." nothing at all would follow and he himself would be quite oblivious to the fact that he had not finished his thought, supposing he had said all that was necessary.

"What is it?" said Petrovich, and at the same time with his solitary eye he scrutinized his whole uniform from the collar to the sleeves, the back, the skirts, the buttonholes — with all of which he was very familiar since they were all his own work. Such scrutiny is habitual with tailors; it is the first thing they do on meeting one.

"It's like this, Petrovich . . . the overcoat, the cloth . . . you see everywhere else it is quite strong; it's a little dusty and looks as though it were old, but it is new and it is only in one place just a little . . . on the back, and just a little worn on one shoulder and on this shoulder, too, a little . . . do you see? that's all, and it's not much work . . ."

Petrovich took the "dressing gown," first spread it out over the table, examined it for a long time, shook his head, and put his hand out to the window sill for a round snuffbox with a portrait on the lid of some general — which general I can't exactly say, for a finger had been thrust through the spot where a face should have been, and the hole had been pasted over with a square piece of paper. After taking a pinch of snuff, Petrovich held the "dressing gown" up in his hands and looked at it against the light, and again he shook his head; then he turned it with the lining upward and once more shook his head; again he took off the lid with the general pasted up with paper and snuffed a pinch into his nose, shut the box, put it away, and at last said: "No, it can't be repaired; a wretched garment!" Akaky Akakievich's heart sank at those words.

"Why can't it, Petrovich?" he said, almost in the imploring voice of a child. "Why, the only thing is, it is a bit worn on the shoulders; why, you have got some little pieces . . ."

"Yes, the pieces will be found all right," Petrovich, "but it can't be patched, the stuff is rotten; if you put a needle in it, it would give way."

"Let it give way, but you just put a patch on it."

"There is nothing to put a patch on. There is nothing for it to hold on to; there is a great strain on it; it is not worth calling cloth; it would fly away at a breath of wind."

"Well, then, strengthen it with something — I'm sure, really, this is . . ."

"No," said Petrovich resolutely, "there is nothing that can be done, the thing is no good at all. You had far better, when the cold winter weather comes, make yourself leg wrappings out of it, for there is no warmth in stockings; the Germans invented them just to make money." (Petrovich enjoyed a dig at the Germans occasionally.) "And as for the overcoat, it is obvious that you will have to have a new one."

At the word "new" there was a mist before Akaky Akakievich's eyes, and everything in the room seemed blurred. He could see nothing clearly but the general with the piece of paper over his face on the lid of Petrovich's snuffbox.

"A new one?" he said, still feeling as though he were in a dream; "why, I haven't the money for it."

"Yes, a new one," Petrovich repeated with barbarous composure.

"Well, and if I did have a new one, how much would it . . . ?"

"You mean what will it cost?"

"Yes."

"Well, at least one hundred and fifty rubles," said Petrovich, and he compressed his lips meaningfully. He was very fond of making an effect; he was fond of suddenly disconcerting a man completely and then squinting sideways to see what sort of a face he made.

"A hundred and fifty rubles for an overcoat!" screamed poor Akaky Akakievich — it was perhaps the first time he had screamed in his life, for he was always distinguished by the softness of his voice.

"Yes," said Petrovich, "and even then it depends on the coat. If I were to put marten on the collar, and add a hood with silk linings, it would come to two hundred."

"Petrovich, please," said Akaky Akakievich in an imploring voice, not hearing and not trying to hear what Petrovich said, and missing all his effects, "repair it somehow, so that it will serve a little longer."

"No, that would be wasting work and spending money for nothing," said Petrovich, and after that Akaky Akakievich went away completely crushed, and when he had gone Petrovich remained standing for a long time with his lips pursed up meaningfully before he began his work again, feeling pleased that he had not demeaned himself or lowered the dignity of the tailor's art.

When he got into the street, Akaky Akakievich felt as though he was in a dream. "So that is how it is," he said to himself. "I really did not think it would be this way . . ." and then after a pause he added, "So that's it! So that's how it is at last! and I really could never have supposed it would be this way. And there . . ." There followed another long silence, after which he said: "So that's it! well, it really is so utterly unexpected . . . who would have thought . . . what a circumstance . . ." Saying this, instead of going home he walked off in quite the opposite direction without suspecting what he was doing. On the way a clumsy chimney sweep brushed the whole of his sooty side against him and blackened his entire shoulder; a whole hatful of plaster scattered upon him from the top of a house that was being built.

He noticed nothing of this, and only after he had jostled against a police-man who had set his halberd down beside him and was shaking some snuff out of his horn into his rough fist, he came to himself a little and then only because the policeman said: "Why are you poking yourself right in one's face, haven't you enough room on the street?" This made him look around and turn homeward; only there he began to collect his thoughts, to see his position in a clear and true light, and began talking to himself no longer in-coherently but reasonably and openly as with a sensible friend with whom one can discuss the most intimate and vital matters. "No," said Akaky Akakievich, "it is no use talking to Petrovich now; just now he really is . . . his wife must have been giving it to him. I had better go to him on Sunday morning; after Saturday night he will have a crossed eye and be sleepy, so he'll want a little drink and his wife won't give him a kopek. I'll slip ten kopeks into his hand and then he will be more accommodating and maybe take the overcoat . . ."

So reasoning with himself, Akaky Akakievich cheered up and waited until the next Sunday; then, seeing from a distance Petrovich's wife leaving the house, he went straight in. Petrovich certainly had a crossed eye after Saturday. He could hardly hold his head up and was very drowsy; but, de-spite all that, as soon as he heard what Akaky Akakievich was speaking about, it seemed as though the devil had nudged him. "I can't," he said, "you must order a new one." Akaky Akakievich at once slipped a ten-kopek piece into his hand. "I thank you, sir, I will have just a drop to your health, but don't trouble yourself about the overcoat; it is no good for anything. I'll make you a fine new coat; you can have faith in me for that."

Akaky Akakievich would have said more about repairs, but Petrovich, without listening, said: "A new one I'll make you without fail; you can rely on that; I'll do my best. It could even be like the fashion that is popular, with the collar to fasten with silver-plated hooks under a flap."

Then Akaky Akakievich saw that there was no escape from a new overcoat and he was utterly depressed. How indeed, for what, with what money could he get it? Of course he could to some extent rely on the bonus for the coming holiday, but that money had long been appropriated and its use determined beforehand. It was needed for new trousers and to pay the cobbler an old debt for putting some new tops on some old boots, and he had to order three shirts from a seamstress as well as two items of undergar-ments which it is indecent to mention in print; in short, all that money ab-solutely must be spent, and even if the director were to be so gracious as to give him a holiday bonus of forty-five or even fifty, instead of forty rubles, there would be still left a mere trifle, which would be but a drop in the ocean compared to the fortune needed for an overcoat. Though, of course, he knew that Petrovich had a strange craze for suddenly demanding the devil knows what enormous price, so that at times his own wife could not help crying out: "Why, you are out of your wits, you idiot! Another time he'll undertake a job for nothing, and here the devil has bewitched him to ask more than he is worth himself." Though, of course, he knew that Petrovich would undertake to make it for eighty rubles, still where would he get those eighty rubles? He might manage half of that sum; half of it could be found, perhaps even a little more; but where could he get the other half? . . . But, first of all, the reader ought to know where that first half was to be found. Akaky Akakievich had the habit every time he spent a ruble of putting aside two kopeks in a little box which he kept locked, with a slit in the lid for dropping in the money. At the end of every six months he would inspect the pile of coppers there and change them for small silver. He had done this for a long time, and in the course of many years the sum had mounted up to forty rubles and so he had half the money in his hands, but where was he to get the other half; where was he to get another forty rubles? Akaky Akakievich thought and thought and decided at last that he would have to diminish his ordinary expenses, at least for a year; give up burning candles in the evening, and if he had to do any work he must go into the landlady's room and work by her candle; that as he walked along the streets he must walk as lightly and carefully as possible, almost on tiptoe, on the cobbles and flagstones, so that his soles might last a little longer than usual; that he must send his linen to the wash less frequently, and that, to preserve it from being worn, he must take if off every day when he came home and sit in a thin cotton dressing gown, a very ancient garment which Time itself had spared. To tell the truth, he found it at first rather difficult to get used to these privations, but after a while it became a habit and went smoothly enough — he even became quite accustomed to being hungry in the evening; on the other hand, he had spiritual nourishment, for he carried ever in his thoughts the idea of his future overcoat. His whole existence had in a sense become fuller, as though he had married, as though some other person were present with him, as though he were no longer alone but an agreeable companion had consented to walk the path of life hand in hand with him, and that companion was none other than the new overcoat with its thick padding and its strong, durable lining. He became, as it were, more alive, even more strong-willed, like a man who has set before himself a definite goal. Uncertainty, indecision, in fact all the hesitating and vague characteristics, vanished from his face and his manners. At times there was a gleam in his eyes; indeed, the most bold and audacious ideas flashed through his mind. Why not really have marten on the collar? Meditation on the subject always made him absent-minded. On one occasion when he was copying a document, he very nearly made a mistake, so that he almost cried out "ough" aloud and crossed himself. At least once every month he went to Petrovich to talk about the overcoat: where it would be best to buy the cloth, and what color it should be, and what price; and, though he returned home a little anxious, he was always pleased at the thought that at last the time was at hand when everything would be bought and the overcoat would be made. Things moved even faster than he had anticipated. Contrary to all expectations, the director bestowed on Akaky Akakievich a bonus of no less than sixty rubles. Whether it was that he had an inkling that Akaky Akakievich needed a coat, or whether it happened by luck, owing to this he found he had twenty rubles extra. This circumstance hastened the course of affairs. Another two or three months of partial starvation and Akaky Akakievich had actually saved up nearly eighty rubles. His heart, as a rule very tranquil, began to throb.

The very first day he set out with Petrovich for the shops. They bought some very good cloth, and no wonder, since they had been thinking of it for more than six months, and scarcely a month had passed without their going out to the shop to compare prices; now Petrovich himself declared that there was no better cloth to be had. For the lining they chose calico, but of such good quality, that in Petrovich's words it was even better than silk, and actually as strong and handsome to look at. Marten they did not buy, because it was too expensive, but instead they chose cat fur, the best to be found in the shop — cat which in the distance might almost be taken for marten. Petrovich was busy making the coat for two weeks, because there was a great deal of quilting; otherwise it would have been ready sooner. Petrovich charged twelve rubles for the work; less than that it hardly could have been; everything was sewn with silk, with fine double seams, and Petrovich went over every seam afterwards with his own teeth, imprinting various patterns with them. It was . . . it is hard to say precisely on what day, but probably on the most triumphant day in the life of Akaky Akakievich, that Petrovich at last brought the overcoat. He brought it in the morning, just before it was time to set off for the department. The overcoat could not have arrived at a more opportune time, because severe frosts were just beginning and seemed threatening to become even harsher. Petrovich brought the coat himself as a good tailor should. There was an expression of importance on his face, such as Akaky Akakievich had never seen there before. He seemed fully conscious of having completed a work of no little importance and of having shown by his own example the gulf that separates tailors who only put in linings and do repairs from those who make new coats. He took the coat out of the huge handkerchief in which he had brought it (the handkerchief had just come home from the wash); he then folded it up and put it in his pocket for future use. After taking out the overcoat, he looked at it with much pride and holding it in both hands, threw it very deftly over Akaky Akakievich's shoulders, then pulled it down and smoothed it out behind with his hands; then draped it about Akaky Akakievich somewhat jauntily. Akaky Akakievich, a practical man, wanted to try it with his arms in the sleeves. Petrovich helped him to put it on, and it looked splendid with his arms in the sleeves, too. In fact, it turned out that the overcoat was completely and entirely successful. Petrovich did not let slip the occasion for observing that it was only because he lived in a small street and had no signboard, and because he had known Akaky Akakievich so long, that he had done it so cheaply, and that on Nevsky Prospekt they would have asked him seventy-five rubles for the tailoring alone. Akaky Akakievich had no inclination to discuss this with Petrovich; besides he was frightened of the big sums that Petrovich was fond of flinging airily about in conversation. He paid him, thanked him, and went off, with his new overcoat on, to the department. Petrovich followed him out and stopped in the street, staring for a long time at the coat from a distance and then purposely turned off and, taking a short cut through a side street, came back into the street, and got another view of the coat from the other side, that is, from the front.

Meanwhile Akaky Akakievich walked along in a gay holiday mood. Every second he was conscious that he had a new overcoat on his shoulders, and several times he actually laughed from inward satisfaction. Indeed, it had two advantages: one that it was warm and the other that it was good. He did not notice how far he had walked at all and he suddenly found himself in the department; in the porter's room he took off the overcoat, looked it over, and entrusted it to the porter's special care. I cannot tell how it happened, but all at once everyone in the department learned that Akaky Akakievich had a new overcoat and that the "dressing gown" no longer existed. They all ran out at once into the cloakroom to look at Akaky Akakievich's new overcoat; they began welcoming him and congratulating him so that at first he could do nothing but smile and then felt positively embarrassed. When, coming up to him, they all began saying that he must "sprinkle" the new overcoat and that he ought at least to buy them all a supper, Akaky Akakievich lost his head completely and did not know what to do, how to get out of it, nor what to answer. A few minutes later, flushing crimson, he even began assuring them with great simplicity that it was not a new overcoat at all, that it wasn't much, that it was an old overcoat. At last one of the clerks, indeed the assistant of the head clerk of the room, probably in order to show that he wasn't too proud to mingle with those beneath him, said: "So be it, I'll give a party instead of Akaky Akakievich and invite you all to tea with me this evening; as luck would have it, it is my birthday." The clerks naturally congratulated the assistant head clerk and eagerly accepted the invitation. Akaky Akakievich was beginning to make excuses, but they all declared that it was uncivil of him, that it would be simply a shame and a disgrace that he could not possibly refuse. So, he finally relented, and later felt pleased about it when he remembered that through this he would have the opportunity of going out in the evening, too, in his new overcoat. That whole day was for Akaky Akakievich the most triumphant and festive day in his life. He returned home in the happiest frame of mind, took off the overcoat, and hung it carefully on the wall, admiring the cloth and lining once more, and then pulled out his old "dressing gown," now completely falling apart, and put it next to his new overcoat to compare the two. He glanced at it and laughed: the difference was enormous! And long afterwards he went on laughing at dinner, as the position in which the "dressing gown" was placed recurred to his mind. He dined in excellent spirits and after dinner wrote nothing, no papers at all, but just relaxed for a little while on his bed, till it got dark; then, without putting things off, he dressed, put on his overcoat, and went out into the street. Where precisely the clerk who had invited him lived we regret to say we cannot tell; our memory is beginning to fail sadly, and everything there in Petersburg, all the streets and houses, are so blurred and muddled in our head that it is a very difficult business to put anything in orderly fashion. Regardless of that, there is no doubt that the clerk lived in the better part of the town and consequently a very long distance from Akaky Akakievich. At first Akaky Akakievich had to walk through deserted streets, scantily lighted, but as he approached his destination the streets became more lively, more full of people, and more brightly lighted; passers-by began to be more frequent, ladies began to appear, here and there beautifully dressed, and beaver collars were to be seen on the men. Cabmen with wooden, railed sledges, studded with brass-topped nails, were less frequently seen; on the other hand, jaunty drivers in raspberry-colored velvet caps, with lacquered sledges and bearskin rugs, appeared and carriages with decorated boxes dashed along the streets, their wheels crunching through the snow.

Akaky Akakievich looked at all this as a novelty; for several years he had not gone out into the streets in the evening. He stopped with curiosity before a lighted shop window to look at a picture in which a beautiful woman was represented in the act of taking off her shoe and displaying as she did so the whole of a very shapely leg, while behind her back a gentleman with whiskers and a handsome imperial on his chin was sticking his head in at the door. Akaky Akakievich shook his head and smiled and then went on his way. Why did he smile? Was it because he had come across something quite unfamiliar to him, though every man retains some instinctive feeling on the subject, or was it that he reflected, like many other clerks, as follows: "Well, those Frenchmen! It's beyond anything! If they go in for anything of the sort, it really is . . . !" Though possibly he did not even think that; there is no creeping into a man's soul and finding out all that he thinks. At last he reached the house in which the assistant head clerk lived in fine style; there was a lamp burning on the stairs, and the apartment was on the second floor. As he went into the hall Akaky Akakievich saw rows of galoshes. Among them in the middle of the room stood a hissing samovar puffing clouds of steam. On the walls hung coats and cloaks among which some actually had beaver collars or velvet lapels. From the other side of the wall there came noise and talk, which suddenly became clear and loud when the door opened and the footman came out with a tray full of empty glasses, a jug of cream, and a basket of biscuits. It was evident that the clerks had arrived long before and had already drunk their first glass of tea. Akaky Akakievich, after hanging up his coat with his own hands, went into the room, and at the same moment there flashed before his eyes a vision of candles, clerks, pipes, and card tables, together with the confused sounds of conversation rising up on all sides and the noise of moving chairs. He stopped very awkwardly in the middle of the room, looking about and trying to think of what to do, but he was noticed and received with a shout and they all went at once into the hall and again took a look at his overcoat. Though Akaky Akakievich was somewhat embarrassed, yet, being a simple-hearted man, he could not help being pleased at seeing how they all admired his coat. Then of course they all abandoned him and his coat, and turned their attention as usual to the tables set for whist. All this — the noise, the talk, and the crowd of people — was strange and wonderful to Akaky Akakievich. He simply did not know how to behave, what to do with his arms and legs and his whole body; at last he sat down beside the players, looked at the cards, stared first at one and then at another of the faces, and in a little while, feeling bored, began to yawn — especially since it was long past the time at which he usually went to bed. He tried to say goodbye to his hosts, but they would not let him go, saying that he absolutely must have a glass of champagne in honor of the new coat. An hour later supper was served, consisting of salad, cold veal, pastry and pies from the bakery, and champagne. They made Akaky Akakievich drink two glasses, after which he felt that things were much more cheerful, though he could not forget that it was twelve o'clock, and that he ought to have been home long ago. That his host might not take it into his head to detain him, he slipped out of the room, hunted in the hall for his coat, which he found, not without regret, lying on the floor, shook it, removed some fluff from it, put it on, and went down the stairs into the street. It was still light in the streets. Some little grocery shops, those perpetual clubs for servants and all sorts of people, were open; others which were closed showed, however, a long streak of light at every crack of the door, proving that they were not yet deserted, and probably maids and menservants were still finishing their conversation and discussion, driving their masters to utter perplexity as to their whereabouts. Akaky Akakievich walked along in a cheeful state of mind; he was even on the point of running, goodness knows why, after a lady of some sort who passed by like lightning with every part of her frame in violent motion. He checked himself at once, however, and again walked along very gently, feeling positively surprised at the inexplicable impulse that had seized him. Soon the deserted streets, which are not particularly cheerful by day and even less so in the evening, stretched before him. Now they were still more dead and deserted; the light of street lamps was scantier, the oil evidently running low; then came wooden houses and fences; not a soul anywhere; only the snow gleamed on the streets and the low-pitched slumbering hovels looked black and gloomy with their closed shutters. He approached the spot where the street was intersected by an endless square, which looked like a fearful desert with its houses scarcely visible on the far side.

In the distance, goodness knows where, there was a gleam of light from some sentry box which seemed to be at the end of the world. Akaky Akakievich's lightheartedness faded. He stepped into the square, not without uneasiness, as though his heart had a premonition of evil. He looked behind him and to both sides — it was as though the sea were all around him. "No, better not look," he thought, and walked on, shutting his eyes, and when he opened them to see whether the end of the square was near, he suddenly saw standing before him, almost under his very nose, some men with mustaches; just what they were like he could not even distinguish. There was a mist before his eyes, and a throbbing in his chest. "Why, that overcoat is mine!" said one of them in a voice like a clap of thunder, seizing him by the collar. Akaky Akakievich was on the point of shouting

"Help" when another put a fist the size of a clerk's head against his lips, saying: "You just shout now." Akaky Akakievich felt only that they took the overcoat off, and gave him a kick with their knees, and he fell on his face in the snow and was conscious of nothing more. A few minutes later he recovered consciousness and got up on his feet, but there was no one there. He felt that it was cold on the ground and that he had no overcoat, and began screaming, but it seemed as though his voice would not carry to the end of the square. Overwhelmed with despair and continuing to scream, he ran across the square straight to the sentry box beside which stood a policeman leaning on his halberd and, so it seemed, looking with curiosity to see who the devil the man was who was screaming and running toward him from the distance. As Akaky Akakievich reached him, he began breathlessly shouting that he was asleep and not looking after his duty not to see that a man was being robbed. The policeman answered that he had seen nothing, that he had only seen him stopped in the middle of the square by two men, and supposed that they were his friends, and that, instead of abusing him for nothing, he had better go the next day to the police inspector, who would certainly find out who had taken the overcoat. Akaky Akakievich ran home in a terrible state: his hair, which was still comparatively abundant on his temples and the back of his head, was completely disheveled; his sides and chest and his trousers were all covered with snow. When his old landlady heard a fearful knock at the door, she jumped hurriedly out of bed and, with only one slipper on, ran to open it, modestly holding her chemise over her bosom; but when she opened it she stepped back, seeing in what a state Akaky Akakievich was. When he told her what had happened, she clasped her hands in horror and said that he must go straight to the district commissioner, because the local police inspector would deceive him, make promises, and lead him a dance; that it would be best of all to go to the district commissioner, and that she knew him, because Anna, the Finnish girl who was once her cook, was now in service as a nurse at the commissioner's; and that she often saw him himself when he passed by their house, and that he used to be every Sunday at church too, saying his prayers and at the same time looking good-humoredly at everyone, and that therefore by every token he must be a kindhearted man. After listening to this advice, Akaky Akakievich made his way very gloomily to his room, and how he spent that night I leave to the imagination of those who are in the least able to picture the position of others.

Early in the morning he set off to the police commissioner's but was told that he was asleep. He came at ten o'clock, he was told again that he was asleep; he came at eleven and was told that the commissioner was not at home; he came at dinnertime, but the clerks in the anteroom would not let him in, and insisted on knowing what was the matter and what business had brought him and exactly what had happened; so that at last Akaky Akakievich for the first time in his life tried to show the strength of his character and said curtly that he must see the commissioner himself, and they dare not refuse to admit him, that he had come from the department on

government business, and that if he made complaint of them they would
see. The clerks dared say nothing to this, and one of them went to summon
the commissioner. The latter received his story of being robbed of his overcoat in an extremely peculiar manner. Instead of attending to the main
point, he began asking Akaky Akakievich questions: why had he been coming home so late? wasn't he going, or hadn't he been, to some bawdy house?
so that Akaky Akakievich was overwhelmed with confusion, and went away
without knowing whether or not the proper measures would be taken regarding his overcoat. He was absent from the office all that day (the only
time that it had happened in his life). Next day he appeared with a pale
face, wearing his old "dressing gown," which had become a still more pitiful sight. The news of the theft of the overcoat — though there were clerks
who did not let even this chance slip of jeering at Akaky Akakievich —
touched many of them. They decided on the spot to get up a collection for
him, but collected only a very trifling sum, because the clerks had already
spent a good deal contributing to the director's portrait and on the purchase
of a book, at the suggestion of the head of their department, who was a
friend of the author, and so the total realized was very insignificant. One of
the clerks, moved by compassion, ventured at any rate to assist Akaky Akakievich with good advice, telling him not to go to the local police inspector,
because, though it might happen that the latter might succeed in finding
his overcoat because he wanted to impress his superiors, it would remain in
the possession of the police unless he presented legal proofs that it belonged
to him; he urged that by far the best thing would be to appeal to a Person of
Consequence; that the Person of Consequence, by writing and getting into
communication with the proper authorities, could push the matter through
more successfully. There was nothing else to do. Akaky Akakievich made
up his mind to go to the Person of Consequence. What precisely was the
nature of the functions of the Person of Consequence has remained a matter of uncertainty. It must be noted that this Person of Consequence had
only lately become a person of consequence, and until recently had been a
person of no consequence. Though, indeed, his position even now was not
reckoned of consequence in comparison with others of still greater consequence. But there is always to be found a circle of persons to whom a person of little consequence in the eyes of others is a person of consequnce. It
is true that he did his utmost to increase the consequence of his position in
various ways, for instance by insisting that his subordinates should come
out onto the stairs to meet him when he arrived at his office; that no one
should venture to approach him directly but all proceedings should follow
the strictest chain of command; that a collegiate registrar should report the
matter to the governmental secretary; and the governmental secretary to the
titular councilors or whomsoever it might be, and that business should only
reach him through this channel. Everyone in Holy Russia has a craze for
imitation; everyone apes and mimics his superiors. I have actually been told
that a titular councilor who was put in charge of a small separate office, immediately partitioned off a special room for himself, calling it the head of-

fice, and posted lackeys at the door with red collars and gold braid, who took hold of the handle of the door and opened it for everyone who went in, though the "head office" was so tiny that it was with difficulty that an ordinary writing desk could be put into it. The manners and habits of the Person of Consequence were dignified and majestic, but hardly subtle. The chief foundation of his system was strictness; "strictness, strictness, and — strictness!" he used to say, and at the last word he would look very significantly at the person he was addressing, though, indeed, he had no reason to do so, for the dozen clerks who made up the whole administrative mechanism of his office stood in appropriate awe of him; any clerk who saw him in the distance would leave his work and remain standing at attention till his superior had left the room. His conversation with his subordinates was usually marked by severity and almost confined to three phrases: "How dare you? Do you know to whom you are speaking? Do you understand who I am?" He was, however, at heart a good-natured man, pleasant and obliging with his colleagues; but his advancement to a high rank had completely turned his head. When he received it, he was perplexed, thrown off his balance, and quite at a loss as to how to behave. If he chanced to be with his equals, he was still quite a decent man, a very gentlemanly man, in fact, and in many ways even an intelligent man; but as soon as he was in company with men who were even one grade below him, there was simply no doing anything with him: he sat silent and his position excited compassion, the more so as he himself felt that he might have been spending his time to so much more advantage. At times there could be seen in his eyes an intense desire to join in some interesting conversation, but he was restrained by the doubt whether it would not be too much on his part, whether it would not be too great a familiarity and lowering of his dignity, and in consequence of these reflections he remained everlastingly in the same mute condition, only uttering from time to time monosyllabic sounds, and in this way he gained the reputation of being a terrible bore.

So this was the Person of Consequence to whom our friend Akaky Akakievich appealed, and he appealed to him at a most unpropitious moment, very unfortunate for himself, though fortunate, indeed, for the Person of Consequence. The latter happened to be in his study, talking in the very best of spirits with an old friend of his childhood who had only just arrived and whom he had not seen for several years. It was at this moment that he was informed that a man called Bashmachkin was asking to see him. He asked abruptly, "What sort of man is he?" and received the answer, "A government clerk." "Ah! he can wait. I haven't time now," said the Person of Consequence. Here I must observe that this was a complete lie on the part of the Person of Consequence; he had time; his friend and he had long ago said all they had to say to each other and their conversation had begun to be broken by very long pauses during which they merely slapped each other on the knee, saying, "So that's how things are, Ivan Abramovich!" — "So that's it, Stepan Varlamovich!" but, despite that, he told the clerk to wait in order to show his friend, who had left the civil service some years before and was living at home in the country, how long clerks had to wait for him. At last, after they had talked or rather been silent, to their heart's content and had smoked a cigar in very comfortable armchairs with sloping backs, he seemed suddenly to recollect, and said to the secretary, who was standing at the door with papers for his signature: "Oh, by the way, there is a clerk waiting, isn't there? tell him he can come in." When he saw Akaky Akakievich's meek appearance and old uniform, he turned to him at once and said: "What do you want?" in a firm and abrupt voice, which he had purposely rehearsed in his own room in solitude before the mirror for a week before receiving his present post and the grade of a general. Akaky Akakievich, who was overwhelmed with appropriate awe beforehand, was somewhat confused and, as far as his tongue would allow him, explained to the best of his powers, with even more frequent "ers" than usual, that he had had a perfectly new overcoat and now he had been robbed of it in the most inhuman way, and that now he had come to beg him by his intervention either to correspond with his honor, the head police commissioner, or anybody else, and find the overcoat. This mode of proceeding struck the general for some reason as too familiar. "What next, sir?" he went on abruptly. "Don't you know the way to proceed? To whom are you addressing yourself? Don't you know how things are done? You ought first to have handed in a petition to the office; it would have gone to the head clerk of the room, and to the head clerk of the section; then it would have been handed to the secretary and the secretary would have brought it to me . . . ."

"But, your Excellency," said Akaky Akakievich, trying to gather the drop of courage he possessed and feeling at the same time that he was perspiring all over, "I ventured, your Excellency, to trouble you because secretaries . . . er . . . are people you can't depend on . . ."

"What? what? what?" said the Person of Consequence, "where did you get hold of that attitude? where did you pick up such ideas? What insubordination is spreading among young men against their superiors and their chiefs!" The Person of Consequence did not apparently observe that Akaky Akakievich was well over fifty, and therefore if he could have been called a young man it would only have been in comparison to a man of seventy. "Do you know to whom you are speaking? Do you understand who I am? Do you understand that, I ask you?" At this point he stamped, and raised his voice to such a powerful note that Akaky Akakievich was not the only one to be terrified. Akaky Akakievich was positively petrified; he staggered, trembling all over, and could not stand; if the porters had not run up to support him, he would have flopped on the floor; he was led out almost unconscious. The Person of Consequence, pleased that the effect had surpassed his expectations and enchanted at the idea that his words could even deprive a man of consciousness, stole a sideway glance at his friend to see how he was taking it, and perceived not without satisfaction that his friend was feeling very uncertain and even beginning to be a little terrified himself.

How he got downstairs, how he went out into the street — of all that Akaky Akakievich remembered nothing; he had no feeling in his arms or his legs. In all his life he had never been so severely reprimanded by a general, and this was by one of another department, too. He went out into the snowstorm that was whistling through the streets, with his mouth open, and as he went he stumbled off the pavement; the wind, as its way is in Petersburg, blew upon him from all points of the compass and from every side street. In an instant it had blown a quinsy into his throat, and when he got home he was not able to utter a word; he went to bed with a swollen face and throat. That's how violent the effects of an appropriate reprimand can be!

Next day he was in a high fever. Thanks to the gracious assistance of the Petersburg climate, the disease made more rapid progress than could have been expected, and when the doctor came, after feeling his pulse he could find nothing to do but prescribe a poultice, and that simply so that the patient might not be left without the benefit of medical assistance; however, two days later he informed him that his end was at hand, after which he turned to Akaky Akakievich's landlady and said: "And you had better lose no time, my good woman, but order him now a pine coffin, for an oak one will be too expensive for him." Whether Akaky Akakievich heard these fateful words or not, whether they produced a shattering effect upon him, and whether he regretted his pitiful life, no one can tell, for he was constantly in delirium and fever. Apparitions, each stranger than the one before, were continually haunting him: first he saw Petrovich and was ordering him to make an overcoat trimmed with some sort of traps for robbers, who were, he believed, continually under the bed, and he was calling his landlady every minute to pull out a thief who had even got under the quilt; then he kept asking why his old "dressing gown" was hanging before him when he had a new overcoat; then he thought he was standing before the general listening to the appropriate reprimand and saying, "I am sorry, your Excellency"; then finally he became abusive, uttering the most awful language, so that his old landlady positively crossed herself, having never heard anything of the kind from him before, and the more horrified because these dreadful words followed immediately upon the phrase "your Excellency." Later on, his talk was merely a medley of nonsense, so that it was quite unintelligible; all that was evident was that his incoherent words and thoughts were concerned with nothing but the overcoat. At last poor Akaky Akakievich gave up the ghost. No seal was put upon his room nor upon his things, because, in the first place, he had no heirs and, in the second, the property left was very small, to wit, a bundle of quills, a quire of white government paper, three pairs of socks, two or three buttons that had come off his trousers, and the "dressing gown" with which the reader is already familiar. Who came into all this wealth God only knows; even I who tell the tale must admit that I have not bothered to inquire. And Petersburg carried on without Akaky Akakievich, as though, indeed, he had never been in the city. A creature had vanished and departed whose cause no one had championed, who was dear to no one, of interest to no one, who never attracted the attention of a naturalist, though the latter does not disdain to fix a common fly upon a pin and look at him under the microscope — a creature who bore patiently the jeers of the office and for no particular reason went to his grave, though even he at the very end of his life was visited by an exalted guest in the form of an overcoat that for one instant brought color into his poor, drab life — a creature on whom disease fell as it falls upon the heads of the mighty ones of this world . . . !

Several days after his death, a messenger from the department was sent to his lodgings with instructions that he should go at once to the office, for his chief was asking for him; but the messenger was obliged to return without him, explaining that he could not come, and to the inquiry "Why?" he added, "Well, you see, the fact is he is dead; he was buried three days ago." This was how they learned at the office of the death of Akaky Akakievich, and the next day there was sitting in his seat a new clerk who was very much taller and who wrote not in the same straight handwriting but made his letters more slanting and crooked.

But who could have imagined that this was not all there was to tell about Akaky Akakievich, that he was destined for a few days to make his presence felt in the world after his death, as though to make up for his life having been unnoticed by anyone? But so it happened, and our little story unexpectedly finishes with a fantastic ending.

Rumors were suddenly floating about Petersburg that in the neighborhood of the Kalinkin Bridge and for a little distance beyond, a corpse[5] had begun appearing at night in the form of a clerk looking for a stolen overcoat, and stripping from the shoulders of all passers-by, regardless of grade and calling, overcoats of all descriptions — trimmed with cat fur or beaver or padded, lined with raccoon, fox, and bear — made, in fact of all sorts of skin which men have adapted for the covering of their own. One of the clerks of the department saw the corpse with his own eyes and at once recognized it as Akaky Akakievich; but it excited in him such terror that he ran away as fast as his legs could carry him and so could not get a very clear view of him, and only saw him hold up his finger threateningly in the distance.

From all sides complaints were continually coming that backs and shoulders, not of mere titular councilors, but even of upper court councilors, had been exposed to catching cold, as a result of being stripped of their overcoats. Orders were given to the police to catch the corpse regardless of trouble or expense, dead or alive, and to punish him severely, as an example to others, and, indeed, they very nearly succeeded in doing so. The policeman of one district in Kiryushkin Alley snatched a corpse by the collar on the spot of the crime in the very act of attempting to snatch a frieze overcoat from a retired musician, who used, in his day, to play the flute. Having

[5] Mrs. Garnett excepted, this is often translated "ghost," but there is no doubt of Gogol's intention. He uses the word *mertverts* ("corpse") and not *prividenye* ("ghost"). To confuse the two is damaging to Gogol's delight in the fantastic, and seriously alters the tone of the story. (Kent, ed.)

caught him by the collar, he shouted until he had brought two other policemen whom he ordered to hold the corpse while he felt just a minute in
his boot to get out a snuffbox in order to revive his nose which had six times
in his life been frostbitten, but the snuff was probably so strong that not
even a dead man could stand it. The policeman had hardly had time to put
his finger over his right nostril and draw up some snuff in the left when the
corpse sneezed violently right into the eyes of all three. While they were
putting their fists up to wipe their eyes, the corpse completely vanished, so
that they were not even sure whether he had actually been in their hands.
From that time forward, the policemen had such a horror of the dead that
they were even afraid to seize the living and confined themselves to shouting from the distance: "Hey, you! Move on!" and the clerk's body began to
appear even on the other side of the Kalinkin Bridge, terrorizing all timid
people.

We have, however, quite neglected the Person of Consequence, who
may in reality almost be said to be the cause of the fantastic ending of this
perfectly true story. To begin with, my duty requires me to do justice to the
Person of Consequence by recording that soon after poor Akaky Akakievich
had gone away crushed to powder, he felt something not unlike regret.
Sympathy was a feeling not unknown to him; his heart was open to many
kindly impulses, although his exalted grade very often prevented them from
being shown. As soon as his friend had gone out of his study, he even began
brooding over poor Akaky Akakievich, and from that time forward, he was
almost every day haunted by the image of the poor clerk who had been unable to survive the official reprimand. The thought of the man so worried
him that a week later he actually decided to send a clerk to find out how he
was and whether he really could help him in any way. And when they
brought him word that Akaky Akakievich had died suddenly in a delirium
and fever, it made a great impression on him; his conscience reproached
him and he was depressed all day. Anxious to distract his mind and to forget
the unpleasant incident, he went to spend the evening with one of his
friends, where he found respectable company, and what was best of all, almost everyone was of the same grade so that he was able to be quite unin-
hibited. This had a wonderful effect on his spirits. He let himself go, became affable and genial — in short, spent a very agreeable evening. At
supper he drank a couple of glasses of champagne — a proceeding which
we all know is not a bad recipe for cheerfulness. The champagne made him
inclined to do something unusual, and he decided not to go home yet but to
visit a lady of his acquaintance, a certain Karolina Ivanovna — a lady apparently of German extraction, for whom he entertained extremely friendly
feelings. It must be noted that the Person of Consequence was a man no
longer young. He was an excellent husband, and the respectable father of a
family. He had two sons, one already serving in an office, and a nice-looking
daughter of sixteen with a rather turned-up, pretty little nose, who used to
come every morning to kiss his hand, saying: "Bon jour, Papa." His wife,
who was still blooming and decidedly good-looking, indeed, used first to

give him her hand to kiss and then turning his hand over would kiss it. But
though the Person of Consequence was perfectly satisfied with the pleasant
amenities of his domestic life, he thought it proper to have a lady friend in
another quarter of the town. This lady friend was not a bit better looking
nor younger than his wife, but these puzzling things exist in the world and
it is not our business to criticize them. And so the Person of Consequence
went downstairs, got into his sledge, and said to his coachman, "To Karolina Ivanovna." While luxuriously wrapped in his warm fur coat he remained in that agreeable frame of mind sweeter to a Russian than anything
that could be invented, that is, when one thinks of nothing while thoughts
come into the mind by themselves, one pleasanter than the other, without
your having to bother following them or looking for them. Full of satisfaction, he recalled all the amusing moments of the evening he had spent, all
the phrases that had started the intimate circle of friends laughing; many of
them he repeated in an undertone and found them as amusing as before,
and so, very naturally, laughed very heartily at them again. From time to
time, however, he was disturbed by a gust of wind which, blowing suddenly,
God knows why or where from, cut him in the face, pelting him with flakes
of snow, puffing out his coat collar like a sail, or suddenly flinging it with
unnatural force over his head and giving him endless trouble to extricate
himself from it. All at once, the Person of Consequence felt that someone
had clutched him very tightly by the collar. Turning around he saw a short
man in a shabby old uniform, and not without horror recognized him as
Akaky Akakievich. The clerk's face was white as snow and looked like that
of a corpse, but the horror of the Person of Consequence was beyond all
bounds when he saw the mouth of the corpse distorted into speech, and
breathing upon him the chill of the grave, it uttered the following words:
"Ah, so here you are at last! At last I've . . . er . . . caught you by the collar.
It's your overcoat I want; you refused to help me and abused me in the bargain! So now give me yours!" The poor Person of Consequence very nearly
dropped dead. Resolute and determined as he was in his office and before
subordinates in general, and though anyone looking at his manly air and figure would have said: "Oh, what a man of character!" yet in this situation he
felt, like very many persons of heroic appearance, such terror that not without reason he began to be afraid he would have some sort of fit. He actually
flung his overcoat off his shoulders as far as he could and shouted to his
coachman in an unnatural voice: "Drive home! Let's get out of here!" The
coachman, hearing the tone which he had only heard in critical moments
and then accompanied by something even more tangible, hunched his
shoulders up to his ears in case of worse following, swung his whip, and flew
on like an arrow. In a little over six minutes, the Person of Consequence
was at the entrance of his own house. Pale, panic-stricken, and without his
overcoat, he arrived home instead of at Karolina Ivanovna's, dragged himself to his own room, and spent the night in great distress, so that next
morning his daughter said to him at breakfast, "You look very pale today,
Papa"; but her papa remained mute and said not a word to anyone of what

had happened to him, where he had been, and where he had been going. The incident made a great impression upon him. Indeed, it happened far more rarely that he said to his subordinates, "How dare you? Do you understand who I am?" and he never uttered those words at all until he had first heard all the facts of the case.

What was even more remarkable is that from that time on the apparition of the dead clerk ceased entirely; apparently the general's overcoat had fitted him perfectly; anyway nothing more was heard of overcoats being snatched from anyone. Many restless and anxious people refused, however, to be pacified, and still maintained that in remote parts of the town the dead clerk went on appearing. One policeman, in Kolomna, for instance, saw with his own eyes an apparition appear from behind a house; but, being by natural constitution somewhat frail — so much so that on one occasion an ordinary grown-up suckling pig, making a sudden dash out of some private building, knocked him off his feet to the great amusement of the cabmen standing around, whom he fined two kopeks each for snuff for such disrespect — he did not dare to stop it, and so followed it in the dark until the apparition suddenly looked around and, stopping, asked him: "What do you want?" displaying a huge fist such as you never see among the living. The policeman said: "Nothing," and turned back on the spot. This apparition, however, was considerably taller and adorned with immense mustaches, and, directing its steps apparently toward Obukhov Bridge, vanished into the darkness of the night.

[1840]

HERMAN MELVILLE (1819–1891) published his first attempt at the short story form in "Bartleby, the Scrivener: A Story of Wall Street." Behind him were seven years of writing novels, which began with a burst of creative energy that produced his early novels of sea adventure: Typee (1846), Omoo (1847), Mardi (1849), Redburn (1849), and White-Jacket (1850). All of these were based on his experiences on board ship. Melville had been left in poverty at the age of fifteen when his father went bankrupt, and in 1839 he went to sea as a cabin boy. Two years later he sailed on a whaler bound for the Pacific, but he deserted in the Marquesas Islands and lived for a time with cannibals. Having little formal education, Melville later boasted that "a whale ship was my Yale College and my Harvard." His most ambitious book was Moby Dick (1851), a work of romantic and allegorical complexity heavily indebted to the influence of Nathaniel Hawthorne, Melville's neighbor in the Berkshires at the time he wrote it. Moby Dick was not as great a commercial success as Melville's earlier books, however, and the novel that followed it, Pierre (1852), was dismissed as incomprehensible trash by the critics, one of whom protested that Melville was allowing his mind to "run riot amid remote analogies, where the chain of association is invisible to mortal minds."

It was at this point that Melville turned to the short story. Between 1853 and 1856 he published fifteen sketches and stories and a serialized historical novel, promising the popular magazines that his stories would "contain nothing of any sort to shock the fastidious." But when these pieces, and another novel (The Confidence Man, 1857), failed to restore interest in him as a writer, Melville ceased trying to make his living by his pen. He left his farm in the Berkshires, moved with his family to a house in New York City bought for them by his father-in-law, and worked from 1866 to 1888 as an inspector of customs. He published a few books of poems in his later years, and wrote a short novel, Billy Budd, which critics acclaimed as one of his greatest works when it was published — thirty years after his death.

Melville stood at the crossroads in the early history of American short fiction. When he began to publish in magazines, Hawthorne and Poe had already done their best work in the romantic vein of tales and sketches, and the realistic local-color school of short stories had hardly begun to appear. Experimenting with forms that he hoped would have popular appeal, Melville created something new in "Bartleby, the Scrivener," a fully developed, if discursive, short story firmly embedded in a contemporary social context. It baffled readers of Putnam's Monthly Magazine in November and December 1853, when it was published in two installments. One reviewer called it "a Poeish tale with an infusion of more natural sentiment." For the remainder of his magazine fiction, Melville concentrated on producing old-

fashioned tales mostly set in remote times or places. He never commented on the meaning of his stories or analyzed the way he wrote short fiction. (See Melville's Commentary about Hawthorne on page 1223.)

Herman Melville

෨෬

BARTLEBY, THE SCRIVENER

A Story of Wall Street

I am a rather elderly man. The nature of my avocations, for the last thirty years, has brought me into more than ordinary contact with what would seem an interesting and somewhat singular set of men, of whom, as yet, nothing, that I know of, has ever been written — I mean, the law-copyists, or scriveners. I have known very many of them, professionally and privately, and, if I pleased, could relate divers histories, at which good-natured gentlemen might smile, and sentimental souls might weep. But I waive the biographies of all other scriveners, for a few passages in the life of Bartleby, who was a scrivener, the strangest I ever saw, or heard of. While, of other law-copyists, I might write the complete life, of Bartleby nothing of that sort can be done. I believe that no materials exist, for a full and satisfactory biography of this man. It is an irreparable loss to literature. Bartleby was one of those beings of whom nothing is ascertainable, except from the original sources, and, in his case, those are very small. What my own astonished eyes saw of Bartleby, *that* is all I know of him, except, indeed, one vague report, which will appear in the sequel.

Ere introducing the scrivener, as he first appeared to me, it is fit I make some mention of myself, my *employés*, my business, my chambers, and general surroundings, because some such description is indispensable to an adequate understanding of the chief character about to be presented. Imprimis:[1] I am a man who, from his youth upwards, has been filled with a profound conviction that the easiest way of life is the best. Hence, though I belong to a profession proverbially energetic and nervous, even to turbulence, at times, yet nothing of that sort have I ever suffered to invade my peace. I am one of those unambitious lawyers who never address a jury, or in any way draw down public applause; but, in the cool tranquillity of a snug retreat, do a snug business among rich men's bonds, and mortgages,

---

[1] in the first place (Latin).

and title-deeds. All who know me, consider me an eminently *safe* man. The late John Jacob Astor, a personage little given to poetic enthusiasm, had no hesitation in pronouncing my first grand point to be prudence; my next, method. I do not speak it in vanity, but simply record the fact, that I was not unemployed in my profession by the late John Jacob Astor; a name which, I admit, I love to repeat; for it hath a rounded and orbicular sound to it, and rings like unto bullion. I will freely add, that I was not insensible to the late John Jacob Astor's good opinion.

Some time prior to the period at which this little history begins, my avocations had been largely increased. The good old office, now extinct in the State of New York, of a Master in Chancery, had been conferred upon me. It was not a very arduous office, but very pleasantly remunerative. I seldom lose my temper; much more seldom indulge in dangerous indignation at wrongs and outrages; but I must be permitted to be rash here and declare, that I consider the sudden and violent abrogation of the office of Master in Chancery, by the new Constitution, as a —— premature act; inasmuch as I had counted upon a life-lease of the profits, whereas I only received those of a few short years. But this is by the way.

My chambers were up stairs, at No. — Wall Street. At one end, they looked upon the white wall of the interior of a spacious skylight shaft, penetrating the building from top to bottom.

This view might have been considered rather tame than otherwise, deficient in what landscape painters call "life." But, if so, the view from the other end of my chambers offered, at least, a contrast, if nothing more. In that direction, my windows commanded an unobstructed view of a lofty brick wall, black by age and everlasting shade; which wall required no spyglass to bring out its lurking beauties, but, for the benefit of all near-sighted spectators, was pushed up to within ten feet of my window-panes. Owing to the great height of the surrounding buildings, and my chambers being on the second floor, the interval between this wall and mine not a little resembled a huge square cistern.

At the period just preceding the advent of Bartleby, I had two persons as copyists in my employment, and a promising lad as an office-boy. First, Turkey; second, Nippers; third, Ginger Nut. These may seem names, the like of which are not usually found in the Directory. In truth, they were nicknames, mutually conferred upon each other by my three clerks, and were deemed expressive of their respective persons or characters. Turkey was a short, pursy Englishman, of about my own age — that is, somewhere not far from sixty. In the morning, one might say, his face was of a fine florid hue, but after twelve o'clock, meridian — his dinner hour — it blazed like a grate full of Christmas coals; and continued blazing — but, as it were, with a gradual wane — till six o'clock, P.M., or thereabouts; after which, I saw no more of the proprietor of the face, which, gaining its meridian with the sun, seemed to set with it, to rise, culminate, and decline the following day, with the like regularity and undiminished glory. There are many singular coincidences I have known in the course of my life, not the least among which was the fact, that, exactly when Turkey displayed his fullest beams from his red and radiant countenance, just then, too, at that critical moment, began the daily period when I considered his business capacities as seriously disturbed for the remainder of the twenty-four hours. Not that he was absolutely idle, or averse to business then; far from it. The difficulty was, he was apt to be altogether too energetic. There was a strange, inflamed, flurried, flighty recklessness of activity about him. He would be incautious in dipping his pen into his inkstand. All his blots upon my documents were dropped there after twelve o'clock, meridian. Indeed, not only would he be reckless, and sadly given to making blots in the afternoon, but, some days, he went further, and was rather noisy. At such times, too, his face flamed with augmented blazonry, as if cannel coal had been heaped on anthracite. He made an unpleasant racket with his chair; spilled his sand-box; in mending his pens, impatiently split them all to pieces, and threw them on the floor in a sudden passion; stood up, and leaned over his table, boxing his papers about in a most indecorous manner, very sad to behold in an elderly man like him. Nevertheless, as he was in many ways a most valuable person to me, and all the time before twelve o'clock, meridian, was the quickest, steadiest creature, too, accomplishing a great deal of work in a style not easily to be matched — for these reasons, I was willing to overlook his eccentricities, though, indeed, occasionally, I remonstrated with him. I did this very gently, however, because, though the civilest, nay, the blandest and most reverential of men in the morning, yet, in the afternoon, he was disposed, upon provocation, to be slightly rash with his tongue — in fact, insolent. Now, valuing his morning services as I did, and resolved not to lose them — yet, at the same time, made uncomfortable by his inflamed ways after twelve o'clock — and being a man of peace, unwilling by my admonitions to call forth unseemly retorts from him, I took upon me, one Saturday noon (he was always worse on Saturdays) to hint to him, very kindly, that, perhaps, now that he was growing old, it might be well to abridge his labors; in short, he need not come to my chambers after twelve o'clock, but, dinner over, had best go home to his lodgings, and rest himself till tea-time. But no; he insisted upon his afternoon devotions. His countenance became intolerably fervid, as he oratorically assured me — gesticulating with a long ruler at the other end of the room — that if his services in the morning were useful, how indispensable, then, in the afternoon?

"With submission, sir," said Turkey, on this occasion, "I consider myself your right-hand man. In the morning I but marshal and deploy my columns; but in the afternoon I put myself at their head, and gallantly charge the foe, thus" — and he made a violent thrust with the ruler.

"But the blots, Turkey," intimated I.

"True; but, with submission, sir, behold these hairs! I am getting old. Surely, sir, a blot or two of a warm afternoon is not to be severely urged against gray hairs. Old age — even if it blot the page — is honorable. With submission, sir, we *both* are getting old."

This appeal to my fellow-feeling was hardly to be resisted. At all events, I saw that go he would not. So, I made up my mind to let him stay, resolving, nevertheless, to see to it that, during the afternoon, he had to do with my less important papers.

Nippers, the second on my list, was a whiskered, sallow, and, upon the whole, rather piratical-looking young man, of about five-and-twenty. I always deemed him the victim of two evil powers — ambition and indigestion. The ambition was evinced by a certain impatience of the duties of a mere copyist, an unwarrantable usurpation of strictly professional affairs such as the original drawing up of legal documents. The indigestion seemed betokened in an occasional nervous testiness and grinning irritability, causing the teeth to audibly grind together over mistakes committed in copying; unnecessary maledictions, hissed, rather than spoken, in the heat of business; and especially by a continual discontent with the height of the table where he worked. Though of a very ingenious mechanical turn, Nippers could never get this table to suit him. He put chips under it, blocks of various sorts, bits of pasteboard, and at last went so far as to attempt an exquisite adjustment, by final pieces of folded blotting-paper. But no invention would answer. If, for the sake of easing his back, he brought the table-lid at a sharp angle well up towards his chin, and wrote there like a man using the steep roof of a Dutch house for his desk, then he declared that it stopped the circulation in his arms. If now he lowered the table to his waistbands, and stooped over it in writing, then there was a sore aching in his back. In short, the truth of the matter was, Nippers knew not what he wanted. Or, if he wanted anything, it was to be rid of a scrivener's table altogether. Among the manifestations of his diseased ambition was a fondness he had for receiving visits from certain ambiguous-looking fellows in seedy coats, whom he called his clients. Indeed, I was aware that not only was he, at times, considerable of a ward-politician, but he occasionally did a little business at the justices' courts, and was not unknown on the steps of the Tombs.[2] I have good reason to believe, however, that one individual who called upon him at my chambers, and who, with a grand air, he insisted was his client, was no other than a dun, and the alleged title-deed, a bill. But, with all his failings, and the annoyances he caused me, Nippers, like his compatriot Turkey, was a very useful man to me; wrote a neat, swift hand; and, when he chose, was not deficient in a gentlemanly sort of deportment. Added to this, he always dressed in a gentlemanly sort of way; and so, incidentally, reflected credit upon my chambers. Whereas, with respect to Turkey, I had much ado to keep him from being a reproach to me. His clothes were apt to look oily, and smell of eating-houses. He wore his pantaloons very loose and baggy in summer. His coats were execrable, his hat not to be handled. But

---

[2] maximum-security prison in New York City.

while the hat was a thing of indifference to me, inasmuch as his natural civility and deference, as a dependent Englishman, always led him to doff it the moment he entered the room, yet his coat was another matter. Concerning his coats, I reasoned with him; but with no effect. The truth was, I suppose, that a man with so small an income could not afford to sport such a lustrous face and a lustrous coat at one and the same time. As Nippers once observed, Turkey's money went chiefly for red ink. One winter day, I presented Turkey with a highly respectable-looking coat of my own — a padded gray coat, of a most comfortable warmth, and which buttoned straight up from the knee to the neck. I thought Turkey would appreciate the favor, and abate his rashness and obstreperousness of afternoons. But no; I verily believe that buttoning himself up in so downy and blanket-like a coat had a pernicious effect upon him — upon the same principle that too much oats are bad for horses. In fact, precisely as a rash, restive horse is said to feel his oats, so Turkey felt his coat. It made him insolent. He was a man whom prosperity harmed.

Though, concerning the self-indulgent habits of Turkey, I had my own private surmises, yet, touching Nippers, I was well persuaded that, whatever might be his faults in other respects, he was, at least, a temperate young man. But, indeed, nature herself seemed to have been his vintner, and, at his birth, charged him so thoroughly with an irritable, brandy-like disposition, that all subsequent potations were needless. When I consider how, amid the stillness of my chambers, Nippers would sometimes impatiently rise from his seat, and stooping over his table, spread his arms wide apart, seize the whole desk, and move it, and jerk it, with a grim, grinding motion on the floor, as if the table were a perverse voluntary agent, intent on thwarting and vexing him, I plainly perceive that, for Nippers, brandy-and-water were altogether superfluous.

It was fortunate for me that, owing to its peculiar cause — indigestion — the irritability and consequent nervousness of Nippers were mainly observable in the morning, while in the afternoon he was comparatively mild. So that, Turkey's paroxysms only coming on about twelve o'clock, I never had to do with their eccentricities at one time. Their fits relieved each other, like guards. When Nippers' was on, Turkey's was off; and *vice versa*. This was a good natural arrangement, under the circumstances.

Ginger Nut, the third on my list, was a lad, some twelve years old. His father was a carman, ambitious of seeing his son on the bench instead of a cart, before he died. So he sent him to my office, as student at law, errand-boy, cleaner, and sweeper, at the rate of one dollar a week. He had a little desk to himself, but he did not use it much. Upon inspection, the drawer exhibited a great array of the shells of various sorts of nuts. Indeed, to this quick-witted youth, the whole noble science of the law was contained in a nutshell. Not the least among the employments of Ginger Nut, as well as one which he discharged with the most alacrity, was his duty as cake and apple purveyor for Turkey and Nippers. Copying lawpapers being proverbially a dry, husky sort of business, my two scriveners were fain to moisten their mouths very often with Spitzenbergs, to be had at the numerous stalls nigh the Custom House and Post Office. Also, they sent Ginger Nut very frequently for that peculiar cake — small, flat, round, and very spicy — after which he had been named by them. Of a cold morning, when business was but dull, Turkey would gobble up scores of these cakes, as if they were mere wafers — indeed, they sell them at the rate of six or eight for a penny — the scrape of his pen blending with the crunching of the crisp particles in his mouth. Of all the fiery afternoon blunders and flurried rashness of Turkey, was his once moistening a ginger-cake between his lips, and clapping it on to a mortgage, for a seal. I came within an ace of dismissing him then. But he mollified me by making an oriental bow, and saying —

"With submission, sir, it was generous of me to find you in stationery on my own account."

Now my original business — that of a conveyancer and title hunter, and drawer-up of recondite documents of all sorts — was considerably increased by receiving the Master's office. There was now great work for scriveners. Not only must I push the clerks already with me, but I must have additional help.

In answer to my advertisement, a motionless young man one morning stood upon my office threshold, the door being open, for it was summer. I can see that figure now — pallidly neat, pitiably respectable, incurably forlorn! It was Bartleby.

After a few words touching his qualifications, I engaged him, glad to have among my corps of copyists a man of so singularly sedate an aspect, which I thought might operate beneficially upon the flighty temper of Turkey, and the fiery one of Nippers.

I should have stated before that ground-glass folding-doors divided my premises into two parts, one of which was occupied by my scriveners, the other by myself. According to my humor, I threw open these doors, or closed them. I resolved to assign Bartleby a corner by the folding-doors, but on my side of them, so as to have this quiet man within easy call, in case any trifling thing was to be done. I placed his desk close up to a small side-window in that part of the room, a window which originally had afforded a lateral view of certain grimy brickyards and bricks, but which, owing to subsequent erections, commanded at present no view at all, though it gave some light. Within three feet of the panes was a wall, and the light came down from far above, between two lofty buildings, as from a very small opening in a dome. Still further to a satisfactory arrangement, I procured a high green folding screen, which might entirely isolate Bartleby from my sight, though not remove him from my voice. And thus, in a manner, privacy and society were conjoined.

At first, Bartleby did an extraordinary quantity of writing. As if long famishing for something to copy, he seemed to gorge himself on my documents. There was no pause for digestion. He ran a day and night line, copying by sunlight and by candle-light. I should have been quite delighted with his application, had he been cheerfully industrious. But he wrote on silently, palely, mechanically.

It is, of course, an indispensable part of a scrivener's business to verify the accuracy of his copy, word by word. Where there are two or more scriveners in an office, they assist each other in this examination, one reading from the copy, the other holding the original. It is a very dull, wearisome, and lethargic affair. I can readily imagine that, to some sanguine temperaments, it would be altogether intolerable. For example, I cannot credit that the mettlesome poet, Byron, would have contentedly sat down with Bartleby to examine a law document of, say five hundred pages, closely written in a crimpy hand.

Now and then, in the haste of business, it had been my habit to assist in comparing some brief document myself, calling Turkey or Nippers for this purpose. One object I had, in placing Bartleby so handy to me behind the screen, was, to avail myself of his services on such trivial occasions. It was on the third day, I think, of his being with me, and before any necessity had arisen for having his own writing examined, that, being much hurried to complete a small affair I had in hand, I abruptly called to Bartleby. In my haste and natural expectancy of instant compliance, I sat with my head bent over the original on my desk, and my right hand sideways, and somewhat nervously extended with the copy, so that, immediately upon emerging from his retreat, Bartleby might snatch it and proceed to business without the least delay.

In this very attitude did I sit when I called to him, rapidly stating what it was I wanted him to do — namely, to examine a small paper with me. Imagine my surprise, nay, my consternation, when, without moving from his privacy, Bartleby, in a singularly mild, firm voice, replied, "I would prefer not to."

I sat awhile in perfect silence, rallying my stunned faculties. Immediately it occurred to me that my ears had deceived me, or Bartleby had entirely misunderstood my meaning. I repeated my request in the clearest tone I could assume; but in quite as clear a one came the previous reply, "I would prefer not to."

"Prefer not to," echoed I, rising in high excitement, and crossing the room with a stride. "What do you mean? Are you moonstruck? I want you to help me compare this sheet here — take it," and I thrust it towards him.

"I would prefer not to," said he.

I looked at him steadfastly. His face was leanly composed; his gray eye dimly calm. Not a wrinkle of agitation rippled him. Had there been the least uneasiness, anger, impatience, or impertinence in his manner; in other words, had there been anything ordinarily human about him, doubtless I should have violently dismissed him from the premises. But as it was, I should have as soon thought of turning my pale plaster-of-paris bust of Cicero out of doors. I stood gazing at him awhile, as he went on with his own writing, and then reseated myself at my desk. This is very strange, thought I. What had one best do? But my business hurried me. I concluded to forget the matter for the present, reserving it for my future leisure. So, calling Nippers from the other room, the paper was speedily examined.

A few days after this, Bartleby concluded four lengthy documents, being quadruplicates of a week's testimony taken before me in my High Court of Chancery. It became necessary to examine them. It was an important suit, and great accuracy was imperative. Having all things arranged, I called Turkey, Nippers, and Ginger Nut, from the next room, meaning to place the four copies in the hands of my four clerks, while I should read from the original. Accordingly, Turkey, Nippers, and Ginger Nut had taken their seats in a row, each with his document in his hand, when I called to Bartleby to join this interesting group.

"Bartleby! quick, I am waiting."

I heard a slow scrape of his chair legs on the uncarpeted floor, and soon he appeared standing at the entrance of his hermitage.

"What is wanted?" said he, mildly.

"The copies, the copies," said I, hurriedly. "We are going to examine them. There" — and I held towards him the fourth quadruplicate.

"I would prefer not to," he said, and gently disappeared behind the screen.

For a few moments I was turned into a pillar of salt, standing at the head of my seated column of clerks. Recovering myself, I advanced towards the screen, and demanded the reason for such extraordinary conduct.

"*Why* do you refuse?"

"I would prefer not to."

With any other man I should have flown outright into a dreadful passion, scorned all further words, and thrust him ignominiously from my presence. But there was something about Bartleby that not only strangely disarmed me, but, in a wonderful manner, touched and disconcerted me. I began to reason with him.

"These are your own copies we are about to examine. It is labor saving to you, because one examination will answer for your four papers. It is common usage. Every copyist is bound to help examine his copy. Is it not so? Will you not speak? Answer!"

"I prefer not to," he replied in a flute-like tone. It seemed to me that, while I had been addressing him, he carefully revolved every statement that I made; fully comprehended the meaning; could not gainsay the irresistible conclusion; but, at the same time, some paramount consideration prevailed with him to reply as he did.

"You are decided, then, not to comply with my request — a request made according to common usage and common sense?"

He briefly gave me to understand, that on that point my judgment was sound. Yes: his decision was irreversible.

It is not seldom the case that, when a man is browbeaten in some unprecedented and violently unreasonable way, he begins to stagger in his own plainest faith. He begins, as it were, vaguely to surmise that, wonderful as it may be, all the justice and all the reason is on the other side. Accordingly, if any disinterested persons are present, he turns to them for some reinforcement for his own faltering mind.

"Turkey," said I, "what do you think of this? Am I not right?"

"With submission, sir," said Turkey, in his blandest tone, "I think that you are."

"Nippers," said I, "what do *you* think of it?"

"I think I should kick him out of the office."

(The reader of nice perceptions will have perceived that, it being morning, Turkey's answer is couched in polite and tranquil terms, but Nippers replies in ill-tempered ones. Or, to repeat a previous sentence, Nippers' ugly mood was on duty, and Turkey's off.)

"Ginger Nut," said I, willing to enlist the smallest suffrage in my behalf, "what do *you* think of it?"

"I think, sir, he's a little *luny*," replied Ginger Nut, with a grin.

"You hear what they say," said I, turning towards the screen, "come forth and do your duty."

But he vouchsafed no reply. I pondered a moment in sore perplexity. But once more business hurried me. I determined again to postpone the consideration of this dilemma to my future leisure. With a little trouble we made out to examine the papers without Bartleby, though at every page or two Turkey deferentially dropped his opinion, that this proceeding was quite out of the common; while Nippers, twitching in his chair with a dyspeptic nervousness, ground out, between his set teeth, occasional hissing maledictions against the stubborn oaf behind the screen. And for his (Nippers') part, this was the first and the last time he would do another man's business without pay.

Meanwhile Bartleby sat in his hermitage, oblivious to everything but his own peculiar business there.

Some days passed, the scrivener being employed upon another lengthy work. His late remarkable conduct led me to regard his ways narrowly. I observed that he never went to dinner; indeed, that he never went anywhere. As yet I had never, of my personal knowledge, known him to be outside of my office. He was a perpetual sentry in the corner. At about eleven o'clock though, in the morning, I noticed that Ginger Nut would advance towards the opening in Bartleby's screen, as if silently beckoned thither by a gesture invisible to me where I sat. The boy would then leave the office, jingling a few pence, and reappear with a handful of ginger-nuts, which he delivered in the hermitage, receiving two of the cakes for his trouble.

He lives, then, on ginger-nuts, thought I; never eats a dinner, properly speaking; he must be a vegetarian, then; but no; he never eats even vegetables, he eats nothing but ginger-nuts. My mind then ran on in reveries concerning the probable effects upon the human constitution of living entirely on ginger-nuts. Ginger-nuts are so called, because they contain ginger as one of their peculiar constituents, and the final flavoring one. Now, what was ginger? A hot, spicy thing. Was Bartleby hot and spicy? Not at all. Ginger, then, had no effect upon Bartleby. Probably he preferred it should have none.

Nothing so aggravates an earnest person as a passive resistance. If the individual so resisted be of a not inhumane temper, and the resisting one perfectly harmless in his passivity, then, in the better moods of the former, he will endeavor charitably to construe to his imagination what proves impossible to be solved by his judgment. Even so, for the most part, I regarded Bartleby and his ways. Poor fellow! thought I, he means no mischief; it is plain he intends no insolence; his aspect sufficiently evinces that his eccentricities are involuntary. He is useful to me. I can get along with him. If I turn him away, the chances are he will fall in with some less indulgent employer, and then he will be rudely treated, and perhaps driven forth miserably to starve. Yes. Here I can cheaply purchase a delicious self-approval. To befriend Bartleby; to humor him in his strange wilfulness, will cost me little or nothing, while I lay up in my soul what will eventually prove a sweet morsel for my conscience. But this mood was not invariable with me. The passiveness of Bartleby sometimes irritated me. I felt strangely goaded on to encounter him in new opposition — to elicit some angry spark from him answerable to my own. But, indeed, I might as well have essayed to strike fire with my knuckles against a bit of Windsor soap. But one afternoon the evil impulse in me mastered me, and the following little scene ensued:

"Bartleby," said I, "when those papers are all copied, I will compare them with you."

"I would prefer not to."

"How? Surely you do not mean to persist in that mulish vagary?"

No answer.

I threw open the folding-doors nearby, and turning upon Turkey and Nippers, exclaimed:

"Bartleby a second time says, he won't examine his papers. What do you think of it, Turkey?"

It was afternoon, be it remembered. Turkey sat glowing like a brass boiler; his bald head steaming; his hands reeling among his blotted papers.

"Think of it?" roared Turkey. "I think I'll just step behind his screen, and black his eyes for him!"

So saying, Turkey rose to his feet and threw his arms into a pugilistic position. He was hurrying away to make good his promise, when I detained him, alarmed at the effect of incautiously rousing Turkey's combativeness after dinner.

"Sit down, Turkey," said I, "and hear what Nippers has to say. What do you think of it, Nippers? Would I not be justified in immediately dismissing Bartleby?"

"Excuse me, that is for you to decide, sir. I think his conduct quite unusual, and, indeed, unjust, as regards Turkey and myself. But it may only be a passing whim."

"Ah," exclaimed I, "you have strangely changed your mind, then — you speak very gently of him now."

"All beer," cried Turkey; "gentleness is effects of beer — Nippers and I dined together to-day. You see how gentle *I* am, sir. Shall I go and black his eyes?"

"You refer to Bartleby, I suppose. No, not to-day, Turkey," I replied; "pray, put up your fists."

I closed the doors, and again advanced towards Bartleby. I felt additional incentives tempting me to my fate. I burned to be rebelled against again. I remembered that Bartleby never left the office.

"Bartleby," said I, "Ginger Nut is away; just step around to the Post Office, won't you?" (it was but a three minutes' walk) "and see if there is anything for me."

"I would prefer not to."

"You *will* not?"

"I *prefer* not."

I staggered to my desk, and sat there in a deep study. My blind inveteracy returned. Was there any other thing in which I could procure myself to be ignominiously repulsed by this lean, penniless wight? — my hired clerk? What added thing is there, perfectly reasonable, that he will be sure to refuse to do?

"Bartleby!"

No answer.

"Bartleby," in a louder tone.

No answer.

"Bartleby," I roared.

Like a very ghost, agreeably to the laws of magical invocation, at the third summons, he appeared at the entrance of his hermitage.

"Go to the next room, and tell Nippers to come to me."

"I prefer not to," he respectfully and slowly said, and mildy disappeared.

"Very good, Bartleby," said I, in a quiet sort of serenely-severe self-possessed tone, intimating the unalterable purpose of some terrible retribution very close at hand. At the moment I half intended something of the kind. But upon the whole, as it was drawing towards my dinner-hour, I thought it best to put on my hat and walk home for the day, suffering much from perplexity and distress of mind.

Shall I acknowledge it? The conclusion of this whole business was, that it soon became a fixed fact of my chambers, that a pale young scriv-

ener, by the name of Bartleby, had a desk there; that he copied for me at
the usual rate of four cents a folio (one hundred words); but he was permanently exempt from examining the work done by him, that duty being
transferred to Turkey and Nippers, out of compliment, doubtless, to their
superior acuteness; moreover, said Bartleby was never, on any account, to
be dispatched on the most trivial errand of any sort; and that even if entreated to take upon him such a matter, it was generally understood that he
would "prefer not to" — in other words, that he would refuse point-blank.

As days passed on, I became considerably reconciled to Bartleby. His
steadiness, his freedom from all dissipation, his incessant industry (except
when he chose to throw himself into a standing revery behind his screen),
his great stillness, his unalterableness of demeanor under all circumstances,
made him a valuable acquisition. One prime thing was this — *he was always there* — first in the morning, continually through the day, and the last
at night. I had a singular confidence in his honesty. I felt my most precious
papers perfectly safe in his hands. Sometimes, to be sure, I could not, for
the very soul of me, avoid falling into sudden spasmodic passions with him.
For it was exceeding difficult to bear in mind all the time those strange peculiarities, privileges, and unheard-of exemptions, forming the tacit stipula-
tions on Bartleby's part under which he remained in my office. Now and
then, in the eagerness of dispatching pressing business, I would inadvertently summon Bartleby, in a short, rapid tone, to put his finger, say, on the
incipient tie of a bit of red tape with which I was about compressing some
papers. Of course, from behind the screen the usual answer, "I prefer not
to," was sure to come; and then, how could a human creature, with the
common infirmities of our nature, refrain from bitterly exclaiming upon
such perverseness — such unreasonableness? However, every added repulse
of this sort which I received only tended to lessen the probability of my repeating the inadvertence.

Here it must be said, that, according to the custom of most legal gentlemen occupying chambers in densely populated law buildings, there were
several keys to my door. One was kept by a woman residing in the attic,
which person weekly scrubbed and daily swept and dusted my apartments.
Another was kept by Turkey for convenience sake. The third I sometimes
carried in my own pocket. The fourth I knew not who had.

Now, one Sunday morning I happened to go to Trinity Church, to
hear a celebrated preacher, and finding myself rather early on the ground I
thought I would walk round to my chambers for a while. Luckily I had my
key with me; but upon applying it to the lock, I found it resisted by something inserted from the inside. Quite surprised, I called out; when to my
consternation a key was turned from within; and thrusting his lean visage at
me, and holding the door ajar, the apparition of Bartleby appeared, in his
shirt-sleeves, and otherwise in a strangely tattered *deshabille*, saying quietly
that he was sorry, but he was deeply engaged just then, and — preferred not

admitting me at present. In a brief word or two, he moreover added, that perhaps I had better walk round the block two or three times, and by that time he would probably have concluded his affairs.

Now, the utterly unsurmised appearance of Bartleby, tenanting my law-chambers of a Sunday morning, with his cadaverously gentlemanly *nonchalance*, yet withal firm and self-possessed, had such a strange effect upon me, that incontinently I slunk away from my own door, and did as desired. But not without sundry twinges of impotent rebellion against the mild effrontery of this unaccountable scrivener. Indeed, it was his wonderful mildness chiefly, which not only disarmed me, but unmanned me, as it were. For I consider that one, for the time, is a sort of unmanned when he tranquilly permits his hired clerk to dictate to him, and order him away from his own premises. Furthermore, I was full of uneasiness as to what Bartleby could possibly be doing in my office in his shirt-sleeves, and in an otherwise dismantled condition of a Sunday morning. Was anything amiss going on? Nay, that was out of the question. It was not to be thought of for a moment that Bartleby was an immoral person. But what could he be doing there? — copying? Nay again, whatever might be his eccentricities, Bartleby was an eminently decorous person. He would be the last man to sit down to his desk in any state approaching to nudity. Besides, it was Sunday; and there was something about Bartleby that forbade the supposition that he would by any secular occupation violate the proprieties of the day.

Nevertheless, my mind was not pacified; and full of a restless curiosity, at last I returned to the door. Without hindrance I inserted my key, opened it, and entered. Bartleby was not to be seen. I looked round anxiously, peeped behind his screen; but it was very plain that he was gone. Upon more closely examining the place, I surmised that for an indefinite period Bartleby must have ate, dressed, and slept in my office, and that too without plate, mirror, or bed. The cushioned seat of a rickety old sofa in one corner bore the faint impress of a lean, reclining form. Rolled away under his desk, I found a blanket; under the empty grate, a blacking box and brush; on a chair, a tin basin, with soap and a ragged towel; in a newspaper a few crumbs of ginger-nuts and a morsel of cheese. Yes, thought I, it is evident enough that Bartleby has been making his home here, keeping bachelor's hall all by himself. Immediately then the thought came sweeping across me, what miserable friendlessness and loneliness are here revealed! His poverty is great; but his solitude, how horrible! Think of it. Of a Sunday, Wall Street is deserted as Petra;[3] and every night of every day it is an emptiness. This building, too, which of week-days hums with industry and life, at nightfall echoes with sheer vacancy, and all through Sunday is forlorn. And here Bartleby makes his home; sole spectator of a solitude which he has

---

[3] A city in what is now Jordan, once the center of an Arab kingdom. It was deserted for more than ten centuries, until its rediscovery by explorers in 1812.

seen all populous — a sort of innocent and transformed Marius[4] brooding
among the ruins of Carthage!

For the first time in my life a feeling of overpowering stinging melancholy seized me. Before, I had never experienced aught but a not unpleas-
ing sadness. The bond of a common humanity now drew me irresistibly to
gloom. A fraternal melancholy! For both I and Bartleby were sons of Adam.
I remembered the bright silks and sparkling faces I had seen that day, in
gala trim, swan-like sailing down the Mississippi of Broadway; and I contrasted them with the pallid copyist, and thought to myself, Ah, happiness
courts the light, so we deem the world is gay; but misery hides aloof, so we
deem that misery there is none. These sad fancyings — chimeras, doubtless, of a sick and silly brain — led on to other and more special thoughts,
concerning the eccentricities of Bartleby. Presentiments of strange discoveries hovered round me. The scrivener's pale form appeared to me laid out,
among uncaring strangers, in its shivering winding-sheet.

Suddenly I was attracted by Bartleby's closed desk, the key in open
sight left in the lock.

I mean no mischief, seek the gratification of no heartless curiosity,
thought I; besides, the desk is mine, and its contents, too, so I will make
bold to look within. Everything was methodically arranged, the papers
smoothly placed. The pigeon-holes were deep, and removing the files of
documents, I groped into their recesses. Presently I felt something there,
and dragged it out. It was an old bandanna handkerchief, heavy and knotted. I opened it, and saw it was a saving's bank.

I now recalled all the quiet mysteries which I had noted in the man. I
remembered that he never spoke but to answer; that, though at intervals he
had considerable time to himself, yet I had never seen him reading — no,
not even a newspaper; that for long periods he would stand looking out, at
his pale window behind the screen, upon the dead brick wall; I was quite
sure he never visited any refectory or eating-house; while his pale face
clearly indicated that he never drank beer like Turkey; or tea and coffee
even, like other men; that he never went anywhere in particular that I could
learn; never went out for a walk, unless, indeed, that was the case at present;
that he had declined telling who he was, or whence he came, or whether he
had any relatives in the world; that though so thin and pale, he never complained of ill-health. And more than all, I remembered a certain unconscious air of pallid — how shall I call it? — of pallid haughtiness, say, or
rather an austere reserve about him, which has positively awed me into my
tame compliance with his eccentricities, when I had feared to ask him to do
the slightest incidental thing for me, even though I might know, from his

---

[4] Gaius Marius (157?–86 B.C.), a Roman general, several times elected consul.
Marius's greatest military successes came in the Jugurthine War, in Africa. Later, when his
opponents gained power and he was banished, he fled to Africa. Carthage was a city in North
Africa.

long-continued motionlessness, that behind his screen he must be standing in one of those dead-wall reveries of his.

Revolving all these things, and coupling them with the recently discovered fact, that he made my office his constant abiding place and home, and not forgetful of his morbid moodiness; revolving all these things, a prudential feeling began to steal over me. My first emotions had been those of pure melancholy and sincerest pity; but just in proportion as the forlornness of Bartleby grew and grew to my imagination, did that same melancholy merge into fear, that pity into repulsion. So true it is, and so terrible, too, that up to a certain point the thought or sight of misery enlists our best affections; but, in certain special cases, beyond that point it does not. They err who would assert that invariably this is owing to the inherent selfishness of the human heart. It rather proceeds from a certain hopelessness of remedying excessive and organic ill. To a sensitive being, pity is not seldom pain. And when at last it is perceived that such pity cannot lead to effectual succor, common sense bids the soul be rid of it. What I saw that morning persuaded me that the scrivener was the victim of innate and incurable disorder. I might give alms to his body; but his body did not pain him; it was his soul that suffered, and his soul I could not reach.

I did not accomplish the purpose of going to Trinity Church that morning. Somehow, the things I had seen disqualified me for the time from church-going. I walked homeward, thinking what I would do with Bartleby. Finally, I resolved upon this — I would put certain calm questions to him the next morning, touching his history, etc., and if he declined to answer them openly and unreservedly (and I supposed he would prefer not), then to give him a twenty dollar bill over and above whatever I might owe him, and tell him his services were no longer required; but that if in any other way I could assist him, I would be happy to do so, especially if he desired to return to his native place, wherever that might be, I would willingly help to defray the expenses. Moreover, if, after reaching home, he found himself at any time in want of aid, a letter from him would be sure of a reply.

The next morning came.

"Bartleby," said I, gently calling to him behind his screen.

No reply.

"Bartleby," said I, in a still gentler tone, "come here; I am not going to ask you to do anything you would prefer not to do — I simply wish to speak to you."

Upon this he noiselessly slid into view.

"Will you tell me, Bartleby, where you were born?"

"I would prefer not to."

"Will you tell me *anything* about yourself?"

"I would prefer not to."

"But what reasonable objection can you have to speak to me? I feel friendly towards you."

He did not look at me while I spoke, but kept his glance fixed upon my bust of Cicero, which, as I then sat, was directly behind me, some six inches above my head.

"What is your answer, Bartleby?" said I, after waiting a considerable time for a reply, during which his countenance remained immovable, only there was the faintest conceivable tremor of the white attenuated mouth.

"At present I prefer to give no answer," he said, and retired into his hermitage.

It was rather weak in me I confess, but his manner, on this occasion, nettled me. Not only did there seem to lurk in it a certain calm disdain, but his perverseness seemed ungrateful, considering the undeniable good usage and indulgence he had received from me.

Again I sat ruminating what I should do. Mortified as I was at his behavior, and resolved as I had been to dismiss him when I entered my office, nevertheless I strangely felt something superstitious knocking at my heart, and forbidding me to carry out my purpose, and denouncing me for a villain if I dared to breathe one bitter word against this forlornest of mankind. At last, familiarly drawing my chair behind his screen, I sat down and said: "Bartleby, never mind, then, about revealing your history; but let me entreat you, as a friend, to comply as far as may be with the usages of this office. Say now, you will help to examine papers tomorrow or next day: in short, say now, that in a day or two you will begin to be a little reasonable: — say so, Bartleby."

"At present I would prefer not to be a little reasonable," was his mildly cadaverous reply.

Just then the folding-doors opened, and Nippers approached. He seemed suffering from an unusually bad night's rest, induced by severer indigestion than common. He overheard those final words of Bartleby.

"*Prefer not*, eh?" gritted Nippers — "I'd *prefer* him, if I were you, sir," addressing me — "I'd *prefer* him; I'd give him preferences, the stubborn mule! What is it, sir, pray, that he *prefers* not to do now?"

Bartleby moved not a limb.

"Mr. Nippers," said I, "I'd prefer that you would withdraw for the present."

Somehow, of late, I had got into the way of involuntarily using this word "prefer" upon all sorts of not exactly suitable occasions. And I trembled to think that my contact with the scrivener had already and seriously affected me in a mental way. And what further and deeper aberration might it not yet produce? This apprehension had not been without efficacy in determining me to summary measures.

As Nippers, looking very sour and sulky, was departing, Turkey blandly and deferentially approached.

"With submission, sir," said he, "yesterday I was thinking about Bartleby here, and I think that if he would but prefer to take a quart of good ale every day, it would do much towards mending him, and enabling him to assist in examining his papers."

"So you have got the word, too," said I, slightly excited.

"With submission, what word, sir?" asked Turkey, respectfully crowding himself into the contracted space behind the screen, and by so doing, making me jostle the scrivener. "What word, sir?"

"I would prefer to be left alone here," said Bartleby, as if offended at being mobbed in his privacy.

"That's the word, Turkey," said I — *"that's* it."

"Oh, *prefer?* oh yes — queer word. I never use it myself. But, sir, as I was saying, if he would but prefer — "

"Turkey," interrupted I, "you will please withdraw."

"Oh certainly, sir, if you prefer that I should."

As he opened the folding-door to retire, Nippers at his desk caught a glimpse of me, and asked whether I would prefer to have a certain paper copied on blue paper or white. He did not in the least roguishly accent the word "prefer." It was plain that it involuntarily rolled from his tongue. I thought to myself, surely I must get rid of a demented man, who already has in some degree turned the tongues, if not the heads of myself and clerks. But I thought it prudent not to break the dismission at once.

The next day I noticed that Bartleby did nothing but stand at his window in his dead-wall revery. Upon asking him why he did not write, he said that he had decided upon doing no more writing.

"Why, how now? what next?" exclaimed I, "do no more writing?"

"No more."

"And what is the reason?"

"Do you not see the reason for yourself?" he indifferently replied.

I looked steadfastly at him, and perceived that his eyes looked dull and glazed. Instantly it occurred to me, that his unexampled diligence in copying by his dim window for the first few weeks of his stay with me might have temporarily impaired his vision.

I was touched. I said something in condolence with him. I hinted that of course he did wisely in abstaining from writing for a while; and urged him to embrace that opportunity of taking wholesome exercise in the open air. This, however, he did not do. A few days after this, my other clerks being absent, and being in a great hurry to dispatch certain letters by the mail, I thought that, having nothing else earthly to do, Bartleby would surely be less inflexible than usual, and carry these letters to the Post Office. But he blankly declined. So, much to my inconvenience, I went myself.

Still added days went by. Whether Bartleby's eyes improved or not, I could not say. To all appearance, I thought they did. But when I asked him if they did, he vouchsafed no answer. At all events, he would do no copying. At last, in replying to my urgings, he informed me that he had permanently given up copying.

"What!" exclaimed I; "suppose your eyes should get entirely well — better than ever before — would you not copy then?"

"I have given up copying," he answered, and slid aside.

He remained as ever, a fixture in my chamber. Nay — if that were possible — he became still more of a fixture than before. What was to be done? He would do nothing in the office; why should he stay there? In plain fact, he had now become a millstone to me, not only useless as a necklace, but afflictive to bear. Yet I was sorry for him. I speak less than truth when I say that, on his own account, he occasioned me uneasiness. If he would but have named a single relative or friend, I would instantly have written, and urged their taking the poor fellow away to some convenient retreat. But he seemed alone, absolutely alone in the universe. A bit of wreck in the mid-Atlantic. At length, necessities connected with my business tyrannized over all other considerations. Decently as I could, I told Bartleby that in six days' time he must unconditionally leave the office. I warned him to take measures, in the interval, for procuring some other abode. I offered to assist him in this endeavor, if he himself would but take the first step towards a removal. "And when you finally quit me, Bartleby," added I, "I shall see that you go not away entirely unprovided. Six days from this hour, remember."

At the expiration of that period, I peeped behind the screen, and lo! Bartleby was there.

I buttoned up my coat, balanced myself; advanced slowly towards him, touched his shoulder, and said, "The time has come; you must quit this place; I am sorry for you; here is money; but you must go."

"I would prefer not," he replied, with his back still towards me.

"You *must*."

He remained silent.

Now I had an unbounded confidence in this man's common honesty. He had frequently restored to me sixpences and shillings carelessly dropped upon the floor, for I am apt to be very reckless in such shirt-button affairs. The proceeding, then, which followed will not be deemed extraordinary.

"Bartleby," said I, "I owe you twelve dollars on account; here are thirty-two; the odd twenty are yours — Will you take it?" and I handed the bills towards him.

But he made no motion.

"I will leave them here, then," putting them under a weight on the table. Then taking my hat and cane and going to the door, I tranquilly turned and added — "After you have removed your things from these offices, Bartleby, you will of course lock the door — since every one is now gone for the day but you — and if you please, slip your key underneath the mat, so that I may have it in the morning. I shall not see you again; so good-bye to you. If, hereafter, in your new place of abode, I can be of any service to you, do not fail to advise me by letter. Good-bye, Bartleby, and fare you well."

But he answered not a word; like the last column of some ruined temple, he remained standing mute and solitary in the middle of the otherwise deserted room.

As I walked home in a pensive mood, my vanity got the better of my pity. I could not but highly plume myself on my masterly management in getting rid of Bartleby. Masterly I call it, and such it must appear to any dispassionate thinker. The beauty of my procedure seemed to consist in its perfect quietness. There was no vulgar bullying, no bravado of any sort, no choleric hectoring, and striding to and fro across the apartment, jerking out vehement commands for Bartleby to bundle himself off with his beggarly traps. Nothing of the kind. Without loudly bidding Bartleby depart — as an inferior genius might have done — I *assumed* the ground that depart he must; and upon that assumption built all I had to say. The more I thought over my procedure, the more I was charmed with it. Nevertheless, next morning, upon awakening, I had my doubts — I had somehow slept off the fumes of vanity. One of the coolest and wisest hours a man has, is just after he awakes in the morning. My procedure seemed as sagacious as ever — but only in theory. How it would prove in practice — there was the rub. It was truly a beautiful thought to have assumed Bartleby's departure; but, after all, that assumption was simply my own, and none of Bartleby's. The great point was, not whether I had assumed that he would quit me, but whether he would prefer to do so. He was more a man of preferences than assumptions.

After breakfast, I walked down town, arguing the probabilities *pro* and *con.* One moment I thought it would prove a miserable failure, and Bartleby would be found all alive at my office as usual; the next moment it seemed certain that I should find his chair empty. And so I kept veering about. At the corner of Broadway and Canal Street, I saw quite an excited group of people standing in earnest conversation.

"I'll take odds he doesn't," said a voice as I passed.

"Doesn't go? — done!" said I, "put up your money."

I was instinctively putting my hand in my pocket to produce my own, when I remembered that this was an election day. The words I had overheard bore no reference to Bartleby, but to the success or non-success of some candidate for the mayoralty. In my intent frame of mind, I had, as it were, imagined that all Broadway shared in my excitement, and were debating the same question with me. I passed on, very thankful that the uproar of the street screened my momentary absent-mindedness.

As I had intended, I was earlier than usual at my office door. I stood listening for a moment. All was still. He must be gone. I tried the knob. The door was locked. Yes, my procedure had worked to a charm; he indeed must be vanished. Yet a certain melancholy mixed with this: I was almost sorry for my brilliant success. I was fumbling under the door mat for the key, which Bartleby was to have left there for me, when accidentally my knee knocked against a panel, producing a summoning sound, and in response a voice came to me from within — "Not yet; I am occupied."

It was Bartleby.

I was thunderstruck. For an instant I stood like the man who, pipe in mouth, was killed one cloudless afternoon long ago in Virginia, by summer lightning; at his own warm open window he was killed, and remained leaning out there upon the dreamy afternoon, till some one touched him, when he fell.

"Not gone!" I murmured at last. But again obeying that wondrous ascendancy which the inscrutable scrivener had over me, and from which ascendancy, for all my chafing, I could not completely escape, I slowly went down stairs and out into the street, and while walking round the block, considered what I should next do in this unheard-of perplexity. Turn the man out by an actual thrusting I could not; to drive him away by calling him hard names would not do; calling in the police was an unpleasant idea; and yet, permit him to enjoy his cadaverous triumph over me — this, too, I could not think of. What was to be done? or, if nothing could be done, was there anything further that I could *assume* in the matter? Yes, as before I had prospectively assumed that Bartleby would depart, so now I might retrospectively assume that departed he was. In the legitimate carrying out of this assumption, I might enter my office in a great hurry, and pretending not to see Bartleby at all, walk straight against him as if he were air. Such a proceeding would in a singular degree have the appearance of a home-thrust. It was hardly possible that Bartleby could withstand such an application of the doctrine of assumption. But upon second thoughts the success of the plan seemed rather dubious. I resolved to argue the matter over with him again.

"Bartleby," said I, entering the office, with a quietly severe expression, "I am seriously displeased. I am pained, Bartleby. I had thought better of you. I had imagined you of such a gentlemanly organization, that in any delicate dilemma a slight hint would suffice — in short, an assumption. But it appears I am deceived. Why," I added, unaffectedly starting, "you have not even touched that money yet," pointing to it, just where I had left it the evening previous.

He answered nothing.

"Will you, or will you not, quit me?" I now demanded in a sudden passion, advancing close to him.

"I would prefer *not* to quit you," he replied, gently emphasizing the *not*.

"What earthly right have you to stay here? Do you pay any rent? Do you pay my taxes? Or is this property yours?"

He answered nothing.

"Are you ready to go on and write now? Are your eyes recovered? Could you copy a small paper for me this morning? or help examine a few lines? or step round to the Post Office? In a word, will you do anything at all, to give a coloring to your refusal to depart the premises?"

He silently retired into his hermitage.

I was now in such a state of nervous resentment that I thought it but prudent to check myself at present from further demonstrations. Bartleby and I were alone. I remembered the tragedy of the unfortunate Adams and the still more unfortunate Colt in the solitary office of the latter; and how poor Colt, being dreadfully incensed by Adams, and imprudently permitting himself to get wildly excited, was at unawares hurried into his fatal act — an act which certainly no man could possibly deplore more than the actor himself.[5] Often it had occurred to me in my ponderings upon the subject that had that altercation taken place in the public street, or at a private residence, it would not have terminated as it did. It was the circumstance of being alone in a solitary office, up stairs, of a building entirely unhallowed by humanizing domestic associations — an uncarpeted office, doubtless, of a dusty, haggard sort of appearance — this it must have been, which greatly helped to enhance the irritable desperation of the hapless Colt.

But when this old Adam of resentment rose in me and tempted me concerning Bartleby, I grappled him and threw him. How? Why, simply by recalling the divine injunction: "A new commandment give I unto you, that ye love one another." Yes, this it was that saved me. Aside from higher considerations, charity often operates as a vastly wise and prudent principle — a great safeguard to its possessor. Men have committed murder for jealousy's sake, and anger's sake, and hatred's sake, and selfishness' sake, and spiritual pride's sake; but no man, that ever I heard of, ever committed a diabolical murder for sweet charity's sake. Mere self-interest, then, if no better motive can be enlisted, should, especially with high-tempered men, prompt all beings to charity and philanthropy. At any rate, upon the occasion in question, I strove to drown my exasperated feelings towards the scrivener by benevolently construing his conduct. Poor fellow, poor fellow! thought I, he don't mean anything; and besides, he has seen hard times, and ought to be indulged.

I endeavored, also, immediately to occupy myself, and at the same time to comfort my despondency. I tried to fancy, that in the course of the morning, at such time as might prove agreeable to him, Bartleby, of his own free accord, would emerge from his hermitage and take up some decided line of march in the direction of the door. But no. Half-past twelve o'clock came; Turkey began to glow in the face, overturn his inkstand, and become generally obstreperous; Nippers abated down into quietude and courtesy; Ginger Nut munched his noon apple; and Bartleby remained standing at his window in one of his profoundest dead-wall reveries. Will it be credited? Ought I to acknowledge it? That afternoon I left the office without saying one further word to him.

---

[5] John C. Colt murdered Samuel Adams in January 1842. Later that year, after his conviction, Colt committed suicide a half-hour before he was to be hanged. The case received wide and sensationalistic press coverage at the time.

Some days now passed, during which, at leisure intervals I looked a little into "Edwards[6] on the Will," and "Priestley[7] on Necessity." Under the circumstances, those books induced a salutary feeling. Gradually I slid into the persuasion that these troubles of mine, touching the scrivener, had been all predestined from eternity, and Bartleby was billeted upon me for some mysterious purpose of an all-wise Providence, which it was not for a mere mortal like me to fathom. Yes, Bartleby, stay there behind your screen, thought I; I shall persecute you no more; you are harmless and noiseless as any of these old chairs; in short, I never feel so private as when I know you are here. At last I see it, I feel it; I penetrate to the predestined purpose of my life. I am content. Others may have loftier parts to enact; but my mission in this world, Bartleby, is to furnish you with office-room for such period as you may see fit to remain.

I believe that this wise and blessed frame of mind would have contin-ued with me, had it not been for the unsolicited and uncharitable remarks obtruded upon me by my professional friends who visited the rooms. But thus it often is, that the constant friction of illiberal minds wears out at last the best resolves of the more generous. Though to be sure, when I reflected upon it, it was not strange that people entering my office should be struck by the peculiar aspect of the unaccountable Bartleby, and so be tempted to throw out some sinister observations concerning him. Sometimes an attor-ney, having business with me, and calling at my office, and finding no one but the scrivener there, would undertake to obtain some sort of precise in-formation from him touching my whereabouts; but without heeding his idle talk, Bartleby would remain standing immovable in the middle of the room. So after contemplating him in that position for a time, the attorney would depart, no wiser than he came.

Also, when a reference was going on, and the room full of lawyers and witnesses, and business driving fast, some deeply-occupied legal gentleman present, seeing Bartleby wholly unemployed, would request him to run round to his (the legal gentleman's) office and fetch some papers for him. Thereupon, Bartleby would tranquilly decline, and yet remain idle as be-fore. Then the lawyer would give a great stare, and turn to me. And what could I say? At last I was made aware that all through the circle of my pro-fessional acquaintance, a whisper of wonder was running round, having ref-erence to the strange creature I kept at my office. This worried me very

---

[6] Jonathan Edwards, *Freedom of the Will* (1754). Edwards was an important Ameri-can theologian, a rigidly orthodox Calvinist who believed in the doctrine of predestination, and a leader of the Great Awakening, the religious revival that swept the North American colonies in the 1740s.

[7] Joseph Priestley, eighteenth-century English scientist and clergyman. Priestley began as a Unitarian, but developed his own radical ideas on "natural determinism." As a scientist, he did early experiments with electricity and was one of the first to discover the existence of oxygen. As a political philosopher, he championed the French Revolution — a cause so un-popular in England that he had to flee that country and spend the last decade of his life in the United States.

much. And as the idea came upon me of his possibly turning out a long-lived man, and keeping occupying my chambers, and denying my authority; and perplexing my visitors; and scandalizing my professional reputation; and casting a general gloom over the premises; keeping soul and body together to the last upon his savings (for doubtless he spent but half a dime a day), and in the end perhaps outlive me, and claim possession of my office by right of his perpetual occupancy: as all these dark anticipations crowded upon me more and more, and my friends continually intruded their relentless remarks upon the apparition in my room; a great change was wrought in me. I resolved to gather all my faculties together, and forever rid me of this intolerable incubus.

Ere revolving any complicated project, however, adapted to this end, I first simply suggested to Bartleby the propriety of his permanent departure. In a calm and serious tone, I commended the idea to his careful and mature consideration. But, having taken three days to meditate upon it, he apprised me, that his original determination remained the same; in short, that he still preferred to abide with me.

What shall I do? I now said to myself, buttoning up my coat to the last button. What shall I do? what ought I to do? what does conscience say I *should* do with this man, or, rather, ghost. Rid myself of him, I must; go, he shall. But how? You will not thrust him, the poor, pale, passive mortal — you will not thrust such a helpless creature out of your door? you will not dishonor yourself by such cruelty? No, I will not, I cannot do that. Rather would I let him live and die here, and then mason up his remains in the wall. What, then, will you do? For all your coaxing, he will not budge. Bribes he leaves under your own paper-weight on your table; in short, it is quite plain that he prefers to cling to you.

Then something severe, something unusual must be done. What! surely you will not have him collared by a constable, and commit his innocent pallor to the common jail? And upon what ground could you procure such a thing to be done? — a vagrant, is he? What! he a vagrant, a wanderer, who refuses to budge? It is because he will *not* be a vagrant, then, that you seek to count him *as* a vagrant. That is too absurd. No visible means of support: there I have him. Wrong again: for indubitably he *does* support himself, and that is the only unanswerable proof that any man can show of his possessing the means so to do. No more, then. Since he will not quit me, I must quit him. I will change my offices; I will move elsewhere, and give him fair notice, that if I find him on my new premises I will then proceed against him as a common trespasser.

Acting accordingly, next day I thus addressed him: "I find these chambers too far from the City Hall; the air is unwholesome. In a word, I propose to remove my offices next week, and shall no longer require your services. I tell you this now, in order that you may seek another place."

He made no reply, and nothing more was said.

On the appointed day I engaged carts and men, proceeded to my chambers, and, having but little furniture, everything was removed in a few hours. Throughout, the scrivener remained standing behind the screen, which I directed to be removed the last thing. It was withdrawn; and, being folded up like a huge folio, left him the motionless occupant of a naked room. I stood in the entry watching him a moment, while something from within me upbraided me.

I re-entered, with my hand in my pocket — and — and my heart in my mouth.

"Good-bye, Bartleby; I am going — good-bye, and God some way bless you; and take that," slipping something in his hand. But it dropped upon the floor, and then — strange to say — I tore myself from him whom I had so longed to be rid of.

Established in my new quarters, for a day or two I kept the door locked, and started at every footfall in the passages. When I returned to my rooms, after any little absence, I would pause at the threshold for an instant, and attentively listen, ere applying my key. But these fears were needless. Bartleby never came nigh me.

I thought all was going well, when a perturbed-looking stranger visited me, inquiring whether I was the person who had recently occupied rooms at No. — Wall Street.

Full of forebodings, I replied that I was.

"Then, sir," said the stranger, who proved a lawyer, "you are responsible for the man you left there. He refuses to do any copying; he refuses to do anything; he says he prefers not to; and he refuses to quit the premises."

"I am very sorry, sir," said I, with assumed tranquillity, but an inward tremor, "but, really, the man you allude to is nothing to me — he is no relation or apprentice of mine, that you should hold me responsible for him."

"In mercy's name, who is he?"

"I certainly cannot inform you. I know nothing about him. Formerly I employed him as a copyist; but he has done nothing for me now for some time past."

"I shall settle him, then — good morning, sir."

Several days passed, and I heard nothing more; and, though I often felt a charitable prompting to call at the place and see poor Bartleby, yet a certain squeamishness, of I know not what, withheld me.

All is over with him, by this time, thought I, at last, when, through another week, no further intelligence reached me. But, coming to my room the day after, I found several persons waiting at my door in a high state of nervous excitement.

"That's the man — here he comes," cried the foremost one, whom I recognized as the lawyer who had previously called upon me alone.

"You must take him away, sir, at once," cried a portly person among them, advancing upon me, and whom I knew to be the landlord of No. — Wall Street. "These gentlemen, my tenants, cannot stand it any longer; Mr. B——," pointing to the lawyer, "has turned him out of his room, and he now persists in haunting the building generally, sitting upon the banisters of the stairs by day, and sleeping in the entry by night. Everybody is concerned; clients are leaving the offices; some fears are entertained of a mob; something you must do, and that without delay."

Aghast at this torrent, I fell back before it, and would fain have locked myself in my new quarters. In vain I persisted that Bartleby was nothing to me — no more than to any one else. In vain — I was the last person known to have anything to do with him, and they held me to the terrible account. Fearful, then, of being exposed in the papers (as one person present obscurely threatened), I considered the matter, and, at length, said, that if the lawyer would give me a confidential interview with the scrivener, in his (the lawyer's) own room, I would, that afternoon, strive my best to rid them of the nuisance they complained of.

Going up stairs to my old haunt, there was Bartleby silently sitting upon the banister at the landing.

"What are you doing here, Bartleby?" said I.

"Sitting upon the banister," he mildly replied.

I motioned him into the lawyer's room, who then left us.

"Bartleby," said I, "are you aware that you are the cause of great tribulation to me, by persisting in occupying the entry after being dismissed from the office?"

No answer.

"Now one of two things must take place. Either you must do something, or something must be done to you. Now what sort of business would you like to engage in? Would you like to re-engage in copying for some one?"

"No; I would prefer not to make any change."

"Would you like a clerkship in a dry-goods store?"

"There is too much confinement about that. No, I would not like a clerkship; but I am not particular."

"Too much confinement," I cried, "why, you keep yourself confined all the time!"

"I would prefer not to take a clerkship," he rejoined, as if to settle that little item at once.

"How would a bar-tender's business suit you? There is no trying of the eye-sight in that."

"I would not like it at all; though, as I said before, I am not particular."

His unwonted wordiness inspirited me. I returned to the charge.

"Well, then, would you like to travel through the country collecting bills for the merchants? That would improve your health."

"No, I would prefer to be doing something else."

"How, then, would going as a companion to Europe, to entertain some young gentleman with your conversation — how would that suit you?"

"Not at all. It does not strike me that there is anything definite about that. I like to be stationary. But I am not particular."

"Stationary you shall be, then," I cried, now losing all patience, and, for the first time in all my exasperating connection with him, fairly flying into a passion. "If you do not go away from these premises before night, I shall feel bound — indeed, I *am* bound — to — to — to quit the premises myself!" I rather absurdly concluded, knowing not with what possible threat to try to frighten his immobility into compliance. Despairing of all further efforts, I was precipitately leaving him, when a final thought occurred to me — one which had not been wholly unindulged before.

"Bartleby," said I, in the kindest tone I could assume under such exciting circumstances, "will you go home with me now — not to my office, but my dwelling — and remain there till we can conclude upon some convenient arrangement for you at our leisure? Come, let us start now, right away."

"No: at present I would prefer not to make any change at all."

I answered nothing; but, effectually dodging every one by the suddenness and rapidity of my flight, rushed from the building, ran up Wall Street towards Broadway, and, jumping into the first omnibus, was soon removed from pursuit. As soon as tranquillity returned, I distinctly perceived that I had now done all that I possibly could, both in respect to the demands of the landlord and his tenants, and with regard to my own desire and sense of duty, to benefit Bartleby, and shield him from rude persecution. I now strove to be entirely care-free and quiescent; and my conscience justified me in the attempt; though, indeed, it was not so successful as I could have wished. So fearful was I of being again hunted out by the incensed landlord and his exasperated tenants, that, surrendering my business to Nippers, for a few days, I drove about the upper part of the town and through the suburbs, in my rockaway; crossed over to Jersey City and Hoboken, and paid fugitive visits to Manhattanville and Astoria. In fact, I almost lived in my rockaway for the time.

When again I entered my office, lo, a note from the landlord lay upon the desk. I opened it with trembling hands. It informed me that the writer had sent to the police, and had Bartleby removed to the Tombs as a vagrant. Moreover, since I knew more about him than any one else, he wished me to appear at that place, and make a suitable statement of the facts. These tidings had a conflicting effect upon me. At first I was indignant; but, at last, almost approved. The landlord's energetic, summary disposition, had led him to adopt a procedure which I do not think I would have decided upon myself; and yet, as a last resort, under such peculiar circumstances, it seemed the only plan.

As I afterwards learned, the poor scrivener, when told that he must be conducted to the Tombs, offered not the slightest obstacle, but, in his pale, unmoving way, silently acquiesced.

Some of the compassionate and curious by-standers joined the party;

and headed by one of the constables arm-in-arm with Bartleby, the silent procession filed its way through all the noise, and heat, and joy of the roaring thoroughfares at noon.

The same day I received the note, I went to the Tombs, or, to speak more properly, the Halls of Justice. Seeking the right officer, I stated the purpose of my call, and was informed that the individual I described was, indeed, within. I then assured the functionary that Bartleby was a perfectly honest man, and greatly to be compassionated, however unaccountably eccentric. I narrated all I knew, and closed by suggesting the idea of letting him remain in as indulgent confinement as possible, till something less harsh might be done — though, indeed, I hardly knew what. At all events, if nothing else could be decided upon, the alms-house must receive him. I then begged to have an interview.

Being under no disgraceful charge, and quite serene and harmless in all his ways, they had permitted him freely to wander about the prison, and, especially, in the inclosed grass-platted yards thereof. And so I found him there, standing all alone in the quietest of the yards, his face towards a high wall, while all around, from the narrow slits of the jail windows, I thought I saw peering out upon him the eyes of murderers and thieves.

"Bartleby!"

"I know you," he said, without looking round — "and I want nothing to say to you."

"It was not I that brought you here, Bartleby," said I, keenly pained at his implied suspicion. "And to you, this should not be so vile a place. Nothing reproachful attaches to you by being here. And see, it is not so sad a place as one might think. Look, there is the sky, and here is the grass."

"I know where I am," he replied, but would say nothing more, and so I left him.

As I entered the corridor again, a broad meat-like man, in an apron, accosted me, and, jerking his thumb over his shoulder, said — "Is that your friend?"

"Yes."

"Does he want to starve? If he does, let him live on the prison fare, that's all."

"Who are you?" asked I, not knowing what to make of such an unofficially speaking person in such a place.

"I am the grub-man. Such gentlemen as have friends here, hire me to provide them with something good to eat."

"Is this so?" said I, turning to the turnkey.

He said it was.

"Well, then," said I, slipping some silver into the grub-man's hands (for so they called him), "I want you to give particular attention to my friend there; let him have the best dinner you can get. And you must be as polite to him as possible."

"Introduce me, will you?" said the grub-man, looking at me with an expression which seemed to say he was all impatience for an opportunity to give a specimen of his breeding.

Thinking it would prove of benefit to the scrivener, I acquiesced; and, asking the grub-man his name, went up with him to Bartleby.

"Bartleby, this is a friend; you will find him very useful to you."

"Your sarvant, sir, your sarvant," said the grub-man, making a low salutation behind his apron. "Hope you find it pleasant here, sir; nice grounds — cool apartments — hope you'll stay with us some time — try to make it agreeable. What will you have for dinner to-day?"

"I prefer not to dine to-day," said Bartleby, turning away. "It would disagree with me; I am unused to dinners." So saying, he slowly moved to the other side of the inclosure, and took up a position fronting the dead-wall.

"How's this?" said the grub-man, addressing me with a stare of astonishment. "He's odd, ain't he?"

"I think he is a little deranged," said I, sadly.

"Deranged? deranged is it? Well, now, upon my word, I thought that friend of yourn was a gentleman forger; they are always pale and genteel-like, them forgers. I can't help pity 'em — can't help it, sir. Did you know Monroe Edwards?" he added, touchingly, and paused. Then, laying his hand piteously on my shoulder, sighed, "he died of consumption at Sing-Sing. So you weren't acquainted with Monroe?"

"No, I was never socially acquainted with any forgers. But I cannot stop longer. Look to my friend yonder. You will not lose by it. I will see you again."

Some few days after this, I again obtained admission to the Tombs, and went through the corridors in quest of Bartleby; but without finding him.

"I saw him coming from his cell not long ago," said a turnkey, "may be he's gone to loiter in the yards."

So I went in that direction.

"Are you looking for the silent man?" said another turnkey, passing me. "Yonder he lies — sleeping in the yard there. 'Tis not twenty minutes since I saw him lie down."

The yard was entirely quiet. It was not accessible to the common prisoners. The surrounding walls, of amazing thickness, kept off all sounds behind them. The Egyptian character of the masonry weighed upon me with its gloom. But a soft imprisoned turf grew under foot. The heart of the eternal pyramids, it seemed, wherein, by some strange magic, through the clefts, grass-seed, dropped by birds, had sprung.

Strangely huddled at the base of the wall, his knees drawn up, and lying on his side, his head touching the cold stones, I saw the wasted Bartleby. But nothing stirred. I paused; then went close up to him; stooped over, and saw that his dim eyes were open; otherwise he seemed profoundly sleeping. Something prompted me to touch him. I felt his hand, when a tingling shiver ran up my arm and down my spine to my feet.

The round face of the grub-man peered upon me now. "His dinner is ready. Won't he dine to-day, either? Or does he live without dining?"

"Lives without dining," said I, and closed the eyes.

"Eh! — He's asleep, ain't he?"

"With kings and counselors,"[8] murmured I.

There would seem little need for proceeding further in this history. Imagination will readily supply the meagre recital of poor Bartleby's interment. But, ere parting with the reader, let me say, that if this little narrative has sufficiently interested him, to awaken curiosity as to who Bartleby was, and what manner of life he led prior to the present narrator's making his acquaintance, I can only reply, that in such curiosity I fully share, but am wholly unable to gratify it. Yet here I hardly know whether I should divulge one little item of rumor, which came to my ear a few months after the scrivener's decease. Upon what basis it rested, I could never ascertain; and hence, how true it is I cannot now tell. But, inasmuch as this vague report has not been without a certain suggestive interest to me, however sad, it may prove the same with some others; and so I will briefly mention it. The report was this: that Bartleby had been a subordinate clerk in the Dead Letter Office at Washington, from which he had been suddenly removed by a change in the administration. When I think over this rumor, hardly can I express the emotions which seize me. Dead letters! does it not sound like dead men? Conceive a man by nature and misfortune prone to a pallid hopelessness, can any business seem more fitted to heighten it than that of continually handling these dead letters, and assorting them for the flames? For by the cart-load they are annually burned. Sometimes from out the folded paper the pale clerk takes a ring — the finger it was meant for, perhaps, moulders in the grave; a bank-note sent in swiftest charity — he whom it would relieve, nor eats nor hungers any more; pardon for those who died despairing; hope for those who died unhoping; good tidings for those who died stifled by unrelieved calamities. On errands of life, these letters speed to death.

Ah, Bartleby! Ah, humanity!

[1853]

---

[8] A reference to Job 3:14. Job, who has lost his family and all his property and been stricken by a terrible disease, wishes he had never been born: "then had I been at rest with kings and counselors of the earth, which built desolate places for themselves."

GUSTAVE FLAUBERT (1821–1880) *said that in writing, everything is a matter of style, of the particular turn and aspect one gives to things. Flaubert led a singularly uneventful life, remarkable mostly for the intensity with which he devoted himself to writing fiction. He once told a friend, "I have more imagination than heart." Born into a prosperous bourgeois family in Rouen, Flaubert was the son of a surgeon. His mother encouraged him to read literature and write plays while he was still a child. He attended school in Rouen and began to study law in Paris, but in 1844 his health failed and he suffered the first of many attacks of unconsciousness — possibly epilepsy. Like many of his contemporaries, including the poet Charles Baudelaire and his relative Guy de Maupassant, he was afflicted with syphilis; in his Dictionary of Accepted Opinions, Flaubert defined syphilis as being in his time as common as the cold.*

Returning to live with his widowed mother in the family home on the Seine, Flaubert began to write his books. His most famous novel is Madame Bovary (1857), which he worked on with complete absorption for more than four years, struggling to rewrite and polish it. His prose set a new standard of perfection for writers in the period when the style of the novel was evolving from romanticism to realism. Flaubert knew that "the public wants works which flatter its illusions," yet he insisted on gazing at the truth and not shrinking from the consequences: "You don't make art out of good intentions."

After his mother's death, Flaubert wrote "A Simple Heart," for the pleasure of remembering his own childhood in a provincial household. He intended the story to be the legend of a modern saint. It was one of the Three Tales *he published in 1877. Flaubert's aim as a writer was to show that "there are no noble subjects or ignoble subjects; from the standpoint of pure Art one might almost establish the axiom that there is no such thing as subject — style in itself being an absolute manner of seeing things." In his fiction he included no detail that did not have an idea behind it and no physical fact that did not help to establish a psychological mood. Letting the tale speak for itself, he believed that "the artist ought not to appear in the work any more than God in nature."*

Although Flaubert wrote few short stories, he experimented with different prose forms during his lifetime. He always sought the most exact use of language, trying to make his prose "as rhythmical as verse and as precise as the language of science." His self-discipline was an example to later writers, teaching what the novelist Julian Barnes has called "the virtue of being able to remain by yourself in your own room." Flaubert died of a sudden cerebral hemorrhage at age fifty-nine and was buried in the cemetery at Rouen.

Gustave Flaubert

ཨༀ

A SIMPLE HEART

—translated by Robert Baldick

I

For half a century the women of Pont-l'Évêque envied Mme Aubain her maidservant Félicité.

In return for a hundred francs a year she did all the cooking and the housework, the sewing, the washing, and the ironing. She could bridle a horse, fatten poultry, and churn butter, and she remained faithful to her mistress, who was by no means an easy person to get on with.

Mme Aubain had married a young fellow who was good-looking but badly-off, and who died at the beginning of 1809, leaving her with two small children and a pile of debts. She then sold all her property except for the farms of Toucques and Geffosses, which together brought in five thousand francs a year at the most, and left her house at Saint-Melaine for one behind the covered market which was cheaper to run and had belonged to her family.

This house had a slate roof and stood between the alley-way and a lane leading down to the river. Inside there were differences in level which were the cause of many a stumble. A narrow entrance-hall separated the kitchen from the parlor, where Mme Aubain sat all day long in a wicker easy-chair by the window. Eight mahogany chairs were lined up against the white-painted wainscoting, and under the barometer stood an old piano loaded with a pyramid of boxes and cartons. On either side of the chimney-piece, which was carved out of yellow marble in the Louis Quinze style, there was a tapestry-covered arm-chair, and in the middle was a clock designed to look like a temple of Vesta.[1] The whole room smelt a little musty, as the floor was on a lower level than the garden.

On the first floor was "Madame's" bedroom — very spacious, with a patterned wallpaper of pale flowers and a portrait of "Monsieur" dressed in

---

[1] Roman goddess of the hearth.

what had once been the height of fashion. It opened into a smaller room in which there were two cots, without mattresses. Then came the drawing-room, which was always shut up and full of furniture covered with dust-sheets. Next there was a passage leading to the study, where books and papers filled the shelves of a book-case in three sections built round a big writing-table of dark wood. The two end panels were hidden under pen-and-ink drawings, landscapes in gouache, and etchings by Audran,[2] souvenirs of better days and bygone luxury. On the second floor a dormer window gave light to Félicité's room, which looked out over the fields.

Every day Félicité got up at dawn, so as not to miss Mass, and worked until evening without stopping. Then, once dinner was over, the plates and dishes put away, and the door bolted, she piled ashes on the log fire and went to sleep in front of the hearth, with her rosary in her hands. Nobody could be more stubborn when it came to haggling over prices, and as for cleanliness, the shine on her saucepans was the despair of all the other servants. Being of a thrifty nature, she ate slowly, picking up from the table the crumbs from her loaf of bread — a twelve pound loaf which was baked specially for her and lasted twenty days.

All the year round she wore a kerchief of printed calico fastened behind with a pin, a bonnet which covered her hair, grey stockings, a red skirt, and over her jacket a bibbed apron such as hospital nurses wear.

Her face was thin and her voice was sharp. At twenty-five she was often taken for forty; once she reached fifty, she stopped looking any age in particular. Always silent and upright and deliberate in her movements, she looked like a wooden doll driven by clock-work.

II

Like everyone else, she had had her love-story.

Her father, a mason, had been killed when he fell off some scaffolding. Then her mother died, and when her sisters went their separate ways, a farmer took her in, sending her, small as she was, to look after the cows out in the fields. She went about in rags, shivering with cold, used to lie flat on the ground to drink water out of the ponds, would be beaten for no reason at all, and was finally turned out of the house for stealing thirty sous, a theft of which she was innocent. She found work at another farm, looking after the poultry, and as she was liked by her employers the other servants were jealous of her.

One August evening — she was eighteen at the time — they took her off to the fête at Colleville. From the start she was dazed and bewildered by the noise of the fiddles, the lamps in the trees, the medley of gaily colored dresses, the gold crosses and lace, and the throng of people jigging up and down. She was standing shyly on one side when a smart young fellow, who

[2] family name of several famous French engravers.

had been leaning on the shaft of a cart, smoking his pipe, came up and asked her to dance. He treated her to cider, coffee, griddle-cake, and a silk neckerchief, and imagining that she knew what he was after, offered to see her home. At the edge of a field of oats, he pushed her roughly to the ground. Thoroughly frightened, she started screaming for help. He took to his heels.

Another night, on the road to Beaumont, she tried to get past a big, slow-moving wagon loaded with hay, and as she was squeezing by she recognized Théodore.

He greeted her quite calmly, saying that she must forgive him for the way he had behaved to her, as "it was the drink that did it."

She did not know what to say in reply and felt like running off.

Straight away he began talking about the crops and the notabilities of the commune, saying that his father had left Colleville for the farm at Les Écots, so that they were now neighbors.

"Ah!" she said.

He added that his family wanted to see him settle but that he was in no hurry and was waiting to find a wife to suit his fancy. She lowered her head. Then he asked her if she was thinking of getting married. She answered with a smile that it was mean of him to make fun of her.

"But I'm not making fun of you!" he said. "I swear I'm not!"

He put his left arm round her waist, and she walked on supported by his embrace. Soon they slowed down. There was a gentle breeze blowing, the stars were shining, the huge load of hay was swaying about in front of them, and the four horses were raising clouds of dust as they shambled along. Then, without being told, they turned off to the right. He kissed her once more and she disappeared into the darkness.

The following week Théodore got her to grant him several rendezvous.

They would meet at the bottom of a farm-yard, behind a wall, under a solitary tree. She was not ignorant of life as young ladies are, for the animals had taught her a great deal; but her reason and an instinctive sense of honor prevented her from giving way. The resistance she put up inflamed Théodore's passion to such an extent that in order to satisfy it (or perhaps out of sheer naïveté) he proposed to her. At first she refused to believe him, but he swore that he was serious.

Soon afterwards he had a disturbing piece of news to tell her: the year before, his parents had paid a man to do his military service for him, but now he might be called up again any day, and the idea of going into the army frightened him. In Félicité's eyes this cowardice of his appeared to be a proof of his affection, and she loved him all the more for it. Every night she would steal out to meet him, and every night Théodore would plague her with his worries and entreaties.

In the end he said that he was going to the Prefecture himself to make inquiries, and that he would come and tell her how matters stood the following Sunday, between eleven and midnight.

At the appointed hour she hurried to meet her sweetheart, but found one of his friends waiting for her instead.

He told her that she would not see Théodore again. To make sure of avoiding conscription, he had married a very rich old woman, Mme Lehoussais of Toucques.

Her reaction was an outburst of frenzied grief. She threw herself on the ground, screaming and calling on God, and lay moaning all alone in the open until sunrise. Then she went back to the farm and announced her intention of leaving. At the end of the month, when she had received her wages, she wrapped her small belongings up in a kerchief and made her way to Pont-l'Évêque.

In front of the inn there, she sought information from a woman in a widow's bonnet, who, as it happened, was looking for a cook. The girl did not know much about cooking, but she seemed so willing and expected so little that finally Mme Aubain ended up by saying: "Very well, I will take you on."

A quarter of an hour later Félicité was installed in her house.

At first she lived there in a kind of fearful awe caused by "the style of the house" and the memory of "Monsieur" brooding over everything. Paul and Virginie, the boy aged seven and the girl barely four, seemed to her to be made of some precious substance. She used to carry them about pick-a-back, and when Mme Aubain told her not to keep on kissing them she was cut to the quick. All the same, she was happy now, for her pleasant surroundings had dispelled her grief.

On Thursdays, a few regular visitors came in to play Boston, and Félicité got the cards and the foot-warmers ready beforehand. They always arrived punctually at eight, and left before the clock struck eleven.

Every Monday morning the second-hand dealer who lived down the alley put all his junk out on the pavement. Then the hum of voices began to fill the town, mingled with the neighing of horses, the bleating of lambs, the grunting of pigs, and the rattle of carts in the streets.

About midday, when the market was in full swing, a tall old peasant with a hooked nose and his cap on the back of his head would appear at the door. This was Robelin, the farmer from Geffosses. A little later, and Liébard, the farmer from Toucques, would arrive — a short, fat, red-faced fellow in a grey jacket and leather gaiters fitted with spurs.

Both men had hens or cheeses they wanted to sell to "Madame." But Félicité was up to all their tricks and invariably outwitted them, so that they went away full of respect for her.

From time to time Mme Aubain had a visit from an uncle of hers, the Marquis de Grémanville, who had been ruined by loose living and was now living at Falaise on his last remaining scrap of property. He always turned up at lunch-time, accompanied by a hideous poodle who dirtied all the furniture with its paws. However hard he tried to behave like a gentleman, even going so far as to raise his hat every time he mentioned "my late father" the force of habit was usually too much for him, for he would start pouring himself one glass after another and telling bawdy stories. Félicité used to push him gently out of the house, saying politely: "You've had quite enough, Monsieur de Grémanville. See you another time!" and shutting the door on him.

She used to open it with pleasure to M. Bourais, who was a retired solicitor. His white tie and his bald head, his frilled shirt-front and his ample brown frock-coat, the way he had of rounding his arm to take a pinch of snuff, and indeed everything about him made an overwhelming impression on her such as we feel when we meet some outstanding personality.

As he looked after "Madame's" property, he used to shut himself up with her for hours in "Monsieur's" study. He lived in dread of compromising his reputation, had a tremendous respect for the Bench, and laid claim to some knowledge of Latin.

To give the children a little painless instruction, he made them a present of a geography book with illustrations. These represented scenes in different parts of the world, such as cannibals wearing feather head-dresses, a monkey carrying off a young lady, Bedouins in the desert, a whale being harpooned, and so on.

Paul explained these pictures to Félicité, and that indeed was all the education she ever had. As for the children, they were taught by Guyot, a poor devil employed at the Town Hall, who was famous for his beautiful handwriting, and who had a habit of sharpening his penknife on his boots.

When the weather was fine the whole household used to set off early for a day on the Geffosses farm.

The farm-yard there was on a slope, with the house in the middle; and the sea, in the distance, looked like a streak of grey. Félicité would take some slices of cold meat out of her basket, and they would have their lunch in a room adjoining the dairy. It was all that remained of a country house which had fallen into ruin, and the wallpaper hung in shreds, fluttering in the draught. Mme Aubain used to sit with bowed head, absorbed in her memories, so that the children were afraid to talk. "Why don't you run along and play?" she would say, and away they went.

Paul climbed up into the barn, caught birds, played ducks and drakes on the pond, or banged with a stick on the great casks, which sounded just like drums.

Virginie fed the rabbits, or scampered off to pick cornflowers, showing her little embroidered knickers as she ran.

One autumn evening they came home through the fields. The moon, which was in its first quarter, lit up part of the sky, and there was some mist floating like a scarf over the winding Toucques. The cattle, lying out in the middle of the pasture, looked peacefully at the four people walking by. In the third field a few got up and made a half circle in front of them.

"Don't be frightened!" said Félicité, and crooning softly, she stroked the back of the nearest animal. It turned about and the others did the same. But while they were crossing the next field they suddenly heard a dreadful bellowing. It came from a bull which had been hidden by the mist, and which now came towards the two women.

Mme Aubain started to run.

"No! No!" said Félicité. "Not so fast!"

All the same they quickened their pace, hearing behind them a sound of heavy breathing which came nearer and nearer. The bull's hooves thudded like hammers on the turf, and they realized that it had broken into a gallop. Turning round, Félicité tore up some clods of earth and flung them at its eyes. It lowered its muzzle and thrust its horns forward, trembling with rage and bellowing horribly.

By now Mme Aubain had got to the end of the field with her two children and was frantically looking for a way over the high bank. Félicité was still backing away from the bull, hurling clods of turf which blinded it, and shouting: "Hurry! Hurry!"

Mme Aubain got down into the ditch, pushed first Virginie and then Paul up the other side, fell once or twice trying to climb the bank, and finally managed it with a valiant effort.

The bull had driven Félicité back against a gate, and its slaver was spurting into her face. In another second it would have gored her, but she just had time to slip between two of the bars, and the great beast halted in amazement.

This adventure was talked about at Pont-l'Évêque for a good many years, but Félicité never prided herself in the least on what she had done, as it never occurred to her that she had done anything heroic.

Virginie claimed all her attention, for the fright had affected the little girl's nerves, and M. Poupart, the doctor, recommended sea-bathing at Trouville.

In those days the resort had few visitors. Mme Aubain made inquiries, consulted Bourais, and got everything ready as though for a long journey.

Her luggage went off in Liébard's cart the day before she left. The next morning he brought along two horses, one of which had a woman's saddle with a velvet back, while the other carried a cloak rolled up to make a kind of seat on its crupper. Mme Aubain sat on this, with Liébard in front. Félicité looked after Virginie on the other horse, and Paul mounted M. Lechaptois's donkey, which he had lent them on condition they took great care of it.

The road was so bad that it took two hours to travel the five miles to Toucques. The horses sank into the mud up to their pasterns and had to jerk their hind-quarters to get out; often they stumbled in the ruts, or else they had to jump. In some places, Liébard's mare came to a sudden stop, and while he waited patiently for her to move off again, he talked about the people whose properties bordered the road, adding moral reflections to each story. For instance, in the middle of Toucques, as they were passing underneath some windows set in a mass of nasturtiums, he shrugged his shoulders and said:

"There's a Madame Lehoussais lives here. Now instead of taking a young man, she. . . ."

Félicité did not hear the rest, for the horses had broken into a trot and the donkey was galloping along. All three turned down a bridle-path, a gate swung open, a couple of boys appeared, and everyone dismounted in front of a manure-heap right outside the farm-house door.

Old Mother Liébard welcomed her mistress with every appearance of pleasure. She served up a sirloin of beef for lunch, with tripe and black pudding, a fricassee of chicken, sparkling cider, a fruit tart and brandy-plums, garnishing the whole meal with compliments to Madame, who seemed to be enjoying better health, to Mademoiselle, who had turned into a "proper little beauty," and to Monsieur Paul, who had "filled out a lot." Nor did she forget their deceased grandparents, whom the Liébards had known personally, having been in the family's service for several generations.

Like its occupants, the farm had an air of antiquity. The ceiling-beams were worm-eaten, the walls black with smoke, and the window-panes grey with dust. There was an oak dresser laden with all sorts of odds and ends — jugs, plates, pewter bowls, wolf-traps, sheep-shears, and an enormous syringe which amused the children. In the three yards outside there was not a single tree without either mushrooms at its base or mistletoe in its branches. Several had been blown down and had taken root again in the middle; all of them were bent under the weight of their apples. The thatched roofs, which looked like brown velvet and varied in thickness, weathered the fiercest winds, but the cart-shed was tumbling down. Mme Aubain said that she would have it seen to, and ordered the animals to be reharnessed.

It took them another half-hour to reach Trouville. The little caravan dismounted to make their way along the Écores, a cliff jutting right out over the boats moored below; and three minutes later they got to the end of the quay and entered the courtyard of the Golden Lamb, the inn kept by Mère David.

After the first few days Virginie felt stronger, as a result of the change of air and the sea-bathing. Not having a costume, she went into the water in her chemise and her maid dressed her afterwards in a customs officer's hut which was used by the bathers.

In the afternoons they took the donkey and went off beyond the Roches-Noires, in the direction of Hennequeville. To begin with, the path went uphill between gentle slopes like the lawns in a park, and then came out on a plateau where pastureland and ploughed fields alternated. On either side there were holly-bushes standing out from the tangle of brambles, and here and there a big dead tree spread its zigzag branches against the blue sky.

They almost always rested in the same field, with Deauville on their left, Le Havre on their right, and the open sea in front. The water glittered in the sunshine, smooth as a mirror, and so still that the murmur it made was scarcely audible; unseen sparrows could be heard twittering, and the sky covered the whole scene with its huge canopy. Mme Aubain sat doing her needlework, Virginie plaited rushes beside her, Félicité gathered lavender, and Paul, feeling profoundly bored, longed to get up and go.

Sometimes they crossed the Toucques in a boat and hunted for shells. When the tide went out, sea-urchins, ormers, and jelly-fish were left behind; and the children scampered around, snatching at the foam-flakes carried on the wind. The sleepy waves, breaking on the sand, spread themselves out along the shore. The beach stretched as far as the eye could see, bounded on the land side by the dunes which separated it from the Marais, a broad meadow in the shape of an arena. When they came back that way, Trouville, on the distant hillside, grew bigger at every step, and with its medley of oddly assorted houses seemed to blossom out in gay disorder.

On exceptionally hot days they stayed in their room. The sun shone in dazzling bars of light between the slats of the blind. There was not a sound to be heard in the village, and not a soul to be seen down in the street. Everything seemed more peaceful in the prevailing silence. In the distance caulkers were hammering away at the boats, and the smell of tar was wafted along by a sluggish breeze.

The principal amusement consisted in watching the fishingboats come in. As soon as they had passed the buoys, they started tacking. With their canvas partly lowered and their foresails blown out like balloons they glided through the splashing waves as far as the middle of the harbor, where they suddenly dropped anchor. Then each boat came alongside the quay, and the crew threw ashore their catch of quivering fish. A line of carts stood waiting, and women in cotton bonnets rushed forward to take the baskets and kiss their men.

One day one of these women spoke to Félicité, who came back to the inn soon after in a state of great excitement. She explained that she had found one of her sisters — and Nastasie Barette, now Leroux, made her appearance, with a baby at her breast, another child holding her right hand, and on her left a little sailor-boy, his arms akimbo and his cap over one ear.

Mme Aubain sent her off after a quarter of an hour. From then on they were forever hanging round the kitchen or loitering about when the family went for a walk, though the husband kept out of sight.

Félicité became quite attached to them. She bought them a blanket, several shirts, and a stove; and it was clear that they were bent on getting all they could out of her.

This weakness of hers annoyed Mme Aubain, who in any event disliked the familiar way in which the nephew spoke to Paul. And so, as Virginie had started coughing and the good weather was over, she decided to go back to Pont-l'Évêque.

M. Bourais advised her on the choice of a school; Caen was considered the best, so it was there that Paul was sent. He said good-bye bravely, feeling really rather pleased to be going to a place where he would have friends of his own.

Mme Aubain resigned herself to the loss of her son, knowing that it was unavoidable. Virginie soon got used to it. Félicité missed the din he used to make, but she was given something new to do which served as a distraction; from Christmas onwards she had to take the little girl to catechism every day.

III

After genuflecting at the door, she walked up the center aisle under the nave, opened the door of Mme Aubain's pew, sat down, and started looking about her.

The choir stalls were all occupied, with the boys on the right and the girls on the left, while the curé stood by the lectern. In one of the stained-glass windows in the apse the Holy Ghost looked down on the Virgin; another window showed her kneeling before the Infant Jesus; and behind the tabernacle there was a wood-carving of St. Michael slaying the dragon.

The priest began with a brief outline of sacred history. Listening to him, Félicité saw in imagination the Garden of Eden, the Flood, the Tower of Babel, cities burning, peoples dying, and idols being overthrown; and his dazzling vision left her with a great respect for the Almighty and profound fear of His wrath.

Then she wept as she listened to the story of the Passion. Why had they crucified Him, when He loved children, fed the multitudes, healed the blind, and had chosen out of humility to be born among the poor, on the litter of a stable? The sowing of the seed, the reaping of the harvest, the pressing of the grapes — all those familiar things of which the Gospels speak had their place in her life. God had sanctified them in passing, so that she loved the lambs more tenderly for love of the Lamb of God, and the doves for the sake of the Holy Ghost.

She found it difficult, however, to imagine what the Holy Ghost looked like, for it was not just a bird but a fire as well, and sometimes a breath. She wondered whether that was its light she had seen flitting about the edge of the marshes at night, whether that was its breath she had felt driving the clouds across the sky, whether that was its voice she had heard in the sweet music of the bells. And she sat in silent adoration, delighting in the coolness of the walls and the quiet of the church.

Of dogma she neither understood nor even tried to understand anything. The curé discoursed, the children repeated their lesson, and she finally dropped off to sleep, waking up suddenly at the sound of their sabots[3] clattering across the flagstones as they left the church.

It was in this manner, simply by hearing it expounded, that she learnt her catechism, for her religious education had been neglected in her youth. From then on she copied all Virginie's observances, fasting when she did and going to confession with her. On the feast of Corpus Christi the two of them made an altar of repose together.

The preparations for Virginie's first communion caused her great anxiety. She worried over her shoes, her rosary, her missal, and her gloves. And how she trembled as she helped Mme Aubain to dress the child!

All through the Mass her heart was in her mouth. One side of the choir was hidden from her by M. Bourais, but directly opposite her she could see the flock of maidens, looking like a field of snow with their white crowns perched on top of their veils; and she recognized her little darling from a distance by her dainty neck and her rapt attitude. The bell tinkled. Every head bowed low, and there was a silence. Then, to the thunderous accompaniment of the organ, choir and congregation joined in singing the *Agnus Dei*. Next the boys' procession began, and after that the girls got up from their seats. Slowly, their hands joined in prayer, they went towards the brightly lit altar, knelt on the first step, received the Host one by one, and went back to their places in the same order. When it was Virginie's turn, Félicité leant forward to see her, and in one of those imaginative flights born of real affection, it seemed to her that she herself was in the child's place. Virginie's face became her own, Virginie's dress clothed her, Virginie's heart was beating in her breast; and as she closed her eyes and opened her mouth, she almost fainted away.

Early next morning she went to the sacristy and asked M. le Curé to give her communion. She received the sacrament with all due reverence, but did not feel the same rapture as she had the day before.

Mme Aubain wanted her daughter to possess every accomplishment, and since Guyot could not teach her English or music, she decided to send her as a boarder to the Ursuline Convent at Honfleur.

Virginie raised no objection, but Félicité went about sighing at Madame's lack of feeling. Then she thought that perhaps her mistress was right: such matters, after all, lay outside her province.

Finally the day arrived when an old wagonette stopped at their door, and a nun got down from it who had come to fetch Mademoiselle. Félicité hoisted the luggage up on top, gave the driver some parting instructions, and put six pots of jam, a dozen pears, and a bunch of violets in the boot.

At the last moment Virginie burst into a fit of sobbing. She threw her arms round her mother, who kissed her on the forehead, saying: "Come now, be brave, be brave." The step was pulled up and the carriage drove away.

[3] wooden shoes.

Then Mme Aubain broke down, and that evening all her friends, M. and Mme Lormeau, Mme Lechaptois, the Rochefeuille sisters, M. de Houppeville, and Bourais, came in to console her.

To begin with she missed her daughter badly. But she had a letter from her three times a week, wrote back on the other days, walked round her garden, did a little reading, and thus contrived to fill the empty hours.

As for Félicité, she went into Virginie's room every morning from sheer force of habit and looked round it. It upset her not having to brush the child's hair any more, tie her bootlaces, or tuck her up in bed; and she missed seeing her sweet face all the time and holding her hand when they went out together. For want of something to do, she tried making lace, but her fingers were too clumsy and broke the threads. She could not settle to anything, lost her sleep, and, to use her own words, was "eaten up inside."

To "occupy her mind," she asked if her nephew Victor might come and see her, and permission was granted.

He used to arrive after Mass on Sunday, his cheeks flushed, his chest bare, and smelling of the countryside through which he had come. She laid a place for him straight away, opposite hers, and they had lunch together. Eating as little as possible herself, in order to save the expense, she stuffed him so full of food that he fell asleep after the meal. When the first bell for vespers rang, she woke him up, brushed his trousers, tied his tie, and set off for church, leaning on his arm with all a mother's pride.

His parents always told him to get something out of her — a packet of brown sugar perhaps, some soap, or a little brandy, sometimes even money. He brought her his clothes to be mended, and she did the work gladly, thankful for anything that would force him to come again.

In August his father took him on a coasting trip. The children's holidays were just beginning, and it cheered her up to have them home again. But Paul was turning capricious and Virginie was getting too old to be addressed familiarly — a state of affairs which put a barrier of constraint between them.

Victor went to Morlaix, Dunkirk, and Brighton in turn, and brought her a present after each trip. The first time it was a box covered with shells, the second a coffee cup, the third a big gingerbread man. He was growing quite handsome, with his trim figure, his little moustache, his frank open eyes, and the little leather cap that he wore on the back of his head like a pilot. He kept her amused by telling her stories full of nautical jargon.

One Monday — it was the fourteenth of July 1819, a date she never forgot — Victor told her that he had signed on for an ocean voyage, and that on the Wednesday night he would be taking the Honfleur packet to join his schooner, which was due to sail shortly from Le Havre. He might be away, he said, for two years.

The prospect of such a long absence made Félicité extremely unhappy, and she felt she must bid him godspeed once more. So on the

Wednesday evening, when Madame's dinner was over, she put on her clogs and swiftly covered the ten miles between Pont-l'Évêque and Honfleur.

When she arrived at the Calvary she turned right instead of left, got lost in the shipyards, and had to retrace her steps. Some people she spoke to advised her to hurry. She went right round the harbor, which was full of boats, constantly tripping over moorings. Then the ground fell away, rays of light criss-crossed in front of her, and for a moment, she thought she was going mad, for she could see horses up in the sky.

On the quayside more horses were neighing, frightened by the sea. A derrick was hoisting them into the air and dropping them into one of the boats, which was already crowded with passengers elbowing their way between barrels of cider, baskets of cheese, and sacks of grain. Hens were cackling and the captain swearing, while a cabin-boy stood leaning on the cats-head, completely indifferent to it all. Félicité, who had not recognized him, shouted: "Victor!" and he raised his head. She rushed forward, but at that very moment the gangway was pulled ashore.

The packet moved out of the harbor with women singing as they hauled it along, its ribs creaking and heavy waves lashing its bows. The sail swung round, hiding everyone on board from view, and against the silvery, moonlit sea the boat appeared as a dark shape that grew ever fainter, until at last it vanished in the distance.

As Félicité was passing the Calvary, she felt a longing to commend to God's mercy all that she held most dear; and she stood there praying for a long time, her face bathed in tears, her eyes fixed upon the clouds. The town was asleep, except for the customs officers walking up and down. Water was pouring ceaselessly through the holes in the sluice-gate, making as much noise as a torrent. The clocks struck two.

The convent parlor would not be open before daybreak, and Madame would be annoyed if she were late; so, although she would have liked to give a kiss to the other child, she set off for home. The maids at the inn were just waking up as she got to Pont-l'Évêque.

So the poor lad was going to be tossed by the waves for months on end! His previous voyages had caused her no alarm. People came back from England and Brittany; but America, the Colonies, the Islands, were all so far away, somewhere at the other end of the world.

From then on Félicité thought of nothing but her nephew. On sunny days she hoped he was not too thirsty, and when there was a storm she was afraid he would be struck by lightning. Listening to the wind howling in the chimney or blowing slates off the roof, she saw him being buffeted by the very same storm, perched on the top of a broken mast, with his whole body bent backwards under a sheet of foam; or again — and these were reminiscences of the illustrated geography book — he was being eaten by savages, captured by monkeys in the forest, or dying on a desert shore. But she never spoke of her worries.

Mme Aubain had worries of her own about her daughter. The good nuns said that she was an affectionate child, but very delicate. The slightest emotion upset her, and she had to give up playing the piano.

Her mother insisted on regular letters from the convent. One morning when the postman had not called, she lost patience and walked up and down the room, between her chair and the window. It was really extraordinary! Four days without any news!

Thinking her own example would comfort her, Félicité said:

"I've been six months, Madame, without news."

"News of whom?"

The servant answered gently:

"Why — of my nephew."

"Oh, your nephew!" And Mme Aubain started pacing up and down again, with a shrug of her shoulders that seemed to say: "I wasn't thinking of him — and indeed, why should I? Who cares about a young, good-for-nothing cabin-boy? Whereas my daughter — why, just think!"

Although she had been brought up the hard way, Félicité was indignant with Madame, but she soon forgot. It struck her as perfectly natural to lose one's head where the little girl was concerned. For her, the two children were of equal importance; they were linked together in her heart by a single bond, and their destinies should be the same.

The chemist told her that Victor's ship had arrived at Havana: he had seen this piece of information in a newspaper.

Because of its association with cigars, she imagined Havana as a place where nobody did anything but smoke, and pictured Victor walking about among crowds of Negroes in a cloud of tobacco-smoke. Was it possible, she wondered, "in case of need" to come back by land? And how far was it from Pont-l'Évêque? To find out she asked M. Bourais.

He reached for his atlas, and launched forth into an explanation of latitudes and longitudes, smiling like the pedant he was at Félicité's bewilderment. Finally he pointed with his pencil at a minute black dot inside a ragged oval patch, saying:

"There it is."

She bent over the map, but the network of colored lines meant nothing to her and only tired her eyes. So when Bourais asked her to tell him what was puzzling her, she begged him to show her the house where Victor was living. He threw up his hands, sneezed, and roared with laughter, delighted to come across such simplicity. And Félicité — whose intelligence was so limited that she probably expected to see an actual portrait of her nephew — could not make out why he was laughing.

It was a fortnight later that Liébard came into the kitchen at market-time, as he usually did, and handed her a letter from her brother-in-law. As neither of them could read, she turned to her mistress for help.

Mme Aubain, who was counting the stitches in her knitting, put it down and unsealed the letter. She gave a start, and, looking hard at Félicité, said quietly:

"They have some bad news for you. . . . Your nephew. . . ."

He was dead. That was all the letter had to say.

Félicité dropped on to a chair, leaning her head against the wall and closing her eyelids, which suddenly turned pink. Then, with her head bowed, her hands dangling, and her eyes set, she kept repeating:

"Poor little lad! Poor little lad!"

Liébard looked at her and sighed. Mme Aubain was trembling slightly. She suggested that she should go and see her sister at Trouville, but Félicité shook her head to indicate that there was no need for that.

There was a silence. Old Liébard thought it advisable to go.

Then Félicité said:

"It doesn't matter a bit, not to them it doesn't."

Her head fell forward again, and from time to time she unconsciously picked up the knitting needles lying on the work table.

Some women went past carrying a tray full of dripping linen.

Catching sight of them through the window, she remembered her own washing; she had passed the lye through it the day before and today it needed rinsing. So she left the room.

Her board and tub were on the bank of the Toucques. She threw a pile of chemises down by the water's edge, rolled up her sleeves, and picked up her battledore. The lusty blows she gave with it could be heard in all the neighboring gardens.

The fields were empty, the river rippling in the wind; at the bottom long weeds were waving to and fro, like the hair of corpses floating in the water. She held back her grief, and was very brave until the evening; but in her room she gave way to it completely, lying on her mattress with her face buried in the pillow and her fists pressed against her temples.

Long afterwards she learnt the circumstances of Victor's death from the captain of his ship. He had gone down with yellow fever, and they had bled him too much at the hospital. Four doctors had held him at once. He had died straight away, and the chief doctor had said:

"Good! There goes another!"

His parents had always treated him cruelly. She preferred not to see them again, and they made no advances, either because they had forgotten about her or out of the callousness of the poor.

Meanwhile Virginie was growing weaker. Difficulty in breathing, fits of coughing, protracted bouts of fever, and mottled patches on the cheek-bones all indicated some deepseated complaint. M. Poupart had advised a stay in Provence. Mme Aubain decided to follow this suggestion, and, if it had not been for the weather at Pont-l'Évêque, she would have brought her daughter home at once.

She arranged with a jobmaster to drive her out to the convent every Tuesday. There was a terrace in the garden, overlooking the Seine, and there Virginie, leaning on her mother's arm, walked up and down over the fallen vineleaves. Sometimes, while she was looking at the sails in the distance, or at the long stretch of horizon from the Château de Tancarville to the lighthouses of Le Havre, the sun would break through the clouds and make her blink. Afterwards they would rest in the arbor. Her mother had secured a little cask of excellent Malaga, and, laughing at the idea of getting tipsy, Virginie used to drink a thimbleful, but no more.

Her strength revived. Autumn slipped by, and Félicité assured Mme Aubain that there was nothing to fear. But one evening, coming back from some errand in the neighborhood, she found M. Poupart's gig standing at the door. He was in the hall, and Mme Aubain was trying on her bonnet.

"Give me my foot-warmer, purse, gloves. Quickly now!"

Virginie had pneumonia and was perhaps past recovery.

"Not yet!" said the doctor; and the two of them got into the carriage with snowflakes swirling around them. Night was falling and it was very cold.

Félicité rushed into the church to light a candle, and then ran after the gig. She caught up with it an hour later, jumped lightly behind, and hung on to the fringe. But then a thought struck her: the courtyard had not been locked up, the burglars might get in. So she jumped down again.

At dawn the next day she went to the doctor's. He had come home and gone out again on his rounds. Then she waited at the inn, thinking that somebody who was a stranger to the district might call there with a letter. Finally, when it was twilight, she got into the coach for Lisieux.

The convent was at the bottom of a steep lane. When she was halfway down the hill, she heard a strange sound which she recognized as a death-bell tolling.

"It's for somebody else," she thought, as she banged the door-knocker hard.

After a few minutes she heard the sound of shuffling feet, the door opened a little way, and a nun appeared.

The good sister said with an air of compunction that "she had just passed away." At that moment the bell of Saint-Léonard was tolled more vigorously than ever.

Félicité went up to the second floor. From the doorway of the room she could see Virginie lying on her back, her hands clasped together, her mouth open, her head tilted back under a black crucifix that leant over her, her face whiter than the curtains that hung motionless on either side. Mme Aubain was clinging to the foot of the bed and sobbing desperately. The Mother Superior stood on the right. Three candlesticks on the chest of drawers added touches of red to the scene, and fog was whitening the windows. Some nuns led Mme Aubain away.

For two nights Félicité never left the dead girl. She said the same prayers over and over again, sprinkled holy water on the sheets, then sat down again to watch. At the end of her first vigil she noticed that the child's face had gone yellow, the lips were turning blue, the nose looked sharper, and the eyes were sunken. She kissed them several times, and would not have been particularly surprised if Virginie had opened them again: to minds like hers the supernatural is a simple matter. She laid her out, wrapped her in a shroud, put her in her coffin, placed a wreath on her, and spread out her hair. It was fair and amazingly long for her age. Félicité cut off a big lock, half of which she slipped into her bosom, resolving never to part with it.

The body was brought back to Pont-l'Évêque at the request of Mme Aubain, who followed the hearse in a closed carriage.

After the Requiem Mass, it took another three-quarters of an hour to reach the cemetery. Paul walked in front, sobbing. Then came M. Bourais, and after him the principal inhabitants of the town, the women all wearing long black veils, and Félicité. She was thinking about her nephew; and since she had been unable to pay him these last honors, she felt an added grief, just as if they were burying him with Virginie.

Mme Aubain's despair passed all bounds. First of all she rebelled against God, considering it unfair of Him to have taken her daughter from her — for she had never done any harm, and her conscience was quite clear. But was it? She ought to have taken Virginie to the south; other doctors would have saved her life. She blamed herself, wished she could have joined her daughter, and cried out in anguish in her dreams. One dream in particular obsessed her. Her husband, dressed like a sailor, came back from a long voyage, and told her amid tears that he had been ordered to take Virginie away — whereupon they put their heads together to discover somewhere to hide her.

One day she came in from the garden utterly distraught. A few minutes earlier — and she pointed to the spot — father and daughter had appeared to her, doing nothing, but simply looking at her.

For several months she stayed in her room in a kind of stupor. Félicité scolded her gently, telling her that she must take care of herself for her son's sake, and also in remembrance of "her."

"Her?" repeated Mme Aubain, as if she were waking from a sleep. "Oh, yes, of course! You don't forget her, do you!" This was an allusion to the cemetery, where she herself was strictly forbidden to go.

Félicité went there every day. She would set out on the stroke of four, going past the houses, up the hill, and through the gate, until she came to Virginie's grave. There was a little column of pink marble with a tablet at its base, and a tiny garden enclosed by chains. The beds were hidden under a carpet of flowers. She watered their leaves and changed the sand, going down on her knees to fork the ground thoroughly. The result was that when Mme Aubain was able to come here, she experienced a feeling of relief, a kind of consolation.

Then the years slipped by, each one like the last, with nothing to vary the rhythm of the great festivals: Easter, the Assumption, All Saints' Day. Domestic events marked dates that later served as points of reference. Thus in 1825 a couple of glaziers whitewashed the hall; in 1827 a piece of the roof fell into the courtyard and nearly killed a man; and in the summer of 1828 it was Madame's turn to provide the bread for consecration. About this time Bourais went away in a mysterious fashion; and one by one the old acquaintances disappeared: Guyot, Liébard, Mme Lechaptois, Robelin, and Uncle Grémanville, who had been paralyzed for a long time.

One night the driver of the mail-coach brought Pont-l'Évêque news of the July Revolution.[4] A few days later a new subprefect was appointed. This was the Baron de Larsonnière, who had been a consul in America, and who brought with him, besides his wife, his sister-in-law and three young ladies who were almost grown-up. They were to be seen on their lawn, dressed in loose-fitting smocks; and they had a Negro servant and a parrot. They paid a call on Mme Aubain, who made a point of returning it. As soon as Félicité saw them coming, she would run and tell her mistress. But only one thing could really awaken her interest, and that was her son's letters.

He seemed to be incapable of following any career and spent all his time in taverns. She paid his debts, but he contracted new ones, and the sighs Mme Aubain heaved as she knitted by the window reached Félicité at her spinning wheel in the kitchen.

The two women used to walk up and down together beside the espalier,[5] forever talking of Virginie and debating whether such and such a thing would have appealed to her, or what she would have said on such and such an occasion.

All her little belongings were in a cupboard in the children's bedroom. Mme Aubain went through them as seldom as possible. One summer day she resigned herself to doing so, and the moths were sent fluttering out of the cupboard.

Virginie's frocks hung in a row underneath a shelf containing three dolls, a few hoops, a set of toy furniture, and the wash-basin she had used. Besides the frocks, they took out her petticoats, her stockings, and her handkerchiefs, and spread them out on the two beds before folding them up again. The sunlight streamed in on these pathetic objects, bringing out the stains and showing up the creases made by the child's movements. The air was warm, the sky was blue, a blackbird was singing, and everything seemed to be utterly at peace.

They found a little chestnut-colored hat, made of plush with a long nap; but the moths had ruined it. Félicité asked if she might have it. The two women looked at each other and their eyes filled with tears. Then the mistress opened her arms, the maid threw herself into them, and they clasped each other in a warm embrace, satisfying their grief in a kiss which made them equal.

[4] Popular rebellion of July and August 1830 in response to the attempt of King Charles X to dissolve the elected Chamber of Deputies and repeal certain freedoms granted in the Charter of 1814. It took just over a week for the rebels to force Charles to abdicate and to replace him with Louis-Philippe, the duke of Orleans.
[5] a trellis against which shrubs and fruit trees grow flat.

It was the first time that such a thing had happened, for Mme Aubain was not of a demonstrative nature. Félicité was as grateful as if she had received a great favor, and henceforth loved her mistress with dog-like devotion and religious veneration.

Her heart grew softer as time went by.

When she heard the drums of a regiment coming down the street she stood at the door with a jug of cider and offered the soldiers a drink. She looked after the people who went down with cholera. She watched over the Polish refugees, and one of them actually expressed a desire to marry her. But they fell out, for when she came back from the Angelus one morning, she found that he had got into her kitchen and was calmly eating an oil-and-vinegar salad.

After the Poles it was Père Colmiche, an old man who was said to have committed fearful atrocities in '93.[6] He lived by the river in a ruined pig-sty. The boys of the town used to peer at him through the cracks in the walls, and threw pebbles at him which landed on the litter where he lay, constantly shaken by fits of coughing. His hair was extremely long, his eyelids inflamed, and on one arm there was a swelling bigger than his head. Félicité brought him some linen, tried to clean out his filthy hovel, and even wondered if she could install him in the wash-house without annoying Madame. When the tumor had burst, she changed his dressings every day, brought him some cake now and then, and put him out in the sun on a truss of hay. The poor old fellow would thank her in a faint whisper, slavering and trembling all the while, fearful of losing her and stretching his hands out as soon as he saw her moving away.

He died, and she had a Mass said for the repose of his soul.

That same day a great piece of good fortune came her way. Just as she was serving dinner, Mme de Larsonnière's Negro appeared carrying the parrot in its cage, complete with perch, chain, and padlock. The Baroness had written a note informing Mme Aubain that her husband had been promoted to a Prefecture and they were leaving that evening; she begged her to accept the parrot as a keepsake and a token of her regard.

This bird had engrossed Félicité's thoughts for a long time, for it came from America, and that word reminded her of Victor. So she had asked the Negro all about it, and once she had even gone so far as to say:

"How pleased Madame would be if it were hers!"

The Negro had repeated this remark to his mistress, who, unable to take the parrot with her, was glad to get rid of it in this way.

IV

His name was Loulou. His body was green, the tips of his wings were pink, his poll blue, and his breast golden.

[6] in 1793, during the Reign of Terror in the French Revolution.

Unfortunately he had a tiresome mania for biting his perch, and also used to pull his feathers out, scatter his droppings everywhere, and upset his bath water. He annoyed Mme Aubain, and so she gave him to Félicité for good.

Félicité started training him, and soon he could say: "Nice boy! Your servant, sir! Hail, Mary!" He was put near the door, and several people who spoke to him said how strange it was that he did not answer to the name of Jacquot, as all parrots were called Jacquot. They likened him to a turkey or a block of wood, and every sneer cut Félicité to the quick. How odd, she thought, that Loulou should be so stubborn, refusing to talk whenever anyone looked at him!

For all that, he liked having people around him, because on Sundays, while the Rochefeuille sisters, M. Houppeville, and some new friends — the apothecary Onfroy, M. Varin, and Captain Mathieu — were having their game of cards, he would beat on the window-panes with his wings and make such a din that it was impossible to hear oneself speak.

Bourais's face obviously struck him as terribly funny, for as soon as he saw it he was seized with uncontrollable laughter. His shrieks rang round the courtyard, the echo repeated them, and the neighbors came to their windows and started laughing too. To avoid being seen by the bird, M. Bourais used to creep along by the wall, hiding his face behind his hat, until he got to the river, and then come into the house from the garden. The looks he gave the parrot were far from tender.

Loulou had once been cuffed by the butcher's boy for poking his head into his basket; and since then he was always trying to give him a nip through his shirt. Fabu threatened to wring his neck, although he was not a cruel fellow, in spite of his tattooed arms and bushy whiskers. On the contrary, he rather liked the parrot, so much so indeed that in a spirit of jovial camaraderie he tried to teach him a few swear-words. Félicité, alarmed at this development, put the bird in the kitchen. His little chain was removed and he was allowed to wander all over the house.

Coming downstairs, he used to rest the curved part of his beak on each step and then raise first his right foot, then his left; and Félicité was afraid that this sort of gymnastic performance would make him giddy. He fell ill and could neither talk nor eat for there was a swelling under his tongue such as hens sometimes have. She cured him by pulling this pellicule[7] out with her finger-nails. One day M. Paul was silly enough to blow the smoke of his cigar at him; another time Mme Lormeau started teasing him with the end of her parasol, and he caught hold of the ferrule with his beak. Finally he got lost.

Félicité had put him down on the grass in the fresh air, and left him there for a minute. When she came back, the parrot had gone. First of all she looked for him in the bushes, by the river, and on the rooftops, paying

[7] a thin skin or piece of skin.

no attention to her mistress's shouts of: "Be careful, now! You must be mad!" Next she went over all the gardens in Pont-l'Évêque, stopping passersby and asking them: "You don't happen to have seen my parrot by any chance?" Those who did not know him already were given a description of the bird. Suddenly she thought she could make out something green flying about behind the mills at the foot of the hill. But up on the hill there was nothing to be seen. A pedlar told her that he had come upon the parrot a short time before in Mère Simon's shop at Saint-Melaine. She ran all the way there, but no one knew what she was talking about. Finally she came back home, worn out, her shoes falling to pieces, and death in her heart. She was sitting beside Madame on the garden-seat and telling her what she had been doing, when she felt something light drop on her shoulder. It was Loulou! What he had been up to, no one could discover: perhaps he had just gone for a little walk round the town.

Félicité was slow to recover from this fright, and indeed never really got over it.

As the result of a chill she had an attack of quinsy, and soon after that her ears were affected. Three years later she was deaf, and she spoke at the top of her voice, even in church. Although her sins could have been proclaimed over the length and breadth of the diocese without dishonor to her or offense to others, M. le Curé thought it advisable to hear her confession in the sacristy.

Imaginary buzzings in the head added to her troubles. Often her mistress would say: "Heavens, how stupid you are!" and she would reply: "Yes, Madame," at the same time looking all around her for something.

The little circle of her ideas grew narrower and narrower, and the pealing of bells and the lowing of cattle went out of her life. Every living thing moved about in a ghostly silence. Only one sound reached her ears now, and that was the voice of the parrot.

As if to amuse her, he would reproduce the click-clack of the turn-spit, the shrill call of a man selling fish, and the noise of the saw at the joiner's across the way; and when the bell rang he would imitate Mme Aubain's "Félicité! The door, the door!"

They held conversations with each other, he repeating *ad nauseam* the three phrases in his repertory, she replying with words which were just as disconnected but which came from the heart. In her isolation, Loulou was almost a son or a lover to her. He used to climb up her fingers, peck at her lips, and hang on to her shawl; and as she bent over him, wagging her head from side to side as nurses do, the great wings of her bonnet and the wings of the bird quivered in unison.

When clouds banked up in the sky and there was a rumbling of thunder, he would utter piercing cries, no doubt remembering the sudden downpours in his native forests. The sound of the rain falling roused him to frenzy. He would flap excitedly around, shoot up to the ceiling, knocking everything over, and fly out of the window to splash about in the garden. But he would soon come back to perch on one of the firedogs, hopping about to dry his feathers and showing tail and beak in turn.

One morning in the terrible winter of 1837, when she had put him in front of the fire because of the cold she found him dead in the middle of his cage, hanging head down with his claws caught in the bars. He had probably died of a stroke, but she thought he had been poisoned with parsley, and despite the absence of any proof, her suspicions fell on Fabu.

She wept so much that her mistress said to her: "Why don't you have him stuffed?"

Félicité asked the chemist's advice, remembering that he had always been kind to the parrot. He wrote to Le Havre, and a man called Fellacher agreed to do the job. As parcels sometimes went astray on the mail-coach, she decided to take the parrot as far as Honfleur herself.

On either side of the road stretched an endless succession of apple trees, all stripped of their leaves, and there was ice in the ditches. Dogs were barking around the farms; and Félicité, with her hands tucked under her mantlet, her little black sabots, and her basket, walked briskly along the middle of the road.

She crossed the forest, passed Le Haut-Chêne, and got as far as Saint-Gatien.

Behind her, in a cloud of dust, and gathering speed as the horses galloped downhill, a mail-coach swept along like a whirlwind. When he saw this woman making no attempt to get out of the way, the driver poked his head out above the hood, and he and the postilion shouted at her. His four horses could not be held in and galloped faster, the two leaders touching her as they went by. With a jerk of the reins the driver threw them to one side, and then, in a fury, he raised his long whip and gave her such a lash, from head to waist, that she fell flat on her back.

The first thing she did on regaining consciousness was to open her basket. Fortunately nothing had happened to Loulou. She felt her right cheek burning, and when she touched it her hand turned red; it was bleeding.

She sat down on a heap of stones and dabbed her face with her handkerchief. Then she ate a crust of bread which she had taken the precaution of putting in her basket, and tried to forget her wound by looking at the bird.

As she reached the top of the hill at Ecquemauville, she saw the lights of Honfleur twinkling in the darkness like a host of stars, and the shadowy expanse of the sea beyond. Then a sudden feeling of faintness made her stop; and the misery of her childhood, the disappointment of her first love, the departure of her nephew, and the death of Virginie all came back to her at once like the waves of a rising tide, and, welling up in her throat, choked her.

When she got to the boat she insisted on speaking to the captain, and without telling him what was in her parcel, asked him to take good care of it.

Fellacher kept the parrot a long time. Every week he promised it for the next; after six months he announced that a box had been sent off, and nothing more was heard of it. It looked as though Loulou would never come back, and Félicité told herself: "They've stolen him for sure!"

At last he arrived — looking quite magnificent, perched on a branch screwed into a mahogany base, one foot in the air, his head cocked to one side, and biting a nut which the taxidermist, out of love of the grandiose, had gilded.

Félicité shut him up in her room.

This place, to which few people were ever admitted, contained such a quantity of religious bric-à-brac and miscellaneous oddments that it looked like a cross between a chapel and a bazaar.

A big wardrobe prevented the door from opening properly. Opposite the window that overlooked the garden was a little round one looking on to the courtyard. There was a table beside the bed, with a water-jug, a couple of combs, and a block of blue soap in a chipped plate. On the walls there were rosaries, medals, several pictures of the Virgin, and a holy-water stoup made out of a coconut. On the chest of drawers, which was draped with a cloth just like an altar, was the shell box Victor had given her, and also a watering-can and a ball, some copy-books, the illustrated geography book, and a pair of ankle-boots. And on the nail supporting the looking-glass, fastened by its ribbons, hung the little plush hat.

Félicité carried this form of veneration to such lengths that she even kept one of Monsieur's frock-coats. All the old rubbish Mme Aubain had no more use for, she carried off to her room. That was how there came to be artificial flowers along the edge of the chest of drawers, and a portrait of the Comte d'Artois in the window-recess.

With the aid of a wall-bracket, Loulou was installed on a chimney-breast that jutted out into the room. Every morning when she awoke, she saw him in the light of the dawn, and then she remembered the old days, and the smallest details of insignificant actions, not in sorrow but in absolute tranquillity.

Having no intercourse with anyone, she lived in the torpid state of a sleep-walker. The Corpus Christi processions roused her from this condition, for she would go round the neighbors collecting candlesticks and mats to decorate the altar of repose which they used to set up in the street.

In church she was forever gazing at the Holy Ghost, and one day she noticed that it had something of the parrot about it. This resemblance struck her as even more obvious in a colorprint depicting the baptism of Our Lord. With its red wings and its emerald-green body, it was the very image of Loulou.

She bought the print and hung it in the place of the Comte d'Artois, so that she could include them both in a single glance. They were linked together in her mind, the parrot being sanctified by this connection with the Holy Ghost, which itself acquired new life and meaning in her eyes. God the Father could not have chosen a dove as a means of expressing Himself, since doves cannot talk, but rather one of Loulou's ancestors. And although Félicité used to say her prayers with her eyes on the picture, from time to time she would turn slightly towards the bird.

She wanted to join the Children of Mary, but Mme Aubain dissuaded her from doing so.

An important event now loomed up — Paul's wedding.

After starting as a lawyer's clerk, he had been in business, in the Customs, and in Inland Revenue, and had even begun trying to get into the Department of Woods and Forests, when, at the age of thirty-six, by some heaven-sent inspiration, he suddenly discovered his real vocation — in the Wills and Probate Department. There he proved so capable that one of the auditors had offered him his daughter in marriage and promised to use his influence on his behalf.

Paul, grown serious-minded, brought her to see his mother. She criticized the way things were done at Pont-l'Évêque, put on airs, and hurt Félicité's feelings. Mme Aubain was relieved to see her go.

The following week came news of M. Bourais's death in an inn in Lower Brittany. Rumors that he had committed suicide were confirmed, and doubts arose as to his honesty. Mme Aubain went over her accounts and was soon conversant with the full catalogue of his misdeeds — embezzlement of interest, secret sales of timber, forged receipts, etc. Besides all this, he was the father of an illegitimate child, and had had "relations with a person at Dozule."

These infamies upset Mme Aubain greatly. In March 1853 she was afflicted with a pain in the chest; her tongue seemed to be covered with a film; leeches failed to make her breathing any easier; and on the ninth evening of her illness she died. She had just reached the age of seventy-two.

She was thought to be younger because of her brown hair, worn in bandeaux round her pale, pock-marked face. There were few friends to mourn her, for she had a haughty manner which put people off. Yet Félicité wept for her as servants rarely weep for their masters. That Madame should die before her upset her ideas, seemed to be contrary to the order of things, monstrous and unthinkable.

Ten days later — the time it took to travel hot-foot from Besançon — the heirs arrived. The daughter-in-law ransacked every drawer, picked out some pieces of furniture, and sold the rest; and then back they went to the Wills and Probate Department.

Madame's arm-chair, her pedestal table, her foot-warmer, and the eight chairs had all gone. Yellow squares in the center of the wall-panels showed where the pictures had hung. They had carried off the two cots with their mattresses, and no trace remained in the cupboard of all Virginie's things. Félicité climbed the stairs to her room, numbed with sadness.

The next day there was a notice on the door, and the apothecary shouted in her ear that the house was up for sale.

She swayed on her feet, and was obliged to sit down.

What distressed her most of all was the idea of leaving her room, which was so suitable for poor Loulou. Fixing an anguished look on him as she appealed to the Holy Ghost, she contracted the idolatrous habit of kneeling in front of the parrot to say her prayers. Sometimes the sun, as it came through the little window, caught his glass eye, so that it shot out a great luminous ray which sent her into ecstasies.

She had a pension of three hundred and eighty francs a year which her mistress had left her. The garden kept her in vegetables. As for clothes, she had enough to last her till the end of her days, and she saved on lighting by going to bed as soon as darkness fell.

She went out as little as possible, to avoid the second-hand dealer's shop where some of the old furniture was on display. Ever since her fit of giddiness, she had been dragging one leg; and as her strength was failing, Mère Simon, whose grocery business had come to grief, came in every morning to chop wood and pump water for her.

Her eyes grew weaker. The shutters were not opened any more. Years went by, and nobody rented the house and nobody bought it.

For fear of being evicted, Félicité never asked for any repairs to be done. The laths in the roof rotted, and all through one winter her bolster was wet. After Easter she began spitting blood.

When this happened Mère Simon called in a doctor. Félicité wanted to know what was the matter with her, but she was so deaf that only one word reached her: "Pneumonia." It was a word she knew, and she answered gently: "Ah! like Madame," thinking it natural that she should follow in her mistress's footsteps.

The time to set up the altars of repose was drawing near.

The first altar was always at the foot of the hill, the second in front of the post office, the third about halfway up the street. There was some argument as to the siting of this one, and finally the women of the parish picked on Mme Aubain's courtyard.

The fever and the tightness of the chest grew worse. Félicité fretted over not doing anything for the altar. If only she could have something put on it! Then she thought of the parrot. The neighbors protested that it would not be seemly, but the curé gave his permission, and this made her so happy that she begged him to accept Loulou, the only thing of value she possessed, when she died.

From Tuesday to Saturday, the eve of Corpus Christi, she coughed more and more frequently. In the evening her face looked pinched and drawn, her lips stuck to her gums, and she started vomiting. At dawn the next day, feeling very low, she sent for a priest.

Three good women stood by her while she was given extreme unction. Then she said that she had to speak to Fabu.

He arrived in his Sunday best, very ill at ease in this funereal atmosphere.

"Forgive me," she said, making an effort to stretch out her arm. "I thought it was you who had killed him."

What could she mean by such nonsense? To think that she had suspected a man like him of murder! He got very indignant and was obviously going to make a scene.

"Can't you see," they said, "that she isn't in her right mind any more?"

From time to time Félicité would start talking to shadows. The women went away. Mère Simon had her lunch.

A little later she picked Loulou up and held him out to Félicité, saying:

"Come now, say good-bye to him."

Although the parrot was not a corpse, the worms were eating him up. One of his wings was broken, and the stuffing was coming out of his stomach. But she was blind by now, and she kissed him on the forehead and pressed him against her cheek. Mère Simon took him away from her to put him on the altar.

V

The scents of summer came up from the meadows; there was a buzzing of flies; the sun was glittering in the river and warming the slates of the roof. Mère Simon had come back into the room and was gently nodding off to sleep.

The noise of church bells woke her up; the congregation was coming out from vespers. Félicité's delirium abated. Thinking of the procession, she could see it as clearly as if she had been following it.

All the school-children, the choristers, and the firemen were walking along the pavements, while advancing up the middle of the street came the church officer armed with his halberd, the beadle carrying a great cross, the schoolmaster keeping an eye on the boys, and the nun fussing over her little girls — three of the prettiest, looking like curly-headed angels, were throwing rose-petals into the air. Then came the deacon, with both arms outstretched, conducting the band, and a couple of censer-bearers who turned round at every step to face the Holy Sacrament, which the curé, wearing his splendid chasuble, was carrying under a canopy of poppy-red velvet held aloft by four churchwardens. A crowd of people surged along behind, between the white cloths covering the walls of the houses, and eventually they got to the bottom of the hill.

A cold sweat moistened Félicité's temples. Mère Simon sponged it up with a cloth, telling herself that one day she would have to go the same way.

The hum of the crowd increased in volume, was very loud for a moment, then faded away.

A fusillade shook the window-panes. It was the postilions saluting the monstrance. Félicité rolled her eyes and said as loud as she could: "Is he all right?" — worrying about the parrot.

She entered into her death-agony. Her breath, coming ever faster, with a rattling sound, made her sides heave. Bubbles of froth appeared at the corners of her mouth, and her whole body trembled.

Soon the booming of the ophicleides,[8] the clear voices of the children, and the deep voices of the men could be heard near at hand. Now and then everything was quiet, and the tramping of feet, deadened by a carpet of flowers, sounded like a flock moving across pasture-land.

The clergy appeared in the courtyard. Mère Simon climbed on to a chair to reach the little round window, from which she had a full view of the altar below.

It was hung with green garlands and adorned with a flounce in English needlepoint lace. In the middle was a little frame containing some relics, there were two orange-trees at the corners, and all the way along stood silver candlesticks and china vases holding sunflowers, lilies, peonies, foxgloves, and bunches of hydrangea. This pyramid of bright colors stretched from the first floor right down to the carpet which was spread out over the pavement. Some rare objects caught the eye: a silver-gilt sugar-basin wreathed in violets, some pendants of Alençon gems gleaming on a bed of moss, and two Chinese screens with landscape decorations. Loulou, hidden under roses, showed nothing but his blue poll, which looked like a plaque of lapis lazuli.

The churchwardens, the choristers, and the children lined up along the three sides of the courtyard. The priest went slowly up the steps and placed his great shining gold sun on the lace altar-cloth. Everyone knelt down. There was a deep silence. And the censers, swinging at full tilt, slid up and down their chains.

A blue cloud of incense was wafted up into Félicité's room. She opened her nostrils wide and breathed it in with a mystical, sensuous fervor. Then she closed her eyes. Her lips smiled. Her heart-beats grew slower and slower, each a little fainter and gentler, like a fountain running dry, an echo fading away. And as she breathed her last, she thought she could see, in the opening heavens, a gigantic parrot hovering above her head.

[1877]

---

[8] an early brass wind instrument.

LEO TOLSTOY (1828–1910) *is generally considered the greatest Russian writer of prose fiction. His supreme quality as a storyteller was a narrative gift that enabled him to describe with minute fidelity and richness exactly what his characters are doing and thinking.*

Tolstoy was born on his parents' estate in the province of Tula, Russia. His early years were unpromising. Like most noblemen, he spent his time at the university drinking and gambling; but in his twenties he joined the Russian Army, and he began writing sketches of military life during the Crimean War (1853–1856). After he left the army and traveled in Europe, he settled down to writing. He married in 1862, and produced his two great novels, War and Peace *in 1869 and* Anna Karenina *in 1877.*

As Tolstoy grew older, he lost the temporary peace of mind he had possessed while absorbed in his writing and his family life. He began to live according to strict principles of his own view of rational Christian morality. Dissatisfied with literature, he reached the conclusion that art is ungodly because it is founded on imagination. Vladimir Nabokov has described Tolstoy's obsession thus: "Somehow, the process of seeking the Truth seemed more important to him than the easy, vivid, brilliant discovery of the illusion of truth through the medium of his artistic genius." In his eighties, Tolstoy decided that by continuing to live with his wife and family on his country estate he was betraying his idea of simple, saintly existence, which he dramatized in his parable "The Three Hermits." Finally Tolstoy left his family and wandered away, his destination a monastery that he never reached. He died in the waiting room of a little railway station near his home.

Tolstoy's fiction is so powerfully written that it usually transcends the sermon that motivated it, but he insisted that it is always the writer's obligation to tell the reader how to live. Describing "The Soul of the Artist" in an essay about Maupassant in 1896, he wrote:

> *The cement which binds together every work of art into a whole and thereby produces the effect of lifelike illusion, is not the unity of persons and places, but that of the author's independent moral relation to the subject. In reality, when we read or examine the work of a new author, the fundamental questions which arise in our mind are always of this kind: "Well, what sort of a man are you? What distinguishes you from all the people I know, and what information can you give me, as to how we must look upon our life?" Whatever the artist depicts, whether it be saints or robbers, kings or lackeys, we seek and see only the soul of the artist himself. And if he is an established writer, with whom we are already acquainted, the question is no longer "Who are you?" but "Well, what more can you tell me that is new? From what standpoint will you now illuminate life for me?" Therefore, a writer who has not a clear, definite, and*

fresh view of the universe, and especially a writer who does not even con-
sider this necessary, cannot produce a work of art. He may write much and
beautifully, but a work of art will not result.

The chief theme of Tolstoy's writing, as in his great story "The Death
of Ivan Ilych," is that the only certain happiness in life is to live for others.
This helps to explain the tragedy of Ivan Ilych, who just before his death
concludes that he has not lived as he ought to have. The story took Tolstoy
two years to finish. In its first version, it was mostly told in the first person
singular by one of Ivan Ilych's colleagues, who was given the diary Ivan
Ilych kept during his fatal illness. The narrator begins, "It is impossible, ab-
solutely impossible, to live as I have lived, and as we all live. I realized that
as a result of the death of an acquaintance of mine, Ivan Ilych, and of the
diary he left behind." Ultimately, however, Tolstoy changed his approach
to the story and told it in the third person, without using the form of a
diary.

Leo Tolstoy

ಬಬ

THE DEATH OF IVAN ILYCH

–translated by Louise and
Aylmer Maude

I

During an interval in the Melvinski trial in the large building of the
Law Courts, the members and public prosecutor met in Ivan Egorovich
Shebek's private room, where the conversation turned on the celebrated
Krasovski case. Fëdor Vasilievich warmly maintained that it was not subject
to their jurisdiction, Ivan Egorovich maintained the contrary, while Peter
Ivanovich, not having entered into the discussion at the start, took no part
in it but looked through the *Gazette* which had just been handed in.

"Gentlemen," he said, "Ivan Ilych has died!"

"You don't say so!"

"Here, read it yourself," replied Peter Ivanovich, handing Fëdor Vasilievich the paper still damp from the press. Surrounded by a black border
were the words: "Praskovya Fëdorovna Golovina, with profound sorrow, informs relatives and friends of the demise of her beloved husband
Ivan Ilych Golovin, Member of the Court of Justice, which occurred on

February the 4th of this year 1882. The funeral will take place on Friday at one o'clock in the afternoon."

Ivan Ilych had been a colleague of the gentlemen present and was liked by them all. He had been ill for some weeks with an illness said to be incurable. His post had been kept open for him, but there had been conjectures that in case of his death Alexeev might receive his appointment, and that either Vinnikov or Shtabel would succeed Alexeev. So on receiving the news of Ivan Ilych's death the first thought of each of the gentlemen in that private room was of the changes and promotions it might occasion among themselves or their acquaintances.

"I shall be sure to get Shtabel's place or Vinnikov's," thought Fëdor Vasilievich. "I was promised that long ago, and the promotion means an extra eight hundred rubles a year for me besides the allowance."

"Now I must apply for my brother-in-law's transfer from Kaluga," thought Peter Ivanovich. "My wife will be very glad, and then she won't be able to say that I never do anything for her relations."

"I thought he would never leave his bed again," said Peter Ivanovich aloud. "It's very sad."

"But what really was the matter with him?"

"The doctors couldn't say — at least they could, but each of them said something different. When last I saw him I thought he was getting better."

"And I haven't been to see him since the holidays. I always meant to go."

"Had he any property?"

"I think his wife had a little — but something quite trifling."

"We shall have to go to see her, but they live so terribly far away."

"Far away from you, you mean. Everything's far away from your place."

"You see, he never can forgive my living on the other side of the river," said Peter Ivanovich, smiling at Shebek. Then, still talking of the distances between different parts of the city, they returned to the Court.

Besides considerations as to the possible transfers and promotions likely to result from Ivan Ilych's death, the mere fact of the death of a near acquaintance aroused, as usual, in all who heard of it the complacent feeling that, "it is he who is dead and not I."

Each one thought or felt, "Well, he's dead but I'm alive!" But the more intimate of Ivan Ilych's acquaintances, his so-called friends, could not help thinking also that they would now have to fulfill the very tiresome demands of propriety by attending the funeral service and paying a visit of condolence to the widow.

Fëdor Vasilievich and Peter Ivanovich had been his nearest acquaintances. Peter Ivanovich had studied law with Ivan Ilych and had considered himself to be under obligations to him.

Having told his wife at dinner-time of Ivan Ilych's death and of his conjecture that it might be possible to get her brother transferred to their circuit, Peter Ivanovich sacrificed his usual nap, put on his evening clothes, and drove to Ivan Ilych's house.

At the entrance stood a carriage and two cabs. Leaning against the wall in the hall downstairs near the cloak-stand was a coffin-lid covered with cloth of gold, ornamented with gold cord and tassels, that had been polished up with metal powder. Two ladies in black were taking off their fur cloaks. Peter Ivanovich recognized one of them as Ivan Ilych's sister, but the other was a stranger to him. His colleague Schwartz was just coming downstairs, but on seeing Peter Ivanovich enter he stopped and winked at him, as if to say: "Ivan Ilych has made a mess of things — not like you and me."

Schwartz's face, with his Piccadilly whiskers and his slim figure in evening dress, had as usual an air of elegant solemnity which contrasted with the playfulness of his character and had a special piquancy here, or so it seemed to Peter Ivanovich.

Peter Ivanovich allowed the ladies to precede him and slowly followed them upstairs. Schwartz did not come down but remained where he was, and Peter Ivanovich understood that he wanted to arrange where they should play bridge that evening. The ladies went upstairs to the widow's room, and Schwartz, with seriously compressed lips but a playful look in his eyes, indicated by a twist of his eyebrows the room to the right where the body lay.

Peter Ivanovich, like everyone else on such occasions, entered feeling uncertain what he would have to do. All he knew was that at such times it is always safe to cross oneself. But he was not quite sure whether one should make obeisances while doing so. He therefore adopted a middle course. On entering the room he began crossing himself and made a slight movement resembling a bow. At the same time, as far as the motion of his head and arm allowed, he surveyed the room. Two young men — apparently nephews, one of whom was a high-school pupil — were leaving the room, crossing themselves as they did so. An old woman was standing motionless, and a lady with strangely arched eyebrows was saying something to her in a whisper. A vigorous, resolute Church Reader, in a frock-coat, was reading something in a loud voice with an expression that precluded any contradiction. The butler's assistant, Gerasim, stepping lightly in front of Peter Ivanovich, was strewing something on the floor. Noticing this, Peter Ivanovich was immediately aware of a faint odor of a decomposing body.

The last time he had called on Ivan Ilych, Peter Ivanovich had seen Gerasim in the study. Ivan Ilych had been particularly fond of him and he was performing the duty of a sick nurse.

Peter Ivanovich continued to make the sign of the cross, slightly inclining his head in an intermediate direction between the coffin, the Reader, and the icons on the table in a corner of the room. Afterwards, when it seemed to him that this movement of his arm in crossing himself had gone on too long, he stopped and began to look at the corpse.

The dead man lay, as dead men always lie, in a specially heavy way, his rigid limbs sunk in the soft cushions of the coffin, with the head forever bowed on the pillow. His yellow waxen brow with bald patches over his sunken temples was thrust up in the way peculiar to the dead, the protruding nose seeming to press on the upper lip. He was much changed and had grown even thinner since Peter Ivanovich had last seen him, but, as is always the case with the dead, his face was handsomer and above all more dignified than when he was alive. The expression on the face said that what was necessary had been accomplished, and accomplished rightly. Besides this there was in that expression a reproach and a warning to the living. This warning seemed to Peter Ivanovich out of place, or at least not applicable to him. He felt a certain discomfort and so he hurriedly crossed himself once more and turned and went out the door — too hurriedly and too regardless of propriety, as he himself was aware.

Schwartz was waiting for him in the adjoining room with legs spread wide apart and both hands toying with his top-hat behind his back. The mere sight of that playful, well-groomed, and elegant figure refreshed Peter Ivanovich. He felt that Schwartz was above all these happenings and would not surrender to any depressing influences. His very look said that this incident of a church service for Ivan Ilych could not be a sufficient reason for infringing the order of the session — in other words, that it would certainly not prevent his unwrapping a new pack of cards and shuffling them that evening while a footman placed four fresh candles on the table: in fact, that there was no reason for supposing that this incident would hinder their spending the evening agreeably. Indeed he said this in a whisper as Peter Ivanovich passed him, proposing that they should meet for a game at Fëdor Vasilievich's. But apparently Peter Ivanovich was not destined to play bridge that evening. Praskovya Fëdorovna (a short, fat woman who despite all efforts to the contrary had continued to broaden steadily from her shoulders downwards and who had the same extraordinarily arched eyebrows as the lady who had been standing by the coffin), dressed all in black, her head covered with lace, came out of her own room with some other ladies, conducted them to the room where the dead body lay, and said: "The service will begin immediately. Please go in."

Schwartz, making an indefinite bow, stood still, evidently neither accepting nor declining this invitation. Praskovya Fëdorovna, recognizing Peter Ivanovich, sighed, went close up to him, took his hand, and said: "I know you were a true friend to Ivan Ilych . . ." and looked at him awaiting some suitable response. And Peter Ivanovich knew that, just as it had been the right thing to cross himself in that room, so what he had to do here was to press her hand, sigh, and say, "Believe me. . . ." So he did all this and as he did it felt that the desired result had been achieved: that both he and she were touched.

"Come with me. I want to speak to you before it begins," said the widow. "Give me your arm."

Peter Ivanovich gave her his arm and they went to the inner rooms, passing Schwartz, who winked at Peter Ivanovich compassionately.

"That does for our bridge! Don't object if we find another player. Perhaps you can cut in when you do escape," said his playful look.

Peter Ivanovich sighed still more deeply and despondently, and Praskovya Fëdorovna pressed his arm gratefully. When they reached the drawing-room, upholstered in pink cretonne and lighted by a dim lamp, they sat down at the table — she on a sofa and Peter Ivanovich on a low pouffe, the springs of which yielded spasmodically under his weight. Praskovya Fëdorovna had been on the point of warning him to take another seat, but felt that such a warning was out of keeping with her present condition and so changed her mind. As he sat down on the pouffe Peter Ivanovich recalled how Ivan Ilych had arranged this room and had consulted him regarding this pink cretonne with green leaves. The whole room was full of furniture and knick-knacks, and on her way to the sofa the lace of the widow's black shawl caught on the carved edge of the table. Peter Ivanovich rose to detach it, and the springs of the pouffe, relieved of his weight, rose also and gave him a push. The widow began detaching her shawl herself, and Peter Ivanovich again sat down, suppressing the rebellious springs of the pouffe under him. But the widow had not quite freed herself and Peter Ivanovich got up again, and again the pouffe rebelled and even creaked. When this was all over she took out a clean cambric handkerchief and began to weep. The episode with the shawl and the struggle with the pouffe had cooled Peter Ivanovich's emotions and he sat there with a sullen look on his face. This awkward situation was interrupted by Sokolov, Ivan Ilych's butler, who came to report that the plot in the cemetery that Praskovya Fëdorovna had chosen would cost two hundred rubles. She stopped weeping and, looking at Peter Ivanovich with the air of a victim, remarked in French that it was very hard for her. Peter Ivanovich made a silent gesture signifying his full conviction that it must indeed be so.

"Please smoke," she said in a magnanimous yet crushed voice, and turned to discuss with Sokolov the price of the plot for the grave.

Peter Ivanovich while lighting his cigarette heard her inquiring very circumstantially into the price of different plots in the cemetery and finally decided which she would take. When that was done she gave instructions about engaging the choir. Sokolov then left the room.

"I look after everything myself," she told Peter Ivanovich, shifting the albums that lay on the table; and noticing that the table was endangered by his cigarette-ash, she immediately passed him an ashtray, saying as she did so: "I consider it an affectation to say that my grief prevents my attending to practical affairs. On the contrary, if anything can — I won't say console me, but — distract me, it is seeing to everything concerning him." She again took out her handkerchief as if preparing to cry, but suddenly, as if mastering her feeling, she shook herself and began to speak calmly. "But there is something I want to talk to you about."

Peter Ivanovich bowed, keeping control of the springs of the pouffe, which immediately began quivering under him.

"He suffered terribly the last few days."

"Did he?" said Peter Ivanovich.

"Oh, terribly! He screamed unceasingly, not for minutes but for hours. For the last three days he screamed incessantly. It was unendurable. I cannot understand how I bore it; you could hear him three rooms off. Oh, what I have suffered!"

"Is it possible that he was conscious all that time?" asked Peter Ivanovich.

"Yes," she whispered. "To the last moment. He took leave of us a quarter of an hour before he died, and asked us to take Vasya away."

The thought of the sufferings of this man he had known so intimately, first as a merry little boy, then as a school-mate, and later as a grown-up colleague, suddenly struck Peter Ivanovich with horror, despite an unpleasant consciousness of his own and this woman's dissimulation. He again saw that brow, and that nose pressing down on the lip, and felt afraid for himself.

"Three days of frightful suffering and then death! Why, that might suddenly, at any time, happen to me," he thought, and for a moment felt terrified. But — he did not himself know how — the customary reflection at once occurred to him that this had happened to Ivan Ilych and not to him, and that it should not and could not happen to him, and that to think that it could would be yielding to depression which he ought not to do, as Schwartz's expression plainly showed. After which reflection Peter Ivanovich felt reassured, and began to ask with interest about the details of Ivan Ilych's death, as though death was an accident natural to Ivan Ilych but certainly not to himself.

After many details of the really dreadful physical sufferings Ivan Ilych had endured (which details he learnt only from the effect those sufferings had produced on Praskovya Fëdorovna's nerves) the widow apparently found it necessary to get to business.

"Oh, Peter Ivanovich, how hard is it! How terribly, terribly hard!" and she again began to weep.

Peter Ivanovich sighed and waited for her to finish blowing her nose. When she had done so he said, "Believe me . . ." and she again began talking and brought out what was evidently her chief concern with him — namely, to question him as to how she could obtain a grant of money from the government on the occasion of her husband's death. She made it appear that she was asking Peter Ivanovich's advice about her pension, but he soon saw that she already knew about that to the minutest detail, more even than he did himself. She knew how much could be got out of the government in consequence of her husband's death, but wanted to find out whether she could not possibly extract something more. Peter Ivanovich tried to think of some means of doing so, but after reflecting for a while and, out of propriety, condemning the government for its niggardliness, he said he thought that nothing more could be got. Then she sighed and evidently began to devise means of getting rid of her visitor. Noticing this, he put out his cigarette, rose, pressed her hand, and went out into the anteroom.

In the dining-room where the clock stood that Ivan Ilych had liked so much and had bought at an antique shop, Peter Ivanovich met a priest and a few acquaintances who had come to attend the service, and he recognized Ivan Ilych's daughter, a handsome young woman. She was in black and her slim figure appeared slimmer than ever. She had a gloomy, determined, almost angry expression, and bowed to Peter Ivanovich as though he were in some way to blame. Behind her, with the same offended look, stood a wealthy young man, an examining magistrate, whom Peter Ivanovich also knew and who was her fiancé, as he had heard. He bowed mournfully to them and was about to pass into the death-chamber, when from under the stairs appeared the figure of Ivan Ilych's schoolboy son, who was extremely like his father. He seemed a little Ivan Ilych, such as Peter Ivanovich remembered when they studied law together. His tear-stained eyes had in them the look that is seen in the eyes of boys of thirteen or fourteen who are not pure-minded. When he saw Peter Ivanovich he scowled morosely and shamefacedly. Peter Ivanovich nodded to him and entered the death-chamber. The service began: candles, groans, incense, tears, and sobs. Peter Ivanovich stood looking gloomily down at his feet. He did not look once at the dead man, did not yield to any depressing influence, and was one of the first to leave the room. There was no one in the anteroom, but Gerasim darted out of the dead man's room, rummaged with his strong hands among the fur coats to find Peter Ivanovich's, and helped him on with it.

"Well, friend Gerasim," said Peter Ivanovich, so as to say something. "It's a sad affair, isn't it?"

"It's God's will. We shall all come to it some day," said Gerasim, displaying his teeth — the even, white teeth of a healthy peasant — and, like a man in the thick of urgent work, he briskly opened the front door, called the coachman, helped Peter Ivanovich into the sledge, and sprang back to the porch as if in readiness for what he had to do next.

Peter Ivanovich found the fresh air particularly pleasant after the smell of incense, the dead body, and carbolic acid.

"Where to, sir?" asked the coachman.

"It's not too late even now. . . . I'll call round on Fëdor Vasilievich."

He accordingly drove there and found them just finishing the first rubber, so that it was quite convenient for him to cut in.

II

Ivan Ilych's life had been most simple and most ordinary and therefore most terrible.

He had been a member of the Court of Justice, and died at the age of forty-five. His father had been an official who after serving in various ministries and departments in Petersburg had made the sort of career which brings men to positions from which by reason of their long service they cannot be dismissed, though they were obviously unfit to hold any responsible position, and for whom therefore posts are specially created, which though fictitious carry salaries of from six to ten thousand rubles that are not fictitious, and in receipt of which they live on to a great age.

Such was the Privy Councillor and superfluous member of various superfluous institutions, Ilya Epimovich Golovin.

He had three sons, of whom Ivan Ilych was the second. The eldest son was following in his father's footsteps only in another department, and was already approaching that stage in the service at which a similar sinecure would be reached. The third son was a failure. He had ruined his prospects in a number of positions and was now serving in the railway department. His father and brothers, and still more their wives, not merely disliked meeting him, but avoided remembering his existence unless compelled to do so. His sister had married Baron Greff, a Petersburg official of her father's type. Ivan Ilych was *le phénix de la famille*[1] as people said. He was neither as cold and formal as his elder brother nor as wild as the younger, but was a happy mean between them — an intelligent, polished, lively, and agreeable man. He had studied with his younger brother at the School of Law, but the latter had failed to complete the course and was expelled when he was in the fifth class. Ivan Ilych finished the course well. Even when he was at the School of Law he was just what he remained for the rest of his life: a capable, cheerful, good-natured, and sociable man, though strict in the fulfillment of what he considered to be his duty: and he considered his duty to be what was so considered by those in authority. Neither as a boy nor as a man was he a toady, but from early youth was by nature attracted to people of high station as a fly is drawn to the light, assimilating their ways and views of life and establishing friendly relations with them. All the enthusiasms of childhood and youth passed without leaving much trace on him; he succumbed to sensuality, to vanity, and latterly among the highest classes to liberalism, but always within limits which his instinct unfailingly indicated to him as correct.

At school he had done things which had formerly seemed to him very horrid and made him feel disgusted with himself when he did them; but when later on he saw that such actions were done by people of good position and that they did not regard them as wrong, he was able not exactly to regard them as right, but to forget about them entirely or not be at all troubled at remembering them.

Having graduated from the School of Law and qualified for the tenth rank of the civil service, and having received money from his father for his equipment, Ivan Ilych ordered himself clothes at Scharmer's, the fashionable tailor, hung a medallion inscribed *respice finem*[2] on his watch-chain, took leave of his professor and the prince who was patron of the school, had a farewell dinner with his comrades at Donon's first-class restaurant, and with his new and fashionable portmanteau, linen, clothes, shaving and

---

[1] the pride of the family. (Unless otherwise indicated, all foreign phrases are in French — often the everyday language of middle-class and upper-class Russians of Tolstoy's time.)

[2] "Consider your end," that is, your death (Latin).

other toilet appliances, and a traveling rug, all purchased at the best shops, he set off for one of the provinces where, through his father's influence, he had been attached to the Governor as an official for special service.

In the province Ivan Ilych soon arranged as easy and agreeable a position for himself as he had had at the School of Law. He performed his official tasks, made his career, and at the same time amused himself pleasantly and decorously. Occasionally he paid official visits to country districts, where he behaved with dignity both to his superiors and inferiors, and performed the duties entrusted to him, which related chiefly to the sectarians,[3] with an exactness and incorruptible honesty of which he could not but feel proud.

In official matters, despite his youth and taste for frivolous gaiety, he was exceedingly reserved, punctilious, and even severe; but in society he was often amusing and witty, and always good-natured, correct in his manner, and *bon enfant*,[4] as the governor and his wife — with whom he was like one of the family — used to say of him.

In the province he had an affair with a lady who made advances to the elegant young lawyer, and there was also a milliner; and there were carousals with aides-de-camp who visited the district, and after-supper visits to a certain outlying street of doubtful reputation; and there was too some obsequiousness to his chief and even to his chief's wife, but all this was done with such a tone of good breeding that no hard names could be applied to it. It all came under the heading of the French saying: *"Il faut que jeunesse se passe."*[5] It was all done with clean hands, in clean linen, with French phrases, and above all among people of the best society and consequently with the approval of people of rank.

So Ivan Ilych served for five years and then came a change in his official life. The new and reformed judicial institutions were introduced, and new men were needed. Ivan Ilych became such a new man. He was offered the post of examining magistrate, and he accepted it though the post was in another province and obliged him to give up the connections he had formed and to make new ones. His friends met to give him a send-off; they had a group-photograph taken and presented him with a silver cigarette-case, and he set off to his new post.

As examining magistrate Ivan Ilych was just as *comme il faut*[6] and decorous a man, inspiring general respect and capable of separating his official duties from his private life, as he had been when acting as an official on special service. His duties now as examining magistrate were far more interesting and attractive than before. In his former position it had been pleasant to wear an undress uniform made by Scharmer, and to pass through the crowd of petitioners and officials who were timorously awaiting an audience with the governor, and who envied him as with free and easy gait he went

[3] "Old Believers," dissenters from the Orthodox Church.
[4] one of the boys (literally, "a good child").
[5] "Youth will have its day."
[6] proper (literally, "as it should be").

straight into his chief's private room to have a cup of tea and a cigarette with him. But not many people had then been directly dependent on him — only police officials and the sectarians when he went on special missions — and he liked to treat them politely, almost as comrades, as if he were letting them feel that he who had the power to crush them was treating them in this simple, friendly way. There were then but few such people. But now, as an examining magistrate, Ivan Ilych felt that everyone without exception, even the most important and self-satisfied, was in his power, and that he need only write a few words on a sheet of paper with a certain heading, and this or that important, self-satisfied person would be brought before him in the role of an accused person or a witness, and if he did not choose to allow him to sit down, would have to stand before him and answer his questions. Ivan Ilych never abused his power; he tried on the contrary to soften its expression, but the consciousness of it and of the possibility of softening its effect, supplied the chief interest and attraction of his office. In his work itself, especially in his examinations, he very soon acquired a method of eliminating all considerations irrelevant to the legal aspect of the case, and reducing even the most complicated case to a form in which it would be presented on paper only in its externals, completely excluding his personal opinion of the matter, while above all observing every prescribed formality. The work was new and Ivan Ilych was one of the first men to apply the new Code of 1864.[7]

On taking up the post of examining magistrate in a new town, he made new acquaintances and connections, placed himself on a new footing, and assumed a somewhat different tone. He took up an attitude of rather dignified aloofness towards the provincial authorities, but picked out the best circle of legal gentlemen and wealthy gentry living in the town and assumed a tone of slight dissatisfaction with the government, of moderate liberalism, and of enlightened citizenship. At the same time, without at all altering the elegance of his toilet, he ceased shaving his chin and allowed his beard to grow as it pleased.

Ivan Ilych settled down very pleasantly in this new town. The society there, which inclined towards opposition to the Governor, was friendly, his salary was larger, and he began to play *vint*,[8] which he found added not a little to the pleasure of life, for he had a capacity for cards, played good-humoredly, and calculated rapidly and astutely, so that he usually won.

After living there for two years he met his future wife, Praskovya Fëdorovna Mikhel, who was the most attractive, clever, and brilliant girl of the set in which he moved, and among other amusements and relaxations from his labors as examining magistrate, Ivan Ilych established light and playful relations with her.

While he had been an official on special service he had been accustomed to dance, but now as an examining magistrate it was exceptional for

---

[7] The emancipation of the serfs in 1861 was followed by a thorough all-round reform of judicial proceedings. [Translators' note]

[8] a form of bridge. [Translators' note]

him to do so. If he danced now, he did it as if to show that though he served under the reformed order of things, and had reached the fifth official rank, yet when it came to dancing he could do it better than most people. So at the end of an evening he sometimes danced with Praskovya Fëdorovna, and it was chiefly during these dances that he captivated her. She fell in love with him. Ivan Ilych had at first no definite intention of marrying, but when the girl fell in love with him he said to himself: "Really, why shouldn't I marry?"

Praskovya Fëdorovna came of a good family, was not bad looking, and had some little property. Ivan Ilych might have aspired to a more brilliant match, but even this was good. He had his salary, and she, he hoped, would have an equal income. She was well connected, and was a sweet, pretty, and thoroughly correct young woman. To say that Ivan Ilych married because he fell in love with Praskovya Fëdorovna and found that she sympathized with his views of life would be as incorrect as to say that he married because his social circle approved of the match. He was swayed by both these considerations: the marriage gave him personal satisfaction, and at the same time it was considered the right thing by the most highly placed of his associates.

So Ivan Ilych got married.

The preparations for marriage and the beginning of married life, with its conjugal caresses, the new furniture, new crockery, and new linen, were very pleasant until his wife became pregnant — so that Ivan Ilych had begun to think that marriage would not impair the easy, agreeable, gay, and always decorous character of his life, approved of by society and regarded by himself as natural, but would even improve it. But from the first months of his wife's pregnancy, something new, unpleasant, depressing, and unseemly, and from which there was no way of escape, unexpectedly showed itself.

His wife, without any reason — *de gaieté de coeur*[9] as Ivan Ilych expressed it to himself — began to disturb the pleasure and propriety of their life. She began to be jealous without any cause, expected him to devote his whole attention to her, found fault with everything, and made coarse and ill-mannered scenes.

At first Ivan Ilych hoped to escape from the unpleasantness of this state of affairs by the same easy and decorous relation to life that had served him heretofore: he tried to ignore his wife's disagreeable moods, continued to live in his usual easy and pleasant way, invited friends to his house for a game of cards, and also tried going out to his club or spending his evenings with friends. But one day his wife began upbraiding him so vigorously, using such coarse words, and continued to abuse him every time he did not fulfil her demands, so resolutely and with such evident determination not to give way till he submitted — that is, till he stayed at home and was bored

---

[9] from sheer exuberance (literally, "from happiness of heart").

just as she was — that he became alarmed. He now realized that matrimony — at any rate with Praskovya Fëdorovna — was not always conducive to the pleasures and amenities of life, but on the contrary often infringed both comfort and propriety, and that he must therefore entrench himself against such infringement. And Ivan Ilych began to seek for means of doing so. His official duties were the one thing that imposed upon Praskovya Fëdorovna, and by means of his official work and the duties attached to it he began struggling with his wife to secure his own independence.

With the birth of their child, the attempts to feed it and the various failures in doing so, and with the real and imaginary illnesses of mother and child, in which Ivan Ilych's sympathy was demanded but about which he understood nothing, the need of securing for himself an existence outside his family life became still more imperative.

As his wife grew more irritable and exacting and Ivan Ilych transferred the center of gravity of his life more and more to his official work so did he grow to like his work better and became more ambitious than before.

Very soon, within a year of his wedding, Ivan Ilych had realized that marriage, though it may add some comforts to life, is in fact a very intricate and difficult affair towards which in order to perform one's duty, that is, to lead a decorous life approved of by society, one must adopt a definite attitude just as towards one's official duties.

And Ivan Ilych evolved such an attitude towards married life. He only required of it those conveniences — dinner at home, housewife, and bed — which it could give him, and above all that propriety of external forms required by public opinion. For the rest he looked for light-hearted pleasure and propriety, and was very thankful when he found them, but if he met with antagonism and querulousness he at once retired into his separate fenced-off world of official duties, where he found satisfaction.

Ivan Ilych was esteemed a good official, and after three years was made Assistant Public Prosecutor. His new duties, their importance, the possibility of indicting and imprisoning anyone he chose, the publicity his speeches received, and the success he had in all these things made his work still more attractive.

More children came. His wife became more and more querulous and ill-tempered, but the attitude Ivan Ilych had adopted towards his home life rendered him almost impervious to her grumbling.

After seven years' service in that town he was transferred to another province as Public Prosecutor. They moved, but were short of money and his wife did not like the place they moved to. Though the salary was higher the cost of living was greater, besides which two of their children died and family life became still more unpleasant for him.

Praskovya Fëdorovna blamed her husband for every inconvenience they encountered in their new home. Most of the conversations between husband and wife, especially as to the children's education, led to topics which recalled former disputes, and those disputes were apt to flare up again at any moment. There remained only those rare periods of amorousness which still came to them at times but did not last long. These were islets at which they anchored for a while and then again set out upon that ocean of veiled hostility which showed itself in their aloofness from one another. This aloofness might have grieved Ivan Ilych had he considered that it ought not to exist, but he now regarded the position as normal, and even made it the goal at which he aimed in family life. His aim was to free himself more and more from those unpleasantnesses and to give them a semblance of harmlessness and propriety. He attained this by spending less and less time with his family, and when obliged to be at home he tried to safeguard his position by the presence of outsiders. The chief thing however was that he had his official duties. The whole interest of his life now centered in the official world and that interest absorbed him. The consciousness of his power, being able to ruin anybody he wished to ruin, the importance, even the external dignity of his entry into court, or meetings with his subordinates, his success with superiors and inferiors, and above all his masterly handling of cases, of which he was conscious — all this gave him pleasure and filled his life, together with chats with his colleagues, dinners, and bridge. So that on the whole Ivan Ilych's life continued to flow as he considered it should do — pleasantly and properly.

So things continued for another seven years. His eldest daughter was already sixteen, another child had died, and only one son was left, a schoolboy and a subject of dissension. Ivan Ilych wanted to put him in the School of Law, but to spite him Praskovya Fëdorovna entered him at the High School. The daughter had been educated at home and had turned out well: the boy did not learn badly either.

III

So Ivan Ilych lived for seventeen years after his marriage. He was already a Public Prosecutor of long standing, and had declined several proposed transfers while awaiting a more desirable post, when an unanticipated and unpleasant occurrence quite upset the peaceful course of his life. He was expecting to be offered the post of presiding judge in a University town, but Happe somehow came to the front and obtained the appointment instead. Ivan Ilych became irritable, reproached Happe, and quarreled both with him and with his immediate superiors — who became colder to him and again passed him over when other appointments were made.

This was in 1880, the hardest year of Ivan Ilych's life. It was then that it became evident on the one hand that his salary was insufficient for them to live on, and on the other that he had been forgotten, and not only this, but that what was for him the greatest and most cruel injustice appeared to others a quite ordinary occurrence. Even his father did not consider it his duty to help him. Ivan Ilych felt himself abandoned by everyone, and that they regarded his position with a salary of 3,500 rubles as quite normal and even fortunate. He alone knew that with the consciousness of the injustices done him, with his wife's incessant nagging, and with the debts he had contracted by living beyond his means, his position was far from normal.

In order to save money that summer he obtained leave of absence and went with his wife to live in the country at her brother's place.

In the country, without his work, he experienced *ennui* for the first time in his life, and not only *ennui* but intolerable depression, and he decided that it was impossible to go on living like that, and that it was necessary to take energetic measures.

Having passed a sleepless night pacing up and down the veranda, he decided to go to Petersburg and bestir himself, in order to punish those who had failed to appreciate him and to get transferred to another ministry.

Next day, despite many protests from his wife and her brother, he started for Petersburg with the sole object of obtaining a post with a salary of five thousand rubles a year. He was no longer bent on any particular department, or tendency, or kind of activity. All he now wanted was an appointment to another post with a salary of five thousand rubles, either in the administration, in the banks, with the railways, in one of the Empress Marya's Institutions,[10] or even in the customs — but it had to carry with it a salary of five thousand rubles and be in a ministry other than that in which they had failed to appreciate him.

And this quest of Ivan Ilych's was crowned with remarkable and unexpected success. At Kursk an acquaintance of his, F. I. Ilyin, got into the first-class carriage, sat down beside Ivan Ilych, and told him of a telegram just received by the Governor of Kursk announcing that a change was about to take place in the ministry: Peter Ivanovich was to be superseded by Ivan Semënovich.

The proposed change, apart from its significance for Russia, had a special significance for Ivan Ilych, because by bringing forward a new man, Peter Petrovich, and consequently his friend Zachar Ivanovich, it was highly favorable for Ivan Ilych, since Zachar Ivanovich was a friend and colleague of his.

In Moscow this news was confirmed, and on reaching Petersburg Ivan Ilych found Zachar Ivanovich and received a definite promise of an appointment in his former department of Justice.

A week later he telegraphed to his wife: "Zachar in Miller's place. I shall receive appointment on presentation of report."

Thanks to this change of personnel, Ivan Ilych had unexpectedly obtained an appointment in his former ministry which placed him two stages above his former colleagues besides giving him five thousand rubles salary and three thousand five hundred rubles for expenses connected with his removal. All his ill humor towards his former enemies and the whole department vanished, and Ivan Ilych was completely happy.

He returned to the country more cheerful and contented than he had been for a long time. Praskovya Fëdorovna also cheered up and a truce was

---

[10] orphanages founded by the wife of Tsar Paul I, who ruled from 1796 to 1801.

arranged between them. Ivan Ilych told of how he had been fêted by every-body in Petersburg, how all those who had been his enemies were put to shame and now fawned on him, how envious they were of his appointment, and how much everybody in Petersburg had liked him.

Praskovya Fëdorovna listened to all this and appeared to believe it. She did not contradict anything, but only made plans for their life in the town to which they were going. Ivan Ilych saw with delight that these plans were his plans, that he and his wife agreed, and that, after a stumble, his life was regaining its due and natural character of pleasant lightheartedness and decorum.

Ivan Ilych had come back for a short time only, for he had to take up his new duties on the 10th of September. Moreover, he needed time to set-tle into the new place, to move all his belongings from the province, and to buy and order many additional things: in a word, to make such arrange-ments as he had resolved on, which were almost exactly what Praskovya Fëdorovna too had decided on.

Now that everything had happened so fortunately, and that he and his wife were at one in their aims and moreover saw so little of one another, they got on together better than they had done since the first years of mar-riage. Ivan Ilych had thought of taking his family away with him at once, but the insistence of his wife's brother and her sister-in-law, who had sud-denly become particularly amiable and friendly to him and his family, in-duced him to depart alone.

So he departed, and the cheerful state of mind induced by his success and by the harmony between his wife and himself, the one intensifying the other, did not leave him. He found a delightful house, just the thing both he and his wife had dreamt of. Spacious, lofty reception rooms in the old style, a convenient and dignified study, rooms for his wife and daughter, a study for his son — it might have been specially built for them. Ivan Ilych himself superintended the arrangements, chose the wallpapers, supple-mented the furniture (preferably with antiques which he considered par-ticularly *comme il faut*), and supervised the upholstering. Everything progressed and progressed and approached the ideal he had set himself: even when things were only half completed they exceeded his expectations. He saw what a refined and elegant character, free from vulgarity, it would all have when it was ready. On falling asleep he pictured to himself how the reception-room would look. Looking at the yet unfinished drawing-room he could see the fireplace, the screen, the what-not, the little chairs dotted here and there, the dishes and plates on the walls, and the bronzes, as they would be when everything was in place. He was pleased by the thought of how his wife and daughter, who shared his taste in this matter, would be impressed by it. They were certainly not expecting as much. He had been particularly successful in finding, and buying cheaply, antiques which gave a particu-larly aristocratic character to the whole place. But in his letters he inten-tionally understated everything in order to be able to surprise them. All this so absorbed him that his new duties — though he liked his official work —

interested him less than he had expected. Sometimes he even had moments of absent-mindedness during the Court Sessions, and would consider whether he should have straight or curved cornices for his curtains. He was so interested in it all that he often did things himself, rearranging the furniture, or rehanging the curtains. Once when mounting a step-ladder to show the upholsterer, who did not understand, how he wanted the hangings draped, he made a false step and slipped, but being a strong and agile man he clung on and only knocked his side against the knob of the window frame. The bruised place was painful but the pain soon passed, and he felt particularly bright and well just then. He wrote: "I feel fifteen years younger." He thought he would have everything ready by September, but it dragged on till mid-October. But the result was charming not only in his eyes but to everyone who saw it.

In reality it was just what is usually seen in the houses of people of moderate means who want to appear rich, and therefore succeed only in resembling others like themselves: there were damasks, dark wood, plants, rugs, and dull and polished bronzes — all the things people of a certain class have in order to resemble other people of that class. His house was so like the others that it would never have been noticed, but to him it all seemed to be quite exceptional. He was very happy when he met his family at the station and brought them to the newly furnished house all lit up, where a footman in a white tie opened the door into the hall decorated with plants, and when they went on into the drawing-room, and the study uttering exclamations of delight. He conducted them everywhere, drank in their praises eagerly, and beamed with pleasure. At tea that evening, when Praskovya Fëdorovna among other things asked him about his fall, he laughed and showed them how he had gone flying and had frightened the upholsterer.

"It's a good thing I'm a bit of an athlete. Another man might have been killed, but I merely knocked myself, just here; it hurts when it's touched, but it's passing off already — it's only a bruise."

So they began living in their new home — in which, as always happens, when they got thoroughly settled in they found they were just one room short — and with the increased income, which as always was just a little (some five hundred rubles) too little, but it was all very nice.

Things went particularly well at first, before everything was finally arranged and while something had still to be done: this thing bought, that thing ordered, another thing moved, and something else adjusted. Though there were some disputes between husband and wife, they were both so well satisfied and had so much to do that it all passed off without any serious quarrels. When nothing was left to arrange it became rather dull and something seemed to be lacking, but they were then making acquaintances, forming habits, and life was growing fuller.

Ivan Ilych spent his mornings at the law court and came home to dinner, and at first he was generally in a good humor, though he occasionally became irritable just on account of his house. (Every spot on the tablecloth or the upholstery, and every broken windowblind string, irritated him. He had devoted so much trouble to arranging it all that every disturbance of it distressed him.) But on the whole his life ran its course as he believed life should do: easily, pleasantly, and decorously.

He got up at nine, drank his coffee, read the paper, and then put on his undress uniform and went to the law courts. There the harness in which he worked had already been stretched to fit him and he donned it without a hitch: petitioners, inquiries at the chancery, the chancery itself, and the sittings public and administrative. In all this the thing was to exclude everything fresh and vital, which always disturbs the regular course of official business, and to admit only official relations with people, and then only on official grounds. A man would come, for instance, wanting some information. Ivan Ilych, as one in whose sphere the matter did not lie, would have nothing to do with him: but if the man had some business with him in his official capacity, something that could be expressed on officially stamped paper, he would do everything, positively everything he could within the limits of such relations, and in doing so would maintain the semblance of friendly human relations, that is, would observe the courtesies of life. As soon as the official relations ended, so did everything else. Ivan Ilych possessed this capacity to separate his real life from the official side of affairs and not mix the two, in the highest degree, and by long practice and natural aptitude had brought it to such a pitch that sometimes, in the manner of a virtuoso, he would even allow himself to let the human and official relations mingle. He let himself do this just because he felt that he could at any time he chose resume the strictly official attitude again and drop the human relation. And he did it all easily, pleasantly, correctly, and even artistically. In the intervals between the sessions he smoked, drank tea, chatted a little about politics, a little about general topics, a little about cards, but most of all about official appointments. Tired, but with the feelings of a virtuoso — one of the first violins who has played his part in an orchestra with precision — he would return home to find that his wife and daughter had been out paying calls, or had a visitor, and that his son had been to school, had done his homework with his tutor, and was duly learning what is taught at High Schools. Everything was as it should be. After dinner, if they had no visitors, Ivan Ilych sometimes read a book that was being much discussed at the time, and in the evening settled down to work, that is, read official papers, compared the depositions of witnesses, and noted paragraphs of the Code applying to them. This was neither dull nor amusing. It was dull when he might have been playing bridge, but if no bridge was available it was at any rate better than doing nothing or sitting with his wife. Ivan Ilych's chief pleasure was giving little dinners to which he invited men and women of good social position, and just as his drawing-room resembled all other drawing-rooms so did his enjoyable little parties resemble all other such parties.

Once they even gave a dance. Ivan Ilych enjoyed it and everything went off well, except that it led to a violent quarrel with his wife about the cakes and sweets. Praskovya Fëdorovna had made her own plans, but Ivan Ilych insisted on getting everything from an expensive confectioner and ordered too many cakes, and the quarrel occurred because some of those cakes were left over and the confectioner's bill came to forty-five rubles. It was a great and disagreeable quarrel. Praskovya Fëdorovna called him "a fool and an imbecile," and he clutched at his head and made angry allusions to divorce.

But the dance itself had been enjoyable. The best people were there, and Ivan Ilych had danced with Princess Trufonova, a sister of the distinguished founder of the Society "Bear My Burden."

The pleasures connected with his work were pleasures of ambition; his social pleasures were those of vanity; but Ivan Ilych's greatest pleasure was playing bridge. He acknowledged that whatever disagreeable incident happened in his life, the pleasure that beamed like a ray of light above everything else was to sit down to bridge with good players, not noisy partners, and of course to four-handed bridge (with five players it was annoying to have to stand out, though one pretended not to mind), to play a clever and serious game (when the cards allowed it), and then to have supper and drink a glass of wine. After a game of bridge, especially if he had won a little (to win a large sum was unpleasant), Ivan Ilych went to bed in specially good humor.

So they lived. They formed a circle of acquaintances among the best people and were visited by people of importance and by young folk. In their views as to their acquaintances, husband, wife, and daughter were entirely agreed, and tacitly and unanimously kept at arm's length and shook off the various shabby friends and relations who, with much show of affection, gushed into the drawing-room with its Japanese plates on the walls. Soon these shabby friends ceased to obtrude themselves and only the best people remained in the Golovins' set.

Young men made up to Lisa, and Petrishchev, an examining magistrate and Dmitri Ivanovich Petrishchev's son and sole heir, began to be so attentive to her that Ivan Ilych had already spoken to Praskovya Fëdorovna about it, and considered whether they should not arrange a party for them, or get up some private theatricals.

So they lived, and all went well, without change, and life flowed pleasantly.

IV

They were all in good health. It could not be called ill health if Ivan Ilych sometimes said that he had a queer taste in his mouth and felt some discomfort in his left side.

But this discomfort increased and, though not exactly painful, grew into a sense of pressure in his side accompanied by ill humor. And his irritability became worse and worse and began to mar the agreeable, easy, and correct life that had established itself in the Golovin family. Quarrels between husband and wife became more and more frequent, and soon the ease and amenity disappeared and even the decorum was barely maintained. Scenes again became frequent, and very few of those islets remained on which husband and wife could meet without an explosion. Praskovya Fëdorovna now had good reason to say that her husband's temper was trying. With characteristic exaggeration she said he had always had a dreadful temper, and that it had needed all her good nature to put up with it for twenty years. It was true that now the quarrels were started by him. His bursts of temper always came just before dinner, often just as he began to eat his soup. Sometimes he noticed that a plate or dish was chipped, or the food was not right, or his son put his elbow on the table, or his daughter's hair was not done as he liked it, and for all this he blamed Praskovya Fëdorovna. At first she retorted and said disagreeable things to him, but once or twice he fell into such a rage at the beginning of dinner that she realized it was due to some physical derangement brought on by taking food, and so she restrained herself and did not answer, but only hurried to get the dinner over. She regarded this self-restraint as highly praiseworthy. Having come to the conclusion that her husband had a dreadful temper and made her life miserable, she began to feel sorry for herself, and the more she pitied herself the more she hated her husband. She began to wish he would die; yet she did not want him to die because then his salary would cease. And this irritated her against him still more. She considered herself dreadfully unhappy just because not even his death could save her, and though she concealed her exasperation, that hidden exasperation of hers increased his irritation also.

After one scene in which Ivan Ilych had been particularly unfair and after which he had said in explanation that he certainly was irritable but that it was due to his not being well, she said that if he was ill it should be attended to, and insisted on his going to see a celebrated doctor.

He went. Everything took place as he had expected and as it always does. There was the usual waiting and the important air assumed by the doctor, with which he was so familiar (resembling that which he himself assumed in court), and the sounding and listening, and the questions which called for answers that were foregone conclusions and were evidently unnecessary, and the look of importance which implied that "if only you put yourself in our hands we will arrange everything — we know indubitably how it has to be done, always in the same way for everybody alike." It was all just as it was in the law courts. The doctor put on just the same air towards him as he himself put on towards an accused person.

The doctor said that so-and-so indicated that there was so-and-so inside the patient, but if the investigation of so-and-so did not confirm this, then he must assume that and that. If he assumed that and that, then . . . and so on. To Ivan Ilych only one question was important: was his case serious or not? But the doctor ignored that inappropriate question. From his point of view it was not the one under consideration, the real question was to decide between a floating kidney, chronic catarrh, or appendicitis. It was not a question of Ivan Ilych's life or death, but one between a floating kidney and appendicitis. And that question the doctor solved brilliantly, as it seemed to Ivan Ilych, in favor of the appendix, with the reservation that should an examination of the urine give fresh indications the matter would be reconsidered. All this was just what Ivan Ilych had himself brilliantly accomplished a thousand times in dealing with men on trial. The doctor summed up just as brilliantly, looking over his spectacles triumphantly and even gaily at the accused. From the doctor's summing up Ivan Ilych concluded that things were bad, but that for the doctor, and perhaps for everybody else, it was a matter of indifference, though for him it was bad. And this conclusion struck him painfully, arousing in him a great feeling of pity for himself and of bitterness towards the doctor's indifference to a matter of such importance.

He said nothing of this, but rose, placed the doctor's fee on the table, and remarked with a sigh: "We sick people probably often put inappropriate questions. But tell me, in general, is this complaint dangerous, or not? . . ."

The doctor looked at him sternly over his spectacles with one eye, as if to say: "Prisoner, if you will not keep to the questions put to you, I shall be obliged to have you removed from the court."

"I have already told you what I consider necessary and proper. The analysis may show something more." And the doctor bowed.

Ivan Ilych went out slowly, seated himself disconsolately in his sledge, and drove home. All the way home he was going over what the doctor had said, trying to translate those complicated, obscure, scientific phrases into plain language and find in them an answer to the question: "Is my condition bad? Is it very bad? Or is there as yet nothing much wrong?" And it seemed to him that the meaning of what the doctor had said was that it was very bad. Everything in the streets seemed depressing. The cabmen, the houses, the passers-by, and the shops, were dismal. His ache, this dull gnawing ache that never ceased for a moment, seemed to have acquired a new and more serious significance from the doctor's dubious remarks. Ivan Ilych now watched it with a new and oppressive feeling.

He reached home and began to tell his wife about it. She listened, but in the middle of his account his daughter came in with her hat on, ready to go out with her mother. She sat down reluctantly to listen to this tedious story, but could not stand it long, and her mother too did not hear him to the end.

"Well, I am very glad," she said. "Mind now to take your medicine regularly. Give me the prescription and I'll send Gerasim to the chemist's." And she went to get ready to go out.

While she was in the room Ivan Ilych had hardly taken time to breathe, but he sighed deeply when she left it.

"Well," he thought, "perhaps it isn't so bad after all."

He began taking his medicine and following the doctor's directions, which had been altered after the examination of the urine. But then it happened that there was a contradiction between the indications drawn from the examination of the urine and the symptoms that showed themselves. It turned out that what was happening differed from what the doctor had told him, and that he had either forgotten, or blundered, or hidden something from him. He could not, however, be blamed for that, and Ivan Ilych still obeyed his orders implicitly and at first derived some comfort from doing so.

From the time of his visit to the doctor, Ivan Ilych's chief occupation was the exact fulfilment of the doctor's instructions regarding hygiene and the taking of medicine, and the observation of his pain and his excretions. His chief interests came to be people's ailments and people's health. When sickness, deaths, or recoveries were mentioned in his presence, especially when the illness resembled his own, he listened with agitation which he tried to hide, asked questions, and applied what he heard to his own case.

The pain did not grow less, but Ivan Ilych made efforts to force himself to think that he was better. And he could do this so long as nothing agitated him. But as soon as he had any unpleasantness with his wife, any lack of success in his official work, or held bad cards at bridge, he was at once acutely sensible of his disease. He had formerly borne such mischances, hoping soon to adjust what was wrong, to master it and attain success, or make a grand slam. But now every mischance upset him and plunged him into despair. He would say to himself: "There now, just as I was beginning to get better and the medicine had begun to take effect, comes this accursed misfortune, or unpleasantness. . . ." And he was furious with the mishap, or with the people who were causing the unpleasantness and killing him, for he felt that this fury was killing him but could not restrain it. One would have thought that it should have been clear to him that this exasperation with circumstances and people aggravated his illness, and that he ought therefore to ignore unpleasant occurrences. But he drew the very opposite conclusion: he said that he needed peace, and he watched for everything that might disturb it and became irritable at the slightest infringement of it. His condition was rendered worse by the fact that he read medical books and consulted doctors. The progress of his disease was so gradual that he could deceive himself when comparing one day with another — the difference was so slight. But when he consulted the doctors it seemed to him that he was getting worse, and even very rapidly. Yet despite this he was continually consulting them.

That month he went to see another celebrity, who told him almost the same as the first had done but put his questions rather differently, and the interview with this celebrity only increased Ivan Ilych's doubts and fears. A friend of a friend of his, a very good doctor, diagnosed his illness again quite differently from the others, and though he predicted recovery, his questions and suppositions bewildered Ivan Ilych still more and increased his doubts. A homoeopathist diagnosed the disease in yet another way, and prescribed medicine which Ivan Ilych took secretly for a week. But after a week, not feeling any improvement and having lost confidence both in the former doctor's treatment and in this one's, he became still more despondent. One day a lady acquaintance mentioned a cure effected by a wonder-working icon. Ivan Ilych caught himself listening attentively and beginning to believe that it had occurred. This incident alarmed him. "Has my mind really weakened to such an extent?" he asked himself. "Nonsense! It's all rubbish. I mustn't give way to nervous fears but having chosen a doctor must keep strictly to his treatment. That is what I will do. Now it's all settled. I won't think about it, but will follow the treatment seriously till summer, and then we shall see. From now there must be no more of this wavering!" This was easy to say but impossible to carry out. The pain in his side oppressed him and seemed to grow worse and more incessant, while the taste in his mouth grew stranger and stranger. It seemed to him that his breath had a disgusting smell, and he was conscious of a loss of appetite and strength. There was no deceiving himself: something terrible, new, and more important than anything before in his life, was taking place within him of which he alone was aware. Those about him did not understand or would not understand it, but thought everything in the world was going on as usual. That tormented Ivan Ilych more than anything. He saw that his household, especially his wife and daughter who were in a perfect whirl of visiting, did not understand anything of it and were annoyed that he was so depressed and so exacting, as if he were to blame for it. Though they tried to disguise it he saw that he was an obstacle in their path, and that his wife had adopted a definite line in regard to his illness and kept to it regardless of anything he said or did. Her attitude was this: "You know," she would say to her friends, "Ivan Ilych can't do as other people do, and keep to the treatment prescribed for him. One day he'll take his drops and keep strictly to his diet and go to bed in good time, but the next day unless I watch him he'll suddenly forget his medicine, eat sturgeon — which is forbidden — and sit up playing cards till one o'clock in the morning."

"Oh, come, when was that?" Ivan Ilych would ask in vexation. "Only once at Peter Ivanovich's."

"And yesterday with Shebek."

"Well, even if I hadn't stayed up, this pain would have kept me awake."

"Be that as it may you'll never get well like that, but will always make us wretched."

Praskovya Fëdorovna's attitude to Ivan Ilych's illness, as she expressed it both to others and to him, was that it was his own fault and was another of the annoyances he caused her. Ivan Ilych felt that this opinion escaped her involuntarily — but that did not make it easier for him.

At the law courts too, Ivan Ilych noticed, or thought he noticed, a strange attitude towards himself. It sometimes seemed to him that people were watching him inquisitively as a man whose place might soon be vacant. Then again, his friends would suddenly begin to chaff him in a friendly way about his low spirits, as if the awful, horrible, and unheard-of thing that was going on within him, incessantly gnawing at him and irresistibly drawing him away, was a very agreeable subject for jests. Schwartz in

particular irritated him by his jocularity, vivacity, and *savoir-faire*, which reminded him of what he himself had been ten years ago.

Friends came to make up a set and they sat down to cards. They dealt,
bending the new cards to soften them, and he sorted the diamonds in his
hand and found he had seven. His partner said "No trumps" and supported
him with two diamonds. What more could be wished for? It ought to be
jolly and lively. They would make a grand slam. But suddenly Ivan Ilych
was conscious of that gnawing pain, that taste in his mouth, and it seemed
ridiculous that in such circumstances he should be pleased to make a grand
slam.

He looked at his partner Mikhail Mikhaylovich, who rapped the table
with his strong hand and instead of snatching up the tricks pushed the cards
courteously and indulgently towards Ivan Ilych that he might have the
pleasure of gathering them up without the trouble of stretching out his
hand for them. "Does he think I am too weak to stretch out my arm?"
thought Ivan Ilych, and forgetting what he was doing he over-trumped his
partner, missing the grand slam by three tricks. And what was most awful of
all was that he saw how upset Mikhail Mikhaylovich was about it but did
not himself care. And it was dreadful to realize why he did not care.

They all saw that he was suffering, and said: "We can stop if you are
tired. Take a rest." Lie down? No, he was not at all tired, and he finished
the rubber. All were gloomy and silent. Ivan Ilych felt that he had diffused
this gloom over them and could not dispel it. They had supper and went
away, and Ivan Ilych was left alone with the consciousness that his life was
poisoned and was poisoning the lives of others, and that this poison did not
weaken but penetrated more and more deeply into his whole being.

With this consciousness, and with physical pain besides the terror, he
must go to bed, often to lie awake the greater part of the night. Next morning he had to get up again, dress, go to the law courts, speak, and write; or if
he did not go out, spend at home those twenty-four hours a day each of
which was a torture. And he had to live thus all alone on the brink of an
abyss, with no one who understood or pitied him.

V

So one month passed and then another. Just before the New Year his
brother-in-law came to town and stayed at their house. Ivan Ilych was at the
law courts and Praskovya Fëdorovna had gone shopping. When Ivan Ilych
came home and entered his study he found his brother-in-law there — a
healthy, florid man — unpacking his portmanteau himself. He raised his
head on hearing Ivan Ilych's footsteps and looked up at him for a moment
without a word. That stare told Ivan Ilych everything. His brother-in-law
opened his mouth to utter an exclamation of surprise but checked himself,
and that action confirmed it all.

"I have changed, eh?"

"Yes, there is a change."

And after that, try as he would to get his brother-in-law to return to the subject of his looks, the latter would say nothing about it. Praskovya Fëdorovna came home and her brother went out to her. Ivan Ilych locked the door and began to examine himself in the glass, first full face, then in profile. He took up a portrait of himself taken with his wife, and compared it with what he saw in the glass. The change in him was immense. Then he bared his arms to the elbow, looked at them, drew the sleeves down again, sat down on an ottoman, and grew blacker than night.

"No, no, this won't do!" he said to himself, and jumped up, went to the table, took up some law papers and began to read them, but could not continue. He unlocked the door and went into the reception-room. The door leading to the drawing-room was shut. He approached it on tiptoe and listened.

"No, you are exaggerating!" Praskovya Fëdorovna was saying.

"Exaggerating! Don't you see it? Why, he's a dead man! Look at his eyes—there's no light in them. But what is it that is wrong with him?"

"No one knows. Nikolaevich said something, but I don't know what. And Leshchetitsky[11] said quite the contrary. . . ."

Ivan Ilych walked away, went to his own room, lay down, and began musing: "The kidney, a floating kidney." He recalled all the doctors had told him of how it detached itself and swayed about. And by an effort of imagination he tried to catch that kidney and arrest it and support it. So little was needed for this, it seemed to him. "No, I'll go to see Peter Ivanovich again." He rang, ordered the carriage, and got ready to go.

"Where are you going, Jean?" asked his wife, with a specially sad and exceptionally kind look.

This exceptionally kind look irritated him. He looked morosely at her. "I must go to see Peter Ivanovich."[12]

He went to see Peter Ivanovich, and together they went to see his friend, the doctor. He was in, and Ivan Ilych had a long talk with him.

Reviewing the anatomical and physiological details of what in the doctor's opinion was going on inside him, he understood it all.

There was something, a small thing, in the vermiform appendix. It might all come right. Only stimulate the energy of one organ and check the activity of another, then absorption would take place and everything would come right. He got home rather late for dinner, ate his dinner, and conversed cheerfully, but could not for a long time bring himself to go back to work in his room. At last, however, he went to his study and did what was necessary, but the consciousness that he had put something aside — an important, intimate matter which he would revert to when his work was done — never left him. When he had finished his work he remembered that this intimate matter was the thought of his vermiform appendix. But he did not give himself up to it, and went to the drawing-room for tea.

---

[11] two doctors, the latter a celebrated specialist. [Translators' note]

[12] That was the friend whose friend was a doctor. [Translators' note]

There were callers there, including the examining magistrate who was a desirable match for his daughter, and they were conversing, playing the piano, and singing. Ivan Ilych, as Praskovya Fëdorovna remarked, spent that evening more cheerfully than usual, but he never for a moment forgot that he had postponed the important matter of the appendix. At eleven o'clock he said good-night and went to his bedroom. Since his illness he had slept alone in a small room next to his study. He undressed and took up a novel by Zola,[13] but instead of reading it he fell into thought, and in his imagination that desired improvement in the vermiform appendix occurred. There were the absorption and evacuation and the re-establishment of normal activity. "Yes, that's it!" he said to himself. "One need only assist nature, that's all." He remembered his medicine, rose, took it, and lay down on his back watching for the beneficent action of the medicine and for it to lessen the pain. "I need only take it regularly and avoid all injurious influences. I am already feeling better, much better." He began touching his side: it was not painful to the touch. "There, I really don't feel it. It's much better already." He put out the light and turned on his side. . . . "The appendix is getting better, absorption is occurring." Suddenly he felt the old, familiar, dull, gnawing pain, stubborn and serious. There was the same familiar loathsome taste in his mouth. His heart sank and he felt dazed. "My God! My God!" he muttered. "Again, again! and it will never cease." And suddenly the matter presented itself in a quite different aspect. "Vermiform appendix! Kidney!" he said to himself. "It's not a question of appendix or kidney, but of life and . . . death. Yes, life was there and now it is going, going and I cannot stop it. Yes. Why deceive myself? Isn't it obvious to everyone but me that I'm dying, and that it's only a question of weeks, days . . . it may happen this moment. There was light and now there is darkness. I was here and now I'm going there! Where?" A chill came over him, his breathing ceased, and he felt only the throbbing of his heart.

"When I am not, what will there be? There will be nothing. Then where shall I be when I am no more? Can this be dying? No, I don't want to!" He jumped up and tried to light the candle, felt for it with trembling hands, dropped candle and candlestick on the floor, and fell back on his pillow.

"What's the use? It makes no difference," he said to himself, staring with wide-open eyes into the darkness. "Death. Yes, death. And none of them know or wish to know it, and they have no pity for me. Now they are playing." (He heard through the door the distant sound of a song and its accompaniment.) "It's all the same to them, but they will die too! Fools! I first, and they later, but it will be the same for them. And now they are merry . . . the beasts!"

Anger choked him and he was agonizingly, unbearably miserable. "It is impossible that all men have been doomed to suffer this awful horror!" He raised himself.

"Something must be wrong. I must calm myself — must think it all

[13] Émile Zola (1840–1902), French novelist.

over from the beginning." And he again began thinking. "Yes, the beginning of my illness: I knocked my side, but I was still quite well that day and the next. It hurt a little, then rather more. I saw the doctors, then followed despondency and anguish, more doctors, and I drew nearer to the abyss. My strength grew less and I kept coming nearer and nearer, and now I have wasted away and there is no light in my eyes. I think of the appendix — but this is death! I think of mending the appendix, and all the while here is death! Can it really be death?" Again terror seized him and he gasped for breath. He leant down and began feeling for the matches, pressing with his elbow on the stand beside the bed. It was in his way and hurt him, he grew furious with it, pressed on it still harder, and upset it. Breathless and in despair he fell on his back, expecting death to come immediately.

Meanwhile the visitors were leaving. Praskovya Fëdorovna was seeing them off. She heard something fall and came in.

"What has happened?"

"Nothing. I knocked it over accidentally."

She went out and returned with a candle. He lay there panting heavily, like a man who has run a thousand yards, and stared upwards at her with a fixed look.

"What is it, Jean?"

"No . . . no . . . thing. I upset it." ("Why speak of it? She won't understand," he thought.)

And in truth she did not understand. She picked up the stand, lit his candle, and hurried away to see another visitor off. When she came back he still lay on his back, looking upwards.

"What is it? Do you feel worse?"

"Yes."

She shook her head and sat down.

"Do you know, Jean, I think we must ask Leshchetitsky to come and see you here."

This meant calling in the famous specialist, regardless of expense. He smiled malignantly and said "No." She remained a little longer and then went up to him and kissed his forehead.

While she was kissing him he hated her from the bottom of his soul and with difficulty refrained from pushing her away.

"Good-night. Please God you'll sleep."

"Yes."

VI

Ivan Ilych saw that he was dying, and he was in continual despair.

In the depth of his heart he knew he was dying, but not only was he not accustomed to the thought, he simply did not and could not grasp it.

The syllogism he had learnt from Kiezewetter's Logic:[14] "Caius is a

---

[14] Klaus Kiezewetter (1766–1819), *The Outline of Logic According to Kantian Principles,* a popular text in Russia, based on the teachings of German philosopher Immanuel Kant (1722–1804).

man, men are mortal, therefore Caius is mortal," had always seemed to him correct as applied to Caius, but certainly not as applied to himself. That Caius — man in the abstract — was mortal, was perfectly correct, but he was not Caius, not an abstract man, but a creature quite, quite separate from all others. He had been little Vanya, with a mama and a papa, with Mitya and Volodya, with the toys, a coachman and a nurse, afterwards with Katenka and with all the joys, griefs, and delights of childhood, boyhood, and youth. What did Caius know of the smell of that striped leather ball Vanya had been so fond of? Had Caius kissed his mother's hand like that, and did the silk of her dress rustle so for Caius? Had he rioted like that at school when the pastry was bad? Had Caius been in love like that? Could Caius preside at a session as he did? "Caius really was mortal, and it was right for him to die; but for me, little Vanya, Ivan Ilych, with all my thoughts and emotions, it's altogether a different matter. It cannot be that I ought to die. That would be too terrible."

Such was his feeling.

"If I had to die like Caius I should have known it was so. An inner voice would have told me so, but there was nothing of the sort in me and I and all my friends felt that our case was quite different from that of Caius. And now here it is!" he said to himself. "It can't be. It's impossible! But here it is. How is this? How is one to understand it?"

He could not understand it, and tried to drive this false, incorrect, morbid thought away and to replace it by other proper and healthy thoughts. But that thought, and not the thought only but the reality itself, seemed to come and confront him.

And to replace that thought he called up a succession of others, hoping to find in them some support. He tried to get back into the former current of thoughts that had once screened the thought of death from him. But strange to say, all that formerly shut off, hidden, and destroyed, his consciousness of death, no longer had that effect. Ivan Ilych now spent most of his time in attempting to re-establish that old current. He would say to himself: "I will take up my duties again — after all I used to live by them." And banishing all doubts he would go to the law courts, enter into conversation with his colleagues, and sit carelessly as was his wont, scanning the crowd with a thoughtful look and leaning both his emaciated arms on the arms of his oak chair; bending over as usual to a colleague and drawing his papers nearer he would interchange whispers with him, and then suddenly raising his eyes and sitting erect would pronounce certain words and open the proceedings. But suddenly in the midst of those proceedings the pain in his side, regardless of the stage the proceedings had reached, would begin its own gnawing work. Ivan Ilych would turn his attention to it and try to drive the thought of it away, but without success. *It* would come and stand before him and look at him, and he would be petrified and the light would die out of his eyes, and he would again begin asking himself whether *It* alone was true. And his colleagues and subordinates would see with surprise and distress that he, the brilliant and subtle judge, was becoming confused and making mistakes. He would shake himself, try to pull himself together, manage somehow to bring the sitting to a close, and return home with the sorrowful consciousness that his judicial labors could not as formerly hide from him what he wanted them to hide, and could not deliver him from *It*. And what was worst of all was that *It* drew his attention to itself not in order to make him take some action but only that he should look at *It*, look it straight in the face: look at it and without doing anything, suffer inexpressibly.

And to save himself from this condition Ivan Ilych looked for consolations — new screens — and new screens were found and for a while seemed to save him, but then they immediately fell to pieces or rather became transparent, as if *It* penetrated them and nothing could veil *It*.

In these latter days he would go into the drawing-room he had arranged — that drawing-room where he had fallen and for the sake of which (how bitterly ridiculous it seemed) he had sacrificed his life — for he knew that his illness originated with that knock. He would enter and see that something had scratched the polished table. He would look for the cause of this and find that it was the bronze ornamentation of an album, that had got bent. He would take up the expensive album which he had lovingly arranged, and feel vexed with his daughter and her friends for their untidiness — for the album was torn here and there and some of the photographs turned upside down. He would put it carefully in order and bend the ornamentation back into position. Then it would occur to him to place all those things in another corner of the room, near the plants. He could call the footman, but his daughter or wife would come to help him. They would not agree, and his wife would contradict him, and he would dispute and grow angry. But that was all right, for then he did not think about *It*. *It* was invisible.

But then, when he was moving something himself, his wife would say: "Let the servants do it. You will hurt yourself again." And suddenly *It* would flash through the screen and he would see it. It was just a flash, and he hoped it would disappear, but he would involuntarily pay attention to his side. "It sits there as before, gnawing just the same!" And he could no longer forget *It*, but could distinctly see it looking at him from behind the flowers. "What is it all for?"

"It really is so! I lost my life over that curtain as I might have done when storming a fort. Is that possible? How terrible and how stupid. It can't be true! It can't, but it is."

He would go to his study, lie down, and again be alone with *It*: face to face with *It*. And nothing could be done with *It* except to look at it and shudder.

VII

How it happened it is impossible to say because it came about step by step, unnoticed, but in the third month of Ivan Ilych's illness, his wife, his daughter, his son, his acquaintances, the doctors, the servants, and above all he himself, were aware that the whole interest he had for other people was whether he would soon vacate his place, and at last release the living from the discomfort caused by his presence and be himself released from his sufferings.

He slept less and less. He was given opium and hypodermic injections of morphine, but this did not relieve him. The dull depression he experienced in a somnolent condition at first gave him a little relief, but only as something new, afterwards it became as distressing as the pain itself or even more so.

Special foods were prepared for him by the doctors' orders, but all those foods became increasingly distasteful and disgusting to him.

For his excretions also special arrangements had to be made, and this was a torment to him every time — a torment from the uncleanliness, the unseemliness, and the smell, and from knowing that another person had to take part in it.

But just through this most unpleasant matter, Ivan Ilych obtained comfort. Gerasim, the butler's young assistant, always came in to carry the things out. Gerasim was a clean, fresh peasant lad, grown stout on town food and always cheerful and bright. At first the sight of him, in his clean Russian peasant costume, engaged on that disgusting task embarrassed Ivan Ilych.

Once when he got up from the commode too weak to draw up his trousers, he dropped into a soft armchair and looked with horror at his bare, enfeebled thighs with the muscles so sharply marked on them.

Gerasim with a firm light tread, his heavy boots emitting a pleasant smell of tar and fresh winter air, came in wearing a clean Hessian apron, the sleeves of his print shirt tucked up over his strong bare young arms; and refraining from looking at his sick master out of consideration for his feelings, and restraining the joy of life that beamed from his face, he went up to the commode.

"Gerasim!" said Ivan Ilych in a weak voice.

Gerasim started, evidently afraid he might have committed some blunder, and with a rapid movement turned his fresh, kind, simple young face which just showed the first downy signs of a beard.

"Yes, sir?"

"That must be very unpleasant for you. You must forgive me. I am helpless."

"Oh, why, sir," and Gerasim's eyes beamed and he showed his glistening white teeth, "what's a little trouble? It's a case of illness with you, sir."

And his deft strong hands did their accustomed task, and he went out of the room stepping lightly. Five minutes later he as lightly returned.

Ivan Ilych was still sitting in the same position in the armchair.

"Gerasim," he said when the latter had replaced the freshly-washed utensil. "Please come here and help me." Gerasim went up to him. "Lift me up. It is hard for me to get up, and I have sent Dmitri away."

Gerasim went up to him, grasped his master with his strong arms deftly but gently, in the same way that he stepped — lifted him, supported him with one hand, and with the other drew up his trousers and would have set him down again, but Ivan Ilych asked to be led to the sofa. Gerasim, without an effort and without apparent pressure, led him, almost lifting him, to the sofa and placed him on it.

"Thank you. How easily and well you do it all!"

Gerasim smiled again and turned to leave the room. But Ivan Ilych felt his presence such a comfort that he did not want to let him go.

"One thing more, please move up that chair. No, the other one — under my feet. It is easier for me when my feet are raised."

Gerasim brought the chair, set it down gently in place, and raised Ivan Ilych's legs on to it. It seemed to Ivan Ilych that he felt better while Gerasim was holding up his legs.

"It's better when my legs are higher," he said. "Place that cushion under them."

Gerasim did so. He again lifted the legs and placed them, and again Ivan Ilych felt better while Gerasim held his legs. When he set them down Ivan Ilych fancied he felt worse.

"Gerasim," he said. "Are you busy now?"

"Not at all, sir," said Gerasim, who had learnt from the townsfolk how to speak to gentlefolk.

"What have you still to do?"

"What have I to do? I've done everything except chopping the logs for tomorrow."

"Then hold my legs up a bit higher, can you?"

"Of course I can. Why not?" And Gerasim raised his master's legs higher and Ivan Ilych thought that in that position he did not feel any pain at all.

"And how about the logs?"

"Don't trouble about that, sir. There's plenty of time."

Ivan Ilych told Gerasim to sit down and hold his legs, and began to talk to him. And strange to say it seemed to him that he felt better while Gerasim held his legs up.

After that Ivan Ilych would sometimes call Gerasim and get him to hold his legs on his shoulders, and he liked talking to him. Gerasim did it all easily, willingly, simply, and with a good nature that touched Ivan Ilych. Health, strength, and vitality in other people were offensive to him, but Gerasim's strength and vitality did not mortify but soothed him.

What tormented Ivan Ilych most was the deception, the lie, which for some reason they all accepted, that he was not dying but was simply ill, and that he only need keep quiet and undergo a treatment and then something very good would result. He however knew that do what they would nothing would come of it, only still more agonizing suffering and death. This deception tortured him — their not wishing to admit what they all knew and what he knew, but wanting to lie to him concerning his terrible condition, and wishing and forcing him to participate in that lie. Those lies — lies enacted over him on the eve of his death and destined to degrade this awful, solemn act to the level of their visitings, their curtains, their sturgeon for dinner — were a terrible agony for Ivan Ilych. And strangely enough, many times when they were going through their antics over him he had been within a hairbreadth of calling out to them: "Stop lying! You know and I know that I am dying. Then at least stop lying about it!" But he had never had the spirit to do it. The awful, terrible act of his dying was, he could see, reduced by those about him to the level of a casual, unpleasant, and almost indecorous incident (as if someone entered a drawing-room diffusing an unpleasant odor) and this was done by that very decorum which he had served all his life long. He saw that no one felt for him, because no one even wished to grasp his position. Only Gerasim recognized it and pitied him. And so Ivan Ilych felt at ease only with him. He felt comforted when Gerasim supported his legs (sometimes all night long) and refused to go to bed, saying: "Don't you worry, Ivan Ilych. I'll get sleep enough later on," or when he suddenly became familiar and exclaimed: "If you weren't sick it would be another matter, but as it is, why should I grudge a little trouble?" Gerasim alone did not lie; everything showed that he alone understood the facts of the case and did not consider it necessary to disguise them, but simply felt sorry for his emaciated and enfeebled master. Once when Ivan Ilych was sending him away he even said straight out: "We shall all of us die, so why should I grudge a little trouble?" — expressing the fact that he did not think his work burdensome, because he was doing it for a dying man and hoped someone would do the same for him when his time came.

Apart from this lying, or because of it, what most tormented Ivan Ilych was that no one pitied him as he wished to be pitied. At certain moments after prolonged suffering he wished most of all (though he would have been ashamed to confess it) for someone to pity him as a sick child is pitied. He longed to be petted and comforted. He knew he was an important functionary, that he had a beard turning grey, and that therefore what he longed for was impossible, but still he longed for it. And in Gerasim's attitude towards him there was something akin to what he wished for, and so that attitude comforted him. Ivan Ilych wanted to weep, wanted to be petted and cried over, and then his colleague Shebek would come, and instead of weeping and being petted, Ivan Ilych would assume a serious, severe, and profound air, and by force of habit would express his opinion on a decision of the Court of Cassation and would stubbornly insist on that view. This falsity around him and within him did more than anything else to poison his last days.

VIII

It was morning. He knew it was morning because Gerasim had gone, and Peter the footman had come and put out the candles, drawn back one of the curtains, and begun quietly to tidy up. Whether it was morning or evening, Friday or Sunday, made no difference, it was all just the same: the gnawing, unmitigated, agonizing pain, never ceasing for an instant, the consciousness of life inexorably waning but not yet extinguished, the approach of that ever dreaded and hateful Death which was the only reality, and always the same falsity. What were days, weeks, hours, in such a case?

"Will you have some tea, sir?"

"He wants things to be regular, and wishes the gentlefolk to drink tea in the morning," thought Ivan Ilych, and only said "No."

"Wouldn't you like to move onto the sofa, sir?"

"He wants to tidy up the room, and I'm in the way. I am uncleanliness and disorder," he thought, and said only:

"No, leave me alone."

The man went on bustling about. Ivan Ilych stretched out his hand. Peter came up, ready to help.

"What is it, sir?"

"My watch."

Peter took the watch which was close at hand and gave it to his master.

"Half-past eight. Are they up?"

"No, sir, except Vasily Ivanich" (the son) "who has gone to school. Praskovya Fëdorovna ordered me to wake her if you asked for her. Shall I do so?"

"No, there's no need to." "Perhaps I'd better have some tea," he thought, and added aloud: "Yes, bring me some tea."

Peter went to the door, but Ivan Ilych dreaded being left alone. "How can I keep him here? Oh yes, my medicine." "Peter, give me my medicine." "Why not? Perhaps it may still do me some good." He took a spoonful and swallowed it. "No, it won't help. It's all tomfoolery, all deception," he decided as soon as he became aware of the familiar, sickly, hopeless taste. "No, I can't believe in it any longer. But the pain, why this pain? If it would only cease just for a moment!" And he moaned. Peter turned towards him. "It's all right. Go and fetch me some tea."

Peter went out. Left alone Ivan Ilych groaned not so much with pain, terrible though that was, as from mental anguish. Always and for ever the same, always these endless days and nights. If only it would come quicker! If only what would come quicker? Death, darkness? . . . No, no! Anything rather than death!

When Peter returned with the tea on a tray, Ivan Ilych stared at him for a time in perplexity, not realizing who and what he was. Peter was disconcerted by that look and his embarrassment brought Ivan Ilych to himself.

"Oh, tea! All right, put it down. Only help me to wash and put on a clean shirt."

And Ivan Ilych began to wash. With pauses for rest, he washed his hands and then his face, cleaned his teeth, brushed his hair, and looked in the glass. He was terrified by what he saw, especially by the limp way in which his hair clung to his pallid forehead.

While his shirt was being changed he knew that he would be still more frightened at the sight of his body, so he avoided looking at it. Finally he was ready. He drew on a dressing-gown, wrapped himself in a plaid, and sat down in the armchair to take his tea. For a moment he felt refreshed, but as soon as he began to drink the tea he was again aware of the same taste, and the pain also returned. He finished it with an effort, and then lay down stretching out his legs, and dismissed Peter.

Always the same. Now a spark of hope flashes up, then a sea of despair rages, and always pain; always pain, always despair, and always the same. When alone he had a dreadful and distressing desire to call someone, but he knew beforehand that with others present it would be still worse. "Another dose of morphine — to lose consciousness. I will tell him, the doctor, that he must think of something else. It's impossible, impossible, to go on like this."

An hour and another pass like that. But now there is a ring at the door bell. Perhaps it's the doctor? It is. He comes in fresh, hearty, plump, and cheerful, with that look on his face that seems to say: "There now, you're in a panic about something, but we'll arrange it all for you directly!" The doctor knows this expression is out of place here, but he has put it on once for all and can't take it off — like a man who has put on a frock-coat in the morning to pay a round of calls.

The doctor rubs his hands vigorously and reassuringly.

"Brr! How cold it is! There's such a sharp frost; just let me warm myself!" he says, as if it were only a matter of waiting till he was warm, and then he would put everything right.

"Well now, how are you?"

Ivan Ilych feels that the doctor would like to say: "Well, how are our affairs?" but that even he feels that this would not do, and says instead: "What sort of a night have you had?"

Ivan Ilych looks at him as much as to say: "Are you really never ashamed of lying?" But the doctor does not wish to understand this question, and Ivan Ilych says: "Just as terrible as ever. The pain never leaves me and never subsides. If only something. . . ."

"Yes, you sick people are always like that. . . . There, now I think I am warm enough. Even Praskovya Fëdorovna, who is so particular, could find no fault with my temperature. Well, now I can say good-morning," and the doctor presses his patient's hand.

Then, dropping his former playfulness, he begins with a most serious face to examine the patient, feeling his pulse and taking his temperature, and then begins the sounding and auscultation.

Ivan Ilych knows quite well and definitely that all this is nonsense and pure deception, but when the doctor, getting down on his knee, leans over him, putting his ear first higher then lower, and performs various gymnastic movements over him with a significant expression on his face, Ivan Ilych submits to it all as he used to submit to the speeches of the lawyers, though he knew very well that they were all lying and why they were lying.

The doctor, kneeling on the sofa, is still sounding him when Praskovya Fëdorovna's silk dress rustles at the door and she is heard scolding Peter for not having let her know of the doctor's arrival.

She comes in, kisses her husband, and at once proceeds to prove that she has been up a long time already, and only owing to a misunderstanding failed to be there when the doctor arrived.

Ivan Ilych looks at her, scans her all over, sets against her the whiteness and plumpness and cleanness of her hands and neck, the gloss of her hair, and the sparkle of her vivacious eyes. He hates her with his whole soul. And the thrill of hatred he feels for her makes him suffer from her touch.

Her attitude towards him and his disease is still the same. Just as the doctor had adopted a certain relation to his patient which he could not abandon, so had she formed one towards him — that he was not doing something he ought to do and was himself to blame, and that she reproached him lovingly for this — and she could not now change that attitude.

"You see he doesn't listen to me and doesn't take his medicine at the proper time. And above all he lies in a position that is no doubt bad for him — with his legs up."

She described how he made Gerasim hold his legs up.

The doctor smiled with a contemptuous affability that said: "What's to be done? These sick people do have foolish fancies of that kind, but we must forgive them."

When the examination was over the doctor looked at his watch, and then Praskovya Fëdorovna announced to Ivan Ilych that it was of course as he pleased, but she had sent today for a celebrated specialist who would examine him and have a consultation with Michael Danilovich (their regular doctor).

"Please don't raise any objections. I am doing this for my own sake," she said ironically, letting it be felt that she was doing it all for his sake and only said this to leave him no right to refuse. He remained silent, knitting his brows. He felt that he was so surrounded and involved in a mesh of falsity that it was hard to unravel anything.

Everything she did for him was entirely for her own sake, and she told him she was doing for herself what she actually was doing for herself, as if that was so incredible that he must understand the opposite.

At half-past eleven the celebrated specialist arrived. Again the sounding began and the significant conversations in his presence and in another room, about the kidneys and the appendix, and the questions and answers, with such an air of importance that again, instead of the real question of life and death which now alone confronted him, the question arose of the kidney and appendix which were not behaving as they ought to and would now be attacked by Michael Danilovich and the specialist and forced to amend their ways.

The celebrated specialist took leave of him with a serious though not hopeless look, and in reply to the timid question Ivan Ilych, with eyes glistening with fear and hope, put to him as to whether there was a chance of recovery, said that he could not vouch for it but there was a possibility. The look of hope with which Ivan Ilych watched the doctor out was so pathetic that Praskovya Fëdorovna, seeing it, even wept as she left the room to hand the doctor his fee.

The gleam of hope kindled by the doctor's encouragement did not last long. The same room, the same pictures, curtains, wallpaper, medicine bottles, were all there, and the same aching suffering body, and Ivan Ilych began to moan. They gave him a subcutaneous injection and he sank into oblivion.

It was twilight when he came to. They brought him his dinner and he swallowed some beef tea with difficulty, and then everything was the same again and night was coming on.

After dinner, at seven o'clock, Praskovya Fëdorovna came into the room in evening dress, her full bosom pushed up by her corset, and with traces of powder on her face. She had reminded him in the morning that they were going to the theater. Sarah Bernhardt was visiting the town and they had a box, which he had insisted on their taking. Now he had forgotten about it and her toilet offended him, but he concealed his vexation when he remembered that he had himself insisted on their securing a box and going because it would be an instructive and aesthetic pleasure for the children.

Praskovya Fëdorovna came in, self-satisfied but yet with a rather guilty air. She sat down and asked how he was, but, as he saw, only for the sake of asking and not in order to learn about it, knowing that there was nothing to learn — and then went on to what she really wanted to say: that she would not on any account have gone but that the box had been taken and Helen and their daughter were going, as well as Petrishchev (the examining magistrate, their daughter's fiancé) and that it was out of the question to let them go alone; but that she would have much preferred to sit with him for a while; and he must be sure to follow the doctor's orders while she was away.

"Oh, and Fëdor Petrovich" (the fiancé) "would like to come in. May he? And Lisa?"

"All right."

Their daughter came in in full evening dress, her fresh young flesh exposed (making a show of that very flesh which in his own case caused so much suffering), strong, healthy, evidently in love, and impatient with illness, suffering, and death, because they interfered with her happiness.

Fëdor Petrovich came in too, in evening dress, his hair curled *à la Capoul*,[15] a tight stiff collar round his long sinewy neck, an enormous white shirt-front and narrow black trousers tightly stretched over his strong thighs. He had one white glove tightly drawn on, and was holding his opera hat in his hand.

Following him the schoolboy crept in unnoticed, in a new uniform,

[15] An elaborate hair styling for men. Capoul was a famous French singer.

poor little fellow, and wearing gloves. Terribly dark shadows showed under his eyes, the meaning of which Ivan Ilych knew well.

His son had always seemed pathetic to him, and now it was dreadful to see the boy's frightened look of pity. It seemed to Ivan Ilych that Vasya was the only one besides Gerasim who understood and pitied him.

They all sat down and again asked how he was. A silence followed. Lisa asked her mother about the opera-glasses, and there was an altercation between mother and daughter as to who had taken them and where they had been put. This occasioned some unpleasantness.

Fëdor Petrovich inquired of Ivan Ilych whether he had ever seen Sarah Bernhardt. Ivan Ilych did not at first catch the question, but then replied: "No, have you seen her before?"

"Yes, in *Adrienne Lecouvreur*."[16]

Praskovya Fëdorovna mentioned some rôles in which Sarah Bernhardt was particularly good. Her daughter disagreed. Conversation sprang up as to the elegance and realism of her acting — the sort of conversation that is always repeated and is always the same.

In the midst of the conversation Fëdor Petrovich glanced at Ivan Ilych and became silent. The others also looked at him and grew silent. Ivan Ilych was staring with glittering eyes straight before him, evidently indignant with them. This had to be rectified, but it was impossible to do so. The silence had to be broken, but for a time no one dared to break it and they all became afraid that the conventional deception would suddenly become obvious and the truth become plain to all. Lisa was the first to pluck up courage and break that silence, but by trying to hide what everybody was feeling, she betrayed it.

"Well, if we are going it's time to start," she said, looking at her watch, a present from her father, and with a faint and significant smile at Fëdor Petrovich relating to something known only to them. She got up with a rustle of her dress.

They all rose, said good-night, and went away.

When they had gone it seemed to Ivan Ilych that he felt better; the falsity had gone with them. But the pain remained — that same pain and that same fear that made everything monotonously alike, nothing harder and nothing easier. Everything was worse.

Again minute followed minute and hour followed hour. Everything remained the same and there was no cessation. And the inevitable end of it all became more and more terrible.

"Yes, send Gerasim here," he replied to a question Peter asked.

IX

His wife returned late at night. She came in on tiptoe, but he heard her, opened his eyes, and made haste to close them again. She wished to send Gerasim away and to sit with him herself, but he opened his eyes and said: "No, go away."

---

[16] comedy by French playwrights Eugène Scribe and Ernest Legouvé.

"Are you in great pain?"

"Always the same."

"Take some opium."

He agreed and took some. She went away.

Till about three in the morning he was in a state of stupefied misery. It seemed to him that he and his pain were being thrust into a narrow, deep black sack, but though they were pushed further and further in they could not be pushed to the bottom. And this, terrible enough in itself, was accompanied by suffering. He was frightened yet wanted to fall through the sack, he struggled but yet co-operated. And suddenly he broke through, fell, and regained consciousness. Gerasim was sitting at the foot of the bed dozing quietly and patiently, while he himself lay with his emaciated stockinged legs resting on Gerasim's shoulders; the same shaded candle was there and the same unceasing pain.

"Go away, Gerasim," he whispered.

"It's all right, sir. I'll stay a while."

"No. Go away."

He removed his legs from Gerasim's shoulders, turned sideways onto his arm, and felt sorry for himself. He only waited till Gerasim had gone into the next room and then restrained himself no longer but wept like a child. He wept on account of his helplessness, his terrible loneliness, the cruelty of man, the cruelty of God, and the absence of God.

"Why hast Thou done all this? Why hast Thou brought me here? Why, why dost Thou torment me so terribly?"

He did not expect an answer and yet wept because there was no answer and could be none. The pain again grew more acute, but he did not stir and did not call. He said to himself: "Go on! Strike me! But what is it for? What have I done to Thee? What is it for?"

Then he grew quiet and not only ceased weeping but even held his breath and became all attention. It was as though he were listening not to an audible voice but to the voice of his soul, to the current of thoughts arising within him.

"What is it you want?" was the first clear conception capable of expression in words, that he heard.

"What do you want? What do you want?" he repeated to himself.

"What do I want? To live and not to suffer," he answered.

And again he listened with such concentrated attention that even his pain did not distract him.

"To live? How?" asked his inner voice.

"Why, to live as I used to — well and pleasantly."

"As you lived before, well and pleasantly?" the voice repeated.

And in imagination he began to recall the best moments of his pleasant life. But strange to say none of those best moments of his pleasant life now seemed at all what they had then seemed — none of them except the first recollections of childhood. There, in childhood, there had been something really pleasant with which it would be possible to live if it could return. But the child who had experienced that happiness existed no longer, it was like a reminiscence of somebody else.

As soon as the period began which had produced the present Ivan Ilych, all that had then seemed joys now melted before his sight and turned into something trivial and often nasty.

And the further he departed from childhood and the nearer he came to the present the more worthless and doubtful were the joys. This began with the School of Law. A little that was really good was still found there — there was lightheartedness, friendship, and hope. But in the upper classes there had already been fewer of such good moments. Then during the first years of his official career, when he was in the service of the Governor, some pleasant moments again occurred: they were the memories of love for a woman. Then all became confused and there was still less of what was good; later on again there was still less that was good, and the further he went the less there was. His marriage, a mere accident, then the disenchantment that followed it, his wife's bad breath and the sensuality and hypocrisy: then the deadly official life and those preoccupations about money, a year of it, and two, and ten, and twenty, and always the same thing. And the longer it lasted the more deadly it became. "It is as if I had been going downhill while I imagined I was going up. And that is really what it was. I was going up in public opinion, but to the same extent life was ebbing away from me. And now it is all done and there is only death."

"Then what does it mean? Why? It can't be that life is so senseless and horrible. But if it really has been so horrible and senseless, why must I die and die in agony? There is something wrong!"

"Maybe I did not live as I ought to have done," it suddenly occurred to him. "But how could that be, when I did everything properly?" he replied, and immediately dismissed from his mind this, the sole solution of all the riddles of life and death, as something quite impossible.

"Then what do you want now? To live? Live how? Live as you lived in the law courts when the usher proclaimed 'The judge is coming!' The judge is coming, the judge!" he repeated to himself. "Here he is, the judge. But I am not guilty!" he exclaimed angrily. "What is it for?" And he ceased crying, but turning his face to the wall continued to ponder on the same question: Why, and for what purpose, is there all this horror? But however much he pondered he found no answer. And whenever the thought occurred to him, as it often did, that it all resulted from his not having lived as he ought to have done, he at once recalled the correctness of his whole life and dismissed so strange an idea.

X

Another fortnight passed. Ivan Ilych now no longer left his sofa. He would not lie in bed but lay on the sofa, facing the wall nearly all the time. He suffered ever the same unceasing agonies and in his loneliness pondered always on the same insoluble question: "What is this? Can it be that it is Death?" And the inner voice answered: "Yes, it is Death."

"Why these sufferings?" And the voice answered, "For no reason — they just are so." Beyond and besides this there was nothing.

From the very beginning of his illness, ever since he had first been to see the doctor, Ivan Ilych's life had been divided between two contrary and alternating moods: now it was despair and the expectation of this uncomprehended and terrible death, and now hope and an intently interested observation of the functioning of his organs. Now before his eyes there was only a kidney or an intestine that temporarily evaded its duty, and now only that incomprehensible and dreadful death from which it was impossible to escape.

These two states of mind had alternated from the very beginning of his illness, but the further it progressed the more doubtful and fantastic became the conception of the kidney, and the more real the sense of impending death.

He had but to call to mind what he had been three months before and what he was now, to call to mind with what regularity he had been going downhill, for every possibility of hope to be shattered.

Latterly during that loneliness in which he found himself as he lay facing the back of the sofa, a loneliness in the midst of a populous town and surrounded by numerous acquaintances and relations but that yet could not have been more complete anywhere — either at the bottom of the sea or under the earth — during that terrible loneliness Ivan Ilych had lived only in memories of the past. Pictures of his past rose before him one after another. They always began with what was nearest in time and then went back to what was most remote — to his childhood — and rested there. If he thought of the stewed prunes that had been offered him that day, his mind went back to the raw shrivelled French plums of his childhood, their peculiar flavor and the flow of saliva when he sucked their stones, and along with the memory of that taste came a whole series of memories of those days: his nurse, his brother, and their toys. "No, I mustn't think of that. . . . It is too painful," Ivan Ilych said to himself, and brought himself back to the present — to the button on the back of the sofa and the creases in its morocco. "Morocco is expensive, but it does not wear well: there had been a quarrel about it. It was a different kind of quarrel and a different kind of morocco that time when we tore father's portfolio and were punished, and mama brought us some tarts. . . ." And again his thoughts dwelt on his childhood, and again it was painful and he tried to banish them and fix his mind on something else.

Then again together with that chain of memories another series passed through his mind — of how his illness had progressed and grown worse. There also the further back he looked the more life there had been. There had been more of what was good in life and more of life itself. The two merged together. "Just as the pain went on getting worse and worse, so my life grew worse and worse," he thought. "There is one bright spot there at the back, at the beginning of life, and afterwards all becomes blacker and blacker and proceeds more and more rapidly — in inverse ratio to the square of the distance from death," thought Ivan Ilych. And the example of a stone falling downwards with increasing velocity entered his mind. Life, a series of increasing sufferings, flies further and further towards its end — the most terrible suffering. "I am flying. . . ." He shuddered, shifted himself, and tried to resist, but was already aware that resistance was impossible, and again with eyes weary of gazing but unable to cease seeing what was before them, he stared at the back of the sofa and waited — awaiting that dreadful fall and shock and destruction.

"Resistance is impossible!" he said to himself. "If I could only understand what it is all for! But that too is impossible. An explanation would be possible if it could be said that I have not lived as I ought to. But it is impossible to say that," and he remembered all the legality, correctitude, and propriety of his life. "That at any rate can certainly not be admitted," he thought, and his lips smiled ironically as if someone could see that smile and be taken in by it. "There is no explanation! Agony, death. . . . What for?"

XI

Another two weeks went by in this way and during that fortnight an event occurred that Ivan Ilych and his wife had desired. Petrishchev formally proposed. It happened in the evening. The next day Praskovya Fëdorovna came into her husband's room considering how best to inform him of it, but that very night there had been a fresh change for the worse in his condition. She found him still lying on the sofa but in a different position. He lay on his back, groaning and staring fixedly straight in front of him.

She began to remind him of his medicines, but he turned his eyes towards her with such a look that she did not finish what she was saying; so great an animosity, to her in particular, did that look express.

"For Christ's sake let me die in peace!" he said.

She would have gone away, but just then their daughter came in and went up to say good morning. He looked at her as he had done at his wife, and in reply to her inquiry about his health said dryly that he would soon free them all of himself. They were both silent and after sitting with him for a while went away.

"Is it our fault?" Lisa said to her mother. "It's as if we were to blame! I am sorry for papa, but why should we be tortured?"

The doctor came at his usual time. Ivan Ilych answered "Yes" and "No," never taking his angry eyes from him, and at last said: "You know you can do nothing for me, so leave me alone."

"We can ease your sufferings."

"You can't even do that. Let me be."

The doctor went into the drawing-room and told Praskovya Fëdorovna that the case was very serious and that the only resource left was opium to allay her husband's sufferings, which must be terrible.

It was true, as the doctor said, that Ivan Ilych's physical sufferings were terrible, but worse than the physical sufferings were his mental sufferings, which were his chief torture.

His mental sufferings were due to the fact that that night, as he looked at Gerasim's sleepy, good-natured face with its prominent cheek-bones, the question suddenly occurred to him: "What if my whole life has really been wrong?"

It occurred to him that what had appeared perfectly impossible before, namely that he had not spent his life as he should have done, might after all be true. It occurred to him that his scarcely perceptible attempts to struggle against what was considered good by the most highly placed people, those scarcely noticeable impulses which he had immediately suppressed, might have been the real thing, and all the rest false. And his professional duties and the whole arrangement of his life and of his family, and all his social and official interests, might all have been false. He tried to defend all those things to himself and suddenly felt the weakness of what he was defending. There was nothing to defend.

"But if that is so," he said to himself, "and I am leaving this life with the consciousness that I have lost all that was given me and it is impossible to rectify it — what then?"

He lay on his back and began to pass his life in review in quite a new way. In the morning when he saw first his footman, then his wife, then his daughter, and then the doctor, their every word and movement confirmed to him the awful truth that had been revealed to him during the night. In them he saw himself — all that for which he had lived — and saw clearly that it was not real at all, but a terrible and huge deception which had hidden both life and death. This consciousness intensified his physical suffering tenfold. He groaned and tossed about, and pulled at his clothing which choked and stifled him. And he hated them on that account.

He was given a large dose of opium and became unconscious, but at noon his sufferings began again. He drove everybody away and tossed from side to side.

His wife came to him and said:

"Jean, my dear, do this for me. It can't do any harm and often helps. Healthy people often do it."

He opened his eyes wide.

"What? Take communion? Why? It's unnecessary! However. . . ."

She began to cry.

"Yes, do, my dear. I'll send for our priest. He is such a nice man."

"All right. Very well," he muttered.

When the priest came and heard his confession, Ivan Ilych was softened and seemed to feel a relief from his doubts and consequently from his sufferings, and for a moment there came a ray of hope. He again began to think of the vermiform appendix and the possibility of correcting it. He received the sacrament with tears in his eyes.

When they laid him down again afterwards he felt a moment's ease, and the hope that he might live awoke in him again. He began to think of the operation that had been suggested to him. "To live! I want to live!" he said to himself.

His wife came in to congratulate him after his communion, and when uttering the usual conventional words she added:

"You feel better, don't you?"

Without looking at her he said "Yes."

Her dress, her figure, the expression of her face, the tone of her voice, all revealed the same thing. "This is wrong, it is not as it should be. All you have lived for and still live for is falsehood and deception, hiding life and death from you." And as soon as he admitted that thought, his hatred and his agonizing physical suffering again sprang up, and with that suffering a consciousness of the unavoidable, approaching end. And to this was added a new sensation of grinding shooting pain and a feeling of suffocation.

The expression of his face when he uttered that "yes" was dreadful. Having uttered it, he looked her straight in the eyes, turned on his face with a rapidity extraordinary in his weak state and shouted:

"Go away! Go away and leave me alone!"

XII

From that moment the screaming began that continued for three days, and was so terrible that one could not hear it through two closed doors without horror. At the moment he answered his wife he realized that he was lost, that there was no return, that the end had come, the very end, and his doubts were still unsolved and remained doubts.

"Oh! Oh! Oh!" he cried in various intonations. He had begun by screaming "I won't!" and continued screaming on the letter O.

For three whole days, during which time did not exist for him, he struggled in that black sack into which he was being thrust by an invisible, resistless force. He struggled as a man condemned to death struggles in the hands of the executioner, knowing that he cannot save himself. And every moment he felt that despite all his efforts he was drawing nearer and nearer to what terrified him. He felt that his agony was due to his being thrust into that black hole and still more to his not being able to get right into it. He was hindered from getting into it by his conviction that his life had been a good one. That very justification of his life held him fast and prevented his moving forward, and it caused him most torment of all.

Suddenly some force struck him in the chest and side, making it still harder to breathe, and he fell through the hole and there at the bottom was a light. What had happened to him was like the sensation one sometimes experiences in a railway carriage when one thinks one is going backwards while one is really going forwards and suddenly becomes aware of the real direction.

"Yes, it was all not the right thing," he said to himself, "but that's no matter. It can be done. But what is the right thing?" he asked himself, and suddenly grew quiet.

This occurred at the end of the third day, two hours before his death. Just then his schoolboy son had crept softly in and gone up to the bedside. The dying man was still screaming desperately and waving his arms. His hand fell on the boy's head, and the boy caught it, pressed it to his lips, and began to cry.

At that very moment Ivan Ilych fell through and caught sight of the light, and it was revealed to him that though his life had not been what it should have been, this could still be rectified. He asked himself, "What *is* the right thing?" and grew still, listening. Then he felt that someone was kissing his hand. He opened his eyes, looked at his son, and felt sorry for him. His wife came up to him and he glanced at her. She was gazing at him open-mouthed, with undried tears on her nose and cheek and a despairing look on her face. He felt sorry for her too.

"Yes, I am making them wretched," he thought. "They are sorry, but it will be better for them when I die." He wished to say this but had not the strength to utter it. "Besides, why speak? I must act," he thought. With a look at his wife he indicated his son and said: "Take him away . . . sorry for him . . . sorry for you too. . . ." He tried to add, "forgive me," but said "forgo" and waved his hand, knowing that He whose understanding mattered would understand.

And suddenly it grew clear to him that what had been oppressing him and would not leave him was all dropping away at once from two sides, from ten sides, and from all sides. He was sorry for them, he must act so as not to hurt them: release them and free himself from these sufferings. "How good and how simple!" he thought. "And the pain?" he asked himself. "What has become of it? Where are you, pain?"

He turned his attention to it.

"Yes, here it is. Well, what of it? Let the pain be."

"And death . . . where is it?"

He sought his former accustomed fear of death and did not find it. "Where is it? What death?" There was no fear because there was no death.

In place of death there was light.

"So that's what it is!" he suddenly exclaimed aloud. "What joy!"

To him all this happened in a single instant, and the meaning of that instant did not change. For those present his agony continued for another two hours. Something rattled in his throat, his emaciated body twitched, then the gasping and rattle became less and less frequent.

"It is finished!" said someone near him.

He heard these words and repeated them in his soul.

"Death is finished," he said to himself. "It is no more!"

He drew in a breath, stopped in the midst of a sigh, stretched out, and died.

[1886]

Leo Tolstoy

∽∾

THE THREE HERMITS

–translated by Louise and
Aylmer Maude

An Old Legend Current in the Volga District

"And in praying use not vain repetitions, as the Gentiles do: for they think
that they shall be heard for their much speaking. Be not therefore like
unto them: for your Father knoweth what things ye have need of, before
ye ask Him." — Matt. 6:7, 8.

A Bishop was sailing from Archangel to the Solovétsk Monastery, and
on the same vessel were a number of pilgrims on their way to visit the
shrines at that place. The voyage was a smooth one; the wind favourable
and the weather fair. The pilgrims lay on deck, eating, or sat in groups talking to one another. The Bishop, too, came on deck, and as he was pacing up
and down he noticed a group of men standing near the prow and listening
to a fisherman, who was pointing to the sea and telling them something.
The Bishop stopped, and looked in the direction in which the man was
pointing. He could see nothing, however, but the sea glistening in the sunshine. He drew nearer to listen, but when the man saw him, he took off his
cap and was silent. The rest of the people also took off their caps and
bowed.

"Do not let me disturb you, friends," said the Bishop. "I came to hear
what this good man was saying."

"The fisherman was telling us about the hermits," replied one, a
tradesman, rather bolder than the rest.

"What hermits?" asked the Bishop, going to the side of the vessel and
seating himself on a box. "Tell me about them. I should like to hear. What
were you pointing at?"

"Why, that little island you can just see over there," answered the
man, pointing to a spot ahead and a little to the right. "That is the island
where the hermits live for the salvation of their souls."

"Where is the island?" asked the Bishop. "I see nothing."

"There, in the distance, if you will please look along my hand. Do you
see that little cloud? Below it, and a bit to the left, there is just a faint
streak. That is the island."

The Bishop looked carefully, but his unaccustomed eyes could make
out nothing but the water shimmering in the sun.

"I cannot see it," he said. "But who are the hermits that live there?"

"They are holy men," answered the fisherman. "I had long ago heard tell of them, but never chanced to see them myself till the year before last."

And the fisherman related how once, when he was out fishing, he had been stranded at night upon that island, not knowing where he was. In the morning, as he wandered about the island, he came across an earth hut, and met an old man standing near it. Presently two others came out, and after having fed him and dried his things they helped him mend his boat.

"And what are they like?" asked the Bishop.

"One is a small man and his back is bent. He wears a priest's cassock and is very old; he must be more than a hundred, I should say. He is so old that the white of his beard is taking a greenish tinge, but he is always smiling, and his face is as bright as an angel's from heaven. The second is taller, but he also is very old. He wears a tattered peasant coat. His beard is broad, and of a yellowish-grey colour. He is a strong man. Before I had time to help him, he turned my boat over as if it were only a pail. He too is kindly and cheerful. The third is tall, and has a beard as white as snow and reaching to his knees. He is stern, with overhanging eyebrows; and he wears nothing but a piece of matting tied around his waist."

"And did they speak to you?" asked the Bishop.

"For the most part they did everything in silence, and spoke but little even to one another. One of them would just give a glance, and the others would understand him. I asked the tallest whether they had lived there long. He frowned, and muttered something as if he were angry; but the oldest one took his hand and smiled, and then the tall one was quiet. The oldest one only said: 'Have mercy upon us,' and smiled."

While the fisherman was talking, the ship had drawn nearer to the island.

"There, now you can see it plainly, if your Lordship will please to look," said the tradesman, pointing with his hand.

The Bishop looked, and now he really saw a dark streak — which was the island. Having looked at it a while, he left the prow of the vessel, and going to the stern, asked the helmsman:

"What island is that?"

"That one," replied the man, "has no name. There are many such in this sea."

"Is it true that there are hermits who live there for the salvation of their souls?"

"So it is said, your Lordship, but I don't know if it's true. Fishermen say they have seen them; but of course they may only be spinning yarns."

"I should like to land on the island and see these men," said the Bishop. "How could I manage it?"

"The ship cannot get close to the island," replied the helmsman, "but you might be rowed there in a boat. You had better speak to the captain."

The captain was sent for and came.

"I should like to see these hermits," said the Bishop. "Could I not be rowed ashore?"

The captain tried to dissuade him.

"Of course it could be done," said he, "but we should lose much time. And if I might venture to say so to your Lordship, the old men are not worth your pains. I have heard say that they are foolish old fellows, who understand nothing, and never speak a word, any more than the fish in the sea."

"I wish to see them," said the Bishop, "and I will pay you for your trouble and loss of time. Please let me have a boat."

There was no help for it; so the order was given. The sailors trimmed the sails, the steersman put up the helm, and the ship's course was set for the island. A chair was placed at the prow for the Bishop, and he sat there, looking ahead. The passengers all collected at the prow and gazed at the island. Those who had the sharpest eyes could presently make out the rocks on it, and then a mud hut was seen. At last one man saw the hermits themselves. The captain brought a telescope and, after looking through it, handed it to the Bishop.

"It's right enough. There are three men standing on the shore. There, a little to the right of that big rock."

The Bishop took the telescope, got it into position, and he saw the three men: a tall one, a shorter one, and one very small and bent, standing on the shore and holding each other by the hand.

The captain turned to the Bishop.

"The vessel can get no nearer in than this, your Lordship. If you wish to go ashore, we must ask you to go in the boat, while we anchor here.

The cable was quickly let out, the anchor cast, and the sails furled. There was a jerk, and the vessel shook. Then, a boat having been lowered, the oarsmen jumped in, and the Bishop descended the ladder and took his seat. The men pulled at their oars and the boat moved rapidly towards the island. When they came within a stone's throw, they saw three old men: a tall one with only a piece of matting tied round his waist; a shorter one in a tattered peasant coat; and a very old one bent with age and wearing an old cassock — all three standing hand in hand.

The oarsmen pulled into the shore, and held on with the boathook while the Bishop got out.

The old men bowed to him, and he gave them his blessing, at which they bowed still lower. Then the Bishop began to speak to them.

"I have heard," he said, "that you, godly men, live here saving your own souls and praying to our Lord Christ for your fellow-men. I, an unworthy servant of Christ, am called, by God's mercy, to keep and teach His flock. I wished to see you, servants of God, and to do what I can to teach you also."

The old men looked at each other, smiling, but remained silent.

"Tell me," said the Bishop, "what you are doing to save your souls, and how you serve God on this island."

The second hermit sighed, and looked at the oldest, the very ancient one. The latter smiled, and said:

"We do not know how to serve God. We only serve and support ourselves, servant of God."

"But how do you pray to God?" asked the Bishop.

"We pray in this way," replied the hermit. "Three are ye, three are we, have mercy upon us."

And when the old man said this, all three raised their eyes to heaven, and repeated:

"Three are ye, three are we, have mercy upon us!"

The Bishop smiled.

"You have evidently heard something about the Holy Trinity," said he. "But you do not pray aright. You have won my affection, godly men. I see you wish to please the Lord, but you do not know how to serve Him. That is not the way to pray; but listen to me, and I will teach you. I will teach you, not a way of my own, but the way in which God in the Holy Scriptures has commanded all men to pray to Him."

And the Bishop began explaining to the hermits how God had revealed Himself to men; telling them of God the Father, and God the Son, and God the Holy Ghost.

"God the Son came down on earth," said he, "to save men, and this is how He taught us all to pray. Listen, and repeat after me: 'Our Father.'"

And the first old man repeated after him, "Our Father," and the second said, "Our Father," and the third said, "Our Father."

"Which art in heaven," continued the Bishop.

The first hermit repeated, "Which art in heaven," but the second blundered over the words, and the tall hermit could not say them properly. His hair had grown over his mouth so that he could not speak plainly. The very old hermit, having no teeth, also mumbled indistinctly.

The Bishop repeated the words again, and the old men repeated them after him. The Bishop sat down on a stone, and the old men stood before him, watching his mouth, and repeating the words as he uttered them. And all day long the Bishop laboured, saying a word twenty, thirty, a hundred times over, and the old men repeated it after him. They blundered, and he corrected them, and made them begin again.

The Bishop did not leave off till he had taught them the whole of the Lord's Prayer so that they could not only repeat it after him, but could say it by themselves. The middle one was the first to know it, and to repeat the whole of it alone. The Bishop made him say it again and again, and at last the others could say it too.

It was getting dark and the moon was appearing over the water before the Bishop rose to return to the vessel. When he took leave of the old men they all bowed down to the ground before him. He raised them, and kissed each of them, telling them to pray as he had taught them. Then he got into the boat and returned to the ship.

And as he sat in the boat and was rowed to the ship he could hear the three voices of the hermits loudly repeating the Lord's Prayer. As the boat drew near the vessel their voices could no longer be heard, but they could still be seen in the moonlight, standing as he had left them on the shore, the shortest in the middle, the tallest on the right, the middle one on the left. As soon as the Bishop had reached the vessel and got on board, the anchor was weighed and the sails unfurled. The wind filled them and the ship sailed away, and the Bishop took a seat in the stern and watched the island they had left. For a time he could still see the hermits, but presently they disappeared from sight, though the island was still visible. At last it too vanished, and only the sea was to be seen, rippling in the moonlight.

The pilgrims lay down to sleep, and all was quiet on deck. The Bishop did not wish to sleep, but sat alone at the stern, gazing at the sea where the island was no longer visible, and thinking of the good old men. He thought how pleased they had been to learn the Lord's Prayer; and he thanked God for having sent him to teach and help such godly men.

So the Bishop sat, thinking, and gazing at the sea where the island had disappeared. And the moonlight flickered before his eyes, sparkling, now here, now there, upon the waves. Suddenly he saw something white and shining, on the bright path which the moon cast across the sea. Was it a seagull, or the little gleaming sail of some small boat? The Bishop fixed his eyes upon it, wondering.

"It must be a boat sailing after us," thought he, "but it is overtaking us very rapidly. It was far, far away a minute ago, but now it is much nearer. It cannot be a boat, for I can see no sail; but whatever it may be, it is following us and catching us up."

And he could not make out what it was. Not a boat, nor a bird, nor a fish! It was too large for a man, and, besides, a man could not be out here in the midst of the sea. The Bishop rose, and said to the helmsman:

"Look there, what is that, my friend? What is it?" the Bishop repeated, though he could now see plainly what it was — the three hermits running upon the water, all gleaming white, their grey beards shining, and approaching the ship as quickly as though it were not moving.

The steersman looked, and let go the helm in terror.

"O Lord! The hermits are running after us on the water as though it were dry land!"

The passengers, hearing him, jumped and crowded to the stern. They saw the hermits coming along hand in hand, and the two outer ones beckoning the ship to stop. All three were gliding along upon the water without moving their feet. Before the ship could be stopped, the hermits had reached it, and raising their heads, all three as with one voice began to say:

"We have forgotten your teaching, servant of God. As long as we kept repeating it we remembered, but when we stopped saying it for a time, a word dropped out, and now it has all gone to pieces. We can remember nothing of it. Teach us again."

The Bishop crossed himself, and leaning over the ship's side, said:

"Your own prayer will reach the Lord, men of God. It is not for me to teach you. Pray for us sinners."

And the Bishop bowed low before the old men; and they turned and went back across the sea. And a light shone until daybreak on the spot where they were lost to sight.

[1886]

MARK TWAIN was the name under which Samuel Langhorne Clemens (1835–1910) published his works. Clemens was born in the village of Florida, Missouri, the son of a lawyer from Virginia. When he was five, the family moved to Hannibal, Missouri, on the west bank of the Mississippi River — "a heavenly place for a boy," he later remembered. His formal schooling ended at age twelve, when his father died and he was apprenticed to his brother Orion, who edited a country newspaper. At this time he saw his first story printed — "The Dandy Frightening the Squatter," a typical piece of frontier humor. For years he worked as a journeyman printer in St. Louis, New York City, Philadelphia, and Cincinnati. Then he became an apprentice steamboat pilot on the Mississippi in 1857, and he remained on the river until the Civil War. In his book Life on the Mississippi (1883), Twain wrote that on the river he became "acquainted with all the different types of human nature that are to be found in fiction, biography or history." After considering enlisting in the Confederate Army, he joined his brother Orion in the Nevada Territory, first prospecting for gold and then working for the Virginia City Enterprise. It was in his writing for this newspaper that he first used the pseudonym Mark Twain, a call of the Mississippi pilots signifying a depth of two fathoms (twelve feet), just barely safe water for riverboats.

Twain's early work for newspapers was influenced by the topical humorists of his time. He first achieved recognition as a writer in 1865 with a tall tale, "The Notorious Jumping Frog of Calaveras County." Twain later said he didn't think much of the story, but it was published in book form with other sketches in 1867. Two years later his career was established with the travel book The Innocents Abroad. He achieved further fame (and fortune) with the popular success of his novels, The Adventures of Tom Sawyer (1876), The Prince and the Pauper (1882), A Connecticut Yankee in King Arthur's Court (1889), and many other books, including his masterpiece, The Adventures of Huckleberry Finn (1884). Twain's life was a strange compound of public glory and private tragedy, but he was one of the greatest American writers. "I am persuaded," the Irish dramatist Bernard Shaw wrote to him, "that the future historian of America will find your works as indispensable to him as a French historian finds the political tracts of Voltaire."

Twain had a sensitive ear for the varied riches of American regional dialects, and he was our first author to write great works using a genuinely colloquial and native American speech. He published collections of short stories throughout his life, beginning with his first book, The Notorious Jumping Frog of Calaveras County and Other Sketches, and including such titles as Mark Twain's Sketches (1875), Merry Tales (1892), and My Debut as a Literary Person, with Other Essays and Stories (1903). The Complete Stories of Mark Twain, sixty in all, was published in 1957.

Mark Twain

 භාෂ

THE NOTORIOUS JUMPING FROG
OF CALAVERAS COUNTY

In compliance with the request of a friend of mine, who wrote me from the East, I called on good-natured, garrulous old Simon Wheeler, and inquired after my friend's friend, Leonidas W. Smiley, as requested to do, and I hereunto append the result. I have a lurking suspicion that *Leonidas W.* Smiley is a myth; that my friend never knew such a personage; and that he only conjectured that if I asked old Wheeler about him, it would remind him of his infamous *Jim* Smiley, and he would go on to work and bore me to death with some exasperating reminiscence of him as long and as tedious as it should be useless to me. If that was the design, it succeeded.

I found Simon Wheeler dozing comfortably by the bar-room stove of the dilapidated tavern in the decayed mining camp of Angel's, and I noticed that he was fat and bald-headed, and had an expression of winning gentleness and simplicity upon his tranquil countenance. He roused up, and gave me good day. I told him that a friend of mine had commissioned me to make some inquiries about a cherished companion of his boyhood named *Leonidas W.* Smiley — *Rev. Leonidas W.* Smiley, a young minister of the Gospel, who he had heard was at one time a resident of Angel's Camp. I added that if Mr. Wheeler could tell me anything about his Rev. Leonidas W. Smiley, I would feel under many obligations to him.

Simon Wheeler backed me into a corner and blockaded me there with his chair, and then sat down and reeled off the monotonous narrative which follows this paragraph. He never smiled, he never frowned, he never changed his voice from the gentle-flowing key to which he tuned his initial sentence, he never betrayed the slightest suspicion of enthusiasm: but all through the interminable narrative there ran a vein of impressive earnestness and sincerity, which showed me plainly that, so far from his imagining that there was anything ridiculous or funny about his story, he regarded it as a really important matter, and admired its two heroes as men of transcendent genius in *finesse.* I let him go on in his own way, and never interrupted him once.

"Rev. Leonidas W. H'm, Reverend Le — well, there was a feller here once by the name of *Jim* Smiley, in the winter of '49 — or maybe it was the spring of '50 — I don't recollect exactly, somehow, though what makes me think it was one or the other is because I remember the big flume warn't finished when he first come to the camp; but anyway, he was the curiousest man about always betting on anything that turned up you ever see, if he could get anybody to bet on the other side; and if he couldn't he'd change sides. Any way that suited the other man would suit *him* — any way just so's he got a bet, *he* was satisfied. But still he was lucky, uncommon lucky; he most always come out winner. He was always ready and laying for a chance; there couldn't be no solit'ry thing mentioned but that feller'd offer to bet on it, and take ary side you please, as I was just telling you. If there was a horse-race, you'd find him flush or you'd find him busted at the end of it; if there was a dog-fight, he'd bet on it; if there was a cat-fight, he'd bet on it; if there was a chicken-fight, he'd bet on it; why, if there was two birds setting on a fence, he would bet you which one would fly first; or if there was a camp-meeting, he would be there reg'lar to bet on Parson Walker, which he judged to be the best exhorter about here, and so he was too, a good man. If he even see a straddle-bug start to go anywheres, he would bet you how long it would take him to get to — to wherever he was going to, and if you took him up, he would foller that straddle-bug to Mexico but what he would find out where he was bound for and how long he was on the road. Lots of the boys here has seen that Smiley, and can tell you about him. Why, it never made no difference to *him* — he'd bet on *any* thing — the dangdest feller. Parson Walker's wife laid very sick once, for a good while, and it seemed as if they weren't going to save her; but one morning he come in, and Smiley up and asked him how she was, and he said she was considerable better — thank the Lord for his inf'nite mercy — and coming on so smart that with the blessing of Prov'dence she'd got well yet; and Smiley, before he thought, says, 'Well, I'll resk two-and-a-half she don't anyway.'

"Thish-yer Smiley had a mare — the boys called her the fifteen-minute nag, but that was only in fun, you know, because of course she was faster than that — and he used to win money on that horse, for all she was so slow and always had the asthma, or the distemper, or the consumption, or something of that kind. They used to give her two or three hundred yards' start, and then pass her under way; but always at the fag end of the race she'd get excited and desperate like, and came cavorting and straddling up, and scattering her legs around limber, sometimes in the air, and sometimes out to one side among the fences, and kicking up m-o-r-e dust and raising m-o-r-e racket with her coughing and sneezing and blowing her nose — and always fetch up at the stand just about a neck ahead, as near as you could cipher it down.

"And he had a little small bull-pup, that to look at him you'd think he warn't worth a cent but to set around and look ornery and lay for a chance to steal something. But as soon as money was up on him he was a different dog; his under-jaw'd begin to stick out like the fo'castle of a steamboat, and his teeth would uncover and shine like the furnaces. And a dog might tackle him and bully-rag him, and bite him, and throw him over his shoulder two

or three times, and Andrew Jackson — which was the name of the pup —
Andrew Jackson would never let on but what *he* was satisfied, and hadn't
expected nothing else — and the bets being doubled and doubled on the
other side all the time, till the money was all up; and then all of a sudden he
would grab that other dog jest by the j'int of his hind leg and freeze to it —
not chaw, you understand, but only just grip and hang on till they throwed
up the sponge, if it was a year. Smiley always come out winner on that pup,
till he harnessed a dog once that didn't have no hind legs, because they'd
been sawed off in a circular saw, and when the thing had gone along far
enough, and the money was all up, and he come to make a snatch for his
pet holt, he see in a minute how he'd been imposed on, and how the other
dog had him in the door, so to speak, and he 'peared surprised, and then he
looked sorter discouraged-like, and didn't try no more to win the fight, and
so he got shucked out bad. He give Smiley a look, as much as to say his
heart was broke, and it was *his* fault, for putting up a dog that hadn't no
hind legs for him to take holt of, which was his main dependence in a fight,
and then he limped off a piece and laid down and died. It was a good pup,
was that Andrew Jackson, and would have made a name for hisself if he'd
lived, for the stuff was in him and he had genius — I know it, because he
hadn't no opportunities to speak of, and it don't stand to reason that a dog
could make such a fight as he could under them circumstances if he hadn't
no talent. It always makes me feel sorry when I think of that last fight of
his'n, and the way it turned out.

"Well, thish-yer Smiley had rat-tarriers, and chicken cocks, and tom-
cats and all of them kind of things, till you couldn't rest, and you couldn't
fetch nothing for him to bet on but he'd match you. He ketched a frog one
day, and took him home, and said he cal'lated to educate him; and so he
never done nothing for three months but set in his back yard and learn that
frog to jump. And you bet you he *did* learn him, too. He'd give him a little
punch behind, and the next minute you'd see that frog whirling in the air
like a doughnut — see him turn one summerset, or maybe a couple, if he
got a good start, and come down flat-footed and all right, like a cat. He got
him up so in the matter of ketching flies, and kep' him in practice so constant, that he'd nail a fly every time as fur as he could see him. Smiley said
all a frog wanted was education, and he could do 'most anything — and I
believe him. Why, I've seen him set Dan'l Webster down here on this
floor — Dan'l Webster was the name of the frog — and sing out, "Flies,
Dan'l, flies!" and quicker'n you could wink he'd spring straight up and
snake a fly off'n the counter there, and flop down on the floor ag'in as solid
as a gob of mud, and fall to scratching the side of his head with his hind
foot as indifferent as he hadn't no idea he'd been doin' any more'n any frog
might do. You never see a frog so modest and straighfor'ard as he was, for
all he was so gifted. And when it come to fair and square jumping on a dead
level, he could get over more ground at one straddle than any animal of his
breed you ever see. Jumping on a dead level was his strong suit, you understand; and when it come to that, Smiley would ante up money on him as

long as he had a red. Smiley was monstrous proud of his frog, and well he might be, for fellers that had traveled and been everywheres all said he laid over any frog that ever *they* see.

"Well, Smiley kep' the beast in a little lattice box, and he used to fetch him down-town sometimes and lay for a bet. One day a feller — a stranger in the camp, he was — come acrost him with his box, and says:

" 'What might it be that you've got in the box?'

"And Smiley says, sorter indifferent-like, 'It might be a parrot, or it might be a canary, maybe, but it ain't — it's only just a frog.'

"And the feller took it, and looked at it careful, and turned it round this way and that, and says, 'H'm — so 'tis. Well, what's *he* good for?'

" 'Well,' Smiley says, easy and careless, 'he's good enough for *one* thing, I should judge — he can outjump any frog in Calaveras County.'

"The feller took the box again, and took another long, particular look, and give it back to Smiley, and says, very deliberate, 'Well,' he says, 'I don't see no p'ints about that frog that's any better'n any other frog.'

" 'Maybe you don't,' Smiley says. 'Maybe you understand frogs and maybe you don't understand 'em; maybe you've had experience, and maybe you ain't only a amature, as it were. Anyways, I've got *my* opinion, and I'll resk forty dollars that he can outjump any frog in Calaveras County.'

"And the feller studied a minute, and then says, kinder sadlike, 'Well, I'm only a stranger here, and I ain't got no frog; but if I had a frog, I'd bet you.'

"And then Smiley says, 'That's all right — that's all right — if you'll hold my box a minute, I'll go and get you a frog.' And so the feller took the box, and put up his forty dollars along with Smiley's, and set down to wait.

"So he set there a good while thinking and thinking to himself, and then he got the frog out and prized his mouth open and took a teaspoon and filled him full of quail-shot — filled him pretty near up to his chin — and set him on the floor. Smiley he went to the swamp and slopped around in the mud for a long time, and finally he ketched a frog, and fetched him in, and give him to this feller, and says:

" 'Now, if you're ready, set him alongside of Dan'l, with his fore paws just even with Dan'l's, and I'll give the word.' Then he says, 'One — two — three — *git!*' and him and the feller touched up the frogs from behind, and the new frog hopped off lively, but Dan'l give a heave, and hysted up his shoulders — so — like a Frenchman, but it warn't no use — he couldn't budge; he was planted as solid as a church, and he couldn't no more stir than if he was anchored out. Smiley was a good deal surprised, and he was disgusted too, but he didn't have no idea what the matter was, of course.

"The feller took the money and started away; and when he was going out at the door, he sorter jerked his thumb over his shoulder — so — at Dan'l, and says again, very deliberate, 'Well,' he says, 'I don't see no p'ints about that frog that's any better'n any other frog.'

"Smiley he stood scratching his head and looking down at Dan'l a long time, and at last he says, 'I do wonder what in the nation that frog throw'd off for — I wonder if there ain't something the matter with him — he pears to look mighty baggy, somehow.' And he ketched Dan'l by the nap of the neck, and hefted him, and says, "Why blame my cats if he don't weigh five pound!' and turned him upside down and he belched out a double handful of shot. And then he see how it was, and he was the maddest man — he set the frog down and took out after the feller, but he never ketched him. And —"

[Here Simon Wheeler heard his name called from the front yard, and got up to see what was wanted.] And turning to me as he moved away, he said: "Just set where you are, stranger, and rest easy — I ain't going to be gone a second."

But, by your leave, I did not think that a continuation of the history of the enterprising vagabond *Jim* Smiley would be likely to afford me much information concerning the Rev. *Leonidas* W. Smiley, and so I started away.

At the door I met the sociable Wheeler returning, and he buttonholed me and recommenced:

"Well, thish-yer Smiley had a yaller one-eyed cow that didn't have no tail, only just a short stump like a bannanner, and —"

However, lacking both time and inclination, I did not wait to hear about the afflicted cow, but took my leave.

[1865]

AMBROSE BIERCE (1842–1914?) was born in a log cabin in Horse Cave Creek, Meigs County, Ohio, the youngest of nine children. His father was a poverty-stricken farmer, and Bierce had only one year of formal education at the Kentucky Military Institute when he was seventeen. During the Civil War he enlisted with the 9th Indiana Infantry as a drummer boy. He fought bravely all through the war, was wounded at Kenesaw Mountain, Georgia, in 1864, and was discharged with the title of major. Then Bierce lived with a brother in San Francisco, working briefly as a night watchman at the United States Mint there. He also began his career as a newspaper writer at this time, and published his first story, "The Haunted Valley," in the Overland Magazine in 1871. When Bierce married the daughter of a wealthy Nevada miner, his father-in-law gave the young couple a wedding gift of $10,000, and they settled in London for five years. There Bierce worked as a journalist, an experience that turned him from a rough western humorist to a wit who wrote with great stylistic finish. Homesick for California, he returned with his wife and wrote columns and short stories for various newspapers, including William Randolph Hearst's San Francisco Examiner. In the 1880s he became very influential in his profession, although in literary circles outside California he was not widely known. Then his wife separated from him, his two sons died tragically, and he became embittered. In his seventies, Bierce supervised publication of the twelve volumes of his Collected Works, revisited the Civil War battlefields of his youth, and then disappeared across the Mexican border, leaving the facts of his life after 1914 to trail off into legend.

Bierce is well known as the author of the philosophical epigrams in The Devil's Dictionary (1906), but his two volumes of short stories are his finest achievement as a writer. He is considered a notable forerunner of such American realists as Stephen Crane. "An Occurrence at Owl Creek Bridge" was included in Bierce's first story collection, In the Midst of Life, published privately in San Francisco under the title Tales of Soldiers and Civilians (1891). The second collection, Can Such Things Be?, was published in New York two years later. Bierce preferred the short story to the novel, defining the novel as a "short story padded" and saying that it lacks the story's totality of effect. He modeled his technique of creating suspense that leads up to a dramatic crisis on Poe's stories, but Bierce gave a more realistic motivation to his horrors. His obsession with sudden, violent death cuts through the twists of conventional magazine fiction to give a darker reality to his stories. Dreams, flashbacks, and hallucinations, as in "An Occurrence at Owl Creek Bridge," provide irony and vivid imagery, but offer no escape. After four years in Civil War, Bierce was fascinated with death, although he came to doubt the justice of the cause for which he had fought.

180

He declined a large sum of back pay from the United States government, saying, "When I hired out as an assassin for my country, that wasn't part of the contract." Bierce seems entirely indifferent to human suffering in his stories, but his unemotional depictions of the horrors of war have a strong effect on most readers.

Ambrose Bierce

ตฉ

AN OCCURRENCE
AT OWL CREEK BRIDGE

I

A man stood upon a railroad bridge in Northern Alabama, looking down into the swift waters twenty feet below. The man's hands were behind his back, the wrists bound with a cord. A rope loosely encircled his neck. It was attached to a stout cross-timber above his head, and the slack fell to the level of his knees. Some loose boards laid upon the sleepers supporting the metals of the railway supplied a footing for him and his executioners — two private soldiers of the Federal army, directed by a sergeant, who in civil life may have been a deputy sheriff. At a short remove upon the same temporary platform was an officer in the uniform of his rank, armed. He was a captain. A sentinel at each end of the bridge stood with his rifle in the position known as "support," that is to say, vertical in front of the left shoulder, the hammer resting on the forearm thrown straight across the chest — a formal and unnatural position, enforcing an erect carriage of the body. It did not appear to be the duty of these two men to know what was occurring at the centre of the bridge; they merely blockaded the two ends of the foot plank which traversed it.

Beyond one of the sentinels nobody was in sight; the railroad ran straight away into a forest for a hundred yards, then, curving, was lost to view. Doubtless there was an outpost further along. The other bank of the stream was open ground — a gentle acclivity crowned with a stockade of vertical tree trunks, loop-holed for rifles, with a single embrasure through which protruded the muzzle of a brass cannon commanding the bridge. Midway of the slope between bridge and fort were the spectators — a single company of infantry in line, at "parade rest," the butts of the rifles on the ground, the barrels inclining slightly backward against the right shoulder, the hands crossed upon the stock. A lieutenant stood at the right of the line, the point of his sword upon the ground, his left hand resting upon his right. Excepting the group of four at the centre of the bridge not a man moved. The company faced the bridge, staring stonily, motionless. The sentinels, facing the banks of the stream, might have been statues to adorn the bridge. The captain stood with folded arms, silent, observing the work of his subordinates but making no sign. Death is a dignitary who, when he comes announced, is to be received with formal manifestations of respect, even by those most familiar with him. In the code of military etiquette silence and fixity are forms of deference.

The man who was engaged in being hanged was apparently about thirty-five years of age. He was a civilian, if one might judge from his dress, which was that of a planter. His features were good — a straight nose, firm mouth, broad forehead, from which his long, dark hair was combed straight back, falling behind his ears to the collar of his well-fitting frock coat. He wore a moustache and pointed beard, but no whiskers; his eyes were large and dark grey and had a kindly expression which one would hardly have expected in one whose neck was in the hemp. Evidently this was no vulgar assassin. The liberal military code makes provision for hanging many kinds of people, and gentlemen are not excluded.

The preparations being complete, the two private soldiers stepped aside and each drew away the plank upon which he had been standing. The sergeant turned to the captain, saluted and placed himself immediately behind that officer, who in turn moved apart one pace. These movements left the condemned man and the sergeant standing on the two ends of the same plank, which spanned three of the cross-ties of the bridge. The end upon which the civilian stood almost, but not quite, reached a fourth. This plank had been held in place by the weight of the captain; it was now held by that of the sergeant. At a signal from the former, the latter would step aside, the plank would tilt and the condemned man go down between two ties. The arrangement commended itself to his judgment as simple and effective. His face had not been covered nor his eyes bandaged. He looked a moment at his "unsteadfast footing," then let his gaze wander to the swirling water of the stream racing madly beneath his feet. A piece of dancing driftwood caught his attention and his eyes followed it down the current. How slowly it appeared to move! What a sluggish stream!

He closed his eyes in order to fix his last thoughts upon his wife and children. The water, touched to gold by the early sun, the brooding mists under the banks at some distance down the stream, the fort, the soldiers, the piece of drift — all had distracted him. And now he became conscious of a new disturbance. Striking through the thought of his dear ones was a sound which he could neither ignore nor understand, a sharp, distinct, metallic percussion like the stroke of a blacksmith's hammer upon the anvil; it had the same ringing quality. He wondered what it was, and whether immeasurably distant or near by — it seemed both. Its recurrence was regular, but as slow as the tolling of a death knell. He awaited each stroke with impatience and — he knew not why — apprehension. The intervals of silence grew progressively longer; the delays became maddening. With their greater infrequency the sounds increased in strength and sharpness. They hurt his ear like the thrust of a knife; he feared he would shriek. What he heard was the ticking of his watch.

He unclosed his eyes and saw again the water below him. "If I could free my hands," he thought, "I might throw off the noose and spring into the stream. By diving I could evade the bullets, and, swimming vigorously, reach the bank, take to the woods, and get away home. My home, thank God, is as yet outside their lines; my wife and little ones are still beyond the invader's farthest advance."

As these thoughts, which have here to be set down in words, were flashed into the doomed man's brain rather than evolved from it, the captain nodded to the sergeant. The sergeant stepped aside.

II

Peyton Farquhar was a well-to-do planter, of an old and highly-respected Alabama family. Being a slave owner, and, like other slave owners, a politician, he was naturally an original secessionist and ardently devoted to the Southern cause. Circumstances of an imperious nature which it is unnecessary to relate here, had prevented him from taking service with the gallant army which had fought the disastrous campaigns ending with the fall of Corinth, and he chafed under the inglorious restraint, longing for the release of his energies, the larger life of the soldier, the opportunity for distinction. That opportunity, he felt, would come, as it comes to all in war time. Meanwhile he did what he could. No service was too humble for him to perform in aid of the South, no adventure too perilous for him to undertake if consistent with the character of a civilian who was at heart a soldier, and who in good faith and without too much qualification assented to at least a part of the frankly villainous dictum that all is fair in love and war.

One evening while Farquhar and his wife were sitting on a rustic bench near the entrance to his grounds, a grey-clad soldier rode up to the gate and asked for a drink of water. Mrs. Farquhar was only too happy to serve him with her own white hands. While she was gone to fetch the water, her husband approached the dusty horseman and inquired eagerly for news from the front.

"The Yanks are repairing the railroads," said the man, "and are getting ready for another advance. They have reached the Owl Creek bridge, put it in order, and built a stockade on the other bank. The commandant has issued an order, which is posted everywhere, declaring that any civilian caught interfering with the railroad, its bridges, tunnels, or trains, will be summarily hanged. I saw the order."

"How far is it to the Owl Creek bridge?" Farquhar asked.

"About thirty miles."

"Is there no force on this side the creek?"

"Only a picket post half a mile out, on the railroad, and a single senti-nel at this end of the bridge."

"Suppose a man — a civilian and student of hanging — should elude the picket post and perhaps get the better of the sentinel," said Farquhar, smiling, "what could he accomplish?"

The soldier reflected. "I was there a month ago," he replied. "I ob-served that the flood of last winter had lodged a great quantity of driftwood against the wooden pier at this end of the bridge. It is now dry and would burn like tow."

The lady had now brought the water, which the soldier drank. He thanked her ceremoniously, bowed to her husband, and rode away. An hour later, after nightfall, he repassed the plantation, going northward in the di-rection from which he had come. He was a Federal scout.

III

As Peyton Farquhar fell straight downward through the bridge, he lost consciousness and was as one already dead. From this state he was awak-ened — ages later, it seemed to him — by the pain of a sharp pressure upon his throat, followed by a sense of suffocation. Keen, poignant agonies seemed to shoot from his neck downward through every fibre of his body and limbs. These pains appeared to flash along well-defined lines of ramifi-cation, and to beat with an inconceivably rapid periodicity. They seemed like streams of pulsating fire heating him to an intolerable temperature. As to his head, he was conscious of nothing but a feeling of fullness — of con-gestion. These sensations were unaccompanied by thought. The intellec-tual part of his nature was already effaced; he had power only to feel, and feeling was torment. He was conscious of motion. Encompassed in a lumi-nous cloud, of which he was now merely the fiery heart, without material substance, he swung through unthinkable arcs of oscillation, like a vast pendulum. Then all at once, with terrible suddenness, the light about him shot upward with the noise of a loud plash; a frightful roaring was in his ears, and all was cold and dark. The power of thought was restored; he knew that the rope had broken and he had fallen into the stream. There was no additional strangulation; the noose about his neck was already suffocating him, and kept the water from his lungs. To die of hanging at the bottom of a river — the idea seemed to him ludicrous. He opened his eyes in the blackness and saw above him a gleam of light, but how distant, how inac-cessible! He was still sinking, for the light became fainter and fainter until it was a mere glimmer. Then it began to grow and brighten, and he knew that he was rising toward the surface — knew it with reluctance, for he was now very comfortable. "To be hanged and drowned," he thought, "that is not so bad; but I do not wish to be shot. No; I will not be shot; that is not fair."

He was not conscious of an effort, but a sharp pain in his wrist apprised him that he was trying to free his hands. He gave the struggle his attention, as an idler might observe the feat of a juggler, without interest in the outcome. What splendid effort! — what magnificent, what superhuman strength! Ah, that was a fine endeavor! Bravo! The cord fell away; his arms parted and floated upward, the hands dimly seen on each side in the growing light. He watched them with a new interest as first one and then the other pounced upon the noose at his neck. They tore it away and thrust it fiercely aside, its undulations resembling those of a water-snake. "Put it back, put it back!" He thought he shouted these words to his hands, for the undoing of the noose had been succeeded by the direst pang which he had yet experienced. His neck arched horribly; his brain was on fire; his heart, which had been fluttering faintly, gave a great leap, trying to force itself out at his mouth. His whole body was racked and wrenched with an insupportable anguish! But his disobedient hands gave no heed to the command. They beat the water vigorously with quick, downward strokes, forcing him to the surface. He felt his head emerge; his eyes were blinded by the sunlight; his chest expanded convulsively, and with a supreme and crowning agony his lungs engulfed a great draught of air, which instantly he expelled in a shriek!

He was now in full possession of his physical senses. They were, indeed, preternaturally keen and alert. Something in the awful disturbance of his organic system had so exalted and refined them that they made record of things never before perceived. He felt the ripples upon his face and heard their separate sounds as they struck. He looked at the forest on the bank of the stream, saw the individual trees, the leaves and the veining of each leaf — saw the very insects upon them, the locusts, the brilliant-bodied flies, the grey spiders stretching their webs from twig to twig. He noted the prismatic colors in all the dewdrops upon a million blades of grass. The humming of the gnats that danced above the eddies of the stream, the beating of the dragon flies' wings, the strokes of the water spiders' legs, like oars which had lifted their boat — all these made audible music. A fish slid along beneath his eyes and he heard the rush of its body parting the water.

He had come to the surface facing down the stream; in a moment the visible world seemed to wheel slowly round, himself the pivotal point, and he saw the bridge, the fort, the soldiers upon the bridge, the captain, the sergeant, the two privates, his executioners. They were in silhouette against the blue sky. They shouted and gesticulated, pointing at him; the captain had drawn his pistol, but did not fire; the others were unarmed. Their movements were grotesque and horrible, their forms gigantic.

Suddenly he heard a sharp report and something struck the water smartly within a few inches of his head, spattering his face with spray. He heard a second report, and saw one of the sentinels with his rifle at his shoulder, a light cloud of blue smoke rising from the muzzle. The man in the water saw the eye of the man on the bridge gazing into his own through the sights of the rifle. He observed that it was a grey eye, and remembered having read that grey eyes were keenest and that all famous marksmen had them. Nevertheless, this one had missed.

A counter swirl had caught Farquhar and turned him half round; he was again looking into the forest on the bank opposite the fort. The sound of a clear, high voice in a monotonous singsong now rang out behind him and came across the water with a distinctness that pierced and subdued all other sounds, even the beating of the ripples in his ears. Although no soldier, he had frequented camps enough to know the dread significance of that deliberate, drawling, aspirated chant; the lieutenant on shore was taking a part in the morning's work. How coldly and pitilessly — with what an even, calm intonation, presaging and enforcing tranquillity in the men — with what accurately-measured intervals fell those cruel words:

"Attention, company.... Shoulder arms.... Ready.... Aim.... Fire."

Farquhar dived — dived as deeply as he could. The water roared in his ears like the voice of Niagara, yet he heard the dulled thunder of the volley, and rising again toward the surface, met shining bits of metal, singularly flattened, oscillating slowly downward. Some of them touched him on the face and hands, then fell away, continuing their descent. One lodged between his collar and neck; it was uncomfortably warm, and he snatched it out.

As he rose to the surface, gasping for breath, he saw that he had been a long time under water; he was perceptibly farther down stream — nearer to safety. The soldiers had almost finished reloading; the metal ramrods flashed all at once in the sunshine as they were drawn from the barrels, turned in the air, and thrust into their sockets. The two sentinels fired again, independently and ineffectually.

The hunted man saw all this over his shoulder; he was now swimming vigorously with the current. His brain was as energetic as his arms and legs; he thought with the rapidity of lightning.

"The officer," he reasoned, "will not make the martinet's error a second time. It is as easy to dodge a volley as a single shot. He has probably already given the command to fire at will. God help me, I cannot dodge them all!"

An appalling plash within two yards of him, followed by a loud rushing sound, *diminuendo*, which seemed to travel back through the air to the fort and died in explosion which stirred the very river to its deeps! A rising sheet of water, which curved over him, fell down upon him, blinded him, strangled him! The cannon had taken a hand in the game. As he shook his head free from the commotion of the smitten water, he heard the deflected shot humming through the air ahead, and in an instant it was cracking and smashing the branches in the forest beyond.

"They will not do that again," he thought; "the next time they will use a charge of grape. I must keep my eye upon the gun; the smoke will apprise me — the report arrives too late; it lags behind the missile. It is a good gun."

Suddenly he felt himself whirled round and round — spinning like a top. The water, the banks, the forest, the now distant bridge, fort and men — all were commingled and blurred. Objects were represented by their colors only; circular horizontal streaks of color — that was all he saw. He had been caught in a vortex and was being whirled on with a velocity of advance and gyration which made him giddy and sick. In a few moments he was flung upon the gravel at the foot of the left bank of the stream — the southern bank — and behind a projecting point which concealed him from his enemies. The sudden arrest of his motion, the abrasion of one of his hands on the gravel, restored him and he wept with delight. He dug his fingers into the sand, threw it over himself in handfuls and audibly blessed it. It looked like gold, like diamonds, rubies, emeralds; he could think of nothing beautiful which it did not resemble. The trees upon the bank were giant garden plants; he noted a definite order in their arrangement, inhaled the fragrance of their blooms. A strange, roseate light shone through the spaces among their trunks, and the wind made in their branches the music of æolian harps. He had no wish to perfect his escape, was content to remain in that enchanting spot until retaken.

A whizz and rattle of grapeshot among the branches high above his head roused him from his dream. The baffled cannoneer had fired him a random farewell. He sprang to his feet, rushed up the sloping bank, and plunged into the forest.

All that day he travelled, laying his course by the rounding sun. The forest seemed interminable; nowhere did he discover a break in it, not even a woodman's road. He had not known that he lived in so wild a region. There was something uncanny in the revelation.

By nightfall he was fatigued, footsore, famishing. The thought of his wife and children urged him on. At last he found a road which led him in what he knew to be the right direction. It was as wide and straight as a city street, yet it seemed untravelled. No fields bordered it, no dwelling anywhere. Not so much as the barking of a dog suggested human habitation. The black bodies of the great trees formed a straight wall on both sides, terminating on the horizon in a point, like a diagram in a lesson in perspective. Overhead, as he looked up through this rift in the wood, shone great golden stars looking unfamiliar and grouped in strange constellations. He was sure they were arranged in some order which had a secret and malign significance. The wood on either side was full of singular noises, among which — once, twice, and again — he distinctly heard whispers in an unknown tongue.

His neck was in pain, and, lifting his hand to it, he found it horribly swollen. He knew that it had a circle of black where the rope had bruised it.

His eyes felt congested; he could no longer close them. His tongue was swollen with thirst; he relieved its fever by thrusting it forward from between his teeth into the cool air. How softly the turf had carpeted the untravelled avenue! He could no longer feel the roadway beneath his feet!

Doubtless, despite his suffering, he fell asleep while walking, for now he sees another scene — perhaps he has merely recovered from a delirium. He stands at the gate of his own home. All is as he left it, and all bright and beautiful in the morning sunshine. He must have travelled the entire night. As he pushes open the gate and passes up the wide white walk, he sees a flutter of female garments; his wife, looking fresh and cool and sweet, steps down from the verandah to meet him. At the bottom of the steps she stands waiting, with a smile of ineffable joy, an attitude of matchless grace and dignity. Ah, how beautiful she is! He springs forward with extended arms. As he is about to clasp her, he feels a stunning blow upon the back of the neck; a blinding white light blazes all about him, with a sound like a shock of a cannon — then all is darkness and silence!

Peyton Farquhar was dead; his body, with a broken neck, swung gently from side to side beneath the timbers of the Owl Creek bridge.

[1891]

HENRY JAMES *(1843–1916) was born in New York City. His father was a religious philosopher, and his brother William James was a noted physician, philosopher, and psychologist. Educated mostly by tutors in the United States and Europe, James published his first story at the age of twenty-one. In 1875 he chose to live permanently in England. He formed friendships with several European writers, including Gustave Flaubert, and Guy de Maupassant. During the first phase of James's long career, he explored personal relationships, most notably in the novel* The Portrait of a Lady *(1881). Then he turned to themes of social reform, as in* The Bostonians *(1886). He constantly experimented with ways to refine his writing and commented on his "art of fiction" in many essays, prefaces, letters, and notebooks. The dense, symbolic style of his later work, whose fundamental theme is the innocence and exuberance of the New World clashing with the experience and corruption of the Old, can be seen in his three last novels,* The Wings of the Dove *(1902),* The Ambassadors *(1903), and* The Golden Bowl *(1904).*

In his lifetime James wrote more than seventy stories. He began as a modest imitator of Nathaniel Hawthorne and ended as a great creative writer of fiction and literary criticism; the progression was the result of his professionalism, his constant self-examination, his self-knowledge, and his self-control. He felt that experience assumes meaning only when the proper form for its expression is found. One of his favorite words was "awareness," and he tried to make his own awareness encompass everything he could observe, relate, weigh, and judge. Thus, his was a world of connections continually subjected to a controlled and harmonious ordering. In the essay "The Art of Fiction," he said that the source of fiction is not mere raw experience but "the power to guess the unseen from the seen, to trace the implication of things, to judge the whole piece by the pattern, the condition of feeling life in general so completely that you are well on your way to knowing any particular corner of it."

James's stories lack the characteristic compression and dramatic action typical of this literary form. Instead, through the device he called a "central intelligence," he revealed the world through the silent thought of one of his characters, proceeding at a stately, leisurely pace. Yet in 1891, when James wrote in his notebook the idea that was the genesis of the story "The Real Thing," he apparently had in mind something else, a compressed short story in the manner of Guy de Maupassant, which he hoped would be easier to sell to a magazine than a longer work. He regarded this story as a great challenge: "To look at a thing hard and straight and seriously — to fix it." (See James's Commentary on page 1232.)

Henry James

ဇာ

THE REAL THING

I

When the porter's wife, who used to answer the house-bell, announced "A gentleman and a lady, sir," I had, as I often had in those days — the wish being father to the thought — an immediate vision of sitters. Sitters my visitors in this case proved to be; but not in the sense I should have preferred. There was nothing at first however to indicate that they mightn't have come for a portrait. The gentleman, a man of fifty, very high and very straight, with a moustache slightly grizzled and a dark grey walking-coat admirably fitted, both of which I noted professionally — I don't mean as a barber or yet as a tailor — would have struck me as a celebrity if celebrities often were striking. It was a truth of which I had for some time been conscious that a figure with a good deal of frontage was, as one might say, almost never a public institution. A glance at the lady helped to remind me of this paradoxical law: she also looked too distinguished to be a "personality." Moreover one would scarcely come across two variations together.

Neither of the pair immediately spoke — they only prolonged the preliminary gaze suggesting that each wished to give the other a chance. They were visibly shy; they stood there letting me take them in — which, as I afterwards perceived, was the most practical thing they could have done. In this way their embarrassment served their cause. I had seen people painfully reluctant to mention that they desired anything so gross as to be represented on canvas; but the scruples of my new friends appeared almost insurmountable. Yet the gentleman might have said "I should like a portrait of my wife," and the lady might have said "I should like a portrait of my husband." Perhaps they weren't husband and wife — this naturally would make the matter more delicate. Perhaps they wished to be done together — in which case they ought to have brought a third person to break the news.

"We come from Mr. Rivet," the lady finally said with a dim smile that had the effect of a moist sponge passed over a "sunk" piece of painting, as well as of a vague allusion to vanished beauty. She was as tall and straight, in her degree, as her companion, and with ten years less to carry. She looked as sad as a woman could look whose face was not charged with expression; that is her tinted oval mask showed waste as an exposed surface shows friction. The hand of time had played over her freely, but to an effect of elimination. She was slim and stiff, and so well-dressed, in dark blue cloth, with lappets and pockets and buttons, that it was clear she employed the same tailor as her husband. The couple had an indefinable air of prosperous thrift — they evidently got a good deal of luxury for their money. If I was to be one of their luxuries it would behoove me to consider my terms.

"Ah Claude Rivet recommended me?" I echoed; and I added that it was very kind of him, though I could reflect that, as he only painted landscape, this wasn't a sacrifice.

The lady looked very hard at the gentleman, and the gentleman looked round the room. Then staring at the floor a moment and stroking his moustache, he rested his pleasant eyes on me with the remark: "He said you were the right one."

"I try to be, when people want to sit."

"Yes, we should like to," said the lady anxiously.

"Do you mean together?"

My visitors exchanged a glance. "If you could do anything with *me* I suppose it would be double," the gentleman stammered.

"Oh yes, there's naturally a higher charge for two figures than for one."

"We should like to make it pay," the husband confessed.

"That's very good of you," I returned, appreciating so unwonted a sympathy — for I supposed he meant pay the artist.

A sense of strangeness seemed to dawn on the lady. "We mean for the illustrations — Mr. Rivet said you might put one in."

"Put in — an illustration?" I was equally confused.

"Sketch her off, you know," said the gentleman, coloring.

It was only then that I understood the service Claude Rivet had rendered me; he had told them how I worked in black-and-white, for magazines, for storybooks, for sketches of contemporary life, and consequently had copious employment for models. These things were true, but it was not less true — I may confess it now; whether because the aspiration was to lead to everything or to nothing I leave the reader to guess — that I couldn't get the honors, to say nothing of the emoluments, of a great painter of portraits out of my head. My "illustrations" were my pot-boilers; I looked to a different branch of art — far and away the most interesting it had always seemed to me — to perpetuate my fame. There was no shame in looking to it also to make my fortune; but that fortune was by so much further from being made from the moment my visitors wished to be "done" for nothing. I was disappointed; for in the pictorial sense I had immediately *seen* them. I had seized their type — I had already settled what I would do with it. Something that wouldn't absolutely have pleased them, I afterwards reflected.

"Ah you're — you're — a?" I began as soon as I had mastered my surprise. I couldn't bring out the dingy word "models": it seemed so little to fit the case.

"We haven't had much practice," said the lady.

"We've got to *do* something, and we've thought that an artist in your line might perhaps make something of us," her husband threw off. He further mentioned that they didn't know many artists and that they had gone first, on the off-chance — he painted views of course, but sometimes put in figures; perhaps I remembered — to Mr. Rivet, whom they had met a few years before at a place in Norfolk where he was sketching.

"We used to sketch a little ourselves," the lady hinted.

"It's very awkward, but we absolutely *must* do something," her husband went on.

"Of course we're not so *very* young," she admitted with a wan smile.

With the remark that I might as well know something more about them the husband had handed me a card extracted from a neat new pocket-book — their appurtenances were all of the freshest — and inscribed with the words "Major Monarch." Impressive as these words were they didn't carry my knowledge much further; but my visitor presently added: "I've left the army and we've had the misfortune to lose our money. In fact our means are dreadfully small."

"It's awfully trying — a regular strain," said Mrs. Monarch.

They evidently wished to be discreet — to take care not to swagger because they were gentlefolk. I felt them willing to recognize this as something of a drawback, at the same time that I guessed at an underlying sense — their consolation in adversity — that they *had* their points. They certainly had; but these advantages struck me as preponderantly social; such for instance as would help to make a drawing-room look well. However, a drawing-room was always, or ought to be, a picture.

In consequence of his wife's allusion to their age Major Monarch observed: "Naturally, it's more for the figure that we thought of going in. We can still hold ourselves up." On the instant I saw that the figure was indeed their strong point. His "naturally" didn't sound vain, but it lighted up the question. "*She* has got the best," he continued, nodding at his wife, with a pleasant after-dinner absence of circumlocution. I could only reply, as if we were in fact sitting over our wine, that this didn't prevent his own from being very good; which led him in turn to rejoin: "We thought that if you ever have to do people like us, we might be something like it. *She*, particularly — for a lady in a book, you know."

I was so amused by them that, to get more of it, I did my best to take their point of view; and though it was an embarrassment to find myself appraising physically, as if they were animals on hire or useful blacks, a pair whom I should have expected to meet only in one of the relations in which criticism is tacit, I looked at Mrs. Monarch judicially enough to be able to exclaim, after a moment, with conviction: "Oh yes, a lady in a book!" She was singularly like a bad illustration.

"We'll stand up, if you like," said the Major; and he raised himself before me with a really grand air.

I could take his measure at a glance — he was six feet two and a perfect gentleman. It would have paid any club in process of formation and in want of a stamp to engage him at a salary to stand in the principal window. What struck me immediately was that in coming to me they had rather missed their vocation; they could surely have been turned to better account for advertising purposes. I couldn't of course see the thing in detail, but I could see them make someone's fortune — I don't mean their own. There was something in them for a waistcoat-maker, an hotel-keeper, or a soap-vendor. I could imagine "We always use it" pinned on their bosoms with the greatest effect; I had a vision of the promptitude with which they would launch a table d'hôte.

Mrs. Monarch sat still, not from pride but from shyness, and presently her husband said to her: "Get up my dear and show how smart you are." She obeyed, but she had no need to get up to show it. She walked to the end of the studio, and then she came back blushing, with her fluttered eyes on her husband. I was reminded of an incident I had accidentally had a glimpse of in Paris — being with a friend there, a dramatist about to produce a play — when an actress came to him to ask to be intrusted with a part. She went through her paces before him, walked up and down as Mrs. Monarch was doing. Mrs. Monarch did it quite as well, but I abstained from applauding. It was very odd to see such people apply for such poor pay. She looked as if she had ten thousand a year. Her husband had used the word that described her: she was in the London current jargon essentially and typically "smart." Her figure was, in the same order of ideas, conspicuously and irreproachably "good." For a woman of her age her waist was surprisingly small; her elbow moreover had the orthodox crook. She held her head at the conventional angle, but why did she come to *me*? She ought to have tried on jackets at a big shop. I feared my visitors were not only destitute but "artistic" — which would be a great complication. When she sat down again I thanked her, observing that what a draughtsman most valued in his model was the faculty of keeping quiet.

"Oh *she* can keep quiet," said Major Monarch. Then he added jocosely: "I've always kept her quiet."

"I'm not a nasty fidget, am I?" It was going to wring tears from me, I felt, the way she hid her head, ostrich-like, in the other broad bosom.

The owner of this expanse addressed his answer to me. "Perhaps it isn't out of place to mention — because we ought to be quite businesslike, oughtn't we? — that when I married her she was known as the Beautiful Statue."

"Oh dear!" said Mrs. Monarch ruefully.

"Of course I should want a certain amount of expression," I rejoined.

"Of *course!*" — and I had never heard such unanimity.

"And then I suppose you know that you'll get awfully tired."

"Oh, we *never* get tired!" they eagerly cried.

"Have you had any kind of practice?"

They hesitated — they looked at each other. "We've been photo-graphed — *immensely,*" said Mrs. Monarch.

"She means the fellows have asked us themselves," added the Major.

"I see — because you're so good-looking."

"I don't know what they thought, but they were always after us."

"We always got our photographs for nothing," smiled Mrs. Monarch.

"We might have brought some, my dear," her husband remarked.

"I'm not sure we have any left. We've given quantities away," she explained to me.

"With our autographs and that sort of thing," said the Major.

"Are they to be got in the shops?" I enquired as a harmless pleasantry.

"Oh yes, *hers* — they used to be."

"Not now," said Mrs. Monarch, with her eyes on the floor.

II

I could fancy the "sort of thing" they put on the presentation copies of their photographs, and I was sure they wrote a beautiful hand. It was odd how quickly I was sure of everything that concerned them. If they were now so poor as to have to earn shillings and pence they could never have had much of a margin. Their good looks had been their capital, and they had good-humoredly made the most of the career that this resource marked out for them. It was in their faces, the blankness, the deep intellectual repose of the twenty years of country-house visiting that had given them pleasant in-tonations. I could see the sunny drawing-rooms, sprinkled with periodicals she didn't read, in which Mrs. Monarch had continually sat; I could see the wet shrubberies in which she had walked, equipped to admiration for either exercise. I could see the rich covers the Major had helped to shoot and the wonderful garments in which, late at night, he repaired to the smoking-room to talk about them. I could imagine their leggings and waterproofs, their knowing tweeds and rugs, their rolls of sticks and cases of tackle and neat umbrellas; and I could evoke the exact appearance of their servants and the compact variety of their luggage on the platforms of country sta-tions.

They gave small tips, but they were liked; they didn't do anything themselves, but they were welcome. They looked so well everywhere; they gratified the general relish for stature, complexion, and "form." They knew it without fatuity or vulgarity, and they respected themselves in conse-quence. They weren't superficial; they were thorough and kept themselves

up — it had been their line. People with such a taste for activity had to
have some line. I could feel how even in a dull house they could have been
counted on for the joy of life. At present something had happened — it
didn't matter what, their little income had grown less, it had grown
least — and they had to do something for pocket-money. Their friends
could like them, I made out, without liking to support them. There was
something about them that represented credit — their clothes, their manners, their type; but if credit is a large empty pocket in which an occasional
chink reverberates, the chink at least must be audible. What they wanted of
me was to help to make it so. Fortunately they had no children — I soon
divined that. They would also perhaps wish our relations to be kept secret:
this was why it was "for the figure" — the reproduction of the face would
betray them.

I liked them — I felt, quite as their friends must have done — they
were so simple; and I had no objection to them if they would suit. But
somehow with all their perfections I didn't easily believe in them. After all
they were amateurs, and the ruling passion of my life was the detestation of
the amateur. Combined with this was another perversity — an innate preference for the represented subject over the real one: the defect of the real
one was so apt to be a lack of representation. I like things that appeared;
then one was sure. Whether they *were* or not was a subordinate and almost
always a profitless question. There were other considerations, the first of
which was that I already had two or three recruits in use, notably a young
person with big feet, in alpaca, from Kilburn, who for a couple of years had
come to me regularly for my illustrations and with whom I was still — perhaps ignobly — satisfied. I frankly explained to my visitors how the case
stood, but they had taken more precautions than I supposed. They had reasoned out their opportunity, for Claude Rivet had told them of the projected *édition de luxe* of one of the writers of our day — the rarest of the
novelists — who, long neglected by the multitudinous vulgar and dearly
prized by the attentive (need I mention Philip Vincent?), had had the
happy fortune of seeing, late in life, the dawn and then the full light of a
higher criticism; an estimate in which on the part of the public there was
something really of expiation. The edition preparing, planned by a publisher of taste, was practically an act of high reparation; the wood-cuts with
which it was to be enriched were the homage of English art to one of the
most independent representatives of English letters. Major and Mrs. Monarch confessed to me they had hoped I might be able to work *them* into my
branch of the enterprise. They knew I was to do the first of the books,
"Rutland Ramsay," but I had to make clear to them that my participation
in the rest of the affair — this first book was to be a test — must depend on
the satisfaction I should give. If this should be limited my employers would
drop me with scarce common forms. It was therefore a crisis for me, and
naturally I was making special preparations, looking about for new people,

should they be necessary, and securing the best types. I admitted however that I should like to settle down to two or three good models who would do for everything.

"Should we have often to — a — put on special clothes?" Mrs. Monarch timidly demanded.

"Dear yes — that's half the business."

"And should we be expected to supply our own costumes?"

"Oh no; I've got a lot of things. A painter's models put on — or put off — anything he likes."

"And you mean — a — the same?"

"The same?"

Mrs. Monarch looked at her husband again.

"Oh she was just wondering," he explained, "if the costumes are in *general* use." I had to confess that they were, and I mentioned further that some of them — I had a lot of genuine greasy last-century things — had served their time, a hundred years ago, on living world-stained men and women; on figures not perhaps so far removed, in that vanished world, from *their* type, the Monarchs', *quoi!* of a breeched and bewigged age. "We'll put on anything that *fits*," said the Major.

"Oh I arrange that — they fit in the pictures."

"I'm afraid I should do better for the modern books. I'd come as you like," said Mrs. Monarch.

"She has got a lot of clothes at home: they might do for contemporary life," her husband continued.

"Oh I can fancy scenes in which you'd be quite natural." And indeed I could see the slipshod rearrangements of stale properties — the stories I tried to produce pictures for without the exasperation of reading them — whose sandy tracts the good lady might help to people. But I had to return to the fact that for this sort of work — the daily mechanical grind — I was already equipped: the people I was working with were fully adequate.

"We only thought we might be more like *some* characters," said Mrs. Monarch mildly, getting up.

Her husband also rose; he stood looking at me with a dim wistfulness that was touching in so fine a man. "Wouldn't it be rather a pull sometimes to have — a — to have — ?" He hung fire; he wanted me to help him by phrasing what he meant. But I couldn't — I didn't know. So he brought it out awkwardly: "The *real* thing; a gentleman, you know, or a lady." I was quite ready to give a general assent — I admitted that there was a great deal in that. This encouraged Major Monarch to say, following up his appeal with an unacted gulp: "It's awfully hard — we've tried everything." The gulp was communicative; it proved too much for his wife. Before I knew it Mrs. Monarch had dropped again upon a divan and burst into tears. Her husband sat down beside her, holding one of her hands; whereupon she quickly dried her eyes with the other, while I felt embarrassed as she looked up at me. "There isn't a confounded job I haven't applied for — waited for — prayed for. You can fancy we'd be pretty bad first. Secretaryships and that sort of thing? You might as well ask for a peerage. I'd be *anything* — I'm strong; a messenger or a coalheaver. I'd put on a gold-laced cap and open carriage-doors in front of the haberdasher's; I'd hang about a station to carry portmanteaux; I'd be a postman. But they won't *look* at you; there are thousands as good as yourself already on the ground. *Gentlemen*, poor beggars, who've drunk their wine, who've kept their hunters!"

I was as reassuring as I knew how to be, and my visitors were presently on their feet again while, for the experiment, we agreed on an hour. We were discussing it when the door opened and Miss Churm came in with a wet umbrella. Miss Churm had to take the omnibus to Maida Vale and then walk half a mile. She looked a trifle blowsy and slightly splashed. I scarcely ever saw her come in without thinking afresh how odd it was that, being so little in herself, she should yet be so much in others. She was a meagre little Miss Churm, but was such an ample heroine of romance. She was only a freckled cockney, but she could represent everything, from a fine lady to a shepherdess; she had the faculty as she might have had a fine voice or long hair. She couldn't spell and she loved beer, but she had two or three "points," and practice, and a knack, and mother-wit, and a whimsical sensibility, and a love of the theatre, and seven sisters, and not an ounce of respect, especially for the *h*. The first thing my visitors saw was that her umbrella was wet, and in their spotless perfection they visibly winced at it. The rain had come on since their arrival.

"I'm all in a soak; there *was* a mess of people in the 'bus. I wish you lived near a stytion," said Miss Churm. I requested her to get ready as quickly as possible, and she passed into the room in which she always changed her dress. But before going out she asked me what she was to get into this time.

"It's the Russian princess, don't you know?" I answered; "the one with the 'golden eyes,' in black velvet, for the long thing in the *Cheapside*."

"Golden eyes? I *say!*" cried Miss Churm, while my companions watched her with intensity as she withdrew. She always arranged herself, when she was late, before I could turn round; and I kept my visitors a little on purpose, so that they might get an idea, from seeing her, what would be expected of themselves. I mentioned that she was quite my notion of an excellent model — she was really very clever.

"Do you think she looks like a Russian princess?" Major Monarch asked with lurking alarm.

"When I make her, yes."

"Oh if you have to *make* her — !" he reasoned, not without point.

"That's the most you can ask. There are so many who are not makeable."

"Well now, *here's* a lady" — and with a persuasive smile he passed his arm into his wife's — "who's already made!"

"Oh I'm not a Russian princess," Mrs. Monarch protested a little coldly. I could see she had known some and didn't like them. There at once was a complication of a kind I never had to fear with Miss Churm.

This young lady came back in black velvet — the gown was rather rusty and very low on her lean shoulders — and with a Japanese fan in her red hands. I reminded her that in the scene I was doing she had to look over some one's head. "I forget whose it is; but it doesn't matter. Just look over a head."

"I'd rather look over a stove," said Miss Churm; and she took her station near the fire. She fell into position, settled herself into a tall attitude, gave a certain backward inclination to her head and a certain forward droop to her fan, and looked, at least to my prejudiced sense, distinguished and charming, foreign and dangerous. We left her looking so while I went downstairs with Major and Mrs. Monarch.

"I believe I could come about as near it as that," said Mrs. Monarch.

"Oh you think she's shabby, but you must allow for the alchemy of art."

However, they went off with an evident increase of comfort founded on their demonstrable advantage in being the real thing. I could fancy them shuddering over Miss Churm. She was very droll about them when I went back, for I told her what they wanted.

"Well, if *she* can sit I'll tyke to book-keeping," said my model.

"She's very ladylike," I replied as an innocent form of aggravation.

"So much the worse for *you*. That means she can't turn round."

"She'll do for the fashionable novels."

"Oh yes, she'll *do* for them!" my model humorously declared. "Ain't they bad enough without her?" I had often sociably denounced them to Miss Churm.

III

It was for the elucidation of a mystery in one of these works that I first tried Mrs. Monarch. Her husband came with her, to be useful if necessary — it was sufficiently clear that as a general thing he would prefer to come with her. At first I wondered if this were for "propriety's" sake — if he were going to be jealous and meddling. The idea was too tiresome, and if it had been confirmed it would speedily have brought our acquaintance to a close. But I soon saw there was nothing in it and that if he accompanied Mrs. Monarch it was — in addition to the chance of being wanted — simply because he had nothing else to do. When they were separate his occupation was gone and they never *had* been separate. I judged rightly that in their awkward situation their close union was their main comfort and that this union had no weak spot. It was a real marriage, an encouragement to the hesitating, a nut for pessimists to crack. Their address was humble — I remember afterwards thinking it had been the only thing about them that was really professional — and I could fancy the lamentable lodgings in which the Major would have been left alone. He could sit there more or less grimly with his wife — he couldn't sit there anyhow without her.

He had too much tact to try and make himself agreeable when he couldn't be useful; so when I was too absorbed in my work to talk he simply sat and waited. But I liked to hear him talk — it made my work, when not interrupting it, less mechanical, less special. To listen to him was to combine the excitement of going out with the economy of staying at home. There was only one hindrance — that I seemed not to know any of the people this brilliant couple had known. I think he wondered extremely, during the term of our intercourse, whom the deuce I *did* know. He hadn't a stray sixpence of an idea to fumble for, so we didn't spin it very fine; we confined ourselves to questions of leather and even of liquor — saddlers and breeches-makers and how to get excellent claret cheap — and matters like "good trains" and the habits of small game. His lore on these last subjects was astonishing — he managed to interweave the station-master with the ornithologist. When he couldn't talk about greater things he could talk cheerfully about smaller, and since I couldn't accompany him into reminiscences of the fashionable world he could lower the conversation without a visible effort to my level.

So earnest a desire to please was touching in a man who could so easily have knocked one down. He looked after the fire and had an opinion on the draught of the stove without my asking him, and I could see that he thought many of my arrangements not half knowing. I remember telling him that if I were only rich I'd offer him a salary to come and teach me how to live. Sometimes he gave a random sigh of which the essence might have been: "Give me even such a bare old barrack as *this*, and I'd do something with it!" When I wanted to use him he came alone; which was an illustration of the superior courage of women. His wife could bear her solitary second floor, and she was in general more discreet; showing by various small reserves that she was alive to the propriety of keeping our relations markedly professional — not letting them slide into sociability. She wished it to remain clear that she and the Major were employed, not cultivated, and if she approved of me as a superior, who could be kept in his place, she never thought me quite good enough for an equal.

She sat with great intensity, giving the whole of her mind to it, and was capable of remaining for an hour almost as motionless as before a photographer's lens. I could see she had been photographed often, but somehow the very habit that made her good for that purpose unfitted her for mine. At first I was extremely pleased with her ladylike air, and it was a satisfaction, on coming to follow her lines, to see how good they were and how far they could lead the pencil. But after a little skirmishing I began to find her too insurmountably stiff; do what I would with it my drawing looked like a photograph or a copy of a photograph. Her figure had no variety of expression — she herself had no sense of variety. You may say that this was my business and was only a question of placing her. Yet I placed her in every conceivable position and she managed to obliterate their differences. She was always a lady certainly, and into the bargain was always the same lady. She was the real thing, but always the same thing. There were moments when I rather writhed under the serenity of her confidence that she *was* the real thing. All her dealings with me and all her husband's were an implication that this was lucky for *me*. Meanwhile I found myself trying to invent types that approached her own, instead of making her own transform itself — in the clever way that was not impossible for instance to poor Miss Churm. Arrange as I would and take the precautions I would, she always came out, in my pictures, too tall — landing me in the dilemma of having represented a fascinating woman as seven feet high, which (out of respect perhaps to my own very much scantier inches) was far from my idea of such a personage.

The case was worse with the Major — nothing I could do would keep *him* down, so that he became useful only for the representation of brawny giants. I adored variety and range, I cherished human accidents, the illustrative note; I wanted to characterize closely, and the thing in the world I most hated was the danger of being ridden by a type. I had quarreled with some of my friends about it; I had parted company with them for maintaining that one *had* to be, and that if the type was beautiful — witness Raphael and Leonardo — the servitude was only a gain. I was neither Leonardo nor Raphael — I might only be a presumptuous young modern searcher; but I held that everything was to be sacrificed sooner than character. When they claimed that the obsessional form could easily *be* character I retorted, perhaps superficially, "Whose?" It couldn't be everybody's — it might end in being nobody's.

After I had drawn Mrs. Monarch a dozen times I felt surer even than before that the value of such a model as Miss Churm resided precisely in the fact that she had no positive stamp, combined of course with the other fact that what she did have was a curious and inexplicable talent for imitation. Her usual appearance was like a curtain which she could draw up at request for a capital performance. This performance was simply suggestive; but it was a word to the wise — it was vivid and pretty. Sometimes even I thought it, though she was plain herself, too insipidly pretty; I made it a reproach to her that the figures drawn from her were monotonously (*bêtement*, as we used to say) graceful. Nothing made her more angry; it was so much her pride to feel she could sit for characters that had nothing in common with each other. She would accuse me at such moments of taking away her "reputytion."

It suffered a certain shrinkage, this queer quantity, from the repeated visits of my new friends. Miss Churm was greatly in demand, never in want of employment, so I had no scruple in putting her off occasionally, to try them more at my ease. It was certainly amusing at first to do the real thing — it was amusing to do Major Monarch's trousers. They *were* the real thing, even if he did come out colossal. It was amusing to do his wife's back hair — it was so mathematically neat — and the particular "smart" tension of her tight stays. She lent herself especially to positions in which the face was somewhat averted or blurred; she abounded in ladylike back views and *profils perdus.*[1] When she stood erect she took naturally one of the attitudes in which court-painters represent queens and princesses; so that I found myself wondering whether, to draw out this accomplishment, I couldn't get the editor of the *Cheapside* to publish a really royal romance, "A Tale of Buckingham Palace." Sometimes however the real thing and the make-believe came into contact; by which I mean that Miss Churm, keeping an appointment or coming to make one on days when I had much work in hand, encountered her invidious rivals. The encounter was not on their part, for they noticed her no more than if she had been the housemaid; not from intentional loftiness, but simply because as yet, professionally, they didn't know how to fraternize, as I could imagine they would have liked — or at least that the Major would. They couldn't talk about the omnibus — they always walked; and they didn't know what else to try — she wasn't interested in good trains or cheap claret. Besides, they must have felt — in the air — that she was amused at them, secretly derisive of their ever knowing how. She wasn't a person to conceal the limits of her faith if she had had a chance to show them. On the other hand Mrs. Monarch didn't think her tidy; for why else did she take pains to say to me — it was going out of the way, for Mrs. Monarch — that she didn't like dirty women?

One day when my young lady happened to be present with my other sitters — she even dropped in, when it was convenient, for a chat — I asked her to be so good as to lend a hand in getting tea, a service with which she was familiar and which was one of a class that, living as I did in a small way, with slender domestic resources, I often appealed to my models to render. They liked to lay hands on my property, to break the sitting, and sometimes the china — it made them feel Bohemian. The next time I saw Miss Churm after this incident she surprised me greatly by making a scene about it — she accused me of having wished to humiliate her. She hadn't resented the outrage at the time, but had seemed obliging and amused, enjoying the comedy of asking Mrs. Monarch, who sat vague and silent, whether she would have cream and sugar, and putting an exaggerated simper into the question. She had tried intonations — as if she too wished to pass for the real thing — till I was afraid my other visitors would take offense.

Oh they were determined not to do this, and their touching patience was the measure of their great need. They would sit by the hour, uncomplaining, till I was ready to use them; they would come back on the chance of being wanted and would walk away cheerfully if it failed. I used to go to the door with them to see in what magnificent order they retreated. I tried to find other employment for them — I introduced them to several artists.

---

[1] profiles in which the face is averted and its features remain unseen.

But they didn't "take," for reasons I could appreciate, and I became rather anxiously aware that after such disappointments they fell back upon me with a heavier weight. They did me the honor to think me most *their* form. They weren't romantic enough for the painters, and in those days there were few serious workers in black-and-white. Besides, they had an eye to the great job I had mentioned to them — they had secretly set their hearts on supplying the right essence for my pictorial vindication of our fine novelist. They knew that for this undertaking I should want no costume-effects, none of the frippery of past ages — that it was a case in which everything would be contemporary and satirical and presumably genteel. If I could work them into it their future would be assured, for the labor would of course be long and the occupation steady.

One day Mrs. Monarch came without her husband — she explained his absence by his having had to go to the City. While she sat there in her usual relaxed majesty there came at the door a knock which I immediately recognized as the subdued appeal of a model out of work. It was followed by the entrance of a young man whom I at once saw to be a foreigner and who proved in fact an Italian acquainted with no English word but my name, which he uttered in a way that made it seem to include all others. I hadn't then visited his country, nor was I proficient in his tongue; but as he was not so meanly constituted — what Italian is? — as to depend only on that member for expression he conveyed to me, in familiar but graceful mimicry, that he was in search of exactly the employment in which the lady before me was engaged. I was not struck with him at first, and while I continued to draw I dropped few signs of interest or encouragement. He stood his ground however — not importunately, but with a dumb dog-like fidelity in his eyes that amounted to innocent impudence, the manner of a devoted servant — he might have been in the house for years — unjustly suspected. Suddenly it struck me that this very attitude and expression made a picture; whereupon I told him to sit down and wait till I should be free. There was another picture in the way he obeyed me, and I observed as I worked that there were others still in the way he looked wonderingly, with his head thrown back, about the high studio. He might have been crossing himself in Saint Peter's. Before I finished I said to myself "The fellow's a bankrupt orange-monger, but a treasure."

When Mrs. Monarch withdrew he passed across the room like a flash to open the door for her, standing there with the rapt pure gaze of the young Dante spellbound by the young Beatrice. As I never insisted, in such situations, on the blankness of the British domestic, I reflected that he had the making of a servant — and I needed one, but couldn't pay him to be only that — as well as of a model; in short I resolved to adopt my bright adventurer if he would agree to officiate in the double capacity. He jumped at my offer, and in the event my rashness — for I had really known nothing about him — wasn't brought home to me. He proved a sympathetic though a desultory ministrant, and had in a wonderful degree the *sentiment de la pose.* It was uncultivated, instinctive, a part of the happy instinct that had guided him to my door and helped him to spell out my name on the card nailed to it. He had had no other introduction to me than a guess, from the shape of my high north window, seen outside, that my place was a studio and that as a studio it would contain an artist. He had wandered to England in search of fortune, like other itinerants, and had embarked, with a partner and a small green hand-cart, on the sale of penny ices. The ices had melted away and the partner had dissolved in their train. My young man wore tight yellow trousers with reddish stripes and his name was Oronte. He was sallow but fair, and when I put him into some old clothes of my own he looked like an Englishman. He was as good as Miss Churm, who could look, when requested, like an Italian.

IV

I thought Mrs. Monarch's face slightly convulsed when, on her coming back with her husband, she found Oronte installed. It was strange to have to recognize in a scrap of a lazzarone[2] a competitor to her magnificent Major. It was she who scented danger first, for the Major was anecdotically unconscious. But Oronte gave us tea, with a hundred eager confusions — he had never been concerned in so queer a process — and I think she thought better of me for having at last an "establishment." They saw a couple of drawings that I had made of the establishment, and Mrs. Monarch hinted that it never would have struck her he had sat for them. "Now the drawings you make from *us*, they look exactly like us," she reminded me, smiling in triumph; and I recognized that this was indeed just their defect. When I drew the Monarchs I couldn't anyhow get away from them — get into the character I wanted to represent; and I hadn't the least desire my model should be discoverable in my picture. Miss Churm never was, and Mrs. Monarch thought I hid her, very properly, because she was vulgar; whereas if she was lost it was only as the dead who go to heaven are lost — in the gain of an angel the more.

By this time I had got a certain start with "Rutland Ramsay," the first novel in the great projected series; that is I had produced a dozen drawings, several with the help of the Major and his wife, and I had sent them in for approval. My understanding with the publishers, as I have already hinted, had been that I was to be left to do my work, in this particular case, as I liked, with the whole book committed to me; but my connection with the rest of the series was only contingent. There were moments when, frankly, it *was* a comfort to have the real thing under one's hand; for there were characters in "Rutland Ramsay" that were very much like it. There were people presumably as erect as the Major and women of as good a fashion as Mrs. Monarch. There was a great deal of country-house life — treated, it is

---

[2] the name given to homeless beggars in Naples.

true, in a fine fanciful ironical generalized way — and there was a considerable implication of knickerbockers and kilts. There were certain things I
had to settle at the outset; such things for instance as the exact appearance
of the hero and the particular bloom and figure of the heroine. The author
of course gave me a lead, but there was a margin for interpretation. I took
the Monarchs into my confidence, I told them frankly what I was about, I
mentioned my embarrassments and alternatives. "Oh take *him!*" Mrs.
Monarch murmured sweetly, looking at her husband; and "What could you
want better than my wife?" the Major enquired with the comfortable candor that now prevailed between us.

I wasn't obliged to answer these remarks — I was only obliged to place
my sitters. I wasn't easy in mind, and I postponed a little timidly perhaps
the solving of my question. The book was a large canvas, the other figures
were numerous, and I worked off at first some of the episodes in which the
hero and the heroine were not concerned. When once I had set *them* up I
should have to stick to them — I couldn't make my young man seven feet
high in one place and five feet nine in another. I inclined on the whole to
the latter measurement, though the Major more than once reminded me
that *he* looked about as young as any one. It was indeed quite possible to
arrange him, for the figure, so that it would have been difficult to detect his
age. After the spontaneous Oronte had been with me a month, and after I
had given him to understand several times over that his native exuberance
would presently constitute an insurmountable barrier to our further intercourse, I waked to a sense of his heroic capacity. He was only five feet seven,
but the remaining inches were latent. I tried him almost secretly at first, for
I was really rather afraid of the judgment my other models would pass on
such a choice. If they regarded Miss Churm as little better than a snare
what would they think of the representation by a person so little the
real thing as an Italian street-vendor of a protagonist formed by a public
school?

If I went a little in fear of them it wasn't because they bullied me, because they had got an oppressive foothold, but because in their really pathetic decorum and mysteriously permanent newness they counted on me
so intensely. I was therefore very glad when Jack Hawley came home: he
was always of such good counsel. He painted badly himself, but there was
no one like him for putting his finger on the place. He had been absent
from England for a year; he had been somewhere — I don't remember
where — to get a fresh eye. I was in a good deal of dread of any such organ,
but we were old friends; he had been away for months and a sense of emptiness was creeping into my life. I hadn't dodged a missile for a year.

He came back with a fresh eye, but with the same old black velvet
blouse, and the first evening he spent in my studio we smoked cigarettes till
the small hours. He had done no work himself, he had only got the eye; so
the field was clear for the production of my little things. He wanted to see
what I had produced for the *Cheapside,* but he was disappointed in the ex-

hibition. That at least seemed the meaning of two or three comprehensive groans which, as he lounged on my big divan, his leg folded under him, looking at my latest drawings, issued from his lips with the smoke of the cigarette.

"What's the matter with you?" I asked.

"What's the matter with *you*?"

"Nothing save that I'm mystified."

"You are indeed. You're quite off the hinge. What's the meaning of this new fad?" And he tossed me, with visible irreverence, a drawing in which I happened to have depicted both my elegant models. I asked if he didn't think it good, and he replied that it struck him as execrable, given the sort of thing I had always represented myself to him as wishing to arrive at; but I let that pass — I was so anxious to see exactly what he meant. The two figures in the picture looked colossal, but I supposed this was *not* what he meant, inasmuch as, for aught he knew to the contrary, I might have been trying for some such effect. I maintained that I was working exactly in the same way as when he last had done me the honor to tell me I might do something some day. "Well, there's a screw loose somewhere," he answered; "wait a bit and I'll discover it." I depended upon him to do so: where else was the fresh eye? But he produced at last nothing more luminous than "I don't know — I don't like your types." This was lame for a critic who had never consented to discuss with me anything but the question of execution, the direction of strokes, and the mystery of values.

"In the drawings you've been looking at I think my types are very handsome."

"Oh they won't do!"

"I've been working with new models."

"I see you have. *They* won't do."

"Are you very sure of that?"

"Absolutely — they're stupid."

"You mean *I* am — for I ought to get round that."

"You *can't* — with such people. Who are they?"

I told him, so far as was necessary, and he concluded heartlessly: "*Ce sont des gens qu'il faut mettre à la porte.*"[3]

"You've never seen them; they're awfully good" — I flew to their defense.

"Not seen them? Why all this recent work of yours drops to pieces with them. It's all I want to see of them."

"No one else has said anything against it — the *Cheapside* people are pleased."

"Every one else is an ass, and the *Cheapside* people the biggest asses of all. Come, don't pretend at this time of day to have pretty illusions about the public, especially about publishers and editors. It's not for *such* animals

---

[3] "You'll have to throw them out" (French).

you work — it's for those you know, *coloro che sanno;*[4] so keep straight for *me* if you can't keep straight for yourself. There was a certain sort of thing you used to try for — and a very good thing it was. But this twaddle isn't *in* it." When I talked with Hawley later about "Rutland Ramsay" and its possible successors he declared that I must get back into my boat again or I should go to the bottom. His voice in short was the voice of warning.

I noted the warning, but I didn't turn my friends out of doors. They bored me a good deal; but the very fact that they bored me admonished me not to sacrifice them — if there was anything to be done with them — simply to irritation. As I look back at this phase they seem to me to have pervaded my life not a little. I have a vision of them as most of the time in my studio, seated against the wall on an old velvet bench to be out of the way, and resembling the while a pair of patient courtiers in a royal ante-chamber. I'm convinced that during the coldest weeks of the winter they held their ground because it saved them fire. Their newness was losing its gloss, and it was impossible not to feel them objects of charity. Whenever Miss Churm arrived they went away, and after I was fairly launched in "Rutland Ramsay" Miss Churm arrived pretty often. They managed to express to me tacitly that they supposed I wanted her for the low life of the book, and I let them suppose it, since they had attempted to study the work — it was lying about the studio — without discovering that it dealt only with the highest circles. They had dipped into the most brilliant of our novelists without deciphering many passages. I still took an hour from them, now and again, in spite of Jack Hawley's warning: it would be time enough to dismiss them, if dismissal should be necessary, when the rigor of the season was over. Hawley had made their acquaintance — he had met them at my fireside — and thought them a ridiculous pair. Learning that he was a painter they tried to approach him, to show him too that they were the real thing; but he looked at them, across the big room, as if they were miles away: they were a compendium of everything he most objected to in the social system of his country. Such people as that, all convention and patent-leather, with ejaculations that stopped conversation, had no business in a studio. A studio was a place to learn to see, and how could you see through a pair of feather-beds?

The main inconvenience I suffered at their hands was that at first I was shy of letting it break upon them that my artful little servant had begun to sit to me for "Rutland Ramsay." They knew I had been odd enough — they were prepared by this time to allow oddity to artists — to pick a foreign vagabond out of the streets when I might have had a person with whiskers and credentials; but it was some time before they learned how high I rated his accomplishments. They found him in an attitude more than once, but they never doubted I was doing him as an organ-grinder. There were several things they never guessed, and one of them was that for a

---

[4] "the ones who understand" (Italian).

striking scene in the novel, in which a footman briefly figured, it occurred to me to make use of Major Monarch as the menial. I kept putting this off, I didn't like to ask him to don the livery — besides the difficulty of finding a livery to fit him. At last, one day late in the winter, when I was at work on the despised Oronte, who caught one's idea on the wing, and was in the glow of feeling myself go very straight, they came in, the Major and his wife, with their society laugh about nothing (there was less and less to laugh at); came in like country-callers — they always reminded me of that — who have walked across the park after church and are presently persuaded to stay to luncheon. Luncheon was over, but they could stay to tea — I knew they wanted it. The fit was on me, however, and I couldn't let my ardor cool and my work wait, with the fading daylight, while my model prepared it. So I asked Mrs. Monarch if she would mind laying it out — a request which for an instant brought all the blood to her face. Her eyes were on her husband's for a second, and some mute telegraphy passed between them. Their folly was over the next instant; his cheerful shrewdness put an end to it. So far from pitying their wounded pride, I must add, I was moved to give it as complete a lesson as I could. They bustled about together and got out the cups and saucers and made the kettle boil. I know they felt as if they were waiting on my servant, and when the tea was prepared I said: "He'll have a cup, please — he's tired." Mrs. Monarch brought him one where he stood, and he took it from her as if he had been a gentleman at a party squeezing a crush-hat with an elbow.

Then it came over me that she had made a great effort for me — made it with a kind of nobleness — and that I owed her a compensation. Each time I saw her after this I wondered what the compensation could be. I couldn't go on doing the wrong thing to oblige them. Oh it *was* the wrong thing, the stamp of the work for which they sat — Hawley was not the only person to say it now. I sent in a large number of the drawings I had made for "Rutland Ramsay," and I received a warning that was more to the point than Hawley's. The artistic adviser of the house for which I was working was of opinion that many of my illustrations were not what had been looked for. Most of these illustrations were the subjects in which the Monarchs had figured. Without going into the question of what *had* been looked for, I had to face the fact that at this rate I shouldn't get the other books to do. I hurled myself in despair on Miss Churm — I put her through all her paces. I not only adopted Oronte publicly as my hero, but one morning when the Major looked in to see if I didn't require him to finish a *Cheapside* figure for which he had begun to sit the week before, I told him I had changed my mind — I'd do the drawing from my man. At this my visitor turned pale and stood looking at me. "Is *he* your idea of an English gentleman?" he asked.

I was disappointed, I was nervous, I wanted to get on with my work; so I replied with irritation: "Oh my dear Major — I can't be ruined for *you!*"

It was a horrid speech, but he stood another moment — after which, without a word, he quitted the studio. I drew a long breath, for I said to myself that I shouldn't see him again. I hadn't told him definitely that I was in danger of having my work rejected, but I was vexed at his not having felt the catastrophe in the air, read with me the moral of our fruitless collaboration, the lesson that in the deceptive atmosphere of art even the highest respectability may fail of being plastic.

I didn't owe my friends money, but I did see them again. They reappeared together three days later; and, given all the other facts, there was something tragic in that one. It was a clear proof they could find nothing else in life to do. They had threshed the matter out in a dismal conference — they had digested the bad news that they were not in for the series. If they weren't useful to me for the *Cheapside* their function seemed difficult to determine, and I could only judge at first that they had come, forgivingly, decorously, to take a last leave. This made me rejoice in secret that I had little leisure for a scene; for I had placed both my other models in position together and I was pegging away at a drawing from which I hoped to derive glory. It had been suggested by the passage in which Rutland Ramsay, drawing up a chair to Artemisia's piano-stool, says extraordinary things to her while she ostensibly fingers out a difficult piece of music. I had done Miss Churm at the piano before — it was an attitude in which she knew how to take on an absolutely poetic grace. I wished the two figures to "compose" together with intensity, and my little Italian had entered perfectly into my conception. The pair were vividly before me, the piano had been pulled out; it was a charming show of blended youth and murmured love, which I had only to catch and keep. My visitors stood and looked at it, and I was friendly to them over my shoulder.

They made no response, but I was used to silent company and went on with my work, only a little disconcerted — even though exhilarated by the sense that *this* was at least the ideal thing — at not having got rid of them after all. Presently I heard Mrs. Monarch's sweet voice beside or rather above me: "I wish her hair were a little better done." I looked up and she was staring with a strange fixedness at Miss Churm, whose back was turned to her. "Do you mind my just touching it?" she went on — a question which made me spring up for an instant as with the instinctive fear that she might do the young lady a harm. But she quieted me with a glance I shall never forget — I confess I should like to have been able to paint *that* — and went for a moment to my model. She spoke to her softly, laying a hand on her shoulder and bending over her; and as the girl, understanding, gratefully assented, she disposed her rough curls, with a few quick passes, in such a way as to make Miss Churm's head twice as charming. It was one of the most heroic personal services I've ever seen rendered. Then Mrs. Monarch turned away with a low sigh and, looking about her as if for something to do, stooped to the floor with a noble humility and picked up a dirty rag that had dropped out of my paint-box.

The Major meanwhile had also been looking for something to do, and, wandering to the other end of the studio, saw before him my breakfast-things neglected, unremoved. "I say, can't I be useful *here?*" he called out to me with an irrepressible quaver. I assented with a laugh that I fear was awkward, and for the next ten minutes, while I worked, I heard the light clatter of china and the tinkle of spoons and glass. Mrs. Monarch assisted her husband — they washed up my crockery, they put it away. They wandered off into my little scullery, and I afterwards found that they had cleaned my knives and that my slender stock of plate had an unprecedented surface. When it came over me, the latent eloquence of what they were doing, I confess that my drawing was blurred for a moment — the picture swam. They had accepted their failure, but they couldn't accept their fate. They had bowed their heads in bewilderment to the perverse and cruel law in virtue of which the real thing could be so much less precious than the unreal; but they didn't want to starve. If my servants were my models, then my models might be my servants. They would reverse the parts — the others would sit for the ladies and gentlemen and *they* would do the work. They would still be in the studio — it was an intense dumb appeal to me not to turn them out. "Take us on," they wanted to say — "we'll do *anything.*"

My pencil dropped from my hand; my sitting was spoiled and I got rid of my sitters, who were also evidently rather mystified and awestruck. Then, alone with the Major and his wife I had a most uncomfortable moment. He put their prayer into a single sentence: "I say, you know — just let *us* do for you, can't you?" I couldn't — it was dreadful to see them emptying my slops; but I pretended I could, to oblige them, for about a week. Then I gave them a sum of money to go away, and I never saw them again. I obtained the remaining books, but my friend Hawley repeats that Major and Mrs. Monarch did me a permanent harm, got me into false ways. If it be true I'm content to have paid the price — for the memory.

[1891]

SARAH ORNE JEWETT (1849–1909) *was born in South Berwick, Maine. Her father was a country doctor, and she often accompanied him on his horse-and-buggy rounds among sick people on the local farms. She later said that she got her real education from these trips, rather than from her classes at Miss Rayne's School and the Berwick Academy. She had a fine ear for local speech and the native idiom, which she used to good effect in her stories. Impressed as a girl by the sympathetic depiction of* local color *(the people and life of a particular geographical setting) in the fiction of Harriet Beecher Stowe, she began to write stories herself, publishing her earliest one, "Jenny Garrow's Lovers," in a Boston weekly when she was eighteen years old. Shortly after her twentieth birthday her work was accepted by the prestigious* Atlantic Monthly, *and her career was launched. Jewett published her first collection of stories,* Deephaven, *in 1877. She read Gustave Flaubert, Émile Zola, Leo Tolstoy, and Henry James, and her style gradually matured, as is evident in the stories that make up the 1886 volume,* The White Heron and Other Stories. *Her masterpiece,* The Country of the Pointed Firs *(1896), is a book of short sketches linked by the narrator's account of her stay in a Maine seacoast village and her growing involvement in the quiet lives of the people there.*

Many stories were written about New England in Jewett's time, but hers have a unique quality, stemming from her deep sympathy not just for the landscape but for the native characters. She was able to suggest a mysterious depth in her characters, and she insisted that the personal point of view is essential to writers of fiction. Once she laughingly told the younger writer Willa Cather that her head was full of dear old houses and dear old women, and when an old house and an old woman came together in her brain with a click, she knew a story was under way.

While it is true that Jewett's realism heightens the attractive aspects of the rural New England character at the same time that it diminishes the harsher qualities, her literary technique is so candid and true to the larger aspects of human nature that the darker undercurrents of deprivation, both physical and psychological, are also evident beneath the surface of her descriptions. Henry James recognized that Jewett was "surpassed only by Hawthorne as producer of the most finished and penetrating of the numerous 'short stories' that have the domestic life of New England for their general and their doubtless somewhat lean subject." In her time she was lauded for possessing an exquisitely simple, natural, and graceful style. More recently, readers have responded to the serenity and honesty in stories like "The White Heron," with its hint of tragedy in the young girl's conflict between her admiration for the ornithologist and her love for the wild bird.

Sarah Orne Jewett

A White Heron

I

The woods were already filled with shadows one June evening, just before eight o'clock, though a bright sunset still glimmered faintly among the trunks of the trees. A little girl was driving home her cow, a plodding, dilatory, provoking creature in her behavior, but a valued companion for all that. They were going away from the western light, and striking deep into the dark woods, but their feet were familiar with the path, and it was no matter whether their eyes could see it or not.

There was hardly a night the summer through when the old cow could be found waiting at the pasture bars; on the contrary, it was her greatest pleasure to hide herself away among the high huckleberry bushes, and though she wore a loud bell she had made the discovery that if one stood perfectly still it would not ring. So Sylvia had to hunt for her until she found her, and call Co'! Co'! with never an answering Moo, until her childish patience was quite spent. If the creature had not given good milk and plenty of it, the case would have seemed very different to her owners. Besides, Sylvia had all the time there was, and very little use to make of it. Sometimes in pleasant weather it was a consolation to look upon the cow's pranks as an intelligent attempt to play hide and seek, and as the child had no playmates she lent herself to this amusement with a good deal of zest. Though this chase had been so long that the wary animal herself had given an unusual signal of her whereabouts, Sylvia had only laughed when she came upon Mistress Moolly at the swamp-side, and urged her affectionately homeward with a twig of birch leaves. The old cow was not inclined to wander farther, she even turned in the right direction for once as they left the pasture, and stepped along the road at a good pace. She was quite ready to be milked now, and seldom stopped to browse. Sylvia wondered what her grandmother would say because they were so late. It was a great while since she had left home at half past five o'clock, but everybody knew the difficulty of making this errand a short one. Mrs. Tilley had chased the horned torment too many summer evenings herself to blame any one else for lingering, and was only thankful as she waited that she had Sylvia, nowadays,

to give such valuable assistance. The good woman suspected that Sylvia loi-
tered occasionally on her own account; there never was such a child for
straying about out-of-doors since the world was made! Everybody said that
it was a good change for a little maid who had tried to grow for eight years
in a crowded manufacturing town, but, as for Sylvia herself, it seemed as if
she never had been alive at all before she came to live at the farm. She
thought often with wistful compassion of a wretched dry geranium that belonged to a town neighbor.

" 'Afraid of folks,' " old Mrs. Tilley said to herself, with a smile, after
she had made the unlikely choice of Sylvia from her daughter's houseful of
children, and was returning to the farm. " 'Afraid of folks,' they said! I
guess she won't be troubled no great with 'em up to the old place!" When
they reached the door of the lonely house and stopped to unlock it, and the
cat came to purr loudly, and rub against them, a deserted pussy, indeed, but
fat with young robins, Sylvia whispered that this was a beautiful place to
live in, and she never should wish to go home.

The companions followed the shady wood-road, the cow taking slow
steps, and the child very fast ones. The cow stopped long at the brook to
drink, as if the pasture were not half a swamp, and Sylvia stood still and
waited, letting her bare feet cool themselves in the shoal water, while the
great twilight moths struck softly against her. She waded on through the
brook as the cow moved away, and listened to the thrushes with a heart that
beat fast with pleasure. There was a stirring in the great boughs overhead.
They were full of little birds and beasts that seemed to be wide-awake, and
going about their world, or else saying good-night to each other in sleepy
twitters. Sylvia herself felt sleepy as she walked along. However, it was not
much farther to the house, and the air was soft and sweet. She was not
often in the woods so late as this, and it made her feel as if she were a part
of the gray shadows and the moving leaves. She was just thinking how long
it seemed since she first came to the farm a year ago, and wondering if
everything went on in the noisy town just the same as when she was there;
the thought of the great red-faced boy who used to chase and frighten her
made her hurry along the path to escape from the shadow of the trees.

Suddenly this little woods-girl is horror-stricken to hear a clear whistle
not very far away. Not a bird's whistle, which would have a sort of friendli-
ness, but a boy's whistle, determined, and somewhat aggressive. Sylvia left
the cow to whatever sad fate might await her, and stepped discreetly aside
into the bushes, but she was just too late. The enemy had discovered her,
and called out in a very cheerful and persuasive tone, "Halloa, little girl,
how far is it to the road?" and trembling Sylvia answered almost inaudibly,
"A good ways."

She did not dare to look boldly at the tall young man, who carried a
gun over his shoulder, but she came out of her bush and again followed the
cow, while he walked alongside.

"I have been hunting for some birds," the stranger said kindly, "and I have lost my way, and need a friend very much. Don't be afraid," he added gallantly. "Speak up and tell me what your name is, and whether you think I can spend the night at your house, and go out gunning early in the morning."

Sylvia was more alarmed than before. Would not her grandmother consider her much to blame? But who could have foreseen such an accident as this? It did not appear to be her fault, and she hung her head as if the stem of it were broken, but managed to answer, "Sylvy," with much effort when her companion again asked her name.

Mrs. Tilley was standing in the doorway when the trio came into view. The cow gave a loud moo by way of explanation.

"Yes, you'd better speak up for yourself, you old trial! Where'd she tucked herself away this time, Sylvy?" Sylvia kept an awed silence; she knew by instinct that her grandmother did not comprehend the gravity of the situation. She must be mistaking the stranger for one of the farmer-lads of the region.

The young man stood his gun beside the door, and dropped a heavy game-bag beside it; then he bade Mrs. Tilley good-evening, and repeated his wayfarer's story, and asked if he could have a night's lodging.

"Put me anywhere you like," he said. "I must be off early in the morning, before day; but I am very hungry, indeed. You can give me some milk at any rate, that's plain."

"Dear sakes, yes," responded the hostess, whose long slumbering hospitality seemed to be easily awakened. "You might fare better if you went out on the main road a mile or so, but you're welcome to what we've got. I'll milk right off, and you make yourself at home. You can sleep on husks or feathers," she proffered graciously. "I raised them all myself. There's good pasturing for geese just below here towards the ma'sh. Now step round and set a plate for the gentleman, Sylvy!" And Sylvia promptly stepped. She was glad to have something to do, and she was hungry herself.

It was a surprise to find so clean and comfortable a little dwelling in this New England wilderness. The young man had known the horrors of its most primitive housekeeping, and the dreary squalor of that level of society which does not rebel at the companionship of hens. This was the best thrift of an old-fashioned farmstead, though on such a small scale that it seemed like a hermitage. He listened eagerly to the old woman's quaint talk, he watched Sylvia's pale face and shining gray eyes with ever growing enthusiasm, and insisted that this was the best supper he had eaten for a month; then, afterward, the new-made friends sat down in the doorway together while the moon came up.

Soon it would be berry-time, and Sylvia was a great help at picking. The cow was a good milker, though a plaguy thing to keep track of, the hostess gossiped frankly, adding presently that she had buried four children, so that Sylvia's mother, and a son (who might be dead) in California were all the children she had left. "Dan, my boy, was a great hand to go gunning," she explained sadly. "I never wanted for pa'tridges or gray squer'ls while he was to home. He's been a great wand'rer, I expect, and he's no hand to write letters. There, I don't blame him, I'd ha' seen the world myself if it had been so I could.

"Sylvia takes after him," the grandmother continued affectionately, after a minute's pause. "There ain't a foot o' ground she don't know her way over, and the wild creatur's counts her one o' themselves. Squer'ls she'll tame to come an' feed right out o' her hands, and all sorts o' birds. Last winter she got the jay-birds to bangeing here, and I believe she'd 'a' scanted herself of her own meals to have plenty to throw out amongst 'em, if I hadn't kep' watch. Anything but crows, I tell her, I'm willin' to help support, — though Dan he went an' tamed one o' them that did seem to have reason same as folks. It was round here a good spell after he went away. Dan an' his father they didn't hitch, — but he never held up his head ag'in after Dan had dared him an' gone off."

The guest did not notice this hint of family sorrows in his eager interest in something else.

"So Sylvy knows all about birds, does she?" he exclaimed, as he looked round at the little girl who sat, very demure but increasingly sleepy, in the moonlight. "I am making a collection of birds myself. I have been at it ever since I was a boy." (Mrs. Tilley smiled.) "There are two or three very rare ones I have been hunting for these five years. I mean to get them on my own ground if they can be found."

"Do you cage 'em up?" asked Mrs. Tilley doubtfully, in response to this enthusiastic announcement.

"Oh, no, they're stuffed and preserved, dozens and dozens of them," said the ornithologist, "and I have shot or snared every one myself. I caught a glimpse of a white heron three miles from here on Saturday, and I have followed it in this direction. They have never been found in this district at all. The little white heron, it is," and he turned again to look at Sylvia with the hope of discovering that the rare bird was one of her acquaintances.

But Sylvia was watching a hop-toad in the narrow footpath.

"You would know the heron if you saw it," the stranger continued eagerly. "A queer tall white bird with soft feathers and long thin legs. And it would have a nest perhaps in the top of a high tree, made of sticks, something like a hawk's nest."

Sylvia's heart gave a wild beat; she knew that strange white bird, and had once stolen softly near where it stood in some bright green swamp grass, away over at the other side of the woods. There was an open place where the sunshine always seemed strangely yellow and hot, where tall, nodding rushes grew, and her grandmother had warned her that she might sink in the soft black mud underneath and never be heard of more. Not far beyond were the salt marshes and beyond those was the sea, the sea which

Sylvia wondered and dreamed about, but never had looked upon, though its great voice could often be heard above the noise of the woods on stormy nights.

"I can't think of anything I should like so much as to find that heron's nest," the handsome stranger was saying. "I would give ten dollars to anybody who could show it to me," he added desperately, "and I mean to spend my whole vacation hunting for it if need be. Perhaps it was only migrating, or had been chased out of its own region by some bird of prey."

Mrs. Tilley gave amazed attention to all this, but Sylvia still watched the toad, not divining, as she might have done at some calmer time, that the creature wished to get to its hole under the doorstep, and was much hindered by the unusual spectators at that hour of the evening. No amount of thought, that night, could decide how many wished-for treasures the ten dollars, so lightly spoken of, would buy.

The next day the young sportsman hovered about the woods, and Sylvia kept him company, having lost her first fear of the friendly lad, who proved to be most kind and sympathetic. He told her many things about the birds and what they knew and where they lived and what they did with themselves. And he gave her a jack-knife, which she thought as great a treasure as if she were a desert-islander. All day long he did not once make her troubled or afraid except when he brought down some unsuspecting singing creature from its bough. Sylvia would have liked him vastly better without his gun; she could not understand why he killed the very birds he seemed to like so much. But as the day waned, Sylvia still watched the young man with loving admiration. She had never seen anybody so charming and delightful; the woman's heart, asleep in the child, was vaguely thrilled by a dream of love. Some premonition of that great power stirred and swayed these young foresters who traversed the solemn woodlands with soft-footed silent care. They stopped to listen to a bird's song; they pressed forward again eagerly, parting the branches — speaking to each other rarely and in whispers; the young man going first and Sylvia following, fascinated, a few steps behind, with her gray eyes dark with excitement.

She grieved because the longed-for white heron was elusive, but she did not lead the guest, she only followed, and there was no such thing as speaking first. The sound of her own unquestioned voice would have terrified her — it was hard enough to answer yes or no when there was need of that. At last evening began to fall, and they drove the cow home together, and Sylvia smiled with pleasure when they came to the place where she heard the whistle and was afraid only the night before.

II

Half a mile from home, at the farther edge of the woods, where the land was highest, a great pine-tree stood, the last of its generation. Whether it was left for a boundary mark, or for what reason, no one could say; the woodchoppers who had felled its mates were dead and gone long ago, and a whole forest of sturdy trees, pines and oaks and maples, had grown again. But the stately head of this old pine towered above them all and made a landmark for sea and shore miles and miles away. Sylvia knew it well. She had always believed that whoever climbed to the top of it could see the ocean; and the little girl had often laid her hand on the great rough trunk and looked up wistfully at those dark boughs that the wind always stirred, no matter how hot and still the air might be below. Now she thought of the tree with a new excitement, for why, if one climbed it at break of day, could not one see all the world, and easily discover whence the white heron flew, and mark the place, and find the hidden nest?

What a spirit of adventure, what wild ambition! What fancied triumph and delight and glory for the later morning when she could make known the secret! It was almost too real and too great for the childish heart to bear.

All night the door of the little house stood open, and the whippoorwills came and sang upon the very step. The young sportsman and his old hostess were sound asleep, but Sylvia's great design kept her broad awake and watching. She forgot to think of sleep. The short summer night seemed as long as the winter darkness, and at last when the whippoorwills ceased, and she was afraid the morning would after all come too soon, she stole out of the house and followed the pasture path through the woods, hastening toward the open ground beyond, listening with a sense of comfort and companionship to the drowsy twitter of a half-awakened bird, whose perch she had jarred in passing. Alas, if the great wave of human interest which flooded for the first time this dull little life should sweep away the satisfactions of an existence heart to heart with nature and the dumb life of the forest!

There was the huge tree asleep yet in the paling moonlight, and small and hopeful Sylvia began with utmost bravery to mount to the top of it, with tingling, eager blood coursing the channels of her whole frame, with her bare feet and fingers, that pinched and held like bird's claws to the monstrous ladder reaching up, up, almost to the sky itself. First she must mount the white oak tree that grew alongside, where she was almost lost among the dark branches and the green leaves heavy and wet with dew; a bird fluttered off its nest, and a red squirrel ran to and fro and scolded pettishly at the harmless housebreaker. Sylvia felt her way easily. She had often climbed there, and knew that higher still one of the oak's upper branches chafed against the pine trunk, just where its lower boughs were set close together. There, when she made the dangerous pass from one tree to the other, the great enterprise would really begin.

She crept out along the swaying oak limb at last, and took the daring step across into the old pine-tree. The way was harder than she thought; she must reach far and hold fast, the sharp dry twigs caught and held her and scratched her like angry talons, the pitch made her thin little fingers clumsy and stiff as she went round and round the tree's great stem, higher and higher upward. The sparrows and robins in the woods below were beginning to wake and twitter to the dawn, yet it seemed much lighter there aloft in the pine-tree, and the child knew that she must hurry if her project were to be of any use.

The tree seemed to lengthen itself out as she went up, and to reach farther and farther upward. It was like a great main-mast to the voyaging earth; it must truly have been amazed that morning through all its ponderous frame as it felt this determined spark of human spirit creeping and climbing from higher branch to branch. Who knows how steadily the least twigs held themselves to advantage this light, weak creature on her way! The old pine must have loved his new dependent. More than all the hawks, and bats, and moths, and even the sweet-voiced thrushes, was the brave, beating heart of the solitary gray-eyed child. And the tree stood still and held away the winds that June morning while the dawn grew bright in the east.

Sylvia's face was like a pale star, if one had seen it from the ground, when the last thorny bough was past, and she stood trembling and tired but wholly triumphant, high in the tree-top. Yes, there was the sea with the dawning sun making a golden dazzle over it, and toward that glorious east flew two hawks with slow-moving pinions. How low they looked in the air from that height when before one had only seen them far up, and dark against the blue sky. Their gray feathers were as soft as moths; they seemed only a little way from the tree, and Sylvia felt as if she too could go flying away among the clouds. Westward, the woodlands and farms reached miles and miles into the distance; here and there were church steeples, and white villages; truly it was a vast and awesome world.

The birds sang louder and louder. At last the sun came up bewilderingly bright. Sylvia could see the white sails of ships out at sea, and the clouds that were purple and rose-colored and yellow at first began to fade away. Where was the white heron's nest in the sea of green branches, and was this wonderful sight and pageant of the world the only reward for having climbed to such a giddy height? Now look down again, Sylvia, where the green marsh is set among the shining birches and dark hemlocks; there where you saw the white heron once you will see him again; look, look! a white spot of him like a single floating feather comes up from the dead hemlock and grows larger, and rises, and comes close at last, and goes by the landmark pine with steady sweep of wing and outstretched slender neck and crested head. And wait! wait! do not move a foot or a finger, little girl, do not send an arrow of light and consciousness from your two eager eyes, for the heron has perched on a pine bough not far beyond yours, and cries back to his mate on the nest, and plumes his feathers for the new day!

The child gives a long sigh a minute later when a company of shouting cat-birds comes also to the tree, and vexed by their fluttering and lawless-ness the solemn heron goes away. She knows his secret now, the wild, light, slender bird that floats and wavers, and goes back like an arrow presently to his home in the green world beneath. Then Sylvia, well satisfied, makes her perilous way down again, not daring to look far below the branch she stands on, ready to cry sometimes because her fingers ache and her lamed feet slip. Wondering over and over again what the stranger would say to her, and what he would think when she told him how to find his way straight to the heron's nest.

"Sylvy, Sylvy!" called the busy old grandmother again and again, but nobody answered, and the small husk bed was empty, and Sylvia had disappeared.

The guest waked from a dream, and remembering his day's pleasure hurried to dress himself that it might sooner begin. He was sure from the way the shy little girl looked once or twice yesterday that she had at least seen the white heron, and now she must really be persuaded to tell. Here she comes now, paler than ever, and her worn old frock is torn and tattered, and smeared with pine pitch. The grandmother and the sportsman stand in the door together and question her, and the splendid moment has come to speak of the dead hemlock-tree by the green marsh.

But Sylvia does not speak after all, though the old grandmother fretfully rebukes her, and the young man's kind appealing eyes are looking straight in her own. He can make them rich with money; he has promised it, and they are poor now. He is so well worth making happy, and he waits to hear the story she can tell.

No, she must keep silence! What is it that suddenly forbids her and makes her dumb? Has she been nine years growing, and now, when the great world for the first time puts out a hand to her, must she thrust it aside for a bird's sake? The murmur of the pine's green branches is in her ears, she remembers how the white heron came flying through the golden air and how they watched the sea and the morning together, and Sylvia cannot speak; she cannot tell the heron's secret and give its life away.

Dear loyalty, that suffered a sharp pang as the guest went away disappointed later in the day, that could have served and followed him and loved him as a dog loves! Many a night Sylvia heard the echo of his whistle haunting the pasture path as she came home with the loitering cow. She forgot even her sorrow at the sharp report of his gun and the piteous sight of thrushes and sparrows dropping silent to the ground, their songs hushed and their pretty feathers stained and wet with blood. Were the birds better friends than their hunter might have been, — who can tell? Whatever treasures were lost to her, woodlands and summer-time, remember! Bring your gifts and graces and tell your secrets to this lonely country child!

[1886]

GUY DE MAUPASSANT (1850–1893) *was born in Normandy, the son of a wealthy stockbroker. Rebellious in school, he learned to accept army discipline during the Franco-Prussian War of 1870–1871. Then for seven years he apprenticed himself to Gustave Flaubert, a distant relative, who attempted to teach his young disciple how to write. Maupassant remembered, "I wrote verses, short stories, longer stories, even a wretched play. Nothing survived. The master read everything. Then, the following Sunday at lunch, he developed his criticisms." Flaubert taught Maupassant that talent "is nothing other than a long patience. Work."*

The essence of Flaubert's now famous teaching was exactness of observation. The writer must look at everything to find some aspect of the object that no one has yet seen or expressed. As Maupassant wrote in his preface to Pierre and Jean *in 1888, "Everything contains some element of the unexplored because we are accustomed to use our eyes only with the memory of what other people before us have thought about the object we are looking at. The least thing has a bit of the unknown about it. Let us find this. In order to describe a fire burning or a tree in a field, let us stand in front of that fire and that tree until they no longer look to us like any other fire or any other tree." Flaubert taught Maupassant that "when you pass a grocer sitting at his door, or a concierge smoking his pipe, or a cab-stand, you must show me that grocer and that concierge, their attitude, their whole physical appearance, including as well — indicated by the aptness of your image — their entire moral nature, in such a way that I shan't confuse them with any other grocer or any other concierge, and you must make me see, with a single word, in what way one cab-horse is totally unlike fifty others that go before and after it."*

In 1880 Maupassant's career was launched with the publication of a single story, "Boule de Suif" ("Ball of Fat"), an uncompromising picture of bourgeois hypocrisy. During the next decade, before his gradual incapacitation and death from syphilis, he published nearly three hundred stories. Characterized by a compact and dramatic narrative line, they are modern short stories, eliminating the long explanations and digressions used by many earlier writers. Along with his younger contemporary Anton Chekhov, Maupassant is responsible for technical advances that moved the short story toward austerity. They influenced nearly every writer of the short story who came after them. As Joseph Conrad wrote about "The String," "Facts, and again facts, are his [Maupassant's] unique concern. That is why he is not always properly understood." Maupassant's stories are like sections of life prepared for the microscope, and in looking at them we are led to believe that we have clearer eyes than usual. His lack of sentimentality toward his characters laid him open to charges of cynicism and hardness. In a story like "Miss Harriet," he presented the Englishwoman's sexual frustration honestly, without romanticizing her situation. Both Maupassant and Chekhov wrote with compassion about a wide spectrum of ordinary characters and everyday situations, shunning "fine" subjects. If Maupassant's stories display a greater distance from his characters and a less sympathetic irony than Chekhov's, both writers were the most accomplished of narrators, equal in their powers of exact observation and independent judgment, and in their supple, practiced knowledge of their craft. (See the Commentaries on pages 1235, 1238, and 1240.)

Guy de Maupassant

ᔕᙢ

THE STRING

– translated by Ernest Boyd

Along all the roads around Goderville the peasants and their wives were coming toward the little town, for it was market-day. The men walked with slow steps, their whole bodies bent forward at each movement of their long twisted legs, deformed by their hard work, by the weight on the plough which, at the same time, raises the left shoulder and distorts the figure, by the reaping of the wheat which forces the knees apart to get a firm stand, by all the slow and painful labors of the country. Their blouses, blue, starched, shining as if varnished, ornamented with a little design in white at the neck and wrists, puffed about their bony bodies, seemed like balloons ready to carry them off. From each of them a head, two arms, and two feet protruded.

Some led a cow or a calf at the end of a rope, and their wives, walking behind the animal, whipped its haunches with a leafy branch to hasten its progress. They carried on their arms large wicker-baskets, out of which a chicken here, a duck there, thrust out its head. And they walked with a quicker, livelier step than their husbands. Their spare, straight figures were wrapped in a scanty little shawl, pinned over their flat bosoms, and their heads were enveloped in a piece of white linen tightly pressed on the hair and surmounted by a cap.

Then a wagon passed, its nag's jerky trot shaking up and down two men seated side by side and a woman in the bottom of the vehicle, the latter holding on to the sides to lessen the hard jolts.

In the square of Goderville there was a crowd, a throng of human beings and animals mixed together. The horns of the cattle, the rough-napped top-hats of the rich peasants, and the head-gear of the peasant women rose above the surface of the crowd. And the clamorous, shrill, screaming voices made a continuous and savage din which sometimes was dominated by the robust lungs of some countryman's laugh, of the long lowing of a cow tied to the wall of a house.

It all smacked of the stable, the dairy, and the dung-heap, of hay and sweat, giving forth that sharp, unpleasant odor, human and animal, peculiar to the people of the fields.

Maître Hauchecorne, of Bréauté, had just arrived at Goderville, and was directing his steps toward the square, when he perceived upon the ground a little piece of string. Maître Hauchecorne, economical like a true Norman, thought that everything useful ought to be picked up, and he stooped painfully, for he suffered from rheumatism. He took the bit of thin cord from the ground and was beginning to roll it carefully when he noticed Maître Malandain, the harness-maker, on the threshold of his door, looking at him. They had once had a quarrel together on the subject of a halter, and they had remained on bad terms, being both good haters. Maître Hauche-corne was seized with a sort of shame to be seen thus by his enemy, picking a bit of string out of the dirt. He concealed his find quickly under his blouse, then in his trousers pocket; then he pretended to be still looking on the ground for something which he did not find, and he went towards the market, his head thrust forward, bent double by his pains.

He was soon lost in the noisy and slowly moving crowd, which was busy with interminable bargainings. The peasants looked at cows, went away, came back, perplexed, always in fear of being cheated, not daring to decide, watching the vendor's eye, ever trying to find the trick in the man and the flaw in the beast.

The women, having placed their great baskets at their feet, had taken out the poultry, which lay upon the ground, tied together by the feet, with terrified eyes and scarlet crests.

They heard offers, stated their prices with a dry air and impassive face, or perhaps, suddenly deciding on some proposed reduction, shouted to the customer who was slowly going away: "All right, Maître Anthime, I'll give it to you for that."

Then little by little the square was deserted, the Angelus rang for noon, and those who lived too far away went to the different inns.

At Jourdain's the great room was full of people eating, as the big yard was full of vehicles of all kinds, carts, gigs, wagons, nondescript carts, yellow with dirt, mended and patched, raising their shafts to the sky like two arms, or perhaps with their shafts on the ground and their backs in the air.

Right against the diners seated at the table, the immense fireplace, filled with bright flames, cast a lively heat on the backs of the row on the right. Three spits were turning on which were chickens, pigeons, and legs of mutton; and an appetizing odor of roast meat and gravy dripping over the nicely browned skin rose from the hearth, lightened hearts, and made mouths water.

All the aristocracy of the plough ate there, at Maître Jourdain's, tavern keeper and horse dealer, a clever fellow who had money.

The dishes were passed and emptied, as were the jugs of yellow cider. Everyone told his affairs, his purchases, and sales. They discussed the crops. The weather was favorable for the greens but rather damp for the wheat.

Suddenly the drum began to beat in the yard, before the house. Everybody rose, except a few indifferent persons, and ran to the door, or to the windows, their mouths still full, their napkins in their hands.

After the public crier had stopped beating his drum, he called out in a jerky voice, speaking his phrases irregularly:

"It is hereby made known to the inhabitants of Goderville, and in general to all persons present at the market, that there was lost this morning, on the road to Benzeville, between nine and ten o'clock, a black leather pocket-book containing five hundred francs and some business papers. The finder is requested to return same to the Mayor's office or to Maître Fortuné Houlbrèque of Manneville. There will be twenty francs reward."

Then the man went away. The heavy roll of the drum and the crier's voice were again heard at a distance.

Then they began to talk of this event discussing the chances that Maître Houlbrèque had of finding or not finding his pocket-book.

And the meal concluded. They were finishing their coffee when the chief of the gendarmes appeared upon the threshold.

He inquired:

"Is Maître Hauchecorne, of Bréauté, here?"

Maître Hauchecorne, seated at the other end of the table, replied: "Here I am."

And the officer resumed:

"Maître Hauchecorne, will you have the goodness to accompany me to the Mayor's office? The Mayor would like to talk to you."

The peasant, surprised and disturbed, swallowed at a draught his tiny glass of brandy, rose, even more bent than in the morning, for the first steps after each rest were specially difficult, and set out, repeating: "Here I am, here I am."

The Mayor was awaiting him, seated in an armchair. He was the local lawyer, a stout, serious man, fond of pompous phrases.

"Maître Hauchecorne," said he, "you were seen this morning picking up, on the road to Benzeville, the pocket-book lost by Maître Houlbrèque, of Manneville."

The countryman looked at the Mayor in astonishment, already terrified by this suspicion resting on him without his knowing why.

"Me? Me? I picked up the pocket-book?"

"Yes, you, yourself."

"On my word of honor, I never heard of it."

"But you were seen."

"I was seen, me? Who says he saw me?"

"Monsieur Malandain, the harness-maker."

The old man remembered, understood, and flushed with anger.

"Ah, he saw me, the clodhopper, he saw me pick up this string, here, Mayor." And rummaging in his pocket he drew out the little piece of string.

But the Mayor, incredulous, shook his head.

"You will not make me believe, Maître Hauchecorne, that Monsieur Malandain, who is a man we can believe, mistook this cord for a pocketbook."

The peasant, furious, lifted his hand, spat at one side to attest his honor, repeating:

"It is nevertheless God's own truth, the sacred truth. I repeat it on my soul and my salvation."

The Mayor resumed:

"After picking up the object, you stood like a stilt, looking a long while in the mud to see if any piece of money had fallen out."

The old fellow choked with indignation and fear.

"How anyone can tell — how anyone can tell — such lies to take away an honest man's reputation! How can anyone —— "

There was no use in his protesting, nobody believed him. He was confronted with Monsieur Malandain, who repeated and maintained his affirmation. They abused each other for an hour. At his own request, Maître Hauchecorne was searched. Nothing was found on him.

Finally the Mayor, very much perplexed, discharged him with the warning that he would consult the Public Prosecutor and ask for further orders.

The news had spread. As he left the Mayor's office, the old man was surrounded and questioned with a serious or bantering curiosity, in which there was no indignation. He began to tell the story of the string. No one believed him. They laughed at him.

He went along, stopping his friends, beginning endlessly his statement and his protestations, showing his pockets turned inside out, to prove that he had nothing.

They said:

"Ah, you old devil!"

And he grew angry, becoming exasperated, hot, and distressed at not being believed, not knowing what to do and always repeating himself.

Night came. He had to leave. He started on his way with three neighbors to whom he pointed out the place where he had picked up the bit of string; and all along the road he spoke of his adventure.

In the evening he took a turn in the village of Bréauté, in order to tell it to everybody. He only met with incredulity.

It made him ill all night.

The next day about one o'clock in the afternoon, Marius Paumelle, a hired man in the employ of Maître Breton, husbandman at Ymauville, returned the pocket-book and its contents to Maître Houlbrèque of Manneville.

This man claimed to have found the object in the road; but not knowing how to read, he had carried it to the house and given it to his employer.

The news spread through the neighborhood. Maître Hauchecorne was informed of it. He immediately went the circuit and began to recount his story completed by the happy climax. He triumphed.

"What grieved me so much was not the thing itself, as the lying. There is nothing so shameful as to be placed under a cloud on account of a lie."

He talked of his adventure all day long, he told it on the highway to people who were passing by, in the inn to people who were drinking there, and to persons coming out of church the following Sunday. He stopped strangers to tell them about it. He was calm now, and yet something disturbed him without his knowing exactly what it was. People had the air of joking while they listened. They did not seem convinced. He seemed to feel that remarks were being made behind his back.

On Tuesday of the next week he went to the market at Goderville, urged solely by the necessity he felt of discussing the case.

Malandain, standing at his door, began to laugh on seeing him pass. Why?

He approached a farmer from Criquetot, who did not let him finish, and giving him a thump in the stomach said to his face:

"You clever rogue."

Then he turned his back on him.

Maître Hauchecorne was confused, why was he called a clever rogue?

When he was seated at the table, in Jourdain's tavern he commenced to explain "the affair."

A horse dealer from Monvilliers called to him:

"Come, come, old sharper, that's an old trick; I know all about your piece of string!"

Hauchecorne stammered:

"But the pocket-book was found."

But the other man replied:

"Shut up, papa, there is one that finds, and there is one that brings back. No one is any the wiser, so you get out of it."

The peasant stood choking. He understood. They accused him of having had the pocket-book returned by a confederate, by an accomplice.

He tried to protest. All the table began to laugh.

He could not finish his dinner and went away, in the midst of jeers.

He went home ashamed and indignant, choking with anger and confusion, the more dejected that he was capable with his Norman cunning of doing what they had accused him of, and even of boasting of it as a good trick. His innocence seemed to him, in a confused way, impossible to prove, as his sharpness was known. And he was stricken to the heart by the injustice of the suspicion.

Then he began to recount the adventure again, enlarging his story every day, adding each time new reasons, more energetic protestations, more solemn oaths which he imagined and prepared in his hours of solitude, his whole mind given up to the story of the string. He was believed so much the less as his defense was more complicated and his arguing more subtle.

"Those are lying excuses," they said behind his back.

He felt it, consumed his heart over it, and wore himself out with useless efforts. He was visibly wasting away.

The wags now made him tell about the string to amuse them, as they make a soldier who has been on a campaign tell about his battles. His mind, seriously affected, began to weaken.

Towards the end of December he took to his bed.

He died in the first days of January, and in the delirium of his death struggles he kept claiming his innocence, reiterating:

"A piece of string, a piece of string — look — here it is."

[1884]

Guy de Maupassant

ຉຉ

Miss Harriet

– translated by Ernest Boyd

There were seven of us in the drag, four women, and three men, one of whom was on the box-seat beside the coachman. We were following, at a walking pace, the winding coast road up the hill.

Having set out from Étretat at daybreak to visit the ruins of Tancarville, we were still half asleep, benumbed by the fresh air of the morning. The women, especially, who were little accustomed to early rising, let their eyelids fall every moment, nodding their heads or yawning, quite insensible to the glory of the dawn.

It was autumn. On both sides of the road the bare fields stretched out, yellowed by the stubble of oats and wheat which covered the soil like a badly shaved beard. The misty earth looked as if it were steaming. Larks were singing in the air, while other birds piped in the bushes.

At length the sun rose in front of us, a bright red on the edge of the horizon; and as it ascended, growing clearer from minute to minute, the country seemed to awake, to smile, to stretch itself, to slip off its night-gown of white mist, like a young girl leaving her bed. The Comte d'Etraille, who was seated on the box, cried:

"Look! look! a hare!" and he stretched out his arm to the left, pointing to a patch of clover. The animal scurried along, almost concealed by the field, only its large ears visible. Then it swerved across a deep furrow, stopped, started off again at top speed, changed its course, stopped anew, uneasy, spying out every danger, and undecided as to the route it should take. Suddenly it began to run, with great bounds of its hind legs, disappearing finally in a large patch of beetroot. All the men had wakened up to watch the animal's movements.

René Lemanoir then exclaimed:

"We are not at all gallant this morning," and looking at his neighbor, the little Baroness de Sérennes, who was struggling with drowsiness, he said to her in a subdued voice: "You are thinking of your husband, Baroness. Reassure yourself; he will not return before Saturday, so you still have four days."

She replied, with a sleepy smile:

"How silly you are." Then, shaking off her torpor, she added: "Now, let somebody say something that will make us all laugh. You, Monsieur Chenal, who have the reputation of having more successes than the Duc de Richelieu, tell us a love-story in which you have been involved, anything you like."

Léon Chenal, an old painter, who had once been very handsome, very strong, very proud of his physique, and very popular, took his long white beard in his hand and smiled; then, after a few moments' reflection, he became suddenly grave.

"Ladies, it will not be an amusing tale; for I am going to relate to you the most lamentable love-affair of my life, and I sincerely hope that none of my friends may ever inspire a similar passion."

I

"At that time I was twenty-five years old, and I was daubing along the coast of Normandy. I mean by 'daubing' wandering about, with a knapsack on one's back, from inn to inn, under the pretext of making studies and sketches from nature. I know nothing more enjoyable than that happy-go-lucky wandering life, in which you are perfectly free, without shackles of any kind, without a care, without a single preoccupation, without even a thought of tomorrow. You go in any direction you please, without any guide save your fancy, without any counsellor save what pleases your eyes. You pull up, because a running brook seduces you, or because you are attracted, in front of an inn, by the smell of fried potatoes. Sometimes it is the perfume of clematis which decides you in your choice, or the glance of the servant at an inn. Do not despise these rustic affections. These girls have souls as well as bodies, firm cheeks and fresh lips; their vigorous kisses are strong and fragrant, like wild fruits. Love is always worth while, come whence it may. A heart that beats when you make your appearance, an eye that weeps when you go away, these are things so rare, so sweet, so precious, that they must never be despised.

"I have had rendezvous in ditches full of primroses, behind the stable in which the cattle slept, and among the straw in garrets still warm from the heat of the day. I have memories of coarse grey linen on supple, strong bodies, and of hearty, fresh, free kisses, more delicate, in their sincere brutality, than the subtle joys accorded by charming and distinguished women.

"But what one chiefly loves in these pilgrimages of adventure is the country, the woods, the sunrises, the twilights, the light of the moon. For the painter these are honeymoon trips with Nature. You are alone with her in a long, quiet rendezvous. You go to bed in the fields amid marguerites and wild poppies, and, with eyes wide open, under the bright sunlight, you regard far away some little village, with pointed clock-tower which sounds the hour of noon.

"You sit down by the side of a spring which gushes out from the foot of an oak, amid a covering of tall, fragile weeds, glistening with life. You go down on your knees, bend forward, and drink the cold and pellucid water, wetting your moustache and nose; you drink it with a physical pleasure, as though you were kissing the spring, lip to lip. Sometimes, when you find a deep hole along the course of these tiny brooks, you plunge into it, quite naked, and on your skin, from head to foot, like an icy and delicious caress, you feel the swift and gentle quivering of the current.

"You are gay on the hills, melancholy on the shores of the lagoons, exalted when the sun is drowned in an ocean of blood-red clouds and wakes red reflections in the rivers. And at night, under the moon, as she passes across the roof of heaven, you think of things, singular things, which would never have occurred to your mind under the brilliant light of day.

"So, in wandering through this same country where we are this year, I came one day to the little village of Bénouville, on the rocky coast between Yport and Étretat. I came from Fécamp, following the cliff, the tall cliff, perpendicular as a wall, with its bastions of chalk falling sheer down into the sea. I had walked since morning on the close-clipped grass, as smooth and yielding as a carpet, which grows along the edge of the cliff, fanned by the salt breezes of the ocean. Singing lustily, I walked with long strides, looking sometimes at the slow, curving flight of a gull, with its sweep of white wings sailing over the blue heavens, sometimes at the green sea, or at the brown sails of a fishing bark. In short, I had passed a happy day, a day of liberty and freedom from care.

"I was told there was a little farmhouse where travellers were put up, a kind of inn kept by a peasant, which stood in a Normandy courtyard, surrounded by a double row of beeches.

"Leaving the cliff, I reached the hamlet, which was shut in by great trees, and I presented myself at the house of Mother Lecacheur.

"She was an old country woman, wrinkled and austere, who always seemed to receive customers reluctantly, with a kind of contempt.

"It was the month of May: the flowering apple-trees covered the court with a roof of perfumed flowers, with a whirling shower of pink blossoms which rained unceasingly upon the people and upon the grass.

"I said:

" 'Well, Madame Lecacheur, have you a room for me?'

"Astonished to find that I knew her name, she answered:

" 'That depends; everything is let; but all the same, there will be no harm in looking.'

"In five minutes we had come to an agreement, and I deposited my bag upon the earthen floor of a rustic room, furnished with a bed, two chairs, a table, and a wash-stand. The room opened into the large, smoky kitchen, where the lodgers took their meals with the people of the farm and with the woman herself, who was a widow.

"I washed my hands, after which I went out. The old woman was making a chicken fricassee for dinner in a large fireplace, in which hung the stew-pot, black with smoke.

" 'You have visitors, then, at the present time?' I said to her.

"She answered in an offended tone of voice:

" 'I have a lady, an English lady, of a certain age. She is occupying the other room.'

"For an extra five sous a day, I obtained the privilege of dining out in the court when the weather was fine.

"My place was accordingly set in front of the door, and I began to champ the lean limbs of the Normandy chicken, to drink the clear cider, and to munch the hunk of white bread, which, though four days old, was excellent.

"Suddenly the wooden gate which opened on to the highway was opened, and a strange person walked toward the house. She was very thin, very tall, enveloped in a Scotch shawl with red checks. You would have believed that she had no arms, if you had not seen a long hand appear just above the hips, holding a white tourist's umbrella. The face of a mummy, surrounded with sausage-rolls of plaited grey hair, which shook at every step she took, made me think, I know not why, of a pickled herring adorned with curling-papers. Lowering her eyes, she passed quickly in front of me, and entered the house.

"This singular apparition amused me. She undoubtedly was my neighbor, the 'English lady of a certain age' of whom our hostess had spoken.

"I did not see her again that day. The next day, when I had begun to paint at the end of the beautiful valley which you know, which extends as far as Étretat, lifting my eyes suddenly, I perceived something singularly attired standing on the crest of the declivity; it looked like a pole decked out with flags. It was she. On seeing me, she disappeared.

"I returned to the house at midday for lunch, and took my seat at the common table, so as to make the acquaintance of this eccentric old creature. But she did not respond to my polite advances, was insensible even to my little attentions. I perseveringly poured water out for her, I passed her the dishes with an air. A slight, almost imperceptible movement of the head, and an English word, murmured so low that I did not understand it, were her only acknowledgments.

"I ceased taking any notice of her, although she had disturbed my thoughts. At the end of three days, I knew as much about her as Madame Lecacheur did herself.

"She was called Miss Harriet. Seeking a secluded village in which to pass the summer, she had stopped at Bénouville, some six weeks before, and did not seem disposed to leave it. She never spoke at table, ate rapidly, reading all the while a small book of Protestant propaganda. She gave a copy of this book to everybody. The curé himself had received no less than four copies, at the hands of an urchin to whom she had paid two sous' commission. She said sometimes to our hostess, abruptly, without the slightest preliminary leading up to this declaration:

" 'I love the Savior above all; I worship Him in all creation; I adore Him in all nature; I carry Him always in my heart.'

"And she would immediately present the old woman with one of her brochures destined to convert the universe.

"In the village she was not liked. In fact, the schoolmaster had declared that she was an atheist, and a kind of stigma attached to her. The curé, who had been consulted by Madame Lecacheur, responded:

" 'She is a heretic, but God does not wish the death of the sinner, and I believe her to be a person of pure morals.'

"These words, 'atheist,' 'heretic,' words which no one could precisely define, threw doubts into some minds. It was asserted further, that this Englishwoman was rich, and that she had passed her life in travelling through every country in the world, because her family had thrown her off. Why had her family thrown her off? Because of her impiety, of course.

"She was, in reality, one of those people of exalted principles, one of those obstinate puritans of whom England produces so many, one of those good and insupportable old women who haunt the tables d'hôte of every hotel in Europe, who spoil Italy, poison Switzerland, render the charming cities of the Mediterranean uninhabitable, carry everywhere their fantastic manias, their petrified vestal morals, their indescribable toilettes, and a certain odor of india-rubber, which makes one believe that at night they slip themselves into a case of that material. When I met one of these people in a hotel, I used to flee like the birds when they see a scarecrow in a field.

"This woman, however, appeared so singular that she did not displease me.

"Madame Lecacheur, hostile by instinct to everything that was not peasant, felt in her narrow soul a kind of hatred for the ecstatic extravagances of the old maid. She had found a phrase by which to describe her, a phrase assuredly contemptuous, which had sprung to her lips I know not how, invented probably by some confused and mysterious travail of soul. She said: 'That woman is a demoniac.' This phrase, applied to the austere and sentimental creature, seemed to me irresistibly comic. I, myself, never called her now anything else but 'the demoniac,' feeling a singular pleasure in pronouncing this word aloud on seeing her.

"I would ask Mother Lecacheur: 'Well, what is our demoniac doing today?' To which the peasant would respond with a scandalized air:

" 'What do you think, sir? She picked up a toad with a crushed paw, carried it to her room, put it in her wash-stand, and dressed its wound as if it were a human. If that is not profanation, I should like to know what is!'

"On another occasion, when walking along the shore, she had bought a large fish which had just been caught, simply to throw it back into the sea again. The sailor, from whom she had bought it, though paid handsomely, was greatly provoked at this act — more exasperated, indeed, than if she had put her hand into his pocket and taken his money. For a whole month he could not speak of the circumstance without getting into a fury and denouncing it as an outrage. Oh yes! She was indeed a demoniac, this Miss Harriet, and Mother Lecacheur must have had an inspiration of genius in thus christening her.

"The stable-boy, who was called Sapeur, because he had served in Africa in his youth, entertained other opinions. He said, with a knowing air: 'She is an old hag who has had her day.' If the poor woman had but known.

"Céleste, the little servant, did not like waiting on her, but I was never able to understand why. Probably her only reason was that she was a stranger, of another race, of a different tongue, and of another religion. She was a demoniac, in brief!

"She passed her time wandering about the country, adoring and searching for God in nature. I found her one evening on her knees in a cluster of bushes. Having discovered something red through the leaves, I brushed aside the branches, and Miss Harriet at once rose to her feet, confused at having been found thus, looking at me with eyes as frightened as those of an owl surprised in open day.

"Sometimes, when I was working among the rocks, I would suddenly see her on the edge of the cliff, standing like a semaphore signal. She gazed passionately at the vast sea, glittering in the sunlight, and the boundless sky empurpled with fire. Sometimes I would distinguish her at the bottom of a valley, walking quickly, with her elastic English step; and I would go toward her, mysteriously attracted, simply to see her visionary expression, her dried-up, ineffable features, full of an inward and profound happiness.

"Often I would encounter her in the corner of a field sitting on the grass, under the shadow of an apple-tree, with her little Bible lying open on her knee, while she looked meditatively into the distance.

"I could no longer tear myself away from that quiet country neighborhood, bound to it as I was by a thousand links of love for its soft and sweeping landscapes. I was happy at this farm, which was out of the world, far removed from everything, but in close proximity to the soil, the good, healthy, beautiful green soil, which we ourselves shall fertilize with our bodies some day. And, I must confess, there was perhaps a certain amount of curiosity which kept me at Mother Lecacheur's. I wished to become acquainted a little with this strange Miss Harriet, and to learn what passes in the solitary souls of those wandering old English dames."

II

"We became acquainted in a rather singular manner. I had just finished a study which I thought good, and so it was. It was sold for ten thousand francs, fifteen years later. It was as simple as twice two make four, and had nothing to do with academic rules. The whole of the right side of my canvas represented a rock, an enormous jagged rock, covered with sea-wrack, brown, yellow, and red, across which the sun poured like a stream of oil. The light fell upon the stone, and gilded it as if with fire, but the sun itself was behind me and could not be seen. That was all. A foreground dazzling with light, blazing, superb.

"On the left was the sea, not the blue sea, the slate-colored sea, but a sea of jade, greenish, milky, and hard under the deep sky.

"I was so pleased with my work that I danced as I carried it back to the inn. I wished that the whole world could have seen it at one and the same moment. I can remember that I showed it to a cow which was browsing by the wayside, exclaiming, at the same time: 'Look at that, my old beauty; you will not often see its like again.'

"When I had reached the front of the house, I immediately called out to Mother Lecacheur, bawling with all my might:

"'Look at this! You won't see anything like it in a hurry.'

"The woman came and looked at my work with stupid eyes, which distinguished nothing, and did not even recognize whether the picture represented an ox or a house.

"Miss Harriet was coming into the house, and she passed behind me just at the moment when, holding out my canvas at arm's length, I was exhibiting it to the old innkeeper. The 'demoniac' could not help but see it, for I took care to exhibit the thing in such a way that it could not escape her notice. She stopped abruptly and stood motionless, stupefied. It was her rock which was depicted, the one which she usually climbed to dream away her time undisturbed.

"She uttered a British 'Oh,' which was at once so accentuated and so flattering, that I turned round to her, smiling, and said:

" 'This is my latest study, Mademoiselle.'

"She murmured ecstatically, comically, and tenderly:

" 'Oh! Monsieur, you understand nature in a most thrilling way!'

"I colored up, indeed I did, and was more excited by that compliment than if it had come from a queen. I was seduced, conquered, vanquished. I could have embraced her — upon my honor.

"I took my seat at the table beside her, as I had always done. For the first time, she spoke, following out her thought aloud:

" 'Oh! I love nature so much.'

"I offered her bread, water, wine. She now accepted these with a slight, dry smile. I then began to converse with her about the scenery.

"After the meal, we rose from the table together and walked leisurely across the court; then, attracted by the fiery glow which the setting sun cast over the surface of the sea, I opened the outside gate which faced in the direction of the cliff, and we walked on side by side, happy as two persons are who have just learned to understand and penetrate each other's motives and feelings.

"It was a misty, relaxing evening, one of those enjoyable evenings which impart happiness to mind and body alike. All is joy, all is charm. The luscious and balmy air, loaded with the perfume of grass, with the tang of seaweed, with the odor of the wild flowers, caresses the nostrils with its wild perfume, the palate with its salty savor, the soul with a penetrating sweetness. We were walking as on the brink of the abyss which overlooked the vast sea, which rolled its little waves a hundred yards below our feet.

"We drank, with open mouth and expanded chest, that fresh breeze from the ocean which glides slowly over the skin, salted by long contact with the waves.

"Wrapped in her plaid shawl, with a look of inspiration as she faced the breeze, the Englishwoman gazed fixedly at the great sun ball as it descended toward the horizon. Far off in the distance a three-master in full sail was outlined on the blood-red sky and a steamship, somewhat nearer, passed along, leaving behind it a trail of smoke on the horizon. The red sun-globe sank slowly lower and lower and presently touched the water just behind the motionless vessel, which, in its dazzling effulgence, looked as though framed in a flame of fire. We saw it plunge, grow smaller, and disappear, swallowed up by the ocean.

"Miss Harriet gazed in rapture at the last gleams of the dying day. She seemed longing passionately to embrace the sky, the sea, the whole landscape.

"She murmured: 'Ah! I love — I love ——— ' I saw a tear in her eye.

She went on: 'I wish I were a little bird, so that I could mount up into the firmament.'

"She remained standing as I had often before seen her, perched on the cliff, her face as red as her shawl. I should have liked to have sketched her in my album. It would have been a caricature of ecstasy.

"I turned away so as not to laugh.

"I then spoke to her of painting as I would have done to a fellow-artist, using the technical terms common among the devotees of the profession. She listened attentively, eagerly seeking to divine the meaning of the terms, so as to understand my thoughts. From time to time she would exclaim: 'Oh! I understand, I understand. It is very interesting.'

"We returned home.

"The next day, on seeing me, she approached me, cordially holding out her hand; and we at once became firm friends.

"She was a good creature who had a kind of soul on springs, which became enthusiastic at a bound. She lacked equilibrium, like all women who are spinsters at the age of fifty. She seemed to be preserved in vinegary innocence, but her heart still retained something of youth and of girlish effervescence. She loved both nature and animals with a fervent ardor, a love like old wine, mellow through age, a sensual love that she had never bestowed on men.

"One thing is certain: a bitch feeding her pups, a mare roaming in a meadow with a foal at its side, a bird's nest full of young ones, squeaking, with their open mouths and enormous heads, and no feathers, made her quiver with the most violent emotion.

"Poor solitary beings! Sad wanderers from table d'hôte to table d'hôte, poor beings, ridiculous and lamentable, I love you ever since I became acquainted with Miss Harriet!

"I soon discovered that she had something she would like to tell me, but dared not, and I was amused at her timidity. When I started out in the morning with my box on my back, she would accompany me to the end of the village, silent, but evidently struggling inwardly to find words with which to begin a conversation. Then she would leave me abruptly, and walk away quickly with her jaunty step.

"One day, however, she plucked up courage:

" 'I would like to see how you paint pictures. Will you show me? I have been very curious.'

"And she colored up as though she had given utterance to words of extreme audacity.

"I conducted her to the bottom of the Petit-Val, where I had commenced a large picture.

"She remained standing near me, following all my gestures with concentrated attention. Then, suddenly, fearing, perhaps, that she was disturbing me, she said to me: 'Thank you,' and walked away.

"But in a short time she became more familiar, and accompanied me every day, with visible pleasure. She carried her folding-stool under her arm, would not consent to my carrying it, and she sat by my side. She would remain there for hours immovable and mute, following with her eye the point of my brush in its every movement. When I would obtain, by a large splotch of color spread on with a knife, a striking and unexpected effect, she would, in spite of herself, give vent to a half-suppressed 'Oh!' of astonishment, of joy, of admiration. She had the most tender respect for my canvases, an almost religious respect for that human reproduction of a part of Nature's divine work. My studies appeared to her as a species of holy pictures, and sometimes she spoke to me of God, with the idea of converting me.

"Oh! He was a queer creature, this God of hers. He was a sort of village philosopher without any great resources, and without great power; for she always pictured him to herself as being in despair over injustices committed under his eyes, as if he were helpless to prevent them.

"She was, however, on excellent terms with him, affecting even to be the confidante of his secrets and of his whims. She said: 'God wills,' or 'God does not will,' just like a sergeant announcing to a recruit: 'The colonel has commanded.'

"At the bottom of her heart she deplored my ignorance of the intentions of the Eternal, which she strove to impart to me.

"Every day I found in my pockets, in my hat when I lifted it from the ground, in my box of colors, in my polished shoes, standing in the mornings in front of my door, those little pious brochures, which she, no doubt, received directly from Paradise.

"I treated her as one would an old friend, with unaffected cordiality. But I soon perceived that she had changed somewhat in her manner, though, for a while, I paid little attention to it.

"When I was painting, whether in my valley or in some country lane, I would see her suddenly appear with her rapid, springy walk. She would then sit down abruptly, out of breath, as though she had been running or were overcome by some profound emotion. Her face would be red, that English red which is denied to the people of all other countries; then, without any reason, she would turn ashy pale and seem about to faint away. Gradually, however, her natural color would return and she would begin to speak.

"Then, without warning, she would break off in the middle of a sentence, spring up from her seat and walk away so rapidly and so strangely that I was at my wits' ends to discover whether I had done or said anything to displease or wound her.

"I finally came to the conclusion that those were her normal manners, somewhat modified no doubt in my honor during the first days of our acquaintance.

"When she returned to the farm, after walking for hours on the windy coast, her long curls often hung straight down, as if their springs had been broken. This had hitherto seldom given her any concern, and she would come to dinner without embarrassment, all dishevelled by her sister, the breeze.

"But now she would go up to her room in order to adjust what I called her lamp-glasses. When I would say to her, with familiar gallantry, which, however, always offended her: 'You are as beautiful as a star today, Miss Harriet,' a little blood would immediately mount into her cheeks, the blood of a young maiden, the blood of sweet fifteen.

"Then she became very shy, and ceased coming to watch me paint. I thought:

" 'This is only a fit of temper. It will pass.'

"But it did not pass away. When I spoke to her now, she would answer me, either with an air of affected indifference, or in a sullen anger; and she became by turns rude, impatient, and nervous. I never saw her except at meals, and we spoke but little. I concluded, at length, that I must have offended her in something: and, accordingly, I said to her one evening:

" 'Miss Harriet, why have you changed towards me? What have I done to displease you? You are causing me much pain!'

"She responded in an angry tone, which was very funny: 'I have not changed towards you. It is not true, not true,' and she ran upstairs and shut herself up in her room.

"At times she would look upon me with strange eyes. Since that time I have often said to myself that those condemned to death must look thus when informed that their last day has come. In her eye there lurked a species of madness, an insanity at once mystical and violent — something more, a fever, an exasperated desire, impatient and impotent, for the unrealized and unrealizable!

"It seemed to me that there was also going on within her a combat, in which her heart struggled against an unknown force that she wished to overcome — perhaps, even, something else. But what could I know? What could I know?"

III

"It was indeed a singular revelation.

"For some time I had been working as soon as it got light on a picture the subject of which was as follows:

"A deep ravine, enclosed, surmounted by two thickets of rushes and trees, extended into the distance and was lost, submerged in that milky vapor, in that cloud-like cotton-down that sometimes floats over valleys at daybreak. And at the extreme end of that heavy, transparent fog one saw, or rather guessed, two human figures, a youth and a maiden, their arms interlaced, embracing, she with her head raised towards him, he bending over her, their lips joined.

"A first ray of the sun, glistening through the branches, pierced that fog of the dawn, illuminated it with a rosy reflection just behind the rustic lovers, framing their vague shadows in a silvery background. It was good; really good.

"I was working on the declivity which led to the valley of Étretat. On this particular morning I had, by chance, the sort of floating vapor which I needed.

"Suddenly something rose up in front of me like a phantom; it was Miss Harriet. On seeing me she was about to flee. But I called after her, saying: 'Come here, come here, Mademoiselle. I have a nice little picture for you.'

"She came forward, though with seeming reluctance. I handed her my sketch. She said nothing, but stood for a long time motionless, looking at it. Suddenly she burst into tears. She wept spasmodically, like men who have been struggling hard against shedding tears, but who can do so no longer, and abandon themselves to grief, resisting still. I got up, trembling, moved myself by the sight of a sorrow I did not understand, and I took her by the hand with a gesture of brusque affection, a real French impulse, in which action outruns thought.

"She let her hands rest in mine for a few seconds, and I felt them quiver, as if her whole nervous system were on the rack. Then she withdrew her hands abruptly, or, rather, tore them out of mine.

"I recognized that shiver as soon as I had felt it; I knew it perfectly. Ah! the love-thrill of a woman, whether she is fifteen or fifty years of age, whether she is of the people or in society, goes so straight to my heart that I never have any difficulty in understanding it!

"Her whole frail being trembled, vibrated, swooned. I knew it. She walked away before I had time to say a word, leaving me as surprised as if I had witnessed a miracle, and as troubled as if I had committed a crime.

"I did not go in to breakfast. I took a walk on the edge of the cliff, feeling that I could just as soon weep as laugh, looking on the adventure as both comic and deplorable, and my position as ridiculous, believing her unhappy enough to go mad.

"I asked myself what I ought to do. I decided that my only course was to leave the place, and at once made up my mind to do so.

"Somewhat sad and perplexed, I wandered about until dinner-time, and entered the farmhouse just when the soup had been served.

"I sat down at the table as usual. Miss Harriet was there, eating away solemnly, without speaking to anyone, without even lifting her eyes. Her manner and expression were the same as usual.

"I waited patiently till the meal had been finished, then, turning toward the landlady, I said: 'Well, Madame Lecacheur, it will not be long now before I shall have to take my leave of you.'

"The good woman, surprised and troubled, replied in her drawling voice: 'My dear sir, what's this? You are going to leave us after I have become so accustomed to you?'

"I glanced at Miss Harriet out of the corner of my eye. Her countenance did not change in the least. But Céleste, the little servant, looked up at me. She was a fat girl of about eighteen, rosy, fresh, as strong as a horse, and possessing the rare attribute of cleanliness. I had kissed her at odd times in out-of-the-way corners, after the manner of travellers — nothing more.

"The dinner being at length over, I went to smoke my pipe under the apple-trees, walking up and down from one end of the enclosure to the other. All the reflections which I had made during the day, the strange discovery of the morning, that passionate and grotesque attachment for me, the recollections which that revelation had suddenly called up, recollections at once charming and perplexing, perhaps also that look which the servant had cast on me at the announcement of my departure — all these things, mixed up and combined, put me now in a reckless humor, gave me a tickling sensation of kisses on the lips, and in my veins a something which urged me on to commit some folly.

"Night was coming on, casting its dark shadows under the trees, when I descried Céleste, who had gone to fasten up the poultry-yard at the other end of the enclosure. I darted towards her, running so noiselessly that she heard nothing, and as she got up from closing the small trap-door by which the chickens got in and out, I clasped her in my arms and rained on her coarse, fat face a shower of kisses. She struggled, laughing all the same, as she was accustomed to do in such circumstances. Why did I suddenly loose my grip of her? Why did I at once experience a shock? What was it that I heard behind me?

"It was Miss Harriet, who had come upon us, who had seen us and who stood in front of us motionless as a specter. Then she disappeared in the darkness.

"I was ashamed, embarrassed, more sorry at having been thus surprised by her than if she had caught me committing some criminal act.

"I slept badly that night. I was completely unnerved and haunted by sad thoughts. I seemed to hear loud weeping, but in this I was no doubt deceived. Moreover, I thought several times that I heard someone walking up and down in the house and opening the hall-door.

"Toward morning I was overcome by fatigue and fell asleep. I got up late and did not go downstairs until the late breakfast, being still in a bewildered state, not knowing what kind of expression to put on.

"No one had seen Miss Harriet. We waited for her at table, but she did not appear. At length, Mother Lecacheur went to her room. The Englishwoman had gone out. She must have set out at break of day, as she often did to see the sun rise.

"Nobody seemed surprised at this and we began to eat in silence.

"The weather was hot, very hot, one of those still, sultry days when not a leaf stirs. The table had been placed out of doors, under an apple-tree; and we drank so much that Sapeur had to go constantly to the cellar to replenish the cider-jug. Céleste brought the dishes from the kitchen, a ragout of mutton with potatoes, a cold rabbit, and a salad. Afterwards she placed before us a dish of cherries, the first of the season.

"As I wanted to wash and freshen these, I begged the servant to go and bring a pitcher of cold water.

"In about five minutes she returned, declaring that the well was dry. She had lowered the pitcher to the full extent of the cord, and had touched the bottom, but on drawing the pitcher up again, it was empty. Mother Lecacheur, anxious to examine the thing for herself, went and looked down the hole. She returned announcing that there must be something in the well, something altogether unusual. Doubtless a neighbor had thrown some bundles of straw down, out of spite.

"I wanted to look down the well, too, thinking I could better make out what it was. I leaned over the brink. I perceived, indistinctly, a white object. What could it be? I then conceived the idea of lowering a lantern at the end of a cord. The yellow flame danced on the stone walls, and gradually sank deeper. All four of us were leaning over the opening, Sapeur and Céleste having now joined us. The lantern rested on a black and white, indistinct mass, singular, incomprehensible. Sapeur exclaimed:

" 'It is a horse. I see the hoofs. It must have escaped from the meadow during the night, and fallen in.'

"But suddenly a cold shiver attacked my spine, I first recognized a foot, then a leg which protruded; the whole body and the other leg were submerged.

"I groaned and trembled so violently that the light of the lamp danced hither and thither over the object.

" 'It is a woman, who — who — is down there! It is Miss Harriet.'

"Sapeur alone did not flinch. He had witnessed worse things in Africa.

"Mother Lecacheur and Céleste began to scream piercingly, and ran away.

"But the corpse had to be recovered. I attached the boy securely by the loins, then I lowered him slowly, by means of the pulley, and watched him disappear in the darkness. In his hands he had a lantern, and another rope. Soon his voice, seeming to come from the center of the earth, cried:

" 'Stop.'

"I then saw him fish something out of the water. It was the other leg. He bound the two feet together and shouted anew:

" 'Haul up.'

"I commenced to wind him up, but I felt as if my arms were broken, my muscles relaxed, and I was in terror lest I should let the boy fall to the bottom. When his head appeared over the brink, I asked:

" 'Well,' as if I expected he had a message from the woman lying at the bottom.

"We both got on to the stone slab at the edge of the well, and, face to face, leaning over the aperture, hoisted the body.

"Mother Lecacheur and Céleste watched us from a distance, hidden behind the wall of the house. When they saw the black slippers and white stockings of the corpse emerge from the hole, they disappeared.

"Sapeur seized the ankles, and we pulled up that poor, chaste woman in the most immodest posture. The head was in a shocking state, bruised and black; and the long, grey hair, hanging down, out of curl for ever, was muddy and dripping with water.

"'Good Lord, how thin she is!' exclaimed Sapeur, in a contemptuous tone.

"We carried her into the room, and as the women did not put in an appearance, I, with the assistance of the lad, dressed the corpse for burial.

"I washed her sad, disfigured face. By the touch of my hand an eye was slightly opened; it fixed me with that pale stare, with that cold, that terrible look which corpses have, a look which seems to come from the beyond. I plaited up, as well as I could, her dishevelled hair, and I arranged on her forehead a novel and singular coiffure. Then I took off her dripping wet garments, baring, not without a feeling of shame, as though I had been guilty of some profanation, her shoulders and her chest, and her long arms, slim as the twigs of branches.

"Then I went to fetch some flowers, poppies, corn-flowers, marguerites, and fresh, sweet-smelling grass, with which to strew her funeral couch.

"Being the only person near her, it was necessary for me to fulfil the usual formalities. In a letter found in her pocket written at the last moment, she asked that her body be buried in the village in which she had passed the last days of her life. A frightful thought then oppressed my heart. Was it not on my account that she wished to be laid at rest in this place?

"Toward evening, all the female gossips of the locality came to view the remains of the deceased; but I would not allow a single person to enter; I wanted to be alone; and I watched by the corpse the whole night.

"By the light of the candles, I looked at the body of this miserable woman, wholly unknown, who had died so lamentably and so far away from home. Had she left no friends, no relatives behind her? What had her infancy been? What had been her life? Whence had she come, all alone, a wanderer, like a dog driven from home? What secrets of suffering and of despair were sealed up in that uncouth body, like a shameful defect, concealed all her life beneath that ridiculous exterior, which had driven away from her all affection and all love?

"What unhappy beings there are! I felt that upon that human creature weighed the eternal injustice of implacable nature! Life was over with her, without her ever having experienced, perhaps, that which sustains the most miserable of us all — the hope of being once loved! Otherwise, why should she thus have concealed herself, have fled from others? Why did she love everything so tenderly and so passionately, everything living that was not a man?

"I understood, also, why she believed in a God, and hoped for compensation from him for the miseries she had endured. She had now begun to decompose, and to become, in turn, a plant. She would blossom in the sun, and be eaten up by the cattle, carried away in seed by the birds, and as flesh by the beasts, again to become human flesh. But that which is called the soul had been extinguished at the bottom of the dark well. She suffered no longer. She had changed her life for that of others yet to be born.

"Hours passed away in this silent and sinister communion with the dead. A pale light announced the dawn of a new day, and a bright ray glistened on the bed, casting a line of fire on the bed-clothes and on her hands. This was the hour she had so much loved, when the waking birds began to sing in the trees.

"I opened the window wide, I drew back the curtains, so that the whole heavens might look in upon us. Then bending toward the glassy corpse, I took in my hands the mutilated head, and slowly, without terror or disgust, imprinted a long, long kiss upon those lips, which had never before received the salute of love."

Léon Chenal was silent. The women wept. We heard the Comte d'Etraille on the box-seat blow his nose several times in succession. Only the coachman nodded. The horses, no longer feeling the sting of the whip, had slackened their pace and were dragging us slowly along. And the brake hardly moved at all, having become suddenly heavy, as if laden with sorrow.

[1884]

KATE CHOPIN (1851–1904) *was born in St. Louis, the daughter of an Irish immigrant father who was killed in a train wreck when she was four. She was raised by her Creole mother's family and educated at a convent. In 1870 she married Oscar Chopin, a cotton broker. They lived in Louisiana, first in New Orleans and then on a large plantation her husband's family owned on the Crane River among the French-speaking Acadians, in a section of the country that later gave her the physical locale and the Creole, Cajun, and Negro characters portrayed in many of her short stories. When her husband died in 1882, Chopin moved back to St. Louis with her six children. Friends encouraged her to write, and when she was nearly forty years old she published her first novel,* At Fault *(1890). Her stories began to appear in* Century *and* Harper's, *and two collections followed:* Bayou Folk *(1894) and* A Night in Arcadie *(1897). Her last work, the novel* The Awakening *(1899), is her masterpiece, but its sympathetic treatment of adultery shocked reviewers and readers throughout America. In St. Louis the novel was taken out of circulation in the libraries, and Chopin was denied membership in the St. Louis Fine Arts Club. When her third collection of stories was rejected by her publisher at the end of 1899, Chopin felt herself a literary outcast; she wrote very little in the last years of her life.*

What affronted the genteel readers of the 1890s in Chopin's fiction was her attempt to write frankly about women's emotions in their relations with men, children, and their own sexuality. After her mother's death in 1885 she stopped being a practicing Catholic, believing that no author could be true to life who did not accept the Darwinian view of human evolution. Seeking God in nature rather than through the church, Chopin expressed herself freely on the subjects of sex and love, but she said she learned to her sorrow that for American authors "the limitations imposed upon their art by their environment hamper a full and spontaneous expression." She dealt in her fiction with such problems as adultery, slavery, miscegenation, and integration, but she was interested more in the psychology of the individual than in social issues. Magazine editors turned down her writing if it challenged conventional social behavior, as in the case of "The Story of an Hour," which feminist critics championed more than half a century after Chopin's death.

Chopin took her writing seriously, adopting Guy de Maupassant for a model after translating his stories from the French. She felt, "Here was life, not fiction; for where were the plots, the old fashioned mechanism and stage trappings that in a vague, unthinking way I had fancied were essential to the art of story making?" Since she didn't need to depend on writing for her income, she wrote as she pleased and rarely revised, claiming she was

241

*guarding her literary integrity in both subject and form. The result is that
her stories are sometimes marred by stilted language or improbable coincidences. At her best she wrote with control and objectivity, usually emphasizing character rather than plot. In the story "Regret" she centered on a
small event, taking the reader right into the story, and developing it logically toward its conclusion where she dramatically revealed the emotional
cost of her heroine's apparent freedom in choosing an independent life as
her destiny. (See Chopin's Commentary about Maupassant on page 1238.)*

Kate Chopin

∽

REGRET

Mamzelle Aurélie possessed a good strong figure, ruddy cheeks, hair
that was changing from brown to gray, and a determined eye. She wore a
man's hat about the farm, and an old blue army overcoat when it was cold,
and sometimes topboots.

Mamzelle Aurélie had never thought of marrying. She had never been
in love. At the age of twenty she had received a proposal, which she had
promptly declined, and at the age of fifty she had not yet lived to regret it.

So she was quite alone in the world, except for her dog Ponto, and the
negroes who lived in her cabins and worked her crops, and the fowls, a few
cows, a couple of mules, her gun (with which she shot chicken-hawks), and
her religion.

One morning Mamzelle Aurélie stood upon her gallery, contemplating, with arms akimbo, a small band of very small children who, to all intents and purposes, might have fallen from the clouds, so unexpected and
bewildering was their coming, and so unwelcome. They were the children
of her nearest neighbor, Odile, who was not such a near neighbor, after all.

The young woman had appeared but five minutes before, accompanied by these four children. In her arms she carried little Elodie; she
dragged Ti Nomme by an unwilling hand; while Marcéline and Marcélette
followed with irresolute steps.

Her face was red and disfigured from tears and excitement. She had
been summoned to a neighboring parish by the dangerous illness of her
mother; her husband was away in Texas — it seemed to her a million miles
away; and Valsin was waiting with the mule-cart to drive her to the station.

"It's no question, Mamzelle Aurélie; you jus' got to keep those youngsters fo' me tell I come back. Dieu sait,[1] I would n' botha you with 'em if it was any otha way to do! Make 'em mine you, Mamzelle Aurélie; don' spare 'em. Me, there, I'm half crazy between the chil'ren, an' Léon not home, an' maybe not even to fine po' maman alive encore!" — a harrowing possibility which drove Odile to take a final hasty and convulsive leave of her disconsolate family.

She left them crowded into the narrow strip of shade on the porch of the long, low house; the white sunlight was beating in on the white old boards; some chickens were scratching in the grass at the foot of the steps, and one had boldly mounted, and was stepping heavily, solemnly, and aimlessly across the gallery. There was a pleasant odor of pinks in the air, and the sound of negroes' laughter was coming across the flowering cotton-field.

Mamzelle Aurélie stood contemplating the children. She looked with a critical eye upon Marcéline, who had been left staggering beneath the weight of the chubby Elodie. She surveyed with the same calculating air Marcélette mingling her silent tears with the audible grief and rebellion of Ti Nomme. During those few contemplative moments she was collecting herself, determining upon a line of action which should be identical with a line of duty. She began by feeding them.

If Mamzelle Aurélie's responsibilities might have begun and ended there, they could easily have been dismissed; for her larder was amply provided against an emergency of this nature. But little children are not little pigs; they require and demand attentions which were wholly unexpected by Mamzelle Aurélie, and which she was ill prepared to give.

She was, indeed, very inapt in her management of Odile's children during the first few days. How could she know that Marcélette always wept when spoken to in a loud and commanding tone of voice? It was a peculiarity of Marcélette's. She became acquainted with Ti Nomme's passion for flowers only when he had plucked all the choicest gardenias and pinks for the apparent purpose of critically studying their botanical construction.

" 'Tain't enough to tell 'im, Mamzelle Aurélie," Marcéline instructed her; "you got to tie 'im in a chair. It's w'at maman all time do w'en he's bad: she tie 'im in a chair." The chair in which Mamzelle Aurélie tied Ti Nomme was roomy and comfortable, and he seized the opportunity to take a nap in it, the afternoon being warm.

At night, when she ordered them one and all to bed as she would have shooed the chickens into the hen-house, they stayed uncomprehending before her. What about the little white nightgowns that had to be taken from the pillow-slip in which they were brought over, and shaken by some strong hand till they snapped like ox-whips? What about the tub of water which had to be brought and set in the middle of the floor, in which the little tired, dusty, sunbrowned feet had every one to be washed sweet and clean? And it made Marcéline and Marcélette laugh merrily — the idea that

---

[1] "God knows."

Mamzelle Aurélie should for a moment have believed that Ti Nomme could fall asleep without being told the story of *Croque-mitaine*[2] or *Loup-garou*,[3] or both; or that Elodie could fall asleep at all without being rocked and sung to.

"I tell you, Aunt Ruby," Mamzelle Aurélie informed her cook in confidence; "me, I'd rather manage a dozen plantation' than fo' chil'ren. It's terrassent! Bonté! Don't talk to me about chil'ren!"

" 'Tain' ispected sich as you would know airy thing 'bout 'em, Mamzelle Aurélie. I see dat plainly yistiddy w'en I spy dat li'le chile playin' wid yo' baskit o' keys. You don' know dat makes chillun grow up hard-headed, to play wid keys? Des like it make 'em teeth hard to look in a lookin'-glass. Them's the things you got to know in the raisin' an' manigement o' chillun."

Mamzelle Aurélie certainly did not pretend or aspire to such subtle and far-reaching knowledge on the subject as Aunt Ruby possessed, who had "raised five an' bared (buried) six" in her day. She was glad enough to learn a few little mother-tricks to serve the moment's need.

Ti Nomme's sticky fingers compelled her to unearth white aprons that she had not worn for years, and she had to accustom herself to his moist kisses — the expressions of an affectionate and exuberant nature. She got down her sewing-basket, which she seldom used, from the top shelf of the armoire, and placed it within the ready and easy reach which torn slips and buttonless waists demanded. It took her some days to become accustomed to the laughing, the crying, the chattering that echoed through the house and around it all day long. And it was not the first or the second night that she could sleep comfortably with little Elodie's hot, plump body pressed close against her, and the little one's warm breath beating her cheek like the fanning of a bird's wing.

But at the end of two weeks Mamzelle Aurélie had grown quite used to these things, and she no longer complained.

It was also at the end of two weeks that Mamzelle Aurélie, one evening, looking away toward the crib where the cattle were being fed, saw Valsin's blue cart turning the bend of the road. Odile sat beside the mulatto, upright and alert. As they drew near, the young woman's beaming face indicated that her homecoming was a happy one.

But this coming, unannounced and unexpected, threw Mamzelle Aurélie into a flutter that was almost agitation. The children had to be gathered. Where was Ti Nomme? Yonder in the shed, putting an edge on his knife at the grindstone. And Marcéline and Marcélette? Cutting and fashioning doll-rags in the corner of the gallery. As for Elodie, she was safe enough in Mamzelle Aurélie's arms; and she had screamed with delight at sight of the familiar blue cart which was bringing her mother back to her.

[2] the bogey-man.
[3] the werewolf.

The excitement was all over, and they were gone. How still it was when they were gone! Mamzelle Aurélie stood upon the gallery, looking and listening. She could no longer see the cart; the red sunset and the blue-gray twilight had together flung a purple mist across the fields and road that hid it from her view. She could no longer hear the wheezing and creaking of its wheels. But she could still faintly hear the shrill, glad voices of the children.

She turned into the house. There was much work awaiting her, for the children had left a sad disorder behind them; but she did not at once set about the task of righting it. Mamzelle Aurélie seated herself beside the table. She gave one slow glance through the room, into which the evening shadows were creeping and deepening around her solitary figure. She let her head fall down upon her bended arm, and began to cry. Oh, but she cried! Not softly, as women often do. She cried like a man, with sobs that seemed to tear her very soul. She did not notice Ponto licking her hand.

[1894]

Kate Chopin

✂

THE STORY OF AN HOUR

Knowing that Mrs. Mallard was afflicted with a heart trouble, great care was taken to break to her as gently as possible the news of her husband's death.

It was her sister Josephine who told her, in broken sentences; veiled hints that revealed in half concealing. Her husband's friend Richards was there, too, near her. It was he who had been in the newspaper office when intelligence of the railroad disaster was received, with Brently Mallard's name leading the list of "killed." He had only taken the time to assure himself of its truth by a second telegram, and had hastened to forestall any less careful, less tender friend in bearing the sad message.

She did not hear the story as many women have heard the same, with a paralyzed inability to accept its significance. She wept at once, with sudden, wild abandonment, in her sister's arms. When the storm of grief had spent itself she went away to her room alone. She would have no one follow her.

There stood, facing the open window, a comfortable, roomy armchair. Into this she sank, pressed down by a physical exhaustion that haunted her body and seemed to reach into her soul.

She could see in the open square before her house the tops of trees that were all aquiver with the new spring life. The delicious breath of rain was in the air. In the street below a peddler was crying his wares. The notes of a distant song which some one was singing reached her faintly, and countless sparrows were twittering in the eaves.

There were patches of blue sky showing here and there through the clouds that had met and piled one above the other in the west facing her window.

She sat with her head thrown back upon the cushion of the chair, quite motionless, except when a sob came up into her throat and shook her, as a child who had cried itself to sleep continues to sob in its dreams.

She was young, with a fair, calm face, whose lines bespoke repression and even a certain strength. But now there was a dull stare in her eyes, whose gaze was fixed away off yonder on one of those patches of blue sky. It was not a glance of reflection, but rather indicated a suspension of intelligent thought.

There was something coming to her and she was waiting for it, fearfully. What was it? She did not know; it was too subtle and elusive to name. But she felt it, creeping out of the sky, reaching toward her through the sounds, the scents, the color that filled the air.

Now her bosom rose and fell tumultuously. She was beginning to recognize this thing that was approaching to possess her, and she was striving to beat it back with her will — as powerless as her two white slender hands would have been.

When she abandoned herself a little whispered word escaped her slightly parted lips. She said it over and over under her breath: "free, free, free!" The vacant stare and the look of terror that had followed it went from her eyes. They stayed keen and bright. Her pulses beat fast, and the coursing blood warmed and relaxed every inch of her body.

She did not stop to ask if it were or were not a monstrous joy that held her. A clear and exalted perception enabled her to dismiss the suggestion as trivial.

She knew that she would weep again when she saw the kind, tender hands folded in death; the face that had never looked save with love upon her, fixed and gray and dead. But she saw beyond that bitter moment a long procession of years to come that would belong to her absolutely. And she opened and spread her arms out to them in welcome.

There would be no one to live for her during those coming years: she would live for herself. There would be no powerful will bending hers in that blind persistence with which men and women believe they have a right to impose a private will upon a fellow-creature. A kind intention or a cruel intention made the act seem no less a crime as she looked upon it in that brief moment of illumination.

And yet she had loved him — sometimes. Often she had not. What did it matter! What could love, the unsolved mystery, count for in face of this possession of self-assertion which she suddenly recognized as the strongest impulse of her being!

"Free! Body and soul free!" she kept whispering.

Josephine was kneeling before the closed door with her lips to the keyhole, imploring for admission. "Louise, open the door! I beg; open the door — you will make yourself ill. What are you doing, Louise? For heaven's sake open the door."

"Go away. I am not making myself ill." No; she was drinking in a very elixir of life through that open window.

Her fancy was running riot along those days ahead of her. Spring days, and summer days, and all sorts of days that would be her own. She breathed a quick prayer that life might be long. It was only yesterday she had thought with a shudder that life might be long.

She arose at length and opened the door to her sister's importunities. There was a feverish triumph in her eyes, and she carried herself unwittingly like a goddess of Victory. She clasped her sister's waist, and together they descended the stairs. Richards stood waiting for them at the bottom.

Some one was opening the front door with a latchkey. It was Brently Mallard who entered, a little travel-stained, composedly carrying his gripsack and umbrella. He had been far from the scene of accident, and did not even know there had been one. He stood amazed at Josephine's piercing cry; at Richards' quick motion to screen him from the view of his wife.

But Richards was too late.

When the doctors came they said she had died of heart disease — of joy that kills.

[1894]

MARY ELEANOR WILKINS FREEMAN (1852–1930) *was born in Randolph, Massachusetts, the daughter of a carpenter. When she was fifteen her family moved to Brattleboro, Vermont, where she graduated from high school. After a year at Mt. Holyoke Female Seminary in 1870, which she said "combined a thorough intellectual training with careful religious culture," she — like the poet Emily Dickinson before her — returned home. She lived with her parents in Brattleboro and turned to writing for periodicals to try to earn some money. In 1881, after years of rejection slips, she sold her first poem to a children's magazine. A year later she wrote her first stories and sold them to magazines, and her career was launched. She felt she had succeeded because she wrote about things she knew best, a village like the one in which she lived and people like the ones she had grown up with. Later she advised a young writer to "follow the safe course of writing only about those subjects she knows thoroughly, and concerning which she trusts her own convictions."*

After the deaths of her parents and sister, Freeman returned to Randolph, Massachusetts, where she resided with a friend and made her living writing for magazines and publishing three books for young readers. In 1887 her first book of adult fiction, a collection of stories she had written for Harper's New Monthly *and* Harper's Bazaar, *appeared; it was titled* A Humble Romance and Other Stories. *This was one of her most successful and enduring books, along with her 1891 collection,* A New England Nun and Other Stories, *in which "The Revolt of 'Mother' " appeared. As the critic Perry Westbrook has observed, these two collections contain stories that she never surpassed "either in narrative skill or in psychological insight," although she continued writing and publishing books of fiction nearly every year until 1918. In 1902 she married Dr. Charles Freeman and moved to Metuchen, New Jersey, where she resided until the end of her life.*

Along with Sarah Orne Jewett, whose stories she read and admired when she was an aspiring young writer, Freeman is considered a member of the local-color school because she created tales of New England rural life from her experiences in Vermont and Massachusetts. Although she published several novels, Freeman's talent lay in writing conventional magazine fiction. She usually focused her realistic depiction of repressed people in a confining social system on a dominant characteristic of personality, as in "The Revolt of 'Mother,' " her most widely acclaimed story. She wrote it as a comic fantasy, later asserting that no woman with the courage and imagination of her central character, Sarah Penn, ever existed in real life. Freeman was angry when President Theodore Roosevelt commented in a speech that American women would do well to emulate the independence of Sarah Penn. She said she never intended "The Revolt of 'Mother' " to be read as a serious tract on women's rights. Yet her local-color stories abound in strong-minded women, and if the plot of "The Revolt of 'Mother' " is improbable, it is true to the spirit of the fierce individuality Freeman depicted within the nineteenth-century New England village character, both male and female.

Mary E. Wilkins Freeman

∽ঞ৹

THE REVOLT OF "MOTHER"

"Father!"

"What is it?"

"What are them men diggin' over there in the field for?"

There was a sudden dropping and enlarging of the lower part of the old man's face, as if some heavy weight had settled therein; he shut his mouth tight, and went on harnessing the great bay mare. He hustled the collar on to her neck with a jerk.

"Father!"

The old man slapped the saddle upon the mare's back.

"Look here, father, I want to know what them men are diggin' over in the field for, an' I'm goin' to know."

"I wish you'd go into the house, mother, an' 'tend to your own affairs," the old man said then. He ran his words together, and his speech was almost as inarticulate as a growl.

But the woman understood; it was her most native tongue. "I ain't goin' into the house till you tell me what them men are doin' over there in the field," said she.

Then she stood waiting. She was a small woman, short and straight-waisted like a child in her brown cotton gown. Her forehead was mild and benevolent between the smooth curves of gray hair; there were meek downward lines about her nose and mouth; but her eyes, fixed upon the old man, looked as if the meekness had been the result of her own will, never of the will of another.

They were in the barn, standing before the wide open doors. The spring air, full of the smell of growing grass and unseen blossoms, came in their faces. The deep yard in front was littered with farm wagons and piles of wood; on the edges, close to the fence and the house, the grass was a vivid green, and there were some dandelions.

The old man glanced doggedly at his wife as he tightened the last buckles on the harness. She looked as immovable to him as one of the rocks in his pasture-land, bound to the earth with generations of blackberry vines. He slapped the reins over the horse, and started forth from the barn.

"*Father!*" said she.

The old man pulled up. "What is it?"

"I want to know what them men are diggin' over there in the field for."

"They're diggin' a cellar, I s'pose, if you've got to know."

"A cellar for what?"

"A barn."

"A barn? You ain't goin' to build a barn over there where we was goin' to have a house, father?"

The old man said not another word. He hurried the horse into the farm wagon, and clattered out of the yard, jouncing as sturdily on his seat as a boy.

The woman stood a moment looking after him, then she went out of the barn across a corner of the yard to the house. The house, standing at right angles with the great barn and a long reach of sheds and out-buildings, was infinitesimal compared with them. It was scarcely as commodious for people as the little boxes under the barn eaves were for doves.

A pretty girl's face, pink and delicate as a flower, was looking out of one of the house windows. She was watching three men who were digging over in the field which bounded the yard near the road line. She turned quietly when the woman entered.

"What are they digging for, mother?" said she. "Did he tell you?"

"They're diggin' for — a cellar for a new barn."

"Oh, mother, he ain't going to build another barn?"

"That's what he says."

A boy stood before the kitchen glass combing his hair. He combed slowly and painstakingly, arranging his brown hair in a smooth hillock over his forehead. He did not seem to pay any attention to the conversation.

"Sammy, did you know father was going to build a new barn?" asked the girl.

The boy combed assiduously.

"Sammy!"

He turned, and showed a face like his father's under his smooth crest of hair. "Yes, I s'pose I did," he said, reluctantly.

"How long have you known it?" asked his mother.

"'Bout three months, I guess."

"Why didn't you tell of it?"

"Didn't think 'twould do no good."

"I don't see what father wants another barn for," said the girl, in her sweet, slow voice. She turned again to the window, and stared out at the digging men in the field. Her tender, sweet face was full of a gentle distress. Her forehead was as bald and innocent as a baby's, with the light hair strained back from it in a row of curl-papers. She was quite large, but her soft curls did not look as if they covered muscles.

Her mother looked sternly at the boy. "Is he goin' to buy more cows?" said she.

The boy did not reply; he was tying his shoes.

"Sammy, I want you to tell me if he's goin' to buy more cows."

"I s'pose he is."

"How many?"

"Four, I guess."

His mother said nothing more. She went into the pantry, and there was a clatter of dishes. The boy got his cap from a nail behind the door, took an old arithmetic from the shelf, and started for school. He was lightly built, but clumsy. He went out of the yard with a curious spring in the hips, that made his loose home-made jacket tilt up in the rear.

The girl went to the sink, and began to wash the dishes that were piled up there. Her mother came promptly out of the pantry, and shoved her aside. "You wipe 'em," said she; "I'll wash. There's a good many this mornin'."

The mother plunged her hands vigorously into the water, the girl wiped the plates slowly and dreamily. "Mother," said she, "don't you think it's too bad father's going to build that new barn, much as we need a decent house to live in?"

Her mother scrubbed a dish fiercely. "You ain't found out yet we're women-folks, Nanny Penn," said she. "You ain't seen enough of men-folks yet to. One of these days you'll find it out, an' then you'll know that we know only what men-folks think we do, so far as any use of it goes, an' how we'd ought to reckon men-folks in with Providence, an' not complain of what they do any more than we do of the weather."

"I don't care; I don't believe George is anything like that, anyhow," said Nanny. Her delicate face flushed pink, her lips pouted softly, as if she were going to cry.

"You wait an' see. I guess George Eastman ain't no better than other men. You hadn't ought to judge father, though. He can't help it, 'cause he don't look at things jest the way we do. An' we've been pretty comfortable here, after all. The roof don't leak — ain't never but once — that's one thing. Father's kept it shingled right up."

"I do wish we had a parlor."

"I guess it won't hurt George Eastman any to come to see you in a nice clean kitchen. I guess a good many girls don't have as good a place as this. Nobody's ever heard me complain."

"I ain't complained either, mother."

"Well, I don't think you'd better, a good father an' a good home as you've got. S'pose your father made you go out an' work for your livin'? Lots of girls have to that ain't no stronger an' better able to than you be."

Sarah Penn washed the frying-pan with a conclusive air. She scrubbed the outside of it as faithfully as the inside. She was a masterly keeper of her box of a house. Her one living-room never seemed to have in it any of the dust which the friction of life with inanimate matter produces. She swept, and there seemed to be no dirt to go before the broom; she cleaned, and one could see no difference. She was like an artist so perfect that he has apparently no art. To-day she got out a mixing bowl and a board, and rolled some pies, and there was no more flour upon her than upon her daughter who was doing finer work. Nanny was to be married in the fall, and she was sewing on some white cambric and embroidery. She sewed industriously while her mother cooked, her soft milk-white hands and wrists showed whiter than her delicate work.

"We must have the stove moved out in the shed before long," said Mrs. Penn. "Talk about not havin' things, it's been a real blessin' to be able to put a stove up in that shed in hot weather. Father did one good thing when he fixed that stove-pipe out there."

Sarah Penn's face as she rolled her pies had that expression of meek vigor which might have characterized one of the New Testament saints. She was making mince-pies. Her husband, Adoniram Penn, liked them better than any other kind. She baked twice a week. Adoniram often liked a piece of pie between meals. She hurried this morning. It had been later than usual when she began, and she wanted to have a pie baked for dinner. However deep a resentment she might be forced to hold against her husband, she would never fail in sedulous attention to his wants.

Nobility of character manifests itself at loop-holes when it is not provided with large doors. Sarah Penn's showed itself to-day in flaky dishes of pastry. So she made the pies faithfully, while across the table she could see, when she glanced up from her work, the sight that rankled in her patient and steadfast soul — the digging of the cellar of the new barn in the place where Adoniram forty years ago had promised her their new house should stand.

The pies were done for dinner. Adoniram and Sammy were home a few minutes after twelve o'clock. The dinner was eaten with serious haste. There was never much conversation at the table in the Penn family. Adoniram asked a blessing, and they ate promptly, then rose up and went about their work.

Sammy went back to school, taking soft sly lopes out of the yard like a rabbit. He wanted a game of marbles before school, and feared his father would give him some chores to do. Adoniram hastened to the door and called after him, but he was out of sight.

"I don't see what you let him go for, Mother," said he. "I wanted him to help me unload that wood."

Adoniram went to work out in the yard unloading wood from the wagon. Sarah put away the dinner dishes, while Nanny took down her curl-papers and changed her dress. She was going down to the store to buy some more embroidery and thread.

When Nanny was gone, Mrs. Penn went to the door. "Father!" she called.

"Well, what is it!"

"I want to see you jest a minute."

"I can't leave this wood nohow. I've got to git it unloaded an' go for a load of gravel afore two o'clock. Sammy had ought to helped me. You hadn't ought to let him go to school so early."

"I want to see you jest a minute."

"I tell ye I can't, nohow, mother."

"Father, you come here." Sarah Penn stood in the door like a queen; she held her head as if it bore a crown; there was that patience which makes authority royal in her voice. Adoniram went.

Mrs. Penn led the way into the kitchen, and pointed to a chair. "Sit down, father," said she; "I've got somethin' I want to say to you."

He sat down heavily; his face was quite stolid, but he looked at her with restive eyes. "Well, what is it, mother?"

"I want to know what you're buildin' that new barn for, father?"

"I ain't got nothin' to say about it."

"It can't be you think you need another barn?"

"I tell ye I ain't got nothin' to say about it, mother; an' I ain't goin' to say nothin'."

"Be you goin' to buy more cows?"

Adoniram did not reply; he shut his mouth tight.

"I know you be, as well as I want to. Now, father, look here" — Sarah Penn had not sat down; she stood before her husband in the humble fashion of a Scripture woman — "I'm goin' to talk real plain to you; I never have sence I married you, but I'm goin' to now. I ain't never complained, an' I ain't goin' to complain now, but I'm goin' to talk plain. You see this room here, father; you look at it well. You see there ain't no carpet on the floor, an' you see the paper is all dirty, an' droppin' off the walls. We ain't had no new paper on it for ten year, an' then I put it on myself, an' it didn't cost but ninepence a roll. You see this room, father; it's all the one I've had to work in an' eat in an' sit in sence we was married. There ain't another woman in the whole town whose husband ain't got half the means you have but what's got better. It's all the room Nanny's got to have her company in; an' there ain't one of her mates but what's got better, an' their fathers not so able as hers is. It's all the room she'll have to be married in. What would you have thought, father, if we had had our weddin' in a room no better than this? I was married in my mother's parlor, with a carpet on the floor, an' stuffed furniture, an' a mahogany card-table. An' this is all the room my daughter will have to be married in. Look here, father!"

Sarah Penn went across the room as though it were a tragic stage. She flung open a door and disclosed a tiny bedroom, only large enough for a bed and bureau, with a path between. "There, father," said she — "there's all the room I've had to sleep in forty year. All my children were born there — the two that died, an' the two that's livin.' I was sick with a fever there."

She stepped into another door and opened it. It led into the small, ill-lighted pantry. "Here," said she, "is all the buttery I've got — every place I've got for my dishes, to set away my victuals in, an' to keep my milk-pans in. Father, I've been takin' care of the milk of six cows in this place, an' now you're goin' to build a new barn, an' keep more cows, an' give me more to do in it."

She threw open another door. A narrow crooked flight of stairs wound upward from it. "There, father," said she. "I want you to look at the stairs that go up to them two unfinished chambers that are all the places our son an' daughter have had to sleep in all their lives. There ain't a prettier girl in town nor a more ladylike one than Nanny, an' that's the place she has to sleep in. It ain't so good as your horse's stall; it ain't so warm an' tight."

Sarah Penn went back and stood before her husband. "Now, father," said she, "I want to know if you think you're doin' right an' accordin' to what you profess. Here, when we was married, forty year ago, you promised me faithful that we should have a new house built in that lot over in the field before the year was out. You said you had money enough, an' you wouldn't ask me to live in no such place as this. It is forty year now, an' you've been makin' more money, an' I've been savin' of it for you ever since, an' you ain't built no house yet. You've built sheds an' cow-houses an' one new barn, an' now you're goin' to build another. Father, I want to know if you think it's right. You're lodgin' your dumb beasts better than you are your own flesh an' blood. I want to know if you think it's right."

"I ain't got nothin' to say."

"You can't say nothin' without ownin' it ain't right, father. An' there's another thing — I ain't complained; I've got along forty year, an' I s'pose I should forty more, if it wa'n't for that — if we don't have another house. Nanny she can't live with us after she's married. She'll have to go some-wheres else to live away from us, an' it don't seem as if I could have it so, noways, father. She wa'n't ever strong. She's got considerable color, but there wa'n't never any backbone to her. I've always took the heft of every-thing off her, an' she ain't fit to keep house an' do everything herself. She'll be all worn out inside of a year. Think of her doin' all the washin' an' ironin' an' bakin' with them soft white hands an' arms, an' sweepin'! I can't have it so, noways, father."

Mrs. Penn's face was burning; her mild eyes gleamed. She had pleaded her little cause like a Webster;[1] she had ranged from severity to pathos; but her opponent employed that obstinate silence which makes eloquence futile with mocking echoes. Adoniram arose clumsily.

"Father, ain't you got nothin' to say?" said Mrs. Penn.

"I've got to go off after that load of gravel. I can't stan' here talkin' all day."

"Father, won't you think it over, an' have a house built there instead of a barn?"

"I ain't got nothin' to say."

Adoniram shuffled out. Mrs. Penn went into her bedroom. When she came out, her eyes were red. She had a roll of unbleached cotton cloth. She spread it out on the kitchen table, and began cutting out some shirts for her

---

[1] Daniel Webster (1782–1852) was an American orator, lawyer, and statesman.

husband. The men over in the field had a team to help them this afternoon; she could hear their halloos. She had a scanty pattern for the shirts; she had to plan and piece the sleeves.

Nanny came home with her embroidery, and sat down with her needlework. She had taken down her curl-papers, and there was a soft roll of fair hair like an aureole over her forehead; her face was as delicately fine and clear as porcelain. Suddenly she looked up, and the tender red flamed all over her face and neck. "Mother," said she.

"What say?"

"I've been thinking — I don't see how we're goin' to have any — wedding in this room. I'd be ashamed to have his folks come if we didn't have anybody else."

"Mebbe we can have some new paper before then; I can put it on. I guess you won't have no call to be ashamed of your belongin's."

"We might have the wedding in the new barn," said Nanny, with gentle pettishness. "Why, mother, what makes you look so?"

Mrs. Penn had started, and was staring at her with a curious expression. She turned again to her work, and spread out a pattern carefully on the cloth. "Nothin'," said she.

Presently Adoniram clattered out of the yard in his two-wheeled dump cart, standing as proudly upright as a Roman charioteer. Mrs. Penn opened the door and stood there a minute looking out; the halloos of the men sounded louder.

It seemed to her all through the spring months that she heard nothing but the halloos and the noises of saws and hammers. The new barn grew fast. It was a fine edifice for this little village. Men came on pleasant Sundays, in their meeting suits and clean shirt bosoms, and stood around it admiringly. Mrs. Penn did not speak of it, and Adoniram did not mention it to her, although sometimes, upon a return from inspecting it, he bore himself with injured dignity.

"It's a strange thing how your mother feels about the new barn," he said, confidentially, to Sammy one day.

Sammy only grunted after an odd fashion for a boy; he had learned it from his father.

The barn was all completed ready for use by the third week in July. Adoniram had planned to move his stock in on Wednesday; on Tuesday he received a letter which changed his plans. He came in with it early in the morning. "Sammy's been to the post-office," said he, "an' I've got a letter from Hiram." Hiram was Mrs. Penn's brother, who lived in Vermont.

"Well," said Mrs. Penn, "what does he say about the folks?"

"I guess they're all right. He says he thinks if I come up country right off there's a chance to buy jest the kind of a horse I want." He stared reflectively out of the window at the new barn.

Mrs. Penn was making pies. She went on clapping the rolling-pin into the crust, although she was very pale, and her heart beat loudly.

"I dun' know but what I'd better go," said Adoniram. "I hate to go off jest now, right in the midst of hayin', but the ten-acre lot's cut, an' I guess Rufus an' the others can git along without me three or four days. I can't get a horse round here to suit me, nohow, an' I've got to have another for all that wood-haulin' in the fall. I told Hiram to watch out, an' if he got wind of a good horse to let me know. I guess I'd better go."

"I'll get your clean shirt an' collar," said Mrs. Penn calmly.

She laid out Adoniram's Sunday suit and his clean clothes on the bed in the little bedroom. She got his shaving-water and razor ready. At last she buttoned on his collar and fastened his black cravat.

Adoniram never wore his collar and cravat except on extra occasions. He held his head high, with a rasped dignity. When he was all ready, with his coat and hat brushed, and a lunch of pie and cheese in a paper bag, he hesitated on the threshold of the door. He looked at his wife, and his manner was defiantly apologetic. "*If* them cows come to-day, Sammy can drive 'em into the new barn," said he; "an' when they bring the hay up, they can pitch it in there."

"Well," replied Mrs. Penn.

Adoniram set his shaven face ahead and started. When he had cleared the door-step, he turned and looked back with a kind of nervous solemnity. "I shall be back by Saturday if nothin' happens," said he.

"Do be careful, father," returned his wife.

She stood at the door with Nanny at her elbow and watched him out of sight. Her eyes had a strange, doubtful expression in them; her peaceful forehead was contracted. She went in, and about her baking again. Nanny sat sewing. Her wedding-day was drawing nearer, and she was getting pale and thin with her steady sewing. Her mother kept glancing at her.

"Have you got that pain in your side this mornin'?" she asked.

"A little."

Mrs. Penn's face, as she worked, changed, her perplexed forehead smoothed, her eyes were steady, her lips firmly set. She formed a maxim for herself, although incoherently with her unlettered thoughts. "Unsolicited opportunities are the guide-posts of the Lord to the new roads of life," she repeated in effect, and she made up her mind to her course of action.

"S'posin' I *had* wrote to Hiram," she muttered once, when she was in the pantry — "s'posin' I had wrote, an' asked him if he knew of any horse? But I didn't, an' father's goin' wa'n't none of my doin'. It looks like a providence." Her voice rang out quite loud at the last.

"What are you talkin' about, mother?" called Nanny.

"Nothin'."

Mrs. Penn hurried her baking; at eleven o'clock it was all done. The load of hay from the west field came slowly down the cart track, and drew up at the new barn. Mrs. Penn ran out. "Stop!" she screamed — "stop!"

The men stopped and looked; Sammy upreared from the top of the load, and stared at his mother.

"Stop!" she cried out again. "Don't you put the hay in that barn; put it in the old one."

"Why, he said to put it in here," returned one of the haymakers, won-deringly. He was a young man, a neighbor's son, whom Adoniram hired by the year to help on the farm.

"Don't you put the hay in the new barn; there's room enough in the old one, aint there?" said Mrs. Penn.

"Room enough," returned the hired man, in his thick, rustic tones. "Didn't need the new barn, nohow, far as room's concerned. Well, I s'pose he changed his mind." He took hold of the horses' bridles.

Mrs. Penn went back to the house. Soon the kitchen windows were darkened, and a fragrance like warm honey came into the room.

Nanny laid down her work. "I thought father wanted them to put the hay into the new barn?" she said, wonderingly.

"It's all right," replied her mother.

Sammy slid down from the load of hay, and came in to see if dinner was ready.

"I ain't goin' to get a regular dinner to-day, as long as father's gone," said his mother. "I've let the fire go out. You can have some bread an' milk an' pie. I thought we could get along." She set out some bowls of milk, some bread, and a pie on the kitchen table. "You'd better eat your dinner now," said she. "You might jest as well get through with it. I want you to help me afterward."

Nanny and Sammy stared at each other. There was something strange in their mother's manner. Mrs. Penn did not eat anything herself. She went into the pantry, and they heard her moving dishes while they ate. Presently she came out with a pile of plates. She got the clothes-basket out of the shed, and packed them in it. Nanny and Sammy watched. She brought out cups and saucers, and put them in with the plates.

"What you goin' to do, mother?" inquired Nanny, in a timid voice. A sense of something unusual made her tremble, as if it were a ghost. Sammy rolled his eyes over his pie.

"You'll see what I'm goin' to do," replied Mrs. Penn. "If you're through, Nanny, I want you to go upstairs an' pack up your things; an' I want you, Sammy, to help me take down the bed in the bedroom."

"Oh, mother, what for?" gasped Nanny.

"You'll see."

During the next few hours a feat was performed by this simple, pious New England mother which was equal in its way to Wolfe's storming of the Heights of Abraham.[2] It took no more genius and audacity of bravery for Wolfe to cheer his wondering soldiers up those steep precipices, under the sleeping eyes of the enemy, than for Sarah Penn, at the head of her chil-dren, to move all their little household goods into the new barn while her husband was away.

Nanny and Sammy followed their mother's instructions without a

[2] James Wolfe (1727–1759) was a British general whose troops stormed the French army on the Plains of Abraham above Quebec.

murmur; indeed, they were overawed. There is a certain uncanny and superhuman quality about all such purely original undertakings as their
mother's was to them. Nanny went back and forth with her light loads, and
Sammy tugged with sober energy.

At five o'clock in the afternoon the little house in which the Penns had
lived for forty years had emptied itself into the new barn.

Every builder builds somewhat for unknown purposes, and is in a
measure a prophet. The architect of Adoniram Penn's barn, while he designed it for the comfort of four-footed animals, had planned better than he
knew for the comfort of humans. Sarah Penn saw at a glance its possibilities. Those great box-stalls, with quilts hung before them, would make better bedrooms than the one she had occupied for forty years, and there was a
tight carriage-room. The harness-room, with its chimney and shelves, would
make a kitchen of her dreams. The great middle space would make a parlor,
by-and-by, fit for a palace. Upstairs there was as much room as down. With
partitions and windows, what a house would there be! Sarah looked at the
row of stanchions before the allotted space for cows, and reflected that she
would have her front entry there.

At six o'clock the stove was up in the harness-room, the kettle was
boiling, and the table set for tea. It looked almost as home-like as the abandoned house across the yard had ever done. The young hired man milked,
and Sarah directed him calmly to bring the milk to the new barn. He came
gaping, dropping little blots of foam from the brimming pails on the grass.
Before the next morning he had spread the story of Adoniram Penn's wife
moving into the new barn all over the little village. Men assembled in the
store and talked it over, women with shawls over their heads scuttled into
each other's houses before their work was done. Any deviation from the ordinary course of life in this quiet town was enough to stop all progress in it.
Everybody paused to look at the staid, independent figure on the side track.
There was a difference of opinion with regard to her. Some held her to be
insane; some, of a lawless and rebellious spirit.

Friday the minister went to see her. It was in the forenoon, and she
was at the barn door shelling pease[3] for dinner. She looked up and returned
his salutation with dignity, then she went on with her work. She did not invite him in. The saintly expression of her face remained fixed, but there was
an angry flush over it.

The minister stood awkwardly before her, and talked. She handled the
pease as if they were bullets. At last she looked up, and her eyes showed the
spirit that her meek front had covered for a lifetime.

"There ain't no use talkin', Mr. Hersey," she said. "I've thought it all
over an' over, an' I believe I'm doin' what's right. I've made it the subject of
prayer, an' it's betwixt me an' the Lord an' Adoniram. There ain't no call
for anybody else to worry about it."

---

[3] old or variant spelling of "peas."

"Well, of course, if you have brought it to the Lord in prayer, and feel satisfied that you are doing right, Mrs. Penn," said the minister, helplessly. His thin gray-bearded face was pathetic. He was a sickly man; his youthful confidence had cooled; he had to scourge himself up to some of his pastoral duties as relentlessly as a Catholic ascetic, and then he was prostrated by the smart.

"I think it's right jest as much as I think it was right for our forefathers to come over from the old country 'cause they didn't have what belonged to 'em," said Mrs. Penn. She arose. The barn threshold might have been Plymouth Rock from her bearing. "I don't doubt you mean well, Mr. Hersey," said she, "but there are things people hadn't ought to interfere with. I've been a member of the church for over forty year. I've got my own mind an' my own feet, an' I'm goin' to think my own thoughts an' go my own ways, an' nobody but the Lord is goin' to dictate to me unless I've a mind to have him. Won't you come in an' set down? How is Mis' Hersey?"

"She is well, I thank you," replied the minister. He added some more perplexed apologetic remarks; then he retreated.

He could expound the intricacies of every character study in the Scriptures, he was competent to grasp the Pilgrim Fathers and all historical innovators, but Sarah Penn was beyond him. He could deal with primal causes, but parallel ones worsted him. But, after all, although it was aside from his province, he wondered more how Adoniram Penn would deal with his wife than how the Lord would. Everybody shared the wonder. When Adoniram's four new cows arrived, Sarah ordered three to be put in the old barn, the other in the house shed where the cooking-stove had stood. That added to the excitement. It was whispered that all four cows were domiciled in the house.

Towards sunset on Saturday, when Adoniram was expected home, there was a knot of men in the road near the new barn. The hired man had milked, but he still hung around the premises. Sarah Penn had supper all ready. There were brown-bread and baked beans and a custard pie; it was the supper that Adoniram loved on a Saturday night. She had on a clean calico, and she bore herself imperturbably. Nanny and Sammy kept close at her heels. Their eyes were large, and Nanny was full of nervous tremors. Still there was to them more pleasant excitement than anything else. An inborn confidence in their mother over their father asserted itself.

Sammy looked out of the harness-room window. "There he is," he announced, in an awed whisper. He and Nanny peeped around the casing. Mrs. Penn kept on about her work. The children watched Adoniram leave the new horse standing in the drive while he went to the house door. It was fastened. Then he went around to the shed. That door was seldom locked, even when the family was away. The thought how her father would be confronted by the cow flashed upon Nanny. There was a hysterical sob in her throat. Adoniram emerged from the shed and stood looking about in a dazed fashion. His lips moved; he was saying something, but they could not hear what it was. The hired man was peeping around a corner of the old barn, but nobody saw him.

Adoniram took the new horse by the bridle and led him across the yard to the new barn. Nanny and Sammy slunk close to their mother. The barn doors rolled back, and there stood Adoniram, with the long mild face of the great Canadian farm horse looking over his shoulder.

Nanny kept behind her mother, but Sammy stepped suddenly forward, and stood in front of her.

Adoniram stared at the group. "What on airth you all down here for?" said he. "What's the matter over to the house?"

"We've come here to live, father," said Sammy. His shrill voice quavered out bravely.

"What" — Adoniram sniffed — "what is it smells like cooking?" said he. He stepped forward and looked in the open door of the harness-room. Then he turned to his wife. His old bristling face was pale and frightened. "What on airth does this mean, mother?" he gasped.

"You come in here, father," said Sarah. She led the way into the harness-room and shut the door. "Now, father," said she, "you needn't be scared. I ain't crazy. There ain't nothin' to be upset over. But we've come here to live, an' we're goin' to live here. We've got jest as good a right here as new horses an' cows. The house wa'n't fit for us to live in any longer, an' I made up my mind I wa'n't goin' to stay there. I've done my duty by you forty year, an' I'm goin' to do it now; but I'm goin' to live here. You've got to put in some windows and partitions; an' you'll have to buy some furniture."

"Why, mother!" the old man gasped.

"You'd better take your coat off an' get washed — there's the wash-basin — an' then we'll have supper."

"Why, mother!"

Sammy went past the window, leading the new horse to the old barn. The old man saw him, and shook his head speechlessly. He tried to take off his coat, but his arms seemed to lack the power. His wife helped him. She poured some water into the tin basin, and put in a piece of soap. She got the comb and brush, and smoothed his thin gray hair after he had washed. Then she put the beans, hot bread, and tea on the table. Sammy came in, and the family drew up. Adoniram sat looking dazedly at his plate, and they waited.

"Ain't you goin' to ask a blessin', father?" said Sarah.

And the old man bent his head and mumbled.

All through the meal he stopped eating at intervals, and stared furtively at his wife; but he ate well. The home food tasted good to him, and his old frame was too sturdily healthy to be affected by his mind. But after supper he went out, and sat down on the step of the smaller door at the right of the barn, through which he had meant his Jerseys to pass in stately file, but which Sarah designed for her front house door, and he leaned his head on his hands.

After the supper dishes were cleared away and the milk-pans washed, Sarah went out to him. The twilight was deepening. There was a clear green glow in the sky. Before them stretched the smooth level of field; in the distance was a cluster of hay-stacks like the huts of a village; the air was very cool and calm and sweet. The landscape might have been an ideal one of peace.

Sarah bent over and touched her husband on one of his thin, sinewy shoulders. "Father!"

The old man's shoulders heaved: he was weeping.

"Why, don't do so, father," said Sarah.

"I'll — put up the — partitions, an' — everything you — want, mother."

Sarah put her apron up to her face; she was overcome by her own triumph.

Adoniram was like a fortress whose walls had no active resistance, and went down the instant the right besieging tools were used. "Why, mother," he said, hoarsely, "I hadn't no idee you was so set on't as all this comes to."

[1891]

JOSEPH CONRAD *(1857–1924) was born Jozef Teodore Konrad Nalecz Korzeniowski near Kiev, in what was then Russian Poland. His parents died when he was young, and he was raised by a strict, aristocratic uncle. At the age of seventeen he persuaded his uncle to let him go to sea, and for many years he sailed in the French and British navies. He then accepted a post as steamboat captain on the Congo River, an experience that matured him: "Before I went to the Congo I was just a mere animal," he wrote. After his stint in the Congo, he settled in England to become a professional writer. Although Conrad did not learn English until after he was twenty (Polish was his native tongue and French his second language), he is considered one of the supreme English stylists. In 1895 he published his first novel,* Almayer's Folly, *followed in quick succession by the great books of his early period:* An Outcast of the Islands *(1896),* The Nigger of the "Narcissus" *(1897),* Lord Jim *(1902), and* Nostromo *(1904). His later novels include* The Secret Agent *(1907),* Chance *(1913), and* Victory *(1915).*

Conrad believed that a freely ranging imagination was his most precious possession as a writer, and he did not consider himself bound by the "fettering dogmas of some romantic, realistic, or naturalistic creed." The avowed aim of his fiction was "to make you hear, to make you feel, above all to make you see." His tales are never simple adventure stories, although they contain a great deal of adventure. His epic descriptions of vast natural forces and limited human fortitude were recognized in his own time as reminiscent of the work of his Russian predecessor Leo Tolstoy, but Conrad added his special poetic sense of the scene as a whole, with the human drama played against the surrounding, often menacing forces of nature. In his themes, his use of rich symbolism, and his subtle exploration of human psychology, he anticipated the direction that modern fiction would take.

Conrad experimented with a new approach to narrative in "Heart of Darkness." He structured it as a "frame story" to conform to a formula often used in Blackwood's, *the English magazine for which he wrote it. But the depth of his psychological insight and the grandeur of his prose lifts "Heart of Darkness" far above a formula story. Conrad showed Kurtz betrayed by the enormous power imperialism gives to the white man, and by the heart of darkness he finds in the "orgiastic" native rites of the Africans. In Marlow's identification with Kurtz, Conrad explored another twist to the "double" theme, the idea that a good and honorable man might be attracted to his opposite. As the critic Tony Tanner has said, Conrad showed "that a hidden part of a man committed to order and the rules of society might suddenly embrace and identify itself with a being, a presence, an apparition which seems most antithetic to his own conscious self, a walking reminder of all that inner darkness and weakness which civilized man has suppressed in order to make group life possible."*

Conrad felt that he might have made Kurtz "too symbolic" and that his story "pushed a little (but only very little)" beyond the actual facts of his four-month experience in the Congo. He justified his exaggeration, however, by his strong desire to give a political dimension to "Heart of Darkness." When the story was published in 1902, it gave literary expression to an entire age's perception of the Congo as a place of horror and human degradation resulting from ruthless colonialism. In the story, the "Company" collecting "ivory" from the natives is a thinly disguised reference to the Anglo-Belgium India-Rubber Company. During the twenty years of King Leopold of Belgium's control of the company (he personally owned 50 percent of its stock), its agents killed an estimated 5 million people in the Congo, terrorizing and murdering the natives who failed to meet rubber quotas. Leopold himself cleared at least $20 million in profit before he lost his monopoly control of the trade as a result of the reform movement sparked by "Heart of Darkness" and other eyewitness reports.

Joseph Conrad

ဢ

HEART OF DARKNESS

I

The *Nellie*, a cruising yawl, swung to her anchor without a flutter of the sails, and was at rest. The flood had made, the wind was nearly calm, and being bound down the river, the only thing for it was to come to and wait for the turn of the tide.

The sea-reach of the Thames stretched before us like the beginning of an interminable waterway. In the offing the sea and the sky were welded together without a joint, and in the luminous space the tanned sails of the barges drifting up with the tide seemed to stand still in red clusters of canvas sharply peaked, with gleams of varnished sprits. A haze rested on the low shores that ran out to sea in vanishing flatness. The air was dark above Gravesend, and farther back still seemed condensed into a mournful gloom, brooding motionless over the biggest, and the greatest, town on earth.

The Director of Companies was our captain and our host. We four affectionately watched his back as he stood in the bows looking to seaward. On the whole river there was nothing that looked half so nautical. He resembled a pilot, which to a seaman is trustworthiness personified. It was difficult to realize his work was not out there in the luminous estuary, but behind him, within the brooding gloom.

Between us there was, as I have already said somewhere, the bond of the sea. Besides holding our hearts together through long periods of separation, it had the effect of making us tolerant of each other's yarns — and even convictions. The Lawyer — the best of old fellows — had, because of his many years and many virtues, the only cushion on deck, and was lying on the only rug. The accountant had brought out already a box of dominoes, and was toying architecturally with the bones. Marlow sat cross-legged right aft, leaning against the mizzen-mast. He had sunken cheeks, a yellow complexion, a straight back, and ascetic aspect, and, with his arms dropped, the palms of hands outwards, resembled an idol. The director, satisfied the anchor had good hold, made his way aft and sat down amongst us. We exchanged a few words lazily. Afterwards there was silence on board the yacht. For some reason or other we did not begin that game of dominoes. We felt meditative, and fit for nothing but placid staring. The day was ending in a serenity of still and exquisite brilliance. The water shone pacifically; the sky, without a speck, was a benign immensity of unstained light; the very mist on the Essex marshes was like a gauzy and radiant fabric, hung from the wooded rises inland, and draping the low shores in diaphanous folds. Only the gloom to the west, brooding over the upper reaches, became more somber every minute, as if angered by the approach of the sun.

And at last, in its curved and imperceptible fall, the sun sank low, and from glowing white changed to a dull red without rays and without heat, as if about to go out suddenly, stricken to death by the touch of that gloom brooding over a crowd of men.

Forthwith a change came over the water, and the serenity became less brilliant but more profound. The old river in its broad reach rested unruffled at the decline of day, after ages of good service done to the race that peopled its banks, spread out in the tranquil dignity of a waterway leading to the uttermost ends of the earth. We looked at the venerable stream not in the vivid flush of a short day that comes and departs forever, but in the august light of abiding memories. And indeed nothing is easier for a man who has, as the phrase goes, "followed the sea" with reverence and affection, than to evoke the great spirit of the past upon the lower reaches of the Thames. The tidal current runs to and fro in its unceasing service, crowded with memories of men and ships it had borne to the rest of home or to the battles of the sea. It had known and served all the men of whom the nation is proud, from Sir Francis Drake[1] to Sir John Franklin,[2] knights all, titled

---

[1] Sir Francis Drake (1540–1596), English navigator and pirate, sailed around the world (1577–1580) and led the fleet that defeated the Spanish Armada in 1588. The *Golden Hind* was his ship.

[2] Sir John Franklin (1786–1847), English explorer of the Arctic. His ships the *Erebus*

and untitled — the knights-errant of the sea. It had borne all the ships whose names are like jewels flashing in the night of time, from the *Golden Hind* returning with her round flanks full of treasure, to be visited by the Queen's Highness and thus pass out of the gigantic tale, to the *Erebus* and *Terror*, bound on other conquests — and that never returned. It had known the ships and the men. They had sailed from Deptford, from Greenwich, from Erith — the adventurers and the settlers; kings' ships and the ships of men on 'Change;[3] captains, admirals, the dark "interlopers" of the Eastern trade, and the commissioned "Generals" of East India fleets. Hunters for gold or pursuers of fame, they all had gone out on that stream, bearing the sword, and often the torch, messengers of the might within the land, bearers of a spark from the sacred fire. What greatness had not floated on the ebb of that river into the mystery of an unknown earth! . . . The dreams of men, the seed of commonwealths, the germs of empires.

The sun set; the dusk fell on the stream, and lights began to appear along the shore. The Chapman lighthouse, a three-legged thing erect on a mud-flat, shone strongly. Lights of ships moved in the fairway — a great stir of lights going up and going down. And farther west on the upper reaches the place of the monstrous town was still marked ominously on the sky, a brooding gloom in sunshine, a lurid glare under the stars.

"And this also," said Marlow suddenly, "has been one of the dark places on the earth."

He was the only man of us who still "followed the sea." The worst that could be said of him was that he did not represent his class. He was a seaman, but he was a wanderer, too, while most seamen lead, if one may so express it, a sedentary life. Their minds are of the stay-at-home order, and their home is always with them — the ship; and so is their country — the sea. One ship is very much like another, and the sea is always the same. In the immutability of their surroundings the foreign shores, the foreign faces, the changing immensity of life, glide past, veiled not by a sense of mystery but by a slightly disdainful ignorance; for there is nothing mysterious to a seaman unless it be the sea itself, which is the mistress of his existence and as inscrutable as Destiny. For the rest, after his hours of work, a casual stroll or a casual spree on shore suffices to unfold for him the secret of a whole continent, and generally he finds the secret not worth knowing. The yarns of seamen have a direct simplicity, the whole meaning of which lies within the shell of a cracked nut. But Marlow was not typical (if his propensity to spin yarns be excepted), and to him the meaning of an episode was not inside like a kernel but outside, enveloping the tale which brought it out only as a glow brings out a haze, in the likeness of one of these misty halos that sometimes are made visible by the special illumination of moonshine.

---

and the *Terror* were lost in an expedition to find the Northwest Passage from the Atlantic to the Pacific.
[3] investors at the London Stock Exchange.

His remark did not seem at all surprising. It was just like Marlow. It was accepted in silence. No one took the trouble to grunt even; and presently he said, very slow —

"I was thinking of very old times, when the Romans first came here, nineteen hundred years ago — the other day.... Light came out of this river since — you say Knights? Yes; but it is like a running blaze on a plain, like a flash of lightning in the clouds. We live in the flicker — may it last as long as the old earth keeps rolling! But darkness was here yesterday. Imagine the feelings of a commander of a fine — what d'ye call 'em? — trireme in the Mediterranean, ordered suddenly to the north; run overland across the Gauls in a hurry; put in charge of one of these craft the legionaries — a wonderful lot of handy men they must have been, too — used to build, apparently by the hundred, in a month or two, if we may believe what we read. Imagine him here — the very end of the world, a sea the color of lead, a sky the color of smoke, a kind of ship about as rigid as a concertina — and going up this river with stores, or orders, or what you like. Sandbanks, marshes, forests, savages — precious little to eat fit for a civilized man, nothing but Thames water to drink. No Falernian wine[4] here, no going ashore. Here and there a military camp lost in a wilderness, like a needle in a bundle of hay — cold, fog, tempests, disease, exile, and death — death skulking in the air, in the water, in the bush. They must have been dying like flies here. Oh, yes — he did it. Did it very well, too, no doubt, and without thinking much about it either, except afterwards to brag of what he had gone through in his time, perhaps. They were men enough to face the darkness. And perhaps he was cheered by keeping his eye on a chance of promotion to the fleet at Ravenna by and by, if he had good friends in Rome and survived the awful climate. Or think of a decent young citizen in a toga — perhaps too much dice, you know — coming out here in the train of some prefect, or taxgatherer, or trader even, to mend his fortunes. Land in a swamp, march through the woods, and in some inland post feel the savagery, the utter savagery, had closed round him — all that mysterious life of the wilderness that stirs in the forest, in the jungles, in the hearts of wild men. There's no initiation either into such mysteries. He has to live in the midst of the incomprehensible, which is also detestable. And it has a fascination, too, that goes to work upon him. The fascination of the abomination — you know, imagine the growing regrets, the longing to escape, the powerless digust, the surrender, the hate."

He paused.

"Mind," he began again, lifting one arm from the elbow, the palm of the hand outwards, so that, with his legs folded before him, he had the pose of a Buddha preaching in European clothes and without a lotus-flower — "Mind, none of us would feel exactly like this. What saves us is efficiency — the devotion to efficiency. But these chaps were not much ac-

[4] legendary Roman wine.

count, really. They were no colonists; their administration was merely a squeeze, and nothing more, I suspect. They were conquerors, and for that you want only brute force — nothing to boast of, when you have it, since your strength is just an accident arising from the weakness of others. They grabbed what they could get for the sake of what was to be got. It was just robbery with violence, aggravated murder on a great scale, and men going at it blind — as is very proper for those who tackle a darkness. The conquest of the earth, which mostly means the taking it away from those who have a different complexion or slightly flatter noses than ourselves, is not a pretty thing when you look into it too much. What redeems it is the idea only. An idea at the back of it; not a sentimental pretense but an idea; and an unselfish belief in the idea — something you can set up, and bow down before, and offer a sacrifice to. . . ."

He broke off. Flames glided in the river, small green flames, red flames, white flames, pursuing, overtaking, joining, crossing each other — then separating slowly or hastily. The traffic of the great city went on in the deepening night upon the sleepless river. We looked on, waiting patiently — there was nothing else to do till the end of the flood; but it was more after a long silence, when he said, in a hesitating voice, "I suppose you fellows remember I did once turn fresh-water sailor for a bit," that we knew we were fated, before the ebb began to run, to hear one of Marlow's inconclusive experiences.

"I don't want to bother you much with what happened to me personally," he began, showing in this remark the weakness of many tellers of tales who seem so often unaware of what their audience would best like to hear; "yet to understand the effect of it on me you ought to know how I got out there, what I saw, how I went up that river to the place where I first met the poor chap. It was the farthest point of navigation and the culminating point of my experience. It seemed somehow to throw a kind of light on everything about me — and into my thoughts. It was somber enough, too — and pitiful — not extraordinary in any way — not very clear either. No, not very clear. And yet it seemed to throw a kind of light.

"I had then, as you remember, just returned to London after a lot of Indian Ocean, Pacific, China Seas — a regular dose of the East — six years or so, and I was loafing about, hindering you fellows in your work and invading your homes, just as though I had got a heavenly mission to civilize you. It was very fine for a time, but after a bit I did get tired of resting. Then I began to look for a ship — I should think the hardest work on earth. But the ships wouldn't even look at me. And I got tired of that game, too.

"Now when I was a little chap I had a passion for maps. I would look for hours at South America, or Africa, or Australia, and lose myself in all the glories of exploration. At that time there were many blank spaces on the earth, and when I saw one that looked particularly inviting on a map (but they all look that) I would put my finger on it and say, When I grow up I will go there. The North Pole was one of these places, I remember. Well, I haven't been there yet, and shall not try now. The glamour's off. Other places were scattered about the Equator, and in every sort of latitude all over the two hemispheres. I have been in some of them, and . . . well, we won't talk about that. But there was one yet — the biggest, the most blank, so to speak — that I had a hankering after.

"True, by this time it was not a blank space any more. It had got filled since my childhood with rivers and lakes and names. It had ceased to be a blank space of delightful mystery—a white patch for a boy to dream gloriously over. It had become a place of darkness. But there was in it one river especially, a mighty big river, that you could see on the map, resembling an immense snake uncoiled, with its head in the sea, its body at rest curving afar over a vast country, and its tail lost in the depths of the land. And as I looked at the map of it in a shop-window, it fascinated me as a snake would a bird — a silly little bird. Then I remembered there was a big concern, a Company for trade on that river. Dash it all! I thought to myself, they can't trade without using some kind of craft on that lot of fresh water — steamboats! Why shouldn't I try to get charge of one? I went on along Fleet Street, but could not shake off the idea. The snake had charmed me.

"You understand it was a Continental concern, that Trading society; but I have a lot of relations living on the Continent, because it's cheap and not so nasty as it looks, they say.

"I am sorry to own I began to worry them. This was already a fresh departure for me. I was not used to getting things that way, you know. I always went my own road and on my own legs where I had a mind to go. I wouldn't have believed it of myself; but, then — you see — I felt somehow I must get there by hook or by crook. So I worried them. The men said 'My dear fellow,' and did nothing. Then — would you believe it? — I tried the women. I, Charlie Marlow, set the women to work — to get a job. Heavens! Well, you see, the notion drove me. I had an aunt, a dear enthusiastic soul. She wrote: 'It will be delightful. I am ready to do anything, anything for you. It is a glorious idea. I know the wife of a very high personage in the Administration, and also a man who has lots of influence with,' etc., etc. She was determined to make no end of fuss to get me appointed skipper of a river steamboat, if such was my fancy.

"I got my appointment — of course; and I got it very quick. It appears the Company had received news that one of their captains had been killed in a scuffle with the natives. This was my chance, and it made me the more anxious to go. It was only months and months afterwards, when I made the attempt to recover what was left of the body, that I heard the original quarrel arose from a misunderstanding about some hens. Yes, two black hens. Fresleven — that was the fellow's name, a Dane — thought himself wronged somehow in the bargain, so he went ashore and started to hammer the chief of the village with a stick. Oh, it didn't surprise me in the least to hear this, and at the same time to be told that Fresleven was the gentlest, quietest creature that ever walked on two legs. No doubt he was; but he had been a couple of years already out there engaged in the noble cause, you know, and he probably felt the need at last of asserting his self-respect in some way. Therefore he whacked the old nigger mercilessly, while a big crowd of his people watched him, thunderstruck, till some man — I was told the chief's son — in desperation at hearing the old chap yell, made a tentative jab with a spear at the white man — and of course it went quite easy between the shoulder blades. Then the whole population cleared into the forest, expecting all kinds of calamities to happen, while, on the other hand, the steamer Fresleven commanded left also in a bad panic, in charge of the engineer, I believe. Afterwards nobody seemed to trouble much about Fresleven's remains, till I got out and stepped into his shoes. I couldn't let it rest, though; but when an opportunity offered at last to meet my predecessor, the grass growing through his ribs was tall enough to hide his bones. They were all there. The supernatural being had not been touched after he fell. And the village was deserted, the huts gaped black, rotting, all askew within the fallen enclosures. A calamity had come to it, sure enough. The people had vanished. Mad terror had scattered them, men, women, and children, through the bush, and they had never returned. What became of the hens I don't know either. I should think the cause of progress got them, anyhow. However, through this glorious affair I got my appointment, before I had fairly begun to hope for it.

"I flew around like mad to get ready, and before forty-eight hours I was crossing the Channel to show myself to my employers, and sign the contract. In a very few hours I arrived in a city that always makes me think of a whited sepulcher. Prejudice no doubt. I had no difficulty in finding the Company's offices. It was the biggest thing in the town, and everybody I met was full of it. They were going to run an over-sea empire, and make no end of coin by trade.

"A narrow and deserted street in deep shadow, high houses, innumerable windows with venetian blinds, a dead silence, grass sprouting between the stones, imposing carriage archways right and left, immense double doors standing ponderously ajar. I slipped through one of these cracks, went up a swept and ungarnished staircase, as arid as a desert, and opened the first door I came to. Two women, one fat and the other slim, sat on straw-bottomed chairs, knitting black wool. The slim one got up and walked straight at me — still knitting with downcast eyes — and only just as I began to think of getting out of her way, as you would for a somnambulist, stood still, and looked up. Her dress was as plain as an umbrella-cover, and she turned round without a word and preceded me into a waiting-room. I gave my name, and looked about. Deal table in the middle, plain chairs all around the walls, on one end a large shining map, marked with all the colors of a rainbow. There was a vast amount of red — good to see at any time, because one knows that some real work is done in there, a deuce of a lot of blue, a little green, smears of orange, and, on the East Coast, a purple patch, to show where the jolly pioneers of progress drink the jolly lagerbeer. However, I wasn't going into any of these. I was going into the yellow. Dead in the center. And the river was there — fascinating — deadly — like a snake. Ough! A door opened, a white-haired secretarial head, but wearing a compassionate expression, appeared, and a skinny forefinger beckoned me into the sanctuary. Its light was dim, and a heavy writing-desk squatted in the middle. From behind that structure came out an impression of pale plumpness in a frock-coat. The great man himself. He was five feet six, I should judge, and had his grip on the handle-end of ever so many millions. He shook hands, I fancy, murmured vaguely, was satisfied with my French. *Bon voyage.*

"In about forty-five seconds I found myself again in the waiting-room with the compassionate secretary, who, full of desolation and sympathy, made me sign some document. I believe I undertook amongst other things not to disclose any trade secrets. Well, I am not going to.

"I began to feel slightly uneasy. You know I am not used to such cere-monies, and there was something ominous in the atmosphere. It was just as though I had been let into some conspiracy — I don't know — something not quite right; and I was glad to get out. In the outer room the two women knitted black wool feverishly. People were arriving, and the younger one was walking back and forth introducing them. The old one sat on her chair. Her flat cloth slippers were propped up on a footwarmer, and a cat reposed on her lap. She wore a starched white affair on her head, had a wart on one cheek, and silver-rimmed spectacles hung on the tip of her nose. She glanced at me above the glasses. The swift and indifferent placidity of that look troubled me. Two youths with foolish and cheery countenances were being piloted over, and she threw at them the same quick glance of uncon-cerned wisdom. She seemed to know all about them and about me, too. An eerie feeling came over me. She seemed uncanny and fateful. Often far away there I thought of these two, guarding the door of Darkness, knitting black wool as for a warm pall, one introducing, introducing continuously to the unknown, the other scrutinizing the cheery and foolish faces with un-concerned old eyes. *Ave!* Old knitter of black wool. *Morituri te salutant.*[5] Not many of those she looked at ever saw her again — not half, by a long way.

"There was yet a visit to the doctor. 'A simple formality,' assured me the secretary, with an air of taking an immense part in all my sorrows. Ac-cordingly a young chap wearing his hat over the left eyebrow, some clerk I suppose — there must have been clerks in the business, though the house was as still as a house in a city of the dead — came from somewhere up-stairs, and led me forth. He was shabby and careless, with inkstains on the sleeves of his jacket, and his cravat was large and billowy, under a chin shaped like the toe of an old boot. It was a little too early for the doctor, so I

---

[5] "Those who are about to die salute you" (Latin).

proposed a drink, and thereupon he developed a vein of joviality. As we sat over our vermouths he glorified the Company's business, and by and by I expressed casually my surprise at him not going out there. He became very cool and collected all at once. 'I am not such a fool as I look, quoth Plato to his disciples,' he said sententiously, emptied his glass with great resolution, and we rose.

"The old doctor felt my pulse, evidently thinking of something else the while. 'Good, good for there,' he mumbled, and then with a certain eagerness asked me whether I would let him measure my head. Rather surprised, I said Yes, when he produced a thing like calipers and got the dimensions back and front and every way, taking notes carefully. He was an unshaven little man in a threadbare coat like a gaberdine, with his feet in slippers, and I thought him a harmless fool. 'I always ask leave, in the interests of science, to measure the crania of those going out there,' he said. 'And when they come back, too?' I asked, 'Oh, I never see them,' he remarked; 'and, moreover, the changes take place inside, you know.' He smiled, as if at some quiet joke. 'So you are going out there. Famous. Interesting, too.' He gave me a searching glance, and made another note. 'Ever any madness in your family?' he asked, in a matter-of-fact tone. I felt very annoyed. 'Is that question in the interests of science, too?' 'It would be,' he said, without taking notice of my irritation, 'interesting for science to watch the mental changes of individuals, on the spot, but. . . .' 'Are you an alienist?' I interrupted. 'Every doctor should be — a little,' answered that original, imperturbably. 'I have a little theory which you Messieurs who go out there must help me to prove. This is my share in the advantages my country shall reap from the possession of such a magnificent dependency. The mere wealth I leave to others. Pardon my questions, but you are the first Englishman coming under my observation. . . .' I hastened to assure him I was not in the least typical. 'If I were,' said I 'I wouldn't be talking like this with you.' 'What you say is rather profound, and probably erroneous,' he said, with a laugh. 'Avoid irritation more than exposure to the sun. Adieu. How do you English say, eh? Good-by. Ah! Good-by. Adieu. In the tropics one must before everything keep calm.' . . . He lifted a warning forefinger. . . . 'Du calme, du calme. Adieu.'

"One thing more remained to do — say good-by to my excellent aunt. I found her triumphant. I had a cup of tea — the last decent cup of tea for many days — and in a room that most soothingly looked just as you would expect a lady's drawing-room to look, we had a long quiet chat by the fireside. In the course of these confidences it became quite plain to me I had been represented to the wife of the high dignitary, and goodness knows to how many more people besides, as an exceptional and gifted creature — a piece of good fortune for the Company — a man you don't get hold of every day. Good heavens! and I was going to take charge of a two-penny-half-penny river-steamboat with a penny whistle attached! It appeared, however, I was also one of the Workers, with a capital — you know. Something like an emissary of light, something like a lower sort of apostle. There had been a lot of such rot let loose in print and talk just about that time, and the excellent woman, living right in the rush of all that humbug, got carried off her feet. She talked about 'weaning those ignorant millions from their horrid ways,' till, upon my word, she made me quite uncomfortable. I ventured to hint that the Company was run for profit.

" 'You forget, dear Charlie, that the laborer is worthy of his hire,' she said, brightly. It's queer how out of touch with truth women are. They live in a world of their own, and there has never been anything like it, and never can be. It is too beautiful altogether, and if they were to set it up it would go to pieces before the first sunset. Some confounded fact we men have been living contentedly with ever since the day of creation would start up and knock the whole thing over.

"After this I got embraced, told to wear flannel, be sure to write often, and so on — and I left. In the street — I don't know why — a queer feeling came to me that I was an impostor. Odd thing that I, who used to clear out for any part of the world at twenty-four hours' notice, with less thought than most men give to the crossing of a street, had a moment — I won't say of hesitation, but of startled pause, before this commonplace affair. The best way I can explain it to you is by saying that, for a second or two, I felt as though, instead of going to the center of a continent, I were about to set off for the center of the earth.

"I left in a French steamer, and she called in every blamed port they have out there, for, as far as I could see, the sole purpose of landing soldiers and custom-house officers. I watched the coast. Watching a coast as it slips by the ship is like thinking about an enigma. There it is before you — smiling, frowning, inviting, grand, mean, insipid, or savage, and always mute with an air of whispering, Come and find out. This one was almost featureless, as if still in the making, with an aspect of monotonous grimness. The edge of a colossal jungle, so dark-green as to be almost black, fringed with white surf, ran straight, like a ruled line, far, far away along a blue sea whose glitter was blurred by a creeping mist. The sun was fierce, the land seemed to glisten and drip with steam. Here and there grayish-whitish specks showed up clustered inside the white surf, with a flag flying above them perhaps. Settlements some centuries old, and still no bigger than pinheads on the untouched expanse of their background. We pounded along, stopped, landed soldiers; went on, landed custom-house clerks to levy toll in what looked like a God-forsaken wilderness, with a tin shed and a flag-pole lost in it; landed more soldiers — to take care of the custom-house clerks, presumably. Some, I heard, got drowned in the surf; but whether they did or not, nobody seemed particularly to care. They were just flung out there, and on we went. Every day the coast looked the same, as though we had not moved; but we passed various places — trading places — with names like Gran' Bassam, Little Popo; names that seemed to belong to some sordid farce acted in front of a sinister backcloth. The idleness of a passenger, my isolation amongst all these men with whom I had no point of contact, the oily and languid sea, the uniform somberness of the coast, seemed to keep me away from the truth of things, within the toil of a mournful and sense-less delusion. The voice of the surf heard now and then was a positive plea-sure, like the speech of a brother. It was something natural, that had its reason, that had a meaning. Now and then a boat from the shore gave one a momentary contact with reality. It was paddled by black fellows. You could see from afar the white of their eyeballs glistening. They shouted, sang; their bodies streamed with perspiration; they had faces like grotesque masks — these chaps; but they had bone, muscle, a wild vitality, an intense energy of movement, that was as natural and true as the surf along their coast. They wanted no excuse for being there. They were a great comfort to look at. For a time I would feel I belonged still to a world of straightforward facts, but the feeling would not last long. Something would turn up to scare it away. Once, I remember, we came upon a man-of-war anchored off the coast. There wasn't even a shed there, and she was shelling the bush. It ap-pears the French had one of their wars going on thereabouts. Her ensign dropped limp like a rag; the muzzles of the long six-inch guns stuck out all over the low hull; the greasy, slimy swell swung her up lazily and let her down, swaying her thin masts. In the empty immensity of earth, sky, and water, there she was, incomprehensible, firing into a continent. Pop, would go one of the six-inch guns; a small flame would dart and vanish, a little white smoke would disappear, a tiny projectile would give a feeble screech — and nothing happened. Nothing could happen. There was a touch of insanity in the proceeding, a sense of lugubrious drollery in the sight; and it was not dissipated by somebody on board assuring me earnestly there was a camp of natives — he called them enemies! — hidden out of sight somewhere.

"We gave her her letters (I heard the men in that lonely ship were dying of fever at the rate of three a day) and went on. We called at some more places with farcical names, where the merry dance of death and trade goes on in a still and earthy atmosphere as of an overheated catacomb; all along the formless coast bordered by dangerous surf, as if Nature herself had tried to ward off intruders; in and out of rivers, streams of death in life, whose banks were rotting into mud, whose waters, thickened into slime, in-vaded the contorted mangroves, that seemed to writhe at us in the extrem-ity of an impotent despair. Nowhere did we stop long enough to get a par-ticularized impression, but the general sense of vague and oppressive wonder grew upon me. It was like a weary pilgrimage amongst hints for nightmares.

"It was upward of thirty days before I saw the mouth of the big river. We anchored off the seat of the government. But my work would not begin till some two hundred miles farther on. So as soon as I could I made a start for a place thirty miles higher up.

"I had my passage on a little sea-going steamer. Her captain was a

Swede, and knowing me for a seaman, invited me on the bridge. He was a young man, lean, fair, and morose, with lanky hair and a shuffling gait. As we left the miserable little wharf, he tossed his head contemptuously at the shore. 'Been living there?' he asked. I said, 'Yes.' 'Fine lot these government chaps — are they not?' he went on, speaking English with great precision and considerable bitterness. 'It is funny what some people will do for a few francs a month. I wonder what becomes of that kind when it goes upcountry?' I said to him I expected to see that soon. 'So-o-o!' he exclaimed. He shuffled athwart, keeping one eye ahead vigilantly. 'Don't be too sure,' he continued. 'The other day I took up a man who hanged himself on the road. He was a Swede, too.' 'Hanged himself! Why, in God's name?' I cried. I kept on looking out watchfully. 'Who knows? The sun was too much for him, or the country perhaps.'

"At last we opened a reach. A rocky cliff appeared, mounds of turned-up earth by the shore, houses on a hill, others with iron roofs, amongst a waste of excavations, or hanging to the declivity. A continuous noise of the rapids above hovered over this scene of inhabited devastation. A lot of people, mostly black and naked, moved about like ants. A jetty projected into the river. A blinding sunlight drowned all this at times in a sudden recrudescence of glare. 'There's your Company's station,' said the Swede, pointing to three wooden barrack-like structures on the rocky slope. 'I will send your things up. Four boxes did you say? So. Farewell.'

"I came upon a boiler wallowing in the grass, then found a path leading up the hill. It turned aside for the boulders, and also for an undersized railway-truck lying there on its back with its wheels in the air. One was off. The thing looked as dead as the carcass of some animal. I came upon more pieces of decaying machinery, a stack of rusty rails. To the left a clump of trees made a shady spot, where dark things seemed to stir feebly. I blinked, the path was steep. A horn tooted to the right, and I saw the black people run. A heavy and dull detonation shook the ground, a puff of smoke came out of the cliff, and that was all. No change appeared on the face of the rock. They were building a railway. The cliff was not in the way of anything; but the objectless blasting was all the work going on.

"A slight clinking behind me made me turn my head. Six black men advanced in a file, toiling up the path. They walked erect and slow, balancing small baskets full of earth on their heads, and the clink kept time with their footsteps. Black rags were wound round their loins, and the short ends behind waggled to and fro like tails. I could see every rib, the joints of their limbs were like knots in a rope; each had an iron collar on his neck, and all were connected together with a chain whose bights[6] swung between them, rhythmically clinking. Another report from the cliff made me think suddenly of that ship of war I had seen firing into a continent. It was the same kind of ominous voice; but these men could by no stretch of imagination be

---

[6] loops.

called enemies. They were called criminals, and the outraged law, like the bursting shells, had come to them, an insoluble mystery from the sea. All their meager breasts panted together, the violently dilated nostrils quivered, the eyes stared stonily uphill. They passed me within six inches, without a glance, with that complete, deathlike indifference of unhappy savages. Behind this raw matter one of the reclaimed, the product of the new forces at work, strolled despondently, carrying a rifle by its middle. He had a uniform jacket with one button off, and seeing a white man on the path, hoisted his weapon to his shoulder with alacrity. This was simple prudence, white men being so much alike at a distance that he could not tell who I might be. He was speedily reassured, and with a large, white, rascally grin, and a glance at his charge, seemed to take me into partnership in his exalted trust. After that, I also was a part of the great cause of these high and just proceedings.

"Instead of going up, I turned and descended to the left. My idea was to let that chain-gang get out of sight before I climbed the hill. You know I am not particularly tender, I've had to strike and to fend off. I've had to resist and to attack sometimes — that's only one way of resisting — without counting the exact cost, according to the demands of such sort of life as I had blundered into. I've seen the devil of violence, and the devil of greed, and the devil of hot desire; but, by all the stars! these were strong, lusty, red-eyed devils, that swayed and drove men — men, I tell you. But as I stood on this hillside, I foresaw that in the blinding sunshine of that land I would become acquainted with a flabby, pretending, weak-eyed devil of a rapacious and pitiless folly. How insidious he could be, too, I was only to find out several months later and a thousand miles farther. For a moment I stood appalled, as though by a warning. Finally I descended the hill, obliquely, towards the trees I had seen.

"I avoided a vast artificial hole somebody had been digging on the slope, the purpose of which I found it impossible to divine. It wasn't a quarry or a sandpit, anyhow. It was just a hole. It might have been connected with the philanthropic desire of giving the criminals something to do. I don't know. Then I nearly fell into a very narrow ravine, almost no more than a scar in the hillside. I discovered that a lot of imported drainage-pipes for the settlement had been tumbled in there. There wasn't one that was not broken. It was a wanton smash-up. At last I got under the trees. My purpose was to stroll into the shade for a moment; but no sooner within than it seemed to me I had stepped into the gloomy circle of some Inferno. The rapids were near, and an uninterrupted, uniform, headlong, rushing noise filled the mournful stillness of the grove, where not a breath stirred, not a leaf moved, with a mysterious sound — as though the tearing pace of the launched earth had suddenly become audible.

"Black shapes crouched, lay, sat between the trees leaning against the trunks, clinging to the earth, half coming out, half effaced within the dim light, in all the attitudes of pain, abandonment, and despair. Another mine on the cliff went off, followed by a slight shudder of the soil under my feet.

The work was going on. The work! and this was the place where some of
the helpers had withdrawn to die.

"They were dying slowly — it was very clear. They were not enemies,
they were not criminals, they were nothing earthly now — nothing but
black shadows of disease and starvation, lying confusedly in the greenish
gloom. Brought from all the recesses of the coast in all the legality of time
contracts, lost in uncongenial surroundings, fed on unfamiliar food, they
sickened, became inefficient, and were then allowed to crawl away and rest.
These moribund shapes were free as air — and nearly as thin. I began to
distinguish the gleam of the eyes under the trees. Then, glancing down, I
saw a face near my hand. The black bones reclined at full length with one
shoulder against the tree, and slowly the eyelids rose and the sunken eyes
looked up at me, enormous and vacant, a kind of blind, white flicker in the
depths of the orbs, which died out slowly. The man seemed young — almost a boy — but you know with them it's hard to tell. I found nothing else
to do but to offer him one of my good Swede's ship's biscuits I had in my
pocket. The fingers closed slowly on it and held — there was no other
movement and no other glance. He had tied a bit of white worsted round
his neck — Why? Where did he get it? Was it a badge — an ornament —
a charm — a propitiatory act? Was there any idea at all connected with it?
It looked startling round his black neck, this bit of white thread from beyond the seas.

"Near the same tree two more bundles of acute angles sat with their
legs drawn up. One, with his chin propped on his knees, stared at nothing,
in an intolerable and appalling manner: his brother phantom rested its
forehead, as if overcome with a great weariness; and all about others were
scattered in every pose of contorted collapse, as in some picture of a massacre or a pestilence. While I stood horror-struck, one of these creatures
rose to his hands and knees, and went off on all-fours towards the river to
drink. He lapped out of his hand, then sat up in the sunlight, crossing his
shins in front of him, and after a time let his woolly head fall on his breast-
bone.

"I didn't want any more loitering in the shade, and I made haste towards the station. When near the buildings I met a white man, in such an
unexpected elegance of get-up that in the first moment I took him for a sort
of vision. I saw a high starched collar, white cuffs, a light alpaca jacket,
snowy trousers, a clean necktie, and varnished boots. No hat. Hair parted,
brushed, oiled, under a green-lined parasol held in a big white hand. He was
amazing, and had a penholder behind his ear.

"I shook hands with this miracle, and I learned he was the Company's
chief accountant, and that all the bookkeeping was done at this station. He
had come out for a moment, he said, 'to get a breath of fresh air.' The expression sounded wonderfully odd, with its suggestion of sedentary desk-
life. I wouldn't have mentioned the fellow to you at all, only it was from his
lips that I first heard the name of the man who is so indissolubly connected

with the memories of that time. Moreover, I respected the fellow. Yes; I respected his collars, his vast cuffs, his brushed hair. His appearance was certainly that of a hairdresser's dummy; but in the great demoralization of the land he kept up his appearance. That's backbone. His starched collars and got-up shirt-fronts were achievements of character. He had been out nearly three years; and, later, I could not help asking him how he managed to sport such linen. He had just the faintest blush, and said modestly, 'I've been teaching one of the native women about the station. It was difficult. She had a distaste for the work.' Thus this man had verily accomplished something. And he was devoted to his books, which were in apple-pie order.

"Everything else in the station was in a muddle — heads, things, buildings. Strings of dusty niggers with splay feet arrived and departed; a stream of manufactured goods, rubbishy cottons, beads, and brass-wire set into the depths of darkness, and in return came a precious trickle of ivory.

"I had to wait in the station for ten days — an eternity. I lived in a hut in the yard, but to be out of the chaos I would sometimes get into the accountant's office. It was built of horizontal planks, and so badly put together that, as he bent over his high desk, he was barred from neck to heels with narrow strips of sunlight. There was no need to open the big shutter to see. It was hot there, too; big flies buzzed fiendishly, and did not sting, but stabbed. I sat generally on the floor, while, of faultless appearance (and even slightly scented), perching on a high stool, he wrote, he wrote. Sometimes he stood up for exercise. When a trucklebed with a sick man (some invalid agent from up-country) was put in there, he exhibited a gentle annoyance. 'The groans of this sick person,' he said, 'distract my attention. And without that it is extremely difficult to guard against clerical errors in this climate.'

"One day he remarked, without lifting his head, 'In the interior you will no doubt meet Mr. Kurtz.' On my asking who Mr. Kurtz was, he said he was a first-class agent; and seeing my disappointment at this information, he added slowly, laying down his pen, 'He is a very remarkable person.' Further questions elicited from him that Mr. Kurtz was at present in charge of a trading-post, a very important one, in the true ivory-country, at 'the very bottom of there. Sends in as much ivory as all the others put together. . . .' He began to write again. The sick man was too ill to groan. The flies buzzed in a great peace.

"Suddenly there was a growing murmur of voices and a great tramping of feet. A caravan had come in. A violent babble of uncouth sounds burst out on the other side of the planks. All the carriers were speaking together, and in the midst of the uproar the lamentable voice of the chief agent was heard 'giving it up' tearfully for the twentieth time that day. . . . He rose slowly. 'What a frightful row,' he said. He crossed the room gently to look at the sick man, and returning, said to me, 'He does not hear.' 'What! Dead?' I asked, startled. 'No, not yet,' he answered, with great composure. Then, alluding with a toss of the head to the tumult in the station-yard,

'When one has got to make correct entries, one comes to hate those savages — hate them to the death.' He remained thoughtful for a moment. 'When you see Mr. Kurtz,' he went on, 'tell him for me that everything here' — he glanced at the desk — 'is very satisfactory. I don't like to write to him — with those messengers of ours you never know who may get hold of your letter — at that Central Station.' He stared at me for a moment with his mild, bulging eyes. 'Oh, he will go far, very far,' he began again. 'He will be a somebody in the Administration before long. They, above — the Council in Europe, you know — mean him to be.'

"He turned to his work. The noise outside had ceased, and presently in going out I stopped at the door. In the steady buzz of flies the homeward-bound agent was lying flushed and insensible; the other, bent over his books, was making correct entries of perfectly correct transactions; and fifty feet below the doorstep I could see the still tree-tops of the grove of death.

"Next day I left the station at last, with a caravan of sixty men, for a two-hundred-mile tramp.

"No use telling you much about that. Paths, paths, everywhere; a stamped-in network of paths spreading over the empty land, through long grass, through burnt grass, through thickets, down and up chilly ravines, up and down stony hills ablaze with heat; and a solitude, a solitude, nobody, not a hut. The population had cleared out a long time ago. Well, if a lot of mysterious niggers armed with all kinds of fearful weapons suddenly took to traveling on the road between Deal and Gravesend, catching the yokels right and left to carry heavy loads for them, I fancy every farm and cottage thereabouts would get empty very soon. Only here the dwellings were gone, too. Still I passed through several abandoned villages. There's something pathetically childish in the ruins of grass walls. Day after day, with the stamp and shuffle of sixty pair of bare feet behind me, each pair under a sixty-pound load. Camp, cook, sleep, strike camp, march. Now and then a carrier dead in harness, at rest in the long grass near the path, with an empty water-gourd and his long staff lying by his side. A great silence around and above. Perhaps on some quiet night the tremor of far-off drums, sinking, swelling, a tremor vast, faint; a sound weird, appealing, suggestive, and wild — and perhaps with as profound a meaning as the sound of bells in a Christian country. Once a white man in an unbuttoned uniform, camping on the path with an armed escort of lank Zanzibaris, very hospitable and festive — not to say drunk. Was looking after the upkeep of the road, he declared. Can't say I saw any road or any upkeep, unless the body of a middle-aged Negro, with a bullet-hole in the forehead, upon which I absolutely stumbled three miles farther on, may be considered as a permanent improvement. I had a white companion, too, not a bad chap, but rather too fleshy and with the exasperating habit of fainting on the hot hillsides, miles away from the least bit of shade and water. Annoying, you know, to hold your own coat like a parasol over a man's head while he is coming to. I couldn't help asking him once what he meant by coming there at all. 'To make money, of course. What do you think?' he said, scornfully. Then he got fever, and had to be carried in a hammock slung under a pole. As he weighed sixteen stone[7] I had no end of rows with the carriers. They jibbed, ran away, sneaked off with their loads in the night — quite a mutiny. So, one evening, I made a speech in English with gestures, not one of which was lost to the sixty pairs of eyes before me, and the next morning I started the hammock off in front all right. An hour afterwards I came upon the whole concern wrecked in a bush — man, hammock, groans, blankets, horrors. The heavy pole had skinned his poor nose. He was very anxious for me to kill somebody, but there wasn't the shadow of a carrier near. I remember the old doctor—'It would be interesting for science to watch the mental changes of individuals, on the spot.' I felt I was becoming scientifically interesting. However, all that is to no purpose. On the fifteenth day I came in sight of the big river again, and hobbled into the Central Station. It was a backwater surrounded by scrub and forest, with a pretty border of smelly mud on one side, and on the three others enclosed by a crazy fence of rushes. A neglected gap was all the gate it had, and the first glance at the place was enough to let you see the flabby devil was running that show. White men with long staves in their hands appeared languidly from amongst the buildings, strolling up to take a look at me, and then retired out of sight somewhere. One of them, a stout, excitable chap with black mustaches, informed me with great volubility and many digressions, as soon as I told him who I was, that my steamer was at the bottom of the river. I was thunderstruck. What, how, why? Oh, it was 'all right.' The 'manager himself' was there. All quite correct. 'Everybody had behaved splendidly! splendidly!' — 'you must,' he said in agitation, 'go and see the general manager at once. He is waiting!'

"I did not see the real significance of that wreck at once. I fancy I see it now, but I am not sure — not at all. Certainly the affair was too stupid — when I think of it — to be altogether natural. Still. . . . But at the moment it presented itself simply as a confounded nuisance. The steamer was sunk. They had started two days before in a sudden hurry up the river with the manager on board, in charge of some volunteer skipper, and before they had been out three hours they tore the bottom out of her on stones, and she sank near the south bank. I asked myself what I was to do there, now my boat was lost. As a matter of fact, I had plenty to do in fishing my command out of the river. I had to set about it the very next day. That, and the repairs when I brought the pieces to the station, took some months.

"My first interview with the manager was curious. He did not ask me to sit down after my twenty-mile walk that morning. He was commonplace in complexion, in feature, in manners, and in voice. He was of middle size and of ordinary build. His eyes, of the usual blue, were perhaps remarkably cold, and he certainly could make his glance fall on one as trenchant and

---

[7] 224 pounds (a *stone* is the equivalent of fourteen pounds).

heavy as an ax. But even at these times the rest of his person seemed to dis-
claim the intention. Otherwise there was only an indefinable, faint expression of his lips, something stealthy — a smile — not a smile — I remember
it, but I can't explain. It was unconscious, this smile was, though just after
he had said something it got intensified for an instant. It came at the end of
his speeches like a seal applied on the words to make the meaning of the
commonest phrase appear absolutely inscrutable. He was a common trader,
from his youth up employed in these parts — nothing more. He was
obeyed, yet he inspired neither love nor fear, nor even respect. He inspired
uneasiness. That was it! Uneasiness. Not a definite mistrust — just uneasiness — nothing more. You have no idea how effective such a . . . a . . . faculty can be. He had no genius for organizing, for initiative, or for order
even. That was evident in such things as the deplorable state of the station.
He had no learning, and no intelligence. His position had come to him —
why? Perhaps because he was never ill. . . . He had served three terms of
three years out there. . . . Because triumphant health in the general rout of
constitutions is a kind of power in itself. When he went home on leave he
rioted on a large scale — pompously. Jack ashore — with a difference — in
externals only. This one could gather from his casual talk. He originated
nothing, he could keep the routine going — that's all. But he was great. He
was great by this little thing that it was impossible to tell what could control
such a man. He never gave the secret away. Perhaps there was nothing
within him. Such a suspicion made one pause — for out there there were
no external checks. Once when various tropical diseases had laid low almost
every 'agent' in the station, he was heard to say, 'Men who come out here
should have no entrails.' He sealed the utterance with that smile of his, as
though it had been a door opening into a darkness he had in his keeping.
You fancied you had seen things — but the seal was on. When annoyed at
meal-times by the constant quarrels of the white men about precedence, he
ordered an immense round table to be made, for which a special house had
to be built. This was the station's messroom. Where he sat was the first
place — the rest were nowhere. One felt this to be his unalterable conviction. He was neither civil nor uncivil. He was quiet. He allowed his
'boy' — an overfed young Negro from the coast — to treat the white men,
under his very eyes, with provoking insolence.

　　"He began to speak as soon as he saw me. I had been very long on the
road. He could not wait. Had to start without me. The upriver stations had
to be relieved. There had been so many delays already that he did not know
who was dead and who was alive, and how they got on — and so on, and so
on. He paid no attention to my explanations, and, playing with a stick of
sealing-wax, repeated several times that the situation was 'very grave, very
grave.' There were rumors that a very important station was in jeopardy,
and its chief, Mr. Kurtz, was ill. Hoped it was not true. Mr. Kurtz was. . . . I
felt weary and irritable. Hang Kurtz, I thought. I interrupted him by saying
I had heard of Mr. Kurtz on the coast. 'Ah! So they talk of him down there,'

he murmured to himself. Then he began again, assuring me Mr. Kurtz was the best agent he had, an exceptional man, of the greatest importance to the Company; therefore I could understand his anxiety. He was, he said, 'very, very uneasy.' Certainly he fidgeted on his chair a good deal, exclaimed, 'Ah, Mr. Kurtz!' broke the stick of sealing-wax and seemed dumfounded by the accident. Next thing he wanted to know 'how long it would take to. . . .' I interrupted him again. Being hungry, you know, and kept on my feet too, I was getting savage. 'How can I tell?' I said. 'I haven't even seen the wreck yet — some months, no doubt.' All this talk seemed to me so futile. 'Some months,' he said. 'Well, let us say three months before we can make a start. Yes. That ought to do the affair.' I flung out of his hut (he lived all alone in a clay hut with a sort of veranda) muttering to myself my opinion of him. He was a chattering idiot. Afterwards I took it back when it was borne in upon me startlingly with what extreme nicety he had estimated the time requisite for the 'affair.'

"I went to work the next day, turning, so to speak, my back on that station. In that way only it seemed to me I could keep my hold on the redeeming facts of life. Still, one must look about sometimes; and then I saw this station, these men strolling aimlessly about in the sunshine of the yard. I asked myself sometimes what it all meant. They wandered here and there with their absurd long staves in their hands, like a lot of faithless pilgrims bewitched inside a rotten fence. The word 'ivory' rang in the air, was whispered, was sighed. You would think they were praying to it. A taint of imbecile rapacity blew through it all, like a whiff from some corpse. By Jove! I've never seen anything so unreal in my life. And outside, the silent wilderness surrounding this cleared speck on the earth struck me as something great and invincible, like evil or truth, waiting patiently for the passing away of this fantastic invasion.

"Oh, these months! Well, never mind. Various things happened. One evening a grass shed full of calico, cotton prints, beads, and I don't know what else, burst into a blaze so suddenly that you would have thought the earth had opened to let an avenging fire consume all the trash. I was smoking my pipe quietly by my dismantled steamer, and saw them all cutting capers in the light, with their arms lifted high, when the stout man with mustaches came tearing down to the river, a tin pail in his hand, assured me that everybody was 'behaving splendidly, splendidly,' dipped about a quart of water and tore back again. I noticed there was a hole in the bottom of his pail.

"I strolled up. There was no hurry. You see the thing had gone off like a box of matches. It had been hopeless from the very first. The flame had leaped high, driven everybody back, lighted up everything — and collapsed. The shed was already a heap of embers glowing fiercely. A nigger was being beaten near by. They said he had caused the fire in some way; be that as it may, he was screeching most horribly. I saw him, later, for several days, sitting in a bit of shade looking very sick and trying to recover himself:

afterwards he arose and went out — and the wilderness without a sound took him into its bosom again. As I approached the glow from the dark I found myself at the back of two men, talking. I heard the name of Kurtz pronounced, then the words, 'take advantage of this unfortunate accident.' One of the men was the manager. I wished him a good evening. 'Did you ever see anything like it — eh? it is incredible,' he said, and walked off. The other man remained. He was a first-class agent, young, gentlemanly, a bit reserved, with a forked little beard and a hooked nose. He was standoffish with the other agents, and they on their side said he was the manager's spy among them. As to me, I had hardly ever spoken to him before. We got into talk, and by and by we strolled away from the hissing ruins. Then he asked me to his room, which was in the main building of the station. He struck a match, and I perceived that this young aristocrat had not only a silver-mounted dressing-case but also a whole candle all to himself. Just at that time the manager was the only man supposed to have any right to candles. Native mats covered the clay walls; a collection of spears, assegais, shields, knives was hung up in trophies. The business intrusted to this fellow was the making of bricks — so I had been informed; but there wasn't a fragment of a brick anywhere in the station, and he had been there more than a year — waiting. It seems he could not make bricks without something, I don't know what — straw, maybe. Anyways, it could not be found there, and as it was not likely to be sent from Europe, it did not appear clear to me what he was waiting for. An act of special creation perhaps. However, they were all waiting — all the sixteen or twenty pilgrims of them — for something; and upon my word it did not seem an uncongenial occupation, from the way they took it, though the only thing that ever came to them was disease — as far as I could see. They beguiled the time by backbiting and intriguing against each other in a foolish kind of way. There was an air of plotting about that station, but nothing came of it, of course. It was as unreal as everything else — as the philanthropic pretense of the whole concern, as their talk, as their government, as their show of work. The only real feeling was a desire to get appointed to a trading-post where ivory was to be had, so that they could earn percentages. They intrigued and slandered and hated each other only on that account — but as to effectually lifting a little finger — oh, no. By heavens! there is something after all in the world allowing one man to steal a horse while another must not look at the halter. Steal a horse straight out. Very well. He has done it. Perhaps he can ride. But there is a way of looking at a halter that would provoke the most charitable of saints into a kick.

"I had no idea why he wanted to be sociable, but as we chatted in there it suddenly occurred to me the fellow was trying to get at something — in fact, pumping me. He alluded constantly to Europe, to the people I was supposed to know there — putting leading questions as to my acquaintances in the sepulchral city, and so on. His little eyes glittered like mica discs — with curiosity — though he tried to keep up a bit of superciliousness. At first I was astonished, but very soon I became awfully curious to see what he would find out from me. I couldn't possibly imagine what I had in me to make it worth his while. It was very pretty to see how he baffled himself, for in truth my body was full only of chills, and my head had nothing in it but that wretched steamboat business. It was evident he took me for a perfectly shameless prevaricator. At last he got angry, and, to conceal a movement of furious annoyance, he yawned. I rose. Then I noticed a small sketch in oils, on a panel, representing a woman, draped and blindfolded, carrying a lighted torch. The background was somber — almost black. The movement of the woman was stately, and the effect of the torchlight on the face was sinister.

"It arrested me, and he stood by civilly, holding an empty half-pint champagne bottle (medical comforts) with the candle stuck in it. To my question he said Mr. Kurtz had painted this — in this very station more than a year ago — while waiting for means to go to his trading-post. 'Tell me, pray,' said I, 'who is this Mr. Kurtz?'

" 'The chief of the Inner Station,' he answered in a short tone, looking away. 'Much obliged,' I said, laughing. 'And you are the brickmaker of the Central Station. Everyone knows that.' He was silent for a while. 'He is a prodigy,' he said at last. 'He is an emissary of pity, and science, and progress, and devil knows what else. We want,' he began to declaim suddenly, 'for the guidance of the cause intrusted to us by Europe, so to speak, higher intelligence, wide sympathies, a singleness of purpose.' 'Who says that?' I asked. 'Lots of them,' he replied. 'Some even write that; and so *he* comes here, a special being, as you ought to know.' 'Why ought I to know?' I interrupted, really surprised. He paid no attention. 'Yes. Today he is chief of the best station, next year he will be assistant-manager, two years more and . . . but I daresay you know what he will be in two years' time. You are of the new gang — the gang of virtue. The same people who sent him specially also recommended you. Oh, don't say no. I've my own eyes to trust.' Light dawned upon me. My dear aunt's influential acquaintances were producing an unexpected effect upon that young man. I nearly burst into a laugh. 'Do you read the Company's confidential correspondence?' I asked. He hadn't a word to say. It was great fun. 'When Mr. Kurtz,' I continued, severely, 'is General Manager, you won't have the opportunity.'

"He blew the candle out suddenly, and we went outside. The moon had risen. Black figures strolled about listlessly, pouring water on the glow, whence proceeded a sound of hissing; steam ascended in the moonlight, the beaten nigger groaned somewhere. 'What a row the brute makes!' said the indefatigable man with the mustaches, appearing near us. 'Serves him right. Transgression — punishment — bang! Pitiless, pitiless. That's the only way. This will prevent all conflagrations for the future. I was just telling the manager. . . .' He noticed my companion, and became crestfallen all at once. 'Not in bed yet,' he said, with a kind of servile heartiness; 'it's so natural. Ha! Danger — agitation.' He vanished. I went on to the riverside, and the other followed me. I heard a scathing murmur at my ear, 'Heap of muffs — go to.' The pilgrims could be seen in knots gesticulating, discussing. Several had still their staves in their hands. I verily believe they took these sticks to bed with them. Beyond the fence the forest stood up spectrally in the moonlight, and through the dim stir, through the faint sounds of that lamentable courtyard, the silence of the land went home to one's very heart — its mystery, its greatness, the amazing reality of its concealed life. The hurt nigger moaned feebly somewhere near by, and then fetched a deep sigh that made me mend my pace away from there. I felt a hand introducing itself under my arm. 'My dear sir,' said the fellow, 'I don't want to be misunderstood, and especially by you, who will see Mr. Kurtz long before I can have that pleasure. I wouldn't like him to get a false idea of my disposition. . . .'

"I let him run on, this papier-mâché Mephistopheles, and it seemed to me that if I tried I could poke my forefinger through him, and would find nothing inside but a little loose dirt, maybe. He, don't you see, had been planning to be assistant-manager by and by under the present man, and I could see that the coming of that Kurtz had upset them both not a little. He talked precipitately, and I did not try to stop him. I had my shoulders against the wreck of my steamer, hauled up on the slope like a carcass of some big river animal. The smell of mud, of primeval mud, by Jove! was in my nostrils, the high stillness of primeval forest was before my eyes; there were shiny patches on the black creek. The moon had spread over everything a thin layer of silver — over the rank grass, over the mud, upon the wall of matted vegetation standing higher than the wall of a temple, over the great river I could see through a somber gap glittering, glittering, as it flowed broadly by without a murmur. All this was great, expectant, mute, while the man jabbered about himself. I wondered whether the stillness on the face of the immensity looking at us two were meant as an appeal or as a menace. What were we who had strayed in here? Could we handle that dumb thing, or would it handle us? I felt how big, how confoundedly big, was that thing that couldn't talk, and perhaps was deaf as well. What was in there? I could see a little ivory coming out from there, and I had heard Mr. Kurtz was in there. I had heard enough about it, too — God knows! Yet somehow it didn't bring any image with it — no more than if I had been told an angel or a fiend was in there. I believed it in the same way one of you might believe there are inhabitants in the planet Mars. I knew once a Scotch sailmaker who was certain, dead sure, there were people in Mars. If you asked him for some idea how they looked and behaved, he would get shy and mutter something about 'walking on all-fours.' If you as much as smiled, he would — though a man of sixty — offer to fight you. I would not have gone so far as to fight for Kurtz, but I went for him near enough to a lie. You know I hate, detest, and can't bear a lie, not because I am straighter than the rest of us, but simply because it appalls me. There is a taint of death, a flavor of mortality in lies — which is exactly what I hate and detest in the world — what I want to forget. It makes me miserable and sick, like biting something rotten would do. Temperament, I suppose. Well, I went near enough to it by letting the young fool there believe anything he liked to imagine as to my influence in Europe. I became in an instant as much of a pretense as the rest of the bewitched pilgrims. This simply because I had a notion it somehow would be of help to that Kurtz whom at the time I did not see — you understand. He was just a word for me. I did not see the man in the name any more than you do. Do you see him? Do you see the story? Do you see anything? It seems to me I am trying to tell you a dream — making a vain attempt, because no relation of a dream can convey the dream-sensation, that commingling of absurdity, surprise, and bewilderment in a tremor of struggling revolt, that notion of being captured by the incredible which is of the very essence of dreams. . . ."

He was silent for a while.

". . . No, it is impossible; it is impossible to convey the life-sensation of any given epoch of one's existence — that which makes its truth, its meaning — its subtle and penetrating essence. It is impossible. We live, as we dream — alone. . . ."

He paused again as if reflecting, then added —

"Of course in this you fellows see more than I could then. You see me, whom you know. . . ."

It had become so pitch dark that we listeners could hardly see one another. For a long time already he, sitting apart, had been no more to us than a voice. There was not a word from anybody. The others might have been asleep, but I was awake. I listened, I listened on the watch for the sentence, for the word, that would give me the clew of the faint uneasiness inspired by this narrative that seemed to shape itself without human lips in the heavy night-air of the river.

". . . Yes — I let him run on," Marlow began again, "and think what he pleased about the powers that were behind me. I did! And there was nothing behind me! There was nothing but that wretched, old, mangled steamboat I was leaning against, while he talked fluently about 'the necessity for every man to get on.' 'And when one comes out here, you conceive, it is not to gaze at the moon.' Mr. Kurtz was a 'universal genius,' but even a genius would find it easier to work with 'adequate tools — intelligent men.' He did not make bricks — why, there was a physical impossibility in the way — as I was well aware; and if he did secretarial work for the manager, it was because 'no sensible man rejects wantonly the confidence of his superiors.' Did I see it? I saw it. What more did I want? What I really wanted was rivets, by heavens! Rivets. To get on with the work — to stop the hole. Rivets I wanted. There were cases of them down at the coast — cases — piled up — burst — split! You kicked a loose rivet at every second step in that station yard on the hillside. Rivets had rolled into the grove of death. You could fill your pockets with rivets for the trouble of stooping down — and there wasn't one rivet to be found where it was wanted. We had plates that would do, but nothing to fasten them with. And every week the messenger, a lone Negro, letter-bag on shoulder and staff in hand, left our station for the coast. And several times a week a coast caravan came in with trade goods — ghastly glazed calico that made you shudder only to look at it; glass beads, valued about a penny a quart, confounded spotted cotton handkerchiefs. And no rivets. Three carriers could have brought all that was wanted to set that steamboat afloat.

"He was becoming confidential now, but I fancy my unresponsive attitude must have exasperated him at last, for he judged it necessary to inform me he feared neither God nor devil, let alone any mere man. I said I could see that very well, but what I wanted was a certain quantity of rivets — and rivets were what really Mr. Kurtz wanted, if he had only known it. Now letters went to the coast every week. . . . 'My dear sir,' he cried, 'I write from dictation.' I demanded rivets. There was a way — for an intelligent man. He changed his manner; became very cold, and suddenly began to talk about a hippopotamus; wondered whether sleeping on board the steamer (I stuck to my salvage night and day) I wasn't disturbed. There was an old hippo that had the bad habit of getting out on the bank and roaming at night over the station grounds. The pilgrims used to turn out in a body and empty every rifle they could lay hands on at him. Some even had sat up o' nights for him. All this energy was wasted, though. 'That animal had a charmed life,' he said; 'but you can say this only of brutes in this country. No man — you apprehend me? — no man here bears a charmed life.' He stood there for a moment in the moonlight with his delicate hooked nose set a little askew, and his mica eyes glittering without a wink, then, with a curt good night, he strode off. I could see he was disturbed and considerably puzzled, which made me feel more hopeful than I had been for days. It was a great comfort to turn from that chap to my influential friend, the battered, twisted, ruined, tin-pot steamboat. I clambered on board. She rang under my feet like an empty Huntley & Palmer biscuit-tin kicked along a gutter; she was nothing so solid in make, and rather less pretty in shape, but I had expended enough hard work on her to make me love her. No influential friend would have served me better. She had given me a chance to come out a bit — to find out what I could do. No, I don't like work. I had rather laze about and think of all the fine things that can be done. I don't like work — no man does — but I like what is in the work — the chance to find yourself. Your own reality — for yourself, not for others — what no other man can ever know. They can only see the mere show, and never tell me what it really means.

"I was not surprised to see somebody sitting aft, on the deck, with his legs dangling over the mud. You see I rather chummed with the few mechanics there were in that station, whom the other pilgrims naturally despised — on account of their imperfect manners, I suppose. This was the foreman — a boiler-maker by trade — a good worker. He was a lank, bony, yellow-faced man, with big intense eyes. His aspect was worried, and his head was as bald as the palm of my hand; but his hair in falling seemed to have stuck to his chin, and had prospered in the new locality, for his beard hung down to his waist. He was a widower with six young children (he had left them in charge of a sister of his to come out there), and the passion of his life was pigeon-flying. He was an enthusiast and a connoisseur. He would rave about pigeons. After work hours he used sometimes to come over from his hut for a talk about his children and his pigeons; at work, when he had to crawl in the mud under the bottom of the steamboat, he would tie up that beard of his in a kind of white serviette he brought for the purpose. It had loops to go over his ears. In the evening he could be seen squatted on the bank rinsing that wrapper in the creek with great care, then spreading it solemnly on a bush to dry.

"I slapped him on the back and shouted, 'We shall have rivets!' He scrambled to his feet exclaiming, 'No! Rivets!' as though he couldn't believe his ears. Then in a low voice, 'You . . . eh?' I don't know why we behaved like lunatics. I put my finger to the side of my nose and nodded mysteriously. 'Good for you!' he cried, snapped his fingers above his head, lifting one foot. I tried a jig. We capered on the iron deck. A frightful clatter came out of that hulk, and the virgin forest on the other bank of the creek sent it back in a thundering roll upon the sleeping station. It must have made some of the pilgrims sit up in their hovels. A dark figure obscured the lighted doorway of the manager's hut, vanished, then, a second or so after, the doorway itself vanished, too. We stopped, and the silence driven away by the stamping of our feet flowed back again from the recesses of the land. The great wall of vegetation, an exuberant and entangled mass of trunks, branches, leaves, boughs, festoons, motionless in the moonlight, was like a rioting invasion of soundless life, a rolling wave of plants, piled up, crested, ready to topple over the creek, to sweep every little man of us out of his little existence. And it moved not. A deadened burst of mighty splashes and snorts reached us from afar as though an ichthyosaurus[8] had been taking a bath of glitter in the great river. 'After all,' said the boilermaker in a reasonable tone, 'why shouldn't we get the rivets?' Why not, indeed! I did not know of any reason why we shouldn't. 'They'll come in three weeks,' I said confidently.

"But they didn't. Instead of rivets there came an invasion, an infliction, a visitation. It came in sections during the next three weeks, each section headed by a donkey carrying a white man in new clothes and tan shoes, bowing from that elevation right and left to the impressed pilgrims. A quarrelsome band of footsore sulky niggers trod on the heels of the donkeys; a lot of tents, campstools, tin boxes, white cases, brown bales would be shot down in the courtyard, and the air of mystery would deepen a little over the muddle of the station. Five such installments came, with their absurd air of disorderly flight with the loot of innumerable outfit shops and provision

---

[8] water-dwelling dinosaur.

stores, that, one would think, they were lugging, after a raid, into the wilderness for equitable division. It was an extricable mess of things decent in themselves but that human folly made look like the spoils of thieving.

"This devoted band called itself the Eldorado Exploring Expedition, and I believe they were sworn to secrecy. Their talk, however, was the talk of sordid buccaneers: it was reckless without hardihood, greedy without audacity, and cruel without courage; there was not an atom of foresight or of serious intention in the whole batch of them, and they did not seem aware these things are wanted for the work of the world. To tear treasure out of the bowels of the land was their desire, with no more moral purpose at the back of it than there is in burglars breaking into a safe. Who paid the expenses of the noble enterprise I don't know; but the uncle of our manager was leader of that lot.

"In exterior he resembled a butcher in a poor neighborhood, and his eyes had a look of sleepy cunning. He carried his fat paunch with ostentation on his short legs, and during the time his gang infested the station spoke to no one but his nephew. You could see these two roaming about all day long with their heads close together in an everlasting confab.

"I had given up worrying myself about the rivets. One's capacity for that kind of folly is more limited than you would suppose. I said Hang! — and let things slide. I had plenty of time for meditation, and now and then I would give some thought to Kurtz. I wasn't very interested in him. No. Still, I was curious to see whether this man, who had come out equipped with moral ideas of some sort, would climb to the top after all and how he would set about his work when there."

II

"One evening as I was lying flat on the deck of my steamboat, I heard voices approaching — and there were the nephew and the uncle strolling along the bank. I laid my head on my arm again, and had nearly lost myself in a doze, when somebody said in my ear, as it were: 'I am as harmless as a little child, but I don't like to be dictated to. Am I the manager — or am I not? I was ordered to send him there. It's incredible.' . . . I became aware that the two were standing on the shore alongside the forepart of the steamboat, just below my head. I did not move; it did not occur to me to move: I was sleepy. 'It *is* unpleasant,' grunted the uncle. 'He has asked the Administration to be sent there,' said the other, 'with the idea of showing what he could do; and I was instructed accordingly. Look at the influence that man must have. Is it not frightful?' They both agreed it was frightful, then made several bizarre remarks: 'Make rain and fine weather — one man — the Council — by the nose' — bits of absurd sentences that got the better of my drowsiness, so that I had pretty near the whole of my wits about me when the uncle said, 'The climate may do away with this difficulty for you. Is he alone there?' 'Yes,' answered the manager; 'he sent his assistant down the river with a note to me in these terms: "Clear this poor devil out of the country, and don't bother sending more of that sort. I had rather be alone than have the kind of men you can dispose of with me." It was more than a year ago. Can you imagine such impudence!' 'Anything since then?' asked the other, hoarsely. 'Ivory,' jerked the nephew; 'lots of it — prime sort — lots — most annoying, from him.' 'And with that?' questioned the heavy rumble. 'Invoice,' was the reply fired out, so to speak. Then silence. They had been talking about Kurtz.

"I was broad awake by this time, but, lying perfectly at ease, remained still, having no inducement to change my position. 'How did that ivory come all this way?' growled the elder man, who seemed very vexed. The other explained that it had come with a fleet of canoes in charge of an English half-caste clerk Kurtz had with him; that Kurtz had apparently intended to return himself, the station being by that time bare of goods and stores, but after coming three hundred miles, had suddenly decided to go back, which he started to do alone in a small dugout with four paddlers, leaving the half-caste to continue down the river with the ivory. The two fellows there seemed astounded at anybody attempting such a thing. They were at a loss for an adequate motive. As to me, I seemed to see Kurtz for the first time. It was a distinct glimpse: the dugout, four paddling savages, and the lone white man turning his back suddenly on the headquarters, on relief, on thoughts of home — perhaps; setting his face towards the depths of the wilderness, towards his empty and desolate station. I did not know the motive. Perhaps he was just simply a fine fellow who stuck to his work for its own sake. His name, you understand, had not been pronounced once. He was 'that man.' The half-caste, who, as far as I could see, had conducted a difficult trip with great prudence and pluck, was invariably alluded to as 'that scoundrel.' The 'scoundrel' had reported that the 'man' had been very ill — had recovered imperfectly. . . . The two below me moved away then a few paces, and strolled back and forth at some little distance. I heard: 'Military post — doctor — two hundred miles — quite alone now — unavoidable delays — nine months — no news — strange rumors.' They approached again, just as the manager was saying, 'No one, as far as I know, unless a species of wandering trader — a pestilential fellow, snapping ivory from the natives.' Who was it they were talking about now? I gathered in snatches that this was some man supposed to be in Kurtz's district, and of whom the manager did not approve. 'We will not be free from unfair competition till one of these fellows is hanged for an example,' he said. 'Certainly,' grunted the other; 'get him hanged! Why not? Anything — anything can be done in this country. That's what I say; nobody here, you understand, here, can endanger your position. And why? You stand the climate — you outlast them all. The danger is in Europe; but there before I left I took care to — ' They moved off and whispered, then their voices rose again. 'The extraordinary series of delays is not my fault. I did my best.' The fat man sighed. 'Very sad.' 'And the pestiferous absurdity of his talk,' continued the other; 'he bothered me enough when he was here. "Each station should be like a beacon on the road towards better things, a center for trade, of course, but also for humanizing, improving, instructing." Conceive you — that ass! And he wants to be manager! No it's — ' Here he got choked by excessive indignation, and I lifted my head the least bit. I was surprised to see how near they were — right under me. I could have spat upon their hats. They were looking on the ground, absorbed in thought. The manager was switching his leg with a slender twig: his sagacious relative lifted his head. 'You have been well since you came out this time?' he asked. The other gave a start. 'Who? I? Oh! Like a charm — like a charm. But the rest — oh, my goodness! All sick. They die so quick, too, that I haven't the time to send them out of the country—it's incredible!' 'H'm. Just so,' grunted the uncle. 'Ah! my boy, trust to this — I say, trust to this.' I saw him extend his short flipper of an arm for a gesture that took in the forest, the creek, the mud, the river — seemed to beckon with a dishonoring flourish before the sunlit face of the land a treacherous appeal to the lurking death, to the hidden evil, to the profound darkness of its heart. It was so startling that I leaped to my feet and looked back at the edge of the forest, as though I had expected an answer of some sort to that black display of confidence. You know the foolish notions that come to one sometimes. The high stillness confronted these two figures with its ominous patience, waiting for the passing away of a fantastic invasion.

"They swore aloud together — out of sheer fright, I believe — then pretending not to know anything of my existence, turned back to the station. The sun was low; and leaning forward side by side, they seemed to be tugging painfully uphill their two ridiculous shadows of unequal length, that trailed behind them slowly over the tall grass without bending a single blade.

"In a few days the Eldorado Expedition went into the patient wilderness, that closed upon it as the sea closes over a diver. Long afterwards the news came that all the donkeys were dead. I know nothing as to the fate of the less valuable animals. They, no doubt, like the rest of us, found what they deserved. I did not inquire. I was then rather excited at the prospect of meeting Kurtz very soon. When I say very soon I mean it comparatively. It was just two months from the day we left the creek when we came to the bank below Kurtz's station.

"Going up that river was like traveling back to the earliest beginnings of the world, when vegetation rioted on the earth and the big trees were kings. An empty stream, a great silence, an impenetrable forest. The air was warm, thick, heavy, sluggish. There was no joy in the brilliance of sunshine. The long stretches of the waterway ran on, deserted, into the gloom of overshadowed distances. On silvery sandbanks hippos and alligators sunned themselves side by side. The broadening waters flowed through a mob of wooded islands; you lost your way on that river as you would in a desert, and butted all day long against shoals, trying to find the channel, till you thought yourself bewitched and cut off forever from everything you had known once — somewhere — far away — in another existence perhaps. There were moments when one's past came back to one, as it will sometimes when you have not a moment to spare to yourself; but it came in the shape of an unrestful and noisy dream, remembered with wonder amongst the overwhelming realities of this strange world of plants, and water, and silence. And this stillness of life did not in the least resemble a peace. It was the stillness of an implacable force brooding over an inscrutable intention. It looked at you with a vengeful aspect. I got used to it afterwards; I did not see it any more; I had no time. I had to keep guessing at the channel; I had to discern, mostly by inspiration, the signs of hidden banks; I watched for sunken stones; I was learning to clap my teeth smartly before my heart flew out, when I shaved by a fluke some infernal sly old snag that would have ripped the life out of the tin-pot steamboat and drowned all the pilgrims; I had to keep a lookout for the signs of dead wood we could cut up in the night for next day's steaming. When you have to attend to things of that sort, to the mere incidents of the surface, the reality — the reality, I tell you — fades. The inner truth is hidden — luckily, luckily. But I felt it all the same; I felt often its mysterious stillness watching me at my monkey tricks, just as it watches you fellows performing on your respective tight-ropes for — what is it? half-a-crown a tumble — "

"Try to be civil, Marlow," growled a voice, and I knew there was at least one listener awake besides myself.

"I beg your pardon. I forgot the heartache which makes up the rest of the price. And indeed what does the price matter, if the trick be well done? You do your tricks very well. And I didn't do badly either, since I managed not to sink that steamboat on my first trip. It's a wonder to me yet. Imagine a blindfolded man set to drive a van over a bad road. I sweated and shivered over the business considerably, I can tell you. After all, for a seaman, to scrape the bottom of the thing that's supposed to float all the time under his care is the unpardonable sin. No one may know of it, but you never forget the thump — eh? A blow on the very heart. You remember it, you dream of it, you wake up at night and think of it — years after — and go hot and cold all over. I don't pretend to say that steamboat floated all the time. More than once she had to wade for a bit, with twenty cannibals splashing around and pushing. We had enlisted some of these chaps on the way for a crew. Fine fellows — cannibals — in their place. They were men one could work with, and I am grateful to them. And, after all, they did not eat each other before my face: they had brought along a provision of hippo-meat which went rotten, and made the mystery of the wilderness stink in my nostrils. Phoo! I can sniff it now. I had the manager on board and three or four pilgrims with their staves — all complete. Sometimes we came upon a station close by the bank, clinging to the skirts of the unknown, and the white men rushing out of a tumble-down hovel, with great gestures of joy and surprise and welcome, seemed very strange — had the appearance of being held there captive by a spell. The word ivory would ring in the air for a while — and on we went again into the silence, along empty reaches, round the still bends, between the high walls of our winding way, reverberating in hollow claps the ponderous beat of the stern-wheel. Trees, trees, millions of trees, massive, immense, running up high; and at their foot, hugging the bank against the stream, crept the little begrimed steamboat, like a sluggish beetle crawling on the floor of a lofty portico. It made you feel very small, very lost, and yet it was not altogether depressing, that feeling. After all, if you were small, the grimy beetle crawled on — which was just what you wanted it to do. Where the pilgrims imagined it crawled to I don't know. To some place where they expected to get something, I bet! For me it crawled towards Kurtz — exclusively; but when the steam-pipes started leaking we crawled very slow. The reaches opened before us and closed behind, as if the forest had stepped leisurely across the water to bar the way for our return. We penetrated deeper and deeper into the heart of darkness. It was very quiet there. At night sometimes the roll of drums behind the curtain of trees would run up the river and remain sustained faintly, as if hovering in the air high over our heads, till the first break of day. Whether it meant war, peace, or prayer we could not tell. The dawns were heralded by the descent of a chill stillness; the wood-cutters slept, their fires burned low; the snapping of a twig would make you start. We were wanderers on a prehistoric earth, on an earth that wore the aspect of an unknown planet. We could have fancied ourselves the first men taking possession of an accursed inheritance, to be subdued at the cost of profound anguish and of excessive toil. But suddenly, as we struggled round a bend, there would be a glimpse of rush walls, of peaked grass-roofs, a burst of yells, a whirl of black limbs, a mass of hands clapping, of feet stamping, of bodies swaying, of eyes rolling, under the droop of heavy and motionless foliage. The steamer toiled along slowly on the edge of a black and incomprehensible frenzy. The prehistoric man was cursing us, praying to us, welcoming us — who could tell? We were cut off from the comprehension of our surroundings; we glided past like phantoms, wondering and secretly appalled, as sane men would be before an enthusiastic outbreak in a madhouse. We could not understand because we were too far and could not remember, because we were traveling in the night of first ages, of those ages that are gone, leaving hardly a sign — and no memories.

"The earth seemed unearthly. We are accustomed to look upon the shackled form of a conquered monster, but there — there you could look at a thing monstrous and free. It was unearthly, and the men were — No, they were not inhuman. Well, you know, that was the worst of it — this suspicion of their not being inhuman. It would come slowly to one. They howled and leaped, and spun, and made horrid faces; but what thrilled you was just the thought of their humanity — like yours — the thought of your remote kinship with this wild and passionate uproar. Ugly. Yes, it was ugly enough; but if you were man enough you would admit to yourself that there was in you just the faintest trace of a response to the terrible frankness of that noise, a dim suspicion of there being a meaning in it which you — you so remote from the night of first ages — could comprehend. And why not? The mind of man is capable of anything — because everything is in it, all the past as well as all the future. What was there after all? Joy, fear, sorrow, devotion, valor, rage — who can tell? — but truth — truth stripped of its cloak of time. Let the fool gape and shudder — the man knows, and can look on without a wink. But he must at least be as much of a man as these on the shore. He must meet the truth with his own true stuff — with his own inborn strength. Principles won't do. Acquisitions, clothes, pretty rags — rags that would fly off at the first good shake. No; you want a deliberate belief. An appeal to me in this fiendish row — is there? Very well; I hear; I admit, but I have a voice, too, and for good or evil mine is the speech that cannot be silenced. Of course, a fool, what with sheer fright and fine sentiments, is always safe. Who's that grunting? You wonder I didn't go ashore for a howl and a dance? Well, no — I didn't. Fine sentiments, you say? Fine sentiments, be hanged! I had no time. I had to mess about with white-lead and strips of woolen blanket helping to put bandages on those leaky steam-pipes — I tell you. I had to watch the steering, and circumvent those snags, and get the tin-pot along by hook or by crook. There was surface-truth enough in these things to save a wiser man. And between whiles I had to look after the savage who was fireman. He was an improved specimen; he could fire up a vertical boiler. He was there below me, and, upon my word, to look at him was as edifying as seeing a dog in a parody of breeches and a feather hat, walking on his hindlegs. A few months of training had done for that really fine chap. He squinted at the steam-gauge and at the water-gauge with an evident effort of intrepidity — and he had filed teeth, too, the poor devil, and the wool of his pate shaved into queer patterns, and three ornamental scars on each of his cheeks. He ought to have been clapping his hands and stamping his feet on the bank, instead of which he was hard at work, a thrall to strange witchcraft, full of improving knowledge. He was useful because he had been instructed; and what he knew was this — that should the water in that transparent thing disappear, the evil spirit inside the boiler would get angry through the greatness of his thirst, and take a terrible vengeance. So he sweated and fired up and watched the glass fearfully (with an impromptu charm, made of rags, tied to his arm, and a piece of polished bone, as big as a watch, stuck flatways through his lower lip), while the wooden banks slipped past us slowly, the short noise was left behind, the interminable miles of silence — and we crept on, towards Kurtz. But the snags were thick, the water was treacherous and shallow, the boiler seemed indeed to have a sulky devil in it, and thus neither that fireman nor I had any time to peer into our creepy thoughts.

"Some fifty miles below the Inner Station we came upon a hut of reeds, an inclined and melancholy pole, with the unrecognizable tatters of what had been a flag of some sort flying from it, and a neatly stacked wood-pile. This was unexpected. We came to the bank, and on the stack of fire-wood found a flat piece of board with some faded pencil-writing on it. When deciphered it said: 'Wood for you. Hurry up. Approach cautiously.' There was a signature, but it was illegible — not Kurtz — a much longer word. 'Hurry up.' Where? Up the river? 'Approach cautiously.' We had not done so. But the warning could not have been meant for the place where it could be only found after approach. Something was wrong above. But what — and how much? That was the question. We commented adversely upon the imbecility of that telegraphic style. The bush around said nothing, and would not let us look very far, either. A torn curtain of red twill hung in the doorway of the hut, and flapped sadly in our faces. The dwelling was dismantled; but we could see a white man had lived there not very long ago. There remained a rude table — a plank on two posts; a heap of rubbish re-posed in a dark corner, and by the door I picked up a book. It had lost its covers, and the pages had been thumbed into a state of extremely dirty softness; but the back had been lovingly stitched afresh with white cotton thread, which looked clean yet. It was an extraordinary find. Its title was, *An Inquiry into Some Points of Seamanship*, by a man Towser, Towson — some such name — Master in his Majesty's Navy. The matter looked dreary reading enough, with illustrative diagrams and repulsive tables of fig-ures, and the copy was sixty years old. I handled this amazing antiquity with the greatest possible tenderness, lest it should dissolve in my hands. Within, Towson or Towser was inquiring earnestly into the breaking strain of ships' chains and tackle, and other such matters. Not a very enthralling book; but at the first glance you could see there a singleness of intention, an honest concern for the right way of going to work, which made these humble pages, thought out so many years ago, luminous with another than a pro-fessional light. The simple old sailor, with his talk of chains and purchases, made me forget the jungle and the pilgrims in a delicious sensation of hav-ing come upon something unmistakably real. Such a book being there was wonderful enough; but still more astounding were the notes penciled in the margin, and plainly referring to the text. I couldn't believe my eyes! They were in cipher! Yes, it looked like cipher. Fancy a man lugging with him a book of that description into this nowhere and studying it — and making notes — in cipher at that! It was an extravagant mystery.

"I had been dimly aware for some time of a worrying noise, and when I lifted my eyes I saw the woodpile was gone, and the manager, aided by all the pilgrims, was shouting at me from the riverside. I slipped the book into my pocket. I assure you to leave off reading was like tearing myself away from the shelter of an old and solid friendship.

"I started the lame engine ahead. 'It must be this miserable trader — this intruder,' exclaimed the manager, looking back malevolently at the place we had left. 'He must be English,' I said. 'It will not save him from getting into trouble if he is not careful,' muttered the manager darkly. I observed with assumed innocence that no man was safe from trouble in this world.

"The current was more rapid now, the steamer seemed at her last gasp, the stern-wheel flopped languidly, and I caught myself listening on tiptoe for the next beat of the float, for in sober truth I expected the wretched thing to give up every moment. It was like watching the last flickers of a life. But still we crawled. Sometimes I would pick out a tree a little way ahead to measure our progress towards Kurtz by, but I lost it invariably before we got abreast. To keep the eyes so long on one thing was too much for human patience. The manager displayed a beautiful resignation. I fretted and fumed and took to arguing with myself whether or not I would talk openly with Kurtz; but before I could come to any conclusion it occurred to me that my speech or my silence, indeed any action of mine, would be a mere futility. What did it matter what anyone knew or ignored? What did it matter who was manager? One gets sometimes such a flash of insight. The essentials of this affair lay deep under the surface, beyond my reach, and beyond my power of meddling.

"Towards the evening of the second day we judged ourselves about eight miles from Kurtz's station. I wanted to push on; but the manager looked grave, and told me the navigation up there was so dangerous that it would be advisable, the sun being very low already, to wait where we were till next morning. Moreover, he pointed out that if the warning to approach cautiously were to be followed, we must approach in daylight — not at dusk, or in the dark. This was sensible enough. Eight miles meant nearly three hours' steaming for us, and I could also see suspicious ripples at the upper end of the reach. Nevertheless, I was annoyed beyond expression at the delay, and most unreasonably, too, since one night more could not matter much after so many months. As we had plenty of wood, and caution was the word, I brought up in the middle of the stream. The reach was narrow, straight, with high sides like a railway cutting. The dusk came gliding into it long before the sun had set. The current ran smooth and swift, but a dumb immobility sat on the banks. The living trees, lashed together by the creepers and every living bush of the undergrowth, might have been changed into stone, even to the slenderest twig, to the lightest leaf. It was not sleep — it seemed unnatural, like a state of trance. Not the faintest sound of any kind could be heard. You looked on amazed, and began to suspect yourself of being deaf — then the night came suddenly, and struck you blind as well. About three in the morning some large fish leaped, and the loud splash made me jump as though a gun had been fired. When the sun rose there was a white fog, very warm and clammy, and more blinding than the night. It did not shift or drive; it was just there, standing all around you like something solid. At eight or nine, perhaps, it lifted as a shutter lifts. We had a glimpse of the towering multitude of trees, of the immense matted jungle, with the blazing little ball of the sun hanging over it — all perfectly still — and then the white shutter came down again, smoothly, as if sliding in greased grooves. I ordered the chain, which we had begun to heave in, to be paid out again. Before it stopped running with a muffled rattle, a cry, a very loud cry, as of infinite desolation, soared slowly in the opaque air. It ceased. A complaining clamor, modulated in savage discords, filled our ears. The sheer unexpectedness of it made my hair stir under my cap. I don't know how it struck the others: to me it seemed as though the mist itself had screamed, so suddenly, and apparently from all sides at once, did this tumultuous and mournful uproar arise. It culminated in a hurried outbreak of almost intolerably excessive shrieking, which stopped short, leaving us stiffened in a variety of silly attitudes, and obstinately listening to the nearly as appalling and excessive silence. 'Good God! What is the meaning — ' stammered at my elbow one of the pilgrims — a little fat man, with sandy hair and red whiskers, who wore side-spring boots, and pink pajamas tucked into his socks. Two others remained open-mouthed a whole minute, then dashed into the little cabin, to rush out incontinently and stand darting scared glances, with Winchesters at 'ready' in their hands. What we could see was just the steamer we were on, her outlines blurred as though she had been on the point of dissolving, and a misty strip of water, perhaps two feet broad, around her — and that was all. The rest of the world was nowhere, as far as our eyes and ears were concerned. Just nowhere. Gone, disappeared; swept off without leaving a whisper or a shadow behind.

"I went forward, and ordered the chain to be hauled in short, so as to be ready to trip the anchor and move the steamboat at once if necessary. 'Will they attack?' whispered an awed voice. 'We will be all butchered in this fog,' murmured another. The faces twitched with the strain, the hands trembling slightly, the eyes forgot to wink. It was very curious to see the contrast of expressions of the white men and of the black fellows of our crew, who were as much strangers to that part of the river as we, though their homes were only eight hundred miles away. The whites, of course, greatly discomposed, had besides a curious look of being painfully shocked by such an outrageous row. The others had an alert, naturally interested expression; but their faces were essentially quiet, even those of the one or two who grinned as they hauled at the chain. Several exchanged short, grunting phrases, which seemed to settle the matter to their satisfaction. Their headman, a young, broad-chested black, severely draped in dark-blue fringed cloths, with fierce nostrils and his hair all done up artfully in oily ringlets, stood near me. 'Aha!' I said, just for good fellowship's sake. 'Catch 'em,' he snapped, with a bloodshot widening of his eyes and a flash of sharp teeth — 'catch 'im. Give 'im to us.' 'To you, eh?' I asked; 'what would you do with them?' 'Eat 'em!' he said, curtly, and, leaning his elbow on the rail, looked out into the fog in a dignified and profoundly pensive attitude. I would no doubt have been properly horrified, had it not occurred to me that he and his chaps must be very hungry: that they must have been growing increasingly hungry for at least this month past. They had been engaged for six months (I don't think a single one of them had any clear idea of time, as we at the end of countless ages have. They still belonged to the beginnings of time — had no inherited experience to teach them as it were), and of course, as long as there was a piece of paper written over in accordance with some farcical law or other made down the river, it didn't enter anybody's head to trouble how they would live. Certainly they had brought with them some rotten hippo-meat, which couldn't have lasted very long, anyway, even if the pilgrims hadn't, in the midst of a shocking hullabaloo, thrown a considerable quantity of it overboard. It looked like a high-handed proceeding; but it was really a case of legitimate self-defense. You can't breathe dead hippo waking, sleeping, and eating, and at the same time keep your precarious grip on existence. Besides that, they had given them every week three pieces of brass wire, each about nine inches long; and the theory was they were to buy their provisions with that currency in riverside villages. You can see how *that* worked. There were either no villages, or the people were hostile, or the director, who like the rest of us fed out of tins, with an occasional old he-goat thrown in, didn't want to stop the steamer for some more or less recondite reason. So, unless they swallowed the wire itself, or made loops of it to snare the fishes with, I don't see what good their extravagant salary could be to them. I must say it was paid with a regularity worthy of a large and honorable trading company. For the rest, the only thing to eat — though it didn't look eatable in the least — I saw in their possession was a few lumps of some stuff like half-cooked dough, of a dirty lavender color, they kept wrapped in leaves, and now and then swallowed a piece of, but so small that it seemed done more for the looks of the thing than for any serious purpose of sustenance. Why in the name of all the gnawing devils of hunger they didn't go for us — they were thirty to five — and have a good tuck-in for once, amazes me now when I think of it. They were big powerful men, with not much capacity to weigh the consequences, with courage, with strength, even yet, though their skins were no longer glossy and their muscles no longer hard. And I saw that something restraining, one of those human secrets that baffle probability, had come into play there. I looked at them with a swift quickening of interest — not because it occurred to me I might be eaten by them before very long, though I own to you that just then I perceived — in a new light, as it were — how unwholesome the pilgrims looked, and I hoped, yes, I positively hoped, that my aspect was not so — what shall I say? — so — unappetizing: a touch of fantastic vanity which fitted well with the dream-sensation that pervaded all my days at that time. Perhaps I had a little fever, too. One can't live with one's finger everlastingly on one's pulse. I had often 'a little fever,' or a little touch of other things — the playful paw-strokes of the wilderness, the preliminary trifling before the more serious onslaught which came in due course. Yes; I looked at them as you would on any human being, with a curiosity of their impulses, motives, capacities, weaknesses, when brought to the test of an inexorable physical necessity. Restraint! What possible restraint? Was it superstition, disgust, patience, fear — or some kind of primitive honor? No fear can stand up to hunger, no patience can wear it out, disgust simply does not exist where hunger is; and as to superstition, beliefs, and what you may call principles, they are less than chaff in a breeze. Don't you know the devilry of lingering starvation, its exasperating torment, its black thoughts, its somber and brooding ferocity? Well, I do. It takes a man all his inborn strength to fight hunger properly. It's really easier to face bereavement, dishonor, and the perdition of one's soul — than this kind of prolonged hunger. Sad, but true. And these chaps, too, had no earthly reason for any kind of scruple. Restraint! I would just as soon have expected restraint from a hyena prowling amongst the corpses of a battlefield. But there was the fact facing me — the fact dazzling, to be seen, like the foam on the depths of the sea, like a ripple on an unfathomable enigma, a mystery greater — when I thought of it — than the curious, inexplicable note of desperate grief in this savage clamor that had swept by us on the riverbank, behind the blind whiteness of the fog.

"Two pilgrims were quarreling in hurried whispers as to which bank. 'Left.' 'No, no; how can you? Right, right, of course.' 'It is very serious,' said the manager's voice behind me; 'I would be desolated if anything should happen to Mr. Kurtz before we came up.' I looked at him, and had not the slightest doubt he was sincere. He was just the kind of man who would wish to preserve appearances. That was his restraint. But when he muttered something about going on at once, I did not even take the trouble to answer him. I knew, and he knew, that it was impossible. Were we to let go our hold of the bottom, we would be absolutely in the air — in space. We wouldn't be able to tell where we were going to — whether up or down stream, or across — till we fetched against one bank or the other — and then we wouldn't know at first which it was. Of course I made no move. I had no mind for a smash-up. You couldn't imagine a more deadly place for a shipwreck. Whether drowned at once or not, we were sure to perish speedily in one way or another. 'I authorize you to take all the risks,' he said, after a short silence. 'I refuse to take any,' I said, shortly; which was just the answer he expected, though its tone might have surprised him. 'Well, I must defer to your judgment. You are captain,' he said, with marked civility. I turned my shoulder to him in sign of my appreciation, and looked into the fog. How long would it last? It was the most hopeless lookout. The approach to this Kurtz grubbing for ivory in the wretched bush was beset by as many dangers as though he had been an enchanted princess sleeping in a fabulous castle. 'Will they attack, do you think?' asked the manager, in a confidential tone.

"I did not think they would attack, for several obvious reasons. The thick fog was one. If they left the bank in their canoes they would get lost in it, as we would be if we attempted to move. Still, I had also judged the jungle of both banks quite impenetrable — and yet eyes were in it, eyes that had seen us. The riverside bushes were certainly very thick; but the undergrowth behind was evidently penetrable. However, during the short lift I had seen no canoes anywhere in the reach — certainly not abreast of the steamer. But what made the idea of attack inconceivable to me was the nature of the noise — of the cries we had heard. They had not the fierce character boding immediate hostile intention. Unexpected, wild, and violent as they had been, they had given me an irresistible impression of sorrow. The glimpse of the steamboat had for some reason filled those savages with unrestrained grief. The danger, if any, I expounded, was from our proximity to a great human passion let loose. Even extreme grief may ultimately vent itself in violence — but more generally takes the form of apathy. . . .

"You should have seen the pilgrims stare! They had no heart to grin, or even to revile me: but I believe they thought me gone mad — with fright, maybe. I delivered a regular lecture. My dear boys, it was no good bothering. Keep a lookout? Well, you may guess I watched the fog for the signs of lifting as a cat watches a mouse; but for anything else our eyes were of no more use to us than if we had been buried miles deep in a heap of cotton-wool. It felt like it, too — choking, warm, stifling. Besides, all I said, though it sounded extravagant, was absolutely true to fact. What we afterwards alluded to as an attack was really an attempt at repulse. The action was very far from being aggressive — it was not even defensive, in the usual sense: it was undertaken under the stress of desperation, and in its essence was purely protective.

"It developed itself, I should say, two hours after the fog lifted, and its commencement was at a spot, roughly speaking, about a mile and a half below Kurtz's station. We had just floundered and flopped round a bend, when I saw an islet, a mere grassy hummock of bright green, in the middle of the stream. It was the only thing of the kind; but as we opened the reach more, I perceived it was the head of a long sandbank, or rather of a chain of shallow patches stretching down the middle of the river. They were discolored, just awash, and the whole lot was seen just under the water, exactly as a man's backbone is seen running down the middle of his back under the skin. Now, as far as I did see, I could go to the right or to the left of this. I didn't know either channel, of course. The banks looked pretty well alike, the depth appeared the same; but as I had been informed the station was on the west side, I naturally headed for the western passage.

"No sooner had we fairly entered it than I became aware it was much narrower than I had supposed. To the left of us there was the long uninterrupted shoal, and to the right a high, steep bank heavily overgrown with bushes. Above the bush the trees stood in serried ranks. The twigs overhung the current thickly, and from distance to distance a large limb of some tree projected rigidly over the stream. It was then well on in the afternoon, the face of the forest was gloomy, and a broad strip of shadow had already fallen on the water. In this shadow we steamed up — very slowly, as you may imagine. I sheered her well inshore — the water being deepest near the bank, as the sounding-pole informed me.

"One of my hungry and forbearing friends was sounding in the bows just below me. This steamboat was exactly like a decked scow. On the deck, there were two little teak-wood houses, with doors and windows. The boiler was in the fore-end, and the machinery right astern. Over the whole there was a light roof, supported on stanchions. The funnel projected through that roof, and in front of the funnel a small cabin built of light planks served for a pilot-house. It contained a couch, two campstools, a loaded Martini-Henry[9] leaning in one corner, a tiny table, and the steering-wheel. It had a wide door in front and a broad shutter at each side. All these were always thrown open, of course. I spent my days perched up there on the extreme fore-end of that roof, before the door. At night I slept, or tried to, on the couch. An athletic black belonging to some coast tribe, and educated by my poor predecessor, was the helmsman. He sported a pair of brass earrings, wore a blue cloth wrapper from the waist to the ankles, and thought all the world of himself. He was the most unstable kind of fool I had ever seen. He steered with no end to a swagger while you were by; but if he lost sight of you, he became instantly the prey of an abject funk, and would let that cripple of a steamboat get the upper hand of him in a minute.

"I was looking down at the sounding-pole, and feeling much annoyed to see at each try a little more of it stick out that river, when I saw my pole-man give up the business suddenly, and stretch himself flat on the deck, without even taking the trouble to haul his pole in. He kept hold on it though, and it trailed in the water. At the same time the fireman, whom I could also see below me, sat down abruptly before his furnace and ducked his head. I was amazed. Then I had to look at the river mighty quick, because there was a snag in the fairway. Sticks, little sticks, were flying about — thick: they were whizzing before my nose, dropping below me, striking behind me against my pilot-house. All this time the river, the shore, the woods, were very quiet — perfectly quiet. I could only hear the heavy splashing thump of the stern-wheel and the patter of these things. We cleared the snag clumsily. Arrows, by Jove! We were being shot at! I stepped in quickly to close the shutter on the land-side. That fool-helmsman, his hands on the spokes, was lifting his knees high, stamping his feet, champing his mouth, like a reined-in horse. Confound him! And we were staggering within ten feet of the bank. I had to lean right out to swing the heavy shutter, and I saw a face amongst the leaves on the level with my own, looking at me very fierce and steady; and then suddenly, as though a veil had been removed from my eyes, I made out, deep in the tangled gloom, naked breasts, arms, legs, glaring eyes — the bush was swarming with human limbs in movement, glistening, of bronze color. The twigs shook, swayed, and rustled, the arrows flew out of them, and then the shutter came to. 'Steer her straight,' I said to the helmsman. He held his head rigid, face forward; but his eyes rolled, he kept on lifting and setting down his feet gently, his mouth foamed a little. 'Keep quiet!' I said in a fury. I

---

[9] a heavy military rifle.

might just as well have ordered a tree not to sway in the wind. I darted out. Below me there was a great scuffle of feet on the iron deck; confused exclamations; a voice screamed, 'Can you turn back?' I caught sight of a V-shaped ripple on the water ahead. What? Another snag! A fusillade burst out under my feet. The pilgrims had opened with their Winchesters, and were simply squirting lead into that bush. A deuce of a lot of smoke came up and drove slowly forward. I swore at it. Now I couldn't see the ripple or the snag either. I stood in the doorway, peering, and the arrows came in swarms. They might have been poisoned, but they looked as though they wouldn't kill a cat. The bush began to howl. Our wood-cutters raised a war-like whoop; the report of a rifle just at my back deafened me. I glanced over my shoulder, and the pilot-house was yet full of noise and smoke when I made a dash at the wheel. The fool-nigger had dropped everything to throw the shutter open and let off that Martini-Henry. He stood before the wide opening, glaring, and I yelled at him to come back, while I straightened the sudden twist out of that steamboat. There was no room to turn even if I had wanted to, the snag was somewhere very near ahead in that confounded smoke, there was no time to lose, so I just crowded her into the bank — right into the bank, where I knew the water was deep.

"We tore slowly along the overhanging bushes in a whirl of broken twigs and flying leaves. The fusillade below stopped short, as I had foreseen it would when the squirts got empty. I threw my head back to a glinting whizz that traversed the pilot-house, in at one shutter-hole and out at the other. Looking past that mad helmsman, who was shaking the empty rifle and yelling at the shore, I saw vague forms of men running bent double, leaping, gliding, distinct, incomplete, evanescent. Something big appeared in the air before the shutter, the rifle went overboard, and the man stepped back swiftly, looked at me over his shoulder in an extraordinary, profound, familiar manner, and fell upon my feet. The side of his head hit the wheel twice, and the end of what appeared a long cane clattered round and knocked over a little campstool. It looked as though after wrenching that thing from somebody ashore he had lost his balance in the effort. The thin smoke had blown away, we were clear of the snag, and looking ahead I could see that in another hundred yards or so I would be free to sheer off, away from the bank; but my feet felt so very warm and wet that I had to look down. The man had rolled on his back and stared straight up at me; both his hands clutched that cane. It was the shaft of a spear that, either thrown or lunged through the opening, had caught him in the side just below the ribs; the blade had gone in out of sight, after making a frightful gash; my shoes were full; a pool of blood lay very still, gleaming dark-red under the wheel; his eyes shone with an amazing luster. The fusillade burst out again. He looked at me anxiously, gripping the spear like something precious, with an air of being afraid I would try to take it away from him. I had to make an effort to free my eyes from his gaze and attend to steering. With one hand I felt above my head for the line of the steam-whistle, and jerked out screech after screech hurriedly. The tumult of angry and warlike yells was checked instantly, and then from the depths of the woods went out such a tremulous and prolonged wail of mournful fear and utter despair as may be imagined to follow the flight of the last hope from the earth. There was a great commotion in the bush; the shower of arrows stopped, a few dropping shots rang out sharply — then silence, in which the languid beat of the stern-wheel came plainly to my ears. I put the helm hard a-starboard at the moment when the pilgrim in pink pajamas, very hot and agitated, appeared in the doorway. 'The manager sends me — ' he began in an official tone, and stopped short. 'Good God!' he said, glaring at the wounded man.

"We two whites stood over him, and his lustrous and inquiring glance enveloped us both. I declare it looked as though he would presently put to us some question in an understandable language; but he died without uttering a sound, without moving a limb, without twitching a muscle. Only in the very last moment, as though in response to some sign we could not see, to some whisper we could not hear, he frowned heavily, and that frown gave to his black death-mask an inconceivably somber, brooding, and menacing expression. The luster of inquiring glance faded swiftly into vacant glassiness. 'Can you steer?' I asked the agent eagerly. He looked very dubious; but I made a grab at his arm, and he understood at once I meant him to steer whether or no. To tell you the truth, I was morbidly anxious to change my shoes and socks. 'He is dead,' murmured the fellow, immensely impressed. 'No doubt about it,' said I tugging like mad at the shoe-laces. 'And by the way, I suppose Mr. Kurtz is dead as well by this time.'

"For the moment that was the dominant thought. There was a sense of extreme disappointment, as though I had found out I had been striving after something altogether without a substance. I couldn't have been more disgusted if I had traveled all this way for the sole purpose of talking with Mr. Kurtz. Talking with. . . . I flung one shoe overboard, and became aware that that was exactly what I had been looking forward to — a talk with Kurtz. I made the strange discovery that I had never imagined him as doing, you know, but as discoursing. I didn't say to myself, 'Now I will never see him,' or 'Now I will never shake him by the hand,' but, 'Now I will never hear him.' The man presented himself as a voice. Not of course that I did not connect him with some sort of action. Hadn't I been told in all the tones of jealousy and admiration that he had collected, bartered, swindled, or stolen more ivory than all the other agents together? That was not the point. The point was in his being a gifted creature, and that of all his gifts the one that stood out preeminently, that carried with it a sense of real presence, was his ability to talk, his words — the gift of expression, the bewildering, the illuminating, the most exalted and the most contemptible, the pulsating stream of light, or the deceitful flow from the heart of an impenetrable darkness.

"The other shoe went flying unto the devil-god of that river. I thought, by Jove! it's all over. We are too late; he has vanished — the gift has vanished, by means of some spear, arrow, or club. I will never hear that chap speak after all — and my sorrow had a startling extravagance of emotion, even such as I had noticed in the howling sorrow of these savages in the bush. I couldn't have felt more lonely desolation somehow, had I been robbed of a belief or had missed my destiny in life. . . . Why do you sigh in this beastly way, somebody? Absurd? Well, absurd. Good Lord! mustn't a man ever — Here, give me some tobacco." . . .

There was a pause of profound stillness, then a match flared, and Marlow's lean face appeared, worn, hollow, with downward folds and drooped eyelids, with an aspect of concentrated attention; and as he took vigorous draws at his pipe, it seemed to retreat and advance out of the night in the regular flicker of the tiny flame. The match went out.

"Absurd!" he cried. "This is the worst of trying to tell. . . . Here you all are, each moored with two good addresses, like a hulk with two anchors, a butcher round one corner, a policeman round another, excellent appetites, and temperature normal — you hear — normal from year's end to year's end. And you say, Absurd! Absurd be — exploded! Absurd! My dear boys, what can you expect from a man who out of sheer nervousness had just flung overboard a pair of new shoes! Now I think of it, it is amazing I did not shed tears. I am, upon the whole, proud of my fortitude. I was cut to the quick at the idea of having lost the inestimable privilege of listening to the gifted Kurtz. Of course I was wrong. The privilege was waiting for me. Oh, yes, I heard more than enough. And I was right, too. A voice. He was very little more than a voice. And I heard — him — it — this voice — other voices — all of them were so little more than voices — and the memory of that time itself lingers around me, impalpable, like a dying vibration of one immense jabber, silly, atrocious, sordid, savage, or simply mean, without any kind of sense. Voices, voices — even the girl herself — now —"

He was silent for a long time.

"I laid the ghost of his gifts at last with a lie," he began, suddenly. "Girl! What? Did I mention a girl? Oh, she is out of it — completely. They — the women I mean — are out of it — should be out of it. We must help them to stay in that beautiful world of their own, lest ours gets worse. Oh, she had to be out of it. You should have heard the disinterred body of Mr. Kurtz saying, 'My Intended.' You would have perceived directly then how completely she was out of it. And the lofty frontal bone of Mr. Kurtz! They say the hair goes on growing sometimes, but this — ah — specimen, was impressively bald. The wilderness had patted him on the head, and, behold, it was like a ball — an ivory ball; it had caressed him, and — lo! — he had withered; it had taken him, loved him, embraced him, got into his veins, consumed his flesh, and sealed his soul to its own by the inconceivable ceremonies of some devilish initiation. He was its spoiled and pampered favorite. Ivory? I should think so. Heaps of it, stacks of it. The old mud shanty was bursting with it. You would think here was not a single tusk left either above or below the ground in the whole country. 'Mostly fossil,' the manager had remarked, disparagingly. It was no more fossil than I am; but they call it fossil when it is dug up. It appears these niggers do bury the tusks sometimes — but evidently they couldn't bury this parcel deep enough to save the gifted Mr. Kurtz from his fate. We filled the steamboat with it, and had to pile a lot on the deck. Thus he could see and enjoy as long as he could see, because the appreciation of this favor had remained with him to the last. You should have heard him say, 'My ivory.' Oh, yes, I heard him. 'My Intended, my ivory, my station, my river, my — ' everything belonged to him. It made me hold my breath in expectation of hearing the wilderness burst into a prodigious peal of laughter that would shake the fixed stars in their places. Everything belonged to him — but that was a trifle. The thing was to know what he belonged to, how many powers of darkness claimed him for their own. That was the reflection that made you creepy all over. It was impossible — it was not good for one either — trying to imagine. He had taken a high seat amongst the devils of the land — I mean literally. You can't understand. How could you? — with solid pavement under your feet, surrounded by kind neighbors ready to cheer you or to fall on you, stepping delicately between the butcher and the policeman, in the holy terror of scandal and gallows and lunatic asylums — how can you imagine what particular region of the first ages a man's untrammeled feet may take him into by the way of solitude — utter solitude without a policeman — by the way of silence — utter silence, where no warning voice of a kind neighbor can be heard whispering of public opinion? These little things make all the great difference. When they are gone you must fall back upon your own innate strength, upon your own capacity for faithfulness. Of course you may be too much of a fool to go wrong — too dull even to know you are being assaulted by the powers of darkness. I take it, no fool ever made a bargain for his soul with the devil: the fool is too much of a fool, or the devil too much of a devil — I don't know which. Or you may be such a thunderingly exalted creature as to be altogether deaf and blind to anything but heavenly sights and sounds. Then the earth for you is only a standing place — and whether to be like this is your loss or your gain I won't pretend to say. But most of us are neither one nor the other. The earth for us is a place to live in, where we must put up with sights, with sounds, with smells, too, by Jove! — breathe dead hippo, so to speak and not be contaminated. And there, don't you see? your strength comes in, the faith in your ability for the digging of unostentatious holes to bury the stuff in — your power of devotion, not to yourself, but to an obscure, back-breaking business. And that's difficult enough. Mind, I am not trying to excuse or even explain — I am trying to account to myself for — for — Mr. Kurtz — for the shade of Mr. Kurtz. This initiated wraith from the back of Nowhere honored me with its amazing confidence before it vanished altogether. This was because it could speak English to me. The original Kurtz had been educated partly in England, and — as he was good enough to say himself — his sympathies were in the right place. His mother was half-English, his father was half-French. All Europe contributed to the making of Kurtz; and by and by I learned that, most appropriately, the International Society for the Suppression of Savage Customs had intrusted him with the making of a report, for its future guidance. And he had written it, too. I've seen it. I've read it. It was eloquent, vibrating with eloquence, but too high-strung, I think. Seventeen pages of close writing he had found time for! But this must have been before his — let us say — nerves, went wrong, and caused him to preside at certain midnight dances ending with unspeakable rites, which — as far as I reluctantly gathered from what I heard at various times — were offered up to him — do you understand? — to Mr. Kurtz himself. But it was a beautiful piece of writing. The opening paragraph, however, in the light of later information, strikes me now as ominous. He began with the argument that we whites, from the point of development we had arrived at, 'must necessarily appear to them [savages] in the nature of supernatural beings — we approach them with the might as of a deity,' and so on, and so on. 'By the simple exercise of our will we can exert a power for good practically unbounded,' etc., etc. From that point he soared and took me with him. The peroration was magnificent, though difficult to remember, you know. It gave me the notion of an exotic Immensity ruled by an august Benevolence. It made me tingle with enthusiasm. This was the unbounded power of eloquence — of words — of burning noble words. There were no practical hints to interrupt the magic current of phrases, unless a kind of note at the foot of the last page, scrawled evidently much later, in an unsteady hand, may be regarded as the exposition of a method. It was very simple, and at the end of that moving appeal to every altruistic sentiment it blazed at you, luminous and terrifying, like a flash of lightning in a serene sky: 'Exterminate all the brutes!' The curious part was that he had apparently forgotten all about that valuable postscriptum, because, later on, when he in a sense came to himself, he repeatedly entreated me to take good care of 'my pamphlet' (he called it), as it was sure to have in the future a good influence upon his career. I had full information about all these things, and, besides, as it turned out, I was to have the care of his memory. I've done enough for it to give me the indisputable right to lay it, if I choose, for an everlasting rest in the dust-bin of progress, amongst all the sweepings and, figuratively speaking, all the dead cats of civilization. But then, you see, I can't choose. He won't be forgotten. Whatever he was, he was not common. He had the power to charm or frighten rudimentary souls into an aggravated witch-dance in his honor; he could also fill the small souls of the pilgrims with bitter misgivings: he had one devoted friend at least, and he had conquered one soul in the world that was neither rudimentary nor tainted with self-seeking. No; I can't forget him, though I am not prepared to affirm the fellow was exactly worth the life we lost in getting to him. I missed my late helmsman awfully — I missed him even while his body was still lying in the pilot-house. Perhaps you will think it passing strange this regret for a savage who was no more account than a grain of sand in a black Sahara. Well, don't you see, he had done something, he had steered; for months I had him at my back — a help — an instrument. It was a kind of partnership. He steered for me — I had to look after him, I worried about his deficiencies, and thus a subtle bond had been created, of which I only became aware when it was suddenly broken. And the intimate profundity of that look he gave me when he received his hurt remains to this day in my memory — like a claim of distant kinship affirmed in a supreme moment.

"Poor fool! If he had only left that shutter alone. He had no restraint, no restraint — just like Kurtz — a tree swayed by the wind. As soon as I had put on a dry pair of slippers, I dragged him out, after first jerking the spear out of his side, which operation I confess I performed with my eyes shut tight. His heels leaped together over the little door-step; his shoulders were pressed to my breast; I hugged him from behind desperately. Oh! he was heavy, heavy; heavier than any man on earth, I should imagine. Then without more ado I tipped him overboard. The current snatched him as though he had been a wisp of grass, and I saw the body roll over twice before I lost sight of it forever. All the pilgrims and the manager were then congregated on the awning-deck about the pilot-house, chattering at each other like a flock of excited magpies, and there was a scandalized murmur at my heartless promptitude. What they wanted to keep that body hanging about for I can't guess. Embalm it, maybe. But I had also heard another, and a very ominous, murmur on the deck below. My friends the wood-cutters were likewise scandalized, and with a better show of reason — though I admit that the reason itself was quite inadmissible. Oh, quite! I had made up my mind that if my late helmsman was to be eaten, the fishes alone should have him. He had been a very second-rate helmsman while alive, but now he was dead he might have become a first-class temptation, and possibly cause some startling trouble. Besides, I was anxious to take the wheel, the man in pink pajamas showing himself a hopeless duffer at the business.

"This I did directly the simple funeral was over. We were going half-speed, keeping right in the middle of the stream, and I listened to the talk about me. They had given up Kurtz, they had given up the station; Kurtz was dead, and the station had been burnt — and so on — and so on. The red-haired pilgrim was beside himself with the thought that at least this poor Kurtz had been properly avenged. 'Say! We must have made a glorious slaughter of them in the bush. Eh? What do you think? Say?' He positively danced, the blood-thirsty little gingery beggar. And he had nearly fainted when he saw the wounded man! I could not help saying, 'You made a glorious lot of smoke, anyhow.' I had seen, from the way the tops of the bushes rustled and flew, that almost all the shots had gone too high. You can't hit anything unless you take aim and fire from the shoulder; but these chaps fired from the hip with their eyes shut. The retreat, I maintained — and I was right — was caused by the screeching of the steam-whistle. Upon this they forgot Kurtz, and began to howl at me with indignant protests.

"The manager stood by the wheel murmuring confidentially about the necessity of getting well away down the river before dark at all events, when I saw in the distance a clearing on the riverside and the outlines of some sort of building. 'What's this?' I asked. He clapped his hands in wonder. 'The station!' he cried. I edged in at once, still going half-speed.

Through my glasses I saw the slope of a hill interspersed with rare trees and perfectly free from undergrowth. A long decaying building on the summit was half buried in the high grass; the large holes in the peaked roof gaped black from afar; the jungle and the woods made a background. There was no enclosure or fence of any kind; but there had been one apparently, for near the house half-a-dozen slim posts remained in a row, roughly trimmed, and with their upper ends ornamented with round carved balls. The rails, or whatever there had been between, had disappeared. Of course the forest surrounded all that. The riverbank was clear, and on the water-side I saw a white man under a hat like a cart-wheel beckoning persistently with his whole arm. Examining the edge of the forest above and below, I was almost certain I could see movements — human forms gliding here and there. I steamed past prudently, then stopped the engines and let her drift down. The man on the shore began to shout, urging us to land. 'We have been attacked,' screamed the manager. 'I know — I know. It's all right,' yelled back the other, as cheerful as you please. 'Come along. It's all right, I am glad.'

"His aspect reminded me of something I had seen — something funny I had seen somewhere. As I maneuvered to get alongside, I was asking myself, 'What does this fellow look like?' Suddenly I got it. He looked like a harlequin. His clothes had been made of some stuff that was brown holland probably, but it was covered with patches all over, with bright patches, blue, red, and yellow — patches on the back, patches on the front, patches on elbows, on knees; colored binding around his jacket, scarlet edging at the bottom of his trousers; and the sunshine made him look extremely gay and wonderfully neat withal, because you could see how beautifully all this patching had been done. A beardless, boyish face, very fair, no features to speak of, nose peeling, little blue eyes, smiles and frowns chasing each other over that open countenance like sunshine and shadow on a windswept plain. 'Look out, captain!' he cried; 'there's a snag lodged in here last night.' What! Another snag? I confess I swore shamefully. I had nearly holed my cripple, to finish off that charming trip. The harlequin on the bank turned his little pug-nose up to me. 'You English?' he asked, all smiles. 'Are you?' I shouted from the wheel. The smiles vanished, and he shook his head as if sorry for my disappointment. Then he brightened up. 'Never mind!' he cried, encouragingly. 'Are we in time?' I asked. 'He is up there,' he replied with a toss of the head up the hill, and becoming gloomy all of a sudden. His face was like the autumn sky, overcast one moment and bright the next.

"When the manager, escorted by the pilgrims, all of them armed to the teeth, had gone to the house this chap came on board. 'I say, I don't like this. These natives are in the bush,' I said. He assured me earnestly it was all right. 'They are simple people,' he added; 'well, I am glad you came. It took me all my time to keep them off.' 'But you said it was all right,' I cried. 'Oh, they meant no harm,' he said; and as I stared he corrected himself, 'Not exactly.' Then vivaciously, 'My faith, your pilot-house wants a clean-up!' In the next breath he advised me to keep enough steam on the boiler to blow the whistle in case of any trouble. 'One good screech will do more for you than all your rifles. They are simple people,' he repeated. He rattled away at such a rate he quite overwhelmed me. He seemed to be trying to make up for lots of silence, and actually hinted, laughing, that such was the case. 'Don't you talk with Mr. Kurtz?' I said. 'You don't talk with that man — you listen to him,' he exclaimed with severe exaltation. 'But now — ' He waved his arm, and in the twinkling of an eye was in the utter-most depths of despondency. In a moment he came up again with a jump, possessed himself of both my hands, and shook them continuously, while he gabbled: 'Brother sailor . . . honor . . . pleasure . . . delight . . . introduce myself . . . Russian . . . son of an arch-priest . . . Government of Tambov. . . . What? Tobacco! English tobacco; the excellent English tobacco! Now, that's brotherly. Smoke? Where's a sailor that does not smoke?'

"The pipe soothed him, and gradually I made out he had run away from school, had gone to sea in a Russian ship; ran away again; served some time in English ships; was now reconciled with the arch-priest. He made a point of that. 'But when one is young one must see things, gather experience, ideas; enlarge the mind.' 'Here!' I interrupted. 'You can never tell! Here I met Mr. Kurtz,' he said, youthfully solemn and reproachful. I held my tongue after that. It appears he had persuaded a Dutch trading-house on the coast to fit him out with stores and goods, and had started for the interior with a light heart, and no more idea of what would happen to him than a baby. He had been wandering about that river for nearly two years alone, cut off from everybody and everything. 'I am not so young as I look. I am twenty-five,' he said. 'At first old Van Shuyten would tell me to go to the devil,' he narrated with keen enjoyment; 'but I stuck to him, and talked and talked, till at last he got afraid I would talk the hind-leg off his favorite dog, so he gave me some cheap things and a few guns, and told me he hoped he would never see my face again. Good old Dutchman, Van Shuyten. I've sent him one small lot of ivory a year ago, so that he can't call me a little thief when I get back. I hope he got it. And for the rest I don't care. I had some wood stacked for you. That was my old house. Did you see?'

I gave him Towson's book. He made as though he would kiss me, but restrained himself. 'The only book I had left, and I thought I had lost it,' he said, looking at it ecstatically. 'So many accidents happen to a man going about alone, you know. Canoes get upset sometimes — and sometimes you've got to clear out so quick when the people get angry.' He thumbed the pages. 'You made notes in Russian?' I asked. He nodded. 'I thought they were written in cipher,' I said. He laughed, then became serious. 'I had lots of trouble to keep these people off,' he said. 'Did they want to kill you?' I asked. 'Oh, no!' he cried, and checked himself. 'Why did they attack us?' I pursued. He hesitated, then said shamefacedly, 'They don't want him to go.' 'Don't they?' I said, curiously. He nodded a nod full of mystery and wisdom. 'I tell you,' he cried, 'this man has enlarged my mind.' He opened his arms wide, staring at me with his little blue eyes that were perfectly round."

III

"I looked at him, lost in astonishment. There he was before me, in motley, as though he had absconded from a troupe of mimes, enthusiastic, fabulous. His very existence was improbable, inexplicable, and altogether bewildering. He was an insoluble problem. It was inconceivable how he had existed, how he had succeeded in getting so far, how he had managed to remain — why he did not instantly disappear. 'I went a little farther,' he said, 'then still a little farther — till I had gone so far that I don't know how I'll ever get back. Never mind. Plenty time. I can manage. You take Kurtz away quick — quick — I tell you.' The glamour of youth enveloped his parti-colored rags, his destitution, his loneliness, the essential desolation of his futile wanderings. For months — for years — his life hadn't been worth a day's purchase; and there he was gallantly, thoughtlessly alive, to all appearance indestructible solely by the virtue of his few years and of his unreflecting audacity. I was seduced into something like admiration — like envy. Glamour urged him on, glamour kept him unscathed. He surely wanted nothing from the wilderness but space to breathe in and to push on through. His need was to exist, and to move onwards at the greatest possible risk, and with a maximum of privation. If the absolutely pure, uncalculating, unpractical spirit of adventure had ever ruled a human being, it ruled this be-patched youth. I almost envied him the possession of this modest and clear flame. It seemed to have consumed all thought of self so completely, that even while he was talking to you, you forgot that it was he — the man before your eyes — who had gone through these things. I did not envy him his devotion to Kurtz, though. He had not meditated over it. It came to him and he accepted it with a sort of eager fatalism. I must say that to me it appeared about the most dangerous thing in every way he had come upon so far.

"They had come together unavoidably, like two ships becalmed near each other, and lay rubbing sides at last. I suppose Kurtz wanted an audience, because on a certain occasion, when encamped in the forest, they had

talked all night, or more probably Kurtz had talked. 'We talked of everything,' he said, quite transported at the recollection. 'I forgot there was such
a thing as sleep. The night did not seem to last an hour. Everything! Everything! . . . Of love, too.' 'Ah, he talked to you of love!' I said, much amused.
'It isn't what you think,' he cried, almost passionately. 'It was in general. He
made me see things — things.'

"He threw his arms up. We were on deck at the time, and the headman of my wood-cutters, lounging near by, turned upon him his heavy and
glittering eyes. I looked around, and I don't know why, but I assure you that
never, never before, did this land, this river, this jungle, the very arch of this
blazing sky, appear to me so hopeless and so dark, so impenetrable to
human thought, so pitiless to human weakness. 'And, ever since, you have
been with him, of course?' I said.

"On the contrary. It appears their intercourse had been very much
broken by various causes. He had, as he informed me proudly, managed to
nurse Kurtz through two illnesses (he alluded to it as you would to some
risky feat), but as a rule Kurtz wandered alone far in the depths of the forest. 'Very often coming to this station, I had to wait days and days before he
would turn up,' he said. 'Ah, it was worth waiting for! — sometimes.'
'What was he doing? exploring or what?' I asked. 'Oh, yes, of course'; he
had discovered lots of villages, a lake, too — he did not know exactly in
what direction; it was dangerous to inquire too much — but mostly his ex-
peditions had been for ivory. 'But he had no goods to trade with by that
time,' I objected. 'There's a good lot of cartridges left even yet,' he answered, looking away. 'To speak plainly, he raided the country,' I said. He
nodded. 'Not alone, surely!' He muttered something about the villages
round that lake. 'Kurtz got the tribe to follow him, did he?' I suggested. He
fidgeted a little. 'They adored him,' he said. The tone of these words was so
extraordinary that I looked at him searchingly. It was curious to see his
mingled eagerness and reluctance to speak of Kurtz. The man filled his life,
occupied his thoughts, swayed his emotions. 'What can you expect?' he
burst out; 'he came to them with thunder and lightning, you know — and
they had never seen anything like it — and very terrible. He could be very
terrible. You can't judge Mr. Kurtz as you would an ordinary man. No, no,
no! Now — just to give you an idea — I don't mind telling you, he wanted
to shoot me, too, one day — but I don't judge him.' 'Shoot you!' I cried.
'What for?' 'Well, I had a small lot of ivory the chief of that village near my
house gave me. You see I used to shoot game for them. Well, he wanted it,
and wouldn't hear reason. He declared he would shoot me unless I gave
him the ivory and then cleared out of the country, because he could do so,
and had a fancy for it, and there was nothing on earth to prevent him killing
whom he jolly well pleased. And it was true, too. I gave him the ivory.
What did I care! But I didn't clear out. No, no. I couldn't leave him. I had
to be careful, of course, till we got friendly again for a time. He had his second illness then. Afterwards I had to keep out of the way; but I didn't mind.

He was living for the most part in those villages on the lake. When he came down to the river, sometimes he would take to me, and sometimes it was better for me to be careful. This man suffered too much. He hated all this, and somehow he couldn't get away. When I had a chance I begged him to try and leave while there was time; I offered to go back with him. And he would say yes, and then he would remain; go off on another ivory hunt; disappear for weeks; forget himself amongst these people — forget himself — you know.' 'Why! he's mad,' I said. He protested indignantly. Mr. Kurtz couldn't be mad. If I had heard him talk, only two days ago, I wouldn't dare hint at such a thing. . . . I had taken up my binoculars while we talked, and was looking at the shore, sweeping the limit of the forest at each side and at the back of the house. The consciousness of there being people in that bush, so silent, so quiet — as silent and quiet as the ruined house on the hill — made me uneasy. There was no sign on the face of nature of this amazing tale that was not so much told as suggested to me in desolate exclamations, completed by shrugs, in interrupted phrases, in hints ending in deep sighs. The woods were unmoved, like a mask — heavy, like the closed door of a prison — they looked with their air of hidden knowledge, of patient expectation, of unapproachable silence. The Russian was explaining to me that it was only lately that Mr. Kurtz had come down to the river, bringing along with him all the fighting men of that lake tribe. He had been absent for several months — getting himself adored, I suppose — and had come down unexpectedly, with the intention to all appearance of making a raid either across the river or down stream. Evidently the appetite for more ivory had got the better of the — what shall I say? — less material aspirations. However he had got much worse suddenly. 'I heard he was lying helpless, and so I came up — took my chance,' said the Russian. 'Oh, he is bad, very bad.' I directed my glass to the house. There were no signs of life, but there was the ruined roof, the long mud wall peeping above the grass, with three little square window-holes, no two of the same size; all this brought within reach of my hand, as it were. And then I made a brusque movement, and one of the remaining posts of that vanished fence leaped up in the field of my glass. You remember I told you I had been struck at the distance by certain attempts at ornamentation, rather remarkable in the ruinous aspect of the place. Now I had suddenly a nearer view, and its first result was to make me throw my head back as if before a blow. Then I went carefully from post to post with my glass, and I saw my mistake. These round knobs were not ornamental but symbolic; they were expressive and puzzling, striking and disturbing — food for thought and also for vultures if there had been any looking down from the sky; but at all events for such ants as were industrious enough to ascend the pole. They would have been even more impressive, those heads on the stakes, if their faces had not been turned to the house. Only one, the first I had made out, was facing my way. I was not so shocked as you may think. The start back I had given was really nothing but a movement of surprise. I had expected to see a knob of wood there, you know. I returned deliberately to the first I had seen — and there it was, black, dried, sunken, with closed eyelids — a head that seemed to sleep at the top of that pole, and with the shrunken dry lips showing a narrow white line of the teeth, was smiling, too, smiling continuously at some endless and jocose dream of that eternal slumber.

"I am not disclosing any trade secrets. In fact, the manager said afterwards that Mr. Kurtz's methods had ruined the district. I have no opinion on that point, but I want you clearly to understand that there was nothing exactly profitable in these heads being there. They only showed that Mr. Kurtz lacked restraint in the gratification of his various lusts, that there was something wanting in him — some small matter which, when the pressing need arose, could not be found under his magnificent eloquence. Whether he knew of this deficiency himself I can't say. I think the knowledge came to him at last — only at the very last. But the wilderness had found him out early, and had taken on him a terrible vengeance for the fantastic invasion. I think it had whispered to him things about himself which he did not know, things of which he had no conception till he took counsel with this great solitude — and the whisper had proved irresistibly fascinating. It echoed loudly within him because he was hollow at the core. . . . I put down the glass, and the head that had appeared near enough to be spoken to seemed at once to have leaped away from me into inaccessible distance.

"The admirer of Mr. Kurtz was a bit crestfallen. In a hurried indistinct voice he began to assure me he had not dared to take these — say, symbols — down. He was not afraid of the natives; they would not stir till Mr. Kurtz gave the word. His ascendancy was extraordinary. The camps of these people surrounded the place, and the chiefs came every day to see him. They would crawl. . . . 'I don't want to know anything of the ceremonies used when approaching Mr. Kurtz,' I shouted. Curious, this feeling that came over me that such details would be more intolerable than those heads drying on the stakes under Mr. Kurtz's windows. After all, that was only a savage sight, while I seemed at one bound to have been transported into some lightless region of subtle horrors, where pure, uncomplicated savagery was a positive relief, being something that had a right to exist — obviously — in the sunshine. The young man looked at me with surprise. I suppose it did not occur to him that Mr. Kurtz was no idol of mine. He forgot I hadn't heard any of these splendid monologues on, what was it? on love, justice, conduct of life — or what not. If it had come to crawling before Mr. Kurtz, he crawled as much as the veriest savage of them all. I had no idea of the conditions, he said: these heads were the heads of rebels. I shocked him excessively by laughing. Rebels! What would be the next definition I was to hear? There had been enemies, criminals, workers — and these were rebels. Those rebellious heads looked very subdued to me on their sticks. 'You don't know how such a life tries a man like Kurtz,' cried Kurtz's last disciple. 'Well, and you?' I said. 'I! I! I am a simple man. I have no great thoughts. I want nothing from anybody. How can you compare me to. . . ?' His feelings were too much for speech, and suddenly he broke down. 'I don't understand,' he groaned. 'I've been doing my best to keep him alive, and that's enough. I had no hand in all this. I have no abilities. There hasn't been a drop of medicine or a mouthful of invalid food for months here. He was shamefully abandoned. A man like this, with such ideas. Shamefully! Shamefully! I — I — haven't slept for the last ten nights. . . .'

"His voice lost itself in the calm of the evening. The long shadows of the forest had slipped downhill while we talked, had gone far beyond the ruined hovel, beyond the symbolic row of stakes. All this was in the gloom, while we down there were yet in the sunshine, and the stretch of the river abreast of the clearing glittered in a still and dazzling splendor, with a murky and overshadowed bend above and below. Not a living soul was seen on the shore. The bushes did not rustle.

"Suddenly round the corner of the house a group of men appeared, as though they had come up from the ground. They waded waist-deep in the grass, in a compact body, bearing an improvised stretcher in their midst. Instantly, in the emptiness of the landscape, a cry arose whose shrillness pierced the still air like a sharp arrow flying straight to the very heart of the land; and, as if by enchantment, streams of human beings — of naked human beings — with spears in their hands, with bows, with shields, with wild glances and savage movements, were poured into the clearing by the dark-faced and pensive forest. The bushes shook, the grass swayed for a time, and then everything stood still in attentive immobility.

"'Now, if he does not say the right thing to them we are all done for,' said the Russian at my elbow. The knot of men with the stretcher had stopped, too, halfway to the steamer, as if petrified. I saw the man on the stretcher sit up, lank and with an uplifted arm, above the shoulders of the bearers. 'Let us hope that the man who can talk so well of love in general will find some particular reason to spare us this time,' I said. I resented bitterly the absurd danger of our situation, as if to be at the mercy of that atrocious phantom had been a dishonoring necessity. I could not hear a sound, but through my glasses I saw the thin arm extended commandingly, the lower jaw moving, the eyes of that apparition shining darkly far in its bony head that nodded with grotesque jerks. Kurtz — Kurtz — that means short in Germany — don't it? Well, the name was as true as everything else in his life — and death. He looked at least seven feet long. His covering had fallen off, and his body emerged from it pitiful and appalling as from a winding-sheet. I could see the cage of his ribs all astir, the bones of his arm waving. It was as though an animated image of death carved out of old ivory had been shaking its hand with menaces at a motionless crowd of men made of dark and glittering bronze. I saw him open his mouth wide — it gave him a weirdly voracious aspect, as though he had wanted to swallow all the air, all the earth, all the men before him. A deep voice reached me faintly. He must have been shouting. He fell back suddenly. The stretcher shook as the bearers staggered forward again, and almost at the same time I noticed that the crowd of savages was vanishing without any perceptible movement of retreat, as if the forest that had ejected these beings so suddenly had drawn them in again as the breath is drawn in a long aspiration.

"Some of the pilgrims behind the stretcher carried his arms — two shotguns, a heavy rifle, and a light revolver-carbine — the thunderbolts of that pitiful Jupiter. The manager bent over him murmuring as he walked beside his head. They laid him down in one of the little cabins — just a room for a bedplace and a campstool or two, you know. We had brought his belated correspondence, and a lot of torn envelopes and open letters littered his bed. His hand roamed feebly amongst these papers. I was struck by the fire in his eyes and the composed languor of his expression. It was not so much the exhaustion of disease. He did not seem in pain. This shadow looked satiated and calm, as though for the moment it had had its fill of all the emotions.

"He rustled one of the letters, and looking straight in my face said, 'I am glad.' Somebody had been writing to him about me. These special recommendations were turning up again. The volume of tone he emitted without effort, almost without the trouble of moving his lips, amazed me. A voice! a voice! It was grave, profound, vibrating, while the man did not seem capable of a whisper. However, he had enough strength in him — factitious no doubt — to very nearly make an end of us, as you shall hear directly.

"The manager appeared silently in the doorway; I stepped out at once and he drew the curtain after me. The Russian, eyed curiously by the pilgrims, was staring at the shore. I followed the direction of his glance.

"Dark human shapes could be made out in the distance, flitting indistinctly against the gloomy border of the forest, and near the river two bronze figures, leaning on tall spears, stood in the sunlight under fantastic headdresses of spotted skins, war-like and still in statuesque repose. And from right to left along the lighted shore moved a wild and gorgeous apparition of a woman.

"She walked with measured steps, draped in striped and fringed cloths, treading the earth proudly, with a slight jingle and flash of barbarous ornaments. She carried her head high; her hair was done in the shape of a helmet; she had brass leggings to the knee, brass wire gauntlets to the elbow, a crimson spot on her tawny cheek, innumerable necklaces of glass beads on her neck; bizarre things, charms, gifts of witchmen, that hung about her, glittered and trembled at every step. She must have had the value of several elephant tusks upon her. She was savage and superb, wild-eyed and magnificent; there was something ominous and stately in her deliberate progress. And in the hush that had fallen suddenly upon the whole sorrowful land, the immense wilderness, the colossal body of the fecund and mysterious life seemed to look at her, pensive, as though it had been looking at the image of its own tenebrous and passionate soul.

"She came abreast of the steamer, stood still, and faced us. Her long shadow fell to the water's edge. Her face had a tragic and fierce aspect of wild sorrow and of dumb pain mingled with the fear of some struggling, half-shaped resolve. She stood looking at us without a stir, and like the wilderness itself, with an air of brooding over an inscrutable purpose. A whole minute passed, and then she made a step forward. There was a low jingle, a glint of yellow metal, a sway of fringed draperies, and she stopped as if her heart had failed her. The young fellow by my side growled. The pilgrims murmured at my back. She looked at us all as if her life had depended upon the unswerving steadiness of her glance. Suddenly she opened her bared arms and threw them up rigid above her head, as though in an uncontrollable desire to touch the sky, and at the same time the swift shadows darted out on the earth, swept around on the river, gathering the steamer into a shadowy embrace. A formidable silence hung over the scene.

"She turned away slowly, walked on, following the bank, and passed into the bushes to the left. Once only her eyes gleamed back at us in the dusk of the thickets before she disappeared.

" 'If she had offered to come aboard I really think I would have tried to shoot her,' said the man of patches, nervously. 'I have been risking my life every day for the last fortnight to keep her out of the house. She got in one day and kicked up a row about those miserable rags I picked up in the storeroom to mend my clothes with. I wasn't decent. At least it must have been that, for she talked like a fury to Kurtz for an hour, pointing at me now and then. I don't understand the dialect of this tribe. Luckily for me, I fancy Kurtz felt too ill that day to care, or there would have been mischief. I don't understand. . . . No — it's too much for me. Ah, well, it's all over now.'

"At this moment I heard Kurtz's deep voice behind the curtain: 'Save me! — save the ivory, you mean. Don't tell me. Save *me*! Why, I've had to save you. You are interrupting my plans now. Sick! Sick! Not so sick as you would like to believe. Never mind. I'll carry my ideas out yet — I will return. I'll show you what can be done. You with your little peddling notions — you are interfering with me. I will return. I. . . .'

"The manager came out. He did me the honor to take me under the arm and lead me aside. 'He is very low, very low,' he said. He considered it necessary to sigh, but neglected to be consistently sorrowful. 'We have done all we could for him — haven't we? But there is no disguising the fact, Mr. Kurtz has done more harm than good to the Company. He did not see the time was not ripe for vigorous action. Cautiously, cautiously — that's my principle. We must be cautious yet. The district is closed to us for a time. Deplorable! Upon the whole, the trade will suffer. I don't deny there is a remarkable quantity of ivory — mostly fossil. We must save it, at all events — but look how precarious the position is — and why? Because the method is unsound.' 'Do you,' said I, looking at the shore, 'call it "unsound method"?' 'Without doubt,' he exclaimed, hotly. 'Don't you?' . . . 'No

method at all,' I murmured after a while. 'Exactly,' he exulted. 'I anticipated this. Shows a complete want of judgment. It is my duty to point it out
in the proper quarter.' 'Oh,' said I, 'that fellow — what's his name? — the
brick-maker, will make a readable report for you.' He appeared confounded
for a moment. It seemed to me I had never breathed an atmosphere so vile,
and I turned mentally to Kurtz for relief — positively for relief. 'Nevertheless I think Mr. Kurtz is a remarkable man,' I said with emphasis. He
started, dropped on me a cold heavy glance, said very quietly, 'he *was*,' and
turned his back on me. My hour of favor was over; I found myself lumped
along with Kurtz as a partisan of methods for which the time was not ripe: I
was unsound! Ah! but it was something to have at least a choice of nightmares.

"I had turned to the wilderness really, not to Mr. Kurtz, who, I was
ready to admit, was as good as buried. And for a moment it seemed to me as
if I also were buried in a vast grave full of unspeakable secrets. I felt an intolerable weight oppressing my breast, the smell of the damp earth, the unseen presence of victorious corruption, the darkness of an impenetrable
night. . . . The Russian tapped me on the shoulder. I heard him mumbling
and stammering something about 'brother seaman — couldn't conceal —
knowledge of matters that would affect Mr. Kurtz's reputation.' I waited.
For him evidently Mr. Kurtz was not in his grave; I suspect that for him
Mr. Kurtz was one of the immortals. 'Well!' said I at last, 'speak out. As it
happens, I am Mr. Kurtz's friend — in a way.'

"He stated with a good deal of formality that had we not been 'of the
same profession,' he would have kept the matter to himself without regard
to consequences. 'He suspected there was an active ill will towards him on
the part of these white men that — ' 'You are right,' I said, remembering a
certain conversation I had overheard. 'The manager thinks you ought to be
hanged.' He showed a concern at this intelligence which amused me at
first. 'I had better get out of the way quietly,' he said, earnestly. 'I can do no
more for Kurtz now, and they would soon find some excuse. What's to stop
them? There's a military post three hundred miles from here.' 'Well, upon
my word,' said I, 'perhaps you had better go if you have any friends
amongst the savages near by.' 'Plenty,' he said. 'They are simple people —
and I want nothing, you know.' He stood biting his lip, then: 'I don't want
any harm to happen to these whites here, but of course I was thinking of
Mr. Kurtz's reputation — but you are a brother seaman and — ' 'All right,'
said I, after a time. 'Mr. Kurtz's reputation is safe with me.' I did not know
how truly I spoke.

"He informed me, lowering his voice, that it was Kurtz who had ordered the attack to be made on the steamer. 'He hated sometimes the idea
of being taken away — and then again. . . . But I don't understand these
matters. I am a simple man. He thought it would scare you away — that
you would give it up, thinking him dead. I could not stop him. Oh, I had an
awful time of it this last month.' 'Very well,' I said. 'He is all right now.'

'Ye-e-es,' he muttered, not very convinced apparently. 'Thanks,' said I; 'I shall keep my eyes open.' 'But quiet — eh?' he urged, anxiously. 'It would be awful for his reputation if anybody here — ' I promised a complete discretion with great gravity. 'I have a canoe and three black fellows waiting not very far. I am off. Could you give me a few Martini-Henry cartridges?' I could, and did, with proper secrecy. He helped himself, with a wink at me, to a handful of my tobacco. 'Between sailors — you know — good English tobacco.' At the door of the pilot-house he turned round — 'I say, haven't you a pair of shoes you could spare?' He raised one leg. 'Look.' The soles were tied with knotted strings sandal-wise under his bare feet. I rooted out an old pair, at which he looked with admiration before tucking them under his left arm. One of his pockets (bright red) was bulging with cartridges, from the other (dark blue) peeped 'Towson's Inquiry,' etc., etc. He seemed to think himself excellently well equipped for a renewed encounter with the wilderness. 'Ah! I'll never, never meet such a man again. You ought to have heard him recite poetry — his own, too, it was, he told me. Poetry!' He rolled his eyes at the recollection of these delights. 'Oh, he enlarged my mind!' 'Good-by,' said I. He shook hands and vanished in the night. Sometimes I ask myself whether I had ever really seen him — whether it was possible to meet such a phenomenon! . . .

"When I woke up shortly after midnight his warning came to my mind with its hint of danger that seemed, in the starred darkness, real enough to make me get up for the purpose of having a look round. On the hill a big fire burned, illuminating fitfully a crooked corner of the station-house. One of the agents with a picket of a few of our blacks, armed for the purpose, was keeping guard over the ivory; but deep within the forest, red gleams that wavered, that seemed to sink and rise from the ground amongst confused columnar shapes of intense blackness, showed the exact position of the camp where Mr. Kurtz's adorers were keeping their uneasy vigil. The monotonous beating of a big drum filled the air with muffled shocks and a lingering vibration. A steady droning sound of many men chanting each to himself some weird incantation came out from the black, flat wall of the wood as the humming of bees comes out of a hive, and had a strange narcotic effect upon my half-awake senses. I believe I dozed off leaning over the rail, till an abrupt burst of yells, an overwhelming outbreak of a pent-up and mysterious frenzy, woke me up in a bewildered wonder. It was cut short all at once, and the low droning went on with an effect of audible and soothing silence. I glanced casually into the little cabin. A light was burning within, but Mr. Kurtz was not there.

"I think I would have raised an outcry if I had believed my eyes. But I didn't believe them at first — the thing seemed so impossible. The fact is I was completely unnerved by a sheer blank fright, pure abstract terror, unconnected with any distinct shape of physical danger. What made this emotion so overpowering as — how shall I define it? — the moral shock I received, as if something altogether monstrous, intolerable to thought and odious to the soul, had been thrust upon me unexpectedly. This lasted of course the merest fraction of a second, and then the usual sense of commonplace, deadly danger, the possibility of a sudden onslaught and massacre, or something of the kind, which I saw impending, was positively welcome and composing. It pacified me, in fact, so much, that I did not raise an alarm.

"There was an agent buttoned up inside an ulster and sleeping on a chair on deck within three feet of me. The yells had not awakened him; he snored very slightly; I left him to his slumbers and leaped ashore. I did not betray Mr. Kurtz — it was ordered I should never betray him — it was written I should be loyal to the nightmare of my choice. I was anxious to deal with this shadow by myself alone — and to this day I don't know why I was so jealous of sharing with anyone the peculiar blackness of that experience.

"As soon as I got on the bank I saw a trail — a broad trail through the grass. I remember the exultation with which I said to myself, 'He can't walk — he is crawling on all-fours — I've got him.' The grass was wet with dew. I strode rapidly with clenched fists. I fancy I had some vague notion of falling upon him and giving him a drubbing. I don't know. I had some imbecile thoughts. The knitting old woman with the cat obtruded herself upon my memory as a most improper person to be sitting at the other end of such an affair. I saw a row of pilgrims squirting lead in the air out of Winchesters held to the hip. I thought I would never get back to the steamer, and imagined myself living alone and unarmed in the woods to an advanced age. Such silly things — you know. And I remember I confounded the beat of the drum with the beating of my heart, and was pleased at its calm regularity.

"I kept to the track though — then stopped to listen. The night was very clear; a dark blue space, sparkling with dew and starlight, in which black things stood very still. I thought I could see a kind of motion ahead of me. I was strangely cocksure of everything that night. I actually left the track and ran in a wide semicircle (I verily believe chuckling to myself) so as to get in front of that stir, of that motion I had seen — if indeed I had seen anything. I was circumventing Kurtz as though it had been a boyish game.

"I came upon him, and, if he had not heard me coming, I would have fallen over him, too, but he got up in time. He rose, unsteady, long, pale, indistinct, like a vapor exhaled by the earth, and swayed slightly, misty and silent before me; while at my back the fires loomed between the trees, and the murmur of many voices issued from the forest. I had cut him off cleverly; but when actually confronting him I seemed to come to my senses, I saw the danger in its right proportion. It was by no means over yet. Suppose he began to shout? Though he could hardly stand, there was still plenty of vigor in his voice. 'Go away — hide yourself,' he said, in that profound tone. It was very awful. I glanced back. We were within thirty yards from the nearest fire. A black figure stood up, strode on long black legs, waving long black arms, across the glow. It had horns — antelope horns, I think — on its head. Some sorcerer, some witchman, no doubt: it looked fiend-like enough. 'Do you know what you are doing?' I whispered. 'Perfectly,' he answered, raising his voice for that single word: it sounded to me far off and yet loud, like a hail through a speaking-trumpet. If he makes a row we are lost, I thought to myself. This clearly was not a case for fisticuffs, even apart from the very natural aversion I had to beat that Shadow — this wandering and tormented thing. 'You will be lost,' I said — 'utterly lost.' One gets sometimes such a flash of inspiration, you know. I did say the right thing, though indeed he could not have been more irretrievably lost than he was at this very moment, when the foundations of our intimacy were being laid — to endure — to endure — even to the end — even beyond.

" 'I had immense plans,' he muttered irresolutely. 'Yes,' said I; 'but if you try to shout I'll smash your head with — ' There was not a stick or a stone near. 'I will throttle you for good,' I corrected myself. 'I was on the threshold of great things,' he pleaded, in a voice of longing, with a wistfulness of tone that made my blood run cold. 'And now for this stupid scoundrel — ' 'Your success in Europe is assured in any case,' I affirmed, steadily. I did not want to have the throttling of him, you understand — and indeed it would have been very little use for any practical purpose. I tried to break the spell — the heavy, mute spell of the wilderness — that seemed to draw him to its pitiless breast by the awakening of forgotten and brutal instincts, by the memory of gratified and monstrous passions. This alone, I was convinced, had driven him out to the edge of the forest, to the bush, towards the gleam of fires, the throb of drums, the drone of weird incantations; this alone had beguiled his unlawful soul beyond the bounds of permitted aspirations. And, don't you see, the terror of the position was not in being knocked on the head — though I had a very lively sense of that danger, too — but in this, that I had to deal with a being to whom I could not appeal in the name of anything high or low. I had, even like the niggers, to invoke him — himself — his own exalted and incredible degradation. There was nothing either above or below him, and I knew it. He had kicked himself loose of the earth. Confound the man! he had kicked the very earth to pieces. He was alone, and I before him did not know whether I stood on the ground or floated in the air. I've been telling you what we said — repeating the phrases we pronounced — but what's the good? They were common everyday words — the familiar, vague sounds exchanged on every waking day of life. But what of that? They had behind them, to my mind, the terrific suggestiveness of words heard in dreams, of phrases spoken in nightmares. Soul! If anybody had ever struggled with a soul, I am the man. And I wasn't arguing with a lunatic either. Believe me or not, his intelligence was perfectly clear — concentrated, it is true, upon himself with horrible intensity, yet clear; and therein was my only chance — barring, of course, the killing him there and then, which wasn't so good, on account of unavoidable noise. But his soul was mad. Being alone in the wilderness, it had looked within itself, and, by heavens! I tell you, it had gone mad. I had — for my sins, I suppose — to go through the ordeal of looking into it myself. No eloquence could have been so withering to one's belief in mankind as his final burst of sincerity. He struggled with himself, too. I saw it — I heard it. I saw the inconceivable mystery of a soul that knew no restraint, no faith, and no fear, yet struggling blindly with itself. I kept my head pretty well; but when I had him at last stretched on the couch, I wiped my forehead, while my legs shook under me as though I had carried half a ton on my back down that hill. And yet I had only supported him, his bony arm clasped round my neck — and he was not much heavier than a child.

"When next day we left at noon, the crowd, of whose presence behind the curtain of trees I had been acutely conscious all the time, flowed out of the woods again, filled the clearing, covered the slope with a mass of naked, breathing, quivering, bronze bodies. I steamed up a bit, then swung downstream, and two thousand eyes followed the evolutions of the splashing, thumping, fierce river-demon beating the water with its terrible tail and breathing black smoke into the air. In front of the first rank, along the river, three men, plastered with bright red earth from head to foot, strutted to and fro restlessly. When we came abreast again, they faced the river, stamped their feet, nodded their horned heads, swayed their scarlet bodies; they shook towards the fierce river-demon a bunch of black feathers, a mangy skin with a pendent tail — something that looked like a dried gourd; they shouted periodically together strings of amazing words that resembled no sounds of human language; and the deep murmurs of the crowd, interrupted suddenly, were like the responses of some satanic litany.

"We had carried Kurtz into the pilot-house: there was more air there. Lying on the couch, he stared through the open shutter. There was an eddy in the mass of human bodies, and the woman with helmeted head and tawny cheeks rushed out to the very brink of the stream. She put out her hands, shouted something, and all that wild mob took up the shout in a roaring chorus of articulated, rapid, breathless utterance.

" 'Do you understand this?' I asked.

"He kept on looking out past me with fiery, longing eyes, with a mingled expression of wistfulness and hate. He made no answer, but I saw a smile, a smile of indefinable meaning, appear on his colorless lips that a moment after twitched convulsively. 'Do I not?' he said slowly, gasping, as if the words had been torn out of him by a supernatural power.

"I pulled the string of the whistle, and I did this because I saw the pilgrims on deck getting out their rifles with an air of anticipating a jolly lark. At the sudden screech there was a movement of abject terror through that wedged mass of bodies. 'Don't! don't you frighten them away,' cried someone on deck disconsolately. I pulled the string time after time. They broke and ran, they leaped, they crouched, they swerved, they dodged the flying terror of the sound. The three red chaps had fallen flat, face down on the shore, as though they had been shot dead. Only the barbarous and superb woman did not so much as flinch, and stretched tragically her bare arms after us over the somber and glittering river.

"And then that imbecile crowd down on the deck started their little fun, and I could see nothing more for smoke.

"The brown current ran swiftly out of the heart of darkness, bearing us down towards the sea with twice the speed of our upward progress; and Kurtz's life was running swiftly, too, ebbing, ebbing out of his heart into the sea of inexorable time. The manager was very placid, he had no vital anxieties now, he took us both in with a comprehensive and satisfied glance: the 'affair' had come off as well as could be wished. I saw the time approaching when I would be left alone of the party of 'unsound method.' The pilgrims looked upon me with disfavor. I was, so to speak, numbered with the dead. It is strange how I accepted this unforeseen partnership, this choice of nightmares forced upon me in the tenebrous land invaded by these mean and greedy phantoms.

"Kurtz discoursed. A voice! a voice! It rang deep to the very last. It survived his strength to hide in the magnificent folds of eloquence the barren darkness of his heart. Oh, he struggled! he struggled! The wastes of his weary brain were haunted by shadowy images now — images of wealth and fame revolving obsequiously round his unextinguishable gift of noble and lofty expression. My Intended, my station, my career, my ideas — these were the objects for the occasional utterances of elevated sentiments. The shade of the original Kurtz frequented the bedside of the hollow sham, whose fate it was to be buried presently in the mold of primeval earth. But both the diabolic love and the unearthly hate of the mysteries it had penetrated fought for the possession of that soul satiated with primitive emotions, avid of lying fame, of sham distinction, of all the appearances of success and power.

"Sometimes he was contemptibly childish. He desired to have kings meet him at railway stations on his return from some ghastly Nowhere, where he intended to accomplish great things. 'You show them you have in you something that is really profitable, and then there will be no limits to the recognition of your ability,' he would say. 'Of course you must take care of the motives — right motives — always.' The long reaches that were like one and the same reach, monotonous bends that were exactly alike, slipped past the steamer with their multitude of secular trees looking patiently after this grimy fragment of another world, the forerunner of change, of conquest, of trade, of massacres, of blessings. I looked ahead — piloting. 'Close the shutter,' said Kurtz suddenly one day; 'I can't bear to look at this.' I did so. There was a silence. 'Oh, but I will wring your heart yet!' he cried at the invisible wilderness.

"We broke down — as I had expected — and had to lie up for repairs at the head of an island. This delay was the first thing that shook Kurtz's confidence. One morning he gave me a packet of papers and a photograph — the lot tied together with a shoestring. 'Keep this for me,' he said. 'This noxious fool' (meaning the manager) 'is capable of prying into my boxes when I am not looking.' In the afternoon I saw him. He was lying on his back with closed eyes, and I withdrew quietly, but I heard him mutter, 'Live rightly, die, die. . . .' I listened. There was nothing more. Was he rehearsing some speech in his sleep, or was it a fragment of a phrase from some newspaper article? He had been writing for the papers and meant to do so again, 'for the furthering of my ideas. It's a duty.'

"His was an impenetrable darkness. I looked at him as you peer down at a man who is lying at the bottom of a precipice where the sun never shines. But I had not much time to give him, because I was helping the engine-driver to take to pieces the leaky cylinders, to straighten a bent connecting-rod, and in other such matters. I lived in an infernal mess of rust, filings, nuts, bolts, spanners, hammers, ratchet-drills — things I abominate, because I don't get on with them. I tended the little forge we fortunately had aboard; I toiled wearily in a wretched scrap-heap — unless I had the shakes too bad to stand.

"One evening coming in with a candle I was startled to hear him say a little tremulously, 'I am lying here in the dark waiting for death.' The light was within a foot of his eyes. I forced myself to murmur, 'Oh, nonsense!' and stood over him as if transfixed.

"Anything approaching the change that came over his features I have never seen before, and hope never to see again. Oh, I wasn't touched. I was fascinated. It was as though a veil had been rent. I saw on that ivory face the expression of somber pride, of ruthless power, of craven terror — of an intense and hopeless despair. Did he live his life again in every detail of desire, temptation, and surrender during that supreme moment of complete knowledge? He cried in a whisper at some image, at some vision — he cried out twice, a cry that was no more than a breath —

" 'The horror! The horror!'

"I blew the candle out and left the cabin. The pilgrims were dining in the messroom, and I took my place opposite the manager, who lifted his eyes to give me a questioning glance, which I successfully ignored. He leaned back, serene, with that peculiar smile of his sealing the unexpressed depths of his meanness. A continuous shower of small flies streamed upon the lamp, upon the cloth, upon our hands and faces. Suddenly the manager's boy put his insolent black head in the doorway, and said in a tone of scathing contempt —

" 'Mistah Kurtz — he dead.'

"All the pilgrims rushed out to see. I remained, and went on with my dinner. I believe I was considered brutally callous. However, I did not eat much. There was a lamp in there — light, don't you know — and outside it was so beastly, beastly dark. I went no more near the remarkable man who had pronounced a judgment upon the adventures of his soul on this earth.

The voice was gone. What else had been there? But I am of course aware that next day the pilgrims buried something in a muddy hole.

"And then they very nearly buried me.

"However, as you see, I did not go to join Kurtz there and then. I did not. I remained to dream the nightmare out to the end, and to show my loyalty to Kurtz once more. Destiny. My destiny! Droll thing life is — that mysterious arrangement of merciless logic for a futile purpose. The most you can hope from it is some knowledge of yourself — that comes too late — a crop of unextinguishable regrets. I have wrestled with death. It is the most unexciting contest you can imagine. It takes place in an impalpable grayness, with nothing underfoot, with nothing around, without spectators, without clamor, without glory, without the great desire of victory, without the great fear of defeat, in a sickly atmosphere of tepid skepticism, without much belief in your own right, and still less in that of your adversary. If such is the form of ultimate wisdom, then life is a greater riddle than some of us think it to be. I was within a hair's breadth of the last opportunity for pronouncement, and I found with humiliation that probably I would have nothing to say. This is the reason why I affirm that Kurtz was a remarkable man. He had something to say. He said it. Since I had peeped over the edge myself, I understand better the meaning of his stare, that could not see the flame of the candle, but was wide enough to embrace the whole universe, piercing enough to penetrate all the hearts that beat in the darkness. He had summed up — he had judged. 'The horror!' He was a remarkable man. After all, this was the expression of some sort of belief; it had candor, it had conviction, it had a vibrating note of revolt in its whisper, it had the appalling face of a glimpsed truth — the strange commingling of desire and hate. And it is not my own extremity I remember best — a vision of grayness without form filled with physical pain, and a careless contempt for the evanescence of all things — even of this pain itself. No! It is his extremity that I seem to have lived through. True, he had made that last stride, he had stepped over the edge, while I had been permitted to draw back my hesitating foot. And perhaps in this is the whole difference; perhaps all the wisdom, and all truth, and all sincerity, are just compressed into that inappreciable moment of time in which we step over the threshold of the invisible. Perhaps! I like to think my summing-up would not have been a word of careless contempt. Better his cry — much better. It was an affirmation, a moral victory paid for by innumerable defeats, by abominable terrors, by abominable satisfactions. But it was a victory! That is why I have remained loyal to Kurtz to the last, and even beyond, when a long time after I heard once more, not his own choice, but the echo of his magnificent eloquence thrown to me from a soul as translucently pure as a cliff of crystal.

"No, they did not bury me, though there is a period of time which I remember mistily, with a shuddering wonder, like a passage through some inconceivable world that had no hope in it and no desire. I found myself back in the sepulchral city resenting the sight of people hurrying through the streets to filch a little money from each other, to devour their infamous cookery, to gulp their unwholesome beer, to dream their insignificant and silly dreams. They trespassed upon my thoughts. They were intruders whose knowledge of life was to me an irritating pretense, because I felt so sure they could not possibly know the things I knew. Their bearing, which was simply the bearing of commonplace individuals going about their business in the assurance of perfect safety, was offensive to me like the outrageous flauntings of folly in the face of a danger it is unable to comprehend. I had no particular desire to enlighten them, but I had some difficulty in restraining myself from laughing in their faces, so full of stupid importance. I daresay I was not very well at that time. I tottered about the streets — there were various affairs to settle — grinning bitterly at perfectly respectable persons. I admit my behavior was inexcusable, but then my temperature was seldom normal in these days. My dear aunt's endeavors to 'nurse up my strength' seemed altogether beside the mark. It was not my strength that wanted nursing, it was my imagination that wanted soothing. I kept the bundle of papers given me by Kurtz, not knowing exactly what to do with it. His mother had died lately, watched over, as I was told, by his Intended. A clean-shaven man, with an official manner and wearing gold-rimmed spectacles, called on me one day and made inquiries, at first circuitous, afterwards suavely pressing, about what he was pleased to denominate certain 'documents.' I was not surprised, because I had had two rows with the manager on the subject out there. I had refused to give up the smallest scrap out of that package, and I took the same attitude with the spectacled man. He became darkly menacing at last, and with much heat argued that the Company had the right to every bit of information about its 'territories.' And said he, 'Mr. Kurtz's knowledge of unexplored regions must have been necessarily extensive and peculiar — owing to his great abilities and to the deplorable circumstances in which he had been placed: therefore — ' I assured him Mr. Kurtz's knowledge, however extensive, did not bear upon the problems of commerce or administration. He invoked then the name of science. 'It would be an incalculable loss if,' etc., etc. I offered him the report on the 'Suppression of Savage Customs,' with the postscriptum torn off. He took it up eagerly, but ended by sniffing at it with an air of contempt. 'This is not what we had a right to expect,' he remarked. 'Expect nothing else,' I said. 'There are only private letters.' He withdrew upon some threat of legal proceedings, and I saw him no more; but another fellow, calling himself Kurtz's cousin, appeared two days later, and was anxious to hear all the details about his dear relative's last moments. Incidentally he gave me to understand that Kurtz had been essentially a great musician. 'There was the making of an immense success,' said the man, who was an organist, I believe, with lank gray hair flowing over a greasy coat-collar. I had no reason to doubt his statement; and to this day I am unable to say what was Kurtz's profession, whether he ever had any —

which was the greatest of his talents. I had taken him for a painter who wrote for the papers, or else for a journalist who could paint — but even the cousin (who took snuff during the interview) could not tell me what he had been — exactly. He was a universal genius — on that point I agreed with the old chap, who thereupon blew his nose noisily into a large cotton handkerchief and withdrew in senile agitation, bearing off some family letters and memoranda without importance. Ultimately a journalist anxious to know something of the fate of his 'dear colleague' turned up. This visitor informed me Kurtz's proper sphere ought to have been politics 'on the popular side.' He had furry straight eyebrows, bristly hair cropped short, an eye-glass on a broad ribbon, and, becoming expansive, confessed his opinion that Kurtz really couldn't write a bit — 'But heavens! how that man could talk. He electrified large meetings. He had faith — don't you see? — he had the faith. He could get himself to believe anything — anything. He would have been a splendid leader of an extreme party.' 'What party?' I asked. 'Any party,' answered the other. 'He was an — an — extremist.' Did I not think so? I assented. Did I know, he asked, with a sudden flash of curiosity, 'what it was that had induced him to go out there?' 'Yes,' said I, and forthwith handed him the famous Report for publication, if he thought fit. He glanced through it hurriedly, mumbling all the time, judged 'it would do,' and took himself off with this plunder.

"Thus I was left at last with a slim packet of letters and the girl's portrait. She struck me as beautiful — I mean she had a beautiful expression. I know that the sunlight can be made to lie, too, yet one felt that no manipulation of light and pose could have conveyed the delicate shade of truthfulness upon those features. She seemed ready to listen without mental reservation, without suspicion, without a thought for herself. I concluded I would go and give her back her portrait and those letters myself. Curiosity? Yes; and also some other feeling perhaps. All that had been Kurtz's had passed out of my hands: his soul, his body, his station, his plans, his ivory, his career. There remained only this memory and his Intended — and I wanted to give that up, too, to the past; in a way — to surrender personally all that remained of him with me to that oblivion which is the last word of our common fate. I don't defend myself. I had no clear perception of what it was I really wanted. Perhaps it was an impulse of unconscious loyalty, or the fulfillment of one of those ironic necessities, that lurk in the facts of human existence. I don't know. I can't tell. But I went.

"I thought his memory was like the other memories of the dead that accumulate in every man's life — a vague impress on the brain of shadows that had fallen on it in their swift and final passage; but before the high and ponderous door, between the tall houses of a street as still and decorous as a well-kept alley in a cemetery, I had a vision of him on the stretcher, opening his mouth voraciously, as if to devour all the earth with all its mankind. He lived then before me; he lived as much as he had ever lived — a shadow insatiable of splendid appearances, of frightful realities; a shadow darker than the shadow of the night, and draped nobly in the folds of a gorgeous eloquence. The vision seemed to enter the house with me — the stretcher, the phantom-bearers, the wild crowd of obedient worshipers, the gloom of the forests, the glitter of the reach between the murky bends, the beat of the drum, regular and muffled like the beating of a heart—the heart of a conquering darkness. It was a moment of triumph for the wilderness, an invading and vengeful rush which, it seemed to me, I would have to keep back alone for the salvation of another soul. And the memory of what I had heard him say afar there, with the honored shapes stirring at my back, in the glow of fires, within the patient woods, those broken phrases came back to me, were heard again in their ominous and terrifying simplicity. I remembered his abject pleading, his abject threats, the colossal scale of his vile desires, the meanness, the torment, the tempestuous anguish of his soul. And later on I seem to see his collected languid manner, when he said one day, 'This lot of ivory now is really mine. The Company did not pay for it. I collected it myself at a very great personal risk. I am afraid they will try to claim it as theirs though. H'm. It is a difficult case. What do you think I ought to do — resist? Eh? I want no more than justice.'. . . He wanted no more than justice—no more than justice. I rang the bell before a mahogany door on the first floor, and while I waited he seemed to stare at me out of the glassy panel — stare with that wide and immense stare embracing, condemning, loathing all the universe. I seemed to hear the whispered cry, 'The horror! The horror!'

"The dusk was falling. I had to wait in a lofty drawing-room with three long windows from floor to ceiling that were like three luminous and bedraped columns. The bent gilt legs and backs of the furniture shone in indistinct curves. The tall marble fireplace had a cold and monumental whiteness. A grand piano stood massively in a corner; with dark gleams on the flat surfaces like a somber and polished sarcophagus. A high door opened — closed. I rose.

"She came forward, all in black, with a pale head, floating towards me in the dusk. She was in mourning. It was more than a year since his death, more than a year since the news came; she seemed as though she would remember and mourn forever. She took both my hands in hers and murmured, 'I had heard you were coming.' I noticed she was not very young — I mean not girlish. She had a mature capacity for fidelity, for belief, for suffering. The room seemed to have grown darker, as if all the sad light of the cloudy evening had taken refuge on her forehead. This fair hair, this pale visage, this pure brow, seemed surrounded by an ashy halo from which the dark eyes looked out at me. Their glance was guileless, profound, confident, and trustful. She carried her sorrowful head as though she were proud of that sorrow, as though she would say, I — I alone know how to mourn him as he deserves. But while we were still shaking hands, such a look of awful desolation came upon her face that I perceived she was one of those creatures that are not the playthings of Time. For her he had died only yesterday. And, by Jove! the impression was so powerful that for me, too, he seemed to have died only yesterday — nay, this very minute. I saw her and him in the same instant of time — his death and her sorrow — I saw her sorrow in the very moment of his death. Do you understand? I saw them together—I heard them together. She had said, with a deep catch of the breath, 'I have survived' while my strained ears seemed to hear distinctly, mingled with her tone of despairing regret, the summing up whisper of his eternal condemnation. I asked myself what I was doing there, with a sensation of panic in my heart as though I had blundered into a place of cruel and absurd mysteries not fit for a human being to behold. She motioned me to a chair. We sat down. I laid the packet gently on the little table, and she put her hand over it. . . . 'You knew him well,' she murmured, after a moment of mourning silence.

" 'Intimacy grows quickly out there,' I said. 'I knew him as well as it is possible for one man to know another.'

" 'And you admired him,' she said. 'It was impossible to know him and not to admire him. Was it?'

" 'He was a remarkable man,' I said, unsteadily. Then before the appealing fixity of her gaze, that seemed to watch for more words on my lips, I went on, 'It was impossible not to — '

" 'Love him,' she finished eagerly, silencing me into an appalled dumbness. 'How true! how true! But when you think that no one knew him so well as I! I had all his noble confidence. I knew him best.'

" 'You knew him best,' I repeated. And perhaps she did. But with every word spoken the room was growing darker, and only her forehead, smooth and white, remained illumined by the unextinguishable light of belief and love.

" 'You were his friend,' she went on. 'His friend,' she repeated, a little louder. 'You must have been, if he had given you this, and sent you to me. I feel I can speak to you — and oh! I must speak. I want you — you have heard his last words — to know I have been worthy of him. . . . It is not pride. . . . Yes! I am proud to know I understood him better than anyone on earth — he told me so himself. And since his mother died I have had no one — no one — to — to — '

"I listened. The darkness deepened. I was not even sure he had given me the right bundle. I rather suspect he wanted me to take care of another batch of his papers which, after his death, I saw the manager examining under the lamp. And the girl talked, easing her pain in the certitude of my sympathy; she talked as thirsty men drink. I had heard that her engagement with Kurtz had been disapproved by her people. He wasn't rich enough or something. And indeed I don't know whether he had not been a pauper all his life. He had given me some reason to infer that it was his impatience of comparative poverty that drove him out there.

" '. . . Who was not his friend who had heard him speak once?' she was saying. 'He drew men towards him by what was best in them.' She looked at me with intensity. 'It is the gift of the great,' she went on, and the sound of her low voice seemed to have the accompaniment of all the other sounds, full of mystery, desolation, and sorrow, I had ever heard — the ripple of the river, the soughing of the trees swayed by the wind, the murmurs of the crowds, the faint ring of incomprehensible words cried from afar, the whisper of a voice speaking from beyond the threshold of an eternal darkness. 'But you have heard him! You know!' she cried.

" 'Yes, I know,' I said with something like despair in my heart, but bowing my head before the faith that was in her, before that great and saving illusion that shone with an unearthly glow in the darkness, in the triumphant darkness from which I could not have defended her — from which I could not even defend myself.

" 'What a loss to me — to us!' — she corrected herself with beautiful generosity; then added in a murmur, 'To the world.' By the last gleams of twilight I could see the glitter of her eyes, full of tears — of tears that would not fall.

" 'I have been very happy — very fortunate — very proud,' she went on. 'Too fortunate. Too happy for a little while. And now I am unhappy for — for life.'

"She stood up; her fair hair seemed to catch all the remaining light in a glimmer of gold. I rose, too.

" 'And of all this,' she went on, mournfully, 'of all his promise, and of all his greatness, of his generous mind, of his noble heart, nothing remains — nothing but a memory. You and I —'

" 'We shall always remember him,' I said, hastily.

" 'No!' she cried. "It is impossible that all this should be lost — that such a life should be sacrificed to leave nothing — but sorrow. You know what vast plans he had. I knew of them, too — I could not perhaps understand — but others knew of them. Something must remain. His words, at least, have not died.'

" 'His words will remain,' I said.

" 'And his example,' she whispered to herself. 'Men looked up to him — his goodness shone in every act. His example —'

" 'True,' I said; 'his example, too. Yes, his example. I forgot that.'

" 'But I do not. I cannot — I cannot believe — not yet. I cannot believe that I shall never see him again, that nobody will see him again, never, never, never."

"She put out her arms as if after a retreating figure, stretching them black and with clasped pale hands across the fading and narrow sheen of the window. Never see him! I saw him clearly enough then. I shall see this eloquent phantom as long as I live, and I shall see her, too, a tragic and familiar Shade, resembling in this gesture another one, tragic also, and bedecked with powerless charms, stretching bare brown arms over the glitter of the infernal stream, the stream of darkness. She said suddenly very low, 'He died as he lived.'

" 'His end,' said I, with dull anger stirring in me, 'was in every way worthy of his life.' "

" 'And I was not with him,' she murmured. My anger subsided before a feeling of infinite pity.

" 'Everything that could be done — ' I mumbled.

" 'Ah, but I believed in him more than anyone on earth — more than his own mother, more than — himself. He needed me! Me! I would have treasured every sigh, every word, every sign, every glance.'

"I felt like a chill grip on my chest. 'Don't,' I said, in a muffled voice.

" 'Forgive me. I — I have mourned so long in silence — in silence. . . . You were with him — to the last? I think of his loneliness. Nobody near to understand him as I would have understood. Perhaps no one to hear. . . .'

" 'To the very end,' I said shakily. 'I heard his very last words. . . .' I stopped in a fright.

" 'Repeat them,' she murmured in a heart-broken tone. 'I want — I want — something — something — to — live with.'

"I was on the point of crying at her, 'Don't you hear them?' The dusk was repeating them in a persistent whisper all around us, in a whisper that seemed to swell menacingly like the first whisper of a rising wind. 'The horror! The horror!'

" 'His last word — to live with,' she insisted. 'Don't you understand I loved him — I loved him — I loved him!'

"I pulled myself together and spoke slowly.

" 'The last word he pronounced was — your name.'

"I heard a light sigh and then my heart stood still, stopped dead short by an exulting and terrible cry, by the cry of inconceivable triumph and of unspeakable pain. 'I knew it — I was sure!' . . . She knew. She was sure. I heard her weeping, she had hidden her face in her hands. It seemed to me that the house would collapse before I could escape, that the heavens would fall upon my head. But nothing happened. The heavens do not fall for such a trifle. Would they have fallen, I wonder, if I had rendered Kurtz that justice which was his due? Hadn't he said he wanted only justice? But I couldn't. I could not tell her. It would have been too dark — too dark altogether. . . ."

Marlow ceased, and sat apart, indistinct and silent, in the pose of a meditating Buddha. Nobody moved for a time. "We have lost the first of the ebb," said the Director, suddenly. I raised my head. The offing was barred by a black bank of clouds, and the tranquil waterway leading to the uttermost ends of the earth flowed somber under an overcast sky — seemed to lead into the heart of an immense darkness.

[1902]

ANTON CHEKHOV (1860–1904) *wrote his first stories while he was a medical student at Moscow University, to raise money for his family. His grandfather had been a serf who had bought his freedom. His father was an unsuccessful grocer in Taganrog, in southwestern Russia. After completing his medical training, Chekhov became an assistant to the district doctor in a small provincial town, where he began to accumulate his vast store of observations of the peasants and provincial characters who came to the hospital. His early sketches were mostly humorous stories that he first published in newspapers under different pen names, keeping his true signature for his medical articles. But the popularity of these sketches made him determined to become a serious artist.*

Chekhov's first two collections of short stories, published in 1886 and 1887, were acclaimed by readers, and from that time on he was able to abandon his medical career and give all his time to writing. He bought a small estate near Moscow, where he lived with his family and treated sick peasants in his home at no charge. Chekhov's kindness and good works were not a matter of any political program or religious philosophy, but rather "the natural coloration of his talent," as Vladimir Nabokov put it. Once Chekhov told a visitor, "Do you know how I write my stories? Here's how!" And he glanced at his table, took up the first object that met his eye — it was an ashtray — and said, "If you want it, you'll have a story tomorrow. It will be called 'The Ashtray.'" And it seemed to the visitor that a magical transformation of that ashtray was taking place: "Certain indefinite situations, adventures which had not yet found concrete form, were already beginning to crystallize about the ashtray."

In his short stories, Chekhov conveys an impression of beauty with a disarmingly simple technique, as in "A Trifle from Real Life." The variety of his moods, the flicker of his wit, and the spareness of his characterizations are enhanced because they are suffused with a faintly iridescent verbal haziness. Virginia Woolf said that "as we read these little stories about nothing at all, the horizon widens; the soul gains an astonishing sense of freedom." Chekhov's hard-won artistic control can be seen in a masterpiece like "The Lady with the Pet Dog," with its great compassion for the adulterous couple. He once wrote a self-portrait for the editor who first encouraged him, in which he gave a sense of the depth of his self-knowledge and the extent of his remarkable human decency:

> *Write a story, do, about a young man, the son of a serf, a former grocery boy, a choir singer, a high school pupil and university student, brought up to respect rank, to kiss the hands of priests, to truckle to the ideas of others — a young man who expressed thanks for every piece of bread, who was whipped many times, who went without galoshes to do his*

tutoring, who used his fists, tortured animals, was fond of dining with rich relatives, was a hypocrite in his dealings with God and men, needlessly, solely out of a realization of his own insignificance — write how this young man squeezes the slave out of himself, drop by drop, and how, on awaking one fine morning, he feels that the blood coursing through his veins is no longer that of a slave but that of a real human being.

In his last years, Chekhov — already established as a great writer of short fiction — wrote plays for the Moscow Art Theater, which was then remaking the whole idea of theater in Russia under the direction of Konstantin Stanislavsky. These plays — including The Seagull *(1896),* Uncle Vanya *(1898),* The Three Sisters *(1901), and* The Cherry Orchard *(1904) — established him as a great dramatist as well. In 1901 he married Olga Knipper, one of the leading actresses of the Moscow Art Theater. But he was already dying of tuberculosis, and he lived his last three years as an invalid.*

Chekhov's hundreds of stories have immensely influenced the art of fiction. He was never concerned with giving a social or ethical message in his writing, but the complete integrity and harmony that his work conveys will live in the world, according to Nabokov, "as long as there are birchwoods and sunsets and the urge to write." (See Chekhov's Commentary on page 1242 and Nabokov's Commentary about "The Lady with the Little Dog" on page 1244.)

Anton Chekhov

ဢ

A Trifle from Real Life

– translated by Marian Fell

Nikolai Ilitch Belayeff was a young gentleman of St. Petersburg, aged thirty-two, rosy, well fed, and a patron of the race-tracks. Once, toward evening, he went to pay a call on Olga Ivanovna with whom, to use his own expression, he was dragging through a long and tedious love-affair. And the truth was that the first thrilling, inspiring pages of this romance had long since been read, and that the story was now dragging wearily on, presenting nothing that was either interesting or novel.

Not finding Olga at home, my hero threw himself upon a couch and prepared to await her return.

"Good evening, Nikolai Ilitch!" he heard a child's voice say. "Mamma will soon be home. She has gone to the dressmaker's with Sonia."

On the divan in the same room lay Aliosha, Olga's son, a small boy of eight, immaculately and picturesquely dressed in a little velvet suit and long black stockings. He had been lying on a satin pillow, mimicking the antics of an acrobat he had seen at the circus. First he stretched up one pretty leg, then another; then, when they were tired, he brought his arms into play, and at last jumped up galvanically, throwing himself on all fours in an effort to stand on his head. He went through all these motions with the most serious face in the world, puffing like a martyr, as if he himself regretted that God had given him such a restless little body.

"Ah, good evening, my boy!" said Belayeff. "Is that you? I did not know you were here. Is mamma well?"

Aliosha seized the toe of his left shoe in his right hand, assumed the most unnatural position in the world, rolled over, jumped up, and peeped out at Belayeff from under the heavy fringes of the lampshade.

"Not very," he said shrugging his shoulders. "Mamma is never really well. She is a woman, you see, and women always have something the matter with them."

From lack of anything better to do, Belayeff began scrutinizing Aliosha's face. During all his acquaintance with Olga he had never bestowed any consideration upon the boy or noticed his existence at all. He had seen the child about, but what he was doing there Belayeff, somehow, had never cared to think.

Now, in the dusk of evening, Aliosha's pale face and fixed, dark eyes unexpectedly reminded Belayeff of Olga as she had appeared in the first pages of their romance. He wanted to pet the boy.

"Come here, little monkey," he said, "and let me look at you!"

The boy jumped down from the sofa and ran to Belayeff.

"Well," the latter began, laying his hand on the boy's thin shoulder. "And how are you? Is everything all right with you?"

"No, not very. It used to be much better."

"In what way?"

"That's easy to answer. Sonia and I used to learn only music and reading before, but now we have French verses, too. You have cut your beard!"

"Yes."

"So I noticed. It is shorter than it was. Please let me touch it — does that hurt?"

"No, not a bit."

"Why does it hurt if you pull one hair at a time, and not a bit if you pull lots? Ha! Ha! I'll tell you something. You ought to wear whiskers! You could shave here on the sides, here, and here you could let the hair grow —— "

The boy nestled close to Belayeff and began to play with his watch-chain.

"Mamma is going to give me a watch when I go to school, and I am going to ask her to give me a chain just like yours —— Oh, what a lovely locket! Papa has a locket just like that; only yours has little stripes on it, and papa's has letters. He has a portrait of mamma in his locket. Papa wears another watch-chain now made of ribbon."

"How do you know? Do you ever see your papa?"

"I — n-no — I ——"

Aliosha blushed deeply at being caught telling a fib and began to scratch the locket furiously with his nail. Belayeff looked searchingly into his face and repeated:

"Do you ever see your papa?"

"N-no!"

"Come, tell me honestly! I can see by your face that you are not telling the truth. It's no use quibbling now that the cat is out of the bag. Tell me, do you see him? Now then, as between friends!"

Aliosha reflected.

"You won't tell mamma?" he said.

"What an idea!"

"Honor bright?"

"Honor bright!"

"Promise!"

"Oh, you insufferable child! What do you take me for?"

Aliosha glanced around, opened his eyes wide, and said:

"For heaven's sake don't tell mamma! Don't tell a soul, because it's a secret. I don't know what would happen to Sonia and Pelagia and me if mamma should find out. Now, listen. Sonia and I see papa every Thursday and every Friday. When Pelagia takes us out walking before dinner we go to Anfel's confectionery and there we find papa already waiting for us. He is always sitting in the little private room with the marble table and the ashtray that's made like a goose without a back."

"What do you do in there?"

"We don't do anything. First we say how do you do, and then papa orders coffee and pasties for us. Sonia likes pasties with meat, you know, but I can't abide them with meat. I like mine with cabbage or eggs. We eat so much that we have a hard time eating our dinner afterward so that mamma won't guess anything."

"What do you talk about?"

"With papa? Oh, about everything. He kisses us and hugs us and tells us the funniest jokes. Do you know what? He says that when we grow bigger he is going to take us to live with him. Sonia doesn't want to go, but I wouldn't mind. Of course it would be lonely without mamma, but I could write letters to her. Isn't it funny, we might go and see her then on Sundays, mightn't we? Papa says too, he is going to buy me a pony. He is such a nice man! I don't know why mamma doesn't ask him to live with her and why she won't let us see him. He loves mamma very much. He always asks how she is and what she has been doing. When she was ill he took hold of his head just like this — and ran about the room. He always asks us whether we are obedient and respectful to her. Tell me, is it true that we are unfortunate?"

"H'm — why do you ask?"

"Because papa says we are. He says we are unfortunate children, and that he is unfortunate, and that mamma is unfortunate. He tells us to pray to God for her and for ourselves."

Aliosha fixed his eyes on the figure of a stuffed bird, and became lost in thought.

"Well, I declare —— " muttered Belayeff. "So, that's what you do, you hold meetings at a confectioner's? And your mamma doesn't know it?"

"N-no. How could she? Pelagia wouldn't tell her for the world. Day before yesterday papa gave us pears. They were as sweet as sugar. I ate two!"

"H'm. But — listen to me, does papa ever say anything about me?"

"About you? What shall I say?" Aliosha looked searchingly into Belayeff's face and shrugged his shoulders. "Nothing special," he answered.

"Well, what does he say, for instance?"

"You won't be angry if I tell you?"

"What an idea! Does he abuse me?"

"No, he doesn't abuse you, but, you know, he is angry with you. He says that it is your fault that mamma is unhappy, and that you have ruined mamma. He is such a funny man! I tell him that you are kind and that you never scold mamma, but he only shakes his head."

"So he says I have ruined her?"

"Yes — don't be angry, Nikolai Ilitch!"

Belayeff rose and began pacing up and down the room.

"How strange this is — and how ridiculous!" he muttered shrugging his shoulders and smiling sarcastically. "It is all *his* fault and yet he says *I* have ruined her! What an innocent baby this is! And so he told you I had ruined your mother?"

"Yes, but — you promised not to be angry!"

"I'm not angry and — and it is none of your business anyway. Yes, this is — this is really ridiculous! Here I have been caught like a mouse in a trap, and now it seems it is all my fault!"

The door-bell rang. The boy tore himself from Belayeff's arms and ran out of the room. A moment later a lady entered with a little girl. It was Aliosha's mother, Olga Ivanovna. Aliosha skipped into the room behind her, singing loudly and clapping his hands. Belayeff nodded and continued to walk up and down.

"Of course!" he muttered. "Whom should he blame but me? He has right on his side! He is the injured husband."

"What is that you are saying?" asked Olga Ivanovna.

"What am I saying? Just listen to what your young hopeful here has been preaching. It appears that I am a wicked scoundrel and that I have ruined you and your children. You are all unhappy, and I alone am frightfully happy. Frightfully, frightfully happy!"

"I don't understand you, Nikolai. What is the matter?"

"Just listen to what this young gentleman here has to say!" cried Belayeff pointing to Aliosha.

Aliosha flushed and then grew suddenly pale and his face became distorted with fear.

"Nikolai Ilitch!" he whispered loudly. "Hush!"

Olga Ivanovna looked at Aliosha in surprise, and then at Belayeff, and then back again at Aliosha.

"Ask him!" Belayeff continued. "That idiot of yours, Pelagia, takes them to a confectioner's and arranges meetings there between them and their papa. But that isn't the point. The point is that papa is the victim, and that I am an abandoned scoundrel who has wrecked the lives of both of you!"

"Nikolai Ilitch!" groaned Aliosha. "You gave me your word of honor!"

"Leave me alone!" Belayeff motioned to him impatiently. "This is more important than words of honor. This hypocrisy, these lies are intolerable!"

"I don't understand!" cried Olga Ivanovna, the tears glistening in her eyes. "Listen, Aliosha," she asked, turning to her son. "Do you really see your father?"

But Aliosha did not hear her, his eyes were fixed with horror on Belayeff.

"It cannot be possible!" his mother exclaimed, "I must go and ask Pelagia."

Olga Ivanovna left the room.

"But Nikolai Ilitch, you gave me your word of honor!" cried Aliosha trembling all over.

Belayeff made an impatient gesture and went on pacing the floor. He was absorbed in thoughts of the wrong that had been done him, and, as before, was unconscious of the boy's presence: a serious, grown-up person like him could not be bothered with little boys. But Aliosha crept into a corner and told Sonia with horror how he had been deceived. He trembled and hiccoughed and cried. This was the first time in his life that he had come roughly face to face with deceit; he had never imagined till now that there were things in this world besides pasties and watches and sweet pears, things for which no name could be found in the vocabulary of childhood.

[1888]

Anton Chekhov

ॐ

THE LADY WITH THE PET DOG

– translated by Avrahm Yarmolinsky

I

A new person, it was said, had appeared on the esplanade: a lady with a pet dog. Dmitry Dmitrich Gurov, who had spent a fortnight at Yalta and had got used to the place, had also begun to take an interest in new arrivals. As he sat in Vernet's confectionery shop, he saw, walking on the esplanade, a fair-haired young woman of medium height, wearing a beret; a white Pomeranian was trotting behind her.

And afterwards he met her in the public garden and in the square several times a day. She walked alone, always wearing the same beret and always with the white dog; no one knew who she was and everyone called her simply "the lady with the pet dog."

"If she is here alone without husband or friends," Gurov reflected, "it wouldn't be a bad thing to make her acquaintance."

He was under forty, but he already had a daughter twelve years old, and two sons at school. They had found a wife for him when he was very young, a student in his second year, and by now she seemed half as old again as he. She was a tall, erect woman with dark eyebrows, stately and dignified and, as she said of herself, intellectual. She read a great deal, used simplified spelling in her letters, called her husband, not Dmitry, but Dimitry, while he privately considered her of limited intelligence, narrow-minded, dowdy, was afraid of her, and did not like to be at home. He had begun being unfaithful to her long ago — had been unfaithful to her often and, probably for that reason, almost always spoke ill of women, and when they were talked of in his presence used to call them "the inferior race."

It seemed to him that he had been sufficiently tutored by bitter experience to call them what he pleased, and yet he could not have lived without "the inferior race" for two days together. In the company of men he was bored and ill at ease, he was chilly and uncommunicative with them; but when he was among women he felt free, and knew what to speak to them about and how to comport himself; and even to be silent with them was no strain on him. In his appearance, in his character, in his whole make-up there was something attractive and elusive that disposed women in his favor and allured them. He knew that, and some force seemed to draw him to them, too.

Oft-repeated and really bitter experience had taught him long ago that with decent people — particularly Moscow people — who are irresolute and slow to move, every affair which at first seems a light and charming adventure inevitably grows into a whole problem of extreme complexity, and in the end a painful situation is created. But at every new meeting with an interesting woman this lesson of experience seemed to slip from his memory, and he was eager for life, and everything seemed so simple and diverting.

One evening while he was dining in the public garden the lady in the beret walked up without haste to take the next table. Her expression, her gait, her dress, and the way she did her hair told him that she belonged to the upper class, that she was married, that she was in Yalta for the first time and alone, and that she was bored there. The stories told of the immorality in Yalta are to a great extent untrue; he despised them, and knew that such stories were made up for the most part by persons who would have been glad to sin themselves if they had had the chance; but when the lady sat down at the next table three paces from him, he recalled these stories of easy conquests, of trips to the mountains, and the tempting thought of a swift, fleeting liaison, a romance with an unknown woman of whose very name he was ignorant suddenly took hold of him.

He beckoned invitingly to the Pomeranian, and when the dog approached him, shook his finger at it. The Pomeranian growled; Gurov threatened it again.

The lady glanced at him and at once dropped her eyes.

"He doesn't bite," she said and blushed.

"May I give him a bone?" he asked; and when she nodded he inquired affably, "Have you been in Yalta long?"

"About five days."

"And I am dragging out the second week here."

There was a short silence.

"Time passes quickly, and yet it is so dull here!" she said, not looking at him.

"It's only the fashion to say it's dull here. A provincial will live in Belyov or Zhizdra and not be bored, but when he comes here it's 'Oh, the dullness! Oh, the dust!' One would think he came from Granada."

She laughed. Then both continued eating in silence, like strangers, but after dinner they walked together and there sprang up between them the light banter of people who are free and contented, to whom it does not matter where they go or what they talk about. They walked and talked of the strange light on the sea: the water was a soft, warm, lilac color, and there was a golden band of moonlight upon it. They talked of how sultry it was after a hot day. Gurov told her that he was a native of Moscow, that he had studied languages and literature at the university, but had a post in a bank; that at one time he had trained to become an opera singer but had given it up, that he owned two houses in Moscow. And he learned from her that she had grown up in Petersburg, but had lived in S — since her marriage two years previously, that she was going to stay in Yalta for about another month, and that her husband, who needed a rest, too, might perhaps come to fetch her. She was not certain whether her husband was a member of a Government Board or served on a Zemstvo Council,[1] and this amused her. And Gurov learned too that her name was Anna Sergeyevna.

Afterwards in his room at the hotel he thought about her — and was certain that he would meet her the next day. It was bound to happen. Getting into bed he recalled that she had been a schoolgirl only recently, doing lessons like his own daughter; he thought how much timidity and angularity there was still in her laugh and her manner of talking with a stranger. It must have been the first time in her life that she was alone in a setting in which she was followed, looked at, and spoken to for one secret purpose alone, which she could hardly fail to guess. He thought of her slim, delicate throat, her lovely gray eyes.

"There's something pathetic about her, though," he thought, and dropped off.

II

A week had passed since they had struck up an acquaintance. It was a holiday. It was close indoors, while in the street the wind whirled the dust about and blew people's hats off. One was thirsty all day, and Gurov often went into the restaurant and offered Anna Sergeyevna a soft drink or ice cream. One did not know what to do with oneself.

In the evening when the wind had abated they went out on the pier to watch the steamer come in. There were a great many people walking about the dock; they had come to welcome someone and they were carrying bunches of flowers. And two peculiarities of a festive Yalta crowd stood out: the elderly ladies were dressed like young ones and there were many generals.

Owing to the choppy sea, the steamer arrived late, after sunset, and it was a long time tacking about before it put in at the pier. Anna Sergeyevna peered at the steamer and the passengers through her lorgnette as though looking for acquaintances, and whenever she turned to Gurov her eyes were shining. She talked a great deal and asked questions jerkily, forgetting the next moment what she had asked; then she lost her lorgnette in the crush.

The festive crowd began to disperse; it was now too dark to see people's faces; there was no wind any more, but Gurov and Anna Sergeyevna still stood as though waiting to see someone else come off the steamer.

[1] county council.

Anna Sergeyevna was silent now, and sniffed her flowers without looking at Gurov.

"The weather has improved this evening," he said. "Where shall we go now? Shall we drive somewhere?"

She did not reply.

Then he looked at her intently, and suddenly embraced her and kissed her on the lips, and the moist fragrance of her flowers enveloped him; and at once he looked round him anxiously, wondering if anyone had seen them.

"Let us go to your place," he said softly. And they walked off together rapidly.

The air in her room was close and there was the smell of the perfume she had bought at the Japanese shop. Looking at her, Gurov thought: "What encounters life offers!" From the past he preserved the memory of carefree, good-natured women whom love made gay and who were grateful to him for the happiness he gave them, however brief it might be; and of women like his wife who loved without sincerity, with too many words, affectedly, hysterically, with an expression that it was not love or passion that engaged them but something more significant; and of two or three others, very beautiful, frigid women, across whose faces would suddenly flit a rapacious expression — an obstinate desire to take from life more than it could give, and these were women no longer young, capricious, unreflecting, domineering, unintelligent, and when Gurov grew cold to them their beauty aroused his hatred, and the lace on their lingerie seemed to him to resemble scales.

But here there was the timidity, the angularity of inexperienced youth, a feeling of awkwardness; and there was a sense of embarrassment, as though someone had suddenly knocked at the door. Anna Sergeyevna, "the lady with the pet dog," treated what had happened in a peculiar way, very seriously, as though it were her fall — so it seemed, and this was odd and inappropriate. Her features drooped and faded, and her long hair hung down sadly on either side of her face; she grew pensive and her dejected pose was that of a Magdalene in a picture by an old master.

"It's not right," she said. "You don't respect me now, you first of all."

There was a watermelon on the table. Gurov cut himself a slice and began eating it without haste. They were silent for at least half an hour.

There was something touching about Anna Sergeyevna; she had the purity of a well-bred, naive woman who has seen little of life. The single candle burning on the table barely illumined her face, yet it was clear that she was unhappy.

"Why should I stop respecting you, darling?" asked Gurov. "You don't know what you're saying."

"God forgive me," she said, and her eyes filled with tears. "It's terrible."

"It's as though you were trying to exonerate yourself."

"How can I exonerate myself? No. I am a bad, low woman; I despise myself and I have no thought of exonerating myself. It's not my husband but myself I have deceived. And not only just now; I have been deceiving myself for a long time. My husband may be a good, honest man, but he is a flunkey! I don't know what he does, what his work is, but I know he is a flunkey! I was twenty when I married him. I was tormented by curiosity; I wanted something better. 'There must be a different sort of life,' I said to myself. I wanted to live! To live, to live! Curiosity kept eating at me — you don't understand it, but I swear to God I could no longer control myself; something was going on in me; I could not be held back. I told my husband I was ill, and came here. And here I have been walking about as though in a daze, as though I were mad; and now I have become a vulgar, vile woman whom anyone may despise."

Gurov was already bored with her; he was irritated by her naive tone, by her repentance, so unexpected and so out of place, but for the tears in her eyes he might have thought she was joking or play-acting.

"I don't understand, my dear," he said softly. "What do you want?"

She hid her face on his breast and pressed close to him.

"Believe me, believe me, I beg you," she said, "I love honesty and purity, and sin is loathsome to me; I don't know what I'm doing. Simple people say, 'The Evil One has led me astray.' And I may say of myself now that the Evil One has led me astray."

"Quiet, quiet," he murmured.

He looked into her fixed, frightened eyes, kissed her, spoke to her softly and affectionately, and by degrees she calmed down, and her gaiety returned; both began laughing.

Afterwards when they went out there was not a soul on the esplanade. The town with its cypresses looked quite dead, but the sea was still sounding as it broke upon the beach; a single launch was rocking on the waves and on it a lantern was blinking sleepily.

They found a cab and drove to Oreanda.

"I found out your surname in the hall just now: it was written on the board — von Dideritz," said Gurov. "Is your husband German?"

"No; I believe his grandfather was German, but he is Greek Orthodox himself."

At Oreanda they sat on a bench not far from the church, looked down at the sea, and were silent. Yalta was barely visible through the morning mist; white clouds rested motionlessly on the mountaintops. The leaves did not stir on the trees, cicadas twanged, and the monotonous muffled sound of the sea that rose from below spoke of the peace, the eternal sleep awaiting us. So it rumbled below when there was no Yalta, no Oreanda here; so it rumbles now, and it will rumble as indifferently and as hollowly when we are no more. And in this constancy, in this complete indifference to the life and death of each of us, there lies, perhaps, a pledge of our eternal salvation, of the unceasing advance of life upon earth, of unceasing movement towards perfection. Sitting beside a young woman who in the dawn seemed so lovely, Gurov, soothed and spellbound by these magical surroundings — the sea, the mountains, the clouds, the wide sky — thought how everything is really beautiful in this world when one reflects: everything except what we think or do ourselves when we forget the higher aims of life and our own human dignity.

A man strolled up to them — probably a guard — looked at them and walked away. And this detail, too, seemed so mysterious and beautiful. They saw a steamer arrive from Feodosia, its lights extinguished in the glow of dawn.

"There is dew on the grass," said Anna Sergeyevna, after a silence.

"Yes, it's time to go home."

They returned to the city.

Then they met every day at twelve o'clock on the esplanade, lunched and dined together, took walks, admired the sea. She complained that she slept badly, that she had palpitations, asked the same questions, troubled now by jealousy and now by the fear that he did not respect her sufficiently. And often in the square or the public garden, when there was no one near them, he suddenly drew her to him and kissed her passionately. Complete idleness, these kisses in broad daylight exchanged furtively in dread of someone's seeing them, the heat, the smell of the sea, and the continual flitting before his eyes of idle, well-dressed, well-fed people, worked a complete change in him; he kept telling Anna Sergeyevna how beautiful she was, how seductive, was urgently passionate; he would not move a step away from her, while she was often pensive and continually pressed him to confess that he did not respect her, did not love her in the least, and saw in her nothing but a common woman. Almost every evening rather late they drove somewhere out of town, to Oreanda or to the waterfall; and the excursion was always a success, the scenery invariably impressed them as beautiful and magnificent.

They were expecting her husband, but a letter came from him saying that he had eye-trouble, and begging his wife to return home as soon as possible. Anna Sergeyevna made haste to go.

"It's a good thing I am leaving," she said to Gurov. "It's the hand of Fate!"

She took a carriage to the railway station, and he went with her. They were driving the whole day. When she had taken her place in the express, and when the second bell had rung, she said, "Let me look at you once more — let me look at you again. Like this."

She was not crying but was so sad that she seemed ill and her face was quivering.

"I shall be thinking of you — remembering you," she said. "God bless you; be happy. Don't remember evil against me. We are parting forever — it has to be, for we ought never to have met. Well, God bless you."

The train moved off rapidly, its lights soon vanished, and a minute later there was no sound of it, as though everything had conspired to end as quickly as possible that sweet trance, that madness. Left alone on the platform, and gazing into the dark distance, Gurov listened to the twang of the grasshoppers and the hum of the telegraph wires, feeling as though he had just waked up. And he reflected, musing, that there had now been another episode or adventure in his life, and it, too, was at an end, and nothing was left of it but a memory. He was moved, sad, and slightly remorseful: this young woman whom he would never meet again had not been happy with him; he had been warm and affectionate with her, but yet in his manner, his tone, and his caresses there had been a shade of light irony, the slightly coarse arrogance of a happy male who was, besides, almost twice her age. She had constantly called him kind, exceptional, high-minded; obviously he had seemed to her different from what he really was, so he had involuntarily deceived her.

Here at the station there was already a scent of autumn in the air; it was a chilly evening.

"It is time for me to go north, too," thought Gurov as he left the platform. "High time!"

III

At home in Moscow the winter routine was already established; the stoves were heated, and in the morning it was still dark when the children were having breakfast and getting ready for school, and the nurse would light the lamp for a short time. There were frosts already. When the first snow falls, on the first day the sleighs are out, it is pleasant to see the white earth, the white roofs; one draws easy, delicious breaths, and the season brings back the days of one's youth. The old limes and birches, white with hoar-frost, have a good-natured look; they are closer to one's heart than cypresses and palms, and near them one no longer wants to think of mountains and the sea.

Gurov, a native of Moscow, arrived there on a fine frosty day, and when he put on his fur coat and warm gloves and took a walk along Petrovka, and when on Saturday night he heard the bells ringing, his recent trip and the places he had visited lost all charm for him. Little by little he became immersed in Moscow life, greedily read three newspapers a day, and declared that he did not read the Moscow papers on principle. He already felt a longing for restaurants, clubs, formal dinners, anniversary celebrations, and it flattered him to entertain distinguished lawyers and actors, and to play cards with a professor at the physicians' club. He could eat a whole portion of meat stewed with pickled cabbage and served in a pan, Moscow style.

A month or so would pass and the image of Anna Sergeyevna, it seemed to him, would become misty in his memory, and only from time to time he would dream of her with her touching smile as he dreamed of others. But more than a month went by, winter came into its own, and everything was still clear in his memory as though he had parted from Anna Sergeyevna only yesterday. And his memories glowed more and more vividly. When in the evening stillness the voices of his children preparing their lessons reached his study, or when he listened to a song or to an organ playing in a restaurant, or when the storm howled in the chimney, suddenly everything would rise up in his memory; what had happened on the pier and the early morning with the mist on the mountains, and the steamer coming from Feodosia, and the kisses. He would pace about his room a long time, remembering and smiling; then his memories passed into reveries, and in his imagination the past would mingle with what was to come. He did not dream of Anna Sergeyevna, but she followed him about everywhere and watched him. When he shut his eyes he saw her before him as though she were there in the flesh, and she seemed to him lovelier, younger, tenderer than she had been, and he imagined himself a finer man than he had been in Yalta. Of evenings she peered out at him from the bookcase, from the fireplace, from the corner — he heard her breathing, the caressing rustle of her clothes. In the street he followed the women with his eyes, looking for someone who resembled her.

Already he was tormented by a strong desire to share his memories with someone. But in his home it was impossible to talk of his love, and he had no one to talk to outside; certainly he could not confide in his tenants or in anyone at the bank. And what was there to talk about? He hadn't loved her then, had he? Had there been anything beautiful, poetical, edifying, or simply interesting in his relations with Anna Sergeyevna? And he was forced to talk vaguely of love, of women, and no one guessed what he meant; only his wife would twitch her black eyebrows and say, "The part of a philanderer does not suit you at all, Dimitry."

One evening, coming out of the physicians' club with an official with whom he had been playing cards, he could not resist saying:

"If you only knew what a fascinating woman I became acquainted with at Yalta!"

The official got into his sledge and was driving away, but turned suddenly and shouted:

"Dmitry Dmitrich!"

"What is it?"

"You were right this evening: the sturgeon was a bit high."

These words, so commonplace, for some reason moved Gurov to indignation, and struck him as degrading and unclean. What savage manners, what mugs! What stupid nights, what dull, humdrum days! Frenzied gambling, gluttony, drunkenness, continual talk always about the same thing! Futile pursuits and conversations always about the same topics take up the better part of one's time, the better part of one's strength, and in the end there is left a life clipped and wingless, an absurd mess, and there is no

escaping or getting away from it — just as though one were in a madhouse
or a prison.

Gurov, boiling with indignation, did not sleep all night. And he had a
headache all the next day. And the following nights too he slept badly; he
sat up in bed, thinking, or paced up and down his room. He was fed up with
his children, fed up with the bank; he had no desire to go anywhere or to
talk of anything.

In December during the holidays he prepared to take a trip and told
his wife he was going to Petersburg to do what he could for a young
friend — and he set off for S — . What for? He did not know, himself. He
wanted to see Anna Sergeyevna and talk with her, to arrange a rendezvous if
possible.

He arrived at S — in the morning, and at the hotel took the best room,
in which the floor was covered with gray army cloth, and on the table there
was an inkstand, gray with dust and topped by a figure on horseback, its hat
in its raised hand and its head broken off. The porter gave him the necessary information: von Dideritz lived in a house of his own on Staro-
Goncharnaya Street, not far from the hotel: he was rich and lived well and
kept his own horses; everyone in the town knew him. The porter pronounced the name: "Dridiritz."

Without haste Gurov made his way to Staro-Goncharnaya Street and
found the house. Directly opposite the house stretched a long gray fence
studded with nails.

"A fence like that would make one run away," thought Gurov, looking
now at the fence, now at the windows of the house.

He reflected: this was a holiday, and the husband was apt to be at
home. And in any case, it would be tactless to go into the house and disturb
her. If he were to send her a note, it might fall into her husband's hands,
and that might spoil everything. The best thing was to rely on chance. And
he kept walking up and down the street and along the fence, waiting for the
chance. He saw a beggar go in at the gate and heard the dogs attack him;
then an hour later he heard a piano, and the sound came to him faintly and
indistinctly. Probably it was Anna Sergeyevna playing. The front door
opened suddenly, and an old woman came out, followed by the familiar
white Pomeranian. Gurov was on the point of calling to the dog, but his
heart began beating violently, and in his excitement he could not remember
the Pomeranian's name.

He kept walking up and down, and hated the gray fence more and
more, and by now he thought irritably that Anna Sergeyevna had forgotten
him, and was perhaps already diverting herself with another man, and that
that was very natural in a young woman who from morning till night had to
look at that damn fence. He went back to his hotel room and sat on the
couch for a long while, not knowing what to do, then he had dinner and a
long nap.

"How stupid and annoying all this is!" he thought when he woke and looked at the dark windows: it was already evening. "Here I've had a good sleep for some reason. What am I going to do at night?"

He sat on the bed, which was covered with a cheap gray blanket of the kind seen in hospitals, and he twitted himself in his vexation:

"So there's your lady with the pet dog. There's your adventure. A nice place to cool your heels in."

That morning at the station a playbill in large letters had caught his eye. *The Geisha* was to be given for the first time. He thought of this and drove to the theater.

"It's quite possible that she goes to first nights," he thought.

The theater was full. As in all provincial theaters, there was a haze above the chandelier, the gallery was noisy and restless; in the front row, before the beginning of the performance the local dandies were standing with their hands clasped behind their backs; in the Governor's box the Governor's daughter, wearing a boa, occupied the front seat, while the Governor himself hid modestly behind the portiere and only his hands were visible; the curtain swayed; the orchestra was a long time tuning up. While the audience was coming in and taking their seats, Gurov scanned the faces eagerly.

Anna Sergeyevna, too, came in. She sat down in the third row, and when Gurov looked at her his heart contracted, and he understood clearly that in the whole world there was no human being so near, so precious, and so important to him; she, this little, undistinguished woman, lost in a provincial crowd, with a vulgar lorgnette in her hand, filled his whole life now, was his sorrow and his joy, the only happiness that he now desired for himself, and to the sounds of the bad orchestra, of the miserable local violins, he thought how lovely she was. He thought and dreamed.

A young man with small side-whiskers, very tall and stooped, came in with Anna Sergeyevna and sat down beside her; he nodded his head at every step and seemed to be bowing continually. Probably this was the husband whom at Yalta, in an access of bitter feeling, she had called a flunkey. And there really was in his lanky figure, his side-whiskers, his small bald patch, something of a flunkey's retiring manner; his smile was mawkish, and in his buttonhole there was an academic badge like a waiter's number.

During the first intermission the husband went out to have a smoke; she remained in her seat. Gurov, who was also sitting in the orchestra, went up to her and said in a shaky voice, with a forced smile:

"Good evening!"

She glanced at him and turned pale, then looked at him again in horror, unable to believe her eyes, and gripped the fan and the lorgnette tightly together in her hands, evidently trying to keep herself from fainting. Both were silent. She was sitting, he was standing, frightened by her distress and not daring to take a seat beside her. The violins and the flute that were being tuned up sang out. He suddenly felt frightened: it seemed as if all the people in the boxes were looking at them. She got up and went hurriedly to the exit; he followed her, and both of them walked blindly along the corridors and up and down stairs, and figures in the uniforms prescribed for magistrates, teachers, and officials of the Department of Crown Lands, all wearing badges, flitted before their eyes, as did also ladies, and fur coats on hangers; they were conscious of drafts and the smell of stale tobacco. And Gurov, whose heart was beating violently, thought:

"Oh, Lord! Why are these people here and this orchestra!"

And at that instant he suddenly recalled how when he had seen Anna Sergeyevna off at the station he had said to himself that all was over between them and that they would never meet again. But how distant the end still was!

On the narrow, gloomy staircase over which it said "To the Amphitheatre," she stopped.

"How you frightened me!" she said, breathing hard, still pale and stunned. "Oh, how you frightened me! I am barely alive. Why did you come? Why?"

"But do understand, Anna, do understand — " he said hurriedly, under his breath. "I implore you, do understand — "

She looked at him with fear, with entreaty, with love; she looked at him intently, to keep his features more distinctly in her memory.

"I suffer so," she went on, not listening to him. "All this time I have been thinking of nothing but you; I live only by the thought of you. And I wanted to forget, to forget; but why, oh, why have you come?"

On the landing above them two high school boys were looking down and smoking, but it was all the same to Gurov; he drew Anna Sergeyevna to him and began kissing her face and hands.

"What are you doing, what are you doing!" she was saying in horror, pushing him away. "We have lost our senses. Go away today; go away at once — I conjure you by all that is sacred, I implore you — People are coming this way!"

Someone was walking up the stairs.

"You must leave," Anna Sergeyevna went on in a whisper. "Do you hear, Dmitry Dmitrich? I will come and see you in Moscow. I have never been happy; I am unhappy now, and I never, never shall be happy, never! So don't make me suffer still more! I swear I'll come to Moscow. But now let us part. My dear, good, precious one, let us part!"

She pressed his hand and walked rapidly downstairs, turning to look round at him, and from her eyes he could see that she really was unhappy. Gurov stood for a while, listening, then when all grew quiet, he found his coat and left the theater.

IV

And Anna Sergeyevna began coming to see him in Moscow. Once every two or three months she left S — telling her husband that she was going to consult a doctor about a woman's ailment from which she was suffering — and her husband did and did not believe her. When she arrived in Moscow she would stop at the Slavyansky Bazar Hotel, and at once send a man in a red cap to Gurov. Gurov came to see her, and no one in Moscow knew of it.

Once he was going to see her in this way on a winter morning (the messenger had come the evening before and not found him in). With him walked his daughter, whom he wanted to take to school; it was on the way. Snow was coming down in big wet flakes.

"It's three degrees above zero,[2] and yet it's snowing," Gurov was saying to his daughter. "But this temperature prevails only on the surface of the earth; in the upper layers of the atmosphere there is quite a different temperature."

"And why doesn't it thunder in winter, papa?"

He explained that, too. He talked, thinking all the while that he was on his way to a rendezvous, and no living soul knew of it, and probably no one would ever know. He had two lives, an open one, seen and known by all who needed to know it, full of conventional truth and conventional falsehood, exactly like the lives of his friends and acquaintances; and another life that went on in secret. And through some strange, perhaps accidental, combination of circumstances, everything that was of interest and importance to him, everything that was essential to him, everything about which he felt sincerely and did not deceive himself, everything that constituted the core of his life, was going on concealed from others; while all that was false, the shell in which he hid to cover the truth — his work at the bank, for instance, his discussions at the club, his references to the "inferior race," his appearances at anniversary celebrations with his wife — all that went on in the open. Judging others by himself, he did not believe what he saw, and always fancied that every man led his real, most interesting life under cover of secrecy as under cover of night. The personal life of every individual is based on secrecy, and perhaps it is partly for that reason that civilized man is so nervously anxious that personal privacy should be respected.

Having taken his daughter to school, Gurov went on to the Slavyansky Bazar Hotel. He took off his fur coat in the lobby, went upstairs, and knocked gently at the door. Anna Sergeyevna, wearing his favorite gray dress, exhausted by the journey and by waiting, had been expecting him since the previous evening. She was pale, and looked at him without a smile, and he had hardly entered when she flung herself on his breast. That

---

[2] on the Celsius scale — about thirty-seven degrees Fahrenheit.

kiss was a long, lingering one, as though they had not seen one another for two years.

"Well, darling, how are you getting on there?" he asked. "What news?"

"Wait; I'll tell you in a moment — I can't speak."

She could not speak; she was crying. She turned away from him, and pressed her handkerchief to her eyes.

"Let her have her cry; meanwhile I'll sit down," he thought, and he seated himself in an armchair.

Then he rang and ordered tea, and while he was having his tea she remained standing at the window with her back to him. She was crying out of sheer agitation, in the sorrowful consciousness that their life was so sad; that they could only see each other in secret and had to hide from people like thieves! Was it not a broken life?

"Come, stop now, dear!" he said.

It was plain to him that this love of theirs would not be over soon, that the end of it was not in sight. Anna Sergeyevna was growing more and more attached to him. She adored him, and it was unthinkable to tell her that their love was bound to come to an end some day; besides, she would not have believed it!

He went up to her and took her by the shoulders, to fondle her and say something diverting, and at that moment he caught sight of himself in the mirror.

His hair was already beginning to turn gray. And it seemed odd to him that he had grown so much older in the last few years, and lost his looks. The shoulders on which his hands rested were warm and heaving. He felt compassion for this life, still so warm and lovely, but probably already about to begin to fade and wither like his own. Why did she love him so much? He always seemed to women different from what he was, and they loved in him not himself, but the man whom their imagination created and whom they had been eagerly seeking all their lives; and afterwards, when they saw their mistake, they loved him nevertheless. And not one of them had been happy with him. In the past he had met women, come together with them, parted from them, but he had never once loved; it was anything you please, but not love. And only now when his head was gray he had fallen in love, really, truly — for the first time in his life.

Anna Sergeyevna and he loved each other as people do who are very close and intimate, like man and wife, like tender friends; it seemed to them that Fate itself had meant them for one another, and they could not understand why he had a wife and she a husband; and it was as though they were a pair of migratory birds, male and female, caught and forced to live in different cages. They forgave each other what they were ashamed of in their past, they forgave everything in the present, and felt that this love of theirs had altered them both.

Formerly in moments of sadness he had soothed himself with whatever logical arguments came into his head, but now he no longer cared for logic; he felt profound compassion, he wanted to be sincere and tender.

"Give it up now, my darling," he said. "You've had your cry; that's enough. Let us have a talk now, we'll think up something."

Then they spent a long time taking counsel together, they talked of how to avoid the necessity for secrecy, for deception, for living in different cities, and not seeing one another for long stretches of time. How could they free themselves from these intolerable fetters?

"How? How?" he asked, clutching his head. "How?"

And it seemed as though in a little while the solution would be found, and then a new and glorious life would begin; and it was clear to both of them that the end was still far off, and that what was to be most complicated and difficult for them was only just beginning.

[1899]

CHARLOTTE PERKINS STETSON GILMAN (1860–1935) was born in Hartford, Connecticut. Her father left the family soon after she was born and provided them only meager support. As a teenager she attended the Rhode Island School of Design for a brief period and worked as a commercial artist and teacher. Like her great-aunt Harriet Beecher Stowe, Gilman was concerned at an early age with social injustice and wrote poetry about the difficulty of women's lives.

In 1884 she married the artist Charles Walter Stetson. Suffering extreme depression after the birth of a daughter, she left her husband and moved to California in 1888. They were divorced, and she later married her second husband, George Houghton Gilman, with whom she lived for thirty-four years. In the 1890s Gilman established a reputation as a lecturer and writer of political tracts. The critic William Dean Howells called her "the only optimist reformer" he ever met. Her first book of poetry, published in 1893, did not have a wide success. Her next book, Women and Economics, published five years later, is considered one of the most important works of the early years of the women's movement. As the biographer Mary Beth Pringle has stated, "This book's arguments in behalf of women's rights arise out of a firm and broad philosophical and historical base. Gilman calls American society 'androcentric' and illustrates how traditionally male values have dominated almost every aspect of American life."

Gilman's later books — Concerning Children (1900), The Home (1904), and Human Work (1904) — continue the feminist argument that women should be financially independent so that they can mature intellectually and emotionally and thus contribute more to the development of human progress. From 1909 to 1917 Gilman published her own journal, the Forerunner, for which she wrote voluminously. In her articles and her two novels she usually juxtaposed what she considered typical male and female values, presenting women as peace-loving and concerned with practical issues of living day to day, and showing men as aggressive, competitive, and destructive.

At the end of her life Gilman suffered from cancer. Her autobiography, The Living of Charlotte Perkins Gilman (1935), concludes with a letter left to her survivors, written shortly before she committed suicide with chloroform. In the letter she wrote, "The one predominant duty is to find one's work and do it, and I have striven mightily at that. The religion, the philosophy, set up so early, have seen me through."

Today Gilman's best-known work is her early story, "The Yellow Wallpaper," written around 1890, shortly after her own nervous breakdown. It is part fantasy and part autobiography, a vivid account of her illness and treatment by a hostile physician named Dr. S. Wier Mitchell, who forbade her any activity, especially writing, the thing she most wanted to do. In the *story Gilman uses elements of conventional Gothic romances that were a staple in women's popular fiction—an isolated mansion, a distant but dominating male figure, and a mysterious household—that all force the heroine into the role of the passive victim of circumstances. But Gilman gave her own twist to the form. She narrates her story with clinical precision, avoiding the conventional language of popular romances that are usually written in brief paragraphs and simple sentences to make them pleasant to read. The cumulative effect of Gilman's short paragraphs conveys a different impression, suggesting the desperate isolation and frustration of the narrator and her driving compulsion to tell her story.*

Charlotte Perkins Gilman

ဢ

THE YELLOW WALLPAPER

It is very seldom that mere ordinary people like John and myself secure ancestral halls for the summer.

A colonial mansion, a hereditary estate, I would say a haunted house and reach the height of romantic felicity — but that would be asking too much of fate!

Still I will proudly declare that there is something queer about it.

Else, why should it be let so cheaply? And why have stood so long untenanted?

John laughs at me, of course, but one expects that.

John is practical in the extreme. He has no patience with faith, an intense horror of superstition, and he scoffs openly at any talk of things not to be felt and seen and put down in figures.

John is a physician, and *perhaps* — (I would not say it to a living soul, of course, but this is dead paper and a great relief to my mind) — *perhaps* that is one reason I do not get well faster.

You see, he does not believe I am sick! And what can one do?

If a physician of high standing, and one's own husband, assures friends and relatives that there is really nothing the matter with one but temporary nervous depression — a slight hysterical tendency — what is one to do?

My brother is also a physician, and also of high standing, and he says the same thing.

So I take phosphates or phosphites — whichever it is — and tonics, and air and exercise, and journeys, and am absolutely forbidden to "work" until I am well again.

Personally, I disagree with their ideas.

Personally, I believe that congenial work, with excitement and change, would do me good.

But what is one to do?

I did write for a while in spite of them; but it *does* exhaust me a good deal — having to be so sly about it, or else meet with heavy opposition.

I sometimes fancy that in my condition, if I had less opposition and more society and stimulus — but John says the very worst thing I can do is to think about my condition, and I confess it always makes me feel bad.

So I will let it alone and talk about the house.

The most beautiful place! It is quite alone, standing well back from the road, quite three miles from the village. It makes me think of English places that you read about, for there are hedges and walls and gates that lock, and lots of separate little houses for the gardeners and people.

There is a *delicious* garden! I never saw such a garden — large and shady, full of box-bordered paths, and lined with long grape-covered arbors with seats under them.

There were greenhouses, but they are all broken now.

There was some legal trouble, I believe, something about the heirs and co-heirs; anyhow, the place has been empty for years.

That spoils my ghostliness, I am afraid, but I don't care — there is something strange about the house — I can feel it.

I even said so to John one moonlight evening, but he said what I felt was a draught, and shut the window.

I get unreasonably angry with John sometimes. I'm sure I never used to be so sensitive. I think it is due to this nervous condition.

But John says if I feel so I shall neglect proper self-control; so I take pains to control myself — before him, at least, and that makes me very tired.

I don't like our room a bit. I wanted one downstairs that opened onto the piazza and had roses all over the window, and such pretty old-fashioned chintz hangings! But John would not hear of it.

He said there was only one window and not room for two beds, and no near room for him if he took another.

He is very careful and loving, and hardly lets me stir without special direction.

I have a schedule prescription of each hour in the day; he takes all care from me, and so I feel basely ungrateful not to value it more.

He said he came here solely on my account, that I was to have perfect rest and all the air I could get. "Your exercise depends on your strength, my dear," said he, "and your food somewhat on your appetite; but air you can absorb all the time." So we took the nursery at the top of the house.

It is a big, airy room, the whole floor nearly, with windows that look all ways, and air and sunshine galore. It was nursery first, and then playroom and gymnasium, I should judge, for the windows are barred for little children, and there are rings and things in the walls.

The paint and paper look as if a boys' school had used it. It is stripped off — the paper — in great patches all around the head of my bed, about as far as I can reach, and in a great place on the other side of the room low down. I never saw a worse paper in my life. One of those sprawling, flamboyant patterns committing every artistic sin.

It is dull enough to confuse the eye in following, pronounced enough constantly to irritate and provoke study, and when you follow the lame uncertain curves for a little distance they suddenly commit suicide — plunge off at outrageous angles, destroy themselves in unheard-of contradictions.

The color is repellent, almost revolting: a smouldering unclean yellow, strangely faded by the slow-turning sunlight. It is a dull yet lurid orange in some places, a stickly sulphur tint in others.

No wonder the children hated it! I should hate it myself if I had to live in this room long.

There comes John, and I must put this away — he hates to have me write a word.

We have been here two weeks, and I haven't felt like writing before, since that first day.

I am sitting by the window now, up in this atrocious nursery, and there is nothing to hinder my writings as much as I please, save lack of strength.

John is away all day, and even some nights when his cases are serious.

I am glad my case is not serious!

But these nervous troubles are dreadfully depressing.

John does not know how much I really suffer. He knows there is no reason to suffer, and that satisfies him.

Of course it is only nervousness. It does weigh on me so not to do my duty in any way!

I meant to be such a help to John, such a real rest and comfort, and here I am a comparative burden already!

Nobody would believe what an effort it is to do what little I am able — to dress and entertain, and order things.

It is fortunate Mary is so good with the baby. Such a dear baby!

And yet I *cannot* be with him, it makes me so nervous.

I suppose John never was nervous in his life. He laughs at me so about this wallpaper!

At first he meant to repaper the room, but afterward he said that I was letting it get the better of me, and that nothing was worse for a nervous patient than to give way to such fancies.

He said that after the wallpaper was changed it would be the heavy bedstead, and then the barred windows, and then that gate at the head of the stairs, and so on.

"You know the place is doing you good," he said, "and really, dear, I don't care to renovate the house just for a three months' rental."

"Then do let us go downstairs," I said. "There are such pretty rooms there."

Then he took me in his arms and called me a blessed little goose, and said he would go down cellar, if I wished, and have it whitewashed into the bargain.

But he is right enough about the beds and windows and things.

It is as airy and comfortable a room as anyone need wish, and, of course, I would not be so silly as to make him uncomfortable just for a whim.

I'm really getting quite fond of the big room, all but that horrid paper.

Out of one window I can see the garden — those mysterious deep-shaded arbors, the riotous old-fashioned flowers, and bushes and gnarly trees.

Out of another I get a lovely view of the bay and a little private wharf belonging to the estate. There is a beautiful shaded lane that runs down there from the house. I always fancy I see people walking in these numerous paths and arbors, but John has cautioned me not to give way to fancy in the least. He says that with my imaginative power and habit of story-making, a nervous weakness like mine is sure to lead to all manner of excited fancies, and that I ought to use my will and good sense to check the tendency. So I try.

I think sometimes that if I were only well enough to write a little it would relieve the press of ideas and rest me.

But I find I get pretty tired when I try.

It is so discouraging not to have any advice and companionship about my work. When I get really well, John says we will ask Cousin Henry and Julia down for a long visit; but he says he would as soon put fireworks in my pillow-case as to let me have those stimulating people about now.

I wish I could get well faster.

But I must not think about that. This paper looks to me as if it *knew* what a vicious influence it had!

There is a recurrent spot where the pattern lolls like a broken neck and two bulbous eyes stare at you upside down.

I get positively angry with the impertinence of it and the everlastingness. Up and down and sideways they crawl, and those absurd unblinking eyes are everywhere. There is one place where two breadths didn't match, and the eyes go all up and down the line, one a little higher than the other.

I never saw so much expression in an inanimate thing before, and we all know how much expression they have! I used to lie awake as a child and get more entertainment and terror out of blank walls and plain furniture than most children could find in a toy-store.

I remember what a kindly wink the knobs of our big old bureau used to have, and there was one chair that always seemed like a strong friend.

I used to feel that if any of the other things looked too fierce I could always hop into that chair and be safe.

The furniture in this room is no worse than inharmonious, however, for we had to bring it all from downstairs. I suppose when this was used as a playroom they had to take the nursery things out, and no wonder! I never saw such ravages as the children have made here.

The wallpaper, as I said before, is torn off in spots, and it sticketh closer than a brother — they must have had perseverance as well as hatred.

Then the floor is scratched and gouged and splintered, the plaster it-self is dug out here and there, and this great heavy bed, which is all we found in the room, looks as if it had been through the wars.

But I don't mind it a bit — only the paper.

There comes John's sister. Such a dear girl as she is, and so careful of me! I must not let her find me writing.

She is a perfect and enthusiastic housekeeper, and hopes for no better profession. I verily believe she thinks it is the writing which made me sick!

But I can write when she is out, and see her a long way off from these windows.

There is one that commands the road, a lovely shaded winding road, and one that just looks off over the country. A lovely country, too, full of great elms and velvet meadows.

This wallpaper has a kind of subpattern in a different shade, a particu-larly irritating one, for you can only see it in certain lights, and not clearly then.

But in the places where it isn't faded and where the sun is just so — I can see a strange, provoking, formless sort of figure that seems to skulk about behind that silly and conspicuous front design.

There's sister on the stairs!

Well, the Fourth of July is over! The people are all gone, and I am tired out. John thought it might do me good to see a little company, so we just had Mother and Nellie and the children down for a week.

Of course I didn't do a thing. Jennie sees to everything now.

But it tired me all the same.

John says if I don't pick up faster he shall send me to Weir Mitchell[1] in the fall.

But I don't want to go there at all. I had a friend who was in his hands once, and she says he is just like John and my brother, only more so!

Besides, it is such an undertaking to go so far.

I don't feel as if it was worthwhile to turn my hand over for anything, and I'm getting dreadfully fretful and querulous.

I cry at nothing, and cry most of the time.

Of course I don't when John is here, or anybody else, but when I am alone.

And I am alone a good deal just now. John is kept in town very often by serious cases, and Jennie is good and lets me alone when I want her to.

[1]Dr. S. Weir Mitchell (1829–1914) was an eminent Philadelphia neurologist who ad-vocated "rest cures" for nervous disorders. He was the author of *Diseases of the Nervous System, Especially of Women* (1881).

So I walk a little in the garden or down that lovely lane, sit on the porch under the roses, and lie down up here a good deal.

I'm getting really fond of the room in spite of the wallpaper. Perhaps *because* of the wallpaper.

It dwells in my mind so!

I lie here on this great immovable bed — it is nailed down, I believe — and follow that pattern about by the hour. It is as good as gymnastics, I assure you. I start, we'll say, at the bottom, down in the corner over there where it has not been touched, and I determine for the thousandth time that I *will* follow that pointless pattern to some sort of a conclusion.

I know a little of the principle of design, and I know this thing was not arranged on any laws of radiation, or alternation, or repetition, or symmetry, or anything else that I ever heard of.

It is repeated, of course, by the breadths, but not otherwise.

Looked at in one way, each breadth stands alone; the bloated curves and flourishes — a kind of "debased Romanesque" with dilirium tremens go waddling up and down in isolated columns of fatuity.

But, on the other hand, they connect diagonally, and the sprawling outlines run off in great slanting waves of optic horror, like a lot of wallowing sea-weeds in full chase.

The whole thing goes horizontally, too, at least it seems so, and I exhaust myself trying to distinguish the order of its going in that direction.

They have used a horizontal breadth for a frieze, and that adds wonderfully to the confusion.

There is one end of the room where it is almost intact, and there, when the crosslights fade and the low sun shines directly upon it, I can almost fancy radiation after all — the interminable grotesque seems to form around a common center and rush off in headlong plunges of equal distraction.

It makes me tired to follow it. I will take a nap, I guess.

I don't know why I should write this.

I don't want to.

I don't feel able.

And I know John would think it absurd. But I *must* say what I feel and think in some way — it is such a relief!

But the effort is getting to be greater than the relief.

Half the time now I am awfully lazy, and lie down ever so much. John says I mustn't lose my strength, and has me take cod liver oil and lots of tonics and things, to say nothing of ale and wines and rare meat.

Dear John! He loves me very dearly, and hates to have me sick. I tried to have a real earnest reasonable talk with him the other day, and tell him how I wish he would let me go and make a visit to Cousin Henry and Julia.

But he said I wasn't able to go, nor able to stand it after I got there; and I did not make out a very good case for myself, for I was crying before I had finished.

It is getting to be a great effort for me to think straight. Just this nervous weakness, I suppose.

And dear John gathered me up in his arms, and just carried me upstairs and laid me on the bed, and sat by me and read to me till it tired my head.

He said I was his darling and his comfort and all he had, and that I must take care of myself for his sake, and keep well.

He says no one but myself can help me out of it, that I must use my will and self-control and not let any silly fancies run away with me.

There's one comfort — the baby is well and happy, and does not have to occupy this nursery with the horrid wallpaper.

If we had not used it, that blessed child would have! What a fortunate escape! Why, I wouldn't have a child of mine, an impressionable little thing, live in such a room for worlds.

I never thought of it before, but it is lucky that John kept me here after all; I can stand it so much easier than a baby, you see.

Of course I never mention it to them any more — I am too wise — but I keep watch for it all the same.

There are things in the wallpaper that nobody knows about but me, or ever will.

Behind that outside pattern the dim shapes get clearer every day.

It is always the same shape, only very numerous.

And it is like a woman stooping down and creeping about behind that pattern. I don't like it a bit. I wonder — I begin to think — I wish John would take me away from here!

It is so hard to talk with John about my case, because he is so wise, and because he loves me so.

But I tried it last night.

It was moonlight. The moon shines in all around just as the sun does.

I hate to see it sometimes, it creeps so slowly, and always comes in by one window or another.

John was asleep and I hated to waken him, so I kept still and watched the moonlight on that undulating wallpaper till I felt creepy.

The faint figure behind seemed to shake the pattern, just as if she wanted to get out.

I got up softly and went to feel and see if the paper *did* move, and when I came back John was awake.

"What is it, little girl?" he said. "Don't go walking about like that — you'll get cold."

I thought it was a good time to talk, so I told him that I really was not gaining here, and that I wished he would take me away.

"Why, darling!" said he. "Our lease will be up in three weeks, and I can't see how to leave before.

"The repairs are not done at home, and I cannot possibly leave town just now. Of course, if you were in any danger, I could and would, but you really are better, dear, whether you can see it or not. I am a doctor, dear, and I know. You are gaining flesh and color, your appetite is better, I feel really much easier about you."

"I don't weigh a bit more," said I, "nor as much; and my appetite may be better in the evening when you are here but it is worse in the morning when you are away!"

"Bless her little heart!" said he with a big hug. "She shall be as sick as she pleases! But now let's improve the shining hours by going to sleep, and talk about it in the morning!"

"And you won't go away?" I asked gloomily.

"Why, how can I, dear? It is only three weeks more and then we will take a nice little trip for a few days while Jennie is getting the house ready. Really, dear, you are better!"

"Better in body perhaps — " I began, and stopped short, for he sat up straight and looked at me with such a stern, reproachful look that I could not say another word.

"My darling," said he, "I beg you, for my sake and for our child's sake, as well as for your own, that you will never for one instant let that idea enter your mind! There is nothing so dangerous, so fascinating, to a temperament like yours. It is a false and foolish fancy. Can you trust me as a physician when I tell you so?"

So of course I said no more on that score, and we went to sleep before long. He thought I was asleep first, but I wasn't, and lay there for hours trying to decide whether that front pattern and the back pattern really did move together or separately.

On a pattern like this, by daylight, there is a lack of sequence, a defiance of law, that is a constant irritant to a normal mind.

The color is hideous enough, and unreliable enough, and infuriating enough, but the pattern is torturing.

You think you have mastered it, but just as you get well under way in following, it turns a back-somersault and there you are. It slaps you in the face, knocks you down, and tramples upon you. It is like a bad dream.

The outside pattern is a florid arabesque, reminding one of a fungus. If you can imagine a toadstool in joints, an interminable string of toadstools, budding and sprouting in endless convolutions — why, that is something like it.

That is, sometimes!

There is one marked peculiarity about this paper, a thing nobody seems to notice but myself, and that is that it changes as the light changes.

When the sun shoots in through the east window — I always watch for that first long, straight ray — it changes so quickly that I never can quite believe it.

That is why I watch it always.

By moonlight — the moon shines in all night when there is a moon — I wouldn't know it was the same paper.

At night in any kind of light, in twilight, candlelight, lamplight, and worst of all by moonlight, it becomes bars! The outside pattern, I mean, and the woman behind it is as plain as can be.

I didn't realize for a long time what the thing was that showed behind, that dim subpattern, but now I am quite sure it is a woman.

By daylight she is subdued, quiet. I fancy it is the pattern that keeps her so still. It is so puzzling. It keeps me quiet by the hour.

I lie down ever so much now. John says it is good for me, and to sleep all I can.

Indeed he started the habit by making me lie down for an hour after each meal.

It is a very bad habit, I am convinced, for you see, I don't sleep.

And that cultivates deceit, for I don't tell them I'm awake — oh, no!

The fact is I am getting a little afraid of John.

He seems very queer sometimes, and even Jennie has an inexplicable look.

It strikes me occasionally, just as a scientific hypothesis, that perhaps it is the paper!

I have watched John when he did not know I was looking, and come into the room suddenly on the most innocent excuses, and I've caught him several times *looking at the paper!* And Jennie too. I caught Jennie with her hand on it once.

She didn't know I was in the room, and when I asked her in a quiet, a very quiet voice, with the most restrained manner possible, what she was doing with the paper, she turned around as if she had been caught stealing, and looked quite angry — asked me why I should frighten her so!

Then she said that the paper stained everything it touched, that she had found yellow smooches on all my clothes and John's and she wished we would be more careful!

Did not that sound innocent? But I know she was studying that pattern, and I am determined that nobody shall find it out but myself!

Life is very much more exciting now than it used to be. You see, I have something more to expect, to look forward to, to watch. I really do eat better, and am more quiet than I was.

John is so pleased to see me improve! He laughed a little the other day, and said I seemed to be flourishing in spite of my wallpaper.

I turned it off with a laugh. I had no intention of telling him it was *because* of the wallpaper — he would make fun of me. He might even want to take me away.

I don't want to leave now until I have found it out. There is a week more, and I think that will be enough.

I'm feeling so much better!

I don't sleep much at night, for it is so interesting to watch developments; but I sleep a good deal during the daytime.

In the daytime it is tiresome and perplexing.

There are always new shoots on the fungus, and new shades of yellow all over it. I cannot keep count of them, though I have tried conscientiously.

It is the strangest yellow, that wallpaper! It makes me think of all the yellow things I ever saw — not beautiful ones like buttercups, but old, foul, bad yellow things.

But there is something else about that paper — the smell! I noticed it the moment we came into the room, but with so much air and sun it was not bad. Now we have had a week of fog and rain, and whether the windows are open or not, the smell is here.

It creeps all over the house.

I find it hovering in the dining-room, skulking in the parlor, hiding in the hall, lying in wait for me on the stairs.

It gets into my hair.

Even when I go to ride, if I turn my head suddenly and surprise it — there is that smell!

Such a peculiar odor, too! I have spent hours in trying to analyze it, to find what it smelled like.

It is not bad — at first — and very gentle, but quite the subtlest, most enduring odor I ever met.

In this damp weather it is awful. I wake up in the night and find it hanging over me.

It used to disturb me at first. I thought seriously of burning the house — to reach the smell.

But now I am used to it. The only thing I can think of that it is like is the *color* of the paper! A yellow smell.

There a very funny mark on this wall, low down, near the mopboard. A streak that runs round the room. It goes behind every piece of furniture, except the bed, a long straight, even *smooch*, as if it had been rubbed over and over.

I wonder how it was done and who did it, and what they did it for. Round and round and round — round and round and round — it makes me dizzy!

I really have discovered something at last.

Through watching so much at night, when it changes so, I have finally found out.

The front pattern *does* move — and no wonder! The woman behind shakes it!

Sometimes I think there are a great many women behind, and sometimes only one, and she crawls around fast, and her crawling shakes it all over.

Then in the very bright spots she keeps still, and in the very shady spots she just takes hold of the bars and shakes them hard.

And she is all the time trying to climb through. But nobody could climb through that pattern — it strangles so; I think that is why it has so many heads.

They get through and then the pattern strangles them off and turns them upside down, and makes their eyes white!

If those heads were covered or taken off it would not be half so bad.

I think that woman gets out in the daytime!

And I'll tell you why — privately — I've seen her!

I can see her out of every one of my windows!

It is the same woman, I know, for she is always creeping, and most women do not creep by daylight.

I see her in that long shaded lane, creeping up and down. I see her in those dark grape arbors, creeping all round the garden.

I see her on that long road under the trees, creeping along, and when a carriage comes she hides under the blackberry vines.

I don't blame her a bit. It must be very humiliating to be caught creeping by daylight!

I always lock the door when I creep by daylight. I can't do it at night, for I know John would suspect something at once.

And John is so queer now that I don't want to irritate him. I wish he would take another room! Besides, I don't want anybody to get that woman out at night but myself.

I often wonder if I could see her out of all the windows at once.

But, turn as fast as I can, I can only see out of one at one time.

And though I always see her, she *may* be able to creep faster than I can turn! I have watched her sometimes away off in the open country, creeping as fast as a cloud shadow in a wind.

If only that top pattern could be gotten off from the under one! I mean to try it, little by little.

I have found out another funny thing, but I shan't tell it this time! It does not do to trust people too much.

There are only two more days to get this paper off, and I believe John is beginning to notice. I don't like the look in his eyes.

And I heard him ask Jennie a lot of professional questions about me. She had a very good report to give.

She said I slept a good deal in the daytime.

John knows I don't sleep very well at night, for all I'm so quiet!

He asked me all sorts of questions too, and pretended to be very loving and kind.

As If I couldn't see through him!

Still, I don't wonder he acts so, sleeping under this paper for three months.

It only interests me, but I feel sure John and Jennie are affected by it.

Hurrah! This is the last day, but it is enough. John is to stay in town over night, and won't be out until this evening.

Jennie wanted to sleep with me — the sly thing; but I told her I should undoubtedly rest better for a night all alone.

That was clever, for really I wasn't alone a bit! As soon as it was moonlight and that poor thing began to crawl and shake the pattern, I got up and ran to help her.

I pulled and she shook. I shook and she pulled, and before morning we had peeled off yards of that paper.

A strip about as high as my head and half around the room.

And then when the sun came and that awful pattern began to laugh at me, I declared I would finish it today!

We go away tomorrow, and they are moving all my furniture down again to leave things as they were before.

Jennie looked at the wall in amazement, but I told her merrily that I did it out of pure spite at the vicious thing.

She laughed and said she wouldn't mind doing it herself, but I must not get tired.

How she betrayed herself that time!

But I am here, and no person touches this paper but Me — not *alive!*

She tried to get me out of the room — it was too patent! But I said it was so quiet and empty and clean now that I believed I would lie down again and sleep all I could, and not to wake me even for dinner — I would call when I woke.

So now she is gone, and the servants are gone, and the things are gone, and there is nothing left but that great bedstead nailed down, with the canvas mattress we found on it.

We shall sleep downstairs tonight, and take the boat home tomorrow.

I quite enjoy the room, now it is bare again.

How those children did tear about here!

This bedstead is fairly gnawed!

But I must get to work.

I have locked the door and thrown the key down into the front path.

I don't want to go out, and I don't want to have anybody come in, till John comes.

I want to astonish him.

I've got a rope up here that even Jennie did not find. If that woman does get out, and tries to get away, I can tie her!

But I forgot I could not reach far without anything to stand on!

This bed will *not* move!

I tried to lift and push it until I was lame, and then I got so angry I bit off a little piece at one corner — but it hurt my teeth.

Then I peeled off all the paper I could reach standing on the floor. It sticks horribly and the pattern just enjoys it! All those strangled heads and bulbous eyes and waddling fungus growths just shriek with derision!

I am getting angry enough to do something desperate. To jump out of the window would be admirable exercise, but the bars are too strong even to try.

Besides I wouldn't do it. Of course not. I know well enough that a step like that is improper and might be misconstrued.

I don't like to *look* out of the windows even — there are so many of those creeping women, and they creep so fast.

I wonder if they all come out of that wallpaper as I did!

But I am securely fastened now by my well-hidden rope — you don't get *me* out in the road there!

I suppose I shall have to get back behind the pattern when it comes night, and that is hard!

It it so pleasant to be out in this great room and creep around as I please!

I don't want to go outside. I won't, even if Jennie asks me to.

For outside you have to creep on the ground, and everything is green instead of yellow.

But here I can creep smoothly on the floor, and my shoulder just fits in that long smooch around the wall, so I cannot lose my way.

Why, there's John at the door!

It is no use, young man, you can't open it!

How he does call and pound!

Now he's crying to Jennie for an axe.

It would be a shame to break down that beautiful door!

"John, dear!" said I in the gentlest voice. "The key is down by the front steps, under a plantain leaf!"

That silenced him for a few moments.

Then he said, very quietly indeed, "Open the door, my darling!"

"I can't," said I. "The key is down by the front door under a plantain leaf!" And then I said it again, several times, very gently and slowly, and said it so often that he had to go and see, and he got it of course, and came in. He stopped short by the door.

"What is the matter?" he cried."For God's sake, what are you doing!"

I kept on creeping just the same, but I looked at him over my shoulder.

"I've got out at last," said I, "in spite of you and Jane. And I've pulled off most of the paper, so you can't put me back!"

Now why should that man have fainted? But he did, and right across my path by the wall, so that I had to creep over him every time!

[1892]

HAMLIN GARLAND (1860–1940) *was born in West Salem, Wisconsin, the son of a New England father lured west by the prospect of cheap land. When Garland was nine, his family moved to a farm on the unfenced prairie of northern Iowa, where he was educated at the Cedar Valley Seminary. As a boy Garland loved literature. His biographer B. R. McElderry, Jr., has stated that "Ivanhoe, Scottish Chiefs, The Life of P. T. Barnum, and Franklin's Autobiography, available at home or borrowed from neighbors, along with numerous dime novels, put before the boy a mixture of impractical romance and shrewd materialism. . . . Later he became acquainted with Hawthorne and with Shakespeare, whose great speeches the boy recited as he followed the plow."*

In 1881, after numerous crop failures, the family moved again, this time to South Dakota, where Garland worked as a carpenter and taught school. When he was twenty-five, he sold his claim in the Dakota Territory and used the money to live in Boston, where he began a program of self-directed study at the public library.

In 1885 Garland modeled his first attempt at fiction, the story "Ten Years Dead," on Nathaniel Hawthorne's style, but he was dissatisfied with it. He kept writing, publishing reviews and poems. In 1888 his first magazine story appeared in Harper's Weekly; *it was based on an incident his mother had told him about when he returned to South Dakota to visit his family after three years in Boston and saw the limitations and hardships of prairie life with new eyes. Garland had finally found his subject. He said, "The ugliness, the endless drudgery, and the loneliness of the farmer's lot smote me with stern insistence. I was the militant reformer." Several other realistic stories about prairie life, including "Under the Lion's Paw," were inspired by his visit home and written soon after Garland returned to Boston.*

In 1891 a collection of these prairie stories was published under the title Main-Travelled Roads. *The book caused an uproar. Garland's bitter picture of farmers caught in the grip of relentless capitalism provoked a storm of denials, but the author was established as the voice of the rebellious Populists, a political party urging agricultural reform. The critic William Dean Howells defended the book: "The type caught in Mr. Garland's book is not pretty; it is ugly and often ridiculous; but it is heart-breaking in its despair."*

Main-Travelled Roads *is one of the first important collections of modern short stories closely related by a common theme and location, like* The Country of the Pointed Firs *(1896) by Sarah Orne Jewett,* Dubliners *(1916) by James Joyce, and* Winesburg, Ohio *(1919) by Sherwood Anderson. Garland published four other books of realistic short stories in the 1890s, but he turned to other literary forms for the remainder of his long life, including several memoirs and his autobiography,* A Son of the Middle Border (1917).

Hamlin Garland

ಸಿಂ

UNDER THE LION'S PAW

"Along this main-travelled road trailed an endless line of prairie schooners, coming into sight at the east, and passing out of sight over the swell to the west. We children used to wonder where they were going and why they went."

I

It was the last of autumn and first day of winter coming together. All day long the plowmen on their prairie farms had moved to and fro on their wide level field through the falling snow, which melted as it fell, wetting them to the skin — all day, notwithstanding the frequent squalls of snow, the dripping, desolate clouds, and the muck of the furrows, black and tenacious as tar.

Under their dripping harness the horses swung to and fro silently, with that marvelous uncomplaining patience which marks the horse. All day the wild geese, honking wildly as they sprawled sidewise down the wind, seemed to be fleeing from an enemy behind, and with neck outthrust and wings extended, sailed down the wind, soon lost to sight.

Yet the plowman behind his plow, though the snow lay on his ragged greatcoat and the cold clinging mud rose on his heavy boots, fettering him like gyves, whistled in the very beard of the gale. As day passed, the snow, ceasing to melt, lay along the plowed land and lodged in the depth of the stubble, till on each slow round the last furrow stood out black and shining as jet between the plowed land and the gray stubble.

When night began to fall, and the geese, flying low, began to alight invisibly in the near cornfield, Stephen Council was still at work "finishing a land." He rode on his sulky-plow when going with the wind, but walked when facing it. Sitting bent and cold but cheery under his slouch hat, he talked encouragingly to his four-in-hand.

"Come round there, boys! — round agin! We got t' finish this land.

Come in there, Dan! *Stiddy,* Kate! — stiddy! None o' y'r tantrums, Kittie.
It's purty tuff, but gotta be did. *Tchk! tchk!* Step along, Pete! Don't let
Kate git y'r single tree on the wheel. *Once* more!"

They seemed to know what he meant, and that this was the last round,
for they worked with greater vigor than before.

"Once more, boys, an' sez I oats, an' a nice warm stall, an' sleep f'r
all."

By the time the last furrow was turned on the land it was too dark to
see the house, and the snow changing to rain again. The tired and hungry
man could see the light from the kitchen shining through the leafless hedge,
and lifting a great shout, he yelled, "Sup*per* f'r a half a dozen!"

It was nearly eight o'clock by the time he had finished his chores and
started for supper. He was picking his way carefully through the mud when
the tall form of a man loomed up before him with a premonitory cough.

"Waddy ye want?" was the rather startled question of the farmer.

"Well, ye see," began the stranger in a deprecating tone, "we'd like t'
git in f'r the night. We've tried every house f'r the last two miles, but they
hadn't any room f'r us. My wife's jest about sick, 'n' the children are cold
and hungry — "

"Oh, y' want a stay all night, eh?"

"Yes, sir; it 'ud be a great accom — "

"Waal, I don't make it a practice t' turn anybuddy away hungry, not
on sech nights as this. Drive right in. We ain't got much, but sech as it
is — "

But the stranger had disappeared. And soon his steaming, weary team,
with drooping heads and swinging single trees, moved past the well to the
block beside the path. Council stood at the side of the "schooner" and
helped the children out — two little half-sleeping children — and then a
small woman with a babe in her arms.

"There ye go!" he shouted jovially to the children. "*Now* we're all
right. Run right along to the house there, an' tell M'am Council you wants
sumpthin' t' eat. Right this way, Mis' — keep right off t' the right there. I'll
go an' git a lantern. Come," he said to the dazed and silent group at his
side.

"Mother," he shouted as he neared the fragrant and warmly lighted
kitchen, "here are some wayfarers an' folks who need sumpthin t' eat an' a
place t' snooze." He ended by pushing them all in.

Mrs. Council, a large, jolly, rather coarse-looking woman, took the
children in her arms. "Come right in, you little rabbits. 'Most asleep, hay?
Now here's a drink o' milk f'r each o' ye. I'll have s'm tea in a minute. Take
off y'r things and set up t' the fire."

While she set the children to drinking milk, Council got out his lantern and went out to the barn to help the stranger about his team, where his
loud, hearty voice could be heard as it came and went between the haymow
and the stalls.

The woman came to light as a small, timid, and discouraged-looking woman, but still pretty, in a thin and sorrowful way.

"Land sakes! An' you've travelled all the way from Clear Lake t'day in this mud! Waal! waal! No wonder you're all tired out. Don't wait f'r the men, Mis' — " She hesitated, waiting for the name.

"Haskins."

"Mis' Haskins, set right up to the table an' take a good swig o' tea, whilst I make y' s'm toast. It's green tea, an' it's good. I tell Council as I git older I don't seem t' enjoy Young Hyson n'r Gunpowder. I want the real green tea, jest as it comes off'n the vines. Seems t' have more heart in it some way. Don't s'pose it has. Council says it's all in m' eye."

Going on in this easy way, she soon had the children filled with bread and milk and the woman thoroughly at home, eating some toast and sweet-melon pickles and sipping the tea.

"See the little rats!" she laughed at the children. "They're full as they can stick now, and they want to go to bed. Now don't git up, Mis' Haskins; set right where you are an' let me look after 'em. I know all about young ones, though I am all alone now. Jane went an' married last fall. But, as I tell Council, it's lucky we keep our health. Set right there, Mis' Haskins; I won't have you stir a finger."

It was an unmeasured pleasure to sit there in the warm, homely kitchen, the jovial chatter of the housewife driving out and holding at bay the growl of the impotent, cheated wind.

The little woman's eyes filled with tears which fell down upon the sleeping baby in her arms. The world was not so desolate and cold and hopeless, after all.

"Now I hope Council won't stop out there and talk politics all night. He's the greatest man to talk politics an' read the *Tribune*. How old is it?"

She broke off and peered down at the face of the babe.

"Two months 'n' five days," said the mother, with a mother's exactness.

"Ye don't say! I want t' know! The dear little pudzy-wudzy!" she went on, stirring it up in the neighborhood of the ribs with her fat forefinger.

"Pooty tough on 'oo to go gallivant'n' 'cross lots this way."

"Yes, that's so; a man can't lift a mountain," said Council, entering the door. "Sarah, this is Mr. Haskins from Kansas. He's been eat up 'n' drove out by grasshoppers."

"Glad t' see yeh! Pa, empty that washbasin 'n' give him a chance t'wash."

Haskins was a tall man with a thin, gloomy face. His hair was a reddish brown, like his coat, and seemed equally faded by the wind and sun. And his sallow face, though hard and set, was pathetic somehow. You would have felt that he had suffered much by the line of his mouth showing under his thin, yellow mustache.

"Hain't Ike got home yet, Sairy?"

"Hain't seen 'im."

"W-a-al, set right up, Mr. Haskins; wade right into what we've got; 'tain't much, but we manage to live on it — she gits fat on it," laughed Council, pointing his thumb at his wife.

After supper, while the women put the children to bed, Haskins and Council talked on, seated near the huge cooking stove, the steam rising from their wet clothing. In the Western fashion, Council told as much of his own life as he drew from his guest. He asked but few questions; but by and by the story of Haskins's struggles and defeat came out. The story was a terrible one, but he told it quietly, seated with his elbows on his knees, gazing most of the time at the hearth.

"I didn't like the looks of the country, anyhow," Haskins said, partly rising and glancing at his wife."I was ust t' northern Ingyannie, where we have lots a timber 'n' lots o' rain, 'n' I didn't like the looks o' that dry prairie. What galled me the worst was goin' s' far away acrosst so much fine land layin' all through here vacant."

"And the 'hoppers eat ye four years hand running, did they?"

"Eat! They wiped us out. They chawed everything that was green. They jest set around waitin' f'r us to die t' eat us, too. My God! I ust t' dream of 'em sitt'n' 'round on the bedpost, six feet long, workin' their jaws. They eet the fork handles. They got worse 'n' worse till they jest rolled on one another, piled up like snow in winter. Well, it ain't no use; if I was t' talk all winter I couldn't tell nawthin'. But all the while I couldn't help thinkin' of all that land back here that nobuddy was usin', that I ought a had 'stead o' bein' out there in that cussed country."

"Waal, why didn't ye stop an' settle here?" asked Ike, who had come in and was eating his supper.

"Fer the simple reason that you fellers wantid ten 'r fifteen dollars an acre fer the bare land, and I hadn't no money fer that kind o' thing."

"Yes, I do my own work," Mrs. Council was heard to say in the pause which followed. "I'm a-gettin' purty heavy t' be on m' laigs all day, but we can't afford t' hire, so I keep rackin' around somehow, like a foundered horse. S' lame — I tell Council he can't tell how lame I am f'r I'm jest as lame in one laig as t'other." And the good soul laughed at the joke on herself as she took a handful of flour and dusted the biscuit board to keep the dough from sticking.

"Well, I hain't *never* been very strong," said Mrs. Haskins. "Our folks was Canadians an' small-boned, and then since my last child I hain't got up again fairly. I don't like t' complain — Tim has about all he can bear now — but they was days this week when I jest wanted to lay right down an' die."

"Waal, now, I'll tell ye," said Council from his side of the stove, silencing everybody with his good-natured roar, "I'd go down and *see* Butler, *anyway*, if I was you. I guess he'd let you have his place purty cheap; the farm's all run down. He's ben anxious t' let t' somebuddy next year. It 'ud be a good chance fer you. Anyhow, you go to bed and sleep like a babe. I've got some plowin' t' do anyhow, an' we'll see if somethin' can't be done about your case. Ike, you go out an' see if the horses is all right, an' I'll show the folks t' bed."

When the tired husband and wife were lying under the generous quilts of the spare bed, Haskins listened a moment to the wind in the eaves, and then said with a slow and solemn tone:

"There are people in this world who are good enough t' be angels, an' only haff t' die to *be* angels."

II

Jim Butler was one of those men called in the West "land poor." Early in the history of Rock River he had come into town and started in the grocery business in a small way, occupying a small building in a mean part of the town. At this period of his life he earned all he got, and was up early and late, sorting beans, working over butter, and carting his goods to and from the station. But a change came over him at the end of the second year, when he sold a lot of land for four times what he paid for it. From that time forward he believed in land speculation as the surest way of getting rich. Every cent he could save or spare from his trade he put into land at forced sale, or mortgages on land, which were "just as good as the wheat," he was accustomed to say.

Farm after farm fell into his hands, until he was recognized as one of the leading landowners of the county. His mortgages were scattered all over Cedar County, and as they slowly but surely fell in he sought usually to retain the former owner as tenant.

He was not ready to foreclose; indeed, he had the name of being one of the "easiest" men in town. He let the debtor off again and again, extending the time whenever possible.

"I don't want y'r land," he said. "All I'm after is the int'rest on my money — that's all. Now if y' want 'o stay on the farm, why, I'll give y' a good chance. I can't have the land layin' vacant." And in many cases the owner remained as tenant.

In the meantime he had sold his store; he couldn't spend time in it; he was mainly occupied now with sitting around town on rainy days, smoking and "gassin' with the boys," or in riding to and from his farms. In fishing time he fished a good deal. Doc Grimes, Ben Ashley, and Cal Cheatham were his cronies on these fishing excursions or hunting trips in the time of chickens or partridges. In winter they went to northern Wisconsin to shoot deer.

In spite of all these signs of easy life, Butler persisted in saying he "hadn't money enough to pay taxes on his land," and was careful to convey the impression that he was poor in spite of his twenty farms. At one time he was said to be worth fifty thousand dollars, but land had been a little slow of sale of late, so that he was not worth so much. A fine farm, known as the Higley place, had fallen into his hands in the usual way the previous year, and he had not been able to find a tenant for it. Poor Higley, after working himself nearly to death on it, in the attempt to lift the mortgage, had gone off to Dakota, leaving the farm and his curse to Butler.

This was the farm which Council advised Haskins to apply for; and the next day Council hitched up his team and drove down town to see Butler.

"You jest le' *me* do the talkin'," he said. "We'll find him wearin' out his pants on some salt barrel somew'er's; and if he thought you *wanted* a place, he'd sock it to you hot and heavy. You jest keep quiet; I'll fix 'im."

Butler was seated in Ben Ashley's store, telling "fish yarns," when Council sauntered in casually.

"Hello, But; lyin' agin, hay?"

"Hello, Steve! how goes it?"

"Oh, so-so. Too dang much rain these days. I thought it was goin' t' freeze f'r good last night. Tight squeak if I git m' plowin' done. How's farmin' with *you* these days?"

"Bad. Plowin' ain't half done."

"It 'ud be a religious idee f'r you t' go out and' take a hand y'rself."

"I don't haff to," said Butler with a wink.

"Got anybody on the Higley place?"

"No. Know of anybody?"

"Waal, no; not eggsackly. I've got a relation back t' Michigan who's b'en hot an' cold on the idee o' comin' West f'r some time. *Might* come if he could get a good layout. What do you talk on the farm?"

"Well, I d' know. I'll rent it on shares, or I'll rent it money rent."

"Waal, how much money, say?"

"Well, say ten per cent on the price — two-fifty."

"Waal, that ain't bad. Wait on 'im till 'e thrashes?"

Haskins listened eagerly to this important question, but Council was coolly eating a dried apple which he had speared out of a barrel with his knife. Butler studied him carefully.

"Well, knocks me out of twenty-five dollars interest."

"My relation 'll need all he's got t' git his crops in," said Council in the same indifferent way.

"Well, all right; *say* wait," concluded Butler.

"All right; this is the man. Haskins, this is Mr. Butler — no relation to Ben — the hardest working man in Cedar county."

On the way home Haskins said: "I ain't much better off. I'd like that farm; its a good farm, but it's all run down, an' so'm I. I could make a good farm of it if I had half a show. But I can't stock it n'r seed it."

"Waal, now, don't you worry," roared Council in his ear. "We'll pull y' through somehow till next harvest. He's agreed t' hire it plowed, an' you can earn a hundred dollars ploughin' an' y' c'n git the seed o' me, an' pay me back when y' can."

Haskins was silent with emotion, but at last he said, "I ain't got nothin' t' live on."

"Now don't you worry 'bout that. You jest make your headquarters at ol' Steve Council's. Mother 'll take a pile o' comfort in havin' y'r wife an children 'round. Y' see Jane's married off lately, an' Ike's away a good 'eal, so we'll be darn glad t' have ye stop with us this winter. Nex' spring we'll see if y' can't git a start agin;" and he chirruped to the team, which sprang forward with the rumbling, clattering wagon.

"Say, looky here, Council, you can't do this. I never saw — " shouted Haskins in his neighbor's ear.

Council moved about uneasily in his seat and stopped his stammering gratitude by saying: "Hold on, now; don't make such a fuss over a little thing. When I see a man down, an' things all on top of 'm, I jest like t' kick em off an' help 'm up. That's the kind of religion I got, an' it's about the *only* kind."

They rode the rest of the way home in silence. And when the red light of the lamp shone out into the darkness of the cold and windy night, and he thought of this refuge for his children and wife, Haskins could have put his arm around the neck of his burly companion and squeezed him like a lover; but he contented himself with saying: "Steven Council, you'll git y'r pay f'r this some day."

"Don't want any pay. My religion ain't run on such business principles."

The wind was growing colder, and the ground was covered with a white frost, as they turned into the gate of the Council farm, and the children came rushing out, shouting "Papa's come!" They hardly looked like the same children who had sat at the table the night before. Their torpidity under the influence of sunshine and Mother Council had given way to a sort of spasmodic cheerfulness, as insects in winter revive when laid on the earth.

III

Haskins worked like a fiend, and his wife, like the heroic woman that she was, bore also uncomplainingly the most terrible burdens. They rose early and toiled without intermission till the darkness fell on the plain, then tumbled into bed, every bone and muscle aching with fatigue, to rise with the sun next morning to the same round of the same ferocity of labor.

The eldest boy, now nine years old, drove a team all through the spring, plowing and seeding, milked the cows, and did chores innumerable, in most ways taking the place of a man; an infinitely pathetic but common figure — this boy — on the American farm, where there is no law against child labor. To see him in his coarse clothing, his huge boots, and his ragged cap, as he staggered with a pail of water from the well, or trudged in the cold and cheerless dawn out into the frosty field behind his team, gave the city-bred visitor a sharp pang of sympathetic pain. Yet Haskins loved his boy, and would have saved him from this if he could, but he could not.

By June the first year the result of such Herculean toil began to show on the farm. The yard was cleaned up and sown to grass, the garden plowed and planted, and the house mended. Council had given them four of his cows.

"Take 'em an' run 'em on shares. I don't want a milk s' many. Ike's away s' much now, Sat'd'ys an' Sund'ys, I can't stand the bother anyhow."

Other men, seeing the confidence of Council in the newcomer, had sold him tools on time; and as he was really an able farmer, he soon had round him many evidences of his care and thrift. At the advice of Council he had taken the farm for three years, with the privilege of rerenting or buying at the end of the term.

"It's a good bargain, an' y' want 'o nail it," said Council. "If you have any kind ov a crop, you can pay y'r debts an' keep seed an' bread."

The new hope which now sprang up in the heart of Haskins and his wife grew great almost as a pain by the time the wide field of wheat began to wave and rustle and swirl in the winds of July. Day after day he would snatch a few moments after supper to go and look at it.

"Have ye seen the wheat t'day, Nettie?" he asked one night as he rose from supper.

"No, Tim, I ain't had time."

"Well, take time now. Le's go look at it."

She threw an old hat on her head — Tommy's hat — and looking almost pretty in her thin sad way, went out with her husband to the hedge.

"Ain't it grand, Nettie? Just look at it."

It was grand. Level, russet here and there, heavy-headed, wide as a lake, and full of multitudinous whispers and gleams of wealth, it stretched away before the gazers like the fabled field of the cloth of gold.

"Oh, I think — I *hope* we'll have a good crop, Tim; and oh, how good the people have been to us!"

"Yes; I don't know where we'd be t'day if it hadn't ben f'r Council and his wife."

"They're the best people in the world," said the little woman with a great sob of gratitude.

"We'll be in the field on Monday, sure," said Haskins, gripping the rail on the fence as if already at the work of the harvest.

The harvest came, bounteous, glorious, but the winds came and blew it into tangles, and the rain matted it here and there close to the ground, increasing the work of gathering it threefold.

Oh, how they toiled in those glorious days! Clothing dripping with sweat, arms aching, filled with briers, fingers raw and bleeding, backs broken with the weight of heavy bundles, Haskins and his man toiled on. Tommy drove the harvester while his father and a hired man bound on the machine. In this way they cut ten acres every day, and almost every night after supper, when the hand went to bed, Haskins returned to the field, shocking the bound grain in the light of the moon. Many a night he worked till his anxious wife came out to call him in to rest and lunch.

At the same time she cooked for the men, took care of the children, washed and ironed, milked the cows at night, made the butter, and sometimes fed the horses and watered them while her husband kept at the shocking. No slave in the Roman galleys could have toiled so frightfully and lived, for this man thought himself a free man, and that he was working for his wife and babes.

When he sank into his bed with a deep groan of relief, too tired to change his grimy, dripping clothing, he felt that he was getting nearer and nearer to a home of his own, and pushing the wolf of want a little farther from his door.

There is no despair so deep as the despair of a homeless man or woman. To roam the roads of the country or the streets of the city, to feel there is no rood of ground on which the feet can rest, to halt weary and hungry outside lighted windows and hear laughter and song within — these are the hungers and rebellions that drive men to crime and women to shame.

It was the memory of this homelessness, and the fear of its coming again, that spurred Timothy Haskins and Nettie, his wife, to such ferocious labor during that first year.

IV

"M, yes; 'm, yes; first-rate," said Butler as his eye took in the great garden, the pigpen, and the well-filled barnyard. "You're git'n' quite a stock around yer. Done well, eh?"

Haskins was showing Butler around the place. He had not seen it for a year, having spent the year in Washington and Boston with Ashley, his brother-in-law, who had been elected to Congress.

"Yes, I've laid out a good deal of money during the last three years. I've paid out three hundred dollars f'r fencin'."

"Um — h'm! I see, I see," said Butler while Haskins went on.

"The kitchen there cost two hundred; the barn ain't cost much in money, but I've put o lot o' time on it. I've dug a new well, and I — "

"Yes, yes. I see! You've done well. Stalk worth a thousand dollars," said Butler, picking his teeth with a straw.

"About that," said Haskins modestly. "We begin to feel 's if we wuz git'n' a home f'r ourselves; but we've worked hard. I tell ye we begin to feel it, Mr. Butler, and we're goin' t' begin t' ease up purty soon. We've been kind o' plannin' a trip back t' *her* folks after the fall plowin's done."

"*Eggs*-actly!" said Butler, who was evidently thinking of something else. "I suppose you've kine o' kalklated on stayin' here three years more?"

"Well, yes. Fact is, I think I c'n buy the farm this fall, if you'll give me a reasonable show."

"Um — m! What do you call a reasonable show?"

"Waal; say a quarter down and three years' time."

Butler looked at the huge stacks of wheat which filled the yard, over which the chickens were fluttering and crawling, catching grasshoppers, and out of which the crickets were singing innumerably. He smiled in a peculiar way as he said, "Oh, I won't be hard on yer. But what did you expect to pay f'r the place?"

"Why, about what you offered it for before, two thousand five hundred, or *possibly* the three thousand dollars," he added quickly as he saw the owner shake his head.

"This farm is worth five thousand and five hundred dollars," said Butler in a careless but decided voice.

"*What!*" almost shrieked the astounded Haskins. "What's that? Five thousand? Why, that's double what you offered it for three years ago."

"Of course; and it's worth it. It was all run down then; now it's in good shape. You've laid out fifteen hundred dollars in improvements, according to your own story."

"But *you* had nothin' t' do about that. It's my work an' my money."

"You bet it was; but it's my land."

"But what's to pay me for all my — ?"

"Ain't you had the use of 'em?" replied Butler, smiling calmly into his face.

Haskins was like a man struck on the head with a sandbag; he couldn't think; he stammered as he tried to say: "But — I never 'd git the use — You'd rob me. More'n that: you agreed — you promised that I could buy or rent at the end of three years at — "

"That's all right. But I didn't say I'd let you carry off the improvements, nor that I'd go on renting the farm at two-fifty. The land is doubled in value, it don't matter how; it don't enter into the question; an' now you can pay me five hundred dollars a year rent, or take it on your own terms at fifty-five hundred, or — git out."

He was turning away when Haskins, the sweat pouring from his face, fronted him, saying again:

"But *you've* done nothing to make it so. You hain't added a cent. I put it all there myself, expectin' to buy. I worked an' sweat to improve it. I was working' f'r myself an' babes — "

"Well, why didn't you buy when I offered to sell? What y' kickin' about?"

"I'm kickin' about payin' you twice f'r my own things — my own fences, my own kitchen, my own garden."

Butler laughed. "You're too green t' eat, young feller. *Your* improvements! The law will sing another tune."

"But I trusted your word."

"Never trust anybody, my friend. Besides, I didn't promise not to do this thing. Why, man, don't look at me like that. Don't take me for a thief. It's the law. The reg'lar thing. Everybody does it."

"I don't care if they do. It's stealin' jest the same. You take three thousand dollars of my money. The work o' my hands and my wife's." He broke down at this point. He was not a strong man mentally. He could face hardship, ceaseless toil, but he could not face the cold and sneering face of Butler.

"But I don't take it," said Butler coolly. "All you've got to do is to go on jest as you've been a-doin', or give me a thousand dollars down and a mortgage at ten per cent on the rest."

Haskins sat down blindly on a bundle of oats nearby and, with staring eyes and drooping head, went over the situation. He was under the lion's paw. He felt a horrible numbness in his heart and limbs. He was hid in a mist, and there was no path out.

Butler walked about, looking at the huge stacks of grain and pulling now and again a few handfuls out, shelling the heads in his hands and blowing the chaff away. He hummed a little tune as he did so. He had an accommodating air of waiting.

Haskins was in the midst of the terrible toil of the last year. He was walking again in the rain and the mud behind his plow, he felt the dust and dirt of the threshing. The ferocious husking time, with its cutting wind and biting, clinging snows, lay hard upon him. Then he thought of his wife, how she had cheerfully cooked and baked, without holiday and without rest.

"Well, what do you think of it?" inquired the cool, mocking, insinuating voice of Butler.

"I think you're a thief and a liar!" shouted Haskins, leaping up. "A black-hearted houn'!" Butler's smile maddened him; with a sudden leap he caught a fork in his hands and whirled it in the air. "You'll never rob another man, damn ye!" he grated through his teeth, a look of pitiless ferocity in his accusing eyes.

Butler shrank and quivered, expecting the blow; stood, held hypnotized by the eyes of the man he had a moment before despised — a man transformed into an avenging demon. But in the deadly hush between the lift of the weapon and its fall there came a gush of faint, childish laughter, and then across the range of his vision, far away and dim, he saw the sunbright head of his baby girl as, with the pretty tottering run of a two-year-old, she moved across the grass of the dooryard. His hands relaxed; the fork fell to the ground; his head lowered.

"Make out y'r deed an' morgige, an' git off'n my land, an' don't ye never cross my line agin; if y' do, I'll kill ye."

Butler backed away from the man in wild haste and, climbing into his buggy with trembling limbs, drove off down the road, leaving Haskins seated dumbly on the sunny pile of sheaves, his head sunk into his hands.

[1891]

EDITH WHARTON (1862–1937) was born into a wealthy family in New York City. She later wrote, "My little-girl life, safe, guarded, monotonous, was cradled in the only world about which, according to Goethe, it is impossible to write poetry. The small society into which I was born was 'good' in the most prosaic sense of the term, and its only interest, for the generality of readers, lies in the fact of its sudden and total extinction." She was raised by governesses and tutors in the family homes in Paris, New York City, and Newport, Rhode Island. At an early age she decided to become a writer, and when she was only thirteen she published, at her own expense, a collection of verse. Later she found her chief literary task in adapting the conventional novel of manners, depicting the customs of a definite social class, to reveal the deeper human significance of her seemingly shallow characters. Her family persisted in viewing her literary work as an eccentricity best disregarded and left undiscussed.

After her marriage to Edward Wharton of Boston in 1885, Wharton began to write stories for popular magazines. She was a prolific author, and her first collection of stories, The Greater Inclination (1899), was followed by books of fiction almost every year for more than a quarter of a century. All told, she published eleven collections of stories and sixteen novels. She lived most of her life in Paris, but her photographic memory and her periodic visits to her country estate in the Berkshires, near Lenox, Massachusetts, helped her recall scenes of American life for her fiction. Her best works include the early novel The House of Mirth (1905), Ethan Frome (1911), a laconically powerful New England tragedy, and The Age of Innocence (1920), a novel about Newport society. Wharton's novels tend to be tragic and to concentrate on the presentation of characters, while her short stories, more satiric, emphasize plots. In both forms her point of view is usually poised and distant, and this is reflected in the elegance and clarity of her prose style.

One of Wharton's good friends was another expatriate, Henry James, who also visited her in the Berkshires. James had a profound influence on her writing, as a guiding spirit encouraging her to set a high standard for herself. Both writers are important social historians of their era, keen observers of the society they knew so well. Unlike James, Wharton did not write experimentally, but, like him, she enjoyed defining her artistic methods as a storyteller. In 1925 she published The Writing of Fiction, and in analyzing the French and Russian contributions to the short story form, she recognized that "instead of a loose web spread over the surface of life they have made it, at its best, a shaft driven straight into the heart of human experience." Her carefully crafted story "Roman Fever" has an ending that may strike the reader as "a shaft driven straight into the heart," but every *phrase in the realistic depiction of the characters and the situation is a sign-post that can be trusted for its relevance to the moral drama suddenly re-vealed in the last sentence. (See Wharton's Commentary on page 1252.)*

Edith Wharton

ఴఴ

ROMAN FEVER

I

From the table at which they had been lunching two American ladies of ripe but well-cared-for middle age moved across the lofty terrace of the Roman restaurant and, leaning on its parapet, looked first at each other, and then down on the outspread glories of the Palatine and the Forum, with the same expression of vague but benevolent approval.

As they leaned there a girlish voice echoed up gaily from the stairs leading to the court below. "Well, come along, then," it cried, not to them but to an invisible companion, "and let's leave the young things to their knitting" and a voice as fresh laughed back: "Oh, look here, Babs, not ac-tually *knitting* — " "Well, I mean figuratively," rejoined the first. "After all, we haven't left our poor parents much else to do . . . " and at that point the turn of the stairs engulfed the dialogue.

The two ladies looked at each other again, this time with a tinge of smiling embarrassment, and the smaller and paler one shook her head and colored slightly.

"Barbara!" she murmured, sending an unheard rebuke after the mocking voice in the stairway.

The other lady, who was fuller, and higher in color, with a small de-termined nose supported by vigorous black eyebrows, gave a good-humored laugh. "That's what our daughters think of us!"

Her companion replied by a deprecating gesture. "Not of us individu-ally. We must remember that. It's just the collective modern idea of Moth-ers. And you see — " Half guiltily she drew from her handsomely mounted black hand-bag a twist of crimson silk run through by two fine knitting nee-dles. "One never knows," she murmured. "The new system has certainly given us a good deal of time to kill; and sometimes I get tired just look-ing — even at this." Her gesture was now addressed to the stupendous scene at their feet.

The dark lady laughed again, and they both relapsed upon the view, contemplating it in silence, with a sort of diffused serenity which might have been borrowed from the spring effulgence of the Roman skies. The luncheon-hour was long past, and the two had their end of the vast terrace to themselves. At its opposite extremity a few groups, detained by a lingering look at the outspread city, were gathering up guide-books and fumbling for tips. The last of them scattered, and the two ladies were alone on the air-washed height.

"Well, I don't see why we shouldn't just stay here," said Mrs. Slade, the lady of the high color and energetic brows. Two derelict basket-chairs stood near, and she pushed them into the angle of the parapet, and settled herself in one, her gaze upon the Palatine. "After all, it's still the most beautiful view in the world."

"It always will be, to me," assented her friend Mrs. Ansley, with so slight a stress on the "me" that Mrs. Slade, though she noticed it, wondered if it were not merely accidental, like the random underlinings of old-fashioned letter-writers.

"Grace Ansley was always old-fashioned," she thought; and added aloud, with a retrospective smile: "It's a view we've both been familiar with for a good many years. When we first met here we were younger than our girls are now. You remember?"

"Oh, yes, I remember," murmured Mrs. Ansley, with the same undefinable stress — "There's that head-waiter wondering," she interpolated. She was evidently far less sure than her companion of herself and of her rights in the world.

"I'll cure him of wondering," said Mrs. Slade, stretching her hand toward a bag as discreetly opulent-looking as Mrs. Ansley's. Signing to the head-waiter, she explained that she and her friend were old lovers of Rome, and would like to spend the end of the afternoon looking down on the view — that is, if it did not disturb the service? The head-waiter, bowing over her gratuity, assured her that the ladies were most welcome, and would be still more so if they would condescend to remain for dinner. A full moon night, they would remember. . . .

Mrs. Slade's black brows drew together, as though references to the moon were out-of-place and even unwelcome. But she smiled away her frown as the head-waiter retreated. "Well, why not? We might do worse. There's no knowing, I suppose, when the girls will be back. Do you even know back from *where?* I don't!"

Mrs. Ansley again colored slightly. "I think those young Italian aviators we met at the Embassy invited them to fly to Tarquinia for tea. I suppose they'll want to wait and fly back by moonlight."

"Moonlight — moonlight! What a part it still plays. Do you suppose they're as sentimental as we were?"

"I've come to the conclusion that I don't in the least know what they are," said Mrs. Ansley. "And perhaps we didn't know much more about each other."

"No; perhaps we didn't."

Her friend gave her a shy glance. "I never should have supposed you were sentimental, Alida."

"Well, perhaps I wasn't." Mrs. Slade drew her lids together in retrospect; and for a few moments the two ladies, who had been intimate since childhood, reflected how little they knew each other. Each one, of course, had a label ready to attach to the other's name; Mrs. Delphin Slade, for instance, would have told herself, or any one who asked her, that Mrs. Horace Ansley, twenty-five years ago, had been exquisitely lovely — no, you wouldn't believe it, would you? . . . though, of course, still charming, distinguished. . . . Well, as a girl she had been exquisite; far more beautiful than her daughter Barbara, though certainly Babs, according to the new standards at any rate, was more effective—had more *edge*, as they say. Funny where she got it, with those two nullities as parents. Yes; Horace Ansley was — well, just the duplicate of his wife. Museum specimens of old New York. Good-looking, irreproachable, exemplary. Mrs. Slade and Mrs. Ansley had lived opposite each other — actually as well as figuratively — for years. When the drawing-room curtains in No. 20 East 73rd Street were renewed, No. 23, across the way, was always aware of it. And of all the movings, buyings, travels, anniversaries, illnesses — the tame chronicle of an estimable pair. Little of it escaped Mrs. Slade. But she had grown bored with it by the time her husband made his big *coup* in Wall Street, and when they bought in upper Park Avenue had already begun to think: "I'd rather live opposite a speak-easy for a change; at least one might see it raided." The idea of seeing Grace raided was so amusing that (before the move) she launched it at a woman's lunch. It made a hit, and went the rounds — she sometimes wondered if it had crossed the street, and reached Mrs. Ansley. She hoped not, but didn't much mind. Those were the days when respectability was at a discount, and it did the irreproachable no harm to laugh at them a little.

A few years later, and not many months apart, both ladies lost their husbands. There was an appropriate exchange of wreaths and condolences, and a brief renewal of intimacy in the half-shadow of their mourning; and now, after another interval, they had run across each other in Rome, at the same hotel, each of them the modest appendage of a salient daughter. The similarity of their lot had again drawn them together, lending itself to mild jokes, and the mutual confession that, if in old days it must have been tiring to "keep up" with daughters, it was now, at times, a little dull not to.

No doubt, Mrs. Slade reflected, she felt her unemployment more than poor Grace ever would. It was a big drop from being the wife of Delphin Slade to being his widow. She had always regarded herself (with a certain conjugal pride) as his equal in social gifts, as contributing her full share to the making of the exceptional couple they were: but the difference after his death was irremediable. As the wife of the famous corporation lawyer, al-

ways with an international case or two on hand, every day brought its exciting and unexpected obligation: the impromptu entertaining of eminent colleagues from abroad, the hurried dashes on legal business to London, Paris
or Rome, where the entertaining was so handsomely reciprocated; the
amusement of hearing in her wake: "What, that handsome woman with the
good clothes and the eyes is Mrs. Slade — *the* Slade's wife? Really? Generally the wives of celebrities are such frumps."

Yes; being *the* Slade's widow was a dullish business after that. In living
up to such a husband all her faculties had been engaged; now she had only
her daughter to live up to, for the son who seemed to have inherited his father's gifts had died suddenly in boyhood. She had fought through that
agony because her husband was there, to be helped and to help; now, after
the father's death, the thought of the boy had become unbearable. There
was nothing left but to mother her daughter; and dear Jenny was such a
perfect daughter that she needed no excessive mothering. "Now with Babs
Ansley I don't know that I *should* be so quiet," Mrs. Slade sometimes half-
enviously reflected; but Jenny, who was younger than her brilliant friend,
was that rare accident, an extremely pretty girl who somehow made youth
and prettiness seem as safe as their absence. It was all perplexing — and to
Mrs. Slade a little boring. She wished that Jenny would fall in love — with
the wrong man, even; that she might have to be watched, out-manœuvred,
rescued. And instead, it was Jenny who watched her mother, kept her out of
draughts, made sure that she had taken her tonic. . . .

Mrs. Ansley was much less articulate than her friend, and her mental
portrait of Mrs. Slade was slighter, and drawn with fainter touches. "Alida
Slade's awfully brilliant; but not as brilliant as she thinks," would have
summed it up; though she would have added, for the enlightenment of
strangers, that Mrs. Slade had been an extremely dashing girl; much more
so than her daughter, who was pretty, of course, and clever in a way, but
had none of her mother's — well, "vividness," some one had once called it.
Mrs. Ansley would take up current words like this, and cite them in quotation marks, as unheard-of audacities. No; Jenny was not like her mother.
Sometimes Mrs. Ansley thought Alida Slade was disappointed; on the
whole she had had a sad life. Full of failures and mistakes; Mrs. Ansley had
always been rather sorry for her. . . .

So these two ladies visualized each other, each through the wrong end
of her little telescope.

II

For a long time they continued to sit side by side without speaking. It
seemed as though, to both, there was a relief in laying down their somewhat
futile activities in the presence of the vast Memento Mori which faced
them. Mrs. Slade sat quite still, her eyes fixed on the golden slope of the
Palace of the Caesars, and after a while Mrs. Ansley ceased to fidget with

her bag, and she too sank into meditation. Like many intimate friends, the two ladies had never before had occasion to be silent together, and Mrs. Ansley was slightly embarrassed by what seemed, after so many years, a new stage in their intimacy, and one with which she did not yet know how to deal.

Suddenly the air was full of that deep clangor of bells which periodically covers Rome with a roof of silver. Mrs. Slade glanced at her wristwatch. "Five o'clock already," she said, as though surprised.

Mrs. Ansley suggested interrogatively: "There's bridge at the Embassy at five." For a long time Mrs. Slade did not answer. She appeared to be lost in contemplation, and Mrs. Ansley thought the remark had escaped her. But after a while she said, as if speaking out of a dream: "Bridge, did you say? Not unless you want to. . . . But I don't think I will, you know."

"Oh, no," Mrs. Ansley hastened to assure her. "I don't care to at all. It's so lovely here; and so full of old memories, as you say." She settled herself in her chair, and almost furtively drew forth her knitting. Mrs. Slade took sideway note of this activity, but her own beautifully cared-for hands remained motionless on her knee.

"I was just thinking," she said slowly, "what different things Rome stands for to each generation of travelers. To our grandmothers, Roman fever; to our mothers, sentimental danger — how we used to be guarded! — to our daughters, no more dangers than the middle of Main Street. They don't know it — but how much they're missing!"

The long golden light was beginning to pale, and Mrs. Ansley lifted her knitting a little closer to her eyes. "Yes; how we were guarded!"

"I always used to think," Mrs. Slade continued, "that our mothers had a much more difficult job than our grandmothers. When Roman fever stalked the streets it must have been comparatively easy to gather in the girls at the danger hour; but when you and I were young, with such beauty calling us, and the spice of disobedience thrown in, and no worse risk than catching cold during the cool hour after sunset, the mothers used to be put to it to keep us in — didn't they?"

She turned again toward Mrs. Ansley, but the latter had reached a delicate point in her knitting. "One, two, three — slip two; yes, they must have been," she assented, without looking up.

Mrs. Slade's eyes rested on her with a deepened attention. "She can knit — in the face of this! How like her. . . ."

Mrs. Slade leaned back, brooding, her eyes ranging from the ruins which faced her to the long green hollow of the Forum, the fading glow of the church fronts beyond it, and the outlying immensity of the Colosseum. Suddenly she thought: "It's all very well to say that our girls have done away with sentiment and moonlight. But if Babs Ansley isn't out to catch that young aviator — the one who's a Marchese — then I don't know anything. And Jenny has no chance beside her. I know that too. I wonder if that's why Grace Ansley likes the two girls to go everywhere together? My

poor Jenny as a foil — !" Mrs. Slade gave a hardly audible laugh, and at the
sound Mrs. Ansley dropped her knitting.

"Yes — ?"

"I — oh, nothing. I was only thinking how your Babs carries everything before her. That Campolieri boy is one of the best matches in Rome.
Don't look so innocent, my dear — you know he is. And I was wondering,
ever so respectfully, you understand . . . wondering how two such exemplary
characters as you and Horace had managed to produce anything quite so
dynamic." Mrs. Slade laughed again, with a touch of asperity.

Mrs. Ansley's hands lay inert across her needles. She looked straight
out at the great accumulated wreckage of passion and splendor at her feet.
But her small profile was almost expressionless. At length she said: "I think
you overrate Babs, my dear."

Mrs. Slade's tone grew easier. "No; I don't. I appreciate her. And perhaps envy you. Oh, my girl's perfect; if I were a chronic invalid I'd — well,
I think I'd rather be in Jenny's hands. There must be times . . . but there! I
always wanted a brilliant daughter . . . and never quite understood why I
got an angel instead."

Mrs. Ansley echoed her laugh in a faint murmur. "Babs is an angel
too."

"Of course — of course! But she's got rainbow wings. Well, they're
wandering by the sea with their young men; and here we sit . . . and it all
brings back the past a little too acutely."

Mrs. Ansley had resumed her knitting. One might almost have imagined (if one had known her less well, Mrs. Slade reflected) that, for her also,
too many memories rose from the lengthening shadows of those august
ruins. But no; she was simply absorbed in her work. What was there for her
to worry about? She knew that Babs would almost certainly come back engaged to the extremely eligible Campolieri. "And she'll sell the New York
house, and settle down near them in Rome, and never be in their way . . .
she's much too tactful. But she'll have an excellent cook, and just the right
people in for bridge and cocktails . . . and a perfectly peaceful old age
among her grandchildren."

Mrs. Slade broke off this prophetic flight with a recoil of self-disgust.
There was no one of whom she had less right to think unkindly than of
Grace Ansley. Would she never cure herself of envying her? Perhaps she
had begun too long ago.

She stood up and leaned against the parapet, filling her troubled eyes
with the tranquilizing magic of the hour. But instead of tranquilizing her
the sight seemed to increase her exasperation. Her gaze turned toward the
Colosseum. Already its golden flank was drowned in purple shadow, and
above it the sky curved crystal clear, without light or color. It was the moment when afternoon and evening hang balanced in mid-heaven.

Mrs. Slade turned back and laid her hand on her friend's arm. The
gesture was so abrupt that Mrs. Ansley looked up, startled.

"The sun's set. You're not afraid, my dear?"

"Afraid — ?"

"Of Roman fever or pneumonia? I remember how ill you were that winter. As a girl you had a very delicate throat, hadn't you?"

"Oh, we're all right up here. Down below, in the Forum, it does get deathly cold, all of a sudden . . . but not here."

"Ah, of course you know because you had to be so careful." Mrs. Slade turned back to the parapet. She thought: "I must make one more effort not to hate her." Aloud she said: "Whenever I look at the Forum from up here I remember that story about a great-aunt of yours, wasn't she? A dreadfully wicked great-aunt?"

"Oh yes; Great-aunt Harriet. The one who was supposed to have sent her young sister out to the Forum after sunset to gather a night-blooming flower for her album. All our great-aunts and grandmothers used to have albums of dried flowers."

Mrs. Slade nodded. "But she really sent her because they were in love with the same man — "

"Well, that was the family tradition. They said Aunt Harriet confessed it years afterward. At any rate, the poor little sister caught the fever and died. Mother used to frighten us with the story when we were children."

"And you frightened *me* with it, that winter when you and I were here as girls. The winter I was engaged to Delphin."

Mrs. Ansley gave a faint laugh. "Oh, did I? Really frightened you? I don't believe you're easily frightened."

"Not often; but I was then. I was easily frightened because I was too happy. I wonder if you know what that means?"

"I — yes. . . ." Mrs. Ansley faltered.

"Well, I suppose that was why the story of your wicked aunt made such an impression on me. And I thought: 'There's no more Roman fever, but the Forum is deathly cold after sunset — especially after a hot day. And the Colosseum's even colder and damper'."

"The Colosseum — ?"

"Yes. It wasn't easy to get in, after the gates were locked for the night. Far from easy. Still, in those days it could be managed; it was managed, often. Lovers met there who couldn't meet elsewhere. You knew that?"

"I — I daresay. I don't remember."

"You don't remember? You don't remember going to visit some ruins or other one evening, just after dark, and catching a bad chill? You were supposed to have gone to see the moon rise. People always said that expedition was what caused your illness."

There was a moment's silence; then Mrs. Ansley rejoined: "Did they? It was all so long ago."

"Yes. And you got well again — so it didn't matter. But I suppose it struck your friend — the reason given for your illness, I mean — because everybody knew you were so prudent on account of your throat, and your mother took such care of you. . . . You *had* been out late sight-seeing, hadn't you, that night?"

"Perhaps I had. The most prudent girls aren't always prudent. What made you think of it now?"

Mrs. Slade seemed to have no answer ready. But after a moment she broke out: "Because I simply can't bear it any longer — !"

Mrs. Ansley lifted her head quickly. Her eyes were wide and very pale. "Can't bear what?"

"Why — your not knowing that I've always known why you went."

"Why I went — ?"

"Yes. You think I'm bluffing, don't you? Well, you went to meet the man I was engaged to — and I can repeat every word of the letter that took you there."

While Mrs. Slade spoke Mrs. Ansley had risen unsteadily to her feet. Her bag, her knitting and gloves, slid in a panic-stricken heap to the ground. She looked at Mrs. Slade as though she were looking at a ghost.

"No, no — don't," she faltered out.

"Why not? Listen, if you don't believe me. 'My one darling, things can't go on like this. I must see you alone. Come to the Colosseum immediately after dark tomorrow. There will be somebody to let you in. No one whom you need fear will suspect' — but perhaps you've forgotten what the letter said?"

Mrs. Ansley met the challenge with an unexpected composure. Steadying herself against the chair she looked at her friend, and replied: "No; I know it by heart too."

"And the signature? 'Only *your* D. S.' Was that it? I'm right, am I? That was the letter that took you out that evening after dark?"

Mrs. Ansley was still looking at her. It seemed to Mrs. Slade that a slow struggle was going on behind the voluntarily controlled mask of her small quiet face. "I shouldn't have thought she had herself so well in hand," Mrs. Slade reflected, almost resentfully. But at this moment Mrs. Ansley spoke, "I don't know how you knew. I burnt that letter at once."

"Yes; you would, naturally — you're so prudent!" The sneer was open now. "And if you burnt the letter you're wondering how on earth I know what was in it. That's it, isn't it?"

Mrs. Slade waited, but Mrs. Ansley did not speak.

"Well, my dear, I know what was in that letter because I wrote it!"

"You wrote it?"

"Yes."

The two women stood for a minute staring at each other in the last golden light. Then Mrs. Ansley dropped back into her chair. "Oh," she murmured, and covered her face with her hands.

Mrs. Slade waited nervously for another word or movement. None came, and at length she broke out: "I horrify you."

Mrs. Ansley's hands dropped to her knee. The face they uncovered was streaked with tears. "I wasn't thinking of you. I was thinking — it was the only letter I ever had from him!"

"And I wrote it. Yes; I wrote it! But I was the girl he was engaged to. Did you happen to remember that?"

Mrs. Ansley's head drooped again. "I'm not trying to excuse myself. . . . I remembered. . . ."

"And still you went?"

"Still I went."

Mrs. Slade stood looking down on the small bowed figure at her side. The flame of her wrath had already sunk, and she wondered why she had ever thought there would be any satisfaction in inflicting so purposeless a wound on her friend. But she had to justify herself.

"You do understand? I'd found out — and I hated you, hated you. I knew you were in love with Delphin — and I was afraid; afraid of you, of your quiet ways, your sweetness . . . your . . . well, I wanted you out of the way, that's all. Just for a few weeks; just till I was sure of him. So in a blind fury I wrote that letter. . . . I don't know why I'm telling you now."

"I suppose," said Mrs. Ansley slowly, "it's because you've always gone on hating me."

"Perhaps. Or because I wanted to get the whole thing off my mind." She paused. "I'm glad you destroyed the letter. Of course I never thought you'd die."

Mrs. Ansley relapsed into silence, and Mrs. Slade, leaning above her, was conscious of a strange sense of isolation, of being cut off from the warm current of human communion. "You think me a monster!"

"I don't know. . . . It was the only letter I had, and you say he didn't write it?"

"Ah, how you care for him still!"

"I cared for that memory," said Mrs. Ansley.

Mrs. Slade continued to look down on her. She seemed physically reduced by the blow — as if, when she got up, the wind might scatter her like a puff of dust. Mrs. Slade's jealousy suddenly leapt up again at the sight. All these years the woman had been living on that letter. How she must have loved him, to treasure the mere memory of its ashes! The letter of the man her friend was engaged to. Wasn't it she who was the monster?

"You tried your best to get him away from me, didn't you? But you failed; and I kept him. That's all."

"Yes. That's all."

"I wish now I hadn't told you. I'd no idea you'd feel about it as you do; I thought you'd be amused. It all happened so long ago, as you say; and you must do me the justice to remember that I had no reason to think you'd ever taken it seriously. How could I, when you were married to Horace Ansley two months afterward? As soon as you could get out of bed your mother rushed you off to Florence and married you. People were rather surprised — they wondered at its being done so quickly; but I thought I knew. I had an idea you did it out of *pique* — to be able to say you'd got ahead of Delphin and me. Girls have such silly reasons for doing the most serious things. And your marrying so soon convinced me that you'd never really cared."

"Yes. I suppose it would," Mrs. Ansley assented.

The clear heaven overhead was emptied of all its gold. Dusk spread over it, abruptly darkening the Seven Hills. Here and there lights began to twinkle through the foliage at their feet. Steps were coming and going on the deserted terrace — waiters looking out of the doorway at the head of the stairs, then reappearing with trays and napkins and flasks of wine. Tables were moved, chairs straightened. A feeble string of electric lights flickered out. Some vases of faded flowers were carried away, and brought back replenished. A stout lady in a dust-coat suddenly appeared, asking in broken Italian if any one had seen the elastic band which held together her tattered Baedeker. She poked with her stick under the table at which she had lunched, the waiters assisting.

The corner where Mrs. Slade and Mrs. Ansley sat was still shadowy and deserted. For a long time neither of them spoke. At length Mrs. Slade began again: "I suppose I did it as a sort of joke — "

"A joke?"

"Well, girls are ferocious sometimes, you know. Girls in love especially. And I remember laughing to myself all that evening at the idea that you were waiting around there in the dark, dodging out of sight, listening for every sound, trying to get in — Of course I was upset when I heard you were so ill afterward."

Mrs. Ansley had not moved for a long time. But now she turned slowly toward her companion. "But I didn't wait. He'd arranged everything. He was there. We were let in at once," she said.

Mrs. Slade sprang up from her leaning position. "Delphin there? They let you in? — Ah, now you're lying!" she burst out with violence.

Mrs. Ansley's voice grew clearer, and full of surprise. "But of course he was there. Naturally he came — "

"Came? How did he know he'd find you there? You must be raving!"

Mrs. Ansley hesitated, as though reflecting. "But I answered the letter. I told him I'd be there. So he came."

Mrs. Slade flung her hands up to her face. "Oh, God — you answered! I never thought of your answering. . . ."

"It's odd you never thought of it, if you wrote the letter."

"Yes. I was blind with rage."

Mrs. Ansley rose, and drew her fur scarf about her. "It is cold here. We'd better go. . . . I'm sorry for you," she said as she clasped the fur about her throat.

The unexpected words sent a pang through Mrs. Slade. "Yes; we'd better go." She gathered up her bag and cloak. "I don't know why you should be sorry for me," she muttered.

Mrs. Ansley stood looking away from her toward the dusky secret mass of the Colosseum. "Well — because I didn't have to wait that night."

Mrs. Slade gave an unquiet laugh. "Yes; I was beaten there. But I oughtn't to begrudge it to you, I suppose. At the end of all these years. After all, I had everything; I had him for twenty-five years. And you had nothing but that one letter that he didn't write."

Mrs. Ansley was again silent. At length she turned toward the door of the terrace. She took a step, and turned back, facing her companion.

"I had Barbara," she said, and began to move ahead of Mrs. Slade toward the stairway.

[1936]

STEPHEN CRANE (1871–1900), in his short stories and novels, forecast a new direction in American literature. As the literary critics Carl and Mark Van Doren wrote, "Modern fiction may be said to begin with Stephen Crane." Although he lived only twenty-nine years — a shorter lifetime than Poe's — Crane wrote some of the most memorable fiction and poetry ever created by an American. He published fourteen books in his energetic lifetime, even while striking his contemporaries as a typically irresponsible genius who acted out the legend of the writer as soldier of fortune. The poet John Berryman, who wrote a biography of Crane, observed the essential truth about him, however: "Crane was a writer and nothing else: a man alone in a room with the English language, trying to get human feelings right." Crane's style in his short stories is as intensely personal as Poe's and Hawthorne's, but he did not make use of the techniques of fantasy and allegory. "His eyes remained wide open on his world. He was almost illusionless, whether about his subjects or himself. Perhaps his sole illusion was the heroic one; and not even this, especially if he was concerned in it himself as a man, escaped his irony."

Crane was born in Newark, New Jersey, the youngest of fourteen children. His father, a Methodist minister, died when Crane was just a boy, and his mother supported the family by writing articles for Methodist papers and reporting for the New York Tribune and the Philadelphia Press. Crane briefly attended Lafayette College and Syracuse University before going to work in New York City as a freelance journalist. He became deeply interested in life along the Bowery, one of the worst slums in New York, and he used this setting for his novel Maggie: A Girl of the Streets. Maggie was so grimly naturalistic in its portrayal of slum life and so frank in its treatment of sex that Crane had to publish it at his own expense in 1893. Two years later he sold a long story about the Civil War to a syndicate for less than $100. That work, The Red Badge of Courage, was such a vivid, imaginatively rendered account of wartime experience — even though Crane had never been in a battle himself — that it established his literary reputation. It remains his most famous work. In the last five years of his life, before he died of tuberculosis in Germany, Crane traveled extensively as a reporter, first to the American West, then to Florida. He was en route to Florida on the steamship Commodore when that ship was wrecked on New Year's Day, 1897, and Crane recreated the ordeal after the disaster in one of his finest short stories, "The Open Boat." Next he went to Greece to report on the Greco-Turkish War and finally — after he had moved to England — to Cuba to cover the Spanish-American War. Like Ernest Hemingway after him, Crane couldn't keep away from war or revolution, believing that "the nearer a writer gets to life, the greater he becomes as an artist."

Crane's chief literary importance is as a unique stylist. His short fiction has an affinity with Chekhov's stories, where the plots often build up to a crucial moment of impasse and then collapse. In the final confrontation in "The Bride Comes to Yellow Sky," for example, contrary to the reader's expectations, no violent action occurs. Crane also used language poetically. His patterning of words, which has been termed "prose pointillism," consists of discrete images that coalesce like the points of color in a French Impressionist painting, every word-group making a cross-reference, every seemingly disconnected detail being interrelated to the whole. To be as honest as possible was Crane's supreme ambition; toward the end of his life he told a younger writer, "An artist, I think, is nothing but a powerful memory that can move itself at will through certain experiences sideways, and every artist must be in some things powerless as a dead snake."

Stephen Crane

෨

THE OPEN BOAT

A Tale Intended to Be after the Fact,
Being the Experience of Four Men from
the Sunk Steamer Commodore

I

None of them knew the color of the sky. Their eyes glanced level, and were fastened upon the waves that swept toward them. These waves were of the hue of slate, save for the tops, which were of foaming white, and all of the men knew the colors of the sea. The horizon narrowed and widened, and dipped and rose, and at all times its edge was jagged with waves that seemed thrust up in points like rocks.

Many a man ought to have a bath-tub larger than the boat which here rode upon the sea. These waves were most wrongfully and barbarously abrupt and tall, and each froth-top was a problem in small boat navigation.

The cook squatted in the bottom and looked with both eyes at the six inches of gunwale which separated him from the ocean. His sleeves were rolled over his fat forearms, and the two flaps of his unbuttoned vest dangled as he bent to bail out the boat. Often he said: "Gawd! That was a narrow clip." As he remarked it he invariably gazed eastward over the broken sea.

The oiler, steering with one of the two oars in the boat, sometimes raised himself suddenly to keep clear of water that swirled in over the stern. It was a thin little oar and it seemed often ready to snap.

The correspondent, pulling at the other oar, watched the waves and wondered why he was there.

The injured captain, lying in the bow, was at this time buried in that profound dejection and indifference which comes, temporarily at least, to even the bravest and most enduring when, willy nilly, the firm fails, the army loses, the ship goes down. The mind of the master of a vessel is rooted deep in the timbers of her, though he command for a day or a decade, and this captain had on him the stern impression of a scene in the grays of dawn of seven turned faces, and later a stump of a top-mast with a white ball on it that slashed to and fro at the waves, went low and lower, and down. Thereafter there was something strange in his voice. Although steady, it was deep with mourning, and of a quality beyond oration or tears.

"Keep 'er a little more south, Billie," said he.

" 'A little more south,' sir," said the oiler in the stern.

A seat in this boat was not unlike a seat upon a bucking broncho, and, by the same token, a broncho is not much smaller. The craft pranced and reared, and plunged like an animal. As each wave came, and she rose for it, she seemed like a horse making at a fence outrageously high. The manner of her scramble over these walls of water is a mystic thing, and, moreover, at the top of them were ordinarily these problems in white water, the foam racing down from the summit of each wave, requiring a new leap, and a leap from the air. Then, after scornfully bumping a crest, she would slide, and race, and splash down a long incline and arrive bobbing and nodding in front of the next menace.

A singular disadvantage of the sea lies in the fact that after successfully surmounting one wave you discover that there is another behind it just as important and just as nervously anxious to do something effective in the way of swamping boats. In a ten-foot dingey one can get an idea of the resources of the sea in the line of waves that is not probable to the average experience, which is never at sea in a dingey. As each slaty wall of water approached, it shut all else from the view of the men in the boat, and it was not difficult to imagine that this particular wave was the final outburst of the ocean, the last effort of the grim water. There was a terrible grace in the move of the waves, and they came in silence, save for the snarling of the crests.

In the wan light, the faces of the men must have been gray. Their eyes must have glinted in strange ways as they gazed steadily astern. Viewed from a balcony, the whole thing would doubtlessly have been weirdly picturesque. But the men in the boat had no time to see it, and if they had had leisure there were other things to occupy their minds. The sun swung steadily up the sky, and they knew it was broad day because the color of the sea changed from slate to emerald-green, streaked with amber lights, and the foam was like tumbling snow. The process of the breaking day was un-known to them. They were aware only of this effect upon the color of the waves that rolled toward them.

In disjointed sentences the cook and the correspondent argued as to the difference between a life-saving station and a house of refuge. The cook had said: "There's a house of refuge just north of the Mosquito Inlet Light, and as soon as they see us, they'll come off in their boat and pick us up."

"As soon as who see us?" said the correspondent.

"The crew," said the cook.

"Houses of refuge don't have crews," said the correspondent. "As I understand them, they are only places where clothes and grub are stored for the benefit of shipwrecked people. They don't carry crews."

"Oh, yes, they do," said the cook.

"No, they don't," said the correspondent.

"Well, we're not there yet, anyhow," said the oiler, in the stern.

"Well," said the cook, "perhaps it's not a house of refuge that I'm thinking of as being near Mosquito Inlet Light. Perhaps it's a life-saving station."

"We're not there yet," said the oiler, in the stern.

II

As the boat bounced from the top of each wave, the wind tore through the hair of the hatless men, and as the craft plopped her stern down again the spray slashed past them. The crest of each of these waves was a hill, from the top of which the men surveyed, for a moment, a broad tumultuous expanse, shining and wind-riven. It was probably splendid. It was probably glorious, this play of the free sea, wild with lights of emerald and white and amber.

"Bully good thing it's an on-shore wind," said the cook. "If not where would we be? Wouldn't have a show."

"That's right," said the correspondent.

The busy oiler nodded his assent.

Then the captain, in the bow, chuckled in a way that expressed humor, contempt, tragedy, all in one. "Do you think we've got a show, now, boys?" said he.

Whereupon the three went silent, save for a trifle of hemming and hawing. To express any particular optimism at this time they felt to be chil-dish and stupid, but they all doubtless possessed this sense of the situation in their mind. A young man thinks doggedly at such times. On the other hand, the ethics of their condition was decidedly against any open sugges-tion of hopelessness. So they were silent.

"Oh, well," said the captain, soothing his children, "we'll get ashore all right."

But there was that in his tone which made them think, so the oiler quoth: "Yes! If this wind holds!"

The cook was bailing. "Yes! If we don't catch hell in the surf."

Canton flannel gulls flew near and far. Sometimes they sat down on the sea, near patches of brown sea-weed that rolled over the waves with a movement like carpets on a line in a gale. The birds sat comfortably in groups, and they were envied by some in the dingey, for the wrath of the sea was no more to them than it was to a covey of prairie chickens a thousand miles inland. Often they came very close and stared at the men with black bead-like eyes. At these times they were uncanny and sinister in their un-blinking scrutiny, and the men hooted angrily at them, telling them to be gone. One came, and evidently decided to alight on the top of the captain's head. The bird flew parallel to the boat and did not circle, but made short sidelong jumps in the air in chicken-fashion. His black eyes were wistfully fixed upon the captain's head. "Ugly brute," said the oiler to the bird. "You look as if you were made with a jack-knife." The cook and the correspon-dent swore darkly at the creature. The captain naturally wished to knock it away with the end of the heavy painter, but he did not dare do it, because anything resembling an emphatic gesture would have capsized this freighted boat, and so with his open hand, the captain gently and carefully waved the gull away. After it had been discouraged from the pursuit the captain breathed easier on account of his hair, and others breathed easier because the bird struck their minds at this time as being somehow grue-some and ominous.

In the meantime the oiler and the correspondent rowed. And also they rowed.

They sat together in the same seat, and each rowed an oar. Then the oiler took both oars; then the correspondent took both oars; then the oiler; then the correspondent. They rowed and they rowed. The very ticklish part of the business was when the time came for the reclining one in the stern to take his turn at the oars. By the very last star of truth, it is easier to steal eggs from under a hen than it was to change seats in the dingey. First the man in the stern slid his hand along the thwart and moved with care, as if he were of Sèvres.[1] Then the man in the rowing seat slid his hand along the other thwart. It was all done with the most extraordinary care. As the two sidled past each other, the whole party kept watchful eyes on the coming wave, and the captain cried: "Look out now! Steady there!"

The brown mats of sea-weed that appeared from time to time were like islands, bits of earth. They were travelling, apparently, neither one way nor the other. They were, to all intents, stationary. They informed the men in the boat that it was making progress slowly toward the land.

The captain, rearing cautiously in the bow, after the dingey soared on a great swell, said that he had seen the light-house at Mosquito Inlet. Pres-

[1] a delicate French porcelain.

ently the cook remarked that he had seen it. The correspondent was at the oars, then, and for some reason he too wished to look at the light-house, but his back was toward the far shore and the waves were important, and for some time he could not seize an opportunity to turn his head. But at last there came a wave more gentle than the others, and when at the crest of it he swiftly scoured the western horizon.

"See it?" said the captain.

"No," said the correspondent, slowly, "I didn't see anything."

"Look again," said the captain. He pointed. "It's exactly in that direction."

At the top of another wave, the correspondent did as he was bid, and this time his eyes chanced on a small still thing on the edge of the swaying horizon. It was precisely like the point of a pin. It took an anxious eye to find a light-house so tiny.

"Think we'll make it, Captain?"

"If this wind holds and the boat don't swamp, we can't do much else," said the captain.

The little boat, lifted by each towering sea, and splashed viciously by the crests, made progress that in the absence of sea-weed was not apparent to those in her. She seemed just a wee thing wallowing, miraculously, top-up, at the mercy of five oceans. Occasionally, a great spread of water, like white flames, swarmed into her.

"Bail her, cook," said the captain, serenely.

"All right, Captain," said the cheerful cook.

III

It would be difficult to describe the subtle brotherhood of men that was here established on the seas. No one said that it was so. No one mentioned it. But it dwelt in the boat, and each man felt it warm him. They were a captain, an oiler, a cook, and a correspondent, and they were friends, friends in a more curiously iron-bound degree than may be common. The hurt captain, lying against the water-jar in the bow, spoke always in a low voice and calmly, but he could never command a more ready and swiftly obedient crew than the motley three of the dingey. It was more than a mere recognition of what was best for the common safety. There was surely in it a quality that was personal and heartfelt. And after this devotion to the commander of the boat there was this comradeship that the correspondent, for instance, who had been taught to be cynical of men, knew even at the time was the best experience of his life. But no one said that it was so. No one mentioned it.

"I wish we had a sail," remarked the captain. "We might try my overcoat on the end of an oar and give you two boys a chance to rest." So the cook and the correspondent held the mast and spread wide the overcoat. The oiler steered, and the little boat made good way with her new rig.

Sometimes the oiler had to scull sharply to keep a sea from breaking into the boat, but otherwise sailing was a success.

Meanwhile the light-house had been growing slowly larger. It had now almost assumed color, and appeared like a little gray shadow on the sky. The man at the oars could not be prevented from turning his head rather often to try for a glimpse of this little gray shadow.

At last, from the top of each wave the men in the tossing boat could see land. Even as the light-house was an upright shadow on the sky, this land seemed but a long black shadow on the sea. It certainly was thinner than paper. "We must be about opposite New Smyrna," said the cook, who had coasted this shore often in schooners. "Captain, by the way, I believe they abandoned that life-saving station there about a year ago."

"Did they?" said the captain.

The wind slowly died away. The cook and the correspondent were not now obliged to slave in order to hold high the oar. But the waves continued their old impetuous swooping at the dingey, and the little craft, no longer under way, struggled woundily over them. The oiler or the correspondent took the oars again.

Shipwrecks are *apropos* of nothing. If men could only train for them and have them occur when the men had reached pink condition, there would be less drowning at sea. Of the four in the dingey none had slept any time worth mentioning for two days and two nights previous to embarking in the dingey, and in the excitement of clambering about the deck of a foundering ship they had also forgotten to eat heartily.

For these reasons, and for others, neither the oiler nor the correspondent was fond of rowing at this time. The correspondent wondered ingenuously how in the name of all that was sane could there be people who thought it amusing to row a boat. It was not an amusement; it was a diabolical punishment, and even a genius of mental aberrations could never conclude that it was anything but a horror to the muscles and a crime against the back. He mentioned to the boat in general how the amusement of rowing struck him, and the weary-faced oiler smiled in full sympathy. Previously to the foundering, by the way, the oiler had worked double-watch in the engine-room of the ship.

"Take her easy, now, boys," said the captain. "Don't spend yourselves. If we have to run a surf you'll need all your strength, because we'll sure have to swim for it. Take your time."

Slowly the land arose from the sea. From a black line it became a line of black and a line of white — trees and sand. Finally, the captain said that he could make out a house on the shore. "That's the house of refuge, sure," said the cook. "They'll see us before long, and come out after us."

The distant light-house reared high. "The keeper ought to be able to make us out now, if he's looking through a glass," said the captain. "He'll notify the life-saving people."

"None of those other boats could have got ashore to give word of the wreck," said the oiler, in a low voice. "Else the life-boat would be out hunting us."

Slowly and beautifully the land loomed out of the sea. The wind came again. It had veered from the northeast to the southeast. Finally, a new sound struck the ears of the men in the boat. It was the low thunder of the surf on the shore. "We'll never be able to make the light-house now," said the captain. "Swing her head a little more north, Billie."

" 'A little more north,' sir," said the oiler.

Whereupon the little boat turned her nose once more down the wind, and all but the oarsman watched the shore grow. Under the influence of this expansion doubt and direful apprehension were leaving the minds of the men. The management of the boat was still most absorbing, but it could not prevent a quiet cheerfulness. In an hour, perhaps, they would be ashore.

Their back-bones had become thoroughly used to balancing in the boat and they now rode this wild colt of a dingey like circus men. The correspondent thought that he had been drenched to the skin, but happening to feel in the top pocket of his coat, he found therein eight cigars. Four of them were soaked with sea-water; four were perfectly scatheless. After a search, somebody produced three dry matches, and thereupon the four waifs rode impudently in their little boat, and with an assurance of an impending rescue shining in their eyes, puffed at the big cigars and judged well and ill of all men. Everybody took a drink of water.

IV

"Cook," remarked the captain, "there don't seem to be any signs of life about your house of refuge."

"No," replied the cook. "Funny they don't see us!"

A broad stretch of lowly coast lay before the eyes of the men. It was of dunes topped with dark vegetation. The roar of the surf was plain, and sometimes they could see the white lip of a wave as it spun up the beach. A tiny house was blocked out black upon the sky. Southward, the slim light-house lifted its little gray length.

Tide, wind, and waves were swinging the dingey northward. "Funny they don't see us," said the men.

The surf's roar was here dulled, but its tone was, nevertheless, thunderous and mighty. As the boat swam over the great rollers, the men sat listening to this roar. "We'll swamp sure," said everybody.

It is fair to say here that there was not a life-saving station within twenty miles in either direction, but the men did not know this fact and in consequence they made dark and opprobrious remarks concerning the eyesight of the nation's life-savers. Four scowling men sat in the dingey and surpassed records in the invention of epithets.

"Funny they don't see us."

The light-heartedness of a former time had completely faded. To their sharpened minds it was easy to conjure pictures of all kinds of incompetency and blindness and, indeed, cowardice. There was the shore of the populous land, and it was bitter and bitter to them that from it came no sign.

"Well," said the captain, ultimately, "I suppose we'll have to make a try for ourselves. If we stay out here too long, we'll none of us have strength left to swim after the boat swamps."

And so the oiler, who was at the oars, turned the boat straight for the shore. There was a sudden tightening of muscles. There was some thinking.

"If we don't all get ashore —" said the captain. "If we don't all get ashore, I suppose you fellows know where to send news of my finish?"

They then briefly exchanged some addresses and admonitions. As for the reflections of the men, there was a great deal of rage in them. Perchance they might be formulated thus: "If I am going to be drowned — if I am going to be drowned — if I am going to be drowned, why, in the name of the seven mad gods who rule the sea, was I allowed to come thus far and contemplate sand and trees? Was I brought here merely to have my nose dragged away as I was about to nibble the sacred cheese of life? It is preposterous. If this old ninny-woman, Fate, cannot do better than this, she should be deprived of the management of men's fortunes. She is an old hen who knows not her intention. If she has decided to drown me, why did she not do it in the beginning and save me all this trouble. The whole affair is absurd. . . . But, no, she cannot mean to drown me. She dare not drown me. She cannot drown me. Not after all this work." Afterward the man might have had an impulse to shake his fist at the clouds. "Just you drown me, now, and then hear what I call you!"

The billows that came at this time were more formidable. They seemed always just about to break and roll over the little boat in a turmoil of foam. There was a preparatory and long growl in the speech of them. No mind unused to the sea would have concluded that the dingey could ascend these sheer heights in time. The shore was still afar. The oiler was a wily surfman. "Boys," he said, swiftly, "she won't live three minutes more and we're too far out to swim. Shall I take her to sea again, Captain?"

"Yes! Go ahead!" said the captain.

This oiler, by a series of quick miracles, and fast and steady oarsmanship, turned the boat in the middle of the surf and took her safely to sea again.

There was a considerable silence as the boat bumped over the furrowed sea to deeper water. Then somebody in gloom spoke. "Well, anyhow, they must have seen us from the shore by now."

The gulls went in slanting flight up the wind toward the gray desolate east. A squall, marked by dingy clouds, and clouds brick-red, like smoke from a burning building, appeared from the southeast.

"What do you think of those life-saving people? Ain't they peaches?"

"Funny they haven't seen us."

"Maybe they think we're out here for sport! Maybe they think we're fishin'. Maybe they think we're damned fools."

It was a long afternoon. A changed tide tried to force them southward, but wind and wave said northward. Far ahead, where coast-line, sea, and sky formed their mighty angle, there were little dots which seemed to indicate a city on the shore.

"St. Augustine?"

The captain shook his head. "Too near Mosquito Inlet."

And the oiler rowed, and then the correspondent rowed. Then the oiler rowed. It was a weary business. The human back can become the seat of more aches and pains than are registered in books for the composite anatomy of a regiment. It is a limited area, but it can become the theatre of innumerable muscular conflicts, tangles, wrenches, knots, and other comforts.

"Did you ever like to row, Billie?" asked the correspondent.

"No," said the oiler, "Hang it."

When one exchanged the rowing-seat for a place in the bottom of the boat, he suffered a bodily depression that caused him to be careless of everything save an obligation to wiggle one finger. There was cold sea-water swashing to and fro in the boat, and he lay in it. His head, pillowed on a thwart, was within an inch of the swirl of a wave crest, and sometimes a particularly obstreperous sea came in-board and drenched him once more. But these matters did not annoy him. It is almost certain that if the boat had capsized he would have tumbled comfortably out upon the ocean as if he felt sure that it was a great soft mattress.

"Look! There's a man on the shore!"

"Where?"

"There! See 'im? See 'im?"

"Yes, sure! He's walking along."

"Now he's stopped. Look! He's facing us!"

"He's waving at us!"

"So he is! By thunder!"

"Ah, now, we're all right! There'll be a boat out here for us in half an hour."

"He's going on. He's running. He's going up to that house there."

The remote beach seemed lower than the sea, and it required a searching glance to discern the little black figure. The captain saw a floating stick and they rowed to it. A bath-towel was by some weird chance in the boat, and, tying this on the stick, the captain waved it. The oarsman did not dare turn his head, so he was obliged to ask questions.

"What's he doing now?"

"He's standing still again. He's looking, I think. . . . There he goes again. Toward the house. . . . Now he's stopped again."

"Is he waving at us?"

"No, not now! He was, though."

"Look! There comes another man!"

"He's running."

"Look at him go, would you."

"Why, he's on a bicycle. Now he's met the other man. They're both waving at us. Look!"

"There comes something up the beach."

"What the devil is that thing?"

"Why, it looks like a boat."

"Why, certainly it's a boat."

"No, it's on wheels."

"Yes, so it is. Well, that must be the life-boat. They drag them along shore on a wagon."

"That's the life-boat, sure."

"No, by, it's — it's an omnibus."

"I tell you it's a life-boat."

"It is not! It's an omnibus. I can see it plain. See? One of those big hotel omnibuses."

"By thunder, you're right. It's an omnibus, sure as fate. What do you suppose they are doing with an omnibus? Maybe they are going around collecting the life-crew, hey?"

"That's it, likely. Look! There's a fellow waving a little black flag. He's standing on the steps of the omnibus. There come those other two fellows. Now they're all talking together. Look at the fellow with the flag. Maybe he ain't waving it!"

"That ain't a flag, is it? That's his coat. Why, certainly, that's his coat."

"So it is. It's his coat. He's taken it off and is waving it around his head. But would you look at him swing it!"

"Oh, say, there isn't any life-saving station there. That's just a winter resort hotel omnibus that has brought over some of the boarders to see us drown."

"What's that idiot with the coat mean? What's he signaling, anyhow?"

"It looks as if he were trying to tell us to go north. There must be a life-saving station up there."

"No! He thinks we're fishing. Just giving us a merry hand. See? Ah, there, Willie."

"Well, I wish I could make something out of those signals. What do you suppose he means?"

"He don't mean anything. He's just playing."

"Well, if he'd just signal us to try the surf again, or to go to sea and wait, or go north, or go south, or go to hell — there would be some reason in it. But look at him. He just stands there and keeps his coat revolving like a wheel. The ass!"

"There come more people."

"Now there's quite a mob. Look! Isn't that a boat?"

"Where? Oh, I see where you mean. No, that's no boat."

"That fellow is still waving his coat."

"He must think we like to see him do that. Why don't he quit it. It don't mean anything."

"I don't know. I think he is trying to make us go north. It must be that there's a life-saving station there somewhere."

"Say, he ain't tired yet. Look at 'im wave."

"Wonder how long he can keep that up. He's been revolving his coat ever since he caught sight of us. He's an idiot. Why aren't they getting men to bring a boat out. A fishing boat — one of those big yawls — could come out here all right. Why don't he do something?"

"Oh, it's all right, now."

"They'll have a boat out here for us in less than no time, now that they've seen us."

A faint yellow tone came into the sky over the low land. The shadows on the sea slowly deepened. The wind bore coldness with it, and the men began to shiver.

"Holy smoke!" said one, allowing his voice to express his impious mood, "if we keep on monkeying out here! If we've got to flounder out here all night!"

"Oh, we'll never have to stay here all night! Don't you worry. They've seen us now, and it won't be long before they'll come chasing out after us."

The shore grew dusky. The man waving a coat blended gradually into this gloom, and it swallowed in the same manner the omnibus and the group of people. The spray, when it dashed uproariously over the side, made the voyagers shrink and swear like men who were being branded.

"I'd like to catch the chump who waved the coat. I feel like soaking him one, just for luck."

"Why? What did he do?"

"Oh, nothing, but then he seemed so damned cheerful."

In the meantime the oiler rowed, and then the correspondent rowed, and then the oiler rowed. Gray-faced and bowed forward, they mechanically, turn by turn, plied the leaden oars. The form of the light-house had vanished from the southern horizon, but finally a pale star appeared, just lifting from the sea. The streaked saffron in the west passed before the all-merging darkness, and the sea to the east was black. The land had vanished, and was expressed only by the low and drear thunder of the surf.

"If I am going to be drowned — if I am going to be drowned — if I am going to be drowned, why, in the name of the seven mad gods who rule the sea, was I allowed to come thus far and contemplate sand and trees? Was I brought here merely to have my nose dragged away as I was about to nibble the sacred cheese of life?"

The patient captain, drooped over the water-jar, was sometimes obliged to speak to the oarsman.

"Keep her head up! Keep her head up!"

" 'Keep her head up,' sir." The voices were weary and low.

This was surely a quiet evening. All save the oarsman lay heavily and listlessly in the boat's bottom. As for him, his eyes were just capable of noting the tall black waves that swept forward in a most sinister silence, save for an occasional subdued growl of a crest.

The cook's head was on a thwart, and he looked without interest at the water under his nose. He was deep in other scenes. Finally he spoke. "Billie," he murmured, dreamfully, "what kind of pie do you like best?"

V

"Pie," said the oiler and the correspondent, agitatedly. "Don't talk about those things, blast you!"

"Well," said the cook, "I was just thinking about ham sandwiches, and——"

A night on the sea in an open boat is a long night. As darkness settled finally, the shine of the light, lifting from the sea in the south, changed to full gold. On the northern horizon a new light appeared, a small bluish gleam on the edge of the waters. These two lights were the furniture of the world. Otherwise there was nothing but waves.

Two men huddled in the stern, and distances were so magnificent in the dingey that the rower was enabled to keep his feet partly warmed by thrusting them under his companions. Their legs indeed extended far under the rowing-seat until they touched the feet of the captain forward. Sometimes, despite the efforts of the tired oarsman, a wave came piling into the boat, an icy wave of the night, and the chilling water soaked them anew. They would twist their bodies for a moment and groan, and sleep the dead sleep once more, while the water in the boat gurgled about them as the craft rocked.

The plan of the oiler and the correspondent was for one to row until he lost the ability, and then arouse the other from his sea-water couch in the bottom of the boat.

The oiler plied the oars until his head drooped forward, and the overpowering sleep blinded him. And he rowed yet afterward. Then he touched a man in the bottom of the boat, and called his name. "Will you spell me for a little while?" he said, meekly.

"Sure, Billie," said the correspondent, awakening and dragging himself to a sitting position. They exchanged places carefully, and the oiler, cuddling down in the sea-water at the cook's side, seemed to go to sleep instantly.

The particular violence of the sea had ceased. The waves came without snarling. The obligation of the man at the oars was to keep the boat headed so that the tilt of the rollers would not capsize her, and to preserve her from filling when the crests rushed past. The black waves were silent and hard to be seen in the darkness. Often one was almost upon the boat before the oarsman was aware.

In a low voice the correspondent addressed the captain. He was not sure that the captain was awake, although this iron man seemed to be always awake. "Captain, shall I keep her making for that light north, sir?"

The same steady voice answered him. "Yes. Keep it about two points off the port bow."

The cook had tied a life-belt around himself in order to get even the warmth which this clumsy cork contrivance could donate, and he seemed almost stove-like when a rower, whose teeth invariably chattered wildly as soon as he ceased his labor, dropped down to sleep.

The correspondent, as he rowed, looked down at the two men sleeping under foot. The cook's arm was around the oiler's shoulders, and, with their fragmentary clothing and haggard faces, they were the babes of the sea, a grotesque rendering of the old babes in the wood.

Later he must have grown stupid at his work, for suddenly there was a growling of water, and a crest came with a roar and a swash into the boat, and it was a wonder that it did not set the cook afloat in his life-belt. The cook continued to sleep, but the oiler sat up, blinking his eyes and shaking with the new cold.

"Oh, I'm awful sorry, Billie," said the correspondent, contritely.

"That's all right, old boy," said the oiler, and lay down again and was asleep.

Presently it seemed that even the captain dozed, and the correspondent thought that he was the one man afloat on all the oceans. The wind had a voice as it came over the waves, and it was sadder than the end.

There was a long, loud swishing astern of the boat, and a gleaming trail of phosphorescence, like blue flame, was furrowed on the black waters. It might have been made by a monstrous knife.

Then there came a stillness, while the correspondent breathed with the open mouth and looked at the sea.

Suddenly there was another swish and another long flash of bluish light, and this time it was alongside the boat, and might almost have been reached with an oar. The correspondent saw an enormous fin speed like a shadow through the water, hurling the crystalline spray and leaving the long glowing trail.

The correspondent looked over his shoulder at the captain. His face was hidden, and he seemed to be asleep. He looked at the babes of the sea. They certainly were asleep. So, being bereft of sympathy, he leaned a little way to one side and swore softly into the sea.

But the thing did not then leave the vicinity of the boat. Ahead or astern, on one side or the other, at intervals long or short, fled the long sparkling streak, and there was to be heard the whirroo of the dark fin. The speed and power of the thing were greatly to be admired. It cut the water like a gigantic and keen projectile.

The presence of this biding thing did not affect the man with the same horror that it would if he had been a picnicker. He simply looked at the sea dully and swore in an undertone.

Nevertheless, it is true that he did not wish to be alone with the thing. He wished one of his companions to awaken by chance and keep him company with it. But the captain hung motionless over the water-jar and the oiler and the cook in the bottom of the boat were plunged in slumber.

VI

"If I am going to be drowned — if I am going to be drowned — if I am going to be drowned, why, in the name of the seven mad gods who rule the sea, was I allowed to come thus far and contemplate sand and trees?"

During this dismal night, it may be remarked that a man would conclude that it was really the intention of the seven mad gods to drown him, despite the abominable injustice of it. For it was certainly an abominable injustice to drown a man who had worked so hard, so hard. The man felt it would be a crime most unnatural. Other people had drowned at sea since galleys swarmed with painted sails, but still —

When it occurs to a man that nature does not regard him as important, and that she feels she would not maim the universe by disposing of him, he at first wishes to throw bricks at the temple, and he hates deeply the fact that there are no bricks and no temples. Any visible expression of nature would surely be pelleted with his jeers.

Then, if there be no tangible thing to hoot he feels, perhaps, the desire to confront a personification and indulge in pleas, bowed to one knee, and with hands supplicant, saying: "Yes, but I love myself."

A high cold star on a winter's night is the word he feels that she says to him. Thereafter he knows the pathos of his situation.

The men in the dingey had not discussed these matters, but each had, no doubt, reflected upon them in silence and according to his mind. There was seldom any expression upon their faces save the general one of complete weariness. Speech was devoted to the business of the boat.

To chime the notes of his emotion, a verse mysteriously entered the correspondent's head. He had even forgotten that he had forgotten this verse, but it suddenly was in his mind.

> A soldier of the Legion lay dying in Algiers,
> There was lack of woman's nursing, there was dearth of woman's tears;
> But a comrade stood beside him, and he took that comrade's hand,
> And he said: "I never more shall see my own, my native land."

In his childhood, the correspondent had been made acquainted with the fact that a soldier of the Legion lay dying in Algiers, but he had never

regarded it as important. Myriads of his school-fellows had informed him of
the soldier's plight, but the dinning had naturally ended by making him
perfectly indifferent. He had never considered it his affair that a soldier of
the Legion lay dying in Algiers, nor had it appeared to him as a matter for
sorrow. It was less to him than the breaking of a pencil's point.

Now, however, it quaintly came to him as a human, living thing. It
was no longer merely a picture of a few throes in the breast of a poet,
meanwhile drinking tea and warming his feet at the grate; it was an actuality — stern, mournful, and fine.

The correspondent plainly saw the soldier. He lay on the sand with his
feet out straight and still. While his pale left hand was upon his chest in an
attempt to thwart the going of his life, the blood came between his fingers.
In the far Algerian distance, a city of low square forms was set against a sky
that was faint with the last sunset hues. The correspondent, plying the oars
and dreaming of the slow and slower movements of the lips of the soldier,
was moved by a profound and perfectly impersonal comprehension. He was
sorry for the soldier of the Legion who lay dying in Algiers.

The thing which had followed the boat and waited had evidently
grown bored at the delay. There was no longer to be heard the slash of the
cut-water, and there was no longer the flame of the long trail. The light in
the north still glimmered, but it was apparently no nearer to the boat.
Sometimes the boom of the surf rang in the correspondent's ears, and he
turned the craft seaward then and rowed harder. Southward, some one had
evidently built a watch-fire on the beach. It was too low and too far to be
seen, but it made a shimmering, roseate reflection upon the bluff back of it,
and this could be discerned from the boat. The wind came stronger, and
sometimes a wave suddenly raged out like a mountain-cat and there was to
be seen the sheen and sparkle of a broken crest.

The captain, in the bow, moved on his water-jar and sat erect. "Pretty
long night," he observed to the correspondent. He looked at the shore.
"Those life-saving people take their time."

"Did you see that shark playing around?"

"Yes, I saw him. He was a big fellow, all right."

"Wish I had known you were awake."

Later the correspondent spoke into the bottom of the boat.

"Billie!" There was a slow and gradual disentanglement. "Billie, will
you spell me?"

"Sure," said the oiler.

As soon as the correspondent touched the cold comfortable sea-water
in the bottom of the boat, and had huddled close to the cook's life-belt he
was deep in sleep, despite the fact that his teeth played all the popular airs.
This sleep was so good to him that it was but a moment before he heard a
voice call his name in a tone that demonstrated the last stages of exhaustion. "Will you spell me?"

"Sure, Billie."

The light in the north had mysteriously vanished, but the correspondent took his course from the wide-awake captain.

Later in the night they took the boat farther out to sea, and the captain directed the cook to take one oar at the stern and keep the boat facing the seas. He was to call out if he should hear the thunder of the surf. This plan enabled the oiler and the correspondent to get respite together. "We'll give those boys a chance to get into shape again," said the captain. They curled down and, after a few preliminary chatterings and trembles, slept once more the dead sleep. Neither knew they had bequeathed to the cook the company of another shark, or perhaps the same shark.

As the boat caroused on the waves, spray occasionally bumped over the side and gave them a fresh soaking, but this had no power to break their repose. The ominous slash of the wind and the water affected them as it would have affected mummies.

"Boys," said the cook, with the notes of every reluctance in his voice, "she's drifted in pretty close. I guess one of you had better take her to sea again." The correspondent, aroused, heard the crash of the toppled crests.

As he was rowing, the captain gave him some whiskey and water, and this steadied the chills out of him. "If I ever get ashore and anybody shows me even a photograph of an oar — "

At last there was a short conversation.

"Billie. . . . Billie, will you spell me?"

"Sure," said the oiler.

VII

When the correspondent again opened his eyes, the sea and the sky were each of the gray hue of the dawning. Later, carmine and gold was painted upon the waters. The morning appeared finally, in its splendor, with a sky of pure blue, and the sunlight flamed on the tips of the waves.

On the distant dunes were set many little black cottages, and a tall white wind-mill reared above them. No man, nor dog, nor bicycle appeared on the beach. The cottages might have formed a deserted village.

The voyagers scanned the shore. A conference was held in the boat. "Well," said the captain, "if no help is coming, we might better try a run through the surf right away. If we stay out here much longer we will be too weak to do anything for ourselves at all." The others silently acquiesced in this reasoning. The boat was headed for the beach. The correspondent wondered if none ever ascended the tall wind-tower, and if then they never looked seaward. This tower was a giant, standing with its back to the plight of the ants. It represented in a degree, to the correspondent, the serenity of nature amid the struggles of the individual — nature in the wind, and nature in the vision of men. She did not seem cruel to him then, nor beneficent, nor treacherous, nor wise. But she was indifferent, flatly indifferent. It is, perhaps, plausible that a man in this situation, impressed with the unconcern of the universe, should see the innumerable flaws of his life and have them taste wickedly in his mind and wish for another chance. A distinction between right and wrong seems absurdly clear to him, then, in this new ignorance of the grave-edge, and he understands that if he were given another opportunity he would mend his conduct and his words, and be better and brighter during an introduction, or at a tea.

"Now, boys," said the captain, "she is going to swamp sure. All we can do is to work her in as far as possible, and then when she swamps, pile out and scramble for the beach. Keep cool now, and don't jump until she swamps sure."

The oiler took the oars. Over his shoulders he scanned the surf. "Captain," he said, "I think I'd better bring her about, and keep her head-on to the seas and back her in."

"All right, Billie," said the captain. "Back her in." The oiler swung the boat then and, seated in the stern, the cook and the correspondent were obliged to look over their shoulders to contemplate the lonely and indifferent shore.

The monstrous inshore rollers heaved the boat high until the men were again enabled to see the white sheets of water scudding up the slanted beach. "We won't get in very close," said the captain. Each time a man could wrest his attention from the rollers, he turned his glance toward the shore, and in the expression of the eyes during this contemplation there was a singular quality. The correspondent, observing the others, knew that they were not afraid, but the full meaning of their glances was shrouded.

As for himself, he was too tired to grapple fundamentally with the fact. He tried to coerce his mind into thinking of it, but the mind was dominated at this time by the muscles, and the muscles said they did not care. It merely occurred to him that if he should drown it would be a shame.

There were no hurried words, no pallor, no plain agitation. The men simply looked at the shore. "Now, remember to get well clear of the boat when you jump," said the captain.

Seaward the crest of a roller suddenly fell with a thunderous crash, and the long white comber came roaring down upon the boat.

"Steady now," said the captain. The men were silent. They turned their eyes from the shore to the comber and waited. The boat slid up the incline, leaped at the furious top, bounced over it, and swung down the long back of the wave. Some water had been shipped and the cook bailed it out.

But the next crest crashed also. The tumbling boiling flood of white water caught the boat and whirled it almost perpendicular. Water swarmed in from all sides. The correspondent had his hands on the gunwale at this time, and when the water entered at that place he swiftly withdrew his fingers, as if he objected to wetting them.

The little boat, drunken with this weight of water, reeled and snuggled deeper into the sea.

"Bail her out, cook! Bail her out," said the captain.

"All right, Captain," said the cook.

"Now boys, the next one will do for us, sure," said the oiler. "Mind to jump clear of the boat."

The third wave moved forward, huge, furious, implacable. It fairly swallowed the dingey, and almost simultaneously the men tumbled into the sea. A piece of life-belt had lain in the bottom of the boat, and as the correspondent went overboard he held this to his chest with his left hand.

The January water was icy, and he reflected immediately that it was colder than he had expected to find it off the coast of Florida. This appeared to his dazed mind as a fact important enough to be noted at the time. The coldness of the water was sad; it was tragic. This fact was somehow so mixed and confused with his opinion of his own situation that it seemed almost a proper reason for tears. The water was cold.

When he came to the surface he was conscious of little but the noisy water. Afterward he saw his companions in the sea. The oiler was ahead in the race. He was swimming strongly and rapidly. Off to the correspondent's left, the cook's great white and corked back bulged out of the water, and in the rear the captain was hanging with his one good hand to the keel of the overturned dingey.

There is a certain immovable quality to a shore, and the correspondent wondered at it amid the confusion of the sea.

It seemed also very attractive, but the correspondent knew that it was a long journey, and he paddled leisurely. The piece of life-preserver lay under him, and sometimes he whirled down the incline of a wave as if he were on a hand-sled.

But finally he arrived at a place in the sea where travel was beset with difficulty. He did not pause swimming to inquire what manner of current had caught him, but there his progress ceased. The shore was set before him like a bit of scenery on a stage, and he looked at it and understood with his eyes each detail of it.

As the cook passed, much farther to the left, the captain was calling to him, "Turn over on your back, cook! Turn over on your back and use the oar."

"All right, sir." The cook turned on his back, and, paddling with an oar, went ahead as if he were a canoe.

Presently the boat also passed to the left of the correspondent with the captain clinging with one hand to the keel. He would have appeared like a man raising himself to look over a board fence, if it were not for the extraordinary gymnastics of the boat. The correspondent marvelled that the captain could still hold to it.

They passed on, nearer to shore — the oiler, the cook, the captain — and following them went the water-jar, bouncing gayly over the seas.

The correspondent remained in the grip of this strange new enemy — a current. The shore, with its white slope of sand and its green bluff, topped with little silent cottages, was spread like a picture before him. It was very near to him then, but he was impressed as one who in a gallery looks at a scene from Brittany or Holland.

He thought: "I am going to drown? Can it be possible? Can it be possible? Can it be possible?" Perhaps an individual must consider his own death to be the final phenomenon of nature.

But later a wave perhaps whirled him out of his small deadly current, for he found suddenly that he could again make progress toward the shore. Later still, he was aware that the captain, clinging with one hand to the keel of the dingey, had his face turned away from the shore and toward him, and was calling his name. "Come to the boat! Come to the boat!"

In his struggle to reach the captain and the boat, he reflected that when one gets properly wearied, drowning must really be a comfortable arrangement, a cessation of hostilities accompanied by a large degree of relief, and he was glad of it, for the main thing in his mind for some moments had been the horror of the temporary agony. He did not wish to be hurt.

Presently he saw a man running along the shore. He was undressing with most remarkable speed. Coat, trousers, shirt, everything flew magically off him.

"Come to the boat," called the captain.

"All right, Captain." As the correspondent paddled, he saw the captain let himself down to bottom and leave the boat. Then the correspondent performed his one little marvel of the voyage. A large wave caught him and flung him with ease and supreme speed completely over the boat and far beyond it. It struck him even then as an event in gymnastics, and a true miracle of the sea. An overturned boat in the surf is not a plaything to a swimming man.

The correspondent arrived in water that reached only to his waist, but his condition did not enable him to stand for more than a moment. Each wave knocked him into a heap, and the under-tow pulled at him.

Then he saw the man who had been running and undressing, and undressing and running, come bounding into the water. He dragged ashore the cook, and then waded toward the captain, but the captain waved him away, and sent him to the correspondent. He was naked, naked as a tree in winter, but a halo was about his head, and he shone like a saint. He gave a strong pull, and a long drag, and a bully heave at the correspondent's hand. The correspondent, schooled in the minor formulae, said: "Thanks, old man." But suddenly the man cried: "What's that?" He pointed a swift finger. The correspondent said: "Go."

In the shallows, face downward, lay the oiler. His forehead touched sand that was periodically, between each wave, clear of the sea.

The correspondent did not know all that transpired afterward. When he achieved safe ground he fell, striking the sand with each particular part of his body. It was as if he had dropped from a roof, but the thud was grateful to him.

It seems that instantly the beach was populated with men with blankets, clothes, and flasks, and women with coffee-pots and all the remedies
sacred to their minds. The welcome of the land to the men from the sea was
warm and generous, but a still and dripping shape was carried slowly up the
beach, and the land's welcome for it could only be the different and sinister
hospitality of the grave.

When it came night, the white waves paced to and fro in the moonlight, and the wind brought the sound of the great sea's voice to the men on
shore, and they felt that they could then be interpreters.

[1897]

Stephen Crane

⚡

THE BRIDE COMES TO YELLOW SKY

I

The great Pullman was whirling onward with such dignity of motion
that a glance from the window seemed simply to prove that the plains of
Texas were pouring eastward. Vast flats of green grass, dull-hued spaces of
mesquit and cactus, little groups of frame houses, woods of light and tender
trees, all were sweeping into the east, sweeping over the horizon, a precipice.

A newly married pair had boarded this coach at San Antonio. The
man's face was reddened from many days in the wind and sun, and a direct
result of his new black clothes was that his brick-colored hands were constantly performing in a most conscious fashion. From time to time he
looked down respectfully at his attire. He sat with a hand on each knee, like
a man waiting in a barber's shop. The glances he devoted to other passengers were furtive and shy.

The bride was not pretty, nor was she very young. She wore a dress of
blue cashmere, with small reservations of velvet here and there, and with
steel buttons abounding. She continually twisted her head to regard her
puff sleeves, very stiff, straight, and high. They embarrassed her. It was
quite apparent that she had cooked, and that she expected to cook, dutifully. The blushes caused by the careless scrutiny of some passengers as she
had entered the car were strange to see upon this plain, under-class countenance, which was drawn in placid, almost emotionless lines.

They were evidently very happy. "Ever been in a parlor-car before?" he asked, smiling with delight.

"No," she answered; "I never was. It's fine, ain't it?"

"Great! And then after a while we'll go forward to the diner, and get a big lay-out. Finest meal in the world. Charge a dollar."

"Oh, do they?" cried the bride. "Charge a dollar? Why, that's too much — for us — ain't it, Jack?"

"Not this trip, anyhow," he answered bravely. "We're going to go the whole thing."

Later he explained to her about the trains. "You see, it's a thousand miles from one end of Texas to the other; and this train runs right across it, and never stops but four times." He had the pride of an owner. He pointed out to her the dazzling fittings of the coach; and in truth her eyes opened wider as she contemplated the sea-green figured velvet, the shining brass, silver, and glass, the wood that gleamed as darkly brilliant as the surface of a pool of oil. At one end a bronze figure sturdily held a support for a separated chamber, and at convenient places on the ceiling were frescos in olive and silver.

To the minds of the pair, their surroundings reflected the glory of their marriage that morning in San Antonio; this was the environment of their new estate; and the man's face in particular beamed with an elation that made him appear ridiculous to the negro porter. This individual at times surveyed them from afar with an amused and superior grin. On other occasions he bullied them with skill in ways that did not make it exactly plain to them that they were being bullied. He subtly used all the manners of the most unconquerable kind of snobbery. He oppressed them; but of this oppression they had small knowledge, and they speedily forgot that infrequently a number of travellers covered them with stares of derisive enjoyment. Historically there was supposed to be something infinitely humorous in their situation.

"We are due in Yellow Sky at 3:42," he said, looking tenderly into her eyes.

"Oh, are we?" she said, as if she had not been aware of it. To evince surprise at her husband's statement was part of her wifely amiability. She took from a pocket a little silver watch; and as she held it before her, and stared at it with a frown of attention, the new husband's face shone.

"I bought it in San Anton' from a friend of mine," he told her gleefully.

"It's seventeen minutes past twelve," she said, looking up at him with a kind of shy and clumsy coquetry. A passenger, noting this play, grew excessively sardonic, and winked at himself in one of the numerous mirrors.

At last they went to the dining-car. Two rows of negro waiters, in glowing white suits, surveyed their entrance with the interest, and also the equanimity, of men who had been forewarned. The pair fell to the lot of a waiter who happened to feel pleasure in steering them through their meal. He viewed them with the manner of a fatherly pilot, his countenance radiant with benevolence. The patronage, entwined with the ordinary deference, was not plain to them. And yet, as they returned to their coach, they showed in their faces a sense of escape.

To the left, miles down a long purple slope, was a little ribbon of mist where moved the keening Rio Grande. The train was approaching it at an angle, and the apex was Yellow Sky. Presently it was apparent that, as the distance from Yellow Sky grew shorter, the husband became commensurately restless. His brick-red hands were more insistent in their prominence. Occasionally he was even rather absent-minded and far-away when the bride leaned forward and addressed him.

As a matter of truth, Jack Potter was beginning to find the shadow of a deed weigh upon him like a leaden slab. He, the town marshal of Yellow Sky, a man known, liked, and feared in his corner, a prominent person, had gone to San Antonio to meet a girl he believed he loved, and there, after the usual prayers, had actually induced her to marry him, without consulting Yellow Sky for any part of the transaction. He was now bringing his bride before an innocent and unsuspecting community.

Of course people in Yellow Sky married as it pleased them in accordance with a general custom; but such was Potter's thought of his duty to his friends, or of their idea of his duty, or of an unspoken form which does not control men in these matters, that he felt he was heinous. He had committed an extraordinary crime. Face to face with this girl in San Antonio, and spurred by his sharp impulse, he had gone headlong over all the social hedges. At San Antonio he was like a man hidden in the dark. A knife to sever any friendly duty, any form, was easy to his hand in that remote city. But the hour of Yellow Sky — the hour of daylight — was approaching.

He knew full well that his marriage was an important thing to his town. It could only be exceeded by the burning of the new hotel. His friends could not forgive him. Frequently he had reflected on the advisability of telling them by telegraph, but a new cowardice had been upon him. He feared to do it. And now the train was hurrying him toward a scene of amazement, glee, and reproach. He glanced out of the window at the line of haze swinging slowly in toward the train.

Yellow Sky had a kind of brass band, which played painfully, to the delight of the populace. He laughed without heart as he thought of it. If the citizens could dream of his prospective arrival with his bride, they would parade the band at the station and escort them, amid cheers and laughing congratulations, to his adobe home.

He resolved that he would use all the devices of speed and plainscraft in making the journey from the station to his house. Once within that safe citadel, he could issue some sort of vocal bulletin, and then not go among the citizens until they had time to wear off a little of their enthusiasm.

The bride looked anxiously at him. "What's worrying you, Jack?"

He laughed again. "I'm not worrying, girl; I'm only thinking of Yellow Sky."

She flushed in comprehension.

A sense of mutual guilt invaded their minds and developed a finer tenderness. They looked at each other with eyes softly aglow. But Potter often laughed the same nervous laugh; the flush upon the bride's face seemed quite permanent.

The traitor to the feelings of Yellow Sky narrowly watched the speeding landscape. "We're nearly there," he said.

Presently the porter came and announced the proximity of Potter's home. He held a brush in his hand, and, with all his airy superiority gone, he brushed Potter's new clothes as the latter slowly turned this way and that way. Potter fumbled out a coin and gave it to the porter, as he had seen others do. It was a heavy and muscle-bound business, as that of a man shoeing his first horse.

The porter took their bag, and as the train began to slow they moved forward to the hooded platform of the car. Presently the two engines and their long string of coaches rushed into the station of Yellow Sky.

"They have to take water here," said Potter, from a constricted throat and in mournful cadence, as one announcing death. Before the train stopped his eye had swept the length of the platform, and he was glad and astonished to see there was none upon it but the station-agent, who, with a slightly hurried and anxious air, was walking toward the water-tanks. When the train had halted, the porter alighted first, and placed in position a little temporary step.

"Come on, girl," said Potter, hoarsely. As he helped her down they each laughed on a false note. He took the bag from the negro, and bade his wife cling to his arm. As they slunk rapidly away, his hang-dog glance perceived that they were unloading the two trunks, and also that the station-agent, far ahead near the baggage-car, had turned and was running toward him, making gestures. He laughed, and groaned as he laughed, when he noted the first effect of his marital bliss upon Yellow Sky. He gripped his wife's arm firmly to his side, and they fled. Behind them the porter stood, chuckling fatuously.

II

The California express on the Southern Railway was due at Yellow Sky in twenty-one minutes. There were six men at the bar of the Weary Gentleman saloon. One was a drummer who talked a great deal and rapidly; three were Texans who did not care to talk at that time; and two were Mexican sheep-herders, who did not talk as a general practice in the Weary Gentleman saloon. The barkeeper's dog lay on the board walk that crossed in front of the door. His head was on his paws, and he glanced drowsily here and there with the constant vigilance of a dog that is kicked on occasion.

Across the sandy street were some vivid green grass-plots, so wonderful in appearance, amid the sands that burned near them in a blazing sun, that they caused a doubt in the mind. They exactly resembled the grass mats used to represent lawns on the stage. At the cooler end of the railway station, a man without a coat sat in a tilted chair and smoked his pipe. The fresh-cut bank of the Rio Grande circled near the town, and there could be seen beyond it a great plum-colored plain of mesquit.

Save for the busy drummer and his companions in the saloon, Yellow Sky was dozing. The new-comer leaned gracefully upon the bar, and recited many tales with the confidence of a bard who has come upon a new field.

"— and at the moment that the old man fell downstairs with the bureau in his arms, the old woman was coming up with two scuttles of coal, and of course —"

The drummer's tale was interrupted by a young man who suddenly appeared in the open door. He cried: "Scratchy Wilson's drunk, and has turned loose with both hands." The two Mexicans at once set down their glasses and faded out of the rear entrance of the saloon.

The drummer, innocent and jocular, answered: "All right, old man. S'pose he has? Come in and have a drink, anyhow."

But the information had made such an obvious cleft in every skull in the room that the drummer was obliged to see its importance. All had become instantly solemn. "Say," said he, mystified, "what is this?" His three companions made the introductory gesture of eloquent speech; but the young man at the door forestalled them.

"It means, my friend," he answered, as he came into the saloon, "that for the next two hours this town won't be a health resort."

The barkeeper went to the door, and locked and barred it; reaching out of the window, he pulled in heavy wooden shutters, and barred them. Immediately a solemn, chapel-like gloom was upon the place. The drummer was looking from one to another.

"But, say," he cried, "what is this, anyhow? You don't mean there is going to be a gun-fight?"

"Don't know whether there'll be a fight or not," answered one man, grimly; "but there'll be some shootin' — some good shootin'."

The young man who had warned them waved his hand. "Oh, there'll be a fight fast enough, if any one wants it. Anybody can get a fight out there in the street. There's a fight just waiting."

The drummer seemed to be swayed between the interest of a foreigner and a perception of personal danger.

"What did you say his name was?" he asked.

"Scratchy Wilson," they answered in chorus.

"And will he kill anybody? What are you going to do? Does this happen often? Does he rampage around like this once a week or so? Can he break in that door?"

"No; he can't break down that door," replied the barkeeper. "He's tried it three times. But when he comes you'd better lay down on the floor, stranger. He's dead sure to shoot at it, and a bullet may come through."

Thereafter the drummer kept a strict eye upon the door. The time had not yet called for him to hug the floor, but, as a minor precaution, he sidled near the wall. "Will he kill anybody?" he said again.

The men laughed low and scornfully at the question.

"He's out to shoot, and he's out for trouble. Don't see any good in experimentin' with him."

"But what do you do in a case like this? What do you do?"

A man responded: "Why, he and Jack Potter —"

"But," in chorus the other men interrupted, "Jack Potter's in San Anton'."

"Well, who is he? What's he got to do with it?"

"Oh, he's the town marshal. He goes out and fights Scratchy when he gets on one of these tears."

"Wow!" said the drummer, mopping his brow. "Nice job he's got."

The voices had toned away to mere whisperings. The drummer wished to ask further questions, which were born of an increasing anxiety and bewilderment; but when he attempted them, the men merely looked at him in irritation and motioned him to remain silent. A tense waiting hush was upon them. In the deep shadows of the room their eyes shone as they listened for sounds from the street. One man made three gestures at the barkeeper; and the latter, moving like a ghost, handed him a glass and a bottle. The man poured a full glass of whisky, and set down the bottle noiselessly. He gulped the whisky in a swallow, and turned again toward the door in immovable silence. The drummer saw that the barkeeper, without a sound, had taken a Winchester from beneath the bar. Later he saw this individual beckoning to him, so he tiptoed across the room.

"You better come with me back of the bar."

"No, thanks," said the drummer, perspiring; "I'd rather be where I can make a break for the back door."

Whereupon the man of bottles made a kindly but peremptory gesture. The drummer obeyed it, and, finding himself seated on a box with his head below the level of the bar, balm was laid upon his soul at sight of various zinc and copper fittings that bore a resemblance to armor-plate. The barkeeper took a seat comfortably upon an adjacent box.

"You see," he whispered, "this here Scratchy Wilson is a wonder with a gun — a perfect wonder; and when he goes on the war-trail, we hunt our holes — naturally. He's about the last one of the old gang that used to hang out along the river here. He's a terror when he's drunk. When he's sober he's all right — kind of simple — wouldn't hurt a fly — nicest fellow in town. But when he's drunk — whoo!"

There were periods of stillness. "I wish Jack Potter was back from San Anton'," said the barkeeper. "He shot Wilson up once — in the leg — and he would sail in and pull out the kinks in this thing."

Presently they heard from a distance the sound of a shot, followed by three wild yowls. It instantly removed a bond from the men in the darkened saloon. There was a shuffling of feet. They looked at each other. "Here he comes," they said.

III

A man in a maroon-colored flannel shirt, which had been purchased for purposes of decoration, and made principally by some Jewish women on the East Side of New York, rounded a corner and walked into the middle of the main street of Yellow Sky. In either hand the man held a long, heavy, blue-black revolver. Often he yelled, and these cries rang through a semblance of a deserted village, shrilly flying over the roofs in a volume that seemed to have no relation to the ordinary vocal strength of a man. It was as if the surrounding stillness formed the arch of a tomb over him. These cries of ferocious challenge rang against walls of silence. And his boots had red tops with gilded imprints, of the kind beloved in winter by little sledding boys on the hillsides of New England.

The man's face flamed in a rage begot of whisky. His eyes, rolling, and yet keen for ambush, hunted the still doorways and windows. He walked with the creeping movement of the midnight cat. As it occurred to him, he roared menacing information. The long revolvers in his hands were as easy as straws; they were removed with an electric swiftness. The little fingers of each hand played sometimes in a musician's way. Plain from the low collar of the shirt, the cords of his neck straightened and sank, straightened and sank, as passion moved him. The only sounds were his terrible invitations. The calm adobes preserved their demeanor at the passing of this small thing in the middle of the street.

There was no offer of fight — no offer of fight. The man called to the sky. There were no attractions. He bellowed and fumed and swayed his revolvers here and everywhere.

The dog of the barkeeper of the Weary Gentleman saloon had not appreciated the advance of events. He yet lay dozing in front of his master's door. At sight of the dog, the man paused and raised his revolver humorously. At sight of the man, the dog sprang up and walked diagonally away, with a sullen head, and growling. The man yelled, and the dog broke into a gallop. As it was about to enter the alley, there was a loud noise, a whistling, and something spat the ground directly before it. The dog screamed, and, wheeling in terror, galloped headlong in a new direction. Again there was a noise, a whistling, and sand was kicked viciously before it. Fear-stricken, the dog turned and flurried like an animal in a pen. The man stood laughing, his weapons at his hips.

Ultimately the man was attracted by the closed door of the Weary Gentleman saloon. He went to it and, hammering with a revolver, demanded drink.

The door remaining imperturbable, he picked a bit of paper from the walk, and nailed it to the framework with a knife. He then turned his back contemptuously upon this popular resort and, walking to the opposite side of the street and spinning there on his heel quickly and lithely, fired at the bit of paper. He missed it by a half inch. He swore at himself, and went away. Later he comfortably fusilladed the windows of his most intimate friend. The man was playing with this town; it was a toy for him.

But still there was no offer of fight. The name of Jack Potter, his ancient antagonist, entered his mind, and he concluded that it would be a glad thing if he should go to Potter's house, and by bombardment induce him to come out and fight. He moved in the direction of his desire, chanting Apache scalp-music.

When he arrived at it, Potter's house presented the same still front as had the other adobes. Taking up a strategic position, the man howled a challenge. But this house regarded him as might a great stone god. It gave no sign. After a decent wait, the man howled further challenges, mingling with them wonderful epithets.

Presently there came the spectacle of a man churning himself into deepest rage over the immobility of a house. He fumed at it as the winter wind attacks a prairie cabin in the North. To the distance there should have gone the sound of a tumult like the fighting of two hundred Mexicans. As necessity bade him, he paused for breath or to reload his revolvers.

IV

Potter and his bride walked sheepishly and with speed. Sometimes they laughed together shamefacedly and low.

"Next corner, dear," he said finally.

They put forth the efforts of a pair walking bowed against a strong wind. Potter was about to raise a finger to point the first appearance of the new home when, as they circled the corner, they came face to face with a man in a maroon-colored shirt, who was feverishly pushing cartridges into a large revolver. Upon the instant the man dropped his revolver to the ground and, like lightning, whipped another from its holster. The second weapon was aimed at the bridegroom's chest.

There was a silence. Potter's mouth seemed to be merely a grave for his tongue. He exhibited an instinct to at once loosen his arm from the woman's grip, and he dropped the bag to the sand. As for the bride, her face had gone as yellow as old cloth. She was a slave to hideous rites, gazing at the apparitional snake.

The two men faced each other at a distance of three paces. He of the revolver smiled with a new and quiet ferocity.

"Tried to sneak up on me," he said. "Tried to sneak up on me!" His eyes grew more baleful. As Potter made a slight movement, the man thrust his revolver venomously forward. "No; don't you do it, Jack Potter. Don't you move a finger toward a gun just yet. Don't you move an eyelash. The time has come for me to settle with you and I'm goin' to do it my own way, and loaf along with no interferin'. So if you don't want a gun bent on you, just mind what I tell you."

Potter looked at his enemy. "I ain't got a gun on me, Scratchy," he said. "Honest, I ain't." He was stiffening and steadying, but yet somewhere at the back of his mind a vision of the Pullman floated: the sea-green figured velvet, the shining brass, silver, and glass, the wood that gleamed as darkly brilliant as the surface of a pool of oil — all the glory of marriage, the environment of the new estate. "You know I fight when it comes to fighting, Scratchy Wilson; but I ain't got a gun on me. You'll have to do all the shootin' yourself."

His enemy's face went livid. He stepped forward, and lashed his weapon to and fro before Potter's chest. "Don't you tell me you ain't got no gun on you, you whelp. Don't tell me no lie like that. There ain't a man in Texas ever seen you without no gun. Don't take me for no kid." His eyes blazed with light, and his throat worked like a pump.

"I ain't takin' you for no kid," answered Potter. His heels had not moved an inch backward. "I'm takin' you for a damn fool. I tell you I ain't got a gun, and I ain't. If you're goin' to shoot me up, you better begin now; you'll never get a chance like this again."

So much enforced reasoning had told on Wilson's rage; he was calmer. "If you ain't got a gun, why ain't you got a gun?" he sneered. "Been to Sunday-school?"

"I ain't got a gun because I've just come from San Anton' with my wife. I'm married," said Potter. "And if I'd thought there was going to be any galoots like you prowling around when I brought my wife home, I'd had a gun, and don't you forget it."

"Married!" said Scratchy, not at all comprehending.

"Yes, married. I'm married," said Potter, distinctly.

"Married?" said Scratchy. Seemingly for the first time, he saw the drooping, drowning woman at the other man's side. "No!" he said. He was like a creature allowed a glimpse of another world. He moved a pace backward, and his arm, with the revolver, dropped to his side. "Is this the lady?" he asked.

"Yes; this is the lady," answered Potter.

There was another period of silence.

"Well," said Wilson at last, slowly, "I s'pose it's all off now."

"It's all off if you say so, Scratchy. You know I didn't make the trouble." Potter lifted his valise.

"Well, I 'low it's off, Jack," said Wilson. He was looking at the ground. "Married!" He was not a student of chivalry; it was merely that in the presence of this foreign condition he was a simple child of the earlier plains. He picked up his starboard revolver, and, placing both weapons in their holsters, he went away. His feet made funnel-shaped tracks in the heavy sand.

[1898]

WILLA CATHER *(1873–1947) once wrote that "a creative writer can do his best only with what lies within the range and character of his deepest sympathies." She herself was thirty-nine before her true subject came into focus for her. Born in rural Virginia, she moved to Nebraska with her family nine years later. The oldest of seven children, she was raised in a loving home, but her strongest response to the frontier prairie village of Red Cloud, Nebraska, where her family finally settled, was the urge to escape. She went to a preparatory school in Lincoln, where she also continued at the University of Nebraska, studying classics. After her graduation in 1895 she went to Pittsburgh, where she worked as a journalist for seven years and then for another three years teaching English and Latin in high schools. At this time her stories and poems began to appear in popular magazines. Her first book was a volume of poetry,* April Twilights *(1903), followed in 1905 by* The Troll Gardens, *the first of four collections of short stories. In 1906 she joined the staff of* McClure's *magazine in New York City, assuming the position of managing editor before she left to devote full time to her writing.*

As a university student Cather read the fiction of Gustave Flaubert, whose restraint as a stylist she admired, but the most important influence on her work was Sarah Orne Jewett, who taught her that beautiful writing was a consequence of steady concentration on a thoroughly understood scene. Cather met Jewett in Boston, and Jewett urged her to develop her talents as a writer, advising her to "find your own quiet center of life and write to the human heart, the great consciousness that all humanity goes to make up." It was not until 1912 that Cather found her subject, after a trip home to Red Cloud. She no longer saw her adolescence on the prairie as deprived and stifling, and she was able to feel that her own experience was significant enough to write about. O Pioneers! *(1913), the first of three novels about immigrant life on the western frontier, was followed in 1915 by* The Song of the Lark *and in 1918 by* My Ántonia, *a portrait of a pioneer woman that is generally regarded as her masterpiece.*

Cather went on to publish a total of twelve novels and several collections of stories, many about artists, but she did not value her forty-four stories as highly as her novels, including only three of them in the definitive "Library Edition" that represents her final judgment of her work. She wrote "Paul's Case," a story about a sensitive boy who hungers for art and feels oppressed by everyday life, while she was still a high school teacher in Pittsburgh. Many critics have commented on the purity of Cather's prose style. Her early study of classical languages and her admiration of Flaubert helped form her attitudes toward rigorous control in her realistic fiction. Cather was also a perceptive literary critic. She published a collection of essays, On Writing *(1949), in which she analyzed the subtle magic of the storyteller's* art: *"Whatever is felt on the page without being specifically named there — that, one might say, is created." (See Cather's Commentary about Mansfield on page 1277.)*

Willa Cather

ᔕᙚ

PAUL'S CASE

It was Paul's afternoon to appear before the faculty of the Pittsburgh High School to account for his various misdemeanors. He had been suspended a week ago, and his father had called at the Principal's office and confessed his perplexity about his son. Paul entered the faculty room suave and smiling. His clothes were a trifle outgrown and the tan velvet on the collar of his open overcoat was frayed and worn; but for all that there was something of the dandy about him, and he wore an opal pin in his neatly knotted black four-in-hand, and a red carnation in his buttonhole. This latter adornment the faculty somehow felt was not properly significant of the contrite spirit befitting a boy under the ban of suspension.

Paul was tall for his age and very thin, with high, cramped shoulders and a narrow chest. His eyes were remarkable for a certain hysterical brilliancy and he continually used them in a conscious, theatrical sort of way, peculiarly offensive in a boy. The pupils were abnormally large, as though he were addicted to belladonna, but there was a glassy glitter about them which that drug does not produce.

When questioned by the Principal as to why he was there, Paul stated, politely enough, that he wanted to come back to school. This was a lie, but Paul quite accustomed to lying; found it, indeed, indispensable for overcoming friction. His teachers were asked to state their respective charges against him, which they did with such a rancor and aggrievedness as evinced that this was not a usual case. Disorder and impertinence were among the offenses named, yet each of his instructors felt that it was scarcely possible to put into words the real cause of the trouble, which lay in a sort of hysterically defiant manner of the boy's; in the contempt which they all knew he felt for them, and which he seemingly made not the least effort to conceal. Once, when he had been making a synopsis of a paragraph at the blackboard, his English teacher had stepped to his side and attempted to guide his hand. Paul had started back with a shudder and thrust his hands violently behind him. The astonished woman could scarcely have been more hurt and embarrassed had he struck at her. The insult was so involuntary and definitely personal as to be unforgettable. In one way and another, he had made all his teachers, men and women alike, conscious of the same feeling of physical aversion. In one class he habitually sat with his hand shading his eyes; in another he always looked out of the window during the recitation; in another he made a running commentary on the lecture, with humorous intention.

His teachers felt this afternoon that his whole attitude was symbolized by his shrug and his flippantly red carnation flower, and they fell upon him without mercy, his English teacher leading the pack. He stood through it smiling, his pale lips parted over his white teeth. (His lips were continually twitching, and he had a habit of raising his eyebrows that was contemptuous and irritating to the last degree.) Older boys than Paul had broken down and shed tears under that baptism of fire, but his set smile did not once desert him, and his only sign of discomfort was the nervous trembling of the fingers that toyed with the buttons of his overcoat, and an occasional jerking of the other hand that held his hat. Paul was always smiling, always glancing about him, seeming to feel that people might be watching him and trying to detect something. This conscious expression, since it was as far as possible from boyish mirthfulness, was usually attributed to insolence or "smartness."

As the inquisition proceeded, one of his instructors repeated an impertinent remark of the boy's, and the Principal asked him whether he thought that a courteous speech to have made a woman. Paul shrugged his shoulders slightly and his eyebrows twitched.

"I don't know," he replied. "I didn't mean to be polite or impolite, either. I guess it's a sort of way I have of saying things regardless."

The Principal, who was a sympathetic man, asked him whether he didn't think that a way it would be well to get rid of. Paul grinned and said he guessed so. When he was told that he could go, he bowed gracefully and went out. His bow was but a repetition of the scandalous red carnation.

His teachers were in despair, and his drawing master voiced the feeling of them all when he declared there was something about the boy which none of them understood. He added: "I don't really believe that smile of his comes altogether from insolence; there's something sort of haunted about it. The boy is not strong, for one thing. I happen to know that he was born in Colorado, only a few months before his mother died out there of a long illness. There is something wrong about the fellow."

The drawing master had come to realize that, in looking at Paul, one saw only his white teeth and the forced animation of his eyes. One warm afternoon the boy had gone to sleep at his drawing-board, and his master had noted with amazement what a white, blue-veined face it was; drawn and wrinkled like an old man's about the eyes, the lips twitching even in his sleep, and stiff with a nervous tension that drew them back from his teeth.

His teachers left the building dissatisfied and unhappy; humiliated to have felt so vindictive toward a mere boy, to have uttered this feeling in cutting terms, and to have set each other on, as it were, in the gruesome game of intemperate reproach. Some of them remembered having seen a miserable street cat set at bay by a ring of tormentors.

As for Paul, he ran down the hill whistling the Soldiers' Chorus from *Faust* looking wildly behind him now and then to see whether some of his teachers were not there to writhe under this light-heartedness. As it was now late in the afternoon and Paul was on duty that evening as usher at Carnegie Hall, he decided that he would not go home to supper. When he reached the concert hall the doors were not yet open and, as it was chilly outside, he decided to go up into the picture gallery — always deserted at this hour — where there were some of Raffelli's gay studies of Paris streets and an airy blue Venetian scene or two that always exhilarated him. He was delighted to find no one in the gallery but the old guard, who sat in one corner, a newspaper on his knee, a black patch over one eye and the other closed. Paul possessed himself of the place and walked confidently up and down, whistling under his breath. After a while he sat down before a blue Rico and lost himself. When he bethought him to look at his watch, it was after seven o'clock, and he rose with a start and ran downstairs, making a face at Augustus, peering out from the cast-room, and an evil gesture at the Venus of Milo as he passed her on the stairway.

When Paul reached the ushers' dressing-room half-a-dozen boys were there already, and he began excitedly to tumble into his uniform. It was one of the few that at all approached fitting, and Paul thought it very becoming — though he knew that the tight, straight coat accentuated his narrow chest, about which he was exceedingly sensitive. He was always considerably excited while he dressed, twanging all over to the tuning of the strings and the preliminary flourishes of the horns in the music-room; but to-night he seemed quite beside himself, and he teased and plagued the boys until, telling him that he was crazy, they put him down on the floor and sat on him.

Somewhat calmed by his suppression, Paul dashed out to the front of the house to seat the early comers. He was a model usher; gracious and smiling he ran up and down the aisles; nothing was too much trouble for him; he carried messages and brought programmes as though it were his greatest pleasure in life, and all the people in his section thought him a charming boy, feeling that he remembered and admired them. As the house filled, he grew more and more vivacious and animated, and the color came to his cheeks and lips. It was very much as though this were a great reception and Paul were the host. Just as the musicians came out to take their places, his English teacher arrived with checks for the seats which a prominent manufacturer had taken for the season. She betrayed some embarrassment when she handed Paul the tickets, and a *hauteur* which subsequently made her feel very foolish. Paul was startled for a moment, and had the feeling of wanting to put her out; what business had she here among all these fine people and gay colors? He looked her over and decided that she was not appropriately dressed and must be a fool to sit downstairs in such togs. The tickets had probably been sent her out of kindness, he reflected as he put down a seat for her, and she had about as much right to sit there as he had.

When the symphony began Paul sank into one of the rear seats with a long sigh of relief, and lost himself as he had done before the Rico. It was not that symphonies, as such, meant anything in particular to Paul, but the first sigh of the instruments seemed to free some hilarious and potent spirit within him; something that struggled there like the Genius in the bottle found by the Arab fisherman. He felt a sudden zest of life; the lights danced before his eyes and the concert hall blazed into unimaginable splendor. When the soprano soloist came on, Paul forgot even the nastiness of his teacher's being there and gave himself up to the peculiar stimulus such personages always had for him. The soloist chanced to be a German woman, by no means in her first youth, and the mother of many children; but she wore an elaborate gown and a tiara, and above all she had that indefinable air of achievement, that world-shine upon her, which, in Paul's eyes, made her a veritable queen of Romance.

After a concert was over Paul was always irritable and wretched until he got to sleep, and tonight he was even more than usually restless. He had the feeling of not being able to let down, of its being impossible to give up this delicious excitement which was the only thing that could be called living at all. During the last number he withdrew and, after hastily changing his clothes in the dressing-room, slipped out to the side door where the soprano's carriage stood. Here he began pacing rapidly up and down the walk, waiting to see her come out.

Over yonder the Schenley, in its vacant stretch, loomed big and square through the fine rain, the windows of its twelve stories glowing like those of a lighted cardboard house under a Christmas tree. All the actors and singers of the better class stayed there when they were in the city, and a number of the big manufacturers of the place lived there in the winter. Paul had often hung about the hotel, watching the people go in and out, longing to enter and leave school-masters and dull care behind him forever.

At last the singer came out, accompanied by the conductor, who helped her into her carriage and closed the door with a cordial *auf wiedersehen* which set Paul to wondering whether she were not an old sweetheart of his. Paul followed the carriage over to the hotel, walking so rapidly as not to be far from the entrance when the singer alighted and disappeared behind the swinging glass doors that were opened by a negro in a tall hat and a long coat. In the moment that the door was ajar it seemed to Paul that he, too, entered. He seemed to feel himself go after her up the steps, into the warm, lighted building, into an exotic, a tropical world of shiny, glistening surfaces and basking ease. He reflected upon the mysterious dishes that were brought into the dining-room, the green bottles in buckets of ice, as he had seen them in the supper party pictures of the *Sunday World* supplement. A quick gust of wind brought the rain down with sudden vehemence, and Paul was startled to find that he was still outside in the slush of the gravel driveway; that his boots were letting in the water and his scanty overcoat was clinging wet about him; that the lights in front of the concert hall were out, and that the rain was driving in sheets between him and the orange glow of the windows above him. There it was, what he wanted — tangibly before him, like the fairy world of a Christmas pantomime, but mocking spirits stood guard at the doors, and, as the rain beat in his face, Paul wondered whether he were destined always to shiver in the black night outside, looking up at it.

He turned and walked reluctantly toward the car tracks. The end had to come sometime; his father in his night-clothes at the top of the stairs, explanations that did not explain, hastily improvised fictions that were forever tripping him up, his upstairs room and its horrible yellow wall-paper, the creaking bureau with the greasy plush collar-box, and over his painted wooden bed the pictures of George Washington and John Calvin, and the framed motto, "Feed my Lambs," which had been worked in red worsted by his mother.

Half an hour later, Paul alighted from his car and went slowly down one of the side streets off the main thoroughfare. It was a highly respectable street, where all the houses were exactly alike, and where businessmen of moderate means begot and reared large families of children, all of whom went to Sabbath-school and learned the shorter catechism, and were interested in arithmetic; all of whom were as exactly alike as their homes, and of a piece with the monotony in which they lived. Paul never went up Cordelia Street without a shudder of loathing. His home was next to the house of the Cumberland minister. He approached it tonight with the nerveless sense of defeat, the hopeless feeling of sinking back forever into ugliness and commonness that he had always had when he came home. The moment he turned into Cordelia Street he felt the waters close above his head. After each of these orgies of living, he experienced all the physical depression which follows a debauch; the loathing of respectable beds, of common food, of a house penetrated by kitchen odors; a shuddering repulsion for the flavorless, colorless mass of every-day existence; a morbid desire for cool things and soft lights and fresh flowers.

The nearer he approached the house, the more absolutely unequal Paul felt to the sight of it all; his ugly sleeping chamber; the cold bathroom with the grimy zinc tub, the cracked mirror, the dripping spiggots; his father, at the top of the stairs, his hairy legs sticking out from his night-shirt, his feet thrust into carpet slippers. He was so much later than usual that there would certainly be inquiries and reproaches. Paul stopped short before the door. He felt that he could not be accosted by his father tonight; that he could not toss again on that miserable bed. He would not go in. He would tell his father that he had no car fare, and it was raining so hard he had gone home with one of the boys and stayed all night.

Meanwhile, he was wet and cold. He went around to the back of the house and tried one of the basement windows, found it open, raised it cautiously, and scrambled down the cellar wall to the floor. There he stood, holding his breath, terrified by the noise he had made, but the floor above him was silent, and there was no creak on the stairs. He found a soap-box, and carried it over to the soft ring of light that streamed from the furnace door, and sat down. He was horribly afraid of rats, so he did not try to sleep, but sat looking distrustfully at the dark, still terrified lest he might have awakened his father. In such reactions, after one of the experiences which made days and nights out of the dreary blanks of the calendar, when his senses were deadened, Paul's head was always singularly clear. Suppose his father had heard him getting in at the window and had come down and shot him for a burglar? Then, again, suppose his father had come down, pistol in hand, and he had cried out in time to save himself, and his father had been horrified to think how nearly he had killed him? Then, again, suppose a day should come when his father would remember that night, and wish there had been no warning cry to stay his hand? With this last supposition Paul entertained himself until daybreak.

The following Sunday was fine; the sodden November chill was broken by the last flash of autumnal summer. In the morning Paul had to go to church and Sabbath-school, as always. On seasonable Sunday afternoons the burghers of Cordelia Street always sat out on their front "stoops," and talked to their neighbors on the next stoop, or called to those across the street in neighborly fashion. The men usually sat on gay cushions placed upon the steps that led down to the sidewalk, while the women, in their Sunday "waists," sat in rockers on the cramped porches, pretending to be greatly at their ease. The children played in the streets; there were so many of them that the place resembled the recreation grounds of a kindergarten. The men on the steps — all in their shirt sleeves, their vests unbuttoned — sat with their legs well apart, their stomachs comfortably protruding, and talked of the prices of things, or told anecdotes of the sagacity of their various chiefs and overlords. They occasionally looked over the multitude of squabbling children, listened affectionately to their high-pitched, nasal voices, smiling to see their own proclivities reproduced in their offspring, and interspersed their legends of the iron kings with remarks about their sons' progress at school, their grades in arithmetic, and the amounts they had saved in their toy banks.

On this last Sunday of November, Paul sat all the afternoon on the lowest step of his "stoop," staring into the street, while his sisters, in their rockers, were talking to the minister's daughters next door about how many shirt-waists they had made in the last week, and how many waffles some one had eaten at the last church supper. When the weather was warm, and his father was in a particularly jovial frame of mind, the girls made lemonade, which was always brought out in a red-glass pitcher, ornamented with forget-me-nots in blue enamel. This the girls thought very fine, and the neighbors always joked about the suspicious color of the pitcher.

Today Paul's father sat on the top step, talking to a young man who shifted a restless baby from knee to knee. He happened to be the young man who was daily held up to Paul as a model, and after whom it was his father's dearest hope that he would pattern. This young man was of a ruddy complexion, with a compressed, red mouth, and faded, near-sighted eyes, over which he wore thick spectacles, with gold bows that curved about his ears. He was clerk to one of the magnates of a great steel corporation, and was looked upon in Cordelia Street as a young man with a future. There was a story that, some five years ago — he was now barely twenty-six — he had been a trifle dissipated but in order to curb his appetites and save the loss of time and strength that a sowing of wild oats might have entailed, he had taken his chief's advice, oft reiterated to his employees, and at twenty-one had married the first woman whom he could persuade to share his fortunes. She happened to be an angular school-mistress, much older than he, who also wore thick glasses, and who had now borne him four children, all near-sighted, like herself.

The young man was relating how his chief, now cruising in the Mediterranean, kept in touch with all the details of the business, arranging his office hours on his yacht just as though he were at home, and "knocking off work enough to keep two stenographers busy." His father told, in turn, the plan his corporation was considering, of putting in an electric railway plant at Cairo. Paul snapped his teeth; he had an awful apprehension that they might spoil it all before he got there. Yet he rather liked to hear these legends of the iron kings, that were told and retold on Sundays and holidays; these stories of palaces in Venice, yachts on the Mediterranean, and high play at Monte Carlo appealed to his fancy, and he was interested in the triumphs of these cash boys who had become famous, though he had no mind for the cash-boy stage.

After supper was over, and he had helped to dry the dishes, Paul nervously asked his father whether he could go to George's to get some help in his geometry, and still more nervously asked for car fare. This latter request he had to repeat, as his father, on principle, did not like to hear requests for money, whether much or little. He asked Paul whether he could not go to some boy who lived nearer, and told him that he ought not to leave his school work until Sunday; but he gave him the dime. He was not a poor man, but he had a worthy ambition to come up in the world. His only reason for allowing Paul to usher was, that he thought a boy ought to be earning a little.

Paul bounded upstairs, scrubbed the greasy odor of the dish-water from his hands with the ill-smelling soap he hated, and then shook over his fingers a few drops of violet water from the bottle he kept hidden in his drawer. He left the house with his geometry conspicuously under his arm, and the moment he got out of Cordelia Street and boarded a downtown car, he shook off the lethargy of two deadening days, and began to live again.

The leading juvenile of the permanent stock company which played at one of the downtown theatres was an acquaintance of Paul's, and the boy had been invited to drop in at the Sunday-night rehearsals whenever he could. For more than a year Paul had spent every available moment loitering about Charley Edwards's dressing-room. He had won a place among Edwards's following not only because the young actor, who could not afford to employ a dresser, often found him useful, but because he recognized in Paul something akin to what churchmen term "vocation."

It was at the theatre and at Carnegie Hall that Paul really lived; the rest was but a sleep and a forgetting. This was Paul's fairy tale, and it had for him all the allurement of a secret love. The moment he inhaled the gassy, painty, dusty odor behind the scenes, he breathed like a prisoner set free, and felt within him the possibility of doing or saying splendid, brilliant, poetic things. The moment the cracked orchestra beat out the overture from *Martha*, or jerked at the serenade from *Rigoletto*, all stupid and ugly things slid from him, and his senses were deliciously, yet delicately fired.

Perhaps it was because, in Paul's world, the natural nearly always wore the guise of ugliness, that a certain element of artificiality seemed to him necessary in beauty. Perhaps it was because his experience of life elsewhere was so full of Sabbath-school picnics, petty economies, wholesome advice as to how to succeed in life, and the unescapable odors of cooking, that he found this existence so alluring, these smartly-clad men and women so attractive, that he was so moved by these starry apple orchards that bloomed perennially under the lime-light.

It would be difficult to put it strongly enough how convincingly the stage entrance of that theatre was for Paul the actual portal of Romance. Certainly none of the company ever suspected it, least of all Charley Edwards. It was very like the old stories that used to float about London of fabulously rich Jews, who had subterranean halls there, with palms, and fountains, and soft lamps and richly apparelled women who never saw the disenchanting light of London day. So, in the midst of that smoke-palled city, enamored of figures and grimy toil, Paul had his secret temple, his wishing carpet, his bit of blue-and-white Mediterranean shore bathed in perpetual sunshine.

Several of Paul's teachers had a theory that his imagination had been perverted by garish fiction, but the truth was that he scarcely ever read at all. The books at home were not such as would either tempt or corrupt a youthful mind, and as for reading the novels that some of his friends urged upon him — well, he got what he wanted much more quickly from music; any sort of music, from an orchestra to a barrel organ. He needed only the spark, the indescribable thrill that made his imagination master of his senses, and he could make plots and pictures enough of his own. It was equally true that he was not stage struck — not, at any rate, in the usual acceptation of that expression. He had no desire to become an actor, any more than he had to become a musician. He felt no necessity to do any of these things; what he wanted was to see, to be in the atmosphere, float on the wave of it, to be carried out, blue league after blue league, away from everything.

After a night behind the scenes, Paul found the school-room more than ever repulsive; the bare floors and naked walls; the prosy men who never wore frock coats, or violets in their buttonholes; the women with their dull gowns, shrill voices, and pitiful seriousness about prepositions that govern the dative. He could not bear to have the other pupils think, for a moment, that he took these people seriously; he must convey to them that he considered it all trivial, and was there only by way of a jest, anyway. He had autographed pictures of all the members of the stock company which he showed his classmates, telling them the most incredible stories of his familiarity with these people, of his acquaintance with the soloists who came to Carnegie Hall, his suppers with them and the flowers he sent them. When these stories lost their effect, and his audience grew listless, he became desperate and would bid all the boys good-bye, announcing that he was going to travel for a while; going to Naples, to Venice, to Egypt. Then, next Monday, he would slip back, conscious and nervously smiling; his sister was ill, and he should have to defer his voyage until spring.

Matters went steadily worse with Paul at school. In the itch to let his instructors know how heartily he despised them and their homilies, and how thoroughly he was appreciated elsewhere, he mentioned once or twice that he had no time to fool with theorems; adding — with a twitch of the eyebrows and a touch of that nervous bravado which so perplexed them — that he was helping the people down at the stock company; they were old friends of his.

The upshot of the matter was that the Principal went to Paul's father, and Paul was taken out of school and put to work. The manager at Carnegie Hall was told to get another usher in his stead; the door-keeper at the theatre was warned not to admit him to the house; and Charley Edwards remorsefully promised the boy's father not to see him again.

The members of the stock company were vastly amused when some of Paul's stories reached them — especially the women. They were hard-working women, most of them supporting indigent husbands or brothers, and they laughed rather bitterly at having stirred the boy to such fervid and florid inventions. They agreed with the faculty and with his father that Paul's was a bad case.

The east-bound train was ploughing through a January snow-storm; the dull dawn was beginning to show grey when the engine whistled a mile out of Newark. Paul started up from the seat where he had lain curled in uneasy slumber, rubbed the breath-misted window glass with his hand, and peered out. The snow was whirling in curling eddies above the white bottom lands, and the drifts lay already deep in the fields and along the fences, while here and there the long dead grass and dried weed stalks protruded black above it. Lights shone from the scattered houses, and a gang of laborers who stood beside the track waved their lanterns.

Paul had slept very little, and he felt grimy and uncomfortable. He had made the all-night journey in a day coach, partly because he was ashamed, dressed as he was, to go into a Pullman, and partly because he was afraid of being seen there by some Pittsburgh businessman, who might have noticed him in Denny & Carson's office. When the whistle awoke him, he clutched quickly at his breast pocket, glancing about him with an uncertain smile. But the little, clay-bespattered Italians were still sleeping, the slatternly women across the aisle were in open-mouthed oblivion, and even the crumby, crying babies were for the nonce stilled. Paul settled back to struggle with his impatience as best he could.

When he arrived at the Jersey City station, he hurried through his breakfast, manifestly ill at ease and keeping a sharp eye about him. After he reached the Twenty-third Street station, he consulted a cabman, and had himself driven to a men's furnishing establishment that was just opening for the day. He spent upward of two hours there, buying with endless reconsidering and great care. His new street suit he put on in the fitting-room; the frock coat and dress clothes he had bundled into the cab with his linen. Then he drove to a hatter's and a shoe house. His next errand was at Tiffany's, where he selected his silver and a new scarf-pin. He would not wait to have his silver marked, he said. Lastly, he stopped at a trunk shop on Broadway, and had his purchases packed into various travelling bags.

It was a little after one o'clock when he drove up to the Waldorf, and after settling with the cabman, went into the office. He registered from Washington; said his mother and father had been abroad, and that he had come down to await the arrival of their steamer. He told his story plausibly and had no trouble, since he volunteered to pay for them in advance, in engaging his rooms; a sleeping-room, sitting-room, and bath.

Not once, but a hundred times Paul had planned this entry into New York. He had gone over every detail of it with Charley Edwards, and in his scrap book at home there were pages of description about New York hotels, cut from the Sunday papers. When he was shown to his sitting-room on the eighth floor, he saw at a glance that everything was as it should be; there was but one detail in his mental picture that the place did not realize, so he rang for the bell boy and sent him down for flowers. He moved about nervously until the boy returned, putting away his new linen and fingering it delightedly as he did so. When the flowers came, he put them hastily into water, and then tumbled into a hot bath. Presently he came out of his white bath-room, resplendent in his new silk underwear, and playing with the tassels of his red robe. The snow was whirling so fiercely outside his windows that he could scarcely see across the street, but within the air was deliciously soft and fragrant. He put the violets and jonquils on the taboret beside the couch, and threw himself down, with a long sigh, covering himself with a Roman blanket. He was thoroughly tired; he had been in such haste, he had stood up to such a strain, covered so much ground in the last twenty-four hours, that he wanted to think how it had all come about. Lulled by the sound of the wind, the warm air, and the cool fragrance of the flowers, he sank into deep, drowsy retrospection.

It had been wonderfully simple; when they had shut him out of the theatre and concert hall, when they had taken away his bone, the whole thing was virtually determined. The rest was a mere matter of opportunity. The only thing that at all surprised him was his own courage — for he realized well enough that he had always been tormented by fear, a sort of apprehensive dread that, of late years, as the meshes of the lies he had told closed about him, had been pulling the muscles of his body tighter and tighter. Until now, he could not remember the time when he had not been dreading something. Even when he was a little boy, it was always there — behind him, or before, or on either side. There had always been the shadowed corner, the dark place into which he dared not look, but from which something seemed always to be watching him — and Paul had done things that were not pretty to watch, he knew.

But now he had a curious sense of relief, as though he had at last thrown down the gauntlet to the thing in the corner.

Yet it was but a day since he had been sulking in the traces; but yesterday afternoon that he had been sent to the bank with Denny & Carson's deposit, as usual — but this time he was instructed to leave the book to be balanced. There was above two thousand dollars in checks, and nearly a thousand in the bank notes which he had taken from the book and quietly transferred to his pocket. At the bank he had made out a new deposit slip. His nerves had been steady enough to permit of his returning to the office, where he had finished his work and asked for a full day's holiday tomorrow, Saturday, giving a perfectly reasonable pretext. The bank book, he knew, would not be returned before Monday or Tuesday, and his father would be out of town for the next week. From the time he slipped the bank notes into his pocket until he boarded the night train for New York, he had not known a moment's hesitation. It was not the first time Paul had steered through treacherous waters.

How astonishingly easy it had all been; here he was, the thing done; and this time there would be no awakening, no figure at the top of the stairs. He watched the snow flakes whirling by his window until he fell asleep.

When he awoke, it was three o'clock in the afternoon. He bounded up with a start; half of one of his precious days gone already! He spent more than an hour in dressing, watching every stage of his toilet carefully in the mirror. Everything was quite perfect; he was exactly the kind of boy he had always wanted to be.

When he went downstairs, Paul took a carriage and drove up Fifth Avenue toward the Park. The snow had somewhat abated; carriages and tradesmen's wagons were hurrying soundlessly to and fro in the winter twilight; boys in woollen mufflers were shovelling off the doorsteps; the avenue stages made fine spots of color against the white street. Here and there on the corners were stands, with whole flower gardens blooming under glass cases, against the sides of which the snow flakes stuck and melted; violets, roses, carnations, lilies of the valley — somewhat vastly more lovely and alluring that they blossomed thus unnaturally in the snow. The Park itself was a wonderful stage winterpiece.

When he returned, the pause of the twilight had ceased, and the tune of the streets had changed. The snow was falling faster, lights streamed from the hotels that reared their dozen stories fearlessly up into the storm, defying the raging Atlantic winds. A long, black stream of carriages poured down the avenue, intersected here and there by other streams, tending horizontally. There were a score of cabs about the entrance of his hotel, and his driver had to wait. Boys in livery were running in and out of the awning stretched across the sidewalk, up and down the red velvet carpet laid from the door to the street. Above, about, within it all was the rumble and roar, the hurry and toss of thousands of human beings as hot for pleasure as himself, and on every side of him towered the glaring affirmation of the omnipotence of wealth.

The boy set his teeth and drew his shoulders together in a spasm of realization: the plot of all dramas, the text of all romances, the nerve-stuff of all sensations was whirling about him like the snow flakes. He burnt like a faggot in a tempest.

When Paul went down to dinner, the music of the orchestra came floating up the elevator shaft to greet him. His head whirled as he stepped into the thronged corridor, and he sank back into one of the chairs against the wall to get his breath. The lights, the chatter, the perfumes, the bewildering medley of color — he had, for a moment, the feeling of not being able to stand it. But only for a moment; these were his own people, he told himself. He went slowly about the corridors, through the writing-rooms, smoking-rooms, reception-rooms, as though he were exploring the chambers of an enchanted palace, built and peopled for him alone.

When he reached the dining-room he sat down at a table near a window. The flowers, the white linen, the many-colored wine glasses, the gay toilettes of the women, the low popping of corks, the undulating repetitions of the Blue Danube from the orchestra, all flooded Paul's dream with bewildering radiance. When the roseate tinge of his champagne was added — that cold, precious, bubbling stuff that creamed and foamed in his glass — Paul wondered that there were honest men in the world at all. This was what all the world was fighting for, he reflected; this was what all the struggle was about. He doubted the reality of his past. Had he ever known a place called Cordelia Street, a place where fagged-looking businessmen got on the early car; mere rivets in a machine they seemed to Paul — sickening men, with combings of children's hair always hanging to their coats, and the smell of cooking in their clothes. Cordelia Street — Ah! that belonged to another time and country; had he not always been thus, had he not sat here night after night, from as far back as he could remember, looking pensively over just such shimmering textures, and slowly twirling the stem of a glass like this one between his thumb and middle finger? He rather thought he had.

He was not in the least abashed or lonely. He had no especial desire to meet or to know any of these people; all he demanded was the right to look on and conjecture, to watch the pageant. The mere stage properties were all he contended for. Nor was he lonely later in the evening, in his loge at the Metropolitan. He was now entirely rid of his nervous misgivings, of his forced aggressiveness, of the imperative desire to show himself different from his surroundings. He felt now that his surroundings explained him. Nobody questioned the purple; he had only to wear it passively. He had only to glance down at his attire to reassure himself that here it would be impossible for anyone to humiliate him.

He found it hard to leave his beautiful sitting-room to go to bed that night, and sat long watching the raging storm from his turret window. When he went to sleep it was with the lights turned on in his bedroom; partly because of his old timidity, and partly so that, if he should wake in the night, there would be no wretched moment of doubt, no horrible suspicion of yellow wall-paper, or of Washington and Calvin above his bed.

Sunday morning the city was practically snow-bound. Paul breakfasted late, and in the afternoon he fell in with a wild San Francisco boy, a freshman at Yale, who said he had run down for a "little flyer" over Sunday. The young man offered to show Paul the night side of the town, and the two boys went out together after dinner, not returning to the hotel until seven o'clock the next morning. They had started out in the confiding warmth of a champagne friendship, but their parting in the elevator was singularly cool. The freshman pulled himself together to make his train, and Paul went to bed. He awoke at two o'clock in the afternoon, very thirsty and dizzy, and rang for ice-water, coffee, and the Pittsburgh papers.

On the part of the hotel management, Paul excited no suspicion. There was this to be said for him, that he wore his spoils with dignity and in no way made himself conspicuous. Even under the glow of his wine he was never boisterous, though he found the stuff like a magician's wand for wonder-building. His chief greediness lay in his ears and eyes, and his excesses were not offensive ones. His dearest pleasures were the grey winter twilights in his sitting-room; his quiet enjoyment of his flowers, his clothes, his wide divan, his cigarette, and his sense of power. He could not remember a time when he had felt so at peace with himself. The mere release from the necessity of petty lying, lying every day and every day, restored his self-respect. He had never lied for pleasure, even at school; but to be noticed and admired, to assert his difference from other Cordelia Street boys; and he felt a good deal more manly, more honest, even, now that he had no need for boastful pretensions, now that he could, as his actor friends used to say, "dress the part." It was characteristic that remorse did not occur to him. His golden days went by without a shadow, and he made each as perfect as he could.

On the eighth day after his arrival in New York, he found the whole affair exploited in the Pittsburgh papers, exploited with a wealth of detail which indicated that local news of a sensational nature was at a low ebb. The firm of Denny & Carson announced that the boy's father had refunded the full amount of the theft, and that they had no intention of prosecuting. The Cumberland minister had been interviewed, and expressed his hope of yet reclaiming the motherless lad, and his Sabbath-school teacher declared that she would spare no effort to that end. The rumor had reached Pittsburgh that the boy had been seen in a New York hotel, and his father had gone East to find him and bring him home.

Paul had just come in to dress for dinner; he sank into a chair, weak to the knees, and clasped his head in his hands. It was to be worse than jail, even; the tepid waters of Cordelia Street were to close over him finally and forever. The grey monotony stretched before him in hopeless, unrelieved years; Sabbath-school, Young People's Meeting, the yellow-papered room, the damp dish-towels; it all rushed back upon him with a sickening vividness. He had the old feeling that the orchestra had suddenly stopped, the sinking sensation that the play was over. The sweat broke out on his face, and he sprang to his feet, looked about him with his white, conscious smile, and winked at himself in the mirror. With something of the old childish belief in miracles with which he had so often gone to class, all his lessons unlearned, Paul dressed and dashed whistling down the corridor to the elevator.

He had no sooner entered the dining-room and caught the measure of the music than his remembrance was lightened by his old elastic power of claiming the moment, mounting with it, and finding it all sufficient. The glare and glitter about him, the mere scenic accessories had again, and for the last time, their old potency. He would show himself that he was game, he would finish the thing splendidly. He doubted, more than ever, the existence of Cordelia Street, and for the first time he drank his wine recklessly. Was he not, after all, one of those fortunate beings born to the purple, was he not still himself and in his own place? He drummed a nervous accompaniment to the Pagliacci music and looked about him, telling himself over and over that it had paid.

He reflected drowsily, to the swell of the music and the chill sweetness of his wine, that he might have done it more wisely. He might have caught an outboard steamer and been well out of their clutches before now. But the other side of the world had seemed too far away and too uncertain then; he could not have waited for it; his need had been too sharp. If he had to choose over again, he would do the same thing tomorrow. He looked affectionately about the dining-room, now gilded with a soft mist. Ah, it had paid indeed!

Paul was awakened next morning by a painful throbbing in his head and feet. He had thrown himself across the bed without undressing, and had slept with his shoes on. His limbs and hands were lead heavy, and his tongue and throat were parched and burnt. There came upon him one of those fateful attacks of clear-headedness that never occurred except when he was physically exhausted and his nerves hung loose. He lay still and closed his eyes and let the tide of things wash over him.

His father was in New York; "stopping at some joint or other," he told himself. The memory of successive summers on the front stoop fell upon him like a weight of black water. He had not a hundred dollars left; and he knew now, more than ever, that money was everything, the wall that stood between all he loathed and all he wanted. The thing was winding itself up; he had thought of that on his first glorious day in New York, and had even provided a way to snap the thread. It lay on his dressing-table now; he had got it out last night when he came blindly up from dinner, but the shiny metal hurt his eyes, and he disliked the looks of it.

He rose and moved about with a painful effort, succumbing now and again to attacks of nausea. It was the old depression exaggerated; all the world had become Cordelia Street. Yet somehow he was not afraid of anything, was absolutely calm; perhaps because he had looked into the dark corner at last and knew. It was bad enough, what he saw there, but somehow not so bad as his long fear of it had been. He saw everything clearly now. He had a feeling that he had made the best of it, that he had lived the sort of life he was meant to live, and for half an hour he sat staring at the revolver. But he told himself that was not the way, so he went downstairs and took a cab to the ferry.

When Paul arrived at Newark, he got off the train and took another cab, directing the driver to follow the Pennsylvania tracks out of the town. The snow lay heavy on the roadways and had drifted deep in the open fields. Only here and there the dead grass or dried weed stalks projected, singularly black, above it. Once well into the country, Paul dismissed the carriage and walked, floundering along the tracks, his mind a medley of irrelevant things. He seemed to hold in his brain an actual picture of everything he had seen that morning. He remembered every feature of both his drivers, of the toothless old woman from whom he had bought the red flowers in his coat, the agent from whom he had got his ticket, and all of his fellow-passengers on the ferry. His mind, unable to cope with vital matters near at hand, worked feverishly and deftly at sorting and grouping these images. They made for him a part of the ugliness of the world, of the ache in his head, and the bitter burning on his tongue. He stooped and put a handful of snow into his mouth as he walked, but that, too, seemed hot. When he reached a little hillside, where the tracks ran through a cut some twenty feet below him, he stopped and sat down.

The carnations in his coat were drooping with the cold, he noticed; their red glory all over. It occurred to him that all the flowers he had seen in the glass cases that first night must have gone the same way, long before this. It was only one splendid breath they had, in spite of their brave mockery at the winter outside the glass; and it was a losing game in the end, it seemed, this revolt against the homilies by which the world is run. Paul took one of the blossoms carefully from his coat and scooped a little hole in the snow, where he covered it up. Then he dozed a while, from his weak condition, seemingly insensible to the cold.

The sound of an approaching train awoke him, and he started to his feet, remembering only his resolution, and afraid lest he should be too late. He stood watching the approaching locomotive, his teeth chattering, his lips drawn away from them in a frightened smile; once or twice he glanced nervously sidewise, as though he were being watched. When the right moment came, he jumped. As he fell, the folly of his haste occurred to him with merciless clearness, the vastness of what he had left undone. There flashed through his brain, clearer than ever before, the blue of Adriatic water, the yellow of Algerian sands.

He felt something strike his chest, and that his body was being thrown swiftly through the air, on and on, immeasurably far and fast, while his limbs were gently relaxed. Then, because the picture making mechanism was crushed, the disturbing visions flashed into black, and Paul dropped back into the immense design of things.

[1905]

JACK LONDON (1876–1916), unlike Bret Harte, Mark Twain, and most of the early American writers who wrote stories about the American West, was born in that region — in San Francisco. He had a hard childhood, forced to earn his own living by manual labor in a canning factory starting at age fifteen. Later he worked in a laundry, and still later he was a sailor. Descriptive writing came naturally to him, and two years before he graduated from Oakland High School he won first prize in a local newspaper's article contest for "Story of a Typhoon off the Coast of Japan." He attended the University of California at Berkeley for one semester, but he regarded himself as self-taught, reading Karl Marx and Friedrich Engels, Herbert Spencer, and Friedrich Nietzsche as a young man. He joined the Socialist Labor Party after he had become convinced that it was impossible for workers to secure better conditions without organizing to take over the means of production. In 1897 he joined the Klondike gold rush and spent the winter in the Yukon. Two years later, after his return from Alaska on a 2,000-mile boat trip down the Yukon River, he published his first professional story, "To the Man on the Trail," in the Overland Monthly, and began to write for his living. London's first collection of fiction, Son of the Wolf, appeared in 1900. His novel The Call of the Wild (1903) was his biggest success, selling 1.5 million copies, and he became the highest-paid author of his time. He regarded his adventure stories as inferior to his political writing, however; they were merely a means of making money to meet his expanding interests in social reform as a Socialist speaker and political candidate. He covered the Russian-Japanese War as a correspondent, and wrote articles on the San Francisco earthquake of 1906 and the Mexican revolution of 1914. Shortly before his death at the age of forty, he resigned from the Socialist Party "because of its lack of fire and fight, and its loss of emphasis on the class struggle." London's death, possibly by his own hand, strangely echoed the events of his semiautobiographical novel Martin Eden (1909), in which a writer achieves success, but after rejecting Socialist aims finds his life meaningless and commits suicide.

London produced almost fifty volumes of prose, including several collections of short stories such as Son of the Wolf, South Sea Tales (1911), and The House of Pride and Other Tales of Hawaii (1912). He learned to tell stories, he claimed, when he was bumming across the United States and had to decide exactly the right line to pitch between the moment the housewife opened the door and the moment she asked him what he wanted. He felt that poverty had made him hustle, but that only his good luck had prevented it from destroying him. Claiming "no mentor but myself" as a writer, he placed the highest value on original experience; the stamp of self on a writer's work was "a trademark of far greater value than copyright."

434

London's reputation as a storyteller has declined in the United States in recent times, but he remains one of our most translated authors. His literary style is simple, often journalistic, and his stories are known to countless readers around the world as embodying the theme of social protest and dramatizing this country's rugged pioneer experience. As Jorge Luis Borges has observed, the vitality which permeated London's life is apparent in his best work. "To Build a Fire" tells the story of a man's struggle against nature, trying to survive against impossible odds in a universe indifferent to individual fate.

Jack London

ᐁᐁ

To Build a Fire

Day had broken cold and grey, exceedingly cold and grey, when the man turned aside from the main Yukon trail and climbed the high earth-bank, where a dim and little-travelled trail led eastward through the fat spruce timberland. It was a steep bank, and he paused for breath at the top, excusing the act to himself by looking at his watch. It was nine o'clock. There was no sun nor hint of sun, though there was not a cloud in the sky. It was a clear day, and yet there seemed an intangible pall over the face of things, a subtle gloom that made the day dark, and that was due to the absence of sun. This fact did not worry the man. He was used to the lack of sun. It had been days since he had seen the sun, and he knew that a few more days must pass before that cheerful orb, due south, would just peep above the skyline and dip immediately from view.

The man flung a look back along the way he had come. The Yukon lay a mile wide and hidden under three feet of ice. On top of this ice were as many feet of snow. It was all pure white, rolling in gentle undulations where the ice jams of the freeze-up had formed. North and south, as far as his eye could see, it was unbroken white, save for a dark hairline that curved and twisted from around the spruce-covered island to the south, and that curved and twisted away into the north, where it disappeared behind another spruce-covered island. This dark hairline was the trail — the main trail — that led south five hundred miles to the Chilcoot Pass, Dyea, and salt water; and that led north seventy miles to Dawson, and still on to the north a thousand miles to Nulato, and finally to St. Michael, on Bering Sea, a thousand miles and half a thousand more.

But all this — the mysterious, far-reaching hairline trail, the absence of sun from the sky, the tremendous cold, and the strangeness and weirdness of it all — made no impression on the man. It was not because he was long used to it. He was a newcomer in the land, a *chechaquo*, and this was his first winter. The trouble with him was that he was without imagination. He was quick and alert in the things of life, but only in the things, and not in the significances. Fifty degrees below zero meant eighty-odd degrees of frost. Such fact impressed him as being cold and uncomfortable, and that was all. It did not lead him to meditate upon his frailty as a creature of temperature, and upon man's frailty in general, able only to live within certain narrow limits of heat and cold; and from there on it did not lead him to the conjectural field of immortality and man's place in the universe. Fifty degrees below zero stood for a bite of frost that hurt and that must be guarded against by the use of mittens, ear flaps, warm moccasins, and thick socks. Fifty degrees below zero. That there should be anything more to it than that was a thought that never entered his head.

As he turned to go on, he spat speculatively. There was a sharp explosive crackle that startled him. He spat again. And again, in the air, before it could fall to the snow, the spittle crackled. He knew that at fifty below spittle crackled on the snow, but this spittle had crackled in the air. Undoubtedly it was colder than fifty below — how much colder he did not know. But the temperature did not matter. He was bound for the old claim on the left fork of Henderson Creek, where the boys were already. They had come over across the divide from the Indian Creek country, while he had come the roundabout way to take a look at the possibilities of getting out logs in the spring from the islands in the Yukon. He would be in to camp by six o'clock; a bit after dark, it was true, but the boys would be there, a fire would be going, and a hot supper would be ready. As for lunch, he pressed his hand against the protruding bundle under his jacket. It was also under his shirt, wrapped up in a handkerchief and lying against the naked skin. It was the only way to keep the biscuits from freezing. He smiled agreeably to himself as he thought of those biscuits, each cut open and sopped in bacon grease, and each enclosing a generous slice of fried bacon.

He plunged in among the big spruce trees. The trail was faint. A foot of snow had fallen since the last sled had passed over, and he was glad he was without a sled, travelling light. In fact, he carried nothing but the lunch wrapped in the handkerchief. He was surprised, however, at the cold. It certainly was cold, he concluded, as he rubbed his numb nose and cheekbones with his mittened hand. He was a warm-whiskered man, but the hair on his face did not protect the high cheekbones and the eager nose that thrust itself aggressively into the frosty air.

At the man's heels trotted a dog, a big native husky, the proper wolf-dog, grey-coated and without any visible or temperamental difference from its brother, the wild wolf. The animal was depressed by the tremendous cold. It knew that it was no time for travelling. Its instinct told it a truer tale than was told to the man by the man's judgment. In reality, it was not merely colder than fifty below zero; it was colder than sixty below, than seventy below. It was seventy-five below zero. Since the freezing point is thirty-two above zero, it meant that one hundred and seven degrees of frost obtained. The dog did not know anything about thermometers. Possibly in its brain there was no sharp consciousness of a condition of very cold such as was in the man's brain. But the brute had its instinct. It experienced a vague but menacing apprehension that subdued it and made it slink along at the man's heels, and that made it question eagerly every unwonted movement of the man as if expecting him to go into camp or to seek shelter somewhere and build a fire. The dog had learned fire, and it wanted fire, or else to burrow under the snow and cuddle its warmth away from the air.

The frozen moisture of its breathing had settled on its fur in a fine powder of frost, and especially were its jowls, muzzle, and eyelashes whitened by its crystal breath. The man's red beard and moustache were likewise frosted, but more solidly, the deposit taking the form of ice and increasing with every warm, moist breath he exhaled. Also, the man was chewing tobacco, and the muzzle of ice held his lips so rigidly that he was unable to clear his chin when he expelled the juice. The result was a crystal beard of the color and solidity of amber that was increasing its length on his chin. If he fell down it would shatter itself, like glass, into brittle fragments. But he did not mind the appendage. It was the penalty all tobacco chewers paid in that country, and he had been out before in two cold snaps. They had not been so cold as this, he knew, but by the spirit thermometer at Sixty Mile he knew they had been registered at fifty below and at fifty-five.

He held on through the level stretch of woods for several miles, crossed a wide flat of nigger heads, and dropped down a bank to the frozen bed of a small stream. This was Henderson Creek, and he knew he was ten miles from the forks. He looked at his watch. It was ten o'clock. He was making four miles an hour, and he calculated that he would arrive at the forks at half-past twelve. He decided to celebrate that event by eating his lunch there.

The dog dropped in again at his heels, with a tail drooping discouragement, as the man swung along the creek bed. The furrow of the old sled trail was plainly visible, but a dozen inches of snow covered up the marks of the last runners. In a month no man had come up or down that silent creek. The man held steadily on. He was not much given to thinking, and just then particularly he had nothing to think about save that he would eat lunch at the forks and that at six o'clock he would be in camp with the boys. There was nobody to talk to; and, had there been, speech would have been impossible because of the ice muzzle on his mouth. So he continued monotonously to chew tobacco and to increase the length of his amber beard.

Once in a while the thought reiterated itself that it was very cold and that he had never experienced such cold. As he walked along he rubbed his cheekbones and nose with the back of his mittened hand. He did this automatically, now and again changing hands. But, rub as he would, the instant he stopped his cheekbones went numb, and the following instant the end of his nose went numb. He was sure to frost his cheeks; he knew that, and experienced a pang of regret that he had not devised a nose strap of the sort Bud wore in cold snaps. Such a strap passed across the cheeks, as well, and saved them. But it didn't matter much, after all. What were frosted cheeks? A bit painful, that was all; they were never serious.

Empty as the man's mind was of thoughts, he was keenly observant, and he noticed the changes in the creeks, the curves and bends and timber jams, and always he sharply noted where he placed his feet. Once, coming round a bend, he shied abruptly, like a startled horse, curved away from the place where he had been walking, and retreated several paces back along the trail. The creek he knew was frozen clear to the bottom — no creek could contain water in that arctic winter — but he knew also that there were springs that bubbled out from the hillsides and ran along under the snow and on top of the ice of the creek. He knew that the coldest snaps never froze these springs, and he knew likewise their danger. They were traps. They hid pools of water under the snow that might be three inches deep, or three feet. Sometimes a skin of ice half an inch thick covered them, and in turn was covered by the snow. Sometimes there were alternate layers of water and ice skin, so that when one broke through he kept on breaking through for a while, sometimes wetting himself to the waist.

That was why he had shied in such a panic. He had felt the give under his feet and heard the crackle of a snow-hidden ice skin. And to get his feet wet in such a temperature meant trouble and danger. At the very least it meant delay, for he would be forced to stop and build a fire, and under its protection to bare his feet while he dried his socks and moccasins. He stood and studied the creek bed and its banks, and decided that the flow of water came from the right. He reflected awhile, rubbing his nose and cheeks, then skirted to the left, stepping gingerly and testing the footing for each step. Once clear of the danger, he took a fresh chew of tobacco and swung along at his four-mile gait.

In the course of the next two hours he came upon several similar traps. Usually the snow above the hidden pools had a sunken, candied appearance that advertised the danger. Once again, however, he had a close call; and once, suspecting danger, he compelled the dog to go on in front. The dog did not want to go. It hung back until the man shoved it forward, and then it went quickly across the white, unbroken surface. Suddenly it broke through, floundered to one side, and got away to firmer footing. It had wet its forefeet and legs, and almost immediately the water that clung to it turned to ice. It made quick efforts to lick the ice off its legs, then dropped down in the snow and began to bite out the ice that had formed between the toes. This was a matter of instinct. To permit the ice to remain would mean sore feet. It did not know this. It merely obeyed the mysterious prompting that arose from the deep crypts of its being. But the man knew, having achieved a judgment on the subject, and he removed the mitten from his right hand and helped to tear out the ice particles. He did not expose his fingers more than a minute, and was astonished at the swift numbness that smote them. It certainly was cold. He pulled on the mitten hastily, and beat the hand savagely across his chest.

At twelve o'clock the day was at its brightest. Yet the sun was too far south on its winter journey to clear the horizon. The bulge of the earth intervened between it and Henderson Creek, where the man walked under a clear sky at noon and cast no shadow. At half-past twelve, to the minute, he arrived at the forks of the creek. He was pleased at the speed he had made. If he kept it up, he would certainly be with the boys by six. He unbuttoned his jacket and shirt and drew forth his lunch. The action consumed no more than a quarter of a minute, yet in that brief moment the numbness laid hold of the exposed fingers. He did not put the mitten on, but, instead, struck the fingers a dozen sharp smashes against his leg. Then he sat down on a snow-covered log to eat. The sting that followed upon the striking of his fingers against his leg ceased so quickly that he was startled. He had had no chance to take a bite of biscuit. He struck the fingers repeatedly and returned them to the mitten, baring the other hand for the purpose of eating. He tried to take a mouthful, but the ice muzzle prevented. He had forgotten to build a fire and thaw out. He chuckled at his foolishness, and as he chuckled he noted the numbness creeping into the exposed fingers. Also, he noted that the stinging which had first come to his toes when he sat down was already passing away. He wondered whether the toes were warm or numb. He moved them inside the moccasins and decided that they were numb.

He pulled the mitten on hurriedly and stood up. He was a bit frightened. He stamped up and down until the stinging returned into the feet. It certainly was cold, was his thought. That man from Sulphur Creek had spoken the truth when telling how cold it sometimes got in the country. And he had laughed at him at the time! That showed one must not be too sure of things. There was no mistake about it, it *was* cold. He strode up and down, stamping his feet and threshing his arms, until reassured by the returning warmth. Then he got out matches and proceeded to make a fire. From the undergrowth, where high water of the previous spring had lodged a supply of seasoned twigs, he got his firewood. Working carefully from a small beginning, he soon had a roaring fire, over which he thawed the ice from his face and in the protection of which he ate his biscuits. For the moment the cold of space was outwitted. The dog took satisfaction in the fire, stretching out close enough for warmth and far enough away to escape being singed.

When the man had finished, he filled his pipe and took his comfortable time over a smoke. Then he pulled on his mittens, settled the ear flaps of his cap firmly about his ears, and took the creek trail up the left fork. The dog was disappointed and yearned back towards the fire. This man did not know cold. Possibly all the generations of his ancestry had been ignorant of cold, of real cold, of cold one hundred and seven degrees below freezing point. But the dog knew; all its ancestry knew, and it had inherited the knowledge. And it knew that it was not good to walk abroad in such fearful cold. It was the time to lie snug in a hole in the snow and wait for a curtain of cloud to be drawn across the face of outer space whence this cold came. On the other hand, there was no keen intimacy between the dog and the man. The one was the toil slave of the other, and the only caresses it had ever received were the caresses of the whip lash and of harsh and menacing throat sounds that threatened the whip lash. So the dog made no effort to communicate its apprehension to the man. It was not concerned in the welfare of the man; it was for its own sake that it yearned back towards the fire. But the man whistled, and spoke to it with the sound of whip lashes, and the dog swung in at the man's heels and followed after.

The man took a chew of tobacco and proceeded to start a new amber beard. Also, his moist breath quickly powdered with white his moustache, eyebrows, and lashes. There did not seem to be so many springs on the left fork of the Henderson, and for half an hour the man saw no signs of any. And then it happened. At a place where there were no signs, where the soft, unbroken snow seemed to advertise solidity beneath, the man broke through. It was not deep. He wet himself half-way to the knees before he floundered out of the firm crust.

He was angry, and cursed his luck aloud. He had hoped to get into camp with the boys at six o'clock, and this would delay him an hour, for he would have to build a fire and dry out his footgear. This was imperative at that low temperature — he knew that much; and he turned aside to the bank, which he climbed. On top, tangled in the underbrush about the trunks of several small spruce trees, was a high-water deposit of dry firewood—sticks and twigs, principally, but also larger portions of seasoned branches and fine, dry, last year's grasses. He threw down several large pieces on top of the snow. This served for a foundation and prevented the young flame from drowning itself in the snow it otherwise would melt. The flame he got by touching a match to a small shred of birch bark that he took from his pocket. This burned even more readily than paper. Placing it on the foundation, he fed the young flame with wisps of dry grass and with the tiniest dry twigs.

He worked slowly and carefully, keenly aware of his danger. Gradually, as the flame grew stronger, he increased the size of the twigs with which he fed it. He squatted in the snow pulling the twigs out from their entanglement in the brush and feeding directly to the flame. He knew there must be no failure. When it is seventy-five below zero, a man must not fail in his first attempt to build a fire — that is, if his feet are wet. If his feet are dry, and he fails, he can run along the trail for half a mile and restore his circulation. But the circulation of wet and freezing feet cannot be restored by running when it is seventy-five below. No matter how fast he runs, the wet feet will freeze the harder.

All this the man knew. The old-timer on Sulphur Creek had told him about it the previous fall, and now he was appreciating the advice. Already all sensation had gone out of his feet. To build the fire he had been forced to remove his mittens, and the fingers had quickly gone numb. His pace of four miles an hour had kept his heart pumping blood to the surface of his body and to all the extremities. But the instant he stopped, the action of the pump eased down. The cold of space smote the unprotected tip of the planet, and he, being on that unprotected tip, received the full force of the blow. The blood of his body recoiled before it. The blood was alive, like the dog, and like the dog it wanted to hide away and cover itself up from the fearful cold. So long as he walked four miles an hour, he pumped that blood, willy-nilly, to the surfaces; but now it ebbed away and sank down into the recesses of his body. The extremities were the first to feel its absence. His wet feet froze the faster, and his exposed fingers numbed the faster, though they had not yet begun to freeze. Nose and cheeks were already freezing, while the skin of all his body chilled as it lost its blood.

But he was safe. Toes and nose and cheeks would be only touched by the frost, for the fire was beginning to burn with strength. He was feeding it with twigs the size of his finger. In another minute he would be able to feed it with branches the size of his wrist, and then he could remove his wet footgear, and, while it dried, he could keep his naked feet warm by the fire, rubbing them at first, of course, with snow. The fire was a success. He was safe. He remembered the advice of the old-timer on Sulphur Creek, and smiled. The old-timer had been very serious in laying down the law that no man must travel alone in the Klondike after fifty below. Well, here he was; he had had the accident; he was alone; and he had saved himself. Those old-timers were rather womanish, some of them, he thought. All a man had to do was to keep his head, and he was all right. Any man who was a man could travel alone. But it was surprising, the rapidity with which his cheeks and nose were freezing. And he had not thought his fingers could go lifeless in so short a time. Lifeless they were, for he could scarcely make them move together to grip a twig, and they seemed remote from his body and from him. When he touched a twig, he had to look and see whether or not he had hold of it. The wires were pretty well down between him and his finger ends.

All of which counted for little. There was the fire, snapping and crackling and promising life with every dancing flame. He started to untie his moccasins. They were coated with ice; the thick German socks were like sheaths of iron halfway to the knees; and the moccasin strings were like rods of steel all twisted and knotted as by some conflagration. For a moment he tugged with his numb fingers, then, realizing the folly of it, he drew his sheath knife.

But before he could cut the strings, it happened. It was his own fault or, rather, his mistake. He should not have built the fire under the spruce tree. He should have built it in the open. But it had been easier to pull the twigs from the brush and drop them directly on the fire. Now the tree under which he had done this carried a weight of snow on its boughs. No wind had blown for weeks, and each bough was fully freighted. Each time he had pulled a twig he had communicated a slight agitation to the tree — an imperceptible agitation, so far as he was concerned, but an agitation sufficient to bring about the disaster. High up in the tree one bough capsized its load of snow. This fell on the boughs beneath, capsizing them. This process continued, spreading out and involving the whole tree. It grew like an avalanche, and it descended without warning upon the man and the fire, and the fire was blotted out! Where it had burned was a mantle of fresh and disordered snow.

The man was shocked. It was as though he had just heard his own sentence of death. For a moment he sat and stared at the spot where the fire had been. Then he grew very calm. Perhaps the old-timer on Sulphur Creek was right. If he had only had a trail mate he would have been in no danger now. The trail mate could have built the fire. Well, it was up to him to build the fire over again, and this second time there must be no failure. Even if he succeeded, he would most likely lose some toes. His feet must be badly frozen by now, and there would be some time before the second fire was ready.

Such were his thoughts, but he did not sit and think them. He was busy all the time they were passing through his mind. He made a new foundation for a fire, this time in the open, where no treacherous tree could blot it out. Next he gathered dry grasses and tiny twigs from the high-water flotsam. He could not bring his fingers together to pull them out, but he was able to gather them by the handful. In this way he got many rotten twigs and bits of green moss that were undesirable, but it was the best he could do. He worked methodically, even collecting an armful of the larger branches to be used later when the fire gathered strength. And all the while the dog sat and watched him, a certain yearning wistfulness in its eyes, for it looked upon him as the fire provider, and the fire was slow in coming.

When all was ready, the man reached in his pocket for a second piece of birch bark. He knew the bark was there, and, though he could not feel it with his fingers, he could hear its crisp rustling as he fumbled for it. Try as he would, he could not clutch hold of it. And all the time, in his consciousness, was the knowledge that each instant his feet were freezing. This thought tended to put him in a panic, but he fought against it and kept calm. He pulled on his mittens with his teeth, and threshed his arms back and forth, beating his hands with all his might against his sides. He did this sitting down, and he stood up to do it; and all the while the dog sat in the snow, its wolf brush of a tail curled around warmly over its forefront, its sharp wolf ears pricked forward intently as it watched the man. And the man, as he beat and threshed with his arms and hands, felt a great surge of envy as he regarded the creature that was warm and secure in its natural covering.

After a time he was aware of the first faraway signals of sensation in his beaten fingers. The faint tingling grew stronger till it evolved into a stinging ache that was excruciating, but which the man hailed with satisfaction. He stripped the mitten from his right hand and fetched forth the birch bark. The exposed fingers were quickly going numb again. Next he brought out his bunch of sulphur matches. But the tremendous cold had already driven the life out of his fingers. In his effort to separate one match from the others, the whole bunch fell in the snow. He tried to pick it out of the snow, but failed. The dead fingers could neither touch nor clutch. He was very careful. He drove the thought of his freezing feet, and nose, and cheeks, out of his mind, devoting his whole soul to the matches. He watched, using the sense of vision in place of that touch, and when he saw his fingers on each side the bunch, he closed them — that is, he willed to close them, for the wires were down, and the fingers did not obey. He pulled the mitten on the right hand, and beat it fiercely against his knee. Then with both mittened hands, he scooped the bunch of matches, along with much snow, into his lap. Yet he was no better off.

After some manipulation he managed to get the bunch between the heels of his mittened hands. In this fashion he carried it to his mouth. The ice crackled and snapped when by a violent effort he opened his mouth. He drew the lower jaw in, curled the upper lip out of the way, and scraped the bunch with his upper teeth in order to separate a match. He succeeded in getting one, which he dropped on his lap. He was no better off. He could not pick it up. Then he devised a way. He picked it up in his teeth and scratched it on his leg. Twenty times he scratched before he succeeded in lighting it. As it flamed he held it with his teeth to the birch bark. But the burning brimstone went up his nostrils and into his lungs, causing him to cough spasmodically. The match fell into the snow and went out.

The old-timer on Sulphur Creek was right, he thought in the moment of controlled despair that ensued: after fifty below, a man should travel with a partner. He beat his hands, but failed in exciting any sensation. Suddenly he bared both hands, removing the mittens with his teeth. He caught the whole bunch between the heels of his hands. His arm muscles not being frozen enabled him to press the hand heels tightly against the matches. Then he scratched the bunch along his leg. It flared into flame, seventy sulphur matches at once! There was no wind to blow them out. He kept his head to one side to escape the strangling fumes, and held the blazing bunch to the birch bark. As he so held it, he became aware of sensation in his hand. His flesh was burning. He could smell it. Deep down below the surface he could feel it. The sensation developed into pain that grew acute. And still he endured it, holding the flame of the matches clumsily to the bark that would not light readily because his own burning hands were in the way, absorbing most of the flame.

At last, when he could endure no more, he jerked his hands apart. The blazing matches fell sizzling into the snow, but the birch bark was alight. He began laying dry grasses and the tiniest twigs on the flame. He could not pick and choose, for he had to lift the fuel between the heels of his hands. Small pieces of rotten wood and green moss clung to the twigs, and he bit them off as well as he could with his teeth. He cherished the flame carefully and awkwardly. It meant life, and it must not perish. The withdrawal of blood from the surface of his body now made him begin to shiver, and he grew more awkward. A large piece of green moss fell squarely on the little fire. He tried to poke it out with his fingers, but his shivering frame made him poke too far, and he disrupted the nucleus of the little fire, the burning grasses and tiny twigs separating and scattering. He tried to poke them together again, but in spite of the tenseness of the effort, his shivering got away with him, and the twigs were hopelessly scattered. Each twig gushed a puff of smoke and went out. The fire provider had failed. As he looked apathetically about him, his eyes chanced on the dog, sitting across the ruins of the fire from him, in the snow, making restless, hunching movements, slightly lifting one forefoot and then the other, shifting its weight back and forth on them with wistful eagerness.

The sight of the dog put a wild idea into his head. He remembered the tale of the man, caught in a blizzard, who killed a steer and crawled inside the carcass, and so was saved. He would kill the dog and bury his hands in the warm body until the numbness went out of them. Then he could build another fire. He spoke to the dog, calling it to him; but in his voice was a strange note of fear that frightened the animal, who had never known the man to speak in such a way before. Something was the matter, and its suspicious nature sensed danger — it knew not what danger, but somewhere, somehow, in its brain arose an apprehension of the man. It flattened its ears down at the sound of the man's voice, and its restless, hunching movements and the liftings and shiftings of its forefeet became more pronounced; but it would not come to the man. He got on his hands and knees and crawled towards the dog. This unusual posture again excited suspicion, and the animal sidled mincingly away.

The man sat up in the snow for a moment and struggled for calmness. Then he pulled on his mittens, by means of his teeth, and got upon his feet. He glanced down at first in order to assure himself that he was really standing up, for the absence of sensation in his feet left him unrelated to the earth. His erect position in itself started to drive the webs of suspicion from the dog's mind; and when he spoke peremptorily, with the sound of whip lashes in his voice, the dog rendered its customary allegiance and came to him. As it came within reaching distance, the man lost his control. His arms flashed out to the dog, and he experienced genuine surprise when he discovered that his hands could not clutch, that there was neither bend nor feeling in the fingers. He had forgotten for the moment that they were frozen and that they were freezing more and more. All this happened quickly, and before the animal could get away, he encircled its body with his arms. He sat down in the snow, and in this fashion held the dog, while it snarled and whined and struggled.

But it was all he could do, hold its body encircled in his arms and sit there. He realized he could not kill the dog. There was no way to do it. With his helpless hands he could neither draw nor hold his sheath knife nor throttle the animal. He released it, and it plunged wildly away, with tail between its legs, and still snarling. It halted forty feet away and surveyed him curiously, with ears sharply pricked forward.

The man looked down at his hands in order to locate them, and found them hanging on the ends of his arms. It struck him as curious that one should have to use his eyes in order to find out where his hands were. He began threshing his arms back and forth, beating the mittened hands against his sides. He did this for five minutes, violently, and his heart pumped enough blood up to the surface to put a stop to his shivering. But no sensation was aroused in the hands. He had an impression that they hung like weights on the ends of his arms, but when he tried to run the impression down, he could not find it.

A certain fear of death, dull and oppressive, came to him. This fear quickly became poignant as he realized that it was no longer a mere matter of freezing his fingers and toes, or of losing his hands and feet, but that it was a matter of life and death with the chances against him. This threw him into a panic, and he turned and ran up the creek bed along the old, dim trail. The dog joined in behind him and kept up with him. He ran blindly, without intention, in fear such as he had never known in his life. Slowly, as he ploughed and floundered through the snow, he began to see things again — the banks of the creek, the old timber jams, the leafless aspens, and the sky. The running made him feel better. He did not shiver. Maybe, if he ran on, his feet would thaw out; and, anyway, if he ran far enough, he would reach camp and the boys. Without doubt he would lose some fingers and toes and some of his face; but the boys would take care of him, and save the rest of him when he got there. And at the same time there was another thought in his mind that said he would never get to the camp and the boys; that it was too many miles away, that the freezing had too great a start on him, and that he would soon be stiff and dead. This thought he kept in the background and refused to consider. Sometimes it pushed itself forward and demanded to be heard, but he thrust it back and strove to think of other things.

It struck him as curious that he could run at all on feet so frozen that he could not feel them when they struck the earth and took the weight of his body. He seemed to himself to skim along above the surface, and to have no connection with the earth. Somewhere he had once seen a winged Mercury, and he wondered if Mercury felt as he felt when skimming over the earth.

His theory of running until he reached camp and the boys had one flaw in it: he lacked the endurance. Several times he stumbled, and finally he tottered, crumpled up, and fell. When he tried to rise, he failed. He must sit and rest, he decided, and next time he would merely walk and keep on going. As he sat and regained his breath, he noted that he was feeling quite warm and comfortable. He was not shivering, and it even seemed that a warm glow had come to his chest and trunk. And yet, when he touched his nose or cheeks, there was no sensation. Running would not thaw them out. Nor would it thaw out his hands and feet. Then the thought came to him that the frozen portions of his body must be extending. He tried to keep this thought down, to forget it, to think of something else; he was aware of the panicky feeling that it caused, and he was afraid of the panic. But the thought asserted itself, and persisted, until it produced a vision of his body totally frozen. This was too much, and he made another wild run along the trail. Once he slowed down to a walk, but the thought of the freezing extending itself made him run again.

And all the time the dog ran with him, at his heels. When he fell down a second time, it curled its tail over its forefeet and sat in front of him, facing him, curiously eager and intent. The warmth and security of the animal angered him, and he cursed it till it flattened down its ears appeasingly. This time the shivering came more quickly upon the man. He was losing in his battle with the frost. It was creeping into his body from all sides. The thought of it drove him on, but he ran no more than a hundred feet, when he staggered and pitched headlong. It was his last panic. When he had recovered his breath and control, he sat up and entertained in his mind the conception of meeting death with dignity. However, the conception did not come to him in such terms. His idea of it was that he had been making a fool of himself, running around like a chicken with its head cut off — such was the simile that occurred to him. Well, he was bound to freeze anyway, and he might as well take it decently. With this new-found peace of mind came the first glimmerings of drowsiness. A good idea, he thought, to sleep off to death. It was like taking an anaesthetic. Freezing was not so bad as people thought. There were lots worse ways to die.

He pictured the boys finding his body next day. Suddenly he found himself with them, coming along the trail looking for himself. And, still with them, he came around a turn in the trail and found himself lying in the snow. He did not belong with himself any more, for even then he was out of himself, standing with the boys and looking at himself in the snow. It certainly was cold, was his thought. When he got back to the States he could tell the folks what real cold was. He drifted on from this to a vision of the old-timer on Sulphur Creek. He could see him quite clearly, warm and comfortable, and smoking a pipe.

"You were right, old hoss; you were right," the man mumbled to the old-timer of Sulphur Creek.

Then the man drowsed off into what seemed to him the most comfortable and satisfying sleep he had ever known. The dog sat facing him and waiting. The brief day drew to a close in a long, slow twilight. There were no signs of a fire to be made, and, besides, never in the dog's experience had it known a man to sit like that in the snow and make no fire. As the twilight drew on, its eager yearning for the fire mastered it, and with a great lifting and shifting of forefeet, it whined softly, then flattened its ears down in anticipation of being chidden by the man. But the man remained silent. Later the dog whined loudly. And still later it crept close to the man and caught the scent of death. This made the animal bristle and back away. A little longer it delayed, howling under the stars that leaped and danced and shone brightly in the cold sky. Then it turned and trotted up the trail in the direction of the camp it knew, where were the other food providers and fire providers.

[1908]

SHERWOOD ANDERSON (1876–1941), *born the son of a jack-of-all-trades father in Camden, Ohio, spent his youth drifting with his family from town to town in midwestern America. He did not publish his first book until he was over forty years old. Later, when he analyzed the impulse toward writing fiction that he had experienced after working for many years as a newsboy, farm laborer, stable boy, factory hand, and advertising copywriter, Anderson recalled that he said to himself, "I'll take some fellow, a little like myself, something of the same circumstances, same experiences in life. I'll put him down on paper, his life, his relations with others, the story of the things that happen to him, how he feels — all this on sheets of paper. It seemed to me, when I began to do it, that I could, by writing, push myself, as self, far off. I could get myself, as self, in the unimportant position I deserved. I became, for the nonce, to myself, just a passing thing, just one of a long, long procession of men . . . any one other figure in the procession certainly as important as myself . . . a kind of new gladness inside."*

Dissatisfied with the commercial spirit of the advertising business, Anderson made friends with writers in Chicago and began to publish his own poetry and fiction. The poet Carl Sandburg encouraged him, but Anderson's literary style was most influenced by Three Lives, *an early book of the expatriate American writer Gertrude Stein, which he felt revolutionized the language of narrative. In 1916 he published his first novel,* Windy McPherson's Son. *He followed it with another novel and a volume of poetry, but he did not receive wide recognition until 1919, with the book* Winesburg, Ohio. *This was a collection of related stories, including "Hands," about life in a small town, that developed the theme of youth in revolt against the repressive conventions of a materialistic society. It was followed by other important collections of stories:* The Triumph of the Egg *(1921),* Horses and Men *(1923), and* Death in the Woods and Other Stories *(1933). In his time Anderson was a strong influence on Ernest Hemingway, William Faulkner, and John Steinbeck. The best of his stories, like "Hands," "The Egg," "I'm a Fool," and "Death in the Woods," have an enduring vitality and are important contributions to the achievement of the American short story.*

The characteristic tone of Anderson's short fiction is melancholy reminiscence. His stories are largely autobiographical, often recalling the tales told by his father or other members of his family. In an understated fashion, Anderson weaves carefully selected realistic details into a narrative that moves by apparently formless associations of thought and feeling, but is actually a controlled progression of fully dramatized situations. At the heart of "Death in the Woods," as of all his best work, is Anderson's obsession with the theme of love denied and life destroyed by an uncaring, hostile environ-

ment. His importance in literary history is accurately summed up in William Faulkner's statement that Anderson was "the father of my generation of American writers and the tradition of American writing which our successors will carry on." (See Anderson's Commentary on page 1254.)

Sherwood Anderson

ॐ

HANDS

Upon the half decayed veranda of a small frame house that stood near the edge of a ravine near the town of Winesburg, Ohio, a fat little old man walked nervously up and down. Across a long field that had been seeded for clover but that had produced only a dense crop of yellow mustard weeds, he could see the public highway along which went a wagon filled with berry pickers returning from the fields. The berry pickers, youths and maidens, laughed and shouted boisterously. A boy clad in a blue shirt leaped from the wagon and attempted to drag after him one of the maidens who screamed and protested shrilly. The feet of the boy in the road kicked up a cloud of dust that floated across the face of the departing sun. Over the long field came a thin girlish voice. "Oh, you Wing Biddlebaum, comb your hair, it's falling into your eyes," commanded the voice to the man, who was bald and whose nervous little hands fiddled about the bare white forehead as though arranging a mass of tangled locks.

Wing Biddlebaum, forever frightened and beset by a ghostly band of doubts, did not think of himself as in any way a part of the life of the town where he had lived for twenty years. Among all the people of Winesburg but one had come close to him. With George Willard, son of Tom Willard, the proprietor of the new Willard House, he had formed something like a friendship. George Willard was the reporter on the *Winesburg Eagle* and sometimes in the evenings he walked out along the highway to Wing Biddlebaum's house. Now as the old man walked up and down on the veranda, his hands moving nervously about, he was hoping that George Willard would come and spend the evening with him. After the wagon containing the berry pickers had passed, he went across the field through the tall mustard weeds and climbing a rail fence peered anxiously along the road to the town. For a moment he stood thus, rubbing his hands together and looking up and down the road, and then, fear overcoming him, ran back to walk again upon the porch on his own house.

In the presence of George Willard, Wing Biddlebaum, who for twenty years had been the town mystery, lost something of his timidity, and his shadowy personality, submerged in a sea of doubts, came forth to look at the world. With the young reporter at his side, he ventured in the light of day into Main Street or strode up and down on the rickety front porch of his own house, talking excitedly. The voice that had been low and trembling became shrill and loud. The bent figure straightened. With a kind of wriggle, like a fish returned to the brook by the fisherman, Biddlebaum the silent began to talk, striving to put into words the ideas that had been accumulated by his mind during long years of silence.

Wing Biddlebaum talked much with his hands. The slender expressive fingers, forever active, forever striving to conceal themselves in his pockets or behind his back, came forth and became the piston rods of his machinery of expression.

The story of Wing Biddlebaum is a story of hands. Their restless activity, like unto the beating of the wings of an imprisoned bird, had given him his name. Some obscure poet of the town had thought of it. The hands alarmed their owner. He wanted to keep them hidden away and looked with amazement at the quiet inexpressive hands of other men who worked beside him in the fields, or passed, driving sleepy teams on country roads.

When he talked to George Willard, Wing Biddlebaum closed his fists and beat with them upon a table or on the walls of his house. The action made him more comfortable. If the desire to talk came to him when the two were walking in the fields, he sought out a stump or the top board of a fence and with his hands pounding busily talked with renewed ease.

The story of Wing Biddlebaum's hands is worth a book itself. Sympathetically set forth it would tap many strange, beautiful qualities in obscure men. It is a job for a poet. In Winesburg the hands had attracted attention merely because of their activity. With them Wing Biddlebaum had picked as high as a hundred and forty quarts of strawberries in a day. They became his distinguishing feature, the source of his fame. Also they made more grotesque an already grotesque and elusive individuality. Winesburg was proud of the hands of Wing Biddlebaum in the same spirit in which it was proud of Banker White's new stone house and Wesley Moyer's bay stallion, Tony Tip, that had won the two-fifteen trot at the fall races in Cleveland.

As for George Willard, he had many times wanted to ask about the hands. At times an almost overwhelming curiosity had taken hold of him. He felt that there must be a reason for their strange activity and their inclination to keep hidden away and only a growing respect for Wing Biddlebaum kept him from blurting out the questions that were often in his mind.

Once he had been on the point of asking. The two were walking in the fields on a summer afternoon and had stopped to sit upon a grassy bank. All afternoon Wing Biddlebaum had talked as one inspired. By a fence he had stopped and beating like a giant woodpecker upon the top board had shouted at George Willard, condemning his tendency to be too much influenced by the people about him. "You are destroying yourself," he cried.

"You have the inclination to be alone and to dream and you are afraid of dreams. You want to be like others in town here. You hear them talk and you try to imitate them."

On the grassy bank Wing Biddlebaum had tried again to drive his point home. His voice became soft and reminiscent, and with a sigh of contentment he launched into a long rambling talk, speaking as one lost in a dream.

Out of the dream Wing Biddlebaum made a picture for George Willard. In the picture men lived again in a kind of pastoral golden age. Across a green open country came clean-limbed young men, some afoot, some mounted upon horses. In crowds the young men came to gather about the feet of an old man who sat beneath a tree in a tiny garden and who talked to them.

Wing Biddlebaum became wholly inspired. For once he forgot the hands. Slowly they stole forth and lay upon George Willard's shoulders. Something new and bold came into the voice that talked. "You must try to forget all you have learned," said the old man. "You must begin to dream. From this time on you must shut your ears to the roaring of the voices."

Pausing in his speech, Wing Biddlebaum looked long and earnestly at George Willard. His eyes glowed. Again he raised the hands to caress the boy and then a look of horror swept over his face.

With a convulsive movement of his body, Wing Biddlebaum sprang to his feet and thrust his hands deep into his trousers pockets. Tears came to his eyes. "I must be getting along home. I can talk no more with you," he said nervously.

Without looking back, the old man had hurried down the hillside and across a meadow, leaving George Willard perplexed and frightened upon the grassy slope. With a shiver of dread the boy arose and went along the road toward town. "I'll not ask him about his hands," he thought, touched by the memory of the terror he had seen in the man's eyes. "There's something wrong, but I don't want to know what it is. His hands have something to do with his fear of me and of everyone."

And George Willard was right. Let us look briefly into the story of the hands. Perhaps our talking of them will arouse the poet who will tell the hidden wonder story of the influence for which the hands were but fluttering pennants of promise.

In his youth Wing Biddlebaum had been a school teacher in a town in Pennsylvania. He was not then known as Wing Biddlebaum, but went by the less euphonic name of Adolph Myers. As Adolph Myers he was much loved by the boys of his school.

Adolph Myers was meant by nature to be a rare teacher of youth. He was one of those rare, little-understood men who rule by a power so gentle that it passes as a lovable weakness. In their feeling for the boys under their charge such men are not unlike the finer sort of women in their love of men.

And yet that is but crudely stated. It needs the poet there. With the boys of his school, Adolph Myers had walked in the evening or had sat talking until dusk upon the schoolhouse steps lost in a kind of dream. Here and there went his hands, caressing the shoulders of the boys, playing about the tousled heads. As he talked his voice became soft and musical. There was a caress in that also. In a way the voice and the hands, the stroking of the shoulders and the touching of the hair was a part of the schoolmaster's effort to carry a dream into the young minds. By the caress that was in his fingers he expressed himself. He was one of those men in whom the force that creates life is diffused, not centralized. Under the caress of his hands doubt and disbelief went out of the minds of the boys and they began also to dream.

And then the tragedy. A half-witted boy of the school became enamored of the young master. In his bed at night he imagined unspeakable things and in the morning went forth to tell his dreams as facts. Strange, hideous accusations fell from his loose-hung lips. Through the Pennsylvania town went a shiver. Hidden, shadowy doubts that had been in men's minds concerning Adolph Myers were galvanized into beliefs.

The tragedy did not linger. Trembling lads were jerked out of bed and questioned. "He put his arms about me," said one. "His fingers were always playing in my hair," said another.

One afternoon a man of the town, Henry Bradford, who kept a saloon, came to the schoolhouse door. Calling Adolph Myers into the school yard he began to beat him with his fists. As his hard knuckles beat down into the frightened face of the schoolmaster, his wrath became more and more terrible. Screaming with dismay, the children ran here and there like disturbed insects. "I'll teach you to put your hands on my boy, you beast," roared the saloon keeper, who, tired of beating the master, had begun to kick him about the yard.

Adolph Myers was driven from the Pennsylvania town in the night. With lanterns in their hands a dozen men came to the door of the house where he lived alone and commanded that he dress and come forth. It was raining and one of the men had a rope in his hands. They had intended to hang the schoolmaster, but something in his figure, so small, white, and pitiful, touched their hearts and they let him escape. As he ran away into the darkness they repented of their weakness and ran after him, swearing and throwing sticks and great balls of soft mud at the figure that screamed and ran faster and faster into the darkness.

For twenty years Adolph Myers had lived alone in Winesburg. He was but forty but looked sixty-five. The name Biddlebaum he got from a box of goods seen at a freight station as he hurried through an eastern Ohio town. He had an aunt in Winesburg, a black-toothed old woman who raised chickens, and with her he lived until she died. He had been ill for a year after the experience in Pennsylvania, and after his recovery worked as a day laborer in the fields, going timidly about and striving to conceal his hands. Although he did not understand what had happened he felt that the hands must be to blame. Again and again the fathers of the boys had talked of the hands. "Keep your hands to yourself," the saloon keeper had roared, dancing with fury in the schoolhouse yard.

Upon the veranda of his house by the ravine, Wing Biddlebaum continued to walk up and down until the sun had disappeared and the road beyond the field was lost in the grey shadows. Going into his house he cut slices of bread and spread honey upon them. When the rumble of the evening train that took away the express cars loaded with the day's harvest of berries had passed and restored the silence of the summer night, he went again to walk upon the veranda. In the darkness he could not see the hands and they became quiet. Although he still hungered for the presence of the boy, who was the medium through which he expressed his love of man, the hunger became again a part of his loneliness and his waiting. Lighting a lamp, Wing Biddlebaum washed the few dishes soiled by his simple meal and, setting up a folding cot by the screen door that led to the porch, prepared to undress for the night. A few stray white bread crumbs lay on the cleanly washed floor by the table; putting the lamp upon a low stool he began to pick up the crumbs, carrying them to his mouth one by one with unbelievable rapidity. In the dense blotch of light beneath the table, the kneeling figure looked like a priest engaged in some service of his church. The nervous expressive fingers, flashing in and out of the light, might well have been mistaken for the fingers of the devotee going swiftly through decade after decade of his rosary.

[1919]

Sherwood Anderson

ॐ

DEATH IN THE WOODS

I

She was an old woman and lived on a farm near the town in which I lived. All country and small-town people have seen such old women, but no one knows much about them. Such an old woman comes into town driving an old worn-out horse or she comes afoot carrying a basket. She may own a few hens and have eggs to sell. She brings them in a basket and takes them to a grocer. There she trades them in. She gets some salt pork and some beans. Then she gets a pound or two of sugar and some flour.

Afterwards she goes to the butcher's and asks for some dog-meat. She may spend ten or fifteen cents, but when she does she asks for something. Formerly the butchers gave liver to any one who wanted to carry it away. In our family we were always having it. Once one of my brothers got a whole cow's liver at the slaughter-house near the fairgrounds in our town. We had it until we were sick of it. It never cost a cent. I have hated the thought of it ever since.

The old farm woman got some liver and a soup-bone. She never visited with any one, and as soon as she got what she wanted she lit out for home. It made quite a load for such an old body. No one gave her a lift. People drive right down a road and never notice an old woman like that.

There was such an old woman who used to come into town past our house one Summer and Fall when I was a young boy and was sick with what was called inflammatory rheumatism. She went home later carrying a heavy pack on her back. Two or three large gaunt-looking dogs followed at her heels.

The old woman was nothing special. She was one of the nameless ones that hardly anyone knows, but she got into my thoughts. I have just suddenly now, after all these years, remembered her and what happened. It is a story. Her name was Grimes, and she lived with her husband and son in a small unpainted house on the bank of a small creek four miles from town.

The husband and son were a tough lot. Although the son was but twenty-one, he had already served a term in jail. It was whispered about that the woman's husband stole horses and ran them off to some other county. Now and then, when a horse turned up missing, the man had also disappeared. No one ever caught him. Once, when I was loafing at Tom Whitehead's livery-barn, the man came there and sat on the bench in front. Two or three other men were there, but no one spoke to him. He sat for a few minutes and then got up and went away. When he was leaving he turned around and stared at the men. There was a look of defiance in his eyes. "Well, I have tried to be friendly. You don't want to talk to me. It has been so wherever I have gone in this town. If, some day, one of your fine horses turns up missing, well, then what?" He did not say anything actually. "I'd like to bust one of you on the jaw," was about what his eyes said. I remember how the look in his eyes made me shiver.

The old man belonged to a family that had had money once. His name was Jake Grimes. It all comes back clearly now. His father, John Grimes, had owned a sawmill when the country was new, and had made money. Then he got to drinking and running after women. When he died there wasn't much left.

Jake blew in the rest. Pretty soon there wasn't any more lumber to cut and his land was nearly all gone.

He got his wife off a German farmer, for whom he went to work one June day in the wheat harvest. She was a young thing then and scared to death. You see, the farmer was up to something with the girl — she was, I think, a bound girl and his wife had her suspicions. She took it out on the girl when the man wasn't around. Then, when the wife had to go off to town for supplies, the farmer got after her. She told young Jake that nothing really ever happened, but he didn't know whether to believe it or not.

He got her pretty easy himself, the first time he was out with her. He wouldn't have married her if the German farmer hadn't tried to tell him where to get off. He got her to go riding with him in his buggy one night when he was threshing on the place, and then he came for her the next Sunday night.

She managed to get out of the house without her employer's seeing, but when she was getting into the buggy he showed up. It was almost dark, and he just popped up suddenly at the horse's head. He grabbed the horse by the bridle and Jake got out his buggy-whip.

They had it out all right! The German was a tough one. Maybe he didn't care whether his wife knew or not. Jake hit him over the face and shoulders with the buggy-whip, but the horse got to acting up and he had to get out.

Then the two men went for it. The girl didn't see it. The horse started to run away and went nearly a mile down the road before the girl got him stopped. Then she managed to tie him to a tree beside the road. (I wonder how I know all this. It must have stuck in my mind from small-town tales when I was a boy.) Jake found her there after he got through with the German. She was huddled up in the buggy seat, crying, scared to death. She told Jake a lot of stuff, how the German had tried to get her, how he chased her once into the barn, how another time, when they happened to be alone in the house together, he tore her dress open clear down the front. The German, she said, might have got her that time if he hadn't heard his old woman drive in at the gate. She had been off to town for supplies. Well, she would be putting the horse in the barn. The German managed to sneak off to the fields without his wife seeing. He told the girl he would kill her if she told. What could she do? She told a lie about ripping her dress in the barn when she was feeding the stock. I remember now that she was a bound girl and did not know where her father and mother were. Maybe she did not have any father. You know what I mean.

Such bound children were often enough cruelly treated. They were children who had no parents, slaves really. There were very few orphan homes then. They were legally bound into some home. It was a matter of pure luck how it came out.

II

She married Jake and had a son and daughter, but the daughter died.

Then she settled down to feed stock. That was her job. At the German's place she had cooked the food for the German and his wife. The wife was a strong woman with big hips and worked most of the time in the fields with her husband. She fed them and fed the cows in the barn, fed the pigs, the horses and the chickens. Every moment of every day, as a young girl, was spent feeding something.

Then she married Jake Grimes and he had to be fed. She was a slight thing, and when she had been married for three or four years, and after the two children were born, her slender shoulders became stooped.

Jake always had a lot of big dogs around the house, that stood near the unused sawmill near the creek. He was always trading horses when he wasn't stealing something and had a lot of poor bony ones about. Also he kept three or four pigs and a cow. They were all pastured in the few acres left of the Grimes place and Jake did little enough work.

He went into debt for a threshing outfit and ran it for several years, but it did not pay. People did not trust him. There were afraid he would steal the grain at night. He had to go a long way off to get work and it cost too much to get there. In the Winter he hunted and cut a little firewood, to be sold in some nearby town. When the son grew up he was just like the father. They got drunk together. If there wasn't anything to eat in the house when they came home the old man gave his old woman a cut over the head. She had a few chickens of her own and had to kill one of them in a hurry. When they were all killed she wouldn't have any eggs to sell when she went to town, and then what would she do?

She had to scheme all her life about getting things fed, getting the pigs fed so they would grow fat and could be butchered in the Fall. When they were butchered her husband took most of the meat off to town and sold it. If he did not do it first the boy did. They fought sometimes and when they fought the old woman stood aside trembling.

She had got the habit of silence anyway — that was fixed. Sometimes, when she began to look old — she wasn't forty yet — and when the husband and son were both off, trading horses or drinking or hunting or stealing, she went around the house and the barnyard muttering to herself.

How was she going to get everything fed? — that was her problem. The dogs had to be fed. There wasn't enough hay in the barn for the horses and the cow. If she didn't feed the chickens how could they lay eggs? Without eggs to sell how could she get things in town, things she had to have to keep the life of the farm going? Thank heaven, she did not have to feed her husband — in a certain way. That hadn't lasted long after their marriage and after the babies came. Where he went on his long trips she did not know. Sometimes he was gone from home for weeks, and after the boy grew up they went off together.

They left everything at home for her to manage and she had no money. She knew no one. No one ever talked to her in town. When it was Winter she had to gather sticks of wood for her fire, had to try to keep the stock fed with very little grain.

The stock in the barn cried to her hungrily, the dogs followed her about. In the Winter the hens laid few enough eggs. They huddled in the corners of the barn and she kept watching them. If a hen lays an egg in the barn in the Winter and you do not find it, it freezes and breaks.

One day in Winter the old woman went off to town with a few eggs and the dogs followed her. She did not get started until nearly three o'clock and the snow was heavy. She hadn't been feeling very well for several days and so she went muttering along, scantily clad, her shoulders stooped. She had an old grain bag in which she carried her eggs, tucked away down in the bottom. There weren't many of them, but in Winter the price of eggs is up. She would get a little meat in exchange for the eggs, some salt pork, a little sugar, and some coffee perhaps. It might be the butcher would give her a piece of liver.

When she had got to town and was trading in her eggs the dogs lay by the door outside. She did pretty well, got the things she needed, more than she had hoped. Then she went to the butcher and he gave her some liver and some dog-meat.

It was the first time any one had spoken to her in a friendly way for a long time. The butcher was alone in his shop when she came in and was annoyed by the thought of such a sick-looking old woman out on such a day. It was bitter cold and the snow, that had let up during the afternoon, was falling again. The butcher said something about her husband and her son, swore at them, and the old woman stared at him, a look of mild surprise in her eyes as he talked. He said that if either the husband or the son were going to get any of the liver or the heavy bones with scraps of meat hanging to them that he had put into the grain bag, he'd see him starve first.

Starve, eh? Well, things had to be fed. Men had to be fed, and horses that weren't any good but maybe could be traded off, and the poor thin cow that hadn't given any milk for three months.

Horses, cows, pigs, dogs, men.

III

The old woman had to get back before darkness came if she could. The dogs followed at her heels, sniffing at the heavy grain bag she had fastened on her back. When she got to the edge of town she stopped by a fence and tied the bag on her back with a piece of rope she had carried in her dress-pocket for just that purpose. It was hard when she had to crawl over fences and once she fell over and landed in the snow. The dogs went frisking about. She had to struggle to get to her feet again, but she made it. The point of climbing over the fences was that there was a short cut over a hill and through a woods. She might have gone around by the road, but it was a mile farther that way. She was afraid she couldn't make it. And then, besides, the stock had to be fed. There was a little hay left and a little corn. Perhaps her husband and son would bring some home when they came.

•

They had driven off in the only buggy the Grimes family had, a rickety thing, a rickety horse hitched to the buggy, two other rickety horses led by halters. They were going to trade horses, get a little money if they could. They might come home drunk. It would be well to have something in the house when they came back.

The son had an affair on with a woman at the county seat, fifteen miles away. She was a rough enough woman, a tough one. Once, in the Summer, the son had brought her to the house. Both she and the son had been drinking. Jake Grimes was away and the son and his woman ordered the old woman about like a servant. She didn't mind much; she was used to it. Whatever happened she never said anything. That was her way of getting along. She had managed that way when she was a young girl at the German's and ever since she had married Jake. That time her son brought his woman to the house they stayed all night, sleeping together just as though they were married. It hadn't shocked the old woman, not much. She had got past being shocked early in life.

With the pack on her back she went painfully along across an open field, wading in the deep snow, and got into the woods.

There was a path, but it was hard to follow. Just beyond the top of the hill, where the woods was thickest, there was a small clearing. Had some one once thought of building a house there? The clearing was as large as a building lot in town, large enough for a house and a garden. The path ran along the side of the clearing, and when she got there the old woman sat down to rest at the foot of a tree.

It was a foolish thing to do. When she got herself placed, the pack against the tree's trunk, it was nice, but what about getting up again? She worried about that for a moment and then quietly closed her eyes.

She must have slept for a time. When you are about so cold you can't get any colder. The afternoon grew a little warmer and the snow came thicker than ever. Then after a time the weather cleared. The moon even came out.

There were four Grimes dogs that had followed Mrs. Grimes into town, all tall gaunt fellows. Such men as Jake Grimes and his son always keep just such dogs. They kick and abuse them, but they stay. The Grimes dogs, in order to keep from starving, had to do a lot of foraging for themselves, and they had been at it while the old woman slept with her back to the tree at the side of the clearing. They had been chasing rabbits in the woods and in adjoining fields and in their ranging had picked up three other farm dogs.

After a time all the dogs came back to the clearing. They were excited about something. Such nights, cold and clear and with a moon, do things to dogs. It may be that some old instinct, come down from the time when they were wolves, and ranged the woods in packs on Winter nights, comes back to them.

The dogs in the clearing, before the old woman, had caught two or three rabbits and their immediate hunger had been satisfied. They began to play, running in circles in the clearing. Round and round they ran, each dog's nose at the tail of the next dog. In the clearing, under the snow-laden trees and under the wintry moon they made a strange picture, running thus silently, in a circle their running had beaten in the soft snow. The dogs made no sound. They ran around and around in the circle.

It may have been that the old woman saw them doing that before she died. She may have awakened once or twice and looked at the strange sight with dim old eyes.

She wouldn't be very cold now, just drowsy. Life hangs on a long time. Perhaps the old woman was out of her head. She may have dreamed of her girlhood at the German's, and before that, when she was a child and before her mother lit out and left her.

Her dreams couldn't have been very pleasant. Not many pleasant things had happened to her. Now and then one of the Grimes dogs left the running circle and came to stand before her. The dog thrust his face to her face. His red tongue was hanging out.

The running of the dogs may have been a kind of death ceremony. It may have been that the primitive instinct of the wolf, having been aroused in the dogs by the night and the running, made them somehow, afraid.

"Now we are no longer wolves. We are dogs, the servants of men. Keep alive, man! When man dies we become wolves again." When one of the dogs came to where the old woman sat with her back against the tree and thrust his nose close to her face he seemed satisfied and went back to run with the pack. All the Grimes dogs did it at some time during the evening, before she died. I knew all about it afterward, when I grew to be a man, because once in a woods in Illinois, on another Winter night, I saw a pack of dogs act just like that. The dogs were waiting for me to die as they had waited for the old woman that night when I was a child, but when it happened to me I was a young man and had no intention whatever of dying.

The old woman died softly and quietly. When she was dead and when one of the Grimes dogs had come to her and had found her dead all the dogs stopped running.

They gathered about her.

Well, she was dead now. She had fed the Grimes dogs when she was alive, what about now?

There was the pack on her back, the grain bag containing the piece of salt pork, the liver the butcher had given her, the dog-meat, the soup bones. The butcher in town, having been suddenly overcome with a feeling of pity, had loaded her grain bag heavily. It had been a big haul for the old woman.

It was a big haul for the dogs now.

IV

One of the Grimes dogs sprang suddenly out from among the others and began worrying the pack on the old woman's back. Had the dogs really been wolves that one would have been the leader of the pack. What he did, all the others did.

All of them sank their teeth into the grain bag the old woman had fastened with ropes to her back.

They dragged the old woman's body out into the open clearing. The worn-out dress was quickly torn from her shoulders. When she was found, a day or two later, the dress had been torn from her body clear to the hips, but the dogs had not touched her body. They had got the meat out of the grain bag, that was all. Her body was frozen stiff when it was found, and the shoulders were so narrow and the body so slight that in death it looked like the body of some charming young girl.

Such things happened in towns of the Middle West, on farms near town, when I was a boy. A hunter out after rabbits found the old woman's body and did not touch it. Something, the beaten round path in the little snow-covered clearing, the silence of the place, the place where the dogs had worried the body trying to pull the grain bag away or tear it open — something startled the man and he hurried off to town.

I was in Main Street with one of my brothers who was town newsboy and who was taking the afternoon papers to the stores. It was almost night.

The hunter came into a grocery and told his story. Then he went into a hardware-shop and into a drugstore. Men began to gather on the sidewalks. Then they started out along the road to the place in the woods.

My brother should have gone on about his business of distributing papers but he didn't. Every one was going to the woods. The undertaker went and the town marshal. Several men got on a dray and rode out to where the path left the road and went into the woods, but the horses weren't very sharply shod and slid about on the slippery roads. They made no better time than those of us who walked.

The town marshal was a large man whose leg had been injured in the Civil War. He carried a heavy cane and limped rapidly along the road. My brother and I followed at his heels, and as we went other men and boys joined the crowd.

It had grown dark by the time we got to where the old woman had left the road but the moon had come out. The marshal was thinking there might have been a murder. He kept asking the hunter questions. The hunter went along with his gun across his shoulders, a dog following at his heels. It isn't often a rabbit hunter has a chance to be so conspicuous. He was taking full advantage of it, leading the procession with the town marshal. "I didn't see any wounds. She was a beautiful young girl. Her face was buried in the snow. No, I didn't know her." As a matter of fact, the hunter had not looked closely at the body. He had been frightened. She might have been murdered and some one might spring out from behind a tree and murder him. In a woods, in the late afternoon, when the trees are all bare and there is white snow on the ground, when all is silent, something creepy steals over the mind and body. If something strange or uncanny has happened in the neighborhood all you think about is getting away from there as fast as you can.

The crowd of men and boys had got to where the old woman had crossed the field and went, following the marshal and the hunter, up the slight incline and into the woods.

My brother and I were silent. He had his bundle of papers in a bag slung across his shoulder. When he got back to town he would have to go on distributing his papers before he went home to supper. If I went along, as he had no doubt already determined I should, we would both be late. Either mother or our older sister would have to warm our supper.

Well, we would have something to tell. A boy did not get such a chance very often. It was lucky we just happened to go into the grocery when the hunter came in. The hunter was a country fellow. Neither of us had ever seen him before.

Now the crowd of men and boys had got to the clearing. Darkness comes quickly on such Winter nights, but the full moon made everything clear. My brother and I stood near the tree, beneath which the old woman had died.

She did not look old, lying there in that light, frozen and still. One of the men turned her over in the snow and I saw everything. My body trembled with some strange mystical feeling and so did my brother's. It might have been the cold.

Neither of us had ever seen a woman's body before. It may have been the snow, clinging to the frozen flesh, that made it look so white and lovely, so like marble. No woman had come with the party from town; but one of the men, he was the town blacksmith, took off his overcoat and spread it over her. Then he gathered her into his arms and started off to town, all the others following silently. At that time no one knew who she was.

V

I had seen everything, had seen the oval in the snow, like a miniature race-track, where the dogs had run, had seen how the men were mystified, had seen the white bare young-looking shoulders, had heard the whispered comments of the men.

The men were simply mystified. They took the body to the undertaker's, and when the blacksmith, the hunter, the marshal and several others had got inside they closed the door. If father had been there perhaps he could have got in, but we boys couldn't.

I went with my brother to distribute the rest of his papers and when we got home it was my brother who told the story.

I kept silent and went to bed early. It may have been I was not satisfied with the way he told it.

Later, in the town, I must have heard other fragments of the old woman's story. She was recognized the next day and there was an investigation.

The husband and son were found somewhere and brought to town and there was an attempt to connect them with the woman's death, but it did not work. They had perfect enough alibis.

However, the town was against them. They had to get out. Where they went I never heard.

I remember only the picture there in the forest, the men standing about, the naked girlish-looking figure, face down in the snow, the tracks made by the running dogs and the clear cold Winter sky above. White fragments of clouds were drifting across the sky. They went racing across the little open space among the trees.

The scene in the forest had become for me, without my knowing it, the foundation for the real story I am now trying to tell. The fragments, you see, had to be picked up slowly, long afterwards.

Things happened. When I was a young man I worked on the farm of a German. The hired-girl was afraid of her employer. The farmer's wife hated her.

I saw things at that place. Once later, I had a half-uncanny, mystical adventure with dogs in an Illinois forest on a clear, moon-lit Winter night. When I was a schoolboy, and on a Summer day, I went with a boy friend out along a creek some miles from town and came to the house where the old woman had lived. No one had lived in the house since her death. The doors were broken from the hinges; the window lights were all broken. As the boy and I stood in the road outside, two dogs, just roving farm dogs no doubt, came running around the corner of the house. The dogs were tall, gaunt fellows and came down to the fence and glared through at us, standing in the road.

The whole thing, the story of the old woman's death, was to me as I grew older like music heard from far off. The notes had to be picked up slowly one at a time. Something had to be understood.

The woman who died was one destined to feed animal life. Anyway, that is all she ever did. She was feeding animal life before she was born, as a child, as a young woman working on the farm of the German, after she married, when she grew old and when she died. She fed animal life in cows, in chickens, in pigs, in horses, in dogs, in men. Her daughter had died in childhood and with her one son she had no articulate relations. On the night when she died she was hurrying homeward, bearing on her body food for animal life.

She died in the clearing in the woods and even after her death continued feeding animal life.

You see it is likely that, when my brother told the story, that night when we got home and my mother and sister sat listening, I did not think he got the point. He was too young and so was I. A thing so complete has its own beauty.

I shall not try to emphasize the point. I am only explaining why I was dissatisfied then and have been ever since. I speak of that only that you may understand why I have been impelled to try to tell the simple story over again.

[1933]

EDWARD MORGAN FORSTER (1879–1970) was one of the finest novelists of the twentieth century, and also one of the longest lived. When he died at the age of ninety-two, his longevity had assisted official British recognition of the quality of his work. He was made a Companion of Honor in 1953 and he was appointed to the Order of Merit in 1968. But, as he said in 1940, "By the time writers have become eminent they have usually done their best work." His major fiction is in the form of the novel, and these works belong to the first half of his life. In 1908 Howard's End established his reputation, and A Passage to India, his last and greatest novel, appeared in 1924. The posthumous publication of Maurice (a novel written in 1914) and The Life to Come (stories written up to 1958), shows that Forster had held back some of his fiction because of its homosexual content. As his biographer Philip Gardner has noted, "Forster's recognition of this central aspect of himself seems eventually (for a sense of impatience with conventional human configurations shows itself as early as a diary entry of 1911) to have prevented his imagination from setting it aside in exchange for publication." Forster's situation may be inferred from a sentence in his literary study Aspects of the Novel (1927): "It is a pity that Man cannot be at the same time impressive and truthful."

Forster was born in London, the only son of an architect who died when Forster was little more than a year old. He was raised by his mother, his maternal grandmother, and his paternal great-aunt, who in 1887 left him a substantial fortune, which provided for his education and his travels, and gave him the freedom to write as he pleased. His earliest surviving work is a detailed description from 1894 of the farmhouse in which he lived with his mother in Hertfordshire. He read the classics and history at Cambridge, which he loved for its liberating influence. Most of the time he lived with his mother, who died when he was sixty-six.

Beginning his career as a writer of short fiction, Forster published his first story, "Albergo Empedocle," a mixture of poetry and ironic observation, in 1903. In general he used the short story form for a more fantastic expression of his feelings and ideas than he allowed himself in his realistic novels. Most of Forster's stories, like the fable "Mr. Andrews," celebrate a liberating encounter and are written in a deft blend of whimsy and mysticism. Forster's short fiction is collected in three books: The Celestial Omnibus (1911), The Eternal Moment (1928), and The Life to Come (1972). As the critic V. S. Pritchett has observed, Forster's "voice was the most important thing about him and his prose; it was unofficial, conversational, [and] free of jargon."

E. M. Forster

ॐ

MR. ANDREWS

The souls of the dead were ascending towards the Judgment Seat and the Gate of Heaven. The world soul pressed them on every side, just as the atmosphere presses upon rising bubbles, striving to vanquish them, to break their thin envelope of personality, to mingle their virtue with its own. But they resisted, remembering their glorious individual life on earth, and hoping for an individual life to come.

Among them ascended the soul of a Mr. Andrews who, after a beneficent and honourable life, had recently deceased at his house in town. He knew himself to be kind, upright, and religious, and though he approached his trial with all humility, he could not be doubtful of its result. God was not now a jealous God. He would not deny salvation merely because it was expected. A righteous soul may reasonably be conscious of its own righteousness and Mr. Andrews was conscious of his.

"The way is long," said a voice, "but by pleasant converse the way becomes shorter. Might I travel in your company?"

"Willingly," said Mr. Andrews. He held out his hand, and the two souls floated upwards together.

"I was slain fighting the infidel," said the other exultantly, "and I got straight to those joys of which the Prophet speaks."

"Are you not a Christian?" asked Mr. Andrews gravely.

"No, I am a Believer. But you are a Moslem, surely?"

"I am not," said Mr. Andrews. "I am a Believer."

The two souls floated upwards in silence, but did not release each other's hands. "I am broad church," he added gently. The word "broad" quavered strangely amid the interspaces.

"Relate to me your career," said the Turk at last.

"I was born of a decent middle-class family, and had my education at Winchester and Oxford. I thought of becoming a missionary, but was offered a post in the Board of Trade, which I accepted. At thirty-two I married, and had four children, two of whom have died. My wife survives me. If I had lived a little longer I should have been knighted."

"Now I will relate my career. I was never sure of my father, and my mother does not signify. I grew up in the slums of Salonika. Then I joined a band and we plundered the villages of the infidel. I prospered and had three wives, all of whom survive me. Had I lived a little longer I should have had a band of my own."

"A son of mine was killed travelling in Macedonia. Perhaps you killed him."

"It is very possible."

The two souls floated upwards, hand in hand. Mr. Andrews did not speak again, for he was filled with horror at the approaching tragedy. This man, so godless, so lawless, so cruel, so lustful, believed that he would be admitted into Heaven. And into what a heaven — a place full of the crude pleasures of a ruffian's life on earth! But Mr. Andrews felt neither disgust nor moral indignation. He was only conscious of an immense pity, and his own virtues confronted him not at all. He longed to save the man whose hand he held more tightly, who, he thought, was now holding more tightly on to him. And when he reached the Gate of Heaven, instead of saying, "Can I enter?" as he had intended, he cried out, "Cannot *he* center?"

And at the same moment the Turk uttered the same cry. For the same spirit was working in each of them.

From the gateway a voice replied, "Both can enter." They were filled with joy and pressed forward together.

Then the voice said, "In what clothes will you enter?"

"In my best clothes," shouted the Turk, "the ones I stole." And he clad himself in a splendid turban and waistcoat embroidered with silver, and baggy trousers, and a great belt in which were stuck pipes and pistols and knives.

"And in what clothes will you enter?" said the voice to Mr. Andrews.

Mr. Andrews thought of his best clothes, but he had no wish to wear them again. At last he remembered and said, "Robes."

"Of what colour and fashion?" asked the voice.

Mr. Andrews had never thought about the matter much. He replied, in hesitating tones, "White, I suppose, of some flowing soft material," and he was immediately given a garment such as he had described. "Do I wear it rightly?" he asked.

"Wear it as it pleases you," replied the voice. "What else do you desire?"

"A harp," suggested Mr. Andrews. "A small one."

A small gold harp was placed in his hand.

"And a palm — no, I cannot have a palm, for it is the reward of martyrdom; my life has been tranquil and happy."

"You can have a palm if you desire it."

But Mr. Andrews refused the palm, and hurried in his white robes after the Turk, who had already entered Heaven. As he passed in at the open gate, a man, dressed like himself, passed out with gestures of despair.

"Why is he not happy?" he asked.

The voice did not reply.

"And who are all those figures, seated inside on thrones and mountains? Why are some of them terrible, and sad, and ugly?"

There was no answer. Mr. Andrews entered, and then he saw that those seated figures were all the gods who were then being worshipped on the earth. A group of souls stood round each, singing his praises. But the gods paid no heed, for they were listening to the prayers of living men, which alone brought them nourishment. Sometimes a faith would grow weak, and then the god of that faith also drooped and dwindled and fainted for his daily portion of incense. And sometimes, owing to a revivalist movement, or to a great commemoration, or to some other cause, a faith would grow strong, and the god of that faith grow strong also. And, more frequently still, a faith would alter, so that the features of its god altered and became contradictory, and passed from ecstasy to respectability, or from mildness and universal love to the ferocity of battle. And at times a god would divide into two gods, or three, or more, each with his own ritual and precarious supply of prayer.

Mr. Andrews saw Buddha, and Vishnu, and Allah, and Jehovah, and the Elohim. He saw little ugly determined gods who were worshipped by a few savages in the same way. He saw the vast shadowy outlines of the neo-Pagan Zeus. There were cruel gods, and coarse gods, and tortured gods, and, worse still, there were gods who were peevish, or deceitful, or vulgar. No aspiration of humanity was unfulfilled. There was even an intermediate state for those who wished it, and for the Christian Scientists a place where they could demonstrate that they had not died.

He did not play his harp for long, but hunted vainly for one of his dead friends. And though souls were continually entering Heaven, it still seemed curiously empty. Though he had all that he expected, he was conscious of no great happiness, no mystic contemplation of beauty, no mystic union with good. There was nothing to compare with that moment outside the gate, when he prayed that the Turk might enter and heard the Turk uttering the same prayer for him. And when at last he saw his companion, he hailed him with a cry of human joy.

The Turk was seated in thought, and round him, by sevens, sat the virgins who are promised in the Koran.

"Oh, my dear friend!" he called out. "Come here and we will never be parted, and such as my pleasures are, they shall be yours also. Where are my other friends? Where are the men whom I love, or whom I have killed?"

"I, too, have only found you," said Mr. Andrews. He sat down by the Turk, and the virgins, who were all exactly alike, ogled them with coal black eyes.

"Though I have all that I expected," said the Turk, "I am conscious of no great happiness. There is nothing to compare with that moment outside the gate when I prayed that you might enter, and heard you uttering the same prayer for me. These virgins are as beautiful and good as I had fashioned, yet I could wish that they were better."

As he wished, the forms of the virgins became more rounded, and their eyes grew larger and blacker than before. And Mr. Andrews, by a wish similar in kind, increased the purity and softness of his garment and the glitter of his harp. For in that place their expectations were fulfilled, but not their hopes.

"I am going," said Mr. Andrews at last. "We desire infinity and we cannot imagine it. How can we expect it to be granted? I have never imagined anything infinitely good or beautiful excepting in my dreams."

"I am going with you," said the other.

Together they sought the entrance gate, and the Turk parted with his virgins and his best clothes, and Mr. Andrews cast away his robes and his harp.

"Can we depart?" they asked.

"You can both depart if you wish," said the voice, "but remember what lies outside."

As soon as they passed the gate, they felt again the pressure of the world soul. For a moment they stood hand in hand resisting it. Then they suffered it to break in upon them, and they, and all the experience they had gained, and all the love and wisdom they had generated, passed into it, and made it better.

[1928]

VIRGINIA WOOLF (1882–1941) *is best known as a novelist, critic, and essayist; she published only one book of short stories, early in her career. The daughter of Sir Leslie Stephen, a scholar and editor of the monumental* Dictionary of National Biography, *she was educated at home in her father's library, keenly aware that if she had been born a boy, she would have gone on to Cambridge or Oxford. Later, guided by this sense of injustice, she wrote two enduring feminist works,* A Room of One's Own *(1929) and* Three Guineas *(1938). In frail health all her life, she married the journalist and political philosopher Leonard Woolf in 1912, and they lived in Bloomsbury, the fashionably bohemian section of London. Her first novel,* The Voyage Out, *was published in 1915. Two years later the Woolfs set two stories by "L. and V. Woolf" on an old handpress and published them under the imprint of the Hogarth Press. The little pamphlet was so successful that their press became a thriving enterprise, publishing such authors as Katherine Mansfield and T. S. Eliot. In 1921 the Hogarth Press published* Monday or Tuesday, *Woolf's collection of short stories, and the following year — sustained by the sense of freedom in having her own printing press — she began to publish the unconventional novels that made her reputation:* Jacob's Room *(1922),* Mrs. Dalloway *(1925),* To the Lighthouse *(1927), and* The Waves *(1931). Dissatisfied with realistic fiction, Woolf explained in her* Writer's Diary *her ambition to eliminate "all waste, deadness, superfluity" in her novels in order "to give the moment whole, whatever it includes."*

Most of Woolf's fiction explores the psychological nature of consciousness, depicting her characters' moods and personal attitudes. Her characters pose the questions, "What is life? What is love? What is reality? Who are you? Who am I?" She believed that beneath the appearance of change and disorder that marks daily life is a timeless reality that becomes apparent only during pure "moments of being," when the self is transcended and the individual consciousness becomes an undifferentiated part of a greater whole. For Woolf, the description of the immediate flow of her characters' thoughts and feelings was more important than the realistic depiction of their physical behavior. Some readers, like her good friend E. M. Forster, wondered whether she hadn't gone too far: "She does not tell a story or weave a plot — can she create character?"

Throughout her life, Woolf wrote short stories as a way to relax between the arduous bouts of work on her novels, usually sketching a story out in rough form before putting the draft away in a drawer. She felt that by putting experiences into words, she revealed "some order" about the world, "a token of some real thing behind appearances; and I make it real by put-

ting it into words. It is only by putting it into words that I make it whole ...." Then, if an editor asked her for a short story, she would take out a sketch and rewrite it several times. She discussed with her husband the possibility of republishing Monday or Tuesday *together with her later stories, and after her suicide in 1941, Leonard Woolf saw this book through to publication as* A Haunted House and Other Stories *(1953). "Moments of Being" was included in it as one of the few stories "finally revised by her."*

Virginia Woolf

௹

MOMENTS OF BEING

"Slater's Pins Have No Points"

"Slater's pins have no points — don't you always find that?" said Miss Craye, turning round as the rose fell out of Fanny Wilmot's dress, and Fanny stooped, with her ears full of the music, to look for the pin on the floor.

The words gave her an extraordinary shock, as Miss Craye struck the last chord of the Bach fugue. Did Miss Craye actually go to Slater's and buy pins then, Fanny Wilmot asked herself, transfixed for a moment. Did she stand at the counter waiting like anybody else, and was she given a bill with coppers wrapped in it, and did she slip them into her purse and then, an hour later, stand by her dressing table and take out the pins? What need had she of pins? For she was not so much dressed as cased, like a beetle compactly in its sheath, blue in winter, green in summer. What need had she of pins — Julia Craye — who lived, it seemed in the cool glassy world of Bach fugues, playing to herself what she liked, and only consenting to take one or two pupils at the Archer Street College of Music (so the Principal, Miss Kingston, said) as a special favor to herself, who had "the greatest admiration for her in every way." Miss Craye was left badly off, Miss Kingston was afraid, at her brother's death. Oh, they used to have such lovely things, when they lived at Salisbury, and her brother Julius was, of course, a very well-known man: a famous archaeologist. It was a great privilege to stay with them, Miss Kingston said ("My family had always known them — they were regular Canterbury people," Miss Kingston said), but a little frightening for a child; one had to be careful not to slam the door or bounce into the room unexpectedly. Miss Kingston, who gave little character sketches like this on the first day of term while she received cheques and wrote out receipts for them, smiled here. Yes, she had been rather a tomboy; she had bounced in and set all those green Roman glasses and things jumping in their case. The Crayes were not used to children. The Crayes were none of them married. They kept cats; the cats, one used to feel, knew as much about the Roman urns and things as anybody.

"Far more than I did!" said Miss Kingston brightly, writing her name across the stamp in her dashing, cheerful, full-bodied hand, for she had always been practical. That was how she made her living, after all.

Perhaps then, Fanny Wilmot thought, looking for the pin, Miss Craye said that about "Slater's pins having no points," at a venture. None of the Crayes had ever married. She knew nothing about pins — nothing whatever. But she wanted to break the spell that had fallen on the house; to break the pane of glass which separated them from other people. When Polly Kingston, that merry little girl, had slammed the door and made the Roman vases jump, Julius, seeing that no harm was done (that would be his first instinct) looked, for the case was stood in the window, at Polly skipping home across the fields; looked with the look his sister often had, that lingering, driving look.

"Stars, sun, moon," it seemed to say, "the daisy in the grass, fires, frost on the window pane, my heart goes out to you. But," it always seemed to add, "you break, you pass, you go." And simultaneously it covered the intensity of both these states of mind with "I can't reach you — I can't get at you," spoken wistfully, frustratedly. And the stars faded, and the child went. That was the kind of spell that was the glassy surface, that Miss Craye wanted to break by showing, when she had played Bach beautifully as a reward to a favorite pupil (Fanny Wilmot knew that she was Miss Craye's favorite pupil), that she, too, knew, like other people, about pins. Slater's pins had no points.

Yes, the "famous archaeologist" had looked like that too. "The famous archaeologist" — as she said that, endorsing cheques, ascertaining the day of the month, speaking so brightly and frankly, there was in Miss Kingston's voice an indescribable tone which hinted at something odd; something queer in Julius Craye; it was the very same thing that was odd perhaps in Julia too. One could have sworn, thought Fanny Wilmot, as she looked for the pin, that at parties, meetings (Miss Kingston's father was a clergyman), she had picked up some piece of gossip, or it might only have been a smile, or a tone when his name was mentioned, which had given her "a feeling" about Julius Craye. Needless to say, she had never spoken about it to anybody. Probably she scarcely knew what she meant by it. But whenever she spoke of Julius, or heard him mentioned, that was the first thing that came to mind; and it was a seductive thought; there was something odd about Julius Craye.

It was so that Julia looked too, as she sat half turned on the music stool, smiling. It's on the field, it's on the pane, it's in the sky — beauty;

and I can't get at it; I can't have it — I, she seemed to add, with that little clutch of the hand which was so characteristic, who adore it so passionately, would give the whole world to possess it! And she picked up the carnation which had fallen on the floor, while Fanny searched for the pin. She crushed it, Fanny felt, voluptuously in her smooth veined hands stuck about with water-colored rings set in pearls. The pressure of her fingers seemed to increase all that was most brilliant in the flower; to set it off; to make it more frilled, fresh, immaculate. What was odd in her, and perhaps in her brother, too, was that this crush and grasp of the finger was combined with a perpetual frustration. So it was even now with the carnation. She had her hands on it; she pressed it; but she did not possess it, enjoy it, not entirely and altogether.

None of the Crayes had married, Fanny Wilmot remembered. She had in mind how one evening when the lesson had lasted longer than usual and it was dark, Julia Craye had said "it's the use of men, surely, to protect us," smiling at her that same odd smile, as she stood fastening her cloak, which made her, like the flower, conscious to her finger tips of youth and brilliance, but, like the flower, too, Fanny suspected, made her feel awkward.

"Oh, but I don't want protection," Fanny had laughed, and when Julia Craye, fixing on her that extraordinary look, had said she was not so sure of that, Fanny positively blushed under the admiration in her eyes.

It was the only use of men, she had said. Was it for that reason then, Fanny wondered, with her eyes on the floor, that she had never married? After all, she had not lived all her life in Salisbury. "Much the nicest part of London," she had said once, "(but I'm speaking of fifteen or twenty years ago) is Kensington. One was in the Gardens in ten minutes — it was like the heart of the country. One could dine out in one's slippers without catching cold. Kensington — it was like a village then, you know," she had said.

Here she broke off, to denounce acridly the draughts in the Tubes.

"It was the use of men," she had said, with a queer wry acerbity. Did that throw any light on the problem why she had not married? One could imagine every sort of scene in her youth, when with her good blue eyes, her straight firm nose, her air of cool distinction, her piano playing, her rose flowering with chaste passion in the bosom of her muslin dress, she had attracted first the young men to whom such things, the china tea cups and the silver candlesticks and the inlaid table, for the Crayes had such nice things, were wonderful; young men not sufficiently distinguished; young men of the cathedral town with ambitions. She had attracted them first, and then her brother's friends from Oxford or Cambridge. They would come down in the summer; row her on the river; continue the argument about Browning by letter; and arrange perhaps, on the rare occasions when she stayed in London, to show her — Kensington Gardens?

"Much the nicest part of London — Kensington (I'm speaking of fifteen or twenty years ago)," she had said once. One was in the gardens in ten minutes — in the heart of the country. One could make that yield what one liked, Fanny Wilmot thought, single out, for instance, Mr. Sherman, the painter, an old friend of hers; make him call for her, by appointment, one sunny day in June; take her to have tea under the trees. (They had met, too, at those parties to which one tripped in slippers without fear of catching cold.) The aunt or other elderly relative was to wait there while they looked at the Serpentine. They looked at the Serpentine. He may have rowed her across. They compared it with the Avon. She would have considered the comparison very furiously. Views of rivers were important to her. She sat hunched a little, a little angular, though she was graceful then, steering. At the critical moment, for he had determined that he must speak now — it was his only chance of getting her alone — he was speaking with his head turned at an absurd angle, in his great nervousness, over his shoulder — at that very moment she interrupted fiercely. He would have them into the Bridge, she cried. It was a moment of horror, of disillusionment, of revelation, for both of them. I can't have it, I can't possess it, she thought. He could not see why she had come then. With a great splash of his oar he pulled the boat round. Merely to snub him? He rowed her back and said good-bye to her.

The setting of that scene could be varied as one chose, Fanny Wilmot reflected. (Where had that pin fallen?) It might be Ravenna; or Edinburgh, where she had kept house for her brother. The scene could be changed; and the young man and the exact manner of it all, but one thing was constant — her refusal, and her frown, and her anger with herself afterwards, and her argument, and her relief — yes, certainly her immense relief. The very next day, perhaps, she would get up at six, put on her cloak, and walk all the way from Kensington to the river. She was so thankful that she had not sacrificed her right to go and look at things when they are at their best — before people are up, that is to say she could have her breakfast in bed if she liked. She had not sacrificed her independence.

Yes, Fanny Wilmot smiled, Julia had not endangered her habits. They remained safe; and her habits would have suffered if she had married. "They're ogres," she had said one evening, half laughing, when another pupil, a girl lately married, suddenly bethinking her that she would miss her husband, had rushed off in haste.

"They're ogres," she had said, laughing grimly. An ogre would have interfered perhaps with breakfast in bed; with walks at dawn down to the river. What would have happened (but one could hardly conceive this) had she had children? She took astonishing precautions against chills, fatigue, rich food, the wrong food, draughts, heated rooms, journeys in the Tube, for she could never determine which of these it was exactly that brought on those terrible headaches that gave her life the semblance of a battlefield. She was always engaged in outwitting the enemy, until it seemed as if the pursuit had its interest; could she have beaten the enemy finally she would have found life a little dull. As it was, the tug-of-war was perpetual — on the one side the nightingale or the view which she loved with passion — yes, for views and birds she felt nothing less than passion; on the other the damp path or the horrid long drag up a steep hill which would certainly make her good for nothing next day and bring on one of her headaches. When, therefore, from time to time, she managed her forces adroitly and brought off a visit to Hampton Court the week the crocuses — those glossy bright flowers were her favorite — were at their best, it was a victory. It was something that lasted; something that mattered forever. She strung the afternoon on the necklace of memorable days, which was not too long for her to be able to recall this one or that one; this view, that city; to finger it, to feel it, to savor, sighing, the quality that made it unique.

"It was so beautiful last Friday," she said, "that I determined I must go there." So she had gone off to Waterloo on her great undertaking — to visit Hampton Court — alone. Naturally, but perhaps foolishly, one pitied her for the thing she never asked pity for (indeed she was reticent habitually, speaking of her health only as a warrior might speak of her foe) — one pitied her for always doing everything alone. Her brother was dead. Her sister was asthmatic. She found the climate of Edinburgh good for her. It was too bleak for Julia. Perhaps, too, she found the associations painful, for her brother, the famous archaeologist, had died there; and she had loved her brother. She lived in a little house off the Brompton Road entirely alone.

Fanny Wilmot saw the pin; she picked it up. She looked at Miss Craye. Was Miss Craye so lonely? No, Miss Craye was steadily, blissfully, if only for that moment, a happy woman. Fanny had surprised her in a moment of ecstasy. She sat there, half turned away from the piano, with her hands clasped in her lap holding the carnation upright, while behind her was the sharp square of the window, uncurtained, purple in the evening, intensely purple after the brilliant electric lights which burnt unshaded in the bare music room. Julia Craye, sitting hunched and compact holding her flower, seemed to emerge out of the London night, seemed to fling it like a cloak behind her, it seemed, in its bareness and intensity, the effluence of her spirit, something she had made which surrounded her. Fanny stared.

All seemed transparent, for a moment, to the gaze of Fanny Wilmot, as if looking through Miss Craye, she saw the very fountain of her being spurting its pure silver drops. She saw back and back into the past behind her. She saw the green Roman vases stood in their case; heard the choristers playing cricket; saw Julia quietly descend the curving steps on to the lawn; then saw her pour out tea beneath the cedar tree; softly enclosed the old man's hand in hers; saw her going round and about the corridors of that ancient Cathedral dwelling place with towels in her hand to mark them; lamenting, as she went, the pettiness of daily life; and slowly aging, and putting away clothes when summer came, because at her age they were too bright to wear; and tending her father's sickness; and cleaving her way ever more definitely as her will stiffened toward her solitary goal; travelling frugally; counting the cost and measuring out of her tight shut purse the sum needed for this journey or for that old mirror; obstinately adhering, whatever people might say, in choosing her pleasures for herself. She saw Julia ——

Julia blazed. Julia kindled. Out of the night she burnt like a dead white star. Julia opened her arms. Julia kissed her on the lips. Julia possessed it.

"Slater's pins have no points," Miss Craye said, laughing queerly and relaxing her arms, as Fanny Wilmot pinned the flower to her breast with trembling fingers.

[1921]

JAMES JOYCE (1882-1941) *was born James Augustine Aloysius Joyce in Rathgar, a suburb of Dublin, during a turbulent era of political change in Ireland. His parents sent him at the age of six to the best Jesuit school, Clongowes Wood College, where he spent three years; but in 1891 his father was no longer able to afford the tuition, and he was withdrawn from the school. During the period of his parents' financial decline, Joyce — a brilliant student — was educated at home and then given free tuition at Belvedere College, where he won prizes for his essays. Shortly after taking his bachelor's degree in 1902 from University College, Dublin, he left Ireland for Paris, where he attended one class at the Collège de Médecine but dropped out because he could not afford the fees. Nearly starving, he remained in Paris and wrote some plotless sketches he called "Epiphanies." These were notebook jottings of overheard conversations or passing observations that he later incorporated into his fiction, thinking that they illuminated in a flash the meaning of a group of apparently unrelated phenomena.*

In April 1903 Joyce returned to Dublin because his mother was dying. He remained in Ireland a short time as a teacher, but the following year he went to live abroad again, disillusioned by his home country's political corruption and religious hypocrisy.

Dubliners (1916), a group of fifteen short stories begun in 1904, was Joyce's attempt to "write a chapter of the moral history" of Ireland. He chose Dublin for the setting because that city seemed to him "the center of paralysis," but he also thought of following the book with another entitled "Provincials." As if to prove his perception of the extent of stifling moral repression in his country, he had great difficulties getting the book published — a struggle lasting nine years. This so angered and frustrated Joyce that he never again lived in Ireland, settling in Trieste, Zurich, and Paris and writing the novels that established him as one of the greatest writers of modern times: A Portrait of the Artist as a Young Man *(1916),* Ulysses *(1922), and* Finnegan's Wake *(1939).*

When Joyce wrote his brother Stanislaus about the Dubliner *stories in 1905, he described his struggle against social conventions with a characteristic blend of arrogance and insight: "Maupassant writes very well, of course, but I am afraid that his moral sense is rather obtuse. . . . The struggle against conventions in which I am at present involved was not entered into by me so much as a protest against these conventions as with the intention of living in conformity with my moral nature." Joyce's stories about the lives of young people, servants, politicians, and the complacent middle class were intended to represent a broad spectrum of Dublin life, not "a collection of tourist impressions" but rather a penetrating account of the spiritual waste of his times. Today's reader finds it difficult to believe that*

some stories in Dubliners could have appeared so scandalous to Joyce's pub-
lishers that at one stage in the book's tortuous journey toward publication
the plates were destroyed at the printers.

"The Sisters," "Araby," and "The Dead," represent the spectrum of
the stories in Dubliners, encompassing the periods of youth, adolescence,
and maturity that Joyce included in his book. His technique blends a de-
tached sympathy for his subject with a "scrupulous meanness" of observed
detail. Instead of dramatic plots, he structured his stories around "epiph-
anies" — evanescent moments in the narrative that reveal "a sudden spir-
itual manifestation, whether in the vulgarity of speech or of gesture or in a
memorable expression of the mind itself." The language of the stories goes
beyond pictorial exactness to exhibit a concern for the sound and cadence
of the words as well as the specific details of description. As Frank O'Con-
nor realized, Joyce was not only "insisting that we shall see the scene exactly
as he saw it by his use of Flaubert's 'proper word,' " but also "insisting that
we shall feel it as he felt it by a deliberate though carefully concealed juxta-
position of key words." The "key words" in "The Dead," the final story in
Dubliners, cluster in the often repeated images of light and fire, cold and
snow that appear throughout the story, embodying its meaning. (See
Joyce's Draft of "The Sisters" on page 1257 and O'Connor's Commentary
about "The Dead" on page 1265.)

James Joyce

ೞ

THE SISTERS

There was no hope for him this time: it was the third stroke. Night
after night I had passed the house (it was vacation time) and studied the
lighted square of window: and night after night I had found it lighted in the
same way, faintly and evenly. If he was dead, I thought, I would see the reflection of candles on the darkened blind for I knew that two candles must
be set at the head of a corpse. He had often said to me: *I am not long for*
this world, and I had thought his words idle. Now I knew they were true.
Every night as I gazed up at the window I said softly to myself the word
paralysis. It had always sounded strangely in my ears, like the word *gnomon*
in the Euclid and the word *simony* in the Catechism. But now it sounded
to me like the name of some maleficent and sinful being. It filled me with
fear, and yet I longed to be nearer to it and to look upon its deadly work.

Old Cotter was sitting at the fire, smoking, when I came downstairs to supper. While my aunt was ladling out my stirabout he said, as if returning to some former remark of his:

— No, I wouldn't say he was exactly . . . but there was something queer . . . there was something uncanny about him. I'll tell you my opinion. . . .

He began to puff at his pipe, no doubt arranging his opinion in his mind. Tiresome old fool! When we knew him first he used to be rather interesting, talking of faints and worms; but I soon grew tired of him and his endless stories about the distillery.

— I have my own theory about it, he said. I think it was one of those . . . peculiar cases. . . . But it's hard to say. . . .

He began to puff again at his pipe without giving us his theory. My uncle saw me staring and said to me:

— Well, so your old friend is gone, you'll be sorry to hear.

— Who? said I.

— Father Flynn.

— Is he dead?

— Mr Cotter here has just told us. He was passing by the house.

I knew that I was under observation so I continued eating as if the news had not interested me. My uncle explained to old Cotter.

— The youngster and he were great friends. The old chap taught him a great deal, mind you; and they say he had a great wish for him.

— God have mercy on his soul, said my aunt piously.

Old Cotter looked at me for a while. I felt that his little beady black eyes were examining me but I would not satisfy him by looking up from my plate. He returned to his pipe and finally spat rudely into the grate.

— I wouldn't like children of mine, he said, to have too much to say to a man like that.

— How do you mean, Mr Cotter? asked my aunt.

— What I mean is, said old Cotter, it's bad for children. My idea is: let a young lad run about and play with young lads of his own age and not be . . . Am I right, Jack?

— That's my principle, too, said my uncle. Let him learn to box his corner. That's what I'm always saying to that Rosicrucian there: take exercise. Why, when I was a nipper every morning of my life I had a cold bath, winter and summer. And that's what stands to me now. Education is all very fine and large. . . . Mr. Cotter might take a pick of that leg of mutton, he added to my aunt.

— No, no, not for me, said old Cotter.

My aunt brought the dish from the safe and laid it on the table.

— But why do you think it's not good for children, Mr Cotter? she asked.

— It's bad for children, said old Cotter, because their minds are so impressionable. When children see things like that, you know, it has an effect. . . .

I crammed my mouth with stirabout for fear I might give utterance to my anger. Tiresome old red-nosed imbecile!

It was late when I fell asleep. Though I was angry with old Cotter for alluding to me as a child I puzzled my head to extract meaning from his unfinished sentences. In the dark of my room I imagined that I saw again the heavy grey face of the paralytic. I drew the blankets over my head and tried to think of Christmas. But the grey face still followed me. It murmured; and I understood that it desired to confess something. I felt my soul receding into some pleasant and vicious region; and there again I found it waiting for me. It began to confess to me in a murmuring voice and I wondered why it smiled continually and why the lips were so moist with spittle. But then I remembered that it had died of paralysis and I felt that I too was smiling feebly as if to absolve the simoniac of his sin.

The next morning after breakfast I went down to look at the little house in Great Britain Street. It was an unassuming shop, registered under the vague name of *Drapery*. The drapery consisted mainly of children's bootees and umbrellas; and on ordinary days a notice used to hang in the window, saying: *Umbrellas Re-covered*. No notice was visible now for the shutters were up. A crape bouquet was tied to the door-knocker with ribbon. Two poor women and a telegram boy were reading the card pinned on the crape. I also approached and read:

July 1st, 1895

The Rev. James Flynn (formerly of S. Catherine's Church,
Meath Street), aged sixty-five years.
R.I.P.

The reading of the card persuaded me that he was dead and I was disturbed to find myself at check. Had he not been dead I would have gone into the little dark room behind the shop to find him sitting in his arm-chair by the fire, nearly smothered in his great-coat. Perhaps my aunt would have given me a packet of High Toast for him and this present would have roused him from his stupefied doze. It was always I who emptied the packet into his black snuff-box for his hands trembled too much to allow him to do this without spilling half the snuff about the floor. Even as he raised his large trembling hand to his nose little clouds of smoke dribbled through his fingers over the front of his coat. It may have been these constant showers of snuff which gave his ancient priestly garments their green faded look for the red handkerchief, blackened, as it always was, with the snuff-stains of a week, with which he tried to brush away the fallen grains, was quite inefficacious.

I wished to go in and look at him but I had not the courage to knock. I walked away slowly along the sunny side of the street, reading all the theatrical advertisements in the shop-windows as I went. I found it strange that neither I nor the day seemed in a mourning mood and I felt even annoyed at discovering in myself a sensation of freedom as if I had been freed from something by his death. I wondered at this for, as my uncle had said the night before, he had taught me a great deal. He had studied in the Irish college in Rome and he had taught me to pronounce Latin properly. He had told me stories about the catacombs and about Napoleon Bonaparte, and he had explained to me the meaning of the different ceremonies of the Mass and of the different vestments worn by the priest. Sometimes he had amused himself by putting difficult questions to me, asking me what one should do in certain circumstances or whether such and such sins were mortal or venial or only imperfections. His questions showed me how complex and mysterious were certain institutions of the Church which I had always regarded as the simplest acts. The duties of the priest towards the Eucharist and towards the secrecy of the confessional seemed so grave to me that I wondered how anybody had ever found in himself the courage to undertake them; and I was not surprised when he told me that the fathers of the Church had written books as thick as the *Post Office Directory* and as closely printed as the law notices in the newspaper, elucidating all these intricate questions. Often when I thought of this I could make no answer or only a very foolish and halting one upon which he used to smile and nod his head twice or thrice. Sometimes he used to put me through the responses of the Mass which he had made me learn by heart; and, as I pattered, he used to smile pensively and nod his head, now and then pushing huge pinches of snuff up each nostril alternately. When he smiled he used to uncover his big discoloured teeth and let his tongue lie upon his lower lip — a habit which had made me feel uneasy in the beginning of our acquaintance before I knew him well.

As I walked along in the sun I remembered old Cotter's words and tried to remember what had happened afterwards in the dream. I remembered that I had noticed long velvet curtains and a swinging lamp of antique fashion. I felt that I had been very far away, in some land where the customs were strange — in Persia, I thought. . . . But I could not remember the end of the dream.

In the evening my aunt took me with her to visit the house of mourning. It was after sunset; but the window-panes of the houses that looked to the west reflected the tawny gold of a great bank of clouds. Nannie received us in the hall; and, as it would have been unseemly to have shouted at her, my aunt shook hands with her for all. The old woman pointed upwards interrogatively and, on my aunt's nodding, proceeded to toil up the narrow staircase before us, her bowed head being scarcely above the level of the banister-rail. At the first landing she stopped and beckoned us forward encouragingly towards the open door of the dead-room. My aunt went in and the old woman, seeing that I hesitated to enter, began to beckon to me again repeatedly with her hand.

I went in on tiptoe. The room through the lace end of the blind was suffused with dusky golden light amid which the candles looked like pale thin flames. He had been coffined. Nannie gave the lead and we three knelt down at the foot of the bed. I pretended to pray but I could not gather my thoughts because the old woman's mutterings distracted me. I noticed how clumsily her skirt was hooked at the back and how the heels of her cloth boots were trodden down all to one side. The fancy came to me that the old priest was smiling as he lay there in his coffin.

But no. When we rose and went up to the head of the bed I saw that he was not smiling. There he lay, solemn and copious, vested as for the altar, his large hands loosely retaining a chalice. His face was very truculent, grey and massive, with black cavernous nostrils and circled by a scanty white fur. There was a heavy odour in the room — the flowers.

We blessed ourselves and came away. In the little room downstairs we found Eliza seated in his arm-chair in state. I groped my way towards my usual chair in the corner while Nannie went to the sideboard and brought out a decanter of sherry and some wine-glasses. She set these on the table and invited us to take a little glass of wine. Then, at her sister's bidding, she poured out the sherry into the glasses and passed them to us. She pressed me to take some cream crackers also but I declined because I thought I would make too much noise eating them. She seemed to be somewhat disappointed at my refusal and went over quietly to the sofa where she sat down behind her sister. No one spoke: we all gazed at the empty fireplace.

My aunt waited until Eliza sighed and then said:

— Ah, well, he's gone to a better world.

Eliza sighed again and bowed her head in assent. My aunt fingered the stem of her wine-glass before sipping a little.

— Did he . . . peacefully? she asked.

— O, quite peacefully, ma'am, said Eliza. You couldn't tell when the breath went out of him. He had a beautiful death, God be praised.

— And everything . . . ?

— Father O'Rourke was in with him a Tuesday and anointed him and prepared him and all.

— He knew then?

— He was quite resigned.

— He looks quite resigned, said my aunt.

— That's what the woman we had in to wash him said. She said he just looked as if he was asleep, he looked that peaceful and resigned. No one would think he'd make such a beautiful corpse.

— Yes, indeed, said my aunt.

She sipped a little more from her glass and said:

— Well, Miss Flynn, at any rate it must be a great comfort for you to know that you did all you could for him. You were both very kind to him, I must say.

Eliza smoothed her dress over her knees.

— Ah, poor James! she said. God knows we done all we could, as poor as we are — we wouldn't see him want anything while he was in it.

Nannie had leaned her head against the sofa-pillow and seemed about to fall asleep.

— There's poor Nannie, said Eliza, looking at her, she's wore out. All the work we had, she and me, getting in the woman to wash him and then laying him out and then the coffin and then arranging about the Mass in the chapel. Only for Father O'Rourke I don't know what we'd have done at all. It was him brought us all them flowers and them two candlesticks out of the chapel and wrote out the notice for the *Freeman's General* and took charge of all the papers for the cemetery and poor James's insurance.

— Wasn't that good of him? said my aunt.

Eliza closed her eyes and shook her head slowly.

— Ah, there's no friends like the old friends, she said, when all is said and done, no friends that a body can trust.

— Indeed, that's true, said my aunt. And I'm sure now that he's gone to his eternal reward he won't forget you and all your kindness to him.

— Ah, poor James! said Eliza. He was no great trouble to us. You wouldn't hear him in the house any more than now. Still, I know he's gone and all to that. . . .

— It's when it's all over that you'll miss him, said my aunt.

— I know that, said Eliza. I won't be bringing him in his cup of beef-tea any more, nor you, ma'am, sending him his snuff. Ah, poor James!

She stopped, as if she were communing with the past and then said shrewdly:

— Mind you, I noticed there was something queer coming over him latterly. Whenever I'd bring in his soup to him there I'd find him with his breviary fallen to the floor, lying back in the chair and his mouth open.

She laid a finger against her nose and frowned: then she continued:

— But still and all he kept on saying that before the summer was over he'd go out for a drive one fine day just to see the old house again where we were all born down in Irishtown and take me and Nannie with him. If we could only get one of them new-fangled carriages that makes no noise that Father O'Rourke told him about — them with the rheumatic wheels — for the day cheap, he said, at Johnny Rush's over the way there and drive out the three of us together of a Sunday evening. He had his mind set on that. . . . Poor James!

— The Lord have mercy on his soul! said my aunt.

Eliza took out her handkerchief and wiped her eyes with it. Then she put it back again in her pocket and gazed into the empty grate for some time without speaking.

— He was too scrupulous always, she said. The duties of the priesthood was too much for him. And then his life was, you might say, crossed.

— Yes, said my aunt. He was a disappointed man. You could see that.

A silence took possession of the little room and, under cover of it, I approached the table and tasted my sherry and then returned quietly to my chair in the corner. Eliza seemed to have fallen into a deep revery. We waited respectfully for her to break the silence: and after a long pause she said slowly:

— It was that chalice he broke. . . . That was the beginning of it. Of course, they say it was all right, that it contained nothing, I mean. But still. . . . They say it was the boy's fault. But poor James was so nervous, God be merciful to him!

— And was that it? said my aunt. I heard something. . . . Eliza nodded.

— That affected his mind, she said. After that he began to mope by himself, talking to no one and wandering about by himself. So one night he was wanted for to go on a call and they couldn't find him anywhere. They looked high up and low down; and still they couldn't see a sight of him anywhere. So then the clerk suggested to try the chapel. So then they got the keys and opened the chapel and the clerk and Father O'Rourke and another priest that was there brought in a light for to look for him. . . . And what do you think but there he was, sitting up by himself in the dark in his confession-box, wide-awake and laughing-like softly to himself?

She stopped suddenly as if to listen. I too listened; but there was no sound in the house: and I knew that the old priest was lying still in his coffin as we had seen him, solemn and truculent in death, an idle chalice on his breast.

Eliza resumed:

— Wide-awake and laughing to himself. . . . So then, of course, when they saw that, that made them think that there was something gone wrong with him. . . .

[1916]

James Joyce

∾

ARABY

North Richmond Street, being blind, was a quiet street except at the hour when the Christian Brothers' School set the boys free. An uninhabited house of two storeys stood at the blind end, detached from its neighbours in a square ground. The other houses of the street, conscious of decent lives within them, gazed at one another with brown imperturbable faces.

The former tenant of our house, a priest, had died in the back drawing-room. Air, musty from having been long enclosed, hung in all the rooms, and the waste room behind the kitchen was littered with old useless papers. Among these I found a few paper-covered books, the pages of which were curled and damp: *The Abbot*, by Walter Scott, *The Devout Communicant*, and *The Memoirs of Vidocq*. I liked the last best because its leaves were yellow. The wild garden behind the house contained a central apple-tree and a few straggling bushes under one of which I found the late tenant's rusty bicycle-pump. He had been a very charitable priest; in his will he had left all his money to institutions and the furniture of his house to his sister.

When the short days of winter came dusk fell before we had well eaten our dinners. When we met in the street the houses had grown sombre. The space of sky above us was the colour of ever-changing violet and towards it the lamps of the street lifted their feeble lanterns. The cold air stung us and we played till our bodies glowed. Our shouts echoed in the silent street. The career of our play brought us through the dark muddy lanes behind the houses where we ran the gauntlet of the rough tribes from the cottages, to the back doors of the dark dripping gardens where odours arose from the ashpits, to the dark odorous stables where a coachman smoothed and combed the horse or shook music from the buckled harness. When we returned to the street light from the kitchen windows had filled the areas. If my uncle was seen turning the corner we hid in the shadow until we had seen him safely housed. Or if Mangan's sister came out on the doorstep to call her brother in to his tea we watched her from our shadow peer up and down the street. We waited to see whether she would remain or go in and, if she remained, we left our shadow and walked up to Mangan's steps resignedly. She was waiting for us, her figure defined by the light from the half-opened door. Her brother always teased her before he obeyed and I stood by the railings looking at her. Her dress swung as she moved her body and the soft rope of her hair tossed from side to side.

Every morning I lay on the floor in the front parlour watching her door. The blind was pulled down to within an inch of the sash so that I could not be seen. When she came out on the doorstep my heart leaped. I ran to the hall, seized my books, and followed her. I kept her brown figure always in my eye and, when we came near the point at which our ways diverged, I quickened my pace and passed her. This happened morning after morning. I had never spoken to her, except for a few casual words, and yet her name was like a summons to all my foolish blood.

Her image accompanied me even in places the most hostile to romance. On Saturday evenings when my aunt went marketing I had to go to carry some of the parcels. We walked through the flaring streets, jostled by drunken men and bargaining women, amid the curses of labourers, the shrill litanies of shop-boys who stood on guard by the barrel of pigs' cheeks, the nasal chanting of street-singers, who sang a come-all-you about O'Donovan Rossa, or a ballad about the troubles in our native land. These noises converged in a single sensation of life for me: I imagined that I bore my chalice safely through a throng of foes. Her name sprang to my lips at moments in strange prayers and praises which I myself did not understand. My eyes were often full of tears (I could not tell why) and at times a flood from my heart seemed to pour itself out into my bosom. I thought little of the future. I did not know whether I would ever speak to her or not or, if I spoke to her, how I could tell her of my confused adoration. But my body was like a harp and her words and gestures were like fingers running upon the wires.

One evening I went into the back drawing-room in which the priest had died. It was a dark rainy evening and there was no sound in the house. Through one of the broken panes I heard the rain impinge upon the earth, the fine incessant needles of water playing in the sodden beds. Some distant lamp or lighted window gleamed below me. I was thankful that I could see so little. All my senses seemed to desire to veil themselves and, feeling that I was about to slip from them, I pressed the palms of my hands together until they trembled, murmuring: *"O love! O love!"* many times.

At last she spoke to me. When she addressed the first words to me I was so confused that I did not know what to answer. She asked me was I going to *Araby.* I forgot whether I answered yes or no. It would be a splendid bazaar, she said she would love to go.

"And why can't you?" I asked.

While she spoke she turned a silver bracelet round and round her wrist. She could not go, she said, because there would be a retreat that week in her convent. Her brother and two other boys were fighting for their caps and I was alone at the railings. She held one of the spikes, bowing her head towards me. The light from the lamp opposite our door caught the white curve of her neck, lit up her hair that rested there and, falling, lit up the hand upon the railing. It fell over one side of her dress and caught the white border of a petticoat, just visible as she stood at ease.

"It's well for you," she said.

"If I go," I said, "I will bring you something."

What innumerable follies laid waste my waking and sleeping thoughts after that evening! I wished to annihilate the tedious intervening days. I chafed against the work of school. At night in my bedroom and by day in the classroom her image came between me and the page I strove to read. The syllables of the word *Araby* were called to me through the silence in which my soul luxuriated and cast an Eastern enchantment over me. I asked for leave to go to the bazaar on Saturday night. My aunt was surprised and hoped it was not some Freemason affair. I answered few questions in class. I watched my master's face pass from amiability to sternness; he hoped I was not beginning to idle. I could not call my wandering thoughts together. I had hardly any patience with the serious work of life which, now that it stood between me and my desire, seemed to me child's play, ugly monotonous child's play.

On Saturday morning I reminded my uncle that I wished to go to the bazaar in the evening. He was fussing at the hallstand, looking for the hat-brush, and answered me curtly:

"Yes, boy, I know."

As he was in the hall I could not go into the front parlour and lie at the window. I left the house in bad humour and walked slowly towards the school. The air was pitilessly raw and already my heart misgave me.

When I came home to dinner my uncle had not yet been home. Still it was early. I sat staring at the clock for some time and, when its ticking began to irritate me, I left the room. I mounted the staircase and gained the upper part of the house. The high cold empty gloomy rooms liberated me and I went from room to room singing. From the front window I saw my companions playing below in the street. Their cries reached me weakened and indistinct and, leaning my forehead against the cool glass, I looked over at the dark house where she lived. I may have stood there for an hour, seeing nothing but the brown-clad figure cast by my imagination, touched discreetly by the lamplight at the curved neck, at the hand upon the railings and at the border below the dress.

When I came downstairs again I found Mrs. Mercer sitting at the fire. She was an old garrulous woman, a pawnbroker's widow, who collected used stamps for some pious purpose. I had to endure the gossip of the tea-table. The meal was prolonged beyond an hour and still my uncle did not come. Mrs. Mercer stood up to go: she was sorry she couldn't wait any longer, but it was after eight o'clock and she did not like to be out late, as the night air was bad for her. When she had gone I began to walk up and down the room, clenching my fists. My aunt said:

"I'm afraid you may put off your bazaar for this night of Our Lord."

At nine o'clock I heard my uncle's latchkey in the halldoor. I heard him talking to himself and heard the hallstand rocking when it had received the weight of his overcoat. I could interpret these signs. When he was midway through his dinner I asked him to give me the money to go to the bazaar. He had forgotten.

"The people are in bed and after their first sleep now," he said.

I did not smile. My aunt said to him energetically:

"Can't you give him the money and let him go? You've kept him late enough as it is."

My uncle said he was very sorry he had forgotten. He said he believed in the old saying: "All work and no play makes Jack a dull boy." He asked me where I was going and, when I had told him a second time he asked me did I know *The Arab's Farewell to his Steed.* When I left the kitchen he was about to recite the opening lines of the piece to my aunt.

I held a florin[1] tightly in my hand as I strode down Buckingham Street towards the station. The sight of the streets thronged with buyers and glaring with gas recalled to me the purpose of my journey. I took my seat in a third-class carriage of a deserted train. After an intolerable delay the train moved out of the station slowly. It crept onward among ruinous houses and over the the twinkling river. At Westland Row Station a crowd of people pressed to the carriage doors; but the porters moved them back, saying that it was a special train for the bazaar. I remained alone in the bare carriage. In a few minutes the train drew up beside an improvised wooden platform. I passed out on to the road and saw by the lighted dial of a clock that it was ten minutes to ten. In front of me was a large building which displayed the magical name.

I could not find any sixpenny entrance and, fearing that the bazaar would be closed, I passed in quickly through a turnstile, handing a shilling to a weary-looking man. I found myself in a big hall girdled at half its height by a gallery. Nearly all the stalls were closed and the greater part of the hall

---

[1] a silver coin worth two shillings.

was in darkness. I recognised a silence like that which pervades a church after a service. I walked into the centre of the bazaar timidly. A few people were gathered about the stalls which were still open. Before a curtain, over which the words *Café Chantant* were written in coloured lamps, two men were counting money on a salver. I listened to the fall of the coins.

Remembering with difficulty why I had come I went over to one of the stalls and examined porcelain vases and flowered tea-sets. At the door of the stall a young lady was talking and laughing with two young gentlemen. I remarked their English accents and listened vaguely to their conversation.

"O, I never said such a thing!"

"O, but you did!"

"O, but I didn't!"

"Didn't she say that?"

"Yes. I heard her."

"O, there's a . . . fib!"

Observing me the young lady came over and asked me did I wish to buy anything. The tone of her voice was not encouraging; she seemed to have spoken to me out of a sense of duty. I looked humbly at the great jars that stood like eastern guards at either side of the dark entrance to the stall and murmured:

"No, thank you."

The young lady changed the position of one of the vases and went back to the two young men. They began to talk of the same subject. Once or twice the young lady glanced at me over her shoulder.

I lingered before her stall, though I knew my stay was useless, to make my interest in her wares seem the more real. Then I turned away slowly and walked down the middle of the bazaar. I allowed the two pennies to fall against the sixpence in my pocket. I heard a voice call from one end of the gallery that the light was out. The upper part of the hall was now completely dark.

Gazing up into the darkness I saw myself as a creature driven and derided by vanity; and my eyes burned with anguish and anger.

[1916]

James Joyce

∽∾

THE DEAD

Lily, the caretaker's daughter, was literally run off her feet. Hardly had she brought one gentleman into the little pantry behind the office on the ground floor and helped him off with his overcoat than the wheezy hall-door bell clanged again and she had to scamper along the bare hallway to let in another guest. It was well for her she had not to attend to the ladies also. But Miss Kate and Miss Julia had thought of that and had converted the bathroom upstairs into a ladies' dressing-room. Miss Kate and Miss Julia were there, gossiping and laughing and fussing, walking after each other to the head of the stairs, peering down over the banisters and calling down to Lily to ask her who had come.

It was always a great affair, the Misses Morkan's annual dance. Everybody who knew them came to it, members of the family, old friends of the family, the members of Julia's choir, any of Kate's pupils that were grown up enough and even some of Mary Jane's pupils too. Never once had it fallen flat. For years and years it had gone off in splendid style as long as anyone could remember; ever since Kate and Julia, after the death of their brother Pat, had left the house in Stoney Batter and taken Mary Jane, their only niece, to live with them in the dark gaunt house on Usher's Island, the upper part of which they had rented from Mr Fulham, the corn-factor on the ground floor. That was a good thirty years ago if it was a day. Mary Jane, who was then a little girl in short clothes, was now the main prop of the household for she had the organ in Haddington Road. She had been through the Academy and gave a pupils' concert every year in the upper room of the Antient Concert Rooms. Many of her pupils belonged to better-class families on the Kingstown and Dalkey line. Old as they were, her aunts also did their share. Julia, though she was quite grey, was still the leading soprano in Adam and Eve's, and Kate, being too feeble to go about much, gave music lessons to beginners on the old square piano in the back room. Lily, the caretaker's daughter, did house-maid's work for them. Though their life was modest they believed in eating well; the best of everything: diamond-bone sirloins, three-shilling tea and the best bottled stout. But Lily seldom made a mistake in the orders so that she got on well with her three mistresses. They were fussy, that was all. But the only thing they would not stand was back answers.

Of course they had good reason to be fussy on such a night. And then it was long after ten o'clock and yet there was no sign of Gabriel and his wife. Besides they were dreadfully afraid that Freddy Malins might turn up screwed. They would not wish for worlds that any of Mary Jane's pupils should see him under the influence; and when he was like that it was sometimes very hard to manage him. Freddy Malins always came late but they wondered what could be keeping Gabriel: and that was what brought them every two minutes to the banisters to ask Lily had Gabriel or Freddy come.

— O, Mr Conroy, said Lily to Gabriel when she opened the door for him, Miss Kate and Miss Julia thought you were never coming. Goodnight, Mrs Conroy.

— I'll engage they did, said Gabriel, but they forget that my wife here takes three mortal hours to dress herself.

He stood on the mat, scraping the snow from his goloshes, while Lily led his wife to the foot of the stairs and called out:

— Miss Kate, here's Mrs Conroy.

Kate and Julia came toddling down the dark stairs at once. Both of them kissed Gabriel's wife, said she must be perished alive and asked was Gabriel with her.

— Here I am as right as the mail, Aunt Kate! Go on up. I'll follow, called out Gabriel from the dark.

He continued scraping his feet vigorously while the three women went upstairs, laughing, to the ladies' dressing-room. A light fringe of snow lay like a cape on the shoulders of his overcoat and like toecaps on the toes of his goloshes; and, as the buttons of his overcoat slipped with a squeaking noise through the snow-stiffened frieze, a cold fragrant air from out-of-doors escaped from crevices and folds.

— Is it snowing again, Mr Conroy? asked Lily.

She had preceded him into the pantry to help him off with his overcoat. Gabriel smiled at the three syllables she had given his surname and glanced at her. She was a slim, growing girl, pale in complexion and with hay-coloured hair. The gas in the pantry made her look still paler. Gabriel had known her when she was a child and used to sit on the lowest step nursing a rag doll.

— Yes, Lily, he answered, and I think we're in for a night of it.

He looked up at the pantry ceiling, which was shaking with the stamping and shuffling of feet on the floor above, listened for a moment to the piano and then glanced at the girl, who was folding his overcoat carefully at the end of a shelf.

— Tell me, Lily, he said in a friendly tone, do you still go to school?

— O no, sir, she answered. I'm done schooling this year and more.

— O, then, said Gabriel gaily, I suppose we'll be going to your wedding one of these fine days with your young man, eh?

The girl glanced back at him over her shoulder and said with great bitterness:

— The men that is now is only all palaver and what they can get out of you.

Gabriel coloured as if he felt he had made a mistake and, without looking at her, kicked off his goloshes and flicked actively with his muffler at his patent-leather shoes.

He was a stout tallish young man. The high colour of his cheeks pushed upwards even to his forehead where it scattered itself in a few form-less patches of pale red; and on his hairless face there scintillated restlessly the polished lenses and the bright gilt rims of the glasses which screened his delicate and restless eyes. His glossy black hair was parted in the middle and brushed in a long curve behind his ears where it curled slightly beneath the groove left by his hat.

When he had flicked lustre into his shoes he stood up and pulled his waistcoat down more tightly on his plump body. Then he took a coin rapidly from his pocket.

— O Lily, he said, thrusting it into her hands, it's Christmas-time, isn't it? Just . . . here's a little. . . .

He walked rapidly towards the door.

— O no, sir! cried the girl, following him. Really, sir, I wouldn't take it.

— Christmas-time! Christmas-time! said Gabriel, almost trotting to the stairs and waving his hand to her in deprecation.

The girl, seeing that he had gained the stairs, called out after him:

— Well, thank you, sir.

He waited outside the drawing-room door until the waltz should fin-ish, listening to the skirts that swept against it and to the shuffling of feet. He was still discomposed by the girl's bitter and sudden retort. It had cast a gloom over him which he tried to dispel by arranging his cuffs and the bows of his tie. Then he took from his waistcoat pocket a little paper and glanced at the headings he had made for his speech. He was undecided about the lines from Robert Browning for he feared they would be above the heads of his hearers. Some quotation that they could recognise from Shakespeare or from the Melodies would be better. The indelicate clacking of the men's heels and the shuffling of their soles reminded him that their grade of cul-ture differed from his. He would only make himself ridiculous by quoting poetry to them which they could not understand. They would think that he was airing his superior education. He would fail with them just as he had failed with the girl in the pantry. He had taken up a wrong tone. His whole speech was a mistake from first to last, an utter failure.

Just then his aunts and his wife came out of the ladies' dressing-room. His aunts were two small plainly dressed old women. Aunt Julia was an inch or so the taller. Her hair, drawn low over the tops of her ears, was grey; and grey also, with darker shadows, was her large flaccid face. Though she was stout in build and stood erect her slow eyes and parted lips gave her the ap-pearance of a woman who did not know where she was or where she was going. Aunt Kate was more vivacious. Her face, healthier than her sister's, was all puckers and creases, like a shrivelled red apple, and her hair, braided in the same old-fashioned way, had not lost its ripe nut colour.

They both kissed Gabriel frankly. He was their favourite nephew, the son of their dead elder sister, Ellen, who had married T. J. Conroy of the Port and Docks.

— Gretta tells me you're not going to take a cab back to Monkstown to-night, Gabriel, said Aunt Kate.

— No, said Gabriel, turning to his wife, we had quite enough of that last year, hadn't we? Don't you remember, Aunt Kate, what a cold Gretta got out of it? Cab windows rattling all the way, and the east wind blowing in after we passed Merrion. Very jolly it was. Gretta caught a dreadful cold.

Aunt Kate frowned severely and nodded her head at every word.

— Quite right, Gabriel, quite right, she said. You can't be too careful.

— But as for Gretta there, said Gabriel, she'd walk home in the snow if she were let.

Mrs Conroy laughed.

— Don't mind him, Aunt Kate, she said. He's really an awful bother, what with green shades for Tom's eyes at night and making him do the dumb-bells, and forcing Eva to eat the stirabout. The poor child! And she simply hates the sight of it! . . . O, but you'll never guess what he makes me wear now!

She broke out into a peal of laughter and glanced at her husband, whose admiring and happy eyes had been wandering from her dress to her face and hair. The two aunts laughed heartily too, for Gabriel's solicitude was a standing joke with them.

— Goloshes! said Mrs Conroy. That's the latest. Whenever it's wet underfoot I must put on my goloshes. To-night even he wanted me to put them on, but I wouldn't. The next thing he'll buy me will be a diving suit.

Gabriel laughed nervously and patted his tie reassuringly while Aunt Kate nearly doubled herself, so heartily did she enjoy the joke. The smile soon faded from Aunt Julia's face and her mirthless eyes were directed towards her nephew's face. After a pause she asked:

— And what are goloshes, Gabriel?

— Goloshes, Julia! exclaimed her sister. Goodness me, don't you know what goloshes are? You wear them over your . . . over your boots, Gretta, isn't it?

— Yes, said Mrs Conroy. Guttapercha things. We both have a pair now. Gabriel says everyone wears them on the continent.

— O, on the continent, murmured Aunt Julia, nodding her head slowly.

Gabriel knitted his brows and said, as if he were slightly angered:

— It's nothing very wonderful but Gretta thinks it very funny because she says the word reminds her of Christy Minstrels.

— But tell me, Gabriel, said Aunt Kate, with brisk tact. Of course, you've seen about the room. Gretta was saying . . .

— O, the room is all right, replied Gabriel. I've taken one in the Gresham.

— To be sure, said Aunt Kate, by far the best thing to do. And the children, Gretta, you're not anxious about them?

— O, for one night, said Mrs Conroy. Besides, Bessie will look after them.

— To be sure, said Aunt Kate again. What a comfort it is to have a girl like that, one you can depend on! There's that Lily, I'm sure I don't know what has come over her lately. She's not the girl she was at all.

Gabriel was about to ask his aunt some questions on this point but she broke off suddenly to gaze after her sister who had wandered down the stairs and was craning her neck over the banisters.

— Now, I ask you, she said, almost testily, where is Julia going? Julia! Julia! Where are you going?

Julia, who had gone halfway down one flight, came back and announced blandly:

— Here's Freddy.

At the same moment a clapping of hands and a final flourish of the pianist told that the waltz had ended. The drawing-room door was opened from within and some couples came out. Aunt Kate drew Gabriel aside hurriedly and whispered into his ear:

— Slip down, Gabriel, like a good fellow and see if he's all right, and don't let him up if he's screwed. I'm sure he's screwed. I'm sure he is.

Gabriel went to the stairs and listened over the banisters. He could hear two persons talking in the pantry. Then he recognised Freddy Malins' laugh. He went down the stairs noisily.

— It's such a relief, said Aunt Kate to Mrs Conroy, that Gabriel is here. I always feel easier in my mind when he's here. . . . Julia, there's Miss Daly and Miss Power will take some refreshment. Thanks for your beautiful waltz, Miss Daly. It made lovely time.

A tall wizen-faced man, with a stiff grizzled moustache and swarthy skin, who was passing out with his partner said:

— And may we have some refreshment, too, Miss Morkan?

— Julia, said Aunt Kate summarily, and here's Mr Browne and Miss Furlong. Take them in, Julia, with Miss Daly and Miss Power.

— I'm the man for the ladies, said Mr Browne, pursing his lips until his moustache bristled and smiling in all his wrinkles. You know, Miss Morkan, the reason they are so fond of me is —

He did not finish his sentence, but, seeing that Aunt Kate was out of earshot, at once led the three young ladies into the back room. The middle of the room was occupied by two square tables placed end to end, and on these Aunt Julia and the caretaker were straightening and smoothing a large cloth. On the sideboard were arrayed dishes and plates, and glasses and bundles of knives and forks and spoons. The top of the closed square piano served also as a sideboard for viands and sweets. At a smaller sideboard in one corner two young men were standing, drinking hop-bitters.

Mr Browne led his charges thither and invited them all, in jest, to some ladies' punch, hot, strong and sweet. As they said they never took anything strong he opened three bottles of lemonade for them. Then he asked one of the young men to move aside, and, taking hold of the decanter, filled out for himself a goodly measure of whisky. The young men eyed him respectfully while he took a trial sip.

— God help me, he said, smiling, it's the doctor's orders.

His wizened face broke into a broader smile, and the three young ladies laughed in musical echo to his pleasantry, swaying their bodies to and fro, with nervous jerks of their shoulders. The boldest said:

— O, now, Mr Browne, I'm sure the doctor never ordered anything of the kind.

Mr Browne took another sip of his whisky and said, with sidling mimicry:

— Well, you see, I'm like the famous Mrs Cassidy, who is reported to have said: *Now, Mary Grimes, if I don't take it, make me take it, for I feel I want it.*

His hot face had leaned forward a little too confidentially and he had assumed a very low Dublin accent so that the young ladies, with one instinct, received his speech in silence. Miss Furlong, who was one of Mary Jane's pupils, asked Miss Daly what was the name of the pretty waltz she had played; and Mr Browne, seeing that he was ignored, turned promptly to the two young men who were more appreciative.

A red-faced young woman, dressed in pansy, came into the room, excitedly clapping her hands and crying:

— Quadrilles! Quadrilles!

Close on her heels came Aunt Kate, crying:

— Two gentlemen and three ladies, Mary Jane!

— O, here's Mr Bergin and Mr Kerrigan, said Mary Jane. Mr Kerrigan, will you take Miss Power? Miss Furlong, may I get you a partner, Mr Bergin. O, that'll just do now.

— Three ladies, Mary Jane, said Aunt Kate.

The two young gentlemen asked the ladies if they might have the pleasure, and Mary Jane turned to Miss Daly.

— O, Miss Daly, you're really awfully good, after playing for the last two dances, but really we're so short of ladies to-night.

— I don't mind in the least, Miss Morkan.

— But I've a nice partner for you, Mr Bartell D'Arcy, the tenor. I'll get him to sing later on. All Dublin is raving about him.

— Lovely voice, lovely voice! said Aunt Kate.

As the piano had twice begun the prelude to the first figure Mary Jane led her recruits quickly from the room. They had hardly gone when Aunt Julia wandered slowly into the room, looking behind her at something.

— What is the matter, Julia? asked Aunt Kate anxiously. Who is it?

Julia, who was carrying in a column of table-napkins, turned to her sister and said, simply, as if the question had surprised her:

— It's only Freddy, Kate, and Gabriel with him.

In fact right behind her Gabriel could be seen piloting Freddy Malins across the landing. The latter, a young man of about forty, was of Gabriel's size and build, with very round shoulders. His face was fleshy and pallid, touched with colour only at the thick hanging lobes of his ears and at the wide wings of his nose. He had coarse features, a blunt nose, a convex and receding brow, tumid and protruded lips. His heavy-lidded eyes and the disorder of his scanty hair made him look sleepy. He was laughing heartily in a high key at a story which he had been telling Gabriel on the stairs and at the same time rubbing the knuckles of his left fist backwards and forwards into his left eye.

— Good-evening, Freddy, said Aunt Julia.

Freddy Malins bade the Misses Morkan good-evening in what seemed an offhand fashion by reason of the habitual catch in his voice and then, seeing that Mr Browne was grinning at him from the sideboard, crossed the room on rather shaky legs and began to repeat in an undertone the story he had just told to Gabriel.

— He's not so bad, is he? said Aunt Kate to Gabriel.

Gabriel's brows were dark but he raised them quickly and answered:

— O no, hardly noticeable.

— Now, isn't he a terrible fellow! she said. And his poor mother made him take the pledge on New Year's Eve. But come on, Gabriel, into the drawing-room.

Before leaving the room with Gabriel she signalled to Mr Browne by frowning and shaking her forefinger in warning to and fro. Mr Browne nodded in answer and, when she had gone, said to Freddy Malins:

— Now, then, Teddy, I'm going to fill you out a good glass of lemonade just to buck you up.

Freddy Malins, who was nearing the climax of his story, waved the offer aside impatiently but Mr Browne, having first called Freddy Malins' attention to a disarray in his dress, filled out and handed him a full glass of lemonade. Freddy Malins' left hand accepted the glass mechanically, his right hand being engaged in the mechanical readjustment of his dress. Mr Browne, whose face was once more wrinkling with mirth, poured out for himself a glass of whisky while Freddy Malins exploded, before he had well reached the climax of his story, in a kink of high-pitched bronchitic laughter and, setting down his untasted and overflowing glass, began to rub the knuckles of his left fist backwards and forwards into his left eye, repeating words of his last phrase as well as his fit of laughter would allow him.

Gabriel could not listen while Mary Jane was playing her Academy piece, full of runs and difficult passages, to the hushed drawing-room. He liked music but the piece she was playing had no melody for him and he doubted whether it had any melody for the other listeners, though they had begged Mary Jane to play something. Four young men, who had come from the refreshment-room to stand in the doorway at the sound of the piano, had gone away quietly in couples after a few minutes. The only persons who seemed to follow the music were Mary Jane herself, her hands racing along

the key-board or lifted from it at the pauses like those of a priestess in momentary imprecation, and Aunt Kate standing at her elbow to turn the
page.

Gabriel's eyes, irritated by the floor, which glittered with beeswax
under the heavy chandelier, wandered to the wall above the piano. A picture of the balcony scene in *Romeo and Juliet* hung there and beside it was
a picture of the two murdered princes in the Tower which Aunt Julia had
worked in red, blue and brown wools when she was a girl. Probably in the
school they had gone to as girls that kind of work had been taught, for one
year his mother had worked for him as a birthday present a waistcoat of
purple tabinet, with little foxes' heads upon it, lined with brown satin and
having round mulberry buttons. It was strange that his mother had had no
musical talent though Aunt Kate used to call her the brains carrier of the
Morkan family. Both she and Julia had always seemed a little proud of their
serious and matronly sister. Her photograph stood before the pierglass. She
held an open book on her knees and was pointing out something in it to
Constantine who, dressed in a man-o'-war suit, lay at her feet. It was she
who had chosen the names for her sons for she was very sensible of the dignity of family life. Thanks to her, Constantine was now senior curate in
Balbriggan and, thanks to her, Gabriel himself had taken his degree in the
Royal University. A shadow passed over his face as he remembered her sullen opposition to his marriage. Some slighting phrases she had used still
rankled in his memory; she had once spoken of Gretta as being country cute
and that was not true of Gretta at all. It was Gretta who had nursed her
during all her last long illness in their house at Monkstown.

He knew that Mary Jane must be near the end of her piece for she was
playing again the opening melody with runs of scales after every bar and
while he waited for the end the resentment died down in his heart. The
piece ended with a trill of octaves in the treble and a final deep octave in the
bass. Great applause greeted Mary Jane as, blushing and rolling up her
music nervously, she escaped from the room. The most vigorous clapping
came from the four young men in the doorway who had gone away to the
refreshment-room at the beginning of the piece but had come back when
the piano had stopped.

Lancers were arranged. Gabriel found himself partnered with Miss
Ivors. She was a frank-mannered talkative young lady, with a freckled face
and prominent brown eyes. She did not wear a low-cut bodice and the large
brooch which was fixed in the front of her collar bore on it an Irish device.

When they had taken their places she said abruptly:

— I have a crow to pluck with you.

— With me? said Gabriel.

She nodded her head gravely.

— What is it? asked Gabriel, smiling at her solemn manner.

— Who is G. C.? answered Miss Ivors, turning her eyes upon him.

Gabriel coloured and was about to knit his brows, as if he did not understand, when she said bluntly:

— O, innocent Amy! I have found out that you write for *The Daily Express*. Now, aren't you ashamed of yourself?

— Why should I be ashamed of myself? asked Gabriel, blinking his eyes and trying to smile.

— Well, I'm ashamed of you, said Miss Ivors frankly. To say you'd write for a rag like that. I didn't think you were a West Briton.

A look of perplexity appeared on Gabriel's face. It was true that he wrote a literary column every Wednesday in *The Daily Express*, for which he was paid fifteen shillings. But that did not make him a West Briton surely. The books he received for review were almost more welcome than the paltry cheque. He loved to feel the covers and turn over the pages of newly printed books. Nearly every day when his teaching in the college was ended he used to wander down the quays to the second-hand booksellers, to Hickey's on Bachelor's Walk, to Webb's or Massey's on Aston's Quay, or to O'Clohissey's in the by-street. He did not know how to meet her charge. He wanted to say that literature was above politics. But they were friends of many years' standing and their careers had been parallel, first at the University and then as teachers: he could not risk a grandiose phrase with her. He continued blinking his eyes and trying to smile and murmured lamely that he saw nothing political in writing reviews of books.

When their turn to cross had come he was still perplexed and inattentive. Miss Ivors promptly took his hand in a warm grasp and said in a soft friendly tone:

— Of course, I was only joking. Come, we cross now.

When they were together again she spoke of the University question and Gabriel felt more at ease. A friend of hers had shown her his review of Browning's poems. That was how she had found out the secret: but she liked the review immensely. Then she said suddenly:

— O, Mr Conroy, will you come for an excursion to the Aran Isles this summer? We're going to stay there a whole month. It will be splendid out in the Atlantic. You ought to come. Mr Clancy is coming, and Mr Kilkelly and Kathleen Kearney. It would be splendid for Gretta too if she'd come. She's from Connacht, isn't she?

— Her people are, said Gabriel shortly.

— But you will come, won't you? said Miss Ivors, laying her warm hand eagerly on his arm.

— The fact is, said Gabriel, I have already arranged to go —

— Go where? asked Miss Ivors.

— Well, you know, every year I go for a cycling tour with some fellows and so —

— But where? asked Miss Ivors.

— Well, we usually go to France or Belgium or perhaps Germany, said Gabriel awkwardly.

— And why do you go to France and Belgium, said Miss Ivors, instead of visiting your own land?

— Well, said Gabriel, it's partly to keep in touch with the languages and partly for a change.

— And haven't you your own language to keep in touch with — Irish? asked Miss Ivors.

— Well, said Gabriel, if it comes to that, you know, Irish is not my language.

Their neighbours had turned to listen to the cross-examination. Gabriel glanced right and left nervously and tried to keep his good humour under the ordeal which was making a blush invade his forehead.

— And haven't you your own land to visit, continued Miss Ivors, that you know nothing of, your own people, and your own country?

— O, to tell you the truth, retorted Gabriel suddenly, I'm sick of my own country, sick of it!

— Why? asked Miss Ivors.

Gabriel did not answer for his retort had heated him.

— Why? repeated Miss Ivors.

They had to go visiting together and, as he had not answered her, Miss Ivors said warmly:

— Of course, you've no answer.

Gabriel tried to cover his agitation by taking part in the dance with great energy. He avoided her eyes for he had seen a sour expression on her face. But when they met in the long chain he was surprised to feel his hand firmly pressed. She looked at him from under her brows for a moment quizzically until he smiled. Then, just as the chain was about to start again, she stood on tiptoe and whispered into his ear:

— West Briton!

When the lancers were over Gabriel went away to a remote corner of the room where Freddy Malins' mother was sitting. She was a stout feeble old woman with white hair. Her voice had a catch in it like her son's and she stuttered slightly. She had been told that Freddy had come and that he was nearly all right. Gabriel asked her whether she had had a good crossing. She lived with her married daughter in Glasgow and came to Dublin on a visit once a year. She answered placidly that she had had a beautiful crossing and that the captain had been most attentive to her. She spoke also of the beautiful house her daughter kept in Glasgow, and of all the nice friends they had there. While her tongue rambled on Gabriel tried to banish from his mind all memory of the unpleasant incident with Miss Ivors. Of course the girl or woman, or whatever she was, was an enthusiast but there was a time for all things. Perhaps he ought not to have answered her like that. But she had no right to call him a West Briton before people, even in joke. She had tried to make him ridiculous before people, heckling him and staring at him with her rabbit's eyes.

He saw his wife making her way towards him through the waltzing couples. When she reached him she said into his ear:

— Gabriel, Aunt Kate wants to know won't you carve the goose as usual. Miss Daly will carve the ham and I'll do the pudding.

— All right, said Gabriel.

— She's sending in the younger ones first as soon as this waltz is over so that we'll have the tables to ourselves.

— Were you dancing? asked Gabriel.

— Of course I was. Didn't you see me? What words had you with Molly Ivors?

— No words. Why? Did she say so?

— Something like that. I'm trying to get that Mr D'Arcy to sing. He's full of conceit, I think.

— There were no words, said Gabriel moodily, only she wanted me to go for a trip to the west of Ireland and I said I wouldn't.

His wife clasped her hands excitedly and gave a little jump.

— O, do go, Gabriel, she cried. I'd love to see Galway again.

— You can go if you like, said Gabriel coldly.

She looked at him for a moment, then turned to Mrs Malins and said:

— There's a nice husband for you, Mrs Malins.

While she was threading her way back across the room Mrs Malins, without adverting to the interruption, went on to tell Gabriel what beautiful places there were in Scotland and beautiful scenery. Her son-in-law brought them every year to the lakes and they used to go fishing. Her son-in-law was a splendid fisher. One day he caught a fish, a beautiful big big fish, and the man in the hotel boiled it for their dinner.

Gabriel hardly heard what she said. Now that supper was coming near he began to think again about his speech and about the quotation. When he saw Freddy Malins coming across the room to visit his mother Gabriel left the chair free for him and retired into the embrasure of the window. The room had already cleared and from the back room came the clatter of plates and knives. Those who still remained in the drawing-room seemed tired of dancing and were conversing quietly in little groups. Gabriel's warm trembling fingers tapped the cold pane of the window. How cool it must be outside! How pleasant it would be to walk out alone, first along by the river and then through the park! The snow would be lying on the branches of the trees and forming a bright cap on the top of the Wellington Monument. How much more pleasant it would be there than at the supper-table!

He ran over the headings of his speech: Irish hospitality, sad memories, the Three Graces, Paris, the quotation from Browning. He repeated to himself a phrase he had written in his review: *One feels that one is listening to a thought-tormented music.* Miss Ivors had praised the review. Was she sincere? Had she really any life of her own behind all her propagandism? There had never been any ill-feeling between them until that night. It unnerved him to think that she would be at the supper-table, looking up at him while he spoke with her critical quizzing eyes. Perhaps she would not be sorry to see him fail in his speech. An idea came into his mind and gave him courage. He would say, alluding to Aunt Kate and Aunt Julia: *Ladies and Gentlemen, the generation which is now on the wane among us may have had its faults but for my part I think it had certain qualities of hospitality, of humour, of humanity, which the new and very serious and hypereducated generation that is growing up around us seems to me to lack.*

Very good: that was one for Miss Ivors. What did he care that his aunts were only two ignorant old women?

A murmur in the room attracted his attention. Mr Browne was advancing from the door, gallantly escorting Aunt Julia, who leaned upon his arm, smiling and hanging her head. An irregular musketry of applause escorted her also as far as the piano and then, as Mary Jane seated herself on the stool, and Aunt Julia, no longer smiling, half turned so as to pitch her voice fairly into the room, gradually ceased. Gabriel recognised the prelude. It was that of an old song of Aunt Julia's — *Arrayed for the Bridal*. Her voice, strong and clear in tone, attacked with great spirit the runs which embellish the air and though she sang very rapidly she did not miss even the smallest of the grace notes. To follow the voice, without looking at the singer's face, was to feel and share the excitement of swift and secure flight. Gabriel applauded loudly with all the others at the close of the song and loud applause was borne in from the invisible supper-table. It sounded so genuine that a little colour struggled into Aunt Julia's face as she bent to replace in the music-stand the old leather-bound song-book that had her initials on the cover. Freddy Malins, who had listened with his head perched sideways to hear her better, was still applauding when everyone else had ceased and talking animatedly to his mother who nodded her head gravely and slowly in acquiescence. At last, when he could clap no more, he stood up suddenly and hurried across the room to Aunt Julia whose hand he seized and held in both his hands, shaking it when words failed him or the catch in his voice proved too much for him.

— I was just telling my mother, he said, I never heard you sing so well, never. No, I never heard your voice so good as it is to-night. Now! Would you believe that now? That's the truth. Upon my word and honour that's the truth. I never heard your voice sound so fresh and so . . . so clear and fresh, never.

Aunt Julia smiled broadly and murmured something about compliments as she released her hand from his grasp. Mr Browne extended his open hand towards her and said to those who were near him in the manner of a showman introducing a prodigy to an audience:

— Miss Julia Morkan, my latest discovery!

He was laughing very heartily at this himself when Freddy Malins turned to him and said:

— Well, Browne, if you're serious you might make a worse discovery. All I can say is I never heard her sing half so well as long as I am coming here. And that's the honest truth.

— Neither did I, said Mr Browne. I think her voice has greatly improved.

Aunt Julia shrugged her shoulders and said with meek pride:

— Thirty years ago I hadn't a bad voice as voices go.

— I often told Julia, said Aunt Kate emphatically, that she was simply thrown away in that choir. But she never would be said by me.

She turned as if to appeal to the good sense of the others against a refractory child while Aunt Julia gazed in front of her, a vague smile of reminiscence playing on her face.

— No, continued Aunt Kate, she wouldn't be said or led by anyone, slaving there in that choir night and day, night and day. Six o'clock on Christmas morning! And all for what?

— Well, isn't it for the honour of God, Aunt Kate? asked Mary Jane, twisting round on the piano-stool and smiling.

Aunt Kate turned fiercely on her niece and said:

— I know all about the honour of God, Mary Jane, but I think it's not at all honourable for the pope to turn out the women out of the choirs that have slaved there all their lives and put little whipper-snappers of boys over their heads. I suppose it is for the good of the Church if the pope does it. But it's not just, Mary Jane, and it's not right.

She had worked herself into a passion and would have continued in defence of her sister for it was a sore subject with her but Mary Jane, seeing that all the dancers had come back, intervened pacifically:

— Now, Aunt Kate, you're giving scandal to Mr Browne who is of the other persuasion.

Aunt Kate turned to Mr Browne, who was grinning at this allusion to his religion, and said hastily:

— O, I don't question the pope's being right. I'm only a stupid old woman and I wouldn't presume to do such a thing. But there's such a thing as common everyday politeness and gratitude. And if I were in Julia's place I'd tell that Father Healy straight up to his face. . . .

— And besides, Aunt Kate, said Mary Jane, we really are all hungry and when we are hungry we are all very quarrelsome.

— And when we are thirsty we are also quarrelsome, added Mr Browne.

— So that we had better go to supper, said Mary Jane, and finish the discussion afterwards.

On the landing outside the drawing-room Gabriel found his wife and Mary Jane trying to persuade Miss Ivors to stay for supper. But Miss Ivors, who had put on her hat and was buttoning her cloak, would not stay. She did not feel in the least hungry and she had already overstayed her time.

— But only for ten minutes, Molly, said Mrs Conroy. That won't delay you.

— To take a pick itself, said Mary Jane, after all your dancing.

— I really couldn't, said Miss Ivors.

— I am afraid you didn't enjoy yourself at all, said Mary Jane hopelessly.

— Ever so much, I assure you, said Miss Ivors, but you really must let me run off now.

— But how can you get home? asked Mrs Conroy.

— O, it's only two steps up the quay.

Gabriel hesitated a moment and said:

— If you will allow me, Miss Ivors, I'll see you home if you really are obliged to go.

But Miss Ivors broke away from them.

— I won't hear of it, she cried. For goodness sake go in to your suppers and don't mind me. I'm quite well able to take care of myself.

— Well, you're the comical girl, Molly, said Mrs Conroy frankly.

— *Beannacht libh*,[1] cried Miss Ivors, with a laugh, as she ran down the staircase.

Mary Jane gazed after her, a moody puzzled expression on her face, while Mrs Conroy leaned over the banisters to listen for the hall-door. Gabriel asked himself was he the cause of her abrupt departure. But she did not seem to be in ill humour: she had gone away laughing. He stared blankly down the staircase.

At that moment Aunt Kate came toddling out of the supper-room, almost wringing her hands in despair.

— Where is Gabriel? she cried. Where on earth is Gabriel? There's everyone waiting in there, stage to let, and nobody to carve the goose!

— Here I am, Aunt Kate! cried Gabriel, with sudden animation, ready to carve a flock of geese, if necessary.

A fat brown goose lay at one end of the table and at the other end, on a bed of creased paper strewn with sprigs of parsley, lay a great ham, stripped of its outer skin and peppered over with crust crumbs, a neat paper frill round its shin and beside this was a round of spiced beef. Between these rival ends ran parallel lines of side-dishes: two little minsters of jelly, red and yellow; a shallow dish full of blocks of blancmange and red jam, a large green leaf-shaped dish with a stalk-shaped handle, on which lay bunches of purple raisins and peeled almonds, a companion dish on which lay a solid rectangle of Smyrna figs, a dish of custard topped with grated nutmeg, a small bowl full of chocolates and sweets wrapped in gold and silver papers and a glass vase in which stood some tall celery stalks. In the centre of the table there stood, as sentries to a fruit-stand which upheld a pyramid of oranges and American apples, two squat old-fashioned decanters of cut glass, one containing port and the other dark sherry. On the closed square piano a pudding in a huge yellow dish lay in waiting and behind it were three squads of bottles of stout and ale and minerals, drawn up according to the colours of their uniforms, the first two black, with brown and red labels, the third and smallest squad white, with transverse green sashes.

Gabriel took his seat boldly at the head of the table and, having looked to the edge of the carver, plunged his fork firmly into the goose. He felt quite at ease now for he was an expert carver and liked nothing better than to find himself at the head of a well-laden table.

— Miss Furlong, what shall I send you? he asked. A wing or a slice of the breast?

— Just a small slice of the breast.

— Miss Higgins, what for you?

— O, anything at all, Mr Conroy.

While Gabriel and Miss Daly exchanged plates of goose and plates

[1] "A blessing on you" (Irish — traditional way of saying "farewell").

of ham and spiced beef Lily went from guest to guest with a dish of hot
floury potatoes wrapped in a white napkin. This was Mary Jane's idea and
she had also suggested apple sauce for the goose but Aunt Kate had said
that plain roast goose without apple sauce had always been good enough for
her and she hoped she might never eat worse. Mary Jane waited on her
pupils and saw that they got the best slices and Aunt Kate and Aunt Julia
opened and carried across from the piano bottles of stout and ale for the
gentlemen and bottles of minerals for the ladies. There was a great deal of
confusion and laughter and noise, the noise of orders and counter-orders, of
knives and forks, of corks and glass-stoppers. Gabriel began to carve second
helpings as soon as he had finished the first round without serving himself.
Everyone protested loudly so that he compromised by taking a long draught
of stout for he had found the carving hot work. Mary Jane settled down
quietly to her supper but Aunt Kate and Aunt Julia were still toddling
round the table, walking on each other's heels, getting in each other's way
and giving each other unheeded orders. Mr Browne begged of them to sit
down and eat their suppers and so did Gabriel but they said there was time
enough so that, at last, Freddy Malins stood up and, capturing Aunt Kate,
plumped her down on her chair amid general laughter.

When everyone had been well served Gabriel said, smiling:

— Now, if anyone wants a little more of what vulgar people call stuffing let him or her speak.

A chorus of voices invited him to begin his own supper and Lily came
forward with three potatoes which she had reserved for him.

— Very well, said Gabriel amiably, as he took another preparatory
draught, kindly forget my existence, ladies and gentlemen, for a few minutes.

He set to his supper and took no part in the conversation with which
the table covered Lily's removal of the plates. The subject of talk was the
opera company which was then at the Theatre Royal. Mr Bartell D'Arcy,
the tenor, a dark-complexioned young man with a smart moustache, praised
very highly the leading contralto of the company but Miss Furlong thought
she had a rather vulgar style of production. Freddy Malins said there was a
negro chieftain singing in the second part of the Gaiety pantomime who
had one of the finest tenor voices he had ever heard.

— Have you heard him? he asked Mr Bartell D'Arcy across the table.

— No, answered Mr Bartell D'Arcy carelessly.

— Because, Freddy Malins explained, now I'd be curious to hear your
opinion of him. I think he has a grand voice.

— It takes Teddy to find out the really good things, said Mr Browne
familiarly to the table.

— And why couldn't he have a voice too? asked Freddy Malins
sharply. Is it because he's only a black?

Nobody answered this question and Mary Jane led the table back to
the legitimate opera. One of her pupils had given her a pass for *Mignon*. Of
course it was very fine, she said, but it made her think of poor Georgina

Burns. Mr Browne could go back farther still, to the old Italian companies that used to come to Dublin — Tietjens, Ilma de Murzka, Campanini, the great Trebelli, Giuglini, Ravelli, Aramburo. Those were the days, he said, when there was something like singing to be heard in Dublin. He told too of how the top gallery of the old Royal used to be packed night after night, of how one night an Italian tenor had sung five encores to *Let Me Like a Soldier Fall*, introducing a high C every time, and of how the gallery boys would sometimes in their enthusiasm unyoke the horses from the carriage of some great *prima donna* and pull her themselves through the streets to her hotel. Why did they never play the grand old operas now, he asked, *Dinorah, Lucrezia Borgia*? Because they could not get the voices to sing them: that was why.

— O, well, said Mr Bartell D'Arcy, I presume there are as good singers to-day as there were then.

— Where are they? asked Mr Browne defiantly.

— In London, Paris, Milan, said Mr Bartell D'Arcy warmly. I suppose Caruso, for example, is quite as good, if not better than any of the men you have mentioned.

— Maybe so, said Mr Browne. But I may tell you I doubt it strongly.

— O, I'd give anything to hear Caruso sing, said Mary Jane.

— For me, said Aunt Kate, who had been picking a bone, there was only one tenor. To please me, I mean. But I suppose none of you ever heard of him.

— Who was he, Miss Morkan? asked Mr Bartell D'Arcy politely.

— His name, said Aunt Kate, was Parkinson. I heard him when he was in his prime and I think he had then the purest tenor voice that was ever put into a man's throat.

— Strange, said Mr Bartell D'Arcy. I never even heard of him.

— Yes, yes, Miss Morkan is right, said Mr. Browne. I remember hearing of old Parkinson but he's too far back for me.

— A beautiful pure sweet mellow English tenor, said Aunt Kate with enthusiasm.

Gabriel having finished, the huge pudding was transferred to the table. The clatter of forks and spoons began again. Gabriel's wife served out spoonfuls of the pudding and passed the plates down the table. Midway down they were held up by Mary Jane, who replenished them with raspberry or orange jelly or with blancmange and jam. The pudding was of Aunt Julia's making and she received praises for it from all quarters. She herself said that it was not quite brown enough.

— Well, I hope, Miss Morkan, said Mr Browne, that I'm brown enough for you because, you know, I'm all brown.

All the gentlemen, except Gabriel, ate some of the pudding out of compliment to Aunt Julia. As Gabriel never ate sweets the celery had been left for him. Freddy Malins also took a stalk of celery and ate it with his pudding. He had been told that celery was a capital thing for the blood and he was just then under the doctor's care. Mrs Malins, who had been silent

all through the supper, said that her son was going down to Mount Melleray in a week or so. The table then spoke of Mount Melleray, how bracing
the air was down there, how hospitable the monks were and how they never
asked for a penny-piece from their guests.

— And do you mean to say, asked Mr Browne incredulously, that a
chap can go down there and put up there as if it were a hotel and live on the
fat of the land and then come away without paying a farthing?

— O, most people give some donation to the monastery when they
leave, said Mary Jane.

— I wish we had an institution like that in our Church, said Mr
Browne candidly.

He was astonished to hear that the monks never spoke, got up at two
in the morning and slept in their coffins. He asked what they did it for.

— That's the rule of the order, said Aunt Kate firmly.

— Yes, but why? asked Mr Browne.

Aunt Kate repeated that it was the rule, that was all. Mr Browne still
seemed not to understand. Freddy Malins explained to him, as best he
could, that the monks were trying to make up for the sins committed by all
the sinners in the outside world. The explanation was not very clear for Mr
Browne grinned and said:

— I like that idea very much but wouldn't a comfortable spring bed do
them as well as a coffin?

— The coffin, said Mary Jane, is to remind them of their last end.

As the subject had grown lugubrious it was buried in a silence of the
table during which Mrs Malins could be heard saying to her neighbour in
an indistinct undertone:

— They are very good men, the monks, very pious men.

The raisins and almonds and figs and apples and oranges and chocolates and sweets were now passed about the table and Aunt Julia invited all
the guests to have either port or sherry. At first Mr Bartell D'Arcy refused
to take either but one of his neighbours nudged him and whispered something to him upon which he allowed his glass to be filled. Gradually as the
last glasses were being filled the conversation ceased. A pause followed,
broken only by the noise of the wine and by unsettlings of chairs. The
Misses Morkan, all three, looked down at the tablecloth. Someone coughed
once or twice and then a few gentlemen patted the table gently as a signal
for silence. The silence came and Gabriel pushed back his chair and
stood up.

The patting at once grew louder in encouragement and then ceased altogether. Gabriel leaned his ten trembling fingers on the tablecloth and
smiled nervously at the company. Meeting a row of upturned faces he
raised his eyes to the chandelier. The piano was playing a waltz tune and he
could hear the skirts sweeping against the drawing-room door. People, perhaps, were standing in the snow on the quay outside, gazing up at the
lighted windows and listening to the waltz music. The air was pure there. In
the distance lay the park where the trees were weighted with snow. The

Wellington Monument wore a gleaming cap of snow that flashed westward over the white field of Fifteen Acres.

He began:

— Ladies and Gentlemen.

— It has fallen to my lot this evening, as in years past, to perform a very pleasing task but a task for which I am afraid my poor powers as a speaker are all too inadequate.

— No, no! said Mr Browne.

— But, however that may be, I can only ask you to-night to take the will for the deed and to lend me your attention for a few moments while I endeavour to express to you in words what my feelings are on this occasion.

— Ladies and Gentlemen. It is not the first time that we have gathered together under this hospitable roof, around this hospitable board. It is not the first time that we have been the recipients — or perhaps, I had better say, the victims — of the hospitality of certain good ladies.

He made a circle in the air with his arm and paused. Everyone laughed or smiled at Aunt Kate and Aunt Julia and Mary Jane who all turned crimson with pleasure. Gabriel went on more boldly:

— I feel more strongly with every recurring year that our country has no tradition which does it so much honour and which it should guard so jealously as that of its hospitality. It is a tradition that is unique as far as my experience goes (and I have visited not a few places abroad) among the modern nations. Some would say, perhaps, that with us it is rather a failing than anything to be boasted of. But granted even that, it is, to my mind, a princely failing, and one that I trust will long be cultivated among us. Of one thing, at least, I am sure. As long as this one roof shelters the good ladies aforesaid — and I wish from my heart it may do so for many and many a long year to come — the tradition of genuine warm-hearted courteous Irish hospitality, which our forefathers have handed down to us and which we in turn must hand down to our descendants, is still alive among us.

A hearty murmur of assent ran round the table. It shot through Gabriel's mind that Miss Ivors was not there and that she had gone away discourteously: and he said with confidence in himself:

— Ladies and Gentlemen.

— A new generation is growing up in our midst, a generation actuated by new ideas and new principles. It is serious and enthusiastic for these new ideas and its enthusiasm, even when it is misdirected, is, I believe, in the main sincere. But we are living in a sceptical and, if I may use the phrase, a thought-tormented age: and sometimes I fear that this new generation, educated or hypereducated as it is, will lack those qualities of humanity, of hospitality, of kindly humour which belonged to an older day. Listening to-night to the names of all those great singers of the past it seemed to me, I must confess, that we were living in a less spacious age. Those days might, without exaggeration, be called spacious days: and if they are gone beyond recall let us hope, at least, that in gatherings such as this we shall still speak of them with pride and affection, still cherish in our hearts the memory of those dead and gone great ones whose fame the world will not willingly let die.

— Hear, hear! said Mr Browne loudly.

— But yet, continued Gabriel, his voice falling into a softer inflection, there are always in gatherings such as this sadder thoughts that will recur to our minds: thoughts of the past, of youth, of changes, of absent faces that we miss here to-night. Our path through life is strewn with many such sad memories: and were we to brood upon them always we could not find the heart to go on bravely with our work among the living. We have all of us living duties and living affections which claim, and rightly claim, our strenuous endeavours.

— Therefore, I will not linger on the past. I will not let any gloomy moralising intrude upon us here to-night. Here we are gathered together for a brief moment from the bustle and rush of our everyday routine. We are met here as friends, in the spirit of good-fellowship, as colleagues, also to a certain extent, in the true spirit of *camaraderie*, and as the guests of — what shall I call them? — the Three Graces of the Dublin musical world.

The table burst into applause and laughter at this sally. Aunt Julia vainly asked each of her neighbours in turn to tell her what Gabriel had said.

— He says we are the Three Graces, Aunt Julia, said Mary Jane.

Aunt Julia did not understand but she looked up, smiling, at Gabriel, who continued in the same vein:

— Ladies and Gentlemen.

— I will not attempt to play to-night the part that Paris played on another occasion. I will not attempt to choose between them. The task would be an invidious one and one beyond my poor powers. For when I view them in turn, whether it be our chief hostess herself, whose good heart, whose too good heart, has become a byword with all who know her, or her sister, who seems to be gifted with perennial youth and whose singing must have been a surprise and a revelation to us all to-night, or, last but not least, when I consider our youngest hostess, talented, cheerful, hard-working and the best of nieces, I confess, Ladies and Gentlemen, that I do not know to which of them I should award the prize.

Gabriel glanced down at his aunts and, seeing the large smile on Aunt Julia's face and the tears which had risen to Aunt Kate's eyes, hastened to close. He raised his glass of port gallantly, while every member of the company fingered a glass expectantly, and said loudly:

— Let us toast them all three together. Let us drink to their health, wealth, long life, happiness and prosperity and may they long continue to hold the proud and self-won position which they hold in their profession and the position of honour and affection which they hold in our hearts.

All the guests stood up, glass in hand, and, turning towards the three seated ladies, sang in unison, with Mr Browne as leader:

For they are jolly gay fellows,
For they are jolly gay fellows,
For they are jolly gay fellows,
Which nobody can deny.

Aunt Kate was making frank use of her handkerchief and even Aunt Julia seemed moved. Freddy Malins beat time with his pudding-fork and the singers turned towards one another, as if in melodious conference, while they sang, with emphasis:

Unless he tells a lie,
Unless he tells a lie.

Then, turning once more towards their hostesses, they sang:

For they are jolly gay fellows,
For they are jolly gay fellows,
For they are jolly gay fellows,
Which nobody can deny.

The acclamation which followed was taken up beyond the door of the supper-room by many of the other guests and renewed time after time, Freddy Malins acting as officer with his fork on high.

The piercing morning air came into the hall where they were standing so that Aunt Kate said:

— Close the door, somebody. Mrs Malins will get her death of cold.

— Browne is out there, Aunt Kate, said Mary Jane.

— Browne is everywhere, said Aunt Kate, lowering her voice.

Mary Jane laughed at her tone.

— Really, she said archly, he is very attentive.

— He has been laid on here like the gas, said Aunt Kate in the same tone, all during the Christmas.

She laughed herself this time good-humouredly and then added quickly:

— But tell him to come in, Mary Jane, and close the door. I hope to goodness he didn't hear me.

At that moment the hall-door was opened and Mr Browne came in from the doorstep, laughing as if his heart would break. He was dressed in a long green overcoat with mock astrakhan cuffs and collar and wore on his head an oval fur cap. He pointed down the snow-covered quay from where the sound of shrill prolonged whistling was borne in.

— Teddy will have all the cabs in Dublin out, he said.

Gabriel advanced from the little pantry behind the office, struggling into his overcoat and, looking round the hall, said:

— Gretta not down yet?

— She's getting on her things, Gabriel, said Aunt Kate.

— Who's playing up there? asked Gabriel.

— Nobody. They're all gone.

— O no, Aunt Kate, said Mary Jane. Bartell D'Arcy and Miss O'Callaghan aren't gone yet.

— Someone is strumming at the piano, anyhow, said Gabriel.

Mary Jane glanced at Gabriel and Mr Browne and said with a shiver:

— It makes me feel cold to look at you two gentlemen muffled up like that. I wouldn't like to face your journey home at this hour.

— I'd like nothing better this minute, said Mr Browne stoutly, than a rattling fine walk in the country or a fast drive with a good spanking goer between the shafts.

— We used to have a very good horse and trap at home, said Aunt Julia sadly.

— The never-to-be-forgotten Johnny, said Mary Jane, laughing.

Aunt Kate and Gabriel laughed too.

— Why, what was wonderful about Johnny? asked Mr Browne.

— The late lamented Patrick Morkan, our grandfather, that is, explained Gabriel, commonly known in his later years as the old gentleman, was a glue-boiler.

— O, now, Gabriel, said Aunt Kate, laughing, he had a starch mill.

— Well, glue or starch, said Gabriel, the old gentleman had a horse by the name of Johnny. And Johnny used to work in the old gentleman's mill, walking round and round in order to drive the mill. That was all very well; but now comes the tragic part about Johnny. One fine day the old gentleman thought he'd like to drive out with the quality to a military review in the park.

— The Lord have mercy on his soul, said Aunt Kate compassionately.

— Amen, said Gabriel. So the old gentleman, as I said, harnessed Johnny and put on his very best tall hat and his very best stock collar and drove out in grand style from his ancestral mansion somewhere near Back Lane, I think.

Everyone laughed, even Mrs Malins, at Gabriel's manner and Aunt Kate said:

— O now, Gabriel, he didn't live in Back Lane, really. Only the mill was there.

— Out from the mansion of his forefathers, continued Gabriel, he drove with Johnny. And everything went on beautifully until Johnny came in sight of King Billy's statue: and whether he fell in love with the horse King Billy sits on or whether he thought he was back again in the mill, anyhow he began to walk round the statue.

Gabriel paced in a circle round the hall in his goloshes amid the laughter of the others.

— Round and round he went, said Gabriel, and the old gentleman, who was a very pompous old gentleman, was highly indignant. *Go on, sir! What do you mean, sir? Johnny! Johnny! Most extraordinary conduct! Can't understand the horse!*

The peals of laughter which followed Gabriel's imitation of the incident were interrupted by a resounding knock at the hall-door. Mary Jane ran to open it and let in Freddy Malins. Freddy Malins, with his hat well back on his head and his shoulders humped with cold, was puffing and steaming after his exertions.

— I could only get one cab, he said.

— O, we'll find another along the quay, said Gabriel.

— Yes, said Aunt Kate. Better not keep Mrs Malins standing in the draught.

Mrs Malins was helped down the front steps by her son and Mr Browne and, after many manœuvres, hoisted into the cab. Freddy Malins clambered in after her and spent a long time settling her on the seat, Mr Browne helping him with advice. At last she was settled comfortably and Freddy Malins invited Mr Browne into the cab. There was a good deal of confused talk, and then Mr Browne got into the cab. The cabman settled his rug over his knees, and bent down for the address. The confusion grew greater and the cabman was directed differently by Freddy Malins and Mr Browne, each of whom had his head out through a window of the cab. The difficulty was to know where to drop Mr Browne along the route and Aunt Kate, Aunt Julia and Mary Jane helped the discussion from the doorstep with cross-directions and contradictions and abundance of laughter. As for Freddy Malins he was speechless with laughter. He popped his head in and out of the window every moment, to the great danger of his hat, and told his mother how the discussion was progressing till at last Mr Browne shouted to the bewildered cabman above the din of everybody's laughter:

— Do you know Trinity College?

— Yes, sir, said the cabman.

— Well, drive bang up against Trinity College gates, said Mr Browne, and then we'll tell you where to go. You understand now?

— Yes, sir, said the cabman.

— Make like a bird for Trinity College.

— Right, sir, cried the cabman.

The horse was whipped up and the cab rattled off along the quay amid a chorus of laughter and adieus.

Gabriel had not gone to the door with the others. He was in a dark part of the hall gazing up the staircase. A woman was standing near the top of the first flight, in the shadow also. He could not see her face but he could see the terracotta and salmonpink panels of her skirt which the shadow made appear black and white. It was his wife. She was leaning on the banisters, listening to something. Gabriel was surprised at her stillness and strained his ear to listen also. But he could hear little save the noise of laughter and dispute on the front steps, a few chords struck on the piano and a few notes of a man's voice singing.

He stood still in the gloom of the hall, trying to catch the air that the voice was singing and gazing up at his wife. There was grace and mystery in her attitude as if she were a symbol of something. He asked himself what is a woman standing on the stairs in the shadow, listening to distant music, a symbol of. If he were a painter he would paint her in that attitude. Her blue felt hat would show off the bronze of her hair against the darkness and the dark panels of her skirt would show off the light ones. *Distant Music* he would call the picture if he were a painter.

The hall-door closed; and Aunt Kate, Aunt Julia and Mary Jane came down the hall, still laughing.

— Well, isn't Freddy terrible? said Mary Jane. He's really terrible.

Gabriel said nothing but pointed up the stairs towards where his wife was standing. Now that the hall-door was closed the voice and the piano could be heard more clearly. Gabriel held up his hand for them to be silent. The song seemed to be in the old Irish tonality and the singer seemed uncertain both of his words and of his voice. The voice, made plaintive by distance and by the singer's hoarseness, faintly illuminated the cadence of the air with words expressing grief:

> *O, the rain falls on my heavy locks*
> *And the dew wets my skin,*
> *My babe lies cold . . .*

— O, exclaimed Mary Jane. It's Bartell D'Arcy singing and he wouldn't sing all the night. O, I'll get him to sing a song before he goes.

— O do, Mary Jane, said Aunt Kate.

Mary Jane brushed past the others and ran to the staircase but before she reached it the singing stopped and the piano was closed abruptly.

— O, what a pity! she cried. Is he coming down, Gretta?

Gabriel heard his wife answer yes and saw her come down towards them. A few steps behind her were Mr Bartell D'Arcy and Miss O'Callaghan.

— O, Mr D'Arcy, cried Mary Jane, it's downright mean of you to break off like that when we were all in raptures listening to you.

— I have been at him all the evening, said Miss O'Callaghan, and Mrs Conroy too and he told us he had a dreadful cold and couldn't sing.

— O, Mr D'Arcy, said Aunt Kate, now that was a great fib to tell.

— Can't you see that I'm as hoarse as a crow? said Mr D'Arcy roughly.

He went into the pantry hastily and put on his overcoat. The others, taken aback by his rude speech, could find nothing to say. Aunt Kate wrinkled her brows and made signs to the others to drop the subject. Mr D'Arcy stood swathing his neck carefully and frowning.

— It's the weather, said Aunt Julia, after a pause.

— Yes, everybody has colds, said Aunt Kate readily, everybody.

— They say, said Mary Jane, we haven't had snow like it for thirty years; and I read this morning in the newspapers that the snow is general all over Ireland.

— I love the look of snow, said Aunt Julia sadly.

— So do I, said Miss O'Callaghan. I think Christmas is never really Christmas unless we have the snow on the ground.

— But poor Mr D'Arcy doesn't like the snow, said Aunt Kate, smiling.

Mr D'Arcy came from the pantry, fully swathed and buttoned, and in a repentant tone told them the history of the cold. Everyone gave him advice and said it was a great pity and urged him to be very careful of his throat in the night air. Gabriel watched his wife who did not join in the conversation. She was standing right under the dusty fanlight and the flame of the gas lit up the rich bronze of her hair which he had seen her drying at the fire a few days before. She was in the same attitude and seemed unaware of the talk about her. At last she turned towards them and Gabriel saw that there was colour on her cheeks and that her eyes were shining. A sudden tide of joy went leaping out of his heart.

— Mr D'Arcy, she said, what is the name of that song you were singing?

— It's called The Lass of Aughrim, said Mr D'Arcy, but I couldn't remember it properly. Why? Do you know it?

— The Lass of Aughrim, she repeated. I couldn't think of the name.

— It's a very nice air, said Mary Jane. I'm sorry you were not in voice to-night.

— Now, Mary Jane, said Aunt Kate, don't annoy Mr D'Arcy. I won't have him annoyed.

Seeing that all were ready to start she shepherded them to the door where good-night was said:

— Well, good-night, Aunt Kate, and thanks for the pleasant evening.

— Good-night, Gabriel. Good-night, Gretta!

— Good-night, Aunt Kate, and thanks ever so much. Good-night, Aunt Julia.

— O, good-night, Gretta, I didn't see you.

— Good-night, Mr D'Arcy. Good-night, Miss O'Callaghan.

— Good-night, Miss Morkan.

— Good-night, again.

— Good-night, all. Safe home.

— Good-night. Good-night.

The morning was still dark. A dull yellow light brooded over the houses and the river; and the sky seemed to be descending. It was slushy underfoot; and only streaks and patches of snow lay on the roofs, on the parapets of the quay and on the area railings. The lamps were still burning redly in the murky air and, across the river, the palace of the Four Courts stood out menacingly against the heavy sky.

She was walking on before him with Mr Bartell D'Arcy, her shoes in a brown parcel tucked under one arm and her hands holding her skirt up from the slush. She had no longer any grace of attitude but Gabriel's eyes were still bright with happiness. The blood went bounding along his veins;

and the thoughts were rioting through his brain, proud, joyful, tender, valorous.

She was walking on before him so lightly and so erect that he longed to run after her noiselessly, catch her by the shoulders and say something foolish and affectionate into her ear. She seemed to him so frail that he longed to defend her against something and then to be alone with her. Moments of their secret life together burst like stars upon his memory. A heliotrope envelope was lying beside his breakfast-cup and he was caressing it with his hand. Birds were twittering in the ivy and the sunny web of the curtain was shimmering along the floor: he could not eat for happiness. They were standing on the crowded platform and he was placing a ticket inside the warm palm of her glove. He was standing with her in the cold, looking in through a grated window at a man making bottles in a roaring furnace. It was very cold. Her face, fragrant in the cold air, was quite close to his; and suddenly she called out to the man at the furnace.

— Is the fire hot, sir?

But the man could not hear her with the noise of the furnace. It was just as well. He might have answered rudely.

A wave of yet more tender joy escaped from his heart and went coursing in warm flood along his arteries. Like the tender fires of stars moments of their life together, that no one knew of or would ever know of, broke upon and illumined his memory. He longed to recall to her those moments, to make her forget the years of their dull existence together and remember only their moments of ecstasy. For the years, he felt, had not quenched his soul or hers. Their children, his writing, her household cares had not quenched all their souls' tender fire. In one letter that he had written to her then he had said: *Why is it that words like these seem to me so dull and cold? Is it because there is no word tender enough to be your name?*

Like distant music these words that he had written years before were borne towards him from the past. He longed to be alone with her. When the others had gone away, when he and she were in their room in the hotel, then they would be alone together. He would call her softly:

— Gretta!

Perhaps she would not hear at once: she would be undressing. Then something in his voice would strike her. She would turn and look at him. . . .

At the corner of Winetavern Street they met a cab. He was glad of its rattling noise as it saved him from conversation. She was looking out of the window and seemed tired. The others spoke only a few words, pointing out some building or street. The horse galloped along wearily under the murky morning sky, dragging his old rattling box after his heels, and Gabriel was again in a cab with her, galloping to catch the boat, galloping to their honeymoon.

As the cab drove across O'Connell Bridge Miss O'Callaghan said:

— They say you never cross O'Connell Bridge without seeing a white horse.

— I see a white man this time, said Gabriel.

— Where? asked Mr Bartell D'Arcy.

Gabriel pointed to the statue, on which lay patches of snow. Then he nodded familiarly to it and waved his hand.

— Good-night, Dan, he said gaily.

When the cab drew up before the hotel Gabriel jumped out and, in spite of Mr Bartell D'Arcy's protest, paid the driver. He gave the man a shilling over his fare. The man saluted and said:

— A prosperous New Year to you, sir.

— The same to you, said Gabriel cordially.

She leaned for a moment on his arm in getting out of the cab and while standing at the curbstone, bidding the others good-night. She leaned lightly on his arm, as lightly as when she had danced with him a few hours before. He had felt proud and happy then, happy that she was his, proud of her grace and wifely carriage. But now, after the kindling again of so many memories, the first touch of her body, musical and strange and perfumed, sent through him a keen pang of lust. Under cover of her silence he pressed her arm closely to his side; and, as they stood at the hotel door, he felt that they had escaped from their lives and duties, escaped from home and friends and run away together with wild and radiant hearts to a new adventure.

An old man was dozing in a great hooded chair in the hall. He lit a candle in the office and went before them to the stairs. They followed him in silence, their feet falling in soft thuds on the thickly carpeted stairs. She mounted the stairs behind the porter, her head bowed in the ascent, her frail shoulders curved as with a burden, her skirt girt tightly about her. He could have flung his arms about her hips and held her still for his arms were trembling with desire to seize her and only the stress of his nails against the palms of his hands held the wild impulse of his body in check. The porter halted on the stairs to settle his guttering candle. They halted too on the steps below him. In the silence Gabriel could hear the falling of the molten wax into the tray and the thumping of his own heart against his ribs.

The porter led them along a corridor and opened a door. Then he set his unstable candle down on a toilet-table and asked at what hour they were to be called in the morning.

— Eight, said Gabriel.

The porter pointed to the tap of the electric-light and began a muttered apology but Gabriel cut him short.

— We don't want any light. We have enough light from the street. And I say, he added, pointing to the candle, you might remove that handsome article, like a good man.

The porter took up his candle again, but slowly for he was surprised by such a novel idea. Then he mumbled good-night and went out. Gabriel shot the lock to.

A ghostly light from the street lamp lay in a long shaft from one window to the door. Gabriel threw his overcoat and hat on a couch and crossed the room towards the window. He looked down into the street in order that his emotion might calm a little. Then he turned and leaned against a chest of drawers with his back to the light. She had taken off her hat and cloak and was standing before a large swinging mirror, unhooking her waist. Gabriel paused for a few moments, watching her, and then said:

— Gretta!

She turned away from the mirror slowly and walked along the shaft of light towards him. Her face looked so serious and weary that the words would not pass Gabriel's lips. No, it was not the moment yet.

— You look tired, he said.

— I am a little, she answered.

— You don't feel ill or weak?

— No, tired: that's all.

She went on to the window and stood there, looking out. Gabriel waited again and then, fearing that diffidence was about to conquer him, he said abruptly:

— By the way, Gretta!

— What is it?

— You know that poor fellow Malins? he said quickly.

— Yes. What about him?

— Well, poor fellow, he's a decent sort of chap after all, continued Gabriel in a false voice. He gave me back that sovereign I lent him and I didn't expect it really. It's a pity he wouldn't keep away from that Browne, because he's not a bad fellow at heart.

He was trembling now with annoyance. Why did she seem so abstracted? He did not know how he could begin. Was she annoyed, too, about something? If she would only turn to him or come to him of her own accord! To take her as she was would be brutal. No, he must see some ardour in her eyes first. He longed to be master of her strange mood.

— When did you lend him the pound? she asked, after a pause.

Gabriel strove to restrain himself from breaking out into brutal language about the sottish Malins and his pound. He longed to cry to her from his soul, to crush her body against his, to overmaster her. But he said:

— O, at Christmas, when he opened that little Christmas-card shop in Henry Street.

He was in such a fever of rage and desire that he did not hear her come from the window. She stood before him for an instant, looking at him strangely. Then, suddenly raising herself on tiptoe and resting her hands lightly on his shoulders, she kissed him.

— You are a very generous person, Gabriel, she said.

Gabriel, trembling with delight at her sudden kiss and at the quaintness of her phrase, put his hands on her hair and began smoothing it back, scarcely touching it with his fingers. The washing had made it fine and brilliant. His heart was brimming over with happiness. Just when he was wishing for it she had come to him of her own accord. Perhaps her thoughts had been running with his. Perhaps she had felt the impetuous desire that was in him and then the yielding mood had come upon her. Now that she had fallen to him so easily he wondered why he had been so diffident.

He stood, holding her head between his hands. Then, slipping one arm swiftly about her body and drawing her towards him, he said softly:

— Gretta dear, what are you thinking about?

She did not answer nor yield wholly to his arm. He said again, softly:

— Tell me what it is, Gretta. I think I know what is the matter. Do I know?

She did not answer at once. Then she said in an outburst of tears:

— O, I am thinking about that song, *The Lass of Aughrim.*

She broke loose from him and ran to the bed and, throwing her arms across the bed-rail, hid her face. Gabriel stood stock-still for a moment in astonishment and then followed her. As he passed in the way of the cheval-glass he caught sight of himself in full length, his broad, well-filled shirt-front, the face whose expression always puzzled him when he saw it in a mirror and his glimmering gilt-rimmed eyeglasses. He halted a few paces from her and said:

— What about the song? Why does that make you cry?

She raised her head from her arms and dried her eyes with the back of her hand like a child. A kinder note than he had intended went into his voice.

— Why, Gretta? he asked.

— I am thinking about a person long ago who used to sing that song.

— And who was the person long ago? asked Gabriel, smiling.

— It was a person I used to know in Galway when I was living with my grandmother, she said.

The smile passed away from Gabriel's face. A dull anger began to gather again at the back of his mind and the dull fires of his lust began to glow angrily in his veins.

— Someone you were in love with? he asked ironically.

— It was a young boy I used to know, she answered, named Michael Furey. He used to sing that song, *The Lass of Aughrim*. He was very delicate.

Gabriel was silent. He did not wish her to think that he was interested in this delicate boy.

— I can see him so plainly, she said after a moment. Such eyes as he had: big dark eyes! And such an expression in them — an expression!

— O then, you were in love with him? said Gabriel.

— I used to go out walking with him, she said, when I was in Galway.

A thought flew across Gabriel's mind.

— Perhaps that was why you wanted to go to Galway with that Ivors girl? he said coldly.

She looked at him and asked in surprise:

— What for?

Her eyes made Gabriel feel awkward. He shrugged his shoulders and said:

— How do I know? To see him perhaps.

She looked away from him along the shaft of light towards the window in silence.

— He is dead, she said at length. He died when he was only seventeen. Isn't that a terrible thing to die so young as that?

— What was he? asked Gabriel, still ironically.

— He was in the gasworks, she said.

Gabriel felt humiliated by the failure of his irony and by the evocation of this figure from the dead, a boy in the gasworks. While he had been full of memories of their secret life together, full of tenderness and joy and desire, she had been comparing him in her mind with another. A shameful consciousness of his own person assailed him. He saw himself as a ludicrous figure, acting as a pennyboy for his aunts, a nervous well-meaning sentimentalist, orating to vulgarians and idealising his own clownish lusts, the pitiable fatuous fellow he had caught a glimpse of in the mirror. Instinctively he turned his back more to the light lest she might see the shame that burned upon his forehead.

He tried to keep up his tone of cold interrogation but his voice when he spoke was humble and indifferent.

— I suppose you were in love with this Michael Furey, Gretta, he said.

— I was great with him at that time, she said.

Her voice was veiled and sad. Gabriel, feeling now how vain it would be to try to lead her whither he had purposed, caressed one of her hands and said, also sadly:

— And what did he die of so young, Gretta? Consumption, was it?

— I think he died for me, she answered.

A vague terror seized Gabriel at this answer as if, at that hour when he had hoped to triumph, some impalpable and vindictive being was coming against him, gathering forces against him in its vague world. But he shook himself free of it with an effort of reason and continued to caress her hand. He did not question her again for he felt that she would tell him of herself. Her hand was warm and moist: it did not respond to his touch but he continued to caress it just as he had caressed her first letter to him that spring morning.

— It was in the winter, she said, about the beginning of the winter when I was going to leave my grandmother's and come up here to the convent. And he was ill at the time in his lodgings in Galway and wouldn't be let out and his people in Oughterard were written to. He was in decline, they said, or something like that. I never knew rightly.

She paused for a moment and sighed.

— Poor fellow, she said. He was very fond of me and he was such a gentle boy. We used to go out together, walking, you know, Gabriel, like the way they do in the country. He was going to study singing only for his health. He had a very good voice, poor Michael Furey.

— Well; and then? asked Gabriel.

— And then when it came to the time for me to leave Galway and come up to the convent he was much worse and I wouldn't be let see him so I wrote a letter saying I was going up to Dublin and would be back in the summer and hoping he would be better then.

She paused for a moment to get her voice under control and then went on:

— Then the night before I left I was in my grandmother's house in Nuns' Island, packing up, and I heard gravel thrown up against the window. The window was so wet I couldn't see so I ran downstairs as I was and slipped out the back into the garden and there was the poor fellow at the end of the garden, shivering.

— And did you not tell him to go back? asked Gabriel.

— I implored of him to go home at once and told him he would get his death in the rain. But he said he did not want to live. I can see his eyes as well as well! He was standing at the end of the wall where there was a tree.

— And did he go home? asked Gabriel.

— Yes, he went home. And when I was only a week in the convent he died and he was buried in Oughterard where his people came from. O, the day I heard that, that he was dead!

She stopped, choking with sobs, and, overcome by emotion, flung herself face downward on the bed, sobbing in the quilt. Gabriel held her hand for a moment longer, irresolutely, and then, shy of intruding on her grief, let it fall gently and walked quietly to the window.

She was fast asleep.

Gabriel, leaning on his elbow, looked for a few moments unresentfully on her tangled hair and half-open mouth, listening to her deep-drawn breath. So she had had that romance in her life: a man had died for her sake. It hardly pained him now to think how poor a part he, her husband, had played in her life. He watched her while she slept as though he and she had never lived together as man and wife. His curious eyes rested long upon her face and on her hair: and, as he thought of what she must have been then, in that time of her first girlish beauty, a strange friendly pity for her entered his soul. He did not like to say even to himself that her face was no longer beautiful but he knew that it was no longer the face for which Michael Furey had braved death.

Perhaps she had not told him all the story. His eyes moved to the chair over which she had thrown some of her clothes. A petticoat string dangled to the floor. One boot stood upright, its limp upper fallen down: the fellow of it lay upon its side. He wondered at his riot of emotions of an hour before. From what had it proceeded? From his aunt's supper, from his own foolish speech, from the wine and dancing, the merry-making when saying good-night in the hall, the pleasure of the walk along the river in the snow. Poor Aunt Julia! She, too, would soon be a shade with the shade of Patrick Morkan and his horse. He had caught that haggard look upon her face for a moment when she was singing *Arrayed for the Bridal*. Soon, perhaps, he would be sitting in that same drawing-room, dressed in black, his silk hat on his knees. The blinds would be drawn down and Aunt Kate would be sitting beside him, crying and blowing her nose and telling him how Julia had died. He would cast about his mind for some words that might console her, and would find only lame and useless ones. Yes, yes: that would happen very soon.

The air of the room chilled his shoulders. He stretched himself cautiously along under the sheets and lay down beside his wife. One by one they were all becoming shades. Better pass boldly into that other world, in the full glory of some passion, than fade and wither dismally with age. He thought of how she who lay beside him had locked in her heart for so many years that image of her lover's eyes when he had told her that he did not wish to live.

Generous tears filled Gabriel's eyes. He had never felt like that himself towards any woman but he knew that such a feeling must be love. The tears gathered more thickly in his eyes and in the partial darkness he imagined he saw the form of a young man standing under a dripping tree. Other forms were near. His soul had approached that region where dwell the vast hosts of the dead. He was conscious of, but could not apprehend, their wayward and flickering existence. His own identity was fading out into a grey impalpable world: the solid world itself which these dead had one time reared and lived in was dissolving and dwindling.

A few light taps upon the pane made him turn to the window. It had begun to snow again. He watched sleepily the flakes, silver and dark, falling obliquely against the lamplight. The time had come for him to set out on his journey westward. Yes, the newspapers were right: snow was general all over Ireland. It was falling on every part of the dark central plain, on the treeless hills, falling softly upon the Bog of Allen and, farther westward, softly falling into the dark mutinous Shannon waves. It was falling, too, upon every part of the lonely churchyard on the hill where Michael Furey lay buried. It lay thickly drifted on the crooked crosses and headstones, on the spears of the little gate, on the barren thorns. His soul swooned slowly as he heard the snow falling faintly through the universe and faintly falling, like the descent of their last end, upon all the living and the dead.

[1916]

FRANZ KAFKA (1883–1924) *led a life whose events are simple and* sad. *He was born into a Jewish family in the city of Prague, and from youth onward he feared his authoritarian father so much that he stuttered in his presence, although he spoke easily with others. In 1906 he received a doc- torate in jurisprudence, and for many years he worked a tedious job as a civil service lawyer investigating claims at the state Worker's Accident In- surance Institute. He never married and lived for the most part at home, where he wrote fiction at night (he was an insomniac), publishing only a few slim volumes of stories during his lifetime.* Meditation, *a collection of sketches, appeared in 1912;* The Stoker: A Fragment *in 1913;* The Meta- morphosis *in 1915;* The Judgment *in 1916;* In the Penal Colony *in 1919; and* A Country Doctor *in 1920. Only a few of his friends knew that he was also at work on the great novels that were published after his death from tuberculosis:* Amerika, The Trial, *and* The Castle. *(He asked his literary ex- ecutor, Max Brod, to burn these novels in manuscript, but Brod refused.) Kafka's despair with his writing, with his job, with his father, and with his life was complete, and like Gustave Flaubert — whom he admired — he used his fiction as a "rock" to which he clung in order not to be drowned in the waves of the world around him. With typical irony, however, he saw the effort as futile: "By scribbling I run ahead of myself in order to catch myself up at the finishing post. I cannot run away from myself."*

In his diaries, Kafka recorded his obsession with literature. "What will be my fate as a writer is very simple. My talent for portraying my dreamlike inner life has thrust all other matters into the background. . . ." The "dreamlike" quality of his imagination is apparent in all his work. He is perhaps best known as the author of the waking nightmare "The Metamor- phosis," whose remarkable first sentence is one of the most famous in short story literature. The hero of the story, Gregor Samsa (pronounced Zamsa), is the son of philistine, middle-class parents in Prague, as was Kafka, and literary critics have tended to interpret the story as an autobiographical fic- tion, using the "monstrous insect" as a Freudian symbol that characterizes Kafka's sense of inadequacy before his demanding father. Kafka himself considered psychoanalysis "a helpless error," regarding Freud's theories as very rough pictures which do not do justice to either the details or the es- sence of life. The greatest literary influence upon Kafka was Flaubert; both writers used language with similar ironic precision and without explicit in- trusion of their private sentiments.

At the center of "The Metamorphosis" is Kafka's portrayal of the cru- elty of the family and Gregor Samsa's feelings of isolation and sacrifice that result from the conflict. The visionary, nightmarish quality of the story is in striking contrast to its precise and formal style, the clarity of which intensifies the dark richness of the fantasy. In 1922 Kafka wrote Brod that to be a writer meant for him a "descent to the dark powers" of the night, when anxiety kept him from sleeping. "And what is devilish in it seems to me quite clear. It is the vanity and the craving for enjoyment, which is forever whirring around oneself. . . . The wish that a naive person sometimes has: 'I would like to die and watch the others crying over me' is what such a writer constantly experiences: he dies (or he does not live) and continually cries over himself." (See Janouch's Commentary about "The Metamorphosis" on page 1267 and Updike's Commentary about Kafka on page 1270.)

Franz Kafka

ふふ

THE METAMORPHOSIS

– translated by Willa and Edwin Muir

I

As Gregor Samsa awoke one morning from uneasy dreams he found himself transformed in his bed into a gigantic insect. He was lying on his hard, as it were armor-plated, back and when he lifted his head a little he could see his dome-like brown belly divided into stiff arched segments on top of which the bed quilt could hardly keep in position and was about to slide off completely. His numerous legs, which were pitifully thin compared to the rest of his bulk, waved helplessly before his eyes.

What has happened to me? he thought. It was no dream. His room, a regular human bedroom, only rather too small, lay quiet between the four familiar walls. Above the table on which a collection of cloth samples was unpacked and spread out — Samsa was a commercial traveler — hung the picture which he had recently cut out of an illustrated magazine and put into a pretty gilt frame. It showed a lady, with a fur cap on and a fur stole, sitting upright and holding out to the spectator a huge fur muff into which the whole of her forearm had vanished!

Gregor's eyes turned next to the window, and the overcast sky — one could hear rain drops beating on the window gutter — made him quite melancholy. What about sleeping a little longer and forgetting all this nonsense, he thought, but it could not be done, for he was accustomed to sleep on his right side and in his present condition he could not turn himself over. However violently he forced himself towards his right side he always rolled on to his back again. He tried it at least a hundred times, shutting his eyes to keep from seeing his struggling legs, and only desisted when he began to feel in his side a faint dull ache he had never experienced before.

Oh God, he thought, what an exhausting job I've picked on! Traveling about day in, day out. It's much more irritating work than doing the actual business in the office, and on top of that there's the trouble of constant traveling, of worrying about train connections, the bed and irregular meals, casual acquaintances that are always new and never become intimate friends. The devil take it all! He felt a slight itching up on his belly; slowly pushed himself on his back nearer to the top of the bed so that he could lift his head more easily; identified the itching place which was surrounded by many small white spots the nature of which he could not understand and made to touch it with a leg, but drew the leg back immediately, for the contact made a cold shiver run through him.

He slid down again into his former position. This getting up early, he thought, makes one quite stupid. A man needs his sleep. Other commercials live like harem women. For instance, when I come back to the hotel of a morning to write up the orders I've got, these others are only sitting down to breakfast. Let me just try that with my chief; I'd be sacked on the spot. Anyhow, that might be quite a good thing for me, who can tell? If I didn't have to hold my hand because of my parents I'd have given notice long ago, I'd have gone to the chief and told him exactly what I think of him. That would knock him endways from his desk! It's a queer way of doing, too, this sitting on high at a desk and talking down to employees, especially when they have to come quite near because the chief is hard of hearing. Well, there's still hope; once I've saved enough money to pay back my parents' debts to him — that should take another five or six years — I'll do it without fail. I'll cut myself completely loose then. For the moment, though, I'd better get up, since my train goes at five.

He looked at the alarm clock ticking on the chest. Heavenly Father! he thought. It was half-past six o'clock and the hands were quietly moving on, it was even past the half-hour, it was getting on toward a quarter to seven. Had the alarm clock not gone off? From the bed one could see that it had been properly set for four o'clock; of course it must have gone off. Yes, but was it possible to sleep quietly through that ear-splitting noise? Well, he had not slept quietly, yet apparently all the more soundly for that. But what was he to do now? The next train went at seven o'clock; to catch that he would need to hurry like mad and his samples weren't even packed up, and he himself wasn't feeling particularly fresh and active. And even if he did catch the train he wouldn't avoid a row with the chief, since the firm's porter would have been waiting for the five o'clock train and would have long since reported his failure to turn up. The porter was a creature of the chief's, spineless and stupid. Well, supposing he were to say he was sick? But that would be most unpleasant and would look suspicious, since during his five years' employment he had not been ill once. The chief himself would be sure to come with the sick-insurance doctor, would reproach his parents with their son's laziness and would cut all excuses short by referring to the insurance doctor, who of course regarded all mankind as perfectly healthy malingerers. And would he be so far wrong on this occasion? Gregor really felt quite well, apart from a drowsiness that was utterly superfluous after such a long sleep, and he was even unusually hungry.

As all this was running through his mind at top speed without his being able to decide to leave his bed — the alarm clock had just struck a quarter to seven — there came a cautious tap at the door behind the head of his bed. "Gregor," said a voice — it was his mother's — "it's a quarter to seven. Hadn't you a train to catch?" That gentle voice! Gregor had a shock as he heard his own voice answering hers, unmistakably his own voice, it was true, but with a persistent horrible twittering squeak behind it like an undertone, that left the words in their clear shape only for the first moment and then rose up reverberating round them to destroy their sense, so that one could not be sure one had heard them rightly. Gregor wanted to answer at length and explain everything, but in the circumstances he confined himself to saying: "Yes, yes, thank you, Mother, I'm getting up now." The wooden door between them must have kept the change in his voice from being noticeable outside, for his mother contented herself with this statement and shuffled away. Yet this brief exchange of words had made the other members of the family aware that Gregor was still in the house, as they had not expected, and at one of the side doors his father was already knocking, gently, yet with his fist. "Gregor, Gregor," he called, "what's the matter with you?" And after a little while he called again in a deeper voice: "Gregor! Gregor!" At the other side door his sister was saying in a low, plaintive tone: "Gregor? Aren't you well? Are you needing anything?" He answered them both at once: "I'm just ready," and did his best to make his voice sound as normal as possible by enunciating the words very clearly and leaving long pauses between them. So his father went back to his breakfast, but his sister whispered: "Gregor, open the door, do." However, he was not thinking of opening the door, and felt thankful for the prudent habit he had acquired in traveling of locking all doors during the night, even at home.

His immediate intention was to get up quietly without being disturbed, to put on his clothes and above all eat his breakfast, and only then to consider what else was to be done, since in bed, he was well aware, his meditations would come to no sensible conclusion. He remembered that often enough in bed he had felt small aches and pains, probably caused by awkward postures, which had proved purely imaginary once he got up, and he looked forward eagerly to seeing this morning's delusions gradually fall away. That the change in his voice was nothing but the precursor of a severe chill, a standing ailment of commercial travelers, he had not the least possible doubt.

To get rid of the quilt was quite easy; he had only to inflate himself a little and it fell off by itself. But the next move was difficult, especially because he was so uncommonly broad. He would have needed arms and hands to hoist himself up; instead he had only the numerous little legs which never stopped waving in all directions and which he could not control in the least. When he tried to bend one of them it was the first to stretch itself straight; and did he succeed at last in making it do what he wanted, all the other legs meanwhile waved the more wildly in a high degree of unpleasant agitation. "But what's the use of lying idle in bed," said Gregor to himself.

He thought that he might get out of bed with the lower part of his body first, but this lower part, which he had not yet seen and of which he could form no clear conception, proved too difficult to move; it shifted so slowly; and when finally, almost wild with annoyance, he gathered his forces together and thrust out recklessly, he had miscalculated the direction and bumped heavily against the lower end of the bed, and the stinging pain he felt informed him that precisely this lower part of his body was at the moment probably the most sensitive.

So he tried to get the top part of himself out first, and cautiously moved his head towards the edge of the bed. That proved easy enough, and despite its breadth and mass the bulk of his body at last slowly followed the movement of his head. Still, when he finally got his head free over the edge of the bed he felt too scared to go on advancing, for after all if he let himself fall in this way it would take a miracle to keep his head from being injured. And at all costs he must not lose consciousness now, precisely now; he would rather stay in bed.

But when after a repetition of the same efforts he lay in his former position again, sighing, and watched his little legs struggling against each other more wildly than ever, if that were possible, and saw no way of bringing any order into this arbitrary confusion, he told himself again that it was impossible to stay in bed and that the most sensible course was to risk everything for the smallest hope of getting away from it. At the same time he did not forget meanwhile to remind himself that cool reflection, the coolest possible, was much better than desperate resolves. In such moments he focused his eyes as sharply as possible on the window, but, unfortunately, the prospect of the morning fog, which muffled even the other side of the narrow street, brought him little encouragement and comfort. "Seven o'clock already," he said to himself when the alarm clock chimed again, "seven o'clock already and still such a thick fog." And for a little while he lay quiet, breathing lightly, as if perhaps expecting such complete repose to restore all things to their real and normal condition.

But then he said to himself: "Before it strikes a quarter past seven I must be quite out of this bed, without fail. Anyhow, by that time someone will have come from the office to ask for me, since it opens before seven." And he set himself to rocking his whole body at once in a regular rhythm, with the idea of swinging it out of the bed. If he tipped himself out in that way he could keep his head from injury by lifting it at an acute angle when he fell. His back seemed to be hard and was not likely to suffer from a fall on the carpet. His biggest worry was the loud crash he would not be able to help making, which would probably cause anxiety, if not terror, behind all the doors. Still, he must take the risk.

When he was already half out of the bed — the new method was more a game than an effort, for he needed only to hitch himself across by rocking to and fro — it struck him how simple it would be if he could get help. Two strong people — he thought of his father and the servant girl — would be amply sufficient; they would only have to thrust their arms under his convex back, lever him out of the bed, bend down with their burden and then be patient enough to let him turn himself right over on to the floor, where it was to be hoped his legs would then find their proper function. Well, ignoring the fact that the doors were all locked, ought he really to call for help? In spite of his misery he could not suppress a smile at the very idea of it.

He had got so far that he could barely keep his equilibrium when he rocked himself strongly, and he would have to nerve himself very soon for the final decision since in five minutes' time it would be a quarter past seven — when the front doorbell rang. "That's someone from the office," he said to himself, and grew almost rigid, while his little legs only jigged about all the faster. For a moment everything stayed quiet. "They're not going to open the door," said Gregor to himself, catching at some kind of irrational hope. But then of course the servant girl went as usual to the door with her heavy tread and opened it. Gregor needed only to hear the first good morning of the visitor to know immediately who it was — the chief clerk himself. What a fate, to be condemned to work for a firm where the smallest omission at once gave rise to the gravest suspicion! Were all employees in a body nothing but scoundrels, was there not among them one single loyal devoted man who, had he wasted only an hour or so of the firm's time in a morning, was so tormented by conscience as to be driven out of his mind and actually incapable of leaving his bed? Wouldn't it really have been sufficient to send an apprentice to inquire — if any inquiry were necessary at all — did the chief clerk himself have to come and thus indicate to the entire family, an innocent family, that this suspicious circumstance could be investigated by no one less versed in affairs than himself? And more through the agitation caused by these reflections than through any act of will Gregor swung himself out of bed with all his strength. There was a loud thump, but it was not really a crash. His fall was broken to some extent by the carpet, his back, too, was less stiff then he thought, and so there was merely a dull thud, not so very startling. Only he had not lifted his head carefully enough and had hit it; he turned it and rubbed it on the carpet in pain and irritation.

"That was something falling down in there," said the chief clerk in the next room to the left. Gregor tried to suppose to himself that something like what had happened to him today might some day happen to the chief clerk; one really could not deny that it was possible. But as if in brusque reply to this supposition the chief clerk took a couple of firm steps in the next-door room and his patent leather boots creaked. From the right-hand room his sister was whispering to inform him of the situation: "Gregor, the chief clerk's here." "I know," muttered Gregor to himself; but he didn't dare to make his voice loud enough for his sister to hear it.

"Gregor," said his father now from the left-hand room, "the chief clerk has come and wants to know why you didn't catch the early train. We don't know what to say to him. Besides, he wants to talk to you in person. So open the door, please. He will be good enough to excuse the untidiness of your room." "Good morning, Mr. Samsa," the chief clerk was calling amiably meanwhile. "He's not well," said his mother to the visitor, while his father was still speaking through the door, "he's not well, sir, believe me. What else would make him miss a train! The boy thinks about nothing but his work. It makes me almost cross the way he never goes out in the evenings; he's been here the last eight days and has stayed at home every single evening. He just sits there quietly at the table reading a newspaper or looking through railway timetables. The only amusement he gets is doing fretwork. For instance, he spent two or three evenings cutting out a little picture frame; you would be surprised to see how pretty it is; it's hanging in his room; you'll see it in a minute when Gregor opens the door. I must say I'm glad you've come, sir; we should never have got him to unlock the door by ourselves; he's so obstinate; and I'm sure he's unwell, though he wouldn't have it to be so this morning." "I'm just coming," said Gregor slowly and carefully, not moving an inch for fear of losing one word of the conversation. "I can't think of any other explanation, madam," said the chief clerk, "I hope it's nothing serious. Although on the other hand I must say that we men of business — fortunately or unfortunately — very often simply have to ignore any slight indisposition, since business must be attended to." "Well, can the chief clerk come in now?" asked Gregor's father impatiently, again knocking on the door. "No," said Gregor. In the left-hand room a painful silence followed this refusal, in the right-hand room his sister began to sob.

Why didn't his sister join the others? She was probably newly out of bed and hadn't even begun to put on her clothes yet. Well, why was she crying? Because he wouldn't get up and let the chief clerk in, because he was in danger of losing his job, and because the chief would begin dunning his parents again for the old debts? Surely these were things one didn't need to worry about for the present. Gregor was still at home and not in the least thinking of deserting the family. At the moment, true, he was lying on the carpet and no one who knew the condition he was in could seriously expect him to admit the chief clerk. But for such a small discourtesy, which could plausibly be explained away somehow later on, Gregor could hardly be dismissed on the spot. And it seemed to Gregor that it would be much more sensible to leave him in peace for the present than to trouble him with tears and entreaties. Still, of course, their uncertainty bewildered them all and excused their behavior.

"Mr. Samsa," the chief clerk called now in a louder voice, "what's the matter with you? Here you are, barricading yourself in your room, giving only 'yes' and 'no' for answers, causing your parents a lot of unnecessary trouble and neglecting — I mention this only in passing — neglecting your business duties in an incredible fashion. I am speaking here in the name of your parents and of your chief, and I beg you quite seriously to give me an immediate and precise explanation. You amaze me, you amaze me. I thought you were a quiet, dependable person, and now all at once you seem bent on making a disgraceful exhibition of yourself. The chief did hint to me early this morning a possible explanation for your disappearance — with reference to the cash payments that were entrusted to you recently — but I almost pledged my solemn word of honor that this could not be so. But now that I see how incredibly obstinate you are, I no longer have the slightest desire to take your part at all. And your position in the firm is not so unassailable. I came with the intention of telling you all this in private, but since you are wasting my time so needlessly I don't see why your parents shouldn't hear it too. For some time past your work has been most unsatisfactory; this is not the season of the year for a business boom, of course, we admit that, but a season of the year for doing no business at all, that does not exist, Mr. Samsa, must not exist."

"But, sir," cried Gregor, beside himself and in his agitation forgetting everything else, "I'm just going to open the door this very minute. A slight illness, an attack of giddiness, has kept me from getting up. I'm still lying in bed. But I feel all right again. I'm getting out of bed now. Just give me a moment or two longer! I'm not quite so well as I thought. But I'm all right, really. How a thing like that can suddenly strike one down! Only last night I was quite well, my parents can tell you, or rather I did have a slight presentiment. I must have showed some sign of it. Why didn't I report it at the office! But one always thinks that an indisposition can be got over without staying in the house. Oh sir, do spare my parents! All that you're reproaching me with now has no foundation; no one has ever said a word to me about it. Perhaps you haven't looked at the last orders I sent in. Anyhow, I can still catch the eight o'clock train, I'm much the better for my few hours' rest. Don't let me detain you here, sir; I'll be attending to business very soon, and do be good enough to tell the chief so and to make my excuses to him!"

And while all this was tumbling out pell-mell and Gregor hardly knew what he was saying, he had reached the chest quite easily, perhaps because of the practice he had had in bed, and was now trying to lever himself upright by means of it. He meant actually to open the door, actually to show himself and speak to the chief clerk; he was eager to find out what the others, after all their insistence, would say at the sight of him. If they were horrified then the responsibility was no longer his and he could stay quiet.

But if they took it calmly, then he had no reason either to be upset, and could really get to the station for the eight o'clock train if he hurried. At first he slipped down a few times from the polished surface of the chest, but at length with a last heave he stood upright; he paid no more attention to the pains in the lower part of his body, however they smarted. Then he let himself fall against the back of a near-by chair, and clung with his little legs to the edges of it. That brought him into control of himself again and he stopped speaking, for now he could listen to what the chief clerk was saying.

"Did you understand a word of it?" the chief clerk was asking; "surely he can't be trying to make fools of us?" "Oh dear," cried his mother, in tears, "perhaps he's terribly ill and we're tormenting him. Grete! Grete!" she called out then. "Yes Mother?" called his sister from the other side. They were calling to each other across Gregor's room. "You must go this minute for the doctor. Gregor is ill. Go for the doctor, quick. Did you hear how he was speaking?" "That was no human voice," said the chief clerk in a voice noticeably low beside the shrillness of the mother's. "Anna! Anna!" his father was calling through the hall to the kitchen, clapping his hands, "get a locksmith at once!" And the two girls were already running through the hall with a swish of skirts — how could his sister have got dressed so quickly? — and were tearing the front door open. There was no sound of its closing again; they had evidently left it open, as one does in houses where some great misfortune has happened.

But Gregor was now much calmer. The words he uttered were no longer understandable, apparently, although they seemed clear enough to him, even clearer than before, perhaps because his ear had grown accustomed to the sound of them. Yet at any rate people now believed that something was wrong with him, and were ready to help him. The positive certainty with which these first measures had been taken comforted him. He felt himself drawn once more into the human circle and hoped for great and remarkable results from both the doctor and the locksmith, without really distinguishing precisely between them. To make his voice as clear as possible for the decisive conversation that was now imminent he coughed a little, as quietly as he could, of course, since this noise too might not sound like a human cough for all he was able to judge. In the next room meanwhile there was complete silence. Perhaps his parents were sitting at the table with the chief clerk, whispering, perhaps they were all leaning against the door and listening.

Slowly Gregor pushed the chair towards the door, then let go of it, caught hold of the door for support — the soles at the end of his little legs were somewhat sticky — and rested against it for a moment after his efforts. Then he set himself to turning the key in the lock with his mouth. It seemed, unhappily, that he hadn't really any teeth — what could he grip the key with? — but on the other hand his jaws were certainly very strong; with their help he did manage to set the key in motion, heedless of the fact that he was undoubtedly damaging them somewhere, since a brown fluid issued from his mouth, flowed over the key and dripped on the floor. "Just listen to that," said the chief clerk next door; "he's turning the key." That was a great encouragement to Gregor; but they should all have shouted encouragement to him, his father and mother too: "Go on, Gregor," they should have called out, "keep going, hold on to that key!" And in the belief that they were all following his efforts intently, he clenched his jaws recklessly on the key with all the force at his command. As the turning of the key progressed he circled round the lock, holding on now only with his mouth, pushing on the key, as required, or pulling it down again with all the weight of his body. The louder click of the finally yielding lock literally quickened Gregor. With a deep breath of relief he said to himself: "So I didn't need the locksmith," and laid his head on the handle to open the door wide.

Since he had to pull the door towards him, he was still invisible when it was really wide open. He had to edge himself slowly round the near half of the double door, and to do it very carefully if he was not to fall plump upon his back just on the threshold. He was still carrying out this difficult manoeuvre, with no time to observe anything else, when he heard the chief clerk utter a loud "Oh!" — it sounded like a gust of wind — and now he could see the man, standing as he was nearest to the door, clapping one hand before his open mouth and slowly backing away as if driven by some invisible steady pressure. His mother — in spite of the chief clerk's being there her hair was still undone and sticking up in all directions — first clasped her hands and looked at his father, then took two steps towards Gregor and fell on the floor among her outspread skirts, her face hidden on her breast. His father knotted his fist with a fierce expression on his face as if he meant to knock Gregor back into his room, then looked uncertainly round the living room, covered his eyes with his hands and wept till his great chest heaved.

Gregor did not go now into the living room, but leaned against the inside of the firmly shut wing of the door, so that only half his body was visible and his head above it bending sideways to look at the others. The light had meanwhile strengthened; on the other side of the street one could see clearly a section of the endlessly long, dark gray building opposite — it was a hospital — abruptly punctuated by its row of regular windows; the rain was still falling, but only in large singly discernible and literally singly splashing drops. The breakfast dishes were set out on the table lavishly, for breakfast was the most important meal of the day to Gregor's father, who lingered it out for hours over various newspapers. Right opposite Gregor on the wall hung a photograph of himself on military service, as a lieutenant, hand on sword, a carefree smile on his face, inviting one to respect his uniform and military bearing. The door leading to the hall was open, and one could see that the front door stood open too, showing the landing beyond and the beginning of the stairs going down.

"Well," said Gregor, knowing perfectly that he was the only one who had retained any composure, "I'll put my clothes on at once, pack up my samples and start off. Will you only let me go? You see, sir, I'm not obstinate, and I'm willing to work; traveling is a hard life, but I couldn't live without it. Where are you going, sir? To the office? Yes? Will you give a true account of all this? One can be temporarily incapacitated, but that's just the moment for remembering former services and bearing in mind that later on, when the incapacity has been got over, one will certainly work with all the more industry and concentration. I'm loyally bound to serve the chief, you know that very well. Besides, I have to provide for my parents and my sister. I'm in great difficulties, but I'll get out of them again. Don't make things any worse for me than they are. Stand up for me in the firm. Travelers are not popular there, I know. People think they earn sacks of money and just have a good time. A prejudice there's no particular reason for revising. But you, sir, have a more comprehensive view of affairs than the rest of the staff, yes, let me tell you in confidence, a more comprehensive view than the chief himself, who, being the owner, lets his judgment easily be swayed against one of his employees. And you know very well that the traveler, who is never seen in the office almost the whole year round, can so easily fall a victim to gossip and ill luck and unfounded complaints, which he mostly knows nothing about, except when he comes back exhausted from his rounds, and only then suffers in person from their evil consequences, which he can no longer trace back to the original causes. Sir, sir, don't go away without a word to me to show that you think me in the right at least to some extent!"

But at Gregor's very first words the chief clerk had already backed away and only stared at him with parted lips over one twitching shoulder. And while Gregor was speaking he did not stand still one moment but stole away towards the door, without taking his eyes off Gregor, yet only an inch at a time, as if obeying some secret injunction to leave the room. He was already at the hall, and the suddenness with which he took his last step out of the living room would have made one believe he had burned the sole of his foot. Once in the hall he stretched his right arm before him towards the staircase, as if some supernatural power were waiting there to deliver him.

Gregor perceived that the chief clerk must on no account be allowed to go away in this frame of mind if his position in the firm were not to be endangered to the utmost. His parents did not understand this so well; they had convinced themselves in the course of years that Gregor was settled for life in this firm, and besides they were so occupied with their immediate troubles that all foresight had forsaken them. Yet Gregor had this foresight. The chief clerk must be detained, soothed, persuaded and finally won over; the whole future of Gregor and his family depended on it! If only his sister had been there! She was intelligent; she had begun to cry while Gregor was still lying quietly on his back. And no doubt the chief clerk, so partial to ladies, would have been guided by her; she would have shut the door of the flat and in the hall talked him out of his horror. But she was not there, and

Gregor would have to handle the situation himself. And without remembering that he was still unaware what powers of movement he possessed, without even remembering that his words in all possibility, indeed in all likelihood, would again be unintelligible, he let go the wing of the door, pushed himself through the opening, started to walk towards the chief clerk, who was already ridiculously clinging with both hands to the railing on the landing; but immediately, as he was feeling for a support, he fell down with a little cry upon all his numerous legs. Hardly was he down when he experienced for the first time this morning a sense of physical comfort; his legs had firm ground under them; they were completely obedient, as he noted with joy; they even strove to carry him forward in whatever direction he chose; and he was inclined to believe that a final relief from all his sufferings was at hand. But in the same moment as he found himself on the floor, rocking with suppressed eagerness to move, not far from his mother, indeed just in front of her, she, who had seemed so completely crushed, sprang all at once to her feet, her arms and fingers outspread, cried: "Help, for God's sake, help!" bent her head down as if to see Gregor better, yet on the contrary kept backing senselessly away; had quite forgotten that the laden table stood behind her; sat upon it hastily, as if in absence of mind, when she bumped into it; and seemed altogether unaware that the big coffee pot beside her was upset and pouring coffee in a flood over the carpet.

"Mother, Mother," said Gregor in a low voice, and looked up at her. The chief clerk, for the moment, had quite slipped from his mind; instead, he could not resist snapping his jaws together at the sight of the streaming coffee. That made his mother scream again, she fled from the table and fell into the arms of his father, who hastened to catch her. But Gregor had now no time to spare for his parents; the chief clerk was already on the stairs; with his chin on the banisters he was taking one last backward look. Gregor made a spring, to be as sure as possible of overtaking him; the chief clerk must have divined his intention, for he leaped down several steps and vanished; he was still yelling "Ugh!" and it echoed through the whole staircase.

Unfortunately, the flight of the chief clerk seemed completely to upset Gregor's father, who had remained relatively calm until now, for instead of running after the man himself, or at least not hindering Gregor in his pursuit, he seized in his right hand the walking stick which the chief clerk had left behind on a chair, together with a hat and greatcoat, snatched in his left hand a large newspaper from the table and began stamping his feet and flourishing the stick and the newspaper to drive Gregor back into his room. No entreaty of Gregor's availed, indeed no entreaty was even understood, however humbly he bent his head his father only stamped on the floor the more loudly. Behind his father his mother had torn open a window, despite the cold weather, and was leaning far out of it with her face in her hands. A strong draught set in from the street to the staircase, the window curtains blew in, the newspapers on the table fluttered, stray pages whisked over the floor. Pitilessly Gregor's father drove him back, hissing and crying "Shoo!" like a savage. But Gregor was quite unpracticed in walking backwards, it really was a slow business. If he only had a chance to turn round he could get back to his room at once, but he was afraid of exasperating his father by the slowness of such a rotation and at any moment the stick in his father's hand might hit him a fatal blow on the back or on the head. In the end, however, nothing else was left for him to do since to his horror he observed that in moving backwards he could not even control the direction he took; and so, keeping an anxious eye on his father all the time over his shoulder, he began to turn round as quickly as he could, which was in reality very slowly. Perhaps his father noted his good intentions, for he did not interfere except every now and then to help him in the manoeuvre from a distance with the point of the stick. If only he would have stopped making that unbearable hissing noise! It made Gregor quite lose his head. He had turned almost completely round when the hissing noise so distracted him that he even turned a little the wrong way again. But when at last his head was fortunately right in front of the doorway, it appeared that his body was too broad simply to get through the opening. His father, of course, in his present mood was far from thinking of such a thing as opening the other half of the door, to let Gregor have enough space. He had merely the fixed idea of driving Gregor back into his room as quickly as possible. He would never have suffered Gregor to make the circumstantial preparations for standing up on end and perhaps slipping his way through the door. Maybe he was now making more noise than ever to urge Gregor forward, as if no obstacle impeded him; to Gregor, anyhow, the noise in his rear sounded no longer like the voice of one single father; this was really no joke, and Gregor thrust himself — come what might — into the doorway. One side of his body rose up, he was tilted at an angle in the doorway, his flank was quite bruised, horrid blotches stained the white door, soon he was stuck fast and, left to himself, could not have moved at all, his legs on one side fluttered trembling to the air, those on the other were crushed painfully to the floor — when from behind his father gave him a strong push which was literally a deliverance and he flew far into the room, bleeding freely. The door was slammed behind him with the stick, and then at last there was silence.

II

Not until it was twilight did Gregor awake out of a deep sleep, more like a swoon than a sleep. He would certainly have waked up of his own accord not much later, for he felt himself sufficiently rested and well-slept, but it seemed to him as if a fleeting step and a cautious shutting of the door leading into the hall had aroused him. The electric lights in the street cast a pale sheen here and there on the ceiling and the upper surfaces of the furniture, but down below, where he lay, it was dark. Slowly, awkwardly trying out his feelers, which he now first learned to appreciate, he pushed his way to the door to see what had been happening there. His left side felt like one single long, unpleasant tense scar, and he had actually to limp on his two rows of legs. One little leg, moreover, had been severely damaged in the course of that morning's events — it was almost a miracle that only one had been damaged — and trailed uselessly behind him.

He had reached the door before he discovered what had really drawn him to it: the smell of food. For there stood a basin filled with fresh milk in which floated little sops of white bread. He could almost have laughed with joy, since he was now still hungrier than in the morning, and he dipped his head almost over the eyes straight into the milk. But soon in disappointment he withdrew it again; not only did he find it difficult to feed because of his tender left side — and he could only feed with the palpitating collaboration of his whole body — he did not like the milk either, although milk had been his favorite drink and that was certainly why his sister had set it there for him, indeed it was almost with repulsion that he turned away from the basin and crawled back to the middle of the room.

He could see through the crack of the door that the gas was turned on in the living room, but while usually at this time his father made a habit of reading the afternoon newspaper in a loud voice to his mother and occasionally to his sister as well, not a sound was now to be heard. Well, perhaps his father had recently given up this habit of reading aloud, which his sister had mentioned so often in conversation and in her letters. But there was the same silence all around, although the flat was certainly not empty of occupants. "What a quiet life our family has been leading," said Gregor to himself, and as he sat there motionless staring into the darkness he felt great pride in the fact that he had been able to provide such a life for his parents and sister in such a fine flat. But what if all the quiet, the comfort, the contentment were now to end in horror? To keep himself from being lost in such thoughts Gregor took refuge in movement and crawled up and down the room.

Once during the long evening one of the side doors was opened a little and quickly shut again, later the other side door too; someone had apparently wanted to come in and then thought better of it. Gregor now stationed himself immediately before the living room door, determined to persuade any hesitating visitor to come in or at least to discover who it might be; but the door was not opened again and he waited in vain. In the early morning, when the doors were locked, they had all wanted to come in, now that he had opened one door and the other had apparently been opened during the day, no one came in and even the keys were on the other side of the doors.

It was late at night before the gas went out in the living room, and Gregor could easily tell that his parents and his sister had all stayed awake until then, for he could clearly hear the three of them stealing away on tiptoe. No one was likely to visit him, not until the morning, that was certain;

so he had plenty of time to meditate at his leisure on how he was to arrange his life afresh. But the lofty, empty room in which he had to lie flat on the floor filled him with an apprehension he could not account for, since it had been his very own room for the past five years — and with a half-unconscious action, not without a slight feeling of shame, he scuttled under the sofa, where he felt comfortable at once, although his back was a little cramped and he could not lift his head up, and his only regret was that his body was too broad to get the whole of it under the sofa.

He stayed there all night, spending the time partly in a light slumber, from which his hunger kept waking him up with a start, and partly in worrying and sketching vague hopes, which all led to the same conclusion, that he must lie low for the present and, by exercising patience, and the utmost consideration, help the family to bear the inconvenience he was bound to cause them in his present condition.

Very early in the morning, it was still almost night, Gregor had the chance to test the strength of his new resolutions, for his sister, nearly fully dressed, opened the door from the hall and peered in. She did not see him at once, yet when she caught sight of him under the sofa — well, he had to be somewhere, he couldn't have flown away, could he? — she was so startled that without being able to help it she slammed the door shut again. But as if regretting her behavior she opened the door again immediately and came in on tiptoe, as if she were visiting an invalid or even a stranger. Gregor had pushed his head forward to the very edge of the sofa and watched her. Would she notice that he had left the milk standing, and not for lack of hunger, and would she bring in some other kind of food more to his taste? If she did not do it of her own accord, he would rather starve than draw her attention to the fact, although he felt a wild impulse to dart out from under the sofa, throw himself at her feet and beg her for something to eat. But his sister at once noticed, with surprise, that the basin was still full, except for a little milk that had been spilt all around it, she lifted it immediately, not with her bare hands, true, but with a cloth and carried it away. Gregor was wildly curious to know what she would bring instead, and made various speculations about it. Yet what she actually did next, in the goodness of her heart, he could never have guessed at. To find out what he liked she brought him a whole selection of food, all set out on an old newspaper. There were old, half-decayed vegetables, bones from last night's supper covered with a white sauce that had thickened; some raisins and almonds; a piece of cheese that Gregor would have called uneatable two days ago; a dry roll of bread, a buttered roll, and a roll both buttered and salted. Besides all that, she set down again the same basin, into which she had poured some water, and which was apparently to be reserved for his exclusive use. And with fine tact, knowing that Gregor would not eat in her presence, she withdrew quickly and even turned the key, to let him understand that he could take his ease as much as he liked. Gregor's legs all whizzed towards the food. His wounds must have healed completely, moreover, for he felt no disability, which amazed him and made him reflect how more than a month ago he had cut one finger a little with a knife and had still suffered pain from the wound only the day before yesterday. Am I less sensitive now? he thought, and sucked greedily at the cheese, which above all the other edibles attracted him at once and strongly. One after another and with tears of satisfaction in his eyes he quickly devoured the cheese, the vegetables and the sauce; the fresh food, on the other hand, had no charms for him, he could not even stand the smell of it and actually dragged away to some little distance the things he could eat. He had long finished his meal and was only lying lazily on the same spot when his sister turned the key slowly as a sign for him to retreat. That roused him at once, although he was nearly asleep, and he hurried under the sofa again. But it took considerable self-control for him to stay under the sofa, even for the short time his sister was in the room, since the large meal had swollen his body somewhat and he was so cramped he could hardly breathe. Slight attacks of breathlessness afflicted him and his eyes were starting a little out of his head as he watched his unsuspecting sister sweeping together with a broom not only the remains of what he had eaten but even the things he had not touched, as if these were now of no use to anyone, and hastily shoveling it all into a bucket, which she covered with a wooden lid and carried away. Hardly had she turned her back when Gregor came from under the sofa and stretched and puffed himself out.

In this manner Gregor was fed, once in the early morning while his parents and the servant girl were still asleep, and a second time after they had all had their midday dinner, for then his parents took a short nap and the servant girl could be sent out on some errand or other by his sister. Not that they would have wanted him to starve, of course, but perhaps they could not have borne to know more about his feeding than from hearsay, perhaps too his sister wanted to spare them such little anxieties wherever possible, since they had quite enough to bear as it was.

Under what pretext the doctor and the locksmith had been got rid of on that first morning Gregor could not discover, for since what he had said was not understood by the others it never struck any of them, not even his sister, that he could understand what they said, and so whenever his sister came into his room he had to content himself with hearing her utter only a sigh now and then and an occasional appeal to the saints. Later on, when she had got a little used to the situation — of course she could never get completely used to it — she sometimes threw out a remark which was kindly meant or could be so interpreted. "Well, he liked his dinner today," she would say when Gregor had made a good clearance of his food; and when he had not eaten, which gradually happened more and more often, she would say almost sadly: "Everything's been left standing again."

But although Gregor could get no news directly, he overheard a lot from the neighboring rooms, and as soon as voices were audible, he would run to the door of the room concerned and press his whole body against it.

In the first few days especially there was no conversation that did not refer to him somehow, even if only indirectly. For two whole days there were family consultations at every mealtime about what should be done; but also between meals the same subject was discussed, for there were always at least two members of the family at home, since no one wanted to be alone in the flat and to leave it quite empty was unthinkable. And on the very first of these days the household cook — it was not quite clear what and how much she knew of the situation — went down on her knees to his mother and begged leave to go, and when she departed, a quarter of an hour later, gave thanks for her dismissal with tears in her eyes as if for the greatest benefit that could have been conferred on her, and without any prompting swore a solemn oath that she would never say a single word to anyone about what had happened.

Now Gregor's sister had to cook too, helping her mother; true, the cooking did not amount to much, for they ate scarcely anything. Gregor was always hearing one of the family vainly urging another to eat and getting no answer but: "Thanks, I've had all I want," or something similar. Perhaps they drank nothing either. Time and again his sister kept asking his father if he wouldn't like some beer and offered kindly to go and fetch it herself, and when he made no answer suggested that she could ask the concierge to fetch it, so that he need feel no sense of obligation, but then a round "No" came from his father and no more was said about it.

In the course of that very first day Gregor's father explained the family's financial position and prospects to both his mother and his sister. Now and then he rose from the table to get some voucher or memorandum out of the small safe he had rescued from the collapse of his business five years earlier. One could hear him opening the complicated lock and rustling papers out and shutting it again. This statement made by his father was the first cheerful information Gregor had heard since his imprisonment. He had been of the opinion that nothing at all was left over from his father's business, at least his father had never said anything to the contrary, and of course he had not asked him directly. At the time Gregor's sole desire was to do his utmost to help the family to forget as soon as possible the catastrophe which had overwhelmed the business and thrown them all into a state of complete despair. And so he had set to work with unusual ardor and almost overnight had become a commercial traveler instead of a little clerk, with of course much greater chances of earning money, and his success was immediately translated into good round coin which he could lay on the table for his amazed and happy family. These had been fine times, and they had never recurred, at least not with the same sense of glory, although later on Gregor had earned so much money that he was able to meet the expenses of the whole household and did so. They had simply got used to it, both the family and Gregor; the money was gratefully accepted and gladly given, but there was no special uprush of warm feeling. With his sister alone had he remained intimate, and it was a secret plan of his that she,

who loved music, unlike himself, and could play movingly on the violin,
should be sent next year to study at the Conservatorium, despite the great
expense that would entail, which must be made up in some other way.
During his brief visits home the Conservatorium was often mentioned in
the talks he had with his sister, but always merely as a beautiful dream
which could never come true, and his parents discouraged even these innocent references to it; yet Gregor had made up his mind firmly about it and
meant to announce the fact with due solemnity on Christmas Day.

Such were the thoughts, completely futile in his present condition,
that went through his head as he stood clinging upright to the door and listening. Sometimes out of sheer weariness he had to give up listening and let
his head fall negligently against the door, but he always had to pull himself
together again at once, for even the slight sound his head made was audible
next door and brought all conversation to a stop. "What can he be doing
now?" his father would say after a while, obviously turning towards the
door, and only then would the interrupted conversation gradually be set
going again.

Gregor was now informed as amply as he could wish — for his father
tended to repeat himself in his explanations, partly because it was a long
time since he had handled such matters and partly because his mother
could not always grasp things at once — that a certain amount of investments, a very small amount it was true, had survived the wreck of their fortunes and had even increased a little because the dividends had not been
touched meanwhile. And besides that, the money Gregor brought home
every month — he had kept only a few dollars for himself — had never
been quite used up and now amounted to a small capital sum. Behind the
door Gregor nodded his head eagerly, rejoiced at this evidence of unexpected thrift and foresight. True, he could really have paid off some more of
his father's debts to the chief with his extra money, and so brought much
nearer the day on which he could quit his job, but doubtless it was better
the way his father had arranged it.

Yet this capital was by no means sufficient to let the family live on the
interest of it; for one year, perhaps, or at the most two, they could live on
the principal, that was all. It was simply a sum that ought not to be touched
and should be kept for a rainy day; money for living expenses would have to
be earned. Now his father was still hale enough but an old man, and he had
done no work for the past five years and could not be expected to do much;
during these five years, the first years of leisure in his laborious though unsuccessful life, he had grown rather fat and become sluggish. And Gregor's
old mother, how was she to earn a living with her asthma, which troubled
her even when she walked through the flat and kept her lying on a sofa
every other day panting for breath beside an open window? And was his sister to earn her bread, she who was still a child of seventeen and whose life
hitherto had been so pleasant, consisting as it did in dressing herself nicely,
sleeping long, helping in the housekeeping, going out to a few modest en-

tertainments and above all playing the violin? At first whenever the need for
earning money was mentioned Gregor let go his hold on the door and threw
himself down on the cool leather sofa beside it, he felt so hot with shame
and grief.

Often he just lay there the long nights through without sleeping at all,
scrabbling for hours on the leather. Or he nerved himself to the great effort
of pushing an armchair to the window, then crawled up over the window
sill and, braced against the chair, leaned against the windowpanes, obviously in some recollection of the sense of freedom that looking out of a
window always used to give him. For in reality day by day things that were
even a little way off were growing dimmer to his sight; the hospital across
the street, which he used to execrate for being all too often before his eyes,
was now quite beyond his range of vision, and if he had not known that he
lived in Charlotte Street, a quiet street but still a city street, he might have
believed that his window gave on a desert waste where gray sky and gray
land blended indistinguishably into each other. His quick-witted sister only
needed to observe twice that the armchair stood by the window; after that
whenever she had tidied the room she always pushed the chair back to the
same place at the window and even left the inner casements open.

If he could have spoken to her and thanked her for all she had to do
for him, he could have borne her ministrations better; as it was, they oppressed him. She certainly tried to make as light as possible of whatever was
disagreeable in her task, and as time went on she succeeded, of course, more
and more, but time brought more enlightenment to Gregor too. The very
way she came in distressed him. Hardly was she in the room when she
rushed to the window, without even taking time to shut the door, careful as
she was usually to shield the sight of Gregor's room from the others, and as
if she were almost suffocating tore the casements open with hasty fingers,
standing then in the open draught for a while even in the bitterest cold and
drawing deep breaths. This noisy scurry of hers upset Gregor twice a day; he
would crouch trembling under the sofa all the time, knowing quite well that
she would certainly have spared him such a disturbance had she found it at
all possible to stay in his presence without opening a window.

On one occasion, about a month after Gregor's metamorphosis, when
there was surely no reason for her to be still startled at his appearance, she
came a little earlier than usual and found him gazing out of the window,
quite motionless, and thus well placed to look like a bogey. Gregor would
not have been surprised had she not come in at all, for she could not immediately open the window while he was there, but not only did she retreat,
she jumped back as if in alarm and banged the door shut; a stranger might
well have thought that he had been lying in wait for her there meaning to
bite her. Of course he hid himself under the sofa at once, but he had to wait
until midday before she came again, and she seemed more ill at ease than
usual. This made him realize how repulsive the sight of him still was to her,
and that it was bound to go on being repulsive, and what an effort it must

cost her not to run away even from the sight of the small portion of his body that stuck out from under the sofa. In order to spare her that, therefore, one day he carried a sheet on his back to the sofa — it cost him four hours' labor — and arranged it there in such a way as to hide him completely, so that even if she were to bend down she could not see him. Had she considered the sheet unnecessary, she would certainly have stripped it off the sofa again, for it was clear enough that this curtaining and confining of himself was not likely to conduce Gregor's comfort, but she left it where it was, and Gregor even fancied that he caught a thankful glance from her eye when he lifted the sheet carefully a very little with his head to see how she was taking the new arrangement.

For the first fortnight his parents could not bring themselves to the point of entering his room, and he often heard them expressing their appreciation of his sister's activities, whereas formerly they had frequently scolded her for being as they thought a somewhat useless daughter. But now, both of them often waited outside the door, his father and his mother, while his sister tidied his room, and as soon as she came out she had to tell them exactly how things were in the room, what Gregor had eaten, how he had conducted himself this time and whether there was not perhaps some slight improvement in his condition. His mother, moreover, began relatively soon to want to visit him, but his father and sister dissuaded her at first with arguments which Gregor listened to very attentively and altogether approved. Later, however, she had to be held back by main force, and when she cried out: "Do let me in to Gregor, he is my unfortunate son! Can't you understand that I must go to him?" Gregor thought that it might be well to have her come in, not every day, of course, but perhaps once a week; she understood things, after all, much better than his sister, who was only a child despite the efforts she was making and had perhaps taken on so difficult a task merely out of childish thoughtlessness.

Gregor's desire to see his mother was soon fulfilled. During the daytime he did not want to show himself at the window, out of consideration for his parents, but he could not crawl very far around the few square yards of floor space he had, nor could he bear lying quietly at rest all during the night, while he was fast losing any interest he had ever taken in food, so that for mere recreation he had formed the habit of crawling crisscross over the walls and ceiling. He especially enjoyed hanging suspended from the ceiling; it was much better than lying on the floor; one could breathe more freely; one's body swung and rocked lightly; and in the almost blissful absorption induced by this suspension it could happen to his own surprise that he let go and fell plump on the floor. Yet he now had his body much better under control than formerly, and even such a big fall did him no harm. His sister at once remarked the new distraction Gregor had found for himself — he left traces behind him of the sticky stuff on his soles wherever he crawled — and she got the idea in her head of giving him as wide a field as possible to crawl in and of removing the pieces of furniture that hindered him, above all the chest of drawers and the writing desk. But that was more than she could manage all by herself; she did not dare ask her father to help her; and as for the servant girl, a young creature of sixteen who had had the courage to stay on after the cook's departure, she could not be asked to help, for she had begged as an especial favor that she might keep the kitchen door locked and open it only on a definite summons; so there was nothing left but to apply to her mother at an hour when her father was out. And the old lady did come, with exclamations of joyful eagerness, which, however, died away at the door of Gregor's room. Gregor's sister, of course, went in first, to see that everything was in order before letting his mother enter. In great haste Gregor pulled the sheet lower and rucked it more in folds so that it really looked as if it had been thrown accidentally over the sofa. And this time he did not peer out from under it; he renounced the pleasure of seeing his mother on this occasion and was only glad that she had come at all. "Come in, he's out of sight," said his sister, obviously leading her mother in by the hand. Gregor could now hear the two women struggling to shift the heavy old chest from its place, and his sister claiming the greater part of the labor for herself, without listening to the admonitions of her mother who feared she might overstrain herself. It took a long time. After at least a quarter of an hour's tugging his mother objected that the chest had better be left where it was, for in the first place it was too heavy and could never be got out before his father came home, and standing in the middle of the room like that it would only hamper Gregor's movements, while in the second place it was not at all certain that removing the furniture would be doing a service to Gregor. She was inclined to think to the contrary; the sight of the naked walls made her own heart heavy, and why shouldn't Gregor have the same feeling, considering that he had been used to his furniture for so long and might feel forlorn without it. "And doesn't it look," she concluded in a low voice — in fact she had been almost whispering all the time as if to avoid letting Gregor, whose exact whereabouts she did not know, hear even the tones of her voice, for she was convinced that he could not understand her words — "doesn't it look as if we were showing him, by taking away his furniture, that we have given up hope of his ever getting better and are just leaving him coldly to himself? I think it would be best to keep his room exactly as it has always been, so that when he comes back to us he will find everything unchanged and be able all the more easily to forget what has happened in between."

On hearing these words from his mother Gregor realized that the lack of all direct human speech for the past two months together with the monotony of family life must have confused his mind, otherwise he could not account for the fact that he had quite earnestly looked forward to having his room emptied of furnishing. Did he really want his warm room, so comfortably fitted with old family furniture, to be turned into a naked den in which he would certainly be able to crawl unhampered in all directions but at the price of shedding simultaneously all recollection of his human background? He had indeed been so near the brink of forgetfulness that only the voice of his mother, which he had not heard for so long, had drawn him back from it. Nothing should be taken out of his room; everything must stay as it was; he could not dispense with the good influence of the furniture on his state of mind; and even if the furniture did hamper him in his sense-less crawling round and round, that was no drawback but a great advantage.

Unfortunately his sister was of the contrary opinion; she had grown accustomed, and not without reason, to consider herself an expert in Gregor's affairs as against her parents, and so her mother's advice was now enough to make her determined on the removal not only of the chest and the writing desk, which had been her first intention, but of all the furniture except the indispensable sofa. This determination was not, of course, merely the outcome of childish recalcitrance and of the self-confidence she had recently developed so unexpectedly and at such cost; she had in fact perceived that Gregor needed a lot of space to crawl about in, while on the other hand he never used the furniture at all, so far as could be seen. Another factor might have been also the enthusiastic temperament of an adolescent girl, which seeks to indulge itself on every opportunity and which now tempted Grete to exaggerate the horror of her brother's circumstances in order that she might do all the more for him. In a room where Gregor lorded it all alone over empty walls no one save herself was likely ever to set foot.

And so she was not to be moved from her resolve by her mother who seemed moreover to be ill at ease in Gregor's room and therefore unsure of herself, was soon reduced to silence and helped her daughter as best she could to push the chest outside. Now, Gregor could do without the chest, if need be, but the writing desk he must retain. As soon as the two women had got the chest out of his room, groaning as they pushed it, Gregor stuck his head out from under the sofa to see how he might intervene as kindly and cautiously as possible. But as bad luck would have it, his mother was the first to return, leaving Grete clasping the chest in the room next door where she was trying to shift it all by herself, without of course moving it from the spot. His mother however was not accustomed to the sight of him, it might sicken her and so in alarm Gregor backed quickly to the other end of the sofa, yet could not prevent the sheet from swaying a little in front. That was enough to put her on the alert. She paused, stood still for a moment and then went back to Grete.

Although Gregor kept reassuring himself that nothing out of the way was happening, but only a few bits of furniture were being changed round, he soon had to admit that all this trotting to and fro of the two women, their little ejaculations and the scraping of furniture along the floor affected him like a vast disturbance coming from all sides at once, and however much he tucked in his head and legs and cowered to the very floor he was bound to confess that he would not be able to stand it for long. They were clearing his room out; taking away everything he loved; the chest in which he kept his fret saw and other tools was already dragged off; they were now loosening the writing desk which had almost sunk into the floor, the desk at which he had done all his homework when he was at the commercial academy, at the grammar school before that, and, yes, even at the primary school — he had no more time to waste in weighing the good intentions of the two women, whose existence he had by now almost forgotten, for they were so exhausted that they were laboring in silence and nothing could be heard but the heavy scuffling of their feet.

And so he rushed out — the women were just leaning against the writing desk in the next room to give themselves a breather — and four times changed his direction, since he really did not know what to rescue first, then on the wall opposite, which was already otherwise cleared, he was struck by the picture of the lady muffled in so much fur and quickly crawled up to it and pressed himself to the glass, which was a good surface to hold on to and comforted his hot belly. This picture at least, which was entirely hidden beneath him, was going to be removed by nobody. He turned his head towards the door of the living room so as to observe the women when they came back.

They had not allowed themselves much of a rest and were already coming; Grete had twined her arm round her mother and was almost supporting her. "Well, what shall we take now?" said Grete, looking round. Her eyes met Gregor's from the wall. She kept her composure, presumably because of her mother, bent her head down to her mother, to keep her from looking up, and said, although in a fluttering, unpremeditated voice: "Come, hadn't we better go back to the living room for a moment?" Her intentions were clear enough to Gregor, she wanted to bestow her mother in safety and then chase him down from the wall. Well, just let her try it! He clung to his picture and would not give it up. He would rather fly in Grete's face.

But Grete's words had succeeded in disquieting her mother, who took a step to one side, caught sight of the huge brown mass on the flowered wallpaper, and before she was really conscious that what she saw was Gregor screamed in a loud, hoarse voice: "Oh God, oh God!" fell with outspread arms over the sofa as if giving up and did not move. "Gregor!" cried his sister, shaking her fist and glaring at him. This was the first time she had directly addressed him since his metamorphosis. She ran into the next room for some aromatic essence with which to rouse her mother from her fainting fit. Gregor wanted to help too — there was still time to rescue the picture — but he was stuck fast to the glass and had to tear himself loose; he then ran after his sister into the next room as if he could advise her, as he used to do; but then had to stand helplessly behind her; she meanwhile searched among various small bottles and when she turned round started in alarm at the sight of him; one bottle fell on the floor and broke; a splinter of glass cut Gregor's face and some kind of corrosive medicine splashed him; without pausing a moment longer Grete gathered up all the bottles she could carry and ran to her mother with them; she banged the door shut with her foot. Gregor was now cut off from his mother, who was perhaps nearly dying because of him; he dared not open the door for fear of frightening away his sister, who had to stay with her mother; there was nothing he could do but wait; and harassed by self-reproach and worry he began now to crawl to and fro, over everything, walls, furniture and ceiling, and finally in his despair, when the whole room seemed to be reeling round him, fell down on to the middle of the big table.

A little while elapsed, Gregor was still lying there feebly and all around was quiet, perhaps that was a good omen. Then the doorbell rang. The servant girl was of course locked in her kitchen, and Grete would have to open the door. It was his father. "What's been happening?" were his first words; Grete's face must have told him everything. Grete answered in a muffled voice, apparently hiding her head on his breast: "Mother has been fainting, but she's better now. Gregor's broken loose." "Just what I expected," said his father, "just what I've been telling you, but you women would never listen." It was clear to Gregor that his father had taken the worst interpretation of Grete's all too brief statement and was assuming that Gregor had been guilty of some violent act. Therefore Gregor must now try to propitiate his father, since he had neither time nor means for an explanation. And so he fled to the door of his own room and crouched against it, to let his father see as soon as he came in from the hall that his son had the good intention of getting back into his room immediately and that it was not necessary to drive him there, but that if only the door were opened he would disappear at once.

Yet his father was not in the mood to perceive such fine distinctions. "Ah!" he cried as soon as he appeared, in a tone which sounded at once angry and exultant. Gregor drew his head back from the door and lifted it to look at his father. Truly, this was not the father he had imagined to himself; admittedly he had been too absorbed of late in his new recreation of crawling over the ceiling to take the same interest as before in what was happening elsewhere in the flat, and he ought really to be prepared for some changes. And yet, and yet, could that be his father? The man who used to lie wearily sunk in bed whenever Gregor set out on a business journey; who welcomed him back of an evening lying in a long chair in a dressing gown; who could not really rise to his feet but only lifted his arms in greeting, and on the rare occasions when he did go out with his family, on one or two Sundays a year and on high holidays, walked between Gregor and his mother, who were slow walkers anyhow, even more slowly than they did, muffled in his old greatcoat, shuffling laboriously forward with the help of his crook-handled stick which he set down most cautiously at every step and, whenever he wanted to say anything, nearly always came to a full stop and gathered his escort around him? Now he was standing there in fine shape; dressed in a smart blue uniform with gold buttons, such as bank messengers wear; his strong double chin bulged over the stiff high collar of his jacket; from under his bushy eyebrows his black eyes darted fresh and pene- trating glances; his onetime tangled white hair had been combed flat on either side of a shining and carefully exact parting. He pitched his cap, which bore a gold monogram, probably the badge of some bank, in a wide sweep across the whole room on to a sofa and with the tail-ends of his jacket thrown back, his hands in his trouser pockets, advanced with a grim visage towards Gregor. Likely enough he did not himself know what he meant to do; at any rate he lifted his feet uncommonly high, and Gregor was dumb- founded at the enormous size of his shoe soles. But Gregor could not risk standing up to him, aware as he had been from the very first day of his new life that his father believed only the severest measures suitable for dealing with him. And so he ran before his father, stopping when he stopped and scuttling forward again when his father made any kind of move. In this way they circled the room several times without anything decisive happening; indeed the whole operation did not even look like a pursuit because it was carried out so slowly. And so Gregor did not leave the floor, for he feared that his father might take as a piece of peculiar wickedness any excursion of his over the walls or the ceiling. All the same, he could not stay this course much longer, for while his father took one step he had to carry out a whole series of movements. He was already beginning to feel breathless, just as in his former life his lungs had not been very dependable. As he was staggering along, trying to concentrate his energy on running, hardly keeping his eyes open; in his dazed state never even thinking of any other escape than simply going forward; and having almost forgotten that the walls were free to him, which in this room were well provided with finely carved pieces of furniture full of knobs and crevices — suddenly something lightly flung landed close behind him and rolled before him. It was an apple; a second apple followed immediately; Gregor came to a stop in alarm; there was no point in running on, for his father was determined to bombard him. He had filled his pockets with fruit from the dish on the sideboard and was now shying apple after apple, without taking particularly good aim for the moment. The small red apples rolled about the floor as if magnetized and cannoned into each other. An apple thrown without much force grazed Gregor's back and glanced off harmlessly. But another following immediately landed right on his back and sank in; Gregor wanted to drag himself forward, as if this startling, incredi- ble pain could be left behind him: but he felt as if nailed to the spot and flattened himself out in a complete derangement of all his senses. With his last conscious look he saw the door of his room being torn open and his mother rushing out ahead of his screaming sister, in her underbodice, for her daughter had loosened her clothing to let her breathe more freely and recover from her swoon, he saw his mother rushing towards his father, leaving one after another behind her on the floor her loosened petticoats, stumbling over her petticoats straight to his father and embracing him, in complete union with him — but here Gregor's sight began to fail — with her hands clasped round his father's neck as she begged for her son's life.

III

The serious injury done to Gregor, which disabled him for more than a month — the apple went on sticking in his body as a visible reminder, since no one ventured to remove it — seemed to have made even his father recollect that Gregor was a member of the family, despite his present unfortunate and repulsive shape, and ought not to be treated as an enemy, that, on the contrary, family duty required the suppression of disgust and the exercise of patience, nothing but patience.

And although his injury had impaired, probably for ever, his power of movement, and for the time being it took him long, long minutes to creep across his room like an old invalid — there was no question now of crawling up the wall — yet in his own opinion he was sufficiently compensated for this worsening of his condition by the fact that towards evening the living-room door, which he used to watch intently for an hour or two beforehand, was always thrown open, so that lying in the darkness of his room, invisible to the family, he could see them all at the lamp-lit table and listen to their talk, by general consent as it were, very different from his earlier eavesdropping.

True, their intercourse lacked the lively character of former times, which he had always called to mind with a certain wistfulness in the small hotel bedrooms where he had been wont to throw himself down, tired out, on damp bedding. They were now mostly very silent. Soon after supper his father would fall asleep in his armchair; his mother and sister would admonish each other to be silent; his mother, bending low over the lamp, stitched at fine sewing for an underwear firm; his sister, who had taken a job as a salesgirl, was learning shorthand and French in the evenings on the chance of bettering herself. Sometimes his father woke up, and as if quite unaware that he had been sleeping said to his mother: "What a lot of sewing you're doing today!" and at once fell asleep again, while the two women exchanged a tired smile.

With a kind of mulishness his father persisted in keeping his uniform on even in the house; his dressing gown hung uselessly on its peg and he slept fully dressed where he sat, as if he were ready for service at any moment and even here only at the beck and call of his superior. As a result, his uniform, which was not brand-new to start with, began to look dirty, despite all the loving care of the mother and sister to keep it clean, and Gregor often spent whole evenings gazing at the many greasy spots on the garment, gleaming with gold buttons always in a high state of polish, in which the old man sat sleeping in extreme discomfort and yet quite peacefully.

As soon as the clock struck ten his mother tried to rouse his father with gentle words and to persuade him after that to get into bed, for sitting there he could not have a proper sleep and that was what he needed most, since he had to go to duty at six. But with the mulishness that had obsessed him since he became a bank messenger he always insisted on staying longer at the table, although he regularly fell asleep again and in the end only with the greatest trouble could be got out of his armchair and into his bed. However insistently Gregor's mother and sister kept urging him with gentle reminders, he would go on slowly shaking his head for a quarter of an hour, keeping his eyes shut, and refuse to get to his feet. The mother plucked at his sleeve, whispering endearments in his ear, the sister left her lessons to come to her mother's help, but Gregor's father was not to be caught. He would only sink down deeper in his chair. Not until the two women hoisted him up by the armpits did he open his eyes and look at them both, one after the other, usually with the remark: "This is a life. This is the peace and quiet of my old age." And leaning on the two of them he would heave himself up, with difficulty, as if he were a great burden to himself, suffer them to lead him as far as the door and then wave them off and go on alone, while the mother abandoned her needlework and the sister her pen in order to run after him and help him farther.

Who could find time, in this overworked and tired-out family, to bother about Gregor more than was absolutely needful? The household was reduced more and more; the servant girl was turned off; a gigantic bony charwoman with white hair flying round her head came in morning and evening to do the rough work; everything else was done by Gregor's mother, as well as great piles of sewing. Even various family ornaments, which his mother and sister used to wear with pride at parties and celebrations, had to be sold, as Gregor discovered of an evening from hearing them all discuss the prices obtained. But what they lamented most was the fact that they could not leave the flat which was much too big for their present circumstances, because they could not think of any way to shift Gregor. Yet Gregor saw well enough that consideration for him was not the main difficulty preventing the removal, for they could have easily shifted him in some suitable box with a few air holes in it; what really kept them from moving into another flat was rather their own complete hopelessness and the belief that they had been singled out for a misfortune such as had never happened to any of their relations or acquaintances. They fulfilled to the uttermost all that the world demands of poor people, the father fetched breakfast for the small clerks in the bank, the mother devoted her energy to making underwear for strangers, the sister trotted to and fro behind the counter at the behest of customers, but more than this they had not the strength to do. And the wound in Gregor's back began to nag at him afresh when his mother and sister, after getting his father into bed, came back again, left their work lying, drew close to each other and sat cheek by cheek; when his mother, pointing towards his room, said: "Shut that door now, Grete," and he was left again in darkness, while next door the women mingled their tears or perhaps sat dry-eyed staring at the table.

Gregor hardly slept at all by night or by day. He was often haunted by the idea that next time the door opened he would take the family's affairs in hand again just as he used to do; once more, after this long interval, there appeared in his thoughts the figures of the chief and the chief clerk, the commercial travelers and the apprentices, the porter who was so dull-witted, two or three friends in other firms, a chambermaid in one of the rural hotels, a sweet and fleeting memory, a cashier in a milliner's shop, whom he had wooed earnestly but too slowly — they all appeared, together with strangers or people he had quite forgotten, but instead of helping him and his family they were one and all unapproachable and he was glad when they vanished. At other times he would not be in the mood to bother about his family, he was only filled with rage at the way they were neglecting him, and although he had no clear idea of what he might care to eat he would make plans for getting into the larder to take the food that was after all his due, even if he were not hungry. His sister no longer took thought to bring him what might especially please him, but in the morning and at noon before she went to business hurriedly pushed into his room with her foot any food that was available, and in the evening cleared it out again with one sweep of the broom, heedless of whether it had been merely tasted, or — as most frequently happened — left untouched. The cleaning of his room, which she now did always in the evenings, could not have been more hastily done. Streaks of dirt stretched along the walls, here and there lay balls of dust and filth. At first Gregor used to station himself in some particularly filthy corner when his sister arrived, in order to reproach her with it, so to speak. But he could have sat there for weeks without getting her to make any improvements; she could see the dirt as well as he did, but she had simply made up her mind to leave it alone. And yet, with a touchiness that was new to her, which seemed anyhow to have infected the whole family, she jealously guarded her claim to be the sole caretaker of Gregor's room. His mother once subjected his room to a thorough cleaning, which was achieved only by means of several buckets of water — all this dampness of course upset Gregor too and he lay widespread, sulky and motionless on the sofa — but she was well punished for it. Hardly had his sister noticed the changed aspect of his room than she rushed in high dudgeon into the living room and, despite the imploringly raised hands of her mother, burst into a storm of weeping, while her parents — her father had of course been startled out of his chair — looked on at first in helpless amazement; then they too began to go into action; the father reproached the mother on his right for not having left the cleaning of Gregor's room to his sister; shrieked at the sister on his left that never again was she to be allowed to clean Gregor's room; while the mother tried to pull the father into his bedroom, since he was beyond himself with agitation; the sister, shaken with sobs, then beat upon the table with her small fists; and Gregor hissed loudly with rage because not one of them thought of shutting the door to spare him such a spectacle and so much noise.

Still, even if the sister, exhausted by her daily work, had grown tired of looking after Gregor as she did formerly, there was no need for his mother's intervention or for Gregor's being neglected at all. The charwoman was there. This old widow, whose strong bony frame had enabled her to survive the worst a long life could offer, by no means recoiled from Gregor. Without being in the least curious she had once by chance opened the door of his room and at the sight of Gregor, who, taken by surprise, began to rush to and fro although no one was chasing him, merely stood there with her arms folded. From that time she never failed to open his door a little for a moment, morning and evening, to have a look at him. At first she even used to call him to her, with words which apparently she took to be friendly, such as: "Come along, then, you old dung beetle!" or "Look at the old dung beetle, then!" To such allocutions Gregor made no answer, but stayed motionless where he was, as if the door had never been opened. Instead of being allowed to disturb him so senselessly whenever the whim took her, she should rather have been ordered to clean out his room daily, that charwoman! Once, early in the morning — heavy rain was lashing on the windowpanes, perhaps a sign that spring was on the way — Gregor was so exasperated when she began addressing him again that he ran at her, as if to attack her, although slowly and feebly enough. But the charwoman instead of showing fright merely lifted high a chair that happened to be beside the door, and as she stood there with her mouth wide open it was clear that she meant to shut it only when she brought the chair down on Gregor's back. "So you're not coming any nearer?" she asked, as Gregor turned away again, and quietly put the chair back into the corner.

Gregor was now eating hardly anything. Only when he happened to pass the food laid out for him did he take a bit of something in his mouth as a pastime, kept it there for an hour at a time and usually spat it out again. At first he thought it was chagrin over the state of his room that prevented him from eating, yet he soon got used to the various changes in his room. It had become a habit in the family to push into his room things there was no room for elsewhere, and there were plenty of these now, since one of the rooms had been let to three lodgers. These serious gentlemen — all three of them with full beards, as Gregor once observed through a crack in the door — had a passion for order, not only in their own room but, since they were now members of the household, in all its arrangements, especially in the kitchen. Superfluous, not to say dirty, objects they could not bear. Besides, they had brought with them most of the furnishings they needed. For this reason many things could be dispensed with that it was no use trying to sell but that should not be thrown away either. All of them found their way into Gregor's room. The ash can likewise and the kitchen garbage can. Anything that was not needed for the moment was simply flung into Gregor's room by the charwoman, who did everything in a hurry; fortunately Gregor usually saw only the object, whatever it was, and the hand that held it. Perhaps she intended to take the things away again as time and opportunity offered, or to collect them until she could throw them all out in a heap, but in fact they just lay wherever she happened to throw them, except when Gregor pushed his way through the junk heap and shifted it somewhat, at first out of necessity, because he had not room enough to crawl, but later with increasing enjoyment, although after such excursions, being sad and weary to death, he would lie motionless for hours. And since the lodgers often ate their supper at home in the common living room, the living room door stayed shut many an evening, yet Gregor reconciled himself quite easily to the shutting of the door, for often enough on evenings when it was opened he had disregarded it entirely and lain in the darkest corner of his room, quite unnoticed by the family. But on one occasion the charwoman left the door open a little and it stayed ajar even when the lodgers came in for supper and the lamp was lit. They set themselves at the top end of the table where formerly Gregor and his father and mother had eaten their meals, unfolded their napkins and took knife and fork in hand. At once his mother appeared in the other doorway with a dish of meat and close behind her his sister with a dish of potatoes piled high. The food steamed with a thick vapor. The lodgers bent over the food set before them as if to scrutinize it before eating, in fact the man in the middle, who seemed to pass for an authority with the other two, cut a piece of meat as it lay on the dish, obviously to discover if it were tender or should be sent back to the kitchen. He showed satisfaction, and Gregor's mother and sister, who had been watching anxiously, breathed freely and began to smile.

The family itself took its meals in the kitchen. Nonetheless, Gregor's father came into the living room before going into the kitchen and with one prolonged bow, cap in hand, made a round of the table. The lodgers all stood up and murmured something in their beards. When they were alone again they ate their food in almost complete silence. It seemed remarkable to Gregor that among the various noises coming from the table he could always distinguish the sound of their masticating teeth, as if this were a sign to Gregor that one needed teeth in order to eat, and that with toothless jaws even of the finest make one could do nothing. "I'm hungry enough," said Gregor sadly to himself, "but not for that kind of food. How these lodgers are stuffing themselves, and here am I dying of starvation!"

On that very evening — during the whole of his time there Gregor could not remember ever having heard the violin — the sound of violin-playing came from the kitchen. The lodgers had already finished their supper, the one in the middle had brought out a newspaper and given the other two a page apiece, and now they were leaning back at ease reading and smoking. When the violin began to play they pricked up their ears, got to their feet, and went on tiptoe to the hall door where they stood huddled together. Their movements must have been heard in the kitchen, for Gregor's father called out: "Is the violin-playing disturbing you, gentlemen? It can be stopped at once." "On the contrary," said the middle lodger, "could not Fräulein Samsa come and play in this room, beside us, where it is much more convenient and comfortable?" "Oh certainly," cried Gregor's father, as if he were the violin-player. The lodgers came back into the living room and waited. Presently Gregor's father arrived with the music stand, his mother carrying the music and his sister with the violin. His sister quietly made everything ready to start playing; his parents, who had never let rooms before and so had an exaggerated idea of the courtesy due to lodgers, did not venture to sit down on their own chairs; his father leaned against the door, the right hand thrust between two buttons of his livery coat, which was formally buttoned up; but his mother was offered a chair by one of the lodgers and, since she left the chair just where he had happened to put it, sat down in a corner to one side.

Gregor's sister began to play; the father and mother, from either side, intently watched the movements of her hands. Gregor, attracted by the playing, ventured to move forward a little until his head was actually inside the living room. He felt hardly any surprise at his growing lack of consideration for the others; there had been a time when he prided himself on being considerate. And yet just on this occasion he had more reason than ever to hide himself, since owing to the amount of dust which lay thick in his room and rose into the air at the slightest movement, he too was covered with dust; fluff and hair and remnants of food trailed with him, caught on his back and along his sides; his indifference to everything was much too great for him to turn on his back and scrape himself clean on the carpet, as once he had done several times a day. And in spite of his condition, no shame deterred him from advancing a little over the spotless floor of the living room.

To be sure, no one was aware of him. The family was entirely absorbed in the violin-playing; the lodgers, however, who first of all had stationed themselves, hands in pockets, much too close behind the music stand so that they could all have read the music, which must have bothered his sister, had soon retreated to the window, half-whispering with downbent heads, and stayed there while his father turned an anxious eye on them. Indeed, they were making it more than obvious that they had been disappointed in their expectation of hearing good or enjoyable violin-playing, that they had had more than enough of the performance and only out of courtesy suffered a continued disturbance of their peace. From the way they all kept blowing the smoke of their cigars high in the air through nose and mouth one could divine their irritation. And yet Gregor's sister was playing so beautifully. Her face leaned sideways, intently and sadly her eyes followed the notes of music. Gregor crawled a little farther forward and lowered his head to the ground so that it might be possible for his eyes to meet hers. Was he an animal, that music had such an effect upon him? He felt as if the way were opening before him to the unknown nourishment he craved. He was determined to push forward till he reached his sister, to pull at her skirt and so let her know that she was to come into his room with her violin, for no one here appreciated her playing as he would appreciate it. He would never let her out of his room, at least, not so long as he lived; his frightful appearance would become, for the first time, useful to him; he would watch all the doors of his room at once and spit at intruders; but his sister should need no constraint, she should stay with him of her own free will; she should sit beside him on the sofa, bend down her ear to him and hear him confide that he had had the firm intention of sending her to the Conservatorium, and that, but for his mishap, last Christmas — surely Christmas was long past? — he would have announced it to everybody without allowing a single objection. After this confession his sister would be so touched that she would burst into tears, and Gregor would then raise himself to her shoulder and kiss her on the neck, which, now that she went to business, she kept free of any ribbon or collar.

"Mr. Samsa!" cried the middle lodger, to Gregor's father, and pointed, without wasting any more words, at Gregor, now working himself slowly forwards. The violin fell silent, the middle lodger first smiled to his friends with a shake of the head and then looked at Gregor again. Instead of driving Gregor out, his father seemed to think it more needful to begin by soothing down the lodgers, although they were not at all agitated and apparently found Gregor more entertaining than the violin-playing. He hurried toward them and, spreading out his arms, tried to urge them back into their own room and at the same time to block their view of Gregor. They now began to be really a little angry, one could not tell whether because of the old man's behavior or because it had just dawned on them that all unwittingly they had such a neighbor as Gregor next door. They demanded explanations of his father, they waved their arms like him, tugged uneasily at their beards, and only with reluctance backed towards their room. Meanwhile Gregor's sister, who stood there as if lost when her playing was so abruptly broken off, came to life again, pulled herself together all at once after standing for a while holding violin and bow in nervelessly hanging hands and staring at her music, pushed her violin into the lap of her mother, who was still sitting in her chair fighting asthmatically for breath, and ran into the lodgers' room to which they were now being shepherded by her father rather more quickly than before. One could see the pillows and blankets on the beds flying under her accustomed fingers and being laid in order. Before the lodgers had actually reached their room she had finished making the beds and slipped out.

The old man seemed once more to be so possessed by his mulish self-assertiveness that he was forgetting all the respect he should show to his lodgers. He kept driving them on and driving them on until in the very door of the bedroom the middle lodger stamped his foot loudly on the floor and so brought him to a halt. "I beg to announce," said the lodger, lifting one hand and looking also at Gregor's mother and sister, "that because of the disgusting conditions prevailing in this household and family" — here he spat on the floor with emphatic brevity — "I give you notice on the spot. Naturally I won't pay you a penny for the days I have lived here, on the contrary I shall consider bringing an action for damages against you, based on claims — believe me — that will be easily susceptible of proof." He ceased and stared straight in front of him, as if he expected something. In fact his two friends at once rushed into the breach with these words: "And we too give notice on the spot." On that he seized the door-handle and shut the door with a slam.

Gregor's father, groping with his hands, staggered forward and fell into his chair; it looked as if he were stretching himself there for his ordinary evening nap, but the marked jerkings of his head, which was as if uncontrollable, showed that he was far from asleep. Gregor had simply stayed quietly all the time on the spot where the lodgers had espied him. Disappointment at the failure of his plan, perhaps also the weakness arising from extreme hunger, made it impossible for him to move. He feared, with a fair degree of certainty, that at any moment the general tension would discharge itself in a combined attack upon him, and he lay waiting. He did not react even to the noise made by the violin as it fell off his mother's lap from under her trembling fingers and gave out a resonant note.

"My dear parents," said his sister, slapping her hand on the table by way of introduction, "things can't go on like this. Perhaps you don't realize that, but I do. I won't utter my brother's name in the presence of this creature, and so all I say is: we must try to get rid of it. We've tried to look after it and to put up with it as far as is humanly possible, and I don't think anyone could reproach us in the slightest."

"She is more than right," said Gregor's father to himself. His mother, who was still choking for lack of breath, began to cough hollowly into her hand with a wild look in her eyes.

His sister rushed over to her and held her forehead. His father's thoughts seemed to have lost their vagueness at Grete's words, he sat more upright, fingering his service cap that lay among the plates still lying on the table from the lodgers' supper, and from time to time looked at the still form of Gregor.

"We must try to get rid of it," his sister now said explicitly to her father, since her mother was coughing too much to hear a word, "it will be the death of both of you, I can see that coming. When one has to work as hard as we do, all of us, one can't stand this continual torment at home on top of it. At least I can't stand it any longer." And she burst into such a passion of sobbing that her tears dropped on her mother's face, where she wiped them off mechanically.

"My dear," said the old man sympathetically, and with evident understanding, "but what can we do?"

Gregor's sister merely shrugged her shoulders to indicate the feeling of helplessness that had now overmastered her during her weeping fit, in contrast to her former confidence.

"If he could understand us," said her father, half questioningly; Grete, still sobbing, vehemently waved a hand to show how unthinkable that was.

"If he could understand us," repeated the old man, shutting his eyes to consider his daughter's conviction that understanding was impossible, "then perhaps we might come to some agreement with him. But as it is — "

"He must go," cried Gregor's sister. "That's the only solution, Father. You must just try to get rid of the idea that this is Gregor. The fact that we've believed it for so long is the root of all our trouble. But how can it be Gregor? If this were Gregor, he would have realized long ago that human beings can't live with such a creature, and he'd have gone away on his own accord. Then we wouldn't have any brother, but we'd be able to go on living and keep his memory in honor. As it is, this creature persecutes us, drives away our lodgers, obviously wants the whole apartment to himself and would have us all sleep in the gutter. Just look, Father," she shrieked all at once, "he's at it again!" And in an access of panic that was quite incomprehensible to Gregor she even quitted her mother, literally thrusting the chair from her as if she would rather sacrifice her mother than stay so near to Gregor, and rushed behind her father, who also rose up, being simply upset by her agitation, and half-spread his arms out as if to protect her.

Yet Gregor had not the slightest intention of frightening anyone, far less his sister. He had only begun to turn round in order to crawl back to his room, but it was certainly a startling operation to watch, since because of his disabled condition he could not execute the difficult turning movements except by lifting his head and then bracing it against the floor over and over again. He paused and looked round. His good intentions seemed to have been recognized; the alarm had only been momentary. Now they were all watching him in melancholy silence. His mother lay in her chair, her legs stiffly outstretched and pressed together, her eyes almost closing for sheer weariness; his father and his sister were sitting beside each other, his sister's arm around the old man's neck.

Perhaps I can go on turning round now, thought Gregor, and began his labors again. He could not stop himself from panting with the effort, and had to pause now and then to take breath. Nor did anyone harass him, he was left entirely to himself. When he had completed the turn-round he began at once to crawl straight back. He was amazed at the distance separating him from his room and could not understand how in his weak state he had managed to accomplish the same journey so recently, almost without remarking it. Intent on crawling as fast as possible, he barely noticed that not a single word, not an ejaculation from his family, interfered with his progress. Only when he was already in the doorway did he turn his head round, not completely, for his neck muscles were getting stiff, but enough

to see that nothing had changed behind him except that his sister had risen
to her feet. His last glance fell on his mother, who was not quite overcome
by sleep.

Hardly was he well inside his room when the door was hastily pushed
shut, bolted and locked. The sudden noise in his rear startled him so much
that his little legs gave beneath him. It was his sister who had shown such
haste. She had been standing ready waiting and had made a light spring
forward, Gregor had not even heard her coming, and she cried "At last!" to
her parents as she turned the key in the lock.

"And what now?" said Gregor to himself, looking round in the darkness. Soon he made the discovery that he was now unable to stir a limb.
This did not surprise him, rather it seemed unnatural that he should ever
actually have been able to move on these feeble little legs. Otherwise he felt
relatively comfortable. True, his whole body was aching, but it seemed that
the pain was gradually growing less and would finally pass away. The rotting
apple in his back and the inflamed area around it, all covered with soft dust,
already hardly troubled him. He thought of his family with tenderness and
love. The decision that he must disappear was one that he held to even
more strongly than his sister, if that were possible. In this state of vacant
and peaceful meditation he remained until the tower clock struck three in
the morning. The first broadening of light in the world outside the window
entered his consciousness once more. Then his head sank to the floor
of its own accord and from his nostrils came the last faint flicker of his
breath.

When the charwoman arrived early in the morning — what between
her strength and her impatience she slammed all the doors so loudly, never
mind how often she had been begged not to do so, that no one in the whole
apartment could enjoy any quiet sleep after her arrival — she noticed nothing unusual as she took her customary peep into Gregor's room. She
thought he was lying motionless on purpose, pretending to be in the sulks;
she credited him with every kind of intelligence. Since she happened to
have the long-handed broom in her hand she tried to tickle him up with it
from the doorway. When that too produced no reaction she felt provoked
and poked at him a little harder, and only when she had pushed him along
the floor without meeting any resistance was her attention aroused. It did
not take her long to establish the truth of the matter, and her eyes widened,
she let out a whistle, yet did not waste much time over it but tore open the
door of the Samsas' bedroom and yelled into the darkness at the top of her
voice: "Just look at this, it's dead; it's lying here dead and done for!"

Mr. and Mrs. Samsa started up in their double bed and before they
realized the nature of the charwoman's announcement had some difficulty
in overcoming the shock of it. But then they got out of bed quickly, one on
either side, Mr. Samsa throwing a blanket over his shoulders, Mrs. Samsa in
nothing but her nightgown; in this array they entered Gregor's room.
Meanwhile the door of the living room opened, too, where Grete had been

sleeping since the advent of the lodgers; she was completely dressed as if she had not been to bed, which seemed to be confirmed also by the paleness of her face. "Dead?" said Mrs. Samsa, looking questioningly at the charwoman, although she could have investigated for herself, and the fact was obvious enough without investigation. "I should say so," said the charwoman, proving her words by pushing Gregor's corpse a long way to one side with her broomstick. Mrs. Samsa made a movement as if to stop her, but checked it. "Well," said Mr. Samsa, "now thanks be to God." He crossed himself, and the three women followed his example. Grete, whose eyes never left the corpse, said: "Just see how thin he was. It's such a long time since he's eaten anything. The food came out again just as it went in." Indeed, Gregor's body was completely flat and dry, as could only now be seen when it was no longer supported by the legs and nothing prevented one from looking closely at it.

"Come in beside us, Grete, for a little while," said Mrs. Samsa with a tremulous smile, and Grete, not without looking back at the corpse, followed her parents into their bedroom. The charwoman shut the door and opened the window wide. Although it was so early in the morning a certain softness was perceptible in the fresh air. After all, it was already the end of March.

The three lodgers emerged from their room and were surprised to see no breakfast; they had been forgotten. "Where's our breakfast?" said the middle lodger peevishly to the charwoman. But she put her finger to her lips and hastily, without a word, indicated by gestures that they should go into Gregor's room. They did so and stood, their hands in the pockets of their somewhat shabby coats, around Gregor's corpse in the room where it was now fully light.

At that the door of the Samsas' bedroom opened and Mr. Samsa appeared in his uniform, his wife on one arm, his daughter on the other. They all looked a little as if they had been crying; from time to time Grete hid her face on her father's arm.

"Leave my house at once!" said Mr. Samsa, and pointed to the door without disengaging himself from the women. "What do you mean by that?" said the middle lodger, taken somewhat aback, with a feeble smile. The two others put their hands behind them and kept rubbing them together, as if in gleeful expectation of a fine set-to in which they were bound to come off the winners. "I mean just what I say," answered Mr. Samsa, and advanced in a straight line with his two companions towards the lodger. He stood his ground at first quietly, looking at the floor as if his thoughts were taking a new pattern in his head. "Then let us go, by all means," he said, and looked up at Mr. Samsa as if in a sudden access of humility he were expecting some renewed sanction for this decision. Mr. Samsa merely nodded briefly once or twice with meaning eyes. Upon that the lodger really did go with long strides into the hall, his two friends had been listening and had quite stopped rubbing their hands for some moments and now went scuttling after him as if afraid that Mr. Samsa might get into the hall before them and cut them off from their leader. In the hall they all three took their hats from the rack, their sticks from the umbrella stand, bowed in silence and quitted the apartment. With a suspiciousness which proved quite unfounded Mr. Samsa and the two women followed them out to the landing; leaning over the banister they watched the three figures slowly but surely going down the long stairs, vanishing from sight at a certain turn of the staircase on every floor and coming into view again after a moment or so; the more they dwindled, the more the Samsa family's interest in them dwindled, and when a butcher's boy met them and passed them on the stairs coming up proudly with a tray on his head, Mr. Samsa and the two women soon left the landing and as if a burden had been lifted from them went back into their apartment.

They decided to spend this day in resting and going for a stroll; they had not only deserved such a respite from work, but absolutely needed it. And so they sat down at the table and wrote three notes of excuse, Mr. Samsa to his board of management, Mrs. Samsa to her employer and Grete to the head of her firm. While they were writing, the charwoman came in to say that she was going now, since her morning's work was finished. At first they only nodded without looking up, but as she kept hovering there they eyed her irritably. "Well?" said Mr. Samsa. The charwoman stood grinning in the doorway as if she had good news to impart to the family but meant not to say a word unless properly questioned. The small ostrich feather standing upright on her hat, which had annoyed Mr. Samsa ever since she was engaged, was waving gaily in all directions. "Well, what is it then?" asked Mrs. Samsa, who obtained more respect from the charwoman than the others. "Oh," said the charwoman, giggling so amiably that she could not at once continue, "just this, you don't need to bother about how to get rid of the thing next door. It's been seen to already." Mrs. Samsa and Grete bent over their letters again, as if preoccupied; Mr. Samsa, who perceived that she was eager to begin describing it all in detail, stopped her with a decisive hand. But since she was not allowed to tell her story, she remembered the great hurry she was in, being obviously deeply huffed: "Bye, everybody," she said, whirling off violently, and departed with a frightful slamming of doors.

"She'll be given notice tonight," said Mr. Samsa, but neither from his wife nor his daughter did he get any answer, for the charwoman seemed to have shattered again the composure they had barely achieved. They rose, went to the window and stayed there, clasping each other tight. Mr. Samsa turned in his chair to look at them and quietly observed them for a little. Then he called out: "Come along, now, do. Let bygones be bygones. And you might have some consideration for me." The two of them complied at once, hastened to him, caressed him and quickly finished their letters.

Then they all three left the apartment together, which was more than they had done for months, and went by tram into the open country outside the town. The tram, in which they were the only passengers, was filled with warm sunshine. Leaning comfortably back in their seats they canvassed their prospects for the future, and it appeared on closer inspection that these were not at all bad, for the jobs they had got, which so far they had never really discussed with each other, were all three admirable and likely to lead to better things later on. The greatest immediate improvement in their condition would of course arise from moving to another house; they wanted to take a smaller and cheaper but also better situated and more easily run apartment than the one they had, which Gregor had selected. While they were thus conversing, it struck both Mr. and Mrs. Samsa, almost at the same moment, as they became aware of their daughter's increasing vivacity, that in spite of all the sorrow of recent times, which had made her cheeks pale, she had bloomed into a pretty girl with a good figure. They grew quieter and half unconsciously exchanged glances of complete agreement, having come to the conclusion that it would soon be time to find a good husband for her. And it was like a confirmation of their new dreams and excellent intentions that at the end of their journey their daughter sprang to her feet first and stretched her young body.

[1915]

WILLIAM CARLOS WILLIAMS (1883–1963), the poet, novelist, playwright, and short story writer, was born in Rutherford, New Jersey. After graduating from the University of Pennsylvania Medical School, he returned to Rutherford, where he practiced as a pediatrician for the rest of his life. While still an undergraduate, he began to write poetry, influenced by his friends the poets Ezra Pound and Hilda Doolittle. Williams published his first book, Poems, in 1909. Initially he devoted himself to poetry, but his experimental writing in the 1920s led him to the novel and the short story. The story became for him a way to emphasize his social and humanitarian concerns, which influenced the gritty, down-to-earth realism of his literary style.

Williams wrote most of his stories during the Depression, when his patients in Rutherford were the poor people characterized by President Franklin Delano Roosevelt in 1933 as "ill-fed, ill-housed, and ill-clothed." Williams's patients were often down and out, but he saw them as splendidly vital people. When asked how he managed the two careers of medicine and writing, Williams answered, "It's no strain. In fact, the one [medicine] nourishes the other [writing], even if at times I've groaned to the contrary."

Like the doctor-writer Anton Chekhov before him, Williams understood the moral responsibility of his calling, and he was vigilant against his feelings of arrogance and self-importance. "There's nothing like a difficult patient to show us ourselves," he once told a medical student. "I would learn so much on my rounds, or making home visits. At times I felt like a thief because I heard words, lines, saw people and places — and used it all in my writing. I guess I've told people that, and no one's so surprised! There was something deeper going on, though — the force of all those encounters. I was put off guard again and again, and the result was — well, a descent into myself."

Williams collected his stories in four volumes: The Knife of the Times (1932), Life along the Passaic River (1938), Make Light of It (1950), and The Farmers' Daughters (1961). Recently Robert Coles compiled The Doctor Stories (1984). As Coles understands, in "A Night in June" Williams "extends to us, really, moments of a doctor's self-recognition — rendered in such a way that the particular becomes the universal, and the instantly recognizable: the function, the great advantage of all first-rate art." Williams used vernacular American speech and direct observation in all his writing. His work includes twenty books of poetry, four novels, several books of nonfiction, a collection of plays, and an autobiography.

William Carlos Williams

૨૦૨

A Night in June

a doctor delivering a child next door,

I was a young man then — full of information and tenderness. It was her first baby. She lived just around the corner from her present abode, one room over a small general store kept by an old man.

It was a difficult forceps delivery and I lost the child, to my disgust; though without nurse, anesthetist, or even enough hot water in the place, I shouldn't have been overmuch blamed. I must have been fairly able not to have done worse. But I won a friend and I found another — to admire, a sort of love for the woman.

She was slightly older than her husband, a heavy-looking Italian boy. Both were short. A peasant woman who could scarcely talk a word of English, being recently come from the other side, a woman of great simplicity of character — docility, patience, with a fine direct look in her grey eyes. And courageous. Devoted to her instincts and convictions and to me.

Sometimes she'd cry out at her husband, as I got to know her later, with some high pitched animalistic sound when he would say something to her in Italian that I couldn't understand and I knew that she was holding out for me.

Usually though, she said very little, looking me straight in the eye with a smile, her voice pleasant and candid though I could scarcely understand her few broken words. Her sentences were seldom more than three or four words long. She always acted as though I must naturally know what was in her mind and her smile with a shrug always won me.

Apart from the second child, born a year after the first, during the absence of the family from town for a short time, I had delivered Angelina of all her children. This one would make my eighth attendance on her, her ninth labor.

Three A.M., June the 10th, I noticed the calendar as I flashed on the light in my office to pick up my satchel, the same, by the way, my uncle had given me when I graduated from Medical School. One gets not to deliver women at home nowadays. The hospital is the place for it. The equipment is far better.

Smiling, I picked up the relic from where I had tossed it two or three years before under a table in my small laboratory hoping never to have to use it again. In it I found a brand new hypodermic syringe with the manu-

558

facturer's name still shiny with black enamel on the barrel. Also a pair of curved scissors I had been looking for for the last three years, thinking someone had stolen them.

I dusted off the top of the Lysol bottle when I took it from the shelf and quickly checking on the rest of my necessities, I went off, without a coat or necktie, wearing the same shirt I had had on during the day preceding, soiled but — better so.

It was a beautiful June night. The lighted clock in the tower over the factory said 3:20. The clock in the facade of the Trust Company across the track said it also. Paralleling the railroad I recognized the squat figure of the husband returning home ahead of me — whistling as he walked. I put my hand out of the car in sign of recognition and kept on, rounding the final triangular block a little way ahead to bring my car in to the right in front of the woman's house for parking.

The husband came up as I was trying to decide which of the two steep cobbled entry-ways to take. Got you up early, he said.

Where ya been? his sister said to him when we had got into the house from the rear.

I went down to the police to telephone, he said, that's the surest way.

I told you to go next door, you dope. What did you go away down there for? Leaving me here alone.

Aw, I didn't want to wake nobody up.

I got two calls, I broke in.

Yes, he went away and left me alone. I got scared so I waked him up anyway to call you.

The kitchen where we stood was lighted by a somewhat damaged Welsbach mantel gaslight. Everything was quiet. The husband took off his cap and sat along the wall. I put my satchel on the tubs and began to take things out.

There was just one sterile umbilical tie left, two, really, in the same envelope, as always, for possible twins, but that detail aside, everything was ample and in order. I complimented myself. Even the Argyrol was there, in tablet form, insuring the full potency of a fresh solution. Nothing so satisfying as a kit of any sort prepared and in order even when picked up in an emergency after an interval of years.

I selected out two artery clamps and two scissors. One thing, there'd be no need of sutures afterward in this case.

You want hot water?

Not yet, I said. Might as well take my shirt off, though. Which I did, throwing it on a kitchen chair and donning the usual light rubber apron.

I'm sorry we ain't got no light in there. The electricity is turned off. Do you think you can see with a candle?

Sure. Why not? But it was very dark in the room where the woman lay on a low double bed. A three-year-old boy was asleep on the sheet beside her. She wore an abbreviated nightgown, to her hips. Her short thick legs had, as I knew, bunches of large varicose veins about them like vines. Everything was clean and in order. The sister-in-law held the candle. Few words were spoken.

I made the examination and found the head high but the cervix fully dilated. Oh yeah. It often happens in women who have had many children; pendulous abdomen, lack of muscular power resulting in a slight misdirection of the forces of labor and the thing may go on for days.

When I finished, Angelina got up and sat on the edge of the bed. I went back to the kitchen, the candle following me, leaving the room dark again.

Do you need it any more? the sister-in-law said, I'll put it out.

Then the husband spoke up, Ain't you got but that one candle?

No, said the sister.

Why didn't you get some at the store when you woke him up; use your head.

The woman had the candle in a holder on the cold coal range. She leaned over to blow it out but misdirecting her aim, she had to blow three times to do it. Three or four times.

What's the matter? said her brother, getting weak? Old age counts, eh Doc? he said and got up finally to go out.

We could hear an engineer signaling outside in the still night — with short quick blasts of his whistle — very staccato — not, I suppose, to make any greater disturbance than necessary with people sleeping all about.

Later on the freights began to roar past shaking the whole house.

She doesn't seem to be having many strong pains, I said to my companion in the kitchen, for there wasn't a sound from the labor room and hadn't been for the past half hour.

She don't want to make no noise and wake the kids.

How old is the oldest now? I asked.

He's sixteen. The girl would have been eighteen this year. You know the first one you took from her.

Where are they all?

In there, with a nod of the head toward the other room of the apartment, such as it was, the first floor of an old two-story house, the whole thing perhaps twenty-five feet each way.

I sat in a straight chair by the kitchen table, my right arm, bare to the shoulder, resting on the worn oil cloth.

She says she wants an enema, said the woman. O.K. But I don't know how to give it to her. She ain't got a bed-pan or nothing. I don't want to get the bed all wet.

Has she had a movement today?

Yeah, but she thinks an enema will help her.

Well, have you got a bag?

Yeah, she says there's one here somewhere.

Get it. She's got a chamber pot here, hasn't she?

Sure.

So the woman got the equipment, a blue rubber douche bag, the rubber of it feeling rather stiff to the touch. She laid it on the stove in its open box and looked at it holding her hands out helplessly. I'm afraid, she said.

All right, you hold the candle. Mix up a little warm soapy water. We'll need some Vaseline.

The woman called out to us where to find it, having overheard our conversation.

Lift up, till I put these newspapers under you, said my assistant. I don't want to wet the bed.

That's nothing, Angelina answered smiling. But she raised her buttocks high so we could fix her.

Returning ten minutes later to my chair, I saw the woman taking the pot out through the kitchen and upstairs to empty it. I crossed my legs, crossed my bare arms in my lap also, and let my head fall forward. I must have slept, for when I opened my eyes again, both my legs and my arms were somewhat numb. I felt deliciously relaxed though somewhat bewildered. I must have snored, waking myself with a start. Everything was quiet as before. The peace of the room was unchanged. Delicious.

I heard the woman and her attendant making some slight sounds in the next room and went in to her.

Examining her, I found things unchanged. It was about half past four. *nervous*
What to do? Do you mind if I give you the needle? I asked her gently. We'd been through this many times before. She shrugged her shoulders as much as to say, It's up to you. So I gave her a few minims of pituitrin to intensify the strength of the pains. I was cautious since the practice is not without danger. It is possible to get a ruptured uterus where the muscle has been stretched by many pregnancies if one does not know what one is doing. Then I returned to the kitchen to wait once more.

This time I took out the obstetric gown I had brought with me; it was in a roll as it had come from the satchel, and covering it with my shirt to make a better surface and a little more bulk, I placed it at the edge of the table and leaning forward, laid my face sidewise upon it, my arms resting on the table before me, my nose and mouth at the table edge between my arms. I could breathe freely. It was a pleasant position and as I lay there content, I thought as I often do of what painting it was in which I had seen men sleeping that way.

Then I fell asleep and, in my half sleep began to argue with myself — or some imaginary power — of science and humanity. Our exaggerated ways will have to pull in their horns, I said. We've learned from one teacher and neglected another. Now that I'm older, I'm finding the older school.

The pituitary extract and other simple devices represent science. Science, I dreamed, has crowded the stage more than is necessary. The process of selection will simplify the application. It touches us too crudely now, all newness is overcomplex. I couldn't tell whether I was asleep or awake.

But without science, without pituitrin, I'd be here till noon or maybe — what? Some others wouldn't wait so long but rush her now. A *unsure of what he's doing*

carefully guarded shot of pituitrin — ought to save her at least much exhaustion — if not more. But I don't want to have anything happen to her.

morning

Now when I lifted my head, there was beginning to be a little light outside. The woman was quiet. No progress. This time I increased the dose of pituitrin. She had stronger pains but without effect.

Maybe I'd better give you a still larger dose, I said. She made no demur. Well, let me see if I can help you first. I sat on the edge of the bed while the sister-in-law held the candle again glancing at the window where the daylight was growing. With my left hand steering the child's head, I used my ungloved right hand outside on her bare abdomen to press upon the fundus. The woman and I then got to work. Her two hands grabbed me at first a little timidly about the right wrist and forearm. Go ahead, I said. Pull hard. I welcomed the feel of her hands and the strong pull. It quieted me in the way the whole house had quieted me all night.

This woman in her present condition would have seemed repulsive to me ten years ago — now, poor soul, I see her to be as clean as a cow that calves. The flesh of my arm lay against the flesh of her knee gratefully. It was I who was being comforted and soothed.

Finally the head began to move. I wasn't sorry, thinking perhaps I'd have to do something radical before long. We kept at it till the head was born and I could leave her for a moment to put on my other glove. It was almost light now. What time is it? I asked the other woman. Six o'clock, she said.

something's wrong

Just after I had tied the cord, cut it, and lifted the baby, a girl, to hand it to the woman, I saw the mother clutch herself suddenly between her thighs and give a cry. I was startled.

The other woman turned with a flash and shouted, Get out of here, you damned kids! I'll slap your damned face for you. And the door through which a head had peered was pulled closed. The three-year-old on the bed beside the mother stirred when the baby cried at first shrilly but had not wakened.

Oh yes, the drops in the baby's eyes. No need. She's as clean as a beast. How do I know? Medical discipline says every case must have drops in the eyes. No chance of gonorrhoea though here — but — Do it.

I heard her husband come into the kitchen now so we gave him the afterbirth in a newspaper to bury. Keep them damned kids out of here, his sister told him. Lock that door. Of course, there was no lock on it.

How do you feel now? I asked the mother after everything had been cleaned up. All right, she said with the peculiar turn of her head and smile by which I knew her.

How many is that? I asked the other woman. Five boys and three girls, she said. I've forgotten how to fix a baby, she went on. What shall I do? Put a little boric acid powder on the belly button to help dry it up?

[1938]

ISAK DINESEN is the name under which the Danish Baroness Karen Blixen (1885–1962) published her writings. She was born Karen Christentze Dinesen near Elsinore, Denmark, and grew up in her family's ancestral home close to the sea. When she was a child her father committed suicide, and she felt that a part of herself had also died. Dinesen had such an "intuitive fear of being trapped" that she decided not to become a professional writer after publishing some short stories at the age of twenty. She felt that every profession invariably assigns a definite role in life, which would cut her off from the infinite possibilities of her life itself. In 1914 she married her cousin, Baron Bror Blixen, and went with him to British East Africa (now Kenya) to manage a large coffee plantation. In 1921 she and her husband divorced and she took over the management of the plantation. When coffee prices dropped in 1931 she had to give it up — a severe blow, because the seventeen years she spent in Africa had been the happiest of her life. She also lost her lover, the Englishman Denys Finch-Hatton, in a plane crash at this time. With a sense that her life was over, she returned to Denmark.

Grief over having lost her farm and her lover in Africa made Karen Blixen a writer. She decided that the chief trap in life was not a single profession, as she had feared as a girl, but rather a single identity, so she created another one for herself as a writer. "Slowly the center of gravity of my being will shift over from the world of day . . . into the world of Imagination." She chose to write in English out of loyalty to her dead lover, and she took the male pseudonym Isak, meaning "the one who laughs," in the spirit of the saying "God loves a joke." In her first collection of short stories, Seven Gothic Tales — published in 1934 when she was nearly fifty years old — Dinesen's genius was so immediately apparent that she became world famous. That collection was followed by Out of Africa (1937), a reminiscence of her years in Africa, and a second book of stories, Winter's Tales (1942). Both were best-sellers. Her imaginative brilliance as a teller of spellbinding tales prompted Ernest Hemingway to say in his acceptance speech for the Nobel Prize that it should have been given to "that beautiful writer Isak Dinesen." In the final years of her life she published Last Tales (1957) and Anecdotes of Destiny (1958).

Dinesen's fiction does not fit any literary or ideological formula. She said, "I am a storyteller and nothing else. What interests me is the story and the way to tell it." As Eudora Welty recognized, her tales are "glimpses out of, rather than into, an extraordinary mind." Dinesen spun her stories out of the impulse to bring to life a world of marvels and enchantments, as in her fairy tale "The Blue Stones." Discovering that "all sorrows can be borne if you put them into a story or tell a story about them," Dinesen showed that the storyteller can make meaning out of what otherwise would *remain an unbearable sequence of events or sheer happenings. In the repetition and selection performed by the imagination, the happenings become part of a pattern, what she called a "destiny." Her creation of that destiny in a work of fiction like "The Blue Jar" reveals meaning in life without committing the error of defining it. For Dinesen, the answer to the question "Who are you?" is given in the reply "Let me tell you a story."*

Isak Dinesen

�753

THE BLUE STONES

There was once a skipper who named his ship after his wife. He had the figure-head of it beautifully carved, just like her, and the hair of it gilt. But his wife was jealous of the ship. "You think more of the figure-head than of me," she said to him. "No," he answered, "I think so highly of her because she is like you, yes, because she is you yourself. Is she not gallant, full-bosomed; does she not dance in the waves, like you at our wedding? In a way she is really even kinder to me than you are. She gallops along where I tell her to go, and she lets her long hair hang down freely, while you put up yours under a cap. But she turns her back to me, so that when I want a kiss I come home to Elsinore." Now once, when this skipper was trading at Trankebar, he chanced to help an old native King to flee traitors in his own country. As they parted the King gave him two big blue, precious stones, and these he had set into the face of his figure-head, like a pair of eyes to it. When he came home he told his wife of his adventure, and said: "Now she has your blue eyes too." "You had better give me the stones for a pair of earrings," said she. "No," he said again, "I cannot do that, and you would not ask me to if you understood." Still the wife could not stop fretting about the blue stones, and one day, when her husband was with the skippers' corporation, she had a glazier of the town take them out, and put two bits of blue glass into the figure-head instead, and the skipper did not find out, but sailed off to Portugal. But after some time the skipper's wife found that her eyesight was growing bad, and that she could not see to thread a needle. She went to a wise woman, who gave her ointments and waters, but they did not help her and in the end the old woman shook her head, and told her that this was a rare and incurable disease, and that she was going blind. "Oh, God," the wife then cried, "that the ship was back in the harbor of Elsinore. Then I should have the glass taken out, and the jewels put back. For did he not say that they were my eyes?" But the ship did not come back. Instead the skipper's wife had a letter from the Consul of Portugal, who informed her that she had been wrecked, and gone to the bottom with all hands. And it was a very strange thing, the Consul wrote, that in broad daylight she had run straight into a tall rock, rising out of the sea.

[1942]

Isak Dinesen

ია

THE BLUE JAR

There was once an immensely rich old Englishman who had been a courtier and a councillor to the Queen and who now, in his old age, cared for nothing but collecting ancient blue china. To that end he travelled to Persia, Japan, and China, and he was everywhere accompanied by his daughter, the Lady Helena. It happened, as they sailed in the Chinese Sea, that the ship caught fire on a still night, and everybody went into the lifeboats and left her. In the dark and the confusion the old peer was separated from his daughter. Lady Helena got up on deck late, and found the ship quite deserted. In the last moment a young English sailor carried her down into a lifeboat that had been forgotten. To the two fugitives it seemed as if fire was following them from all sides, for the phosphorescence played in the dark sea, and, as they looked up, a falling star ran across the sky, as if it was going to drop into the boat. They sailed for nine days, till they were picked up by a Dutch merchantman, and came home to England.

The old lord had believed his daughter to be dead. He now wept with joy, and at once took her off to a fashionable watering-place so that she might recover from the hardships she had gone through. And as he thought it must be unpleasant to her that a young sailor, who made his bread in the merchant service, should tell the world that he had sailed for nine days alone with a peer's daughter, he paid the boy a fine sum, and made him promise to go shipping in the other hemisphere and never come back. "For what," said the old nobleman, "would be the good of that?"

When Lady Helena recovered, and they gave her the news of the Court and of her family, and in the end also told her how the young sailor had been sent away never to come back, they found that her mind had suffered from her trials, and that she cared for nothing in all the world. She would not go back to her father's castle in its park, nor go to Court, nor travel to any gay town of the continent. The only thing which she now wanted to do was to go, like her father before her, to collect rare blue china.

So she began to sail, from one country to the other, and her father went with her.

In her search she told the people, with whom she dealt, that she was looking for a particular blue color, and would pay any price for it. But although she bought many hundred blue jars and bowls, she would always after a time put them aside and say: "Alas, alas, it is not the right blue." Her father, when they had sailed for many years, suggested to her that perhaps the color which she sought did not exist. "O God, Papa," said she, "how can you speak so wickedly? Surely there must be some of it left from the time when all the world was blue."

Her two old aunts in England implored her to come back, still to make a great match. But she answered them: "Nay, I have got to sail. For you must know, dear aunts, that it is all nonsense when learned people tell you that the seas have got a bottom to them. On the contrary, the water, which is the noblest of the elements, does, of course, go all through the earth, so that our planet really floats in the ether, like a soapbubble. And there, on the other hemisphere, a ship sails, with which I have got to keep pace. We two are like the reflection of one another, in the deep sea, and the ship of which I speak is always exactly beneath my own ship, upon the opposite side of the globe. You have never seen a big fish swimming underneath a boat, following it like a dark-blue shade in the water. But in that way this ship goes, like the shadow of my ship, and I draw it to and fro wherever I go, as the moon draws the tides, all through the bulk of the earth. If I stopped sailing, what would these poor sailors who make their bread in the merchant service do? But I shall tell you a secret," she said. "In the end my ship will go down, to the center of the globe, and at the very same hour the other ship will sink as well—for people call it sinking, although I can assure you that there is no up and down in the sea—and there, in the midst of the world, we two shall meet."

Many years passed, the old lord died and Lady Helena became old and deaf, but she still sailed. Then it happened, after the plunder of the summer palace of the Emperor of China, that a merchant brought her a very old blue jar. The moment she set eyes on it she gave a terrible shriek. "There it is!" she cried. "I have found it at last. This is the true blue. Oh, how light it makes one. Oh, it is as fresh as a breeze, as deep as a deep secret, as full as I say not what." With trembling hands she held the jar to her bosom, and sat for six hours sunk in contemplation of it. Then she said to her doctor and her lady-companion: "Now I can die. And when I am dead you will cut out my heart and lay it in the blue jar. For then everything will be as it was then. All shall be blue round me, and in the midst of the blue world my heart will be innocent and free, and will beat gently, like a wake that sings, like the drops that fall from an oar blade." A little later she asked them: "Is it not a sweet thing to think that, if only you have patience, all that has ever been, will come back to you?" Shortly afterwards the old lady died.

[1942]

DAVID HERBERT LAWRENCE (1885–1930) *was born the son of a miner in the industrial town of Eastwood, in Nottinghamshire, the coal-mining country of England. His mother had been a schoolteacher, and she was frustrated by the hard existence of a coal miner's wife. She harbored great ambitions for her son, whom she was determined to keep out of the mines. Through his mother's financial sacrifices, Lawrence was able to attend Nottingham High School; then he studied to become a teacher. He also wrote poetry and started a novel, and in 1909 — shortly after he began teaching in South London — his work was published for the first time; a group of his poems appeared in the* English Review. *His first novel,* The White Peacock, *appeared later that year, but he was not established as a major literary figure until the publication of the novel* Sons and Lovers *(1913), based on the tensions in his own family and his struggle to escape his mother's possessiveness. Much of his fiction, like the story "Odour of Chrysanthemums," focuses on characters caught between an attempt to relate to others and a struggle to break free. Lawrence sought an ideal balance or, as he wrote in the novel* Women in Love *(1920), a "star equilibrium," where two beings are attracted to each other but never lose their individuality. As he wrote in his essay "Morality and the Novel," "No emotion is supreme, or exclusively worth living for. All emotions go to the achieving of a living relationship between a human being and the other human being or creature or thing he becomes purely related to."*

Lawrence, who was a prolific writer, suffered from tuberculosis and spent most of his life wandering in Italy, Australia, Mexico, New Mexico, and southern France, seeking a warm, dry climate. He also fled to primitive societies to escape the industrialization and commercialism of Western life, which he despised. A virulent social critic, he was frequently harassed by censorship, because his short stories, novels, and poetry flouted conventional notions of correct behavior. He wrote stories all his life, publishing his first collection, The Prussian Officer, *in 1914; it was followed by* England, My England *in 1922,* The Ladybird *in 1923,* Glad Ghosts *in 1926, and* The Woman Who Rode Away *in 1928. In 1961 his stories were collected in a three-volume edition that has gone through numerous reprintings. The style of the early stories is harshly realistic, but Lawrence's depiction of his characters' emotional situations matured in his later work, in which he created fantasies that explore deeper strata of the unconscious. Among these is his famous story "The Rocking Horse Winner," which shows him in the role of moralist and preacher against materialist values.*

As a writer, Lawrence found the detachment of Gustave Flaubert antithetical to his talent. Lawrence is closer to Leo Tolstoy in expressing an explicit "moral relation" to his subjects. Lawrence's conception of art was that it must be concrete and true to life: "The business of art is to reveal the

*relation between man and his circumambient universe, at the living mo-
ment. As mankind is always struggling in the toils of old relationships, art is
always ahead of the 'times,' which themselves are always far in the rear of
the living moment." Literature, for Lawrence, was always connected to life,
because art has two great functions: It provides an emotional experience,
and then, if the reader has the courage of his or her own feelings and can
live imaginatively, it becomes "a mine of practical truth." (See Lawrence's
Commentary about Poe on page 1228.)*

D. H. Lawrence

ODOUR OF CHRYSANTHEMUMS

I

The small locomotive engine, Number 4, came clanking, stumbling down from Selston with seven full wagons. It appeared round the corner with loud threats of speed, but the colt that it startled from among the gorse, which still flickered indistinctly in the raw afternoon, out-distanced it at a canter. A woman, walking up the railway line to Underwood, drew back into the hedge, held her basket aside, and watched the footplate[1] of the engine advancing. The trucks thumped heavily past, one by one, with slow inevitable movement, as she stood insignificantly trapped between the jolting black wagons and the hedge; then they curved away towards the coppice where the withered oak leaves dropped noiselessly, while the birds, pulling at the scarlet hips beside the track, made off into the dusk that had already crept into the spinney. In the open, the smoke from the engine sank and cleaved to the rough grass. The fields were dreary and forsaken, and in the marshy strip that led to the whimsey, a reedy pit-pond, the fowls had already abandoned their run among the alders, to roost in the tarred fowlhouse. The pit-bank loomed up beyond the pond, flames like red sores licking its ashy sides, in the afternoon's stagnant light. Just beyond rose the tapering chimneys and the clumsy black headstocks of Brinsley Colliery. The two wheels were spinning fast up against the sky, and the winding engine rapped out its little spasms. The miners were being turned up.

The engine whistled as it came into the wide bay of railway lines beside the colliery, where rows of trucks stood in harbour.

Miners, single, trailing and in groups, passed like shadows diverging home. At the edge of the ribbed level of sidings squat a low cottage, three steps down from the cinder track. A large bony vine clutched at the house,

[1] Platform on early locomotives for the engineer to stand on.

as if to claw down the tiled roof. Round the bricked yard grew a few wintry primroses. Beyond, the long garden sloped down to a bush-covered brook course. There were some twiggy apple trees, winter-crack trees, and ragged cabbages. Beside the path hung dishevelled pink chrysanthemums, like pink cloths hung on bushes. A woman came stooping out of the felt-covered fowl-house, half-way down the garden. She closed and padlocked the door, then drew herself erect, having brushed some bits from her white apron.

She was a tall woman of imperious mien, handsome, with definite black eyebrows. Her smooth black hair was parted exactly. For a few moments she stood steadily watching the miners as they passed along the railway: then she turned towards the brook course. Her face was calm and set, her mouth was closed with disillusionment. After a moment she called:

"John!" There was no answer. She waited, and then said distinctly:

"Where are you?"

"Here!" replied a child's sulky voice from among the bushes. The woman looked piercingly through the dusk.

"Are you at that brook?" she asked sternly.

For answer the child showed himself before the raspberry-canes that rose like whips. He was a small, sturdy boy of five. He stood quite still, defiantly.

"Oh!" said the mother, conciliated. "I thought you were down at that wet brook — and you remember what I told you — "

The boy did not move or answer.

"Come, come on in," she said more gently, "it's getting dark. There's your grandfather's engine coming down the line!"

The lad advanced slowly, with resentful, taciturn movement. He was dressed in trousers and waistcoat of cloth that was too thick and hard for the size of the garments. They were evidently cut down from a man's clothes.

As they went slowly towards the house he tore at the ragged wisps of chrysanthemums and dropped the petals in handfuls among the path.

"Don't do that — it does look nasty," said his mother. He refrained, and she, suddenly pitiful, broke off a twig with three or four wan flowers and held them against her face. When mother and son reached the yard her hand hesitated, and instead of laying the flower aside, she pushed it in her apron-band. The mother and son stood at the foot of the three steps looking across the bay of lines at the passing home of the miners. The trundle of the small train was imminent. Suddenly the engine loomed past the house and came to a stop opposite the gate.

The engine-driver, a short man with round grey beard, leaned out of the cab high above the woman.

"Have you got a cup of tea?" he said in a cheery, hearty fashion.

It was her father. She went in, saying she would mash. Directly, she returned.

"I didn't come to see you on Sunday," began the little grey-bearded man.

"I didn't expect you," said his daughter.

The engine-driver winced; then, reassuming his cheery, airy manner, he said:

"Oh, have you heard then? Well, and what do you think —?"

"I think it is soon enough," she replied.

At her brief censure the little man made an impatient gesture, and said coaxingly, yet with dangerous coldness:

"Well, what's a man to do? It's no sort of life for a man of my years, to sit at my own hearth like a stranger. And if I'm going to marry again it may as well be soon as late — what does it matter to anybody?"

The woman did not reply, but turned and went into the house. The man in the engine-cab stood assertive, till she returned with a cup of tea and a piece of bread and butter on a plate. She went up the steps and stood near the footplate of the hissing engine.

"You needn't 'a' brought me bread an' butter," said her father. "But a cup of tea" — he sipped appreciatively — "it's very nice." He sipped for a moment or two, then: "I hear as Walter's got another bout on," he said.

"When hasn't he?" said the woman bitterly.

"I heerd tell of him in the 'Lord Nelson' braggin' as he was going to spend that b —— afore he went: half a sovereign that was."

"When?" asked the woman.

"A' Sat'day night — I know that's true."

"Very likely," she laughed bitterly. "He gives me twenty-three shillings."

"Aye, it's a nice thing, when a man can do nothing with his money but make a beast of himself!" said the grey-whiskered man. The woman turned her head away. Her father swallowed the last of his tea and handed her the cup.

"Aye," he sighed, wiping his mouth. "It's a settler, it is —— "

He put his hand on the lever. The little engine strained and groaned, and the train rumbled towards the crossing. The woman again looked across the metals. Darkness was settling over the spaces of the railway and trucks: the miners, in grey sombre groups, were still passing home. The winding engine pulsed hurriedly, with brief pauses. Elizabeth Bates looked at the dreary flow of men, then she went indoors. Her husband did not come.

The kitchen was small and full of firelight; red coals piled glowing up the chimney mouth. All the life of the room seemed in the white, warm hearth and the steel fender reflecting the red fire. The cloth was laid for tea; cups glinted in the shadows. At the back, where the lowest stairs protruded into the room, the boy sat struggling with a knife and a piece of white wood. He was almost hidden in the shadow. It was half-past four. They had but to await the father's coming to begin tea. As the mother watched her son's sullen little struggle with the wood, she saw herself in his silence and pertinacity; she saw the father in her child's indifference to all but himself. She seemed to be occupied by her husband. He had probably gone past his home, slunk past his own door, to drink before he came in, while his dinner spoiled and wasted in waiting. She glanced at the clock, then took the potatoes to strain them in the yard. The garden and fields beyond the brook were closed in uncertain darkness. When she rose with the saucepan, leaving the drain steaming into the night behind her, she saw the yellow lamps were lit along the high road that went up the hill away beyond the space of the railway lines and the field.

Then again she watched the men trooping home, fewer now and fewer.

Indoors the fire was sinking and the room was dark red. The woman put her saucepan on the hob, and set a batter-pudding near the mouth of the oven. Then she stood unmoving. Directly, gratefully, came quick young steps to the door. Someone hung on the latch a moment, then a little girl entered and began pulling off her outdoor things, dragging a mass of curls, just ripening from gold to brown, over her eyes with her hat.

Her mother chid her for coming late from school, and said she would have to keep her at home the dark winter days.

"Why, mother, it's hardly a bit dark yet. The lamp's not lighted, and my father's not home."

"No, he isn't. But it's a quarter to five! Did you see anything of him?"

The child became serious. She looked at her mother with large, wistful blue eyes.

"No, mother, I've never seen him. Why? Has he come up an' gone past, to Old Brinsley? He hasn't, mother, 'cos I never saw him."

"He'd watch that," said the mother bitterly, "he'd take care as you didn't see him. But you may depend upon it, he's seated in the 'Prince o' Wales.' He wouldn't be this late."

The girl looked at her mother piteously.

"Let's have our teas, mother, should we?" said she.

The mother called John to table. She opened the door once more and looked out across the darkness of the lines. All was deserted: she could not hear the winding-engines.

"Perhaps," she said to herself, "he's stopped to get some ripping done."

They sat down to tea. John, at the end of the table near the door, was almost lost in the darkness. Their faces were hidden from each other. The girl crouched against the fender slowly moving a thick piece of bread before the fire. The lad, his face a dusky mark on the shadow, sat watching her who was transfigured in the red glow.

"I do think it's beautiful to look in the fire," said the child.

"Do you?" said her mother. "Why?"

"It's so red, and full of little caves — and it feels so nice, and you can fair smell it."

"It'll want mending directly," replied her mother, "and then if your father comes he'll carry on and say there never is a fire when a man comes home sweating from the pit. A public house is always warm enough."

There was silence till the boy said complainingly: "Make haste, our Annie."

"Well, I am doing! I can't make the fire do it no faster, can I?"

"She keeps wafflin' it about so's to make 'er slow," grumbled the boy.

"Don't have such an evil imagination, child," replied the mother.

Soon the room was busy in the darkness with the crisp sound of crunching. The mother ate very little. She drank her tea determinedly, and sat thinking. When she rose her anger was evident in the stern unbending of her head. She looked at the pudding in the fender and broke out:

"It is a scandalous thing as a man can't even come home to his dinner! If it's crozzled up to a cinder I don't see why I should care. Past his very door he goes to get to a public-house, and here I sit with his dinner waiting for him — "

She went out. As she dropped piece after piece of coal on the red fire, the shadows fell on the walls, till the room was almost in total darkness.

"I canna see," grumbled the invisible John. In spite of herself, the mother laughed.

"You know the way to your mouth," she said. She set the dust-pan outside the door. When she came again like a shadow on the hearth, the lad repeated, complaining sulkily:

"I canna see."

"Good gracious!" cried the mother irritably, "you're as bad as your father if it's a bit dusk!"

Nevertheless, she took a paper spill from a sheaf on the mantelpiece and proceeded to light the lamp that hung from the ceiling in the middle of the room. As she reached up, her figure displayed itself just rounding with maternity.

"Oh, mother —— !" exclaimed the girl.

"What?" said the woman, suspended in the act of putting the lamp-glass over the flame. The copper reflector shone handsomely on her, as she stood with uplifted arm, turning to face her daughter.

"You've got a flower in your apron!" said the child, in a little rapture at this unusual event.

"Goodness me!" exclaimed the woman, relieved. "One would think the house was afire." She replaced the glass and waited a moment before turning up the wick. A pale shadow was seen floating vaguely on the floor.

"Let me smell!" said the child, still rapturously, coming forward and putting her face to her mother's waist.

"Go along, silly!" said the mother, turning up the lamp. The light revealed their suspense so that the woman felt it almost unbearable. Annie was still bending at her waist. Irritably, the mother took the flowers out from her apron-band.

"Oh, mother — don't take them out!" Annie cried, catching her hand and trying to replace the sprig.

"Such nonsense!" said the mother, turning away. The child put the pale chrysanthemums to her lips, murmuring:

"Don't they smell beautiful!"

Her mother gave a short laugh.

"No," she said, "not to me. It was chrysanthemums when I married him, and chrysanthemums when you were born, and the first time they ever brought him home drunk, he'd got brown chrysanthemums in his button-hole."

She looked at the children. Their eyes and their parted lips were wondering. The mother sat rocking in silence for some time. Then she looked at the clock.

"Twenty minutes to six!" In a tone of fine bitter carelessness she continued: "Eh, he'll not come now till they bring him. There he'll stick! But he needn't come rolling in here in his pit-dirt, for *I* won't wash him. He can lie on the floor —— Eh, what a fool I've been, what a fool! And this is what I came here for, to this dirty hole, rats and all, for him to slink past his very door. Twice last week — he's begun now ——"

She silenced herself, and rose to clear the table.

While for an hour or more the children played, subduedly intent, fertile of imagination, united in fear of the mother's wrath, and in dread of their father's home-coming, Mrs. Bates sat in her rocking-chair making a "singlet" of thick cream-coloured flannel, which gave a dull wounded sound as she tore off the grey edge. She worked at her sewing with energy, listening to the children, and her anger wearied itself, lay down to rest, opening its eyes from time to time and steadily watching, its ears raised to listen. Sometimes even her anger quailed and shrank, and the mother suspended her sewing, tracing the footsteps that thudded along the sleepers outside: she would lift her head sharply to bid the children "hush," but she recovered herself in time, and the footsteps went past the gate, and the children were not flung out of their play-world.

But at last Annie sighed, and gave in. She glanced at her wagon of slippers, and loathed the game. She turned plaintively to her mother.

"Mother!" — but she was inarticulate.

John crept out like a frog from under the sofa. His mother glanced up.

"Yes," she said, "just look at those shirt-sleeves!"

The boy held them out to survey them, saying nothing. Then somebody called in a hoarse voice away down the line, and suspense bristled in the room, till two people had gone by outside, talking.

"It is time for bed," said the mother.

"My father hasn't come," wailed Annie plaintively. But her mother was primed with courage.

"Never mind. They'll bring him when he does come — like a log." She meant there would be no scene. "And he may sleep on the floor till he wakes himself. I know he'll not go to work to-morrow after this!"

The children had their hands and faces wiped with a flannel. They were very quiet. When they had put on their night-dresses, they said their prayers, the boy mumbling. The mother looked down at them, at the brown silken bush of intertwining curls in the nape of the girl's neck, at the little black head of the lad, and her heart burst with anger at their father, who caused all three such distress. The children hid their faces in her skirts for comfort.

When Mrs. Bates came down, the room was strangely empty, with a tension of expectancy. She took up her sewing and stitched for some time without raising her head. Meantime her anger was tinged with fear.

II

The clock struck eight and she rose suddenly, dropping her sewing on her chair. She went to the stair-foot door, opened it, listening. Then she went out, locking the door behind her.

Something scuffled in the yard, and she started, though she knew it was only the rats with which the place was over-run. The night was very dark. In the great bay of railway lines, bulked with trucks, there was no trace of light, only away back she could see a few yellow lamps at the pit-top, and the red smear of the burning pit-bank on the night. She hurried along the edge of the track, then, crossing the converging lines, came to the stile by the white gates, whence she emerged on the road. Then the fear which had led her shrank. People were walking up to New Brinsley; she saw the lights in the houses; twenty yards farther on were the broad windows of the "Prince of Wales," very warm and bright, and the loud voices of men could be heard distinctly. What a fool she had been to imagine that anything had happened to him! He was merely drinking over there at the "Prince of Wales." She faltered. she had never yet been to fetch him, and she never would go. So she continued her walk towards the long straggling line of houses, standing back on the highway. She entered a passage between the dwellings.

"Mr. Rigley? — Yes! Did you want him? No, he's not in at this minute."

The raw-boned woman leaned forward from her dark scullery and peered at the other, upon whom fell a dim light through the blind of the kitchen window.

"Is it Mrs. Bates?" she asked in a tone tinged with respect.

"Yes. I wondered if your Master was at home. Mine hasn't come yet."

" 'Asn't 'e! Oh, Jack's been 'ome an' 'ad 'is dinner an' gone out. 'E's just gone for 'alf an hour afore bed-time. Did you call at the 'Prince of Wales'?"

"No ——"

"No, you didn't like ——! It's not very nice." The other woman was indulgent. There was an awkward pause. "Jack never said nothink about — about your Master," she said.

"No! — I expect he's stuck in there!"

Elizabeth Bates said this bitterly, and with recklessness. She knew that the woman across the yard was standing at her door listening, but she did not care. As she turned:

"Stop a minute! I'll just go an' ask Jack if 'e knows anythink," said Mrs. Rigley.

"Oh no — I wouldn't like to put ——!"

"Yes, I will, if you'll just step inside an' see as th' childer doesn't come downstairs and set theirselves afire."

Elizabeth Bates, murmuring a remonstrance, stepped inside. The other woman apologised for the state of the room.

The kitchen needed apology. There were little frocks and trousers and childish undergarments on the squab and on the floor, and a litter of playthings everywhere. On the black American cloth of the table were pieces of bread and cake, crusts, slops, and a teapot with cold tea.

"Eh, ours is just as bad," said Elizabeth Bates, looking at the woman, not at the house. Mrs. Rigley put a shawl over her head and hurried out, saying:

"I shanna be a minute."

The other sat, noting with faint disapproval the general untidiness of the room. Then she fell to counting the shoes of various sizes scattered over the floor. There were twelve. She sighed and said to herself: "No wonder!" — glancing at the litter. There came the scratching of two pairs of feet on the yard, and the Rigleys entered. Elizabeth Bates rose. Rigley was a big man, with very large bones. His head looked particularly bony. Across his temple was a blue scar, caused by a wound got in the pit, a wound in which the coal-dust remained blue like tattooing.

"'Asna 'e come whoam yit?" asked the man, without any form of greeting, but with deference and sympathy. "I couldna say wheer he is — 'e's non ower theer!" — he jerked his head to signify the "Prince of Wales."

"'E's 'appen gone up to th' 'Yew,'" said Mrs. Rigley.

There was another pause. Rigley had evidently something to get off his mind:

"Ah left 'im finishin' a stint,' he began. "Loose-all 'ad bin gone about ten minutes when we com'n away, an' I shouted: 'Are ter comin', Walt?' an' 'e said: 'Go on, Ah shanna be but a'ef a minnit,' so we com'n ter th' bottom, me an' Bowers, thinkin' as 'e wor just behint, an' 'ud come up i' th' next bantle —— "

He stood perplexed, as if answering a charge of deserting his mate. Elizabeth Bates, now again certain of disaster, hastened to reassure him:

"I expect 'e's gone up to th' 'Yew Tree,' as you say. It' not the first time. I've fretted myself into a fever before now. He'll come home when they carry him."

"Ay, isn't it too bad!" deplored the other woman.

"I'll just step up to Dick's an' see if 'e is theer," offered the man, afraid of appearing alarmed, afraid of taking liberties.

"Oh, I wouldn't think of bothering you that far," said Elizabeth Bates, with emphasis, but he knew she was glad of his offer.

As they stumbled up the entry, Elizabeth Bates heard Rigley's wife run across the yard and open her neighbour's door. At this, suddenly all the blood in her body seemed to switch away from her heart.

"Mind!" warned Rigley. "Ah've said many a time as Ah'd fill up them ruts in this entry, sumb'dy 'll be breakin' their legs yit."

She recovered herself and walked quickly along with the miner.

"I don't like leaving the children in bed, and nobody in the house," she said.

"No, you dunna!" he replied courteously. They were soon at the gate of the cottage.

"Well, I shanna be many minnits. Dunna you be frettin' now, 'e'll be all right," said the butty.[2]

"Thank you very much, Mr. Rigley," she replied.

"You're welcome!" he stammered, moving away. "I shanna be many minnits."

The house was quiet. Elizabeth Bates took off her hat and shawl, and rolled back the rug. When she had finished, she sat down. It was a few minutes past nine. She was startled by the rapid chuff of the winding-engine at the pit, and the sharp whirr of the brakes on the rope as it descended. Again she felt the painful sweep of her blood, and she put her hand to her side, saying aloud: "Good gracious! — it's only the nine o'clock deputy going down," rebuking herself.

She sat still listening. Half an hour of this, and she was wearied out.

"What am I working myself up like this for?" she said pitiably to herself, "I s'll only be doing myself some damage."

She took out her sewing again.

At a quarter to ten there were footsteps. One person! She watched for the door to open. It was an elderly woman, in a black bonnet and a black woollen shawl — his mother. She was about sixty years old, pale, with blue eyes, and her face all wrinkled and lamentable. She shut the door and turned to her daughter-in-law peevishly.

"Eh, Lizzie, whatever shall we do, whatever shall we do!" she cried.

Elizabeth drew back a little, sharply.

"What is it, mother?" she said.

The elder woman seated herself on the sofa.

"I don't know, child, I can't tell you!" — she shook her head slowly. Elizabeth sat watching her, anxious and vexed.

"I don't know," replied the grandmother, sighing very deeply. "There's no end to my troubles, there isn't. The things I've gone through, I'm sure it's enough —— !" She wept without wiping her eyes, the tears running.

"But, mother," interrupted Elizabeth, "what do you mean? What is it?"

The grandmother slowly wiped her eyes. The fountains of her tears were stopped by Elizabeth's directness. She wiped her eyes slowly.

"Poor child! Eh, you poor thing!" she moaned. "I don't know what we're going to do, I don't — and you as you are — it's a thing, it is indeed!"

Elizabeth waited.

"Is he dead?" she asked, and at the words her heart swung violently,

[2] a fellow workman in a colliery.

though she felt a slight flush of shame at the ultimate extravagance of the question. Her words sufficiently frightened the old lady, almost brought her to herself.

"Don't say so, Elizabeth! We'll hope it's not as bad as that; no, may the Lord spare us that, Elizabeth. Jack Rigley came just as I was sittin' down to a glass afore going to bed, an' 'e said: ' 'Appen you'll go down th' line, Mrs. Bates. Walt's had an accident. 'Appen you'll go an' sit wi' 'er till we can get him home.' I hadn't time to ask him a word afore he was gone. An' I put my bonnet on an' come straight down, Lizzie. I thought to myself: 'Eh, that poor blessed child, if anybody should come an' tell her of a sudden, there's no knowing' what'll 'appen to 'er.' You mustn't let it upset you, Lizzie — or you know what to expect. How long is it, six months — or is it five, Lizzie? Ay!" — the old woman shook her head — "time slips on, it slips on! Ay!"

Elizabeth's thoughts were busy elsewhere. If he was killed — would she be able to manage on the little pension and what she could earn? — she counted up rapidly. If he was hurt — they wouldn't take him to the hospital — how tiresome he would be to nurse! — but perhaps she'd be able to get him away from the drink and his hateful ways. She would — while he was ill. The tears offered to come to her eyes at the picture. But what sentimental luxury was this she was beginning? She turned to consider the children. At any rate she was absolutely necessary for them. They were her business.

"Ay!" repeated the old woman, "it seems but a week or two since he brought me his first wages. Ay — he was a good lad, Elizabeth, he was, in his way. I don't know why he got to be such a trouble, I don't. He was a happy lad at home, only full of spirits. But there's no mistake he's been a handful of trouble, he has! I hope the Lord'll spare him to mend his ways. I hope so, I hope so. You've had a sight o' trouble with him, Elizabeth, you have indeed. But he was a jolly enough lad wi' me, he was, I can assure you. I don't know how it is. ...."

The old woman continued to muse aloud, a monotonous irritating sound, while Elizabeth thought concentratedly, startled once, when she heard the winding-engine chuff quickly, and the brakes skirr with a shriek. Then she heard the engine more slowly, and the brakes made no sound. The old woman did not notice. Elizabeth waited in suspense. The mother-in-law talked, with lapses into silence.

"But he wasn't your son, Lizzie, an' it makes a difference. Whatever he was, I remember him when he was little, an' I learned to understand him and to make allowances. You've got to make allowances for them —— "

It was half-past ten, and the old woman was saying: "But it's trouble from beginning to end; you're never too old for trouble, never too old for that —— " when the gate banged back, and there were heavy feet on the steps.

"I'll go, Lizzie, let me go," cried the old woman, rising. But Elizabeth was at the door. It was a man in pit-clothes.

"They're bringin' 'im, Missis," he said. Elizabeth's heart halted a moment. Then it surged on again, almost suffocating her.

"Is he — is it bad?" she asked.

The man turned away, looking at the darkness:

"The doctor says 'e'd been dead hours. 'E saw 'im i' th' lamp-cabin."

The old woman, who stood just behind Elizabeth, dropped into a chair, and folded her hands, crying: "Oh, my boy, my boy!"

"Hush!" said Elizabeth, with a sharp twitch of a frown. "Be still, mother, don't waken th' children: I wouldn't have them down for anything!"

The old woman moaned softly, rocking herself. The man was drawing away. Elizabeth took a step forward.

"How was it?" she asked.

"Well, I couldn't say for sure," the man replied, very ill at ease. " 'E wor finishin' a stint an' th' butties 'ad gone, an' a lot o' stuff come down atop 'n 'im."

"And crushed him?" cried the widow, with a shudder.

"No," said the man, "it fell at th' back of 'im. 'E wor under th' face, an' it niver touched 'im. It shut 'im in. It seems 'e wor smothered."

Elizabeth shrank back. She heard the old woman behind her cry:

"What? — what did 'e say it was?"

The man replied, more loudly: " 'E wor smothered!"

Then the old woman wailed aloud, and this relieved Elizabeth.

"Oh, mother," she said, putting her hand on the old woman, "don't waken th' children, don't waken th' children."

She wept a little, unknowing, while the old mother rocked herself and moaned. Elizabeth remembered that they were bringing him home, and she must be ready. "They'll lay him in the parlour," she said to herself, standing a moment pale and perplexed.

Then she lighted a candle and went into the tiny room. The air was cold and damp, but she could not make a fire, there was no fireplace. She set down the candle and looked round. The candlelight glittered on the lustre-glasses, on the two vases that held some of the pink chrysanthemums, and on the dark mahogany. There was a cold, deathly smell of chrysanthemums in the room. Elizabeth stood looking at the flowers. She turned away, and calculated whether there would be room to lay him on the floor, between the couch and the chiffonier. She pushed the chairs aside. There would be room to lay him down and to step round him. Then she fetched the old red tablecloth, and another old cloth, spreading them down to save her bit of carpet. She shivered on leaving the parlour; so, from the dresser drawer she took a clean shirt and put it at the fire to air. All the time her mother-in-law was rocking herself in the chair and moaning.

"You'll have to move from there, mother," said Elizabeth. "They'll be bringing him in. Come in the rocker."

The old mother rose mechanically, and seated herself by the fire, continuing to lament. Elizabeth went into the pantry for another candle, and there, in the little pent-house under the naked tiles, she heard them coming. She stood still in the pantry doorway, listening. She heard them pass the end of the house, and come awkwardly down the three steps, a jumble of shuffling footsteps and muttering voices. The old woman was silent. The men were in the yard.

Then Elizabeth heard Matthews, the manager of the pit, say: "You go in first, Jim. Mind!"

The door came open, and the two women saw a collier backing into the room, holding one end of a stretcher, on which they could see the nailed pit-boots of the dead man. The two carriers halted, the man at the head stooping to the lintel of the door.

"Wheer will you have him?" asked the manager, a short, white-bearded man.

Elizabeth roused herself and came from the pantry carrying the un-lighted candle.

"In the parlour," she said.

"In there, Jim!" pointed the manager, and the carriers backed round into the tiny room. The coat with which they had covered the body fell off as they awkwardly turned through the two doorways, and the women saw their man, naked to the waist, lying stripped for work. The old woman began to moan in a low voice of horror.

"Lay th' stretcher at th' side," snapped the manager, "an' put 'im on th' cloths. Mind now, mind! Look you now —— !"

One of the men had knocked off a vase of chrysanthemums. He stared awkwardly, then they set down the stretcher. Elizabeth did not look at her husband. As soon as she could get in the room, she went and picked up the broken vase and the flowers.

"Wait a minute!" she said.

The three men waited in silence while she mopped up the water with a duster.

"Eh, what a job, what a job, to be sure!" the manager was saying, rubbing his brow with trouble and perplexity. "Never knew such a thing in my life, never! He'd no business to ha' been left. I never knew such a thing in my life! Fell over him clean as a whistle, an' shut him in. Not four foot of space, there wasn't — yet it scarce bruised him."

He looked down at the dead man, lying prone, half naked, all grimed with coal-dust.

" ' 'Sphyxiated,' the doctor said. It *is* the most terrible job I've ever known. Seems as if it was done o' purpose. Clean over him, an' shut 'im in, like a mouse-trap"— he made a sharp, descending gesture with his hand.

The colliers standing by jerked aside their heads in hopeless comment.

The horror of the thing bristled upon them all.

Then they heard the girl's voice upstairs calling shrilly: "Mother, mother — who is it? Mother, who is it?"

Elizabeth hurried to the foot of the stairs and opened the door:

"Go to sleep!" she commanded sharply. "What are you shouting about? Go to sleep at once — there's nothing —— "

Then she began to mount the stairs. They could hear her on the boards, and on the plaster floor of the little bedroom. They could hear her distinctly:

"What's the matter now? — what's the matter with you, silly thing?" — her voice was much agitated, with an unreal gentleness.

"I thought it was some men come," said the plaintive voice of the child. "Has he come?"

"Yes, they've brought him. There's nothing to make a fuss about. Go to sleep now, like a good child."

They could hear her voice in the bedroom, they waited whilst she covered the children under the bedclothes.

"Is he drunk?" asked the girl, timidly, faintly.

"No! No — he's not! He — he's asleep."

"Is he asleep downstairs?"

"Yes — and don't make a noise."

There was silence for a moment, then the men heard the frightened child again:

"What's that noise?"

"It's nothing, I tell you, what are you bothering for?"

The noise was the grandmother moaning. She was oblivious of everything, sitting on her chair rocking and moaning. The manager put his hand on her arm and bade her "Sh — sh!!"

The old woman opened her eyes and looked at him. She was shocked by this interruption, and seemed to wonder.

"What time is it?" the plaintive thin voice of the child, sinking back unhappily into sleep, asked this last question.

"Ten o'clock," answered the mother more softly. Then she must have bent down and kissed the children.

Matthews beckoned to the men to come away. They put on their caps and took up the stretcher. Stepping over the body, they tiptoed out of the house. None of them spoke till they were far from the wakeful children.

When Elizabeth came down she found her mother alone on the parlour floor, leaning over the dead man, the tears dropping on him.

"We must lay him out," the wife said. She put on the kettle, then returning knelt at the feet, and began to unfasten the knotted leather laces. The room was clammy and dim with only one candle, so that she had to bend her face almost to the floor. At last she got off the heavy boots and put them away.

"You must help me now," she whispered to the old woman. Together they stripped the man.

When they arose, saw him lying in the naïve dignity of death, the women stood arrested in fear and respect. For a few moments they remained still, looking down, the old mother whimpering. Elizabeth felt countermanded. She saw him, how utterly inviolable he lay in himself. She had nothing to do with him. She could not accept it. Stooping, she laid her hand on him, in claim. He was still warm, for the mine was hot where he had died. His mother had his face between her hands, and was murmuring incoherently. The old tears fell in succession as drops from wet leaves; the mother was not weeping, merely her tears flowed. Elizabeth embraced the body of her husband, with cheek and lips. She seemed to be listening, inquiring, trying to get some connection. But she could not. She was driven away. He was impregnable.

She rose, went into the kitchen, where she poured warm water into a bowl, brought soap and flannel and a soft towel.

"I must wash him," she said.

Then the old mother rose stiffly, and watched Elizabeth as she carefully washed his face, carefully brushing the big blond moustache from his mouth with the flannel. She was afraid with a bottomless fear, so she ministered to him. The old woman, jealous, said:

"Let me wipe him!" — and she kneeled on the other side drying slowly as Elizabeth washed, her big black bonnet sometimes brushing the dark head of her daughter-in-law. They worked thus in silence for a long time. They never forgot it was death, and the touch of the man's dead body gave them strange emotions, different in each of the women; a great dread possessed them both, the mother felt the lie was given to her womb, she was denied; the wife felt the utter isolation of the human soul, the child within her was a weight apart from her.

At last it was finished. He was a man of handsome body, and his face showed no traces of drink. He was blond, full-fleshed, with fine limbs. But he was dead.

"Bless him," whispered his mother, looking always at his face, and speaking out of sheer terror. "Dear lad — bless him!" She spoke in a faint, sibilant ecstasy of fear and mother love.

Elizabeth sank down again to the floor, and put her face against his neck, and trembled and shuddered. But she had to draw away again. He was dead, and her living flesh had no place against his. A great dread and weariness held her: she was so unavailing. Her life was gone like this.

"White as milk he is, clear as a twelve-month baby, bless him, the darling!" the old mother murmured to herself. "Not a mark on him, clear and clean and white, beautiful as ever a child was made," she murmured with pride. Elizabeth kept her face hidden.

"He went peaceful, Lizzie — peaceful as sleep. Isn't he beautiful, the lamb? Ay — he must ha' made his peace, Lizzie. 'Appen he made it all right, Lizzie, shut in there. He'd have time. He wouldn't look like this if he hadn't made his peace. The lamb, the dear lamb. 'Eh, but he had a hearty laugh. I loved to hear it. He had the heartiest laugh, Lizzie, as a lad —— "

Elizabeth looked up. The man's mouth was fallen back, slightly open under the cover of the moustache. The eyes, half shut, did not show glazed in the obscurity. Life with its smoky burning gone from him, had left him apart and utterly alien to her. And she knew what a stranger he was to her. In her womb was ice of fear, because of this separate stranger with whom she had been living as one flesh. Was this what it all meant — utter, intact separateness, obscured by heat of living? In dread she turned her face away. The fact was too deadly. There had been nothing between them, and yet they had come together, exchanging their nakedness repeatedly. Each time he had taken her, they had been two isolated beings, far apart as now. He was no more responsible than she. The child was like ice in her womb. For as she looked at the dead man, her mind, cold and detached, said clearly: "Who am I? What have I been doing? I have been fighting a husband who did not exist. *He* existed all the time. What wrong have I done? What was that I have been living with? There lies the reality, this man." And her soul died in her for fear: she knew she had never seen him, he had never seen her, they had met in the dark and had fought in the dark, not knowing whom they met nor whom they fought. And now she saw, and turned silent in seeing. For she had been wrong. She had said he was something he was not; she had felt familiar with him. Whereas he was apart all the while, living as she never lived, feeling as she never felt.

In fear and shame she looked at his naked body, that she had known falsely. And he was the father of her children. Her soul was torn from her body and stood apart. She looked at his naked body and was ashamed, as if she had denied it. After all, it was itself. It seemed awful to her. She looked at his face, and she turned her own face to the wall. For his look was other than hers, his way was not her way. She had denied him what he was — she saw it now. She had refused him as himself. And this had been her life, and his life. She was grateful to death, which restored the truth. And she knew she was not dead.

And all the while her heart was bursting with grief and pity for him. What had he suffered? What stretch of horror for this helpless man! She was rigid with agony. She had not been able to help him. He had been cruelly injured, this naked man, this other being, and she could make no reparation. There were the children — but the children belonged to life. This dead man had nothing to do with them. He and she were only channels through which life had flowed to issue in the children. She was a mother — but how awful she knew it now to have been a wife. And he, dead now, how awful he must have felt it to be a husband. She felt that in the next world he would be a stranger to her. If they met there, in the beyond, they would only be ashamed of what had been before. The children had come, for some mysterious reason, out of both of them. But the children did not unite them. Now he was dead, she knew how eternally he was apart from her, how eternally he had nothing more to do with her. She saw this episode of her life closed. They had denied each other in life. Now he had withdrawn. An anguish came over her. It was finished then: it had become hopeless between them long before he died. Yet he had been her husband. But how little!

"Have you got his shirt, 'Lizabeth?"

Elizabeth turned without answering, though she strove to weep and behave as her mother-in-law expected. But she could not, she was silenced. She went into the kitchen and returned with the garment.

"It is aired," she said, grasping the cotton shirt here and there to try. She was almost ashamed to handle him; what right had she or anyone to lay hands on him; but her touch was humble on his body. It was hard work to clothe him. He was so heavy and inert. A terrible dread gripped her all the while: that he could be so heavy and utterly inert, unresponsive, apart. The horror of the distance between them was almost too much for her — it was so infinite a gap she must look across.

At last it was finished. They covered him with a sheet and left him lying, with his face bound. And she fastened the door of the little parlour, lest the children should see what was lying there. Then, with peace sunk heavy on her heart, she went about making tidy the kitchen. She knew she submitted to life, which was her immediate master. But from death, her ultimate master, she winced with fear and shame.

[1909]

D. H. Lawrence

தை

THE ROCKING HORSE WINNER

There was a woman who was beautiful, who started with all the advantages, yet she had no luck. She married for love, and the love turned to dust. She had bonny children, yet she felt they had been thrust upon her, and she could not love them. They looked at her coldly, as if they were finding fault with her. And hurriedly she felt she must cover up some fault in herself. Yet what it was that she must cover up she never knew. Nevertheless, when her children were present, she always felt the center of her heart go hard. This troubled her, and in her manner she was all the more gentle and anxious for her children, as if she loved them very much. Only she herself knew that at the center of her heart was a hard little place that could not feel love, no, not for anybody. Everybody else said of her: "She is such a good mother. She adores her children." Only she herself, and her children themselves, knew it was not so. They read it in each other's eyes.

There were a boy and two little girls. They lived in a pleasant house, with a garden, and they had discreet servants, and felt themselves superior to anyone in the neighborhood.

Although they lived in style, they felt always an anxiety in the house. There was never enough money. The mother had a small income, and the father had a small income, but not nearly enough for the social position which they had to keep up. The father went into town to some office. But though he had good prospects, these prospects never materialized. There was always the grinding sense of the shortage of money, though the style was always kept up.

At last the mother said: "I will see if *I* can't make something." But she did not know where to begin. She racked her brains, and tried this thing and the other, but could not find anything successful. The failure made deep lines come into her face. Her children were growing up, they would have to go to school. There must be more money, there must be more money. The father, who was always very handsome and expensive in his tastes, seemed as if he never *would* be able to do anything worth doing. And the mother, who had a great belief in herself, did not succeed any better, and her tastes were just as expensive.

And so the house came to be haunted by the unspoken phrase: *There must be more money! There must be more money!* The children could hear it all the time, though nobody said it aloud. They heard it at Christmas, when the expensive and splendid toys filled the nursery. Behind the shining modern rocking horse, behind the smart doll's house, a voice would start whispering: "There *must* be more money! There *must* be more money!" And the children would stop playing, to listen for a moment. They would look into each other's eyes, to see if they had all heard. And each one saw in the eyes of the other two that they too had heard. "There *must* be more money! There *must* be more money!"

It came whispering from the springs of the still-swaying rocking horse, and even the horse, bending his wooden, champing head, heard it. The big doll, sitting so pink and smirking in her new pram, could hear it quite plainly, and seemed to be smirking all the more self-consciously because of it. The foolish puppy, too, that took the place of the teddy bear, he was looking so extraordinarily foolish for no other reason but that he heard the secret whisper all over the house: "There *must* be more money!"

Yet nobody ever said it aloud. The whisper was everywhere, and therefore no one spoke it. Just as no one ever says: "We are breathing!" in spite of the fact that breath is coming and going all the time.

"Mother," said the boy Paul one day, "why don't we keep a car of our own? Why do we always use Uncle's, or else a taxi?"

"Because we're the poor members of the family," said the mother.

"But why *are* we, Mother?"

"Well — I suppose," she said slowly and bitterly, "it's because your father has no luck."

The boy was silent for some time.

"Is luck money, Mother?" he asked rather timidly.

"No, Paul. Not quite. It's what causes you to have money."

"Oh!" said Paul vaguely. "I thought when Uncle Oscar said *filthy lucker*, it meant money."

"*Filthy lucre* does mean money," said the mother. "But it's lucre, not luck."

"Oh!" said the boy. "Then what *is* luck, Mother?"

"It's what causes you to have money. If you're lucky you have money. That's why it's better to be born lucky than rich. If you're rich, you may lose your money. But if you're lucky, you will always get more money."

"Oh! Will you? And is Father not lucky?"

"Very unlucky, I should say," she said bitterly.

The boy watched her with unsure eyes.

"Why?" he asked.

"I don't know. Nobody ever knows why one person is lucky and another unlucky."

"Don't they? Nobody at all? Does *nobody* know?"

"Perhaps God. But He never tells."

"He ought to, then. And aren't you lucky either, Mother?"

"I can't be, if I married an unlucky husband."

"But by yourself, aren't you?"

"I used to think I was, before I married. Now I think I am very unlucky indeed."

"Why?"

"Well — never mind! Perhaps I'm not really," she said.

The child looked at her, to see if she meant it. But he saw, by the lines of her mouth, that she was only trying to hide something from him.

"Well, anyhow," he said stoutly, "I'm a lucky person."

"Why?" said his mother, with a sudden laugh.

He stared at her. He didn't even know why he had said it.

"God told me," he asserted, brazening it out.

"I hope He did, dear!" she said, again with a laugh, but rather bitter.

"He did, Mother!"

"Excellent!" said the mother.

The boy saw she did not believe him; or, rather, that she paid no attention to his assertion. This angered him somewhat, and made him want to compel her attention.

He went off by himself, vaguely, in a childish way, seeking for the clue to "luck." Absorbed, taking no heed of other people, he went about with a sort of stealth, seeking inwardly for luck. He wanted luck, he wanted it, he wanted it. When the two girls were playing dolls in the nursery, he would sit on his big rocking horse, charging madly into space, with a frenzy that made the little girls peer at him uneasily. Wildly the horse careered, the waving dark hair of the boy tossed, his eyes had a strange glare in them. The little girls dared not speak to him.

When he had ridden to the end of his mad little journey, he climbed down and stood in front of his rocking horse, staring fixedly into its lowered face. Its red mouth was slightly open, its big eye was wide and glassy-bright.

Now! he would silently command the snorting steed. Now, take me to where there is luck! Now take me!

And he would slash the horse on the neck with the little whip he had asked Uncle Oscar for. He *knew* the horse could take him to where there was luck, if only he forced it. So he would mount again, and start on his furious ride, hoping at last to get there. He knew he could get there.

"You'll break your horse, Paul!" said the nurse.

"He's always riding like that! I wish he'd leave off!" said his elder sister Joan.

But he only glared down on them in silence. Nurse gave him up. She could make nothing of him. Anyhow he was growing beyond her.

One day his mother and his uncle Oscar came in when he was on one of his furious rides. He did not speak to them.

"Hallo, you young jockey! Riding a winner?" said his uncle.

"Aren't you growing too big for a rocking horse? You're not a very little boy any longer, you know," said his mother.

But Paul only gave a blue glare from his big, rather close-set eyes. He would speak to nobody when he was in full tilt. His mother watched him with an anxious expression on her face.

At last he suddenly stopped forcing his horse into the mechanical gallop, and slid down.

"Well, I got there!" he announced fiercely, his blue eyes still flaring, and his sturdy long legs straddling apart.

"Where did you get to?" asked his mother.

"Where I wanted to go," he flared back at her.

"That's right, son!" said Uncle Oscar. "Don't you stop till you get there. What's the horse's name?"

"He doesn't have a name," said the boy.

"Gets on without all right?" asked the uncle.

"Well, he has different names. He was called Sansovino last week."

"Sansovino, eh? Won the Ascot. How did you know his name?"

"He always talks about horse races with Bassett," said Joan.

The uncle was delighted to find that his small nephew was posted with all the racing news. Bassett, the young gardener, who had been wounded in the left foot in the war and had got his present job through Oscar Cresswell, whose batman he had been, was a perfect blade of the "turf." He lived in the racing events, and the small boy lived with him.

Oscar Cresswell got it all from Bassett.

"Master Paul comes and asks me, so I can't do more than tell him, sir," said Bassett, his face terribly serious, as if he were speaking of religious matters.

"And does he ever put anything on a horse he fancies?"

"Well — I don't want to give him away — he's a young sport, a fine sport, sir. Would you mind asking him himself? He sort of takes a pleasure in it, and perhaps he'd feel I was giving him away, sir, if you don't mind."

Bassett was serious as a church.

The uncle went back to his nephew and took him off for a ride in the car.

"Say, Paul, old man, do you ever put anything on a horse?" the uncle asked.

The boy watched the handsome man closely.

"Why, do you think I oughtn't to?" he parried.

"Not a bit of it! I thought perhaps you might give me a tip for the Lincoln."

The car sped on into the country, going down to Uncle Oscar's place in Hampshire.

"Honor bright?" said the nephew.

"Honor bright, son!" said the uncle.

"Well, then, Daffodil."

"Daffodil! I doubt it, sonny. What about Mirza?"

"I only know the winner," said the boy. "That's Daffodil."

"Daffodil, eh?"

There was a pause. Daffodil was an obscure horse comparatively.

"Uncle!"

"Yes, son?"

"You won't let it go any further, will you? I promised Bassett."

"Bassett be damned, old man! What's he got to do with it?"

"We're partners. We've been partners from the first. Uncle, he lent me my first five shillings, which I lost. I promised him, honor bright, it was only between me and him; only you gave me that ten-shilling note I started winning with, so I thought you were lucky. You won't let it go any further, will you?"

The boy gazed at his uncle from those big, hot, blue eyes, set rather close together. The uncle stirred and laughed uneasily.

"Right you are, son! I'll keep your tip private. Daffodil, eh? How much are you putting on him?"

"All except twenty pounds," said the boy. "I keep that in reserve."

The uncle thought it a good joke.

"You keep twenty pounds in reserve, do you, you young romancer? What are you betting, then?"

"I'm betting three hundred," said the boy gravely. "But it's between you and me, Uncle Oscar! Honor bright?"

The uncle burst into a roar of laughter.

"It's between you and me all right, you young Nat Gould," he said, laughing. "But where's your three hundred?"

"Bassett keeps it for me. We're partners."

"You are, are you! And what is Bassett putting on Daffodil?"

"He won't go quite as high as I do, I expect. Perhaps he'll go a hundred and fifty."

"What, pennies?" laughed the uncle.

"Pounds," said the child, with a surprised look at his uncle. "Bassett keeps a bigger reserve than I do."

Between wonder and amusement Uncle Oscar was silent. He pursued the matter no further, but he determined to take his nephew with him to the Lincoln races.

"Now, son," he said, "I'm putting twenty on Mirza, and I'll put five for you on any horse you fancy. What's your pick?"

"Daffodil, Uncle."

"No, not the fiver on Daffodil!"

"I should if it was my own fiver," said the child.

"Good! Good! Right you are! A fiver for me and a fiver for you on Daffodil."

The child had never been to a race meeting before, and his eyes were blue fire. He pursed his mouth tight, and watched. A Frenchman just in front had put his money on Lancelot. Wild with excitement, he flailed his arms up and down, yelling *"Lancelot! Lancelot!"* in his French accent.

Daffodil came in first, Lancelot second, Mirza third. The child, flushed and with eyes blazing, was curiously serene. His uncle brought him four five-pound notes, four to one.

"What am I to do with these?" he cried, waving them before the boy's eyes.

"I suppose we'll talk to Bassett," said the boy. "I expect I have fifteen hundred now; and twenty in reserve; and this twenty."

His uncle studied him for some moments.

"Look here, son!" he said. "You're not serious about Bassett and that fifteen hundred, are you?"

"Yes, I am. But it's between you and me, Uncle. Honor bright!"

"Honor bright all right, son! But I must talk to Bassett."

"If you'd like to be a partner, Uncle, with Bassett and me, we could all be partners. Only, you'd have to promise, honor bright, Uncle, not to let it go beyond us three. Bassett and I are lucky, and you must be lucky, because it was your ten shillings I started winning with. . . ."

Uncle Oscar took both Bassett and Paul into Richmond Park for an afternoon, and there they talked.

"It's like this, you see, sir," Bassett said. "Master Paul would get me talking about racing events, spinning yarns, you know, sir. And he was always keen on knowing if I'd made or if I'd lost. It's about a year since, now, that I put five shillings on Blush of Dawn for him — and we lost. Then the luck turned, with that ten shillings he had from you, that we put on Singhalese. And since then, it's been pretty steady, all things considering. What do you say, Master Paul?"

"We're all right when we're sure," said Paul. "It's when we're not quite sure that we go down."

"Oh, but we're careful then," said Bassett.

"But when are you *sure*?" Uncle Oscar smiled.

"It's Master Paul, sir," said Bassett, in a secret, religious voice. "It's as if he had it from heaven. Like Daffodil, now, for the Lincoln. That was as sure as eggs."

"Did you put anything on Daffodil?" asked Oscar Cresswell.

"Yes, sir. I made my bit."

"And my nephew?"

Bassett was obstinately silent, looking at Paul.

"I made twelve hundred, didn't I, Bassett? I told Uncle I was putting three hundred on Daffodil."

"That's right," said Bassett, nodding.

"But where's the money?" asked the uncle.

"I keep it safe locked up, sir. Master Paul he can have it any minute he likes to ask for it.

"What, fifteen hundred pounds?"

"And twenty! And *forty*, that is, with the twenty he made on the course."

"It's amazing!" said the uncle.

"If Master Paul offers you to be partners, sir, I would, if I were you; if you'll excuse me," said Bassett.

Oscar Cresswell thought about it.

"I'll see the money," he said.

They drove home again, and sure enough, Bassett came round to the garden house with fifteen hundred pounds in notes. The twenty pounds reserve was left with Joe Glee, in the Turf Commission deposit.

"You see, it's all right, Uncle, when I'm *sure!* Then we go strong, for all we're worth. Don't we, Bassett?"

"We do that, Master Paul."

"And when are you sure?" said the uncle, laughing.

"Oh, well, sometimes I'm *absolutely* sure, like about Daffodil," said the boy; "and sometimes I have an idea; and sometimes I haven't even an idea, have I, Bassett? Then we're careful, because we mostly go down."

"You do, do you! And when you're sure, like about Daffodil, what makes you sure, sonny?"

"Oh, well, I don't know," said the boy uneasily. "I'm sure, you know, Uncle; that's all."

"It's as if he had it from heaven, sir," Bassett reiterated.

"I should say so!" said the uncle.

But he became a partner. And when the Leger was coming on, Paul was "sure" about Lively Spark, which was a quite inconsiderable horse. The boy insisted on putting a thousand on the horse, Bassett went for five hundred, and Oscar Cresswell two hundred. Lively Spark came in first, and the betting had been ten to one against him. Paul had made ten thousand.

"You see," he said, "I was absolutely sure of him."

Even Oscar Cresswell had cleared two thousand.

"Look here, son," he said, "this sort of thing makes me nervous."

"It needn't, Uncle! Perhaps I shan't be sure again for a long time."

"But what are you going to do with your money?" asked the uncle.

"Of course," said the boy. "I started it for Mother. She said she had no luck, because Father is unlucky, so I thought if *I* was lucky, it might stop whispering."

"What might stop whispering?"

"Our house. I *hate* our house for whispering."

"What does it whisper?"

"Why — why" — the boy fidgeted — "why, I don't know. But it's always short of money, you know, Uncle."

"I know it, son, I know it."

"You know people send Mother writs, don't you, Uncle?"

"I'm afraid I do," said the uncle.

"And then the house whispers, like people laughing at you behind your back. It's awful, that is! I thought if I was lucky. . . ."

"You might stop it," added the uncle.

The boy watched him with big blue eyes, that had an uncanny cold fire in them, and he said never a word.

"Well, then!" said the uncle. "What are we doing?"

"I shouldn't like Mother to know I was lucky," said the boy.

"Why not, son?"

"She'd stop me."

"I don't think she would."

"Oh!" — and the boy writhed in an odd way — "I *don't* want her to know, Uncle."

"All right, son! We'll manage it without her knowing."

They managed it very easily. Paul, at the other's suggestion, handed over five thousand pounds to his uncle, who deposited it with the family lawyer, who was then to inform Paul's mother that a relative had put five thousand pounds into his hands, which sum was to be paid out a thousand pounds at a time, on the mother's birthday, for the next five years.

"So she'll have a birthday present of a thousand pounds for five successive years," said Uncle Oscar. "I hope it won't make it all the harder for her later."

Paul's mother had her birthday in November. The house had been "whispering" worse than ever lately, and, even in spite of his luck, Paul could not bear up against it. He was very anxious to see the effect of the birthday letter, telling his mother about the thousand pounds.

When there were no visitors, Paul now took his meals with his parents, as he was beyond the nursery control. His mother went into town nearly every day. She had discovered that she had an odd knack of sketching furs and dress materials, so she worked secretly in the studio of a friend who was the chief artist for the leading drapers. She drew the figures of ladies in furs and ladies in silk and sequins for the newspaper advertisements. This young woman artist earned several thousand pounds a year, but Paul's mother only made several hundreds, and she was again dissatisfied. She so wanted to be first in something, and she did not succeed, even in making sketches for drapery advertisements.

She was down to breakfast on the morning of her birthday. Paul watched her face as she read her letters. He knew the lawyer's letter. As his mother read it, her face hardened and became more expressionless. Then a cold, determined look came on her mouth. She hid the letter under the pile of others, and said not a word about it.

"Didn't you have anything nice in the post for your birthday, Mother?" said Paul.

"Quite moderately nice," she said, her voice cold and absent.

She went away to town without saying more.

But in the afternoon Uncle Oscar appeared. He said Paul's mother had had a long interview with the lawyer, asking if the whole five thousand could not be advanced at once, as she was in debt.

"What do you think, Uncle?" said the boy.

"I leave it to you, son."

"Oh, let her have it, then! We can get some more with the other," said the boy.

"A bird in the hand is worth two in the bush, laddie!" said Uncle Oscar.

"But I'm sure to *know* for the Grand National; or the Lincolnshire; or else the Derby. I'm sure to know for *one* of them," said Paul.

So Uncle Oscar signed the agreement, and Paul's mother touched the whole five thousand. Then something very curious happened. The voices in the house suddenly went mad, like a chorus of frogs on a spring evening. There were certain new furnishings, and Paul had a tutor. He was *really* going to Eton, his father's school, in the following autumn. There were flowers in the winter, and a blossoming of the luxury Paul's mother had been used to. And yet the voices in the house, behind the sprays of mimosa and almond blossom, and from under the piles of iridescent cushions, simply trilled and screamed in a sort of ecstasy: "There *must* be more money! Oh-h-h; there *must* be more money. Oh, now, now-w! Now-w-w — there *must* be more money! — more than ever! More than ever!"

It frightened Paul terribly. He studied away at his Latin and Greek. But his intense hours were spent with Bassett. The Grand National had gone by; he had not "known," and had lost a hundred pounds. Summer was at hand. He was in agony for the Lincoln. But even for the Lincoln he didn't "know," and he lost fifty pounds. He became wild-eyed and strange, as if something were going to explode in him.

"Let it alone, son! Don't you bother about it!" urged Uncle Oscar. But it was as if the boy couldn't really hear what his uncle was saying.

"I've got to know for the Derby! I've got to know for the Derby!" the child reiterated, his big blue eyes blazing with a sort of madness.

His mother noticed how overwrought he was.

"You'd better go to the seaside. Wouldn't you like to go now to the seaside, instead of waiting? I think you'd better," she said, looking down at him anxiously, her heart curiously heavy because of him.

But the child lifted his uncanny blue eyes. "I couldn't possibly go before the Derby, Mother!" he said. "I couldn't possibly!"

"Why not?" she said, her voice becoming heavy when she was opposed. "Why not? You can still go from the seaside to see the Derby with your uncle Oscar, if that's what you wish. No need for you to wait here. Besides, I think you care too much about these races. It's a bad sign. My family has been a gambling family, and you won't know till you grow up how much damage it has done. But it has done damage. I shall have to send Bassett away, and ask Uncle Oscar not to talk racing to you, unless you promise to be reasonable about it; go away to the seaside and forget it. You're all nerves!"

"I'll do what you like, Mother, so long as you don't send me away till after the Derby," the boy said.

"Send you away from where? Just from this house?"

"Yes," he said, gazing at her.

"Why, you curious child, what makes you care about this house so much, suddenly? I never knew you loved it."

He gazed at her without speaking. He had a secret within a secret, something he had not divulged, even to Bassett or to his uncle Oscar.

But his mother, after standing undecided and a little bit sullen for some moments, said:

"Very well, then! Don't go to the seaside till after the Derby, if you don't wish it. But promise me you won't let your nerves go to pieces. Promise you won't think so much about horse racing and *events*, as you call them!"

"Oh, no," said the boy casually. "I won't think much about them, Mother. You needn't worry. I wouldn't worry, Mother, if I were you."

"If you were me and I were you," said his mother, "I wonder what we *should* do!"

"But you know you needn't worry, Mother, don't you?" the boy repeated.

"I should be awfully glad to know it," she said wearily.

"Oh, well, you *can*, you know. I mean, you *ought* to know you needn't worry," he insisted.

"Ought I? Then I'll see about it," she said.

Paul's secret of secrets was his wooden horse, that which had no name. Since he was emancipated from a nurse and a nursery governess, he had had his rocking horse removed to his own bedroom at the top of the house.

"Surely, you're too big for a rocking horse!" his mother had remonstrated.

"Well, you see, Mother, till I can have a *real* horse, I like to have *some* sort of animal about," had been his quaint answer.

"Do you feel he keeps you company?" She laughed.

"Oh, yes! He's very good, he always keeps me company, when I'm there," said Paul.

So the horse, rather shabby, stood in an arrested prance in the boy's bedroom.

The Derby was drawing near, and the boy grew more and more tense. He hardly heard what was spoken to him, he was very frail, and his eyes were really uncanny. His mother had sudden strange seizures of uneasiness about him. Sometimes, for half an hour, she would feel a sudden anxiety about him that was almost anguish. She wanted to rush to him at once, and know he was safe.

Two nights before the Derby, she was at a big party in town, when one of her rushes of anxiety about her boy, her firstborn, gripped her heart till she could hardly speak. She fought with the feeling, might and main, for she believed in common sense. But it was too strong. She had to leave the dance and go downstairs to telephone to the country. The children's nursery governess was terribly surprised and startled at being rung up in the night.

"Are the children all right, Miss Wilmot?"

"Oh, yes, they are quite all right."

"Master Paul? Is he all right?"

"He went to bed as right as a trivet. Shall I run up and look at him?"

"No," said Paul's mother reluctantly. "No! Don't trouble. It's all right. Don't sit up. We shall be home fairly soon." She did not want her son's privacy intruded upon.

"Very good," said the governess.

It was about one o'clock when Paul's mother and father drove up to their house. All was still. Paul's mother went to her room and slipped off her white fur cloak. She had told her maid not to wait up for her. She heard her husband downstairs, mixing a whisky and soda.

And then, because of the strange anxiety at her heart, she stole upstairs to her son's room. Noiselessly she went along the upper corridor. Was there a faint noise? What was it?

She stood, with arrested muscles, outside his door, listening. There was a strange, heavy, and yet not loud noise. Her heart stood still. It was a soundless noise, yet rushing and powerful. Something huge, in violent, hushed motion. What was it? What in God's name was it? She ought to know. She felt that she knew the noise. She knew what it was.

Yet she could not place it. She couldn't say what it was. And on and on it went, like a madness.

Softly, frozen with anxiety and fear, she turned the door handle.

The room was dark. Yet in the space near the window, she heard and saw something plunging to and fro. She gazed in fear and amazement.

Then suddenly she switched on the light, and saw her son, in his green pajamas, madly surging on the rocking horse. The blaze of light suddenly lit him up, as he urged the wooden horse, and lit her up, as she stood, blonde, in her dress of pale green and crystal, in the doorway.

"Paul!" she cried. "Whatever are you doing?"

"It's Malabar!" he screamed, in a powerful, strange voice. "It's Malabar!"

His eyes blazed at her for one strange and senseless second, as he ceased urging his wooden horse. Then he fell with a crash to the ground, and she, all her tormented motherhood flooding upon her, rushed to gather him up.

But he was unconscious, and unconscious he remained, with some brain fever. He talked and tossed, and his mother sat stonily by his side.

"Malabar! It's Malabar! Bassett, Bassett, I *know!* It's Malabar!"

So the child cried, trying to get up and urge the rocking horse that gave him his inspiration.

"What does he mean by Malabar?" asked the heart-frozen mother.

"I don't know," said the father stonily.

"What does he mean by Malabar?" she asked her brother Oscar.

"It's one of the horses running for the Derby," was the answer.

And, in spite of himself, Oscar Cresswell spoke to Bassett, and himself put a thousand on Malabar: at fourteen to one.

The third day of the illness was critical: they were waiting for a change. The boy, with his rather long, curly hair, was tossing ceaselessly on the pillow. He neither slept nor regained consciousness, and his eyes were like blue stones. His mother sat, feeling her heart had gone, turned actually into a stone.

In the evening, Oscar Cresswell did not come, but Bassett sent a message, saying could he come up for one moment, just one moment? Paul's mother was very angry at the intrusion, but on second thought she agreed. The boy was the same. Perhaps Bassett might bring him to consciousness.

The gardener, a shortish fellow with a little brown mustache, and sharp little brown eyes, tiptoed into the room, touched his imaginary cap to Paul's mother, and stole to the bedside, staring with glittering, smallish eyes at the tossing, dying child.

"Master Paul!" he whispered. "Master Paul! Malabar came in first all right, a clean win. I did as you told me. You've made over seventy thousand pounds, you have; you've got over eighty thousand. Malabar came in all right, Master Paul."

"Malabar! Malabar! Did I say Malabar, Mother? Did I say Malabar? Do you think I'm lucky, Mother? I knew Malabar, didn't I? Over eighty thousand pounds! I call that lucky, don't you, Mother? Over eighty thousand pounds! I knew, didn't I know I knew? Malabar came in all right. If I ride my horse till I'm sure, then I tell you, Bassett, you can go as high as you like. Did you go for all you were worth, Bassett?"

"I went a thousand on it, Master Paul."

"I never told you, Mother, that if I can ride my horse, and *get there,* then I'm absolutely sure — oh, absolutely! Mother, did I ever tell you? I *am* lucky!"

"No, you never did," said the mother.

But the boy died in the night.

And even as he lay dead, his mother heard her brother's voice saying to her: "My God, Hester, you're eighty-odd thousand to the good, and a poor devil of a son to the bad. But, poor devil, poor devil, he's best gone out of a life where he rides his rocking horse to find a winner."

[1926]

KATHERINE MANSFIELD (1888–1923) *was born Kathleen Mansfield Beauchamp in Wellington, New Zealand. She persuaded her father, a banker and industrialist, to send her to London in 1903 to study the cello. After a brief return to New Zealand, which she hated for its provincialism and isolation, she went back to London with a small allowance from her family, deciding to become a writer instead of a musician after meeting such literary people as D. H. Lawrence and Virginia Woolf. Mansfield's first book of short stories,* In a German Pension, *was published in 1911. In the same year she met the literary critic and journalist John Middleton Murry, who became her husband in 1918.* Bliss and Other Stories (1920) *established her reputation and was followed by* The Garden Party (1922). *Mansfield took Anton Chekhov as her model, but after she was stricken with tuberculosis in 1918 she found it difficult to continue to work. In her posthumously published* Journal (1927), *she often upbraided herself when her vitality waned and she felt too ill to write: "Look at the stories that wait and wait just at the threshold. Why don't I let them in? And their place would be taken by others who are lurking beyond just there—waiting for the chance." Finally she sought a cure for her illness at the Gurdjieff Institute in France, an establishment run by the noted Armenian mystic Georges Ivanovitch Gurdjieff, whose methods combined spiritual and physical healing. She died at the institute a few months after her thirty-fourth birthday.*

Eighty-eight of Mansfield's stories have been published (including fifteen left unfinished), and they have had a great influence on the development of the literary form. Like Chekhov and James Joyce, she simplified her plot to intensify the story's emotional impact, dramatizing small moments to reveal the larger significance in the lives of people, or, as Willa Cather observed, approaching "the major forces of life through comparatively trivial incidents." Mansfield developed her own technique of prose narration. She presented a decisive psychological moment when a character's life is illuminated in an unforgettable manner. Her stories affected later writers as powerfully as Chekhov's stories had affected her. "Bliss," in which she depicts the secret and passionate lives of individuals flowing treacherously beneath the seemingly smooth and harmonious surface of a marriage, shows the purity of her style.

The setting of most of Mansfield's stories is Europe, but the death of her beloved younger brother in World War I made her reconsider her memories of New Zealand and dedicate herself to recreating life as she remembered it there as a child. Mansfield was triumphant when she heard that the local printer who set the type for her first work based on her New Zealand memories exclaimed on reading the manuscript, "My! But these kids are real." *"The Doll's House" is set in New Zealand, and its details about the village school where children from all the social classes mingle is true to the experience Mansfield herself had in a small township called Karori, a few miles from Wellington, where she attended school. (See Cather's Commentary about Mansfield on page 1277.)*

Katherine Mansfield

ᔕᔓ

Bliss

Although Bertha Young was thirty she still had moments like this when she wanted to run instead of walk, to take dancing steps on and off the pavement, to bowl a hoop, to throw something up in the air and catch it again, or to stand still and laugh at—nothing—at nothing, simply.

What can you do if you are thirty and, turning the corner of your own street, you are overcome, suddenly, by a feeling of bliss—absolute bliss!—as though you'd suddenly swallowed a bright piece of that late afternoon sun and it burned in your bosom, sending out a little shower of sparks into every particle, into every finger and toe? . . .

Oh, is there no way you can express it without being "drunk and disorderly"? How idiotic civilization is! Why be given a body if you have to keep it shut up in a case like a rare, rare fiddle?

"No, that about the fiddle is not quite what I mean," she thought, running up the steps and feeling in her bag for the key—she's forgotten it, as usual—and rattling the letter-box. "It's not what I mean, because—— Thank you, Mary"—she went into the hall. "Is nurse back?"

"Yes, M'm."

"And has the fruit come?"

"Yes, M'm. Everything's come."

"Bring the fruit up to the dining-room, will you? I'll arrange it before I go upstairs."

It was dusky in the dining-room and quite chilly. But all the same Bertha threw off her coat; she could not bear the tight clasp of it another moment, and the cold air fell on her arms.

But in her bosom there was still that bright glowing place—that shower of little sparks coming from it. It was almost unbearable. She hardly dared to breathe for fear of fanning it higher, and yet she breathed deeply, deeply. She hardly dared to look into the cold mirror—but she did look, and it gave her back a woman, radiant, with smiling, trembling lips, with big, dark eyes and an air of listening, waiting for something . . . divine to happen . . . that she knew must happen . . . infallibly.

Mary brought in the fruit on a tray and with it a glass bowl, and a blue dish, very lovely, with a strange sheen on it as though it had been dipped in milk.

"Shall I turn on the light, M'm?"

"No, thank you. I can see quite well."

There were tangerines and apples stained with strawberry pink. Some yellow pears, smooth as silk, some white grapes covered with a silver bloom and a big cluster of purple ones. These last she had bought to tone in with the new dining-room carpet. Yes, that did sound rather far-fetched and absurd, but it was really why she had bought them. She had thought in the shop: "I must have some purple ones to bring the carpet up to the table." And it had seemed quite sense at the time.

When she had finished with them and had made two pyramids of these bright round shapes, she stood away from the table to get the effect — and it really was most curious. For the dark table seemed to melt into the dusky light and the glass dish and the blue bowl to float in the air. This, of course in her present mood, was so incredibly beautiful. . . . She began to laugh.

"No, no. I'm getting hysterical." And she seized her bag and coat and ran upstairs to the nursery.

Nurse sat at a low table giving Little B her supper after her bath. The baby had on a white flannel gown and a blue woollen jacket, and her dark, fine hair was brushed up into a funny little peak. She looked up when she saw her mother and began to jump.

"Now, my lovey, eat it up like a good girl," said Nurse, setting her lips in a way that Bertha knew, and that meant she had come into the nursery at another wrong moment.

"Has she been good, Nanny?"

"She's been a little sweet all the afternoon," whispered Nanny. "We went to the park and I sat down on a chair and took her out of the pram and a big dog came along and put his head on my knee and she clutched its ear, tugged it. Oh, you should have seen her."

Bertha wanted to ask if it wasn't rather dangerous to let her clutch at a strange dog's ear. But she did not dare to. She stood watching them, her hands by her side, like the poor little girl in front of the rich little girl with the doll.

The baby looked up at her again, stared, and then smiled so charmingly that Bertha couldn't help crying:

"Oh, Nanny, do let me finish giving her her supper while you put the bath things away."

"Well, M'm, she oughtn't to be changed hands while she's eating," said Nanny, still whispering. "It unsettles her; it's very likely to upset her."

How absurd it was. Why have a baby if it has to be kept — not in a case like a rare, rare fiddle — but in another woman's arms?

"Oh, I must!" said she.

Very offended, Nanny handed her over.

"Now, don't excite her after her supper. You know you do, M'm. And I have such a time with her after!"

Thank heaven! Nanny went out of the room with the bath towels.

"Now I've got you to myself, my little precious," said Bertha, as the baby leaned against her.

She ate delightfully, holding up her lips for the spoon and then waving her hands. Sometimes she wouldn't let the spoon go; and sometimes, just as Bertha had filled it, she waved it away to the four winds.

When the soup was finished Bertha turned round to the fire.

"You're nice — you're very nice!" said she, kissing her warm baby. "I'm fond of you. I like you."

And, indeed, she loved Little B so much — her neck as she bent forward, her exquisite toes as they shone transparent in the firelight — that all her feeling of bliss came back again, and again she didn't know how to express it — what to do with it.

"You're wanted on the telephone," said Nanny, coming back in triumph and seizing *her* Little B.

Down she flew. It was Harry.

"Oh, is that you, Ber? Look here. I'll be late. I'll take a taxi and come along as quickly as I can, but get dinner put back ten minutes — will you? All right?"

"Yes, perfectly. Oh, Harry!"

"Yes?"

What had she to say? She'd nothing to say. She only wanted to get in touch with him for a moment. She couldn't absurdly cry: "Hasn't it been a divine day!"

"What is it?" rapped out the little voice.

"Nothing. *Entendu*," said Bertha, and hung up the receiver, thinking how more than idiotic civilization was.

They had people coming to dinner. The Norman Knights — a very sound couple — he was about to start a theater, and she was awfully keen on interior decoration, a young man, Eddie Warren, who had just published a little book of poems and whom everybody was asking to dine, and a "find" of Bertha's called Pearl Fulton. What Miss Fulton did, Bertha didn't know. They had met at the club and Bertha had fallen in love with her, as she always did fall in love with beautiful women who had something strange about them.

The provoking thing was that, though they had been about together and met a number of times and really talked, Bertha couldn't yet make her out. Up to a certain point Miss Fulton was rarely, wonderfully frank, but the certain point was there, and beyond that she would not go.

Was there anything beyond it? Harry said "No." Voted her dullish, and "cold like all blond women, with a touch, perhaps, of anæmia of the brain." But Bertha wouldn't agree with him; not yet, at any rate.

"No, the way she has of sitting with her head a little on one side, and smiling, has something behind it, Harry, and I must find out what that something is."

"Most likely it's a good stomach," answered Harry.

He made a point of catching Bertha's heels with replies of that kind ... "liver frozen, my dear girl," or "pure flatulence," or "kidney disease," ... and so on. For some strange reason Bertha liked this, and almost admired it in him very much.

She went into the drawing-room and lighted the fire; then, picking up the cushions, one by one, that Mary had disposed so carefully, she threw them back on to the chairs and the couches. That made all the difference; the room came alive at once. As she was about to throw the last one she surprised herself by suddenly hugging it to her, passionately, passionately. But it did not put out the fire in her bosom. Oh, on the contrary!

The windows of the drawing-room opened on to a balcony overlooking the garden. At the far end, against the wall, there was a tall, slender pear tree in fullest, richest bloom; it stood perfect, as though becalmed against the jade-green sky. Bertha couldn't help feeling, even from this distance, that it had not a single bud or a faded petal. Down below, in the garden beds, the red and yellow tulips, heavy with flowers, seemed to lean upon the dusk. A grey cat, dragging its belly, crept across the lawn, and a black one, its shadow, trailed after. The sight of them, so intent and so quick, gave Bertha a curious shiver.

"What creepy things cats are!" she stammered, and she turned away from the window and began walking up and down. . . .

How strong the jonquils smelled in the warm room. Too strong? Oh, no. And yet, as though overcome, she flung down on a couch and pressed her hands to her eyes.

"I'm too happy — too happy!" she murmured.

And she seemed to see on her eyelids the lovely pear tree with its wide open blossoms as a symbol of her own life.

Really — really — she had everything. She was young. Harry and she were as much in love as ever, and they got on together splendidly and were really good pals. She had an adorable baby. They didn't have to worry about money. They had this absolutely satisfactory house and garden. And friends — modern, thrilling friends, writers and painters and poets or people keen on social questions — just the kind of friends they wanted. And then there were books, and there was music, and she had found a wonderful little dressmaker, and they were going abroad in the summer, and their new cook made the most superb omelettes. . . .

"I'm absurd! Absurd!" She sat up; but she felt quite dizzy, quite drunk. It must have been the spring.

Yes, it was the spring. Now she was so tired she could not drag herself upstairs to dress.

A white dress, a string of jade beads, green shoes and stockings. It wasn't intentional. She had thought of this scheme hours before she stood at the drawing-room window.

Her petals rushed softly into the hall, and she kissed Mrs. Norman Knight, who was taking off the most amusing orange coat with a procession of black monkeys round the hem and up the fronts.

". . . Why! Why! Why is the middle-class so stodgy — so utterly without a sense of humor! My dear, it's only a fluke that I am here at all — Norman being the protective fluke. For my darling monkeys so upset the train that it rose to a man and simply ate me with its eyes. Didn't laugh — wasn't amused — that I should have loved. No, just stared — and bored me through and through."

"But the cream of it was," said Norman, pressing a large tortoiseshell-rimmed monocle into his eye, "you don't mind me telling this, Face, do you?" (In their home and among their friends they called each other Face and Mug.) "The cream of it was when she, being full fed, turned to the woman beside her and said: 'Haven't you cvcr sccn a monkey before?'"

"Oh, yes!" Mrs. Norman Knight joined in the laughter. "Wasn't that too absolutely creamy?"

And a funnier thing still was that now her coat was off she did look like a very intelligent monkey — who had even made that yellow silk dress out of scraped banana skins. And her amber earrings; they were like little dangling nuts.

"This is a sad, sad fall!" said Mug, pausing in front of Little B's perambulator. "When the perambulator comes into the hall ——" and he waved the rest of the quotation away.

The bell rang. It was lean, pale Eddie Warren (as usual) in a state of acute distress.

"It *is* the right house, *isn't* it?" he pleaded.

"Oh, I think so — I hope so," said Bertha brightly.

"I have had such a *dreadful* experience with a taxi-man; he was *most* sinister. I couldn't get him to *stop*. The *more* I knocked and called the *faster* he went. And *in* the moonlight this *bizarre* figure with the *flattened* head *crouching* over the *lit-tle* wheel. . . ."

He shuddered, taking off an immense white silk scarf. Bertha noticed that his socks were white, too — most charming.

"But how dreadful!" she cried.

"Yes, it really was," said Eddie, following her into the drawing-room. "I saw myself *driving* through Eternity in a *timeless* taxi."

He knew the Norman Knights. In fact, he was going to write a play for N. K. when the theater scheme came off.

"Well, Warren, how's the play?" said Norman Knight, dropping his monocle and giving his eye a moment in which to rise to the surface before it was screwed down again.

And Mrs. Norman Knight: "Oh, Mr. Warren, what happy socks!"

"I *am* so glad you like them," said he, staring at his feet. "They seem to have got so *much* whiter since the moon rose." And he turned his lean sorrowful young face to Bertha. "There *is* a moon, you know."

She wanted to cry: "I am sure there is — often — often!"

He really was a most attractive person. But so was Face, crouched before the fire in her banana skins, and so was Mug, smoking a cigarette and saying as he flicked the ash: "Why doth the bridegroom tarry?"

"There he is, now."

Bang went the front door open and shut. Harry shouted: "Hullo, you people. Down in five minutes." And they heard him swarm up the stairs. Bertha couldn't help smiling; she knew how he loved doing things at high pressure. What, after all, did an extra five minutes matter? But he would pretend to himself that they mattered beyond measure. And then he would make a great point of coming into the drawing-room, extravagantly cool and collected.

Harry had such a zest for life. Oh, how she appreciated it in him. And his passion for fighting — for seeking in everything that came up against him another test of his power and of his courage — that, too, she understood. Even when it made him just occasionally, to other people, who didn't know him well, a little ridiculous perhaps. . . . For there were moments when he rushed into battle where no battle was. . . . She talked and laughed and positively forgot until he had come in (just as she had imagined) that Pearl Fulton had not turned up.

"I wonder if Miss Fulton has forgotten?"

"I expect so," said Harry. "Is she on the 'phone?"

"Ah! There's a taxi, now." And Bertha smiled with that little air of proprietorship that she always assumed while her women finds were new and mysterious. "She lives in taxis."

"She'll run to fat if she does," said Harry coolly, ringing the bell for dinner. "Frightful danger for blond women."

"Harry — don't," warned Bertha, laughing up at him.

Came another tiny moment, while they waited, laughing and talking, just a trifle too much at their ease, a trifle too unaware. And then Miss Fulton, all in silver, with a silver fillet binding her pale blond hair, came in smiling, her head a little on one side.

"Am I late?"

"No, not at all," said Bertha. "Come along." And she took her arm and they moved into the dining-room.

What was there in the touch of that cool arm that could fan — fan —

start blazing — blazing — the fire of bliss that Bertha did not know what to do with?

Miss Fulton did not look at her; but then she seldom did look at people directly. Her heavy eyelids lay upon her eyes and the strange half smile came and went upon her lips as though she lived by listening rather than seeing. But Bertha knew, suddenly, as if the longest, most intimate look had passed between them — as if they had said to each other: "You, too?" — that Pearl Fulton, stirring the beautiful red soup in the grey plate, was feeling just what she was feeling.

And the others? Face and Mug, Eddie and Harry, their spoons rising and falling — dabbing their lips with their napkins, crumbling bread, fiddling with the forks and glasses and talking.

"I met her at the Alpha shore — the weirdest little person. She'd not only cut off her hair, but she seemed to have taken a dreadfully good snip off her legs and arms and her neck and her poor little nose as well."

"Isn't she very *liée*[1] with Michael Oat?"

"The man who wrote *Love in False Teeth?*"

"He wants to write a play for me. One act. One man. Decides to commit suicide. Gives all the reasons why he should and why he shouldn't. And just as he has made up his mind either to do it or not to do it — curtain. Not half a bad idea."

"What's he going to call it — 'Stomach Trouble'?"

"I *think* I've come across the *same* idea in a lit-tle French review, *quite* unknown in England."

No, they didn't share it. They were dears — dears — and she loved having them there, at her table, and giving them delicious food and wine. In fact, she longed to tell them how delightful they were, and what a decorative group they made, how they seemed to set one another off and how they reminded her of a play by Tchekof!

Harry was enjoying his dinner. It was part of his — well, not his nature, exactly, and certainly not his pose — his — something or other — to talk about food and to glory in his "shameless passion for the white flesh of the lobster" and "the green of pistachio ices — green and cold like the eyelids of Egyptian dancers."

When he looked up at her and said: "Bertha, this is a very admirable *soufflée!*" she almost could have wept with child-like pleasure.

Oh, why did she feel so tender toward the whole world tonight? Everything was good — was right. All that happened seemed to fill again her brimming cup of bliss.

And still, in the back of her mind, there was the pear tree. It would be silver now, in the light of poor dear Eddie's moon, silver as Miss Fulton, who sat there turning a tangerine in her slender fingers that were so pale a light seemed to come from them.

---

[1] linked or connected with; friendly with (the implication being that they are more than just "friends").

What she simply couldn't make out — what was miraculous — was how she should have guessed Miss Fulton's mood so exactly and so instantly. For she never doubted for a moment that she was right, and yet what had she to go on? Less than nothing.

"I believe this does happen very, very rarely between women. Never between men," thought Bertha. "But while I am making coffee in the drawing-room perhaps she will 'give a sign.'"

What she meant by that she did not know, and what would happen after that she could not imagine.

While she thought like this she saw herself talking and laughing. She had to talk because of her desire to laugh.

"I must laugh or die."

But when she noticed Face's funny little habit of tucking something down the front of her bodice — as if she kept a tiny, secret hoard of nuts there, too — Bertha had to dig her nails into her hands — so as not to laugh too much.

It was over at last. And: "Come and see my new coffee machine," said Bertha.

"We only have a new coffee machine once a fortnight," said Harry. Face took her arm this time; Miss Fulton bent her head and followed after.

The fire had died down in the drawing-room to a red, flickering "nest of baby phoenixes," said Face.

"Don't turn up the light for a moment. It is so lovely." And down she crouched by the fire again. She was always cold . . . "without her little red flannel jacket, of course," thought Bertha.

At that moment Miss Fulton "gave the sign."

"Have you a garden?" said the cool, sleepy voice.

This was so exquisite on her part that all Bertha could do was to obey. She crossed the room, pulled the curtains apart, and opened those long windows.

"There!" she breathed.

And the two women stood side by side looking at the slender, flowering tree. Although it was so still it seemed, like the flame of a candle, to stretch up, to point, to quiver in the bright air, to grow taller and taller as they gazed — almost to touch the rim of the round, silver moon.

How long did they stand there? Both, as it were, caught in that circle of unearthly light, understanding each other perfectly, creatures of another world, and wondering what they were to do in this one with all this blissful treasure that burned in their bosoms and dropped, in silver flowers, from their hair and hands?

Forever — for a moment? And did Miss Fulton murmur: "Yes. Just *that*." Or did Bertha dream it?

Then the light was snapped on and Face made the coffee and Harry said: "My dear Mrs. Knight, don't ask me about my baby. I never see her. I shan't feel the slightest interest in her until she has a lover," and Mug took his eye out of the conservatory for a moment and then put it under glass again and Eddie Warren drank his coffee and set down the cup with a face of anguish as though he had drunk and seen the spider.

"What I want to do is to give the young men a show. I believe London is simply teeming with first-chop, unwritten plays. What I want to say to 'em is: 'Here's the theater. Fire ahead.' "

"You know, my dear, I am going to decorate a room for the Jacob Nathans. Oh, I am so tempted to do a fried-fish scheme, with the backs of the chairs shaped like frying pans and lovely chip potatoes embroidered all over the curtains."

"The trouble with our young writing men is that they are still too romantic. You can't put out to sea without being seasick and wanting a basin. Well, why won't they have the courage of those basins?"

"A *dreadful* poem about a *girl* who was *violated* by a beggar *without* a nose in a lit-tle wood. . . ."

Miss Fulton sank into the lowest, deepest chair and Harry handed round the cigarettes.

From the way he stood in front of her shaking the silver box and saying abruptly: "Egyptian? Turkish? Virginian? They're all mixed up," Bertha realized that she not only bored him; he really disliked her. And she decided from the way Miss Fulton said: "No, thank you, I won't smoke," that she felt it, too, and was hurt.

"Oh, Harry, don't dislike her. You are quite wrong about her. She's wonderful, wonderful. And, besides, how can you feel so differently about someone who means so much to me? I shall try to tell you when we are in bed tonight what has been happening. What she and I have shared."

At those last words something strange and almost terrifying darted into Bertha's mind. And this something blind and smiling whispered to her: "Soon these people will go. The house will be quiet — quiet. The lights will be out. And you and he will be alone together in the dark room — the warm bed. . . ."

She jumped up from her chair and ran over to the piano.

"What a pity someone does not play!" she cried. "What a pity somebody does not play."

For the first time in her life Bertha Young desired her husband.

Oh, she loved him — she'd been in love with him, of course, in every other way, but just not in that way. And, equally, of course, she'd understood that he was different. They'd discussed it so often. It had worried her dreadfully at first to find that she was so cold, but after a time it had not seemed to matter. They were so frank with each other — such good pals. That was the best of being modern.

But now — ardently! ardently! The word ached in her ardent body! Was this what that feeling of bliss had been leading up to? But then — then ——

"My dear," said Mrs. Norman Knight, "you know our shame. We are the victims of time and train. We live in Hampstead. It's been so nice."

"I'll come with you into the hall," said Bertha. "I love having you. But you must not miss the last train. That's so awful, isn't it?"

"Have a whisky, Knight, before you go?" called Harry.

"No, thanks, old chap."

Bertha squeezed his hand for that as she shook it.

"Good night, good-bye," she cried from the top step, feeling that this self of hers was taking leave of them forever.

When she got back into the drawing-room the others were on the move.

". . . Then you can come part of the way in my taxi."

"I shall be *so* thankful *not* to have to face *another* drive *alone* after my *dreadful* experience."

"You can get a taxi at the rank just at the end of the street. You won't have to walk more than a few yards."

"That's comfort. I'll go and put on my coat."

Miss Fulton moved toward the hall and Bertha was following when Harry almost pushed past.

"Let me help you."

Bertha knew that he was repenting his rudeness — she let him go. What a boy he was in some ways — so impulsive — so — simple.

And Eddie and she were left by the fire.

"I *wonder* if you have seen Bilks' *new* poem called *Table d'Hôte*," said Eddie softly. "It's *so* wonderful. In the last Anthology. Have you got a copy? I'd *so* like to *show* it to you. It begins with an *incredibly* beautiful line: 'Why Must it Always be Tomato Soup?' "

"Yes," said Bertha. And she moved noiselessly to a table opposite the drawing-room door and Eddie glided noiselessly after her. She picked up the little book and gave it to him; they had not made a sound.

While he looked it up she turned her head toward the hall. And she saw . . . Harry with Miss Fulton's coat in his arms and Miss Fulton with her back turned to him and her head bent. He tossed the coat away, put his hands on her shoulders and turned her violently to him. His lips said: "I adore you," and Miss Fulton laid her moonbeam fingers on his cheeks and smiled her sleepy smile. Harry's nostrils quivered; his lips curled back in a hideous grin while he whispered: "Tomorrow," and with her eyelids Miss Fulton said: "Yes."

"Here it is," said Eddie. " 'Why Must it Always be Tomato Soup?' It's so *deeply* true, don't you feel? Tomato soup is so *dreadfully* eternal."

"If you prefer," said Harry's voice, very loud, from the hall, "I can 'phone you a cab to come to the door."

"Oh, no. It's not necessary," said Miss Fulton, and she came up to Bertha and gave her the slender fingers to hold.

"Good-bye. Thank you so much."

"Good-bye," said Bertha.

Miss Fulton held her hand a moment longer.

"Your lovely pear tree!" she murmured.

And then she was gone, with Eddie following, like the black cat following the grey cat.

"I'll shut up shop," said Harry, extravagantly cool and collected.

"Your lovely pear tree — pear tree — pear tree!"

Bertha simply ran over to the long windows.

"Oh, what is going to happen now?" she cried.

But the pear tree was as lovely as ever and as full of flower and as still.

[1920]

Katherine Mansfield

ကာ

THE DOLL'S HOUSE

When dear old Mrs. Hay went back to town after staying with the Burnells she sent the children a doll's house. It was so big that the carter and Pat carried it into the courtyard, and there it stayed, propped up on two wooden boxes beside the feed-room door. No harm could come to it; it was summer. And perhaps the smell of paint would have gone off by the time it had to be taken in. For, really, the smell of paint coming from that doll's house ("Sweet of old Mrs. Hay, of course; most sweet and generous!") — but the smell of paint was quite enough to make anyone seriously ill, in Aunt Beryl's opinion. Even before the sacking was taken off. And when it was. . . .

There stood the doll's house, a dark, oily, spinach green, picked out with bright yellow. Its two solid little chimneys, glued on to the roof, were painted red and white, and the door, gleaming with yellow varnish, was like a little slab of toffee. Four windows, real windows, were divided into panes by a broad streak of green. There was actually a tiny porch, too, painted yellow, with big lumps of congealed paint hanging along the edge.

But perfect, perfect little house! Who could possibly mind the smell? It was part of the joy, part of the newness.

"Open it quickly, some one!"

The hook at the side was stuck fast. Pat pried it open with his pen-knife, and the whole house-front swung back, and — there you were, gazing at one and the same moment into the drawing-room and dining-room, the kitchen and two bedrooms. That is the way for a house to open! Why don't all houses open like that? How much more exciting than peering through the slit of a door into a mean little hall with a hatstand and two umbrellas! That is — isn't it? — what you long to know about a house when you put your hand on the knocker. Perhaps it is the way God opens houses at dead of night when He is taking a quiet turn with an angel. . . .

"O-oh!" The Burnell children sounded as though they were in despair. It was too marvelous; it was too much for them. They had never seen anything like it in their lives. All the rooms were papered. There were pictures on the walls, painted on the paper, with gold frames complete. Red carpet covered all the floors except the kitchen; red plush chairs in the drawing-room, green in the dining-room; tables, beds with real bedclothes, a cradle, a stove, a dresser with tiny plates and one big jug. But what Kezia liked more than anything, what she liked frightfully, was the lamp. It stood in the middle of the dining-room table, an exquisite little amber lamp with a white globe. It was even filled all ready for lighting, though, of course, you couldn't light it. But there was something inside that looked like oil, and that moved when you shook it.

The father and mother dolls, who sprawled very stiff as though they had fainted in the drawing-room, and their two little children asleep up-stairs, were really too big for the doll's house. They didn't look as though they belonged. But the lamp was perfect. It seemed to smile at Kezia, to say, "I live here." The lamp was real.

The Burnell children could hardly walk to school fast enough the next morning. They burned to tell everybody, to describe, to — well — to boast about their doll's house before the school-bell rang.

"I'm to tell," said Isabel, "because I'm the eldest. And you two can join in after. But I'm to tell first."

There was nothing to answer. Isabel was bossy, but she was always right, and Lottie and Kezia knew too well the powers that went with being eldest. They brushed through the thick buttercups at the road edge and said nothing.

"And I'm to choose who's to come and see it first. Mother said I might."

For it had been arranged that while the doll's house stood in the court-yard they might ask the girls at school, two at a time, to come and look. Not to stay to tea, of course, or to come traipsing through the house. But just to stand quietly in the courtyard while Isabel pointed out the beauties, and Lottie and Kezia looked pleased. . . .

But hurry as they might, by the time they had reached the tarred pal-ings of the boys' playground the bell had begun to jangle. They only just

had time to whip off their hats and fall into line before the roll was called.
Never mind. Isabel tried to make up for it by looking very important and
mysterious and by whispering behind her hand to the girls near her, "Got
something to tell you at playtime."

Playtime came and Isabel was surrounded. The girls of her class nearly
fought to put their arms round her, to walk away with her, to beam flatter-
ingly, to be her special friend. She held quite a court under the huge pine
trees at the side of the playground. Nudging, giggling together, the little
girls pressed up close. And the only two who stayed outside the ring were
the two who were always outside, the little Kelveys. They knew better than
to come anywhere near the Burnells.

For the fact was, the school the Burnell children went to was not at all
the kind of place their parents would have chosen if there had been any
choice. But there was none. It was the only school for miles. And the consequence was all the children in the neighborhood, the Judge's little girls,
the doctor's daughters, the storekeeper's children, the milkman's, were
forced to mix together. Not to speak of there being an equal number of
rude, rough little boys as well. But the line had to be drawn somewhere. It
was drawn at the Kelveys. Many of the children, including the Burnells,
were not allowed even to speak to them. They walked past the Kelveys with
their heads in the air, and as they set the fashion in all matters of behavior,
the Kelveys were shunned by everybody. Even the teacher had a special
voice for them, and a special smile for the other children when Lil Kelvey
came up to her desk with a bunch of dreadfully common-looking flowers.

They were the daughters of a spry, hardworking little washerwoman,
who went about from house to house by the day. This was awful enough.
But where was Mr. Kelvey? Nobody knew for certain. But everybody said
he was in prison. So they were the daughters of a washerwoman and a gaol-
bird. Very nice company for other people's children! And they looked it.
Why Mrs. Kelvey made them so conspicuous was hard to understand. The
truth was they were dressed in "bits" given to her by the people for whom
she worked. Lil, for instance, who was a stout, plain child, with big freckles,
came to school in a dress made from a green art-serge table-cloth of the
Burnells', with red plush sleeves from the Logans' curtains. Her hat,
perched on top of her high forehead, was a grown-up woman's hat, once the
property of Miss Lecky, the postmistress. It was turned up at the back and
trimmed with a large scarlet quill. What a little guy she looked! It was impossible not to laugh. And her little sister, our Else, wore a long white dress,
rather like a nightgown, and a pair of little boy's boots. But whatever our
Else wore she would have looked strange. She was a tiny wishbone of a
child, with cropped hair and enormous solemn eyes — a little white owl.
Nobody had ever seen her smile; she scarcely ever spoke. She went through
life holding on to Lil, with a piece of Lil's skirt screwed up in her hand.
Where Lil went our Else followed. In the playground, on the road going to
and from school, there was Lil marching in front and our Else holding on

behind. Only when she wanted anything, or when she was out of breath, our Else gave Lil a tug, a twitch, and Lil stopped and turned around. The Kelveys never failed to understand each other.

Now they hovered at the edge; you couldn't stop them listening. When the little girls turned round and sneered, Lil, as usual, gave her silly, shamefaced smile, but our Else only looked.

And Isabel's voice, so very proud, went on telling. The carpet made a great sensation, but so did the beds with real bedclothes, and the stove with an oven door.

When she finished Kezia broke in. "You've forgotten the lamp, Isabel."

"Oh, yes," said Isabel, "and there's a teeny little lamp, all made of yellow glass, with a white globe that stands on the dining-room table. You couldn't tell it from a real one."

"The lamp's best of all," cried Kezia. She thought Isabel wasn't making half enough of the little lamp. But nobody paid any attention. Isabel was choosing the two who were to come back with them that afternoon and see it. She chose Emmie Cole and Lena Logan. But when the others knew they were all to have a chance, they couldn't be nice enough to Isabel. One by one they put their arms round Isabel's waist and walked her off. They had something to whisper to her, a secret. "Isabel's *my* friend."

Only the little Kelveys moved away forgotten; there was nothing more for them to hear.

Days passed, and as more children saw the doll's house, the fame of it spread. It became the one subject, the rage. The one question was, "Have you seen Burnells' doll's house? Oh, ain't it lovely!" "Haven't you seen it? Oh, I say!"

Even the dinner hour was given up to talking about it. The little girls sat under the pines eating their thick mutton sandwiches and big slabs of johnny cake spread with butter. While always, as near as they could get, sat the Kelveys, our Else holding on to Lil, listening too, while they chewed their jam sandwiches out of a newspaper soaked with large red blobs. . . .

"Mother," said Kezia, "can't I ask the Kelveys just once?"

"Certainly not, Kezia."

"But why not?"

"Run away, Kezia; you know quite well why not."

At last everybody had seen it except them. On that day the subject rather flagged. It was the dinner hour. The children stood together under the pine trees, and suddenly, as they looked at the Kelveys eating out of their paper, always by themselves, always listening, they wanted to be horrid to them. Emmie Cole started the whisper.

"Lil Kelvey's going to be a servant when she grows up."

"O-oh, how awful!" said Isabel Burnell, and she made eyes at Emmie.

Emmie swallowed in a very meaning way and nodded to Isabel as she'd seen her mother do on those occasions.

"It's true — it's true — it's true," she said.

Then Lena Logan's little eyes snapped. "Shall I ask her?" she whispered.

"Bet you don't," said Jessie May.

"Pooh, I'm not frightened," said Lena. Suddenly she gave a little squeal and danced in front of the other girls. "Watch! Watch me! Watch me now!" said Lena. And sliding, gliding, dragging one foot, giggling behind her hand, Lena went over to the Kelveys.

Lil looked up from her dinner. She wrapped the rest quickly away. Our Else stopped chewing. What was coming now?

"Is it true you're going to be a servant when you grow up, Lil Kelvey?" shrilled Lena.

Dead silence. But instead of answering, Lil only gave her silly, shamefaced smile. She didn't seem to mind the question at all. What a sell for Lena! The girls began to titter.

Lena couldn't stand that. She put her hands on her hips; she shot forward. "Yah, yer father's in prison!" she hissed, spitefully.

This was such a marvelous thing to have said that the little girls rushed away in a body, deeply, deeply excited, wild with joy. Some one found a long rope, and they began skipping. And never did they skip so high, run in and out so fast, or do such daring things as on that morning.

In the afternoon Pat called for the Burnell children with the buggy and they drove home. There were visitors. Isabel and Lottie, who liked visitors, went upstairs to change their pinafores. But Kezia thieved out at the back. Nobody was about; she began to swing on the big white gates of the courtyard. Presently, looking along the road, she saw two little dots. They grew bigger, they were coming toward her. Now she could see that one was in front and one close behind. Now she could see that they were the Kelveys. Kezia stopped swinging. She slipped off the gate as if she was going to run away. Then she hesitated. The Kelveys came nearer, and beside them walked their shadows, very long, stretching right across the road with their heads in the buttercups. Kezia clambered back on the gate; she had made up her mind; she swung out.

"Hullo," she said to the passing Kelveys.

They were so astounded that they stopped. Lil gave her silly smile. Our Else stared.

"You can come and see our doll's house if you want to," said Kezia, and she dragged one toe on the ground. But at that Lil turned red and shook her head quickly.

"Why not?" asked Kezia.

Lil gasped, then she said, "Your ma told our ma you wasn't to speak to us."

"Oh, well," said Kezia. She didn't know what to reply. "It doesn't matter. You can come and see our doll's house all the same. Come on. Nobody's looking."

But Lil shook her head still harder.

"Don't you want to?" asked Kezia.

Suddenly there was a twitch, a tug at Lil's skirt. She turned round. Our Else was looking at her with big, imploring eyes; she was frowning; she wanted to go. For a moment Lil looked at our Else very doubtfully. But then our Else twitched her skirt again. She started forward. Kezia led the way. Like two little stray cats they followed across the courtyard to where the doll's house stood.

"There it is," said Kezia.

There was a pause. Lil breathed loudly, almost snorted; our Else was still as a stone.

"I'll open it for you," said Kezia kindly. She undid the hook and they looked inside.

"There's the drawing-room and the dining-room, and that's the — "

"Kezia!"

Oh, what a start they gave!

"Kezia!"

It was Aunt Beryl's voice. They turned round. At the back door stood Aunt Beryl, staring as if she couldn't believe what she saw.

"How dare you ask the little Kelveys into the courtyard?" said her cold, furious voice. "You know as well as I do, you're not allowed to talk to them. Run away, children, run away at once. And don't come back again," said Aunt Beryl. And she stepped into the yard and shooed them out as if they were chickens.

"Off you go immediately!" she called, cold and proud.

They did not need telling twice. Burning with shame, shrinking together, Lil huddling along like her mother, our Else dazed, somehow they crossed the big courtyard and squeezed through the white gate.

"Wicked, disobedient little girl!" said Aunt Beryl bitterly to Kezia, and she slammed the doll's house to.

The afternoon had been awful. A letter had come from Willie Brent, a terrifying, threatening letter, saying if she did not meet him that evening in Pulman's Bush, he'd come to the front door and ask the reason why! But now that she had frightened those little rats of Kelveys and given Kezia a good scolding, her heart felt lighter. That ghastly pressure was gone. She went back to the house humming.

When the Kelveys were well out of sight of Burnells', they sat down to rest on a big red drainpipe by the side of the road. Lil's cheeks were still burning; she took off the hat with the quill and held it on her knee. Dreamily they looked over the hay paddocks, past the creek, to the group of wattles where Logan's cows stood waiting to be milked. What were their thoughts?

Presently our Else nudged up close to her sister. But now she had for-

gotten the cross lady. She put out a finger and stroked her sister's quill; she
smiled her rare smile.

"I seen the little lamp," she said, softly.

Then both were silent once more.

[1923]

KATHERINE ANNE PORTER (1890–1980) *was born Callie Russell Porter in Indian Creek, Texas. When she was only two years old her mother died, and then the family moved to Kyle, Texas, where they lived until her grandmother's death in 1901. Porter attended boarding schools and an Ursuline convent. She married for the first time in 1906, and after her divorce five years later she worked briefly as a reporter in Chicago and Denver. As a child she had wanted to be a writer, but it took fifteen years once she started writing seriously before she trusted herself enough as a stylist to approach a publisher. Most of her life during this time was a financial struggle; she spent only 10 percent of her energies on writing, and "the other 90 percent went to keeping my head above water." She nearly lost her life in the influenza epidemic that swept the United States at the end of World War I, and when she recovered she went to Mexico to study Aztec and Mayan art. There she found herself "smack into the Obregón revolution" of 1921, the setting of her story "Flowering Judas." She published her first story in* Century *magazine two years later and achieved acclaim as a writer with her first collection of short stories,* Flowering Judas and Other Stories, *in 1930. Her most productive decade as a writer was the 1930s, when she published* Noon Wine *(1937) and* Pale Horse, Pale Rider: Three Short Novels *(1939). After World War II she supported herself by lecture tours and teaching jobs at various universities while she worked on her novel* Ship of Fools *(1962), which took more than two decades to complete. In 1965 her* Collected Stories *won both the Pulitzer Prize and the National Book Award.*

Porter's style is not so recognizably "southern" as William Faulkner's or Flannery O'Connor's. She was a southerner by tradition and inheritance, but she had thought of herself since childhood as being "always restless, always a roving spirit." She was very conscious of her own art as a storyteller, and of the art of fiction in general, writing personal essays on Willa Cather, Katherine Mansfield, Virginia Woolf, Eudora Welty, and Flannery O'Connor, among others. Particularly indebted in her best stories to Mansfield, Porter attempted to dramatize a character's state of mind, rather than develop a complicated plot. The analysis Porter gave of Mansfield's literary practice in her essay "The Art of Katherine Mansfield" can also be applied to a story like "Flowering Judas": "With fine objectivity, she bares a moment of experience, real experience, in the life of some one human being; she states no belief, gives no motives, airs no theories, but simply presents to the reader a situation, a place, and a character, and there it is; and the emotional content is present as implicitly as the germ is in the grain of wheat."

Porter was a highly disciplined writer whose craftsmanship triumphed over the confusions of her personal life. "Flowering Judas," a complex story about a girl who "was not able to face her own nature and who was afraid of everything," was based on a sudden intuition about an American girl living, like herself, in Mexico during the revolution. "I started 'Flowering Judas' at seven P.M. and at one-thirty I was standing on a snowy windy corner putting it in the mailbox." (See Porter's Interview on page 1282.)

Katherine Anne Porter

෨෨

FLOWERING JUDAS

Braggioni sits heaped upon the edge of a straight-backed chair much too small for him, and sings to Laura in a furry, mournful voice. Laura has begun to find reasons for avoiding her own house until the latest possible moment, for Braggioni is there almost every night. No matter how late she is, he will be sitting there with a surly, waiting expression, pulling at his kinky yellow hair, thumbing the strings of his guitar, snarling a tune under his breath. Lupe the Indian maid meets Laura at the door, and says with a flicker of a glance towards the upper room, "He waits."

Laura wishes to lie down, she is tired of her hairpins and the feel of her long tight sleeves, but she says to him, "Have you a new song for me this evening?" If he says yes, she asks him to sing it. If he says no, she remembers his favorite one, and asks him to sing it again. Lupe brings her a cup of chocolate and a plate of rice, and Laura eats at the small table under the lamp, first inviting Braggioni, whose answer is always the same: "I have eaten, and besides, chocolate thickens the voice."

Laura says, "Sing, then," and Braggioni heaves himself into song. He scratches the guitar familiarly as though it were a pet animal, and sings passionately off key, taking the high notes in a prolonged painful squeal. Laura, who haunts the markets listening to the ballad singers, and stops every day to hear the blind boy playing his reed-flute in Sixteenth of September Street, listens to Braggioni with pitiless courtesy, because she dares not smile at his miserable performance. Nobody dares to smile at him. Braggioni is cruel to everyone, with a kind of specialized insolence, but he is so vain of his talents, and so sensitive to slights, it would require a cruelty and vanity greater than his own to lay a finger on the vast cureless wound of his self-esteem. It would require courage, too, for it is dangerous to offend him, and nobody has this courage.

Braggioni loves himself with such tenderness and amplitude and eternal charity that his followers — for he is a leader of men, a skilled revolutionist, and his skin has been punctured in honorable warfare — warm themselves in the reflected glow, and say to each other: "He has a real nobility, a love of humanity raised above mere personal affections." The excess of this self-love has flowed out, inconveniently for her, over Laura, who, with so many others, owes her comfortable situation and her salary to him. When he is in a very good humor, he tells her, "I am tempted to forgive you for being a *gringa, gringita!*" and Laura, burning, imagines herself leaning forward suddenly, and with a sound back-handed slap wiping the suety smile from his face. If he notices her eyes at these moments he gives no sign.

She knows what Braggioni would offer her, and she must resist tenaciously without appearing to resist, and if she could avoid it she would not admit even to herself the slow drift of his intention. During these long evenings which have spoiled a long month for her, she sits in her deep chair with an open book on her knees, resting her eyes on the consoling rigidity of the printed page when the sight and sound of Braggioni singing threaten to identify themselves with all her remembered afflictions and to add their weight to her uneasy premonitions of the future. The gluttonous bulk of Braggioni has become a symbol of her many disillusions, for a revolutionist should be lean, animated by heroic faith, a vessel of abstract virtues. This is nonsense, she knows it now and is ashamed of it. Revolution must have leaders, and leadership is a career for energetic men. She is, her comrades tell her, full of romantic error, for what she defines as cynicism in them is merely "a developed sense of reality." She is almost too willing to say, "I am wrong, I suppose I don't really understand the principles," and afterward she makes a secret truce with herself, determined not to surrender her will to such expedient logic. But she cannot help feeling that she has been betrayed irreparably by the disunion between her way of living and her feeling of what life should be, and at times she is almost contented to rest in this sense of grievance as a private store of consolation. Sometimes she wishes to run away, but she stays. Now she longs to fly out of this room, down the narrow stairs, and into the street where the houses lean together like conspirators under a single mottled lamp, and leave Braggioni singing to himself.

Instead she looks at Braggioni, frankly and clearly, like a good child who understands the rules of behavior. Her knees cling together under sound blue serge, and her round white collar is not purposely nun-like. She wears the uniform of an idea, and has renounced vanities. She was born Roman Catholic, and in spite of her fear of being seen by someone who might make a scandal of it, she slips now and again into some crumbling little church, kneels on the chilly stone, and says a Hail Mary on the gold rosary she bought in Tehuantepec. It is no good and she ends by examining the altar with its tinsel flowers and ragged brocades, and feels tender about the battered doll-shape of some male saint whose white, lace-trimmed drawers hang limply around his ankles below the hieratic dignity of his velvet robe. She has encased herself in a set of principles derived from her early training, leaving no detail of gesture or of personal taste untouched, and for this reason she will not wear lace made on machines. This is her private heresy, for in her special group the machine is sacred, and will be the salvation of the workers. She loves fine lace, and there is a tiny edge of fluted cobweb on this collar, which is one of twenty precisely alike, folded in blue tissue paper in the upper drawer of her clothes chest.

Braggioni catches her glance solidly as if he had been waiting for it, leans forward, balancing his paunch between his spread knees, and sings with tremendous emphasis, weighing his words. He has, the song relates, no father and no mother, nor even a friend to console him; lonely as a wave of the sea he comes and goes, lonely as a wave. His mouth opens round and yearns sideways, his balloon cheeks grow oily with the labor of song. He bulges marvelously in his expensive garments. Over his lavender collar, crushed upon a purple necktie, held by a diamond hoop: over his ammunition belt of tooled leather worked in silver, buckled cruelly around his gasping middle: over the tops of his glossy yellow shoes Braggioni swells with ominous ripeness, his mauve silk hose stretched taut, his ankles bound with the stout leather thongs of his shoes.

When he stretches his eyelids at Laura she notes again that his eyes are the true tawny yellow cat's eyes. He is rich, not in money, he tells her, but in power, and this power brings with it the blameless ownership of things, and the right to indulge his love of small luxuries. "I have a taste for the elegant refinements," he said once, flourishing a yellow silk handkerchief before her nose. "Smell that? It is Jockey Club, imported from New York." Nonetheless he is wounded by life. He will say so presently. "It is true everything turns to dust in the hand, to gall on the tongue." He sighs and his leather belt creaks like a saddle girth. "I am disappointed in everything as it comes. Everything." He shakes his head. "You, poor thing, you will be disappointed too. You are born for it. We are more alike than you realize in some things. Wait and see. Some day you will remember what I have told you, you will know that Braggioni was your friend."

Laura feels a slow chill, a purely physical sense of danger, a warning in her blood that violence, mutilation, a shocking death, wait for her with lessening patience. She has translated this fear into something homely, immediate, and sometimes hesitates before crossing the street. "My personal fate is nothing, except as the testimony of a mental attitude," she reminds herself, quoting from some forgotten philosophic primer, and is sensible enough to add, "Anyhow, I shall not be killed by an automobile if I can help it."

"It may be true I am as corrupt, in another way, as Braggioni," she thinks in spite of herself, "as callous, as incomplete," and if this is so, any kind of death seems preferable. Still she sits quietly, she does not run. Where could she go? Uninvited she has promised herself to this place; she can no longer imagine herself as living in another country, and there is no pleasure in remembering her life before she came here.

Precisely what is the nature of this devotion, its true motives, and what are its obligations? Laura cannot say. She spends part of her days in Xochimilco, near by, teaching Indian children to say in English, "The cat is on the mat." When she appears in the classroom they crowd about her with smiles on their wise, innocent, clay-colored faces, crying, "Good morning, my titcher!" in immaculate voices, and they make of her desk a fresh garden of flowers every day.

During her leisure she goes to union meetings and listens to busy important voices quarreling over tactics, methods, internal politics. She visits the prisoners of her own political faith in their cells, where they entertain themselves with counting cockroaches, repenting of their indiscretions, composing their memoirs, writing out manifestoes and plans for their comrades who are still walking about free, hands in pockets, sniffing fresh air. Laura brings them food and cigarettes and a little money, and she brings messages disguised in equivocal phrases from the men outside who dare not set foot in the prison for fear of disappearing into the cells kept empty for them. If the prisoners confuse night and day, and complain, "Dear little Laura, time doesn't pass in this infernal hole, and I won't know when it is time to sleep unless I have a reminder," she brings them their favorite narcotics, and says in a tone that does not wound them with pity, "Tonight will really be night for you," and though her Spanish amuses them they find her comforting, useful. If they lose patience and all faith, and curse the slowness of their friends in coming to their rescue with money and influence, they trust her not to repeat everything, and if she inquires, "Where do you think we can find money, or influence?" they are certain to answer, "Well, there is Braggioni, why doesn't he do something?"

She smuggles letters from headquarters to men hiding from firing squads in back streets in mildewed houses, where they sit in tumbled beds and talk bitterly as if all Mexico were at their heels, when Laura knows positively they might appear at the band concert in the Alameda[1] on Sunday morning, and no one would notice them. But Braggioni says, "Let them sweat a little. The next time they may be careful. It is very restful to have them out of the way for a while." She is not afraid to knock on any door in any street after midnight, and enter in the darkness, and say to one of these men who is really in danger: "They will be looking for you — seriously — tomorrow morning after six. Here is some money from Vicente. Go to Vera Cruz and wait."

She borrows money from the Rumanian agitator to give to his bitter enemy the Polish agitator. The favor of Braggioni is their disputed territory, and Braggioni holds the balance nicely, for he can use them both. The Polish agitator talks love to her over café tables, hoping to exploit what he believes is her secret sentimental preference for him, and he gives her misinformation which he begs her to repeat as the solemn truth to certain persons. The Rumanian is more adroit. He is generous with his money in all good causes, and lies to her with an air of ingenuous candor, as if he were her good friend and confidant. She never repeats anything they may say.

[1] a public square in Mexico City.

Braggioni never asks questions. He has other ways to discover all that he wishes to know about them.

Nobody touches her, but all praise her gray eyes, and the soft, round under lip which promises gaiety, yet is always grave, nearly always firmly closed: and they cannot understand why she is in Mexico. She walks back and forth on her errands, with puzzled eyebrows, carrying her little folder of drawings and music and school papers. No dancer dances more beautifully than Laura walks, and she inspires some amusing, unexpected ardors, which cause little gossip, because nothing comes of them. A young captain who had been a soldier in Zapata's[2] army attempted, during a horseback ride near Cuernavaca, to express his desire for her with the noble simplicity befitting a rude folk-hero; but gently, because he was gentle. This gentleness was his defeat, for when he alighted, and removed her foot from the stirrup, and essayed to draw her down into his arms, her horse, ordinarily a tame one, shied fiercely, reared, and plunged away. The young hero's horse careened blindly after his stable-mate, and the hero did not return to the hotel until rather late that evening. At breakfast he came to her table in full charro dress, gray buckskin jacket and trousers with strings of silver buttons down the leg, and he was in a humorous, careless mood. "May I sit with you?" and "You are a wonderful rider. I was terrified that you might be thrown and dragged. I should never have forgiven myself. But I cannot admire you enough for your riding."

"I learned to ride in Arizona," said Laura.

"If you will ride with me again this morning, I promise you a horse that will not shy with you," he said. But Laura remembered that she must return to Mexico City at noon.

Next morning the children made a celebration and spent their playtime writing on the blackboard, "We lov ar titcher," and with tinted chalks they drew wreaths of flowers around the words. The young hero wrote her a letter: "I am a very foolish, wasteful, impulsive man. I should have first said I love you, and then you would not have run away. But you shall see me again." Laura thought, "I must sent him a box of colored crayons," but she was trying to forgive herself for having spurred her horse at the wrong moment.

A brown shock-haired youth came and stood in her patio one night and sang like a lost soul for two hours, but Laura could think of nothing to do about it. The moonlight spread a wash of gauzy silver over the clear spaces of the garden, and the shadows were cobalt blue. The scarlet blossoms of the Judas tree were dull purple, and the names of the colors repeated themselves automatically in her mind, while she watched not the boy, but his shadow, fallen like a dark garment across the fountain rim, trailing in the water. Lupe came silently and whispered expert counsel in

---

[2] Emiliano Zapata (1883–1919), rebel general who was a leader in the Mexican revolution of 1910–1917.

her ear: "If you will throw him one little flower, he will sing another song or two and go away." Laura threw the flower, and he sang a last song and went away with the flower tucked in the band of his hat. Lupe said, "He is one of the organizers of the Typographers Union, and before that he sold corridos[3] in the Merced market, and before that, he came from Guanajuato, where I was born. I would not trust any man, but I trust least those from Guanajuato."

She did not tell Laura that he would be back again the next day, and the next, nor that he would follow her at a certain fixed distance around the Merced market, through the Zocolo, up Francesco I. Madero Avenue, and so along the Paseo de la Reforma to Chapultepec Park, and into the Philosopher's Footpath, still with that flower withering in his hat, and an indivisible attention in his eyes.

Now Laura is accustomed to him, it means nothing except that he is nineteen years old and is observing a convention with all propriety, as though it were founded on a law of nature, which in the end it might very well prove to be. He is beginning to write poems which he prints on a wooden press, and he leaves them stuck like handbills in her door. She is pleasantly disturbed by the abstract, unhurried watchfulness of his black eyes which will in time turn easily toward another object. She tells herself that throwing the flower was a mistake, for she is twenty-two years old and knows better; but she refuses to regret it, and persuades herself that her negation of all external events as they occur is a sign that she is gradually perfecting herself in the stoicism she strives to cultivate against that disaster she fears, though she cannot name it.

She is not at home in the world. Every day she teaches children who remain strangers to her, though she loves their tender round hands and their charming opportunistic savagery. She knocks at unfamiliar doors not knowing whether a friend or a stranger shall answer, and even if a known face emerges from the sour gloom of that unknown interior, still it is the face of a stranger. No matter what this stranger says to her, nor what her message to him, the very cells of her flesh reject knowledge and kinship in one monotonous word. No. No. No. She draws her strength from this one holy talismanic word which does not suffer her to be led into evil. Denying everything, she may walk anywhere in safety, she looks at everything without amazement.

No, repeats this firm unchanging voice of her blood; and she looks at Braggioni without amazement. He is a great man, he wishes to impress this simple girl who covers her great round breasts with thick dark cloth, and who hides long, invaluably beautiful legs under a heavy skirt. She is almost thin except for the incomprehensible fullness of her breasts, like a nursing mother's, and Braggioni, who considers himself a judge of women, speculates again on the puzzle of her notorious virginity, and takes the liberty of

[3] tickets to bullfights.

speech which she permits without a sign of modesty, indeed, without any
sort of sign, which is disconcerting.

"You think you are so cold, *gringita!* Wait and see. You will surprise
yourself someday! May I be there to advise you!" He stretches his eyelids at
her, and his ill-humored cat's eyes waver in a separate glance for the two
points of light marking the opposite ends of a smoothly drawn path between the swollen curve of her breasts. He is not put off by that blue serge,
nor by her resolutely fixed gaze. There is all the time in the world. His
cheeks are bellying with the wind of song. "O girl with the dark eyes," he
sings, and reconsiders. "But yours are not dark. I can change all that. O girl
with the green eyes, you have stolen my heart away." Then his mind wanders to the song, and Laura feels the weight of his attention being shifted
elsewhere. Singing thus, he seems harmless, he is quite harmless, there is
nothing to do but sit patiently and say "No," when the moment comes. She
draws a full breath, and her mind wanders also, but not far. She dares not
wander too far.

Not for nothing has Braggioni taken pains to be a good revolutionist
and a professional lover of humanity. He will never die of it. He has the
malice, the cleverness, the wickedness, the sharpness of wit, the hardness of
heart, stipulated for loving the world profitably. He *will never die of it.* He
will live to see himself kicked out from his feeding trough by other hungry
world-saviors. Traditionally he must sing in spite of his life which drives
him to bloodshed, he tells Laura, for his father was a Tuscany peasant who
drifted to Yucatan and married a Maya woman: a woman of race, an aristocrat. They gave him the love and knowledge of music, thus: and under the
rip of his thumbnail, the strings of the instrument complain like exposed
nerves.

Once he was called Delgadito[4] by all the girls and married women who
ran after him; he was so scrawny all his bones showed under his thin cotton
clothing, and he could squeeze his emptiness to the very backbone with his
two hands. He was a poet and the revolution was only a dream then; too
many women loved him and sapped away his youth, and he could never
find enough to eat anywhere, anywhere! Now he is a leader of men, crafty
men who whisper in his ear, hungry men who wait for hours outside his office for a word with him, emaciated men with wild faces who waylay him at
the street gate with a timid, "Comrade, let me tell you . . ." and they blow
the foul breath from their empty stomachs in his face.

He is always sympathetic. He gives them handfuls of small coins from
his own pockets, he promises them work, there will be demonstrations, they
must join the unions and attend the meetings, above all they must be on
the watch for spies. They are closer to him than his own brothers, without
them he can do nothing — until tomorrow, comrade!

---

[4] "the little skinny one" (Spanish).

Until tomorrow. "They are stupid, they are lazy, they are treacherous, they would cut my throat for nothing," he says to Laura. He has good food and abundant drink, he hires an automobile and drives in the Paseo on Sunday morning, and enjoys plenty of sleep in a soft bed beside a wife who dares not disturb him; and he sits pampering his bones in easy billows of fat, singing to Laura, who knows and thinks these things about him. When he was fifteen, he tried to drown himself because he loved a girl, his first love, and she laughed at him. "A thousand women have paid for that," and his tight little mouth turns down at the corners. Now he perfumes his hair with Jockey Club, and confides to Laura: "One woman is really as good as another for me in the dark. I prefer them all."

His wife organizes unions among the girls in the cigarette factories, and walks in picket lines, and even speaks at meetings in the evening. But she cannot be brought to acknowledge the benefits of true liberty. "I tell her I must have my freedom, net. She does not understand my point of view." Laura has heard this many times. Braggioni scratches the guitar and meditates. "She is an instinctively virtuous woman, pure gold, no doubt of that. If she were not, I should lock her up, and she knows it."

His wife, who works so hard for the good of the factory girls, employs part of her leisure lying on the floor weeping because there are so many women in the world, and only one husband for her, and she never knows where nor when to look for him. He told her: "Unless you can learn to cry when I am not here, I must go away for good." That day he went away and took a room at the Hotel Madrid.

It is this month of separation for the sake of higher principles that has been spoiled not only for Mrs. Braggioni, whose sense of reality is beyond criticism, but for Laura, who feels herself bogged in a nightmare. Tonight Laura envies Mrs. Braggioni, who is alone, and free to weep as much as she pleases about a concrete wrong. Laura has just come from a visit to the prison, and she is waiting for tomorrow with a bitter anxiety as if tomorrow may not come, but time may be caught immovably in this hour, with herself transfixed, Braggioni singing on forever, and Eugenio's body not yet discovered by the guard.

Braggioni says: "Are you going to sleep?" Almost before she can shake her head, he begins telling her about the May-day disturbances coming on in Morelia, for the Catholics hold a festival in honor of the Blessed Virgin, and the Socialists celebrate their martyrs on that day. "There will be two independent processions, starting from either end of town, and they will march until they meet, and the rest depends. . . ." He asks her to oil and load his pistols. Standing up, he unbuckles his ammunition belt, and spreads it laden across her knees. Laura sits with the shells slipping through the cleaning cloth dipped in oil, and he says again he cannot understand why she works so hard for the revolutionary idea unless she loves some man who is in it. "Are you not in love with someone?" "No," says Laura. "And no one is in love with you?" "No." "Then it is your own fault. No woman need go begging. Why, what is the matter with you? The legless beggar woman in the Alameda has a perfectly faithful lover. Did you know that?"

Laura peers down the pistol barrel and says nothing, but a long, slow faintness rises and subsides in her; Braggioni curves his swollen fingers around the throat of the guitar and softly smothers the music out of it, and when she hears him again he seems to have forgotten her, and is speaking in the hypnotic voice he uses when talking in small rooms to a listening, close-gathered crowd. Some day this world, now seemingly so composed and eternal, to the edges of every sea shall be merely a tangle of gaping trenches, of crashing walls and broken bodies. Everything must be torn from its accustomed place where it has rotted for centuries, hurled skyward and distributed, cast down again clean as rain, without separate identity. Nothing shall survive that the stiffened hands of poverty have created for the rich and no one shall be left alive except the elect spirits destined to pro-create a new world cleansed of cruelty and injustice, ruled by benevolent anarchy: "Pistols are good, I love them, cannon are even better, but in the end I pin my faith to good dynamite," he concludes, and strokes the pistol lying in her hands. "Once I dreamed of destroying this city, in case it offered re-sistance to General Ortiz,[5] but it fell into his hands like an overripe pear."

He is made restless by his own words, rises and stands waiting. Laura holds up the belt to him: "Put that on, and go kill somebody in Morelia, and you will be happier," she says softly. The presence of death in the room makes her bold. "Today, I found Eugenio going into a stupor. He refused to allow me to call the prison doctor. He had taken all the tablets I brought him yesterday. He said he took them because he was bored."

"He is a fool, and his death is his own business," says Braggioni, fastening his belt carefully.

"I told him if he had waited only a little while longer, you would have got him set free," says Laura. "He said he did not want to wait."

"He is a fool and we are well rid of him," says Braggioni, reaching for his hat.

He goes away. Laura knows his mood has changed, she will not see him any more for a while. He will send word when he needs her to go on errands into strange streets, to speak to the strange faces that will appear, like clay masks with the power of human speech, to mutter their thanks to Braggioni for his help. Now she is free, and she thinks, I must run while there is time. But she does not go.

Braggioni enters his own house where for a month his wife has spent many hours every night weeping and tangling her hair upon her pillow. She is weeping now, and she weeps more at the sight of him, the cause of all her sorrows. He looks about the room. Nothing is changed, the smells are good

---

[5] Pascual Ortiz Rubio (1877–1963), a revolutionary general who later, from 1930 to 1932, served as president of Mexico.

and familiar, he is well acquainted with the woman who comes toward him with no reproach except grief on her face. He says to her tenderly: "You are so good, please don't cry any more, you dear good creature." She says, "Are you tired, my angel? Sit here and I will wash your feet." She brings a bowl of water, and kneeling, unlaces his shoes, and when from her knees she raises her sad eyes under her blackened lids, he is sorry for everything, and bursts into tears. "Ah, yes, I am hungry, I am tired, let us eat something together," he says, between sobs. His wife leans her head on his arm and says, "Forgive me!" and this time he is refreshed by the solemn, endless rain of her tears.

Laura takes off her serge dress and puts on a white linen nightgown and goes to bed. She turns her head a little to one side, and lying still, reminds herself that it is time to sleep. Numbers tick in her brain like little clocks, soundless doors close of themselves around her. If you would sleep, you must not remember anything, the children will say tomorrow, good morning, my teacher, the poor prisoners who come every day bringing flowers to their jailer. 1–2–3–4–5 — it is monstrous to confuse love with revolution, night with day, life with death — ah Eugenio!

The tolling of the midnight bell is a signal, but what does it mean? Get up, Laura, and follow me: come out of your sleep, out of your bed, out of this strange house. What are you doing in this house? Without a word, without fear she rose and reached for Eugenio's hand, but he eluded her with a sharp, sly smile and drifted away. This is not all, you shall see — Murderer, he said, follow me, I will show you a new country, but it is far away and we must hurry. No, said Laura, not unless you take my hand, no; and she clung first to the stair rail, and then to the topmost branch of the Judas tree that bent down slowly and set her upon the earth, and then to the rocky ledge of a cliff, and then to the jagged wave of a sea that was not water but a desert of crumbling stone. Where are you taking me? she asked in wonder but without fear. To death, and it is a long way off, and we must hurry, said Eugenio. No, said Laura, not unless you take my hand. Then eat these flowers, poor prisoner, said Eugenio in a voice of pity, take and eat: and from the Judas tree he stripped the warm bleeding flowers, and held them to her lips. She saw that his hand was fleshless, a cluster of small white petrified branches, and his eye sockets were without light, but she ate the flowers greedily for they satisfied both hunger and thirst. Murderer! said Eugenio, and Cannibal! This is my body and my blood. Laura cried No! and at the sound of her own voice, she awoke trembling, and was afraid to sleep again.

[1930]

ISAAC BABEL (1894–1939?) was born in the Moldavanka district of Odessa, in Russia. His father, a Jewish businessman, made him study Yiddish, the Bible, and the Talmud, but his favorite subject was French, because the teacher was a native of Brittany who loved literature. By the time Babel was fifteen he began to write stories in French "à la Maupassant," and his later story, "Guy de Maupassant" (1932), is a tribute to the influence of this writer. In 1915 Babel moved to St. Petersburg and tried unsuccessfully to publish his stories. His only encouragement came from the Russian writer Maxim Gorky, who advised him to get more life experience: "Go to the people." For six years Babel took Gorky at his word. He became a soldier on the Romanian Front in World War I, worked as a press correspondent attached to the Soviet Cavalry, and found other jobs as a reporter and a printer during the chaotic period of civil war that followed the Russian Revolution of 1917. In 1923 Babel decided that he had learned enough to express his thoughts clearly and concisely. The following year he began to publish his stories in Left, a Soviet avant-garde literary magazine devoted to revolution in politics and the arts. A year later he published a collection of his tales, The Story of My Dove-Cote, and in 1925 his best work appeared — Red Cavalry, thirty-four sketches depicting scenes of bravery and suffering during the Polish campaign of 1920, when Babel was with the Soviet Cavalry.

Babel's literary style has been called "as terse as algebra," but its lyricism is also unmistakable. His plots are often episodic or anecdotal. He juxtaposed poetic and natural details in his descriptions, often stressing the grotesque and sensual to assault the reader with a barrage of sights, sounds, and smells, as in "My First Goose." These tactics are Babel's way of catching us off guard and breaking down our defenses, so we will be more receptive to his main theme as a writer, the complex relation between our illusions about life and the truth of life.

Babel was an exacting critic of his own work and often revised his stories several times before he was satisfied. When his books first appeared in the 1920s, he was hailed in the Soviet Union as a master prose stylist, but during Stalin's purges in the 1930s he was attacked for his ideological shortcomings. In 1937 he told his Soviet critics, who asked him why he wrote so little, that he could only manage short things: "Let me put it this way; the point is that Tolstoy was able to describe what happened to him minute by minute, he remembered it all, whereas I, evidently, only have it in me to describe the most interesting five minutes I've experienced in twenty-four hours." The tone of Babel's reply is joking, but underneath is a sense of his bitterness and frustration. He also wrote, "No steel can pierce the human heart so chillingly as a period at the right moment," a pun on

Stalin's name as "the man of steel." Babel's brave affirmation of individuality was unacceptable to the Soviet authorities, however, and in May 1939
he was arrested and disappeared into a concentration camp.

Isaac Babel

ॐ

MY FIRST GOOSE

– translated by Walter Morison

Savitsky, Commander of the VI Division, rose when he saw me, and
I wondered at the beauty of his giant's body. He rose, the purple of his
riding-breeches and the crimson of his little tilted cap and the decorations
stuck on his chest cleaving the hut as a standard cleaves the sky. A smell of
scent and sickly sweet freshness of soap emanated from him. His long legs
were like girls sheathed to the neck in shining riding-boots.

He smiled at me, struck his riding-whip on the table, and drew toward
him an order that the Chief of Staff had just finished dictating. It was an
order for Ivan Chesnokov to advance on Chugunov-Dobryvodka with the
regiment entrusted to him, to make contact with the enemy and destroy the
same.

"For which destruction," the Commander began to write, smearing
the whole sheet, "I make this same Chesnokov entirely responsible, up to
and including the supreme penalty, and will if necessary strike him down on
the spot; which you, Chesnokov, who have been working with me at the
front for some months now, cannot doubt."

The Commander signed the order with a flourish, tossed it to his or-
derlies, and turned upon me grey eyes that danced with merriment.

I handed him a paper with my appointment to the Staff of the Division.

"Put it down in the Order of the Day," said the Commander. "Put
him down for every satisfaction save the front one. Can you read and
write?"

"Yes, I can read and write," I replied, envying the flower and iron of
that youthfulness. "I graduated in law from St. Petersburg University."

"Oh, are you one of those grinds?" he laughed. "Specs on your nose,
too! What a nasty little object! They've sent you along without making any
inquiries; and this is a hot place for specs. Think you'll get on with us?"

"I'll get on all right," I answered, and went off to the village with the
quartermaster to find a billet for the night.

The quartermaster carried my trunk on his shoulder. Before us stretched the village street. The dying sun, round and yellow as a pumpkin, was giving up its roseate ghost to the skies.

We went up to a hut painted over with garlands. The quartermaster stopped, and said suddenly, with a guilty smile:

"Nuisance with specs. Can't do anything to stop it, either. Not a life for the brainy type here. But you go and mess up a lady, and a good lady too, and you'll have the boys patting you on the back."

He hesitated, my little trunk on his shoulder; then he came quite close to me, only to dart away again despairingly and run to the nearest yard. Cossacks were sitting there, shaving one another.

"Here, you soldiers," said the quartermaster, setting my little trunk down on the ground. "Comrade Savitsky's orders are that you're to take this chap in your billets, so no nonsense about it, because the chap's been through a lot in the learning line."

The quartermaster, purple in the face, left us without looking back. I raised my hand to my cap and saluted the Cossacks. A lad with long straight flaxen hair and the handsome face of the Ryazan Cossacks went over to my little trunk and tossed it out at the gate. Then he turned his back on me and with remarkable skill emitted a series of shameful noises.

"To your guns — number double-zero!" an older Cossack shouted at him, and burst out laughing. "Running fire!"

His guileless art exhausted, the lad made off. Then, crawling over the ground, I began to gather together the manuscripts and tattered garments that had fallen out of the trunk. I gathered them up and carried them to the other end of the yard. Near the hut, on a brick stove, stood a cauldron in which pork was cooking. The steam that rose from it was like the far-off smoke of home in the village, and it mingled hunger with desperate loneliness in my head. Then I covered my little broken trunk with hay, turning it into a pillow, and lay down on the ground to read in *Pravda* Lenin's speech at the Second Congress of the Comintern. The sun fell upon me from behind the toothed hillocks, the Cossacks trod on my feet, the lad made fun of me untiringly, the beloved lines came toward me along a thorny path and could not reach me. Then I put aside the paper and went out to the landlady, who was spinning on the porch.

"Landlady," I said, "I've got to eat."

The old woman raised to me the diffused whites of her purblind eyes and lowered them again.

"Comrade," she said, after a pause, "what with all this going on, I want to go and hang myself."

"Christ!" I muttered, and pushed the old woman in the chest with my fist. "You don't suppose I'm going to go into explanations with you, do you?"

And turning around I saw somebody's sword lying within reach. A severe-looking goose was waddling about the yard, inoffensively preening its feathers. I overtook it and pressed it to the ground. Its head cracked beneath my boot, cracked and emptied itself. The white neck lay stretched out in the dung, the wings twitched.

"Christ!" I said, digging into the goose with my sword. "Go and cook it for me, landlady."

Her blind eyes and glasses glistening, the old woman picked up the slaughtered bird, wrapped it in her apron, and started to bear it off toward the kitchen.

"Comrade," she said to me, after a while. "I want to go and hang myself." And she closed the door behind her.

The Cossacks in the yard were already sitting around their cauldron. They sat motionless, stiff as heathen priests at a sacrifice, and had not looked at the goose.

"The lad's all right," one of them said, winking and scooping up the cabbage soup with his spoon.

The Cossacks commenced their supper with all the elegance and restraint of peasants who respect one another. And I wiped the sword with sand, went out at the gate, and came in again, depressed. Already the moon hung above the yard like a cheap earring.

"Hey, you," suddenly said Surovkov, an older Cossack. "Sit down and feed with us till your goose is done."

He produced a spare spoon from his boot and handed it to me. We supped up the cabbage soup they had made, and ate the pork.

"What's in the newspaper?" asked the flaxen-haired lad, making room for me.

"Lenin writes in the paper," I said, pulling out *Pravda*. "Lenin writes that there's a shortage of everything."

And loudly, like a triumphant man hard of hearing, I read Lenin's speech out to the Cossacks.

Evening wrapped about me the quickening moisture of its twilight sheets; evening laid a mother's hand upon my burning forehead. I read on and rejoiced, spying out exultingly the secret curve of Lenin's straight line.

"Truth tickles everyone's nostrils," said Surovkov, when I had come to the end. "The question is, how's it to be pulled from the heap. But he goes and strikes at it straight off like a hen pecking at a grain!"

This remark about Lenin was made by Surovkov, platoon commander of the Staff Squadron; after which we lay down to sleep in the hayloft. We slept, all six of us, beneath a wooden roof that let in the stars, warming one another, our legs intermingled. I dreamed: and in my dreams saw women. But my heart, stained with bloodshed, grated and brimmed over.

[1925]

JAMES THURBER (1894–1961), the humorist, was born in Columbus, Ohio. When he was a boy he lost an eye, which kept him from military service in World War I. His eyesight failed him entirely later in life. After his graduation from Ohio State University, he worked as a newspaper reporter in Columbus and New York and lived in Paris. He came back to New York in 1926 to submit his humorous sketches to a new magazine The New Yorker, where he also served briefly as managing editor. The New Yorker printed his cartoons as well as his fables, stories, and essays for many years. In 1940 he wrote a successful play, The Male Animal, with Elliott Nugent. Among his many books of stories, fables, essays, and cartoons are Fables for Our Time (1940), My World — And Welcome to It (1942), The Thurber Carnival (1945), and Thurber Country (1953).

In discussing how he wrote stories, Thurber once quoted a definition of the difference between English and American humor: "The English treat the commonplace as if it were remarkable and the Americans treat the remarkable as if it were commonplace." In his best work, as in "The Secret Life of Walter Mitty," his stories venture into fantasy while still treating the remarkable as commonplace. He felt at home in the genre of the short story, never wanting to write a longer work, yet he recognized that there could also be serious elements in his fiction. "In anything funny you write that isn't close to serious you've missed something along the line." To Thurber, humor was "emotional chaos remembered in tranquility," and although the chaos provoked the immediate comic response, the power of ordered remembering gave the incident its deeper meaning. Resisting comparisons between his funny stories and Mark Twain's humorous sketches, Thurber said he began to write as a young man in "a rather curious style . . . tight journalese laced with heavy doses of Henry James." But his contact with E. B. White and Harold Ross at The New Yorker taught him to value clarity above all else in a literary style. After he matured as a writer he reflected on why James's way of writing no longer worked for him: "James is like — well, I had a bulldog once who used to drag rails around, enormous ones. . . . Once he brought home a chest of drawers — without the drawers in it. Found it on an ash-heap. Well, he'd start to get these things in the garden gate, everything finely balanced, you see, and then crash, he'd come up against the gate posts. He'd get it through finally, but I had that feeling in some of James's novels: that he was trying to get that rail through a gate not wide enough for it."

Thurber wrote his stories very slowly, often revising them several times in an attempt to make the finished version seem smooth and effortless. It was only in his cartoons and drawings that he worked quickly, "sometimes so quickly that the result is an accident, something I hadn't intended at all," but he felt that he did these for relaxation and that they came too fast to be called art. His best fiction and drawings were inspired by his comic view of the perennial battle of the sexes, in which intimidating women try to keep the upper hand over shy, trapped little men like the gentle Waterbury shopper Walter Mitty.

James Thurber

ᔓᔓ

THE SECRET LIFE OF WALTER MITTY

"We're going through!" The Commander's voice was like thin ice breaking. He wore his full-dress uniform, with the heavily braided white cap pulled down rakishly over one cold gray eye. "We can't make it, sir. It's spoiling for a hurricane, if you ask me." "I'm not asking you, Lieutenant Berg," said the Commander. "Throw on the power lights! Rev her up to 8,500! We're going through!" The pounding of the cylinders increased: ta-pocketa-pocketa-pocketa-*pocketa-pocketa*. The Commander stared at the ice forming on the pilot window. He walked over and twisted a row of complicated dials. "Switch on No. 8 auxiliary!" he shouted. "Switch on No. 8 auxiliary!" repeated Lieutenant Berg. "Full strength in No. 3 turret!" shouted the Commander. "Full strength in No. 3 turret!" The crew, bending to their various tasks in the huge, hurtling eight-engined Navy hydroplane, looked at each other and grinned. "The Old Man'll get us through," they said to one another. "The Old Man ain't afraid of Hell!" . . .

"Not so fast! You're driving too fast!" said Mrs. Mitty. "What are you driving so fast for?"

"Hmm?" said Walter Mitty. He looked at his wife, in the seat beside him, with shocked astonishment. She seemed grossly unfamiliar, like a strange woman who had yelled at him in a crowd. "You were up to fifty-five," she said. "You know I don't like to go more than forty. You were up to fifty-five." Walter Mitty drove on toward Waterbury in silence, the roaring of the SN202 through the worst storm in twenty years of Navy flying fading in the remote, intimate airways of his mind. "You're tensed up again," said Mrs. Mitty. "It's one of your days. I wish you'd let Dr. Renshaw look you over."

Walter Mitty stopped the car in front of the building where his wife went to have her hair done. "Remember to get those overshoes while I'm having my hair done," she said. "I don't need overshoes," said Mitty. She put her mirror back into her bag. "We've been all through that," she said, getting out of the car. "You're not a young man any longer." He raced the engine a little. "Why don't you wear your gloves? Have you lost your gloves?" Walter Mitty reached in a pocket and brought out the gloves. He put them on, but after she had turned and gone into the building and he had driven on to a red light, he took them off again. "Pick it up, brother!" snapped a cop as the light changed, and Mitty hastily pulled on his gloves and lurched ahead. He drove around the streets aimlessly for a time, and then he drove past the hospital on his way to the parking lot.

... "It's the millionaire banker, Wellington McMillan," said the pretty nurse. "Yes?" said Walter Mitty, removing his gloves slowly. "Who has the case?" "Dr. Renshaw and Dr. Benbow, but there are two specialists here, Dr. Remington from New York and Dr. Pritchard-Mitford from London. He flew over." A door opened down a long, cool corridor and Dr. Renshaw came out. He looked distraught and haggard. "Hello, Mitty," he said. "We're having the devil's own time with McMillan, the millionaire banker and close personal friend of Roosevelt. Obstreosis of the ductal tract. Tertiary. Wish you'd take a look at him." "Glad to," said Mitty.

In the operating room there were whispered introductions: "Dr. Remington, Dr. Mitty, Mr. Pritchard-Mitford, Dr. Mitty." "I've read your book on streptothricosis," said Pritchard-Mitford, shaking hands. "A brilliant performance, sir." "Thank you," said Walter Mitty. "Didn't know you were in the States, Mitty," grumbled Remington. "Coals to Newcastle, bringing Mitford and me up here for a tertiary." "You are very kind," said Mitty. A huge, complicated machine, connected to the operating table, with many tubes and wires, began at this moment to go pocketa-pocketa-pocketa. "The new anesthetizer is giving way!" shouted an interne. "There is no one in the East who knows how to fix it!" "Quiet, man!" said Mitty, in a low, cool voice. He sprang to the machine, which was now going pocketa-pocketa-queep-pocketa-queep. He began fingering delicately a row of glistening dials. "Give me a fountain pen!" he snapped. Someone handed him a fountain pen. He pulled a faulty piston out of the machine and inserted the pen in its place. "That will hold for ten minutes," he said. "Get on with the operation." A nurse hurried over and whispered to Renshaw, and Mitty saw the man turn pale. "Coreopsis has set in," said Renshaw nervously. "If you would take over, Mitty?" Mitty looked at him and at the craven figure of Benbow, who drank, and at the grave, uncertain faces of the two great specialists. "If you wish," he said. They slipped a white gown on him; he adjusted a mask and drew on thin gloves; nurses handed him shining. . . .

"Back it up, Mac! Look out for that Buick!" Walter Mitty jammed on the brakes. "Wrong lane, Mac," said the parking-lot attendant, looking at Mitty closely. "Gee. Yeh," muttered Mitty. He began cautiously to back out of the lane marked "Exit Only." "Leave her sit there," said the attendant. "I'll put her away." Mitty got out of the car. "Hey, better leave the key." "Oh," said Mitty, handing the man the ignition key. The attendant vaulted into the car, backed it up with insolent skill, and put it where it belonged.

They're so damn cocky, thought Walter Mitty, walking along Main Street; they think they know everything. Once he had tried to take his chains off, outside New Milford, and he had got them wound around the axles. A man had had to come out in a wrecking car and unwind them, a young, grinning garageman. Since then Mrs. Mitty always made him drive to the garage to have the chains taken off. The next time, he thought, I'll wear my right arm in a sling; they won't grin at me then. I'll have my right arm in a sling and they'll see I couldn't possibly take the chains off myself. He kicked at the slush on the sidewalk. "Overshoes," he said to himself, and he began looking for a shoe store.

When he came out into the street again, with the overshoes in a box under his arm, Walter Mitty began to wonder what the other thing was his wife had told him to get. She had told him, twice, before they set out from their house for Waterbury. In a way he hated these weekly trips to town — he was always getting something wrong. Kleenex, he thought, Squibb's, razor blades? No. Toothpaste, toothbrush, bicarbonate, carborundum, initiative and referendum? He gave it up. But she would remember it. "Where's the what's-its-name?" she would ask. "Don't tell me you forgot the what's-its-name." A newsboy went by shouting something about the Waterbury trial.

. . . "Perhaps this will refresh your memory." The District Attorney suddenly thrust a heavy automatic at the quiet figure on the witness stand. "Have you ever seen this before?" Walter Mitty took the gun and examined it expertly. "This is my Webley-Vickers 50.80," he said calmly. An excited buzz ran around the courtroom. The Judge rapped for order. "You are a crack shot with any sort of firearms, I believe?" said the District Attorney, insinuatingly. "Objection!" shouted Mitty's attorney. "We have shown that the defendant could not have fired the shot. We have shown that he wore his right arm in a sling on the night of the fourteenth of July." Walter Mitty raised his hand briefly and the bickering attorneys were stilled. "With any known make of gun," he said evenly, "I could have killed Gregory Fitzhurst at three hundred feet *with my left hand*." Pandemonium broke loose in the courtroom. A woman's scream rose above the bedlam and suddenly a lovely, dark-haired girl was in Walter Mitty's arms. The District Attorney struck at her savagely. Without rising from his chair, Mitty let the man have it on the point of the chin. "You miserable cur!" . . .

"Puppy biscuit," said Walter Mitty. He stopped walking and the buildings of Waterbury rose up out of the misty courtroom and surrounded him again. A woman who was passing laughed. "He said 'Puppy biscuit,'" she said to her companion. "That man said 'Puppy biscuit' to himself." Walter Mitty hurried on. He went into an A. & P., not the first one he came to but a smaller one farther up the street. "I want some biscuit for small, young dogs," he said to the clerk. "Any special brand, sir?" The greatest pistol shot in the world thought a moment. "It says 'Puppies Bark for It' on the box," said Walter Mitty.

His wife would be through at the hairdresser's in fifteen minutes, Mitty saw in looking at his watch, unless they had trouble drying it; sometimes they had trouble drying it. She didn't like to get to the hotel first; she would want him to be there waiting for her as usual. He found a big leather chair in the lobby, facing a window, and he put the overshoes and the puppy biscuit on the floor beside it. He picked up an old copy of *Liberty* and sank down into the chair. "Can Germany Conquer the World through the Air?" Walter Mitty looked at the pictures of bombing planes and of ruined streets.

. . . "The cannonading has got the wind up in young Raleigh, sir," said the sergeant. Captain Mitty looked up at him through tousled hair. "Get him to bed," he said wearily. "With the others. I'll fly alone." "But you can't, sir," said the sergeant anxiously. "It takes two men to handle that bomber and the Archies are pounding hell out of the air. Von Richtman's circus is between here and Saulier." "Somebody's got to get that ammunition dump," said Mitty. "I'm going over. Spot of brandy?" He poured a drink for the sergeant and one for himself. War thundered and whined around the dugout and battered at the door. There was a rending of wood and splinters flew through the room. "A bit of a near thing," said Captain Mitty carelessly. "The box barrage is closing in," said the sergeant. "We only live once, Sergeant," said Mitty, with his faint, fleeting smile. "Or do we?" He poured another brandy and tossed it off. "I never see a man could hold his brandy like you, sir," said the sergeant. "Begging your pardon, sir." Captain Mitty stood up and strapped on his huge Webley-Vickers automatic. "It's forty kilometers through hell, sir," said the sergeant. Mitty finished one last brandy. "After all," he said softly, "what isn't?" The pounding of the cannon increased; there was the rat-tat-tatting of machine guns, and from somewhere came the menacing pocket-pocketa-pocketa of the new flame-throwers. Walter Mitty walked to the door of the dugout humming "Auprès de Ma Blonde." He turned and waved to the sergeant. "Cheerio!" he said. . . .

Something struck his shoulder. "I've been looking all over this hotel for you," said Mrs. Mitty. "Why do you have to hide in this old chair? How did you expect me to find you?" "Things close in," said Walter Mitty vaguely. "What?" Mrs. Mitty said. "Did you get the what's-its-name? The puppy biscuit? What's in that box?" "Overshoes," said Mitty. "Couldn't you have put them on in the store?" "I was thinking," said Walter Mitty. "Does it ever occur to you that I am sometimes thinking?" She looked at him. "I'm going to take your temperature when I get you home," she said.

They went out through the revolving doors that made a faintly derisive whistling sound when you pushed them. It was two blocks to the parking lot. At the drugstore on the corner she said, "Wait here for me. I forgot something. I won't be a minute." She was more than a minute. Walter Mitty lighted a cigarette. It began to rain, rain with sleet in it. He stood up against the wall of the drugstore, smoking. . . . He put his shoulders back and his heels together. "To hell with the handkerchief," said Walter Mitty scornfully. He took one last drag on his cigarette and snapped it away. Then, with that faint, fleeting smile playing about his lips, he faced the firing squad; erect and motionless, proud and disdainful, Walter Mitty the Undefeated, inscrutable to the last.

[1942]

F. SCOTT FITZGERALD (1896–1940), regarded as the literary spokesman for the "Lost Generation" of the 1920s in America, was born in St. Paul, Minnesota. His family had some social standing but little money, and it was only with help from a maiden aunt that he was able to go to an eastern preparatory school and then on to Princeton, where he said his family hoped that he would attend to his studies and stop "wasting his time scribbling." He withdrew from college before graduating to accept a commission as a second lieutenant in the Regular Army during World War I, but he spent most of his time in the service writing his first novel, which he revised several times before it was published in 1920 as This Side of Paradise. The novel was such a success that magazines were eager to print Fitzgerald's stories, and his first story collection, Flappers and Philosophers, was rushed into print later the same year to take advantage of the novel's popularity. Another story collection, Tales of the Jazz Age, followed in 1922. Years later Fitzgerald would say, writing in the third person, that he was grateful to the Jazz Age because "It bore him up, flattered him and gave him more money than he had dreamed of, simply for telling people that he felt as they did, that something had to be done with all the nervous energy stored up and unexpended in the War."

In 1925, with the publication of his novel The Great Gatsby, Fitzgerald reached the peak of his fame as a writer. His reputation declined rapidly in the harsher years of the 1930s. The Great Depression in the United States and around the world coincided with his own emotional and physical collapse, as his marriage and career floundered on his wife's mental illness and his alcoholism. Gertrude Stein had coined the term "Lost Generation" to describe the young men who had served in World War I and were forced to grow up "to find all Gods dead, all wars fought, all faiths in man shaken." But Fitzgerald's last years were truly lost; he confronted the "waste and horror" of his dissipated talent, writing Hollywood screenplays and struggling unsuccessfully to finish his novel The Last Tycoon.

At the time of his death Fitzgerald had written about 160 stories. As one of his editors, Malcolm Cowley, has said, the exact number is hard to set because some of his work was on the borderline between fiction and the informal essay or "magazine piece." Simple and clear in style, Fitzgerald's stories make up an informal history of his career, dating from before the publication of his first novel to after his final crack-up. "Babylon Revisited" (1931) is one of his later stories, perhaps one of the best he ever wrote. It is more complicated emotionally than his earlier short fiction. As Cowley realized, it embodies "less regret for the past and more dignity in the face of real sorrow."

F. Scott Fitzgerald

ကာ

Babylon Revisited

I

"And where's Mr. Campbell?" Charlie asked.

"Gone to Switzerland. Mr. Campbell's a pretty sick man, Mr. Wales."

"I'm sorry to hear that. And George Hardt?" Charlie inquired.

"Back in America, gone to work."

"And where is the Snow Bird?"

"He was in here last week. Anyway, his friend, Mr. Schaeffer, is in Paris."

Two familiar names from the long list of a year and a half ago. Charlie scribbled an address in his notebook and tore out the page.

"If you see Mr. Schaeffer, give him this," he said. "It's my brother-in-law's address. I haven't settled on a hotel yet."

He was not really disappointed to find Paris was so empty. But the stillness in the Ritz bar was strange and portentous. It was not an American bar any more — he felt polite in it, and not as if he owned it. It had gone back into France. He felt the stillness from the moment he got out of the taxi and saw the doorman, usually in a frenzy of activity at this hour, gossiping with a *chasseur*[1] by the servants' entrance.

Passing through the corridor, he heard only a single, bored voice in the once-clamorous women's room. When he turned into the bar he traveled the twenty feet of green carpet with his eyes fixed straight ahead by old habit; and then, with his foot firmly on the rail, he turned and surveyed the room, encountering only a single pair of eyes that fluttered up from a newspaper in the corner. Charlie asked for the head barman, Paul, who in the latter days of the bull market had come to work in his own custom-built car — disembarking, however, with due nicety at the nearest corner. But Paul was at his country house today and Alix giving him information.

"No, no more," Charlie said, "I'm going slow these days."

Alix congratulated him: "You were going pretty strong a couple of years ago."

[1] bellhop.

"I'll stick to it all right," Charlie assured him. "I've stuck to it for over a year and a half now."

"How do you find conditions in America?"

"I haven't been to America for months. I'm in business in Prague, representing a couple of concerns there. They don't know about me down there."

Alix smiled.

"Remember the night of George Hardt's bachelor dinner here?" said Charlie. "By the way, what's become of Claude Fessenden?"

Alix lowered his voice confidentially: "He's in Paris, but he doesn't come here any more. Paul doesn't allow it. He ran up a bill of thirty thousand francs, charging all his drinks and his lunches, and usually his dinner, for more than a year. And when Paul finally told him he had to pay, he gave him a bad check."

Alix shook his head sadly.

"I don't understand it, such a dandy fellow. Now he's all bloated up — " He made a plump apple of his hands.

Charlie watched a group of strident queens installing themselves in a corner.

"Nothing affects them," he thought. "Stocks rise and fall, people loaf or work, but they go on forever." The place oppressed him. He called for the dice and shook with Alix for the drink.

"Here for long, Mr. Wales?"

"I'm here for four or five days to see my little girl."

"Oh-h! You have a little girl?"

Outside, the fire-red, gas-blue, ghost-green signs shone smokily through the tranquil rain. It was late afternoon and the streets were in movement; the *bistros* gleamed. At the corner of the Boulevard des Capucines he took a taxi. The Place de la Concorde moved by in pink majesty; they crossed the logical Seine, and Charlie felt the sudden provincial quality of the Left Bank.

Charlie directed his taxi to the Avenue de l'Opera, which was out of his way. But he wanted to see the blue hour spread over the magnificent façade, and imagine that the cab horns, playing endlessly the first few bars of *La Plus que Lente,*[2] were the trumpets of the Second Empire.[3] They were closing the iron grill in front of Brentano's Book-store, and people were already at dinner behind the trim little bourgeois hedge of Duval's. He had never eaten at a really cheap restaurant in Paris. Five-course dinner, four francs fifty, eighteen cents, wine included. For some odd reason he wished that he had.

As they rolled on to the Left Bank and he felt its sudden provincialism, he thought, "I spoiled this city for myself. I didn't realize it, but the

---

[2] "Slower than Slow," whimsical piano piece by Claude Debussy (1862–1918).
[3] the reign of Napoleon III, 1852–1871.

days came along one after another, and then two years were gone, and everything was gone, and I was gone."

He was thirty-five, and good to look at. The Irish mobility of his face was sobered by a deep wrinkle between his eyes. As he rang his brother-in-law's bell in the Rue Palatine, the wrinkle deepened till it pulled down his brows; he felt a cramping sensation in his belly. From behind the maid who opened the door darted a lovely little girl of nine who shrieked "Daddy!" and flew up, struggling like a fish, into his arms. She pulled his head around by one ear and set her cheek against his.

"My old pie," he said.

"Oh, daddy, daddy, daddy, daddy, dads, dads, dads!"

She drew him into the salon, where the family waited, a boy and a girl his daughter's age, his sister-in-law and her husband. He greeted Marion with his voice pitched carefully to avoid either feigned enthusiasm or dislike, but her response was more frankly tepid, though she minimized her expression of unalterable distrust by directing her regard toward his child. The two men clasped hands in a friendly way and Lincoln Peters rested his for a moment on Charlie's shoulder.

The room was warm and comfortably American. The three children moved intimately about, playing through the yellow oblongs that led to other rooms; the cheer of six o'clock spoke in the eager smacks of the fire and the sounds of French activity in the kitchen. But Charlie did not relax; his heart sat up rigidly in his body and he drew confidence from his daughter, who from time to time came close to him, holding in her arms the doll he had brought.

"Really extremely well," he declared in answer to Lincoln's question. "There's a lot of business there that isn't moving at all, but we're doing even better than ever. In fact, damn well. I'm bringing my sister over from America next month to keep house for me. My income last year was bigger than it was when I had money. You see, the Czechs ———"

His boasting was for a specific purpose; but after a moment, seeing a faint restiveness in Lincoln's eye, he changed the subject:

"Those are fine children of yours, well brought up, good manners."

"We think Honoria's a great little girl too."

Marion Peters came back from the kitchen. She was a tall woman with worried eyes, who had once possessed a fresh American loveliness. Charlie had never been sensitive to it and was always surprised when people spoke of how pretty she had been. From the first there had been an instinctive antipathy between them.

"Well, how do you find Honoria?" she asked.

"Wonderful. I was astonished how much she's grown in ten months. All the children are looking well."

"We haven't had a doctor for a year. How do you like being back in Paris?"

"It seems very funny to see so few Americans around."

"I'm delighted," Marion said vehemently. "Now at least you can go into a store without their assuming you're a millionaire. We've suffered like everybody, but on the whole it's a good deal pleasanter."

"But it was nice while it lasted," Charlie said. "We were a sort of royalty, almost infallible, with a sort of magic around us. In the bar this afternoon" — he stumbled, seeing his mistake — "there wasn't a man I knew."

She looked at him keenly. "I should think you'd have had enough of bars."

"I only stayed a minute. I take one drink every afternoon, and no more."

"Don't you want a cocktail before dinner?" Lincoln asked.

"I take only one drink every afternoon, and I've had that."

"I hope you keep to it," said Marion.

Her dislike was evident in the coldness with which she spoke, but Charlie only smiled; he had larger plans. Her very aggressiveness gave him an advantage, and he knew enough to wait. He wanted them to initiate the discussion of what they knew had brought him to Paris.

At dinner he couldn't decide whether Honoria was most like him or her mother. Fortunate if she didn't combine the traits of both that had brought them to disaster. A great wave of protectiveness went over him. He thought he knew what to do for her. He believed in character; he wanted to jump back a whole generation and trust in character again as the eternally valuable element. Everything else wore out.

He left soon after dinner, but not to go home. He was curious to see Paris by night with clearer and more judicious eyes than those of other days. He bought a *strapontin*[4] for the Casino and watched Josephine Baker go through her chocolate arabesques.

After an hour he left and strolled toward Montmartre, up the Rue Pigalle into the Place Blanche. The rain had stopped and there were a few people in evening clothes disembarking from taxis in front of cabarets, and *cocottes*[5] prowling singly or in pairs, and many Negroes. He passed a lighted door from which issued music, and stopped with the sense of familiarity; it was Bricktop's, where he had parted with so many hours and so much money. A few doors farther on he found another ancient rendezvous and incautiously put his head inside. Immediately an eager orchestra burst into sound, a pair of professional dancers leaped to their feet and a maître d'hôtel swooped toward him, crying, "Crowd just arriving, sir!" But he withdrew quickly.

"You have to be damn drunk," he thought.

Zelli's was closed, the bleak and sinister cheap hotels surrounding it were dark; up in the Rue Blanche there was more light and a local, colloquial French crowd. The Poet's Cave had disappeared, but the two great

---

[4] Cheap seat in the aisle. Josephine Baker was an American black entertainer who gained fame in Paris in the 1920s and 1930s.

[5] prostitutes.

mouths of the Café of Heaven and the Café of Hell still yawned — even devoured, as he watched, the meager contents of a tourist bus — a German, a Japanese, and an American couple who glanced at him with frightened eyes.

So much for the effort and ingenuity of Montmartre. All the catering to vice and waste was on an utterly childish scale, and he suddenly realized the meaning of the word "dissipate" — to dissipate into thin air; to make nothing out of something. In the little hours of the night every move from place to place was an enormous human jump, an increase of paying for the privilege of slower and slower motion.

He remembered thousand-franc notes given to an orchestra for playing a single number, hundred-franc notes tossed to a doorman for calling a cab.

But it hadn't been given for nothing.

It had been given, even the most wildly squandered sum, as an offering to destiny that he might not remember the things most worth remembering, the things that now he would always remember — his child taken from his control, his wife escaped to a grave in Vermont.

In the glare of a *brasserie*[6] a woman spoke to him. He bought her some eggs and coffee, and then, eluding her encouraging stare, gave her a twenty-franc note and took a taxi to his hotel.

II

He woke upon a fine fall day — football weather. The depression of yesterday was gone and he liked the people on the streets. At noon he sat opposite Honoria at Le Grand Vatel, the only restaurant he could think of not reminiscent of champagne dinners and long luncheons that began at two and ended in a blurred and vague twilight.

"Now, how about vegetables? Oughtn't you to have some vegetables?"

"Well, yes."

"Here's *épinards* and *chou-fleur* and carrots and *haricots*."[7]

"I'd like *chou-fleur*."

"Wouldn't you like to have two vegetables?"

"I usually only have one at lunch."

The waiter was pretending to be inordinately fond of children. *"Qu'elle est mignonne la petite! Elle parle exactement comme une Française."*[8]

"How about dessert? Shall we wait and see?"

The waiter disappeared. Honoria looked at her father expectantly.

"What are we going to do?"

"First, we're going to that toy store in the Rue Saint-Honoré and buy

---

[6] small, informal restaurant.

[7] spinach, cauliflower, beans.

[8] "What a cute little girl! She speaks exactly like a French girl."

you anything you like. And then we're going to the vaudeville at the Empire."

She hesitated. "I like it about the vaudeville, but not the toy store."

"Why not?"

"Well, you brought me this doll." She had it with her. "And I've got lots of things. And we're not rich any more, are we?"

"We never were. But today you are to have anything you want."

"All right," she agreed resignedly.

When there had been her mother and a French nurse he had been inclined to be strict; now he extended himself, reached out for a new tolerance; he must be both parents to her and not shut any of her out of communication.

"I want to get to know you," he said gravely. "First let me introduce myself. My name is Charles J. Wales, of Prague."

"Oh, daddy!" her voice cracked with laughter.

"And who are you, please?" he persisted, and she accepted a rôle immediately: "Honoria Wales, Rue Palatine, Paris."

"Married or single?"

"No, not married. Single."

He indicated the doll. "But I see you have a child, madame."

Unwilling to disinherit it, she took it to her heart and thought quickly: "Yes, I've been married, but I'm not married now. My husband is dead."

He went on quickly, "And the child's name?"

"Simone. That's after my best friend at school."

"I'm very pleased that you're doing so well at school."

"I'm third this month," she boasted. "Elsie" — that was her cousin — "is only about eighteenth, and Richard is at the bottom."

"You like Richard and Elsie, don't you?"

"Oh, yes. I like Richard quite well and I like her all right."

Cautiously and casually he asked: "And Aunt Marion and Uncle Lincoln — which do you like best?"

"Oh, Uncle Lincoln, I guess."

He was increasingly aware of her presence. As they came in, a murmur of " . . . adorable" followed them, and now the people at the next table bent all their silences upon her, staring as if she were something no more conscious than a flower.

"Why don't I live with you?" she asked suddenly. "Because mamma's dead?"

"You must stay here and learn more French. It would have been hard for daddy to take care of you so well."

"I don't really need much taking care of any more. I do everything for myself."

Going out of the restaurant, a man and a woman unexpectedly hailed him.

"Well, the old Wales!"

"Hello there, Lorraine. . . . Dunc."

Sudden ghosts out of the past: Duncan Schaeffer, a friend from college. Lorraine Quarrles, a lovely, pale blonde of thirty; one of a crowd who had helped them make months into days in the lavish times of three years ago.

"My husband couldn't come this year," she said, in answer to his question. "We're poor as hell. So he gave me two hundred a month and told me I could do my worst on that. . . . This your little girl?"

"What about coming back and sitting down?" Duncan asked.

"Can't do it." He was glad for an excuse. As always, he felt Lorraine's passionate, provocative attraction, but his own rhythm was different now.

"Well, how about dinner?" she asked.

"I'm not free. Give me your address and let me call you."

"Charlie, I believe you're sober," she said judicially. "I honestly believe he's sober, Dunc. Pinch him and see if he's sober."

Charlie indicated Honoria with his head. They both laughed.

"What's your address?" said Duncan skeptically.

He hesitated, unwilling to give the name of his hotel.

"I'm not settled yet. I'd better call you. We're going to see the vaudeville at the Empire."

"There! That's what I want to do," Lorraine said. "I want to see some clowns and acrobats and jugglers. That's just what we'll do, Dunc."

"We've got to do an errand first," said Charlie. "Perhaps we'll see you there."

"All right, you snob. . . . Good-by, beautiful little girl."

"Good-by."

Honoria bobbed politely.

Somehow, an unwelcome encounter. They liked him because he was functioning, because he was serious; they wanted to see him, because he was stronger than they were now, because they wanted to draw a certain sustenance from his strength.

At the Empire, Honoria proudly refused to sit upon her father's folded coat. She was already an individual with a code of her own, and Charlie was more and more absorbed by the desire of putting a little of himself into her before she crystallized utterly. It was hopeless to try to know her in so short a time.

Between the acts they came upon Duncan and Lorraine in the lobby where the band was playing.

"Have a drink?"

"All right, but not up at the bar. We'll take a table."

"The perfect father."

Listening abstractedly to Lorraine, Charlie watched Honoria's eyes leave their table, and he followed them wistfully about the room, wondering what they saw. He met her glance and she smiled.

"I liked that lemonade," she said.

What had she said? What had he expected? Going home in a taxi afterward, he pulled her over until her head rested against his chest.

"Darling, do you ever think of your mother?"

"Yes, sometimes," she answered vaguely.

"I don't want you to forget her. Have you got a picture of her?"

"Yes, I think so. Anyhow, Aunt Marion has. Why don't you want me to forget her?"

"She loved you very much."

"I loved her too."

They were silent for a moment.

"Daddy, I want to come and live with you," she said suddenly.

His heart leaped; he had wanted it to come like this.

"Aren't you perfectly happy?"

"Yes, but I love you better than anybody. And you love me better than anybody, don't you, now that mummy's dead?"

"Of course I do. But you won't always like me best, honey. You'll grow up and meet somebody your own age and go marry him and forget you ever had a daddy."

"Yes, that's true," she agreed tranquilly.

He didn't go in. He was coming back at nine o'clock and he wanted to keep himself fresh and new for the thing he must say then.

"When you're safe inside, just show yourself in that window."

"All right. Good-by, dads, dads, dads, dads."

He waited in the dark street until she appeared, all warm and glowing, in the window above and kissed her fingers out into the night.

III

They were waiting. Marion sat behind the coffee service in a dignified black dinner dress that just faintly suggested mourning. Lincoln was walking up and down with the animation of one who had already been talking. They were as anxious as he was to get into the question. He opened it almost immediately:

"I suppose you know what I want to see you about — why I really came to Paris."

Marion played with the black stars on her necklace and frowned.

"I'm awfully anxious to have a home," he continued. "And I'm awfully anxious to have Honoria in it. I appreciate your taking in Honoria for her mother's sake, but things have changed now" — he hesitated and then continued more forcibly — "changed radically with me, and I want to ask you to reconsider the matter. It would be silly for me to deny that about three years ago I was acting badly ——— "

Marion looked up at him with hard eyes.

" — but all that's over. As I told you, I haven't had more than a drink a day for over a year, and I take that drink deliberately, so that the idea of alcohol won't get too big in my imagination. You see the idea?"

"No," said Marion succinctly.

"It's a sort of stunt I set myself. It keeps the matter in proportion."

"I get you," said Lincoln. "You don't want to admit it's got any attraction for you."

"Something like that. Sometimes I forget and don't take it. But I try to take it. Anyhow, I couldn't afford to drink in my position. The people I represent are more than satisfied with what I've done, and I'm bringing my sister over from Burlington to keep house for me, and I want awfully to have Honoria too. You know that even when her mother and I weren't getting along well we never let anything that happened touch Honoria. I know she's fond of me and I know I'm able to take care of her and — well, there you are. How do you feel about it?"

He knew that now he would have to take a beating. It would last an hour or two hours, and it would be difficult, but if he modulated his inevitable resentment to the chastened attitude of the reformed sinner, he might win his point in the end.

Keep your temper, he told himself. You don't want to be justified. You want Honoria.

Lincoln spoke first: "We've been talking it over ever since we got your letter last month. We're happy to have Honoria here. She's a dear little thing, and we're glad to be able to help her, but of course that isn't the question —— "

Marion interrupted suddenly. "How long are you going to stay sober, Charlie?" she asked.

"Permanently, I hope."

"How can anybody count on that?"

"You know I never did drink heavily until I gave up business and came over here with nothing to do. Then Helen and I began to run around with —— "

"Please leave Helen out of it. I can't bear to hear you talk about her like that."

He stared at her grimly; he had never been certain how fond of each other the sisters were in life.

"My drinking only lasted about a year and a half — from the time we came over until I — collapsed."

"It was time enough."

"It was time enough," he agreed.

"My duty is entirely to Helen," she said. "I try to think what she would have wanted me to do. Frankly, from the night you did that terrible thing you haven't really existed for me. I can't help that. She was my sister."

"Yes."

"When she was dying she asked me to look out for Honoria. If you hadn't been in a sanitarium then, it might have helped matters."

He had no answer.

"I'll never in my life be able to forget the morning when Helen knocked at my door, soaked to the skin and shivering and said you'd locked her out."

Charlie gripped the sides of the chair. This was more difficult than he expected; he wanted to launch out into a long expostulation and explanation, but he only said: "The night I locked her out — " and she interrupted, "I don't feel up to going over that again."

After a moment's silence Lincoln said: "We're getting off the subject. You want Marion to set aside her legal guardianship and give you Honoria. I think the main point for her is whether she has confidence in you or not."

"I don't blame Marion," Charlie said slowly, "but I think she can have entire confidence in me. I had a good record up to three years ago. Of course, it's within human possibilities I might go wrong any time. But if we wait much longer I'll lose Honoria's childhood and my chance for a home." He shook his head, "I'll simply lose her, don't you see?"

"Yes, I see," said Lincoln.

"Why didn't you think of all this before?" Marion asked.

"I suppose I did, from time to time, but Helen and I were getting along badly. When I consented to the guardianship, I was flat on my back in a sanitarium and the market had cleaned me out. I knew I'd acted badly, and I thought if it would bring any peace to Helen, I'd agree to anything. But now it's different. I'm functioning, I'm behaving damn well, so far as —— "

"Please don't swear at me," Marion said.

He looked at her, startled. With each remark the force of her dislike became more and more apparent. She had built up all her fear of life into one wall and faced it toward him. This trivial reproof was possibly the result of some trouble with the cook several hours before. Charlie became increasingly alarmed at leaving Honoria in this atmosphere of hostility against himself; sooner or later it would come out, in a word here, a shake of the head there, and some of that distrust would be irrevocably implanted in Honoria. But he pulled his temper down out of his face and shut it up inside him; he had won a point, for Lincoln realized the absurdity of Marion's remark and asked her lightly since when she had objected to the word "damn."

"Another thing," Charlie said: "I'm able to give her certain advantages now. I'm going to take a French governess to Prague with me. I've got a lease on a new apartment —— "

He stopped, realizing that he was blundering. They couldn't be expected to accept with equanimity the fact that his income was again twice as large as their own.

"I suppose you can give her more luxuries than we can," said Marion.

"When you were throwing away money we were living along watching every ten francs. . . . I suppose you'll start doing it again."

"Oh, no," he said. "I've learned. I worked hard for ten years, you know — until I got lucky in the market, like so many people. Terribly lucky. It won't happen again."

There was a long silence. All of them felt their nerves straining, and for the first time in a year Charlie wanted a drink. He was sure now that Lincoln Peters wanted him to have his child.

Marion shuddered suddenly; part of her saw that Charlie's feet were planted on the earth now, and her own maternal feeling recognized the naturalness of his desire; but she had lived for a long time with a prejudice — a prejudice founded on a curious disbelief in her sister's happiness, and which, in the shock of one terrible night, had turned to hatred for him. It had all happened at a point in her life where the discouragement of ill health and adverse circumstances made it necessary for her to believe in tangible villainy and a tangible villain.

"I can't help what I think!" she cried out suddenly. "How much you were responsible for Helen's death, I don't know. It's something you'll have to square with your own conscience."

An electric current of agony surged through him; for a moment he was almost on his feet, an unuttered sound echoing in his throat. He hung on to himself for a moment, another moment.

"Hold on there," said Lincoln uncomfortably. "I never thought you were responsible for that."

"Helen died of heart trouble," Charlie said dully.

"Yes, heart trouble." Marion spoke as if the phrase had another meaning for her.

Then, in the flatness that followed her outburst, she saw him plainly and she knew he had somehow arrived at control over the situation. Glancing at her husband, she found no help from him, and as abruptly as if it were a matter of no importance, she threw up the sponge.

"Do what you like!" she cried, springing up from her chair. "She's your child. I'm not the person to stand in your way. I think if it were my child I'd rather see her — " She managed to check herself. "You two decide it. I can't stand this. I'm sick. I'm going to bed."

She hurried from the room; after a moment Lincoln said:

"This has been a hard day for her. You know how strongly she feels — " His voice was almost apologetic: "When a woman gets an idea in her head."

"Of course."

"It's going to be all right. I think she sees now that you — can provide for the child, and so we can't very well stand in your way or Honoria's way."

"Thank you, Lincoln."

"I'd better go along and see how she is."

"I'm going."

He was still trembling when he reached the street, but a walk down the Rue Bonaparte to the *quais* set him up, and as he crossed the Seine, fresh and new by the *quai* lamps, he felt exultant. But back in his room he couldn't sleep. The image of Helen haunted him. Helen whom he had loved so until they had senselessly begun to abuse each other's love, tear it into shreds. On that terrible February night that Marion remembered so vividly, a slow quarrel had gone on for hours. There was a scene at the Florida, and then he attempted to take her home, and then she kissed young Webb at a table; after that there was what she had hysterically said. When he arrived home alone he turned the key in the lock in wild anger. How could he know she would arrive an hour later alone, that there would be a snowstorm in which she wandered about in slippers, too confused to find a taxi? Then the aftermath, her escaping pneumonia by a miracle, and all the attendant horror. They were "reconciled," but that was the beginning of the end, and Marion, who had seen with her own eyes and who imagined it to be one of many scenes from her sister's martyrdom, never forgot.

Going over it again brought Helen nearer, and in the white, soft light that steals upon half sleep near morning he found himself talking to her again. She said that he was perfectly right about Honoria and that she wanted Honoria to be with him. She said she was glad he was being good and doing better. She said a lot of other things — very friendly things — but she was in a swing in a white dress, and swinging faster and faster all the time, so that at the end he could not hear clearly all that she said.

IV

He woke up feeling happy. The door of the world was open again. He made plans, vistas, futures for Honoria and himself, but suddenly he grew sad, remembering all the plans he and Helen had made. She had not planned to die. The present was the thing — work to do and someone to love. But not to love too much, for he knew the injury that a father can do to a daughter or a mother to a son by attaching them too closely: afterward, out in the world, the child would seek in the marriage partner the same blind tenderness and, failing probably to find it, turn against love and life.

It was another bright, crisp day. He called Lincoln Peters at the bank where he worked and asked if he could count on taking Honoria when he left for Prague. Lincoln agreed that there was no reason for delay. One thing — the legal guardianship. Marion wanted to retain that a while longer. She was upset by the whole matter, and it would oil things if she felt that the situation was still in her control for another year. Charlie agreed, wanting only the tangible, visible child.

Then the question of a governess. Charles sat in a gloomy agency and talked to a cross Béarnaise and to a buxom Breton peasant, neither of whom he could have endured. There were others whom he would see tomorrow.

He lunched with Lincoln Peters at Griffons, trying to keep down his exultation.

"There's nothing quite like your own child," Lincoln said. "But you understand how Marion feels too."

"She's forgotten how hard I worked for seven years there," Charlie said. "She just remembers one night."

"There's another thing." Lincoln hesitated. "While you and Helen were tearing around Europe throwing money away, we were just getting along. I didn't touch any of the prosperity because I never got ahead enough to carry anything but my insurance. I think Marion felt there was some kind of injustice in it — you not even working toward the end, and getting richer and richer."

"It went just as quick as it came," said Charlie.

"Yes, a lot of it stayed in the hands of *chasseurs* and saxophone players and maîtres d'hôtel — well, the big party's over now. I just said that to explain Marion's feeling about those crazy years. If you drop in about six o'clock tonight before Marion's too tired, we'll settle the details on the spot."

Back at his hotel, Charlie found a *pneumatique*[9] that had been redirected from the Ritz bar where Charlie had left his address for the purpose of finding a certain man.

> Dear Charlie: You were so strange when we saw you the other day that I wondered if I did something to offend you. If so, I'm not conscious of it. In fact, I have thought about you too much for the last year, and it's always been in the back of my mind that I might see you if I came over here. We *did* have such good times that crazy spring, like the night you and I stole the butcher's tricycle, and the time we tried to call on the president and you had the old derby rim and the wire cane. Everybody seems so old lately, but I don't feel old a bit. Couldn't we get together some time today for old time's sake? I've got a vile hang-over for the moment, but will be feeling better this afternoon and will look for you about five in the sweatshop at the Ritz.
>
> Always devotedly,
> Lorraine

His first feeling was one of awe that he had actually, in his mature years, stolen a tricycle and pedaled Lorraine all over the Étoile between the small hours and dawn. In retrospect it was a nightmare. Locking out Helen didn't fit in with any other act of his life, but the tricycle incident did — it was one of many. How many weeks or months of dissipation to arrive at that condition of utter irresponsibility?

He tried to picture how Lorraine had appeared to him then — very attractive; Helen was unhappy about it, though she said nothing. Yesterday,

[9] message delivered through a citywide system of pneumatic tubes.

in the restaurant, Lorraine had seemed trite, blurred, worn away. He emphatically did not want to see her, and he was glad Alix had not given away his hotel address. It was a relief to think, instead, of Honoria, to think of Sundays spent with her and of saying good morning to her and of knowing she was there in his house at night, drawing her breath in the darkness.

At five he took a taxi and bought presents for all the Peters — a piquant cloth doll, a box of Roman soldiers, flowers for Marion, big linen handkerchiefs for Lincoln.

He saw, when he arrived in the apartment, that Marion had accepted the inevitable. She greeted him now as though he were a recalcitrant member of the family, rather than a menacing outsider. Honoria had been told she was going; Charlie was glad to see that her tact made her conceal her excessive happiness. Only on his lap did she whisper her delight and the question "When?" before she slipped away with the other children.

He and Marion were alone for a minute in the room, and on an impulse he spoke out boldly:

"Family quarrels are bitter things. They don't go according to any rules. They're not like aches or wounds; they're more like splits in the skin that won't heal because there's not enough material. I wish you and I could be on better terms."

"Some things are hard to forget," she answered. "It's a question of confidence." There was no answer to this and presently she asked, "When do you propose to take her?"

"As soon as I can get a governess. I hoped the day after tomorrow."

"That's impossible. I've got to get her things in shape. Not before Saturday."

He yielded. Coming back into the room, Lincoln offered him a drink.

"I'll take my daily whisky," he said.

It was warm here, it was a home, people together by a fire. The children felt very safe and important; the mother and father were serious, watchful. They had things to do for the children more important than his visit here. A spoonful of medicine was, after all, more important than the strained relations between Marion and himself. They were not dull people, but they were very much in the grip of life and circumstances. He wondered if he couldn't do something to get Lincoln out of his rut at the bank.

A long peal at the door-bell; the *bonne d tout faire*[10] passed through and went down the corridor. The door opened upon another long ring, and then voices, and the three in the salon looked up expectantly; Richard moved to bring the corridor within his range of vision, and Marion rose. Then the maid came back along the corridor, closely followed by the voices, which developed under the light into Duncan Schaeffer and Lorraine Quarrles.

They were gay, they were hilarious, they were roaring with laughter.

[10] maid.

For a moment Charlie was astounded; unable to understand how they ferreted out the Peters' address.

"Ah-h-h!" Duncan wagged his finger roguishly at Charlie. "Ah-h-h!"

They both slid down another cascade of laughter. Anxious and at a loss, Charlie shook hands with them quickly and presented them to Lincoln and Marion. Marion nodded, scarcely speaking. She had drawn back a step toward the fire; her little girl stood beside her, and Marion put an arm about her shoulder.

With growing annoyance at the intrusion, Charlie waited for them to explain themselves. After some concentration Duncan said:

"We came to invite you out to dinner. Lorraine and I insist that all this shishi, cagy business 'bout your address got to stop."

Charlie came closer to them, as if to force them backward down the corridor.

"Sorry, but I can't. Tell me where you'll be and I'll phone you in half an hour."

This made no impression. Lorraine sat down suddenly on the side of a chair, and focusing her eyes on Richard, cried, "Oh, what a nice little boy! Come here, little boy." Richard glanced at his mother, but did not move. With a perceptible shrug of her shoulders, Lorraine turned back to Charlie:

"Come and dine. Sure your cousins won' mine. See you so sel'om. Or solemn."

"I can't," said Charlie sharply. "You two have dinner and I'll phone you."

Her voice became suddenly unpleasant. "All right, we'll go. But I remember once when you hammered on my door at four A.M. I was enough of a good sport to give you a drink. Come on, Dunc."

Still in slow motion, with blurred, angry faces, with uncertain feet, they retired along the corridor.

"Good night," Charlie said.

"Good night!" responded Lorraine emphatically.

When he went back into the salon Marion had not moved, only now her son was standing in the circle of her other arm. Lincoln was still swinging Honoria back and forth like a pendulum from side to side.

"What an outrage!" Charlie broke out. "What an absolute outrage!"

Neither of them answered. Charlie dropped into an armchair, picked up his drink, set it down again and said:

"People I haven't seen for two years having the colossal nerve —— "

He broke off. Marion had made the sound "Oh!" in one swift, furious breath, turned her body from him with a jerk and left the room.

Lincoln set down Honoria carefully.

"You children go in and start your soup," he said, and when they obeyed, he said to Charlie:

"Marion's not well and she can't stand shocks. That kind of people make her really physically sick."

"I didn't tell them to come here. They wormed your name out of somebody. They deliberately —— "

"Well, it's too bad. It doesn't help matters. Excuse me a minute."

Left alone, Charlie sat tense in his chair. In the next room he could hear the children eating, talking in monosyllables, already oblivious to the scene between their elders. He heard a murmur of conversation from a farther room and then the ticking bell of a telephone receiver picked up, and in a panic he moved to the other side of the room and out of earshot.

In a minute Lincoln came back. "Look here, Charlie. I think we'd better call off dinner for tonight. Marion's in bad shape."

"Is she angry with me?"

"Sort of," he said, almost roughly. "She's not strong and —— "

"You mean she's changed her mind about Honoria?"

"She's pretty bitter right now. I don't know. You phone me at the bank tomorrow."

"I wish you'd explain to her I never dreamed these people would come here. I'm just as sore as you are."

"I couldn't explain anything to her now."

Charlie got up. He took his coat and hat and started down the corridor. Then he opened the door of the dining room and said in a strange voice, "Good night, children."

Honoria rose and ran around the table to hug him.

"Good night, sweetheart," he said vaguely, and then trying to make his voice more tender, trying to conciliate something, "Good night, dear children."

V

Charlie went directly to the Ritz bar with the furious idea of finding Lorraine and Duncan, but they were not there, and he realized that in any case there was nothing he could do. He had not touched his drink at the Peters', and now he ordered a whisky-and-soda. Paul came over to say hello.

"It's a great change," he said sadly. "We do about half the business we did. So many fellows I hear about back in the States lost everything, maybe not in the first crash, but then in the second. Your friend George Hardt lost every cent, I hear. Are you back in the States?"

"No, I'm in business in Prague."

"I heard that you lost a lot in the crash."

"I did," and he added grimly, "but I lost everything I wanted in the boom."

"Selling short."

"Something like that."

Again the memory of those days swept over him like a nightmare — the people they had met travelling; then people who couldn't add a row of figures or speak a coherent sentence. The little man Helen had consented to dance with at the ship's party, who had insulted her ten feet from the table; the women and girls carried screaming with drink or drugs out of public places ——

—— The men who locked their wives out in the snow, because the snow of twenty-nine wasn't real snow. If you didn't want it to be snow, you just paid some money.

He went to the phone and called the Peters' apartment; Lincoln answered.

"I called up because this thing is on my mind. Has Marion said anything definite?"

"Marion's sick," Lincoln answered shortly. "I know this thing isn't altogether your fault, but I can't have her go to pieces about it. I'm afraid we'll have to let it slide for six months; I can't take the chance of working her up to this state again."

"I see."

"I'm sorry, Charlie."

He went back to his table. His whisky glass was empty, but he shook his head when Alix looked at it questioningly. There wasn't much he could do now except send Honoria some things; he would send her a lot of things tomorrow. He thought rather angrily that this was just money — he had given so many people money. . . .

"No, no more," he said to the waiter. "What do I owe you?"

He would come back some day; they couldn't make him pay forever. But he wanted his child, and nothing was much good now, beside that fact. He wasn't young any more, with a lot of nice thoughts and dreams to have by himself. He was absolutely sure Helen wouldn't have wanted him to be so alone.

[1935]

WILLIAM FAULKNER (1897–1962) *was born in New Albany, Mississippi, into an old southern family that had lost its fortune in the Civil War. When Faulkner was a child, his parents moved to the isolated county-seat town of Oxford, Mississippi, and except for his service in World War I and some time in New Orleans and Hollywood, he spent the rest of his life there. "I discovered my own little postage stamp of native soil was worth writing about and that I would never live long enough to exhaust it." Faulkner went to high school in Oxford and, after serving in the Royal Canadian Air Force during World War I, he attended the University of Mississippi from 1919 to 1921. His literary career began in New Orleans, where he lived for six months and wrote newspaper sketches and stories for the Times-Picayune. He met Sherwood Anderson in New Orleans, and Anderson helped him publish his first novel,* Soldier's Pay, *in 1926. Faulkner's major work was written in the late 1920s and the 1930s, when he created an imaginary county adjacent to Oxford, calling it Yoknapatawpha County and chronicling its history in a series of highly experimental novels, including* The Sound and the Fury *(1929),* As I Lay Dying *(1930),* Sanctuary *(1931),* Light in August *(1932),* Absalom, Absalom! *(1936) and* The Hamlet *(1940). In these works he showed himself to be a writer of genius, although "a willfully and perversely chaotic one," as Jorge Luis Borges has noted, whose "labyrinthine world" required a no less labyrinthine prose technique to describe in epic manner the disintegration of the South through many generations.*

In his short stories, Faulkner wrote about the same themes that obsessed him in his novels. He said in his speech on receiving the Nobel Prize for Literature in 1950 that it is "the problems of the human heart in conflict with itself which alone can make good writing because only that is worth writing about, worth the agony and the sweat." His literary style was less experimental in his stories, where he rarely included poetic imagery or stream-of-consciousness narration. Faulkner wrote nearly a hundred stories, often revising them later to fit as sections into one of his novels. Four books of short stories were published in his lifetime: These Thirteen *(1931),* Doctor Martino and Other Stories *(1934),* Knight's Gambit *(1949), and* Collected Stories *(1950). Faulkner thought of each as a collection possessing a discernible internal organization. He wrote his editor Malcolm Cowley that he believed the only worthwhile purpose of any book is to uplift readers' hearts, "and so even to a collection of short stories, form, integration, is as important as to a novel — an entity of its own, single, set for one pitch, contrapuntal in integration, toward one end, one finale."*

"A Rose for Emily" and "Dry September" were both included in These Thirteen. *They appear in the second section of that book, which is*

devoted to several stories about Yoknapatawpha County. Miss Emily Grierson and Miss Minnie Cooper are similar characters, yet Faulkner resisted having one story follow the other. He sought a "contrapuntal" effect by placing three other stories between them. Although some readers found symbolism in "A Rose for Emily" that suggested Faulkner was implying a battle between the North (the character Homer Barron) and the South (Miss Emily herself), Faulkner denied a schematic interpretation. He said he had intended to write a ghost story, and "I think that the writer is too busy trying to create flesh-and-blood people that will stand up and cast a shadow to have time to be conscious of all the symbolism that he may put into what he does or what people may read into it." (See Faulkner's Commentary about "A Rose for Emily" on page 1285.)

William Faulkner

ཉ

A ROSE FOR EMILY

I

When Miss Emily Grierson died, our whole town went to her funeral: the men through a sort of respectful affection for a fallen monument, the women mostly out of curiosity to see the inside of her house, which no one save an old manservant — a combined gardener and cook — had seen in at least ten years.

It was a big, squarish frame house that had once been white, decorated with cupolas and spires and scrolled balconies in the heavily lightsome style of the seventies, set on what had once been our most select street. But garages and cotton gins had encroached and obliterated even the august names of that neighborhood; only Miss Emily's house was left, lifting its stubborn and coquettish decay above the cotton wagons and the gasoline pumps — an eyesore among eyesores. And now Miss Emily had gone to join the representatives of those august names where they lay in the cedar-bemused cemetery among the ranked and anonymous graves of Union and Confederate soldiers who fell at the battle of Jefferson.

Alive, Miss Emily had been a tradition, a duty, and a care; a sort of hereditary obligation upon the town, dating from that day in 1894 when Colonel Sartoris, the mayor — he who fathered the edict that no Negro woman should appear on the streets without an apron — remitted her taxes, the dispensation dating from the death of her father on into perpetuity. Not that Miss Emily would have accepted charity. Colonel Sartoris invented an involved tale to the effect that Miss Emily's father had loaned money to the town, which the town, as a matter of business, preferred this way of repaying. Only a man of Colonel Sartoris' generation and thought could have invented it, and only a woman could have believed it.

When the next generation, with its more modern ideas, became mayors and aldermen, this arrangement created some little dissatisfaction. On the first of the year they mailed her a tax notice. February came, and there was no reply. They wrote her a formal letter, asking her to call at the sheriff's office at her convenience. A week later the mayor wrote her himself, offering to call or to send his car for her, and received in reply a note on paper of an archaic shape, in a thin, flowing calligraphy in faded ink, to the effect that she no longer went out at all. The tax notice was also enclosed, without comment.

They called a special meeting of the Board of Aldermen. A deputation waited upon her, knocked at the door through which no visitor had passed since she ceased giving china-painting lessons eight or ten years earlier. They were admitted by the old Negro into a dim hall from which a stairway mounted into still more shadow. It smelled of dust and disuse — a close, dank smell. The Negro led them into the parlor. It was furnished in heavy, leather-covered furniture. When the Negro opened the blinds of one window, they could see that the leather was cracked; and when they sat down, a faint dust rose sluggishly about their thighs, spinning with slow motes in the single sun-ray. On a tarnished gilt easel before the fireplace stood a crayon portrait of Miss Emily's father.

They rose when she entered — a small, fat woman in black, with a thin gold chain descending to her waist and vanishing into her belt, leaning on an ebony cane with a tarnished gold head. Her skeleton was small and spare; perhaps that was why what would have been merely plumpness in another was obesity in her. She looked bloated, like a body long submerged in motionless water, and of that pallid hue. Her eyes, lost in the fatty ridges of her face, looked like two small pieces of coal pressed into a lump of dough as they moved from one face to another while the visitors stated their errand.

She did not ask them to sit. She just stood in the door and listened quietly until the spokesman came to a stumbling halt. Then they could hear the invisible watch ticking at the end of the gold chain.

Her voice was dry and cold. "I have no taxes in Jefferson. Colonel Sartoris explained it to me. Perhaps one of you can gain access to the city records and satisfy yourselves."

"But we have. We are the city authorities, Miss Emily. Didn't you get a notice from the sheriff, signed by him?"

"I received a paper, yes," Miss Emily said. "Perhaps he considers himself the sheriff. . . . I have no taxes in Jefferson."

"But there is nothing on the books to show that, you see. We must go by the — "

"See Colonel Sartoris. I have no taxes in Jefferson."

"But, Miss Emily — "

"See Colonel Sartoris." (Colonel Sartoris had been dead almost ten years.) "I have no taxes in Jefferson. Tobe!" The Negro appeared. "Show these gentlemen out."

II

So she vanquished them, horse and foot, just as she had vanquished their fathers thirty years before about the smell. That was two years after her father's death and a short time after her sweetheart — the one we believed would marry her — had deserted her. After her father's death she went out very little; after her sweetheart went away, people hardly saw her at all. A few of the ladies had the temerity to call, but were not received, and the only sign of life about the place was the Negro man — a young man then — going in and out with a market basket.

"Just as if a man — any man — could keep a kitchen properly," the ladies said; so they were not surprised when the smell developed. It was another link between the gross, teeming world and the high and mighty Griersons.

A neighbor, a woman, complained to the mayor, Judge Stevens, eighty years old.

"But what will you have me do about it, madam?" he said.

"Why, send her word to stop it," the woman said. "Isn't there a law?"

"I'm sure that won't be necessary," Judge Stevens said. "It's probably just a snake or a rat that nigger of hers killed in the yard. I'll speak to him about it."

The next day he received two more complaints, one from a man who came in diffident deprecation. "We really must do something about it, Judge. I'd be the last one in the world to bother Miss Emily, but we've got to do something." That night the Board of Aldermen met — three graybeards and one younger man, a member of the rising generation.

"It's simple enough," he said. "Send her word to have her place cleaned up. Give her a certain time to do it in, and if she don't. . . ."

"Dammit, sir," Judge Stevens said, "will you accuse a lady to her face of smelling bad?"

So the next night, after midnight, four men crossed Miss Emily's lawn and slunk about the house like burglars, sniffing along the base of the brickwork and at the cellar openings while one of them performed a regular sowing motion with his hand out of a sack slung from his shoulder. They broke open the cellar door and sprinkled lime there, and in all the outbuildings. As they recrossed the lawn, a window that had been dark was lighted and

Miss Emily sat in it, the light behind her, and her upright torso motionless as that of an idol. They crept quietly across the lawn and into the shadow of the locusts that lined the street. After a week or two the smell went away.

That was when people had begun to feel really sorry for her. People in our town, remembering how old lady Wyatt, her great-aunt, had gone completely crazy at last, believed that the Griersons held themselves a little too high for what they really were. None of the young men were quite good enough for Miss Emily and such. We had long thought of them as a tableau, Miss Emily a slender figure in white in the background, her father a spraddled silhouette in the foreground, his back to her and clutching a horsewhip, the two of them framed by the backflung front door. So when she got to be thirty and was still single, we were not pleased exactly, but vindicated; even with insanity in the family she wouldn't have turned down all of her chances if they had really materialized.

When her father died, it got about that the house was all that was left to her; and in a way, people were glad. At last they could pity Miss Emily. Being left alone, and a pauper, she had become humanized. Now she too would know the old thrill and the old despair of a penny more or less.

The day after his death all the ladies prepared to call at the house and offer condolence and aid, as is our custom. Miss Emily met them at the door, dressed as usual and with no trace of grief on her face. She told them that her father was not dead. She did that for three days, with the ministers calling on her, and the doctors, trying to persuade her to let them dispose of the body. Just as they were about to resort to law and force, she broke down, and they buried her father quickly.

We did not say she was crazy then. We believed she had to do that. We remembered all the young men her father had driven away, and we knew that with nothing left, she would have to cling to that which had robbed her, as people will.

III

She was sick for a long time. When we saw her again, her hair was cut short, making her look like a girl, with a vague resemblance to those angels in colored church windows — sort of tragic and serene.

The town had just let the contracts for paving the sidewalks, and in the summer after her father's death they began the work. The construction company came with niggers and mules and machinery, and a foreman named Homer Barron, a Yankee — a big, dark, ready man, with a big voice and eyes lighter than his face. The little boys would follow in groups to hear him cuss the niggers, and the niggers singing in time to the rise and fall of picks. Pretty soon he knew everybody in town. Whenever you heard a lot of laughing anywhere about the square, Homer Barron would be in the center of the group. Presently, we began to see him and Miss Emily on Sunday afternoons driving in the yellow-wheeled buggy and the matched team of bays from the livery stable.

At first we were glad that Miss Emily would have an interest, because the ladies all said, "Of course a Grierson would not think seriously of a Northerner, a day laborer." But there were still others, older people, who said that even grief could not cause a real lady to forget *noblesse oblige* — without calling it *noblesse oblige.* They just said, "Poor Emily. Her kinsfolk should come to her." She had some kin in Alabama; but years ago her father had fallen out with them over the estate of old lady Wyatt, the crazy woman, and there was no communication between the two families. They had not even been represented at the funeral.

And as soon as the old people said, "Poor Emily," the whispering began. "Do you suppose it's really so?" they said to one another. "Of course it is. What else could. . . ." This behind their hands; rustling of craned silk and satin behind jalousies closed upon the sun of Sunday afternoon as the thin, swift clop-clop-clop of the matched team passed: "Poor Emily."

She carried her head high enough — even when we believed that she was fallen. It was as if she demanded more than ever the recognition of her dignity as the last Grierson; as if it had wanted that touch of earthiness to reaffirm her imperviousness. Like when she bought the rat poison, the arsenic. That was over a year after they had begun to say "Poor Emily," and while the two female cousins were visiting her.

"I want some poison," she said to the druggist. She was over thirty then, still a slight woman, though thinner than usual, with cold, haughty black eyes in a face the flesh of which was strained across the temples and about the eyesockets as you imagine a lighthouse-keeper's face ought to look. "I want some poison," she said.

"Yes, Miss Emily. What kind? For rats and such? I'd recom —— "

"I want the best you have. I don't care what kind."

The druggist named several. "They'll kill anything up to an elephant. But what you want is —— "

"Arsenic," Miss Emily said. "Is that a good one?"

"Is . . . arsenic? Yes, ma'am. But what you want —— "

"I want arsenic."

The druggist looked down at her. She looked back at him, erect, her face like a strained flag. "Why, of course," the druggist said. "If that's what you want. But the law requires you to tell what you are going to use it for."

Miss Emily just stared at him, her head tilted back in order to look him eye for eye, until he looked away and went and got the arsenic and wrapped it up. The Negro delivery boy brought her the package; the druggist didn't come back. When she opened the package at home there was written on the box, under the skull and bones: "For rats."

IV

So the next day we all said, "She will kill herself"; and we said it would be the best thing. When she had first begun to be seen with Homer Barron, we had said, "She will marry him." Then we said, "She will persuade him yet," because Homer himself had remarked — he liked men, and it was known that he drank with the younger men in the Elks' Club — that he was not a marrying man. Later we said, "Poor Emily" behind the jalousies as they passed on Sunday afternoon in the glittering buggy, Miss Emily with her head high and Homer Barron with his hat cocked and a cigar in his teeth, reins and whip in a yellow glove.

Then some of the ladies began to say that it was a disgrace to the town and a bad example to the young people. The men did not want to interfere, but at last the ladies forced the Baptist minister — Miss Emily's people were Episcopal — to call upon her. He would never divulge what happened during that interview, but he refused to go back again. The next Sunday they again drove about the streets, and the following day the minister's wife wrote to Miss Emily's relations in Alabama.

So she had blood-kin under her roof again and we sat back to watch developments. At first nothing happened. Then we were sure that they were to be married. We learned that Miss Emily had been to the jeweler's and ordered a man's toilet set in silver, with the letters H.B. on each piece. Two days later we learned that she had bought a complete outfit of men's clothing, including a nightshirt, and we said, "They are married." We were really glad. We were glad because the two female cousins were even more Grierson than Miss Emily had ever been.

So we were not surprised when Homer Barron — the streets had been finished some time since — was gone. We were a little disappointed that there was not a public blowing-off, but we believed that he had gone on to prepare for Miss Emily's coming, or to give her a chance to get rid of the cousins. (By that time it was a cabal, and we were all Miss Emily's allies to help circumvent the cousins.) Sure enough, after another week they departed. And, as we had expected all along, within three days Homer Barron was back in town. A neighbor saw the Negro man admit him at the kitchen door at dusk one evening.

And that was the last we saw of Homer Barron. And of Miss Emily for some time. The Negro man went in and out with the market basket, but the front door remained closed. Now and then we would see her at the window for a moment, as the men did that night when they sprinkled the lime, but for almost six months she did not appear on the streets. Then we knew that this was to be expected too; as if that quality of her father which had thwarted her woman's life so many times had been too virulent and too furious to die.

When we next saw Miss Emily, she had grown fat and her hair was turning gray. During the next few years it grew grayer and grayer until it attained an even pepper-and-salt iron-gray, when it ceased turning. Up to the day of her death at seventy-four it was still that vigorous iron-gray, like the hair of an active man.

From that time on her front door remained closed, save during a period of six or seven years, when she was about forty, during which she gave lessons in china-painting. She fitted up a studio in one of the downstairs rooms, where the daughters and granddaughters of Colonel Sartoris' contemporaries were sent to her with the same regularity and in the same spirit that they were sent to church on Sundays with a twenty-five-cent piece for the collection plate. Meanwhile her taxes had been remitted.

Then the newer generation became the backbone and the spirit of the town, and the painting pupils grew up and fell away and did not send their children to her with boxes of color and tedious brushes and pictures cut from the ladies' magazines. The front door closed upon the last one and remained closed for good. When the town got free postal delivery, Miss Emily alone refused to let them fasten the metal numbers above her door and attach a mailbox to it. She would not listen to them.

Daily, monthly, yearly we watched the Negro grow grayer and more stooped, going in and out with the market basket. Each December we sent her a tax notice, which would be returned by the post office a week later, unclaimed. Now and then we would see her in one of the downstairs windows — she had evidently shut up the top floor of the house — like the carven torso of an idol in a niche, looking or not looking at us, we could never tell which. Thus she passed from generation to generation — dear, inescapable, impervious, tranquil, and perverse.

And so she died. Fell ill in the house filled with dust and shadows, with only a doddering Negro man to wait on her. We did not even know she was sick; we had long since given up trying to get any information from the Negro. He talked to no one, probably not even to her, for his voice had grown harsh and rusty, as if from disuse.

She died in one of the downstairs rooms, in a heavy walnut bed with a curtain, her gray head propped on a pillow yellow and moldy with age and lack of sunlight.

V

The Negro met the first of the ladies at the front door and let them in, with their hushed, sibilant voices and their quick, curious glances, and then he disappeared. He walked right through the house and out the back and was not seen again.

The two female cousins came at once. They held the funeral on the second day, with the town coming to look at Miss Emily beneath a mass of bought flowers, with the crayon face of her father musing profoundly above the bier and the ladies sibilant and macabre; and the very old men — some in their brushed Confederate uniforms — on the porch and the lawn, talking of Miss Emily as if she had been a contemporary of theirs, believing that they had danced with her and courted her perhaps, confusing time with its mathematical progression, as the old do, to whom all the past is not a diminishing road but, instead, a huge meadow which no winter ever quite touches, divided from them now by the narrow bottleneck of the most recent decade of years.

Already we knew that there was one room in that region above stairs which no one had seen in forty years, and which would have to be forced. They waited until Miss Emily was decently in the ground before they opened it.

The violence of breaking down the door seemed to fill this room with pervading dust. A thin, acrid pall as of the tomb seemed to lie everywhere upon this room decked and furnished as for a bridal: upon the valance curtains of faded rose color, upon the rose-shaded lights, upon the dressing table, upon the delicate array of crystal and the man's toilet things backed with tarnished silver, silver so tarnished that the monogram was obscured. Among them lay a collar and tie, as if they had just been removed, which, lifted, left upon the surface a pale crescent in the dust. Upon a chair hung the suit, carefully folded; beneath it the two mute shoes and the discarded socks.

The man himself lay in the bed.

For a long while we just stood there, looking down at the profound and fleshless grin. The body had apparently once lain in the attitude of an embrace, but now the long sleep that outlasts love, that conquers even the grimace of love, had cuckolded him. What was left of him, rotted beneath what was left of the nightshirt, had become inextricable from the bed in which he lay; and upon him and upon the pillow beside him lay that even coating of the patient and biding dust.

Then we noticed that in the second pillow was the indentation of a head. One of us lifted something from it, and leaning forward, that faint and invisible dust dry and acrid in the nostrils, we saw a long strand of iron-gray hair.

[1931]

William Faulkner

ন্ত্তন্ত

DRY SEPTEMBER

I

Through the bloody September twilight, aftermath of sixty-two rain-less days, it had gone like a fire in dry grass — the rumor, the story, whatever it was. Something about Miss Minnie Cooper and a Negro. Attacked, insulted, frightened: none of them, gathered in the barber shop on that Saturday evening where the ceiling fan stirred, without freshening it, the vitiated air, sending back upon them, in recurrent surges of stale pomade and lotion, their own stale breath and odors, knew exactly what had happened.

"Except it wasn't Will Mayes," a barber said. He was a man of middle age; a thin, sand-colored man with a mild face, who was shaving a client. "I know Will Mayes. He's a good nigger. And I know Miss Minnie Cooper, too."

"What do you know about her?" a second barber said.

"Who is she?" the client said. "A young girl?"

"No," the barber said. "She's about forty, I reckon. She aint married. That's why I dont believe—"

"Believe, hell!" a hulking youth in a sweat-stained silk shirt said. "Wont you take a white woman's word before a nigger's?"

"I dont believe Will Mayes did it," the barber said. "I know Will Mayes."

"Maybe you know who did it, then. Maybe you already got him out of town, you damn niggerlover."

"I dont believe anybody did anything. I dont believe anything happened. I leave it to you fellows if them ladies that get old without getting married dont have notions that a man cant — "

"Then you are a hell of a white man," the client said. He moved under the cloth. The youth had sprung to his feet.

"You dont?" he said. "Do you accuse a white woman of lying?"

The barber held the razor poised above the half-risen client. He did not look around.

"It's this durn weather," another said. "It's enough to make a man do anything. Even to her."

Nobody laughed. The barber said in his mild, stubborn tone: "I aint accusing nobody of nothing. I just know and you fellows know how a woman that never — "

"You damn niggerlover!" the youth said.

"Shut up, Butch," another said. "We'll get the facts in plenty of time to act."

"Who is? Who's getting them?" the youth said. "Facts, hell! I — "

"You're a fine white man," the client said. "Aint you?" In his frothy beard he looked like a desert rat in the moving pictures. "You tell them, Jack," he said to the youth. "If there aint any white men in this town, you can count on me, even if I aint only a drummer and a stranger."

"That's right, boys," the barber said. "Find out the truth first. I know Will Mayes."

"Well, by God!" the youth shouted. "To think that a white man in this town — "

"Shut up, Butch," the second speaker said. "We got plenty of time."

The client sat up. He looked at the speaker. "Do you claim that anything excuses a nigger attacking a white woman? Do you mean to tell me you are a white man and you'll stand for it? You better go back North where you came from. The South dont want your kind here."

"North what?" the second said. "I was born and raised in this town."

"Well, by God!" the youth said. He looked about with a strained, baffled gaze, as if he was trying to remember what it was he wanted to say or to do. He drew his sleeve across his sweating face. "Damn if I'm going to let a white woman — "

"You tell them, Jack," the drummer said. "By God, if they — "

The screen door crashed open. A man stood in the floor, his feet apart and his heavy-set body poised easily. His white shirt was open at the throat; he wore a felt hat. His hot, bold glance swept the group. His name was McLendon. He had commanded troops at the front in France and had been decorated for valor.

"Well," he said, "are you going to sit there and let a black son rape a white woman on the streets of Jefferson?"

Butch sprang up again. The silk of his shirt clung flat to his heavy shoulders. At each armpit was a dark halfmoon. "That's what I been telling them! That's what I — "

"Did it really happen?" a third said. "This aint the first man scare she ever had, like Hawkshaw says. Wasn't there something about a man on the kitchen roof, watching her undress, about a year ago?"

"What?" the client said. "What's that?" The barber had been slowly forcing him back into the chair; he arrested himself reclining, his head lifted, the barber still pressing him down.

McLendon whirled on the third speaker. "Happen? What the hell difference does it make? Are you going to let the black sons get away with it until one really does it?"

"That's what I'm telling them!" Butch shouted. He cursed, long and steady, pointless.

"Here, here," a fourth said. "Not so loud. Dont talk so loud."

"Sure," McLendon said; "no talking necessary at all. I've done my talking. Who's with me?" He poised on the balls of his feet, roving his gaze.

The barber held the drummer's face down, the razor poised. "Find the facts first, boys. I know Willy Mayes. It wasn't him. Let's get the sheriff and do this thing right."

McLendon whirled upon him his furious, rigid face. The barber did not look away. They looked like men of different races. The other barbers had ceased also above their prone clients. "You mean to tell me," McLendon said, "that you'd take a nigger's word before a white woman's? Why, you damn niggerloving — "

The third speaker rose and grasped McLendon's arm; he too had been a soldier. "Now, now. Let's figure this thing out. Who knows anything about what really happened?"

"Figure out hell!" McLendon jerked his arm free. "All that're with me get up from there. The ones that aint — " He roved his gaze, dragging his sleeve across his face.

Three men rose. The drummer in the chair sat up. "Here," he said, jerking at the cloth about his neck; "get this rag off me. I'm with him. I dont live here, but by God, if our mothers and wives and sisters — " He smeared the cloth over his face and flung it to the floor. McLendon stood in the floor and cursed the others. Another rose and moved toward him. The remainder sat uncomfortable, not looking at one another, then one by one they rose and joined him.

The barber picked the cloth from the floor. He began to fold it neatly. "Boys, dont do that. Will Mayes never done it. I know."

"Come on," McLendon said. He whirled. From his hip pocket protruded the butt of a heavy automatic pistol. They went out. The screen door crashed behind them reverberant in the dead air.

The barber wiped the razor carefully and swiftly, and put it away, and ran to the rear, and took his hat from the wall. "I'll be back as soon as I can," he said to the other barbers. "I cant let — " He went out, running. The two other barbers followed him to the door and caught it on the rebound, leaning out and looking up the street after him. The air was flat and dead. It had a metallic taste at the base of the tongue.

"What can he do?" the first said. The second one was saying "Jees Christ, Jees Christ" under his breath. "I'd just as lief be Will Mayes as Hawk, if he gets McLendon riled."

"Jees Christ, Jees Christ," the second whispered.

"You reckon he really done it to her?" the first said.

II

She was thirty-eight or thirty-nine. She lived in a small frame house with her invalid mother and a thin, sallow, unflagging aunt, where each morning between ten and eleven she would appear on the porch in a lace-trimmed boudoir cap, to sit swinging in the porch swing until noon. After dinner she lay down for a while, until the afternoon began to cool. Then, in one of the three or four new voile dresses which she had each summer, she would go downtown to spend the afternoon in the stores with the other ladies, where they would handle the goods and haggle over the prices in cold, immediate voices, without any intention of buying.

She was of comfortable people — not the best in Jefferson, but good people enough — and she was still on the slender side of ordinary looking, with a bright, faintly haggard manner and dress. When she was young she had had a slender, nervous body and a sort of hard vivacity which had enabled her for a time to ride upon the crest of the town's social life as exemplified by the high school party and church social period of her contemporaries while still children enough to be unclassconscious.

She was the last to realize that she was losing ground; that those among whom she had been a little brighter and louder flame than any other were beginning to learn the pleasure of snobbery — male — and retaliation — female. That was when her face began to wear that bright, haggard look. She still carried it to parties on shadowy porticoes and summer lawns, like a mask or a flag, with that bafflement of furious repudiation of truth in her eyes. One evening at a party she heard a boy and two girls, all schoolmates, talking. She never accepted another invitation.

She watched the girls with whom she had grown up as they married and got homes and children, but no man ever called on her steadily until the children of the other girls had been calling her "aunty" for several years, the while their mothers told them in bright voices about how popular Aunt Minnie had been as a girl. Then the town began to see her driving on Sunday afternoons with the cashier in the bank. He was a widower of about forty — a high-colored man, smelling always faintly of the barber shop or of whisky. He owned the first automobile in town, a red runabout; Minnie had the first motoring bonnet and veil the town ever saw. Then the town began to say: "Poor Minnie." "But she is old enough to take care of herself," others said. That was when she began to ask her old schoolmates that their children call her "cousin" instead of "aunty."

It was twelve years now since she had been relegated into adultery by public opinion, and eight years since the cashier had gone to a Memphis bank, returning for one day each Christmas, which he spent at an annual bachelors' party at the hunting club on the river. From behind their curtains the neighbors would see the party pass, and during the over-the-way Christmas day visiting they would tell her about him, about how well he looked, and how they heard that he was prospering in the city, watching with bright, secret eyes her haggard, bright face. Usually by that hour there would be the scent of whisky on her breath. It was supplied her by a youth, a clerk at the soda fountain: "Sure; I buy it for the old gal. I reckon she's entitled to a little fun."

Her mother kept to her room altogether now; the gaunt aunt ran the house. Against that background Minnie's bright dresses, her idle and empty days, had a quality of furious unreality. She went out in the evenings only with women now, neighbors, to the moving pictures. Each afternoon she dressed in one of the new dresses and went downtown alone, where her young "cousins" were already strolling in the late afternoons with their delicate, silken heads and thin, awkward arms and conscious hips, clinging to one another or shrieking and giggling with paired boys in the soda fountain when she passed and went on along the serried store fronts, in the doors of which the sitting and lounging men did not even follow her with their eyes any more.

III

The barber went swiftly up the street where the sparse lights, insect-swirled, glared in rigid and violent suspension in the lifeless air. The day had died in a pall of dust; above the darkened square, shrouded by the spent dust, the sky was as clear as the inside of a brass bell. Below the east was a rumor of the twice-waxed moon.

When he overtook them McLendon and three others were getting into a car parked in an alley. McLendon stooped his thick head, peering out beneath the top. "Changed your mind, did you?" he said. "Damn good thing; by God, tomorrow when this town hears about how you talked to-night —"

"Now, now," the other ex-soldier said. "Hawkshaw's all right. Come on, Hawk; jump in."

"Will Mayes never done it, boys," the barber said. "If anybody done it. Why, you all know well as I do there aint any town where they got better niggers than us. And you know how a lady will kind of think things about men when there aint any reason to, and Miss Minnie anyway —"

"Sure, sure," the soldier said. "We're just going to talk to him a little; that's all."

"Talk hell!" Butch said. "When we're through with the —"

"Shut up, for God's sake!" the soldier said. "Do you want everybody in town —"

"Tell them, by God!" McLendon said. "Tell every one of the sons that'll let a white woman —"

"Let's go; let's go: here's the other car." The second car slid squealing out of a cloud of dust at the alley mouth. McLendon started his car and took the lead. Dust lay like fog in the street. The street lights hung nimbused as in water. They drove on out of town.

A rutted lane turned at right angles. Dust hung above it too, and above all the land. The dark bulk of the ice plant, where the Negro Mayes was night watchman, rose against the sky. "Better stop here, hadn't we?" the soldier said. McLendon did not reply. He hurled the car up and slammed to a stop, the headlights glaring on the blank wall.

"Listen here, boys," the barber said; "if he's here, dont that prove he never done it? Dont it? If it was him, he would run. Dont you see he would?" The second car came up and stopped. McLendon got down; Butch sprang down beside him. "Listen, boys," the barber said.

"Cut the lights off!" McLendon said. The breathless dark rushed down. There was no sound in it save their lungs as they sought air in the parched dust in which for two months they had lived; then the diminishing crunch of McLendon's and Butch's feet, and a moment later McLendon's voice:

"Will! . . . Will!"

Below the east the wan hemorrhage of the moon increased. It heaved above the ridge, silvering the air, the dust, so that they seemed to breathe, live, in a bowl of molten lead. There was no sound of nightbird nor insect, no sound save their breathing and a faint ticking of contracting metal about the cars. Where their bodies touched one another they seemed to sweat dryly, for no more moisture came. "Christ!" a voice said; "let's get out of here."

But they didn't move until vague noises began to grow out of the darkness ahead; then they got out and waited tensely in the breathless dark. There was another sound: a blow, a hissing expulsion of breath and McLendon cursing in undertone. They stood a moment longer, then they ran forward. They ran in a stumbling clump, as though they were fleeing something. "Kill him, kill the son," a voice whispered. McLendon flung them back.

"Not here," he said. "Get him into the car." "Kill him, kill the black son!" the voice murmured. They dragged the Negro to the car. The barber had waited beside the car. He could feel himself sweating and he knew he was going to be sick at the stomach.

"What is it, captains?" the Negro said. "I aint done nothing. 'Fore god, Mr John." Someone produced handcuffs. They worked busily about the Negro as though he were a post, quiet, intent, getting in one another's way. He submitted to the handcuffs, looking swiftly and constantly from dim face to dim face. "Who's here, captains?" he said, leaning to peer into the faces until they could feel his breath and smell his sweaty reek. He spoke a name or two. "What you all say I done, Mr John?"

McLendon jerked the car door open. "Get in!" he said.

The Negro did not move. "What you all going to do with me, Mr John? I aint done nothing. White folks, captains, I aint done nothing: I swear 'fore God." He called another name.

"Get in!" McLendon said. He struck the Negro. The others expelled their breath in a dry hissing and struck him with random blows and he whirled and cursed them, and swept his manacled hands across their faces and slashed the barber upon the mouth, and the barber struck him also. "Get him in there," McLendon said. They pushed at him. He ceased struggling and got in and sat quietly as the others took their places. He sat between the barber and the soldier, drawing his limbs in so as not to touch them, his eyes going swiftly and constantly from face to face. Butch clung to the running board. The car moved on. The barber nursed his mouth with his handkerchief.

"What's the matter, Hawk?" the soldier said.

"Nothing," the barber said. They regained the high road and turned away from town. The second car dropped back out of the dust. They went on, gaining speed; the final fringe of houses dropped behind.

"Goddamn, he stinks!" the soldier said.

"We'll fix that," the drummer in the front beside McLendon said. On the running board Butch cursed into the hot rush of air. The barber leaned suddenly forward and touched McLendon's arm.

"Let me out, John," he said.

"Jump out, niggerlover," McLendon said without turning his head. He drove swiftly. Behind them the sourceless lights of the second car glared in the dust. Presently McLendon turned into a narrow road. It was rutted with disuse. It led back to an abandoned brick kiln — a series of reddish mounds and weed- and vine-choked vats without bottom. It had been used for pasture once, until one day the owner missed one of his mules. Although he prodded carefully in the vats with a long pole, he could not even find the bottom of them.

"John," the barber said.

"Jump out, then," McLendon said, hurling the car along the ruts. Beside the barber the Negro spoke:

"Mr Henry."

The barber sat forward. The narrow tunnel of the road rushed up and past. Their motion was like an extinct furnace blast; cooler, but utterly dead. The car bounded from rut to rut.

"Mr Henry," the Negro said.

The barber began to tug furiously at the door. "Look out, there!" the soldier said, but the barber had already kicked the door open and swung onto the running board. The soldier leaned across the Negro and grasped at him, but he had already jumped. The car went on without checking speed.

The impetus hurled him crashing through dust-sheathed weeds, into the ditch. Dust puffed about him, and in a thin, vicious crackling of sapless stems he lay choking and retching until the second car passed and died away. Then he rose and limped on until he reached the high road and turned toward town, brushing at his clothes with his hands. The moon was higher, riding high and clear of the dust at last, and after a while the town began to glare beneath the dust. He went on, limping. Presently he heard

cars and the glow of them grew in the dust behind him and he left the road
and crouched again in the weeds until they passed. McLendon's car came
last now. There were four people in it and Butch was not on the running
board.

They went on; the dust swallowed them; the glare and the sound died
away. The dust of them hung for a while, but soon the eternal dust absorbed it again. The barber climbed back onto the road and limped on toward town.

IV

As she dressed for supper on that Saturday evening, her own flesh felt
like fever. Her hands trembled among the hooks and eyes and her eyes had
a feverish look, and her hair swirled crisp and crackling under the comb.
While she was still dressing the friends called for her and sat while she
donned her sheerest underthings and stockings and a new voile dress. "Do
you feel strong enough to go out?" they said, their eyes bright too, with a
dark glitter. "When you have had time to get over the shock, you must tell
us what happened. What he said and did; everything."

In the leafed darkness, as they walked toward the square, she began to
breathe deeply, something like a swimmer preparing to dive, until she
ceased trembling, the four of them walking slowly because of the terrible
heat and out of solicitude for her. But as they neared the square she began
to tremble again, walking with her head up, her hands clenched at her sides,
their voices about her murmurous, also with that feverish, glittering quality
of their eyes. They entered the square, she in the center of the group, fragile
in her fresh dress. She was trembling worse. She walked slower and slower,
as children eat ice cream, her head up and her eyes bright in the haggard
banner of her face, passing the hotel and the coatless drummers in chairs
along the curb looking around at her: "That's the one: see? The one in pink
in the middle." "Is that her? What did they do with the nigger? Did
they —?" "Sure. He's all right." "All right, is he?" "Sure. He went on a
little trip." Then the drug store, where even the young men lounging in the
doorway tipped their hats and followed with their eyes the motion of her
hips and legs when she passed.

They went on, passing the lifted hats of the gentlemen, the suddenly
ceased voices, deferent, protective. "Do you see?" the friends said. Their
voices sounded like long, hovering sighs of hissing exultation. "There's not
a Negro on the square. Not one."

They reached the picture show. It was like a miniature fairyland with
its lighted lobby and colored lithographs of life caught in its terrible and
beautiful mutations. Her lips began to tingle. In the dark, when the picture
began, it would be all right; she could hold back the laughing so it would
not waste away so fast and so soon. So she hurried on before the turning
faces, the undertones of low astonishment, and they took their accustomed

places where she could see the aisle against the silver glare and the young men and girls coming in two and two against it.

The lights flicked away; the screen glowed silver, and soon life began to unfold, beautiful and passionate and sad, while still the young men and girls entered, scented and sibilant in the half dark, their paired backs in silhouette delicate and sleek, their slim, quick bodies awkward, divinely young, while beyond them the silver dream accumulated, inevitably on and on. She began to laugh. In trying to suppress it, it made more noise than ever; heads began to turn. Still laughing, her friends raised her and led her out, and she stood at the curb, laughing on a high, sustained note, until the taxi came up and they helped her in.

They removed the pink voile and the sheer underthings and the stockings, and put her to bed, and cracked ice for her temples, and sent for the doctor. He was hard to locate, so they ministered to her with hushed ejaculations, renewing the ice and fanning her. While the ice was fresh and cold she stopped laughing and lay still for a time, moaning only a little. But soon the laughing welled again and her voice rose screaming.

"Shhhhhhhhhhh! Shhhhhhhhhhhhhhh!" they said, freshening the ice-pack, smoothing her hair, examining it for gray; "poor girl!" Then to one another: "Do you suppose anything really happened?" their eyes darkly aglitter, secret and passionate. "Shhhhhhhhhh! Poor girl! Poor Minnie!"

V

It was midnight when McLendon drove up to his neat new house. it was trim and fresh as a birdcage and almost as small, with its clean, green-and-white paint. He locked the car and mounted the porch and entered. His wife rose from a chair beside the reading lamp. McLendon stopped in the floor and stared at her until she looked down.

"Look at that clock," he said, lifting his arm, pointing. She stood before him, her face lowered, a magazine in her hands. Her face was pale, strained, and weary-looking. "Haven't I told you about sitting up like this, waiting to see when I come in?"

"John," she said. She laid the magazine down. Poised on the balls of his feet, he glared at her with his hot eyes, his sweating face.

"Didn't I tell you?" He went toward her. She looked up then. He caught her shoulder. She stood passive, looking at him.

"Don't, John. I couldn't sleep. . . . The heat; something. Please, John. You're hurting me."

"Didn't I tell you?" He released her and half struck, half flung her across the chair, and she lay there and watched him quietly as he left the room.

He went on through the house, ripping off his shirt, and on the dark, screened porch at the rear he stood and mopped his head and shoulders with the shirt and flung it away. He took the pistol from his hip and laid it on the table beside the bed, and sat on the bed and removed his shoes, and rose and slipped his trousers off. He was sweating again already, and he stooped and hunted furiously for the shirt. At last he found it and wiped his body again, and, with his body pressed against the dusty screen, he stood panting. There was no movement, no sound, not even an insect. The dark world seemed to lie stricken beneath the cold moon and the lidless stars.

[1931]

ERNEST HEMINGWAY (1898–1961) was born in Oak Park, Illinois, but he spent most of his boyhood in Michigan, where his father, a doctor, encouraged his enthusiasm for camping and hunting in order to teach him the rudiments of physical courage and endurance. Active as a reporter for his high school newspaper, Hemingway decided not to go on to college. Instead he worked as a reporter on the Kansas City Star for a few months before volunteering to serve in an American ambulance unit in France during World War I. Then he went to Italy, served at the front, and was severely wounded in action just before his nineteenth birthday. After the war he was too restless to settle down in the United States, so, like many American writers of his time, he lived in Paris and supported himself and his young family as a newspaper correspondent. He worked hard at learning how to write fiction; as he later said, "I found the greatest difficulty, aside from knowing what you really felt, rather than what you were supposed to feel, or had been taught to feel, was to put down what really happened in action: what the actual things were which produced the emotion that you experienced." In America he had admired the work of Sherwood Anderson, especially the colloquial, "unliterary" tone of his stories, and in Paris he came under the influence of Gertrude Stein, telling Anderson in a letter of 1922 that "Gertrude Stein and me are just like brothers."

Although Hemingway was unwilling to experiment as radically with his prose style as was Stein — he refused to abandon a narrative plot in his fiction — her technique of the repetition of simple words and ideas for emphasis is evident in his first book, In Our Time (1925), a collection of stories about his boyhood, and in his early novels, The Sun Also Rises (1926) and A Farewell to Arms (1929). With these works Hemingway was established as a master stylist, probably the most influential writer of English prose in the first half of the twentieth century. Yet he was as much identified with the spectacle of such blood sports as hunting and bullfighting, and with the experience of men at war, as he was with literature. He was a reporter sympathetic to the Loyalist side in the Spanish Civil War; one of his most acclaimed novels, For Whom the Bell Tolls (1940), is about that struggle. He also worked as a correspondent during World War II. In 1954, after the publication of The Old Man and the Sea, he was awarded the Nobel Prize for Literature. Seven years later, in poor health and haunted by the memory of the suicide of his father, who had shot himself with a Civil War pistol in 1929, Hemingway killed himself with a shotgun in his Idaho hunting lodge.

Hemingway, unlike his American contemporaries F. Scott Fitzgerald and William Faulkner, achieved the same level of artistry in his short fic-

tion that he did in his novels. His terse way of writing short stories attracted many imitators. He once explained how he achieved this effect of intense compression by comparing his method to the principle of the iceberg. "There is seven-eighths of it under water for every part that shows. Anything you know you can eliminate and it only strengthens your iceberg. It is the part that doesn't show. If a writer omits something because he does not know it then there is a hole in the story." Hemingway's stories often suggest complex meanings because beneath the surface of the apparently simple action and dialogue, as in "The Snows of Kilimanjaro," he presented a skillfully contrived dramatization of his philosophy that the highest human goal is to defy death and preserve one's dignity by acts of courage and integrity. Hemingway's best stories were written before 1938, and he earned a great deal of money from them. Many were anthologized after their first appearance in magazines, or made into motion pictures; his income from "The Snows of Kilimanjaro" alone ran into six figures. He disliked analyzing his method of writing, but, in the preface to his collection of forty-nine stories published in 1938, he justified the way he was living his life, even if it seemed to be at the cost of his fiction: "In going where you have to go, and doing what you have to do, and seeing what you have to see, you dull and blunt the instrument you write with. But I would rather have it bent and dull and know I had to put it on the grindstone again and hammer it into shape and put a whetstone to it, and know that I had something to write about, than to have it bright and shining and nothing to say, or smooth and well-oiled in the closet, but unused."

Ernest Hemingway

෨෬

THE SNOWS OF KILIMANJARO

Kilimanjaro is a snow covered mountain 19,710 feet high, and is said to be the highest mountain in Africa. Its western summit is called the Masai "Ngàje Ngài," the House of God. Close to the western summit there is the dried and frozen carcass of a leopard. No one has explained what the leopard was seeking at that altitude.

"The marvellous thing is that it's painless," he said. "That's how you know when it starts."

"Is it really?"

"Absolutely. I'm awfully sorry about the odor though. That must bother you."

"Don't! Please don't."

"Look at them," he said. "Now is it sight or is it scent that brings them like that?"

The cot the man lay on was in the wide shade of a mimosa tree and as he looked out past the shade onto the glare of the plain there were three of the big birds squatted obscenely, while in the sky a dozen more sailed, making quick-moving shadows as they passed.

"They've been there since the day the truck broke down," he said. "Today's the first time any have lit on the ground. I watched the way they sailed very carefully at first in case I ever wanted to use them in a story. That's funny now."

"I wish you wouldn't," she said.

"I'm only talking," he said. "It's much easier if I talk. But I don't want to bother you."

"You know it doesn't bother me," she said. "It's that I've gotten so very nervous not being able to do anything. I think we might make it as easy as we can until the plane comes."

"Or until the plane doesn't come."

"Please tell me what I can do. There must be something I can do."

"You can take the leg off and that might stop it, though I doubt it. Or you can shoot me. You're a good shot now. I taught you to shoot didn't I?"

"Please don't talk that way. Couldn't I read to you?"

"Read what?"

"Anything in the book bag that we haven't read."

"I can't listen to it," he said. "Talking is the easiest. We quarrel and that makes the time pass."

"I don't quarrel. I never want to quarrel. Let's not quarrel any more. No matter how nervous we get. Maybe they will be back with another truck today. Maybe the plane will come."

"I don't want to move," the man said. "There is no sense in moving now except to make it easier for you."

"That's cowardly."

"Can't you let a man die as comfortably as he can without calling him names? What's the use of slanging me?"

"You're not going to die."

"Don't be silly. I'm dying now. Ask those bastards." He looked over to where the huge, filthy birds sat, their naked heads sunk in the hunched feathers. A fourth planed down, to run quick-legged and then waddle slowly toward the others.

"They are around every camp. You never notice them. You can't die if you don't give up."

"Where did you read that? You're such a bloody fool."

"You might think about some one else."

"For Christ's sake," he said, "That's been my trade."

He lay then and was quiet for a while and looked across the heat shimmer of the plain to the edge of the bush. There were a few Tommies that showed minute and white against the yellow and, far off, he saw a herd of zebra, white against the green of the bush. This was a pleasant camp under big trees against a hill, with good water, and close by, a nearly dry water hole where sand grouse flighted in the mornings.

"Wouldn't you like me to read?" she asked. She was sitting on a canvas chair beside his cot. "There's a breeze coming up."

"No thanks."

"Maybe the truck will come."

"I don't give a damn about the truck."

"I do."

"You give a damn about so many things that I don't."

"Not so many, Harry."

"What about a drink?"

"It's supposed to be bad for you. It said in Black's to avoid all alcohol. You shouldn't drink."

"Molo!" he shouted.

"Yes Bwana."

"Bring whiskey-soda."

"Yes Bwana."

"You shouldn't," she said. "That's what I mean by giving up. It says it's bad for you. I know it's bad for you."

"No," he said. "It's good for me."

So now it was all over, he thought. So now he would never have a chance to finish it. So this was the way it ended in a bickering over a drink. Since the gangrene started in his right leg he had no pain and with the pain the horror had gone and all he felt now was a great tiredness and anger that this was the end of it. For this, that now was coming, he had very little curiosity. For years it had obsessed him; but now it meant nothing in itself. It was strange how easy being tired enough made it.

Now he would never write the things that he had saved to write until he knew enough to write them well. Well, he would not have to fail at trying to write them either. Maybe you could never write them, and that was why you put them off and delayed the starting. Well he would never know, now.

"I wish we'd never come," the woman said. She was looking at him holding the glass and biting her lip. "You never would have gotten anything like this in Paris. You always said you loved Paris. We could have stayed in Paris or gone anywhere. I'd have gone anywhere. I said I'd go anywhere you wanted. If you wanted to shoot we could have gone shooting in Hungary and been comfortable."

"Your bloody money," he said.

"That's not fair," she said. "It was always yours as much as mine. I left everything and I went wherever you wanted to go and I've done what you wanted to do. But I wish we'd never come here."

"You said you loved it."

"I did when you were all right. But now I hate it. I don't see why that had to happen to your leg. What have we done to have that happen to us?"

"I suppose what I did was to forget to put iodine on it when I first scratched it. Then I didn't pay any attention to it because I never infect. Then, later, when it got bad, it was probably using that weak carbolic solution when the other antiseptics ran out that paralyzed the minute blood vessels and started the gangrene." He looked at her, "What else?"

"I don't mean that."

"If we would have hired a good mechanic instead of a half-baked kikuyu driver, he would have checked the oil and never burned out that bearing in the truck."

"I don't mean that."

"If you hadn't left your own people, your goddamned Old Westbury, Saratoga, Palm Beach people to take me on ——— "

"Why, I loved you. That's not fair. I love you now. I'll always love you. Don't you love me?"

"No," said the man. "I don't think so. I never have."

"Harry, what are you saying? You're out of your head."

"No. I haven't any head to go out of."

"Don't drink that," she said. "Darling, please don't drink that. We have to do everything we can."

"You do it," he said. "I'm tired."

Now in his mind he saw a railway station at Karagatch and he was standing with his pack and that was the headlight of the Simplon-Orient cutting the dark now and he was leaving Thrace then after the retreat. That was one of the things he had saved to write, with, in the morning at breakfast, looking out the window and seeing snow on the mountains in Bulgaria and Nansen's Secretary asking the old man if it were snow and the old man looking at it and saying, No, that's not snow. It's too early for snow. And the Secretary repeating to the other girls, No, you see. It's not snow and them all saying, It's not snow we were mistaken. But it was the snow all right and he sent them on into it when he evolved exchange of populations. And it was snow they tramped along in until they died that winter.

It was snow too that fell all Christmas week that year up in the Gauertal, that year they lived in the woodcutter's house with the big square porcelain stove that filled half the room, and they slept on mattresses filled with beech leaves, the time the deserter came with his feet bloody in the snow. He saw the police were right behind him and they gave him woolen socks and held the gendarmes talking until the tracks had drifted over.

In Schrunz, on Christmas day, the snow was so bright it hurt your eyes when you looked out from the weinstube and saw every one coming home from church. That was where they walked up the sleigh-smoothed urine-yellowed road along the river with the steep pine hills, skis heavy on the shoulder, and where they ran that great run down the glacier above the Madlener-haus, the snow as smooth to see as cake frosting and as light as powder and he remembered the noiseless rush the speed made as you dropped down like a bird.

They were snow-bound a week in the Madlener-haus that time in the blizzard playing cards in the smoke by the lantern light and the stakes were higher all the time as Herr Lent lost more. Finally he lost it all. Everything, the skischule money and all the season's profit and then his capital. He could see him with his long nose, picking up the cards and then opening, "Sans Voir." There was always gambling then. When there was no snow you gambled and when there was too much you gambled. He thought of all the time in his life he had spent gambling.

But he had never written a line of that, nor of that cold, bright Christmas day with the mountains showing across the plain that Barker had flown across the lines to bomb the Austrian officer's leave train, machine-gunning them as they scattered and ran. He remembered Barker afterwards coming into the mess and starting to tell about it. And how quiet it got and then somebody saying, "You bloody murderous bastard."

Those were the same Austrians they killed then that he skied with later. No not the same. Hans, that he skied with all that year, had been in the Kaiser-Jägers and when they went hunting hares together up the little valley above the saw-mill they had talked of the fighting on Pasubio and of the attack on Pertica and Asalone and he had never written a word of that. Nor of Monte Corno, nor the Siete Commum, nor of Arsiedo.

How many winters had he lived in the Voralberg and the Arlberg? It was four and then he remembered the man who had the fox to sell when they had walked into Bludenz, that time to buy presents, and the cherry-pit taste of good kirsch, the fast-slipping rush of running powder-snow on crust, singing "Hi! Ho! said Rolly!" as you ran down the last stretch to the steep drop, taking it straight, then running the orchard in three turns and out across the ditch and onto the icy road behind the inn. Knocking your bindings loose, kicking the skis free and leaning them up against the wooden wall of the inn, the lamplight coming from the window, where inside, in the smoky, new-wine smelling warmth, they were playing the accordion.

"Where did we stay in Paris?" he asked the woman who was sitting by him in a canvas chair, now, in Africa.

"At the Crillon. You know that."

"Why do I know that?"

"That's where we always stayed."

"No. Not always."

"There and at the Pavillion Henri-Quatre in St. Germain. You said you loved it there."

"Love is a dunghill," said Harry. "And I'm the cock that gets on it to crow."

"If you have to go away," she said, "is it absolutely necessary to kill off everything you leave behind? I mean do you have to take away everything? Do you have to kill your horse, and your wife and burn your saddle and your armour?"

"Yes," he said. "Your damned money was my armour. My Swift and my Armour."

"Don't."

"All right. I'll stop that. I don't want to hurt you."

"It's a little bit late now."

"All right then. I'll go on hurting you. It's more amusing. The only thing I ever really liked to do with you I can't do now."

"No, that's not true. You liked to do many things and everything you wanted to do I did."

"Oh, for Christ sake stop bragging, will you?"

He looked at her and saw her crying.

"Listen," he said. "Do you think that it is fun to do this? I don't know why I'm doing it. It's trying to kill to keep yourself alive, I imagine. I was all right when we started talking. I didn't mean to start this, and now I'm crazy as a coot and being as cruel to you as I can be. Don't pay any attention, darling, to what I say. I love you, really. You know I love you. I've never loved anyone else the way I love you."

He slipped into the familiar lie he made his bread and butter by.

"You're sweet to me."

"You bitch," he said. "You rich bitch. That's poetry. I'm full of poetry now. Rot and poetry. Rotten poetry."

"Stop it. Harry, why do you have to turn into a devil now?"

"I don't like to leave anything," the man said. "I don't like to leave things behind."

It was evening now and he had been asleep. The sun was gone behind the hill and there was a shadow all across the plain and the small animals were feeding close to camp; quick dropping heads and switching tails, he watched them keeping well out away from the bush now. The birds no longer waited on the ground. They were all perched heavily in a tree. There were many more of them. His personal boy was sitting by the bed.

"Memsahib's gone to shoot," the boy said. "Does Bwana want?"

"Nothing."

She had gone to kill a piece of meat and, knowing how he liked to watch the game, she had gone well away so she would not disturb this little pocket of the plain that he could see. She was always thoughtful, he thought. On anything she knew about, or had read, or that she had ever heard.

It was not her fault that when he went to her he was already over. How could a woman know that you meant nothing that you said; that you spoke only from habit and to be comfortable? After he no longer meant what he said, his lies were more successful with women than when he had told them the truth.

It was not so much that he lied as that there was no truth to tell. He had had his life and it was over and then he went on living it again with different people and more money, with the best of the same places, and some new ones.

You kept from thinking and it was all marvellous. You were equipped with good insides so that you did not go to pieces that way, the way most of them had, and you made an attitude that you cared nothing for the work you used to do, now that you could no longer do it. But, in yourself, you said that you would write about these people; about the very rich; that you were really not of them but a spy in their country; that you would leave it and write of it and for once it would be written by someone who knew what he was writing of. But he would never do it, because each day of not writing, of comfort, of being that which he despised, dulled his ability and softened his will to work so that, finally, he did no work at all. The people he knew now were all much more comfortable when he did not work. Africa was where he had been happiest in the good time of his life, so he had come out here to start again. They had made this safari with the minimum of comfort. There was no hardship; but there was no luxury and he had thought he could get back into training that way. That in some way he could work the fat off his soul the way a fighter went into the mountains to work and train in order to burn it out of his body.

She had liked it. She said she loved it. She loved anything that was exciting, that involved a change of scene, where there were new people and where things were pleasant. And he had felt the illusion of returning strength of will to work. Now if this was how it ended, and he knew it was, he must not turn like some snake biting itself because its back was broken. It wasn't this woman's fault. If it had not been she it would have been another. If he lived by a lie he should try to die by it. He heard a shot beyond the hill.

She shot very well this good, this rich bitch, this kindly caretaker and destroyer of his talent. Nonsense. He had destroyed his talent himself. Why should he blame this woman because she kept him well? He had destroyed his talent by not using it, by betrayals of himself and what he believed in, by drinking so much that he blunted the edge of his perceptions, by laziness, by sloth, and by snobbery, by pride and by prejudice, by hook and by crook. What was this? A catalogue of old books? What was his talent anyway? It was a talent all right but instead of using it, he had traded on it. It was never what he had done, but always what he could do. And he had chosen to make his living with something else instead of a pen or a pencil. It was strange, too, wasn't it, that when he fell in love with another woman, that woman should always have more money than the last one? But when he no longer was in love, when he was only lying, as to this woman, now, who had the most money of all, who had all the money there was, who had had a husband and children, who had taken lovers and been dissatisfied with them, and who loved him dearly as a writer, as a man, as a companion and as a proud possession; it was strange that when he did not love her at all and was lying, that he should be able to give her more for her money than when he had really loved.

We must all be cut out for what we do, he thought. However you make your living is where your talent lies. He had sold vitality, in one form or another, all his life and when your affections are not too involved you give much better value for the money. He had found that out but he would never write that, now, either. No, he would not write that, although it was well worth writing.

Now she came in sight, walking across the open toward the camp. She was wearing jodhpurs and carrying her rifle. The two boys had a Tommie slung and they were coming along behind her. She was still a good-looking woman, he thought, and she had a pleasant body. She had a great talent and appreciation for the bed, she was not pretty, but he liked her face, she read enormously, liked to ride and shoot and, certainly, she drank too much. Her husband had died when she was still a comparatively young woman and for a while she had devoted herself to her two just-grown children, who did not need her and were embarrassed at having her about, to her stable of horses, to books, and to bottles. She liked to read in the evening before dinner and she drank Scotch and soda while she read. By dinner she was fairly drunk and after a bottle of wine at dinner she was usually drunk enough to sleep.

That was before the lovers. After she had the lovers she did not drink so much because she did not have to be drunk to sleep. But the lovers bored her. She had been married to a man who had never bored her and these people bored her very much.

Then one of her two children was killed in a plane crash and after that was over she did not want the lovers, and drink being no anæsthetic she had to make another life. Suddenly, she had been acutely frightened of being alone. But she wanted someone that she respected with her.

It had begun very simply. She liked what he wrote and she had always envied the life he led. She thought he did exactly what he wanted to. The steps by which she had acquired him and the way in which she had finally fallen in love with him were all part of a regular progression in which she had built herself a new life and he had traded away what remained of his old life.

He had traded it for security, for comfort too, there was no denying that, and for what else? He did not know. She would have bought him anything he wanted. He knew that. She was a damned nice woman too. He would as soon be in bed with her as anyone; rather with her, because she was richer, because she was very pleasant and appreciative and because she never made scenes. And now this life that she had built again was coming to a term because he had not used iodine two weeks ago when a thorn had scratched his knee as they moved forward trying to photograph a herd of waterbuck standing, their heads up, peering while their nostrils searched the air, their ears spread wide to hear the first noise that would send them rushing into the bush. They had bolted, too, before he got the picture.

Here she came now.

He turned his head on the cot to look toward her. "Hello," he said.

"I shot a Tommy ram," she told him. "He'll make you good broth and I'll have them mash some potatoes with the Klim. How do you feel?"

"Much better."

"Isn't that lovely? You know I thought perhaps you would. You were sleeping when I left."

"I had a good sleep. Did you walk far?"

"No. Just around behind the hill. I made quite a good shot on the Tommy."

"You shoot marvellously, you know."

"I love it. I've loved Africa. Really. If you're all right it's the most fun that I've ever had. You don't know the fun it's been to shoot with you. I've loved the country."

"I love it too."

"Darling, you don't know how marvellous it is to see you feeling better. I couldn't stand it when you felt that way. You won't talk to me like that again, will you? Promise me?"

"No," he said. "I don't remember what I said."

"You don't have to destroy me. Do you? I'm only a middle-aged woman who loves you and wants to do what you want to do. I've been destroyed two or three times already. You wouldn't want to destroy me again, would you?"

"I'd like to destroy you a few times in bed," he said.

"Yes. That's the good destruction. That's the way we're made to be destroyed. The plane will be here tomorrow."

"How do you know?"

"I'm sure. It's bound to come. The boys have the wood all ready and the grass to make the smudge. I went down and looked at it again today. There's plenty of room to land and we have the smudges ready at both ends."

"What makes you think it will come tomorrow?"

"I'm sure it will. It's overdue now. Then, in town, they will fix up your leg and then we will have some good destruction. Not that dreadful talking kind."

"Should we have a drink? The sun is down."

"Do you think you should?"

"I'm having one."

"We'll have one together. *Molo, letti dui whiskey-soda!*" she called.

"You'd better put on your mosquito boots," he told her.

"I'll wait till I bathe. . . ."

While it grew dark they drank and just before it was dark and there was no longer enough light to shoot, a hyena crossed the open on his way around the hill.

"That bastard crosses there every night," the man said. "Every night for two weeks."

"He's the one makes the noise at night. I don't mind it. They're a filthy animal though."

Drinking together, with no pain now except the discomfort of lying in the one position, the boys lighting a fire, its shadow jumping on the tents, he could feel the return of acquiescence in this life of pleasant surrender. She was very good to him. He had been cruel and unjust in the afternoon. She was a fine woman, marvellous really. And just then it occurred to him that he was going to die.

It came with a rush; not as a rush of water nor of wind; but of a sudden evil-smelling emptiness and the odd thing was that the hyena slipped lightly along the edge of it.

"What is it, Harry?" she asked him.

"Nothing," he said. "You had better move over to the other side. To windward."

"Did Molo change the dressing?"

"Yes. I'm just using the boric now."

"How do you feel?"

"A little wobbly."

"I'm going in to bathe," she said. "I'll be right out. I'll eat with you and then we'll put the cot in."

So, he said to himself, we did well to stop the quarrelling. He had never quarrelled much with this woman, while with the women that he loved he had quarrelled so much they had finally, always, with the corrosion of the quarrelling, killed what they had together. He had loved too much, demanded too much, and he wore it all out.

He thought about alone in Constantinople that time, having quarrelled in Paris before he had gone out. He had whored the whole time and then, when that was over, and he had failed to kill his loneliness, but only made it worse, he had written her, the first one, the one who left him, a letter telling her how he had never been able to kill it. . . . How when he thought he saw her outside the Regence one time it made him go all faint and sick inside, and that he would follow a woman who looked like her in some way, along the Boulevard, afraid to see it was not she, afraid to lose the feeling it gave him. How every one he had slept with had only made him miss her more. How what she had done could never matter since he knew he could not cure himself of loving her. He wrote this letter at the Club, cold sober, and mailed it to New York asking her to write him at the office in Paris. That seemed safe. And that night missing her so much it made him feel hollow sick inside, he wandered up past Taxim's, picked a girl up and took her out to supper. He had gone to a place to dance with her afterward, she danced badly, and left her for a hot Armenian slut, that swung her belly against him so it almost scalded. He took her away from a British gunner subaltern after a row. The gunner asked him outside and they fought in the street on the cobbles in the dark. He'd hit him twice, hard, on the side of the jaw and when he didn't go down he knew he was in for a fight. The gunner hit him in the body, then beside his eye. He swung with his left again and landed and the gunner fell on him and grabbed his coat and tore the sleeve off and he clubbed him twice behind the ear and then smashed him with his right as he pushed him away. When the gunner went down his head hit first and he ran with the girl because they heard the M.P.'s coming. They got into a taxi and drove out to Rimmily Hissa along the Bosphorus, and around, and back in the cool night and went to bed and she felt as over-ripe as she looked but smooth, rose-petal, syrupy, smooth-bellied, big-breasted and needed no pillow under her buttocks, and he left her before she was awake looking blousy enough in the first daylight and turned up at the Pera Palace with a black eye, carrying his coat because one sleeve was missing.

That same night he left for Anatolia and he remembered, later on that trip, riding all day through fields of the poppies that they raised for opium and how strange it made you feel, finally, and all the distances seemed wrong, to where they had made the attack with the newly arrived Constantine officers, that did not know a god-damned thing, and the artillery had fired into the troops and the British observer had cried like a child.

That was the day he'd first seen dead men wearing white ballet skirts and upturned shoes with pompons on them. The Turks had come steadily and lumpily and he had seen the skirted men running and the officers shooting into them and running then themselves and he and the British observer had run too until his lungs ached and his mouth was full of the taste of pennies and they stopped behind some rocks and there were the Turks coming as lumpily as ever. Later he had seen the things that he could never think of and later still he had seen much worse. So when he got back to Paris that time he could not talk about it or stand to have it mentioned. And there in the café as he passed was that American poet with a pile of saucers in front of him and a stupid look on his potato face talking about the Dada movement[1] with a Rumanian who said his name was Tristan Tzara, who always wore a monocle and had a headache, and, back at the apartment with his wife that now he loved again, the quarrel all over, the madness all over, glad to be home, the office sent his mail up to the flat. So

[1] Artistic and literary movement of the 1920s, emphasizing deliberate irrationality and repudiation of earlier artistic values. Leading dadaists included French painter Marcel Duchamp, American painter Man Ray, and Romanian writer Tristan Tzara, all of whom lived in Paris at the time. Tzara invented the name for the movement.

then the letter in answer to the one he'd written came in on a platter one morning and when he saw the handwriting he went cold all over and tried to slip the letter underneath another. But his wife said, "Who is that letter from, dear?" and that was the end of the beginning of that.

He remembered the good times with them all, and the quarrels. They always picked the finest places to have the quarrels. And why had they always quarrelled when he was feeling best? He had never written any of that because, at first, he never wanted to hurt anyone and then it seemed as though there was enough to write without it. But he had always thought that he would write it finally. There was so much to write. He had seen the world change; not just the events; although he had seen many of them and had watched the people, but he had seen the subtler change and he could remember how the people were at different times. He had been in it and he had watched it and it was his duty to write of it; but now he never would.

"How do you feel?" she said. She had come out from the tent now after her bath.

"All right."

"Could you eat now?" He saw Molo behind her with the folding table and the other boy with the dishes.

"I want to write," he said.

"You ought to take some broth to keep your strength up."

"I'm going to die tonight," he said. "I don't need my strength up."

"Don't be melodramatic, Harry, please," she said.

"Why don't you use your nose? I'm rotted half way up my thigh now. What the hell should I fool with broth for? Molo bring whiskey-soda."

"Please take the broth," she said gently.

"All right."

The broth was too hot. He had to hold it in the cup until it cooled enough to take it and then he just got it down without gagging.

"You're a fine woman," he said. "Don't pay any attention to me."

She looked at him with her well-known, well-loved face from *Spur* and *Town and Country*, only a little the worse for drink, only a little the worse for bed, but *Town and Country* never showed those good breasts and those useful thighs and those lightly small-of-back-caressing hands, and as he looked and saw her well-known pleasant smile, he felt death come again. This time there was no rush. It was a puff, as of a wind that makes a candle flicker and the flame go tall.

"They can bring my net out later and hang it from the tree and build the fire up. I'm not going in the tent tonight. It's not worth moving. It's a clear night. There won't be any rain."

So this was how you died, in whispers that you did not hear. Well, there would be no more quarrelling. He could promise that. The one experience that he had never had he was not going to spoil now. He probably would. You spoiled everything. But perhaps he wouldn't.

"You can't take dictation, can you?"

"I never learned," she told him.

"That's all right."

There wasn't time, of course, although it seemed as though it telescoped so that you might put it all into one paragraph if you could get it right.

There was a log house, chinked white with mortar, on a hill above the lake. There was a bell on a pole by the door to call the people in to meals. Behind the house were fields and behind the fields was the timber. A line of Lombardy poplars ran from the house to the dock. Other poplars ran along the point. A road went up to the hills along the edge of the timber and along that road he picked blackberries. Then that log house was burned down and all the guns that had been on deer foot racks above the open fire place were burned and afterwards their barrels, with the lead melted in the magazines, and the stocks burned away, lay out on the heap of ashes that were used to make lye for the big iron soap kettles, and you asked Grandfather if you could have them to play with, and he said, no. You see they were his guns still and he never bought any others. Nor did he hunt any more. The house was rebuilt in the same place out of lumber now and painted white and from its porch you saw the poplars and the lake beyond; but there were never any more guns. The barrels of the guns that had hung on the deer feet on the wall of the log house lay out there on the heap of ashes and no one ever touched them.

In the Black Forest, after the war, we rented a trout stream and there were two ways to walk to it. One was down the valley from Triberg and around the valley road in the shade of the trees that bordered the white road, and then up a side road that went up through the hills past many small farms, with the big Schwarzwald houses, until that road crossed the stream. That was where our fishing began.

The other way was to climb steeply up to the edge of the woods and then go across the top of the hills through the pine woods, and then out to the edge of a meadow and down across this meadow to the bridge. There were birches along the stream and it was not big, but narrow, clear and fast, with pools where it had cut under the roots of the birches. At the Hotel in Triberg the proprietor had a fine season. It was very pleasant and we were all great friends. The next year came the inflation and the money he had made the year before was not enough to buy supplies to open the hotel and he hanged himself.

You could dictate that, but you could not dictate the Place Contrescarpe where the flower sellers dyed their flowers in the street and the dye ran over the paving where the autobus started and the old men and the women, always drunk on wine and bad marc; and the children with their noses running in the cold; the smell of dirty sweat and poverty and drunkenness at the Café des Amateurs and the whores at the Bal Musette they lived above. The Concierge who entertained the trooper of the Garde Re-

publicaine in her loge, his horse-hair-plumed helmet on a chair. The loca-
taire across the hall whose husband was a bicycle racer and her joy that
morning at the Cremerie when she had opened L'Auto and seen where he
placed third in Paris-Tours, his first big race. She had blushed and laughed
and then gone upstairs crying with the yellow sporting paper in her hand.
The husband of the woman who ran the Bal Musette drove a taxi and when
he, Harry, had to take an early plane the husband knocked upon the door to
wake him and they each drank a glass of white wine at the zinc of the bar
before they started. He knew his neighbors in that quarter then because
they all were poor.

Around that Place there were two kinds; the drunkards and the spor-
tifs. The drunkards killed their poverty that way; the sportifs took it out in
exercise. They were the descendants of the Communards[2] and it was no
struggle for them to know their politics. They knew who had shot their fa-
thers, their relatives, their brothers, and their friends when the Versailles
troops came in and took the town after the Commune and executed any
one they could catch with calloused hands, or who wore a cap, or carried
any other sign he was a working man. And in that poverty, and in that quar-
ter across the street from a Boucherie Chevaline and a wine co-operative he
had written the start of all he was to do. There never was another part of
Paris that he loved like that, the sprawling trees, the old white plastered
houses painted brown below, the long green of the autobus in that round
square, the purple flower dye upon the paving, the sudden drop down the
hill of the rue Cardinal Lemoine to the River, and the other way the narrow
crowded world of the rue Mouffetard. The street that ran up toward the
Pantheon and the other that he always took with the bicycle, the only as-
phalted street in all that quarter, smooth under the tires, with the high nar-
row houses and the cheap tall hotel where Paul Verlaine had died. There
were only two rooms in the apartments where they lived and he had a room
on the top floor of that hotel that cost him sixty francs a month where he
did his writing, and from it he could see the roofs and chimney pots and all
the hills of Paris.

From the apartment you could only see the wood and coal man's
place. He sold wine too, bad wine. The golden horse's head outside the
Boucherie Chevaline where the carcasses hung yellow gold and red in the
open window, and the green painted co-operative where they bought their
wine; good wine and cheap. The rest was plaster walls and the windows of
the neighbors. The neighbors who, at night, when some one lay drunk in
the street, moaning and groaning in that typical French ivresse[3] that you
were propaganded to believe did not exist, would open their windows and
then the murmur of talk.

[2] members and supporters of the Commune of Paris, 1871. The commune, a revolutionary council, led a rebellion against the new conservative, rural government and was
quashed in a bloody massacre from May 21 to May 28, 1871.

[3] drunkenness.

"Where is the policeman? When you don't want him the bugger is always there. He's sleeping with some concierge. Get the Agent." Till some one threw a bucket of water from a window and the moaning stopped. "What's that? Water. Ah, that's intelligent." And the windows shutting. Marie, his femme de menage, protesting against the eight-hour day saying, "If a husband works until six he gets only a little drunk on the way home and does not waste too much. If he works only until five he is drunk every night and one has no money. It is the wife of the working man who suffers from this shortening of hours."

"Wouldn't you like some more broth?" the woman asked him now.

"No, thank you very much. It is awfully good."

"Try just a little."

"I would like a whiskey-soda."

"It's not good for you."

"No. It's bad for me. Cole Porter wrote the words and the music. This knowledge that you're going mad for me."

"You know I like you to drink."

"Oh yes. Only it's bad for me."

When she goes, he thought. I'll have all I want. Not all I want but all there is. Ayee he was tired. Too tired. He was going to sleep a little while. He lay still and death was not there. It must have gone around another street. It went in pairs, on bicycles, and moved absolutely silently on the pavements.

No, he had never written about Paris. Not the Paris that he cared about. But what about the rest that he had never written?

What about the ranch and the silvered gray of the sage brush, the quick, clear water in the irrigation ditches, and the heavy green of the alfalfa. The trail went up into the hills and the cattle in the summer were shy as deer. The bawling and the steady noise and slow moving mass raising a dust as you brought them down in the fall. And behind the mountains, the clear sharpness of the peak in the evening light and, riding down along the trail in the moonlight, bright across the valley. Now he remembered coming down through the timber in the dark holding the horse's tail when you could not see and all the stories that he meant to write.

About the half-wit chore boy who was left at the ranch that time and told not to let anyone get any hay, and that old bastard from the Forks who had beaten the boy when he had worked for him stopping to get some feed. The boy refusing and the old man saying he would beat him again. The boy got the rifle from the kitchen and shot him when he tried to come into the barn and when they came back to the ranch he'd been dead a week, frozen in the corral, and the dogs had eaten part of him. But what was left you packed on a sled wrapped in a blanket and roped on and you got the boy to help you haul it, and the two of you took it out over the road on skis, and sixty miles down to town to turn the boy over. He having no idea that he would be arrested. Thinking he had done his duty and that you were his friend and he would be rewarded. He'd helped to haul the old man in so everybody could know how bad the old man had been and how he'd tried to steal some feed that didn't belong to him, and when the sheriff put the handcuffs on the boy he couldn't believe it. Then he'd started to cry. That was one story he had saved to write. He knew at least twenty good stories from out there and he had never written one. Why?

"You tell them why," he said.

"Why what, dear?"

"Why nothing."

She didn't drink so much, now, since she had him. But if he lived he would never write about her, he knew that now. Nor about any of them. The rich were dull and they drank too much, or they played too much backgammon. They were dull and they were repetitious. He remembered poor Julian and his romantic awe of them and how he had started a story once that began, "The very rich are different from you and me." And how someone had said to Julian, Yes, they have more money.[4] But that was not humorous to Julian. He thought they were a special glamorous race and when he found they weren't it wrecked him just as much as any other thing that wrecked him.

He had been contemptuous of those who wrecked. You did not have to like it because you understood it. He could beat anything, he thought, because no thing could hurt him if he did not care.

All right. Now he would not care for death. One thing he had always dreaded was the pain. He could stand pain as well as any man, until it went on too long, and wore him out, but here he had something that had hurt frightfully and just when he had felt it breaking him, the pain had stopped.

He remembered long ago when Williamson, the bombing officer, had been hit by a stick bomb someone in a German patrol had thrown as he was coming in through the wire that night and, screaming, had begged every one to kill him. He was a fat man, very brave, and a good officer, although addicted to fantastic shows. But that night he was caught in the wire, with a flare lighting him up and his bowels spilled out into the wire, so when they brought him in, alive, they had to cut him loose. Shoot me, Harry. For Christ sake shoot me. They had had an argument one time about our Lord never sending you anything you could not bear and someone's theory had been that meant that at a certain time the pain passed you out automati-

---

[4] This exchange is alleged to have actually occurred between Hemingway and F. Scott Fitzgerald, with Fitzgerald speaking the line attributed to "Julian."

cally. But he had always remembered Williamson, that night. Nothing passed out Williamson until he gave him all his morphine tablets that he had always saved to use himself and then they did not work right away.

Still this now, that he had, was very easy; and if it was no worse as it went on there was nothing to worry about. Except that he would rather be in better company.

He thought a little about the company that he would like to have.

No, he thought, when everything you do, you do too long, and do too late, you can't expect to find the people still there. The people all are gone. The party's over and you are with your hostess now.

I'm getting as bored with dying as with everything else, he thought.

"It's a bore," he said out loud.

"What is, my dear?"

"Anything you do too bloody long."

He looked at her face between him and the fire. She was leaning back in the chair and the firelight shone on her pleasantly lined face and he could see that she was sleepy. He heard the hyena make a noise just outside the range of the fire.

"I've been writing," he said. "But I got tired."

"Do you think you will be able to sleep?"

"Pretty sure. Why don't you turn in?"

"I like to sit here with you."

"Do you feel anything strange?" he asked her.

"No. Just a little sleepy."

"I do," he said.

He had just felt death come by again.

"You know the only thing I've never lost is curiosity," he said to her.

"You've never lost anything. You're the most complete man I've ever known."

"Christ," he said. "How little a woman knows. What is that? Your intuition?"

Because, just then, death had come and rested its head on the foot of the cot and he could smell its breath.

"Never believe any of that about a scythe and a skull," he told her. "It can be two bicycle policemen as easily, or be a bird. Or it can have a wide snout like a hyena."

It had moved up on him now, but it had no shape any more. It simply occupied space.

"Tell it to go away."

It did not go away but moved a little closer.

"You've got a hell of a breath," he told it. "You stinking bastard."

It moved up closer to him still and now he could not speak to it, and when it saw he could not speak it came a little closer, and now he tried to send it away without speaking, but it moved in on him so its weight was all upon his chest, and while it crouched there and he could not move, or speak, he heard the woman say, "Bwana is asleep now. Take the cot up very gently and carry it into the tent."

He could not speak to tell her to make it go away and it crouched now, heavier, so he could not breathe. And then, while they lifted the cot, suddenly it was all right and the weight went from his chest.

It was morning and had been morning for some time and he heard the plane. It showed very tiny and then made a wide circle and the boys ran out and lit the fires, using kerosene, and piled on grass so there were two big smudges at each end of the level place and the morning breeze blew them toward the camp and the plane circled twice more, low this time, and then glided down and levelled off and landed smoothly and, coming walking toward him, was old Compton in slacks, a tweed jacket and a brown felt hat.

"What's the matter, old cock?" Compton said.

"Bad leg," he told him. "Will you have some breakfast?"

"Thanks. I'll just have some tea. It's the Puss Moth you know. I won't be able to take the Memsahib. There's only room for one. Your lorry is on the way."

Helen had taken Compton aside and was speaking to him. Compton came back more cheery than ever.

"We'll get you right in," he said. "I'll be back for the Mem. Now I'm afraid I'll have to stop at Arusha to refuel. We'd better get going."

"What about the tea?"

"I don't really care about it you know."

The boys had picked up the cot and carried it around the green tents and down along the rock and out onto the plain and along past the smudges that were burning brightly now, the grass all consumed, and the wind fanning the fire, to the little plane. It was difficult getting him in, but once in he lay back in the leather seat, and the leg was stuck straight out to one side of the seat where Compton sat. Compton started the motor and got in. He waved to Helen and to the boys and, as the clatter moved into the old familiar roar, they swung around with Compie watching for wart-hog holes and roared, bumping, along the stretch between the fires and with the last bump rose and he saw them all standing below, waving, and the camp beside the hill, flattening now, and the plain spreading, clumps of trees, and the bush flattening, while the game trails ran now smoothly to the dry waterholes, and there was a new water that he had never known of. The zebra, small rounded backs now, and the wildebeeste, big-headed dots seeming to climb as they moved in long fingers across the plain, now scattering as the shadow came toward them, they were tiny now, and the movement had no gallop, and the plain as far as you could see, gray-yellow now and ahead old Compie's tweed back and the brown felt hat. Then they were over the first hills and the wildebeeste were trailing up them, and then they were over mountains with sudden depths of green-rising forest and the solid bamboo slopes, and then the heavy forest again, sculptured into peaks and hollows until they crossed, and hills sloped down and then another plain, hot now, and purple brown, bumpy with heat and Compie looking back to see how he was riding. Then there were other mountains dark ahead.

And then instead of going on to Arusha they turned left, he evidently figured that they had the gas, and looking down he saw a pink sifting cloud, moving over the ground, and in the air, like the first snow in a blizzard, that comes from nowhere, and he knew the locusts were coming up from the South. Then they began to climb and they were going to the East it seemed, and then it darkened and they were in a storm, the rain so thick it seemed like flying through a waterfall, and then they were out and Compie turned his head and grinned and pointed and there, ahead, all he could see, as wide as all the world, great, high, and unbelievably white in the sun, was the square top of Kilimanjaro. And then he knew that there was where he was going.

Just then the hyena stopped whimpering in the night and started to make a strange, human, almost crying sound. The woman heard it and stirred uneasily. She did not wake. In her dream she was at the house on Long Island and it was the night before her daughter's début. Somehow her father was there and he had been very rude. Then the noise the hyena made was so loud she woke and for a moment she did not know where she was and she was very afraid. Then she took the flashlight and shone it on the other cot that they had carried in after Harry had gone to sleep. She could see his bulk under the mosquito bar but somehow he had gotten his leg out and it hung down alongside the cot. The dressings had all come down and she could not look at it.

"Molo," she called, "Molo! Molo!"

Then she said, "Harry, Harry!" Then her voice rising, "Harry! Please, Oh Harry!"

There was no answer and she could not hear him breathing.

Outside the tent the hyena made the same strange noise that had awakened her. But she did not hear him for the beating of her heart.

[1936]

ELIZABETH BOWEN *(1899–1973) was born into an upper-class Anglo-Irish family in Dublin, Ireland. Her father, Henry Cole Bowen, was a lawyer and an official of the Land Commission. For the early years of her life, Bowen enjoyed a normal childhood, but when she was twelve her mother died of cancer. Then Bowen was educated at boarding school and raised by her many aunts. As a girl she enjoyed making up stories about imaginary families to amuse herself and her friends. She began writing short stories, studied art, and took a course in journalism, uncomfortable without a specific goal before her. In 1923 she published her first book of short stories and married Alan Charles Cameron, an Oxford graduate who became secretary for education for the city of Oxford. Bowen wrote steadily, and, once she started to publish, she produced a new book of fiction or nonfiction almost every other year for more than fifty years. Her fiction is often compared with the work of Henry James, E. M. Forster, and Virginia Woolf.*

Bowen's short stories are an integral part of her work, not a form of relaxation, as stories were for her friend Virginia Woolf. During Bowen's long career, she usually alternated publishing volumes of long and short fiction. Her story collections include Encounter *(1923),* Ann Lee's and Other Stories *(1926),* Joining Charles *(1929),* The Cat Jumps *(1934),* Look at All These Roses *(1941),* Selected Stories *(1946),* Stories *(1959), and* A Day in the Dark *(1965). In addition, she edited* The Faber Book of Modern Stories *(1937) and* The Stories of Katherine Mansfield *(1956). Her most distinguished novels include* To the North *(1932),* The Death of the Heart *(1938), and* The Heat of the Day *(1949). She is also the author of several books about writing, among them* Why Do I Write? *(1948) and* AfterThought: Pieces about Writing *(1962).*

Literary critics have considered Bowen a social realist, but her fiction is more accurately described as psychological realism or literary impressionism. Many of her short stories are related thematically to her novels, or intended as sketches to explore character, setting, or techniques later used in her longer fiction. She often wrote from a feminine point of view, through which the reader can share the consciousness of a female character, as in "The Demon Lover." In Bowen's preface to the collection of stories about wartime London titled The Demon Lover and Other Stories *(1945), she described the title story as a ghost story, though she considered the ghost "questionable." Bowen intended the character of the "ruthless young soldier lover unheard of since 1916: hostile or not," to be a frightening fantasy projected by her heroine, Mrs. Kathleen Drover, who becomes disoriented under pressure of the catastrophe of war. (See Bowen's Commentary about "The Demon Lover" on page 1287.)*

Elizabeth Bowen

ᔓᕐᕫ

THE DEMON LOVER

Towards the end of her day in London Mrs. Drover went round to her shut-up house to look for several things she wanted to take away. Some belonged to herself, some to her family, who were by now used to their country life. It was late August; it had been a steamy, showery day: at the moment the trees down the pavement glittered in an escape of humid yellow afternoon sun. Against the next batch of clouds, already piling up ink-dark, broken chimneys and parapets stood out. In her once familiar street, as in any unused channel, an unfamiliar queerness had silted up: a cat wove itself in and out of railings, but no human eye watched Mrs. Drover's return. Shifting some parcels under her arm, she slowly forced round her latchkey in an unwilling lock, then gave the door, which had warped, a push with her knee. Dead air came out to meet her as she went in.

The staircase window having been boarded up, no light came down into the hall. But one door, she could just see, stood ajar, so she went quickly through into the room and unshuttered the big window in there. Now the prosaic woman, looking about her, was more perplexed than she knew by everything that she saw, by traces of her long former habit of life — the yellow smoke-stain up the white marble mantelpiece, the ring left by a vase on the top of the escritoire; the bruise in the wallpaper where, on the door being thrown open widely, the china handle had always hit the wall. The piano, having gone away to be stored, had left what looked like claw-marks on its part of the parquet. Though not much dust had seeped in, each object wore a film of another kind; and, the only ventilation being the chimney, the whole drawing-room smelled of the cold hearth. Mrs. Drover put down her parcels on the escritoire and left the room to proceed upstairs; the things she wanted were in a bedroom closet.

She had been anxious to see how the house was — the part-time caretaker she shared with some neighbours was away this week on his holiday, known to be not yet back. At the best of times he did not look in often, and she was never sure that she trusted him. There were some cracks in the structure, left by the last bombing, on which she was anxious to keep an eye. Not that one could do anything —

A shaft of refracted daylight now lay across the hall. She stopped dead and stared at the hall table — on this lay a letter addressed to her.

She thought first — then the caretaker *must* be back. All the same, who, seeing the house shuttered, would have dropped a letter in at the box? It was not a circular, it was not a bill. And the post office redirected, to the address in the country, everything for her that came through the post. The caretaker (even if he *were* back) did not know she was due in London today — her call here had been planned to be a surprise — so his negligence in the manner of this letter, leaving it to wait in the dusk and the dust, annoyed her. Annoyed, she picked up the letter, which bore no stamp. But it cannot be important, or they would know . . . She took the letter rapidly upstairs with her, without a stop to look at the writing till she reached what had been her bedroom, where she let in light. The room looked over the garden and other gardens: the sun had gone in; as the clouds sharpened and lowered, the trees and rank lawns seemed already to smoke with dark. Her reluctance to look again at the letter came from the fact that she felt intruded upon — and by someone contemptuous of her ways. However, in the tenseness preceding the fall of rain she read it: it was a few lines.

> Dear Kathleen: You will not have forgotten that today is our anniversary, and the day we said. The years have gone by at once slowly and fast. In view of the fact that nothing has changed, I shall rely upon you to keep your promise. I was sorry to see you leave London, but was satisfied that you would be back in time. You may expect me, therefore, at the hour arranged. Until then . . .
>
> K.

Mrs. Drover looked for the date: it was today's. She dropped the letter on to the bed-springs, then picked it up to see the writing again — her lips, beneath the remains of lipstick, beginning to go white. She felt so much the change in her own face that she went to the mirror, polished a clear patch in it, and looked at once urgently and stealthily in. She was confronted by a woman of forty-four, with eyes starting out under a hat-brim that had been rather carelessly pulled down. She had not put on any more powder since she left the shop where she ate her solitary tea. The pearls her husband had given her on their marriage hung loose around her now rather thinner throat, slipping in the V of the pink wool jumper her sister knitted last autumn as they sat round the fire. Mrs. Drover's most normal expression was one of controlled worry, but of assent. Since the birth of the third of her little boys, attended by a quite serious illness, she had had an intermittent muscular flicker to the left of her mouth, but in spite of this she could always sustain a manner that was at once energetic and calm.

Turning from her own face as precipitately as she had gone to meet it, she went to the chest where the things were, unlocked it, threw up the lid, and knelt to search. But as rain began to come crashing down she could not keep from looking over her shoulder at the stripped bed on which the letter lay. Behind the blanket of rain the clock of the church that still stood struck six — with rapidly heightening apprehension she counted each of the slow strokes. "The hour arranged . . . My God," she said, "*what* hour? How should I . . . ? After twenty-five years . . ."

The young girl talking to the soldier in the garden had not ever completely seen his face. It was dark; they were saying goodbye under a tree. Now and then — for it felt, from not seeing him at this intense moment, as though she had never seen him at all — she verified his presence for these few moments longer by putting out a hand, which he each time pressed, without very much kindness, and painfully, on to one of the breast buttons of his uniform. That cut of the button on the palm of her hand was, principally, what she was to carry away. This was so near the end of a leave from France that she could only wish him already gone. It was August 1916. Being not kissed, being drawn away from and looked at intimidated Kathleen till she imagined spectral glitters in the place of his eyes. Turning away and looking back up the lawn she saw, through branches of trees, the drawing-room window light: she caught a breath for the moment when she could go running back there into the safe arms of her mother and sister, and cry: "What shall I do, what shall I do? He has gone."

Hearing her catch her breath, her fiancé said, without feeling: "Cold?"

"You're going away such a long way."

"Not so far as you think."

"I don't understand?"

"You don't have to," he said. "You will. You know what we said."

"But that was — suppose you — I mean, suppose."

"I shall be with you," he said, "sooner or later. You won't forget that. You need do nothing but wait."

Only a little more than a minute later she was free to run up the silent lawn. Looking in through the window at her mother and sister, who did not for the moment perceive her, she already felt that unnatural promise drive down between her and the rest of all human kind. No other way of having given herself could have made her feel so apart, lost and foresworn. She could not have plighted a more sinister troth.

Kathleen behaved well when, some months later, her fiancé was reported missing, presumed killed. Her family not only supported her but were able to praise her courage without stint because they could not regret, as a husband for her, the man they knew almost nothing about. They hoped she would, in a year or two, console herself — and had it been only a question of consolation things might have gone much straighter ahead. But her trouble, behind just a little grief, was a complete dislocation from everything. She did not reject other lovers, for these failed to appear: for years she failed to attract men — and with the approach of her thirties she became natural enough to share her family's anxiousness on this score. She began to put herself out, to wonder; and at thirty-two she was very greatly relieved to find herself being courted by William Drover. She married him, and the two of them settled down in this quiet, arboreal part of Kensington: in this house the years piled up, her children were born, and they all lived till they were driven out by the bombs of the next war. Her movements as Mrs. Drover were circumscribed, and she dismissed any idea that they were still watched.

As things were — dead or living the letter-writer sent her only a threat.

Unable, for some minutes, to go on kneeling with her back exposed to the empty room, Mrs. Drover rose from the chest to sit on an upright chair whose back was firmly against the wall. The desuetude of her former bedroom, her married London home's whole air of being a cracked cup from which memory, with its reassuring power, had either evaporated or leaked away, made a crisis — and at just this crisis the letter-writer had, knowledgeably, struck. The hollowness of the house this evening cancelled years on years of voices, habits, and steps. Through the shut windows she only heard rain fall on the roofs around. To rally herself, she said she was in a mood — and for two or three seconds shutting her eyes, told herself that she had imagined the letter. But she opened them — there it lay on the bed.

On the supernatural side of the letter's entrance she was not permitting her mind to dwell. Who, in London, knew she meant to call at the house today? Evidently, however, this had been known. The caretaker, *had* he come back, had had no cause to expect her: he would have taken the letter in his pocket, to forward it, at his own time, through the post. There was no other sign that the caretaker had been in — but, if not? Letters dropped in at doors of deserted houses do not fly or walk to tables in halls. They do not sit on the dust of empty tables with the air of certainty that they will be found. There is needed some human hand — but nobody but the caretaker had a key. Under circumstances she did not care to consider, a house can be entered without a key. It was possible that she was not alone now. She might be being waited for, downstairs. Waited for — until when? Until "the hour arranged." At least that was not six o'clock: six has struck.

She rose from the chair and went over and locked the door.

The thing was, to get out. To fly? No, not that: she had to catch her train. As a woman whose utter dependability was the keystone of her family life she was not willing to return to the country, to her husband, her little boys, and her sister, without the objects she had come up to fetch. Resuming work at the chest she set about making up a number of parcels in a rapid, fumbling-decisive way. These, with her shopping parcels, would be too much to carry; these meant a taxi — at the thought of the taxi her heart went up and her normal breathing resumed. I will ring up the taxi now; the taxi cannot come too soon: I shall hear the taxi out there running its engine, till I walk calmly down to it through the hall. I'll ring up — But no: the telephone is cut off . . . She tugged at a knot she had tied wrong.

The idea of flight . . . He was never kind to me, not really. I don't remember him kind at all. Mother said he never considered me. He was set on me, that was what it was — not love. Not love, not meaning a person well. What did he do, to make me promise like that? I can't remember — But she found that she could.

She remembered with such dreadful acuteness that the twenty-five years since then dissolved like smoke and she instinctively looked for the weal left by the button on the palm of her hand. She remembered not only all that he said and did but the complete suspension of *her* existence during that August week. I was not myself — they all told me so at the time. She remembered — but with one white burning blank as where acid has dropped on a photograph: *under no conditions* could she remember his face.

So, wherever he may be waiting, I shall not know him. You have no time to run from a face you do not expect.

The thing was to get to the taxi before any clock struck what could be the hour. She would slip down the street and round the side of the square to where the square gave on the main road. She would return in the taxi, safe, to her own door, and bring the solid driver into the house with her to pick up the parcels from room to room. The idea of the taxi driver made her decisive, bold: she unlocked her door, went to the top of the staircase, and listened down.

She heard nothing — but while she was hearing nothing the *passé* air of the staircase was disturbed by a draught that travelled up to her face. It emanated from the basement: down there a door or window was being opened by someone who chose this moment to leave the house.

The rain had stopped; the pavements steamily shone as Mrs. Drover let herself out by inches from her own front door into the empty street. The unoccupied houses opposite continued to meet her look with their damaged stare. Making towards the thoroughfare and the taxi, she tried not to keep looking behind. Indeed, the silence was so intense — one of those creeks of London silence exaggerated this summer by the damage of war — that no tread could have gained on hers unheard. Where her street debouched on the square where people went on living, she grew conscious of, and checked, her unnatural pace. Across the open end of the square two buses impassively passed each other: women, a perambulator, cyclists, a man wheeling a barrow signalized, once again, the ordinary flow of life. At the square's most populous corner should be — and was — the short taxi rank. This evening, only one taxi — but this, although it presented its blank rump, appeared already to be alertly waiting for her. Indeed, without looking round the driver started his engine as she panted up from behind and put her hand on the door. As she did so, the clock struck seven. The taxi faced the main road: to make the trip back to her house it would have to turn — she had settled back on the seat and the taxi *had* turned before she, surprised by its knowing movement, recollected that she had not "said where." She leaned forward to scratch at the glass panel that divided the driver's head from her own.

The driver braked to what was almost a stop, turned round, and slid the glass panel back: the jolt of this flung Mrs. Drover forward till her face was almost into the glass. Through the aperture driver and passenger, not six inches between them, remained for an eternity eye to eye. Mrs. Drover's mouth hung open for some seconds before she could issue her first scream. After that she continued to scream freely and to beat with her gloved hands on the glass all round as the taxi, accelerating without mercy, made off with her into the hinterland of deserted streets.

[1946]

JORGE LUIS BORGES (1899–1986), *the Argentinean writer of fiction, poetry, and criticism, was born in Buenos Aires. His father, a professor of psychology, amused him in childhood with various philosophical puzzles which continued to intrigue Borges when he grew up and became a writer. Educated in Europe, he began to write as a member of a Spanish avant-garde literary movement called Ultráisme, a development of expressionism in which image and metaphor were exaggerated to become more important than plot, character, or theme. Borges rejected this extreme view when he matured as an artist, but he remained an antirealist. After his return to Buenos Aires in 1921, he worked in the National Library, rising to the position of its director before the dictator Juan Perón hounded him out of the job for political reasons. Borges published his first book in 1923, but in the 1930s he was most active as an essayist and editor; he also wrote detective stories under other names. Then came* Fictions (1944), *a collection of short, often playful prose assertions in which Borges examined various ideas to show that every human effort is a "fiction."* Labyrinths (1962), The Aleph and Other Stories (1970), *and* Doctor Brodie's Report (1972) *are more collections of sketches and stories.* Borges on Writing (1973) *contains his views on fiction, poetry, and translation. Until his death, Borges lived in Buenos Aires, where his progressive blindness circumscribed his entire life. He continued to write, and he lectured and taught in the United States occasionally.*

Borges has said that he writes stories for the "sheer fun of it. . . . I'm fond of short stories, but I'm far too lazy for novel writing. I'd get tired of the whole thing after writing ten or fifteen pages." He wrote his first short story, "Streetcorner Man," as a literary experiment after seeing a gangster film by Josef von Sternberg. He wanted to write a vivid, visual story, not a realistic one: "I knew quite well it was all unreal, but as I wasn't striving after reality I didn't mind." An erudite man, Borges often bases his stories on anecdotes that he thinks are interesting, as in "The End of the Duel," but the creative process of an anecdote's reappearance in the form of a short story is a slow one: "If you tell me an anecdote today, it wouldn't find its way into print until some four or five years from now. . . . I have to sit back and wait, and then, when the moment comes, I have to be very receptive and try not to tamper or tinker with it."

One of the repeated images in Borges's short fiction is the labyrinth, representing the central paradox that "the rich symmetries" of the mind, and of history and the world, end only in confusion or mystery. Less concerned with character than with plot or situation, Borges works into every story the idea that he, as author, is not sure of all things, "because that's the way reality is." He is equally undogmatic when he speculates on his practices as a writer. From Ralph Waldo Emerson he got the idea that all liter-

ary works are one work and that all writers are one impersonal writer, one single all-knowing "gentleman." Wondering if he has ever created a single original line in his writing, Borges has said that if the reader looks long enough, a source might be found for everything he has written. Invention is just "mixing up memories. I don't think we're capable of creation in the way that God created the world." (See Borges's Commentary about "The End of the Duel" on page 1292.)

Jorge Luis Borges

ဢ

THE END OF THE DUEL

– translated by Anthony Kerrigan

It's a good many years ago now that Carlos Reyles, the son of the Uruguayan novelist, told me the story one summer evening out in Adrogué. In my memory, after all this time, the long chronicle of a feud and its grim ending are mixed up with the medicinal smell of the eucalyptus trees and the babbling voices of birds.

We sat talking, as usual, of the tangled history of our two countries, Uruguay and the Argentine. Reyles said that probably I'd heard of Juan Patricio Nolan, who had won quite a reputation as a brave man, a practical joker, and a rogue. Lying, I answered yes. Though Nolan had died back in the nineties, people still thought of him as a friend. As always happens, however, he had his enemies as well. Reyles gave me an account of one of Nolan's many pranks. The thing had happened a short time before the battle of Manantiales; two gauchos from Cerro Largo, Manuel Cardoso and Carmen Silveira, were the leading characters.

How and why did they begin hating each other? How, after a century, can one unearth the long-forgotten story of two men whose only claim to being remembered is their last duel? A foreman of Reyles' father, whose name was Laderecha and "who had the whiskers of a tiger," had collected from oral accounts certain details that I transcribe now with a good deal of misgiving, since both forgetfulness and memory are apt to be inventive.

Manuel Cardoso and Carmen Silveira had a few acres of land that bordered each other. Like the roots of other passions, those of hatred are mysterious, but there was talk of a quarrel over some unbranded cattle or a free-for-all horse race in which Silveira, who was the stronger of the two, had run Cardoso's horse off the edge of the course. Months afterward, a long two-handed game of *truco*[1] of thirty points was to take place in the local saloon. Following almost every hand, Silveira congratulated his opponent on his skill, but in the end left him without a cent. When he tucked his winnings away in his money belt, Silveira thanked Cardoso for the lesson he had been given. It was then, I believe, that they were at the point of having it out. The game had had its ups and downs. In those rough places and in that day, man squared off against man and steel against steel. But the onlookers, who were quite a few, separated them. A peculiar twist of the story is that Manuel Cardoso and Carmen Silveira must have run across each other out in the hills on more than one occasion at sundown or at dawn, but they never actually faced each other until the very end. Maybe their poor and monotonous lives held nothing else for them than their hatred, and that was why they nursed it. In the long run, without suspecting it, each of the two became a slave to the other.

I no longer know whether the events I am about to relate are effects or causes. Cardoso, less out of love than out of boredom, took up with a neighbor girl, La Serviliana. That was all Silveira had to find out, and, after his manner, he began courting her and brought her to his shack. A few months later, finding her in the way, he threw her out. Full of spite, the woman tried to seek shelter at Cardoso's. Cardoso spent one night with her, and by the next noon packed her off. He did not want the other man's leavings.

It was around that same time, just before or just after La Serviliana, that the incident of Silveira's sheepdog took place. Silveira was very fond of the animal, and had named him Treinta y Tres, after Uruguay's thirty-three founding fathers. When the dog was found dead in a ditch, Silveira was quick to suspect who had given it poison.

Sometime during the winter of 1870, a civil war broke out between the Colorados, or Reds, who were in power, and Aparicio's Blancos, or Whites. The revolution found Silveira and Cardoso in the same crossroads saloon where they had played their game of cards. A Brazilian half-breed, at the head of a detachment of gaucho militiamen, harangued all those present, telling them that the country needed them and that the government oppression was unbearable. He handed around white badges to mark them as Blancos, and at the end of his speech, which nobody understood, everyone in the place was rounded up. They were not allowed even to say goodbye to their families.

Manuel Cardoso and Carmen Silveira accepted their fate; a soldier's life was no harder than a gaucho's. Sleeping in the open on their sheepskin saddle blankets was something to which they were already hardened, and as for killing men, that held no difficulty for hands already in the habit of killing cattle. The clinking of stirrups and weapons is one of the things always heard when cavalry enter into action. The man who is not wounded at the

---

[1] a South American card game.

outset thinks himself invulnerable. A lack of imagination freed Cardoso and Silveira from fear and from pity, although once in a while, heading a charge, fear brushed them. They were never homesick. The idea of patriotism was alien to them, and, in spite of the badges they wore on their hats, one party was to them the same as the other. During the course of marches and countermarches, they learned what a man could do with a spear, and they found out that being companions allowed them to go on being enemies. They fought shoulder to shoulder and, for all we know, did not exchange a single word.

It was in the sultry fall of 1871 that their end was to come. The fight, which would not last an hour, happened in a place whose name they never knew. (Such places are later named by historians.) On the eve of battle, Cardoso crept on all fours into his officer's tent and asked him sheepishly would he save him one of the Reds if the Whites won the next day, because up till then he had not cut anyone's throat and he wanted to know what it was like. His superior promised him that if he handled himself like a man he would be granted that favor.

The Whites outnumbered the enemy, but the Reds were better equipped and cut them down from the crown of a hill. After two unsuccessful charges that never reached the summit, the Whites' commanding officer, badly wounded, surrendered. On the very spot, at his own request, he was put to death by the knife.

The men laid down their arms. Captain Juan Patricio Nolan, who commanded the Reds, arranged the expected execution of the prisoners down to the last detail. He was from Cerro Largo himself, and knew all about the old rivalry between Silveira and Cardoso. He sent for the pair and told them, "I already know you two can't stand the sight of each other, and that for some time now you've been looking for a chance to have it out. I have good news for you. Before sundown, the two of you are going to have that chance to show who's the better man. I'm going to stand you up and have your throats cut, and then you'll run a race. God knows who'll win." The soldier who had brought them took them away.

It was not long before the news spread throughout the camp. Nolan had made up his mind that the race would close the proceedings, but the prisoners sent him a representative to tell him that they, too, wanted to be spectators and to place wagers on the outcome. Nolan, who was an understanding man, let himself be convinced. The bets were laid down — money, riding gear, spears, sabers, and horses. In due time they would be handed over to the widows and next of kin. The heat was unusual. So that no one would miss his siesta, things were delayed until four o'clock. Nolan, in the South American style, kept them waiting another hour. He was probably discussing the campaign with his officers, his aide shuttling in and out with the maté kettle.

Both sides of the dirt road in front of the tents were lined with prisoners, who, to make things easier, squatted on the ground with their hands tied behind their backs. A few of them relieved their feelings in a torrent of swearwords, one went over and over the beginning of the Lord's Prayer, almost all were stunned. Of course, they would not smoke. They no longer cared about the race now, but they all watched.

"They'll be cutting my throat on me, too," one of them said, showing his envy.

"Sure, but along with the mob," said his neighbor.

"Same as you," the first man snapped back.

With his saber, a sergeant drew a line in the dust across the road. Silveira's and Cardoso's wrists had been untied so that they could run freely. A space of some five yards was between them. Each man toed the mark. A couple of the officers asked the two not to let them down because everyone had placed great faith in them, and the sums they had bet on them came to quite a pile.

It fell to Silveira's lot to draw as executioner the mulatto Nolan, whose forefathers had no doubt been slaves of the captain's family and therefore bore his name. Cardoso drew the Reds' official cutthroat, a man from Corrientes well along in years, who, to comfort a condemned man, would pat him on the shoulder and tell him, "Take heart, friend. Women go through far worse when they give birth."

Their torsos bent forward, the two eager men did not look at each other. Nolan gave the signal.

The mulatto, swelling with pride to be at the center of attention, overdid his job and opened a showy slash that ran from ear to ear; the man from Corrientes did his with a narrow slit. Spurts of blood gushed from the men's throats. They dashed forward a number of steps before tumbling face down. Cardoso, as he fell, stretched out his arms. Perhaps never aware of it, he had won.

[1973]

ZORA NEALE HURSTON (1901?–1960) was born in 1901 or 1902 (the records are lost and she gave different birth dates in her writing) in Eatonville, Florida, an all-black town. When her mother died in 1912, her father, a Baptist minister, couldn't raise their eight children, so Hurston was forced to move from one relative's home to another. She never finished grade school, but when she was old enough to support herself, she attended Howard University in Washington, D.C., America's leading black university in the 1920s. In 1921 she published her first story, "John Redding Goes to Sea," in the student literary magazine.

In 1925 Hurston went to New York City and became active in the black cultural renaissance in Harlem, collaborating with Langston Hughes on a folk comedy, Mule Bone. Like Hughes, she was deeply interested in the abiding folk spirit inherent in black life. With several other writers of that time, she tried to express her black cultural heritage. After Hurston studied with the famous anthropologist Franz Boas at Barnard College, she returned to Florida to record the oral traditions of her native community. From this time to the end of her life, she tried to achieve a balance in her literary work between focusing on the folk culture of her racial background and focusing on herself as a developing individual artist. Realizing that average white people used stereotypes to keep blacks, Asians, Mexicans, and Native American Indians in their "place," Hurston insisted that it was "urgent to realize that minorities do think, and think about something other than the race problem. That they are very human and internally, according to natural endowment, are just like everybody else. So long as this is not conceived, there must remain that feeling of unsurmountable difference, and difference to the average man means something bad. If people were made right, they would be just like him."

When the Great Depression of the 1930s ended the Harlem Renaissance, Hurston turned all her energies to writing. She published Mules and Men (1935), based on material from her field trips to Florida, and Their Eyes Were Watching God (1937), a novel about a black woman's search for love and personal identity, in addition to several other books, including an autobiography. Although she published more than any other black woman writer of her time, in the last two decades of her life she earned very little from her writing, and she died penniless in Florida. Fifteen years after Hurston's death, her work was rediscovered by the women's movement, and she is now regarded as an important American black writer. "Spunk" is a story from The Eatonville Anthology (1927), the collection that first brought Hurston to the attention of a national audience.

Zora Neale Hurston

తౌౙ

SPUNK

I

A giant of a brown-skinned man sauntered up the one street of the village and out into the palmetto thickets with a small pretty woman clinging lovingly to his arm.

"Looka theah, folkses!" cried Elijah Mosley, slapping his leg gleefully. "Theah they go, big as life an' brassy as tacks."

All the loungers in the store tried to walk to the door with an air of nonchalance but with small success.

"Now pee-eople!" Walter Thomas gasped. "Will you look at 'em!"

"But that's one thing Ah likes about Spunk Banks — he ain't skeered of nothin' on God's green footstool — *nothin'!* He rides that log down at saw-mill jus' like he struts 'round wid another man's wife — jus' don't give a kitty. When Tes' Miller got cut to giblets on that circle-saw, Spunk steps right up and starts ridin'. The rest of us was skeered to go near it."

A round-shouldered figure in overalls much too large came nervously in the door and the talking ceased. The men looked at each other and winked.

"Gimme some soda-water. Sass'prilla Ah reckon," the newcomer ordered, and stood far down the counter near the open pickled pig-feet tub to drink it.

Elijah nudged Walter and turned with mock gravity to the new-comer. "Say, Joe, how's everything up yo' way? How's yo' wife?"

Joe started and all but dropped the bottle he was holding. He swallowed several times painfully and his lips trembled.

"Aw 'Lige, you oughtn't to do nothin' like that," Walter grumbled. Elijah ignored him.

"She jus' passed heah a few minutes ago goin' thata way," with a wave of his hand in the direction of the woods.

Now Joe knew his wife had passed that way. He knew that the men lounging in the general store had seen her, moreover, he knew that the men knew *he* knew. He stood there silent for a long moment staring blankly, with his Adam's apple twitching nervously up and down his throat. One could actually *see* the pain he was suffering, his eyes, his face, his hands, and even the dejected slump of his shoulders. He set the bottle down upon the counter. He didn't bang it, just eased it out of his hand silently and fiddled with his suspender buckle.

"Well, Ah'm goin' after her to-day. Ah'm goin' an' fetch her back. Spunk's done gone too fur."

He reached deep down into his trouser pocket and drew out a hollow ground razor, large and shiny, and passed his moistened thumb back and forth over the edge.

"Talkin' like a man, Joe. 'Course that's *yo'* fambly affairs, but Ah like to see grit in anybody."

Joe Kanty laid down a nickel and stumbled out into the street.

Dusk crept in from the woods. Ike Clarke lit the swinging oil lamp that was almost immediately surrounded by candle-flies. The men laughed boisterously behind Joe's back as they watched him shamble woodward.

"You oughtn't to said whut you said to him, 'Lige — look how it worked him up," Walter chided.

"And Ah hope it did work him up. Tain't even decent for a man to take and take like he do."

"Spunk will sho' kill him."

"Aw, Ah doan know. You never kin tell. He might turn him up an' spank him fur gettin' in the way, but Spunk wouldn't shoot no unarmed man. Dat razor he carried outa heah ain't gonna run Spunk down an' cut him, an' Joe ain't got the nerve to go to Spunk with it knowing he totes that Army .45. He makes that break outa heah to bluff us. He's gonna hide that razor behind the first palmetto root an' sneak back home to bed. Don't tell me nothin' 'bout that rabbit-foot colored man. Didn't he meet Spunk an' Lena face to face one day las' week an' mumble sumthin' to Spunk 'bout lettin' his wife alone?"

"What did Spunk say?" Walter broke in. "Ah like him fine but tain't right the way he carries on wid Lena Kanty, jus' 'cause Joe's timid 'bout fightin'."

"You wrong theah, Walter. Tain't 'cause Joe's timid at all, it's 'cause Spunk wants Lena. If Joe was a passle of wile cats Spunk would tackle the job just the same. He'd go after *anything* he wanted the same way. As Ah wuz sayin' a minute ago, he tole Joe right to his face that Lena was his. 'Call her and see if she'll come. A woman knows her boss an' she answers when he calls.' 'Lena, ain't I yo' husband?' Joe sorter whines out. Lena looked at him real disgusted but she don't answer and she don't move outa her tracks. Then Spunk reaches out an' takes hold of her arm an' says: 'Lena, youse mine. From now on Ah works for you an' fights for you an' Ah never wants you to look to nobody for a crumb of bread, a stitch of close or a shingle to go over yo' head, but *me* long as Ah live. Ah'll git the lumber foh owah house to-morrow. Go home an' git yo' things together!'

" 'Thass mah house,' Lena speaks up. 'Papa gimme that.'

" 'Well,' says Spunk, 'doan give up whut's yours, but when youse inside doan forgit youse mine, an' let no other man git outa his place wid you!' "

"Lena looked up at him with her eyes so full of love that they wuz runnin' over, an' Spunk seen it an' Joe seen it too, and his lip started to tremblin' and his Adam's apple was galloping up and down his neck like a race horse. Ah bet he's wore out half a dozen Adam's apples since Spunk's been on the job with Lena. That's all he'll do. He'll be back heah after while swallowin' an' workin' his lips like he wants to say somethin' an' can't."

"But didn't he do *nothin'* to stop 'em?"

"Nope, not a frazzlin' thing — jus' stood there. Spunk took Lena's arm and walked off jus' like nothin' ain't happened and he stood there gazin' after them till they was outa sight. Now you know a woman don't want no man like that. I'm jus' waitin' to see whut he's goin' to say when he gits back."

II

But Joe Kanty never came back, never. The men in the store heard the sharp report of a pistol somewhere distant in the palmetto thicket and soon Spunk came walking leisurely, with his big black Stetson set at the same rakish angle and Lena clinging to his arm, came walking right into the general store. Lena wept in a frightened manner.

"Well," Spunk announced calmly, "Joe came out there wid a meat axe an' made me kill him."

He sent Lena home and led the men back to Joe — crumpled and limp with his right hand still clutching his razor.

"See mah back? Mah close cut clear through. He sneaked up an' tried to kill me from the back, but Ah got him, an' got him good, first shot," Spunk said.

The men glared at Elijah, accusingly.

"Take him up an' plant him in Stony Lonesome," Spunk said in a careless voice. "Ah didn't wanna shoot him but he made me do it. He's a dirty coward, jumpin' on a man from behind."

Spunk turned on his heel and sauntered away to where he knew his love wept in fear for him and no man stopped him. At the general store later on, they all talked of locking him up until the sheriff should come from Orlando, but no one did anything but talk.

A clear case of self-defense, the trial was a short one, and Spunk walked out of the court house to freedom again. He could work again, ride the dangerous log-carriage that fed the singing, snarling, biting circle-saw; he could stroll the soft dark lanes with his guitar. He was free to roam the woods again; he was free to return to Lena. He did all of these things.

III

"Whut you reckon, Walt?" Elijah asked one night later. "Spunk's gittin' ready to marry Lena!"

"Naw! Why, Joe ain't had time to git cold yit. Nohow Ah didn't figger Spunk was the marryin' kind."

"Well, he is," rejoined Elijah. "He done moved most of Lena's things — and her along wid 'em — over to the Bradley house. He's buying it. Jus' like Ah told yo' all right in heah the night Joe was kilt. Spunk's crazy 'bout Lena. He don't want folks to keep on talkin' 'bout her — thass reason he's rushin' so. Funny thing 'bout that bob-cat, wan't it?"

"What bob-cat, 'Lige? Ah ain't heered 'bout none."

"Ain't cher? Well, night befo' las' as they was goin' to bed, a big black bob-cat, black all over, you hear me, *black*, walked round and round that house and howled like forty, an' when Spunk got his gun an' went to the winder to shoot it, he says it stood right still an' looked him in the eye, an' howled right at him. The thing got Spunk so nervoused up he couldn't shoot. But Spunk says twan't no bob-cat nohow. He says it was Joe done sneaked back from Hell!"

"Humph!" sniffed Walter, "he oughter be nervous after what he done. Ah reckon Joe come back to dare him to marry Lena, or to come out an' fight. Ah bet he'll be back time and again, too. Know what Ah think? Joe wuz a braver man than Spunk."

There was a general shout of derision from the group.

"Thass a fact," went on Walter. "Lookit whut he done; took a razor an' went out to fight a man he knowed toted a gun an' wuz a crack shot, too; 'nother thing Joe wuz skeered of Spunk, skeered plumb stiff! But he went jes' the same. It took him a long time to get his nerve up. Tain't nothin' for Spunk to fight when he ain't skeered of nothin'. Now, Joe's done come back to have it out wid the man that's got all he ever had. Y'all know Joe ain't never had nothin' nor wanted nothin' besides Lena. It musta been a h'ant cause ain't nobody never seen no black bob-cat."

"'Nother thing," cut in one of the men, "Spunk was cussin' a blue streak to-day 'cause he 'lowed dat saw wuz wobblin' — almos' got 'im once. The machinist come, looked it over an said it wuz alright. Spunk musta been leanin' t'wards it some. Den he claimed somebody pushed 'im but twan't nobody close to 'im. Ah wuz glad when knockin' off time came. I'm skeered of dat man when he gits hot. He'd beat you full of button holes as quick as he's look atcher."

IV

The men gathered the next evening in a different mood, no laughter. No badinage this time.

"Look, 'Lige, you goin' to set up wid Spunk?"

"Naw, Ah reckon not, Walter. Tell yuh the truth, Ah'm a li'l bit skittish. Spunk died too wicket — died cussin' he did. You know he thought he was done outa life."

"Good Lawd, who'd he think done it?"

"Joe."

"Joe Kanty? How come?"

"Walter, Ah b'leeve Ah will walk up thata way an' set. Lena would like it Ah reckon."

"But whut did he say, 'Lige?"

Elijah did not answer until they had left the lighted store and were strolling down the dark street.

"Ah wuz loadin' a wagon wid scantlin' right near the saw when Spunk fell on the carriage but 'fore Ah could git to him the saw got him in the body — awful sight. Me an' Skint Miller got him off but it was too late. Anybody could see that. The fust thing he said wuz: 'He pushed me, 'Lige — the dirty hound pushed me in the back!' — he was spittin' blood at ev'ry breath. We laid him on the sawdust pile with his face to the East so's he could die easy. He helt mah han' till the last, Walter, and said: 'It was Joe, 'Lige ... the dirty sneak shoved me ... he didn't dare come to mah face ... but Ah'll git the son-of-a-wood louse soon's Ah get there an' make hell too hot for him ... Ah felt him shove me ...!' Thass how he died."

"If spirits kin fight, there's a powerful tussle goin' on somewhere ovah Jordan 'cause Ah b'leeve Joe's ready for Spunk an' ain't skeered any more — yas, Ah b'leeve Joe pushed 'im mahself."

They had arrived at the house. Lena's lamentations were deep and loud. She had filled the room with magnolia blossoms that gave off a heavy sweet odor. The keepers of the wake tipped about whispering in frightened tones. Everyone in the village was there, even old Jeff Kanty, Joe's father, who a few hours before would have been afraid to come within ten feet of him, stood leering triumphantly down upon the fallen giant as if his fingers had been the teeth of steel that laid him low.

The cooling board consisted of three sixteen-inch boards on saw horses, a dingy sheet was his shroud.

The women ate heartily of the funeral baked meats and wondered who would be Lena's next. The men whispered coarse conjectures between guzzles of whiskey.

[1927]

LANGSTON HUGHES (1902–1967) was born in Joplin, Missouri. He spent most of his childhood living with his grandmother in Lawrence, Kansas, and his first contact with a large number of other blacks came when he attended high school in Cleveland in 1916. In his high school English classes he read the poetry of Carl Sandburg and Edgar Lee Masters, and he published several poems in the literary magazine. Hughes's father was a college graduate who persuaded him to study engineering at Columbia University in 1921, but after only one year Hughes abandoned his studies and signed on as a mess boy on a ship that took him to Africa and Europe. He was determined to be a writer. He had begun to publish his poetry in the NAACP magazine The Crisis, including what was to become one of his best-known poems, "The Negro Speaks of Rivers" (which he had written as a teenager). His career as a poet was launched a few years later with his book The Weary Blues (1926), which contains poems about a Harlem musician who plays the piano all night and then goes home to sleep. After five years of writing and travel, Hughes took a bachelor's degree from Lincoln University in Pennsylvania, and then settled in New York. He became an important member of the literary coterie including Countee Cullen, Zora Neale Hurston, Nella Larsen, Claude McKay, and Jean Toomer that helped form the Harlem Renaissance of the late 1920s. This group of writers emphasized Negro topics — the African heritage, the slave era, and life in Harlem. Hughes wrote plays as well as poetry and was active in the organization of black theater companies in New York, Los Angeles, and Chicago. His most famous play, Tambourines to Glory, was adapted from his novel of the same name in 1963. Exhibiting an impressive versatility and productivity in his career, Hughes also wrote newspaper columns for the Chicago Defender and the New York Post and edited twenty-eight collections of African and Negro poetry and folklore in addition to writing his own plays, translations, poetry and fiction.

Hughes's interest in fiction developed later than his talent for poetry. As he described it in his autobiography I Wonder As I Wander (1956), he was traveling in the Soviet Union when he picked up a paperback copy of a collection of short stories he had never read before by D. H. Lawrence. He was so impressed with them — especially with "The Rocking Horse Winner" — that a night or two later he sat down at his well-traveled portable typewriter to try to write stories of his own. "If D. H. Lawrence can write such psychologically powerful accounts of folks in England, that send shivers up and down my spine," he reasoned, "maybe I could write stories like his about folks in America." Hughes sent his first three stories from Russia to his literary agent in New York, and by the time he returned to the United States all three had been sold to popular magazines. "The money came in handy. And once started, I wrote almost nothing but short stories."

Hughes found it easy to write conventional short stories — his early stories were published as The Ways of White Folks *in 1934 — but his most original work in this literary form can be seen in his stories about Jesse B. Simple, a character he created in 1942 when he wrote columns for the Chicago Defender. Jesse is a black working man living in Harlem, whose conversations with the middle-class, intellectual narrator are occasions for exhibiting his down-home blend of urban cynicism and genial mother wit on a wide variety of timely topics, such as unemployment, war, divorce, women's rights, education for blacks and the atomic bomb, as in "Radioactive Red Caps."* Simple Speaks His Mind *(1950),* Simple Takes a Wife *(1952),* Simple Stakes a Claim *(1957), and* The Best of Simple *(1961) were the collections of stories about this popular character published in Hughes's lifetime. They were written in a supple blend of Simple's colloquial speech and the narrator's standard English. (See Hughes's Commentary on page 1295.)*

Langston Hughes

෨෨

RADIOACTIVE RED CAPS

"How wonderful," I said, "that Negroes today are being rapidly integrated into every phase of American life from the Army and Navy to schools to industries — advancing, advancing!"

"I have not advanced one step," said Simple. "Still the same old job, same old salary, same old kitchenette, same old Harlem and the same old color."

"You are just one individual," I said. "I am speaking of our race in general. Look how many colleges have opened up to Negroes in the last ten years. Look at the change in restrictive covenants. You can live anywhere."

"You mean *try* to live anywhere."

"Look at the way you can ride unsegregated in interstate travel."

"And get throwed off the bus."

"Look at the ever greater number of Negroes in high places."

"Name me one making an atom bomb."

"That would be top-secret information," I said, "even if I knew. Anyway, you are arguing from supposition, not knowledge. How do you know what our top Negro scientists are doing?"

"I don't," said Simple. "But I bet if one was making an atom bomb, they would have his picture on the cover of *Jet* every other week like Eartha Kitt, just to make Negroes think the atom bomb is an integrated bomb. Then, next thing you know, some old Southern senator would up and move to have that Negro investigated for being subversive, because he would be mad that a Negro ever got anywhere near an atom bomb. Then that Negro would be removed from his job like Miss Annie Lee Moss, and have to hire a lawyer to get halfway back. Then they would put that whitewashed Negro to making plain little old-time ordinary bombs that can only kill a few folks at a time. You know and I know, they don't want no Negroes nowhere near no bomb that can kill a whole state full of folks like an atom bomb can. Just think what would happen to Mississippi. Wow!"

"Your thinking borders on the subversive," I warned. "Do you want to fight the Civil War over again?"

"Not without an atom bomb," said Simple. "If I was in Mississippi, I would be Jim Crowed out of bomb shelters, so I would need some kind of protection. By the time I got the N.A.A.C.P. to take my case to the Supreme Court, the war would be over, else I would be atomized."

"Absurd!" I said. "Bomb shelters will be for everybody."

"Not in Mississippi," said Simple. "Down there they will have some kind of voting test, else loyalty test, in which they will find some way of flunking Negroes out. You can't tell me them Dixiecrats are going to give Negroes free rein of bomb shelters. On the other hand, come to think of it, they might *have* to let us in to save their own skins, because I hear tell that in the next war everything that ain't sheltered will be so charged with atoms a human can't touch it. Even the garbage is going to get radioactive when the bombs start falling. I read last week in the *News* that, in case of a bombing, it will be a problem as to where to put our garbage, because it will be radioactive up to a million years. So you sure can't keep garbage around. If you dump it in the sea, it will make the fish radioactive, too, like them Japanese tunas nobody could eat. I am wondering what the alley cats will eat — because if all the garbage is full of atomic rays, and the cats eat the garbage, and my wife pets a strange cat, Joyce will be radioactive, too. Then if I pet my wife, what will happen to me?"

"You are stretching the long arm of coincidence mighty far," I said. "What is more likely to happen is, if the bombs fall, you will be radioactive long before the garbage will."

"That will worry white folks," said Simple. "Just suppose all the Negroes down South got atomized, charged up like hot garbage, who would serve the white folks' tables, nurse their children, Red Cap their bags, and make up their Pullman berths? Just think! Suppose all the colored Red Caps carrying bags on the Southern Railroad was atom-charged! Suitcases would get atomized, too, and all that is packed in them. Every time a white man took out his toothbrush to wash his teeth on the train, his teeth would get atom-charged. How could he kiss his wife when he got home?"

"I believe you are charged now," I said.

"No," said Simple, "I am only thinking how awful this atom bomb can be! If one fell up North in Harlem and charged me, then I went downtown and punched that time clock where I work, the clock would be charged. Then a white fellow would come along behind me and punch the time clock, and he would be charged. Then both of us would be so full of atoms for the next million years, that at any time we would be liable to explode like firecrackers on the Fourth of July. And from us, everybody else in the plant would get charged. Atoms, they tell me, is catching. What I read in the *News* said that if you even look at an atom bomb going off, the rays are so strong your eyes will water the rest of your life, your blood will turn white, your hair turn gray, and your children will be born backwards. Your breakfast eggs will no longer be sunny-side up, but scrambled, giving off sparks — and people will give off sparks, too. If you walk down the street, every doorbell you pass will ring without your touching it. If you pick up a phone, whoever answers it will be atomized. So if you know somebody you don't like, for example, just phone them — and you can really fix them up! That's what they call a chain reaction. I am getting my chain ready now — the first person I am going to telephone is my former landlady! When she picks up the phone, I hope to atomize her like a Japanese tuna! She will drive a Geiger counter crazy after I say, 'Hello!'"

"My dear boy," I said, "what makes you think you, of all people, would be able to go around transferring atomic radiation to others? you would probably be annihilated yourself by the very first bomb blast."

"Me? Oh, no," said Simple. "Negroes are very hard to annihilate. I am a Negro — so I figure I would live to radiate and, believe me, once charged, I will take charge."

"In other words, come what may, you expect to survive the atom bomb?"

"If Negroes can survive white folks in Mississippi," said Simple, "we can survive anything."

[1957]

JOHN STEINBECK (1902–1968) *was born in Salinas and raised near Monterey in the fertile farm country of the Salinas Valley in California, the locale for his story "The Chrysanthemums." His mother was a former schoolteacher; his father was the county treasurer. In high school Steinbeck wrote for the school newspaper and was president of his class. He enjoyed literature at an early age and read novels by Gustave Flaubert, Fyodor Dostoevsky and Thomas Hardy in the family library. Enrolled at Stanford University as an English major, Steinbeck dropped out before graduating and worked at odd jobs — fruit picker, caretaker, laboratory assistant — while he practiced writing fiction. Several times he took short-term jobs with the Spreckels Sugar Company and gained a perspective on labor problems, which he would later describe in his novels.*

In 1929 Steinbeck began his literary career by publishing Cup of Gold, *a fictionalized biography of Henry Morgan, the seventeenth-century Welsh pirate. His next book,* The Pastures of Heaven (1932), *is a collection of short stories about the people in a farm community in California. The critic Brian Barbour has stated that Steinbeck realized early in his career that the short story form was not congenial to his talents. He needed the more expansive form of the novel to give his fictional characters a chance for what he considered real growth. In 1936 Steinbeck wrote* In Dubious Battle, *his first major political novel. He then published four more novels and another book of short fiction,* The Long Valley (1938), *before his greatest work,* The Grapes of Wrath (1939). *This book, about a family from the Dust Bowl who emigrate to California and struggle to make a living despite agricultural exploitation, won Steinbeck the Pulitzer Prize. Among his many other successful novels are* East of Eden (1952) *and* The Winter of Our Discontent (1961). *He won the Nobel Prize for Literature in 1962.*

In the early nonfiction book Sea of Cortez (1941), *Steinbeck eloquently stated his view of humanity as "a two-legged paradox. [Man] has never become accustomed to the tragic miracle of consciousness. Perhaps, as has been suggested, his species is not set, has not jelled, but is still in a state of becoming, bound by his physical memories to a past of struggle and survival, limited in his future by the uneasiness of thought and consciousness." One of the most accomplished popular novelists in the United States, Steinbeck excelled — like Hemingway — in the creation of exciting conflicts, convincing dialogue, and recognizable characters to dramatize his philosophy of life. Although his production of short stories was relatively slight, his work is often anthologized because of his clear, realistic treatment of social themes as his characters struggle to forge meaningful lives. "The Chrysanthemums" echoes the D. H. Lawrence story "Odour of Chrysanthemums" in its concern with sexual roles and the difficulty of striking a balance between self-interest and the needs of others.*

712

John Steinbeck

⩗

THE CHRYSANTHEMUMS

The high grey-flannel fog of winter closed off the Salinas Valley from the sky and from all the rest of the world. On every side it sat like a lid on the mountains and made of the great valley a closed pot. On the broad, level land floor the gang plows bit deep and left the black earth shining like metal where the shares had cut. On the foothill ranches across the Salinas River, the yellow stubble fields seemed to be bathed in pale cold sunshine, but there was no sunshine in the valley now in December. The thick willow scrub along the river flamed with sharp and positive yellow leaves.

It was a time of quiet and of waiting. The air was cold and tender. A light wind blew up from the southwest so that the farmers were mildly hopeful of a good rain before long; but fog and rain do not go together.

Across the river, on Henry Allen's foothill ranch there was little work to be done, for the hay was cut and stored and the orchards were plowed up to receive the rain deeply when it should come. The cattle on the higher slopes were becoming shaggy and rough-coated.

Elisa Allen, working in her flower garden, looked down across the yard and saw Henry, her husband, talking to two men in business suits. The three of them stood by the tractor shed, each man with one foot on the side of the little Fordson. They smoked cigarettes and studied the machine as they talked.

Elisa watched them for a moment and then went back to her work. She was thirty-five. Her face was lean and strong and her eyes were as clear as water. Her figure looked blocked and heavy in her gardening costume, a man's black hat pulled low down over her eyes, clod-hopper shoes, a figured print dress almost completely covered by a big corduroy apron with four big pockets to hold the snips, the trowel and scratcher, the seeds, and the knife she worked with. She wore heavy leather gloves to protect her hands while she worked.

She was cutting down the old year's chrysanthemum stalks with a pair of short and powerful scissors. She looked down toward the men by the tractor shed now and then. Her face was eager and mature and handsome; even her work with the scissors was overeager, overpowerful. The chrysanthemum stems seemed too small and easy for her energy.

She brushed a cloud of hair out of her eyes with the back of her glove, and left a smudge of earth on her cheek in doing it. Behind her stood the neat white farm house with red geraniums close-banked around it as high as the windows. It was a hard-swept looking little house with hard-polished windows, and a clean mud-mat on the front steps.

Elisa cast another glance toward the tractor shed. The strangers were getting into their Ford coupe. She took off a glove and put her strong fingers down into the forest of new green chrysanthemum sprouts that were growing around the old roots. She spread the leaves and looked down among the close-growing stems. No aphids were there, no sowbugs or snails or cutworms. Her terrier fingers destroyed such pests before they could get started.

Elisa started at the sound of her husband's voice. He had come near quietly, and he leaned over the wire fence that protected her flower garden from cattle and dogs and chickens.

"At it again," he said. "You've got a strong new crop coming."

Elisa straightened her back and pulled on the gardening glove again. "Yes. They'll be strong this coming year." In her tone and on her face there was a little smugness.

"You've got a gift with things," Henry observed. "Some of those yellow chrysanthemums you had this year were ten inches across. I wish you'd work out in the orchard and raise some apples that big."

Her eyes sharpened. "Maybe I could do it, too. I've a gift with things, all right. My mother had it. She could stick anything in the ground and make it grow. She said it was having planters' hands that knew how to do it."

"Well, it sure works with flowers," he said.

"Henry, who were those men you were talking to?"

"Why, sure, that's what I came to tell you. They were from the Western Meat Company. I sold those thirty head of three-year-old steers. Got nearly my own price, too."

"Good," she said. "Good for you."

"And I thought," he continued, "I thought how it's Saturday afternoon, and we might go into Salinas for dinner at a restaurant, and then to a picture show — to celebrate, you see."

"Good," she repeated. "Oh, yes. That will be good."

Henry put on his joking tone. "There's fights tonight. How'd you like to go to the fights?"

"Oh, no," she said breathlessly. "No, I wouldn't like fights."

"Just fooling, Elisa. We'll go to a movie. Let's see. It's two now. I'm going to take Scotty and bring down those steers from the hill. It'll take us maybe two hours. We'll go in town about five and have dinner at the Cominos Hotel. Like that?"

"Of course I'll like it. It's good to eat away from home."

"All right, then. I'll go get up a couple of horses."

She said, "I'll have plenty of time to transplant some of these sets, I guess."

She heard her husband calling Scotty down by the barn. And a little later she saw the two men ride up the pale yellow hillside in search of the steers.

There was a little square sandy bed kept for rooting the chrysanthemums. With her trowel she turned the soil over and over, and smoothed it and patted it firm. Then she dug ten parallel trenches to receive the sets. Back at the chrysanthemum bed she pulled out the little crisp shoots, trimmed off the leaves at each one with her scissors, and laid it on a small orderly pile.

A squeak of wheels and plod of hoofs came from the road. Elisa looked up. The country road ran along the dense bank of willows and cottonwoods that bordered the river, and up this road came a curious vehicle, curiously drawn. It was an old spring-wagon, with a round canvas top on it like the corner of a prairie schooner. It was drawn by an old bay horse and a little grey-and-white burro. A big stubble-bearded man sat between the cover flaps and drove the crawling team. Underneath the wagon, between the hind wheels, a lean and rangy mongrel dog walked sedately. Words were painted on the canvas, in clumsy, crooked letters. "Pots, pans, knives, sisors, lawn mores, Fixed." Two rows of articles, and the triumphantly definitive "Fixed" below. The black paint had run down in little sharp points beneath each letter.

Elisa, squatting on the ground, watched to see the crazy, loose-jointed wagon pass by. But it didn't pass. It turned into the farm road in front of her house, crooked old wheels skirling and squeaking. The rangy dog darted from between the wheels and ran ahead. Instantly the two ranch shepherds flew out at him. Then all three stopped, and with stiff and quivering tails, with taut straight legs, with ambassadorial dignity, they slowly circled, sniffing daintily. The caravan pulled up to Elisa's wire fence and stopped. Now the newcomer dog, feeling outnumbered, lowered his tail and retired under the wagon with raised hackles and bared teeth.

The man on the seat called out, "That's a bad dog in a fight when he gets started."

Elisa laughed. "I see he is. How soon does he generally get started?"

The man caught up her laughter and echoed it heartily. "Sometimes not for weeks and weeks," he said. He climbed stiffly down, over the wheel. The horse and the donkey drooped like unwatered flowers.

Elisa saw that he was a very big man. Although his hair and beard were greying, he did not look old. His worn black suit was wrinkled and spotted with grease. The laughter had disappeared from his face and eyes the moment his laughing voice ceased. His eyes were dark, and they were full of the brooding that gets in the eyes of teamsters and of sailors. The calloused hands he rested on the wire fence were cracked, and every crack was a black line. He took off his battered hat.

"I'm off my general road, ma'am," he said. "Does this dirt road cut over across the river to the Los Angeles highway?"

Elisa stood up and shoved the thick scissors in her apron pocket.

"Well, yes, it does, but it winds around and then fords the river. I don't think your team could pull through the sand."

He replied with some asperity, "It might surprise you what them beasts can pull through."

"When they get started?" she asked.

He smiled for a second. "Yes. When they get started."

"Well," said Elisa, "I think you'll save time if you go back to the Salinas road and pick up the highway there."

He drew a big finger down the chicken wire and made it sing. "I ain't in any hurry, ma'am. I go from Seattle to San Diego and back every year. Takes all my time. About six months each way. I aim to follow nice weather."

Elisa took off her gloves and stuffed them in the apron pocket with the scissors. She touched the under edge of her man's hat, searching for fugitive hairs. "That sounds like a nice kind of a way to live," she said.

He leaned confidentially over the fence. "Maybe you noticed the writing on my wagon. I mend pots and sharpen knives and scissors. You got any of them things to do?"

"Oh, no," she said, quickly. "Nothing like that." Her eyes hardened with resistance.

"Scissors is the worst thing," he explained. "Most people just ruin scissors trying to sharpen 'em, but I know how. I got a special tool. It's a little bobbit kind of thing, and patented. But it sure does the trick."

"No. My scissors are all sharp."

"All right, then. Take a pot," he continued earnestly, "a bent pot, or a pot with a hole. I can make it like new so you don't have to buy no new ones. That's a saving for you."

"No," she said shortly. "I tell you I have nothing like that for you to do."

His face fell to an exaggerated sadness. His voice took on a whining undertone. "I ain't had a thing to do today. Maybe I won't have no supper tonight. You see I'm off my regular road. I know folks on the highway clear from Seattle to San Diego. They save their things for me to sharpen up because they know I do it so good and save them money."

"I'm sorry," Elisa said irritably. "I haven't anything for you to do."

His eyes left her face and fell to searching the ground. They roamed about until they came to the chrysanthemum bed where she had been working. "What's them plants, ma'am?"

The irritation and resistance melted from Elisa's face. "Oh, those are chrysanthemums, giant whites and yellows. I raise them every year, bigger than anybody around here."

"Kind of a long-stemmed flower? Looks like a quick puff of colored smoke?" he asked.

"That's it. What a nice way to describe them."

"They smell kind of nasty till you get used to them," he said.

"It's a good bitter smell," she retorted, "not nasty at all."

He changed his tone quickly, "I like the smell myself."

"I had ten-inch-blooms this year," she said.

The man leaned farther over the fence. "Look. I know a lady down the road a piece, has got the nicest garden you ever seen. Got nearly every kind of flower but no chrysanthemums. Last time I was mending a copper-bottom washtub for her (that's a hard job but I do it good), she said to me, 'If you ever run acrost some nice chrysanthemums I wish you'd try to get me a few seeds.' That's what she told me."

Elisa's eyes grew alert and eager. "She couldn't have known much about chrysanthemums. You *can* raise them from seed, but it's much easier to root the little sprouts you see there."

"Oh," he said. "I s'pose I can't take none to her, then."

"Why yes you can," Elisa cried. "I can put some in damp sand, and you can carry them right along with you. They'll take root in the pot if you keep them damp. And then she can transplant them."

"She'd sure like to have some, ma'am. You say they're nice ones?"

"Beautiful," she said. "Oh, beautiful." Her eyes shone. She tore off the battered hat and shook out her dark pretty hair. "I'll put them in a flower pot, and you can take them right with you. Come into the yard."

While the man came through the picket gate Elisa ran excitedly along the geranium-bordered path to the back of the house. And she returned carrying a big red flower pot. The gloves were forgotten now. She kneeled on the ground by the starting bed and dug up the sandy soil with her fingers and scooped it into the bright new flower pot. Then she picked up the little pile of shoots she had prepared. With her strong fingers she pressed them into the sand and tamped around them with her knuckles. The man stood over her. "I'll tell you what to do," she said. "You remember so you can tell the lady."

"Yes, I'll try to remember."

"Well, look. These will take root in about a month. Then she must set them out, about a foot apart in good rich earth like this, see?" She lifted a handful of dark soil for him to look at. "They'll grow fast and tall. Now remember this: In July tell her to cut them down, about eight inches from the ground."

"Before they bloom?" he asked.

"Yes, before they bloom." Her face was tight with eagerness. "They'll grow right up again. About the last of September the buds will start."

She stopped and seemed perplexed. "It's the budding that takes the most care," she said hesitantly. "I don't know how to tell you." She looked deep into his eyes, searchingly. Her mouth opened a little, and she seemed to be listening. "I'll try to tell you," she said. "Did you ever hear of planting hands?"

"Can't say I have, ma'am."

"Well, I can only tell you what it feels like. It's when you're picking off the buds you don't want. Everything goes right down into your fingertips. You watch your fingers work. They do it themselves. You can feel how it is. They pick and pick the buds. They never make a mistake. They're with the plant. Do you see? Your fingers and the plant. You can feel that, right up your arm. They know. They never make a mistake. You can feel it. When you're like that you can't do anything wrong. Do you see that? Can you understand that?"

She was kneeling on the ground looking up at him. Her breast swelled passionately.

The man's eyes narrowed. He looked away self-consciously. "Maybe I know," he said. "Sometimes in the night in the wagon there — "

Elisa's voice grew husky. She broke in on him, "I've never lived as you do, but I know what you mean. When the night is dark — why, the stars are sharp-pointed, and there's quiet. Why, you rise up and up! Every pointed star gets driven into your body. It's like that. Hot and sharp and — lovely."

Kneeling there, her hand went out toward his legs in the greasy black trousers. Her hesitant fingers almost touched the cloth. Then her hand dropped to the ground. She crouched low like a fawning dog.

He said, "It's nice, just like you say. Only when you don't have no dinner, it ain't."

She stood up then, very straight, and her face was ashamed. She held the flower pot out to him and placed it gently in his arms. "Here. Put it in your wagon, on the seat, where you can watch it. Maybe I can find something for you to do."

At the back of the house she dug in the can pile and found two old and battered aluminum saucepans. She carried them back and gave them to him. "Here, maybe you can fix these."

His manner changed. He became professional. "Good as new I can fix them." At the back of his wagon he set a little anvil, and out of an oily tool box dug a small machine hammer. Elisa came through the gate to watch him while he pounded out the dents in the kettles. His mouth grew sure and knowing. At a difficult part of the work he sucked his underlip.

"You sleep right in the wagon?" Elisa asked.

"Right in the wagon, ma'am. Rain or shine I'm dry as a cow in there."

"It must be nice," she said. "It must be very nice. I wish women could do such things."

"It ain't the right kind of a life for a woman."

Her upper lip raised a little, showing her teeth. "How do you know? How can you tell?" she said.

"I don't know, ma'am," he protested. "Of course I don't know. Now here's your kettles, done. You don't have to buy no new ones."

"How much?"

"Oh, fifty cents'll do. I keep my prices down and my work good. That's why I have all them satisfied customers up and down the highway."

Elisa brought him a fifty-cent piece from the house and dropped it in his hand. "You might be surprised to have a rival some time. I can sharpen scissors, too. And I can beat the dents out of little pots. I could show you what a woman might do."

He put his hammer back in the oily box and shoved the little anvil out of sight. "It would be a lonely life for a woman, ma'am, and a scarey life, too, with animals creeping under the wagon all night." He climbed over the singletree, steadying himself with a hand on the burro's white rump. He settled himself in the seat, picked up the lines. "Thank you kindly, ma'am," he said. "I'll do like you told me; I'll go back and catch the Salinas road."

"Mind," she called, "if you're long in getting there, keep the sand damp."

"Sand, ma'am? . . . Sand? Oh, sure. You mean around the chrysanthemums. Sure I will." He clucked his tongue. The beasts leaned luxuriously into their collars. The mongrel dog took his place between the back wheels. The wagon turned and crawled out the entrance road and back the way it had come, along the river.

Elisa stood in front of her wire fence watching the slow progress of the caravan. Her shoulders were straight, her head thrown back, her eyes half-closed, so that the scene came vaguely into them. Her lips moved silently, forming the words "Good-bye — good-bye." Then she whispered, "That's a bright direction. There's a glowing there." The sound of her whisper startled her. She shook herself free and looked about to see whether anyone had been listening. Only the dogs had heard. They lifted their heads toward her from their sleeping in the dust, and then stretched out their chins and settled asleep again. Elisa turned and ran hurriedly into the house.

In the kitchen she reached behind the stove and felt the water tank. It was full of hot water from the noonday cooking. In the bathroom she tore off her soiled clothes and flung them into the corner. And then she scrubbed herself with a little block of pumice, legs and thighs, loins and chest and arms, until her skin was scratched and red. When she had dried herself she stood in front of a mirror in her bedroom and looked at her body. She tightened her stomach and threw out her chest. She turned and looked over her shoulder at her back.

After a while she began to dress, slowly. She put on her newest underclothing and her nicest stockings and the dress which was the symbol of her prettiness. She worked carefully on her hair, penciled her eyebrows and rouged her lips.

Before she was finished she heard the little thunder of hoofs and the shouts of Henry and his helper as they drove the red steers into the corral. She heard the gate bang shut and set herself for Henry's arrival.

His step sounded on the porch. He entered the house calling, "Elisa, where are you?"

"In my room, dressing. I'm not ready. There's hot water for your bath. Hurry up. It's getting late."

When she heard him splashing in the tub, Elisa laid his dark suit on the bed, and shirt and socks and tie beside it. She stood his polished shoes on the floor beside the bed. Then she went to the porch and sat primly and stiffly down. She looked toward the river road where the willow-line was still yellow with frosted leaves so that under the high grey fog they seemed a thin band of sunshine. This was the only color in the grey afternoon. She sat unmoving for a long time. Her eyes blinked rarely.

Henry came banging out of the door, shoving his tie inside his vest as he came. Elisa stiffened and her face grew tight. Henry stopped short and looked at her. "Why — why, Elisa. You look so nice!"

"Nice? You think I look nice? What do you mean by 'nice'?"

Henry blundered on. "I don't know. I mean you look different, strong and happy."

"I am strong? Yes, strong. What do you mean 'strong'?"

He looked bewildered. "You're playing some kind of a game," he said helplessly. "It's a kind of a play. You look strong enough to break a calf over your knee, happy enough to eat it like a watermelon."

For a second she lost her rigidity. "Henry! Don't talk like that. You didn't know what you said." She grew complete again. "I'm strong," she boasted. "I never knew before how strong."

Henry looked down toward the tractor shed, and when he brought his eyes back to her, they were his own again. "I'll get out the car. You can put on your coat while I'm starting."

Elisa went into the house. She heard him drive to the gate and idle down his motor, and then she took a long time to put on her hat. She pulled it here and pressed it there. When Henry turned the motor off she slipped into her coat and went out.

The little roadster bounced along on the dirt road by the river, raising the birds and driving the rabbits into the brush. Two cranes flapped heavily over the willow-line and dropped into the river-bed.

Far ahead on the road Elisa saw a dark speck. She knew.

She tried not to look as they passed it, but her eyes would not obey. She whispered to herself sadly, "He might have thrown them off the road. That wouldn't have been much trouble, not very much. But he kept the pot," she explained. "He had to keep the pot. That's why he couldn't get them off the road."

The roadster turned a bend and she saw the caravan ahead. She swung full around toward her husband so she could not see the little covered wagon and the mismatched team as the car passed them.

In a moment it was over. The thing was done. She did not look back.

She said loudly, to be heard above the motor. "It will be good, tonight, a good dinner."

"Now you're changed again," Henry complained. He took one hand from the wheel and patted her knee. "I ought to take you in to dinner oftener. It would be good for both of us. We get so heavy out on the ranch."

"Henry," she asked, "could we have wine at dinner?"

"Sure we could. Say! That will be fine."

She was silent for a while; then she said, "Henry, at those prize fights, do the men hurt each other very much?"

"Sometimes a little, not often. Why?"

"Well, I've read how they break noses, and blood runs down their chests. I've read how the fighting gloves get heavy and soggy with blood."

He looked around at her. "What's the matter, Elisa? I didn't know you read things like that." He brought the car to a stop, then turned to the right over the Salinas River bridge.

"Do any women ever go to the fights?" she asked.

"Oh, sure, some. What's the matter Elisa? Do you want to go? I don't think you'd like it, but I'll take you if you really want to go."

She relaxed limply in the seat. "Oh, no. No. I don't want to go. I'm sure I don't." Her face was turned away from him. "It will be enough if we can have wine. It will be plenty." She turned up her coat collar so he could not see that she was crying weakly — like an old woman.

[1938]

FRANK O'CONNOR *was the pseudonym for Michael Francis O'Donovan (1903–1966), who was born in Cork, Ireland. His parents were so poor that he attended school only through the fourth grade, at the Christian Brothers School in Cork. During the Irish struggle for independence from England (1918–1921) he was briefly a member of the Irish Republican Army. For several years thereafter he worked as a librarian in Cork and Dublin; it was at this time that he began using his pseudonym so he would not jeopardize his job as a public official. He had begun to write stories as a boy, and for a while he could not decide whether to be a painter or a writer. "I discovered by the time I was sixteen or seventeen that paints cost too much money, so I became a writer because you could be a writer with a pencil and a penny notebook."*

When O'Connor was twenty-eight years old, The Atlantic Monthly published his story "Guests of the Nation," which he later said was an imitation of Isaac Babel's stories in Red Cavalry. His first collection of stories appeared that same year (1931), and from then on he made his living as a writer. During the 1950s he lived in the United States, teaching at Harvard and Northwestern and publishing two excellent critical works about fiction, The Mirror in the Roadway (1956), a study of the modern novel, and The Lonely Voice (1963), a history of the short story. O'Connor was a prolific writer, editor, critic, and translator, with almost fifty books to his credit, including fourteen volumes of short stories. He often rewrote his stories several times, even after they were published, so many of them appear in different versions in his various volumes.

O'Connor was productive in many literary forms, but his greatest achievement was in the short story. Primarily indebted to Anton Chekhov as his model, he declared himself to be an old-fashioned storyteller, believing that a story should have the sound of a person speaking. This gives his fiction an engaging tone, confirming — as do Chekhov's stories — the author's basically sympathetic attitude toward his characters. In praising O'Connor's stories, the noted Irish poet William Butler Yeats said that he was "doing for Ireland what Chekhov did for Russia." (See O'Connor's Commentary about Joyce's "The Dead" on page 1265 and his Interview on page 1297.)

Frank O'Connor

ॐ

GUESTS OF THE NATION

I

At dusk the big Englishman, Belcher, would shift his long legs out of the ashes and say "Well, chums, what about it?" and Noble or me would say "All right, chum" (for we had picked up some of their curious expressions), and the little Englishman, Hawkins, would light the lamp and bring out the cards. Sometimes Jeremiah Donovan would come up and supervise the game and get excited over Hawkins's cards, which he always played badly, and shout at him as if he was one of our own "Ah, you divil, you, why didn't you play the tray?"

But ordinarily Jeremiah was a sober and contented poor devil like the big Englishman, Belcher, and was looked up to only because he was a fair hand at documents, though he was slow enough even with them. He wore a small cloth hat and big gaiters over his long pants, and you seldom saw him with his hands out of his pockets. He reddened when you talked to him, tilting from toe to heel and back, and looking down all the time at his big farmer's feet. Noble and me used to make fun of his broad accent, because we were from the town.

I couldn't at the time see the point of me and Noble guarding Belcher and Hawkins at all, for it was my belief that you could have planted that pair down anywhere from this to Claregalway and they'd have taken root there like a native weed. I never in my short experience seen two men to take to the country as they did.

They were handed on to us by the Second Battalion when the search for them became too hot, and Noble and myself, being young, took over with a natural feeling of responsibility, but Hawkins made us look like fools when he showed that he knew the country better than we did.

"You're the bloke they calls Bonaparte," he says to me. "Mary Brigid O'Connell told me to ask you what you done with the pair of her brother's socks you borrowed."

For it seemed, as they explained it, that the Second used to have little evenings, and some of the girls of the neighbourhood turned in, and, seeing

723

they were such decent chaps, our fellows couldn't leave the two Englishmen out of them. Hawkins learned to dance "The Walls of Limerick," "The Siege of Ennis," and "The Waves of Tory" as well as any of them, though, naturally, he couldn't return the compliment, because our lads at that time did not dance foreign dances on principle.

So whatever privileges Belcher and Hawkins had with the Second they just naturally took with us, and after the first day or two we gave up all pretense of keeping a close eye on them. Not that they could have got far, for they had accents you could cut with a knife and wore khaki tunics and overcoats with civilian pants and boots. But it's my belief that they never had any idea of escaping and were quite content to be where they were.

It was a treat to see how Belcher got off with the old woman of the house where we were staying. She was a great warrant to scold, and cranky even with us, but before ever she had a chance of giving our guests, as I may call them, a lick of her tongue, Belcher had made her his friend for life. She was breaking sticks, and Belcher, who hadn't been more than ten minutes in the house, jumped up from his seat and went over to her.

"Allow me, madam," he says, smiling his queer little smile, "please allow me"; and he takes the bloody hatchet. She was struck too paralytic to speak, and after that, Belcher would be at her heels, carrying a bucket, a basket, or a load of turf, as the case might be. As Noble said, he got into looking before she leapt, and hot water, or any little thing she wanted, Belcher would have it ready for her. For such a huge man (and though I am five foot ten myself I had to look up at him) he had an uncommon shortness — or should I say lack? — of speech. It took us some time to get used to him, walking in and out, like a ghost, without a word. Especially because Hawkins talked enough for a platoon, it was strange to hear big Belcher with his toes in the ashes come out with a solitary "Excuse me, chum," or "That's right, chum." His one and only passion was cards, and I will say for him that he was a good card-player. He could have fleeced myself and Noble, but whatever we lost to him Hawkins lost to us, and Hawkins played with the money Belcher gave him.

Hawkins lost to us because he had too much old gab, and we probably lost to Belcher for the same reason. Hawkins and Noble would spit at one another about religion into the early hours of the morning, and Hawkins worried the soul out of Noble, whose brother was a priest, with a string of questions that would puzzle a cardinal. To make it worse even in treating of holy subjects, Hawkins had a deplorable tongue. I never in all my career met a man who could mix such a variety of cursing and bad language into an argument. He was a terrible man, and a fright to argue. He never did a stroke of work, and when he had no one else to talk to, he got stuck in the old woman.

He met his match in her, for one day when he tried to get her to complain profanely of the drought, she gave him a great come-down by blaming it entirely on Jupiter Pluvius (a deity neither Hawkins nor I have ever heard of, though Noble said that among the pagans it was believed that he had something to do with the rain). Another day he was swearing at the capitalists for starting the German war when the old lady laid down her iron, puckered up her little crab's mouth, and said: "Mr. Hawkins, you can say what you like about the war, and think you'll deceive me because I'm only a simple poor countrywoman, but I know what started the war. It was the Italian Count that stole the heathen divinity out of the temple in Japan. Believe me, Mr. Hawkins, nothing but sorrow and want can follow the people that disturb the hidden powers."

A queer old girl, all right.

II

We had our tea one evening, and Hawkins lit the lamp and we all sat into cards. Jeremiah Donovan came in too, and sat down and watched us for a while, and it suddenly struck me that he had no great love for the two Englishmen. It came as a great surprise to me, because I hadn't noticed anything about him before.

Late in the evening a really terrible argument blew up between Hawkins and Noble, about capitalists and priests and love of your country.

"The capitalists," says Hawkins with an angry gulp, "pays the priests to tell you about the next world so as you won't notice what the bastards are up to in this."

"Nonsense, man!" says Noble, losing his temper. "Before ever a capitalist was thought of, people believed in the next world."

Hawkins stood up as though he was preaching a sermon.

"Oh, they did, did they?" he says with a sneer. "They believed all the things you believe, isn't that what you mean? And you believe that God created Adam, and Adam created Shem, and Shem created Jehoshophat. You believe all that silly old fairytale about Eve and Eden and the apple. Well, listen to me, chum. If you're entitled to hold a silly belief like that, I'm entitled to hold my silly belief — which is that the first thing your God created was a bleeding capitalist, with morality and Rolls-Royce complete. Am I right, chum?" he says to Belcher.

"You're right, chum," says Belcher with his amused smile, and got up from the table to stretch his long legs into the fire and stroke his moustache. So, seeing that Jeremiah Donovan was going, and that there was no knowing when the argument about religion would be over, I went out with him. We strolled down to the village together, and then he stopped and started blushing and mumbling and saying I ought to be behind, keeping guard on the prisoners. I didn't like the tone he took with me, and anyway I was bored with life in the cottage, so I replied by asking him what the hell we wanted guarding them at all for. I told him I'd talked it over with Noble, and that we'd both rather be out with a fighting column.

"What use are those fellows to us?" says I.

He looked at me in surprise and said: "I thought you knew we were keeping them as hostages."

"Hostages?" I said.

"The enemy have prisoners belonging to us," he says, "and now they're talking of shooting them. If they shoot our prisoners, we'll shoot theirs."

"Shoot them?" I said.

"What else did you think we were keeping them for?" he says.

"Wasn't it very unforeseen of you not to warn Noble and myself of that in the beginning?" I said.

"How was it?" says he. "You might have known it."

"We couldn't know it, Jeremiah Donovan," says I. "How could we when they were on our hands so long?"

"The enemy have our prisoners as long and longer," says he.

"That's not the same thing at all," says I.

"What difference is there?" says he.

I couldn't tell him, because I knew he wouldn't understand. If it was only an old dog that was going to the vet's, you'd try and not get too fond of him, but Jeremiah Donovan wasn't a man that would ever be in danger of that.

"And when is this thing going to be decided?" says I.

"We might hear tonight," he says. "Or tomorrow or the next day at latest. So if it's only hanging round here that's a trouble to you, you'll be free soon enough."

It wasn't the hanging round that was a trouble to me at all by this time. I had worse things to worry about. When I got back to the cottage the argument was still on. Hawkins was holding forth in his best style, maintaining that there was no next world, and Noble was maintaining that there was; but I could see that Hawkins had had the best of it.

"Do you know what, chum?" he was saying with a saucy smile. "I think you're just as big a bleeding unbeliever as I am. You say you believe in the next world, and you know just as much about the next world as I do, which is sweet damn-all. What's heaven? You don't know. Where's heaven? You don't know. You know sweet damn-all! I ask you again, do they wear wings?"

"Very well, then," says Noble, "they do. Is that enough for you? They do wear wings."

"Where do they get them, then? Who makes them? Have they a factory for wings? Have they a sort of store where you hands in your chit and takes your bleeding wings?"

"You're an impossible man to argue with," says Noble. "Now, listen to me — " And they were off again.

It was long after midnight when we locked up and went to bed. As I blew out the candle I told Noble what Jeremiah Donovan was after telling me. Noble took it very quietly. When we'd been in bed about an hour he asked me did I think we ought to tell the Englishmen. I didn't think we should, because it was more than likely that the English wouldn't shoot our men, and even if they did, the brigade officers, who were always up and down with the Second Battalion and knew the Englishmen well, wouldn't be likely to want them plugged. "I think so too," says Noble. "It would be great cruelty to put the wind up them now."

"It was very unforeseen of Jeremiah Donovan anyhow," says I.

It was next morning that we found it so hard to face Belcher and Hawkins. We went about the house all day scarcely saying a word. Belcher didn't seem to notice; he was stretched into the ashes as usual, with his usual look of waiting in quietness for something unforeseen to happen, but Hawkins noticed and put it down to Noble's being beaten in the argument of the night before.

"Why can't you take a discussion in the proper spirit?" he says severely. "You and your Adam and Eve! I'm a Communist, that's what I am. Communist or anarchist, it all comes to much the same thing." And for hours he went round the house, muttering when the fit took him. "Adam and Eve! Adam and Eve! Nothing better to do with their time than picking bleeding apples!"

III

I don't know how we got through that day, but I was very glad when it was over, the tea things were cleared away, and Belcher said in his peaceable way: "Well, chums, what about it?" We sat round the table and Hawkins took out the cards, and just then I heard Jeremiah Donovan's footstep on the path and a dark presentiment crossed my mind. I rose from the table and caught him before he reached the door.

"What do you want?" I asked.

"I want those two soldier friends of yours," he says, getting red.

"Is that the way, Jeremiah Donovan?" I asked.

"That's the way. There were four of our lads shot this morning, one of them a boy of sixteen."

"That's bad," I said.

At that moment Noble followed me out, and the three of us walked down the path together, talking in whispers. Feeney, the local intelligence officer, was standing by the gate.

"What are you going to do about it?" I asked Jeremiah Donovan.

"I want you and Noble to get them out; tell them they're being shifted again; that'll be the quietest way."

"Leave me out of that," says Noble under his breath.

Jeremiah Donovan looks at him hard.

"All right," he says. "You and Feeney get a few tools from the shed and dig a hole by the far end of the bog. Bonaparte and myself will be after you. Don't let anyone see you with the tools. I wouldn't like it to go beyond ourselves."

We saw Feeney and Noble go round to the shed and went in ourselves. I left Jeremiah Donovan to do the explanations. He told them that he had orders to send them back to the Second Battalion. Hawkins let out a mouthful of curses, and you could see that though Belcher didn't say anything, he was a bit upset too. The old woman was for having them stay in spite of us, and she didn't stop advising them until Jeremiah Donovan lost his temper and turned on her. He had a nasty temper, I noticed. It was pitch-dark in the cottage by this time, but no one thought of lighting the lamp, and in the darkness the two Englishmen fetched their topcoats and said good-bye to the old woman.

"Just as a man makes a home of a bleeding place, some bastard at headquarters thinks you're too cushy and shunts you off," says Hawkins, shaking her hand.

"A thousand thanks, madam," says Belcher. "A thousand thanks for everything" — as though he'd made it up.

We went round to the back of the house and down towards the bog. It was only then that Jeremiah Donovan told them. He was shaking with excitement.

"There were four of our fellows shot in Cork this morning and now you're to be shot as a reprisal."

"What are you talking about?" snaps Hawkins. "It's bad enough being mucked about as we are without having to put up with your funny jokes."

"It isn't a joke," says Donovan. "I'm sorry, Hawkins, but it's true," and begins on the usual rigmarole about duty and how unpleasant it is.

I never noticed that people who talk a lot about duty find it much of a trouble to them.

"Oh, cut it out!" says Hawkins.

"Ask Bonaparte," says Donovan, seeing that Hawkins isn't taking him seriously. "Isn't it true, Bonaparte?"

"It is," I say, and Hawkins stops.

"Ah, for Christ's sake, chum!"

"I mean it, chum," I say.

"You don't sound as if you mean it."

"If he doesn't mean it, I do," says Donovan, working himself up.

"What have you against me, Jeremiah Donovan?"

"I never said I had anything against you. But why did your people take out four of our prisoners and shoot them in cold blood?"

He took Hawkins by the arm and dragged him on, but it was impossible to make him understand that we were in earnest. I had the Smith and Wesson in my pocket and I kept fingering it and wondering what I'd do if they put up a fight for it or ran, and wishing to God they'd do one or the other. I knew if they did run for it, that I'd never fire on them. Hawkins wanted to know was Noble in it, and when we said yes, he asked us why Noble wanted to plug him. Why did any of us want to plug him? What had he done to us? Weren't we all chums? Didn't we understand him and didn't he understand us? Did we imagine for an instant that he'd shoot us for all the so-and-so officers in the so-and-so British Army?

By this time we'd reached the bog, and I was so sick I couldn't even answer him. We walked along the edge of it in the darkness, and every now and then Hawkins would call a halt and begin all over again, as if he was wound up, about our being chums, and I knew that nothing but the sight of the grave would convince him that we had to do it. And all the time I was hoping that something would happen; that they'd run for it or that Noble would take over the responsibility from me. I had the feeling that it was worse on Noble than on me.

IV

At last we saw the lantern in the distance and made towards it. Noble was carrying it, and Feeney was standing somewhere in the darkness behind him, and the picture of them so still and silent in the bogland brought it home to me that we were in earnest, and banished the last bit of hope I had.

Belcher, on recognizing Noble, said: "Hallo, chum," in his quiet way, but Hawkins flew at him at once, and the argument began all over again, only this time Noble had nothing to say for himself and stood with his head down, holding the lantern between his legs.

It was Jeremiah Donovan who did the answering. For the twentieth time, as though it was haunting his mind, Hawkins asked if anybody thought he'd shoot Noble.

"Yes, you would," says Jeremiah Donovan.

"No, I wouldn't, damn you!"

"You would, because you'd know you'd be shot for not doing it."

"I wouldn't, not if I was to be shot twenty times over. I wouldn't shoot a pal. And Belcher wouldn't — isn't that right, Belcher?"

"That's right, chum," Belcher said, but more by way of answering the question than of joining in the argument. Belcher sounded as though whatever unforeseen thing he'd always been waiting for had come at last.

"Anyway, who says Noble would be shot if I wasn't? What do you think I'd do if I was in his place, out in the middle of a blasted bog?"

"What would you do?" asks Donovan.

"I'd go with him wherever he was going, of course. Share my last bob with him and stick by him through thick and thin. No one can ever say of me that I let down a pal."

"We had enough of this," says Jeremiah Donovan, cocking his revolver. "Is there any message you want to send?"

"No, there isn't."

"Do you want to say your prayers?"

Hawkins came out with a cold-blooded remark that even shocked me and turned on Noble again.

"Listen to me, Noble," he says. "You and me are chums. You can't come over to my side, so I'll come over to your side. That show you I mean what I say? Give me a rifle and I'll go along with you and the other lads."

Nobody answered him. We knew that was no way out.

"Hear what I'm saying?" he says. "I'm through with it. I'm a deserter or anything else you like. I don't believe in your stuff, but it's no worse than mine. That satisfy you?"

Noble raised his head, but Donovan began to speak and he lowered it again without replying.

"For the last time, have you any messages to send?" says Donovan in a cool, excited sort of voice.

"Shut up, Donovan! You don't understand me, but these lads do. They're not the sort to make a pal and kill a pal. They're not the tools of any capitalist."

I alone of the crowd saw Donovan raise his Webley to the back of Hawkins's neck, and as he did so I shut my eyes and tried to pray. Hawkins had begun to say something else when Donovan fired, and as I opened my eyes at the bang, I saw Hawkins stagger at the knees and lie out flat at Noble's feet, slowly and as quiet as a kid falling asleep, with the lantern-light on his lean legs and bright farmer's boots. We all stood very still, watching him settle out in the last agony.

Then Belcher took out a handkerchief and began to tie it about his own eyes (in our excitement we'd forgotten to do the same for Hawkins), and, seeing it wasn't big enough, turned and asked for the loan of mine. I gave it to him and he knotted the two together and pointed with his foot at Hawkins.

"He's not quite dead," he says. "Better give him another."

Sure enough, Hawkins's left knee is beginning to rise. I bend down and put my gun to his head; then, recollecting myself, I get up again. Belcher understands what's in my mind.

"Give him his first," he says. "I don't mind. Poor bastard, we don't know what's happening to him now."

I knelt and fired. By this time I didn't seem to know what I was doing. Belcher, who was fumbling a bit awkwardly with the handkerchiefs, came out with a laugh as he heard the shot. It was the first time I heard him laugh and it sent a shudder down my back; it sounded so unnatural.

"Poor bugger!" he said quietly. "And last night he was so curious about it all. It's very queer, chums, I always think. Now he knows as much about it as they'll ever let him know, and last night he was all in the dark."

Donovan helped him to tie the handkerchiefs about his eyes. "Thanks, chum," he said. Donovan asked if there were any messages he wanted sent.

"No, chum," he says. "Not for me. If any of you would like to write to Hawkins's mother, you'll find a letter from her in his pocket. He and his mother were great chums. But my missus left me eight years ago. Went away with another fellow and took the kid with her. I like the feeling of a home, as you may have noticed, but I couldn't start again after that."

It was an extraordinary thing, but in those few minutes Belcher said more than in all the weeks before. It was just as if the sound of the shot had started a flood of talk in him and he could go on the whole night like that, quite happily, talking about himself. We stood round like fools now that he couldn't see us any longer. Donovan looked at Noble, and Noble shook his head. Then Donovan raised his Webley, and at that moment Belcher gives his queer laugh again. He may have thought we were talking about him, or perhaps he noticed the same thing I'd noticed and couldn't understand it.

"Excuse me, chums," he says. "I feel I'm talking the hell of a lot, and so silly, about my being so handy about a house and things like that. But this thing came on me suddenly. You'll forgive me, I'm sure."

"You don't want to say a prayer?" asks Donovan.

"No, chum," he says. "I don't think it would help. I'm ready, and you boys want to get it over."

"You understand that we're only doing our duty?" says Donovan.

Belcher's head was raised like a blind man's, so that you could only see his chin and the tip of his nose in the lantern-light.

"I never could make out what duty was myself," he said. "I think you're all good lads, if that's what you mean. I'm not complaining."

Noble, just as if he couldn't bear any more of it, raised his fist at Donovan, and in a flash Donovan raised his gun and fired. The big man went over like a sack of meal, and this time there was no need of a second shot.

I don't remember much about the burying, but that it was worse than all the rest because we had to carry them to the grave. It was all mad lonely with nothing but a patch of lantern-light between ourselves and the dark, and birds hooting and screeching all round, disturbed by the guns. Noble went through Hawkins's belongings to find the letter from his mother, and then joined his hands together. He did the same with Belcher. Then, when we'd filled the grave, we separated from Jeremiah Donovan and Feeney and took our tools back to the shed. All the way we didn't speak a word. The kitchen was dark and cold as we'd left it, and the old woman was sitting over the hearth, saying her beads. We walked past her into the room, and Noble struck a match to light the lamp. She rose quietly and came to the doorway with all her cantankerousness gone.

"What did ye do with them?" she asked in a whisper, and Noble started so that the match went out in his hand.

"What's that?" he asked without turning round.

"I heard ye," she said.

"What did you hear?" asked Noble.

"I heard ye. Do ye think I didn't hear ye, putting the spade back in the houseen?"

Noble struck another match and this time the lamp lit for him.

"Was that what ye did to them?" she asked.

Then, by God, in the very doorway, she fell on her knees and began praying, and after looking at her for a minute or two Noble did the same by the fireplace. I pushed my way out past her and left them at it. I stood at the door, watching the stars and listening to the shrieking of the birds dying out over the bogs. It is so strange what you feel at times like that that you can't describe it. Noble says he saw everything ten times the size, as though there were nothing in the whole world but that little patch of bog with the two Englishmen stiffening into it, but with me it was as if the patch of bog where the Englishmen were was a million miles away, and even Noble and the old woman, mumbling behind me, and the birds and the bloody stars were all far away, and I was somehow very small and very lost and lonely like a child astray in the snow. And anything that happened to me afterwards, I never felt the same about again.

[1931]

*I*SAAC BASHEVIS SINGER *(b. 1904) was born in Radzymin, Poland. After his education at the Tachkemoni Rabbinical Seminary in Warsaw, he worked as a proofreader and translator before emigrating to the United States in 1935. Settling in New York City, he made his living as a journalist for the* Jewish Daily Forward, *a Yiddish-language paper. He also wrote autobiographical sketches, short stories, and novels in Yiddish for many years. In 1950 his writing became available to a wider audience for the first time when he began to publish his work in English translations, starting with the realistic historical chronicle* The Family Moskat. *Singer's first collection of short stories,* Gimpel the Fool and Other Stories *(translated by noted American novelist Saul Bellow and others), appeared in 1957, and during the 1960s and 1970s he alternated novels with books of short fiction, including such popular collections of stories as* The Spinoza of Market Street and Other Stories *(1961),* A Friend of Kafka and Other Stories *(1970),* A Crown of Feathers and Other Stories *(1973),* Passions and Other Stories *(1975), and* Old Love and Other Stories *(1979). In these books, Singer collected stories from different periods in his life without organizing them around a central theme. A prolific writer, he has also published three volumes of autobiographical reminiscences. In 1978 he was awarded the Nobel Prize for Literature. His* Collected Stories *appeared in 1981.*

In all of his work, Singer explores the traditions of Jewish life, past and present, expressing his fascination with the history of his people: "I was born with the feeling that I am part of an unlikely adventure, something that couldn't have happened, but happened all the same." In the best of his short stories, as in "A Crown of Feathers," he dramatizes a complex mysticism in his treatment of Jewish characters, suggesting multiple levels of human existence, both physical and spiritual, and the ambiguous nature of life itself, capable as it is of both natural and supernatural interpretation. Singer's vision of humanity is modern in its treatment of sexuality and insanity, but his interest in mysticism extends back to his roots as the son of a rabbi studying the medieval cabala, *the tradition of Jewish mystical lore. Singer refuses to interpret the mysticism in his stories. He believes that the writer must produce fiction that creates a coherent and self-sustaining illusion of reality, including paradox, to give a true picture of the existence of things in the world. "Everything to me, everything is a paradox. The very existence of things is a paradox."*

Singer has said that in his short stories he is interested in writing about people who are "obsessed by some mania or fixed idea, and everything turns around this idea. . . . Since we don't know really what reality is, whatever we are obsessed with becomes our reality." He believes in demons and the supernatural: "Powers which we don't know take a great part in our life. . . .

*The supernatural for me is not really supernatural; it's powers which we
don't know." His own stories are always based on a realistically observed
setting, however, since "a miracle must be invented among realism, because, if it's one miracle after the other and there's no realism, the miracle
itself becomes nothing." All great literature begins in realism, according to
Singer, who with great clear-sightedness puts the events of our everyday existence in the category of the marvelous too. "Once a man brought me a
story which began with a cut-off head which spoke. And I said to the man,
'Isn't it miracle enough that a head which is not chopped off can talk?' "
(See Singer's Interview on page 1299.)*

Isaac Bashevis Singer

ᔥᔥ

A Crown of Feathers

*– translated by the author
and Laurie Colwin*

Reb Naftali Holishitzer, the community leader in Krasnobród, was left
in his old age with no children. One daughter had died in childbirth and
the other in a cholera epidemic. A son had drowned when he tried to cross
the San River on horseback. Reb Naftali had only one grandchild — a girl,
Akhsa, an orphan. It was not the custom for a female to study at a yeshiva,
because "the King's daughter is all glorious within" and Jewish daughters
are all the daughters of kings. But Akhsa studied at home. She dazzled everyone with her beauty, wisdom, and diligence. She had white skin and
black hair; her eyes were blue.

Reb Naftali managed an estate that had belonged to the Prince Czartoryski. Since he owed Reb Naftali twenty thousand guldens, the prince's
property was a permanent pawn, and Reb Naftali had built for himself a
water mill and a brewery and had sown hundreds of acres with hops. His
wife, Nesha, came from a wealthy family in Prague. They could afford to
hire the finest tutors for Akhsa. One taught her the Bible, another French,
still another the pianoforte, and a fourth dancing. She learned everything
quickly. At eight, she was playing chess with her grandfather. Reb Naftali
didn't need to offer a dowry for her marriage, since she was heir to his entire
fortune.

Matches were sought for her early, but her grandmother was hard to
please. She would look at a boy proposed by the marriage brokers and say,
"He has the shoulders of a fool," or, "He has the narrow forehead of an ignoramus."

One day Nesha died unexpectedly. Reb Naftali was in his late seventies and it was unthinkable that he remarry. Half his day he devoted to religion, the other half to business. He rose at daybreak and pored over the Talmud and the Commentaries and wrote letters to community elders. When a man was sick, Reb Naftali went to comfort him. Twice a week he visited the poorhouse with Akhsa, who carried a contribution of soup and groats herself. More than once, Akhsa, the pampered and scholarly, rolled up her sleeves and made beds there.

In the summer, after midday sleep, Reb Naftali ordered his britska harnessed and he rode around the fields and village with Akhsa. While they rode, he discussed business, and it was known that he listened to her advice just as he had listened to her grandmother's.

But there was one thing that Akhsa didn't have — a friend. Her grandmother had tried to find friends for her; she even lowered her standards and invited girls from Krasnobród. But Akhsa had no patience with their chatter about clothes and household matters. Since the tutors were all men, Akhsa was kept away from them, except for lessons. Now her grandfather became her only companion. Reb Naftali had met famous noblemen in his lifetime. He had been to fairs in Warsaw, Kraków, Danzig, and Koenigsberg. He would sit for hours with Akhsa and tell her about rabbis and miracle workers, about the disciples of the false messiah Sabbatai Zevi, quarrels in the Sejm, the caprices of the Zamojskis, the Radziwills, and the Czartoryskis — their wives, lovers, courtiers. Sometimes Akhsa would cry out, "I wish you were my fiancé, not my grandfather!" and kiss his eyes and his white beard.

Reb Naftali would answer, "I'm not the only man in Poland. There are plenty like me, and young to boot."

"Where, Grandfather? Where?"

After her grandmother's death, Akhsa refused to rely on anyone else's judgment in the choice of a husband — not even her grandfather's. Just as her grandmother saw only bad, Reb Naftali saw only good. Akhsa demanded that the matchmakers allow her to meet her suitor, and Reb Naftali finally consented. The young pair would be brought together in a room, the door would be left open, and a deaf old woman servant would stand at the threshold to watch that the meeting be brief and without frivolity. As a rule, Akhsa stayed with the young man not more than a few minutes. Most of the suitors seemed dull and silly. Others tried to be clever and made undignified jokes. Akhsa dismissed them abruptly. How strange, but her grandmother still expressed her opinion. Once, Akhsa heard her say clearly, "He has the snout of a pig." Another time, she said, "He talks like the standard letter book."

Akhsa knew quite well that it was not her grandmother speaking. The dead don't return from the other world to comment on prospective fiancés. Just the same, it was her grandmother's voice, her style. Akhsa wanted to talk to her grandfather about it, but she was afraid he would think her crazy. Besides, her grandfather longed for his wife, and Akhsa didn't want to stir up his grief.

When Reb Naftali Holishitzer realized that his granddaughter was driving away the matchmakers, he was troubled. Akhsa was now past her eighteenth year. The people in Krasnobród had begun to gossip — she was demanding a knight on a white horse or the moon in heaven; she would stay a spinster. Reb Naftali decided not to give in to her whims any more but to marry her off. He went to a yeshiva and brought back with him a young man named Zemach, an orphan and a devout scholar. He was dark as a gypsy, small, with broad shoulders. His sidelocks were thick. He was nearsighted and studied eighteen hours a day. The moment he reached Krasnobród, he went to the study house and began to sway in front of an open volume of the Talmud. His sidelocks swayed, too. Students came to talk with him, and he spoke without lifting his gaze from the book. He seemed to know the Talmud by heart, since he caught everyone misquoting.

Akhsa demanded a meeting, but Reb Naftali replied that this was conduct befitting tailors and shoemakers, not a girl of good breeding. He warned Akhsa that if she drove Zemach away he would disinherit her. Since men and women were in separate rooms during the engagement party, Akhsa had no chance of seeing Zemach until the marriage contract was to be signed. She looked at him and heard her grandmother say, "They've sold you shoddy goods."

Her words were so clear it seemed to Akhsa that everyone should have heard them, but no one had. The girls and women crowded around her, congratulating her and praising her beauty, her dress, her jewelry. Her grandfather passed her the contract and a quill, and her grandmother cried out, "Don't sign!" She grabbed Akhsa's elbow and a blot formed on the paper.

Reb Naftali shouted, "What have you done!"

Akhsa tried to sign, but the pen fell from her hand. She burst into tears. "Grandfather, I can't."

"Akhsa, you shame me."

"Grandfather, forgive me." Akhsa covered her face with her hands. There was an outcry. Men hissed and women laughed and wept. Akhsa cried silently. They half led, half carried her to her room and put her on her bed.

Zemach exclaimed, "I don't want to be married to this shrew!"

He pushed through the crowd and ran to get a wagon back to the yeshiva. Reb Naftali went after him, trying to pacify him with words and money, but Zemach threw Reb Naftali's banknotes to the ground. Someone brought his wicker trunk from the inn where he had stayed. Before the wagon pulled away, Zemach cried out, "I don't forgive her, and God won't, either."

For days after that, Akhsa was ill. Reb Naftali Holishitzer, who had been successful all his life, was not accustomed to failure. He became sick; his face took on a yellow pallor. Women and girls tried to comfort Akhsa.

Rabbis and elders came to visit Reb Naftali, but he got weaker as the days passed. After a while, Akhsa gained back her strength and left her sickbed. She went to her grandfather's room, bolting the door behind her. The maid who listened and spied through the keyhole reported that she had heard him say, "You are mad!"

Akhsa nursed her grandfather, brought him his medicine and bathed him with a sponge, but the old man developed an inflammation of the lungs. Blood ran from his nose. His urine stopped. Soon he died. He had written his will years before and left one-third of his estate to charity and the rest to Akhsa.

According to the law, one does not sit shivah[1] in mourning after the death of a grandfather, but Akhsa went through the ceremony anyway. She sat on a low stool and read the book of Job. She ordered that no one be let in. She had shamed an orphan — a scholar — and caused the death of her grandfather. She became melancholy. Since she had read the story of Job before, she began search in her grandfather's library for another book to read. To her amazement, she found a Bible translated into Polish — the New Testament as well as the Old. Akhsa knew it was a forbidden book, but she turned the pages anyway. Had her grandfather read it, Akhsa wondered. No, it couldn't be. She remembered that on the Gentile feast days, when holy icons and pictures were carried in processions near the house, she was not allowed to look out of the window. Her grandfather told her it was idolatry. She wondered if her grandmother had read this Bible. Among the pages she found some pressed cornflowers — a flower her grandmother had often picked. Grandmother came from Bohemia; it was said that her father had belonged to the Sabbatai Zevi sect. Akhsa recalled that Prince Czartoryski used to spend time with her grandmother when he visited the estate, and praised the way she spoke Polish. If she hadn't been a Jewish girl, he said, he would have married her — a great compliment.

That night Akhsa read the New Testament to the last page. It was difficult for her to accept that Jesus was God's only begotten son and that He rose from the grave, but she found this book more comforting to her tortured spirit than the castigating words of the prophets, who never mentioned the Kingdom of Heaven or the resurrection of the dead. All they promised was a good harvest for good deeds and starvation and plague for bad ones.

On the seventh night of shivah, Akhsa went to bed. The light was out and she was dozing when she heard footsteps that she recognized as her grandfather's. In the darkness, her grandfather's figure emerged: the light face, the white beard, the mild features, even the skullcap on his high forehead. He said in a quiet voice, "Akhsa, you have committed an injustice."

Akhsa began to cry. "Grandfather, what should I do?"

"Everything can be corrected."

---

[1] Jewish ritual observance to commemorate the memory of the dead.

"How?"

"Apologize to Zemach. Become his wife."

"Grandfather, I hate him."

"He is your destined one."

He lingered for a moment, and Akhsa could smell his snuff, which he used to mix with cloves and smelling salts. Then he vanished and an empty space remained in the darkness. She was too amazed to be frightened. She leaned against the headboard, and after some time she slept.

She woke with a start. She heard her grandmother's voice. This was not a murmuring like Grandfather's but the strong voice of a living person. "Akhsa, my daughter."

Akhsa burst into tears. "Grandmother, where are you?"

"I'm here."

"What should I do?"

"Whatever your heart desires."

"What, Grandmother?"

"Go to the priest. He will advise you."

Akhsa became numb. Fear constricted her throat. She managed to say, "You're not my grandmother. You're a demon."

"I am your grandmother. Do you remember how we went wading in the pond that summer night near the flat hill and you found a gulden in the water?"

"Yes, Grandmother."

"I could give you other proof. Be it known that the Gentiles are right. Jesus of Nazareth is the Son of God. He was born of the Holy Spirit as prophesied. The rebellious Jews refused to accept the truth and therefore they are punished. The Messiah will not come to them because He is here already."

"Grandmother, I'm afraid."

"Akhsa, don't listen!" her grandfather suddenly shouted into her right ear. "This isn't your grandmother. It's an evil spirit disguised to trick you. Don't give in to his blasphemies. He will drag you into perdition."

"Akhsa, that is not your grandfather but a goblin from behind the bathhouse," Grandmother interrupted. "Zemach is a ne'er-do-well, and vengeful to boot. He will torment you, and the children he begets will be vermin like him. Save yourself while there is time. God is with the Gentiles."

"Lilith! She-demon! Daughter of Ketev M'riri!" Grandfather growled. "Liar!"

Grandfather became silent, but Grandmother continued to talk, although her voice faded. She said, "Your real grandfather learned the truth in Heaven and converted. They baptized him with heavenly water and he rests in Paradise. The saints are all bishops and cardinals. Those who remain stubborn are roasted in the fires of Gehenna. If you don't believe me, ask for a sign."

"What sign?"

"Unbutton your pillowcase, rip open the seams of the pillow, and there you will find a crown of feathers. No human hand could make a crown like this."

Her grandmother disappeared, and Akhsa fell into a heavy sleep. At dawn, she awoke and lit a candle. She remembered her grandmother's words, unbuttoned the pillowcase, and ripped open the pillow. What she saw was so extraordinary she could scarcely believe her eyes: down and feathers entwined into a crown, with little ornaments and complex designs no worldly master could have duplicated. On the top of the crown was a tiny cross. It was all so airy that Akhsa's breath made it flutter. Akhsa gasped. Whoever had made this crown — an angel or a demon — had done his work in darkness, in the inside of a pillow. She was beholding a miracle. She extinguished the candle and stretched out on the bed. For a long time she lay without any thoughts. Then she went back to sleep.

In the morning when she awoke, Akhsa thought she had had a dream, but on the night table she saw the crown of feathers. The sun made it sparkle with the colors of the rainbow. It looked as if it were set with the smallest of gems. She sat and contemplated the wonder. Then she put on a black dress and a black shawl and asked that the carriage be brought round for her. She rode to the house where Koscik, the priest, resided. The housekeeper answered her knock. The priest was nearing seventy and he knew Akhsa. He had often come to the estate to bless the peasants' bread at Easter time and to give rites to the dying and conduct weddings and funerals. One of Akhsa's teachers had borrowed a Latin-Polish dictionary from him. Whenever the priest visited, Akhsa's grandmother invited him to her parlor and they conversed over cake and vishniak.

The priest offered Akhsa a chair. She sat down and told him everything. He said, "Don't go back to the Jews. Come to us. We will see to it that your fortune remains intact."

"I forgot to take the crown. I want to have it with me."

"Yes, my daughter, go and bring it."

Akhsa went home, but a maid had cleaned her bedroom and dusted the night table; the crown had vanished. Akhsa searched in the garbage ditch, in the slops, but not a trace could she find.

Soon after that, the terrible news was abroad in Krasnobród that Akhsa had converted.

Six years passed. Akhsa married and became the Squiress Maria Malkowska. The old squire, Wladyslaw Malkowski, had died without direct heir and had left his estate to his nephew Ludwik. Ludwik had remained a bachelor until he was forty-five, and it seemed he would never marry. He lived in his uncle's castle with his spinster sister, Gloria. His love affairs were with peasant girls, and he had sired a number of bastards. He was small and light, with a blond goatee. Ludwik kept to himself, reading old books of history, religion, and genealogy. He smoked a porcelain pipe, drank alone, hunted by himself, and avoided the noblemen's dances. The business of the estate he handled with a strong hand, and he made sure his bailiff never stole from him. His neighbors thought he was a pedant, and some considered him half mad. When Akhsa accepted the Christian faith, he asked her — now Maria — to marry him. Gossips said that Ludwik, the miser, had fallen in love with Maria's inheritance. The priests and others persuaded Akhsa to accept Ludwik's proposal. He was a descendant of the Polish king Leszczynski. Gloria, who was ten years older than Ludwik, opposed the match, but Ludwik for once did not listen to her.

The Jews of Krasnobród were afraid that Akhsa would become their enemy and instigate Ludwik against them, as happened with so many converts, but Ludwik continued to trade with the Jews, selling them fish, grain, and cattle. Zelig Frampoler, a court Jew, delivered all kinds of merchandise to the estate. Gloria remained the lady of the castle.

In the first weeks of the marriage, Akhsa and Ludwik took trips together in a surrey. Ludwik even began to pay visits to neighboring squires, and he talked of giving a ball. He confessed all his past adventures with women to Maria and promised to behave like a God-fearing Christian. But before long he fell back into his old ways; he withdrew from his neighbors, started up his affairs with peasant girls, and began to drink again. An angry silence hung between man and wife. Ludwik ceased coming to Maria's bedroom, and she did not conceive. In time, they stopped dining at the same table, and when Ludwik needed to tell Maria something he sent a note with a servant. Gloria, who managed the finances, allowed her sister-in-law a gulden a week; Maria's fortune now belonged to her husband. It became clear to Akhsa that God was punishing her and that nothing remained but to wait for death. But what would happen to her after she died? Would she be roasted on a bed of needles and be thrown into the waste of the netherworld? Would she be reincarnated as a dog, a mouse, a millstone?

Because she had nothing to occupy her time with, Akhsa spent all day and part of the night in her husband's library. Ludwik had not added to it, and the books were old, bound in leather, in wood, or in moth-eaten velvet and silk. The pages were yellow and foxed. Akhsa read stories of ancient kings, faraway countries, of all sorts of battles and intrigues among princes, cardinals, dukes. She pored over tales of the Crusades and the Black Plague. The world crawled with wickedness, but it was also full of wonders. Stars in the sky warred and swallowed one another. Comets foretold catastrophes. A child was born with a tail; a woman grew scales and fins. In India, fakirs stepped barefooted on red-hot coals without being burned. Others let themselves be buried alive, and then rose from their graves.

It was strange, but after the night Akhsa found the crown of feathers in her pillow she was not given another sign from the powers that rule the universe. She never heard from her grandfather or grandmother. There were times when Akhsa desired to call out to her grandfather, but she did not dare mention his name with her unclean lips. She had betrayed the Jewish God and she no longer believed in the Gentile one, so she refrained from praying. Often when Zelig Frampoler came to the estate and Akhsa saw him from the window, she wanted to ask him about the Jewish community, but she was afraid that he might hold it a sin to speak to her, and that Gloria would denounce her for associating with Jews.

Years rolled by. Gloria's hair turned white and her head shook. Ludwik's goatee became gray. The servants grew old, deaf, and half blind. Akhsa, or Maria, was in her thirties, but she often imagined herself an old woman. With the years she became more and more convinced that it was the Devil who had persuaded her to convert and that it was he who had fashioned the crown of feathers. But the road back was blocked. The Russian law forbade a convert to return to his faith. The bit of information that reached her about the Jews was bad: the synagogue in Krasnobród had burned down, as well as the stores in the marketplace. Dignified householders and community elders hung bags on their shoulders and went begging. Every few months there was an epidemic. There was nowhere to return to. She often contemplated suicide, but how? She lacked the courage to hang herself or cut her veins; she had no poison.

Slowly, Akhsa came to the conclusion that the universe was ruled by the black powers. It was not God holding dominion but Satan. She found a thick book about witchcraft that contained detailed descriptions of spells and incantations, talismans, the conjuring up of demons and goblins, the sacrifices to Asmodeus, Lucifer, and Beelzebub. There were accounts of the Black Mass; and of how the witches anointed their bodies, gathered in the forest, partook of human flesh, and flew in the air riding on brooms, shovels, and hoops, accompanied by bevies of devils and other creatures of the night that had horns and tails, bat's wings, and the snouts of pigs. Often these monsters lay with the witches, who gave birth to freaks.

Akhsa reminded herself of the Yiddish proverb "If you cannot go over, go under." She had lost the world to come; therefore, she decided to enjoy some revelry while she had this life. At night she began to call the Devil, prepared to make a covenant with him as many neglected women had done before.

Once in the middle of the night, after Akhsa had swallowed a potion of mead, spittle, human blood, crow's egg spiced with galbanum and mandrake, she felt a cold kiss on her lips. In the shine of the late-night moon she saw a naked male figure — tall and black, with long elflocks, the horns of a buck, and two protruding teeth, like a boar's. He bent down over her, whispering, "What is your command, my mistress? You may ask for half my kingdom."

His body was as translucent as a spider web. He stank of pitch. Akhsa had been able to reply, "You, my slave, come and have me." Instead, she murmured, "My grandparents."

The Devil burst into laughter. "They are dust!"

"Did you braid the crown of feathers?" Akhsa asked.

"Who else?"

"You deceived me?"

"I am a deceiver," the Devil answered with a giggle.

"Where is the truth?" Akhsa asked.

"The truth is that there is no truth."

The Devil lingered for a while and then disappeared. For the remainder of the night, Akhsa was neither asleep nor awake. Voices spoke to her. Her breasts because swollen, her nipples hard, her belly distended. Pain bored into her skull. Her teeth were on edge, and her tongue enlarged so that she feared it would split her palate. Her eyes bulged from their sockets. There was a knocking in her ears as loud as a hammer on an anvil. Then she felt as if she were in the throes of labor. "I'm giving birth to a demon!" Akhsa cried out. She began to pray to the God she had forsaken. Finally she fell asleep, and when she awoke in the pre-dawn darkness all her pains had ceased. She saw her grandfather standing at the foot of her bed. He wore a white robe and cowl, such as he used to wear on the eve of Yom Kippur when he blessed Akhsa before going to the Kol Nidre prayer. A light shone from his eyes and lit up Akhsa's quilt. "Grandfather," Akhsa murmured.

"Yes, Akhsa. I am here."

"Grandfather, what shall I do?"

"Run away. Repent."

"I'm lost."

"It is never too late. Find the man you shamed. Become a Jewish daughter."

Later, Akhsa did not remember whether her grandfather had actually spoken to her or she had understood him without words. The night was over. Daybreak reddened the window. Birds were twittering. Akhsa examined her sheet. There was no blood. She had not given birth to a demon. For the first time in years, she recited the Hebrew prayer of thanksgiving.

She got out of bed, washed at the basin, and covered her hair with a shawl. Ludwik and Gloria had robbed her of her inheritance, but she still possessed her grandmother's jewelry. She wrapped it in a handkerchief and put it in a basket, together with a shirt and underwear. Ludwik had either stayed the night with one of his mistresses or he had left at dawn to hunt. Gloria lay sick in her boudoir. The maid brought Akhsa her breakfast, but she ate little. Then she left the estate. Dogs barked at her as if she were a stranger. The old servants looked in amazement as the squiress passed through the gates with a basket on her arm and a kerchief on her head like a peasant woman.

Although Malkowski's property was not far from Krasnobród, Akhsa spent most of the day on the road. She sat down to rest and washed her hands in a stream. She recited grace and ate the slice of bread she had brought with her.

Near the Krasnobród cemetery stood the hut of Eber, the gravedigger. Outside, his wife was washing linen in a tub. Akhsa asked her, "Is this the way to Krasnobród?"

"Yes, straight ahead."

"What's the news from the village?"

"Who are you?"

"I'm a relative of Reb Naftali Holishitzer."

The woman wiped her hands on her apron. "Not a soul is left of that family."

"Where is Akhsa?"

The old woman trembled. "She should have been buried head first, Father in Heaven." And she told about Akhsa's conversion. "She's had her punishment already in this world."

"What became of the yeshiva boy she was betrothed to?"

"Who knows? He isn't from around here."

Akhsa asked about the graves of her grandparents, and the old woman pointed to two headstones bent one toward the other, overgrown with moss and weeds. Akhsa prostrated herself in front of them and lay there until nightfall.

For three months, Akhsa wandered from yeshiva to yeshiva, but she did not find Zemach. She searched in community record books, questioned elders and rabbis — without result. Since not every town had an inn, she often slept in the poorhouse. She lay on a pallet of straw, covered with a mat, praying silently that her grandfather would appear and tell her where to find Zemach. He gave no sign. In the darkness, the old and the sick coughed and muttered. Children cried. Mothers cursed. Although Akhsa accepted this as part of her punishment, she could not overcome her sense of indignity. Community leaders scolded her. They made her wait for days to see them. Women were suspicious of her — why was she looking for a man who no doubt had a wife and children, or might even be in his grave? "Grandfather, why did you drive me to this?" Akhsa cried. "Either show me the way or send death to take me."

On a wintry afternoon, while Akhsa was sitting in an inn in Lublin, she asked the innkeeper if he had ever heard of a man called Zemach — small in stature, swarthy, a former yeshiva boy and scholar. One of the other guests said, "You mean Zemach, the teacher from Izbica?"

He described Zemach, and Akhsa knew she had found the one she was looking for. "He was engaged to marry a girl in Krasnobród," she said.

"I know. The convert. Who are you?"

"A relative."

"What do you want with him?" the guest asked. "He's poor, and stubborn to boot. All his pupils have been taken away from him. He's a wild and contrary man."

"Does he have a wife?"

"He's had two already. One he tortured to death and the other left him."

"Does he have children?"

"No, he's sterile."

The guest was about to say more, but a servant came to call for him. Akhsa's eyes filled with tears. Her grandfather had not forsaken her. He had led her in the right direction. She went to arrange conveyance to Izbica, and in front of the inn stood a covered wagon ready to leave. "No, I am not alone," she said to herself. "Every step is known in Heaven."

In the beginning, the roads were paved, but soon they became dirt trails full of holes and ditches. The night was wet and dark. Often the passengers had to climb down and help the coachman push the wagon out of the mud. The others scolded him, but Akhsa accepted her discomfort with grace. Wet snow was falling and a cold wind blew. Every time she got out of the wagon she sank over her ankles in mud. They arrived in Izbica late in the evening. The whole village was a swamp. The huts were dilapidated. Someone showed Akhsa the way to Zemach the Teacher's house — it was on a hill near the butcher shops. Even though it was winter, there was a stench of decay in the air. Butcher-shop dogs were slinking around.

Akhsa looked into the window of Zemach's hut and saw peeling walls, a dirt floor, and shelves of worn books. A wick in a dish of oil gave the only light. At the table sat a little man with a black beard, bushy brows, a yellow face, and a pointed nose. He was bending myopically over a large volume. He wore the lining of a skullcap and a quilted jacket that showed the dirty batting. As Akhsa stood watching, a mouse came out of its hole and scurried over to the bed, which had a pallet of rotting straw, a pillow without a case, and a moth-eaten sheepskin for a blanket. Even though Zemach had aged, Akhsa recognized him. He scratched himself. He spat on his fingertips and wiped them on his forehead. Yes, that was he. Akhsa wanted to laugh and cry at the same time. In a moment she turned her face toward the darkness. For the first time in years, she heard her grandmother's voice. "Akhsa, run away."

"Where to?"

"Back to Esau."

Then she heard her grandfather's voice. "Akhsa, he will save you from the abyss."

Akhsa had never heard her grandfather speak with such fervor. She felt the emptiness that comes before fainting. She leaned against the door and it opened.

Zemach lifted one bushy brow. His eyes were bulging and jaundiced. "What do you want?" he rasped.

"Are you Reb Zemach?"

"Yes, who are you?"

"Akhsa, from Krasnobród. Once your fiancée. . . ."

Zemach was silent. He opened his crooked mouth, revealing a single tooth, black as a hook. "The convert?"

"I have come back to Jewishness."

Zemach jumped up. A terrible cry tore from him. "Get out of my house! Blotted be your name!"

"Reb Zemach, please hear me!"

He ran toward her with clenched fists. The dish of oil fell and the light was extinguished. "Filth!"

The study house in Holishitz was packed. It was the day before the new moon, and a crowd had gathered to recite the supplications. From the women's section came the sound of pious recitation. Suddenly the door opened, and a black-bearded man wearing tattered clothes strode in. A bag was slung over his shoulder. He was leading a woman on a rope as if she were a cow. She wore a black kerchief on her head, a dress made of sackcloth, and rags on her feet. Around her neck hung a wreath of garlic. The worshippers stopped their prayers. The stranger gave a sign to the woman and she prostrated herself on the threshold. "Jews, step on me!" she called. "Jews, spit on me!"

Turmoil rose in the study house. The stranger went up to the reading table, tapped for silence, and intoned, "This woman's family comes from your town. Her grandfather was Reb Naftali Holishitzer. She is the Akhsa who converted and married a squire. She has seen the truth now and wants to atone for her abominations."

Though Holishitz was in the part of Poland that belonged to Austria, the story of Akhsa had been heard there. Some of the worshippers protested that this was not the way of repentance; a human being should not be dragged by a rope, like cattle. Others threatened the stranger with their fists. It was true that in Austria a convert could return to Jewishness according to the law of the land. But if the Gentiles were to learn that one who went over to their faith had been humiliated in such a fashion, harsh edicts and recriminations might result. The old rabbi, Reb Bezalel, approached Akhsa with quick little steps. "Get up, my daughter. Since you have repented, you are one of us."

Akhsa rose. "Rabbi, I have disgraced my people."

"Since you repent, the Almighty will forgive you."

When the worshippers in the women's section heard what was going on, they rushed into the room with the men, the rabbi's wife among them. Reb Bezalel said to her, "Take her home and dress her in decent clothing. Man was created in God's image."

"Rabbi," Akhsa said, "I want to atone for my iniquities."

"I will prescribe a penance for you. Don't torture yourself."

Some of the women began to cry. The rabbi's wife took off her shawl and hung it over Akhsa's shoulders. Another matron offered Akhsa a cape.

They led her into the chamber where in olden times they had kept captive those who sinned against the community — it still contained a block and chain. The women dressed Akhsa there. Someone brought her a skirt and shoes. As they busied themselves about her, Akhsa beat her breast with her fist and recounted her sins: she had spited God, served idols, copulated with a Gentile. She sobbed, "I practiced witchcraft. I conjured up Satan. He braided me a crown of feathers." When Akhsa was dressed, the rabbi's wife took her home.

After prayers, the men began to question the stranger as to who he was and how he was connected with Reb Naftali's granddaughter.

He replied, "My name is Zemach. I was supposed to become her husband, but she refused me. Now she has come to ask my forgiveness."

"A Jew should forgive."

"I forgive her, but the Almighty is a God of vengeance."

"He is also a God of mercy."

Zemach began a debate with the scholars, and his erudition was obvious at once. He quoted the Talmud, the Commentaries, and the Responsa. He even corrected the rabbi when he misquoted.

Reb Bezalel asked him, "Do you have a family?"

"I am divorced."

"In that case, everything can be set right."

The rabbi invited Zemach to go home with him. The women sat with Akhsa out in the kitchen. They urged her to eat bread with chicory. She had been fasting for three days. In the rabbi's study the men looked after Zemach. They brought him trousers, shoes, a coat, and a hat. Since he was infested with lice, they took him to the baths.

In the evening, the seven outstanding citizens of the town and all the important elders gathered. The wives brought Akhsa. The rabbi pronounced that, according to the law, Akhsa was not married. Her union with the squire was nothing but an act of lechery. The rabbi asked, "Zemach, do you desire Akhsa for your wife?"

"I do."

"Akhsa, will you take Zemach for a husband?"

"Yes, Rabbi, but I am not worthy."

The rabbi outlined Akhsa's penance. She must fast each Monday and Thursday, abstain from meat and fish on the weekdays, recite psalms, and rise at dawn for prayers. The rabbi said to her, "The chief thing is not the punishment but the remorse. 'And he will return and be healed,' the prophet says."

"Rabbi, excuse," Zemach interrupted. "This kind of penance is for common sins, not for conversion."

"What do you want her to do?"

"There are more severe forms of contrition."

"What, for example?"

"Wearing pebbles in the shoes. Rolling naked in the snow in winter — in nettles in summer. Fasting from Sabbath to Sabbath."

"Nowadays, people do not have the strength for such rigors," the rabbi said after some hesitation.

"If they have the strength to sin, they should have the strength to expiate."

"Holy Rabbi," said Akhsa, "do not let me off lightly. Let the rabbi give me a harsh penance."

"I have said what is right."

All kept silent. Then Akhsa said, "Zemach, give me my bundle." Zemach had put her bag in a corner. He brought it to the table and she took out a little sack. A sigh could be heard from the group as she poured out settings of pearls, diamonds, and rubies. "Rabbi, this is my jewelry," Akhsa said. "I do not deserve to own it. Let the rabbi dispose of it as he wishes."

"Is it yours or the squire's?"

"Mine, Rabbi, inherited from my sacred grandmother."

"It is written that even the most charitable should never give up more than a fifth part."

Zemach shook his head. "Again I am in disagreement. She disgraced her grandmother in Paradise. She should not be permitted to inherit her jewels."

The rabbi clutched his beard. "If you know better, you become the rabbi." He rose from his chair and then sat down again. "How will you sustain yourselves?"

"I will be a water carrier," Zemach said.

"Rabbi, I can knead dough and wash linen," Akhsa said.

"Well, do as you choose. I believe in the mercy, not in the rigor, of the law."

In the middle of the night Akhsa opened her eyes. Husband and wife lived in a hut with a dirt floor, not far from the cemetery. All day long Zemach carried water. Akhsa washed linen. Except for Saturday and holidays, both fasted every day and ate only in the evening. Akhsa had put sand and pebbles into her shoes and wore a rough woolen skirt next to her skin. At night they slept separately on the floor — he on a mat by the window, she on a straw pallet by the oven. On a rope that stretched from wall to wall hung shrouds she had made for them.

They had been married for three years, but Zemach still had not approached her. He had confessed that he, too, was dipped in sin. While he had a wife, he had lusted for Akhsa. He had spilled his seed like Onan. He had craved revenge upon her, had railed against the Almighty, and had taken out his wrath on his wives, one of whom died. How could he be more defiled?

Even though the hut was near a forest and they could get wood for nothing, Zemach would not allow the stove to be heated at night. They slept in their clothes, covered with sacks and rags. The people of Holishitz maintained that Zemach was a madman; the rabbi had called for man and wife and explained that it is as cruel to torture oneself as it is to torture others, but Zemach quoted from *The Beginning of Wisdom* that repentance without mortification is meaningless.

Akhsa made a confession every night before sleep, and still her dreams were not pure. Satan came to her in the image of her grandmother and described dazzling cities, elegant balls, passionate squires, lusty women. Her grandfather had become silent again.

In Akhsa's dreams, Grandmother was young and beautiful. She sang bawdy songs, drank wine, and danced with charlatans. Some nights she led Akhsa into temples where priests chanted and idolators kneeled before golden statues. Naked courtesans drank wine from horns and gave themselves over to licentiousness.

One night Akhsa dreamed that she stood naked in a round hole. Midgets danced around her in circles. They sang obscene dirges. There was a blast of trumpets and the drumming of drums. When she awoke, the black singing still rang in her ears. "I am lost forever," she said to herself.

Zemach had also wakened. For a time he looked out through the one windowpane he had not boarded up. Then he asked, "Akhsa, are you awake? A new snow has fallen."

Akhsa knew too well what he meant. She said, "I have no strength."

"You had strength to give yourself to the wicked."

"My bones ache."

"Tell that to the Avenging Angel."

The snow and the late-night moon cast a bright glare into the room. Zemach had let his hair grow long, like an ancient ascetic. His beard was wild and his eyes glowed in the night. Akhsa could never understand how he had the power to carry water all day long and still study half the night. He scarcely partook of the evening meal. To keep himself from enjoying the food, he swallowed his bread without chewing it, he oversalted and peppered the soup she cooked for him. Akhsa herself had become emaciated. Often she looked at her reflection in the slops and saw a thin face, sunken cheeks, a sickly pallor. She coughed frequently and spat phlegm with blood. Now she said, "Forgive me, Zemach, I can't get up."

"Get up, adulteress. This may be your last night."

"I wish it were."

"Confess! Tell the truth."

"I have told everything."

"Did you enjoy the lechery?"

"No, Zemach, no."

"Last time you admitted that you did."

Akhsa was silent for a long time. "Very rarely. Perhaps for a second."

"And you forgot God?"

"Not altogether."

"You knew God's law, but you defied Him willfully."

"I thought the truth was with the Gentiles."

"All because Satan braided you a crown of feathers?"

"I thought it was a miracle."

"Harlot, don't defend yourself!"

"I do not defend myself. He spoke with Grandmother's voice."

"Why did you listen to your grandmother and not to your grandfather?"

"I was foolish."

"Foolish? For years you wallowed in utter desecration."

After a while man and wife went out barefoot into the night. Zemach threw himself into the snow first. He rolled over and over with great speed. His skullcap fell off. His body was covered with black hair, like fur. Akhsa waited a minute, and then she too threw herself down. She turned in the snow slowly and in silence while Zemach recited, "We have sinned, we have betrayed, we have robbed, we have lied, we have mocked, we have rebelled." And then he added, "Let it be Thy will that my death shall be the redemption for all my iniquities."

Akhsa had heard this lamentation often, but it made her tremble every time. This was the way the peasants had wailed when her husband, Squire Malkowski, whipped them. She was more afraid of Zemach's wailing than of the cold in winter and the nettles in summer. Occasionally, when he was in a gentler temper, Zemach promised that he would come to her as husband to wife. He even said that he would like to be the father of her children. But when? He kept on searching for new misdeeds in both of them. Akhsa grew weaker from day to day. The shrouds on the rope and the headstones in the graveyard seemed to beckon her. She made Zemach vow that he would recite the Kaddish over her grave.

On a hot day in the month of Tammuz, Akhsa went to gather sorrel leaves from the pasture that bordered the river. She had fasted all day long and she wanted to cook schav[2] for herself and Zemach for their evening meal. In the middle of her gathering she was overcome by exhaustion. She stretched out on the grass and dozed off, intending to rest only a quarter of an hour. But her mind went blank and her legs turned to stone. She fell into a deep sleep. When she opened her eyes, night had fallen. The sky was overcast, the air heavy with humidity. There was a storm coming. The earth steamed with the scent of grass and herbs, and it made Akhsa's head reel. In the darkness she found her basket, but it was empty. A goat or cow had eaten her sorrel. Suddenly she remembered her childhood, when she was pampered by her grandparents, dressed in velvet and silk, and served by maids and butlers. Now coughing choked her, her forehead was hot, and chills flashed through her spine. Since the moon did not shine and the stars were obscured, she scarcely knew her way. Her bare feet stepped on thorns

---

[2] Wild sorrel, a leafy plant.

and cow pats. "What a trap I have fallen into!" something cried out in her. She came to a tree and stopped to rest. At that moment she saw her grandfather. His white beard glowed in the darkness. She recognized his high forehead, his benign smile, and the loving kindness of his gaze. She called out, "Grandfather!" And in a second her face was washed with tears.

"I know everything," her grandfather said. "Your tribulations and your grief."

"Grandfather, what shall I do?"

"My daughter, your ordeal is over. We are waiting for you — I, Grandmother, all who love you. Holy angels will come to meet you."

"When, Grandfather?"

In that instant the image dissolved. Only the darkness remained. Akhsa felt her way home like someone blind. Finally, she reached her hut. As she opened the door she could feel that Zemach was there. He sat on the floor and his eyes were like two coals. He called out, "It's you?"

"Yes, Zemach."

"Why were you so long? Because of you I couldn't say my evening prayers in peace. You confused my thoughts."

"Forgive me, Zemach. I was tired and I fell asleep in the pasture."

"Liar! Convert! Scum!" Zemach screeched. "I searched for you in the pasture. You were whoring with a shepherd."

"What are you saying? God forbid!"

"Tell me the truth!" He jumped up and began to shake her. "Bitch! Demon! Lilith!"

Zemach had never acted so wildly. Akhsa said to him, "Zemach, my husband, I am faithful to you. I fell asleep on the grass. On the way home I saw my grandfather. My time is up." She was seized with such weakness that she sank to the floor.

Zemach's wrath vanished immediately. A mournful wail broke from him. "Sacred soul, where will I be without you? You are a saint. Forgive me my harshness. It was because of my love. I wanted to cleanse you so that you could sit in Paradise with the Holy Mothers."

"As I deserve, so shall I sit."

"Why should this happen to you? Is there no justice in Heaven?" And Zemach wailed in the voice that terrified her. He beat his head against the wall.

The next morning Akhsa did not rise from her bed. Zemach brought porridge he had cooked for her on the tripod. When he fed it to her, it spilled out of her mouth. Zemach fetched the town healer, but the healer did not know what to do. The women of the Burial Society came. Akhsa lay in a state of utter weakness. Her life was draining away. In the middle of the day Zemach went on foot to the town of Jaroslaw to bring a doctor. Evening came and he had not returned. That morning the rabbi's wife had sent a pillow to Akhsa. It was the first time in years she had slept on a pillow. Toward evening, the Burial Society women went home to their families and Akhsa remained alone. A wick burned in a dish of oil. A tepid breeze came through the open window. The moon did not shine, but the stars glittered. Crickets chirped, and frogs croaked with human voices. Once in a while a shadow passed the wall across from her bed. Akhsa knew that her end was near, but she had no fear of death. She took stock of her soul. She had been born rich and beautiful, with more gifts than all the others around her. Bad luck had made everything turn to the opposite. Did she suffer for her own sins or was she a reincarnation of someone who had sinned in a former generation? Akhsa knew that she should be spending her last hours in repentance and prayer. But such was her fate that doubt did not leave her even now. Her grandfather had told her one thing, her grandmother another. Akhsa had read in an old book about the Apostates who denied God, considering the world a random combination of atoms. She had now one desire — that a sign should be given, the pure truth revealed. She lay and prayed for a miracle. She fell into a light sleep and dreamed she was falling into depths that were tight and dark. Each time it seemed that she had reached the bottom, the foundation collapsed under her and she began to sink again with greater speed. The dark became heavier and the abyss even deeper.

She opened her eyes and knew what to do. With her last strength she got up and found a knife. She took off the pillowcase and with numb fingers ripped open the seams of the pillow. From the down stuffing she pulled out a crown of feathers. A hidden hand had braided in its top the four letters of God's name.

Akhsa put the crown beside her bed. In the wavering light of the wick, she could see each letter clearly; the *Yud*, the *Hai*, the *Vov*, and the other *Hai*. But, she wondered, in what way was this crown more a revelation of truth than the other? Was it possible that there were different faiths in Heaven? Akhsa began to pray for a new miracle. In her dismay she remembered the Devil's words: "The truth is that there is no truth."

Late at night, one of the Burial Society women returned. Akhsa wanted to implore her not to step on the crown, but she was too weak. The woman stepped on the crown, and its delicate structure dissolved. Akhsa closed her eyes and never opened them again. At dawn she sighed and gave up her soul.

One of the women lifted a feather and put it to her nostrils, but it did not flutter.

Later in the day, the Burial Society women cleansed Akhsa and dressed her in the shroud that she had sewn for herself. Zemach still had not returned from Jaroslaw and he was never heard of again. There was talk in Holishitz that he had been killed on the road. Some surmised that Zemach was not a man but a demon. Akhsa was buried near the chapel of a holy man, and the rabbi spoke a eulogy for her.

One thing remained a riddle. In her last hours Akhsa had ripped open the pillow that the rabbi's wife had sent her. The women who washed her body found bits of down between her fingers. How could a dying woman have the strength to do this? And what had she been searching for? No matter how much the townspeople pondered and how many explanations they tried to find, they never discovered the truth.

Because if there is such a thing as truth it is as intricate and hidden as a crown of feathers.

[1973]

RASIPURAM KRISNASWAMI NARAYAN (b. 1906) is India's most famous storyteller in English. His published work includes fifteen novels; a memoir, My Days (1974); and several story collections, including An Astrologer's Day (1964), Lawley Road (1967), A Horse and Two Goats (1970), and Under the Banyan Tree and Other Stories (1985). As his traditional middle name implies, he is an elegant, deceptively simple stylist. Narayan has described the way he became a writer in his native city of Madras:

> At an early stage of my life I enjoyed a lot of freedom, no one in our family minding my non-economic style of living. I read a little, also attempted to write, and went out on long walks along the tanks, parks, and avenues, or climbed the hill which looms over our city; and during some part of the day I watched also the crowds at the market — not deliberately and consciously to pick up a subject, but for the sheer pleasure of watching people. The very first story I wrote was about a one-armed beggar who stood in the middle of a narrow street in front of a coffee-house and sailed forth with upheld palm when he spotted young men emerging from the restaurant in a merry, convivial mood. . . . I don't remember much of the story, which is lost in oblivion, originally published in The Hindu of Madras nearly four decades ago. The editor was generous enough to accept it although as I recollect it revolved round a flimsy theme — of the beggar's obsessive desire to acquire an old jacket. Following its publication I became a regular writer for The Hindu. The driving force was the need to write two stories a month to survive.

Narayan is most interested in observing people and telling stories about them filled with gentle humor and compassion. As the critic Alfred Kazin has realized, Narayan's work "derives its charm from the immense calm out of which he writes. It has all happened before, it happens every hour, it will happen again tomorrow." Narayan has created the mythical village of Malgudi for his stories, much like Faulkner created an imaginary Yoknapatawpha County. Yet Narayan's narratives project a unique serenity. If his fiction seems to lack a political edge, its power of invention contains subtle comment meant to show the harsh restrictions of poverty in his characters' environment. There is no economic panic in "Under the Banyan Tree," but the story mentions that the villagers' life is "hard and drab."

Typically, Narayan's stories are accounts of an evolving consciousness, beginning in confusion and ending in wholeness, suggesting the model of attaining peace of mind within the traditional Hindu faith. Perhaps conscious of his own advancing age, Narayan said in 1984 that he meant "Under the Banyan Tree" to have a particularly simple meaning. He realizes that a storyteller "must have the sense to know when to stop, and not wait for others to tell him."

R. K. Narayan

ಌ

Under the Banyan Tree

The village Somal, nestling away in the forest tracts of Mempi, had a population of less than three hundred. It was in every way a village to make the heart of a rural reformer sink. Its tank, a small expanse of water, right in the middle of the village, served for drinking, bathing, and washing the cattle, and it bred malaria, typhoid, and heaven knew what else. The cottages sprawled anyhow and the lanes twisted and wriggled up and down and strangled each other. The population used the highway as the refuse ground and in the backyard of every house drain water stagnated in green puddles.

Such was the village. It is likely that the people of the village were insensitive: but it is more likely that they never noticed their surroundings because they lived in a kind of perpetual enchantment. The enchanter was Nambi the story-teller. He was a man of about sixty or seventy. Or was he eighty or one hundred and eighty? Who could say? In a place so much cut off as Somal (the nearest bus-stop was ten miles away), reckoning could hardly be in the familiar measures of time. If anyone asked Nambi what his age was he referred to an ancient famine or an invasion or the building of a bridge and indicated how high he had stood from the ground at the time.

He was illiterate, in the sense that the written word was a mystery to him; but he could make up a story, in his head, at the rate of one a month; each story took nearly ten days to narrate.

His home was the little temple which was at the very end of the village. No one could say how he had come to regard himself as the owner of the temple. The temple was a very small structure with red-striped walls, with a stone image of the Goddess Shakti in the sanctum. The front portion of the temple was Nambi's home. For aught it mattered any place might be his home; for he was without possessions. All that he possessed was a broom with which he swept the temple; and he had also a couple of dhoties and upper cloth. He spent most of the day in the shade of the banyan which spread out its branches in front of the temple. When he felt hungry he walked into any house that caught his fancy and joined the family at dinner. When he needed new clothes they were brought to him by the villagers. He hardly ever had to go out in search of company; for the banyan shade served as a clubhouse for the village folk. All through the day people came seeking Nambi's company and squatted under the tree. If he was in a mood for it he listened to their talk and entertained them with his own observations and anecdotes. When he was in no mood he looked at the visitors sourly and asked, "What do you think I am? Don't blame me if you get no story at the next moon. Unless I meditate how can the Goddess give me a story? Do you think stories float in the air?" And he moved out to the edge of the forest and squatted there, contemplating the trees.

On Friday evenings the village turned up at the temple for worship, when Nambi lit a score of mud lamps and arranged them around the threshold of the sanctuary. He decorated the image with flowers, which grew wildly in the backyard of the temple. He acted as the priest and offered to the Goddess fruits and flowers brought in by the villagers.

On the nights he had a story to tell he lit a small lamp and placed it in a niche in the trunk of the banyan tree. Villagers as they returned home in the evening saw this, went home, and said to their wives, "Now, now, hurry up with the dinner, the story-teller is calling us." As the moon crept up behind the hillock, men, women, and children gathered under the banyan tree. The story-teller would not appear yet. He would be sitting in the sanctum, before the Goddess, with his eyes shut, in deep meditation. He sat thus as long as he liked and when he came out, with his forehead ablaze with ash and vermilion, he took his seat on a stone platform in front of the temple. He opened the story with a question. Jerking his finger towards a vague, far-away destination, he asked, "A thousand years ago, a stone's throw in that direction, what do you think there was? It was not the weed-covered waste it is now, for donkeys to roll in. It was not the ash-pit it is now. It was the capital of the king. . . ." The king would be Dasaratha, Vikramaditya, Asoka, or anyone that came into the old man's head; the capital was called Kapila, Kridapura, or anything. Opening thus, the old man went on without a pause for three hours. By then brick by brick the palace of the king was raised. The old man described the dazzling durbar hall where sat a hundred vassal kings, ministers, and subjects; in another part of the palace all the musicians in the world assembled and sang; and most of the songs were sung over again by Nambi to his audience; and he described in detail the pictures and trophies that hung on the walls of the palace. . . .

It was story-building on an epic scale. The first day barely conveyed the setting of the tale, and Nambi's audience as yet had no idea who were coming into the story. As the moon slipped behind the trees of Mempi Forest Nambi said, "Now friends, Mother says this will do for the day." He abruptly rose, went in, lay down, and fell asleep long before the babble of the crowd ceased.

The light in the niche would again be seen two or three days later, and again and again throughout the bright half of the month. Kings and heroes, villains and fairy-like women, gods in human form, saints and assassins, jostled each other in that world which was created under the banyan tree. Nambi's voice rose and fell in an exquisite rhythm, and the moonlight and the hour completed the magic. The villagers laughed with Nambi, they wept with him, they adored the heroes, cursed the villains, groaned when the conspirator had his initial success, and they sent up to the gods a heartfelt prayer for a happy ending. . . .

On the day when the story ended, the whole gathering went into the sanctum and prostrated before the Goddess. . . .

By the time the next moon peeped over the hillock Nambi was ready with another story. He never repeated the same kind of story or brought in the same set of persons, and the village folk considered Nambi a sort of miracle, quoted his words of wisdom, and lived on the whole in an exalted plane of their own, though their life in all other respects was hard and drab.

And yet it had gone on for years and years. One moon he lit the lamp in the tree. The audience came. The old man took his seat and began the story. ". . . When King Vikramaditya lived, his minister was . . ." He paused. He could not get beyond it. He made a fresh beginning. "There was the king . . ." he said, repeated it, and then his words trailed off into a vague mumbling. "What has come over me?" he asked pathetically. "Oh, Mother, great Mother, why do I stumble and falter? I know the story. I had the whole of it a moment ago. What was it about? I can't understand what has happened." He faltered and looked so miserable that his audience said, "Take your own time. You are perhaps tired."

"Shut up!" he cried. "Am I tired? Wait a moment; I will tell you the story presently." Following this there was utter silence. Eager faces looked up at him. "Don't look at me!" he flared up. Somebody gave him a tumbler of milk. The audience waited patiently. This was a new experience. Some persons expressed their sympathy aloud. Some persons began to talk among themselves. Those who sat in the outer edge of the crowd silently slipped away. Gradually, as it neared midnight, others followed this example. Nambi sat staring at the ground, his head bowed in thought. For the first time he realized that he was old. He felt he would never more be able to control his thoughts or express them cogently. He looked up. Everyone had gone except his friend Mari the blacksmith. "Mari, why aren't you also gone?"

Mari apologized for the rest: "They didn't want to tire you; so they have gone away."

Nambi got up. "You are right. Tomorrow I will make it up. Age, age. What is my age? It has come on suddenly." He pointed at his head and said, "This says, 'Old fool, don't think I shall be your servant any more. You will be my servant hereafter.' It is disobedient and treacherous."

He lit the lamp in the niche next day. The crowd assembled under the banyan faithfully. Nambi had spent the whole day in meditation. He had been fervently praying to the Goddess not to desert him. He began the story. He went on for an hour without a stop. He felt greatly relieved, so much so that he interrupted his narration to remark, "Oh, friends. The Mother is always kind. I was seized with a foolish fear . . ." and continued the story. In a few minutes he felt dried up. He struggled hard: "And then . . . and then . . . what happened?" He stammered. There followed a pause lasting an hour. The audience rose without a word and went home. The old man sat on the stone brooding till the cock crew. "I can't blame them for it," he muttered to himself. "Can they sit down here and mope all night?" Two days later he gave another instalment of the story, and that, too lasted only a few minutes. The gathering dwindled. Fewer persons began to take notice of the lamp in the niche. Even these came only out of a sense of duty. Nambi realized that there was no use in prolonging the struggle. He brought the story to a speedy and premature end.

He knew what was happening. He was harrowed by the thoughts of his failure. I should have been happier if I had dropped dead years ago, he said to himself. Mother, why have you struck me dumb . . .? He shut himself up in the sanctum, hardly ate any food, and spent the greater part of the day sitting motionless in meditation.

The next moon peeped over the hillock, Nambi lit the lamp in the niche. The villagers as they returned home saw the lamp, but only a handful turned up at night. "Where are the others?" the old man asked. "Let us wait." He waited. The moon came up. His handful of audience waited patiently. And then the old man said, "I won't tell the story today, nor tomorrow unless the whole village comes here. I insist upon it. It is a mighty story. Everyone must hear it." Next day he went up and down the village street shouting, "I have a most wonderful tale to tell tonight. Come one and all; don't miss it. . . ." This personal appeal had a great effect. At night a large crowd gathered under the banyan. They were happy that the storyteller had regained his powers. Nambi came out of the temple when everyone had settled and said: "It is the Mother who gives the gifts; and it is she who takes away the gifts. Nambi is a dotard. He speaks when the Mother has anything to say. He is struck dumb when she has nothing to say. But what is the use of the jasmine when it has lost its scent? What is the lamp for when all the oil is gone? Goddess be thanked. . . . These are my last words on this earth; and this is my greatest story." He rose and went into the sanctum. His audience hardly understood what he meant. They sat there till they became weary. And then some of them got up and stepped into the sanctum. There the story-teller sat with eyes shut. "Aren't you going to tell us a story?" they asked. He opened his eyes, looked at them, and shook his head. He indicated by gesture that he had spoken his last words.

When he felt hungry he walked into any cottage and silently sat down for food, and walked away the moment he had eaten. Beyond this he had hardly anything to demand of his fellow beings. The rest of his life (he lived for a few more years) was one great consummate silence.

[1985]

RICHARD WRIGHT (1908–1960) *was born on a plantation near Natchez, Mississippi, the son of a farmhand and a country schoolteacher. His home life was disrupted when his father deserted the family; after that he lived off and on with his grandmother, a Seventh-Day Adventist whose repressive religious code curbed his early attempts to write fiction, which she labeled "lies" and "the Devil's work." Wright was stubborn, however, and continued to write stories at the Smith-Robinson secondary school in Jackson, Mississippi. After his graduation, he moved north, first to Memphis, then to Chicago, and then to New York City, where he became involved in radical politics. He was a member of the Communist Party from 1932 to 1944. In the 1930s he worked as a reporter for* New Masses, *a correspondent for the Harlem bureau of the* Daily Worker, *and an editor for* New Challenge, *a left-wing magazine.* New Challenge *published his "Blueprint for Negro Writing," an effort to bridge the gap between Marxism and black nationalism, in 1938. He was also writing the stories that appeared in* Uncle Tom's Children, *a book that won first prize in a contest for writers on the Federal Writers' Project sponsored by* Story *magazine during the Depression. Wright's early fiction was strongly influenced by Ernest Hemingway's "simple, direct way" of writing stories, but Wright also set himself the problem of how to use a modernist style to write about social issues:*

> *Practically all of us, young writers, were influenced by Ernest Hemingway. We liked the simple, direct way in which he wrote, but a great many of us wanted to write about social problems. The question came up: How could we write about social problems and use a simple style? Hemingway's style is so concentrated on naturalistic detail that there is no room for social comment. One boy said that one way was to dig deeper into the character and try to get something that will live. I decided to try it.*

The result was the five stories published in Uncle Tom's Children *in 1938. Next Wright turned to his first novel,* Native Son *(1940), an American classic dramatizing a story of racial conflict. This was followed by* Black Boy *(1945), a brilliant autobiography written when he was not yet forty. The next year he left the United States to live the last fourteen years of his life in Paris, feeling himself alienated from the capitalistic goals of American society and looking beyond the scope of racial and political commitment for answers to social problems. In France he wrote the novels* The Outsider *(1953),* Savage Holiday *(1954), and* The Long Dream *(1958). This last was conceived as the first volume of a trilogy depicting the gradual liberation of a black American from the ways of thinking imposed on him* by racial oppression. In 1960, the year Wright died, he gathered for publication his second book of short stories, Eight Men, made up of fiction that had appeared over the years in magazines and anthologies, including "The Man Who Was Almost a Man," written in the 1930s.

Telling stories from a realistic view of black experience, Wright experimented with literary techniques in all his fiction. His short stories dramatize the same themes as his novels and are equally experimental. The story "The Man Who Was Almost a Man" weaves illiterate southern black dialect so skillfully with standard English narration that most readers are unaware of the effect of the deliberate juxtaposition, but the technique brings us closer to the simple farm boy's world while making an implicit social comment about his world's distance from the exploitative white society engulfing him.

Richard Wright

࿊

THE MAN WHO WAS ALMOST A MAN

Dave struck out across the fields, looking homeward through paling light. Whut's the use talkin wid em niggers in the field? Anyhow, his mother was putting supper on the table. Them niggers can't understan nothing. One of these days he was going to get a gun and practice shooting, then they couldn't talk to him as though he were a little boy. He slowed, looking at the ground. Shucks, Ah ain scareda them even ef they are biggern me! Aw, Ah know whut Ahma do. Ahm going by ol Joe's sto n git that Sears Roebuck catlog n look at them guns. Mebbe Ma will lemme buy one when she gits mah pay from ol man Hawkins. Ahma beg her t gimme some money. Ahm ol ernough to hava gun. Ahm seventeen. Almost a man. He strode, feeling his long loose-jointed limbs. Shucks, a man oughta hava little gun aftah he done worked hard all day.

He came in sight of Joe's store. A yellow lantern glowed on the front porch. He mounted steps and went through the screen door, hearing it bang behind him. There was a strong smell of coal oil and mackerel fish. He felt very confident until he saw fat Joe walk in through the rear door, then his courage began to ooze.

"Howdy, Dave! Whutcha want?"

"How yuh, Mistah Joe? Aw, Ah don wanna buy nothing. Ah jus wanted t see ef yuhd lemme look at tha catlog erwhile."

"Sure! You wanna see it here?"

"Nawsuh. Ah wants t take it home wid me. Ah'll bring it back termorrow when Ah come in from the fiels."

"You plannin on buying something?"

"Yessuh."

"Your ma lettin you have your own money now?"

"Shucks. Mistah Joe, Ahm gittin t be a man like anybody else!"

Joe laughed and wiped his greasy white face with a red bandanna.

"Whut you plannin on buyin?"

Dave looked at the floor, scratched his head, scratched his thigh, and smiled. Then he looked up shyly.

"Ah'll tell yuh, Mistah Joe, ef yuh promise yuh won't tell."

"I promise."

"Waal, Ahma buy a gun."

"A gun? What you want with a gun?"

"Ah wanna keep it."

"You ain't nothing but a boy. You don't need a gun."

"Aw, lemme have the catlog, Mistah Joe. Ah'll bring it back."

Joe walked through the rear door. Dave was elated. He looked around at barrels of sugar and flour. He heard Joe coming back. He craned his neck to see if he were bringing the book. Yeah, he's got it. Gawddog, he's got it!

"Here, but be sure you bring it back. It's the only one I got."

"Sho, Mistah Joe."

"Say, if you wanna buy a gun, why don't you buy one from me? I gotta gun to sell."

"Will it shoot?"

"Sure it'll shoot."

"Whut kind is it?"

"Oh, it's kinda old . . . a left-hand Wheeler. A pistol. A big one."

"Is it got bullets in it?"

"It's loaded."

"Kin Ah see it?"

"Where's your money?"

"What yuh wan fer it?"

"I'll let you have it for two dollars."

"Just two dollahs? Shucks, Ah could buy tha when Ah git mah pay."

"I'll have it here when you want it."

"Awright, suh. Ah be in fer it."

He went through the door, hearing it slam again behind him. Ahma git some money from Ma n buy me a gun! Only two dollahs! He tucked the thick catalogue under his arm and hurried.

"Where yuh been, boy?" His mother held a steaming dish of black-eyed peas.

"Aw, Ma, Ah jus stopped down the road t talk wid the boys."

"Yuh know bettah t keep suppah waitin."

He sat down, resting the catalogue on the edge of the table.

"Yuh git up from there and git to the well n wash yosef! Ah ain feedin no hogs in mah house!"

She grabbed his shoulder and pushed him. He stumbled out of the room, then came back to get the catalogue.

"Whut this?"

"Aw, Ma, it's jusa catlog."

"Who yuh git it from?"

"From Joe, down at the sto."

"Waal, thas good. We kin use it in the outhouse."

"Naw, Ma." He grabbed for it. "Gimme ma catlog, Ma."

She held onto it and glared at him.

"Quit hollerin at me! Whut's wrong wid yuh? Yuh crazy?"

"But Ma, please. It ain mine! It's Joe's! He tol me t bring it back t im termorrow."

She gave up the book. He stumbled down the back steps, hugging the thick book under his arm. When he had splashed water on his face and hands, he groped back to the kitchen and fumbled in a corner for the towel. He bumped into a chair; it clattered to the floor. The catalogue sprawled at his feet. When he had dried his eyes he snatched up the book and held it again under his arm. His mother stood watching him.

"Now, ef yuh gonna act a fool over that ol book, Ah'll take it n burn it up."

"Naw, Ma, please."

"Waal, set down n be still!"

He sat down and drew the oil lamp close. He thumbed page after page, unaware of the food his mother set on the table. His father came in. Then his small brother.

"Whutcha got there, Dave?" his father asked.

"Jusa catlog," he answered, not looking up.

"Yeah, here they is!" His eyes glowed at blue-and-black revolvers. He glanced up, feeling sudden guilt. His father was watching him. He eased the book under the table and rested it on his knees. After the blessing was asked, he ate. He scooped up peas and swallowed fat meat without chewing. Buttermilk helped to wash it down. He did not want to mention money before his father. He would do much better by cornering his mother when she was alone. He looked at his father uneasily out of the edge of his eye.

"Boy, how come yuh don quit foolin wid tha book n eat yo suppah?"

"Yessuh."

"How you n ol man Hawkins gitten erlong?"

"Suh?"

"Can't yuh hear? Why don yuh lissen? Ah ast yu how wuz yuh n ol man Hawkins gittin erlong?"

"Oh, swell, Pa. Ah plows mo lan than anybody over there."

"Waal, yuh oughta keep you mind on whut yuh doin."

"Yessuh."

He poured his plate full of molasses and sopped it up slowly with a chunk of cornbread. When his father and brother had left the kitchen, he still sat and looked again at the guns in the catalogue, longing to muster courage enough to present his case to his mother. Lawd, ef Ah only had tha pretty one! He could almost feel the slickness of the weapon with his fingers. If he had a gun like that he would polish it and keep it shining so it would never rust. N Ah'd keep it loaded, by Gawd!

"Ma?" His voice was hesitant.

"Hunh?"

"Ol man Hawkins give yuh mah money yit?"

"Yeah, but ain no usa yuh thinking bout throwin nona it erway. Ahm keeping tha money sos yuh kin have cloes t go to school this winter."

He rose and went to her side with the open catalogue in his palms. She was washing dishes, her head bent low over a pan. Shyly he raised the book. When he spoke, his voice was husky, faint.

"Ma, Gawd knows Ah wans one of these."

"One of whut?" she asked, not raising her eyes.

"One of these," he said again, not daring even to point. She glanced up at the page, then at him with wide eyes.

"Nigger, is yuh gone plumb crazy?"

"Aw, Ma — "

"Git outta here! Don yuh talk t me bout no gun! Yuh a fool!"

"Ma, Ah kin buy one fer two dollahs."

"Not ef Ah knows it, yuh ain!"

"But yuh promised me one — "

"Ah don care what Ah promised! Yuh ain nothing but a boy yit!"

"Ma, ef yuh lemme buy one Ah'll *never* ast yuh fer nothing no mo."

"Ah tol yuh t git outta here! Yuh ain gonna toucha penny of tha money fer no gun! Thas how come Ah has Mistah Hawkins t pay yo wages t me, cause Ah knows yuh ain got no sense."

"But, Ma, we needa gun. Pa ain got no gun. We needa gun in the house. Yuh kin never tell whut might happen."

"Now don yuh try to maka fool outta me, boy! Ef we did hava gun, yuh wouldn't have it!"

He laid the catalogue down and slipped his arm around her waist.

"Aw, Ma, Ah done worked hard alla summer n ain ast yuh fer nothing, is Ah, now?"

"Thas whut yuh spose t do!"

"But Ma, Ah wans a gun. Yuh kin lemme have two dollahs outta mah money. Please, Ma. I kin give it to Pa. . . . Please, Ma! Ah loves yuh, Ma."

When she spoke her voice came soft and low.

"What yu wan wida gun, Dave? Yuh don need no gun. Yuh'll git in trouble. N ef yo pa jus thought Ah let yuh have money t buy a gun he'd hava fit."

"Ah'll hide it, Ma. It ain but two dollahs."

"Lawd, chil, whut's wrong wid yuh?"

"Ain nothin wrong. Ma. Ahm almos a man now. Ah wans a gun."

"Who gonna sell yuh a gun?"

"Ol Joe at the sto."

"N it don cos but two dollahs?"

"Thas all, Ma. Jus two dollahs. Please, Ma."

She was stacking the plates away; her hands moved slowly, reflectively. Dave kept an anxious silence. Finally, she turned to him.

"Ah'll let yuh git tha gun ef yuh promise me one thing."

"What's tha, Ma?"

"Yuh bring it straight back t me, yuh hear? It be fer Pa."

"Yessum! Lemme go now, Ma."

She stooped, turned slightly to one side, raised the hem of her dress, rolled down the top of her stocking, and came up with a slender wad of bills.

"Here," she said. "Lawd knows yuh don need no gun. But yer pa does. Yuh bring it right back t me, yuh hear? Ahma put it up. Now ef yuh don, Ahma have yuh pa lick yuh so hard yuh won fergit it."

"Yessum."

He took the money, ran down the steps, and across the yard.

"Dave! Yuuuuuh Daaaaave!"

He heard, but he was not going to stop now. "Naw, Lawd!"

The first movement he made the following morning was to reach under his pillow for the gun. In the gray light of dawn he held it loosely, feeling a sense of power. Could kill a man with a gun like this. Kill anybody, black or white. And if he were holding his gun in his hand, nobody could run over him; they would have to respect him. It was a big gun, with a long barrel and a heavy handle. He raised and lowered it in his hand, marveling at its weight.

He had not come straight home with it as his mother had asked; instead he had stayed out in the fields, holding the weapon in his hand, aiming it now and then at some imaginary foe. But he had not fired it; he had been afraid that his father might hear. Also he was not sure he knew how to fire it.

To avoid surrendering the pistol he had not come into the house until he knew that they were all asleep. When his mother had tiptoed to his bedside late that night and demanded the gun, he had first played possum; then he had told her that the gun was hidden outdoors, that he would bring it to her in the morning. Now he lay turning it slowly in his hands.

He broke it, took out the cartridges, felt them, and then put them back.

He slid out of bed, got a long strip of old flannel from a trunk, wrapped the gun in it, and tied it to his naked thigh while it was still loaded. He did not go in to breakfast. Even though it was not yet daylight, he started for Jim Hawkins' plantation. Just as the sun was rising he reached the barns where the mules and plows were kept.

"Hey! That you, Dave?"

He turned. Jim Hawkins stood eying him suspiciously.

"What're yuh doing here so early?"

"Ah didn't know Ah wuz gittin up so early, Mistah Hawkins. Ah was fixin t hitch up ol Jenny n take her t the fiels."

"Good. Since you're so early, how about plowing that stretch down by the woods?"

"Suits me, Mistah Hawkins."

"O.K. Go to it!"

He hitched Jenny to a plow and started across the fields. Hot dog! This was just what he wanted. If he could get down by the woods, he could shoot his gun and nobody would hear. He walked behind the plow, hearing the traces creaking, feeling the gun tied tight to his thigh.

When he reached the woods, he plowed two whole rows before he decided to take out the gun. Finally, he stopped, looked in all directions, then untied the gun and held it in his hand. He turned to the mule and smiled.

"Know whut this is, Jenny? Naw, yuh wouldn know! Yuhs jusa ol mule! Anyhow, this is a gun, n it kin shoot, by Gawd!"

He held the gun at arm's length. Whut t hell, Ahma shoot this thing! He looked at Jenny again.

"Lissen here, Jenny! When Ah pull this ol trigger, Ah don wan yuh t run n acka fool now!"

Jenny stood with head down, her short ears pricked straight. Dave walked off about twenty feet, held the gun far out from him at arm's length, and turned his head. Hell, he told himself, Ah ain afraid. The gun felt loose in his fingers; he waved it wildly for a moment. Then he shut his eyes and tightened his forefinger. Bloom! A report half deafened him and he thought his right hand was torn from his arm. He heard Jenny whinnying and galloping over the field, and he found himself on his knees, squeezing his fingers hard between his legs. His hand was numb; he jammed it into his mouth, trying to warm it, trying to stop the pain. The gun lay at his feet. He did not quite know what had happened. He stood up and stared at the gun as though it were a living thing. He gritted his teeth and kicked the gun. Yuh almos broke mah arm! He turned to look for Jenny; she was far over the fields, tossing her head and kicking wildly.

"Hol on there, ol mule!"

When he caught up with her she stood trembling, walling her big white eyes at him. The plow was far away; the traces had broken. Then

Dave stopped short, looking, not believing. Jenny was bleeding. Her left side was red and wet with blood. He went closer. Lawd, have mercy! Wondah did Ah shoot this mule? He grabbed for Jenny's mane. She flinched, snorted, whirled, tossing her head.

"Hol on now! Hol on."

Then he saw the hole in Jenny's side, right between the ribs. It was round, wet, red. A crimson stream streaked down the front leg, flowing fast. Good Gawd! Ah wuzn't shootin at tha mule. He felt panic. He knew he had to stop that blood, or Jenny would bleed to death. He had never seen so much blood in all his life. He chased the mule for half a mile, trying to catch her. Finally she stopped, breathing hard, stumpy tail half arched. He caught her mane and led her back to where the plow and gun lay. Then he stopped and grabbed handfuls of damp black earth and tried to plug the bullet hole. Jenny shuddered, whinnied, and broke from him.

"Hol on! Hol on now!"

He tried to plug it again, but blood came anyhow. His fingers were hot and sticky. He rubbed dirt into his palms, trying to dry them. Then again he attempted to plug the bullet hole, but Jenny shied away, kicking her heels high. He stood helpless. He had to do something. He ran at Jenny; she dodged him. He watched a red stream of blood flow down Jenny's leg and form a bright pool at her feet.

"Jenny . . . Jenny," he called weakly.

His lips trembled. She's bleeding t death! He looked in the direction of home, wanting to go back, wanting to get help. But he saw the pistol lying in the damp black clay. He had a queer feeling that if he only did something, this would not be; Jenny would not be there bleeding to death.

When he went to her this time, she did not move. She stood with sleepy, dreamy eyes; and when he touched her she gave a low-pitched whinny and knelt to the ground, her front knees slopping in blood.

"Jenny . . . Jenny . . . " he whispered.

For a long time she held her neck erect; then her head sank, slowly. Her ribs swelled with a mighty heave and she went over.

Dave's stomach felt empty, very empty. He picked up the gun and held it gingerly between his thumb and forefinger. He buried it at the foot of a tree. He took a stick and tried to cover the pool of blood with dirt — but what was the use? There was Jenny lying with her mouth open and her eyes walled and glassy. He could not tell Jim Hawkins he had shot his mule. But he had to tell something. Yeah, Ah'll tell em Jenny started gittin wil n fell on the joint of the plow. . . . But that would hardly happen to a mule. He walked across the field slowly, head down.

It was sunset. Two of Jim Hawkins' men were over near the edge of the woods digging a hole in which to bury Jenny. Dave was surrounded by a knot of people, all of whom were looking down at the dead mule.

"I don't see how in the world it happened," said Jim Hawkins for the tenth time.

The crowd parted and Dave's mother, father, and small brother pushed into the center.

"Where Dave?" his mother called.

"There he is," said Jim Hawkins.

His mother grabbed him.

"Whut happened, Dave? Whut yuh done?"

"Nothin."

"C mon, boy, talk," his father said.

Dave took a deep breath and told the story he knew nobody believed.

"Waal," he drawled. "Ah brung ol Jenny down here sos Ah could do mah plowin. Ah plowed bout two rows, just like yuh see." He stopped and pointed at the long rows of upturned earth. "Then somethin musta been wrong wid ol Jenny. She wouldn ack right a-tall. She started snortin n kickin her heels. Ah tried t hol her, but she pulled erway, rearin n goin in. Then when the point of the plow was stickin up in the air, she swung erroun n twisted herself back on it. . . . She stuck herself n started t bleed. N fo Ah could do anything, she wuz dead."

"Did you ever hear of anything like that in all your life?" asked Jim Hawkins.

There were white and black standing in the crowd. They murmured. Dave's mother came close to him and looked hard into his face. "Tell the truth, Dave," she said.

"Looks like a bullet hole to me," said one man.

"Dave, whut yuh do wid the gun?" his mother asked.

The crowd surged in, looking at him. He jammed his hands into his pockets, shook his head slowly from left to right, and backed away. His eyes were wide and painful.

"Did he hava gun?" asked Jim Hawkins.

"By Gawd, Ah tol yuh tha wuz a gun wound," said a man, slapping his thigh.

His father caught his shoulders and shook him till his teeth rattled. "Tell whut happened, yuh rascal! Tell whut. . . . "

Dave looked at Jenny's stiff legs and began to cry.

"Whut yuh do wid tha gun?" his mother asked.

"What wuz he doin wida gun?" his father asked.

"Come on and tell the truth," said Hawkins. "Ain't nobody going to hurt you. . . . "

His mother crowded close to him.

"Did yuh shoot tha mule, Dave?"

Dave cried, seeing blurred white and black faces.

"Ahh ddinn gggo tt sshooot hher. . . . Ah ssswear ffo Gawd Ahh ddin. . . . Ah wuz a-tryin t sssee ef the old gggun would sshoot — "

"Where yuh git the gun from?" his father asked.

"Ah got it from Joe, at the sto."

"Where yuh git the money?"

"Ma give it t me."

"He kept worryin me, Bob. Ah had t. Ah tol im t bring the gun right back t me. . . . It was fer yuh, the gun."

"But how yuh happen to shoot that mule?" asked Jim Hawkins.

"Ah wuzn shootin at the mule, Mistah Hawkins. The gun jumped when Ah pulled the trigger. . . . N fo Ah knowed anythin Jenny was there a-bleedin."

Somebody in the crowd laughed. Jim Hawkins walked close to Dave and looked into his face.

"Well, looks like you have bought you a mule, Dave."

"Ah swear fo Gawd, Ah didn go t kill the mule, Mistah Hawkins!"

"But you killed her!"

All the crowd was laughing now. They stood on tiptoe and poked heads over one another's shoulders.

"Well, boy, looks like yuh done bought a dead mule! Hahaha!"

"Ain tha ershame."

"Hohohohoho."

Dave stood, head down, twisting his feet in the dirt.

"Well, you needn't worry about it, Bob," said Jim Hawkins to Dave's father. "Just let the boy keep on working and pay me two dollars a month."

"Whut yuh wan fer yo mule, Mistah Hawkins?"

Jim Hawkins screwed up his eyes.

"Fifty dollars."

"Whut yuh do wid tha gun?" Dave's father demanded.

Dave said nothing.

"Yuh wan me t take a tree n beat yuh till yuh talk!"

"Nawsuh!"

"Whut yuh do wid it?"

"Ah throwed it erway."

"Where?"

"Ah . . . Ah throwed it in the creek."

"Waal, c mon home. N firs thing in the mawnin git to tha creek n fin tha gun."

"Yessuh."

"Whut yuh pay fer it?"

"Two dollahs."

"Take tha gun n git yo money back n carry it to Mistah Hawkins, yuh hear? N don fergit Ahma lam you black bottom good fer this! Now march yosef on home, suh!"

Dave turned and walked slowly. He heard people laughing. Dave glared, his eyes welling with tears. Hot anger bubbled in him. Then he swallowed and stumbled on.

That night Dave did not sleep. He was glad that he had gotten out of killing the mule so easily, but he was hurt. Something hot seemed to turn over inside him each time he remembered how they had laughed. He tossed on his bed, feeling his hard pillow. N Pa says he's gonna beat me. . . . He remembered other beatings, and his back quivered. Naw, naw, Ah sho don wan im t beat me tha way no mo. Dam em all! Nobody ever gave him anything. All he did was work. They treat me like a mule, n then they beat me. He gritted his teeth. N Ma had t tell on me.

Well, if he had to, he would take old man Hawkins that two dollars. But that meant selling the gun. And he wanted to keep that gun. Fifty dollars for a dead mule.

He turned over, thinking how he had fired the gun. He had an itch to fire it again. Ef other men kin shoota gun, by Gawd, Ah kin! He was still, listening. Mebbe they all sleepin now. The house was still. He heard the soft breathing of his brother. Yes, now! He would go down and get that gun and see if he could fire it! He eased out of bed and slipped into overalls.

The moon was bright. He ran almost all the way to the edge of the woods. He stumbled over the ground, looking for the spot where he had buried the gun. Yeah, here it is. Like a hungry dog scratching for a bone, he pawed it up. He puffed his black cheeks and blew dirt from the trigger and barrel. He broke it and found four cartridges unshot. He looked around; the fields were filled with silence and moonlight. He clutched the gun stiff and hard in his fingers. But, as soon as he wanted to pull the trigger, he shut his eyes and turned his head. Naw, Ah can't shoot wid mah eyes closed n mah head turned. With effort he held his eyes open; then he squeezed. *Blooooom!* He was stiff, not breathing. The gun was still in his hands. Dammit, he'd done it! He fired again. *Blooooom!* He smiled. *Blooooom! Blooooom! Click, click.* There! It was empty. If anybody could shoot a gun, he could. He put the gun into his hip pocket and started across the fields.

When he reached the top of a ridge he stood straight and proud in the moonlight, looking at Jim Hawkins' big white house, feeling the gun sagging in his pocket. Lawd, ef Ah had just one mo bullet Ah'd taka shot at tha house. Ah'd like t scare ol man Hawkins jusa little. . . . Jusa enough t let im know Dave Saunders is a man.

To his left the road curved, running to the tracks of the Illinois Central. He jerked his head, listening. From far off came a faint *hoooof-hoooof; hoooof-hoooof.* . . . He stood rigid. Two dollahs a mont. Les see now. . . . Tha means it'll take bout two years. Shucks! Ah'll be dam!

He started down the road, toward the tracks. Yeah, here she comes! He stood beside the track and held himself stiffly. Here she comes, erroun the ben. . . . C mon, yuh slow poke! C mon! He had his hand on his gun; something quivered in his stomach. Then the train thundered past, the gray and brown box cars rumbling and clinking. He gripped the gun tightly; then he jerked his hand out of his pocket. Ah betcha Bill wouldn't do it! Ah betcha. . . . The cars slid past, steel grinding upon steel. Ahm ridin yuh ter-night, so hep me Gawd! He was hot all over. He hesitated just a moment; then he grabbed, pulled atop of a car, and lay flat. He felt his pocket; the gun was still there. Ahead the long rails were glinting in the moonlight, stretching away, away to somewhere, somewhere where he could be a man. . . .

[1961]

EUDORA WELTY (b. 1909) was born in Jackson, Mississippi, where she has spent nearly her whole life. She has a predominately tranquil view of the South, so her stories and novels provide a strong contrast to the turbulent fiction of William Faulkner and Richard Wright, whose geographical terrain somewhat overlaps hers. Welty grew up as one of three children in a close-knit family living two blocks away from the Mississippi state capitol. Her father was the president of an insurance company, and her mother was a thrifty housewife who kept a Jersey cow in a little pasture behind the backyard. Welty regards her personal history as hardly worth mentioning. An insatiable reader as a child, she was also a born writer. She began writing spontaneously and continued, without any particular encouragement or any plan for a profession as a writer, during her years at the Mississippi State College for Women, the University of Wisconsin, and the Columbia University School of Business. In her mid-twenties she began to publish stories in The Southern Review, but she credits the persistence of her New York agent Diarmuid Russell with helping her get a story published in a general-circulation magazine, The Atlantic Monthly, in 1941. This event led directly to the publication of her first book of stories, A Curtain of Green, the same year, when she was a writer "hardly known, true, but in print." During World War II she was a staff member of The New York Times Book Review while she lived at home with her mother and continued to write short fiction. Another collection was published in 1943 as The Wide Net and Other Stories. After leaving her newspaper work, she turned a short story into her first novel, Delta Wedding (1946), on the advice of her agent. She has produced other story collections over the years: The Golden Apples (1949), The Bride of the Innisfallen and Other Stories (1955), and Thirteen Stories (1965). Her novel The Optimist's Daughter won the Pulitzer Prize in 1972. In 1980 The Collected Stories of Eudora Welty appeared, forty-one stories in all. Welty is also a fine critic of the short story. Her essays and reviews of the work of writers like Chekhov, Cather, Porter, Woolf, and Dinesen, as well as some comments on her own work, were collected in The Eye of the Story (1977). Eight years later the book Conversations with Eudora Welty was a best-seller.

In the preface to her collected stories, Welty stated, "I have been told, both in approval and in accusation, that I seem to love all my characters. What I do in writing of any character is to try to enter into the mind, heart, and skin of a human being who is not myself. Whether this happens to be a man or a woman, old or young, with skin black or white, the primary challenge lies in making the jump itself. It is the act of a writer's imagination that I set most high." Although her fiction contains occasional sharp glances at southern people, as in "Lily Daw and the Three Ladies," her usual manner is a calm celebration of the minor victories of her characters,

*in narratives that have some of the willed simplicity of folk tales, catching
the accent, intonation, and rhythms of southern speech with apparent effortlessness.*

*As Katherine Anne Porter recognized in her introduction to A Curtain
of Green, "A Worn Path" is a story "where external act and the internal
voiceless life of the human imagination almost meet and mingle on the
mysterious threshold between dream and waking, one reality refusing to
admit or confirm the existence of the other, yet both conspiring toward the
same end." (See Welty's Commentary about "A Worn Path" on page
1301.)*

Eudora Welty

ୡୡ

Lily Daw and the Three Ladies

Mrs. Watts and Mrs. Carson were both in the post office in Victory
when the letter came from the Ellisville Institute for the Feeble-Minded of
Mississippi. Aimee Slocum, with her hand still full of mail, ran out in front
and handed it straight to Mrs. Watts, and they all three read it together.
Mrs. Watts held it taut between her pink hands, and Mrs. Carson underscored each line slowly with her thimbled finger. Everybody else in the post
office wondered what was up now.

"What will Lily say," beamed Mrs. Carson at last, "when we tell her
we're sending her to Ellisville!"

"She'll be tickled to death," said Mrs. Watts, and added in a guttural
voice to a deaf lady, "Lily Daw's getting in at Ellisville!"

"Don't you all dare go off and tell Lily without me!" called Aimee
Slocum, trotting back to finish putting up the mail.

"Do you suppose they'll look after her down there?" Mrs. Carson
began to carry on a conversation with a group of Baptist ladies waiting in
the post office. She was the Baptist preacher's wife.

"I've always heard it was lovely down there, but crowded," said one.

"Lily lets people walk over her so," said another.

"Last night at the tent show — " said another, and then popped her
hand over her mouth.

"Don't mind me, I know there are such things in the world," said Mrs.
Carson, looking down and fingering the tape measure which hung over her
bosom.

"Oh, Mrs. Carson. Well, anyway, last night at the tent show, why, the
man was just before making Lily buy a ticket to get in."

"A ticket!"

"Till my husband went up and explained she wasn't bright, and so did everybody else."

The ladies all clucked their tongues.

"Oh, it was a very nice show," said the lady who had gone. "And Lily acted so nice. She was a perfect lady — just set in her seat and stared."

"Oh, she can be a lady — she can be," said Mrs. Carson, shaking her head and turning her eyes up. "That's just what breaks your heart."

"Yes'm, she kept her eyes on — what's that thing makes all the commotion? — the xylophone," said the lady. "Didn't turn her head to the right or to the left the whole time. Set in front of me."

"The point is, what did she do after the show?" asked Mrs. Watts practically. "Lily has gotten so she is very mature for her age."

"Oh, Etta!" protested Mrs. Carson, looking at her wildly for a moment.

"And that's how come we are sending her to Ellisville," finished Mrs. Watts.

"I'm ready, you all," said Aimee Slocum, running out with white powder all over her face. "Mail's up. I don't know how good it's up."

"Well, of course, I do hope it's for the best," said several of the other ladies. They did not go at once to take their mail out of their boxes; they felt a little left out.

The three women stood at the foot of the water tank.

"To find Lily is a different thing," said Aimee Slocum.

"Where in the wide world do you suppose she'd be?" It was Mrs. Watts who was carrying the letter.

"I don't see a sign of her either on this side of the street or on the other side," Mrs. Carson declared as they walked along.

Ed Newton was stringing Redbird school tablets on the wire across the store.

"If you're after Lily, she come in here while ago and tole me she was fixin' to get married," he said.

"Ed Newton!" cried the ladies all together, clutching one another. Mrs. Watts began to fan herself at once with the letter from Ellisville. She wore widow's black, and the least thing made her hot.

"Why she is not. She's going to Ellisville, Ed," said Mrs. Carson gently. "Mrs. Watts and I and Aimee Slocum are paying her way out of our own pockets. Besides, the boys of Victory are on their honor. Lily's not going to get married, that's just an idea she's got in her head."

"More power to you, ladies," said Ed Newton, spanking himself with a tablet.

When they came to the bridge over the railroad tracks, there was Estelle Mabers, sitting on a rail. She was slowly drinking an orange Ne-Hi.

"Have you seen Lily?" they asked her.

"I'm supposed to be out here watching for her now," said the Mabers girl, as though she weren't there yet. "But for Jewel — Jewel says Lily came in the store while ago and picked out a two-ninety-eight hat and wore it off. Jewel wants to swap her something else for it."

"Oh, Estelle, Lily says she's going to get married!" cried Aimee Slocum.

"Well, I declare," said Estelle; she never understood anything.

Loralee Adkins came riding by in her Willys-Knight, tooting the horn to find out what they were talking about.

Aimee threw up her hands and ran out into the street. "Loralee, Loralee, you got to ride us up to Lily Daws'. She's up yonder fixing to get married!"

"Hop in, my land!"

"Well, that just goes to show you right now," said Mrs. Watts, groaning as she was helped into the back seat. "What we've got to do is persuade Lily it will be nicer to go to Ellisville."

"Just to think!"

While they rode around the corner Mrs. Carson was going on in her sad voice, sad as the soft noises in the hen house at twilight. "We buried Lily's poor defenseless mother. We gave Lily all her food and kindling and every stitch she had on. Sent her to Sunday school to learn the Lord's teachings, had her baptized a Baptist. And when her old father commenced beating her and tried to cut her head off with the butcher knife, why, we went and took her away from him and gave her a place to stay."

The paintless frame house with all the weather vanes was three stories high in places and had yellow and violet stained-glass windows in front and gingerbread around the porch. It leaned steeply to one side, toward the railroad, and the front steps were gone. The car full of ladies drew up under the cedar tree.

"Now Lily's almost grown up," Mrs. Carson continued. "In fact, she's grown," she concluded, getting out.

"Talking about getting married," said Mrs. Watts disgustedly. "Thanks, Loralee, you run on home."

They climbed over the dusty zinnias onto the porch and walked through the open door without knocking.

"There certainly is always a funny smell in this house. I say it every time I come," said Aimee Slocum.

Lily was there, in the dark of the hall, kneeling on the floor by a small open trunk.

When she saw them she put a zinnia in her mouth, and held still.

"Hello, Lily," said Mrs. Carson reproachfully.

"Hello," said Lily. In a minute she gave a suck on the zinnia stem, that sounded exactly like a jay bird. There she sat, wearing a petticoat for a dress, one of the things Mrs. Carson kept after her about. Her milky-yellow hair streamed freely down from under a new hat. You could see the wavy scar on her throat if you knew it was there.

Mrs. Carson and Mrs. Watts, the two fattest, sat in the double rocker. Aimee Slocum sat on the wire chair donated from the drugstore that burned.

"Well, what are you doing, Lily?" asked Mrs. Watts, who led the rocking.

Lily smiled.

The trunk was old and lined with yellow and brown paper, with an asterisk pattern showing in darker circles and rings. Mutely the ladies indicated to each other that they did not know where in the world it had come from. It was empty except for two bars of soap and a green washcloth, which Lily was now trying to arrange in the bottom.

"Go on and tell us what you're doing, Lily," said Aimee Slocum.

"Packing, silly," said Lily.

"Where are you going?"

"Going to get married, and I bet you wish you was me now," said Lily. But shyness overcame her suddenly, and she popped the zinnia back into her mouth.

"Talk to me, dear," said Mrs. Carson. "Tell old Mrs. Carson why you want to get married."

"No," said Lily, after a moment's hesitation.

"Well, we've thought of something that will be so much nicer," said Mrs. Carson. "Why don't you go to Ellisville!"

"Won't that be lovely?" said Mrs. Watts. "Goodness, yes."

"It's a lovely place," said Aimee Slocum uncertainly.

"You've got bumps on your face," said Lily.

"Aimee, dear, you stay out of this, if you don't mind," said Mrs. Carson anxiously. "I don't know what it is comes over Lily when you come around her."

Lily stared at Aimee Slocum meditatively.

"There! Wouldn't you like to go to Ellisville now?" asked Mrs. Carson.

"No'm," said Lily.

"Why not?" All the ladies leaned down toward her in impressive astonishment.

" 'Cause I'm goin' to get married," said Lily.

"Well, and who are you going to marry, dear?" asked Mrs. Watts. She knew how to pin people down and make them deny what they'd already said.

Lily bit her lip and began to smile. She reached into the trunk and held up both cakes of soap and wagged them.

"Tell us," challenged Mrs. Watts. "Who you're going to marry, now."

"A man last night."

There was a gasp from each lady. The possible reality of a lover descended suddenly like a summer hail over their heads. Mrs. Watts stood up and balanced herself.

"One of those show fellows! A musician!" she cried.

Lily looked up in admiration.

"Did he — did he do anything to you?" In the long run, it was still only Mrs. Watts who could take charge.

"Oh, yes'm," said Lily. She patted the cakes of soap fastidiously with the tips of her small fingers and tucked them in with the washcloth.

"What?" demanded Aimee Slocum, rising up and tottering before her scream. "What?" she called out in the hall.

"Don't ask her what," said Mrs. Carson, coming up behind. "Tell me, Lily — just yes or no — are you the same as you were?"

"He had a red coat," said Lily graciously. "He took little sticks and went *ping-pong! ding-dong!*"

"Oh, I think I'm going to faint," said Aimee Slocum, but they said, "No, you're not."

"The xylophone!" cried Mrs. Watts. "The xylophone player! Why, the coward, he ought to be run out of town on a rail!"

"Out of town? He is out of town, by now," cried Aimee. "Can't you read? — the sign in the café — Victory on the ninth, Como on the tenth? He's in Como. Como!"

"All right! We'll bring him back!" cried Mrs. Watts. "He can't get away from me!"

"Hush," said Mrs. Carson. "I don't think it's any use following that line of reasoning at all. It's better in the long run for him to be gone out of our lives for good and all. That kind of man. He was after Lily's body alone and he wouldn't ever in this world make the poor little thing happy, even if we went out and forced him to marry her like he ought — at the point of a gun."

"Still — " began Aimee, her eyes widening.

"Shut up," said Mrs. Watts. "Mrs. Carson, you're right, I expect."

"This is my hope chest — see?" said Lily politely in the pause that followed. "You haven't even looked at it. I've already got soap and a washrag. And I have my hat — on. What are you all going to give me?"

"Lily," said Mrs. Watts, starting over, "we'll give you lots of gorgeous things if you'll only go to Ellisville instead of getting married."

"What will you give me?" asked Lily.

"I'll give you a pair of hemstitched pillowcases," said Mrs. Carson.

"I'll give you a big caramel cake," said Mrs. Watts.

"I'll give you a souvenir from Jackson — a little toy bank," said Aimee Slocum. "Now will you go?"

"No," said Lily.

"I'll give you a pretty little Bible with your name on it in real gold," said Mrs. Carson.

"What if I was to give you a pink crêpe de Chine brassière with adjustable shoulder straps?" asked Mrs. Watts grimly.

"Oh, Etta."

"Well, she needs it," said Mrs. Watts. "What would they think if she ran all over Ellisville in a petticoat looking like a Fiji?"

"I wish *I* could go to Ellisville," said Aimee Slocum luringly.

"What will they have for me down there?" asked Lily softly.

"Oh! lots of things. You'll have baskets to weave, I expect . . ." Mrs. Carson looked vaguely at the others.

"Oh, yes indeed, they will let you make all sorts of baskets," said Mrs. Watts; then her voice too trailed off.

"No'm, I'd rather get married," said Lily.

"Lily Daw! Now that's just plain stubbornness!" cried Mrs. Watts. "You almost said you'd go and then you took it back!"

"We've all asked God, Lily," said Mrs. Carson finally, "and God seemed to tell us — Mr. Carson, too — that the place where you ought to be, so as to be happy, was Ellisville."

Lily looked reverent, but still stubborn.

"We've really just got to get her there — now!" screamed Aimee Slocum all at once. "Suppose — ! She can't stay here!"

"Oh, no, no, no," said Mrs. Carson hurriedly. "We mustn't think that."

They sat sunken in despair.

"Could I take my hope chest — to go to Ellisville?" asked Lily shyly, looking at them sidewise.

"Why, yes," said Mrs. Carson blankly.

Silently they rose once more to their feet.

"Oh, if I could just take my hope chest!"

"All the time it was just her hope chest," Aimee whispered.

Mrs. Watts struck her palms together. "It's settled!"

"Praise the fathers," murmured Mrs. Carson.

Lily looked up at them, and her eyes gleamed. She cocked her head and spoke out in a proud imitation of someone — someone utterly unknown.

"O.K. — Toots!"

The ladies had been nodding and smiling and backing away toward the door.

"I think I'd better stay," said Mrs. Carson, stopping in her tracks. "Where — where could she have learned that terrible expression?"

"Pack up," said Mrs. Watts. "Lily Daw is leaving for Ellisville on Number One."

In the station the train was puffing. Nearly everyone in Victory was hanging around waiting for it to leave. The Victory Civic Band had assembled without any orders and was scattered through the crowd. Ed Newton gave false signals to start on his bass horn. A crate full of baby chickens got loose on the platform. Everybody wanted to see Lily all dressed up, but Mrs. Carson and Mrs. Watts had sneaked her into the train from the other side of the tracks.

The two ladies were going to travel as far as Jackson to help Lily change trains and be sure she went in the right direction.

Lily sat between them on the plush seat with her hair combed and pinned up into a knot under a small blue hat which was Jewel's exchange for the pretty one. She wore a traveling dress made out of part of Mrs. Watt's last summer's mourning. Pink straps glowed through. She had a purse and a Bible and a warm cake in a box, all in her lap.

Aimee Slocum had been getting the outgoing mail stamped and bundled. She stood in the aisle of the coach now, tears shaking from her eyes. "Good-bye, Lily," she said. She was the one who felt things.

"Good-bye, silly," said Lily.

"Oh, dear, I hope they get our telegram to meet her in Ellisville!" Aimee cried sorrowfully, as she thought how far away it was. "And it was so hard to get it all in ten words, too."

"Get off, Aimee, before the train starts and you break your neck," said Mrs. Watts, all settled and waving her dressy fan gaily. "I declare, it's so hot, as soon as we get a few miles out of town I'm going to slip my corset down."

"Oh, Lily, don't cry down there. Just be good, and do what they tell you — it's all because they love you." Aimee drew her mouth down. She was backing away, down the aisle.

Lily laughed. She pointed across Mrs. Carson's bosom out the window toward a man. He had stepped off the train and just stood there, by himself. He was a stranger and wore a cap.

"Look," she said, laughing softly through her fingers.

"Don't — look," said Mrs. Carson very distinctly, as if, out of all she had ever spoken, she would impress these two solemn words upon Lily's soft little brain. She added, "Don't look at anything till you get to Ellisville."

Outside, Aimee Slocum was crying so hard she almost ran into the stranger. He wore a cap and was short and seemed to have on perfume, if such a thing could be.

"Could you tell me, madam," he said, "where a little lady lives in this burg name of Miss Lily Daw?" He lifted his cap — and he had red hair.

"What do you want to know for?" Aimee asked before she knew it.

"Talk louder," said the stranger. He almost whispered, himself.

"She's gone away — she's gone to Ellisville!"

"Gone?"

"Gone to Ellisville!"

"Well, I like that!" The man stuck out his bottom lip and puffed till his hair jumped.

"What business did you have with Lily?" cried Aimee suddenly.

"We was only going to get married, that's all," said the man.

Aimee Slocum started to scream in front of all those people. She almost pointed to the long black box she saw lying on the ground at the man's feet. Then she jumped back in fright.

"The xylophone! The xylophone!" she cried, looking back and forth from the man to the hissing train. Which was more terrible? The bell began to ring hollowly, and the man was talking.

"Did you say Ellisville? That in the state of Mississippi?" Like light-

ning he had pulled out a red notebook entitled, "Permanent Facts &
Data." He wrote down something. "I don't hear well."

Aimee nodded her head up and down, and circled around him.

Under "Ellis-Ville Miss" he was drawing a line; now he was flicking it
with two little marks. "Maybe she didn't say she would. Maybe she said she
wouldn't." He suddenly laughed very loudly, after the way he had whispered. Aimee jumped back. "Women! — Well, if we play anywheres near
Ellisville, Miss., in the future I may look her up and I may not," he said.

The bass horn sounded the true signal for the band to begin. White
steam rushed out of the engine. Usually the train stopped for only a minute
in Victory, but the engineer knew Lily from waving at her, and he knew this
was her big day.

"Wait!" Aimee Slocum did scream. "Wait, mister! I can get her for
you. Wait, Mister Engineer! Don't go!"

Then there she was back on the train, screaming in Mrs. Carson's and
Mrs. Watts's faces.

"The xylophone player! The xylophone player to marry her! Yonder
he is!"

"Nonsense," murmured Mrs. Watts, peering over the others to look
where Aimee pointed. "If he's there I don't see him. Where is he? You're
looking at One-Eye Beasley."

"The little man with the cap — no, with the red hair! Hurry!"

"Is that really him?" Mrs. Carson asked Mrs. Watts in wonder.
"Mercy! He's small, isn't he?"

"Never saw him before in my life!" cried Mrs. Watts. But suddenly
she shut up her fan.

"Come on! This is a train we're on!" cried Aimee Slocum. Her nerves
were all unstrung.

"All right, don't have a conniption fit, girl," said Mrs. Watts. "Come
on," she said thickly to Mrs. Carson.

"Where are we going now?" asked Lily as they struggled down the
aisle.

"We're taking you to get married," said Mrs. Watts. "Mrs. Carson,
you'd better phone up your husband right there in the station."

"But I don't want to git married," said Lily, beginning to whimper.
"I'm going to Ellisville."

"Hush, and we'll all have some ice-cream cones later," whispered Mrs.
Carson.

Just as they climbed down the steps at the back end of the train, the
band went into "Independence March."

The xylophone player was still there, patting his foot. He came up and
said, "Hello, Toots. What's up — tricks?" and kissed Lily with a smack,
after which she hung her head.

"So you're the young man we've heard so much about," said Mrs.
Watts. Her smile was brilliant. "Here's your little Lily."

"What say?" asked the xylophone player.

"My husband happens to be the Baptist preacher of Victory," said

Mrs. Carson in a loud, clear voice. "Isn't that lucky? I can get him here in five minutes: I know exactly where he is."

They were all in a circle around the xylophone player, all going into the white waiting room.

"Oh, I feel just like crying, at a time like this," said Aimee Slocum. She looked back and saw the train moving slowly away, going under the bridge at Main Street. Then it disappeared around the curve.

"Oh, the hope chest!" Aimee cried in a stricken voice.

"And whom have we the pleasure of addressing?" Mrs. Watts was shouting, while Mrs. Carson was ringing up the telephone.

The band went on playing. Some of the people thought Lily was on the train, and some swore she wasn't. Everybody cheered, though, and a straw hat was thrown into the telephone wires.

[1941]

Eudora Welty

ဢ

A WORN PATH

It was December — a bright frozen day in the early morning. Far out in the country there was an old Negro woman with her head tied in a red rag, coming along a path through the pinewoods. Her name was Phoenix Jackson. She was very old and small and she walked slowly in the dark pine shadows, moving a little from side to side in her steps, with the balanced heaviness and lightness of a pendulum in a grandfather clock. She carried a thin, small cane made from an umbrella, and with this she kept tapping the frozen earth in front of her. This made a grave and persistent noise in the still air, that seemed meditative like the chirping of a solitary little bird.

She wore a dark striped dress reaching down to her shoe tops, and an equally long apron of bleached sugar sacks, with a full pocket: all neat and tidy, but every time she took a step she might have fallen over her shoelaces, which dragged from her unlaced shoes. She looked straight ahead. Her eyes were blue with age. Her skin had a pattern all its own of numberless branching wrinkles and as though a whole little tree stood in the middle of her forehead, but a golden color ran underneath, and the two knobs of her cheeks were illumined by a yellow burning under the dark. Under the red rag her hair came down on her neck in the frailest of ringlets, still black, and with an odor like copper.

Now and then there was a quivering in the thicket. Old Phoenix said, "Out of my way, all you foxes, owls, beetles, jack rabbits, coons and wild animals! . . . Keep out from under these feet, little bobwhites. . . . Keep the big wild hogs out of my path. Don't let none of those come running my direction. I got a long way." Under her small black-freckled hand her cane, limber as a buggy whip, would switch at the brush as if to rouse up any hiding things.

On she went. The woods were deep and still. The sun made the pine needles almost too bright to look at, up where the wind rocked. The cones dropped as light as feathers. Down in the hollow was the mourning dove — it was not too late for him.

The path ran up a hill. "Seem like there is chains about my feet, time I get this far," she said, in the voice of argument old people keep to use with themselves. "Something always take a hold of me on this hill — pleads I should stay."

After she got to the top she turned and gave a full, severe look behind her where she had come. "Up through pines," she said at length. "Now down through oaks."

Her eyes opened their widest, and she started down gently. But before she got to the bottom of the hill a bush caught her dress.

Her fingers were busy and intent, but her skirts were full and long, so that before she could pull them free in one place they were caught in another. It was not possible to allow the dress to tear. "I in the thorny bush," she said. "Thorns, you doing your appointed work. Never want to let folks pass, no sir. Old eyes thought you was a pretty little *green* bush."

Finally, trembling all over, she stood free, and after a moment dared to stoop for her cane.

"Sun so high!" she cried, leaning back and looking, while the thick tears went over her eyes. "The time getting all gone here."

At the foot of this hill was a place where a log was laid across the creek.

"Now comes the trial," said Phoenix.

Putting her right foot out, she mounted the log and shut her eyes. Lifting her skirt, leveling her cane fiercely before her, like a festival figure in some parade, she began to march across. Then she opened her eyes and she was safe on the other side.

"I wasn't as old as I thought," she said.

But she sat down to rest. She spread her skirts on the bank around her and folded her hands over her knees. Up above her was a tree in a pearly cloud of mistletoe. She did not dare to close her eyes, and when a little boy brought her a plate with a slice of marble-cake on it she spoke to him. "That would be acceptable," she said. But when she went to take it there was just her own hand in the air.

So she left that tree, and had to go through a barbed-wire fence. There she had to creep and crawl, spreading her knees and stretching her fingers like a baby trying to climb the steps. But she talked loudly to herself: she could not let her dress be torn now, so late in the day, and she could not pay for having her arm or her leg sawed off if she got caught fast where she was.

At last she was safe through the fence and risen up out in the clearing.

Big dead trees, like black men with one arm, were standing in the purple stalks of the withered cotton field. There sat a buzzard.

"Who you watching?"

In the furrow she made her way along.

"Glad this not the season for bulls," she said, looking sideways, "and the good Lord made his snakes to curl up and sleep in the winter. A pleasure I don't see no two-headed snake coming around that tree, where it come once. It took a while to get by him, back in the summer."

She passed through the old cotton and went into a field of dead corn. It whispered and shook and was taller than her head. "Through the maze now," she said, for there was no path.

Then there was something tall, black, and skinny there, moving before her.

At first she took it for a man. It could have been a man dancing in the field. But she stood still and listened, and it did not make a sound. It was as silent as a ghost.

"Ghost," she said sharply, "who be you the ghost of? For I have heard of nary death close by."

But there was no answer — only the ragged dancing in the wind.

She shut her eyes, reached out her hand, and touched a sleeve. She found a coat and inside that an emptiness, cold as ice.

"You scarecrow," she said. Her face lighted. "I ought to be shut up for good," she said with laughter. "My senses is gone. I too old. I the oldest people I ever know. Dance, old scarecrow," she said, "while I dancing with you."

She kicked her foot over the furrow, and with mouth drawn down, shook her head once or twice in a little strutting way. Some husks blew down and whirled in streamers about her skirts.

Then she went on, parting her way from side to side with the cane, through the whispering field. At last she came to the end, to a wagon track where the silver grass blew between the red ruts. The quail were walking around like pullets, seeming all dainty and unseen.

"Walk pretty," she said. "This the easy place. This the easy going."

She followed the track, swaying through the quiet bare fields, through the little strings of trees silver in their dead leaves, past cabins silver from weather, with the doors and windows boarded shut, all like old women under a spell sitting there. "I walking in their sleep," she said, nodding her head vigorously.

In a ravine she went where a spring was silently flowing through a hollow log. Old Phoenix bent and drank. "Sweet-gum makes the water sweet," she said, and drank more. "Nobody know who made this well, for it was here when I was born."

The track crossed a swampy part where the moss hung as white as lace from every limb. "Sleep on, alligators, and blow your bubbles." Then the track went into the road.

Deep, deep the road went down between the high green-colored banks. Overhead the live-oaks met, and it was as dark as a cave.

A black dog with a lolling tongue came up out of the weeds by the ditch. She was meditating, and not ready, and when he came at her she only hit him a little with her cane. Over she went in the ditch, like a little puff of milkweed.

Down there, her senses drifted away. A dream visited her, and she reached her hand up, but nothing reached down and gave her a pull. So she lay there and presently went to talking. "Old woman," she said to herself, "that black dog come up out of the weeds to stall you off, and now there he sitting on his fine tail, smiling at you."

A white man finally came along and found her — a hunter, a young man, with his dog on a chain.

"Well, Granny!" he laughed. "What are you doing there?"

"Lying on my back like a June-bug waiting to be turned over, mister," she said, reaching up her hand.

He lifted her up, gave her a swing in the air, and set her down. "Anything broken, Granny?"

"No sir, them old dead weeds is springy enough," said Phoenix, when she had got her breath. "I thank you for your trouble."

"Where do you live, Granny?" he asked, while the two dogs were growling at each other.

"Away back yonder, sir, behind the ridge. You can't even see it from here."

"On your way home?"

"No sir, I going to town."

"Why, that's too far! That's as far as I walk when I come out myself, and I get something for my trouble." He patted the stuffed bag he carried, and there hung down a little closed claw. It was one of the bobwhites, with its beak hooked bitterly to show it was dead. "Now you go on home, Granny!"

"I bound to go to town, mister," said Phoenix. "The time come around."

He gave another laugh, filling the whole landscape. "I know you old colored people! Wouldn't miss going to town to see Santa Claus!"

But something held old Phoenix very still. The deep lines in her face went into a fierce and different radiation. Without warning, she had seen with her own eyes a flashing nickel fall out of the man's pocket onto the ground.

"How old are you, Granny?" he was saying.

"There is no telling, mister," she said, "no telling."

Then she gave a little cry and clapped her hands and said, "Git on away from here, dog! Look! Look at that dog!" She laughed as if in admiration. "He ain't scared of nobody. He a big black dog." She whispered, "Sic him!"

"Watch me get rid of that cur," said the man. "Sic him, Pete! Sic him!"

Phoenix heard the dogs fighting, and heard the man running and throwing sticks. She even heard a gunshot. But she was slowly bending forward by that time, further and further forward, the lid stretched down over her eyes, as if she were doing this in her sleep. Her chin was lowered almost to her knees. The yellow palm of her hand came out from the fold of her apron. Her fingers slid down and along the ground under the piece of money with the grace and care they would have in lifting an egg from under a setting hen. Then she slowly straightened up, she stood erect, and the nickel was in her apron pocket. A bird flew by. Her lips moved. "God watching me the whole time. I come to stealing."

The man came back, and his own dog panted about them. "Well, I scared him off that time," he said, and then he laughed and lifted his gun and pointed it at Phoenix.

She stood straight and faced him.

"Doesn't the gun scare you?" he said, still pointing it.

"No, sir, I seen plenty go off closer by, in my day, and for less than what I done," she said, holding utterly still.

He smiled, and shouldered the gun. "Well, Granny," he said, "you must be a hundred years old, and scared of nothing. I'd give you a dime if I had any money with me. But you take my advice and stay home, and nothing will happen to you."

"I bound to go on my way, mister," said Phoenix. She inclined her head in the red rag. Then they went in different directions, but she could hear the gun shooting again and again over the hill.

She walked on. The shadows hung from the oak trees to the road like curtains. Then she smelled wood-smoke, and smelled the river, and she saw a steeple and the cabins on their steep steps. Dozens of little black children whirled around her. There ahead was Natchez shining. Bells were ringing. She walked on.

In the paved city it was Christmas time. There were red and green electric lights strung and crisscrossed everywhere, and all turned on in the daytime. Old Phoenix would have been lost if she had not distrusted her eyesight and depended on her feet to know where to take her.

She paused quietly on the sidewalk where people were passing by. A lady came along in the crowd, carrying an armful of red-, green-, and silver-wrapped presents; she gave off perfume like the red roses in hot summer, and Phoenix stopped her.

"Please, missy, will you lace up my shoe?" She held up her foot.

"What do you want, Grandma?"

"See my shoe," said Phoenix. "Do all right for out in the country, but wouldn't look right to go in a big building."

"Stand still then, Grandma," said the lady. She put her packages down on the sidewalk beside her and laced and tied both shoes tightly.

"Can't lace 'em with a cane," said Phoenix. "Thank you, missy. I doesn't mind asking a nice lady to tie up my shoe, when I gets out on the street."

Moving slowly and from side to side, she went into the big building, and into a tower of steps, where she walked up and around and around until her feet knew to stop.

She entered a door, and there she saw nailed up on the wall the document that had been stamped with the gold seal and framed in the gold frame, which matched the dream that was hung up in her head.

"Here I be," she said. There was a fixed and ceremonial stiffness over her body.

"A charity case, I suppose," said an attendant who sat at the desk before her.

But Phoenix only looked above her head. There was sweat on her face, the wrinkles in her skin shone like a bright net.

"Speak up, Grandma," the woman said. "What's your name? We must have your history, you know. Have you been here before? What seems to be the trouble with you?"

Old Phoenix only gave a twitch to her face as if a fly were bothering her.

"Are you deaf?" cried the attendant.

But then the nurse came in.

"Oh, that's just old Aunt Phoenix," she said. "She doesn't come for herself — she has a little grandson. She makes these trips just as regular as clockwork. She lives away back off the Old Natchez Trace." She bent down. "Well, Aunt Phoenix, why don't you just take a seat? We won't keep you standing after your long trip." She pointed.

The old woman sat down, bolt upright in the chair.

"Now, how is the boy?" asked the nurse.

Old Phoenix did not speak.

"I said, how is the boy?"

But Phoenix only waited and stared straight ahead, her face very solemn and withdrawn into rigidity.

"Is his throat any better?" asked the nurse. "Aunt Phoenix, don't you hear me? Is your grandson's throat any better since the last time you came for the medicine?"

With her hands on her knees, the old woman waited, silent, erect and motionless, just as if she were in armor.

"You mustn't take up our time this way, Aunt Phoenix," the nurse said. "Tell us quickly about your grandson, and get it over. He isn't dead, is he?"

At last there came a flicker and then a flame of comprehension across her face, and she spoke.

"My grandson. It was my memory had left me. There I sat and forgot why I made my long trip."

"Forgot?" The nurse frowned. "After you came so far?"

Then Phoenix was like an old woman begging a dignified forgiveness for waking up frightened in the night. "I never did go to school, I was too old at the Surrender," she said in a soft voice. "I'm an old woman without an education. It was my memory fail me. My little grandson, he is just the same, and I forgot it in the coming."

"Throat never heals, does it?" said the nurse, speaking in a loud, sure voice to old Phoenix. By now she had a card with something written on it, a little list. "Yes. Swallowed lye. When was it? — January — two, three years ago — "

Phoenix spoke unasked now. "No, missy, he not dead, he just the same. Every little while his throat begin to close up again, and he not able to swallow. He not get his breath. He not able to help himself. So the time come around, and I go on another trip for the soothing medicine."

"All right. The doctor said as long as you came to get it, you could have it," said the nurse. "But it's an obstinate case."

"My little grandson, he sit up there in the house all wrapped up, waiting by himself," Phoenix went on. "We is the only two left in the world. He suffer and it don't seem to put him back at all. He got a sweet look. He going to last. He wear a little patch quilt and peep out holding his mouth open like a little bird. I remembers so plain now. I not going to forget him again, no, the whole enduring time. I could tell him from all the others in creation."

"All right." The nurse was trying to hush her now. She brought her a bottle of medicine. "Charity," she said, making a check mark in a book.

Old Phoenix held the bottle close to her eyes, and then carefully put it into her pocket.

"I thank you," she said.

"It's Christmas time, Grandma," said the attendant. "Could I give you a few pennies out of my purse?"

"Five pennies is a nickel," said Phoenix stiffly.

"Here's a nickel," said the attendant.

Phoenix rose carefully and held out her hand. She received the nickel and then fished the other nickel out of her pocket and laid it beside the new one. She stared at her palm closely, with her head on one side.

Then she gave a tap with her cane on the floor.

"This is what come to me to do," she said. "I going to the store and buy my child a little windmill they sells, made out of paper. He going to find it hard to believe there such a thing in the world. I'll march myself back where he waiting, holding it straight up in this hand."

She lifted her free hand, gave a little nod, turned around, and walked out of the doctor's office. Then her slow step began on the stairs, going down.

[1941]

PAUL BOWLES (b. 1910) was born in New York City. When he was very young, his parents encouraged his interest in music, art, and literature, and he began to compose his first opera at the age of eight. After a year at the University of Virginia, he studied music with Aaron Copland in New York and Berlin from 1930 to 1932, and with Virgil Thomson in Paris from 1933 to 1934. In 1938 Bowles married Jane Sydney Auer, who later published fiction under the name Jane Bowles.

As the critic Paul Gray has noted, Bowles is a Renaissance man born into an age that applauds specialization. He has been a distinguished composer, writing music for the plays of his friend Tennessee Williams; he has translated the works of Jean Paul Sartre and founded Antaeus, a literary quarterly; he has been a collector of folklore and legends from North Africa (he has lived in Tangier on and off since the early 1930s); and he has published novels, collections of poetry, travel essays, and an autobiography, Without Stopping. In 1979 he published Collected Stories 1939–1976, a gathering of thirty-nine stories and tales that established him as one of the most accomplished contemporary American writers of short fiction.

"The Hyena" is an animal fable that has contributed to Bowles's reputation as a pitiless chronicler of bizarre and sadistic situations, yet it is no more violent or sadistic than many of Aesop's tales. Bowles used North Africa for its setting and religious context. The subtlety and vigor of the conversational exchange between the two animals impart a classical tone to the literary style that is characteristic of Bowles's best work. In Without Stopping he made clear his attitude toward the difference between life and fiction: "Telling what happened [in autobiography] does not necessarily make a good story. In my tale, for instance, there are no dramatic victories because there was no struggle. I hung on and waited. It seems to me that this must be what most people do; the occasions when there is the possibility of doing more than that are becoming rare indeed."

Paul Bowles

ᔓᔓ

THE HYENA

A stork was passing over desert country on his way north. He was thirsty, and he began to look for water. When he came to the mountains of Khang el Ghar, he saw a pool at the bottom of a ravine. He flew down between the rocks and lighted at the edge of the water. Then he walked in and drank.

At that moment a hyena limped up and, seeing the stork standing in the water, said: "Have you come a long way?" The stork had never seen a hyena before. "So this is what a hyena is like," he thought. And he stood looking at the hyena because he had been told that if the hyena can put a little of his urine on someone, that one will have to walk after the hyena to whatever place the hyena wants him to go.

"It will be summer soon," said the stork. "I am on my way north." At the same time, he walked further out into the pool, so as not to be so near the hyena. The water here was deeper, and he almost lost his balance and had to flap his wings to keep upright. The hyena walked to the other side of the pool and looked at him from there.

"I know what is in your head," said the hyena. "You believe the story about me. You think I have that power? Perhaps long ago hyenas were like that. But now they are the same as everyone else. I could wet you from here with my urine if I wanted to. But what for? If you want to be unfriendly, go to the middle of the pool and stay there."

The stork looked around at the pool and saw that there was no spot in it where he could stand and be out of reach of the hyena.

"I have finished drinking," said the stork. He spread his wings and flapped out of the pool. At the edge he ran quickly ahead and rose into the air. He circled above the pool, looking down at the hyena.

"So you are the one they call the ogre," he said. "The world is full of strange things."

The hyena looked up. His eyes were narrow and crooked. "Allah brought us all here," he said. "You know that. You are the one who knows about Allah."

The stork flew a little lower. "That is true," he said. "But I am surprised to hear you say it. You have a very bad name, as you yourself just said. Magic is against the will of Allah."

The hyena tilted his head. "So you still believe the lies!" he cried.

"I have not seen the inside of your bladder," said the stork. "But why does everyone say you can make magic with it?"

"Why did Allah give you a head, I wonder? You have not learned how to use it." But the hyena spoke in so low a voice that the stork could not hear him.

"Your words got lost," said the stork, and he let himself drop lower.

The hyena looked up again. "I said: 'Don't come too near me. I might lift my leg and cover you with magic!' " He laughed, and the stork was near enough to see that his teeth were brown.

"Still, there must be some reason," the stork began. Then he looked for a rock high above the hyena, and settled himself on it. The hyena sat and stared up at him. "Why does everyone hate you?" the stork went on. "Why do they call you an ogre? What have you done?"

The hyena squinted. "You are very lucky," he told the stork. "Men never try to kill you, because they think you are holy. They call you a saint and a sage. And yet you seem like neither a saint nor a sage."

"What do you mean?" said the stork quickly.

"If you really understood, you would know that magic is a grain of dust in the wind, and that Allah has power over everything. You would not be afraid."

The stork stood for a long time, thinking. He lifted one leg and held it bent in front of him. The ravine grew red as the sun went lower. And the hyena sat quietly looking up at the stork, waiting for him to speak.

Finally the stork put his leg down, opened his bill, and said: "You mean that if there is no magic, the one who sins is the one who believes there is."

The hyena laughed. "I said nothing about sin. But you did, and you are the sage. I am not in the world to tell anyone what is right or wrong. Living from night to night is enough. Everyone hopes to see me dead."

The stork lifted his leg again and stood thinking. The last daylight rose into the sky and was gone. The cliffs at the sides of the ravine were lost in the darkness.

At length the stork said: "You have given me something to think about. That is good. But now night has come. I must go on my way." He raised his wings and started to fly straight out from the boulder where he had stood. The hyena listened. He heard the stork's wings beating the air slowly, and then he heard the sound of the stork's body as it hit the cliff on the other side of the ravine. He climbed up over the rocks and found the stork. "Your wing is broken," he said. "It would have been better for you to go while there was still daylight."

"Yes," said the stork. He was unhappy and afraid.

"Come home with me," the hyena told him. "Can you walk?"

"Yes," said the stork. Together they made their way down the valley. Soon they came to a cave in the side of the mountain. The hyena went in first and called out: "Bend your head." When they were well inside, he said: "Now you can put your head up. The cave is high here."

There was only darkness inside. The stork stood still. "Where are you?" he said.

"I am here," the hyena answered, and he laughed.

"Why are you laughing?" asked the stork.

"I was thinking that the world is strange," the hyena told him. "The saint has come into my cave because he believed in magic."

"I don't understand," said the stork.

"You are confused. But at least now you can believe that I have no magic. I am like anyone else in the world."

The stork did not answer right away. He smelled the stench of the hyena very near him. Then he said, with a sigh: "You are right, of course. There is no power beyond the power of Allah."

"I am happy," said the hyena, breathing into his face. "At last you understand." Quickly he seized the stork's neck and tore it open. The stork flapped and fell on his side.

"Allah gave me something better than magic," the hyena said under his breath. "He gave me a brain."

The stork lay still. He tried to say once more: "There is no power beyond the power of Allah." But his bill merely opened very wide in the dark.

The hyena turned away. "You will be dead in a minute," he said over his shoulder. "In ten days I shall come back. By then you will be ready."

Ten days later the hyena went to the cave and found the stork where he had left him. The ants had not been there. "Good," he said. He devoured what he wanted and went outside to a large flat rock above the entrance to the cave. There in the moonlight he stood a while, vomiting.

He ate some of his vomit and rolled for a long time in the rest of it, rubbing it deep into his coat. Then he thanked Allah for eyes that could see the valley in the moonlight, and for a nose that could smell the carrion on the wind. He rolled some more and licked the rock under him. For a while he lay there panting. Soon he got up and limped on his way.

[1979]

JOHN CHEEVER (1912–1982), *the leading exponent of the kind of carefully fashioned story of modern urban and suburban manners that* The New Yorker *popularized, has been called by the reviewer John Leonard "the Chekhov of the suburbs." Cheever spent most of his life in New York City and in small towns similar to the ones he described in much of his fiction. Born in Quincy, Massachusetts, he was raised by parents who owned a prosperous business that failed after the 1929 stock market crash. His mother then opened a seaside curio shop to support the family. His parents enjoyed reading literature to him, so at an early age he was acquainted with the fiction of Charles Dickens, Jack London, and Robert Louis Stevenson. (Edgar Allan Poe was forbidden, but Cheever read him on the sly.) Cheever began to write when he was about ten years old, and when he was twelve, he said, he was given his parents' permission to write for a living after he had promised that he had "no idea of becoming famous or wealthy." He started his career at an unusually young age. Expelled from Thayer Academy at seventeen for being, by his own account, a "quarrelsome, intractable, . . . and lousy student," he moved to New York City, lived in a cell of a room on a bread-and-buttermilk diet, and wrote stories. When his first one, "Expelled," was accepted for publication by Malcolm Cowley, then editor of* The New Republic, *Cheever was launched as a teenager into a career as a writer of fiction. Earlier Cowley had told him that his stories were too long to get published by magazines that paid, so he made Cheever write a story of not more than a thousand words every day for four days to encourage discipline. As Cowley has remembered, "One of them was a sketch, so I printed it in* The New Republic. *I sent the other three to Katharine White at* The New Yorker, *and she bought two. No one but John could have written those stories in four days."*

In the 1930s Cheever published short fiction in the The New Republic, Collier's, Story, The Atlantic Monthly, *and* The New Yorker. *His first collection of stories,* The Way Some People Live, *appeared in 1942, while he was completing a four-year stint of army duty during World War II. After the war he wrote television scripts, but his main interest was writing stories. In 1953 he strengthened his literary reputation with the book* The Enormous Radio and Other Stories, *a collection of fourteen of his New Yorker pieces. Six years later appeared another story collection,* The Housebreaker of Shady Hill. *His first novel,* The Wapshot Chronicle, *had been published in 1957, and its sequel,* The Wapshot Scandal, *appeared in 1964. In the 1960s and 1970s he published three more books of short stories and two widely acclaimed novels,* Bullet Park *(1969) and* Falconer *(1977). The Stories of John Cheever, published in 1978, won both the Pulitzer Prize and the National Book Critics Circle Award and became one of the few books of short stories ever to make the* New York Times *best-seller list.*

Shortly before his death he published a last short novel and saw a final tele-vision play produced on PBS. In more than fifty years, Cheever published over 200 magazine stories; he figured that he earned "enough money to feed the family and buy a new suit every other year."

Usually a rapid writer, Cheever said he liked best the stories that he wrote in less than a week, although he spent months working on "The Swimmer," a story included in his 1964 collection, The Brigadier and the Golf Widow. He originally wrote a draft of the plot as "a perfectly good" novel, but then he burned it. "I could very easily have sold the book," he said, "but the trick was to get the winter constellations in the midsummer sky without anyone knowing about it, and it didn't take 250 pages to do that." Cheever was a moralist, and most of his stories present a precise dis-section of the values of the ascending American middle class in the years after World War II. The stylistic elegance of stories like "The Enormous Radio" is an ironic contrast to the tensions of contemporary urban life dra-matized in the narrative. (See Cheever's Commentary on page 1304.)

John Cheever

∽∾

THE ENORMOUS RADIO

Jim and Irene Westcott were the kind of people who seem to strike that satisfactory average of income, endeavor, and respectability that is reached by the statistical reports in college alumni bulletins. They were the parents of two young children, they had been married nine years, they lived on the twelfth floor of an apartment house near Sutton Place, they went to the theatre on an average of 10.3 times a year, and they hoped someday to live in Westchester. Irene Westcott was a pleasant, rather plain girl with soft brown hair and a wide, fine forehead upon which nothing at all had been written, and in the cold weather she wore a coat of fitch skins dyed to resemble mink. You could not say that Jim Westcott looked younger than he was, but you could at least say of him that he seemed to feel younger. He wore his graying hair cut very short, he dressed in the kind of clothes his class had worn at Andover, and his manner was earnest, vehement, and in-tentionally naïve. The Westcotts differed from their friends, their class-mates, and their neighbors only in an interest they shared in serious music.

They went to a great many concerts — although they seldom mentioned this to anyone — and they spent a good deal of time listening to music on the radio.

Their radio was an old instrument, sensitive, unpredictable, and beyond repair. Neither of them understood the mechanics of radio — or of any of the other appliances that surrounded them — and when the instrument faltered, Jim would strike the side of the cabinet with his hand. This sometimes helped. One Sunday afternoon, in the middle of a Schubert quartet, the music faded away altogether. Jim struck the cabinet repeatedly, but there was no response; the Schubert was lost to them forever. He promised to buy Irene a new radio, and on Monday when he came home from work he told her that he had got one. He refused to describe it, and said it would be a surprise for her when it came.

The radio was delivered at the kitchen door the following afternoon, and with the assistance of her maid and the handyman Irene uncrated it and brought it into the living room. She was struck at once with the physical ugliness of the large gumwood cabinet. Irene was proud of her living room, she had chosen its furnishings and colors as carefully as she chose her clothes, and now it seemed to her that the new radio stood among her intimate possessions like an aggressive intruder. She was confounded by the number of dials and switches on the instrument panel, and she studied them thoroughly before she put the plug into a wall socket and turned the radio on. The dials flooded with a malevolent green light, and in the distance she heard the music of a piano quintet. The quintet was in the distance for only an instant; it bore down upon her with a speed greater than light and filled the apartment with the noise of music amplified so mightily that it knocked a china ornament from a table to the floor. She rushed to the instrument and reduced the volume. The violent forces that were snared in the ugly gumwood cabinet made her uneasy. Her children came home from school then, and she took them to the Park. It was not until later in the afternoon that she was able to return to the radio.

The maid had given the children their suppers and was supervising their baths when Irene turned on the radio, reduced the volume, and sat down to listen to a Mozart quintet that she knew and enjoyed. The music came through clearly. The new instrument had a much purer tone, she thought, than the old one. She decided that tone was most important and that she could conceal the cabinet behind a sofa. But as soon as she had made her peace with the radio, the interference began. A crackling sound like the noise of a burning powder fuse began to accompany the singing of the strings. Beyond the music, there was a rustling that reminded Irene unpleasantly of the sea, and as the quintet progressed, these noises were joined by many others. She tried all the dials and switches but nothing dimmed the interference, and she sat down, disappointed and bewildered, and tried to trace the flight of the melody. The elevator shaft in her building ran beside the living-room wall, and it was the noise of the elevator that gave her a clue to the character of the static. The rattling of the elevator cables and the opening and closing of the elevator doors were reproduced in her loud-speaker, and, realizing that the radio was sensitive to electrical currents of all sorts, she began to discern through the Mozart the ringing of telephone bells, the dialing of phones, and the lamentation of a vacuum cleaner. By listening more carefully, she was able to distinguish doorbells, elevator bells, electric razors, and Waring mixers, whose sounds had been picked up from the apartments that surrounded hers and transmitted through her loud-speaker. The powerful and ugly instrument, with its mistaken sensitivity to discord, was more than she could hope to master, so she turned the thing off and went into the nursery to see her children.

When Jim Westcott came home that night, he went to the radio con-fidently and worked the controls. He had the same sort of experience Irene had had. A man was speaking on the station Jim had chosen, and his voice swung instantly from the distance into a force so powerful that it shook the apartment. Jim turned the volume control and reduced the voice. Then, a minute or two later, the interference began. The ringing of telephones and doorbells set in, joined by the rasp of the elevator doors and the whir of cooking appliances. The character of the noise had changed since Irene had tried the radio earlier; the last of the electric razors was being unplugged, the vacuum cleaners had all been returned to their closets, and the static reflected that change in pace that overtakes the city after the sun goes down. He fiddled with the knobs but couldn't get rid of the noises, so he turned the radio off and told Irene that in the morning he'd call the people who had sold it to him and give them hell.

The following afternoon, when Irene returned to the apartment from a luncheon date, the maid told her that a man had come and fixed the radio. Irene went into the living room before she took off her hat or her furs and tried the instrument. From the loudspeaker came a recording of the "Missouri Waltz." It reminded her of the thin, scratchy music from an old-fashioned phonograph that she sometimes heard across the lake where she spent her summers. She waited until the waltz had finished, expecting an explanation of the recording, but there was none. The music was fol-lowed by silence, and then the plaintive and scratchy record was repeated. She turned the dial and got a satisfactory burst of Caucasian music — the thump of bare feet in the dust and the rattle of coin jewelry — but in the background she could hear the ringing of bells and a confusion of voices. Her children came home from school then, and she turned off the radio and went to the nursery.

When Jim came home that night, he was tired, and he took a bath and changed his clothes. Then he joined Irene in the living room. He had just turned on the radio when the maid announced dinner, so he left it on, and he and Irene went to the table.

Jim was too tired to make even pretense of sociability, and there was nothing about the dinner to hold Irene's interest, so her attention wandered from the food to the deposits of silver polish on the candlesticks and from there to the music in the other room. She listened for a few minutes to a Chopin prelude and then was surprised to hear a man's voice break in. "For Christ's sake, Kathy," he said, "do you always have to play the piano when I get home?" The music stopped abruptly. "It's the only chance I have," a woman said. "I'm at the office all day." "So am I," the man said. He added something obscene about an upright piano, and slammed a door. The passionate and melancholy music began again.

"Did you hear that?" Irene asked.

"What?" Jim was eating his dessert.

"The radio. A man said something while the music was still going on — something dirty."

"It's probably a play."

"I don't think it *is* a play," Irene said.

They left the table and took their coffee into the living room. Irene asked Jim to try another station. He turned the knob. "Have you seen my garters?" a man asked. "Button me up," a woman said. "Have you seen my garters?" the man said again. "Just button me up and I'll find your garters," the woman said. Jim shifted to another station. "I wish you wouldn't leave apple cores in the ashtrays," a man said. "I hate the smell."

"This is strange," Jim said.

"Isn't it?" Irene said.

Jim turned the knob again. " 'On the coast of Coromandel where the early pumpkins blow,' " a woman with a pronounced English accent said, " 'in the middle of the woods lived the Yonghy-Bonghy-Bò. Two old chairs, and half a candle, one old jug without a handle. . . .' "[1]

"My God!" Irene cried. "That's the Sweeneys' nurse."

" 'These were all his worldly goods,' " the British voice continued.

"Turn that thing off," Irene said. "Maybe they can hear *us*." Jim switched the radio off. "That was Miss Armstrong, the Sweeneys' nurse," Irene said. "She must be reading to the little girl. They live in 17-B. I've talked with Miss Armstrong in the Park. I know her voice very well. We must be getting other people's apartments."

"That's impossible," Jim said.

"Well, that was the Sweeneys' nurse," Irene said hotly. "I know her voice. I know it very well. I'm wondering if they can hear us."

Jim turned the switch. First from a distance and then nearer, nearer, as if borne on the wind, came the pure accents of the Sweeneys' nurse again: " '*Lady Jingly! Lady Jingly!*' " she said, " '*sitting where the pumpkins blow, will you come and be my wife? said the Yonghy-Bonghy-Bò. . . .*' "

Jim went over to the radio and said "Hello" loudly into the speaker.

" '*I am tired of living singly,*' " the nurse went on, " '*on this coast so*

[1] lines from "The Courtship of the Yonghy-Bonghy-Bò," nonsense poem by Edward Lear (1812–1888).

wild and shingly, I'm a-weary of my life; if you'll come and be my wife, quite serene would be my life. . . . ' "

"I guess she can't hear us," Irene said. "Try something else."

Jim turned to another station, and the living room was filled with the uproar of a cocktail party that had overshot its mark. Someone was playing the piano and singing the "Whiffenpoof Song," and the voices that surrounded the piano were vehement and happy. "Eat some more sandwiches," a woman shrieked. There were screams of laughter and a dish of some sort crashed to the floor.

"Those must be the Fullers, in 11-E," Irene said. "I knew they were giving a party this afternoon. I saw her in the liquor store. Isn't this too divine? Try something else. See if you can get those people in 18-C."

The Westcotts overheard that evening a monologue on salmon fishing in Canada, a bridge game, running comments on home movies of what had apparently been a fortnight at Sea Island, and a bitter family quarrel about an overdraft at the bank. They turned off their radio at midnight and went to bed, weak with laughter. Sometime in the night, their son began to call for a glass of water and Irene got one and took it to his room. It was very early. All the lights in the neighborhood were extinguished, and from the boy's window she could see the empty street. She went into the living room and tried the radio. There was some faint coughing, a moan, and then a man spoke. "Are you all right, darling?" he asked. "Yes," a woman said wearily. "Yes, I'm all right, I guess," and then she added with great feeling, "But, you know, Charlie, I don't feel like myself any more. Sometimes there are about fifteen or twenty minutes in the week when I feel like myself. I don't like to go to another doctor, because the doctor's bills are so awful already, but I just don't feel like myself, Charlie. I just never feel like myself." They were not young, Irene thought. She guessed from the timbre of their voices that they were middle-aged. The restrained melancholy of the dialogue and the draft from the bedroom window made her shiver, and she went back to bed.

The following morning, Irene cooked breakfast for the family — the maid didn't come up from her room in the basement until ten — braided her daughter's hair, and waited at the door until her children and her husband had been carried away in the elevator. Then she went into the living room and tried the radio. "I don't want to go to school," a child screamed. "I hate school. I won't go to school. I hate school." "You will go to school," an enraged woman said. "We paid eight hundred dollars to get you into that school and you'll go if it kills you." The next number on the dial produced the worn record of the "Missouri Waltz." Irene shifted the control and invaded the privacy of several breakfast tables. She overheard demonstrations of indigestion, carnal love, abysmal vanity, faith, and despair. Irene's life was nearly as simple and sheltered as it appeared to be, and the forthright and sometimes brutal language that came from the loudspeaker that morning astonished and troubled her. She continued to listen until her maid came in. Then she turned off the radio quickly, since this insight, she realized, was a furtive one.

Irene had a luncheon date with a friend that day, and she left her apartment at a little after twelve. There were a number of women in the elevator when it stopped at her floor. She stared at their handsome and impassive faces, their furs, and the cloth flowers in their hats. Which one of them had been to Sea Island? she wondered. Which one had overdrawn her bank account? The elevator stopped at the tenth floor and a woman with a pair of Skye terriers joined them. Her hair was rigged high on her head and she wore a mink cape. She was humming the "Missouri Waltz."

Irene had two Martinis at lunch, and she looked searchingly at her friend and wondered what her secrets were. They had intended to go shopping after lunch, but Irene excused herself and went home. She told the maid that she was not to be disturbed; then she went into the living room, closed the doors, and switched on the radio. She heard, in the course of the afternoon, the halting conversation of a woman entertaining her aunt, the hysterical conclusion of a luncheon party, and a hostess briefing her maid about some cocktail guests. "Don't give the best Scotch to anyone who hasn't white hair," the hostess said. "See if you can get rid of that liver paste before you pass those hot things, and could you lend me five dollars? I want to tip the elevator man."

As the afternoon waned, the conversations increased in intensity. From where Irene sat, she could see the open sky above the East River. There were hundreds of clouds in the sky, as though the south wind had broken the winter into pieces and were blowing it north, and on her radio she could hear the arrival of cocktail guests and the return of children and businessmen from their schools and offices. "I found a good-sized diamond on the bathroom floor this morning," a woman said. "It must have fallen out of that bracelet Mrs. Dunston was wearing last night." "We'll sell it," a man said. "Take it down to the jeweler on Madison Avenue and sell it. Mrs. Dunston won't know the difference, and we could use a couple of hundred bucks. . . ." " 'Oranges and lemons, say the bells of St. Clement's,' " the Sweeneys' nurse sang. " 'Halfpence and farthings, say the bells of St. Martin's. When will you pay me? say the bells at old Bailey. . . .' " "It's not a hat," a woman cried, and at her back roared a cocktail party. "It's not a hat, it's a love affair. That's what Walter Florell said. He said it's not a hat, it's a love affair," and then, in a lower voice, the same woman added, "Talk to somebody, for Christ's sake, honey, talk to somebody. If she catches you standing here not talking to anybody, she'll take us off her invitation list, and I love these parties."

The Westcotts were going out for dinner that night, and when Jim came home, Irene was dressing. She seemed sad and vague, and he brought her a drink. They were dining with friends in the neighborhood, and they walked to where they were going. The sky was broad and filled with light. It was one of those splendid spring evenings that excite memory and desire, and the air that touched their hands and faces felt very soft. A Salvation Army band was on the corner playing "Jesus Is Sweeter." Irene drew on her husband's arm and held him there for a minute, to hear the music. "They're really such nice people, aren't they?" she said. "They have such nice faces. Actually, they're so much nicer than a lot of the people we know." She took a bill from her purse and walked over and dropped it into the tambourine. There was in her face, when she returned to her husband, a look of radiant melancholy that he was not familiar with. And her conduct at the dinner party that night seemed strange to him, too. She interrupted her hostess rudely and stared at the people across the table from her with an intensity for which she would have punished her children.

It was still mild when they walked home from the party, and Irene looked up at the spring stars. " 'How far that little candle throws its beams,' " she exclaimed. " 'So shines a good deed in a naughty world.' "[2] She waited that night until Jim had fallen asleep, and then went into the living room and turned on the radio.

Jim came home at about six the next night. Emma, the maid, let him in, and he had taken off his hat and was taking off his coat when Irene ran into the hall. Her face was shining with tears and her hair was disordered. "Go up to 16-C, Jim!" she screamed. "Don't take off your coat. Go up to 16-C. Mr. Osborn's beating his wife. They've been quarreling since four o'clock, and now he's hitting her. Go up there and stop him."

From the radio in the living room, Jim heard screams, obscenities, and thuds. "You know you don't have to listen to this sort of thing," he said. He strode into the living room and turned the switch. "It's indecent," he said. "It's like looking in windows. You know you don't have to listen to this sort of thing. You can turn it off."

"Oh, it's so horrible, it's so dreadful," Irene was sobbing. "I've been listening all day, and it's so depressing."

"Well, if it's so depressing, why do you listen to it? I bought this damned radio to give you pleasure," he said. "I paid a great deal of money for it. I thought it might make you happy. I wanted to make you happy."

"Don't, don't, don't, don't quarrel with me," she moaned, and laid her head on his shoulder. "All the others have been quarreling all day. Everybody's been quarreling. They're all worried about money. Mrs. Hutchinson's mother is dying of cancer in Florida and they don't have enough money to send her to the Mayo Clinic. At least, Mr. Hutchinson says they don't have enough money. And some woman in this building is having an affair with the handyman — with that hideous handyman. It's too disgusting. And Mrs. Melville has heart trouble and Mr. Hendricks is going to lose his job in April and Mrs. Hendricks is horrid about the whole thing and that girl who plays the 'Missouri Waltz' is a whore, a common whore, and

[2] Irene is quoting from Shakespeare's The Merchant of Venice, V.i. 101–102.

the elevator man has tuberculosis and Mr. Osborn has been beating Mrs. Osborn." She wailed, she trembled with grief and checked the stream of tears down her face with the heel of her palm.

"Well, why do you have to listen?" Jim asked again. "Why do you have to listen to this stuff if it makes you so miserable?"

"Oh, don't, don't, don't," she cried. "Life is too terrible, too sordid and awful. But we've never been like that, have we, darling? Have we? I mean, we've always been good and decent and loving to one another, haven't we? And we have two children, two beautiful children. Our lives aren't sordid, are they, darling? Are they?" She flung her arms around his neck and drew his face down to hers. "We're happy, aren't we, darling? We are happy, aren't we?"

"Of course we're happy," he said tiredly. He began to surrender his resentment. "Of course we're happy. I'll have that damned radio fixed or taken away tomorrow." He stroked her soft hair. "My poor girl," he said.

"You love me, don't you?" she asked. "And we're not hypercritical or worried about money or dishonest, are we?"

"No, darling," he said.

A man came in the morning and fixed the radio. Irene turned it on cautiously and was happy to hear a California-wine commercial and a recording of Beethoven's Ninth Symphony, including Schiller's "Ode to Joy." She kept the radio on all day and nothing untoward came from the speaker.

A Spanish suite was being played when Jim came home. "Is everything all right?" he asked. His face was pale, she thought. They had some cocktails and went in to dinner to the "Anvil Chorus" from *Il Trovatore*. This was followed by Debussy's "La Mer."

"I paid the bill for the radio today," Jim said. "It cost four hundred dollars. I hope you'll get some enjoyment out of it."

"Oh, I'm sure I will," Irene said.

"Four hundred dollars is a good deal more than I can afford," he went on. "I wanted to get something that you'd enjoy. It's the last extravagance we'll be able to indulge in this year. I see that you haven't paid your clothing bills yet. I saw them on your dressing table." He looked directly at her. "Why did you tell me you'd paid them? Why did you lie to me?"

"I just didn't want you to worry, Jim," she said. She drank some water. "I'll be able to pay my bills out of this month's allowance. There were the slipcovers last month, and that party."

"You've got to learn to handle the money I give you a little more intelligently, Irene," he said. "You've got to understand that we don't have as much money this year as we had last. I had a very sobering talk with Mitchell today. No one is buying anything. We're spending all our time promoting new issues, and you know how long that takes. I'm not getting any younger, you know. I'm thirty-seven. My hair will be gray next year. I haven't done as well as I'd hoped to do. And I don't suppose things will get any better."

"Yes, dear," she said.

"We've got to start cutting down," Jim said. "We've got to think of the children. To be perfectly frank with you, I worry about money a great deal. I'm not at all sure of the future. No one is. If anything should happen to me, there's the insurance, but that wouldn't go very far today. I've worked awfully hard to give you and the children a comfortable life," he said bitterly. "I don't like to see all my energies, all of my youth, wasted in fur coats and radios and slipcovers and — "

"Please, Jim," she said. "Please. They'll hear us."

"*Who'll hear us?* Emma can't hear us."

"The radio."

"Oh, I'm sick!" he shouted. "I'm sick to death of your apprehensiveness. The radio can't hear us. Nobody can hear us. And what if they can hear us? Who cares?"

Irene got up from the table and went into the living room. Jim went to the door and shouted at her from there. "Why are you so Christly all of a sudden? What's turned you overnight into a convent girl? You stole your mother's jewelry before they probated her will. You never gave your sister a cent of that money that was intended for her — not even when she needed it. You made Grace Howland's life miserable, and where was all your piety and your virtue when you went to that abortionist? I'll never forget how cool you were. You packed your bag and went off to have that child murdered as if you were going to Nassau. If you'd had any reasons, if you'd had any good reasons — "

Irene stood for a minute before the hideous cabinet, disgraced and sickened, but she held her hand on the switch before she extinguished the music and the voices, hoping that the instrument might speak to her kindly, that she might hear the Sweeneys' nurse. Jim continued to shout at her from the door. The voice on the radio was suave and noncommittal. "An early-morning railroad disaster in Tokyo," the loudspeaker said, "killed twenty-nine people. A fire in a Catholic hospital near Buffalo for the care of blind children was extinguished early this morning by nuns. The temperature is forty-seven. The humidity is eighty-nine."

[1953]

John Cheever

∾∾

THE SWIMMER

It was one of those midsummer Sundays when everyone sits around saying, "I *drank* too much last night." You might have heard it whispered by the parishioners leaving church, heard it from the lips of the priest himself, struggling with his cassock in the *vestiarium*, heard it from the golf links and the tennis courts, heard it from the wild-life preserve where the leader of the Audubon group was suffering from a terrible hangover. "I *drank* too much," said Donald Westerhazy. "We all *drank* too much," said Lucinda Merrill. "It must have been the wine," said Helen Westerhazy. "I *drank* too much of that claret."

This was the edge of the Westerhazys' pool. The pool, fed by an artesian well with a high iron content, was a pale shade of green. It was a fine day. In the west there was a massive stand of cumulus cloud so like a city seen from a distance — from the bow of an approaching ship — that it might have had a name. Lisbon. Hackensack. The sun was hot. Neddy Merrill sat by the green water, one hand in it, one around a glass of gin. He was a slender man — he seemed to have the especial slenderness of youth — and while he was far from young he had slid down his banister that morning and given the bronze backside of Aphrodite on the hall table a smack, as he jogged toward the smell of coffee in his dining room. He might have been compared to a summer's day, particularly the last hours of one, and while he lacked a tennis racket or a sail bag the impression was definitely one of youth, sport, and clement weather. He had been swimming and now he was breathing deeply, stertorously as if he could gulp into his lungs the components of that moment, the heat of the sun, the intenseness of his pleasure. It all seemed to flow into his chest. His own house stood in Bullet Park, eight miles to the south, where his four beautiful daughters would have had their lunch and might be playing tennis. Then it occurred to him that by taking a dogleg to the southwest he could reach his home by water.

His life was not confining and the delight he took in this observation could not be explained by its suggestion of escape. He seemed to see, with a cartographer's eye, that string of swimming pools, that quasi-subterranean stream that curved across the county. He had made a discovery, a contribution to modern geography; he would name the stream Lucinda after his wife. He was not a practical joker nor was he a fool but he was determinedly original and had a vague and modest idea of himself as a legendary figure. The day was beautiful and it seemed to him that a long swim might enlarge and celebrate its beauty.

He took off a sweater that was hung over his shoulders and dove in. He had an inexplicable contempt for men who did not hurl themselves into pools. He swam a choppy crawl, breathing either with every stroke or every fourth stroke and counting somewhere well in the back of his mind the one-two one-two of a flutter kick. It was not a serviceable stroke for long distances but the domestication of swimming had saddled the sport with some customs and in his part of the world a crawl was customary. To be embraced and sustained by the light green water was less a pleasure, it seemed, than the resumption of a natural condition, and he would have liked to swim without trunks, but this was not possible, considering his project. He hoisted himself up on the far curb — he never used the ladder — and started across the lawn. When Lucinda asked where he was going he said he was going to swim home.

The only maps and charts he had to go by were remembered or imaginary but these were clear enough. First there were the Grahams, the Hammers, the Lears, the Howlands, and the Crosscups. He would cross Ditmar Street to the Bunkers and come, after a short portage, to the Levys, the Welchers, and the public pool in Lancaster. Then there were the Hallorans, the Sachses, the Biswangers, Shirley Adams, the Gilmartins, and the Clydes. The day was lovely, and that he lived in a world so generously supplied with water seemed like a clemency, a beneficence. His heart was high and he ran across the grass. Making his way home by an uncommon route gave him the feeling that he was a pilgrim, an explorer, a man with a destiny, and he knew that he would find friends all along the way; friends would line the banks of the Lucinda River.

He went through a hedge that separated the Westerhazys' land from the Grahams', walked under some flowering apple trees, passed the shed that housed their pump and filter, and came out at the Grahams' pool. "Why, Neddy," Mrs. Graham said, "what a marvelous surprise. I've been trying to get you on the phone all morning. Here, let me get you a drink." He saw then, like any explorer, that the hospitable customs and traditions of the natives would have to be handled with diplomacy if he was ever going to reach his destination. He did not want to mystify or seem rude to the Grahams nor did he have the time to linger there. He swam the length of their pool and joined them in the sun and was rescued, a few minutes later, by the arrival of two carloads of friends from Connecticut. During the uproarious reunions he was able to slip away. He went down by the front of the Grahams' house, stepped over a thorny hedge, and crossed a vacant lot to the Hammers'. Mrs. Hammer, looking up from her roses, saw him swim

by although she wasn't quite sure who it was. The Lears heard him splashing past the open windows of their living room. The Howlands and the
Crosscups were away. After leaving the Howlands' he crossed Ditmar Street
and started for the Bunkers', where he could hear, even at that distance, the
noise of a party.

The water refracted the sound of voices and laughter and seemed to
suspend it in midair. The Bunkers' pool was on a rise and he climbed some
stairs to a terrace where twenty-five or thirty men and women were drinking. The only person in the water was Rusty Towers, who floated there on a
rubber raft. Oh, how bonny and lush were the banks of the Lucinda River!
Prosperous men and women gathered by the sapphire-colored waters while
caterer's men in white coats passed them cold gin. Overhead a red de
Haviland trainer was circling around and around and around in the sky with
something like the glee of a child in a swing. Ned felt a passing affection for
the scene, a tenderness for the gathering, as if it was something he might
touch. In the distance he heard thunder. As soon as Enid Bunker saw him
she began to scream: "Oh, look who's here! What a marvelous surprise!
When Lucinda said you couldn't come I thought I'd *die.*" She made her
way to him through the crowd, and when they had finished kissing she led
him to the bar, a progress that was slowed by the fact that he stopped to kiss
eight or ten other women and shake the hands of as many men. A smiling
bartender he had seen at a hundred parties gave him a gin and tonic and he
stood by the bar for a moment, anxious not to get stuck in any conversation
that would delay his voyage. When he seemed about to be surrounded he
dove in and swam close to the side to avoid colliding with Rusty's raft. At
the far end of the pool he bypassed the Tomlinsons with a broad smile and
jogged up the garden path. The gravel cut his feet but this was only unpleasantness. The party was confined to the pool, and as he went toward the
house he heard the brilliant, watery sound of voices fade, heard the noise of
a radio from the Bunkers' kitchen, where someone was listening to a ball
game. Sunday afternoon. He made his way through the parked cars and
down the grassy border of their driveway to Alewives Lane. He did not want
to be seen on the road in his bathing trunks but there was no traffic and he
made the short distance to the Levys' driveway, marked with a PRIVATE
PROPERTY sign and a green tube for *The New York Times.* All the doors
and windows of the big house were open but there were no signs of life; not
even a dog barked. He went around the side of the house to the pool and
saw that the Levys had only recently left. Glasses and bottles and dishes of
nuts were on a table at the deep end, where there was a bathhouse or gazebo, hung with Japanese lanterns. After swimming the pool he got himself
a glass and poured a drink. It was his fourth or fifth drink and he had swum
nearly half the length of the Lucinda River. He felt tired, clean, and pleased
at that moment to be alone; pleased with everything.

It would storm. The stand of cumulus cloud — that city — had risen
and darkened, and while he sat there he heard the percussiveness of thun-

der again. The de Haviland trainer was still circling overhead and it seemed to Ned that he could almost hear the pilot laugh with pleasure in the afternoon; but when there was another peal of thunder he took off for home. A train whistle blew and he wondered what time it had gotten to be. Four? Five? He thought of the provincial station at that hour, where a waiter, his tuxedo concealed by a raincoat, a dwarf with some flowers wrapped in newspaper, and a woman who had been crying would be waiting for the local. It was suddenly growing dark; it was that moment when the pin-headed birds seemed to organize their song into some acute and knowledgeable recognition of the storm's approach. Then there was a fine noise of rushing water from the crown of an oak at his back, as if a spigot there had been turned. Then the noise of fountains came from the crowns of all the tall trees. Why did he love storms, what was the meaning of his excitement when the door sprang open and the rain wind fled rudely up the stairs, why had the simple task of shutting the windows of an old house seemed fitting and urgent, why did the first watery notes of a storm wind have for him the unmistakable sound of good news, cheer, glad tidings? Then there was an explosion, a smell of cordite, and rain lashed the Japanese lanterns that Mrs. Levy had bought in Kyoto the year before last, or was it the year before that?

He stayed in the Levys' gazebo until the storm had passed. The rain had cooled the air and he shivered. The force of the wind had stripped a maple of its red and yellow leaves and scattered them over the grass and the water. Since it was midsummer the tree must be blighted, and yet he felt a peculiar sadness at this sign of autumn. He braced his shoulders, emptied his glass, and started for the Welchers' pool. This meant crossing the Lindleys' riding ring and he was surprised to find it overgrown with grass and all the jumps dismantled. He wondered if the Lindleys had sold their horses or gone away for the summer and put them out to board. He seemed to remember having heard something about the Lindleys and their horses but the memory was unclear. On he went, barefoot through the wet grass, to the Welchers', where he found their pool was dry.

This breach in his chain of water disappointed him absurdly, and he felt like some explorer who seeks a torrential headwater and finds a dead stream. He was disappointed and mystified. It was common enough to go away for the summer but no one ever drained his pool. The Welchers had definitely gone away. The pool furniture was folded, stacked, and covered with a tarpaulin. The bathhouse was locked. All the windows of the house were shut, and when he went around to the driveway in front he saw a FOR SALE sign nailed to a tree. When had he last heard from the Welchers — when, that is, had he and Lucinda last regretted an invitation to dine with them? It seemed only a week or so ago. Was his memory failing or had he so disciplined it in the repression of unpleasant facts that he had damaged his sense of the truth? Then in the distance he heard the sound of a tennis game. This cheered him, cleared away all his apprehensions and let him regard the overcast sky and the cold air with indifference. This was the day that Neddy Merrill swam across the county. That was the day! He started off then for his most difficult portage.

Had you gone for a Sunday afternoon ride that day you might have seen him, close to naked, standing on the shoulders of Route 424, waiting for a chance to cross. You might have wondered if he was the victim of foul play, had his car broken down, or was he merely a fool. Standing barefoot in the deposits of the highway — beer cans, rags, and blowout patches — exposed to all kinds of ridicule, he seemed pitiful. He had known when he started that this was a part of his journey — it had been on his maps — but confronted with the lines of traffic, worming through the summery light, he found himself unprepared. He was laughed at, jeered at, a beer can was thrown at him, and he had no dignity or humor to bring to the situation. He could have gone back, back to the Westerhazys', where Lucinda would still be sitting in the sun. He had signed nothing, vowed nothing, pledged nothing, not even to himself. Why, believing as he did, that all human obduracy was susceptible to common sense, was he unable to turn back? Why was he determined to complete his journey even if it meant putting his life in danger? At what point had this prank, this joke, this piece of horseplay become serious? He could not go back, he could not even recall with any clearness the green water at the Westerhazys', the sense of inhaling the day's components, the friendly and relaxed voices saying that they had *drunk* too much. In the space of an hour, more or less, he had covered a distance that made his return impossible.

An old man, tooling down the highway at fifteen miles an hour, let him get to the middle of the road, where there was a grass divider. Here he was exposed to the ridicule of the northbound traffic, but after ten or fifteen minutes he was able to cross. From here he had only a short walk to the Recreation Center at the edge of the village of Lancaster, where there were some handball courts and a public pool.

The effect of the water on voices, the illusion of brilliance and suspense, was the same here as it had been at the Bunkers' but the sounds here were louder, harsher, and more shrill, and as soon as he entered the crowded enclosure he was confronted with regimentation. "ALL SWIMMERS MUST TAKE A SHOWER BEFORE USING THE POOL. ALL SWIMMERS MUST USE THE FOOTBATH. ALL SWIMMERS MUST WEAR THEIR IDENTIFICATION DISKS." He took a shower, washed his feet in a cloudy and bitter solution, and made his way to the edge of the water. It stank of chlorine and looked to him like a sink. A pair of lifeguards in a pair of towers blew police whistles at what seemed to be regular intervals and abused the swimmers through a public address system. Neddy remembered the sapphire water at the Bunkers' with longing and thought that he might contaminate himself — damage his own prosperousness and charm — by swimming in this murk, but he reminded himself that he was an explorer, a pilgrim, and that this was merely a stagnant bend in the Lucinda River. He dove, scowling with distaste, into the chlorine and had to swim with his head above water to avoid collisions, but even so he was bumped into, splashed, and jostled. When he got to the shallow end both lifeguards were shouting at him: "Hey, you, you without the identification disk, get outa the water." He did, but they had no way of pursuing him and he went through the reek of suntan oil and chlorine out through the hurricane fence and passed the handball courts. By crossing the road he entered the wooded part of the Halloran estate. The woods were not cleared and the footing was treacherous and difficult until he reached the lawn and the clipped beech hedge that encircled their pool.

The Hallorans were friends, an elderly couple of enormous wealth who seemed to bask in the suspicion that they might be Communists. They were zealous reformers but they were not Communists, and yet when they were accused, as they sometimes were, of subversion, it seemed to gratify and excite them. Their beech hedge was yellow and he guessed this had been blighted like the Levys' maple. He called hullo, hullo, to warn the Hallorans of his approach, to palliate his invasion of their privacy. The Hallorans, for reasons that had never been explained to him, did not wear bathing suits. No explanations were in order, really. Their nakedness was a detail in their uncompromising zeal for reform and he stepped politely out of his trunks before he went through the opening in the hedge.

Mrs. Halloran, a stout woman with white hair and a serene face, was reading the *Times*. Mr. Halloran was taking beech leaves out of the water with a scoop. They seemed not surprised or displeased to see him. Their pool was perhaps the oldest in the county, a fieldstone rectangle, fed by a brook. It had no filter or pump and its waters were the opaque gold of the stream.

"I'm swimming across the county," Ned said.

"Why, I didn't know one could," exclaimed Mrs. Halloran.

"Well, I've made it from the Westerhazys'," Ned said. "That must be about four miles."

He left his trunks at the deep end, walked to the shallow end, and swam this stretch. As he was pulling himself out of the water he heard Mrs. Halloran say, "We've been *terribly* sorry to hear about all your misfortunes, Neddy."

"My misfortunes?" Ned asked. "I don't know what you mean."

"Why we heard that you'd sold the house and that your poor children. . . ."

"I don't recall having sold the house," Ned said, "and the girls are at home."

"Yes," Mrs. Halloran sighed. "Yes. . . ." Her voice filled the air with an unseasonable melancholy and Ned spoke briskly. "Thank you for the swim."

"Well, have a nice trip," said Mrs. Halloran.

Beyond the hedge he pulled on his trunks and fastened them. They were loose and he wondered if, during the space of an afternoon, he could have lost some weight. He was cold and he was tired and the naked Hallorans and their dark water had depressed him. The swim was too much for his strength but how could he have guessed this, sliding down the banister that morning and sitting in the Westerhazys' sun? His arms were lame. His legs felt rubbery and ached at the joints. The worst of it was the cold in his bones and the feeling that he might never be warm again. Leaves were falling down around him and he smelled wood smoke on the wind. Who would be burning wood at this time of the year?

He needed a drink. Whiskey would warm him, pick him up, carry him through the last of his journey, refresh his feeling that it was original and valorous to swim across the county. Channel swimmers took brandy. He needed a stimulant. He crossed the lawn in front of the Hallorans' house and went down a little path to where they had built a house for their only daughter, Helen, and her husband, Eric Sachs. The Sachses' pool was small and he found Helen and her husband there.

"Oh, *Neddy*," Helen said. "Did you lunch at Mother's?"

"Not *really*," Ned said. "I *did* stop to see your parents." This seemed to be explanation enough. "I'm terribly sorry to break in on you like this but I've taken a chill and I wonder if you'd give me a drink."

"Why, I'd *love* to," Helen said, "but there hasn't been anything in this house to drink since Eric's operation. That was three years ago."

Was he losing his memory, had his gift for concealing painful facts let him forget that he had sold his house, that his children were in trouble, and that his friend had been ill? His eyes slipped from Eric's face to his abdomen, where he saw three pale, sutured scars, two of them at least a foot long. Gone was his navel, and what, Neddy thought, would the roving hand, bed-checking one's gifts at 3 A.M., make of a belly with no navel, no link to birth, this breach in the succession?

"I'm sure you can get a drink at the Biswangers'," Helen said. "They're having an enormous do. You can hear it from here. Listen!"

She raised her head and from across the road, the lawns, the gardens, the woods, the fields, he heard again the brilliant noise of voices over water. "Well, I'll get wet," he said, still feeling that he had no freedom of choice about his means of travel. He dove into the Sachses' cold water, and gasping, close to drowning, made his way from one end of the pool to the other. "Lucinda and I want *terribly* to see you," he said over his shoulder, his face set toward the Biswangers'. "We're sorry it's been so long and we'll call you *very* soon."

He crossed some fields to the Biswangers' and the sounds of revelry there. They would be honored to give him a drink, they would be happy to give him a drink. The Biswangers invited him and Lucinda for dinner four times a year, six weeks in advance. They were always rebuffed and yet they continued to send out their invitations, unwilling to comprehend the rigid and undemocratic realities of their society. They were the sort of people who discussed the price of things at cocktails, exchanged market tips during dinner, and after dinner told dirty stories to mixed company. They did not belong to Neddy's set — they were not even on Lucinda's Christmas card list. He went toward their pool with feelings of indifference, charity, and some unease, since it seemed to be getting dark and these were the longest days of the year. The party when he joined it was noisy and large. Grace Biswanger was the kind of hostess who asked the optometrist, the veterinarian, the real-estate dealer, and the dentist. No one was swimming and the twilight, reflected on the water of the pool, had a wintry gleam. There was a bar and he started for this. When Grace Biswanger saw him she came toward him, not affectionately as he had every right to expect, but bellicosely.

"Why, this party has everything," she said loudly, "including a gate crasher."

She could not deal him a social blow — there was no question about this and he did not flinch. "As a gate crasher," he asked politely, "do I rate a drink?"

"Suit yourself," she said. "You don't seem to pay much attention to invitations."

She turned her back on him and joined some guests, and he went to the bar and ordered a whiskey. The bartender served him but he served him rudely. His was a world in which the caterer's men kept the social score, and to be rebuffed by a part-time barkeep meant that he had suffered some loss of social esteem. Or perhaps the man was new and uninformed. Then he heard Grace at his back say: "They went for broke overnight — nothing but income — and he showed up drunk one Sunday and asked us to loan him five thousand dollars. . . ." She was always talking about money. It was worse than eating your peas off a knife. He dove into the pool, swam its length and went away.

The next pool on his list, the last but two, belonged to his old mistress, Shirley Adams. If he had suffered any injuries at the Biswangers' they would be cured here. Love — sexual roughhouse in fact — was the supreme elixir, the pain killer, the brightly colored pill that would put the spring back into his step, the joy of life in his heart. They had had an affair last week, last month, last year. He couldn't remember. It was he who had broken it off, his was the upper hand, and he stepped through the gate of the wall that surrounded her pool with nothing so considered as self-confidence. It seemed in a way to be his pool, as the lover, particularly the illicit lover, enjoys the possessions of his mistress with an authority unknown to holy matrimony. She was there, her hair the color of brass, but her figure, at the edge of the lighted, cerulean water, excited in him no profound memories. It had been, he thought, a lighthearted affair, although she had wept when he broke it off. She seemed confused to see him and he wondered if she was still wounded. Would she, God forbid, weep again?

"What do you want?" she asked.

"I'm swimming across the county."

"Good Christ. Will you ever grow up?"

"What's the matter?"

"If you've come here for money," she said, "I won't give you another cent."

"You could give me a drink."

"I could but I won't. I'm not alone."

"Well, I'm on my way."

He dove in and swam the pool, but when he tried to haul himself up onto the curb he found that the strength in his arms and shoulders had gone, and he paddled to the ladder and climbed out. Looking over his shoulder he saw, in the lighted bathhouse, a young man. Going out onto the dark lawn he smelled chrysanthemums or marigolds — some stubborn autumnal fragrance — on the night air, strong as gas. Looking overhead he saw that the stars had come out, but why should he seem to see Andromeda, Cepheus, and Cassiopeia? What had become of the constellations of midsummer? He began to cry.

It was probably the first time in his adult life that he had ever cried, certainly the first time in his life that he had ever felt so miserable, cold, tired, and bewildered. He could not understand the rudeness of the caterer's barkeep or the rudeness of a mistress who had come to him on her knees and showered his trousers with tears. He had swum too long, he had been immersed too long, and his nose and his throat were sore from the water. What he needed then was a drink, some company, and some clean, dry clothes, and while he could have cut directly across the road to his home he went on to the Gilmartins' pool. Here, for the first time in his life, he did not dive but went down the steps into the icy water and swam a hobbled sidestroke that he might have learned as a youth. He staggered with fatigue on his way to the Clydes' and paddled the length of their pool, stopping again and again with his hand on the curb to rest. He climbed up the ladder and wondered if he had the strength to get home. He had done what he wanted, he had swum the county, but he was so stupefied with exhaustion that his triumph seemed vague. Stooped, holding on to the gateposts for support, he turned up the driveway of his own house.

The place was dark. Was it so late that they had all gone to bed? Had Lucinda stayed at the Westerhazys' for supper? Had the girls joined her there or gone someplace else? Hadn't they agreed, as they usually did on Sunday, to regret all their invitations and stay at home? He tried the garage doors to see what cars were in but the doors were locked and rust came off the handles onto his hands. Going toward the house, he saw the force of the thunderstorm had knocked one of the rain gutters loose. It hung down over the front door like an umbrella rib, but it could be fixed in the morning. The house was locked, and he thought that the stupid cook or the stupid maid must have locked the place up until he remembered that it had been some time since they had employed a maid or a cook. He shouted, pounded on the door, tried to force it with his shoulder, and then, looking in at the windows, saw that the place was empty.

[1964]

TILLIE OLSEN (b. 1913) was born in Omaha, Nebraska, the daughter of political refugees from the Russian Czarist repression after the revolution of 1905. Her father was a farmer, packing-house worker, house painter, and jack-of-all-trades; her mother was a factory worker who also laundered, sewed, and took care of other people's children. At the age of fifteen, Olsen dropped out of high school to help support her family during the Depression. She was a member of the Young Communist League, involved in the Warehouse Union's labor disputes among packing-house workers in Kansas City, and she was jailed briefly. Shortly thereafter she became ill with pleurisy. When she recovered her health at age nineteen, she began to write her first novel, Yonnondio. Four chapters of this book about a poverty-stricken working-class family were completed in the next four years, during which time she married, gave birth to her first child, and was left with the baby by her husband because, as she later wrote in her autobiographical story "I Stand Here Ironing," he "could no longer endure sharing want" with them. In 1934 a section of the first chapter of her novel was published in Partisan Review, but she abandoned the unfinished book in 1937. The year before she had married Jack Olsen, also a political activist, with whom she had three more children; raising the children and working for political causes took up all her time. She also always held a full-time job in addition to the "caring, nurturing, and maintaining of other human beings" as a mother and wife. In the 1940s she was a factory worker, in the 1950s a secretary, and not until 1953, when her youngest daughter started school, could she begin writing again.

That year Olsen enrolled in a class in fiction writing at San Francisco State College. She was awarded a Stanford University creative writing fellowship for 1955 and 1956. During the 1950s she wrote the four stories collected in Tell Me a Riddle, which established her reputation when they were published as a paperback in 1961. Identified as a champion of the reemerging feminist movement, Olsen wrote a biographical introduction to Rebecca Harding Davis's nineteenth-century proletarian novel, Life in the Iron Mills, published by the Feminist Press in 1972. Two years later, after several grants and creative writing fellowships, she published the still-unfinished Yonnondio. In 1978 Silences appeared, a collection of essays exploring the different circumstances that obstruct or silence literary creation.

Olsen cites her own life circumstances as the cause for publishing so little.[1] As the Canadian author Margaret Atwood has understood, "Few writers have gained such wide respect on such a small body of published work. . . . Among women writers in the United States, 'respect' is too pale a word: 'reverence' is more like it. This is presumably because women writers, even more than their male counterparts, recognize what a heroic feat it is to have held down a job, raised four children, and still somehow managed to

810

become and to remain a writer." A radical feminist, Olsen has said that she felt no personal guilt as a single parent over her daughter's predicament, as described in her confessional narrative "I Stand Here Ironing," since "guilt is a word used far too sloppily, to cover up harmful situations in society that must be changed." Her four stories have appeared in over fifty anthologies and have been translated into different languages all over the world.

Tillie Olsen

ೞ

I STAND HERE IRONING

I stand here ironing, and what you asked me moves tormented back and forth with the iron.

"I wish you would manage the time to come in and talk with me about your daughter. I'm sure you can help me understand her. She's a youngster who needs help and whom I'm deeply interested in helping."

"Who needs help." . . . Even if I came, what good would it do? You think because I am her mother I have a key, or that in some way you could use me as a key? She has lived for nineteen years. There is all that life that has happened outside of me, beyond me.

And when is there time to remember, to sift, to weigh, to estimate, to total? I will start and there will be an interruption and I will have to gather it all together again. Or I will become engulfed with all I did or did not do, with what should have been and what cannot be helped.

She was a beautiful baby. The first and only one of our five that was beautiful at birth. You do not guess how new and uneasy her tenancy in her now-loveliness. You did not know her all those years she was thought homely, or see her poring over her baby pictures, making me tell her over and over how beautiful she had been — and would be, I would tell her — and was now, to the seeing eye. But the seeing eyes were few or nonexistent. Including mine.

I nursed her. They feel that's important nowadays. I nursed all the children, but with her, with all the fierce rigidity of first motherhood, I did like the books then said. Though her cries battered me to trembling and my breasts ached with swollenness, I waited till the clock decreed.

Why do I put that first? I do not even know if it matters, or if it explains anything.

She was a beautiful baby. She blew shining bubbles of sound. She loved motion, loved light, loved color and music and textures. She would lie on the floor in her blue overalls patting the surface so hard in ecstasy her hands and feet would blur. She was a miracle to me, but when she was eight months old I had to leave her daytimes with the woman downstairs to whom she was no miracle at all, for I worked or looked for work and for Emily's father, who "could no longer endure" (he wrote in his good-bye note) "sharing want with us."

I was nineteen. It was the pre-relief, pre-WPA world of the depression. I would start running as soon as I got off the streetcar, running up the stairs, the place smelling sour, and awake or asleep to startle awake, when she saw me she would break into a clogged weeping that could not be comforted, a weeping I can hear yet.

After a while I found a job hashing at night so I could be with her days, and it was better. But it came to where I had to bring her to his family and leave her.

It took a long time to raise the money for her fare back. Then she got chicken pox and I had to wait longer. When she finally came, I hardly knew her, walking quick and nervous like her father, looking like her father, thin, and dressed in a shoddy red that yellowed her skin and glared at the pock-marks. All the baby loveliness gone.

She was two. Old enough for nursery school they said, and I did not know then what I know now — the fatigue of the long day, and the lacera-tions of group life in the kinds of nurseries that are only parking places for children.

Except that it would have made no difference if I had known. It was the only place there was. It was the only way we could be together, the only way I could hold a job.

And even without knowing, I knew. I knew the teacher that was evil because all these years it has curdled into my memory, the little boy hunched in the corner, her rasp, "why aren't you outside, because Alvin hits you? that's no reason, go out, scaredy." I knew Emily hated it even if she did not clutch and implore "don't go Mommy" like the other children, mornings.

She always had a reason why we should stay home. Momma, you look sick. Momma, I feel sick. Momma, the teachers aren't there today, they're sick. Momma, we can't go, there was a fire last night. Momma, it's a holi-day today, no school, they told me.

But never a direct protest, never rebellion. I think of our others in their three-, four-year-oldness — the explosions, the tempers, the denunciations, the demands — and I feel suddenly ill. I put the iron down. What in me demanded that goodness in her? And what was the cost, the cost to her of such goodness?

The old man living in the back once said in his gentle way: "You should smile at Emily more when you look at her." What *was* in my face when I looked at her? I loved her. There were all the acts of love.

It was only with the others I remembered what he said, and it was the face of joy, and not of care or tightness or worry I turned to them — too late for Emily. She does not smile easily, let alone almost always as her brothers and sisters do. Her face is closed and sombre, but when she wants, how fluid. You must have seen it in her pantomimes, you spoke of her rare gift for comedy on the stage that rouses laughter out of the audience so dear they applaud and applaud and do not want to let her go.

Where does it come from, that comedy? There was none of it in her when she came back to me that second time, after I had to send her away again. She had a new daddy now to learn to love, and I think perhaps it was a better time.

Except when we left her alone nights, telling ourselves she was old enough.

"Can't you go some other time, Mommy, like tomorrow?" she would ask. "Will it be just a little while you'll be gone? Do you promise?"

The time we came back, the front door open, the clock on the floor in the hall. She rigid awake. "It wasn't just a little while. I didn't cry. Three times I called you, just three times, and then I ran downstairs to open the door so you could come faster. The clock talked loud. I threw it away, it scared me what it talked."

She said the clock talked loud again that night I went to the hospital to have Susan. She was delirious with the fever that comes before red measles, but she was fully conscious all the week I was gone and the week after we were home when she could not come near the new baby or me.

She did not get well. She stayed skeleton thin, not wanting to eat, and night after night she had nightmares. She would call for me, and I would rouse from exhaustion to sleepily call back: "You're all right, darling, go to sleep, it's just a dream," and if she still called, in a sterner voice, "now go to sleep, Emily, there's nothing to hurt you." Twice, only twice, when I had to get up for Susan anyhow, I went in to sit with her.

Now when it is too late (as if she would let me hold her and comfort her like I do the others) I get up and go to her at once at her moan or restless stirring. "Are you awake, Emily? Can I get you something?" And the answer is always the same: "No, I'm all right, go back to sleep, Mother."

They persuaded me at the clinic to send her away to a convalescent home in the country where "she can have the kind of food and care you can't manage for her, and you'll be free to concentrate on the new baby." They still send children to that place. I see pictures on the society page of sleek young women planning affairs to raise money for it, or dancing at the affairs, or decorating Easter eggs or filling Christmas stockings for the children.

They never have a picture of the children so I do not know if the girls still wear those gigantic red bows and the ravaged looks on the every other Sunday when parents can come to visit "unless otherwise notified" — as we were notified the first six weeks.

Oh it is a handsome place, green lawns and tall trees and fluted flower beds. High up on the balconies of each cottage the children stand, the girls in their red bows and white dresses, the boys in white suits and giant red ties. The parents stand below shrieking up to be heard and the children shriek down to be heard, and between them the invisible wall "Not To Be Contaminated by Parental Germs or Physical Affection."

There was a tiny girl who always stood hand in hand with Emily. Her parents never came. One visit she was gone. "They moved her to Rose Cottage" Emily shouted in explanation. "They don't like you to love anybody here."

She wrote once a week, the labored writing of a seven-year-old. "I am fine. How is the baby. If I write my leter nicly I will have a star. Love." There never was a star. We wrote every other day, letters she could never hold or keep but only hear read — once. "We simply do not have room for children to keep any personal possessions," they patiently explained when we pieced one Sunday's shrieking together to plead how much it would mean to Emily, who loved so to keep things, to be allowed to keep her letters and cards.

Each visit she looked frailer. "She isn't eating," they told us.

(They had runny eggs for breakfast or mush with lumps, Emily said later, I'd hold it in my mouth and not swallow. Nothing ever tasted good, just when they had chicken.)

It took us eight months to get her released home, and only the fact that she gained back so little of her seven lost pounds convinced the social worker.

I used to try to hold and love her after she came back, but her body would stay stiff, and after a while she'd push away. She ate little. Food sickened her, and I think much of life too. Oh she had physical lightness and brightness, twinkling by on skates, bouncing like a ball up and down up and down over the jump rope, skimming over the hill; but these were momentary.

She fretted about her appearance, thin and dark and foreign-looking at a time when every little girl was supposed to look or thought she should look a chubby blonde replica of Shirley Temple. The doorbell sometimes rang for her, but no one seemed to come and play in the house or to be a best friend. Maybe because we moved so much.

There was a boy she loved painfully through two school semesters. Months later she told me how she had taken pennies from my purse to buy him candy. "Licorice was his favorite and I brought him some every day, but he still liked Jennifer better'n me. Why, Mommy?" The kind of question for which there is no answer.

School was a worry for her. She was not glib or quick in a world where glibness and quickness were easily confused with ability to learn. To her overworked and exasperated teachers she was an overconscientious "slow learner" who kept trying to catch up and was absent entirely too often.

I let her be absent, though sometimes the illness was imaginary. How different from my now-strictness about attendance with the others. I wasn't working. We had a new baby. I was home anyhow. Sometimes, after Susan grew old enough, I would keep her home from school, too, to have them all together.

Mostly Emily had asthma, and her breathing, harsh and labored, would fill the house with a curiously tranquil sound. I would bring the two old dresser mirrors and her boxes of collections to her bed. She would select beads and single earrings, bottle tops and shells, dried flowers and pebbles, old postcards and scraps, all sorts of oddments; then she and Susan would play Kingdom, setting up landscapes and furniture, peopling them with action.

Those were the only times of peaceful companionship between her and Susan. I have edged away from it, that poisonous feeling between them, that terrible balancing of hurts and needs I had to do between the two, and did so badly, those earlier years.

Oh there were conflicts between the others too, each one human, needing, demanding, hurting, taking — but only between Emily and Susan, no, Emily toward Susan that corroding resentment. It seems so obvious on the surface, yet it is not obvious. Susan, the second child, Susan, golden- and curly-haired and chubby, quick and articulate and assured, everything in appearance and manner Emily was not; Susan, not able to resist Emily's precious things, losing or sometimes clumsily breaking them; Susan telling jokes and riddles to company for applause while Emily sat silent (to say to me later: that was *my* riddle, Mother, I told it to Susan); Susan, who for all the five years' difference in age was just a year behind Emily in developing physically.

I am glad for that slow physical development that widened the difference between her and her contemporaries, though she suffered over it. She was too vulnerable for that terrible world of youthful competition, of preening and parading, of constant measuring of yourself against every other, of envy, "If I had that copper hair," "If I had that skin. . . ." She tormented herself enough about not looking like the others, there was enough of unsureness, the having to be conscious of words before you speak, the constant caring — what are they thinking of me? without having it all magnified by the merciless physical drives.

Ronnie is calling. He is wet and I change him. It is rare there is such a cry now. That time of motherhood is almost behind me when the ear is not one's own but must always be racked and listening for the child cry, the child call. We sit for a while and I hold him, looking out over the city spread in charcoal with its soft aisles of light. *"Shoogily,"* he breathes and curls closer. I carry him back to bed, asleep. *Shoogily.* A funny word, a family word, inherited from Emily, invented by her to say: *comfort.*

In this and other ways she leaves her seal, I say aloud. And startle at my saying it. What do I mean? What did I start to gather together, to try and make coherent? I was at the terrible, growing years. War years. I do not remember them well. I was working, there were four smaller ones now, there was not time for her. She had to help be a mother, and housekeeper, and shopper. She had to get her seal. Mornings of crisis and near hysteria trying to get lunches packed, hair combed, coats and shoes found, everyone to school or Child Care on time, the baby ready for transportation. And always the paper scribbled on by a smaller one, the book looked at by Susan then mislaid, the homework not done. Running out to that huge school where she was one, she was lost, she was a drop; suffering over the unpreparedness, stammering and unsure in her classes.

There was so little time left at night after the kids were bedded down. She would struggle over books, always eating (it was in those years she developed her enormous appetite that is legendary in our family) and I would be ironing, or preparing food for the next day, or writing V-mail to Bill, or tending the baby. Sometimes, to make me laugh, or out of her despair, she would imitate happenings or types at school.

I think I said once: "Why don't you do something like this in the school amateur show?" One morning she phoned me at work, hardly understandable through the weeping: "Mother, I did it. I won, I won; they gave me first prize; they clapped and clapped and wouldn't let me go."

Now suddenly she was Somebody, and as imprisoned in her difference as she had been in anonymity.

She began to be asked to perform at other high schools, even in colleges, then at city and statewide affairs. The first one we went to, I only recognized her that first moment when thin, shy, she almost drowned herself into the curtains. Then: Was this Emily? The control, the command, the convulsing and deadly clowning, the spell, then the roaring, stamping audience, unwilling to let this rare and precious laughter out of their lives.

Afterwards: You ought to do something about her with a gift like that — but without money or knowing how, what does one do? We have left it all to her, and the gift has so often eddied inside, clogged and clotted, as been used and growing.

She is coming. She runs up the stairs two at a time with her light graceful step, and I know she is happy tonight. Whatever it was that occasioned your call did not happen today.

"Aren't you ever going to finish the ironing, Mother? Whistler painted his mother in a rocker. I'd have to paint mine standing over an ironing board." This is one of her communicative nights and she tells me everything and nothing as she fixes herself a plate of food out of the icebox.

She is so lovely. Why did you want me to come in at all? Why were you concerned? She will find her way.

She starts up the stairs to bed. "Don't get me up with the rest in the morning." "But I thought you were having midterms." "Oh, those," she comes back in, kisses me, and says quite lightly, "in a couple of years when we'll all be atom-dead they won't matter a bit."

She has said it before. She *believes* it. But because I have been dredging the past, and all that compounds a human being is so heavy and meaningful in me, I cannot endure it tonight.

I will never total it all. I will never come in to say: She was a child seldom smiled at. Her father left me before she was a year old. I had to work her first six years when there was work, or I sent her home and to his relatives. There were years she had care she hated. She was dark and thin and foreign-looking in a world where the prestige went to blondeness and curly hair and dimples, she was slow where glibness was prized. She was a child of anxious, not proud, love. We were poor and could not afford for her the soil of easy growth. I was a young mother, I was a distracted mother. There were other children pushing up, demanding. Her younger sister seemed all that she was not. There were years she did not want me to touch her. She kept too much in herself, her life was such she had to keep too much in herself. My wisdom came too late. She has much to her and probably little will come of it. She is a child of her age, of depression, of war, of fear.

Let her be. So all that is in her will not bloom — but in how many does it? There is still enough left to live by. Only help her to know — help make it so there is cause for her to know — that she is more than this dress on the ironing board, helpless before the iron.

[1961]

RALPH ELLISON (b. 1914) was born in Oklahoma City, Oklahoma. When he was three his father died, and thereafter his mother worked as a domestic servant to support herself and her son. She often brought home discarded books and phonograph records from the white households where she worked, and as a boy Ellison developed an interest in literature and music. He played trumpet in his high school band, at the same time that he began to relate the works of fiction he was reading to real life. "I began to look at my own life through the lives of fictional characters. When I read Stendhal, I would search until I began to find patterns of a Stendhalian novel within the Negro communities in which I grew up. I began, in other words, quite early to connect the worlds projected in literature . . . with the life in which I found myself."

In 1933 Ellison entered Tuskegee Institute in Alabama, where he studied music for three years. Then he went to New York City and met the black writers Langston Hughes and Richard Wright, whose encouragement helped him to become a writer. Wright turned Ellison's attention to "those works in which writing was discussed as a craft . . . to Henry James's prefaces, to Conrad," and to other authors. In 1939 Ellison's short stories, essays, and reviews began to appear in periodicals. After World War II, aided by a Rosenwald Fellowship, he settled down to work on the novel Invisible Man. Published in 1952, it received the National Book Award for fiction; and, in 1965, a Book Week poll listed it as the most distinguished American novel of the preceding twenty years. In addition to Invisible Man, Ellison has published only a few short stories and a book of essays, Shadow and Act (1964). He has also taught at such universities as Yale, Harvard, and Rutgers, and was Albert Schweitzer Professor of Contemporary Literature and Culture at New York University until his retirement.

"Battle Royal" is an excerpt from Invisible Man, often anthologized in collections of short stories. It appears early in the novel, after the prologue describing the underground chamber to which the protagonist has retreated from the chaos of life above ground. "Battle Royal" is written in a simple, naturalistic style. It is the first step in the quest of an unnamed young black man for personal and community identity as he travels from South to North and from innocence to experience. Ellison meant his central character to dramatize more than just a personal ritual initiation in this story of his encounter with racial prejudice. Believing that modern American writers are handicapped by "the triumph of industrialism . . . with the blatant hypocrisy between its ideals and its acts," Ellison feels that artistic individualism (for example, the amoral violence described by Hemingway) has led writers to reject broad social responsibility. Seeking technical perfection rather *than moral insight, most American writers have forgotten that "art by its nature is social." While Ellison gives no program for the improvement of the situation, his fiction and essays present a depiction of contemporary American social problems remarkable for its intellectual perception, emotional balance, and moral commitment. (See Ellison's Interview about "Battle Royal" on page 1307.)*

Ralph Ellison

৩৩

BATTLE ROYAL

It goes a long way back, some twenty years. All my life I had been looking for something, and everywhere I turned someone tried to tell me what it was. I accepted their answers too, though they were often in contradiction and even self-contradictory. I was naïve. I was looking for myself and asking everyone except myself questions which I, and only I, could answer. It took me a long time and much painful boomeranging of my expectations to achieve a realization everyone else appears to have been born with: That I am nobody but myself. But first I had to discover that I am an invisible man!

And yet I am no freak of nature, nor of history. I was in the cards, other things having been equal (or unequal) eighty-five years ago. I am not ashamed of my grandparents for having been slaves. I am only ashamed of myself for having at one time been ashamed. About eighty-five years ago they were told that they were free, united with others of our country in everything pertaining to the common good, and, in everything social, separate like the fingers of the hand. And they believed it. They exulted in it. They stayed in their place, worked hard, and brought up my father to do the same. But my grandfather is the one. He was an odd old guy, my grandfather, and I am told I take after him. It was he who caused the trouble. On his deathbed he called my father to him and said, "Son, after I'm gone I want you to keep up the good fight. I never told you, but our life is a war and I have been a traitor all my born days, a spy in the enemy's country ever since I give up my gun back in the Reconstruction. Live with your head in the lion's mouth. I want you to overcome 'em with yeses, undermine 'em with grins, agree 'em to death and destruction, let 'em swoller you till they vomit or bust wide open." They thought the old man had gone out of his mind. He had been the meekest of men. The younger children were rushed from the room, the shades drawn and the flame of the lamp turned so low that it sputtered on the wick like the old man's breathing. "Learn it to the younguns," he whispered fiercely; then he died.

But my folks were more alarmed over his last words than over his dying. It was as though he had not died at all, his words caused so much anxiety. I was warned emphatically to forget what he had said and, indeed, this is the first time it has been mentioned outside the family circle. It had a tremendous effect upon me, however. I could never be sure of what he meant. Grandfather had been a quiet old man who never made any trouble, yet on his deathbed he had called himself a traitor and a spy, and he had spoken of his meekness as a dangerous activity. It became a constant puzzle which lay unanswered in the back of my mind. And whenever things went well for me I remembered my grandfather and felt guilty and uncomfortable. It was as though I was carrying out his advice in spite of myself. And to make it worse, everyone loved me for it. I was praised by the most lily-white men of the town. I was considered an example of desirable conduct — just as my grandfather had been. And what puzzled me was that the old man had defined it as *treachery*. When I was praised for my conduct I felt a guilt that in some way I was doing something that was really against the wishes of the white folks, that if they had understood they would have desired me to act just the opposite, that I should have been sulky and mean, and that that really would have been what they wanted, even though they were fooled and thought they wanted me to act as I did. It made me afraid that some day they would look upon me as a traitor and I would be lost. Still I was more afraid to act any other way because they didn't like that at all. The old man's words were like a curse. On my graduation day I delivered an oration in which I showed that humility was the secret, indeed, the very essence of progress. (Not that I believed this — how could I, remembering my grandfather? — I only believed that it worked.) It was a great success. Everyone praised me and I was invited to give the speech at a gathering of the town's leading white citizens. It was a triumph for our whole community.

It was in the main ballroom of the leading hotel. When I got there I discovered that it was on the occasion of a smoker, and I was told that since I was to be there anyway I might as well take part in the battle royal to be fought by some of my schoolmates as part of the entertainment. The battle royal came first.

All of the town's big shots were there in their tuxedoes, wolfing down the buffet foods, drinking beer and whiskey and smoking black cigars. It was a large room with a high ceiling. Chairs were arranged in neat rows around three sides of a portable boxing ring. The fourth side was clear, revealing a gleaming space of polished floor. I had some misgivings over the battle royal, by the way. Not from a distaste for fighting, but because I didn't care too much for the other fellows who were to take part. They were tough guys who seemed to have no grandfather's curse worrying their minds. No one could mistake their toughness. And besides, I suspected that fighting a battle royal might detract from the dignity of my speech. In those pre-invisible days I visualized myself as a potential Booker T. Washington. But the other fellows didn't care too much for me either, and there were nine of them. I felt superior to them in my way, and I didn't like the manner in which we were all crowded together into the servants' elevator. Nor did they like my being there. In fact, as the warmly lighted floors flashed past the elevator we had words over the fact that I, by taking part in the fight, had knocked one of their friends out of a night's work.

odds
to his
environment

We were led out of the elevator through a rococo hall into an ante-room and told to get into our fighting togs. Each of us was issued a pair of boxing gloves and ushered out into the big mirrored hall, which we entered looking cautiously about us and whispering, lest we might accidentally be heard above the noise of the room. It was foggy with cigar smoke. And already the whiskey was taking effect. I was shocked to see some of the most important men of the town quite tipsy. They were all there — bankers, lawyers, judges, doctors, fire chiefs, teachers, merchants. Even one of the more fashionable pastors. Something we could not see was going on up front. A clarinet was vibrating sensuously and the men were standing up and moving eagerly forward. We were a small tight group, clustered together, our bare upper bodies touching and shining with anticipatory sweat; while up front the big shots were becoming increasingly excited over something we still could not see. Suddenly I heard the school superintendent, who had told me to come, yell, "Bring up the shines, gentlemen! Bring up the little shines!"

Excitement

We were rushed up to the front of the ballroom, where it smelled even more strongly of tobacco and whiskey. Then we were pushed into place. I almost wet my pants. A sea of faces, some hostile, some amused, ringed around us, and in the center, facing us, stood a magnificent blonde — stark naked. There was dead silence. I felt a blast of cold air chill me. I tried to back away, but they were behind me and around me. Some of the boys stood with lowered heads, trembling. I felt a wave of irrational guilt and fear. My teeth chattered, my skin turned to goose flesh, my knees knocked. Yet I was strongly attracted and looked in spite of myself. Had the price of looking been blindness, I would have looked. The hair was yellow like that of a circus kewpie doll, the face heavily powdered and rouged, as though to form an abstract mask, the eyes hollow and smeared a cool blue, the color of a baboon's butt. I felt a desire to spit upon her as my eyes brushed slowly over her body. Her breasts were firm and round as the domes of East Indian temples, and I stood so close as to see the fine skin texture and beads of pearly perspiration glistening like dew around the pink and erected buds of her nipples. I wanted at one and the same time to run from the room, to sink through the floor, or go to her and cover her from my eyes and the eyes of the others with my body; to feel the soft thighs, to caress her and destroy her, to love her and murder her, to hide from her, and yet to stroke where below the small American flag tatooed upon her belly her thighs formed a

Degration

Girl was used to create excitement for the white against the narrator.

822   *Ralph Ellison*

capital V. I had a notion that of all in the room she saw only me with her impersonal eyes.

And then she began to dance, a slow sensuous movement; the smoke of a hundred cigars clinging to her like the thinnest of veils. She seemed like a fair bird-girl girdled in veils calling to me from the angry surface of some gray and threatening sea. I was transported. Then I became aware of the clarinet playing and the big shots yelling at us. Some threatened us if we looked and others if we did not. On my right I saw one boy faint. And now a man grabbed a silver pitcher from a table and stepped close as he dashed ice water upon him and stood him up and forced two of us to support him as his head hung and moans issued from his thick bluish lips. Another boy began to plead to go home. He was the largest of the group, wearing dark red fighting trunks much too small to conceal the erection which projected from him as though in answer to the insinuating low-registered moaning of the clarinet. He tried to hide himself with his boxing gloves.

And all the while the blonde continued dancing, smiling faintly at the big shots who watched her with fascination, and faintly smiling at our fear. I noticed a certain merchant who followed her hungrily, his lips loose and drooling. He was a large man who wore diamond studs in a shirtfront which swelled with the ample paunch underneath, and each time the blonde swayed her undulating hips he ran his hand through the thin hair of his bald head and, with his arms upheld, his posture clumsy like that of an intoxicated panda, wound his belly in a slow and obscene grind. This creature was completely hypnotized. The music had quickened. As the dancer flung herself about with a detached expression on her face, the men began reaching out to touch her. I could see their beefy fingers sink into her soft flesh. Some of the others tried to stop them and she began to move around the floor in graceful circles, as they gave chase, slipping and sliding over the polished floor. It was mad. Chairs went crashing, drinks were spilt, as they ran laughing and howling after her. They caught her just as she reached a door, raised her from the floor, and tossed her as college boys are tossed at a hazing, and above her red, fixed-smiling lips I saw the terror and disgust in her eyes, almost like my own terror and that which I saw in some of the other boys. As I watched, they tossed her twice and her soft breasts seemed to flatten against the air and her legs flung wildly as she spun. Some of the more sober ones helped her to escape. And I started off the floor, heading for the anteroom with the rest of the boys.

Some were still crying and in hysteria. But as we tried to leave we were stopped and ordered to get into the ring. There was nothing to do but what we were told. All ten of us climbed under the ropes and allowed ourselves to be blindfolded with broad bands of white cloth. One of the men seemed to feel a bit sympathetic and tried to cheer us up as we stood with our backs against the ropes. Some of us tried to grin. "See that boy over there?" one of the men said. "I want you to run across at the bell and give it to him right in the belly. If you don't get him, I'm going to get you. I don't like his looks." Each of us was told the same. The blindfolds were put on. Yet even then I had been going over my speech. In my mind each word was as bright as flame. I felt the cloth pressed into place, and frowned so that it would be loosened when I relaxed.

But now I felt a sudden fit of blind terror. I was unused to darkness. It was as though I had suddenly found myself in a dark room filled with poisonous cottonmouths. I could hear the bleary voices yelling insistently for the battle royal to begin.

"Get going in there!"

"Let me at that big nigger!"

I strained to pick up the school superintendent's voice, as though to squeeze some security out of that slightly more familiar sound.

"Let me at those black sonsabitches!" someone yelled.

"No, Jackson, no!" another voice yelled. "Here, somebody, help me hold Jack."

"I want to get at that ginger-colored nigger. Tear him limb from limb," the first voice yelled.

I stood against the ropes trembling. For in those days I was what they called ginger-colored, and he sounded as though he might crunch me between his teeth like a crisp ginger cookie.

Quite a struggle was going on. Chairs were being kicked about and I could hear voices grunting as with a terrific effort. I wanted to see, to see more desperately than ever before. But the blindfold was as tight as a thick skin-puckering scab and when I raised my gloved hands to push the layers of white aside a voice yelled, "Oh, no you don't, black bastard! Leave that alone!"

"Ring the bell before Jackson kills him a coon!" someone boomed in the sudden silence. And I heard the bell clang and the sound of the feet scuffling forward.

A glove smacked against my head. I pivoted, striking out stiffly as someone went past, and felt the jar ripple along the length of my arm to my shoulder. Then it seemed as though all nine of the boys had turned upon me at once. Blows pounded me from all sides while I struck out as best I could. So many blows landed upon me that I wondered if I were not the only blindfolded fighter in the ring, or if the man called Jackson hadn't succeeded in getting me after all.

Blindfolded, I could no longer control my motions. I had no dignity. I stumbled about like a baby or a drunken man. The smoke had become thicker and with each new blow it seemed to sear and further restrict my lungs. My saliva became like hot bitter glue. A glove connected with my head, filling my mouth with warm blood. It was everywhere. I could not tell if the moisture I felt upon my body was sweat or blood. A blow landed hard against the nape of my neck. I felt myself going over, my head hitting the floor. Streaks of blue light filled the black world behind the blindfold. I lay prone, pretending that I was knocked out, but felt myself seized by hands and yanked to my feet. "Get going, black boy! Mix it up!" My arms were like lead, my head smarting from blows. I managed to feel my way to the ropes and held on, trying to catch my breath. A glove landed in my mid-section and I went over again, feeling as though the smoke had become a knife jabbed into my guts. Pushed this way and that by the legs milling around me, I finally pulled erect and discovered that I could see the black, sweat-washed forms weaving in the smoky-blue atmosphere like drunken dancers weaving to the rapid drum-like thuds of blows.

Everyone fought hysterically. It was complete anarchy. Everybody fought everybody else. No group fought together for long. Two, three, four, fought one, then turned to fight each other, were themselves attacked. Blows landed below the belt and in the kidney, with the gloves open as well as closed, and with my eye partly opened now there was not so much terror. I moved carefully, avoiding blows, although not too many to attract attention, fighting from group to group. The boys groped about like blind, cautious crabs crouching to protect their mid-sections, their heads pulled in short against their shoulders, their arms stretched nervously before them, with their fists testing the smoke-filled air like the knobbed feelers of hypersensitive snails. In one corner I glimpsed a boy violently punching the air and heard him scream in pain as he smashed his hand against a ring post. For a second I saw him bent over holding his hand, then going down as a blow caught his unprotected head. I played one group against the other, slipping in and throwing a punch then stepping out of range while pushing the others into the melee to take the blows blindly aimed at me. The smoke was agonizing and there were no rounds, no bells at three minute intervals to relieve our exhaustion. The room spun round me, a swirl of lights, smoke, sweating bodies surrounded by tense white faces. I bled from both nose and mouth, the blood spattering upon my chest.

The men kept yelling, "Slug him, black boy! Knock his guts out!"

"Uppercut him! Kill him! Kill that big boy!"

Taking a fake fall, I saw a boy going down heavily beside me as though we were felled by a single blow, saw a sneaker-clad foot shoot into his groin as the two who had knocked him down stumbled upon him. I rolled out of range, feeling a twinge of nausea.

The harder we fought the more threatening the men became. And yet, I had begun to worry about my speech again. How would it go? Would they recognize my ability? What would they give me?

I was fighting automatically and suddenly I noticed that one after another of the boys was leaving the ring. I was surprised, filled with panic, as though I had been left alone with an unknown danger. Then I understood. The boys had arranged it among themselves. It was the custom for the two men left in the ring to slug it out for the winner's prize. I discovered this too late. When the bell sounded two men in tuxedoes leaped into the ring and removed the blindfold. I found myself facing Tatlock, the biggest of the gang. I felt sick at my stomach. Hardly had the bell stopped ringing in my

narrator
a mute fighter

ears than it clanged again and I saw him moving swiftly toward me. Thinking of nothing else to do I hit him smash on the nose. He kept coming, bringing the rank sharp violence of stale sweat. His face was a black blank of a face, only his eyes alive — with hate of me and aglow with a feverish terror from what had happened to us all. I became anxious. I wanted to deliver my speech and he came at me as though he meant to beat it out of me. I smashed him again and again, taking his blows as they came. Then on a sudden impulse I struck him lightly and as we clinched, I whispered, "Fake like I knocked you out, you can have the prize."

"I'll break your behind," he whispered hoarsely.

"For *them?*"

"For *me*, sonofabitch!"

They were yelling for us to break it up and Tatlock spun me half around with a blow, and as a joggled camera sweeps in a reeling scene, I saw the howling red faces crouching tense beneath the cloud of blue-gray smoke. For a moment the world wavered, unraveled, flowed, then my head cleared and Tatlock bounced before me. That fluttering shadow before my eyes was his jabbing left hand. Then falling forward, my head against his damp shoulder, I whispered,

"I'll make it five dollars more."

"Go to hell!"

But his muscles relaxed a trifle beneath my pressure and I breathed, "Seven!"

"Give it to your ma," he said, ripping me beneath the heart.

And while I still held him I butted him and moved away. I felt myself bombarded with punches. I fought back with hopeless desperation. I wanted to deliver my speech more than anything else in the world, because I felt that only these men could judge truly my ability, and now this stupid clown was ruining my chances. I began fighting carefully now, moving in to punch him and out again with my greater speed. A lucky blow to his chin and I had him going too — until I heard a loud voice yell, "I got my money on the big boy."

Hearing this, I almost dropped my guard. I was confused: Should I try to win against the voice out there? Would not this go against my speech, and was not this a moment for humility, for nonresistance? A blow to my head as I danced about sent my right eye popping like a jack-in-the-box and settled my dilemma. The room went red as I fell. It was a dream fall, my body languid and fastidious as to where to land, until the floor became impatient and smashed up to meet me. A moment later I came to. An hypnotic voice said FIVE emphatically. And I lay there, hazily watching a dark red spot of my own blood shaping itself into a butterfly, glistening and soaking into the soiled gray world of the canvas.

When the voice drawled TEN I was lifted up and dragged to a chair. I sat dazed. My eye pained and swelled with each throb of my pounding heart and I wondered if now I would be allowed to speak. I was wringing

Humiliated

wet, my mouth still bleeding. We were grouped along the wall now. The other boys ignored me as they congratulated Tatlock and speculated as to how much they would be paid. One boy whimpered over his smashed hand. Looking up front, I saw attendants in white jackets rolling the portable ring away and placing a small square rug in the vacant space surrounded by chairs. Perhaps, I thought, I will stand on the rug to deliver my speech.

Then the M.C. called to us, "Come on up here boys and get your money."

We ran forward to where the men laughed and talked in their chairs, waiting. Everyone seemed friendly now.

"There it is on the rug," the man said. I saw the rug covered with coins of all dimensions and a few crumpled bills. But what excited me, scattered here and there, were the gold pieces.

"Boys, it's all yours," the man said. "You get all you grab."

"That's right, Sambo," a blond man said, winking at me confidentially.

I trembled with excitement, forgetting my pain. I would get the gold and the bills, I thought. I would use both hands. I would throw my body against the boys nearest me to block them from the gold.

"Get down around the rug now," the man commanded, "and don't anyone touch it until I give the signal."

"This ought to be good," I heard.

As told, we got around the square rug on our knees. Slowly the man raised his freckled hand as we followed it upward with our eyes.

I heard, "These niggers look like they're about to pray!"

Then, "Ready," the man said. "Go!"

Tortured

I lunged for a yellow coin lying on the blue design of the carpet, touching it and sending a surprised shriek to join those rising around me. I tried frantically to remove my hand but could not let go. A hot, violent force tore through my body, shaking me like a wet rat. The rug was electrified. The hair bristled up on my head as I shook myself free. My muscles jumped, my nerves jangled, writhed. But I saw that this was not stopping the other boys. Laughing in fear and embarrassment, some were holding back and scooping up the coins knocked off by the painful contortions of the others. The men roared above us as we struggled.

"Pick it up, goddamnit, pick it up!" someone called like a bass-voiced parrot. "Go on, get it!"

I crawled rapidly around the floor, picking up the coins, trying to avoid the coppers and to get greenbacks and the gold. Ignoring the shock by laughing, as I brushed the coins off quickly, I discovered that I could contain the electricity — a contradiction, but it works. Then the men began to push us onto the rug. Laughing embarrassedly, we struggled out of their hands and kept after the coins. We were all wet and slippery and hard to hold. Suddenly I saw a boy lifted into the air, glistening with sweat like a circus seal, and dropped, his wet back landing flush upon the charged rug, heard him yell and saw him literally dance upon his back, his elbows beating a frenzied tatoo upon the floor, his muscles twitching like the flesh of a horse stung by many flies. When he finally rolled off, his face was gray and no one stopped him when he ran from the floor amid booming laughter.

"Get the money," the M.C. called. "That's good hard American cash!"

And we snatched and grabbed, snatched and grabbed. I was careful not to come too close to the rug now, and when I felt the hot whiskey breath descend upon me like a cloud of foul air I reached out and grabbed the leg of a chair. It was occupied and I held on desperately.

"Leggo, nigger! Leggo!"

The huge face wavered down to mine as he tried to push me free. But my body was slippery and he was too drunk. It was Mr. Colcord, who owned a chain of movie houses and "entertainment palaces." Each time he grabbed me I slipped out of his hands. It became a real struggle. I feared the rug more than I did the drunk, so I held on, surprising myself for a moment by trying to topple *him* upon the rug. It was such an enormous idea that I found myself actually carrying it out. I tried not to be obvious, yet when I grabbed his leg, trying to tumble him out of the chair, he raised up roaring with laughter, and, looking at me with soberness dead in the eye, kicked me viciously in the chest. The chair leg flew out of my hand. I felt myself going and rolled. It was as though I had rolled through a bed of hot coals. It seemed a whole century would pass before I would roll free, a century in which I was seared through the deepest levels of my body to the fearful breath within me and the breath seared and heated to the point of explosion. It'll all be over in a flash, I thought as I rolled clear. It'll all be over in a flash.

But not yet, the men on the other side were waiting, red faces swollen as though from apoplexy as they bent forward in their chairs. Seeing their fingers coming toward me I rolled away as a fumbled football rolls off the receiver's fingertips, back into the coals. That time I luckily sent the rug sliding out of place and heard the coins ringing against the floor and the boys scuffling to pick them up and the M.C. calling, "All right, boys, that's all. Go get dressed and get your money."

I was limp as a dish rag. My back felt as though it had been beaten with wires.

When we had dressed the M.C. came in and gave us each five dollars, except Tatlock, who got ten for being last in the ring. Then he told us to leave. I was not to get a chance to deliver my speech, I thought. I was going out into the dim alley in despair when I was stopped and told to go back. I returned to the ballroom, where the men were pushing back their chairs and gathering in groups to talk.

The M.C. knocked on a table for quiet. "Gentlemen," he said, "we

almost forgot an important part of the program. A most serious part, gentlemen. This boy was brought here to deliver a speech which he made at his
graduation yesterday. . . ."

"Bravo!"

"I'm told that he is the smartest boy we've got out there in Green-
wood. I'm told that he knows more big words than a pocket-sized dictionary."

Much applause and laughter.

"So now, gentlemen, I want you to give him your attention."

There was still laughter as I faced them, my mouth dry, my eye throbbing. I began slowly, but evidently my throat was tense, because they began
shouting, "Louder! Louder!"

"We of the younger generation extol the wisdom of that great leader
and educator," I shouted, "who first spoke these flaming words of wisdom:
'A ship lost at sea for many days suddenly sighted a friendly vessel. From
the mast of the unfortunate vessel was seen a signal: "Water, water; we die
of thirst!" The answer from the friendly vessel came back: "Cast down your
bucket where you are." The captain of the distressed vessel, at last heeding
the injunction, cast down his bucket, and it came up full of fresh sparkling
water from the mouth of the Amazon River.' And like him I say, and in his
words, 'To those of my race who depend upon bettering their condition in a
foreign land, or who underestimate the importance of cultivating friendly
relations with the Southern white man, who is his next-door neighbor, I
would say: "Cast down your bucket where you are" — cast it down in making friends in every manly way of the people of all races by whom we are
surrounded. . . .' "

I spoke automatically and with such fervor that I did not realize that
the men were still talking and laughing until my dry mouth, filling up with
blood from the cut, almost strangled me. I coughed, wanting to stop and go
to one of the tall brass, sand-filled spittoons to relieve myself, but a few of
the men, especially the superintendent, were listening and I was afraid. So I
gulped it down, blood, saliva and all, and continued. (What powers of endurance I had during those days! What enthusiasm! What a belief in the
rightness of things!) I spoke even louder in spite of the pain. But still they
talked and still they laughed, as though deaf with cotton in dirty ears. So I
spoke with greater emotional emphasis. I closed my ears and swallowed
blood until I was nauseated. The speech seemed a hundred times as long as
before, but I could not leave out a single word. All had to be said, each
memorized nuance considered, rendered. Nor was that all. Whenever I uttered a word of three or more syllables a group of voices would yell for me to
repeat it. I used the phrase "social responsibility" and they yelled:

"What's the word you say, boy?"

"Social responsibility," I said.

"What?"

"Social . . ."

"Louder."

". . . responsibility."

"More!"

"Respon —"

"Repeat!"

" — sibility."

The room filled with the uproar of laughter until, no doubt, distracted by having to gulp down my blood, I made a mistake and yelled a phrase I had often seen denounced in newspaper editorials, heard debated in private.

"Social . . ."

"What?" they yelled.

". . . equality —"

The laughter hung smokelike in the sudden stillness. I opened my eyes, puzzled. Sounds of displeasure filled the room. The M.C. rushed forward. They shouted hostile phrases at me. But I did not understand.

A small dry mustached man in the front row blared out, "Say that slowly, son!"

"What sir?"

"What you just said!"

"Social responsibility, sir," I said.

"You weren't being smart, were you, boy?" he said, not unkindly.

"No, sir!"

"You sure that about 'equality' was a mistake?"

"Oh, yes, sir," I said. "I was swallowing blood."

"Well, you had better speak more slowly so we can understand. We mean to do right by you, but you've got to know your place at all times. All right, now, go on with your speech."

I was afraid. I wanted to leave but I wanted also to speak and I was afraid they'd snatch me down.

"Thank you, sir," I said, beginning where I had left off, and having them ignore me as before.

Yet when I finished there was a thunderous applause. I was surprised to see the superintendent come forth with a package wrapped in white tissue paper, and, gesturing for quiet, address the men.

"Gentlemen, you see that I did not overpraise this boy. He makes a good speech and some day he'll lead his people in the proper paths. And I don't have to tell you that that is important in these days and times. This is a good, smart boy, and so to encourage him in the right direction, in the name of the Board of Education I wish to present him a prize in the form of this . . ."

He paused, removing the tissue paper and revealing a gleaming calf-skin brief case.

". . . in the form of this first-class article from Shad Whitmore's shop."

"Boy," he said, addressing me, "take this prize and keep it well. Consider it a badge of office. Prize it. Keep developing as you are and some day it will be filled with important papers that will help shape the destiny of your people."

I was so moved that I could hardly express my thanks. A rope of bloody saliva forming a shape like an undiscovered continent drooled upon the leather and I wiped it quickly away. I felt an importance that I had never dreamed.

"Open it and see what's inside," I was told.

My fingers a-tremble, I complied, smelling the fresh leather and finding an official-looking document inside. It was a scholarship to the state college for Negroes. My eyes filled with tears and I ran awkwardly off the floor.

I was overjoyed; I did not even mind when I discovered that the gold pieces I had scrambled for were brass pocket tokens advertising a certain make of automobile.

When I reached home everyone was excited. Next day the neighbors came to congratulate me. I even felt safe from grandfather, whose deathbed curse usually spoiled my triumphs. I stood beneath his photograph with my brief case in hand and smiled triumphantly into his stolid black peasant's face. It was a face that fascinated me. The eyes seemed to follow everywhere I went.

That night I dreamed I was at a circus with him and that he refused to laugh at the clowns no matter what they did. Then later he told me to open my brief case and read what was inside and I did, finding an official envelope stamped with the state seal; and inside the envelope I found another and another, endlessly, and I thought I would fall of weariness. "Them's years," he said. "Now open that one." And I did and in it I found an engraved document containing a short message in letters of gold. "Read it," my grandfather said. "Out loud."

"To Whom It May Concern," I intoned. "Keep This Nigger-Boy Running."

I awoke with the old man's laughter ringing in my ears.

(It was a dream I was to remember and dream again for many years after. But at the time I had no insight into its meaning. First I had to attend college.)

[1952]

BERNARD MALAMUD (1914–1986), a prominent writer of Jewish-American fiction, was born in Brooklyn, New York, to Max and Bertha Fidelman Malamud, Russian immigrants who ran a mom-and-pop grocery store. Malamud published his earliest stories in Brooklyn's Erasmus Hall High School literary magazine. In 1936 he graduated from City College in New York; in 1942 he earned his M.A. degree from Columbia University with a thesis on the English novelist Thomas Hardy. While teaching English at Erasmus Hall High School in 1945, Malamud married Ann De Chiara, an Italian-American. Throughout his life his stories appeared in a variety of magazines and reflected his interest in minority groups: Jews, Italians, blacks, and others. From 1949 to 1961 Malamud taught English at Oregon State University; then he joined the faculty at Bennington College in Vermont. In his later years he traveled and lectured extensively throughout the world.

Malamud published two novels, The Natural (1952) and The Assistant (1957), before his first collection of short stories, The Magic Barrel, came out in 1958. It won a National Book Award. Idiots First, his second collection, appeared in 1963; Pictures of Fidelman: An Exhibition, a unit of stories published over a period of twelve years, was issued in 1969. Rembrandt's Hat (1973) and The Stories of Bernard Malamud (1983) are his last story collections. He also published five other novels during his long career.

As the critic Leslie Field has recognized, Malamud was "never . . . overly concerned with depicting American Jews in order to discuss Judaism." Malamud said he frequently used Jewish material "because I know it." In the fantasy story "The Jewbird," which blends comedy and pathos, he took the Jew as a symbol for universal humanity. In 1968, while lecturing in Israel, Malamud remarked,

> What has made the Jewish writers conspicuous in American literature is their sensitivity to the value of man. . . . Personally, I handle the Jew as a symbol of the tragic experience of man existentially. I try to see the Jew as universal man. Everyman is a Jew though he may not know it. The Jewish drama is a . . . symbol of the fight for existence in the highest possible human terms. Jewish history is God's gift of drama.

Bernard Malamud

ᔖ

THE JEWBIRD

The window was open so the skinny bird flew in. Flappity-flap with its
frazzled black wings. That's how it goes. It's open, you're in. Closed, you're
out and that's your fate. The bird wearily flapped through the open kitchen
window of Harry Cohen's top-floor apartment on First Avenue near the
lower East River. On a rod on the wall hung an escaped canary cage, its
door wide open, but this black-type long-beaked bird — its ruffled head and
small dull eyes, crossed a little, making it look like a dissipated crow —
landed if not smack on Cohen's thick lamb chop, at least on the table, close
by. The frozen foods salesman was sitting at supper with his wife and young
son on a hot August evening a year ago. Cohen, a heavy man with hairy
chest and beefy shorts; Edie, in skinny yellow shorts and red halter; and
their ten-year-old Morris (after his father) — Maurie, they called him,
a nice kid though not overly bright — were all in the city after two weeks
out, because Cohen's mother was dying. They had been enjoying Kingston, New York, but drove back when Mama got sick in her flat in the
Bronx.

"Right on the table," said Cohen, putting down his beer glass and
swatting at the bird. "Son of a bitch."

"Harry, take care with your language," Edie said, looking at Maurie, Boy
who watched every move.

The bird cawed hoarsely and with a flap of its bedraggled wings —
feathers tufted this way and that — rose heavily to the top of the open
kitchen door, where it perched staring down.

"Gevalt,[1] a pogrom!"

"It's a talking bird," said Edie in astonishment.

"In Jewish," said Maurie.

"Wise guy," muttered Cohen. He gnawed on his chop, then put down
the bone. "So if you can talk, say what's your business. What do you want
here?"

"If you can't spare a lamb chop," said the bird, "I'll settle for a piece
of herring with a crust of bread. You can't live on your nerve forever."

"This ain't a restaurant," Cohen replied. "All I'm asking is what
brings you to this address?"

[1] a cry of surprise.

"The window was open," the bird sighed; adding after a moment, "I'm running. I'm flying but I'm also running."

"From whom?" asked Edie with interest.

"Anti-Semeets."

"Anti-Semites?" they all said.

"That's from who."

"What kind of anti-Semites bother a bird?" Edie asked.

"Any kind," said the bird, "also including eagles, vultures, and hawks. And once in a while some crows will take your eyes out."

"But aren't you a crow?"

"Me? I'm a Jewbird."

Cohen laughed heartily. "What do you mean by that?"

The bird began dovening. He prayed without Book or tallith, but with passion. Edie bowed her head though not Cohen. And Maurie rocked back and forth with the prayer, looking up with one wide-open eye.

When the prayer was done Cohen remarked, "No hat, no phylacteries?"

"I'm an old radical."

"You're sure you're not some kind of a ghost of dybbuk?"

"Not a dybbuk," answered the bird, "though one of my relatives had such an experience once. It's all over now, thanks God. They freed her from a former lover, a crazy jealous man. She's now the mother of two wonderful children."

"Birds?" Cohen asked slyly.

"Why not?"

"What kind of birds?"

"Like me. Jewbirds."

Cohen tipped back in his chair and guffawed. "That's a big laugh. I've heard of a Jewfish but not a Jewbird."

"We're once removed." The bird rested on one skinny leg, then on the other. "Please, could you spare maybe a piece of herring with a small crust of bread?"

Edie got up from the table.

"What are you doing?" Cohen asked her.

"I'll clear the dishes."

Cohen turned to the bird. "So what's your name, if you don't mind saying?"

"Call me Schwartz."

"He might be an old Jew changed into a bird by somebody," said Edie, removing a plate.

"Are you?" asked Harry, lighting a cigar.

"Who knows?" answered Schwartz. "Does God tell us everything?"

Maurie got up on his chair. "What kind of herring?" he asked the bird in excitement.

"Get down, Maurie, or you'll fall," ordered Cohen.

"If you haven't got matjes,[2] I'll take schmaltz,"[3] said Schwartz.

"All we have is marinated, with slices of onion — in a jar," said Edie.

"If you'll open for me the jar I'll eat marinated. Do you have also, if you don't mind, a piece of rye bread — the spitz?"[4]

Edie thought she had.

"Feed him out on the balcony," Cohen said. He spoke to the bird. "After that take off."

Schwartz closed both bird eyes. "I'm tired and it's a long way."

"Which direction are you headed, north or south?"

Schwartz, barely lifting his wings, shrugged.

"You don't know where you're going?"

"Where there's charity I'll go."

"Let him stay, papa," said Maurie. "He's only a bird."

"So stay the night," Cohen said, "but no longer."

In the morning Cohen ordered the bird out of the house but Maurie cried, so Schwartz stayed for a while. Maurie was still on vacation from school and his friends were away. He was lonely and Edie enjoyed the fun he had, playing with the bird.

"He's no trouble at all," she told Cohen, "and besides his appetite is very small."

"What'll you do when he makes dirty?"

"He flies across the street in a tree when he makes dirty, and if nobody passes below, who notices?"

"So all right," said Cohen, "but I'm dead set against it. I warn you he ain't gonna stay here long."

"What have you got against the poor bird?"

"Poor bird, my ass. He's a foxy bastard. He thinks he's a Jew."

"What difference does it make what he thinks?"

"A Jewbird, what a chutzpah. One false move and he's out on his drumsticks."

At Cohen's insistence Schwartz lived out on the balcony in a new wooden birdhouse Edie had bought him.

"With many thanks," said Schwartz, "though I would rather have a human roof over my head. You know how it is at my age. I like the warm, the windows, the smell of cooking. I would also be glad to see once in a while the *Jewish Morning Journal* and have now and then a schnapps because it helps my breathing, thanks God. But whatever you give me, you won't hear complaints."

However, when Cohen brought home a bird feeder full of dried corn, Schwartz said, "Impossible."

Cohen was annoyed. "What's the matter, crosseyes, is your life getting too good for you? Are you forgetting what it means to be migratory? I'll bet

[2] expensive herring.
[3] cheap herring.
[4] the heel of a loaf of bread.

a helluva lot of crows you happen to be acquainted with, Jews or otherwise, would give their eyeteeth to eat this corn."

Schwartz did not answer. What can you say to a grubber yung?[5]

"Not for my digestion," he later explained to Edie. "Cramps. Herring is better even if it makes you thirsty. At least rainwater don't cost anything." He laughed sadly in breathy caws.

And herring, thanks to Edie, who knew where to shop, was what Schwartz got, with an occasional piece of potato pancake, and even a bit of soupmeat when Cohen wasn't looking.

When school began in September, before Cohen would once again suggest giving the bird the boot, Edie prevailed on him to wait a little while until Maurie adjusted.

"To deprive him right now might hurt his school work, and you know what trouble we had last year."

"So okay, but sooner or later the bird goes. That I promise you."

Schwartz, though nobody had asked him, took on full responsibility for Maurie's performance in school. In return for favors granted, when he was let in for an hour or two at night, he spent most of his time overseeing the boy's lessons. He sat on top of the dresser near Maurie's desk as he laboriously wrote out his homework. Maurie was a restless type and Schwartz gently kept him to his studies. He also listened to him practice his screechy violin, taking a few minutes off now and then to rest his ears in the bathroom. And they afterwards played dominoes. The boy was an indifferent checker player and it was impossible to teach him chess. When he was sick, Schwartz read him comic books though he personally disliked them. But Maurie's work improved in school and even his violin teacher admitted his playing was better. Edie gave Schwartz credit for these improvements though the bird pooh-poohed them.

Yet he was proud there was nothing lower than C minuses on Maurie's report card, and on Edie's insistence celebrated with a little schnapps.

"If he keeps up like this," Cohen said, "I'll get him in an Ivy League college for sure."

"Oh I hope so," sighed Edie.

But Schwartz shook his head. "He's a good boy — you don't have to worry. He won't be a shicker[6] or a wifebeater, God forbid, but a scholar he'll never be, if you know what I mean, although maybe a good mechanic. It's no disgrace in these times."

"If I were you," Cohen said, angered, "I'd keep my big snoot out of other people's private business."

"Harry, please," said Edie.

"My goddamn patience is wearing out. That crosseyes butts into everything."

[5] a crude joker.
[6] a drinker.

Though he wasn't exactly a welcome guest in the house, Schwartz gained a few ounces although he did not improve in appearance. He looked bedraggled as ever, his feathers unkempt, as though he had just flown out of a snowstorm. He spent, he admitted, little time taking care of himself. Too much to think about. "Also outside plumbing," he told Edie. Still there was more glow to his eyes so that though Cohen went on calling him cross-eyes he said it less emphatically.

Liking his situation, Schwartz tried tactfully to stay out of Cohen's way, but one night when Edie was at the movies and Maurie was taking a hot shower, the frozen foods salesman began a quarrel with the bird.

"For Christ sake, why don't you wash yourself sometimes? Why must you always stink like a dead fish?"

"Mr. Cohen, if you'll pardon me, if somebody eats garlic he will smell from garlic. I eat herring three times a day. Feed me flowers and I will smell like flowers."

"Who's obligated to feed you anything at all? You're lucky to get herring."

"Excuse me, I'm not complaining," said the bird. "You're complaining."

"What's more," said Cohen, "even from out on the balcony I can hear you snoring away like a pig. It keeps me awake at night."

"Snoring," said Schwartz, "isn't a crime, thanks God."

"All in all you are a goddamn pest and free loader. Next thing you'll want to sleep in bed next to my wife."

"Mr. Cohen," said Schwartz, "on this rest assured. A bird is a bird."

"So you say, but how do I know you're a bird and not some kind of a goddamn devil?"

"If I was a devil you would know already. And I don't mean because your son's good marks."

"Shut up, you bastard bird," shouted Cohen.

"Grubber yung," cawed Schwartz, rising to the tips of his talons, his long wings outstretched.

Cohen was about to lunge for the bird's scrawny neck but Maurie came out of the bathroom, and for the rest of the evening until Schwartz's bedtime on the balcony, there was pretended peace.

But the quarrel had deeply disturbed Schwartz and he slept badly. His snoring woke him, and awake, he was fearful of what would become of him. Wanting to stay out of Cohen's way, he kept to the birdhouse as much as possible. Cramped by it, he paced back and forth on the balcony ledge, or sat on the birdhouse roof, staring into space. In evenings, while overseeing Maurie's lessons, he often fell asleep. Awakening, he nervously hopped around exploring the four corners of the room. He spent much time in Maurie's closet, and carefully examined his bureau drawers when they were left open. And once when he found a large paper bag on the floor, Schwartz poked his way into it to investigate what possibilities were. The boy was amused to see the bird in the paper bag.

"He wants to build a nest," he said to his mother.

Edie, sensing Schwartz's unhappiness, spoke to him quietly.

"Maybe if you did some of the things my husband wants you, you would get along better with him."

"Give me a for instance," Schwartz said.

"Like take a bath, for instance."

"I'm too old for baths," said the bird. "My feathers fall out without baths."

"He says you have a bad smell."

"Everybody smells. Some people smell because of their thoughts or because who they are. My bad smell comes from the food I eat. What does his come from?"

"I better not ask him or it might make him mad," said Edie.

In late November Schwartz froze on the balcony in the fog and cold, and especially on rainy days he woke with stiff joints and could barely move his wings. Already he felt twinges of rheumatism. He would have liked to spend more time in the warm house, particularly when Maurie was in school and Cohen at work. But though Edie was good-hearted and might have sneaked him in in the morning, just to thaw out, he was afraid to ask her. In the meantime Cohen, who had been reading articles about the migration of birds, came out on the balcony one night after work when Edie was in the kitchen preparing pot roast, and peeking into the birdhouse, warned Schwartz to be on his way soon if he knew what was good for him. "Time to hit the flyways."

"Mr. Cohen, why do you hate me so much?" asked the bird. "What did I do to you?"

"Because you're an A-number-one trouble maker, that's why. What's more, whoever heard of a Jewbird! Now scat or it's open war."

But Schwartz stubbornly refused to depart so Cohen embarked on a campaign of harassing him, meanwhile hiding it from Edie and Maurie. Maurie hated violence and Cohen didn't want to leave a bad impression. He thought maybe if he played dirty tricks on the bird he would fly off without being physically kicked out. The vacation was over, let him make his easy living off the fat of somebody else's land. Cohen worried about the effect of the bird's departure on Maurie's schooling but decided to take the chance, first, because the boy now seemed to have the knack of studying — give the black bird-bastard credit — and second, because Schwartz was driving him bats by being there always, even in his dreams.

The frozen foods salesman began his campaign against the bird by mixing watery cat food with the herring slices in Schwartz's dish. He also blew up and popped numerous paper bags outside the birdhouse as the bird slept, and when he got Schwartz good and nervous, though not enough to leave, he brought a full-grown cat into the house, supposedly a gift for little Maurie, who had always wanted a pussy. The cat never stopped springing up at Schwartz whenever he saw him, one day managing to claw out several of his tailfeathers. And even at lesson time, when the cat was usually excluded from Maurie's room, though somehow or other he quickly found his way in at the end of the lesson, Schwartz was desperately fearful of his life and flew from pinnacle to pinnacle — light fixture to clothes-tree to door-top — in order to elude the beast's wet jaws.

Once when the bird complained to Edie how hazardous his existence was, she said, "Be patient, Mr. Schwartz. When the cat gets to know you better he won't try to catch you any more."

"When he stops trying we will both be in Paradise," Schwartz answered. "Do me a favor and get rid of him. He makes my whole life worry. I'm losing feathers like a tree loses leaves."

"I'm awfully sorry but Maurie likes the pussy and sleeps with it."

What could Schwartz do? He worried but came to no decision, being afraid to leave. So he ate the herring garnished with cat food, tried hard not to hear the paper bags bursting like fire crackers outside the birdhouse at night, and lived terror-stricken closer to the ceiling than the floor, as the cat, his tail flicking, endlessly watched him.

Weeks went by. Then on the day after Cohen's mother had died in her flat in the Bronx, when Maurie came home with a zero on an arithmetic test, Cohen, enraged, waited until Edie had taken the boy to his violin lesson, then openly attacked the bird. He chased him with a broom on the balcony and Schwartz frantically flew back and forth, finally escaping into his birdhouse. Cohen triumphantly reached in, and grabbing both skinny legs, dragged the bird out, cawing loudly, his wings wildly beating. He whirled the bird around and around his head. But Schwartz, as he moved in circles, managed to swoop down and catch Cohen's nose in his beak, and hung on for dear life. Cohen cried out in great pain, punched the bird with his fist, and tugging at its legs with all his might, pulled his nose free. Again he swung the yawking Schwartz around until the bird grew dizzy, then with a furious heave, flung him into the night. Schwartz sank like stone into the street. Cohen then tossed the birdhouse and feeder after him, listening at the ledge until they crashed on the sidewalk below. For a full hour, broom in hand, his heart palpitating and nose throbbing with pain, Cohen waited for Schwartz to return but the broken-hearted bird didn't.

That's the end of that dirty bastard, the salesman thought and went in. Edie and Maurie had come home.

"Look," said Cohen, pointing to his bloody nose swollen three times its normal size, "what that sonofabitch bird did. It's a permanent scar."

"Where is he now?" Edie asked, frightened.

"I threw him out and he flew away. Good riddance."

Nobody said no, though Edie touched a handkerchief to her eyes and Maurie rapidly tried the nine times table and found he knew approximately half.

In the spring when the winter's snow had melted, the boy, moved by a memory, wandered in the neighborhood, looking for Schwartz. He found a dead black bird in a small lot near the river, his two wings broken, neck twisted, and both bird-eyes plucked clean.

"Who did it to you, Mr. Schwartz?" Maurie wept.

"Anti-Semeets," Edie said later.   [1963]

PETER TAYLOR (b. 1917) was born in Trenton, Tennessee. His maternal grandfather, Robert L. Taylor, served as governor of Tennessee for three terms and as a United States senator. Taylor's father was the president of a life insurance company in St. Louis. After Taylor's boyhood in Nashville, St. Louis, and Memphis, he studied at Vanderbilt University and Kenyon College, where his desire to become a writer was encouraged by his professor John Crowe Ransom. At Kenyon, Taylor also became friends with the poets Randall Jarrell and Robert Lowell, whose concern for language influenced Taylor's attitude toward his prose.

Taylor served in the army from 1941 to 1945. After the war, he began teaching creative writing at various colleges and universities, including the University of North Carolina, the University of Chicago, Kenyon College, Ohio State University, and the University of Virginia. In 1948 one of his previous professors, the novelist Robert Penn Warren, wrote the introduction to Taylor's first book, A Long Fourth and Other Stories, identifying Taylor's main subject as a writer: "the contemporary, urban, middle-class world of the upper South." During the next fifteen years Taylor published three more books of fiction, The Widows of Thornton (1954), Happy Families Are All Alike (1959), and Miss Leonora When Last Seen and Fifteen Other Stories (1963). In 1969 he secured his reputation as one of the finest short story writers in America with the publication of The Collected Stories of Peter Taylor. Since then he has published two more collections, In the Miro District (1977) and The Old Forest (1985), which recently won the PEN/Faulkner Award for the best work of fiction published in 1985. His short fiction continues to appear in magazines like The New Yorker, and his novels include A Summons to Memphis (1986) and A Woman of Means (1954). Taylor once told an interviewer, "It used to infuriate me, the attitude that you wrote stories until you were good enough to write a novel. I much prefer reading stories; I like James's stories better than his novels, and Faulkner's, and I think D. H. Lawrence's stories are much better than his novels. But people always pressure you, and it does seem like a challenge — the scope of it."

Over the years Taylor has refined his prose technique to the point where he says he now writes the first draft of his stories in verse. "I like it [verse] because you get more emphasis on the groups of words and the language and the rhythms. I can't sustain it very long, but I try to finish a story in verse, then go back and put it into prose. I began writing that way as an effort to compress; in a story you have very limited space, so every sentence has to do more." As the critic Victor Kramer has observed, Taylor has "become more attentive to the complexity of fictional situations, and especially to the intricacies of the individual psyche and to how language reveals this complexity." Taylor is frequently cited as an important influence on the *younger generation of American short story writers. "First Heat" is the story of a man caught between opposing forces and his difficulty in adapting to change.*

Peter Taylor

ෆ

First Heat

He turned up the air conditioning and lay across the bed, wearing only his jockey shorts. But it didn't stop. Two showers already since he came in from the afternoon session! Showers had done no good. Still, he might take another presently if it continued. The flow of perspiration was quite extraordinary. Perhaps it was the extra sleeping pill he took last night. He had never been one to sweat so. It was rather alarming. It really was. And with the air conditioner going full blast he was apt to give himself pneumonia.

What he needed of course was a drink, and that was impossible. He was not going to have a single drink before she arrived. He was determined to be cold sober. She would telephone up from the desk — or from one of the house phones nearby. He always thought of her as telephoning directly from the desk. Somehow that made the warning more official. But she did always telephone, did so out of fear he might not have his regular room. So she said. He knew better, of course. Married for nearly fifteen years, and at home she still knocked on doors — on the door to his study, on the door to the bathroom, even on the door to their bedroom. She even had the children trained to knock on doors, even each other's doors. Couldn't she assume that since he knew she was on the way, knew she was by now wheeling along the Interstate — doing seventy-five and more in her old station wagon — couldn't she assume that whatever kind of fool, whatever kind of philanderer she might suspect him of being, he would have the sense to have set matters right by the time she got there? But what rot! As if he didn't *have* a problem, as if he needed to make one up!

He could hear his own voice in the Senate Chamber that afternoon. Not his words, just his guilty voice. Suddenly he got up off the bed, pulled back the spread, the blanket, the top sheet. He threw himself down on his back, stuck his legs in the air, and pulled off his shorts. They were wringing wet with his damnable perspiration! He wadded them into a ball and, still lying on his back, still holding his legs in the air, he hurled the underwear at the ceiling, where it made a faintly damp spot before falling to the carpeted floor. And she — she would already know what his voice in the Senate

Chamber had said. (His legs still in the air.) And knowing how the voting
went, know who betrayed whom, who let whom down, who let what bill
that was supposed to go through intact be amended. It would all have been
reported on the local six o'clock state news, perhaps even with his taped
voice uttering the words of betrayal. She would have picked it up on the
radio in the station wagon just after she set out, with her evening dress in a
suitbox beside her. Maybe she would even have turned back, feeling she
just couldn't face certain people at the mansion reception tonight . . . or
couldn't face him.

Now — only now — he let his legs drop to the bed, his feet coming
down wide apart on the firm, first-rate-hotel mattress. And he threw out his
arms, one hand palm upward landing on each pillow of the double bed. He
would relax, *would* catch a quick nap. But a new charge of sweat pressed
out through every pore of his skin, on his forehead, on his neck, in the soft
area just above his collarbone, from the exposed inner sides of his thighs
and his ankles, from the exposed armpits and upper arms and forearms,
from the palms of his hands and the soles of his feet. He felt he was aware
of every infinitesimal modicum of sweat that was passing through every
pore of every area of his body. Somehow it made him feel more utterly,
thoroughly naked than he had ever before felt in his entire life. Yes, and this
time the sweat came before the thought — just a little before the thought
this time. The thought of what he had done and left undone concerning the
amendment, said and left unsaid concerning the amendment, the thought
of the discrepancy between his previously announced position and the position he finally took on the floor, all thought of *that* seemed something secondary and consequential to the sweat. Perhaps he was ill, really ill! Perhaps
it was only a coincidence that this sickening sweat had come over his body.
But no, he was not that sort — to claim illness. One thing for certain,
though, the sweat was already like ice water on his skin.

Now he would have to get up and dry himself off again. There was a
scratching sensation in his throat. He even coughed once. He would have to
turn *down* the air conditioner. And he would have to find something else to
focus his mind on. After all, he had not betrayed his country or his family.
And not, God knew, his constituents. Was it only old man Nat Haley he
was worrying about? He had agreed to support Nat Haley's waterways bill,
had been quite outspoken in favor of it. The newspapers all over the state
had quoted him. And then, yesterday, he had received promises from other
sources, promises so much to the interest of his constituents that he could
not resist. By God, it was the sort of thing he — *and* she — had known he
would have to do if he stood for the legislature and got elected, the sort of
thing he would have to face up to if he went into politics, where everybody
had said *he* ought not to go. He and she had looked each other in the eye
one day — before he ever announced — and said as much . . . Well, at the
last minute he had agreed to support the very amendment which Nat Haley
had said would be ruinous, would take all the bite out of his bill. But Nat
Haley was, himself, the damnedest kind of double-dealer. Even *he* had ob-

served that. Ah, he was beginning to know politics. And he was beginning to understand what "everybody" had meant. Old Nat Haley was well known for the deals he arranged and didn't live up to. Everyone knew about Nat Haley. Nat Haley wouldn't have hesitated to fight this bill itself if he had discovered, even at the last minute, that that was to his advantage.

Who, then, was he betraying? And it wasn't a bill of any great import, either.

He sat up and swung his feet over the side of the bed. His hand came down briefly on the moisture his body had left on the otherwise starchy hotel sheet. He glanced backward and saw the wet shadow of himself that his perspiration had left there, and he turned away from it. But as he turned away from his silhouette on the sheet, there he was, in all his nakedness, in the large rectangular mirror above the dresser. And there he was in the mirror on the open bathroom door. He reached to the floor and took up a bath towel he had dropped there earlier and began drying himself — and hiding himself. He stood up and went over his body roughly with the towel; then, his eyes lighting on the mirror on the bathroom door, he wadded up the towel, just as he had the jockey shorts, and hurled it at the door. It came right up against his face there! And when it had fallen, he realized that this time it wasn't — as so often — his face in the mirror that offended him. He didn't care about the face. He knew it too well and what its every line and look meant. The body interested him as never before, or as it had not in years. For a moment, it was like meeting someone from the past, someone he had almost forgotten — an old friend, and old enemy. It was — almost — a young man's body still; he was not forty yet and he exercised as much as he ever had and ate and drank with moderation. The body in the door mirror and in the large mirror over the dresser had good tone, was only a little heavier about the hips than it had once been, and the arm muscles were really better developed than when he was twenty. Taking in the different views he had of the body in the two mirrors he recalled that as late as his college days he had sometimes shadow-boxed before mirrors, usually wearing his ordinary boxer shorts and imagining they were made of silk, with his name, or some title, like *The Killer*, embroidered on them in purple or orange letters. He didn't smile over the recollection. But neither did he take any such stance before the mirrors now. The body in the mirrors was tense, as if prepared to receive a blow; and he looked at it objectively as a painter or a sculptor might, as a physician might. He observed features that particularized it: the modest island of dark hair on the chest, which narrowed into a peninsula pointing down below the navel and over the slightly rounded belly, almost joining the pubic hair above the too-innocent-looking penis; the elongated thighs; the muscular calves; the almost hairless arms; the shoulders, heavy and slightly stooped. Presently, his interest in himself seemed entirely anatomical. And all at once it was as though his eyes were equipped with X-rays. He could see beneath the skin and under the flesh to the veins and tendons and the ropelike muscles, the heart and lungs, the liver, the intestines, the testicles, as well as every bone and joint of the skeleton. And now it was as though a kleig light — no, a supernatural light — shone from behind him and through him. Only when at last he moved one foot, shifting his weight from one leg to the other, did the flesh and the covering skin return. Had it been a dream? A vision? It seemed to him now that he was not naked at all, or that this was not the nakedness he had sought when he removed his clothes. At any rate, his body had ceased to sweat.

He stepped back to the bed and lay down on his side, his back to the mirrors. He experienced momentary relief. It was as though he had seen beyond mere nakedness of body and spirit, had looked beyond all that which particularized him and made his body and his life meaningful, human. Was that the ultimate nakedness? Why, it could just as well have been old Nat Haley's insides he had seen. And he did relax now. He closed his eyes . . . But then it came on again. Only this time there was no sweat. There was just the explicit dread of that moment — soon now, soon — when he would open the door to her. And he thought of how other, older politicians would laugh at his agonizing over so small a matter. *They* would know what a mistake politics was for him. Or perhaps they would know that, like them, he was *made* for politics. Wasn't this merely his baptism — in betrayal? In politics the ends were what mattered, had to matter. In politics that was the only absolute. If you were loyal to other men, you were apt to betray your constituency. Or did he have it all backward? No, he had it right, he was quite sure. And for that very reason, wasn't the state Senate as far as he would go and farther than he should have gone? Friends had warned him against state politics especially. His father had said to him: "You are the unlikeliest-looking political candidate I have ever seen." But it was a decision she and he had made together, and together they had agreed that one's political morality could not always coincide with one's private morality. They had read that somewhere, hadn't they? At any rate, one had to be prepared to face up to that morality . . . And now, though he felt chilled to the bone, the sweat came on again. He rolled over and reached for the towel on the floor, forgetting he had thrown it at the mirror. As he got off the bed, the same hand that had reached for the towel reached out to the wall and turned down the air conditioner. He went into the bathroom and got a dry towel and came back drying himself — or those two hands were drying him. He stopped before the long mirror on the bathroom door, the hands still drying him. He remembered something else his father had said to him once when they were on a fishing trip at Tellico Plains. He had gone for a swim in the river and stood on a rocky slab beside the water afterward, first rubbing his chest and his head with a towel and then fanning his body with it before and aft. His father, watching the way he was fanning himself with the towel, said, "You do cherish that body of yours, don't y'?" But what mistaken notions his father had always had about him. Or perhaps it was only wishful thinking on his father's part. Perhaps he had only *wished* that kind of concern for him. Ah, if only his body *had* been his great care and concern in life — his problem! And no doubt that's what his sweating meant! He *wished* it were only a bodily ill!

He wasn't, as a matter of fact, a man who was given to lolling about this way with no clothes on — either at home or in a hotel room. And it occurred to him now that it wasn't the sweat alone that had made him do so today. As soon as he had walked into the room and closed the door after him he had begun pulling off his clothes. It seemed to him almost that the sweat began *after* he had stripped off his clothes. But he couldn't definitely recall now whether it had begun before or after he got to the room. At any rate, he wasn't *sure* it had begun before. Had it? Else, why had he undressed at once? .... He lay down on the bed again and his eye lit on the black telephone beside the bed. The first thing some men did when alone in a hotel room, he knew, was to take up the telephone and try to arrange for a woman to come up. Or that was what he always understood they did. The point was, he should have *known*. But he — he would hardly know nowadays how to behave with such a woman. He would hardly know what to say or do if one of those hotel creatures came into the room. Or would he know very well, indeed! Yes, how simple it all would be. What a great satisfaction, and how shameful it would seem afterward. How sinful — how clearly sinful — he would know himself to be. There the two of them are, in bed. But suddenly there comes a knock on the door! He will have to hide her. His wife is out there in the passage. The baby-sitter came a little early. And the traffic was not as bad as she had anticipated. With the new Interstate, a forty-mile drive is nothing. He has no choice. There isn't anything else he can do: he will have to hide the creature. She will have to stand naked, her clothes clutched in her arms, behind the drapery or in the closet, while he and his wife dress for the reception at the governor's mansion. If only — But the telephone, the real, black telephone was ringing now, there on the real bedside table.

He let it ring for thirty seconds or so. Finally, he took up the instrument. He said nothing, only lay on his side breathing into the mouthpiece.

"Hello," she said on the house phone. He could hear other voices laughing and talking in the lobby.

"Hello," he managed.

"I'm downstairs," she said, as she always said, waiting for him to invite her to come up. He invited her now, and she replied, "Is everything all right? You sound funny."

"Everything's fine. Come on up," he said. "You've heard the news?"

"I listened in the car, on the way over."

"I changed my mind about the bill," he said.

"Is Mr. Haley pretty angry?"

"He cut me cold on the Capitol steps afterward."

"I thought so," she said. "He was icy to me when I passed him in the lobby just now. Or I imagined he was."

"Do you still want to go to the reception?"

She laughed. "Of course I do. I'm sure you had good reasons."

"Oh, yes, I had good reasons."

"Then, shall I come on up?"

"Do," he said. But then he caught her before she hung up. "Wait," he said. He sat on the bed, pulling the sheet up about his hips. "Why don't you wait down there? Why don't we go somewhere and have a drink and something to eat before we dress for the reception? I'm starved."

"I'm starved, too," she said. "I had only a very small snack with the children at four-thirty."

"I'll be right down," he said.

"Well — " She hesitated and then said, "No, I have my dress with me in a box — my dress for tonight. I want to put it on a hanger. I'll be right up — that is, if you don't mind."

"Good," he said.

"And why don't we have our drink up there? It might be easier."

"Good," he said.

As soon as he had put down the telephone, he sprang from the bed, ran to pick up his sweaty shorts and the sweaty hotel towels. He began straightening the room and pulling on his clothes at the same time, with desperate speed. She must not find him undressed, this way. It would seem too odd. And if he should begin the sweating again, he was lost, he told himself. He would have to try to ignore it, but she would notice, and she would know . . . She would be on the elevator now, riding up with other members of the legislature and their wives, wives who had also come to town for the reception at the mansion. He felt utterly empty, as though not even those veins and tendons and bones and organs were inside him. Wearing only his shirt and fresh shorts and his black socks and supporters, he stopped dressing long enough to give the bed a haphazard making up. He yanked the sheet and blanket and spread about. Fluffed the pillows. But if only there was something besides his body, something else tangible to hide. Catching a glimpse of himself in the mirror, he blushed bashfully and began pulling on his trousers to cover his naked legs. While slipping his tie under his collar, he was also pushing his feet into his shoes. As he tied the necktie and then tied the shoe strings, he was listening for her footsteps in the passage. Oh, if only, if only — if only there were a woman, herself covered with sweat, and still — still panting, for him to hide. What an innocent, simple thing it would be. But there was only himself . . . When the knock came at the door, he was pulling on his jacket. "Just a second," he called. And for no reason at all, before opening the door he went to the glass-topped desk on which lay his open briefcase and closed the lid to the case, giving a quick snap to the lock. Then he threw open the door.

It was as though only a pair of blue eyes — bodiless, even lidless — hung there in the open doorway, suspended by invisible wires from the lintel. He read the eyes as he had not been able to read the voice on the telephone. They were not accusing. They had done their accusing in the car, no doubt, while listening to the radio. Now they were understanding and forgiving . . . He bent forward and kissed the inevitable mouth beneath the eyes. It too was understanding and forgiving. But if only the mouth and eyes would not forgive, not yet. He wanted their censure, first. She entered the room, with the suitbox under her arm, and went straight over to the closet. He held his breath, his eyes fixed on the closet door. She paused with her hand on the doorknob and looked back at him. Suddenly he understood the kind of sympathy she felt for him. Is it the lady or the tiger? her hesitation seemed to say. If only, she seemed to say with him, if only it *were* the lady, naked and clutching her bundle of clothing to her bosom. But he knew of course, as did she, it would be the tiger, the tiger whose teeth they had drawn beforehand, whose claws they had filed with their talk about the difference between things private and things political. The tiger was that very difference, that very discrepancy, and the worst of it was that they could never admit to each other again that the discrepancy existed. They stood facing each other well and fully clothed. When, finally, she would open the closet door, they would see only his formal evening clothes hanging there, waiting to be worn to the governor's mansion tonight. And while he looked over her shoulder, she would open the cardboard box and hang her full-length white evening gown beside his tuxedo. And after a while the tuxedo and the evening gown would leave the hotel room together and go down the elevator to the lobby and ride in a cab across town to the governor's mansion. And there was no denying that when the tuxedo and the evening gown got out of the taxi and went up the steps to the mansion and then moved slowly along in the receiving line, he and she, for better or for worse, would be inside them. But when the reception was over and the gown and the tuxedo came down the steps from the mansion, got into another taxi, and rode back across the town to their empty hotel room, who was it that would be in them then? Who?

[1969]

HEINRICH BÖLL *(1917–1985) was one of postwar Germany's best-known novelists and short story writers. The son of liberal Roman Catholic parents, Böll was born in Cologne. His father was a sculptor, and Böll shared his family's low opinion of the Nazi members of the Hitler Youth, the storm troopers, and the SS, regarding them as "blissful idiots" at the outbreak of the war. He later wrote in his autobiography,* What's to Become of the Boy *(1984), that his "aversion to the Nazis was not revolt: they revolted me, repelled me on every level of my existence, conscious and instinctive, aesthetic and political. To this day I have been unable to find any entertaining, let alone aesthetic, dimension to the Nazis and their era, a fact that makes me shudder when I see certain film and stage productions. I simply could not join the Hitler Youth, I did not join it, and that was that." Under community pressure, Böll's family displayed a small swastika flag, but Böll says that "sentiments could also be deduced from the size of the flags."*

After graduating from high school with a diploma that was called a "certificate of maturity," Böll found a job in a bookstore, but when he was twenty-two he was drafted into the German Army. For six years he fought on various fronts and was wounded before being taken prisoner by the Americans and eventually released. Böll's first book was a war novel, The Train Was on Time, *published in 1949. His reputation in the United States was established later with the success of the novels* Billiards at Half-Past Nine *(1962) and* The Clown *(1965), which was chosen by the American Library Association for its Distinguished Books list. As a writer Böll was regarded as the quasi-official conscience of postwar Germany, a role that was a burden to him since he felt himself primarily a private person. Popular with German readers, Böll had a remarkably balanced view of complicated issues during the Cold War. He believed the basic trouble with contemporary society is anxiety caused by the disparity between the actual and the ideal state of affairs. In 1972 he was awarded the Nobel Prize for Literature for the integrity and seriousness of his moral vision, which probed the schizophrenic contradictions between the realities of the modern world and human reactions based on conscience.*

Böll's stories are less complex than his novels. His short fiction in English translation has been collected in Traveler, If You Come to Spa *(1950),* Eighteen Stories *(1966), and* The Stories of Heinrich Böll *(1986). The husband in "Like a Bad Dream" is a victim of the corruption that surrounds him in an achievement-oriented society, which bears down hard on its victims and offers no escape.*

Heinrich Böll

ೞ

LIKE A BAD DREAM

–translated by Leila Vennewitz

That evening we had invited the Zumpens over for dinner, nice people; it was through my father-in-law that we had got to know them: ever since we have been married he has helped me to meet people who can be useful to me in business, and Zumpen can be useful: he is chairman of a committee which places contracts for large housing projects, and I have married into the excavating business.

I was tense that evening, but Bertha, my wife, reassured me. "The fact," she said, "that he's coming at all is promising. Just try and get the conversation round to the contract. You know it's tomorrow they're going to be awarded."

I stood looking through the net curtains of the glass front door, waiting for Zumpen. I smoked, ground the cigarette butts under my foot, and shoved them under the mat. Next I took up a position at the bathroom window and stood there wondering why Zumpen had accepted the invitation; he couldn't be that interested in having dinner with us, and the fact that the big contract I was involved in was going to be awarded tomorrow must have made the whole thing as embarrassing to him as it was to me.

I thought about the contract too: it was a big one, I would make 20,000 marks on the deal, and I wanted the money.

Bertha had decided what I was to wear: a dark jacket, trousers a shade lighter, and a conservative tie. That's the kind of thing she learned at home, and at boarding school from the nuns. Also what to offer guests: when to pass the cognac, and when the vermouth, how to arrange dessert. It is comforting to have a wife who knows all about such things.

But Bertha was tense too: as she put her hands on my shoulders, they touched my neck, and I felt her thumbs damp and cold against it.

"It's going to be all right," she said. "You'll get the contract."

"Christ," I said, "it means 20,000 marks to me, and you know how we need the money."

"One should never," she said gently, "mention Christ's name in connection with money!"

A dark car drew up in front of our house, a make I didn't recognize, but it looked Italian. "Take it easy," Bertha whispered, "wait till they've rung, let them stand there for a couple of seconds, then walk slowly to the door and open it."

I watched Mr. and Mrs. Zumpen come up the steps: he is slender and tall, with graying temples, the kind of man who fifty years ago would have been known as a "ladies' man"; Mrs. Zumpen is one of those thin dark women who always make me think of lemons. I could tell from Zumpen's face that it was a frightful bore for him to have dinner with us.

Then the doorbell rang, and I waited one second, two seconds, walked slowly to the door and opened it.

"Well," I said, "how nice of you to come!"

Cognac glasses in hand, we went from room to room in our apartment, which the Zumpens wanted to see. Bertha stayed in the kitchen to squeeze some mayonnaise out of a tube onto the appetizers; she does this very nicely: hearts, loops, little houses. The Zumpens complimented us on our apartment; they exchanged smiles when they saw the big desk in my study, at that moment it seemed a bit too big even to me.

Zumpen admired a small rococo cabinet, a wedding present from my grandmother, and a baroque Madonna in our bedroom.

By the time we got back to the dining room, Bertha had dinner on the table; she had done this very nicely too, it was all so attractive yet so natural, and dinner was pleasant and relaxed. We talked about movies and books, about the recent elections, and Zumpen praised the assortment of cheeses, and Mrs. Zumpen praised the coffee and the pastries. Then we showed the Zumpens our honeymoon pictures: photographs of the Breton coast, Spanish donkeys, and street scenes from Casablanca.

After that we had some more cognac, and when I stood up to get the box with the photos of the time when we were engaged, Bertha gave me a sign, and I didn't get the box. For two minutes there was absolute silence, because we had nothing more to talk about, and we all thought about the contract; I thought of the 20,000 marks, and it struck me that I could deduct the bottle of cognac from my income tax. Zumpen looked at his watch and said: "Too bad, it's ten o'clock; we have to go. It' been such a pleasant evening!" And Mrs. Zumpen said: "It was really delightful, and I hope you'll come to us one evening."

"We would love to," Bertha said, and we stood around for another half-minute, all thinking again about the contract, and I felt Zumpen was waiting for me to take him aside and bring up the subject. But I didn't. Zumpen kissed Bertha's hand, and I went ahead, opened the doors, and held the car door open for Mrs. Zumpen down below.

"Why," said Bertha gently, "didn't you mention the contract to him? You know it's going to be awarded tomorrow."

"Well," I said. "I didn't know how to bring the conversation round to it."

"Now look," she said in a quiet voice, "you could have used any excuse to ask him into your study, that's where you should have talked to him. You must have noticed how interested he is in art. You ought to have said: I have an eighteenth-century crucifix in there you might like to have a look at, and then . . ."

I said nothing, and she sighed and tied on her apron. I followed her into the kitchen; we put the rest of the appetizers back in the refrigerator, and I crawled about on the floor looking for the top of the mayonnaise tube. I put away the remains of the cognac, counted the cigars: Zumpen had smoked only one. I emptied the ashtrays, ate another pastry, and looked to see if there was any coffee left in the pot. When I went back to the kitchen, Bertha was standing there with the car key in her hand.

"What's up?" I asked.

"We have to go over there, of course," she said.

"Over where?"

"To the Zumpen's," she said, "where do you think?"

"It's nearly half past ten."

"I don't care if it's midnight," Bertha said, "all I know is, there's 20,000 marks involved. Don't imagine they're squeamish."

She went into the bathroom to get ready, and I stood behind her watching her wipe her mouth and draw in new outlines, and for the first time I noticed how wide and primitive that mouth is. When she tightened the knot of my tie I could have kissed her, the way I always used to when she fixed my tie, but I didn't.

Downtown the cafés and restaurants were brightly lit. People were sitting outside on the terraces, and the light from the street lamps was caught in the silver ice-cream dishes and ice buckets. Bertha gave me an encouraging look; but she stayed in the car when we stopped in front of the Zumpens' house, and I pressed the bell at once and was surprised how quickly the door was opened. Mrs. Zumpen did not seem surprised to see me; she had on some black lounging pajamas with loose full trousers embroidered with yellow flowers, and this made me think more than ever of lemons.

"I beg your pardon," I said, "I would like to speak to your husband."

"He's gone out again," she said, "he'll be back in half an hour."

In the hall I saw a lot of Madonnas, gothic and baroque, even rococo Madonnas, if there is such a thing.

"I see," I said, "well then, if you don't mind, I'll come back in half an hour."

Bertha had bought an evening paper; she was reading it and smoking, and when I sat down beside her she said: "I think you could have talked about it to her too."

"But how do you know he wasn't there?"

"Because I know he is at the Gaffel Club playing chess, as he does every Wednesday evening at this time."

"You might have told me that earlier."

"Please try and understand," said Bertha, folding the newspaper. "I am trying to help you, I want you to find out for yourself how to deal with such things. All we had to do was call up Father and he would have settled the whole thing for you with one phone call, but I want you to get the contract on your own."

"All right," I said, "then what'll we do: wait here half an hour, or go up right away and have a talk with her?"

"We'd better go up right away," said Bertha.

We got out of the car and went up in the elevator together. "Life," said Bertha, "consists of making compromises and concessions."

Mrs. Zumpen was no more surprised now than she had been earlier, when I had come alone. She greeted us, and we followed her into her husband's study. Mrs. Zumpen brought some cognac, poured it out, and before I could say anything about the contract she pushed a yellow folder toward me: "Housing Project Fir Tree Haven," I read, and looked up in alarm at Mrs. Zumpen, at Bertha, but they both smiled, and Mrs. Zumpen said: "Open the folder," and I opened it; inside was another one, pink, and on this I read: "Housing Project Fir Tree Haven — Excavation Work." I opened this too, saw my estimate lying there on top of the pile; along the upper edge someone had written in red: "Lowest bid."

I could feel myself flushing with pleasure, my heart thumping, and I thought of the 20,000 marks.

"Christ," I said softly, and closed the file, and this time Bertha forgot to rebuke me.

"*Prost*," said Mrs. Zumpen with a smile, "let's drink to it then."

We drank, and I stood up and said: "It may seem rude of me, but perhaps you'll understand that I would like to go home now."

"I understand perfectly," said Mrs. Zumpen, "there's just one small item to be taken care of." She took the file, leafed through it, and said: "Your price per square meter is thirty pfennigs below that of the next-lowest bidder. I suggest you raise your price by fifteen pfennigs: that way you'll still be the lowest and you'll have made an extra four thousand five hundred marks. Come on, do it now!" Bertha took her pen out of her purse and offered it to me, but I was in too much of turmoil to write; I gave the file to Bertha and watched her alter the price with a steady hand, rewrite the total, and hand the file back to Mrs. Zumpen.

"And now," said Mrs. Zumpen, "just one more little thing. Get out your check book and write a check for three thousand marks; it must be a cash check and endorsed by you."

She had said this to me, but it was Bertha who pulled our check book out of her purse and made out the check.

"It won't be covered," I said in a low voice.

"When the contract is awarded, there will be an advance, and then it will be covered," said Mrs. Zumpen.

Perhaps I failed to grasp what was happening at the time. As we went down in the elevator, Bertha said she was happy, but I said nothing.

Bertha chose a different way home, we drove through quiet residential districts, I saw lights in open windows, people sitting on balconies drinking wine; it was a clear, warm night.

"I suppose the check was for Zumpen?" was all I said, softly, and Bertha replied, just as softly: "Of course."

I looked at Bertha's small, brown hands on the steering wheel, so confident and quiet. Hands, I thought, that sign checks and squeeze mayonnaise tubes, and I looked higher — at her mouth, and still felt no desire to kiss it.

That evening I did not help Bertha put the car away in the garage, nor did I help her with the dishes. I poured myself a large cognac, went up to my study, and sat down at my desk, which was much too big for me. I was wondering about something. I got up, went into the bedroom, and looked at the baroque Madonna, but even there I couldn't put my finger on the thing I was wondering about.

The ringing of the phone interrupted my thoughts; I lifted the receiver and was not surprised to hear Zumpen's voice.

"Your wife," he said, "made a slight mistake. She raised the price by twenty-five pfennigs instead of fifteen."

I thought for a moment and then said: "That wasn't a mistake, she did it with my consent."

He was silent for a second or two, then said with a laugh: "So you had already discussed the various possibilities?"

"Yes," I said.

"All right, then make out another check for a thousand."

"Five hundred," I said, and I thought: It's like a bad dream — that's what it's like.

"Eight hundred," he said, and I said with a laugh: "Six hundred," and I knew, although I had no experience to go on, that he would now say seven hundred and fifty, and when he did I said "Yes" and hung up.

It was not yet midnight when I went downstairs and over to the car to give Zumpen the check; he was alone and laughed as I reached in to hand him the folded check. When I walked slowly back into the house, there was no sign of Bertha; she didn't appear when I went back into my study; she didn't appear when I went downstairs again for a glass of milk from the refrigerator, and I knew what she was thinking; she was thinking: he has to get over it, and I have to leave him alone; this is something he has to understand.

But I never did understand. It is beyond understanding.

[1966]

ALEKSANDR SOLZHENITSYN (b. 1918) was born in Kislovodsk, Russia, a health resort in the northern Caucasus. His father, a philology student at Moscow University, was killed on the German front during World War I six months before Solzhenitsyn was born. His mother never remarried. She moved with her son to Rostov-on-Don, where she worked as a typist and stenographer. After Solzhenitsyn completed his secondary education, he studied physics and mathematics at Rostov University, graduating with honors in 1941. There was little opportunity to read literature, yet he remembers that "the desire to write, and the unconscious idea (unprompted by anyone) that I ought for some reason to become a writer, arose in me at a very early age, at nine or ten, when I was not even capable of understanding what it was like to be a writer or why one wrote." Because of the poverty of his experience, he had no idea what to write about, and although he "wrote a great deal of nonsense in various genres," it was not until after World War II that he began to write seriously.

Solzhenitsyn served as a commander of a reconnaissance battery in the Russian Army at the front from 1943 to 1945. In 1945 he was arrested suddenly in East Prussia on the charge of criticizing Stalin in a letter to an old friend. He served his full eight-year sentence in hard labor at prison camps, and in 1953 he was sent into "permanent" exile in central Russia to work as a science and mathematics teacher in secondary schools. All through the following years he wrote prose and poetry, but not until 1961 did he attempt to have any of it published. In that year, the short novel One Day in the Life of Ivan Denisovich appeared in the Soviet literary magazine Novy Mir. With this he sprang from obscurity as a provincial teacher to world fame as a writer. Publication of the novel had been ordered by Soviet Premier Nikita Khrushchev himself as part of his anti-Stalinist campaign. The work was a sensation because it gives a realistic account, based on Solzhenitsyn's own experience, of life in a Soviet labor camp. Afterward the only other works by him that were permitted to appear in the Soviet Union were four short stories.

In May 1967 Solzhenitsyn wrote his famous letter to the Fourth National Congress of Soviet Writers, protesting the censorship of his novels, plays, and stories. Two years later he was expelled from the Soviet Writers' Union, and his outspoken letter of protest received worldwide publicity. The authorities cited his publication of two novels abroad (Cancer Ward and The First Circle, in 1968), as well as his criticism of Soviet society, as unacceptable. They also condemned his being awarded the Nobel Prize for Literature in 1970 as a hostile political gesture. In 1971 he published another major novel abroad, August 1914, which had been rejected sight unseen by Soviet publishers. Two years later he authorized publication in the West of his Gulag Archipelago, a factual account, ultimately amounting to three massive volumes, of the "archipelago" system of Soviet prison camps *organized between 1918 and 1956. This literary project has been called "the most heavy and relentless book of our time." Its publication precipitated a major attack on Solzhenitsyn by the Communist Party, and in 1974 he was deprived against his will of his Soviet citizenship and deported. He currently lives with his wife and family in rural Vermont.*

Interested in longer prose forms, Solzhenitsyn has not written many stories, but the construction of his novels is often episodic, dependent on an intricate interlocking of incidents that resemble short stories. "The Right Hand" is based on his own experience in a cancer hospital in the Soviet Union. It was published in the United States in 1971 as part of the book Stories and Prose Poems.

Aleksandr Solzhenitsyn

ೞ

THE RIGHT HAND

–translated by Michael Glenny

When I arrived in Tashkent that winter I was practically a corpse. I came there expecting to die.

But I was given another lease of life.

A month passed, then another and a third. Outside, the vivid Tashkent spring unfolded and advanced into summer; it was already very warm and lush greenery was everywhere when I started to venture out of doors on shaky legs.

I still did not dare to admit to myself that I was getting better; in my wildest dreams I still measured my extra span of life not in years but in months. I would tread slowly along the gravel and asphalt paths in the park which was laid out between the blocks of the clinic. I would often have to sit down for a rest and sometimes, when overcome with nausea, I had to lie down with my head as low as possible.

I was like the sick people all around me, and yet I was different: I had fewer rights than they had and was forced to be more silent. People came to visit them, relatives wept for them, and their one concern, their one aim in life was to get well again. But if I recovered, it would be almost pointless: I was thirty-five years of age and yet in that spring I had no one I could call my own in the whole world. I did not even own a passport, and if I were to recover, I should have to leave this green, abundant land and go back to my desert where I had been exiled "in perpetuity." There I was under open surveillance, reported on every fortnight, and for a long time the local police headquarters had not even allowed me, a dying man, to go away for treatment.

I could not talk about all this to the free patients around me; had I done so, they would not have understood. On the other hand, I had ten years of long and careful reflection behind me and already knew the truth of the saying that the true savour of life is not to be gained by big things but from little ones — things like my ability to shuffle along hesitantly on my weakened legs; my cautious breathing, to avoid stabbing pains in the chest; and a single potato, undamaged by the frost, that I fished out of my soup.

So for me this spring was the most painful and the loveliest of my life.

I was surrounded by things I had either forgotten or had never seen, so everything interested me — even the ice-cream cart, the roadsweeper with his hose, the women selling bunches of long radishes, and especially the foal who had strayed through a gap in the wall onto the grass.

With every passing day I dared to wander farther away from the clinic, through the park, which must have been laid out at the end of the last century, when these good, sturdy buildings, with their ornamental brickwork at the corners, were also put up. From the magnificent sunrise, throughout the long southern day, and deep into the electric-yellow evening, the park was alive with movement. The healthy people would scurry around while the sick would make their unhurried promenade.

At the point where several avenues merged into the one leading to the main gates, there stood a large white alabaster Stalin, grinning sarcastically behind his stone whiskers. Other, smaller statues were spaced out evenly along the path leading to the gates.

Then there was a stationer's kiosk. It sold plastic pencils and tempting notebooks. But I decided it was better to do without them, not merely because I had to keep a strict watch on my spending but also because previous notebooks of mine had fallen into the wrong hands.

A fruit stall and a teahouse were situated right by the gates. We patients in our striped pyjamas were not allowed into the teahouse, but you could watch what was going on through the openwork fence. I had never in my life seen a real teahouse, with those individual pots of green or black tea for each person. The teahouse had a European section with small tables, and an Uzbek section with a large dais. The people at the tables ate and drank quickly, left a small payment in an empty bowl, and departed. But on the dais people sat or sprawled around for hours on end, some of them even for days. On sackcloth mats beneath a rush awning which had been put up at the beginning of the hot weather, they consumed pot after pot of tea while playing dice, as if the whole long day was completely free of cares.

The fruit stall did sell to the patients, but the few kopecks I had earned in exile shied away from the prices. I stared hard at the piles of dried apricots, raisins, and fresh cherries, then walked away.

Farther on there was a high wall; the patients were not allowed beyond the gates. Two or three times a day the strains of a band playing funeral marches would waft over this wall into the hospital grounds.

The city had a million inhabitants, but the cemetery was right next door to us. We could hear the slow funeral processions for about ten minutes, until they had passed the ground. The sound of the drum produced an odd result: its rhythm had no effect on the crowd of mourners, whose jerky movements were always slightly faster than the beat; the healthy bystanders would hardly stop to look around before hurrying off again to wherever they had to go (and they all knew exactly where they had to go); but the patients would stop when they heard these marches, poke their heads out of the windows of the wards, and listen for a long time.

The clearer it grew that I was recovering from the disease, and the more certain I became that I would remain alive, the more wistfully I looked around: I was already sorry to be leaving all this.

In the medical students' sports ground, white figures were hitting white tennis balls to each other. All my life I had wanted to play tennis, but I had never had the chance. Beneath its steep bank, the muddy yellow water of the river Salar was gurgling furiously. Wide-branching oak trees grew in the park, shady maples and delicate Japanese acacias. The octagonal fountain was throwing up fresh, slender streams of silver as high as they could reach. And what grass on the lawns — succulent and mercifully disregarded, unlike the grass in the prison camps, which the authorities ordered to be weeded out like an enemy, while in my place of exile grass could not grow at all. Just to lie in it face downwards, peacefully breathing in its herbal fragrance and its sun-warmed exhalation, was a taste of paradise.

I was not the only one lying there in the grass. Dotted about were students from the Medical Institute, slogging away at their bulky textbooks. Some of them, however, were absorbed in reading short stories which were not part of the examination syllabus, while others, the athletic ones, emerged from the changing rooms swinging their sports hold-alls. In the evening girls, indistinct and therefore three times more attractive, would walk round the fountain in creased or well-ironed frocks, crunching the gravel of the paths under their feet.

My heart was bursting with pity for someone: it might have been for myself and my contemporaries, frozen to death near Demiansk, burnt alive in Auschwitz, harried to exhaustion in Djezkazgan, or dying in the wastes of Siberia, because these girls would never belong to us. Or it might have been for these girls, because of the things I could never tell them and which they would never find out.

The whole day long, women — women, women! — would flow along the gravel and asphalt paths, young doctors, nurses, laboratory assistants, clerks, housekeepers, dispensers, and relatives visiting patients. They would pass me by in their austere white coats and their bright southern dresses, often semi-transparent, the richer ones in bright blues and pinks slowly twirling fashionable bamboo-handled Chinese parasols over their heads. Each one, as she flashed past, momentarily made up a complete plot for a novel: her past, the (nonexistent) chance of my getting to know her.

I was a pitiful wreck. My emaciated face bore the stamp of what I had been through — the wrinkles caused by the enforced gloom of camp life, the ashen colour of death on my leathery skin, the more recent poisoning caused by a venomous disease and toxic medicines which had added a greenish tinge to my cheeks. My back was hunched from the defensive habit of submission and selfeffacement. My clown-like striped jacket barely reached as far as my stomach, my striped trousers ended above my ankles, and the edges of my footcloths, brown from long wear, were hanging out of the canvas uppers of my blunt-toed prison-camp boots.

Not one of these women would have dared to walk beside me. But I could not see myself, and the world impinged upon my consciousness through eyes that were as sensitive as theirs.

One day, towards evening, I was standing by the main gates, looking around me at the usual stream of people rushing past; parasols bobbed along, silk dresses and tussore trouser with bright sashes, embroidered shirts and skullcaps flickered by. There was a buzz of voices. People were selling fruit; behind the fence, others were drinking tea and throwing dice. At the same time, leaning against the fence, a small, ungainly man who looked like a beggar was addressing the crowd from time to time in a voice gasping for breath: "Comrades . . . Comrades . . ."

The busy, gaily-coloured crowd was not listening to him. I went up to him. "What's the matter, brother?"

The man had an enormous belly, larger than a pregnant woman's, which hung down like a sack. It had burst through his dirty khaki tunic and trousers. His shoes, their soles worn away, were clumsy and dusty. His thick, unbuttoned overcoat with its soiled collar and frayed cuffs, unsuitable for this weather, weighed down his shoulders. On his head he wore an ancient, torn peaked cap, fit for a garden scarecrow. His eyes, swollen with dropsy, were glazed.

With great effort he raised one clenched hand, and I pulled a sweaty, crumpled piece of paper out of it. It was an application from citizen Bobrov, written in an angular hand with a pen that had scratched the paper, requesting admission to hospital; slanting across the application were two stamps, one in blue ink and one in red. The one in blue ink was from the Town Health Committee giving reasoned grounds for its refusal to admit him. The one in red ink, however, ordered the clinic of the Medical Institute to accept the man as an in-patient. The blue ink bore yesterday's date; the red ink — today's.

"Look," I explained to him loudly, as if he were deaf. "You've got to go to Reception, in Ward One. So just go straight on past these . . . statues . . ."

But then I noticed that his strength had abandoned him at the very moment that he reached the goal of his journey; not only was he incapable of asking any more questions or dragging his feet over the smooth asphalt path; he was even too weak to carry his shabby bag, which weighed no more than three or four pounds. So I made up my mind and said: "All right, old fellow, I'll take you. Let's go. Give me your bag."

He understood. He handed me his bag with relief, leaned on my proffered arm, and moved forward by dragging his shoes along the asphalt path, hardly lifting his feet off the ground. I guided him by his elbow, holding on to his coat, which was reddish-brown from the dust. His swollen stomach seemed to pull the old man forward and downwards. He frequently heaved a deep sigh.

Thus we advanced, two dishevelled figures, along the same avenue where, in my thoughts, I had linked arms with the most beautiful girls in Tashkent. For a long time we slowly dragged ourselves past the alabaster statues.

At last we turned off. Beside our path stood a bench with a back rest. My companion asked to sit down for a while. I too could feel an attack of nausea coming on, as I had been standing too long. We sat down. From here we could see the fountain.

While we were still walking along, the old man had said a few things to me, and now that he had recovered his breath, he resumed his story. He had to get to the Urals, and the residence permit in his passport was for the Urals, which was the whole trouble. He had been taken ill somewhere near Takhia-Tashem (where, I remember, they had started building a canal). At Urgench they had kept him in hospital for a month, drained the water from his stomach and legs, made him worse, and then discharged him. He had interrupted his journey at Chardzhou and then at Ursatevskaya, but wherever he went for treatment he was turned away; instead, they had sent him on to the Urals, because that was his official place of residence. He had felt too weak to go there by train, and anyway he did not have enough money for the ticket. So two days ago he had managed to get to Tashkent in the hope of being admitted to hospital.

I did not ask what he was doing down south or what had brought him here. His illness was, according to his medical certificates, "advanced," but a glance at the man was enough to tell you that it was terminal. I had seen a lot of patients and I could tell that he no longer had the will to live. He had lost control of his lips, his speech was indistinct, and his eyes had a dull life-lessness about them.

Even his cap was a burden to him. With great difficulty he pulled it off his head, down onto his knees. He struggled to raise his arm again and wiped the sweat off his forehead with his dirty sleeve. The top of his head was bald, though it was ringed by some sparse, untidy hair, still pale red under its coating of dust. It was not old age that had reduced him to this state but disease.

Folds of superfluous skin hung from his neck, which had grown piti-fully thin, like a chicken's, and his triangular Adam's apple protruded visi-bly. I wondered how he held his head up, and we had scarcely sat down when it lolled forward onto his chest, supported by his chin.

There he collapsed, with his cap on his knees and his eyes closed. He seemed to have forgotten that we had only sat down for a moment to re-cover our breath and that he had to go on to Reception.

Before our eyes, the almost noiseless jet of the fountain was casting its silver thread upwards. Beyond it, two girls passed, side by side. I watched them walk away. One was wearing an orange skirt, the other a maroon one. I found both of them extremely attractive.

My neighbour sighed audibly, rolled his head across his chest, and, raising his yellowish-grey lashes, squinted up at me. "Do you happen to have a cigarette, comrade?"

"You can forget that idea, old fellow," I barked at him. "You and I haven't got a hope unless we give up smoking. Take a look at yourself in a mirror. A cigarette! Really!" (I had only just succeeded in breaking myself of the habit a month before.)

Panting for breath, he again raised his eyes and looked at me from underneath his yellow lashes, rather like a dog. "All the same, comrade, give us three roubles."

I thought about whether to give them to him or not. After all, I was still a prisoner, while he was a free man. For all the years I had worked in prison camps I had been paid nothing. And when they did start to pay me they took all of it back in deductions: for the escort, for lighting the perimeter, for police dogs, for the officers, for the prison stew.

I took my oilskin purse out of the small breast pocket of my clown's jacket and inspected the notes in it. I sighed, then handed the old man a three-rouble note.

"Thanks," he said hoarsely. Struggling to hold his arm out, he took the note and put it in his pocket; at once his arm flopped down and slapped against his knee. His chin sagged forward until his head was again resting on his chest.

We fell silent. A woman passed by, then two more girl students. I found all three of them very attractive. It had been years since I had heard girls' voices or the tapping of their stiletto heels.

"Your're lucky they gave you an admission form, otherwise you might have had to hang around here for a week or so. It often happens. Lots of people have to put up with it."

He pulled his chin away from his chest and turned towards me. In his eyes a spark of sense glinted, his voice quivered, and he spoke more distinctly: "They're putting me in here, son, because I'm a deserving case. I'm a veteran of the Revolution. Sergey Mironovich Kirov personally shook me by the hand during the fighting at Tsaritsyn. I should be getting a special pension."

A slight movement of his cheeks and lips — the shadow of a proud smile — registered on his unshaven face.

I examined his rags, then looked him over once more. "Why don't you get it, then?"

"That's life," he sighed. "Now they don't even acknowledge my existence. Some of the records were burnt, others were lost. And I can't get any witnesses. Sergey Mironovich was murdered . . . It's all my fault, I didn't keep my documents . . . I've just one thing here . . ."

He lifted his right hand and fumbled in his pocket with his round, swollen finger joints, but here his burst of activity expired, and he again dropped his arm and his head and sat stock-still.

The sun was already sinking behind the hospital buildings and we would have to hurry to Reception (it was still a hundred paces away). In my experience, getting admitted to hospital is always beset with difficulties.

I took the old man by the shoulder. "Wake up, old fellow. Look, see that door over there? See it? I'm going over there to start persuading them. Come on your own if you can, but if not, wait for me. I'll take your bag."

He nodded as if he understood.

Reception was part of a large, shabby hall, divided off by rough partitions; at one time there had been a communal bathroom, a dressing room, and a hairdresser's here. In the daytime it was always crowded with patients whiling away the long hours until they would be admitted, but now, to my surprise, there was not a soul there. I knocked at the plywood hatch, which was closed. A very young nurse with a snub nose opened it; her lips were painted not red but a thick violet.

"What do you want?" She was sitting at a table reading a spy comic, as far as I could see.

She had very lively eyes.

I gave her the application with the two stamps on it and explained: "He can hardly walk. I've just brought him in."

"How dare you bring anyone in!" she cried sharply, without even looking at the piece of paper. "Don't you know the routine? We only admit patients at nine a.m.!"

She was the one who did not know the "routine." I stuck my head through the hatch and as much of my arm as I could manage, so that she could not slam it shut on me. Twisting my lower lip and pulling a face like a gorilla, I hissed in a menacing voice: "Listen, woman. And get this into your head — I'm not going to be bossed about by you!"

She took fright, moved her chair farther back into her little room, and said: "There's no admission, citizen. Only at nine a.m."

"Look . . . read this bit of paper!" I growled at her in my nastiest voice. She read it.

"Well, so what? The normal routine applies. And there may not be any places tomorrow. There weren't any this morning."

She announced that there had been no places that morning with a sort of satisfaction, as if the remark would puncture me.

"But the man's just passing through, don't you see? He's got nowhere to go."

As I backed out of the hatch and stopped talking in my harsh prison-camp rasp, her face took on its former expression of cheerful callousness. "They're all passing through. Where can we put them? They have to wait. He'll have to find a room somewhere."

"But just come and have a look. You'll see the condition he's in."

"Whatever next? Do you expect me to go round collecting patients? I'm not an orderly, you know!"

And she proudly twitched her snubnose. Her reply was as snappy and as automatic as clockwork.

"Then what the hell are you doing sitting here?"

I banged on the plywood wall with my fist, and a thin layer of white-wash scattered like pollen. "Lock the place up!"

"No one asked for your opinion, you lout!" She exploded with anger, jumped up, ran round, and appeared out of the narrow corridor. "Who do you think you are, anyway? Don't you teach me how to do my job! The ambulance'll bring him in."

Except for her crude violet lips and her matching nail varnish, she would not have been at all bad-looking. Her nose was her attractive feature, and she made great play with her eyebrows. Because it was so stuffy, she had undone the top buttons of her white coat and I could see her nice little pink scarf and Komsomol badge.

"What? If he hadn't come here by himself but had been picked up in the street by an ambulance, you would have admitted him? Is that your rule?"

She stared haughtily at my absurd figure and I stared back at her. I had completely forgotten that my footcloths were poking out of my boots. She snorted, looked at me coldly, and continued: "Yes, *patient*. That *is* the rule."

And she went back behind the partition.

I heard a rustling sound behind me. I looked around. My companion was already standing there. He had heard and understood everything. Clutching onto the wall and hauling himself towards the large bench put there for visitors, he was scarcely able to wave his right hand, which was clutching a tattered piece of paper.

"Here you are," he appealed to me in a faint voice. ". . . Here you are, show her this . . . let her . . . here . . ."

I managed to support him and lowered him onto the bench. With helpless fingers he tried to pull his only certificate out of his wallet but just could not manage it.

I took the top piece of paper from him, which was stuck down along its folds because it was falling apart, and opened it. On it were typed, in violet ink, lines with the letters dancing up and down over the creases:

WORKERS OF THE WORLD UNITE!

This certificate is presented to Comrade Bobrov N.K. for active service in 1921 in the distinguished "World Revolution" Special Detachment of ———— Province for personally eliminating large numbers of counterrevolutionary terrorists.

Signed: Commissar ————

A pale violet seal was attached to it.

Scratching my chest, I asked him quietly: "What's this 'Special Detachment'? What did it do?"

"Aha," he replied, scarcely able to keep his eyes open. "Show it to her."

I noticed his hand, his right hand — so small, with its brown, swollen veins and its round, puffed joints, practically incapable of pulling a certificate out of his wallet. And I remembered the way horsemen used to strike down men on foot with a single, sweeping backhand stroke.

Strange . . . That right hand had once swung a sabre in a full arc and chopped off heads, necks, and shoulders. And now it could not even hold a scrap of paper . . .

I went to up to the plywood hatch and again tried to persuade her to listen. The registrar did not raise her head but continued reading her comic. On the open page I saw a handsome man in uniform leaping onto a windowsill with a pistol.

I quietly placed the torn certificate on top of her book and turned away. I kept rubbing my chest to avoid being sick as I walked towards the door. I had to lie down as quickly as possible.

"What have you put this paper here for? Take it away!" the girl shot at me through the hatch as I walked away.

The veteran shrank into the bench. His head and even his shoulders seemed to sink into his torso. His helpless fingers dangled, outspread. His unbuttoned coat hung down, his bulbous, unbelievably swollen belly sagging into the fold of his thighs.

[1971]

DORIS LESSING (b. 1919) was born in Persia (now Iran), where her father managed a bank. When she was five her family moved to a farm in Rhodesia (now Zimbabwe), in an isolated part of Africa that had not been settled before by white people. "Looking back now at that enormous tract of bush, dotted with lonely farms, it seems as if we all lived on brightly lit stages where the dramas of our lives were played out to a chorus of comment and gossip. As a girl I watched these lives unfolding epically in the logic of their natures — a relentless and pitiless process it seemed then, as it still does." Lessing left school at the age of fourteen in rebellion against her mother, who had conventional ambitions for her. She lived on the farm and wrote two "bad" novels, then married at nineteen and had two children. After this marriage failed, she married again and had one son. She was a Communist for some years in her twenties, when she "learned a great deal, chiefly about the nature of political power, how groups of people operate." Then in 1949 she left her husband in Rhodesia and came with her son to London, where she has lived as a professional writer ever since, "at first rather poor, but now comfortable."

After Lessing left Africa, it remained in her consciousness as "an inexplicable majestic silence lying just over the border of memory or of thought. Africa gives you the knowledge that man is a small creature, among other creatures, in a large landscape." Her first two books, the novel The Grass Is Singing (1950) and a volume of short stories, This Was the Old Chief's Country (1951), are based on her experiences in Rhodesia. They develop the theme of the exploitation of blacks by white people — although Lessing also places racial prejudice in a larger context as being "only one aspect of the atrophy of the imagination that prevents us from seeing ourselves in every creature that breathes under the sun." She was recognized as a gifted young writer, and her next collection of African stories, Five, received the 1953 Somerset Maugham Award. Her third collection of stories, The Habit of Loving (1957), dramatized another of her themes as a writer: the destructive relationship between men and women. While her female characters have achieved a degree of intellectual, professional, and sexual freedom, they are still victims of their own emotional vulnerability to men who continue to exploit them. In 1962 Lessing published the experimental novel The Golden Notebook, which critics read as an exploration of the emotional problems faced by intelligent women who wish to live in the kind of freedom men take for granted. Lessing, however, said that she had shaped the book to explore a theme that goes beyond the status of women: the perilous situation of human beings in a fragmented, materialistic society. Her later novels have included the five volumes in the series Children of Violence, and several recent science-fiction works, Canopus in Argos Archives.

Considered one of the most accomplished novelists now writing in English, Lessing is also praised for her short stories, which have often been compared to those of D. H. Lawrence. Like Lawrence, she is not always confident of rational solutions to the political and sexual problems of modern life. In her fiction she goes beyond Lawrence, however, to explore the possibilities for psychological reorientation that exist in states of temporary insanity and in religious experience. Lessing is highly receptive to emotions that surface during the process of writing fiction: "This question of I, who am I, what different levels there are inside of us, is very relevant to writing, to the process of creative writing about which we know nothing whatsoever. Every writer feels when he, she, hits a different level. A certain kind of writing or emotion comes from it. But you don't know who it is who lives there. It is very frightening to write a story like 'To Room 19,' for instance, a story soaked in emotions that you don't remember as your own."

Doris Lessing

ဆာ

To Room 19

This is a story, I suppose, about a failure in intelligence: the Rawlings' marriage was grounded in intelligence.

They were older when they married than most of their married friends: in their well-seasoned late twenties. Both had had a number of affairs, sweet rather than bitter; and when they fell in love — for they did fall in love — had known each other for some time. They joked that they had saved each other "for the real thing." That they had waited so long (but not too long) for this real thing was to them a proof of their sensible discrimination. A good many of their friends had married young, and now (they felt) probably regretted lost opportunities; while others, still unmarried, seemed to them arid, self-doubting, and likely to make desperate or romantic marriages.

Not only they, but others, felt they were well-matched: their friends' delight was an additional proof of their happiness. They had played the same roles, male and female, in this group or set, if such a wide, loosely connected, constantly changing constellation of people could be called a set. They had both become, by virtue of their moderation, their humour, and their abstinence from painful experience, people to whom others came for advice. They could be, and were, relied on. It was one of those cases of a man and a woman linking themselves whom no one else had ever thought of linking, probably because of their similarities. But then everyone exclaimed: Of course! How right! How was it we never thought of it before!

And so they married amid general rejoicing, and because of their foresight and their sense for what was probable, nothing was a surprise to them.

Both had well-paid jobs. Matthew was a subeditor on a large London newspaper, and Susan worked in an advertising firm. He was not the stuff of which editors or publicised journalists are made, but he was much more than "a subeditor," being one of the essential background people who in fact steady, inspire, and make possible the people in the limelight. He was content with this position. Susan had a talent for commercial drawing. She was humorous about the advertisements she was responsible for, but she did not feel strongly about them one way or the other.

Both, before they married, had had pleasant flats, but they felt it unwise to base a marriage on either flat, because it might seem like a submission of personality on the part of the one whose flat it was not. They moved into a new flat in South Kensington on the clear understanding that when their marriage had settled down (a process they knew would not take long, and was in fact more a humorous concession to popular wisdom than what was due to themselves) they would buy a house and start a family.

And this is what happened. They lived in their charming flat for two years, giving parties and going to them, being a popular young married couple, and then Susan became pregnant, she gave up her job, and they bought a house in Richmond. It was typical of this couple that they had a son first, then a daughter, then twins, son and daughter. Everything right, appropriate, and what everyone would wish for, if they could choose. But people did feel these two had chosen; this balanced and sensible family was no more than what was due to them because of their infallible sense for *choosing* right.

And so they lived with their four children in their gardened house in Richmond and were happy. They had everything they had wanted and had planned for.

And yet. . . .

Well, even this was expected, that there must be a certain flatness. . . .

Yes, yes, of course, it was natural they sometimes felt like this. Like what?

Their life seemed to be like a snake biting its tail. Matthew's job for the sake of Susan, children, house, and garden — which caravanserai needed a well-paid job to maintain it. And Susan's practical intelligence for the sake of Matthew, the children, the house, and the garden — which unit would have collapsed in a week without her.

But there was no point about which either could say: "For the sake of *this* is all at rest." Children? But children can't be a centre of life and a reason for being. They can be a thousand things that are delightful, interesting, satisfying, but they can't be a wellspring to live from. Or they shouldn't be. Susan and Matthew knew that well enough.

Matthew's job? Ridiculous. It was an interesting job, but scarcely a reason for living. Matthew took pride in doing it well, but he could hardly be expected to be proud of the newspaper; the newspaper he read, *his* newspaper, was not the one he worked for.

Their love for each other? Well, that was nearest it. If this wasn't a centre, what was? Yes, it was around this point, their love, that the whole extraordinary structure revolved. For extraordinary it certainly was. Both Susan and Matthew had moments of thinking so, of looking in secret disbelief at this thing they had created: marriage, four children, big house, garden, charwomen, friends, cars . . . and this *thing*, this entity, all of it had come into existence, been blown into being out of nowhere, because Susan loved Matthew and Matthew loved Susan. Extraordinary. So that was the central point, the wellspring.

And if one felt that it simply was not strong enough, important enough, to support it all, well whose fault was that? Certainly neither Susan's nor Matthew's. It was in the nature of things. And they sensibly blamed neither themselves nor each other.

On the contrary, they used their intelligence to preserve what they had created from a painful and explosive world: they looked around them, and took lessons. All around them, marriages collapsing, or breaking, or rubbing along (even worse, they felt). They must not make the same mistakes, they must not.

They had avoided the pitfall so many of their friends had fallen into — of buying a house in the country *for the sake of the children*, so that the husband became a weekend husband, a weekend father, and the wife always careful not to ask what went on in the town flat which they called (in joke) a bachelor flat. No, Matthew was a full-time husband, a full-time father, and at night, in the big married bed in the big married bedroom (which had an attractive view of the river), they lay beside each other talking and he told her about his day, and what he had done, and whom he had met; and she told him about her day (not as interesting, but that was not her fault), for both knew of the hidden resentments and deprivations of the woman who has lived her own life — and above all, has earned her own living — and is now dependent on a husband for outside interests and money.

Nor did Susan make the mistake of taking a job for the sake of her independence, which she might very well have done, since her old firm, missing her qualities of humour, balance, and sense, invited her often to go back. Children needed their mother to a certain age, that both parents knew and agreed on; and when these four healthy wisely brought up children were of the right age, Susan would work again, because she knew, and so did he, what happened to women of fifty at the height of their energy and ability, with grownup children who no longer needed their full devotion.

So here was this couple, testing their marriage, looking after it, treating it like a small boat full of helpless people in a very stormy sea. Well, of course, so it was. . . . The storms of the world were bad, but not too close — which is not to say they were selfishly felt: Susan and Matthew were both well-informed and responsible people. And the inner storms and quicksands were understood and charted. So everything was all right. Everything was in order. Yes, things were under control.

So what did it matter if they felt dry, flat? People like themselves, fed on a hundred books (psychological, anthropological, sociological), could scarcely be unprepared for the dry, controlled wistfulness which is the distinguishing mark of the intelligent marriage. Two people, endowed with education, with discrimination, with judgement, linked together voluntarily from their will to be happy together and to be of use to others — one sees them everywhere, one knows them, one even is that thing oneself: sadness because so much is after all so little. These two, unsurprised, turned towards each other with even more courtesy and gentle love: this was life, that two people, no matter how carefully chosen, could not be everything to each other. In fact, even to say so, to think in such a way, was banal; they were ashamed to do it.

It was banal, too, when one night Matthew came home late and confessed he had been to a party, taken a girl home, and slept with her. Susan forgave him, of course. Except that forgiveness is hardly the word. Understanding, yes. But if you understand something, you don't forgive it, you are the thing itself: forgiveness is for what you *don't* understand. Nor had he *confessed* — what sort of word is that?

The whole thing was not important. After all, years ago they had joked: Of course I'm not going to be faithful to you, no one can be faithful to one other person for a whole lifetime. (And there was the word "faithful" — stupid, all these words, stupid, belonging to a savage old world.) But the incident left both of them irritable. Strange, but they were both bad-tempered, annoyed. There was something unassimilable about it.

Making love splendidly after he had come home that night, both had felt that the idea that Myra Jenkins, a pretty girl met at a party, could be even relevant was ridiculous. They had loved each other for over a decade, would love each other for years more. Who, then, was Myra Jenkins?

Except, thought Susan, unaccountably bad-tempered, she was (is?) the first. In ten years. So either the ten years' fidelity was not important, or she isn't. (No, no, there is something wrong with this way of thinking, there must be.) But if she isn't important, presumably it wasn't important either when Matthew and I first went to bed with each other that afternoon whose delight even now (like a very long shadow at sundown) lays a long, wandlike finger over us. (Why did I say sundown?) Well, if what we felt that afternoon was not important, nothing is important, because if it hadn't been for what we felt, we wouldn't be Mr. and Mrs. Rawlings with four children, et cetera, et cetera. The whole thing is *absurd* — for him to have come home and told me was absurd. For him not to have told me was absurd. For me to care or, for that matter, not to care, is absurd . . . and who is Myra Jenkins? Why, no one at all.

There was only one thing to do, and of course these sensible people did it; they put the thing behind them, and consciously, knowing what they were doing, moved forward into a different phase of their marriage, giving thanks for the past good fortune as they did so.

For it was inevitable that the handsome, blond, attractive, manly man, Matthew Rawlings, should be at times tempted (oh, what a word!) by the attractive girls at parties she could not attend because of the four children; and that sometimes he would succumb (a word even more repulsive, if possible) and that she, a goodlooking woman in the big well-tended garden at Richmond, would sometimes be pierced as by an arrow from the sky with bitterness. Except that bitterness was not in order, it was out of court. Did the casual girls touch the marriage? They did not. Rather it was they who knew defeat because of the handsome Matthew Rawlings' marriage body and soul to Susan Rawlings.

In that case why did Susan feel (though luckily not for longer than a few seconds at a time) as if life had become a desert, and that nothing mattered, and that her children were not her own?

Meanwhile her intelligence continued to assert that all was well. What if her Matthew did have an occasional sweet afternoon, the odd affair? For she knew quite well, except in her moments of aridity, that they were very happy, that the affairs were not important.

Perhaps that was the trouble? It was in the nature of things that the adventures and delights could no longer be hers, because of the four children and the big house that needed so much attention. But perhaps she was secretly wishing, and even knowing that she did, that the wildness and the beauty could be his. But he was married to her. She was married to him. They were married inextricably. And therefore the gods could not strike him with the real magic, not really. Well, was it Susan's fault that after he came home from an adventure he looked harassed rather than fulfilled? (In fact, that was how she knew he had been *unfaithful*, because of his sullen air, and his glances at her, similar to hers at him: What is it that I share with this person that shields all delight from me?) But none of it by anybody's fault. (But what did they feel ought to be somebody's fault?) Nobody's fault, nothing to be at fault, no one to blame, no one to offer or to take it . . . and nothing wrong, either, except that Matthew never was really struck, as he wanted to be, by joy; and that Susan was more and more often threatened by emptiness. (It was usually in the garden that she was invaded by this feeling: she was coming to avoid the garden, unless the children or Matthew were with her.) There was no need to use the dramatic words "unfaithful," "forgive," and the rest: intelligence forbade them. Intelligence barred, too, quarrelling, sulking, anger, silences of withdrawal, accusations, and tears. Above all, intelligence forbids tears.

A high price has to be paid for the happy marriage with the four healthy children in the large white gardened house.

And they were paying it, willingly, knowing what they were doing. When they lay side by side or breast to breast in the big civilised bedroom overlooking the wild sullied river, they laughed, often, for no particular reason; but they knew it was really because of these two small people, Susan and Matthew, supporting such an edifice on their intelligent love. The laugh comforted them; it saved them both, though from what, they did not know.

They were now both fortyish. The older children, boy and girl, were ten and eight, at school. The twins, six, were still at home. Susan did not have nurses or girls to help her: childhood is short; and she did not regret the hard work. Often enough she was bored, since small children can be boring; she was often very tired; but she regretted nothing. In another decade, she would turn herself back into being a woman with a life of her own.

Soon the twins would go to school, and they would be away from home from nine until four. These hours, so Susan saw it, would be the preparation for her own slow emancipation away from the role of hub-of-the-family into woman-with-her-own-life. She was already planning for the hours of freedom when all the children would be "off her hands." That was the phrase used by Matthew and by Susan and by their friends, for the moment when the youngest child went off to school. "They'll be off your hands, darling Susan, and you'll have time to yourself." So said Matthew, the intelligent husband, who had often enough commended and consoled Susan, standing by her in spirit during the years when her soul was not her own, as she said, but her children's.

What it amounted to was that Susan saw herself as she had been at twenty-eight, unmarried; and then again somewhere about fifty, blossoming from the root of what she had been twenty years before. As if the essential Susan were in abeyance, as if she were in cold storage. Matthew said something like this to Susan one night: and she agreed that it was true — she did feel something like that. What, then, was this essential Susan? She did not know. Put like that it sounded ridiculous, and she did not really feel it. Anyway, they had a long discussion about the whole thing before going off to sleep in each other's arms.

So the twins went off to their school, two bright affectionate children who had no problems about it, since their older brother and sister had trodden this path so successfully before them. And now Susan was going to be alone in the big house, every day of the school term, except for the daily woman who came in to clean.

It was now, for the first time in this marriage, that something happened which neither of them had foreseen.

This is what happened. She returned, at nine-thirty, from taking the twins to the school by car, looking forward to seven blissful hours of freedom. On the first morning she was simply restless, worrying about the twins "naturally enough" since this was their first day away at school. She was hardly able to contain herself until they came back. Which they did happily, excited by the world of school, looking forward to the next day. And the next day Susan took them, dropped them, came back, and found herself reluctant to enter her big and beautiful home because it was as if something was waiting for her there that she did not wish to confront. Sensibly, however, she parked the car in the garage, entered the house, spoke to Mrs. Parkes, the daily woman, about her duties, and went up to her bedroom. She was possessed by a fever which drove her out again, downstairs, into the kitchen, where Mrs. Parkes was making cake and did not need her, and into the garden. There she sat on a bench and tried to calm herself looking at trees, at a brown glimpse of the river. But she was filled with tension, like a panic: as if an enemy was in the garden with her. She spoke to herself severely, thus: All this is quite natural. First, I spent twelve years of my adult life working, *living my own life.* Then I married, and from the moment I became pregnant for the first time I signed myself over, so to speak, to other people. To the children. Not for one moment in twelve years have I been alone, had time to myself. So now I have to learn to be myself again. That's all.

And she went indoors to help Mrs. Parkes cook and clean, and found some sewing to do for the children. She kept herself occupied every day. At the end of the first term she understood she felt two contrary emotions. First: secret astonishment and dismay that during those weeks when the house was empty of children she had in fact been more occupied (had been careful to keep herself occupied) than ever she had been when the children were around her needing her continual attention. Second: that now she knew the house would be full of them, and for five weeks, she resented the fact she would never be alone. She was already looking back at those hours of sewing, cooking (but by herself) as at a lost freedom which would not be hers for five long weeks. And the two months of term which would succeed the five weeks stretched alluringly open to her — freedom. But what freedom — when in fact she had been so careful *not* to be free of small duties during the last weeks? She looked at herself, Susan Rawlings, sitting in a big chair by the window in the bedroom, sewing shirts or dresses, which she might just as well have bought. She saw herself making cakes for hours at a time in the big family kitchen: yet usually she bought cakes. What she saw was a woman alone, that was true, but she had not felt alone. For instance, Mrs. Parkes was always somewhere in the house. And she did not like being in the garden at all, because of the closeness there of the enemy — irritation, restlessness, emptiness, whatever it was — which keeping her hands occupied made less dangerous for some reason.

Susan did not tell Matthew of these thoughts. They were not sensible. She did not recognise herself in them. What should she say to her dear friend and husband, Matthew? "When I go into the garden, that is, if the children are not there, I feel as if there is an enemy there waiting to invade me." "What enemy, Susan darling?" "Well I don't know, really. . . ." "Perhaps you should see a doctor?"

No, clearly this conversation should not take place. The holidays began and Susan welcomed them. Four children, lively, energetic, intelligent, demanding: she was never, not for a moment of her day, alone. If she was in a room, they would be in the next room, or waiting for her to do something for them; or it would soon be time for lunch or tea, or to take one of them to the dentist. Something to do: five weeks of it, thank goodness.

On the fourth day of these so welcome holidays, she found she was storming with anger at the twins; two shrinking beautiful children who (and this is what checked her) stood hand in hand looking at her with sheer dismayed disbelief. This was their calm mother, shouting at them. And for what? They had come to her with some game, some bit of nonsense. They looked at each other, moved closer for support, and went off hand in hand, leaving Susan holding on to the windowsill of the livingroom, breathing deep, feeling sick. She went to lie down, telling the older children she had a headache. She heard the boy Harry telling the little ones: "It's all right, Mother's got a headache." She heard that *It's all right* with pain.

That night she said to her husband: "Today I shouted at the twins, quite unfairly." She sounded miserable, and he said gently: "Well, what of it?"

"It's more of an adjustment than I thought, their going to school."

"But Susie, Susie darling. . . . " For she was crouched weeping on the bed. He comforted her: "Susan, what is all this about? You shouted at them? What of it? If you shouted at them fifty times a day it wouldn't be more than the little devils deserve." But she wouldn't laugh. She wept. Soon he comforted her with his body. She became calm. Calm, she wondered what was wrong with her, and why she should mind so much that she might, just once, have behaved unjustly with the children. What did it matter? They had forgotten it all long ago: Mother had a headache and everything was all right.

It was a long time later that Susan understood that that night, when she had wept and Matthew had driven the misery out of her with his big solid body, was the last time, ever in their married life, that they had been — to use their mutual language — with each other. And even that was a lie, because she had not told him of her real fears at all.

The five weeks passed, and Susan was in control of herself, and good and kind, and she looked forward to the holidays with a mixture of fear and longing. She did not know what to expect. She took the twins off to school (the elder children took themselves to school) and she returned to the house determined to face the enemy wherever he was, in the house, or the garden or — where?

She was again restless, she was possessed by restlessness. She cooked and sewed and worked as before, day after day, while Mrs. Parkes remonstrated: "Mrs. Rawlings, what's the need for it? I can do that, it's what you pay me for."

And it was so irrational that she checked herself. She would put the car in the garage, go up to her bedroom, and sit, hands in her lap, forcing herself to be quiet. She listened to Mrs. Parkes moving around the house.

She looked out into the garden and saw the branches shake the trees. She sat defeating the enemy, restlessness. Emptiness. She ought to be thinking about her life, about herself. But she did not. Or perhaps she could not. As soon as she forced her mind to think about Susan (for what else did she want to be alone for?), it skipped off to thoughts of butter or school clothes. Or it thought of Mrs. Parkes. She realised that she sat listening for the movements of the cleaning woman, following her every turn, bend, thought. She followed her in her mind from kitchen to bathroom, from table to oven, and it was as if the duster, the cleaning cloth, the saucepan, were in her own hand. She would hear herself saying: No, not like that, don't put that there. . . . Yet she did not give a damn what Mrs. Parkes did, or if she did it at all. Yet she could not prevent herself from being conscious of her, every minute. Yes, this was what was wrong with her: she needed, when she was alone, to be really alone, with no one near. She could not endure the knowledge that in ten minutes or in half an hour Mrs. Parkes would call up the stairs: "Mrs. Rawlings, there's no silver polish. Madam, we're out of flour."

So she left the house and went to sit in the garden where she was screened from the house by trees. She waited for the demon to appear and claim her, but he did not.

She was keeping him off, because she had not, after all, come to an end of arranging herself.

She was planning how to be somewhere where Mrs. Parkes would not come after her with a cup of tea, or a demand to be allowed to telephone (always irritating, since Susan did not care who she telephoned or how often), or just a nice talk about something. Yes, she needed a place, or a state of affairs, where it would not be necessary to keep reminding herself: In ten minutes I must telephone Matthew about . . . and at half past three I must leave early for the children because the car needs cleaning. And at ten o'clock tomorrow I must remember. . . . She was possessed with resentment that the seven hours of freedom in every day (during weekdays in the school term) were not free, that never, not for one second, ever, was she free from the pressure of time, from having to remember this or that. She could never forget herself; never really let herself go into forgetfulness.

Resentment. It was poisoning her. (She looked at this emotion and thought it was absurd. Yet she felt it.) She was a prisoner. (She looked at this thought too, and it was no good telling herself it was a ridiculous one.) She must tell Matthew — but what? She was filled with emotions that were utterly ridiculous, that she despised, yet that nevertheless she was feeling so strongly she could not shake them off.

The school holidays came round, and this time they were for nearly two months, and she behaved with a conscious controlled decency that nearly drove her crazy. She would lock herself in the bathroom, and sit on the edge of the bath, breathing deep, trying to let go into some kind of calm. Or she went up into the spare room, usually empty, where no one would expect her to be. She heard the children calling "Mother, Mother," and kept silent, feeling guilty. Or she went to the very end of the garden, by herself, and looked at the slow-moving brown river; she looked at the river and closed her eyes and breathed slow and deep, taking it into her being, into her veins.

Then she returned to the family, wife and mother, smiling and responsible, feeling as if the pressure of these people — four lively children and her husband — were a painful pressure on the surface of her skin, a hand pressing on her brain. She did not once break down into irritation during these holidays, but it was like living out a prison sentence, and when the children went back to school, she sat on a white stone near the flowing river, and she thought: It is not even a year since the twins went to school, since *they were off my hands* (What on earth did I think I meant when I used that stupid phrase?), and yet I'm a different person. I'm simply not myself. I don't understand it.

Yet she had to understand it. For she knew that this structure — big white house, on which the mortgage still cost four hundred a year, a husband, so good and kind and insightful; four children, all doing so nicely; and the garden where she sat; and Mrs. Parkes, the cleaning woman — all this depended on her, and yet she could not understand why, or even what it was she contributed to it.

She said to Matthew in their bedroom: "I think there must be something wrong with me."

And he said: "Surely not, Susan? You look marvellous — you're as lovely as ever."

She looked at the handsome blond man, with his clear, intelligent, blue-eyed face, and thought: Why is it I can't tell him? Why not? And she said: "I need to be alone more than I am."

At which he swung his slow blue gaze at her, and she saw what she had been dreading: Incredulity. Disbelief. And fear. An incredulous blue stare from a stranger who was her husband, as close to her as her own breath.

He said: "But the children are at school and off your hands."

She said to herself: I've got to force myself to say: Yes, but do you realize that I never feel free? There's never a moment I can say to myself: There's nothing I have to remind myself about, nothing I have to do in half an hour, or an hour, or two hours. . . .

But she said: "I don't feel well."

He said: "Perhaps you need a holiday."

She said, appalled: "But not without you, surely?" For she could not imagine herself going off without him. Yet that was what he meant. Seeing her face, he laughed, and opened his arms, and she went into them, thinking: Yes, yes, but why can't I say it? And what is it I have to say?

She tried to tell him, about never being free. And he listened and said: "But Susan, what sort of freedom can you possibly want — short of being dead! Am I ever free? I go to the office, and I have to be there at ten — all right, half past ten, sometimes. And I have to do this or that, don't I? Then I've got to come home at a certain time — I don't mean it, you know I don't — but if I'm not going to be back home at six I telephone you. When can I ever say to myself: I have nothing to be responsible for in the next six hours?"

Susan, hearing this, was remorseful. Because it was true. The good marriage, the house, the children, depended just as much on his voluntary bondage as it did on hers. But why did he not feel bound? Why didn't he chafe and become restless? No, there was something really wrong with her and this proved it.

And that word "bondage" — why had she used it? She had never felt marriage, or the children, as bondage. Neither had he, or surely they wouldn't be together lying in each other's arms content after twelve years of marriage.

No, her state (whatever it was) was irrelevant, nothing to do with her real good life with her family. She had to accept the fact that, after all, she was an irrational person and to live with it. Some people had to live with crippled arms, or stammers, or being deaf. She would have to live knowing she was subject to a state of mind she could not own.

Nevertheless, as a result of this conversation with her husband, there was a new regime next holidays.

The spare room at the top of the house now had a cardboard sign saying: PRIVATE! DO NOT DISTURB! on it. (This sign had been drawn in coloured chalks by the children, after a discussion between the parents in which it was decided this was psychologically the right thing.) The family and Mrs. Parkes knew this was "Mother's Room" and that she was entitled to her privacy. Many serious conversations took place between Matthew and the children about not taking Mother for granted. Susan overheard the first, between father and Harry, the older boy, and was surprised at her irritation over it. Surely she could have a room somewhere in that big house and retire into it without such a fuss being made? Without it being so solemnly discussed? Why couldn't she simply have announced: "I'm going to fit out the little top room for myself, and when I'm in it I'm not to be disturbed for anything short of fire"? Just that, and finished; instead of long earnest discussions. When she heard Harry and Matthew explaining it to the twins with Mrs. Parkes coming in — "Yes, well, a family sometimes gets on top of a woman" — she had to go right away to the bottom of the garden until the devils of exasperation had finished their dance in her blood.

But now there was a room, and she could go there when she liked, she used it seldom: she felt even more caged there than in her bedroom. One day she had gone up there after a lunch for ten children she had cooked and served because Mrs. Parkes was not there, and had sat alone for a while looking into the garden. She saw the children stream out from the kitchen and stand looking up at the window where she sat behind the curtains.

They were all — her children and their friends — discussing Mother's Room. A few minutes later, the chase of children in some game came pounding up the stairs, but ended as abruptly as if they had fallen over a ravine, so sudden was the silence. They had remembered she was there, and had gone silent in a great gale of "Hush! Shhhhhh! Quiet, you'll disturb her. . . ." And they went tiptoeing downstairs like criminal conspirators. When she came down to make tea for them, they all apologised. The twins put their arms around her, from front and back, making a human cage of loving limbs, and promised it would never occur again. "We forgot, Mummy, we forgot all about it!"

What it amounted to was that Mother's Room, and her need for privacy, had become a valuable lesson in respect for other people's rights. Quite soon Susan was going up to the room only because it was a lesson it was a pity to drop. Then she took sewing up there, and the children and Mrs. Parkes came in and out: it had become another family room.

She sighed, and smiled, and resigned herself — she made jokes at her own expense with Matthew over the room. That is, she did from the self she liked, she respected. But at the same time, something inside her howled with impatience, with rage. . . . And she was frightened. One day she found herself kneeling by her bed and praying: "Dear God, keep it away from me, keep him away from me." She meant the devil, for she now thought of it, not caring if she was irrational, as some sort of demon. She imagined him, or it, as a youngish man, or perhaps a middleaged man pretending to be young. Or a man young-looking from immaturity? At any rate, she saw the young-looking face which, when she drew closer, had dry lines about mouth and eyes. He was thinnish, meagre in build. And he had a reddish complexion, and ginger hair. That was he — a gingery, energetic man, and he wore a reddish hairy jacket, unpleasant to the touch.

Well, one day she saw him. She was standing at the bottom of the garden, watching the river ebb past, when she raised her eyes and saw this person, or being, sitting on the white stone bench. He was looking at her, and grinning. In his hand was a long crooked stick, which he had picked off the ground, or broken off the tree above him. He was absent-mindedly, out of an absent-minded or freakish impulse of spite, using the stick to stir around in the coils of a blindworm or a grass snake (or some kind of snake-like creature: it was whitish and unhealthy to look at, unpleasant). The snake was twisting about, flinging its coils from side to side in a kind of dance of protest against the teasing prodding stick.

Susan looked at him, thinking: Who is the stranger? What is he doing in our garden? Then she recognised the man around whom her terrors had crystallised. As she did so, he vanished. She made herself walk over to the bench. A shadow from a branch lay across thin emerald grass, moving jerkily over its roughness, and she could see why she had taken it for a snake, lashing and twisting. She went back to the house thinking: Right, then, so I've seen him with my own eyes, so I'm not crazy after all — there *is* a dan-

ger because I've seen him. He is lurking in the garden and sometimes even
in the house, and he wants to *get into me and to take me over.*

She dreamed of having a room or a place, anywhere, where she could
go and sit, by herself, no one knowing where she was.

Once, near Victoria, she found herself outside a news agent that had
Rooms to Let advertised. She decided to rent a room, telling no one. Sometimes she could take the train into Richmond and sit alone in it for an hour
or two. Yet how could she? A room would cost three or four pounds a week,
and she earned no money, and how could she explain to Matthew that she
needed such a sum? What for? It did not occur to her that she was taking it
for granted she wasn't going to tell him about the room.

Well, it was out of the question, having a room; yet she knew she
must.

One day, when a school term was well established, and none of the
children had measles or other ailments, and everything seemed in order, she
did the shopping early, explained to Mrs. Parkes she was meeting an old
school friend, took the train to Victoria, searched until she found a small
quiet hotel, and asked for a room for the day. They did not let rooms by the
day, the manageress said, looking doubtful, since Susan so obviously was
not the kind of woman who needed a room for unrespectable reasons.
Susan made a long explanation about not being well, being unable to shop
without frequent rests for lying down. At last she was allowed to rent the
room provided she paid a full night's price for it. She was taken up by the
manageress and a maid, both concerned over the state of her health . . .
which must be pretty bad if, living at Richmond (she had signed her name
and address in the register), she needed a shelter at Victoria.

The room was ordinary and anonymous, and was just what Susan
needed. She put a shilling in the gas fire, and sat, eyes shut, in a dingy armchair with her back to a dingy window. She was alone. She was alone. She
was alone. She could feel pressures lifting off her. First the sounds of traffic
came very loud; then they seemed to vanish; she might even have slept a
little. A knock on the door: it was Miss Townsend, the manageress, bringing her a cup of tea with her own hands, so concerned was she over Susan's
long silence and possible illness.

Miss Townsend was a lonely woman of fifty, running this hotel with
all the rectitude expected of her, and she sensed in Susan the possibility of
understanding companionship. She stayed to talk. Susan found herself in
the middle of a fantastic story about her illness, which got more and more
impossible as she tried to make it tally with the large house at Richmond,
well-off husband, and four children. Suppose she said instead: Miss Townsend, I'm here in your hotel because I need to be alone for a few hours,
above all *alone and with no one knowing where I am.* She said it mentally,
and saw, mentally, the look that would inevitably come on Miss Townsend's elderly maiden's face. "Miss Townsend, my four children and my
husband are driving me insane, do you understand that? Yes, I can see from
the gleam of hysteria in your eyes that comes from loneliness controlled but

only just contained that I've got everything in the world you've ever longed for. Well, Miss Townsend, I don't want any of it. You can have it, Miss Townsend. I wish I was absolutely alone in the world, like you. Miss Townsend, I'm besieged by seven devils, Miss Townsend, Miss Townsend, let me stay here in your hotel where the devils can't get me. . . . " Instead of saying all this, she described her anaemia, agreed to try Miss Townsend's remedy for it, which was raw liver, minced, between whole-meal bread, and said yes, perhaps it would be better if she stayed at home and let a friend do shopping for her. She paid her bill and left the hotel, defeated.

At home Mrs. Parkes said she didn't really like it, no, not really, when Mrs. Rawlings was away from nine in the morning until five. The teacher had telephoned from school to say Joan's teeth were paining her, and she hadn't known what to say; and what was she to make for the children's tea, Mrs. Rawlings hadn't said.

All this was nonsense, of course. Mrs. Parkes's complaint was that Susan had withdrawn herself spiritually, leaving the burden of the big house on her.

Susan looked back at her day of "freedom" which had resulted in her becoming a friend of the lonely Miss Townsend, and in Mrs. Parkes's remonstrances. Yet she remembered the short blissful hour of being alone, really alone. She was determined to arrange her life, no matter what it cost, so that she could have that solitude more often. An absolute solitude, where no one knew her or cared about her.

But how? She thought of saying to her old employer: I want you to back me up in a story with Matthew that I am doing part-time work for you. The truth is that. . . . But she would have to tell him a lie too, and which lie? She could not say: I want to sit by myself three or four times a week in a rented room. And besides, he knew Matthew, and she could not really ask him to tell lies on her behalf, apart from being bound to think it meant a lover.

Suppose she really took a part-time job, which she could get through fast and efficiently, leaving time for herself. What job? Addressing envelopes? Canvassing?

And there was Mrs. Parkes, working widow, who knew exactly what she was prepared to give to the house, who knew by instinct when her mistress withdrew in spirit from her responsibilities. Mrs. Parkes was one of the servers of this world, but she needed someone to serve. She had to have Mrs. Rawlings, her madam, at the top of the house or in the garden, so that she could come and get support from her: "Yes, the bread's not what it was when I was a girl. . . . Yes, Harry's got a wonderful appetite, I wonder where he puts it all. . . . Yes, it's lucky the twins are so much of a size, they can wear each other's shoes, that's a saving in these hard times. . . . Yes, the cherry jam from Switzerland is not a patch on the jam from Poland, and three times the price. . . . " And so on. That sort of talk Mrs. Parkes must have, every day, or she would leave, not knowing herself why she left.

Susan Rawlings, thinking these thoughts, found that she was prowling through the great thicketed garden like a wild cat: she was walking up the stairs, down the stairs, through the rooms into the garden, along the brown running river, back, up through the house, down again. . . . It was a wonder Mrs. Parkes did not think it strange. But, on the contrary, Mrs. Rawlings could do what she liked, she could stand on her head if she wanted, provided she was *there*. Susan Rawlings prowled and muttered through her house, hating Mrs. Parkes, hating poor Miss Townsend, dreaming of her hour of solitude in the dingy respectability of Miss Townsend's hotel bedroom, and she knew quite well she was mad. Yes, she was mad.

She said to Matthew that she must have a holiday. Matthew agreed with her. This was not as things had been once — how they had talked in each other's arms in the marriage bed. He had, she knew, diagnosed her finally as *unreasonable*. She had become someone outside himself that he had to manage. They were living side by side in this house like two tolerably friendly strangers.

Having told Mrs. Parkes — or rather, asked for her permission — she went off on a walking holiday in Wales. She chose the remotest place she knew of. Every morning the children telephoned her before they went off to school, to encourage and support her, just as they had over Mother's Room. Every evening she telephoned them, spoke to each child in turn, and then to Matthew. Mrs. Parkes, given permission to telephone for instructions or advice, did so every day at lunchtime. When, as happened three times, Mrs. Rawlings was out on the mountainside, Mrs. Parkes asked that she should ring back at such-and-such a time, for she would not be happy in what she was doing without Mrs. Rawlings' blessing.

Susan prowled over wild country with the telephone wire holding her to her duty like a leash. The next time she must telephone, or wait to be telephoned, nailed her to her cross. The mountains themselves seemed trammelled by her unfreedom. Everywhere on the mountains, where she met no one at all, from breakfast time to dusk, excepting sheep, or a shepherd, she came face to face with her own craziness, which might attack her in the broadest valleys, so that they seemed too small, or on a mountain top from which she could see a hundred other mountains and valleys, so that they seemed too low, too small, with the sky pressing down too close. She would stand gazing at a hillside brilliant with ferns and bracken, jewelled with running water, and see nothing but her devil, who lifted inhuman eyes at her from where he leaned negligently on a rock, switching at his ugly yellow boots with a leafy twig.

She returned to her home and family, with the Welsh emptiness at the back of her mind like a promise of freedom.

She told her husband she wanted to have an *au pair* girl.

They were in their bedroom, it was late at night, the children slept. He sat, shirted and slippered, in a chair by the window, looking out. She sat brushing her hair and watching him in the mirror. A time-hallowed scene in the connubial bedroom. He said nothing, while she heard the arguments coming into his mind, only to be rejected because every one was *reasonable*.

"It seems strange to get one now; after all, the children are in school most of the day. Surely the time for you to have help was when you were stuck with them day and night. Why don't you ask Mrs. Parkes to cook for you? She's even offered to — I can understand if you are tired of cooking for six people. But you know that an *au pair* girl means all kinds of problems; it's not like having an ordinary char in during the day. . . ."

Finally he said carefully: "Are you thinking of going back to work?"

"No," she said, "no, not really." She made herself sound vague, rather stupid. She went on brushing her black hair and peering at herself so as to be oblivious of the short uneasy glances her Matthew kept giving her. "Do you think we can't afford it?" she went on vaguely, not at all the old efficient Susan who knew exactly what they could afford.

"It's not that," he said, looking out of the window at dark trees, so as not to look at her. Meanwhile she examined a round, candid, pleasant face with clear dark brows and clear grey eyes. A sensible face. She brushed thick healthy black hair and thought: Yet that's the reflection of a madwoman. How very strange! Much more to the point if what looked back at me was the gingery green-eyed demon with his dry meagre smile. . . . Why wasn't Matthew agreeing? After all, what else could he do? She was breaking her part of the bargain and there was no way of forcing her to keep it: that her spirit, her soul, should live in this house, so that the people in it could grow like plants in water, and Mrs. Parkes remain content in their service. In return for this, he would be a good loving husband, and responsible towards the children. Well, nothing like this had been true of either of them for a long time. He did his duty, perfunctorily; she did not even pretend to do hers. And he had become like other husbands, with his real life in his work and the people he met there, and very likely a serious affair. All this was her fault.

At last he drew heavy curtains, blotting out the trees, and turned to force her attention: "Susan, are you really sure we need a girl?" But she would not meet his appeal at all. She was running the brush over her hair again and again, lifting fine black clouds in a small hiss of electricity. She was peering in and smiling as if she were amused at the clinging hissing hair that followed the brush.

"Yes, I think it would be a good idea, on the whole," she said, with the cunning of a madwoman evading the real point.

In the mirror she could see her Matthew lying on his back, his hands behind his head, staring upwards, his face sad and hard. She felt her heart (the old heart of Susan Rawlings) soften and call out to him. But she set it to be indifferent.

He said: "Susan, the children?" It was an appeal that *almost* reached her. He opened his arms, lifting them palms up, empty. She had only to run across and fling herself into them, onto his hard, warm chest, and melt into herself, into Susan. But she could not. She would not see his lifted arms. She said vaguely: "Well, surely it'll be even better for them? We'll get a French or a German girl and they'll learn the language."

In the dark she lay beside him, feeling frozen, a stranger. She felt as if Susan had been spirited away. She disliked very much this woman who lay here, cold and indifferent beside a suffering man, but she could not change her.

Next morning she set about getting a girl, and very soon came Sophie Traub from Hamburg, a girl of twenty, laughing, healthy, blue-eyed, intending to learn English. Indeed, she already spoke a good deal. In return for a room — "Mother's Room" — and her food, she undertook to do some light cooking, and to be with the children when Mrs. Rawlings asked. She was an intelligent girl and understood perfectly what was needed. Susan said: "I go off sometimes, for the morning or for the day — well, sometimes the children run home from school, or they ring up, or a teacher rings up. I should be here, really. And there's the daily woman. . . ." And Sophie laughed her deep fruity *Fräulein*'s laugh, showed her fine white teeth and her dimples, and said: "You want some person to play mistress of the house sometimes, not so?"

"Yes, that is just so," said Susan, a bit dry, despite herself, thinking in secret fear how easy it was, how much nearer to the end she was than she thought. Healthy Fräulein Traub's instant understanding of their position proved this to be true.

The *au pair* girl, because of her own commonsense, or (as Susan said to herself, with her new inward shudder) because she had been *chosen* so well by Susan, was a success with everyone, the children liking her, Mrs. Parkes forgetting almost at once that she was German, and Matthew finding her "nice to have around the house." For he was now taking things as they came, from the surface of life, withdrawn both as a husband and a father from the household.

One day Susan saw how Sophie and Mrs. Parkes were talking and laughing in the kitchen, and she announced that she would be away until tea time. She knew exactly where to go and what she must look for. She took the District Line to South Kensington, changed to the Circle, got off at Paddington, and walked around looking at the smaller hotels until she was satisfied with one which had FRED'S HOTEL painted on windowpanes that needed cleaning. The facade was a faded shiny yellow, like unhealthy skin. A door at the end of a passage said she must knock; she did, and Fred appeared. He was not at all attractive, not in any way, being fattish, and run-down, and wearing a tasteless striped suit. He had small sharp eyes in a white creased face, and was quite prepared to let Mrs. Jones (she chose the farcical name deliberately, staring him out) have a room three days a week from ten until six. Provided of course that she paid in advance each time she came? Susan produced fifteen shillings (no price had been set by him) and held it out, still fixing him with a bold unblinking challenge she had not known until then she could use at will. Looking at her still, he took up a ten-shilling note from her palm between thumb and forefinger, fingered it; then shuffled up two half-crowns, held out his own palm with these bits of money displayed thereon, and let his gaze lower broodingly at them. They were standing in the passage, a red-shaded light above, bare boards beneath, and a strong smell of floor polish rising about them. He shot his gaze up at her over the still-extended palm, and smiled as if to say: What do you take me for? "I shan't," said Susan, "be using this room for the purposes of making money." He still waited. She added another five shillings, at which he nodded and said: "You pay, and I ask no questions." "Good," said Susan. He now went past her to the stairs, and there waited a moment: the light from the street door being in her eyes, she lost sight of him momentarily. Then she saw a sober-suited, white-faced, white-balding little man trotting up the stairs like a waiter, and she went after him. They proceeded in utter silence up the stairs of this house where no questions were asked — Fred's Hotel, which could afford the freedom for its visitors that poor Miss Townsend's hotel could not. The room was hideous. It had a single window, with thin green brocade curtains, a three-quarter bed that had a cheap green satin bedspread on it, a fireplace with a gas fire and a shilling meter by it, a chest of drawers, and a green wicker armchair.

"Thank you," said Susan, knowing that Fred (if this was Fred, and not George, or Herbert, or Charlie) was looking at her, not so much with curiosity, an emotion he would not own to, for professional reasons, but with a philosophical sense of what was appropriate. Having taken her money and shown her up and agreed to everything, he was clearly disapproving of her for coming here. She did not belong here at all, so his look said. (But she knew, already, how very much she did belong: the room had been waiting for her to join it.) "Would you have me called at five o'clock, please?" and he nodded and went downstairs.

It was twelve in the morning. She was free. She sat in the armchair, she simply sat, she closed her eyes and sat and let herself be alone. She was alone and no one knew where she was. When a knock came on the door she was annoyed, and prepared to show it: but it was Fred himself; it was five o'clock and he was calling her as ordered. He flicked his sharp little eyes over the room — bed, first. It was undisturbed. She might never have been in the room at all. She thanked him, said she would be returning the day after tomorrow, and left. She was back home in time to cook supper, to put the children to bed, to cook a second supper for her husband and herself later. And to welcome Sophie back from the pictures where she had gone with a friend. All these things she did cheerfully, willingly. But she was thinking all the time of the hotel room; she was longing for it with her whole being.

Three times a week. She arrived promptly at ten, looked Fred in the eyes, gave him twenty shillings, followed him up the stairs, went into the room, and shut the door on him with gentle firmness. For Fred, disapproving of her being here at all, was quite ready to let friendship, or at least acquaintanceship, follow his disapproval, if only she would let him. But he was content to go off on her dismissing nod, with the twenty shillings in his hand.

She sat in the armchair and shut her eyes.

What did she *do* in the room? Why, nothing at all. From the chair, when it had rested her, she went to the window, stretching her arms, smiling, treasuring her anonymity, to look out. She was no longer Susan Rawlings, mother of four, wife of Matthew, employer of Mrs. Parkes and of Sophie Traub, with these and those relations with friends, school-teachers, tradesmen. She no longer was mistress of the big white house and garden, owning clothes suitable for this and that activity or occasion. She was Mrs. Jones, and she was alone, and she had no past and no future. Here I am, she thought, after all these years of being married and having children and playing those roles of responsibility — and I'm just the same. Yet there have been times I thought that nothing existed of me except the roles that went with being Mrs. Matthew Rawlings. Yes, here I am, and if I never saw any of my family again, here I would still be . . . how very strange that is! And she leaned on the sill, and looked into the street, loving the men and women who passed, because she did not know them. She looked at the down-trodden buildings over the street, and at the sky, wet and dingy, or sometimes blue, and she felt she had never seen buildings or sky before. And then she went back to the chair, empty, her mind a blank. Sometimes she talked aloud, saying nothing — an exclamation, meaningless, followed by a comment about the floral pattern on the thin rug, or a stain on the green satin coverlet. For the most part, she wool-gathered — what word is there for it? — brooded, wandered, simply went dark, feeling emptiness run deliciously through her veins like the movement of her blood.

This room had become more her own than the house she lived in. One morning she found Fred taking her a flight higher than usual. She stopped, refusing to go up, and demanded her usual room, Number 19. "Well, you'll have to wait half an hour, then," he said. Willingly she descended to the dark disinfectant-smelling hall, and sat waiting until the two, man and woman, came down the stairs, giving her swift indifferent glances before they hurried out into the street, separating at the door. She went up to the room, *her* room, which they had just vacated. It was no less hers, though the windows were set wide open, and a maid was straightening the bed as she came in.

After these days of solitude, it was both easy to play her part as mother and wife, and difficult — because it was so easy: she felt an imposter. She felt as if her shell moved here, with her family, answering to Mummy, Mother, Susan, Mrs. Rawlings. She was surprised no one saw through her, that she wasn't turned out of doors, as a fake. On the contrary, it seemed the children loved her more; Matthew and she "got on" pleasantly, and Mrs. Parkes was happy in her work under (for the most part, it must be confessed) Sophie Traub. At night she lay beside her husband, and they made love again, apparently just as they used to, when they were really married. But she, Susan, or the being who answered so readily and improbably to the name of Susan, was not there: she was in Fred's Hotel, in Paddington, waiting for the easing hours of solitude to begin.

Soon she made a new arrangement with Fred and with Sophie. It was for five days a week. As for the money, five pounds, she simply asked Matthew for it. She saw that she was not even frightened he might ask what for: he would give it to her, she knew that, and yet it was terrifying it could be so, for this close couple, these partners, had once known the destination of every shilling they must spend. He agreed to give her five pounds a week. She asked for just so much, not a penny more. He sounded indifferent about it. It was as if he were paying her, she thought: *paying her off* — yes, that was it. Terror came back for a moment when she understood this, but she stilled it: things had gone too far for that. Now, every week, on Sunday nights, he gave her five pounds, turning away from her before their eyes could meet on the transaction. As for Sophie Traub, she was to be somewhere in or near the house until six at night, after which she was free. She was not to cook, or to clean; she was simply to be there. So she gardened or sewed, and asked friends in, being a person who was bound to have a lot of friends. If the children were sick, she nursed them. If teachers telephoned, she answered them sensibly. For the five daytimes in the school week, she was altogether the mistress of the house.

One night in the bedroom, Matthew asked: "Susan, I don't want to interfere — don't think that, please — but are you sure you are well?"

She was brushing her hair at the mirror. She made two more strokes on either side of her head, before she replied: "Yes, dear, I am sure I am well."

He was again lying on his back, his blond head on his hands, his elbows angled up and part-concealing his face. He said: "Then Susan, I have to ask you this question, though you must understand, I'm not putting any sort of pressure on you." (Susan heard the word "pressure" with dismay, because this was inevitable; of course she could not go on like this.) "Are things going to go on like this?"

"Well," she said, going vague and bright and idiotic again, so as to escape: "Well, I don't see why not."

He was jerking his elbows up and down, in annoyance or in pain, and, looking at him, she saw he had got thin, even gaunt; and restless angry movements were not what she remembered of him. He said: "Do you want a divorce, is that it?"

At this, Susan only with the greatest difficulty stopped herself from laughing: she could hear the bright bubbling laughter she *would* have emitted, had she let herself. He could only mean one thing: she had a lover, and that was why she spent her days in London, as lost to him as if she had vanished to another continent.

Then the small panic set in again: she understood that he hoped she did have a lover, he was begging her to say so, because otherwise it would be too terrifying.

She thought this out as she brushed her hair, watching the fine black stuff fly up to make its little clouds of electricity, hiss, hiss, hiss. Behind her head, across the room, was a blue wall. She realised she was absorbed in watching the black hair making shapes against the blue. She should be answering him. "Do *you* want a divorce, Matthew?"

He said: "That surely isn't the point, is it?"

"You brought it up, I didn't," she said, brightly, suppressing meaningless tinkling laughter.

Next day she asked Fred: "Have enquiries been made for me?"

He hesitated, and she said: "I've been coming here a year now. I've made no trouble, and you've been paid every day. I have a right to be told."

"As a matter of fact, Mrs. Jones, a man did come asking."

"A man from a detective agency?"

"Well, he could have been, couldn't he?"

"I was asking you. . . . Well, what did you tell him?"

"I told him a Mrs. Jones came every weekday from ten until five or six and stayed in Number 19 by herself."

"Describing me?"

"Well, Mrs. Jones, I had no alternative. Put yourself in my place."

"By rights I should deduct what that man gave you for the information."

He raised shocked eyes: she was not the sort of person to make jokes like this! Then he chose to laugh: a pinkish wet slit appeared across his white crinkled face; his eyes positively begged her to laugh, otherwise he might lose some money. She remained grave, looking at him.

He stopped laughing and said: "You want to go up now?" — returning to the familiarity, the comradeship, of the country where no questions are asked, on which (and he knew it) she depended completely.

She went up to sit in her wicker chair. But it was not the same. Her husband had searched her out. (The world had searched her out.) The pressures were on her. She was here with his connivance. He might walk in at any moment, here, into Room 19. She imagined the report from the detective agency: "A woman calling herself Mrs. Jones, fitting the description of your wife (et cetera, et cetera, et cetera), stays alone all day in Room No. 19. She insists on this room, waits for it if it is engaged. As far as the proprietor knows, she receives no visitors there, male or female." A report something on these lines Matthew must have received.

Well, of course he was right: things couldn't go on like this. He had put an end to it all simply by sending a detective after her.

She tried to shrink herself back into the shelter of the room, a snail pecked out of its shell and trying to squirm back. But the peace of the room had gone. She was trying consciously to revive it, trying to let go into the dark creative trance (or whatever it was) that she had found there. It was no use, yet she craved for it, she was as ill as a suddenly deprived addict.

Several times she returned to the room, to look for herself there, but instead she found the unnamed spirit of restlessness, a pricking fevered hunger for movement, an irritable self-consciousness that made her brain feel as if it had coloured lights going on and off inside it. Instead of the soft dark that had been the room's air, were now waiting for her demons that made her dash blindly about, muttering words of hate; she was impelling herself from point to point like a moth dashing itself against a windowpane, sliding to the bottom, fluttering off on broken wings, then crashing into the invisible barrier again. And again and again. Soon she was exhausted, and she told Fred that for a while she would not be needing the room, she was going on a holiday. Home she went, to the big white house by the river. The middle of a weekday, and she felt guilty at returning to her own home when not expected. She stood unseen, looking in at the kitchen window. Mrs. Parkes, wearing a discarded floral overall of Susan's, was stooping to slide something into the oven. Sophie, arms folded, was leaning her back against a cupboard and laughing at some joke made by a girl not seen before by Susan — a dark foreign girl, Sophie's visitor. In an armchair Molly, one of the twins, lay curled, sucking her thumb and watching the grownups. She must have some sickness, to be kept from school. The child's listless face, the dark circles under her eyes, hurt Susan: Molly was looking at the three grownups working and talking in exactly the same way Susan looked at the four through the kitchen window: she was remote, shut off from them.

But then, just as Susan imagined herself going in, picking up the little girl, and sitting in an armchair with her, stroking her probably heated forehead, Sophie did just that: she had been standing on one leg, the other knee flexed, its foot set against the wall. Now she let her foot in its ribbon-tied red shoe slide down the wall, stood solid on two feet, clapping her hands before and behind her, and sang a couple of lines in German, so that the child lifted her heavy eyes at her and began to smile. Then she walked, or rather skipped, over to the child, swung her up, and let her fall into her lap at the same moment she sat herself. She said "Hopla! Hopla! Molly . . ." and began stroking the dark untidy young head that Molly laid on her shoulder for comfort.

Well. . . . Susan blinked the tears of farewell out of her eyes, and went quietly up through the house to her bedroom. There she sat looking at the river through the trees. She felt at peace, but in a way that was new to her. She had no desire to move, to talk, to do anything at all. The devils that had haunted the house, the garden, were not there; but she knew it was because her soul was in Room 19 in Fred's Hotel; she was not really here at all. It was a sensation that should have been frightening: to sit at her own bedroom window, listening to Sophie's rich young voice sing German nursery songs to her child, listening to Mrs. Parkes clatter and move below, and to know that all this had nothing to do with her: she was already out of it.

Later, she made herself go down and say she was home: it was unfair to be here unannounced. She took lunch with Mrs. Parkes, Sophie, Sophie's Italian friend Maria, and her daughter Molly, and felt like a visitor.

A few days later, at bedtime, Matthew said: "Here's your five pounds," and pushed them over at her. Yet he must have known she had not been leaving the house at all.

She shook her head, gave it back to him, and said, in explanation, not in accusation: "As soon as you knew where I was, there was no point."

He nodded, not looking at her. He was turned away from her: thinking, she knew, how best to handle this wife who terrified him.

He said: "I wasn't trying to. . . . It's just that I was worried."

"Yes, I know."

"I must confess that I was beginning to wonder. . . ."

"You thought I had a lover?"

"Yes, I am afraid I did."

She knew that he wished she had. She sat wondering how to say: "For a year now I've been spending all my days in a very sordid hotel room. It's the place where I'm happy. In fact, without it I don't exist." She heard herself saying this, and understood how terrified he was that she might. So instead she said: "Well, perhaps you're not far wrong."

Probably Matthew would think the hotel proprietor lied: he would want to think so.

"Well," he said, and she could hear his voice spring up, so to speak, with relief, "in that case I must confess I've got a bit of an affair on myself."

She said, detached and interested: "Really? Who is she?" and saw Matthew's startled look because of this reaction.

"It's Phil. Phil Hunt."

She had known Phil Hunt well in the old unmarried days. She was thinking: No, she won't do, she's too neurotic and difficult. She's never been happy yet. Sophie's much better. Well, Matthew will see that himself, as sensible as he is.

This line of thought went on in silence, while she said aloud: "It's no point telling you about mine, because you don't know him."

Quick, quick, invent, she thought. Remember how you invented all that nonsense for Miss Townsend.

She began slowly, careful not to contradict herself: "His name is Michael" (*Michael What?*) — "Michael Plant." (What a silly name!) "He's rather like you — in looks, I mean." And indeed, she could imagine herself being touched by no one but Matthew himself. "He's a publisher." (Really? Why?) "He's got a wife already and two children."

She brought out this fantasy, proud of herself.

Matthew said: "Are you two thinking of marrying?"

She said, before she could stop herself: "Good God, *no!*"

She realised, if Matthew wanted to marry Phil Hunt, that this was too emphatic, but apparently it was all right, for his voice sounded relieved as he said: "It is a bit impossible to imagine oneself married to anyone else, isn't it?" With which he pulled her to him, so that her head lay on his shoulder. She turned her face into the dark of his flesh, and listened to the blood pounding through her ears saying: I am alone, I am alone, I am alone.

In the morning Susan lay in bed while he dressed.

He had been thinking things out in the night, because now he said: "Susan, why don't we make a foursome?"

Of course, she said to herself, of course he would be bound to say that. If one is sensible, if one is reasonable, if one never allows oneself a base thought or an envious emotion, naturally one says: Let's make a foursome!

"Why not?" she said.

"We could all meet for lunch. I mean, it's ridiculous, you sneaking off to filthy hotels, and me staying late at the office, and all the lies everyone has to tell."

What on earth did I say his name was? — she panicked, then said: "I think it's a good idea, but Michael is away at the moment. When he comes back, though — and I'm sure you two would like each other."

"He's away, is he? So that's why you've been. . . ." Her husband put his hand to the knot of his tie in a gesture of male coquetry she would not before have associated with him; and he bent to kiss her cheek with the expression that goes with the words: Oh you naughty little puss! And she felt its answering look, naughty and coy, come onto her face.

Inside she was dissolving in horror at them both, at how far they had both sunk from honesty of emotion.

So now she was saddled with a lover, and he had a mistress! How ordinary, how reassuring, how jolly! And now they would make a foursome of it, and go about to theatres and restaurants. After all, the Rawlings could well afford that sort of thing, and presumably the publisher Michael Plant could afford to do himself and his mistress quite well. No, there was nothing to stop the four of them developing the most intricate relationship of civilised tolerance, all enveloped in a charming afterglow of autumnal passion. Perhaps they would all go off on holidays together? She had known people who did. Or perhaps Matthew would draw the line there? Why should he, though, if he was capable of talking about "foursomes" at all?

She lay in the empty bedroom, listening to the car drive off with Matthew in it, off to work. Then she heard the children clattering off to school to the accompaniment of Sophie's cheerfully ringing voice. She slid down into the hollow of the bed, for shelter against her own irrelevance. And she stretched out her hand to the hollow where her husband's body had lain, but found no comfort there: he was not her husband. She curled herself up in a small tight ball under the clothes: she could stay here all day, all week, indeed, all her life.

But in a few days she must produce Michael Plant, and — but how? She must presumably find some agreeable man prepared to impersonate a publisher called Michael Plant. And in return for which she would — what? Well, for one thing they would make love. The idea made her want to cry with sheer exhaustion. Oh no, she had finished with all that — the proof of it was that the words "make love," or even imagining it, trying hard to revive no more than the pleasures of sensuality, let alone affection, or love, made her want to run away and hide from the sheer effort of the thing. . . . Good Lord, why make love at all? Why make love with anyone? Or if you are going to make love, what does it matter who with? Why shouldn't she simply walk into the street, pick up a man, and have a roaring sexual affair with him? Why not? Or even with Fred? What difference did it make?

But she had let herself in for it — an interminable stretch of time with a lover, called Michael, as part of a gallant civilised foursome. Well, she could not, and she would not.

She got up, dressed, went down to find Mrs. Parkes, and asked her for the loan of a pound, since Matthew, she said, had forgotten to leave her money. She exchanged with Mrs. Parkes variations on the theme that husbands are all the same, they don't think, and without saying a word to Sophie, whose voice could be heard upstairs from the telephone, walked to the underground, travelled to South Kensington, changed to the Inner Circle, got out at Paddington, and walked to Fred's Hotel. There she told Fred that she wasn't going on holiday after all, she needed the room. She would have to wait an hour, Fred said. She went to a busy tearoom-cum-restaurant around the corner, and sat watching the people flow in and out the door that kept swinging open and shut, watched them mingle and merge, and separate, felt her being flow into them, into their movement. When the hour was up, she left a half-crown for her pot of tea, and left the place without looking back at it, just as she had left her house, the big, beautiful white house, without another look, but silently dedicating it to Sophie. She returned to Fred, received the key of Number 19, now free, and ascended the grimy stairs slowly, letting floor after floor fall away below her, keeping her eyes lifted, so that floor after floor descended jerkily to her level of vision, and fell away out of sight.

Number 19 was the same. She saw everything with an acute, narrow, checking glance: the cheap shine of the satin spread, which had been replaced carelessly after the two bodies had finished their convulsions under it; a trace of powder on the glass that topped the chest of drawers; an intense green shade in a fold of the curtain. She stood at the window, looking down, watching people pass and pass and pass until her mind went dark from the constant movement. Then she sat in the wicker chair, letting herself go slack. But she had to be careful, because she did not want, today, to be surprised by Fred's knock at five o'clock.

The demons were not here. They had gone forever, because she was buying her freedom from them. She was slipping already into the dark fructifying dream that seemed to caress her inwardly, like the movement of her blood . . . but she had to think about Matthew first. Should she write a letter for the coroner? But what should she say? She would like to leave him with the look on his face she had seen this morning — banal, admittedly, but at least confidently healthy. Well, that was impossible, one did not look like that with a wife dead from suicide. But how to leave him believing she was dying because of a man — because of the fascinating publisher Michael Plant? Oh, how ridiculous! How absurd! How humiliating! But she decided not to trouble about it, simply not to think about the living. If he wanted to believe she had a lover, he would believe it. And he *did* want to believe it. Even when he had found out that there was no publisher in London called Michael Plant, he would think: Oh poor Susan, she was afraid to give me his real name.

And what did it matter whether he married Phil Hunt oi
Though it ought to be Sophie, who was already the mother of tl
dren . . . and what hypocrisy to sit here worrying about the childrei, wnen
she was going to leave them because she had not got the energy to stay.

She had about four hours. She spent them delightfully, darkly,
sweetly, letting herself slide gently, gently, to the edge of the river. Then,
with hardly a break in her consciousness, she got up, pushed the thin rug
against the door, made sure the windows were tight shut, put two shillings
in the meter, and turned on the gas. For the first time since she had been in
the room she lay on the hard bed that smelled stale, that smelled of sweat
and sex.

She lay on her back on the green satin cover, but her legs were chilly.
She got up, found a blanket folded in the bottom of the chest of drawers,
and carefully covered her legs with it. She was quite content lying there, listening to the faint soft hiss of the gas that poured into the room, into her
lungs, into her brain, as she drifted off into the dark river.

[1963]

SHIRLEY JACKSON (1919–1965) *was born in San Francisco, California, her mother a housewife and her father an employee of a lithographing company. Most of her early life was spent in Burlingame, California, which she later used as the setting for her first novel,* The Road Through the Wall *(1948). As a child she was interested in writing; she won a poetry prize at age twelve, and in high school she began keeping a diary to record her writing progress. Her family moved to Rochester, New York, when she was a teenager. After high school she briefly attended the University of Rochester, but left because of an attack of the mental depression that was to recur periodically in her later years. She recovered her health by living quietly at home and writing, conscientiously turning out 1,000 words of prose a day. In 1937 she entered Syracuse University, where she published stories in the student literary magazine. There she also met Stanley Edgar Hyman, who was to become a noted literary critic. They were married in 1940, the year she received her degree from Syracuse. They had four children while both continued active literary careers, settling to raise their family in a large Victorian house in Vermont, where Hyman taught literature at Bennington College.*

Jackson's first national publication was a humorous story written after a job at a department store during the Christmas rush: "My Life with R. H. Macy," which appeared in The New Republic *in 1941. Her first child was born the next year, but she wrote every day on a disciplined schedule, selling stories to* The New Yorker, American Mercury, Harper's, *and* The Hudson Review. *Her work was included in* Best American Stories *of 1944 and 1956. In the 1940s and 1950s she also published many stories in women's magazines, especially* Good Housekeeping *and* Woman's Home Companion, *where her talent for casual, humorous storytelling and her straightforward, conversational prose style turned anecdotes about her own and her husband's eccentricities and the problems of raising four children into blithe domestic narratives. These stories were collected in* Life Among the Savages *(1953) and* Raising Demons *(1957). She regarded these two books as her "potboilers," preferring her psychological suspense novels,* Hangsman *(1951),* The Haunting of Hill House *(1959), and* We Have Always Lived in the Castle *(1962). Jackson refused to take herself too seriously as a writer: "I can't persuade myself that writing is honest work. It is a very personal reaction, but 50 percent of my life is spent washing and dressing the children, cooking, washing dishes and clothes, and mending. After I get it all to bed, I turn around to my typewriter and try to — well, to create concrete things again. It's great fun, and I love it. But it doesn't tie any shoes."*

Best known as a story writer, Jackson published only one collection of short fiction in her lifetime, The Lottery: Or, The Adventures of James

Harris (1949). *After her death her husband issued twenty-five of her stories in two anthologies,* The Magic of Shirley Jackson *(1966) and* Come Along with Me *(1968). "The Lottery" is often anthologized, dramatized, and televised. Jackson regarded it as a tale in the sense that Nathaniel Hawthorne used the term — a moral allegory revealing the hidden evil of the human soul, which in her narrative is illustrated in the injustice performed in blindly observing a social ritual. She wrote later that "explaining just what I had hoped the story to say is very difficult. I supposed, I hoped, by setting a particularly brutal ancient rite in the present and in my own village, to shock the story's readers with a graphic dramatization of the pointless violence and general inhumanity in their own lives." Most of Jackson's best fiction explores extreme psychological states, juxtaposing the familiar and the bizarre. Her work is most absorbing when the reader feels the presence of an inexplicable, genuine sense of evil, as in "The Lottery," which explores the social nature of human evil. (See Jackson's Commentary about "The Lottery" on page 1309.)*

Shirley Jackson

ཟཙ

THE LOTTERY

The morning of June 27th was clear and sunny, with the fresh warmth of a full-summer day; the flowers were blossoming profusely and the grass was richly green. The people of the village began to gather in the square, between the post office and the bank, around ten o'clock; in some towns there were so many people that the lottery took two days and had to be started on June 26th, but in this village, where there were only about three hundred people, the whole lottery took less than two hours, so it could begin at ten o'clock in the morning and still be through in time to allow the villagers to get home for noon dinner.

The children assembled first, of course. School was recently over for the summer, and the feeling of liberty sat uneasily on most of them; they tended to gather together quietly for a while before they broke into boisterous play, and their talk was still of the classroom and the teacher, of books and reprimands. Bobby Martin had already stuffed his pockets full of stones, and the other boys soon followed his example, selecting the smoothest and roundest stones; Bobby and Harry Jones and Dickie Delacroix — the villagers pronounced this name "Dellacroy" — eventually made a great pile of stones in one corner of the square and guarded it against the raids of the other boys. The girls stood aside, talking among themselves, looking over their shoulders at the boys, and the very small children rolled in the dust or clung to the hands of their older brothers or sisters.

Soon the men began to gather, surveying their own children, speaking of planting and rain, tractors and taxes. They stood together, away from the pile of stones in the corner, and their jokes were quiet and they smiled rather than laughed. The women, wearing faded house dresses and sweaters, came shortly after their menfolk. They greeted one another and exchanged bits of gossip as they went to join their husbands. Soon the women, standing by their husbands, began to call to their children, and the children came reluctantly, having to be called four or five times. Bobby Martin ducked under his mother's grasping hand and ran, laughing, back to the pile of stones. His father spoke up sharply, and Bobby came quickly and took his place between his father and his oldest brother.

The lottery was conducted — as were the square dances, the teen-age club, the Halloween program — by Mr. Summers, who had time and energy to devote to civic activities. He was a round-faced, jovial man and he ran the coal business, and people were sorry for him, because he had no children and his wife was a scold. When he arrived in the square, carrying the black wooden box, there was a murmur of conversation among the villagers, and he waved and called, "Little late today, folks." The postmaster, Mr. Graves, followed him, carrying a three-legged stool, and the stool was put in the center of the square and Mr. Summers set the black box down on it. The villagers kept their distance, leaving a space between themselves and the stool, and when Mr. Summers said, "Some of you fellows want to give me a hand?" there was a hesitation before two men, Mr. Martin and his oldest son, Baxter, came forward to hold the box steady on the stool while Mr. Summers stirred up the papers inside it.

The original paraphernalia for the lottery had been lost long ago, and the black box now resting on the stool had been put into use even before Old Man Warner, the oldest man in town, was born. Mr. Summers spoke frequently to the villagers about making a new box, but no one liked to upset even as much tradition as was represented by the black box. There was a story that the present box had been made with some pieces of the box that had preceded it, the one that had been constructed when the first people settled down to make a village here. Every year, after the lottery, Mr. Summers began talking again about a new box, but every year the subject was allowed to fade off without anything's being done. The black box grew shabbier each year; by now it was no longer completely black but splintered badly among one side to show the original wood color, and in some places faded or stained.

Mr. Martin and his oldest son, Baxter, held the black box securely on the stool until Mr. Summers had stirred the papers thoroughly with his hand. Because so much of the ritual had been forgotten or discarded, Mr.

Summers had been successful in having slips of paper substituted for the chips of wood that had been used for generations. Chips of wood, Mr. Summers had argued, had been all very well when the village was tiny, but now that the population was more than three hundred and likely to keep on growing, it was necessary to use something that would fit more easily into the black box. The night before the lottery, Mr. Summers and Mr. Graves made up the slips of paper and put them in the box, and it was then taken to the safe of Mr. Summers's coal company and locked up until Mr. Summers was ready to take it to the square next morning. The rest of the year, the box was put away, sometimes one place, sometimes another; it had spent one year in Mr. Graves's barn and another year underfoot in the post office, and sometimes it was set on a shelf in the Martin grocery and left there.

There was a great deal of fussing to be done before Mr. Summers declared the lottery open. There were the lists to make up — of heads of families, heads of households in each family, members of each household in each family. There was the proper swearing-in of Mr. Summers by the postmaster, as the official of the lottery; at one time, some people remembered, there had been a recital of some sort, performed by the official of the lottery, a perfunctory, tuneless chant that had been rattled off duly each year; some people believed that the official of the lottery used to stand just so when he said or sang it, others believed that he was supposed to walk among the people, but years and years ago this part of the ritual had been allowed to lapse. There had been, also, a ritual salute, which the official of the lottery had had to use in addressing each person who came up to draw from the box, but this also had changed with time, until now it was felt necessary only for the official to speak to each person approaching. Mr. Summers was very good at all this; in his clean white shirt and blue jeans, with one hand resting carelessly on the black box, he seemed very proper and important as he talked interminably to Mr. Graves and the Martins.

Just as Mr. Summers finally left off talking and turned to the assembled villagers, Mrs. Hutchinson came hurriedly along the path to the square, her sweater thrown over her shoulders, and slid into place in the back of the crowd. "Clean forgot what day it was," she said to Mrs. Delacroix, who stood next to her, and they both laughed softly. "Thought my old man was out back stacking wood," Mrs. Hutchinson went on, "and then I looked out the window and the kids was gone, and then I remembered it was the twenty-seventh and came a-running." She dried her hands on her apron, and Mrs. Delacroix said, "You're in time, though. They're still talking away up there."

Mrs. Hutchinson craned her neck to see through the crowd and found her husband and children standing near the front. She tapped Mrs. Delacroix on the arm as a farewell and began to make her way through the crowd. The people separated good-humoredly to let her through; two or three people said, in voices just loud enough to be heard across the crowd,

"Here comes your Missus, Hutchinson," and "Bill, she made it after all." Mrs. Hutchinson reached her husband, and Mr. Summers, who had been waiting, said cheerfully, "Thought we were going to have to get on without you, Tessie." Mrs. Hutchinson said, grinning, "Wouldn't have me leave m'dishes in the sink, now, would you, Joe?" and soft laughter ran through the crowd as the people stirred back into position after Mrs. Hutchinson's arrival.

"Well, now," Mr. Summers said soberly, "guess we better get started, get this over with, so's we can go back to work. Anybody ain't here?"

"Dunbar," several people said. "Dunbar, Dunbar."

Mr. Summers consulted his list. "Clyde Dunbar," he said. "That's right. He's broke his leg, hasn't he? Who's drawing for him?"

"Me, I guess," a woman said, and Mr. Summers turned to look at her. "Wife draws for her husband," Mr. Summers said. "Don't you have a grown boy to do it for you, Janey?" Although Mr. Summers and everyone else in the village knew the answer perfectly well, it was the business of the official of the lottery to ask such questions formally. Mr. Summers waited with an expression of polite interest while Mrs. Dunbar answered.

"Horace's not but sixteen yet," Mrs. Dunbar said regretfully. "Guess I gotta fill in for the old man this year."

"Right," Mr. Summers said. He made a note on the list he was holding. Then he asked, "Watson boy drawing this year?"

A tall boy in the crowd raised his hand. "Here," he said. "I'm drawing for m'mother and me." He blinked his eyes nervously and ducked his head as several voices in the crowd said things like "Good fellow, Jack," and "Glad to see your mother's got a man to do it."

"Well," Mr. Summers said, "guess that's everyone. Old Man Warner make it?"

"Here," a voice said, and Mr. Summers nodded.

A sudden hush fell on the crowd as Mr. Summers cleared his throat and looked at the list. "All ready?" he called. "Now, I'll read the names — heads of families first — and the men come up and take a paper out of the box. Keep the paper folded in your hand without looking at it until everyone has had a turn. Everything clear?"

The people had done it so many times that they only half listened to the directions; most of them were quiet, wetting their lips, not looking around. Then Mr. Summers raised one hand high and said, "Adams." A man disengaged himself from the crowd and came forward. "Hi, Steve," Mr. Summers said, and Mr. Adams said, "Hi, Joe." They grinned at one another humorlessly and nervously. Then Mr. Adams reached into the black box and took out a folded paper. He held it firmly by one corner as he turned and went hastily back to his place in the crowd, where he stood a little apart from his family, not looking down at his hand.

"Allen," Mr. Summers said, "Anderson. . . . Bentham."

"Seems like there's no time at all between lotteries any more," Mrs. Delacroix said to Mrs. Graves in the back row. "Seems like we got through with the last one only last week."

"Time sure goes fast," Mrs. Graves said.

"Clark. . . . Delacroix."

"There goes my old man," Mrs. Delacroix said. She held her breath while her husband went forward.

"Dunbar," Mr. Summers said, and Mrs. Dunbar went steadily to the box while one of the women said, "Go on, Janey," and another said, "There she goes."

"We're next," Mrs. Graves said. She watched while Mr. Graves came around from the side of the box, greeted Mr. Summers gravely, and selected a slip of paper from the box. By now, all through the crowd there were men holding the small folded papers in their large hands, turning them over and over nervously. Mrs. Dunbar and her two sons stood together, Mrs. Dunbar holding the slip of paper.

"Harburt. . . . Hutchinson."

"Get up there, Bill," Mrs. Hutchinson said, and the people near her laughed.

"Jones."

"They do say," Mr. Adams said to Old Man Warner, who stood next to him, "that over in the north village they're talking of giving up the lottery."

Old Man Warner snorted. "Pack of crazy fools," he said. "Listening to the young folks, nothing's good enough for *them*. Next thing you know, they'll be wanting to go back to living in caves, nobody work any more, live *that* way for a while. Used to be a saying about 'Lottery in June, corn be heavy soon.' First thing you know, we'd all be eating stewed chickweed and acorns. There's *always* been a lottery," he added petulantly. "Bad enough to see young Joe Summers up there joking with everybody."

"Some places have already quit lotteries," Mrs. Adams said.

"Nothing but trouble in *that*," Old Man Warner said stoutly. "Pack of young fools."

"Martin." And Bobby Martin watched his father go forward. "Overdyke. . . . Percy."

"I wish they'd hurry," Mrs. Dunbar said to her older son. "I wish they'd hurry."

"They're almost through," her son said.

"You get ready to run tell Dad," Mrs. Dunbar said.

Mr. Summers called his own name and then stepped forward precisely and selected a slip the box. Then he called, "Warner."

"Seventy-seventh year I been in the lottery," Old Man Warner said as he went through the crowd. "Seventy-seventh time."

"Watson." The tall boy came awkwardly through the crowd. Someone said. "Don't be nervous, Jack," and Mr. Summers said, "Take your time, son."

"Zanini."

After that, there was a long pause, a breathless pause, until Mr. Summers, holding his slip of paper in the air, said, "All right, fellows." For a minute, no one moved, and then all the slips of paper were opened. Suddenly, all the women began to speak at once, saying, "Who is it?" "Who's got it?" "Is it the Dunbars?" "Is it the Watsons?" Then the voices began to say, "It's Hutchinson. It's Bill," "Bill Hutchinson's got it."

"Go tell your father," Mrs. Dunbar said to her older son.

People began to look around to see the Hutchinsons. Bill Hutchinson was standing quiet, staring down at the paper in his hand. Suddenly, Tessie Hutchinson shouted to Mr. Summers, "You didn't give him time enough to take any paper he wanted. I saw you. It wasn't fair!"

"Be a good sport, Tessie," Mrs. Delacroix called, and Mrs. Graves said, "All of us took the same chance."

"Shut up, Tessie," Bill Hutchinson said.

"Well, everyone," Mr. Summers said, "that was done pretty fast, and now we've got to be hurrying a little more to get done in time." He consulted his next list. "Bill," he said, "you draw for the Hutchinson family. You got any other households in the Hutchinsons?"

"There's Don and Eva," Mrs. Hutchinson yelled. "Make *them* take their chance!"

"Daughters drew with their husbands' families, Tessie," Mr. Summers said gently. "You know that as well as anyone else."

"It wasn't *fair*," Tessie said.

"I guess not, Joe," Bill Hutchinson said regretfully. "My daughter draws with her husband's family, that's only fair. And I've got no other family except the kids."

"Then, as far as drawing for families is concerned, it's you," Mr. Summers said in explanation, "and as far as drawing for households is concerned, that's you, too. Right?"

"Right," Bill Hutchinson said.

"How many kids, Bill?" Mr. Summers asked formally.

"Three," Bill Hutchinson said. "There's Bill, Jr., and Nancy, and little Dave. And Tessie and me."

"All right, then," Mr. Summers said. "Harry, you got their tickets back?"

Mr. Graves nodded and held up the slips of paper. "Put them in the box, then," Mr. Summers directed. "Take Bill's and put it in."

"I think we ought to start over," Mrs. Hutchinson said, as quietly as she could. "I tell you it wasn't *fair*. You didn't give him time enough to choose. *Every*body saw that."

Mr. Graves had selected the five slips and put them in the box, and he dropped all the papers but those onto the ground, where the breeze caught them and lifted them off.

"Listen, everybody," Mrs. Hutchinson was saying to the people around her.

"Ready, Bill?" Mr. Summers asked, and Bill Hutchinson, with one quick glance around at his wife and children, nodded.

"Remember," Mr. Summers said, "take the slips and keep them folded until each person has taken one. Harry, you help little Dave." Mr. Graves took the hand of the little boy, who came willingly with him up to the box. "Take a paper out of the box, Davy," Mr. Summers said. Davy put his hand into the box and laughed. "Take just *one* paper," Mr. Summers said. "Harry, you hold it for him." Mr. Graves took the child's hand and removed the folded paper from the tight fist and held it while little Dave stood next to him and looked up at him wonderingly.

"Nancy next," Mr. Summers said. Nancy was twelve, and her school friends breathed heavily as she went forward, switching her skirt, and took a slip daintily from the box. "Bill, Jr.," Mr. Summers said, and Billy, his face red and his feet overlarge, nearly knocked the box over as he got a paper out. "Tessie," Mr. Summers said. She hesitated for a minute, looking around defiantly, and then set her lips and went up to the box. She snatched a paper out and held it behind her.

"Bill," Mr. Summers said, and Bill Hutchinson reached into the box and felt around, bringing his hand out at last with the slip of paper in it.

The crowd was quiet. A girl whispered, "I hope it's not Nancy," and the sound of the whisper reached the edges of the crowd.

"It's not the way it used to be," Old Man Warner said clearly. "People ain't the way they used to be."

"All right," Mr. Summers said. "Open the papers. Harry, you open little Dave's."

Mr. Graves opened the slip of paper and there was a general sigh through the crowd as he held it up and everyone could see that it was blank. Nancy and Bill, Jr., opened theirs at the same time, and both beamed and laughed, turning around to the crowd and holding their slips of paper above their heads.

"Tessie," Mr. Summers said. There was a pause, and then Mr. Summers looked at Bill Hutchinson, and Bill unfolded this paper and showed it. It was blank.

"It's Tessie," Mr. Summers said, and his voiced was hushed. "Show us her paper, Bill."

Bill Hutchinson went over to his wife and forced the slip of paper out of her hand. It had a black spot on it, the black spot Mr. Summers had made the night before with the heavy pencil in the coal-company office. Bill Hutchinson held it up and there was a stir in the crowd.

"All right, folks," Mr. Summers said. "Let's finish quickly."

Although the villagers had forgotten the ritual and lost the original black box, they still remembered to use stones. The pile of stones the boys had made earlier was ready; there were stones on the ground with the blowing scraps of paper that had come out of the box. Mrs. Delacroix selected a stone so large she had to pick it up with both hands and turned to Mrs. Dunbar. "Come on," she said. "Hurry up."

Mrs. Dunbar had small stones in both hands, and she said, gasping for breath, "I can't run at all. You'll have to go ahead and I'll catch up with you."

The children had stones already, and someone gave little Davy Hutchinson a few pebbles.

Tessie Hutchinson was in the center of a cleared space by now, and she held her hands out desperately as the villagers moved in on her. "It isn't fair," she said. A stone hit her on the side of the head.

Old Man Warner was saying, "Come on, come on, everyone." Steve Adams was in the front of the crowd of villagers, with Mrs. Graves beside him.

"It isn't fair, it isn't right," Mrs. Hutchinson screamed and then they were upon her.

[1948]

RAY BRADBURY (b. 1920) spent most of his childhood in the small community of Waukegan, Illinois. After his parents moved to California in 1934, he was educated at Los Angeles High School. While still in high school, Bradbury decided to become a professional writer, and at the age of fifteen he began submitting short stories to major national magazines. Two years later he joined the Los Angeles Science Fiction League, which published his first story, "Hollerbochen's Dilemma," in 1938. In his early twenties, he lived at home with his parents, selling newspapers for an income while he developed his literary style and began to place his stories in magazines. By the mid-1940s he was regularly publishing fantasy and horror stories; in 1949 he was voted the best science-fiction author of the year. Now in his sixties, Bradbury has published more than five hundred stories, poems, essays, plays, and film scripts.

Bradbury's best fiction, like his story "August 2026: There Will Come Soft Rains," dramatizes his heightened awareness of the major social problems of our time. His best-known book, The Martian Chronicles (1950), is an accurate reflection of postwar America, with its fear of nuclear war, its problems with racism and book censorship, its confused values, and its longing for a simpler life. The Martian Chronicles is a collection of previously published short stories linked with newly written passages to make a connected narrative. Fahrenheit 451 (1953), Bradbury's first novel, was expanded from an earlier long story, "The Fireman." The firemen of the novel are determined to burn books because they confuse readers with their subtle, contradictory values and their ambivalent portrayals of human behavior.

Among Bradbury's most popular collections of short fiction are The Illustrated Man (1951), Dandelion Wine (1957), I Sing the Body Electric (1969), and The Stories of Ray Bradbury (1980). He credits several American short story writers — Sherwood Anderson, Katherine Anne Porter, and Eudora Welty — with helping him forge his poetic, yet spare, literary style. His style, as the critic Gilbert Highet has realized, is a "curious mixture of poetry and colloquialism." Bradbury has said that "I am not so much a science-fiction writer as I am a magician, an illusionist. From my beginnings as a boy conjurer I grew up frightening myself so as to frighten others so as to cure the midnight in our souls."

Ray Bradbury

ന്ധ

AUGUST 2026:
THERE WILL COME SOFT RAINS

In the living room the voice-clock sang. *Tick-Tock, seven o'clock, time to get up, time to get up, seven o'clock!* as if it were afraid that nobody would. The morning house lay empty. The clock ticked on, repeating and repeating its sounds into the emptiness. *Seven-nine, breakfast time, seven-nine!*

In the kitchen the breakfast stove gave a hissing sigh and ejected from its warm interior eight pieces of perfectly browned toast, eight eggs sunny-side up, sixteen slices of bacon, two coffees, and two cool glasses of milk.

"Today is August 4, 2026," said a second voice from the kitchen ceiling, "in the city of Allendale, California." It repeated the date three times for memory's sake. "Today is Mr. Featherstone's birthday. Today is the anniversary of Tilita's marriage. Insurance is payable, as are the water, gas, and light bills."

Somewhere in the walls, relays clicked, memory tapes glided under electric eyes.

Eight-one, tick-tock, eight-one o'clock, off to school, off to work, run, run, eight-one! But no doors slammed, no carpets took the soft tread of rubber heels. It was raining outside. The weather box on the front door sang quietly: "Rain, rain, go away; rubbers, raincoats for today. . . ." And the rain tapped on the empty house, echoing.

Outside, the garage chimed and lifted its door to reveal the waiting car. After a long wait the door swung down again.

At eight-thirty the eggs were shriveled and toast was like stone. An aluminum wedge scraped them into the sink, where hot water whirled them down a metal throat which digested and flushed them away to the distant sea. The dirty dishes were dropped into a hot washer and emerged twinkling dry.

Nine-fifteen, sang the clock, *time to clean.*

Out of warrens in the wall, tiny robot mice darted. The rooms were acrawl with the small cleaning animals, all rubber and metal. They thudded against chairs, whirling their mustached runners, kneading the rug nap, sucking gently at hidden dust. Then, like mysterious invaders, they popped into their burrows. Their pink electric eyes faded. The house was clean.

Ten o'clock. The sun came out from behind the rain. The house stood alone in a city of rubble and ashes. This was the one house left standing. At night the ruined city gave off a radioactive glow which could be seen for miles.

Ten-fifteen. The garden sprinklers whirled up in golden founts, filling the soft morning air with scatterings of brightness. The water pelted windowpanes, running down the charred west side where the house had been burned evenly free of its white paint. The entire west face of the house was black, save for five places. Here the silhouette in paint of a man mowing a lawn. Here, as in a photograph, a woman bent to pick flowers. Still farther over, their images burned on wood in one titanic instant, a small boy, hands flung into the air; higher up, the image of a thrown ball, and opposite him a girl, hands raised to catch a ball which never came down.

The five spots of paint — the man, the woman, the children, the ball — remained. The rest was a thin charcoaled layer.

The gentle sprinkler rain filled the garden with falling light.

Until this day, how well the house had kept its peace. How carefully it had inquired, "Who goes there? What's the password?" and, getting no answer from lonely foxes and whining cats, it had shut up its windows and drawn shades in an old-maidenly preoccupation with self-protection which bordered on a mechanical paranoia.

It quivered at each sound, the house did. If a sparrow brushed a window, the shade snapped up. The bird, startled, flew off! No, not even a bird must touch the house!

The house was an altar with ten thousand attendants, big, small, servicing, attending, in choirs. But the gods had gone away, and the ritual of the religion continued senselessly, uselessly.

Twelve noon.

A dog whined, shivering, on the front porch.

The front door recognized the dog voice and opened. The dog, once huge and fleshy, but now gone to bone and covered with sores, moved in and through the house, tracking mud. Behind it whirred angry mice, angry at having to pick up mud, angry at inconvenience.

For not a leaf fragment blew under the door but what the wall panels flipped open and the copper scrap rats flashed swiftly out. The offending dust, hair, or paper, seized in miniature steel jaws, was raced back to the burrows. There, down tubes which fed into the cellar, it was dropped into the sighing vent of an incinerator which sat like evil Baal in a dark corner.

The dog ran upstairs, hysterically yelping to each door, at last realizing, as the house realized, that only silence was here.

It sniffed the air and scratched the kitchen door. Behind the door, the stove was making pancakes which filled the house with a rich baked odor and the scent of maple syrup.

The dog frothed at the mouth, lying at the door, sniffing, its eyes turned to fire. It ran wildly in circles, biting at its tail, spun in a frenzy, and died. It lay in the parlor for an hour.

Two o'clock, sang a voice.

Delicately sensing decay at last, the regiments of mice hummed out as softly as blown gray leaves in an electrical wind.

Two-fifteen.

The dog was gone.

In the cellar, the incinerator glowed suddenly and a whirl of sparks leaped up the chimney.

Two thirty-five.

Bridge tables sprouted from patio walls. Playing cards fluttered onto pads in a shower of pips. Martinis manifested on an oaken bench with egg-salad sandwiches. Music played.

But the tables were silent and the cards untouched.

At four o'clock the tables folded like great butterflies back through the paneled walls.

Four-thirty.

The nursery walls glowed.

Animals took shape: yellow giraffes, blue lions, pink antelopes, lilac panthers cavorting in crystal substance. The walls were glass. They looked out upon color and fantasy. Hidden films clocked through well-oiled sprockets, and the walls lived. The nursery floor was woven to resemble a crisp, cereal meadow. Over this ran aluminum roaches and iron crickets, and in the hot still air butterflies of delicate red tissue wavered among the sharp aroma of animal spoors! There was the sound like a great matted yellow hive of bees within a dark bellows, the lazy bumble of a purring lion. And there was the patter of okapi feet and the murmur of a fresh jungle rain, like other hoofs, falling upon the summer-starched grass. Now the walls dissolved into distances of parched weed, mile on mile, and warm endless sky. The animals drew away into thorn brakes and water holes.

It was the children's hour.

Five o'clock. The bath filled with clear hot water.

Six, seven, eight o'clock. The dinner dishes manipulated like magic tricks, and in the study a *click.* In the metal stand opposite the hearth where a fire now blazed up warmly, a cigar popped out, half an inch of soft gray ash on it, smoking, waiting.

Nine o'clock. The beds warmed their hidden circuits, for nights were cool here.

Nine-five. A voice spoke from the study ceiling:

"Mrs. McClellan, which poem would you like this evening?"

The house was silent.

The voice said at last, "Since you express no preference, I shall select a poem at random." Quiet music rose to back the voice. "Sara Teasdale. As I recall, your favorite. . . ."

There will come soft rains and the smell of the ground,
And swallows circling with their shimmering sound;

And frogs in the pools singing at night,
And wild plum trees in tremulous white;

Robins will wear their feathery fire,
Whistling their whims on a low fence-wire;

And not one will know of the war, not one
Will care at last when it is done.

Not one would mind, neither bird nor tree,
If mankind perished utterly;

And Spring herself, when she woke at dawn
Would scarcely know that we were gone."

The fire burned on the stone hearth and the cigar fell away into a mound of quiet ash on its tray. The empty chairs faced each other between the silent walls, and the music played.

At ten o'clock the house began to die.

The wind blew. A falling tree bough crashed through the kitchen window. Cleaning solvent, bottled, shattered over the stove. The room was ablaze in an instant!

"Fire!" screamed a voice. The house lights flashed, water pumps shot water from the ceilings. But the solvent spread on the linoleum, licking, eating, under the kitchen door, while the voices took it up in chorus: "Fire, fire, fire!"

The house tried to save itself. Doors sprang tightly shut, but the windows were broken by the heat and the wind blew and sucked upon the fire.

The house gave ground as the fire in ten billion angry sparks moved with flaming ease from room to room and then up the stairs. While scurrying water rats squeaked from the walls, pistoled their water, and ran for more. And the wall sprays let down showers of mechanical rain.

But too late. Somewhere, sighing, a pump shrugged to a stop. The quenching rain ceased. The reserve water supply which had filled baths and washed dishes for many quiet days was gone.

The fire crackled up the stairs. It fed upon Picassos and Matisses in the upper halls, like delicacies, baking off the oily flesh, tenderly crisping the canvases into black shavings.

Now the fire lay in beds, stood in windows, changed the colors of drapes!

And then, reinforcements.

From attic trapdoors, blind robot faces peered down with faucet mouths gushing green chemical.

The fire backed off, as even an elephant must at the sight of a dead snake. Now there were twenty snakes whipping over the floor, killing the fire with a clear cold venom of green froth.

But the fire was clever. It had sent flames outside the house, up through the attic to the pumps there. An explosion! The attic brain which directed the pumps was shattered into bronze shrapnel on the beams.

The fire rushed back into every closet and felt of the clothes hung there.

The house shuddered, oak bone on bone, its bared skeleton cringing from the heat, its wire, its nerves revealed as if a surgeon had torn the skin off to let the red veins and capillaries quiver in the scalded air. Help, help! Fire! Run, run! Heat snapped mirrors like the brittle winter ice. And the voices wailed Fire, fire, run, run, like a tragic nursery rhyme, a dozen voices, high, low, like children dying in a forest, alone, alone. And the voices fading as the wires popped their sheathings like hot chestnuts. One, two, three, four, five voices died.

In the nursery the jungle burned. Blue lions roared, purple giraffes bounded off. The panthers ran in circles changing color, and ten million animals, running before the fire, vanished off toward a distant steaming river. . . .

Ten more voices died. In the last instant under the fire avalanche, other choruses, oblivious, could be heard announcing the time, playing music, cutting the lawn by remote-control mower, or setting an umbrella frantically out and in the slamming and opening front door, a thousand things happening, like a clock shop when each clock strikes the hour insanely before or after the other, a scene of maniac confusion, yet unity; singing, screaming, a few last cleaning mice darting bravely out to carry the horrid ashes away! And one voice, with sublime disregard for the situation, read poetry aloud in the fiery study, until all the film spools burned, until all the wires withered and the circuits cracked.

The fire burst the house and let it slam flat down, puffing out skirts of spark and smoke.

In the kitchen, an instant before the rain of fire and timber, the stove could be seen making breakfasts at a psychopathic rate, ten dozen eggs, six loaves of toast, twenty dozen bacon strips, which, eaten by fire, started the stove working again, hysterically hissing!

The crash. The attic smashing into kitchen and parlor. The parlor into cellar, cellar into sub-cellar. Deep freeze, armchair, film tapes, circuits, beds, and all like skeletons thrown in a cluttered mound deep under.

Smoke and silence. A great quantity of smoke.

Dawn showed faintly in the east. Among the ruins, one wall stood alone. Within the wall, a last voice said, over and over again and again, even as the sun rose to shine upon the heaped rubble and steam:

"Today is August 5, 2026, today is August 5, 2026, today is . . ."

[1951]

GRACE PALEY (b. 1922) was born in New York City. She studied
at Hunter College and New York University, and in 1942 she married for
the first time. She had two children from that marriage. In the 1950s she
turned from writing poetry to try her hand at short fiction. Her first book of
stories, The Little Disturbances of Man (1959), established her reputation
as a writer with a remarkably supple gift for language. As a reviewer said,
her characters are "delicately manipulated; they approach each other, perhaps touch for an instant, and then back away. [Paley] deals with elaborate
surfaces, scarcely ever with developed interiors. Her characters barely jostle
one another." When the book went out of print in 1965, its reputation survived, strengthened by the infrequent appearances of her new stories in
magazines like The Atlantic Monthly, Esquire, The Noble Savage, Genesis
West, The New American Review, Ararat, and Fiction.

During the 1960s and 1970s Paley was prominent as a nonviolent activist protesting the Vietnam War. She was secretary of the Greenwich
Village Peace Center, spent time in jail for her antiwar activities, and visited Hanoi and Moscow as a member of peace delegations, defining her politics as "anarchist, if that's politics." Courageously speaking out during the
World Peace Congress in Moscow in 1973, she condemned the Soviet
Union for silencing political dissidents; the congress dissociated itself from
her statement. In recent years she has been active in the antinuclear movement. In 1974 her second volume of stories, Enormous Changes at the Last
Minute, was published — it is a quieter, more openly personal collection of
seventeen stories, many of them autobiographical, like "A Conversation
with My Father." Her third book of stories, Later the Same Day, appeared
in 1985.

Although Paley has published only three books of short stories, she refuses to blame her teaching jobs or her involvements as an activist for her
relatively low productivity as a writer. She says she writes "from distress."
What Paley tries to get at in her stories is "a history of everyday life," and
her subject matter and prose style are unmistakable. Living in a New York
apartment close to the Greenwich Village School (P.S. 41), Little Tony's
Unisex Haircutters, the Famous Ray's Pizza, the H & H Fruit and Vegetable Market, and the Jefferson Market Branch of the New York Public Library, Paley observes her neighbors, friends, and family with compassion,
humor, and hope. Her spare dissection of her characters is never performed
at the expense of sympathy for the human condition. It is likely that, as
with her Russian counterpart Isaac Babel, her production of stories will
continue to be limited. As she puts it, "There is a long time in me between
knowing and telling." (See Paley's Interview on page 1313.)

Grace Paley

ᔕᔤ

A CONVERSATION WITH MY FATHER

My father is eighty-six years old and in bed. His heart, that bloody motor, is equally old and will not do certain jobs any more. It still floods his head with brainy light. But it won't let his legs carry the weight of his body around the house. Despite my metaphors, this muscle failure is not due to his old heart, he says, but to a potassium shortage. Sitting on one pillow, leaning on three, he offers last-minute advice and makes a request.

"I would like you to write a simple story just once more," he says, "the kind de Maupassant wrote, or Chekhov, the kind you used to write. Just recognizable people and then write down what happened to them next."

I say, "Yes, why not? That's possible." I want to please him, though I don't remember writing that way. I *would* like to try to tell such a story, if he means the kind that begins: "There was a woman . . ." followed by plot, the absolute line between two points which I've always despised. Not for literary reasons, but because it takes all hope away. Everyone, real or invented, deserves the open destiny of life.

Finally I thought of a story that had been happening for a couple of years right across the street. I wrote it down, then read it aloud. "Pa," I said, "how about this? Do you mean something like this?"

> Once in my time there was a woman and she had a son. They lived nicely, in a small apartment in Manhattan. This boy at about fifteen became a junkie, which is not unusual in our neighborhood. In order to maintain her close friendship with him, she became a junkie too. She said it was part of the youth culture, with which she felt very much at home. After a while, for a number of reasons, the boy gave it all up and left the city and his mother in disgust. Hopeless and alone, she grieved. We all visit her.

"O.K., Pa, that's it," I said, "an unadorned and miserable tale."

"But that's not what I mean," my father said. "You misunderstood me on purpose. You know there's a lot more to it. You know that. You left everything out. Turgenev wouldn't do that. Chekhov wouldn't do that. There are in fact Russian writers you never heard of, you don't have an inkling of, as good as anyone, who can write a plain ordinary story, who would not leave out what you have left out. I object not to facts but to people sitting in trees talking senselessly, voices from who knows where. . . . "

"Forget that one, Pa, what have I left out now? In this one?"

"Her looks, for instance."

"Oh. Quite handsome, I think. Yes."

"Her hair?"

"Dark, with heavy braids, as though she were a girl or a foreigner."

"What were her parents like, her stock? That she became such a person. It's interesting, you know."

"From out of town. Professional people. The first to be divorced in their county. How's that? Enough?" I asked.

"With you, it's all a joke," he said. "What about the boy's father? Why didn't you mention him? Who was he? Or was the boy born out of wedlock?"

"Yes," I said. "He was born out of wedlock."

"For Godsakes, doesn't anyone in your stories get married? Doesn't anyone have the time to run down to City Hall before they jump into bed?"

"No," I said. "In real life, yes. But in my stories, no."

"Why do you answer me like that?"

"Oh, Pa, this is a simple story about a smart woman who came to N.Y.C. full of interest love trust excitement very up to date, and about her son, what a hard time she had in this world. Married or not, it's of small consequence."

"It is of great consequence," he said.

"O.K.," I said.

"O.K. O.K. yourself," he said, "but listen. I believe you that she's good-looking, but I don't think she was so smart."

"That's true," I said. "Actually that's the trouble with stories. People start out fantastic. You think they're extraordinary, but it turns out as the work goes along, they're just average with a good education. Sometimes the other way around, the person's a kind of dumb innocent, but he outwits you and you can't even think of an ending good enough."

"What do you do then?" he asked. He had been a doctor for a couple of decades and then an artist for a couple of decades and he's still interested in details, craft, technique.

"Well, you just have to let the story lie around till some agreement can be reached between you and the stubborn hero."

"Aren't you talking silly now?" he asked. "Start again," he said. "It so happens I'm not going out this evening. Tell the story again. See what you can do this time."

"O.K.," I said. "But it's not a five-minute job." Second attempt:

Once, across the street from us, there was a fine handsome woman, our neighbor. She had a son whom she loved because she'd known him since birth (in helpless chubby infancy, and in the wrestling, hugging ages, seven to ten, as well as earlier and later). This boy, when he fell into the fist of adolescence, became a junkie. He was not a hopeless one. He was in fact hopeful, an ideologue and successful converter. With his busy brilliance, he wrote persuasive articles for his high-school newspaper. Seeking a wider audience, using important connections, he drummed into Lower Manhattan newsstand distribution a periodical called *Oh! Golden Horse!*

In order to keep him from feeling guilty (because guilt is the stony heart of nine tenths of all clinically diagnosed cancers in America today, she said), and because she had always believed in giving bad habits room at home where one could keep an eye on them, she too became a junkie. Her kitchen was famous for a while — a center for intellectual addicts who knew what they were doing. A few felt artistic like Coleridge[1] and others were scientific and revolutionary like Leary.[2] Although she was often high herself, certain good mothering reflexes remained, and she saw to it that there was lots of orange juice around and honey and milk and vitamin pills. However, she never cooked anything but chili, and that no more than once a week. She explained, when we talked to her, seriously, with neighborly concern, that it was her part in the youth culture and she would rather be with the young, it was an honor, than with her own generation.

One week, while nodding through an Antonioni film, this boy was severely jabbed by the elbow of a stern and proselytizing girl, sitting beside him. She offered immediate apricots and nuts for his sugar level, spoke to him sharply, and took him home.

She had heard of him and his work and she herself published, edited, and wrote a competitive journal called *Man Does Live by Bread Alone.* In the organic heat of her continuous presence he could not help but become interested once more in his muscles, his arteries, and nerve connections. In fact he began to love them, treasure them, praise them with funny little songs in *Man Does Live. . . .*

> the fingers of my flesh transcend
> my transcendental soul
> the tightness in my shoulders end
> my teeth have made me whole

To the mouth of his head (that glory of will and determination) he brought hard apples, nuts, wheat germ, and soybean oil. He said to his old friends, From now on, I guess I'll keep my wits about me. I'm going on the natch. He said he was about to begin a spiritual deep-breathing journey. How about you too, Mom? he asked kindly.

His conversion was so radiant, splendid, that neighborhood kids his age began to say that he had never been a real addict at all, only a journalist along for the smell of the story. The mother tried several times to give up what had become without her son and his friends a lonely habit. This effort only brought it to supportable levels. The boy and his girl took their electronic mimeograph and moved to the bushy edge of another borough. They were very strict. They said they would not see her again until she had been off drugs for sixty days.

At home alone in the evening, weeping, the mother read and reread the seven issues of *Oh! Golden Horse!* They seemed to her as truthful as ever. We often crossed the street to visit and console. But if we mentioned any of our children who were at college or in the hospital or dropouts at home, she would cry out, My baby! My baby! and burst into terrible, face-scarring, time-consuming tears. The End.

First my father was silent, then he said, "Number One: You have a nice sense of humor. Number Two: I see you can't tell a plain story. So don't waste time." Then he said sadly, "Number Three: I suppose that means she was alone, she was left like that, his mother. Alone. Probably sick?"

I said, "Yes."

"Poor woman. Poor girl, to be born in a time of fools, to live among fools. The end. The end. You were right to put that down. The end."

I didn't want to argue, but I had to say, "Well, it is not necessarily the end, Pa."

"Yes," he said, "what a tragedy. The end of a person."

"No, Pa," I begged him. "It doesn't have to be. She's only about forty. She could be a hundred different things in this world as time goes on. A teacher or a social worker. An ex-junkie! Sometimes it's better than having a master's in education."

"Jokes," he said. "As a writer that's your main trouble. You don't want to recognize it. Tragedy! Plain tragedy! Historical tragedy! No hope. The end."

"Oh, Pa," I said. "She could change."

"In your own life, too, you have to look it in the face." He took a couple of nitroglycerin. "Turn to five," he said, pointing to the dial on the oxygen tank. He inserted the tubes into his nostrils and breathed deep. He closed his eyes and said, "No."

I had promised the family to always let him have the last word when arguing, but in this case I had a different responsibility. That woman lives across the street. She's my knowledge and my invention. I'm sorry for her. I'm not going to leave her there in that house crying. (Actually neither would Life, which unlike me has no pity.)

Therefore: She did change. Of course her son never came home again. But right now, she's the receptionist in a storefront community clinic in the East Village. Most of the customers are young people, some old friends. The head doctor has said to her, "If we only had three people in this clinic with your experiences. . . ."

"The doctor said that?" My father took the oxygen tubes out of his nostrils and said, "Jokes. Jokes again."

"No, Pa, it could really happen that way, it's a funny world nowadays."

"No," he said. "Truth first. She will slide back. A person must have character. She does not."

"No, Pa," I said. "That's it. She's got a job. Forget it. She's in that storefront working."

"How long will it be?" he asked. "Tragedy! You too. When will you look it in the face?"

[1974]

NADINE GORDIMER (b. 1923) was born in the small town of Springs, near Johannesburg, South Africa. Her mother was English, and her father, a Jewish watchmaker, emigrated to Africa from the Baltic states. Gordimer attended a convent school and studied at the University of Witwatersrand, getting what she has called "a scrappy and uninspiring minimal education." At an early age she turned to books to enrich her experience.

> Life was prefigured in them; without knowing quite how I should bring this about, I felt that I should live it for myself someday. I began, quite unconsciously, through writing; passing from the passive act of reading to the creative act of writing brought me to life. Walls fell down; one of the biggest was the colour bar. I discovered that although the law of my country and the custom of white people kept them huddled together with their skirts drawn up away from what Africa really is, I in myself was free of their prejudices and their fears. . . . This discovery was a joyous personal one, not a political one, at first, but of course, as time has gone by it has hardened into a sense of political opposition to abusive white power. The core of it remains a personal freedom to me.

Gordimer began to write stories before she attempted a novel. She acknowledges three writers as her guides: D. H. Lawrence, who influenced her way of looking at the natural world; Henry James, who gave her a consciousness of form; and Ernest Hemingway, who taught her to hear what is essential in dialogue. Her early stories appeared in The New Yorker, Harper's, and other American magazines, and were first collected in Face to Face (1949) and The Soft Voice of the Serpent (1952). Since her first novel, The Lying Days, was published in 1953, she has continued alternating books of long and short fiction. She rarely experiments beyond the realistic rendering of her subject in her stories, but her decision to write in the form of the short story or the novel depends on the shape the material takes as a narrative.

> Whether it sprawls or neatly bites its own tail, a short story is a concept that the writer can "hold" fully realized in his imagination at one time. A novel is, by comparison, staked out, and must be taken possession of stage by stage; it is impossible to contain, all at once, the proliferation of concepts it ultimately may use. For this reason I cannot understand how people can suppose one makes a conscious choice, after knowing what one wants to write about, between writing a novel or a short story. A short story occurs, in the imaginative sense. To write one is to express from a situation in the exterior or interior world the life-giving drop — sweat, tear, semen, saliva — that will spread an intensity on the page; burn a hole in it.

The pair of linked stories in "Town and Country Lovers" demon-
strates Gordimer's use of fiction over the last thirty years to mirror complex
social attitudes in her beleaguered country. She feels herself "selected" by
her subject. In her latest story collections, A Soldier's Embrace *(1980) and*
Something Out There *(1984) and her latest novels,* Burger's Daughter
(1979) and July's People (1981), she continues to explore the ramifications
of racial strife in South Africa. Gordimer's achievement as a writer is fur-
ther proof of Flaubert's insight, "One is not at all free to write this or that.
One does not choose one's subject. This is what the public and the critics
do not understand. The secret of masterpieces lies in the concordance be-
tween the subject and the temperament of the author." (See Gordimer's
Commentary on page 1318.)

Nadine Gordimer

∞

TOWN AND COUNTRY LOVERS

I

Dr. Franz-Josef von Leinsdorf is a geologist absorbed in his work;
wrapped up in it, as the saying goes — year after year the experience of this
work enfolds him, swaddling him away from the landscapes, the cities, and
the people, wherever he lives: Peru, New Zealand, the United States. He's
always been like that, his mother could confirm from their native Austria.
There, even as a handsome small boy he presented only his profile to her:
turned away to his bits of rock and stone. His few relaxations have not
changed much since then. An occasional skiing trip, listening to music,
reading poetry — Rainer Maria Rilke once stayed in his grandmother's
hunting lodge in the forests of Styria and the boy was introduced to Rilke's
poems while very young.

Layer upon layer, country after country, wherever his work takes
him — and now he has been almost seven years in Africa. First the Côte
d'Ivoire, and for the past five years, South Africa. The shortage of skilled
manpower brought about his recruitment here. He has no interest in the
politics of the countries he works in. His private preoccupation-within-the-
preoccupation of his work has been research into underground water-
courses, but the mining company that employs him in a senior though not
executive capacity is interested only in mineral discovery. So he is much out
in the field — which is the veld, here — seeking new gold, copper, plati-
num, and uranium deposits. When he is at home — on this particular job,

in this particular country, this city — he lives in a two-roomed flat in a suburban block with a landscaped garden, and does his shopping at a supermarket conveniently across the street. He is not married — yet. That is how his colleagues, and the typists and secretaries at the mining company's head office, would define his situation. Both men and women would describe him as a good-looking man, in a foreign way, with the lower half of his face dark and middle-aged (his mouth is thin and curving, and no matter how close-shaven his beard shows like fine shot embedded in the skin round mouth and chin) and the upper half contradictorily young, with deep-set eyes (some would say grey, some black), thick eyelashes and brows. A tangled gaze: through which concentration and gleaming thoughtfulness perhaps appear as fire and languor. It is this that the women in the office mean when they remark he's not unattractive. Although the gaze seems to promise, he has never invited any one of them to go out with him. There is the general assumption he probably has a girl who's been picked for him, he's bespoken by one of his own kind, back home in Europe where he comes from. Many of these well-educated Europeans have no intention of becoming permanent immigrants; neither the remnant of white colonial life nor idealistic involvement with Black Africa appeals to them.

One advantage, at least, of living in underdeveloped or half-developed countries is that flats are serviced. All Dr. von Leinsdorf has to do for himself is buy his own supplies and cook an evening meal if he doesn't want to go to a restaurant. It is simply a matter of dropping in to the supermarket on his way from his car to his flat after work in the afternoon. He wheels a trolley up and down the shelves, and his simple needs are presented to him in the form of tins, packages, plastic-wrapped meat, cheeses, fruit and vegetables, tubes, bottles . . . At the cashier's counters where customers must converge and queue there are racks of small items uncategorized, for last-minute purchase. Here, as the coloured girl cashier punches the adding machine, he picks up cigarettes and perhaps a packet of salted nuts or a bar of nougat. Or razor-blades, when he remembers he's running short. One evening in winter he saw that the cardboard display was empty of the brand of blades he preferred, and he drew the cashier's attention to this. These young coloured girls are usually pretty unhelpful, taking money and punching their machines in a manner that asserts with the time-serving obstinacy of the half-literate the limit of any responsibility towards customers, but this one ran an alert glance over the selection of razor-blades, apologized that she was not allowed to leave her post, and said she would see that the stock was replenished "next time." A day or two later she recognized him, gravely, as he took his turn before her counter — "I ahssed them, but it's out of stock. You can't get it. I did ahss about it." He said this didn't matter. "When it comes in, I can keep a few packets for you." He thanked her.

He was away with the prospectors the whole of the next week. He arrived back in town just before nightfall on Friday, and was on his way from car to flat with his arms full of briefcase, suitcase, and canvas bags when someone stopped him by standing timidly in his path. He was about to dodge round unseeingly on the crowded pavement but she spoke. "We got the blades in now. I didn't see you in the shop this week, but I kept some for when you come. So . . ."

He recognized her. He had never seen her standing before, and she was wearing a coat. She was rather small and finely-made, for one of them. The coat was skimpy but no big backside jutted. The cold brought an apricot-graining of warm colour to her cheekbones, beneath which a very small face was quite delicately hollowed, and the skin was smooth, the subdued satiny colour of certain yellow wood. That crêpey hair, but worn drawn back flat and in a little knot pushed into one of the cheap wool chignons that (he recognized also) hung in the miscellany of small goods along with the razor-blades, at the supermarket. He said thanks, he was in a hurry, he'd only just got back from a trip — shifting the burdens he carried, to demonstrate. "Oh shame." She acknowledged his load. "But if you want I can run in and get it for you quickly. If you want."

He saw at once it was perfectly clear that all the girl meant was that she would go back to the supermarket, buy the blades, and bring the packet to him there where he stood, on the pavement. And it seemed that it was this certainty that made him say, in the kindly tone of assumption used for an obliging underling, "I live just across there — *Atlantis* — that flat building. Could you drop them by, for me — number seven-hundred-and-eighteen, seventh floor — "

She had not before been inside one of these big flat buildings near where she worked. She lived a bus- and train-ride away to the West of the city, but this side of the black townships, in a township for people her tint. There was a pool with ferns, not plastic, and even a little waterfall pumped electrically over rocks, in the entrance of the building *Atlantis*; she didn't wait for the lift marked GOODS but took the one meant for whites and a white woman with one of those sausage-dogs on a lead got in with her but did not pay her any attention. The corridors leading to the flats were nicely glassed-in, not draughty.

He wondered if he should give her a twenty-cent piece for her trouble — ten cents would be right for a black; but she said, "Oh no — please, here — "standing outside his open door and awkwardly pushing back at his hand the change from the money he'd given her for the razor-blades. She was smiling, for the first time, in the dignity of refusing a tip. It was difficult to know how to treat these people, in this country; to know what they expected. In spite of her embarrassing refusal of the coin, she stood there, completely unassuming, fists thrust down the pockets of her cheap coat against the cold she'd come in from, rather pretty thin legs neatly aligned, knee to knee, ankle to ankle.

"Would you like a cup of coffee or something?"

He couldn't very well take her into his study-cum-living-room and offer her a drink. She followed him to his kitchen, but at the sight of her pulling out the single chair to drink her cup of coffee at the kitchen table, he said, "No — bring it in here — " and led the way into the big room where, among his books and his papers, his files of scientific correspondence (and the cigar boxes of stamps from the envelopes), his racks of records, his specimens of minerals and rocks, he lived alone.

It was no trouble to her; she saved him the trips to the supermarket and brought him his groceries two or three times a week. All he had to do was to leave a list and the key under the doormat, and she would come up in her lunch-hour to collect them, returning to put his supplies in the flat after work. Sometimes he was home and sometimes not. He bought a box of chocolates and left it, with a note, for her to find; and that was acceptable, apparently, as a gratuity.

Her eyes went over everything in the flat although her body tried to conceal its sense of being out of place by remaining as still as possible, holding its contours in the chair offered her as a stranger's coat is set aside and remains exactly as left until the owner takes it up to go. "You collect?"

"Well, these are specimens — connected with my work."

"My brother used to collect. Miniatures. With brandy and whisky and that, in them. From all over. Different countries."

The second time she watched him grinding coffee for the cup he had offered her she said, "You always do that? Always when you make coffee?"

"But of course. It is no good, for you. Do I make it too strong?"

"Oh it's just I'm not used to it. We buy it ready — you know, it's in a bottle, you just add a bit to the milk or water."

He laughed, instructive: "That's not coffee, that's a synthetic flavouring. In my country we drink only real coffee, fresh, from the beans — you smell how good it is as it's being ground?"

She was stopped by the caretaker and asked what she wanted in the building? Heavy with the *bona fides* of groceries clutched to her body, she said she was working at number 718, on the seventh floor. The caretaker did not tell her not to use the whites' lift; after all, she was not black; her family was very light-skinned.

There was the item "grey button for trousers" on one of his shopping lists. She said as she unpacked the supermarket carrier, "Give me the pants, so long, then," and sat on his sofa that was always gritty with fragments of pipe tobacco, sewing in and out through the four holes of the button with firm, fluent movements of the right hand, gestures supplying the articulacy missing from her talk. She had a little yokel's, peasant's (he thought of it) gap between her two front teeth when she smiled that he didn't much like, but, face ellipsed to three-quarter angle, eyes cast down in concentration with soft lips almost closed, this didn't matter. He said, watching her sew, "You're a good girl"; and touched her.

She remade the bed every late afternoon when they left it and she dressed again before she went home. After a week there was a day when late afternoon became evening, and they were still in the bed.

"Can't you stay the night?"

"My mother," she said.

"Phone her. Make an excuse." He was a foreigner. He had been in the country five years, but he didn't understand that people don't usually have telephones in their houses, where she lived. She got up to dress. He didn't want that tender body to go out in the night cold and kept hindering her with the interruption of his hands; saying nothing. Before she put on her coat, when the body had already disappeared, he spoke, "But you must make some arrangement."

"Oh my mother!" Her face opened to fear and vacancy he could not read.

He was not entirely convinced the woman would think of her daughter as some pure and unsullied virgin . . . "Why?"

The girl said, "S'e'll be scared. S'e'll be scared we get caught."

"Don't tell her anything. Say I'm employing you." In this country he was working in now there were generally rooms on the roofs of flat buildings for tenants' servants.

She said: "That's what I told the caretaker."

She ground fresh coffee beans every time he wanted a cup while he was working at night. She never attempted to cook anything until she had watched in silence while he did it the way he liked, and she learned to re-produce exactly the simple dishes he preferred. She handled his pieces of rock and stone, at first admiring the colours — "It'd make a beautiful ring or necklace, ay." Then he showed her the striations, the formation of each piece, and explained what each was, and how, in the long life of the earth, it had been formed. He named the mineral it yielded, and what that was used for. He worked at his papers, writing, writing, every night, so it did not matter that they could not go out together to public places. On Sundays she got into his car in the basement garage and they drove to the country and picnicked away up in the Magaliesberg, where there was no one. He read or poked about among the rocks; they climbed together, to the mountain pools. He taught her to swim. She had never seen the sea. She squealed and shrieked in the water, showing the gap between her teeth, as — it crossed his mind — she must do when among her own people. Occasionally he had to go out to dinner at the houses of colleagues from the mining company; she sewed and listened to the radio in the flat and he found her in the bed, warm and already asleep, by the time he came in. He made his way into her body without speaking; she made him welcome without a word. Once he put on evening dress for a dinner at his country's consulate; watching him brush one or two fallen hairs from the shoulders of the dark jacket that sat so well on him, she saw a huge room, all chandeliers and people dancing some dance from a costume film — stately, hand-to-hand. She supposed he was going to fetch, in her place in the car, a partner for the evening. They never kissed when either left the flat; he said, suddenly, kindly, pausing as he picked up cigarettes and keys, "Don't be lonely." And added, "Wouldn't you like to visit your family sometimes, when I have to go out?"

He had told her he was going home to his mother in the forests and mountains of his country near the Italian border (he showed her on the map) after Christmas. She had not told him how her mother, not knowing there was any other variety, assumed he was a medical doctor, so she had talked to her about the doctor's children and the doctor's wife who was a very kind lady, glad to have someone who could help out in the surgery as well as the flat.

She remarked wonderingly on his ability to work until midnight or later, after a day at work. She was so tired when she came home from her cash register at the supermarket that once dinner was eaten she could scarcely keep awake. He explained in a way she could understand that while the work she did was repetitive, undemanding of any real response from her intelligence, requiring little mental or physical effort and therefore unrewarding, his work was his greatest interest, it taxed his mental capacities to their limit, exercised all his concentration, and rewarded him constantly as much with the excitement of a problem presented as with the satisfaction of a problem solved. He said later, putting away his papers, speaking out of a silence: "Have you done other kinds of work?" She said, "I was in a clothing factory before. Sportbeau shirts; you know? But the pay's better in the shop."

Of course. Being a conscientious newspaper-reader in every country he lived in, he was aware that it was only recently that the retail consumer trade in this one had been allowed to employ coloureds as shop assistants; even punching a cash register represented advancement. With the continuing shortage of semi-skilled whites a girl like this might be able to edge a little farther into the white-collar category. He began to teach her to type. He was aware that her English was poor, even though, as a foreigner, in his ears her pronunciation did not offend, nor categorize her as it would in those of someone of his education whose mother tongue was English. He corrected her grammatical mistakes but missed the less obvious ones because of his own sometimes exotic English usage — she continued to use the singular pronoun "it" when what was required was the plural "they." Because he was a foreigner (although so clever, as she saw) she was less inhibited than she might have been by the words she knew she misspelled in her typing. While she sat at the typewriter she thought how one day she would type notes for him, as well as making coffee the way he liked it, and taking him inside her body without saying anything, and sitting (even if only through the empty streets of quiet Sundays) beside him in his car, like a wife.

On a summer night near Christmas — he had already bought and hidden a slightly showy but nevertheless good watch he thought she would like — there was a knocking at the door that brought her out of the bathroom and him to his feet, at his work-table. No one ever came to the flat at night; he had no friends intimate enough to drop in without warning. The summons was an imperious banging that did not pause and clearly would not stop until the door was opened.

She stood in the open bathroom doorway gazing at him across the passage into the living-room; her bare feet and shoulders were free of a big bath-towel. She said nothing, did not even whisper. The flat seemed to shake with the strong unhurried blows.

He made as if to go to the door, at last, but now she ran and clutched him by both arms. She shook her head wildly; her lips drew back but her teeth were clenched, she didn't speak. She pulled him into the bedroom, snatched some clothes from the clean laundry laid out on the bed, and got into the wall-cupboard, thrusting the key at his hand. Although his arms and calves felt weakly cold he was horrified, distastefully embarrassed at the sight of her pressed back crouching there under his suits and coat; it was horrible and ridiculous. *Come out!* he whispered. *No! Come out!* She hissed: *Where? Where can I go?*

Never mind! Get out of there!

He put out his hand to grasp her. At bay, she said with all the force of her terrible whisper, baring the gap in her teeth: *I'll throw myself out the window.*

She forced the key into his hand like the handle of a knife. He closed the door on her face and drove the key home in the lock, then dropped it among coins in his trouser pocket.

He unslotted the chain that was looped across the flat door. He turned the serrated knob of the Yale lock. The three policemen, two in plain clothes, stood there without impatience although they had been banging on the door for several minutes. The big dark one with an elaborate moustache held out in a hand wearing a plaited gilt ring some sort of identity card.

Dr. von Leinsdorf said quietly, the blood coming strangely back to legs and arms, "What is it?"

The sergeant told him they knew there was a coloured girl in the flat. They had had information; "I been watching this flat three months, I know."

"I am alone here." Dr. von Leinsdorf did not raise his voice.

"I know, I know who is here. Come — " And the sergeant and his two assistants went into the living-room, the kitchen, the bathroom (the sergeant picked up a bottle of after-shave cologne, seemed to study the French label), and the bedroom. The assistants removed the clean laundry that was laid upon the bed and then turned back the bedding, carrying the sheets over to be examined by the sergeant under the lamp. They talked to one another in Afrikaans, which the Doctor did not understand. The sergeant himself looked under the bed, and lifted the long curtains at the window. The wall-cupboard was of the kind that has no knobs; he saw that it was locked and began to ask in Afrikaans, then politely changed to English, "Give us the key."

Dr. von Leinsdorf said, "I'm sorry, I left it at my office — I always lock and take my keys with me in the mornings."

"It's no good, man, you better give me the key."

He smiled a little, reasonably. "It's on my office desk."

The assistants produced a screwdriver and he watched while they inserted it where the cupboard doors met, gave it quick, firm but not forceful leverage. He heard the lock give.

She had been naked, it was true, when they knocked. But now she was wearing a long-sleeved T-shirt with an appliquéd butterfly motif on one breast, and a pair of jeans. Her feet were still bare; she had managed, by feel, in the dark, to get into some of the clothing she had snatched from the bed, but she had no shoes. She had perhaps been weeping behind the cupboard door (her cheeks looked stained) but now her face was sullen and she was breathing heavily, her diaphragm contracting and expanding exaggeratedly and her breasts pushing against the cloth. It made her appear angry; it might simply have been that she was half-suffocated in the cupboard and needed oxygen. She did not look at Dr. von Leinsdorf. She would not reply to the sergeant's questions.

They were taken to the police station where they were at once separated and in turn led for examination by the district surgeon. The man's underwear was taken away and examined, as the sheets had been, for signs of his seed. When the girl was undressed, it was discovered that beneath her jeans she was wearing a pair of men's briefs with his name on the neatly-sewn laundry tag; in her haste, she had taken the wrong garment to her hiding-place.

Now she cried, standing there before the district surgeon in a man's underwear.

He courteously pretended not to notice. He handed briefs, jeans, and T-shirt round the door, and motioned her to lie on a white-sheeted high table where he placed her legs apart, resting in stirrups, and put into her where the other had made his way so warmly a cold hard instrument that expanded wider and wider. Her thighs and knees trembled uncontrollably while the doctor looked into her and touched her deep inside with more hard instruments, carrying wafers of gauze.

When she came out of the examining room back to the charge office, Dr. von Leinsdorf was not there; they must have taken him somewhere else. She spent what was left of the night in a cell, as he must be doing; but early in the morning she was released and taken home to her mother's house in the coloured township by a white man who explained he was the clerk of the lawyer who had been engaged for her by Dr. von Leinsdorf. Dr. von Leinsdorf, the clerk said, had also been bailed out that morning. He did not say when, or if she would see him again.

A statement made by the girl to the police was handed in to Court when she and the man appeared to meet charges of contravening the Immorality Act in a Johannesburg flat on the night of — December, 19 — . *I lived with the white man in his flat. He had intercourse with me sometimes. He gave me tablets to take to prevent me becoming pregnant.*

Interviewed by the Sunday papers, the girl said, "I'm sorry for the sadness brought to my mother." She said she was one of nine children of a female laundry worker. She had left school in Standard Three because there was no money at home for gym clothes or a school blazer. She had worked as a machinist in a factory and a cashier in a supermarket. Dr. von Leinsdorf taught her to type his notes.

Dr. Franz-Josef von Leinsdorf, described as the grandson of a baroness, a cultured man engaged in international mineralogical research, said he accepted social distinctions between people but didn't think they should be legally imposed. "Even in my own country it's difficult for a person from a higher class to marry one from a lower class."

The two accused gave no evidence. They did not greet or speak to each other in Court. The Defence argued that the sergeant's evidence that they had been living together as man and wife was heresay. (The woman with the dachshund, the caretaker?) The magistrate acquitted them because the State failed to prove carnal intercourse had taken place on the night of — December, 19 — .

The girl's mother was quoted, with photograph, in the Sunday papers: "I won't let my daughter work as a servant for a white man again."

II

The farm children play together when they are small; but once the white children go away to school they soon don't play together any more, even in the holidays. Although most of the black children get some sort of schooling, they drop every year farther behind the grades passed by the white children; the childish vocabulary, the child's exploration of the adventurous possibilities of dam, koppies, mealie lands, and veld — there comes a time when the white children have surpassed these with the vocabulary of boarding-school and the possibilities of inter-school sports matches and the kind of adventures seen at the cinema. This usefully coincides with the age of twelve or thirteen; so that by the time early adolescence is reached, the black children are making, along with the bodily changes common to all, an easy transition to adult forms of address, beginning to call their old playmates *missus* and *baasie* — little master.

The trouble was Paulus Eysendyck did not seem to realize that Thebedi was now simply one of the crowd of farm children down at the kraal, recognizable in his sisters' old clothes. The first Christmas holidays after he had gone to boarding-school he brought home for Thebedi a painted box he had made in his wood-work class. He had to give it to her secretly because he had nothing for the other children at the kraal. And she gave him, before he went back to school, a bracelet she had made of thin brass wire and the grey-and-white beans of the castor-oil crop his father cultivated. (When they used to play together, she was the one who had taught Paulus how to make clay oxen for their toy spans.) There was a craze, even in the *platteland* towns like the one where he was at school, for boys to wear elephant-hair and other bracelets beside their watch-straps; his was admired, friends asked him to get similar ones for them. He said the natives made them on his father's farm and he would try.

When he was fifteen, six feet tall, and tramping round at school dances with the girls from the "sister" school in the same town; when he had learnt how to tease and flirt and fondle quite intimately these girls who were the daughters of prosperous farmers like his father; when he had even met one who, at a wedding he had attended with his parents on a nearby farm, had let him do with her in a locked storeroom what people did when they made love — when he was as far from his childhood as all this, he still brought home from a shop in town a red plastic belt and gilt hoop ear-rings for the black girl, Thebedi. She told her father the missus had given these to her as a reward for some work she had done — it was true she sometimes was called to help out in the farmhouse. She told the girls in the kraal that she had a sweetheart nobody knew about, far away, away on another farm, and they giggled, and teased, and admired her. There was a boy in the kraal called Njabulo who said he wished he could have brought her a belt and ear-rings.

When the farmer's son was home for the holidays she wandered far from the kraal and her companions. He went for walks alone. They had not arranged this; it was an urge each followed independently. He knew it was she, from a long way off. She knew that his dog would not bark at her. Down at the dried-up river-bed where five or six years ago the children had caught a leguaan one great day — a creature that combined ideally the size and ferocious aspect of the crocodile with the harmlessness of the lizard — they squatted side by side on the earth bank. He told her traveller's tales: about school, about the punishments at school, particularly, exaggerating both their nature and his indifference to them. He told her about the town of Middleburg, which she had never seen. She had nothing to tell but she prompted with many questions, like any good listener. While he talked he twisted and tugged at the roots of white stinkwood and Cape willow trees that looped out of the eroded earth around them. It had always been a good spot for children's games, down there hidden by the mesh of old, ant-eaten trees held in place by vigorous ones, wild asparagus bushing up between the trunks, and here and there prickly-pear cactus sunken-skinned and bristly, like an old man's face, keeping alive sapless until the next rainy season. She punctured the dry hide of a prickly-pear again and again with a sharp stick while she listened. She laughed a lot at what he told her, sometimes dropping her face on her knees, sharing amusement with the cool shady earth beneath her bare feet. She put on her pair of shoes — white sandals, thickly Blanco-ed against the farm dust — when he was on the farm, but these were taken off and laid aside, at the river-bed.

One summer afternoon when there was water flowing there and it was very hot she waded in as they used to do when they were children, her dress bunched modestly and tucked into the legs of her pants. The schoolgirls he went swimming with at dams or pools on neighbouring farms wore bikinis but the sight of their dazzling bellies and thighs in the sunlight had never made him feel what he felt now, when the girl came up the bank and sat beside him, the drops of water beading off her dark legs the only points of light in the earth-smelling, deep shade. They were not afraid of one another, they had known one another always; he did with her what he had done that time in the storeroom at the wedding, and this time it was so lovely, so lovely, he was surprised . . . and she was surprised by it, too — he could see in her dark face that was part of the shade, with her big dark eyes, shiny as soft water, watching him attentively: as she had when they used to huddle over their teams of mud oxen, as she had when he told her about detention weekends at school.

They went to the river-bed often through those summer holidays. They met just before the light went, as it does quite quickly, and each returned home with the dark — she to her mother's hut, he to the farmhouse — in time for the evening meal. He did not tell her about school or town any more. She did not ask questions any longer. He told her, each time, when they would meet again. Once or twice it was very early in the morning; the lowing of the cows being driven to graze came to them where they lay, dividing them with unspoken recognition of the sound read in their two pairs of eyes, opening so close to each other.

He was a popular boy at school. He was in the second, then the first soccer team. The head girl of the "sister" school was said to have a crush on him; he didn't particularly like her, but there was a pretty blonde who put up her long hair into a kind of doughnut with a black ribbon round it, whom he took to see films when the schoolboys and girls had a free Saturday afternoon. He had been driving tractors and other farm vehicles since he was ten years old, and as soon as he was eighteen he got a driver's licence and in the holidays, this last year of his school life, he took neighbours' daughters to dances and to the drive-in cinema that had just opened twenty kilometers from the farm. His sisters were married, by then; his parents often left him in charge of the farm over the weekend while they visited the young wives and grandchildren.

When Thebedi saw the farmer and his wife drive away on a Saturday afternoon, the boot of their Mercedes filled with fresh-killed poultry and vegetables from the garden that it was part of her father's work to tend, she knew that she must come not to the river-bed but up to the house. The house was an old one, thick-walled, dark against the heat. The kitchen was its lively thoroughfare, with servants, food supplies, begging cats and dogs, pots boiling over, washing being damped for ironing, and the big deep-freezer the missus had ordered from town, bearing a crocheted mat and a vase of plastic irises. But the dining-room with the bulging-legged heavy table was shut up in its rich, old smell of soup and tomato sauce. The sitting-room curtains were drawn and the T.V. set silent. The door of the parents' bedroom was locked and the empty rooms where the girls had slept had sheets of plastic spread over the beds. It was in one of these that she and the farmer's son stayed together whole nights— almost: she had to get away before the house servants, who knew her, came in at dawn. There was a risk someone would discover her or traces of her presence if he took her to his own bedroom, although she had looked into it many times when she was helping out in the house and knew well, there, the row of silver cups he had won at school.

When she was eighteen and the farmer's son nineteen and working with his father on the farm before entering a veterinary college, the young man Njabulo asked her father for her. Njabulo's parents met with hers and the money he was to pay in place of the cows it is customary to give a prospective bride's parents was settled upon. He had no cows to offer; he was a labourer on the Eysendyck farm, like her father. A bright youngster; old Eysendyck had taught him brick-laying and was using him for odd jobs in construction, around the place. She did not tell the farmer's son that her parents had arranged for her to marry. She did not tell him, either, before he left for his first term at the veterinary college, that she thought she was going to have a baby. Two months after her marriage to Njabulo, she gave birth to a daughter. There was no disgrace in that; among her people it is customary for a young man to make sure, before marriage, that the chosen girl is not barren, and Njabulo made love to her then. But the infant was very light and did not quickly grow darker as most African babies do. Already at birth there was on its head a quantity of straight, fine floss, like that which carries the seeds of certain weeds in the veld. The unfocused eyes it opened were grey flecked with yellow. Njabulo was the matt, opaque coffee-grounds colour that has always been called black; the colour of Thebedi's legs on which beaded water looked oyster-shell blue, the same colour as Thebedi's face, where the black eyes, with their interested gaze and clear whites, were so dominant.

Njabulo made no complaint. Out of his farm labourer's earnings he bought from the Indian store a cellophane-windowed pack containing a pink plastic bath, six napkins, a card of safety pins, a knitted jacket, cap and bootees, a dress, and a tin of Johnson's Baby Powder, for Thebedi's baby.

When it was two weeks old Paulus Eysendyck arrived home from the veterinary college for the holidays. He drank a glass of fresh, still-warm milk in the childhood familiarity of his mother's kitchen and heard her discussing with the old house-servant where they could get a reliable substitute to help out now that the girl Thebedi had had a baby. For the first time since he was a small boy he came right into the kraal. It was eleven o'clock in the morning. The men were at work in the lands. He looked about him, urgently; the women turned away, each not wanting to be the one approached to point out where Thebedi lived. Thebedi appeared, coming slowly from the hut Njabulo had built in white man's style, with a tin chimney, and a proper window with glass panes set in straight as walls made of unfired bricks would allow. She greeted him with hands brought together and a token movement representing the respectful bob with which she was accustomed to acknowledge she was in the presence of his father or mother. He lowered his head under the doorway of her home and went in. He said, "I want to see. Show me."

She had taken the bundle off her back before she came out into the light to face him. She moved between the iron bedstead made up with Njabulo's checked blankets and the small wooden table where the pink plastic bath stood among food and kitchen pots, and picked up the bundle from the snugly-blanketed grocer's box where it lay. The infant was asleep; she revealed the closed, pale, plump tiny face, with a bubble of spit at the corner of the mouth, the spidery pink hands stirring. She took off the woollen cap and the straight fine hair flew up after it in static electricity, showing gilded strands here and there. He said nothing. She was watching him as she had done when they were little, and the gang of children had trodden down a crop in their games or trangressed in some other way for which he, as the farmer's son, the white one among them, must intercede with the farmer. She disturbed the sleeping face by scratching or tickling gently at a cheek with one finger, and slowly the eyes opened, saw nothing, were still asleep, and then, awake, no longer narrowed, looked out at them, grey with yellowish flecks, his own hazel eyes.

He struggled for a moment with a grimace of tears, anger, and self-pity. She could not put out her hand to him. He said, "You haven't been near the house with it?"

She shook her head.

"Never?"

Again she shook her head.

"Don't take it out. Stay inside. Can't you take it away somewhere. You must give it to someone —"

She moved to the door with him.

He said, "I'll see what I will do. I don't know." And then he said: "I feel like killing myself."

Her eyes began to glow, to thicken with tears. For a moment there was the feeling between them that used to come when they were alone down at the river-bed.

He walked out.

Two days later, when his mother and father had left the farm for the day, he appeared again. The women were away on the lands, weeding, as they were employed to do as casual labour in the summer; only the very old remained, propped up on the ground outside the huts in the flies and the sun. Thebedi did not ask him in. The child had not been well; it had diarrhoea. He asked where its food was. She said, "The milk comes from me." He went into Njabulo's house, where the child lay; she did not follow but stayed outside the door and watched without seeing an old crone who had lost her mind, talking to herself, talking to the fowls who ignored her.

She thought she heard small grunts from the hut, the kind of infant grunt that indicates a full stomach, a deep sleep. After a time, long or short she did not know, he came out and walked away with plodding stride (his father's gait) out of sight, towards his father's house.

The baby was not fed during the night and although she kept telling Njabulo it was sleeping, he saw for himself in the morning that it was dead. He comforted her with words and caresses. She did not cry but simply sat, staring at the door. Her hands were cold as dead chickens' feet to his touch.

Njabulo buried the little baby where farm workers were buried, in the place in the veld the farmer had given them. Some of the mounds had been left to weather away unmarked, others were covered with stones and a few had fallen wooden crosses. He was going to make a cross but before it was finished the police came and dug up the grave and took away the dead baby: someone — one of the other labourers? their women? — had reported that the baby was almost white, that, strong and healthy, it had died suddenly after a visit by the farmer's son. Pathological tests on the infant corpse showed intestinal damage not always consistent with death by natural causes.

Thebedi went for the first time to the country town where Paulus had been to school, to give evidence at the preparatory examination into the charge of murder brought against him. She cried hysterically in the witness box, saying yes, yes (the gilt hoop ear-rings swung in her ears), she saw the accused pouring liquid into the baby's mouth. She said he had threatened to shoot her if she told anyone.

More than a year went by before, in that same town, the case was brought to trial. She came to Court with a new-born baby on her back. She wore gilt hoop ear-rings; she was calm; she said she had not seen what the white man did in the house.

Paulus Eysendyck said he had visited the hut but had not poisoned the child.

The Defence did not contest that there had been a love relationship between the accused and the girl, or that intercourse had taken place, but submitted there was no proof that the child was the accused's.

The judge told the accused there was strong suspicion against him but not enough proof that he had committed the crime. The Court could not accept the girl's evidence because it was clear she had committed perjury either at this trial or at the preparatory examination. There was the suggestion in the mind of the Court that she might be an accomplice in the crime; but, again, insufficient proof.

The judge commended the honourable behaviour of the husband (sitting in court in a brown-and-yellow-quartered golf cap bought for Sundays) who had not rejected his wife and had "even provided clothes for the unfortunate infant out of his slender means."

The verdict on the accused was "not guilty."

The young white man refused to accept the congratulations of press and public and left the Court with his mother's raincoat shielding his face from photographers. His father said to the press, "I will try and carry on as best I can to hold up my head in the district."

Interviewed by the Sunday papers, who spelled her name in a variety of ways, the black girl, speaking in her own language, was quoted beneath her photograph: "It was a thing of our childhood, we don't see each other anymore."

[1980]

YUKIO MISHIMA *(1925–1970) was the pseudonym of Hiraoka Kimitake, the Japanese author whose works are most translated into English. Born in Tokyo and educated at the aristocratic Peer's School and Tokyo Imperial University, Mishima became a legend in his own time after a spectacular ritual suicide. He was obsessed with the idea that Japan was becoming a decadent Western nation after World War II because it had turned away from the classic samurai tradition, which combined spiritual dedication and the martial arts. A bisexual, Mishima was also a physical fitness addict, and he formed the Shield Society with a small private army of young men who were his personal followers. They were united in their desire to protect the country from what they envisioned as a threatened leftist uprising.*

In 1970 Mishima and four of his followers invaded the headquarters of Japan's Eastern Ground Self-Defense Forces. After capturing the troops on the military base, he stood on a roof and exhorted them to return to Japan to the earlier purity of its samurai traditions. The troops jeered him. Recognizing his failure to convince them, Mishima withdrew into a room nearby, knelt on the floor, and stabbed himself in the stomach as a young disciple beheaded him in the ritual of seppuku, a ceremony reserved for samurai warriors.

By the time of his death, Mishima was already established as one of Japan's leading writers. He began to publish fiction when he was in his twenties. His novels published in English are Confessions of a Mask *(1949),* Temple of the Golden Pavilion *(1959),* The Sailor Who Fell from Grace with the Sea *(1965), and* The Sea of Fertility *(1975). "Three Million Yen" is from the story collection* Death in Midsummer, *published in the United States in 1966. In this story Mishima suggested his view of the corruption of contemporary Japanese society and the decay of its moral values.*

Yukio Mishima

ⁿⁿ

THREE MILLION YEN

–translated by Edward G. Seidensticker

"We're to meet her at nine?" asked Kenzō.

"At nine, she said, in the toy department on the ground floor," replied Kiyoko. "But it's too noisy to talk there, and I told her about the coffee shop on the third floor instead."

"That was a good idea."

The young husband and wife looked up at the neon pagoda atop the New World Building, which they were approaching from the rear.

It was a cloudy, muggy night, of a sort common in the early-summer rainy season. Neon lights painted the low sky in rich colors. The delicate pagoda, flashing on and off in the softer of neon tones, was very beautiful indeed. It was particularly beautiful when, after all the flashing neon tubes had gone out together, they suddenly flashed on again, so soon that the afterimage had scarcely disappeared. To be seen from all over Asakusa, the pagoda had replaced Gourd Pond, now filled in, as the main landmark of the Asakusa night.

To Kenzō and Kiyoko the pagoda seemed to encompass in all its purity some grand, inaccessible dream of life. Leaning against the rail of the parking lot, they looked absently up at it for a time.

Kenzō was in an undershirt, cheap trousers, and wooden clogs. His skin was fair but the lines of the shoulders and chest were powerful, and bushes of black hair showed between the mounds of muscle at the armpits. Kiyoko, in a sleeveless dress, always had her own armpits carefully shaved. Kenzō was very fussy. Because they hurt when the hair began to grow again, she had become almost obsessive about keeping them shaved, and there was a faint flush on the white skin.

She had a round little face, the pretty features as though woven of cloth. It reminded one of some earnest, unsmiling little animal. It was a face which a person trusted immediately, but not one on which to read thoughts. On her arms she had a large pink plastic handbag and Kenzō's pale blue sports shirt. Kenzō liked to be empty-handed.

From her modest coiffure and make-up one sensed the frugality of their life. Her eyes were clear and had no time for other men.

They crossed the dark road in front of the parking lot and went into the New World. The big market on the ground floor was filled with myriad-colored mountains of splendid, gleaming, cheap wares, and salesgirls peeped from crevices in the mountains. Cool fluorescent lighting poured over the scene. Behind a grove of antimony models of the Tokyo Tower was a row of mirrors painted with Tokyo scenes, and in them, as the two passed, were rippling, waving images of the mountain of ties and summer shirts opposite.

"I couldn't stand living in a place with so many mirrors," said Kiyoko. "I'd be embarrassed."

"Nothing to be embarrassed about." Though his manner was gruff, Kenzō was not one to ignore what his wife said, and his answers were generally perceptive. The two had come to the toy department.

"She knows how you love the toy department. That's why she said to meet her here."

Kenzō laughed. He was fond of the trains and automobiles and space missiles, and he always embarrassed Kiyoko, getting an explanation for each one and trying each one out, but never buying. She took his arm and steered him some distance from the counter.

"It's easy to see that you want a boy. Look at the toys you pick."

"I don't care whether it's a boy or a girl. I just wish it would come soon."

"Another two years, that's all."

"Everything according to plan."

They had divided the savings account they were so assiduously building up into several parts, labeled Plan X and Plan Y and Plan Z and the like. Children must come strictly according to plan. However much they might want a child now, it would have to wait until sufficient money for Plan X had accumulated. Seeing the inadvisability, for numerous reasons, of installment buying, they waited until the money for Plan A or Plan B or Plan C had accumulated, and then paid cash for an electric washing machine or refrigerator or a television set. Plan A and Plan B had already been carried out. Plan D required little money, but, since it had as its object a low-priority clothes cupboard, it was always being pushed back. Neither of them was much interested in clothes. What they had they could hang in the closet, and all they really needed was enough to keep them warm in the winter.

They were very cautious when making a large purchase. They collected catalogues and looked at various possibilities and asked the advice of people who had already made the purchase, and, when the time for buying finally came, went off to a wholesaler in Okachimachi.

A child was still more serious. First there had to be a secure livelihood and enough money, more than enough money, to see that the child had surroundings of which a parent need not be ashamed, if not, perhaps, enough to see it all the way to adulthood. Kenzō had already made thorough inquiries with friends who had children, and knew what expenditures for powdered milk could be considered reasonable.

With their own plans so nicely formed, the two had nothing but contempt for the thoughtless, floundering ways of the poor. Children were to be produced according to plan in surroundings ideal for rearing them, and the best days were waiting after a child had arrived. Yet they were sensible enough not to pursue their dreams too far. They kept their eyes on the light immediately before them.

There was nothing that enraged Kenzō more than the view of the young that life in contemporary Japan was without hope. He was not a person given to deep thinking, but he had an almost religious faith that if a man respected nature and was obedient to it, and if he but made an effort for himself, the way would somehow open. The first thing was reverence for nature, founded on connubial affection. The greatest antidote for despair was the faith of a man and woman in each other.

Fortunately, he was in love with Kiyoko. To face the future hopefully, therefore, he had only to follow the conditions laid down by nature. Now and then some other woman made a motion in his direction, but he sensed something unnatural in pleasure for the sake of pleasure. It was better to listen to Kiyoko complaining about the dreadful price these days of vegetables and fish.

The two had made a round of the market and were back at the toy department.

Kenzō's eyes were riveted to the toy before him, a station for flying saucers. On the sheet-metal base the complicated mechanism was painted as if viewed through a window, and a revolving light flashed on and off inside the control tower. The flying saucer, of deep-blue plastic, worked on the old principle of the flying top. The station was apparently suspended in space, for the background of the metal base was covered with stars and clouds, among the former the familiar rings of Saturn.

The bright stars of the summer night were splendid. The painted metal surface was indescribably cool, and it was as if all the discomfort of the muggy night would go if a person but gave himself up to that sky.

Before Kiyoko could stop him, Kenzō had resolutely snapped a spring at one corner of the station.

The saucer went spinning toward the ceiling.

The salesgirl reached out and gave a little cry.

The saucer described a gentle arc toward the pastry counter across the aisle and settled square on the million-yen crackers.

"We're in!" Kenzō ran over to it.

"What do you mean, we're in?" Embarrassed, Kiyoko turned quickly away from the salesgirl and started after him.

"Look. Look where it landed. This means good luck. Not a doubt about it."

The oblong crackers were in the shape of decidedly large banknotes, and the baked-in design, again like a banknote, carried the words "One Million Yen." On the printed label of the cellophane wrapper, the figure of a bald shopkeeper took the place of Prince Shōtoku, who decorates most banknotes. There were three large crackers in each package.

Over the objections of Kiyoko, who thought fifty yen for three crackers ridiculous, Kenzō bought a package to make doubly sure of the good luck. He immediately broke the wrapping, gave a cracker to Kiyoko, and took one himself. The third went into her handbag.

As his strong teeth bit into the cracker, a sweet, slightly bitter taste flowed into his mouth. Kiyoko took a little mouselike bite from her own cracker, almost too large for her grasp.

Kenzō brought the flying saucer back to the toy counter. The salesgirl, out of sorts, looked away as she reached to take it.

Kiyoko had high, arched breasts, and, though she was small, her figure was good. When she walked with Kenzō she seemed to be hiding in his shadow. At street crossings he would take her arm firmly, look to the right and the left, and help her across, pleased at the feel of the rich flesh.

Kenzō liked the pliant strength in a woman who, although she could perfectly well do things for herself, always deferred to her husband. Kiyoko had never read a newspaper, but she had an astonishingly accurate knowledge of her surroundings. When she took a comb in her hand or turned over the leaf of a calendar or folded a summer kimono, it was not as if she were engaged in housework, but rather, as if, fresh and alert, she were keeping company with the "things" known as comb and calendar and kimono. She soaked in her world of things as she might soak in a bath.

"There's an indoor amusement park on the fourth floor. We can kill time there," said Kenzō. Kiyoko followed silently into a waiting elevator, but when they reached the fourth floor she tugged at his belt.

"It's a waste of money. Everything seems so cheap, but it's all arranged so that you spend more money than you intend to."

"That's no way to talk. This is our good night, and if you tell yourself it's like a first-run movie it doesn't seem so expensive."

"What's the sense in a first-run movie? If you wait a little while you can see it for half as much."

Her earnestness was most engaging. A brown smudge from the cracker clung to her puckered lips.

"Wipe your mouth," said Kenzō. "You're making a mess of yourself."

Kiyoko looked into a mirror on a near-by pillar and removed the smear with the nail of her little finger. She still had two thirds of a cracker in her hand.

They were at the entrance to "Twenty Thousand Leagues Under the Sea." Jagged rocks reached to the ceiling, and the porthole of a submarine on the sea floor served as the ticket window: forty yen for adults, twenty yen for children.

"But forty yen is too high," said Kiyoko, turning away from the mirror. "You aren't any less hungry after you look at all those cardboard fish, and for forty yen you can get a hundred grams of the best kind of real fish."

"Yesterday they wanted forty for a cut of black snapper. Oh, well. When you're chewing on a million yen you don't talk like a beggar."

The brief debate finished, Kenzō bought the tickets.

"You've let that cracker go to your head."

"But it isn't bad at all. Just right when you're hungry."

"You just ate."

At a landing like a railway platform five or six little boxcars, each large enough for two people, stood at intervals along a track. Three or four other couples were waiting, but the two climbed unabashedly into a car. It was in fact a little tight for two, and Kenzō had to put his arm around his wife's shoulders.

The operator was whistling somewhat disdainfully. Kenzō's powerful arm, on which the sweat had dried, was solid against Kiyoko's naked shoulders and back. Naked skin clung to naked skin like the layers of some intricately folded insect's wing. The car began to shake.

"I'm afraid," said Kiyoko, with the expression of one not in the least afraid.

The cars, each some distance from the rest, plunged into a dark tunnel of rock. Immediately inside there was a sharp curve, and the reverberations were deafening.

A huge shark with shining green scales passed, almost brushing their heads, and Kiyoko ducked away. As she clung to her young husband he gave her a kiss. After the shark had passed, the car ground around a curve in pitch darkness again, but his lips landed unerringly on hers, little fish speared in the dark. The little fish jumped and were still.

The darkness made Kiyoko strangely shy. Only the violent shaking and grinding sustained her. As she slipped deep into the tunnel, her husband's arms around her, she felt naked and flushed crimson. The darkness, dense and impenetrable, had a strength that seemed to render clothes useless. She thought of a dark shed she had secretly played in as a child.

Like a flower springing from the darkness, a red beam of light flashed at them, and Kiyoko cried out once more. It was the wide, gaping mouth of a big angler fish on the ocean floor. Around it, coral fought with the poisonous dark green of seaweed.

Kenzō put his cheek to his wife's — she was still clinging to him — and with the fingers of the arm around her shoulders played with her hair. Compared to the motion of the car the motion of the fingers was slow and deliberate. She knew that he was enjoying the show and enjoying her fright at it as well.

"Will it be over soon? I'm afraid." But her voice was drowned out in the roar.

Once again they were in darkness. Though frightened, Kiyoko had her store of courage. Kenzō's arms were around her, and there was no fright and no shame she could not bear. Because hope had never left them, the state of happiness was for the two of them just such a state of tension.

A big, muddy octopus appeared before them. Once again Kiyoko cried out. Kenzō promptly kissed the nape of her neck. The great tentacles of the octopus filled the cave, and a fierce lightning darted from its eyes.

At the next curve a drowned corpse was standing disconsolately in a seaweed forest.

Finally the light at the far end began to show, the car slowed down, and they were liberated from the unpleasant noise. At the bright platform the uniformed attendant waited to catch the forward handle of the car.

"Is that all?" asked Kenzō.

The man said that it was.

Arching her back, Kiyoko climbed to the platform and whispered in Kenzō's ear: "It makes you feel like a fool, paying forty yen for that."

At the door they compared their crackers. Kiyoko had two thirds left, and Kenzō more than half.

"Just as big as when we came in," said Kenzō. "It was so full of thrills that we didn't have time to eat."

"If you think about it that way, it doesn't seem so bad after all."

Kenzō's eyes were already on the gaudy sign by another door. Electric decorations danced around the word "Magicland," and green and red lights flashed on and off in the startled eyes of a cluster of dwarfs, their domino costumes shining in gold and silver dust. A bit shy about suggesting immediately that they go in, Kenzō leaned against the wall and munched away at his cracker.

"Remember how we crossed the parking lot? The light brought out our shadows on the ground, maybe two feet apart, and a funny idea came to me. I thought to myself how it would be if a little boy's shadow bobbed up and we took it by the hand. And just then a shadow really did break away from ours and come between them."

"No!"

"Then I looked around, and it was someone behind us. A couple of drivers were playing catch, and one of them had dropped the ball and run after it."

"One of these days we really will be out walking, three of us."

"And we'll bring it here." Kenzō motioned toward the sign. "And so we ought to go in and have a look at it first."

Kiyoko said nothing this time as he started for the ticket window.

Possibly because it was a bad time of the day, Magicland was not popular. On both sides of the path as they entered there were flashing banks of artificial flowers. A music box was playing.

"When we build our house this is the way we'll have the path."

"But it's in very bad taste," objected Kiyoko.

How would it feel to go into a house of your own? A building fund had not yet appeared in the plans of the two, but in due course it would. Things they scarely dreamed of would one day appear in the most natural way imaginable. Usually so prudent, they let their dreams run on this evening, perhaps, as Kiyoko said, because the million-yen crackers had gone to their heads.

Great artificial butterflies were taking honey from the artificial flowers. Some were as big as brief cases, and there were yellow and black spots on their translucent red wings. Tiny bulbs flashed on and off in their protuberant eyes. In the light from below, a soft aura as of sunset in a mist bathed the plastic flowers and grasses. It may have been dust rising from the floor.

The first room they came to, following the arrow, was the leaning room. The floor and all the furnishings leaned so that when one entered upright there was a grating, discordant note to the room.

"Not the sort of house I'd want to live in," said Kenzō, bracing himself against a table on which there were yellow wooden tulips. The words were like a command. He was not himself aware of it, but his decisiveness was that of the privileged one whose hope and well-being refuse to admit outsiders. It was not strange that in the hope there was a scorn for the hopes of others and that no one was allowed to lay a finger on the well-being.

Braced against the leaning table, the determined figure in the undershirt made Kiyoko smile. It was a very domestic scene. Kenzō was like an outraged young man who, having built an extra room on his Sunday holidays, had made a mistake somewhere and ended up with the windows and floors all askew.

"You *could* live in a place like this, though," said Kiyoko. Spreading her arms like a mechanical doll, she leaned forward as the room leaned, and her face approached Kenzō's broad left shoulder at the same angle as the wooden tulips.

His brow wrinkled in a serious young frown, Kenzō smiled. He kissed the cheek that leaned toward him and bit roughly into his million-yen cracker.

By the time they had emerged from the wobbly staircases, the shaking passageways, the log bridges from the railings of which monster heads protruded, and numerous other curious places as well, the heat was too much for them. Kenzō finished his own cracker, took what was left of his wife's between his teeth, and set out in search of a cool evening breeze. Beyond a row of rocking horses a door led out to a balcony.

"What time is it?" asked Kiyoko.

"A quarter to nine. Let's go out and cool off till nine."

"I'm thirsty. The cracker was so dry." She fanned at her perspiring white throat with Kenzō's sports shirt.

"In a minute you can have something to drink."

The night breeze was cool on the wide balcony. Kenzō yawned a wide yawn and leaned against the railing beside his wife. Bare young arms caressed the black railing, wet with the night dew.

"It's much cooler than when we came in."

"Don't be silly," said Kenzō. "It's just higher."

Far below, the black machines of the outdoor amusement park seemed to slumber. The bare seats of the merry-go-round, slightly inclined, were exposed to the dew. Between the iron bars of the aerial observation car, suspended chairs swayed gently in the breeze.

The liveliness of the restaurant to the left was in complete contrast. They had a bird's-eye view into all the corners of the wide expanse inside its walls. Everything was there to look at, as if on a stage: the roofs of the separate cottages, the passages joining them, the ponds and brooks in the garden, the stone lanterns, the interiors of the Japanese rooms, some with serving maids whose kimono sleeves were held up by red cords, others with dancing geisha. The strings of lanterns at the eaves were beautiful, and their white lettering was beautiful too.

The wind carried away the noises of the place, and there was something almost mystically beautiful about it, congealed in delicate detail there at the bottom of the murky summer night.

"I'll bet it's expensive." Kiyoko was once more at her favorite romantic topic.

"Naturally. Only a fool would go there."

"I'll bet they say that cucumbers are a great delicacy, and they charge some fantastic price. How much?"

"Two hundred, maybe." Kenzō took his sports shirt and started to put it on.

Buttoning it for him, Kiyoko continued: "They must think their customers are fools. Why, that's ten times what cucumbers are worth. You can get three of the very best for twenty yen."

"Oh? They're getting cheap."

"The price started going down a week or so ago."

It was five to nine. They went out to look for a stairway to the coffee shop on the third floor. Two of the crackers had disappeared. The other was too large for Kiyoko's very large handbag, and protruded from the unfastened clasp.

The old lady, an impatient person, had arrived early and was waiting. The seats from which the loud jazz orchestra could best be seen were all taken, but there were vacant places where the bandstand was out of sight, beside the potted palm probably rented from some gardener. Sitting alone in a summer kimono, the old lady seemed wholly out of place.

She was a small woman not far past middle age, and she had the clean, well-tended face of the plebeian lowlands. She spoke briskly with many delicate gestures. She was proud of the fact that she got along so nicely with young people.

"You'll be treating me, of course, so I ordered something expensive while I was waiting." Even as she spoke the tall glass arrived, pieces of fruit atop a parfait.

"Now that was generous of you. All we needed was soda water."

Her outstretched little finger taut, the old lady plunged in with her spoon and skillfully brought out the cream beneath. Meanwhile she was talking along at her usual brisk pace.

"It's nice that this place is so noisy and no one can hear us. Tonight we go to Nakano — I think I mentioned it over the phone. An ordinary private house and — can you imagine it? — the customers are housewives having a class reunion. There's not much that the rich ladies don't know about these days. And I imagine they walk around pretending the idea never entered their heads. Anyway, I told them about you, and they said they had to have you and no one else. They don't want someone who's all beaten up by the years, you know. And I must say that I can't blame them. So I asked a good stiff price and she said it was low and if they were pleased they'd give you a good tip. They haven't any idea what the market rate is, of course. But I want you to do your best, now. I'm sure I don't need to tell you, but if they're pleased we'll get all sorts of rich customers. There aren't many that go as well together as you two do, of course, and I'm not worried, but don't do anything to make me ashamed of you. Well, anyhow, the woman of the house is the wife of some important person or other, and she'll be waiting for us at the coffee shop in front of Nakano station. You know what will happen next. She'll send the taxi through all sorts of back alleys to get us mixed up. I don't imagine she'll blindfold us, but she'll pull us through the back door, so we don't have a chance to read the sign on the gate. I won't like it any better than you will, but she has herself to consider, after all. Don't let it bother you. Me? Oh, I'll be doing the usual thing, keeping watch in the hall. I can bluff my way through, I don't care who comes in. Well, maybe we ought to get started. And let me say it again, I want a good performance from you."

It was late in the night, and Kiyoko and Kenzō had left the old lady and were back in Asakusa. They were even more exhausted than usual. Kenzō's wooden clogs dragged along the street. The billboards in the park were a poisonous black under the cloudy sky.

Simultaneously, they looked up at the New World. The neon pagoda was dark.

"What a rotten bunch. I don't think I've ever seen such a rotten, stuck-up bunch," said Kenzō.

Her eyes on the ground, Kiyoko did not answer.

"Well? Did you ever see a worse bunch of affected old women?"

"No. But what can you do? The pay was good."

"Playing around with money they pry from their husbands. Don't get to be that way when you have money."

"Silly." Kiyoko's smiling face was sharply white in the darkness.

"A really nasty bunch." Kenzō spat in a strong white arc. "How much?"

"This." Kiyoko reached artlessly into her handbag and pulled out some bills.

"Five thousand? We've never made that much before. And the old woman took three thousand. Damn! I'd like to tear it up, that's what I'd like to do. That would really feel good."

Kiyoko took the money back in some consternation. Her finger touched the last of the million-yen crackers.

"Tear this up in its place," she said softly.

Kenzō took the cracker, wadded the cellophane wrapper, and threw it to the ground. It crackled sharply on the silent, deserted street. Too large for one hand, he took the cracker in both hands and tried to break it. It was damp and soggy, and the sweet surface stuck to his hands. The more it bent the more it resisted. He was in the end unable to break it.

[1966]

FLANNERY O'CONNOR (1925–1964) *was born in Savannah, Georgia, the only child of Roman Catholic parents. When she was thirteen her father was found to have disseminated lupus, an incurable disease in which antibodies in the immune system attack the body's own substances. During her father's medical treatment the family moved to her mother's family home in Milledgeville, Georgia, where her ancestors had lived since before the Civil War. There O'Connor attended high school and began to write. After her father's death in 1941, she finished high school and studied social science and English at the Georgia State College for Women in Milledgeville, where she also published stories and edited the literary magazine. On the strength of these stories, she was awarded a fellowship at the Writer's Workshop at the University of Iowa. In 1946 she sold her first story to* Accent *magazine and earned her M.F.A. degree at Iowa. Two years later she moved to New York City and published chapters of a novel in progress,* Wise Blood, *in magazines. Late in 1950 she became ill with what was diagnosed as lupus, and she returned to Milledgeville to start a series of treatments which temporarily arrested the progress of the disease. Living with her mother on the family's 500-acre dairy farm, she began to work again, writing from nine to twelve in the mornings and spending the rest of the day resting, reading, writing letters, and raising her peacocks, whose proud beauty enthralled her and whose regular cycles of growing, shedding, and regrowing their wondrous plumage served as a symbol to her of Christ's divinity and the resurrection.*

O'Connor's first book, Wise Blood, *a complex comic novel attacking the contemporary secularization of religion, was published in 1952. It was followed in 1955 by her first collection of stories,* A Good Man Is Hard to Find. *O'Connor was able to see a second novel,* The Violent Bear It Away, *through to publication in 1960, but she died of lupus in 1964, having completed enough stories for a second collection,* Everything That Rises Must Converge *(1965). Her total output of just thirty-one stories, collected in her* Complete Stories, *won the National Book Award for fiction in 1972.*

Despite her illness, O'Connor was never a recluse; she accepted as many lecture invitations as her health would permit. A volume of her lectures and occasional pieces was published in 1969 as Mystery and Manners. *It is a valuable companion to her stories and novels, because she often reflected on her writing and interpreted her fiction. As a devout Roman Catholic, O'Connor was uncompromising in her religious views: "For I am no disbeliever in spiritual purpose and no vague believer. This means that for me the meaning of life is centered in our Redemption by Christ and what I see in the world I see in relation to that." As Joyce Carol Oates recognized in her essay "The Visionary Art of Flannery O'Connor," O'Connor is one of the great religious writers of modern times, unique "in her cel-*

ebration of the necessity of succumbing to the divine through violence that is immediate and irreparable. There is no mysticism in her work that is only spiritual; it is physical as well." O'Connor's stories, like the three included here, frequently involve family relationships, but they are not meant to be read as realistic fiction, despite her remarkable ear for dialogue. She wrote them as parables. Her arrangement of the fates of her characters leads to the construction of a vision that is defiantly spiritual. (See O'Connor's Commentary about "A Good Man Is Hard to Find" on page 1322.)

Flannery O'Connor

৯৫২

A GOOD MAN IS HARD TO FIND

> The dragon is by the side of the road, watching those who pass. Beware lest he devour you. We go to the Father of Souls, but it is necessary to pass by the dragon.
>
> – St. Cyril of Jerusalem

The grandmother didn't want to go to Florida. She wanted to visit some of her connections in east Tennessee and she was seizing at every chance to change Bailey's mind. Bailey was the son she lived with, her only boy. He was sitting on the edge of his chair at the table, bent over the orange sports section of the *Journal*. "Now look here, Bailey," she said, "see here, read this," and she stood with one hand on her thin hip and the other rattling the newspaper at his bald head. "Here this fellow that calls himself The Misfit is aloose from the Federal Pen and headed toward Florida and you read here what it says he did to these people. Just you read it. I wouldn't take my children in any direction with a criminal like that aloose in it. I couldn't answer to my conscience if I did."

Bailey didn't look up from his reading so she wheeled around then and faced the children's mother, a young woman in slacks, whose face was as broad and innocent as a cabbage and was tied around with a green headkerchief that had two points on the top like a rabbit's ears. She was sitting on the sofa, feeding the baby his apricots out of a jar. "The children have been to Florida before," the old lady said. "You all ought to take them somewhere else for a change so they would see different parts of the world and be broad. They never have been to east Tennessee."

The children's mother didn't seem to hear her but the eight-year-old boy, John Wesley, a stocky child with glasses, said, "If you don't want to go to Florida, why dontcha stay at home?" He and the little girl, June Star, were reading the funny papers on the floor.

"She wouldn't stay at home to be queen for a day," June Star said without raising her yellow head.

"Yes and what would you do if this fellow, The Misfit, caught you?" the grandmother asked.

"I'd smack his face," John Wesley said.

"She wouldn't stay at home for a million bucks," June Star said. "Afraid she'd miss something. She has to go everywhere we go."

"All right, Miss," the grandmother said. "Just remember that the next time you want me to curl your hair."

June Star said her hair was naturally curly.

The next morning the grandmother was the first one in the car, ready to go. She had her big black valise that looked like the head of a hippopotamus in one corner, and underneath it she was hiding a basket with Pitty Sing, the cat, in it. She didn't intend for the cat to be left alone in the house for three days because he would miss her too much and she was afraid he might brush against one of the gas burners and accidentally asphyxiate himself. Her son, Bailey, didn't like to arrive at a motel with a cat.

She sat in the middle of the back seat with John Wesley and June Star on either side of her. Bailey and the children's mother and the baby sat in front and they left Atlanta at eight forty-five with the mileage on the car at 55890. The grandmother wrote this down because she thought it would be interesting to say how many miles they had been when they got back. It took them twenty minutes to reach the outskirts of the city.

The old lady settled herself comfortably, removing her white cotton gloves and putting them up with her purse on the shelf in front of the back window. The children's mother still had on slacks and still had her head tied up in a green kerchief, but the grandmother had on a navy blue straw sailor hat with a bunch of white violets on the brim and a navy blue dress with a small white dot in the print. Her collars and cuffs were white organdy trimmed with lace and at her neckline she had pinned a purple spray of cloth violets containing a sachet. In case of an accident, anyone seeing her dead on the highway would know at once that she was a lady.

She said she thought it was going to be a good day for driving, neither too hot nor too cold, and she cautioned Bailey that the speed limit was fifty-five miles an hour and that the patrolmen hid themselves behind billboards and small clumps of trees and sped out after you before you had a chance to slow down. She pointed out interesting details of the scenery: Stone Mountain; the blue granite that in some places came up to both sides of the highway; the brilliant red clay banks slightly streaked with purple; and the various crops that made rows of green lace-work on the ground. The trees were full of silver-white sunlight and the meanest of them sparkled. The children were reading comic magazines and their mother had gone back to sleep.

"Let's go through Georgia fast so we won't have to look at it much," John Wesley said.

"If I were a little boy," said the grandmother, "I wouldn't talk about my native state that way. Tennessee has the mountains and Georgia has the hills."

"Tennessee is just a hillbilly dumping ground," John Wesley said, "and Georgia is a lousy state too."

"You said it," June Star said.

"In my time," said the grandmother, folding her thin veined fingers, "children were more respectful of their native states and their parents and everything else. People did right then. Oh look at the cute little pickaninny!" she said and pointed to a Negro child standing in the door of a shack. "Wouldn't that make a picture, now?" she asked and they all turned and looked at the little Negro out of the back window. He waved.

"He didn't have any britches on," June Star said.

"He probably didn't have any," the grandmother explained. "Little niggers in the country don't have things like we do. If I could paint, I'd paint that picture," she said.

The children exchanged comic books.

The grandmother offered to hold the baby and the children's mother passed him over the front seat to her. She set him on her knee and bounced him and told him about the things they were passing. She rolled her eyes and screwed up her mouth and stuck her leathery thin face into his smooth bland one. Occasionally he gave her a faraway smile. They passed a large cotton field with five or six graves fenced in the middle of it, like a small island. "Look at the graveyard!" the grandmother said, pointing it out. "That was the old family burying ground. That belonged to the plantation."

"Where's the plantation?" John Wesley asked.

"Gone with the Wind," said the grandmother. "Ha. Ha."

When the children finished all the comic books they had brought, they opened the lunch and ate it. The grandmother ate a peanut butter sandwich and an olive and would not let the children throw the box and the paper napkins out the window. When there was nothing else to do they played a game by choosing a cloud and making the other two guess what shape it suggested. John Wesley took one the shape of a cow and June Star guessed a cow and John Wesley said, no, an automobile, and June Star said he didn't play fair, and they began to slap each other over the grandmother.

The grandmother said she would tell them a story if they would keep quiet. When she told a story, she rolled her eyes and waved her head and was very dramatic. She said once when she was a maiden lady she had been courted by a Mr. Edgar Atkins Teagarden from Jasper, Georgia. She said he was a very good-looking man and a gentleman and that he brought her a watermelon every Saturday afternoon with his initials cut in it, E. A. T. Well, one Saturday, she said, Mr. Teagarden brought the watermelon and there was nobody at home and he left it on the front porch and returned in his buggy to Jasper, but she never got the watermelon, she said, because a nigger boy ate it when he saw the initials, E. A. T.! This story tickled John Wesley's funny bone and he giggled and giggled but June Star didn't think it was any good. She said she wouldn't marry a man that just brought her a watermelon on Saturday. The grandmother said she would have done well to marry Mr. Teagarden because he was a gentleman and had bought Coca-Cola stock when it first came out and that he had died only a few years ago, a very wealthy man.

They stopped at The Tower for barbecued sandwiches. The Tower was a part stucco and part wood filling station and dance hall set in a clearing outside of Timothy. A fat man named Red Sammy Butts ran it and there were signs stuck here and there on the building and for miles up and down the highway saying, TRY RED SAMMY'S FAMOUS BARBECUE. NONE LIKE FAMOUS RED SAMMY'S! RED SAM! THE FAT BOY WITH THE HAPPY LAUGH. A VETERAN! RED SAMMY'S YOUR MAN!

Red Sammy was lying on the bare ground outside The Tower with his head under a truck while a gray monkey about a foot high, chained to a small chinaberry tree, chattered nearby. The monkey sprang back into the tree and got on the highest limb as soon as he saw the children jump out of the car and run toward him.

Inside, The Tower was a long dark room with a counter at one end and tables at the other and dancing space in the middle. They all sat down at a board table next to the nickelodeon and Red Sam's wife, a tall burnt-brown woman with hair and eyes lighter than her skin, came and took their order. The children's mother put a dime in the machine and played "The Tennessee Waltz," and the grandmother said that tune always made her want to dance. She asked Bailey if he would like to dance but he only glared at her. He didn't have a naturally sunny disposition like she did and trips made him nervous. The grandmother's brown eyes were very bright. She swayed her head from side to side and pretended she was dancing in her chair. June Star said play something she could tap to so the children's mother put in another dime and played a fast number and June Star stepped out onto the dance floor and did her tap routine.

"Ain't she cute?" Red Sam's wife said, leaning over the counter. "Would you like to come be my little girl?"

"No I certainly wouldn't," June Star said. "I wouldn't live in a broken-down place like this for a million bucks!" and she ran back to the table.

"Ain't she cute?" the woman repeated, stretching her mouth politely.

"Aren't you ashamed?" hissed the grandmother.

Red Sam came in and told his wife to quit lounging on the counter and hurry up with these people's order. His khaki trousers reached just to his hip bones and his stomach hung over them like a sack of meal swaying under his shirt. He came over and sat down at a table nearby and let out a combination sigh and yodel. "You can't win," he said. "You can't win," and he wiped his sweating red face off with a gray handkerchief. "These days you don't know who to trust," he said. "Ain't that the truth?"

"People are certainly not nice like they used to be," said the grandmother.

"Two fellers come in here last week," Red Sammy said, "driving a Chrysler. It was a old beat-up car but it was a good one and these boys looked all right to me. Said they worked at the mill and you know I let them fellers charge the gas they bought? Now why did I do that?"

"Because you're a good man!" the grandmother said at once.

"Yes'm, I suppose so," Red Sam said as if he were struck with this answer.

His wife brought the orders, carrying the five plates all at once without a tray, two in each hand and one balanced on her arm. "It isn't a soul in this green world of God's that you can trust," she said. "And I don't count nobody out of that, not nobody," she repeated, looking at Red Sammy.

"Did you read about that criminal, The Misfit, that's escaped?" asked the grandmother.

"I wouldn't be a bit surprised if he didn't attact this place right here," said the woman. "If he hears about it being here, I wouldn't be none surprised to see him. If he hears it's two cent in the cash register, I wouldn't be a tall surprised if he. . . ."

"That'll do," Red Sam said. "Go bring these people their Co'-Colas," and the woman went off to get the rest of the order.

"A good man is hard to find," Red Sammy said. "Everything is getting terrible. I remember the day you could go off and leave your screen door unlatched. Not no more."

He and the grandmother discussed better times. The old lady said that in her opinion Europe was entirely to blame for the way things were now. She said the way Europe acted you would think we were made of money and Red Sam said it was no use talking about it, she was exactly right. The children ran outside into the white sunlight and looked at the monkey in the lacy chinaberry tree. He was busy catching fleas on himself and biting each one carefully between his teeth as if it were a delicacy.

They drove off again into the hot afternoon. The grandmother took cat naps and woke up every few minutes with her own snoring. Outside of Toombsboro she woke up and recalled an old plantation that she had visited in this neighborhood once when she was a young lady. She said the house had six white columns across the front and that there was an avenue of oaks leading up to it and two little wooden trellis arbors on either side in front where you sat down with your suitor after a stroll in the garden. She recalled exactly which road to turn off to get to it. She knew that Bailey would not be willing to lose any time looking at an old house, but the more she talked about it, the more she wanted to see it once again and find out if the little twin arbors were still standing. "There was a secret panel in this house," she said craftily, not telling the truth but wishing that she were, "and the story went that all the family silver was hidden in it when Sherman came through but it was never found. . . ."

"Hey!" John Wesley said. "Let's go see it! We'll find it! We'll poke all the woodwork and find it! Who lives there? Where do you turn off at? Hey Pop, can't we turn off there?"

"We never have seen a house with a secret panel!" June Star shrieked.

"Let's go to the house with the secret panel! Hey Pop, can't we go see the house with the secret panel!"

"It's not far from here, I know," the grandmother said. "It won't take over twenty minutes."

Bailey was looking straight ahead. His jaw was as rigid as a horseshoe. "No," he said.

The children began to yell and scream that they wanted to see the house with the secret panel. John Wesley kicked the back of the front seat and June Star hung over her mother's shoulder and whined desperately into her ear that they never had any fun even on their vacation, that they could never do what THEY wanted to do. The baby began to scream and John Wesley kicked the back of the seat so hard that his father could feel the blows in his kidney.

"All right!" he shouted and drew the car to a stop at the side of the road. "Will you all shut up? Will you all just shut up for one second? If you don't shut up, we won't go anywhere."

"It would be very educational for them," the grandmother murmured.

"All right," Bailey said, "but get this: this is the only time we're going to stop for anything like this. This is the one and only time."

"The dirt road that you have to turn down is about a mile back," the grandmother directed. "I marked it when we passed."

"A dirt road," Bailey groaned.

After they had turned around and were headed toward the dirt road, the grandmother recalled other points about the house, the beautiful glass over the front doorway and the candle-lamp in the hall. John Wesley said that the secret panel was probably in the fireplace.

"You can't go inside this house," Bailey said. "You don't know who lives there."

"While you all talk to the people in front, I'll run around behind and get in a window," John Wesley suggested.

"We'll all stay in the car," his mother said.

They turned onto the dirt road and the car raced roughly along in a swirl of pink dust. The grandmother recalled the times when there were no paved roads and thirty miles was a day's journey. The dirt road was hilly and there were sudden washes in it and sharp curves on dangerous embankments. All at once they would be on a hill, looking down over the blue tops of trees for miles around, then the next minute, they would be in a red depression with the dust-coated trees looking down on them.

"This place had better turn up in a minute," Bailey said, "or I'm going to turn around."

The road looked as if no one had traveled on it for months.

"It's not much farther," the grandmother said and just as she said it, a horrible thought came to her. The thought was so embarrassing that she turned red in the face and her eyes dilated and her feet jumped up, upsetting her valise in the corner. The instant the valise moved, the newspaper top she had over the basket under it rose with a snarl and Pitty Sing, the cat, sprang onto Bailey's shoulder.

The children were thrown to the floor and their mother, clutching the baby, was thrown out the door onto the ground; the old lady was thrown into the front seat. The car turned over once and landed right-side-up in a gulch off the side of the road. Bailey remained in the driver's seat with the cat — gray-striped with a broad white face and an orange nose — clinging to his neck like a caterpillar.

As soon as the children saw they could move their arms and legs, they scrambled out of the car, shouting, "We've had an ACCIDENT!" The grandmother was curled up under the dashboard, hoping she was injured so that Bailey's wrath would not come down on her all at once. The horrible thought she had before the accident was that the house she had remembered so vividly was not in Georgia but in Tennessee.

Bailey removed the cat from his neck with both hands and flung it out the window against the side of a pine tree. Then he got out of the car and started looking for the children's mother. She was sitting against the side of the red gutted ditch, holding the screaming baby, but she only had a cut down her face and a broken shoulder. "We've had an ACCIDENT!" the children screamed in a frenzy of delight.

"But nobody's killed," June Star said with disappointment as the grandmother limped out of the car, her hat still pinned to her head but the broken front brim standing up at a jaunty angle and the violet spray hanging off the side. They all sat down in the ditch, except the children, to recover from the shock. They were all shaking.

"Maybe a car will come along," said the children's mother hoarsely.

"I believe I have injured an organ," said the grandmother, pressing her side, but no one answered her. Bailey's teeth were clattering. He had on a yellow sport shirt with bright blue parrots designed in it and his face was as yellow as the shirt. The grandmother decided that she would not mention that the house was in Tennessee.

The road was about ten feet above and they could see only the tops of the trees on the other side of it. Behind the ditch they were sitting in there were more woods, tall and dark and deep. In a few minutes they saw a car some distance away on top of a hill, coming slowly as if the occupants were watching them. The grandmother stood up and waved both arms dramatically to attract their attention. The car continued to come on slowly, disappeared around a bend and appeared again, moving even slower, on top of the hill they had gone over. It was a big black battered hearse-like automobile. There were three men in it.

It came to a stop just over them and for some minutes, the driver looked down with a steady expressionless gaze to where they were sitting, and didn't speak. Then he turned his head and muttered something to the other two and they got out. One was a fat boy in black trousers and a red sweat shirt with a silver stallion embossed on the front of it. He moved around on the right side of them and stood staring, his mouth partly open in a kind of loose grin. The other had on khaki pants and a blue striped coat and a gray hat pulled down very low, hiding most of his face. He came around slowly on the left side. Neither spoke.

The driver got out of the car and stood by the side of it, looking down at them. He was an older man than the other two. His hair was just beginning to gray and he wore silver-rimmed spectacles that gave him a scholarly look. He had a long creased face and didn't have on any shirt or undershirt. He had on blue jeans that were too tight for him and was holding a black hat and a gun. The two boys also had guns.

"We've had an ACCIDENT!" the children screamed.

The grandmother had the peculiar feeling that the bespectacled man was someone she knew. His face was as familiar to her as if she had known him all her life but she could not recall who he was. He moved away from the car and began to come down the embankment, placing his feet carefully so that he wouldn't slip. He had on tan and white shoes and no socks, and his ankles were red and thin. "Good afternoon," he said. "I see you all had you a little spill."

"We turned over twice!" said the grandmother.

"Oncet," he corrected. "We seen it happen. Try their car and see will it run, Hiram," he said quietly to the boy with the gray hat.

"What you got that gun for?" John Wesley asked. "Whatcha gonna do with that gun?"

"Lady," the man said to the children's mother, "would you mind calling them children to sit down by you? Children make me nervous. I want all you all to sit down right together there where you're at."

"What are you telling US what to do for?" June Star asked.

Behind them the line of woods gaped like a dark open mouth. "Come here," said their mother.

"Look here now," Bailey said suddenly, "we're in a predicament! We're in. . . ."

The grandmother shrieked. She scrambled to her feet and stood staring. "You're The Misfit!" she said. "I recognized you at once!"

"Yes'm," the man said, smiling slightly as if he were pleased in spite of himself to be known, "but it would have been better for all of you, lady, if you hadn't of reckernized me."

Bailey turned his head sharply and said something to his mother that shocked even the children. The old lady began to cry and The Misfit reddened.

"Lady," he said, "don't you get upset. Sometimes a man says things he don't mean. I don't reckon he meant to talk to you thataway."

"You wouldn't shoot a lady, would you?" the grandmother said and removed a clean handkerchief from her cuff and began to slap at her eyes with it.

The Misfit pointed the toe of his shoe into the ground and made a little hole and then covered it up again. "I would hate to have to," he said.

"Listen," the grandmother almost screamed, "I know you're a good man. You don't look a bit like you have common blood. I know you must come from nice people!"

"Yes mam," he said, "finest people in the world." When he smiled he showed a row of strong white teeth. "God never made a finer woman than my mother and my daddy's heart was pure gold," he said. The boy with the red sweat shirt had come around behind them and was standing with his gun at his hip. The Misfit squatted down on the ground. "Watch them children, Bobby Lee," he said. "You know they make me nervous." He looked at the six of them huddled together in front of him and he seemed to be embarrassed as if he couldn't think of anything to say. "Ain't a cloud in the sky," he remarked, looking up at it. "Don't see no sun but don't see no cloud neither."

"Yes, it's a beautiful day," said the grandmother. "Listen," she said, "you shouldn't call yourself The Misfit because I know you're a good man at heart. I can just look at you and tell."

"Hush!" Bailey yelled. "Hush! Everybody shut up and let me handle this!" He was squatting in the position of a runner about to sprint forward but he didn't move.

"I pre-chate that, lady," The Misfit said and drew a little circle in the ground with the butt of his gun.

"It'll take a half a hour to fix this here car," Hiram called, looking over the raised hood of it.

"Well, first you and Bobby Lee get him and that little boy to step over yonder with you," The Misfit said, pointing to Bailey and John Wesley. "The boys want to ast you something," he said to Bailey. "Would you mind stepping back in them woods there with them?"

"Listen," Bailey began, "we're in a terrible predicament! Nobody realizes what this is," and his voice cracked. His eyes were as blue and intense as the parrots in his shirt and he remained perfectly still.

The grandmother reached up to adjust her hat brim as if she were going to the woods with him but it came off in her hand. She stood staring at it and after a second she let it fall to the ground. Hiram pulled Bailey up by the arm as if he were assisting an old man. John Wesley caught hold of his father's hand and Bobby Lee followed. They went off toward the woods and just as they reached the dark edge, Bailey turned and supporting himself against a gray naked pine trunk, he shouted, "I'll be back in a minute, Mamma, wait on me!"

"Come back this instant!" his mother shrilled but they all disappeared into the woods.

"Bailey Boy!" the grandmother called in a tragic voice but she found she was looking at The Misfit squatting on the ground in front of her. "I just know you're a good man," she said desperately. "You're not a bit common!"

"Nome, I ain't a good man," The Misfit said after a second as if he had considered her statement carefully, "but I ain't the worst in the world neither. My daddy said I was a different breed of dog from my brothers and sisters. 'You know,' Daddy said, 'it's some that can live their whole life out without asking about it and it's others has to know why it is, and this boy is one of the latters. He's going to be into everything!'" He put on his black hat and looked up suddenly and then away deep into the woods as if he were embarrassed again. "I'm sorry I don't have on a shirt before you ladies," he said, hunching his shoulders slightly. "We buried our clothes that we had on when we escaped and we're just making do until we can get better. We borrowed these from some folks we met," he explained.

"That's perfectly all right," the grandmother said. "Maybe Bailey has an extra shirt in his suitcase."

"I'll look and see terrectly," The Misfit said.

"Where are they taking him?" the children's mother screamed.

"Daddy was a card himself," The Misfit said. "You couldn't put anything over on him. He never got in trouble with the Authorities though. Just had the knack of handling them."

"You could be honest too if you'd only try," said the grandmother. "Think how wonderful it would be to settle down and live a comfortable life and not have to think about somebody chasing you all the time."

The Misfit kept scratching in the ground with the butt of his gun as if he were thinking about it. "Yes'm, somebody is always after you," he murmured.

The grandmother noticed how thin his shoulder blades were just behind his hat because she was standing up looking down on him. "Do you ever pray?" she asked.

He shook his head. All she saw was the black hat wiggle between his shoulder blades. "Nome," he said.

There was a pistol shot from the woods, followed closely by another. Then silence. The old lady's head jerked around. She could hear the wind move through the tree tops like a long satisfied insuck of breath. "Bailey Boy!" she called.

"I was a gospel singer for a while," The Misfit said. "I been most everything. Been in the arm service, both land and sea, at home and abroad, been twict married, been an undertaker, been with the railroads, plowed Mother Earth, been in a tornado, seen a man burnt alive oncet," and he looked up at the children's mother and the little girl who were sitting close together, their faces white and their eyes glassy; "I even seen a woman flogged," he said.

"Pray, pray," the grandmother began, "pray, pray. . . ."

"I never was a bad boy that I remember of," The Misfit said in an almost dreamy voice, "but somewheres along the line I done something wrong and got sent to the penitentiary. I was buried alive," and he looked up and held her attention to him by a steady stare.

"That's when you should have started to pray," she said. "What did you do to get sent to the penitentiary that first time?"

"Turn to the right, it was a wall," The Misfit said, looking up again at the cloudless sky. "Turn to the left, it was a wall. Look up it was a ceiling, look down it was a floor. I forget what I done, lady. I set there and set there, trying to remember what it was I done and I ain't recalled it to this day. Oncet in a while, I would think it was coming to me, but it never come."

"Maybe they put you in by mistake," the old lady said vaguely.

"Nome," he said. "It wasn't no mistake. They had the papers on me."

"You must have stolen something," she said.

The Misfit sneered slightly. "Nobody had nothing I wanted," he said. "It was a head-doctor at the penitentiary said what I had done was kill my daddy but I known that for a lie. My daddy died in nineteen ought nineteen of the epidemic flu and I never had a thing to do with it. He was buried in the Mount Hopewell Baptist churchyard and you can see for yourself."

"If you would pray," the old lady said, "Jesus would help you."

"That's right," The Misfit said.

"Well then, why don't you pray?" she asked trembling with delight suddenly.

"I don't want no hep," he said. "I'm doing all right by myself."

Bobby Lee and Hiram came ambling back from the woods. Bobby Lee was dragging a yellow shirt with bright blue parrots in it.

"Throw me that shirt, Bobby Lee," The Misfit said. The shirt came flying at him and landed on his shoulder and he put it on. The grandmother couldn't name what the shirt reminded her of. "No, lady," The Misfit said while he was buttoning it up, "I found out the crime don't matter. You can do one thing or you can do another, kill a man or take a tire off his car, because sooner or later you're going to forget what it was you done and just be punished for it."

The children's mother had begun to make heaving noises as if she couldn't get her breath. "Lady," he asked, "would you and that little girl like to step off yonder with Bobby Lee and Hiram and join your husband?"

"Yes, thank you," the mother said faintly. Her left arm dangled helplessly and she was holding the baby, who had gone to sleep, in the other. "Hep that lady up, Hiram," The Misfit said as she struggled to climb out of the ditch, "and Bobby Lee, you hold onto that little girl's hand."

"I don't want to hold hands with him," June Star said. "He reminds me of a pig."

The fat boy blushed and laughed and caught her by the arm and pulled her off into the woods after Hiram and her mother.

Alone with The Misfit, the grandmother found that she had lost her voice. There was not a cloud in the sky nor any sun. There was nothing around her but woods. She wanted to tell him that he must pray. She opened and closed her mouth several times before anything came out. Finally she found herself saying, "Jesus, Jesus," meaning, Jesus will help you, but the way she was saying it, it sounded as if she might be cursing.

"Yes'm," The Misfit said as if he agreed. "Jesus thown everything off balance. It was the same case with Him as with me except He hadn't committed any crime and they could prove I had committed one because they had the papers on me. Of course," he said, "they never shown me my papers. That's why I sign myself now. I said long ago, you get your signature and sign everything you do and keep a copy of it. Then you'll know what you done and you can hold up the crime to the punishment and see do they match and in the end you'll have something to prove you ain't been treated right. I call myself The Misfit," he said, "because I can't make what all I done wrong fit what all I gone through in punishment."

There was a piercing scream from the woods, followed closely by a pistol report. "Does it seem right to you, lady, that one is punished a heap and another ain't punished at all?"

"Jesus!" the old lady cried. "You've got good blood! I know you wouldn't shoot a lady! I know you come from nice people! Pray! Jesus, you ought not to shoot a lady. I'll give you all the money I've got!"

"Lady," The Misfit said, looking beyond her far into the woods, "there never was a body that give the undertaker a tip."

There were two more pistol reports and the grandmother raised her head like a parched old turkey hen crying for water and called, "Bailey Boy, Bailey Boy!" as if her heart would break.

"Jesus was the only One that ever raised the dead," The Misfit continued, "and He shouldn't have done it. He thown everything off balance. If He did what He said, then it's nothing for you to do but throw away everything and follow Him, and if He didn't, then it's nothing for you to do but enjoy the few minutes you got left the best way you can — by killing somebody or burning down his house or doing some other meanness to him. No pleasure but meanness," he said and his voice had become almost a snarl.

"Maybe He didn't raise the dead," the old lady mumbled, not knowing what she was saying and feeling so dizzy that she sank down in the ditch with her legs twisted under her.

"I wasn't there so I can't say He didn't," The Misfit said. "I wisht I had of been there," he said, hitting the ground with his fist. "It ain't right I wasn't there because if I had of been there I would of known. Listen lady," he said in a high voice, "if I had of been there I would of known and I wouldn't be like I am now." His voice seemed about to crack and the grandmother's head cleared for an instant. She saw the man's face twisted close to her own as if he were going to cry and she murmured, "Why you're one of my babies. You're one of my own children!" She reached out and touched him on the shoulder. The Misfit sprang back as if a snake had bitten him and shot her three times through the chest. Then he put his gun down on the ground and took off his glasses and began to clean them.

Hiram and Bobby Lee returned from the woods and stood over the ditch, looking down at the grandmother who half sat and half lay in a puddle of blood with her legs crossed under her like a child's and her face smiling up at the cloudless sky.

Without his glasses, The Misfit's eyes were red-rimmed and pale and defenseless-looking. "Take her off and throw her where you thrown the others," he said, picking up the cat that was rubbing itself against his leg.

"She was a talker, wasn't she?" Bobby Lee said, sliding down the ditch with a yodel.

"She would of been a good woman," The Misfit said, "if it had been somebody there to shoot her every minute of her life."

"Some fun!" Bobby Lee said.

"Shut up, Bobby Lee," The Misfit said. "It's no real pleasure in life."

                                                                    [1955]

Flannery O'Connor

ᔓᔕ

A TEMPLE OF THE HOLY GHOST

All weekend the two girls were calling each other Temple One and Temple Two, shaking with laughter and getting so red and hot that they were positively ugly, particularly Joanne who had spots on her face anyway. They came in the brown convent uniforms they had to wear to Mount St. Scholastica but as soon as they opened their suitcases, they took off the uniforms and put on red skirts and loud blouses. They put on lipstick and their Sunday shoes and walked around in the high heels all over the house, always passing the long mirror in the hall slowly to get a look at their legs. None of their ways were lost on the child. If only one of them had come, that one would have played with her, but since there were two of them, she was out of it and watched them suspiciously from a distance.

They were fourteen — two years older than she was — but neither of them was bright, which was why they had been sent to the convent. If they had gone to a regular school, they wouldn't have done anything but think about boys; at the convent the sisters, her mother said, would keep a grip on their necks. The child decided, after observing them for a few hours, that they were practically morons and she was glad to think that they were only second cousins and she couldn't have inherited any of their stupidity. Susan called herself Su-zan. She was very skinny but she had a pretty pointed face and red hair. Joanne had yellow hair that was naturally curly but she talked through her nose and when she laughed, she turned purple in patches. Neither one of them could say an intelligent thing and all their sentences began, "You know this boy I know well one time he . . ."

They were to stay all weekend and her mother said she didn't see how she would entertain them since she didn't know any boys their age. At this, the child, struck suddenly with genius, shouted, "There's Cheat! Get Cheat to come! Ask Miss Kirby to get Cheat to come show them around!" and she nearly choked on the food she had in her mouth. She doubled over laughing and hit the table with her fist and looked at the two bewildered girls while water started in her eyes and rolled down her fat cheeks and the braces she had in her mouth glared like tin. She had never thought of anything so funny before.

Her mother laughed in a guarded way and Miss Kirby blushed and carried her fork delicately to her mouth with one pea on it. She was a long-faced blonde schoolteacher who boarded with them and Mr. Cheatam was her admirer, a rich old farmer who arrived every Saturday afternoon in a fifteen-year-old baby-blue Pontiac powdered with red clay dust and black inside with Negroes that he charged ten cents apiece to bring into town on Saturday afternoons. After he dumped them he came to see Miss Kirby, always bringing a little gift — a bag of boiled peanuts or a watermelon or a stalk of sugar cane and once a wholesale box of Baby Ruth candy bars. He was bald-headed except for a little fringe of rust-colored hair and his face was nearly the same color as the unpaved roads and washed like them with ruts and gulleys. He wore a pale green shirt with a thin black stripe in it and blue galluses and his trousers cut across a protruding stomach that he pressed tenderly from time to time with his big flat thumb. All his teeth were backed with gold and he would roll his eyes at Miss Kirby in an impish way and say, "Haw haw," sitting in their porch swing with his legs spread apart and his hightopped shoes pointing in opposite directions on the floor.

"I don't think Cheat is going to be in town this weekend," Miss Kirby said, not in the least understanding that this was a joke, and the child was convulsed afresh, threw herself backward in her chair, fell out of it, rolled on the floor, and lay there heaving. Her mother told her if she didn't stop this foolishness she would have to leave the table.

Yesterday her mother had arranged with Alonzo Myers to drive them the forty-five miles to Mayville, where the convent was, to get the girls for the weekend and Sunday afternoon he was hired to drive them back again. He was an eighteen-year-old boy who weighed two hundred and fifty pounds and worked for the taxi company and he was all you could get to drive you anywhere. He smoked or rather chewed a short black cigar and he had a round sweaty chest that showed through the yellow nylon shirt he wore. When he drove all the windows of the car had to be open.

"Well there's Alonzo!" the child roared from the floor. "Get Alonzo to show em around! Get Alonzo!"

The two girls, who had seen Alonzo, began to scream their indignation.

Her mother thought this was funny too but she said, "That'll be about enough out of you," and changed the subject. She asked them why they called each other Temple One and Temple Two and this sent them off into gales of giggles. Finally they managed to explain. Sister Perpetua, the oldest nun at the Sisters of Mercy in Mayville, had given them a lecture on what to do if a young man should — here they laughed so hard they were not able to go on without going back to the beginning — on what to do if a young man should — they put their heads in their laps — on what to do if — they finally managed to shout it out — if he should "behave in an ungentlemanly manner with them in the back of an automobile." Sister Perpetua said they were to say, "Stop sir! I am a Temple of the Holy Ghost!" and that would put an end to it. The child sat up off the floor with a blank face. She didn't see anything so funny in this. What was really funny was the idea of Mr. Cheatam or Alonzo Myers beauing them around. That killed her.

Her mother didn't laugh at what they had said. "I think you girls are pretty silly," she said. "After all, that's what you are — Temples of the Holy Ghost."

The two of them looked up at her, politely concealing their giggles, but with astonished faces as if they were beginning to realize that she was made of the same stuff as Sister Perpetua.

Miss Kirby preserved her set expression and the child thought, it's all over her head anyhow. I am a Temple of the Holy Ghost, she said to herself, and was pleased with the phrase. It made her feel as if somebody had given her a present.

After dinner, her mother collapsed on the bed and said, "Those girls are going to drive me crazy if I don't get some entertainment for them. They're awful."

"I bet I know who you could get," the child started.

"Now listen. I don't want to hear any more about Mr. Cheatam," her mother said. "You embarrass Miss Kirby. He's her only friend. Oh my Lord," and she sat up and looked mournfully out the window, "that poor soul is so lonesome she'll even ride in that car that smells like the last circle in hell."

And she's a Temple of the Holy Ghost too, the child reflected. "I wasn't thinking of him," she said. "I was thinking of those two Wilkinses, Wendell and Cory, that visit old lady Buchell out on her farm. They're her grandsons. They work for her."

"Now that's an idea," her mother murmured and gave her an appreciative look. But then she slumped again. "They're only farm boys. These girls would turn up their noses at them."

"Huh," the child said. "They wear pants. They're sixteen and they got a car. Somebody said they were both going to be Church of God preachers because you don't have to know nothing to be one."

"They would be perfectly safe with those boys all right," her mother said and in a minute she got up and called their grandmother on the telephone and after she had talked to the old woman a half an hour, it was arranged that Wendell and Cory would come to supper and afterwards take the girls to the fair.

Susan and Joanne were so pleased that they washed their hair and rolled it up on aluminum curlers. Hah, thought the child, sitting cross-legged on the bed to watch them undo the curlers, wait'll you get a load of

Wendell and Cory! "You'll like these boys," she said. "Wendell is six feet
tall ands got red hair. Cory is six feet six inches talls got black hair and wears
a sport jacket and they gottem this car with a squirrel tail on the front."

"How does a child like you know so much about these men?" Susan
asked and pushed her face up close to the mirror to watch the pupils in her
eyes dilate.

The child lay back on the bed and began to count the narrow boards
in the ceiling until she lost her place. I know them all right, she said to
someone. We fought in the world war together. They were under me and I
saved them five times from Japanese suicide divers and Wendell said I am
going to marry that kid and the other said oh no you ain't I am and I said
neither one of you is because I will court marshall you all before you can bat
an eye. "I've seen them around is all," she said.

When they came the girls stared at them a second and then began to
giggle and talk to each other about the convent. They sat in the swing together and Wendell and Cory sat on the banisters together. They sat like
monkeys, their knees on a level with their shoulders and their arms hanging
down between. They were short thin boys with red faces and high cheekbones and pale seed-like eyes. They had brought a harmonica and a guitar.
One of them began to blow softly on the mouth organ, watching the girls
over it, and the other started strumming the guitar and then began to sing,
not watching them but keeping his head tilted upward as if he were only
interested in hearing himself. He was singing a hillbilly song that sounded
half like a love song and half like a hymn.

The child was standing on a barrel pushed into some bushes at the
side of the house, her face on a level with the porch floor. The sun was
going down and the sky was turning a bruised violet color that seemed to be
connected with the sweet mournful sound of the music. Wendell began to
smile as he sang and to look at the girls. He looked at Susan with a dog-like
loving look and sang,

> "I've found a friend in Jesus,
> He's everything to me,
> He's the lily of the valley,
> He's the One who's set me free!"

Then he turned the same look on Joanne and sang,

> "A wall of fire about me,
> I've nothing now to fear,
> He's the lily of the valley,
> And I'll always have Him near!"

The girls looked at each other and held their lips stiff so as not to giggle but Susan let out one anyway and clapped her hand on her mouth. The
singer frowned and for a few seconds only strummed the guitar. Then he
began "The Old Rugged Cross" and they listened politely but when he had
finished they said, "Let us sing one!" and before he could start another,
they began to sing with their convent-trained voices,

"Tantum ergo Sacramentum
Veneremur Cernui:
Et antiquum documentum
Novo cedat ritui:"

The child watched the boys' solemn faces turn with perplexed frowning stares at each other as if they were uncertain whether they were being made fun of.

"Praestet fides supplementum
Sensuum defectui.
Genitori, Genitoque
Laus et jubilatio

Salus, honor, virtus quoque . . ."

The boys' faces were dark red in the gray-purple light. They looked fierce and startled.

"Sit et benedictio;
Procedenti ab utroque
Compar sit laudatio.
Amen."

The girls dragged out the Amen and then there was a silence.

"That must be Jew singing," Wendell said and began to tune the guitar.

The girls giggled idiotically but the child stamped her foot on the barrel. "You big dumb ox!" she shouted. "You big dumb Church of God ox!" she roared and fell off the barrel and scrambled up and shot around the corner of the house as they jumped from the banister to see who was shouting.

Her mother had arranged for them to have supper in the back yard and she had a table laid out there under some Japanese lanterns that she pulled out for garden parties. "I ain't eating with them," the child said and snatched her plate off the table and carried it to the kitchen and sat down with the thin blue-gummed cook and ate her supper.

"Howcome you be so ugly sometime?" the cook asked.

"Those stupid idiots," the child said.

The lanterns gilded the leaves of the trees orange on the level where they hung and above them was black-green and below them were different dim muted colors that made the girls sitting at the table look prettier than they were. From time to time, the child turned her head and glared out the kitchen window at the scene below.

"God could strike you deaf dumb and blind," the cook said, "and then you wouldn't be as smart as you is."

"I would still be smarter than some," the child said.

After supper they left for the fair. She wanted to go to the fair but not with them so even if they had asked her she wouldn't have gone. She went upstairs and paced the long bedroom with her hands locked together behind her back and her head thrust forward and an expression, fierce and dreamy both, on her face. She didn't turn on the electric light but let the darkness collect and make the room smaller and more private. At regular intervals a light crossed the open window and threw shadows on the wall. She stopped and stood looking out over the dark slopes, past where the pond glinted silver, past the wall of woods to the speckled sky where a long finger of light was revolving up and around and away, searching the air as if it were hunting for the lost sun. It was the beacon light from the fair.

She could hear the distant sound of the calliope and she saw in her head all the tents raised up in a kind of gold sawdust light and the diamond ring of the ferris wheel going around and around up in the air and down again and the screeking merry-go-round going around and around on the ground. A fair lasted five or six days and there was a special afternoon for school children and a special night for niggers. She had gone last year on the afternoon for school children and had seen the monkeys and the fat man and had ridden on the ferris wheel. Certain tents were closed then because they contained things that would be known only to grown people but she had looked with interest at the advertising on the closed tents, at the faded-looking pictures on the canvas of people in tights, with stiff stretched composed faces like the faces of the martyrs waiting to have their tongues cut out by the Roman soldier. She had imagined that what was inside these tents concerned medicine and she had made up her mind to be a doctor when she grew up.

She had since changed and decided to be an engineer but as she looked out the window and followed the revolving searchlight as it widened and shortened and wheeled in its arc, she felt that she would have to be much more than just a doctor or an engineer. She would have to be a saint because that was the occupation that included everything you could know; and yet she knew she would never be a saint. She did not steal or murder but she was a born liar and slothful and she sassed her mother and was deliberately ugly to almost everybody. She was eaten up also with the sin of Pride, the worst one. She made fun of the Baptist preacher who came to the school at commencement to give the devotional. She would pull down her mouth and hold her forehead as if she were in agony and groan, "Fawther, we thank Thee," exactly the way he did and she had been told many times not to do it. She could never be a saint, but she thought she could be a martyr if they killed her quick.

She could stand to be shot but not to be burned in oil. She didn't know if she could stand to be torn to pieces by lions or not. She began to prepare her martyrdom, seeing herself in a pair of tights in a great arena, lit by the early Christians hanging in cages of fire, making a gold dusty light that fell on her and the lions. The first lion charged forward and fell at her feet, converted. A whole series of lions did the same. The lions liked her so much she even slept with them and finally the Romans were obliged to burn her but to their astonishment she would not burn down and finding she was so hard to kill, they finally cut off her head very quickly with a sword and she went immediately to heaven. She rehearsed this several times, returning each time at the entrance of Paradise to the lions.

Finally she got up from the window and got ready for bed and got in without saying her prayers. There were two heavy double beds in the room. The girls were occupying the other one and she tried to think of something cold and clammy that she could hide in their bed but her thought was fruitless. She didn't have anything she could think of, like a chicken carcass or a piece of beef liver. The sound of the calliope coming through the window kept her awake and she remembered that she hadn't said her prayers and got up and knelt down and began them. She took a running start and went through to the other side of the Apostle's Creed and then hung by her chin on the side of the bed, empty-minded. Her prayers, when she remembered to say them, were usually perfunctory but sometimes when she had done something wrong or heard music or lost something, or sometimes for no reason at all, she would be moved to fervor and would think of Christ on the long journey to Calvary, crushed three times on the rough cross. Her mind would stay on this a while and then get empty and when something roused her, she would find that she was thinking of a different thing entirely, of some dog or some girl or something she was going to do some day. Tonight, remembering Wendell and Cory, she was filled with thanksgiving and almost weeping with delight, she said, "Lord, Lord, thank You that I'm not in the Church of God, thank You Lord, thank You!" and got back in bed and kept repeating it until she went to sleep.

The girls came in at a quarter to twelve and waked her up with their giggling. They turned on the small blue-shaded lamp to see to get undressed by and their skinny shadows climbed up the wall and broke and continued moving about softly on the ceiling. The child sat up to hear what all they had seen at the fair. Susan had a plastic pistol full of cheap candy and Joanne a pasteboard cat with red polka dots on it. "Did you see the monkeys dance?" the child asked. "Did you see that fat man and those midgets?"

"All kinds of freaks," Joanne said. And then she said to Susan, "I enjoyed it all but the you-know-what," and her face assumed a peculiar expression as if she had bit into something that she didn't know if she liked or not.

The other stood still and shook her head once and nodded slightly at the child. "Little pitchers," she said in a low voice but the child heard it and her heart began to beat very fast.

She got out of bed and climbed onto the footboard of theirs. They turned off the light and got in but she didn't move. She sat there, looking hard at them until their faces were well defined in the dark. "I'm not as old as you all," she said, "but I'm about a million times smarter."

"There are some things," Susan said, "that a child of your age doesn't know," and they both began to giggle.

"Go back to your own bed," Joanne said.

The child didn't move. "One time," she said, her voice hollow-sounding in the dark, "I saw this rabbit have rabbits."

There was a silence. Then Susan said, "How?" in an indifferent tone and she knew that she had them. She said she wouldn't tell until they told about the you-know-what. Actually she had never seen a rabbit have rabbits but she forgot this as they began to tell what they had seen in the tent.

It had been a freak with a particular name but they couldn't remember the name. The tent where it was had been divided into two parts by a black curtain, one side for men and one for women. The freak went from one side to the other, talking first to the men and then to the women, but everyone could hear. The stage ran all the way across the front. The girls heard the freak say to the men, "I'm going to show you this and if you laugh, God may strike you the same way." The freak had a country voice, slow and nasal and neither high nor low, just flat. "God made me thisaway and if you laugh He may strike you the same way. This is the way He wanted me to be and I ain't disputing His way. I'm showing you because I got to make the best of it. I expect you to act like ladies and gentlemen. I never done it to myself nor had a thing to do with it but I'm making the best of it. I don't dispute hit." Then there was a long silence on the other side of the tent and finally the freak left the men and came over onto the women's side and said the same thing.

The child felt every muscle strained as if she were hearing the answer to a riddle that was more puzzling than the riddle itself. "You mean it had two heads?" she said.

"No," Susan said, "it was a man and woman both. It pulled up its dress and showed us. It had on a blue dress."

The child wanted to ask how it could be a man and woman both without two heads but she did not. She wanted to get back into her own bed and think it out and she began to climb down off the footboard.

"What about the rabbit?" Joanne asked.

The child stopped and only her face appeared over the footboard, abstracted, absent. "It spit them out of its mouth," she said, "six of them."

She lay in bed trying to picture the tent with the freak walking from side to side but she was too sleepy to figure it out. She was better able to see the faces of the country people watching, the men more solemn than they were in church, and the women stern and polite, with painted-looking eyes, standing as if they were waiting for the first note of the piano to begin the hymn. She could hear the freak saying, "God made me thisaway and I don't dispute hit," and the people saying, "Amen. Amen."

"God done this to me and I praise Him."

"Amen. Amen."

"He could strike you thisaway."

"Amen. Amen."

"But he has not."

"Amen."

"Raise yourself up. A temple of the Holy Ghost. You! You are God's temple, don't you know? Don't you know? God's Spirit has a dwelling in you, don't you know?"

"Amen. Amen."

"If anybody desecrates the temple of God, God will bring him to ruin and if you laugh, He may strike you thisaway. A temple of God is a holy thing. Amen. Amen."

"I am a temple of the Holy Ghost."

"Amen."

The people began to slap their hands without making a loud noise and with a regular beat between the Amens, more and more softly, as if they knew there was a child near, half asleep.

The next afternoon the girls put on their brown convent uniforms again and the child and her mother took them back to Mount St. Scholastica. "Oh glory, oh Pete!" they said. "Back to the salt mines." Alonzo Myers drove them and the child sat in front with him and her mother sat in back between the two girls, telling them such things as how pleased she was to have had them and how they must come back again and then about the good times she and their mothers had had when they were girls at the convent. The child didn't listen to any of this twaddle but kept as close to the locked door as she could get and held her head out the window. They had thought Alonzo would smell better on Sunday but he did not. With her hair blowing over her face she could look directly into the ivory sun which was framed in the middle of the blue afternoon but when she pulled it away from her eyes she had to squint.

Mount St. Scholastica was a red brick house set back in a garden in the center of town. There was a filling station on one side of it and a firehouse on the other. It had a high black grillework fence around it and narrow bricked walks between old trees and japonica bushes that were heavy with blooms. A big moon-faced nun came bustling to the door to let them in and embraced her mother and would have done the same to her but she stuck out her hand and preserved a frigid frown, looking just past the sister's shoes at the wainscoting. They had a tendency to kiss even homely children, but the nun shook her hand vigorously and even cracked her knuckles a little and said they must come to the chapel, that benediction was just beginning. You put your foot in their door and they got you praying, the child thought as they hurried down the polished corridor.

You'd think she had to catch a train, she continued in the same ugly vein as they entered the chapel where the sisters were kneeling on one side and the girls, all in brown uniforms, on the other. The chapel smelled of incense. It was light green and gold, a series of springing arches that ended with the one over the altar where the priest was kneeling in front of the monstrance, bowed low. A small boy in a surplice was standing behind him, swinging the censer. The child knelt down between her mother and the nun and they were well into the *"Tantum Ergo"* before her ugly thoughts stopped and she began to realize that she was in the presence of God. Hep me not to be so mean, she began mechanically. Hep me not to give her so much sass. Hep me not to talk like I do. Her mind began to get quiet and then empty but when the priest raised the monstrance with the Host shining ivory-colored in the center of it, she was thinking of the tent at the fair that had the freak in it. The freak was saying, "I don't dispute hit. This is the way He wanted me to be."

As they were leaving the convent door, the big nun swooped down on her mischievously and nearly smothered her in the black habit, mashing the side of her face into the crucifix hitched onto her belt and then holding her off and looking at her with little periwinkle eyes.

On the way home she and her mother sat in the back and Alonzo drove by himself in the front. The child observed three folds of fat in the back of his neck and noted that his ears were pointed almost like a pig's. Her mother, making conversation, asked him if he had gone to the fair.

"Gone," he said, "and never missed a thing and it was good I gone when I did because they ain't going to have it next week like they said they was."

"Why?" asked her mother.

"They shut it on down," he said. "Some of the preachers from town gone out and inspected it and got the police to shut it on down."

Her mother let the conversation drop and the child's round face was lost in thought. She turned it toward the window and looked out over a stretch of pasture land that rose and fell with a gathering greenness until it touched the dark woods. The sun was a huge red ball like an elevated Host drenched in blood and when it sank out of sight, it left a line in the sky like a red clay road hanging over the trees.

[1955]

Flannery O'Connor

ಬಌ

EVERYTHING THAT RISES MUST CONVERGE

Her doctor had told Julian's mother that she must lose twenty pounds on account of her blood pressure, so on Wednesday nights Julian had to take her downtown on the bus for a reducing class at the Y. The reducing class was designed for working girls over fifty, who weighed from 165 to 200 pounds. His mother was one of the slimmer ones, but she said ladies did not tell their age or weight. She would not ride the buses by herself at night since they had been integrated, and because the reducing class was one of her few pleasures, necessary for her health, and *free*, she said Julian could at least put himself out to take her, considering all she did for him. Julian did not like to consider all she did for him, but every Wednesday night he braced himself and took her.

She was almost ready to go, standing before the hall mirror, putting on her hat, while he, his hands behind him, appeared pinned to the door frame, waiting like Saint Sebastian for the arrows to begin piercing him. The hat was new and had cost her seven dollars and a half. She kept saying, "Maybe I shouldn't have paid that for it. No, I shouldn't have. I'll take it off and return it tomorrow. I shouldn't have bought it."

Julian raised his eyes to heaven. "Yes, you should have bought it," he said. "Put it on and let's go." It was a hideous hat. A purple velvet flap came down on one side of it and stood up on the other; the rest of it was green and looked like a cushion with the stuffing out. He decided it was less comical than jaunty and pathetic. Everything that gave her pleasure was small and depressed him.

She lifted the hat one more time and set it down slowly on top of her head. Two wings of gray hair protruded on either side of her florid face, but her eyes, sky-blue, were as innocent and untouched by experience as they must have been when she was ten. Were it not that she was a widow who had struggled fiercely to feed and clothe and put him through school and who was supporting him still, "until he got on his feet," she might have been a little girl that he had to take to town.

"It's all right, it's all right," he said. "Let's go." He opened the door himself and started down the walk to get her going. The sky was a dying violet and the houses stood out darkly against it, bulbous liver-colored monstrosities of a uniform ugliness though no two were alike. Since this had been a fashionable neighborhood forty years ago, his mother persisted in thinking they did well to have an apartment in it. Each house had a narrow collar of dirt around it in which sat, usually, a grubby child. Julian walked with his hands in his pockets, his head down and thrust forward, and his eyes glazed with the determination to make himself completely numb during the time he would be sacrificed to her pleasure.

The door closed and he turned to find the dumpy figure, surmounted by the atrocious hat, coming toward him. "Well," she said, "you only live once and paying a little more for it, I at least won't meet myself coming and going."

"Some day I'll start making money," Julian said gloomily — he knew he never would — "and you can have one of those jokes whenever you take the fit." But first they would move. He visualized a place where the nearest neighbor would be three miles away on either side.

"I think you're doing fine," she said, drawing on her gloves. "You've only been out of school a year. Rome wasn't built in a day."

She was one of the few members of the Y reducing class who arrived in hat and gloves and who had a son who had been to college. "It takes time," she said, "and the world is in such a mess. This hat looked better on me than any of the others, though when she brought it out I said, 'Take that thing back. I wouldn't have it on my head,' and she said, 'Now wait till you see it on,' and when she put it on me, I said, 'We-ull,' and she said, 'If you ask me, that hat does something for you and you do something for the hat, and besides,' she said, 'with that hat, you won't meet yourself coming and going.' "

Julian thought he could have stood his lot better if she had been selfish, if she had been an old hag who drank and screamed at him. He walked along, saturated in depression, as if in the midst of his martyrdom he had lost his faith. Catching sight of his long, hopeless, irritated face, she stopped suddenly with a grief-stricken look, and pulled back on his arm. "Wait on me," she said. "I'm going back to the house and take this thing off and tomorrow I'm going to return it. I was out of my head. I can pay the gas bill with the seven-fifty."

He caught her arm in a vicious grip. "You are not going to take it back," he said. "I like it."

"Well," she said, "I don't think I ought . . ."

"Shut up and enjoy it," he muttered, more depressed than ever.

"With the world in the mess it's in," she said, "it's a wonder we can enjoy anything. I tell you, the bottom rail is on the top."

Julian sighed.

"Of course," she said, "if you know who you are, you can go anywhere." She said this every time he took her to the reducing class. "Most of them in it are not our kind of people," she said, "but I can be gracious to anybody. I know who I am."

"They don't give a damn for your graciousness," Julian said savagely. "Knowing who you are is good for one generation only. You haven't the foggiest idea where you stand now or who you are."

She stopped and allowed her eyes to flash at him. "I most certainly do know who I am," she said, "and if you don't know who you are, I'm ashamed of you."

"Oh hell," Julian said.

"Your great-grandfather was a former governor of this state," she said. "Your grandfather was a prosperous landowner. Your grandmother was a Godhigh."

"Will you look around you," he said tensely, "and see where you are now?" and he swept his arm jerkily out to indicate the neighborhood, which the growing darkness at least made less dingy.

"You remain what you are," she said. "Your great-grandfather had a plantation and two hundred slaves."

"There are no more slaves," he said irritably.

"They were better off when they were," she said. He groaned to see that she was off on that topic. She rolled onto it every few days like a train on an open track. He knew every stop, every junction, every swamp along the way, and knew the exact point at which her conclusion would roll majestically into the station: "It's ridiculous. It's simply not realistic. They should rise, yes, but on their own side of the fence."

"Let's skip it," Julian said.

"The ones I feel sorry for," she said, "are the ones that are half white. They're tragic."

"Will you skip it?"

"Suppose we were half white. We would certainly have mixed feelings."

"I have mixed feelings now," he groaned.

"Well let's talk about something pleasant," she said. "I remember going to Grandpa's when I was a little girl. Then the house had double stairways that went up to what was really the second floor — all the cooking was done on the first. I used to like to stay down in the kitchen on account of the way the walls smelled. I would sit with my nose pressed against the plaster and take deep breaths. Actually the place belonged to the Godhighs but your grandfather Chestny paid the mortgage and saved it for them. They were in reduced circumstances," she said, "but reduced or not, they never forgot who they were."

"Doubtless that decayed mansion reminded them," Julian muttered. He never spoke of it without contempt or thought of it without longing. He had seen it once when he was a child before it had been sold. The double stairways had rotted and had been torn down. Negroes were living in it. But it remained in his mind as his mother had known it. It appeared in his dreams regularly. He would stand on the wide porch, listening to the rustle of oak leaves, then wander through the high-ceilinged hall into the parlor that opened onto it and gaze at the worn rugs and faded draperies. It occurred to him that it was he, not she, who could have appreciated it. He preferred its threadbare elegance to anything he could name and it was because of it that all the neighborhoods they had lived in had been a torment to him — whereas she had hardly known the difference. She called her insensitivity "being adjustable."

"And I remember the old darky who was my nurse, Caroline. There was no better person in the world. I've always had a great respect for my colored friends," she said. "I'd do anything in the world for them and they'd . . ."

"Will you for God's sake get off that subject?" Julian said. When he got on a bus by himself, he made it a point to sit down beside a Negro, in reparation as it were for his mother's sins.

"You're mighty touchy tonight," she said. "Do you feel all right?"

"Yes I feel all right," he said. "Now lay off."

She pursed her lips. "Well, you certainly are in a vile humor," she observed. "I just won't speak to you at all."

They had reached the bus stop. There was no bus in sight and Julian, his hands still jammed in his pockets and his head thrust forward, scowled down the empty street. The frustration of having to wait on the bus as well as ride on it began to creep up his neck like a hot hand. The presence of his mother was borne in upon him as she gave a pained sigh. He looked at her bleakly. She was holding herself very erect under the preposterous hat, wearing it like a banner of her imaginary dignity. There was in him an evil urge to break her spirit. He suddenly unloosened his tie and pulled it off and put it in his pocket.

She stiffened. "Why must you look like *that* when you take me to town?" she said. "Why must you deliberately embarrass me?"

"If you'll never learn where you are," he said, "you can at least learn where I am."

"You look like a — thug," she said.

"Then I must be one," he murmured.

"I'll just go home," she said. "I will not bother you. If you can't do a little thing like that for me . . ."

Rolling his eyes upward, he put his tie back on. "Restored to my class," he muttered. He thrust his face toward her and hissed, "True culture is in the mind, the *mind*," he said, and tapped his head, "the mind."

"It's in the heart," she said, "and in how you do things and how you do things is because of who you *are*."

"Nobody in the damn bus cares who you are."

"I care who I am," she said icily.

The lighted bus appeared on top of the next hill and as it approached, they moved out into the street to meet it. He put his hand under her elbow and hoisted her up on the creaking step. She entered with a little smile, as if she were going into a drawing room where everyone had been waiting for her. While he put in the tokens, she sat down on one of the broad front seats for three which faced the aisle. A thin woman with protruding teeth and long yellow hair was sitting on the end of it. His mother moved up beside her and left room for Julian beside herself. He sat down and looked at the floor across the aisle where a pair of thin feet in red and white canvas sandals were planted.

His mother immediately began a general conversation meant to attract anyone who felt like talking. "Can it get any hotter?" she said and removed from her purse a folding fan, black with a Japanese scene on it, which she began to flutter before her.

"I reckon it might could," the woman with the protruding teeth said, "but I know for a fact my apartment couldn't get no hotter."

"It must get the afternoon sun," his mother said. She sat forward and looked up and down the bus. It was half filled. Everybody was white. "I see we have the bus to ourselves," she said. Julian cringed.

"For a change," said the woman across the aisle, the owner of the red and white canvas sandals. "I come on one the other day and they were thick as fleas — up front and all through."

"The world is in a mess everywhere," his mother said. "I don't know how we've let it get in this fix."

"What gets my goat is all those boys from good families stealing automobile tires," the woman with the protruding teeth said. "I told my boy, I said you may not be rich but you been raised right and if I ever catch you in any such mess, they can send you on to the reformatory. Be exactly where you belong."

"Training tells," his mother said. "Is your boy in high school?"

"Ninth grade," the woman said.

"My son just finished college last year. He wants to write but he's selling typewriters until he gets started," his mother said.

The woman leaned forward and peered at Julian. He threw her such a malevolent look that she subsided against the seat. On the floor across the aisle there was an abandoned newspaper. He got up and got it and opened it out in front of him. His mother discreetly continued the conversation in a lower tone but the woman across the aisle said in a loud voice, "Well that's nice. Selling typewriters is close to writing. He can go right from one to the other."

"I tell him," his mother said, "that Rome wasn't built in a day."

Behind the newspaper Julian was withdrawing into the inner compartment of his mind where he spent most of his time. This was a kind of mental bubble in which he established himself when he could not bear to be part of what was going on around him. From it he could see out and judge but in it he was safe from any kind of penetration from without. It was the only place where he felt free of the general idiocy of his fellows. His mother had never entered it but from it he could see her with absolute clarity.

The old lady was clever enough and he thought that if she had started from any of the right premises, more might have been expected of her. She lived according to the laws of her own fantasy world, outside of which he had never seen her set foot. The law of it was to sacrifice herself for him after she had first created the necessity to do so by making a mess of things. If he had permitted her sacrifices, it was only because her lack of foresight had made them necessary. All of her life had been a struggle to act like a Chestny without the Chestny goods, and to give him everything she thought a Chestny ought to have; but since, said she, it was fun to struggle, why complain? And when you had won, as she had won, what fun to look back on the hard times! He could not forgive her that she had enjoyed the struggle and that she thought *she* had won.

What she meant when she said she had won was that she had brought him up successfully and had sent him to college and that he had turned out so well — good looking (her teeth had gone unfilled so that his could be straightened), intelligent (he realized he was too intelligent to be a success), and with a future ahead of him (there was of course no future ahead of him). She excused his gloominess on the grounds that he was still growing up and his radical ideas on his lack of practical experience. She said he didn't yet know a thing about "life," that he hadn't even entered the real world — when already he was as disenchanted with it as a man of fifty.

The further irony of all this was that in spite of her, he had turned out so well. In spite of going to only a third-rate college, he had, on his own initiative, come out with a first-rate education; in spite of growing up dominated by a small mind, he had ended up with a large one; in spite of all her foolish views, he was free of prejudice and unafraid to face facts. Most miraculous of all, instead of being blinded by love for her as she was for him, he had cut himself emotionally free of her and could see her with complete objectivity. He was not dominated by his mother.

The bus stopped with a sudden jerk and shook him from his meditation. A woman from the back lurched forward with little steps and barely escaped falling in his newspaper as she righted herself. She got off and a large Negro got on. Julian kept his paper lowered to watch. It gave him a certain satisfaction to see injustice in daily operation. It confirmed his view that with a few exceptions there was no one worth knowing within a radius of three hundred miles. The Negro was well dressed and carried a briefcase. He looked around and then sat down on the other end of the seat where the woman with the red and white canvas sandals was sitting. He immediately unfolded a newspaper and obscured himself behind it. Julian's mother's elbow at once prodded insistently into his ribs. "Now you see why I won't ride on these buses by myself," she whispered.

The woman with the red and white canvas sandals had risen at the same time the Negro sat down and had gone further back in the bus and taken the seat of the woman who had got off. His mother leaned forward and cast her an approving look.

Julian rose, crossed the aisle, and sat down in the place of the woman with the canvas sandals. From this position, he looked serenely across at his mother. Her face had turned an angry red. He stared at her, making his eyes the eyes of a stranger. He felt his tension suddenly lift as if he had openly declared war on her.

He would have liked to get in conversation with the Negro and to talk with him about art or politics or any subject that would be above the comprehension of those around them, but the man remained entrenched behind his paper. He was either ignoring the change of seating or had never noticed it. There was no way for Julian to convey his sympathy.

His mother kept her eyes fixed reproachfully on his face. The woman with the protruding teeth was looking at him avidly as if he were a type of monster new to her.

"Do you have a light?" he asked the Negro.

Without looking away from his paper, the man reached in his pocket and handed him a packet of matches.

"Thanks," Julian said. For a moment he held the matches foolishly. A NO SMOKING sign looked down upon him from over the door. This alone would not have deterred him; he had no cigarettes. He had quit smoking some months before because he could not afford it. "Sorry," he muttered and handed back the matches. The Negro lowered the paper and gave him an annoyed look. He took the matches and raised the paper again.

His mother continued to gaze at him but she did not take the advantage of his momentary discomfort. Her eyes retained their battered look.

Her face seemed to be unnaturally red, as if her blood pressure had risen. Julian allowed no glimmer of sympathy to show on his face. Having got the advantage, he wanted desperately to keep it and carry it through. He would have liked to teach her a lesson that would last her a while, but there seemed no way to continue the point. The Negro refused to come out from behind his paper.

Julian folded his arms and looked stolidly before him, facing her but as if he did not see her, as if he had ceased to recognize her existence. He visualized a scene in which, the bus having reached their stop, he would remain in his seat and when she said, "Aren't you going to get off?" he would look at her as a stranger who had rashly addressed him. The corner they got off on was usually deserted, but it was well lighted and it would not hurt her to walk by herself the four blocks to the Y. He decided to wait until the time came and then decide whether or not he would let her get off by herself. He would have to be at the Y at ten to bring her back, but he could leave her wondering if he was going to show up. There was no reason for her to think she could always depend on him.

He retired again into the high-ceilinged room sparsely settled with large pieces of antique furniture. His soul expanded momentarily but then he became aware of his mother across from him and the vision shriveled. He studied her coldly. Her feet in little pumps dangled like a child's and did not quite reach the floor. She was training on him an exaggerated look of reproach. He felt completely detached from her. At that moment he could with pleasure have slapped her as he would have slapped a particularly obnoxious child in his charge.

He began to imagine various unlikely ways by which he could teach her a lesson. He might make friends with some distinguished Negro professor or lawyer and bring him home to spend the evening. He would be entirely justified but her blood pressure would rise to 300. He could not push her to the extent of making her have a stroke, and moreover, he had never been successful at making any Negro friends. He had tried to strike up an acquaintance on the bus with some of the better types, with ones that looked like professors or ministers or lawyers. One morning he had sat down next to a distinguished-looking dark brown man who had answered his questions with a sonorous solemnity but who had turned out to be an undertaker. Another day he had sat down beside a cigar-smoking Negro with a diamond ring on his finger, but after a few stilted pleasantries, the Negro had rung the buzzer and risen, slipping two lottery tickets into Julian's hand as he climbed over him to leave.

He imagined his mother lying desperately ill and his being able to secure only a Negro doctor for her. He toyed with that idea for a few minutes and then dropped it for a momentary vision of himself participating as a sympathizer in a sit-in demonstration. This was possible but he did not linger with it. Instead, he approached the ultimate horror. He brought home a beautiful suspiciously Negroid woman. Prepare yourself, he said. There is

nothing you can do about it. This is the woman I've chosen. She's intelligent, dignified, even good, and she's suffered and she hasn't thought it *fun*.
Now persecute us, go ahead and persecute us. Drive her out of here, but
remember, you're driving me too. His eyes were narrowed and through the
indignation he had generated, he saw his mother across the aisle, purple-
faced, shrunken to the dwarf-like proportions of her moral nature, sitting
like a mummy beneath the ridiculous banner of her hat.

He was tilted out of his fantasy again as the bus stopped. The door
opened with a sucking hiss and out of the dark a large, gaily dressed, sullen-
looking colored woman got on with a little boy. The child, who might have
been four, had on a short plaid suit and a Tyrolean hat with a blue feather
in it. Julian hoped that he would sit down beside him and that the woman
would push in beside his mother. He could think of no better arrangement.

As she waited for her tokens, the woman was surveying the seating
possibilities — he hoped with the idea of sitting where she was least
wanted. There was something familiar-looking about her but Julian could
not place what it was. She was a giant of a woman. Her face was set not
only to meet opposition but to seek it out. The downward tilt of her large
lower lip was like a warning sign: DON'T TAMPER WITH ME. Her bulging figure was encased in a green crepe dress and her feet overflowed in red shoes.
She had on a hideous hat. A purple velvet flap came down on one side of it
and stood up on the other; the rest of it was green and looked like a cushion
with the stuffing out. She carried a mammoth red pocketbook that bulged
throughout as if it were stuffed with rocks.

To Julian's disappointment, the little boy climbed up on the empty
seat beside his mother. His mother lumped all children, black and white,
into the common category, "cute," and she thought little Negroes were on
the whole cuter than little white children. She smiled at the little boy as he
climbed on the seat.

Meanwhile the woman was bearing down upon the empty seat beside
Julian. To his annoyance, she squeezed herself into it. He saw his mother's
face change as the woman settled herself next to him and he realized with
satisfaction that this was more objectionable to her than it was to him. Her
face seemed almost gray and there was a look of dull recognition in her eyes,
as if suddenly she had sickened at some awful confrontation. Julian saw that
it was because she and the woman had, in a sense, swapped sons. Though
his mother would not realize the symbolic significance of this, she would
feel it. His amusement showed plainly on his face.

The woman next to him muttered something unintelligible to herself.
He was conscious of a kind of bristling next to him, muted growling like
that of an angry cat. He could not see anything but the red pocketbook upright on the bulging green thighs. He visualized the woman as she had
stood waiting for her tokens — the ponderous figure, rising from the red
shoes upward over the solid hips, the mammoth bosom, the haughty face,
to the green and purple hat.

His eyes widened.

The vision of the two hats, identical, broke upon him with the radiance of a brilliant sunrise. His face was suddenly lit with joy. He could not believe that Fate had thrust upon his mother such a lesson. He gave a loud chuckle so that she would look at him and see that he saw. She turned her eyes on him slowly. The blue in them seemed to have turned a bruised purple. For a moment he had an uncomfortable sense of her innocence, but it lasted only a second before principle rescued him. Justice entitled him to laugh. His grin hardened until it said to her as plainly as if he were saying aloud: Your punishment exactly fits your pettiness. This should teach you a permanent lesson.

Her eyes shifted to the woman. She seemed unable to bear looking at him and to find the woman preferable. He became conscious again of the bristling presence at his side. The woman was rumbling like a volcano about to become active. His mother's mouth began to twitch slightly at one corner. With a sinking heart, he saw incipient signs of recovery on her face and realized that this was going to strike her suddenly as funny and was going to be no lesson at all. She kept her eyes on the woman and an amused smile came over her face as if the woman were a monkey that had stolen her hat. The little Negro was looking up at her with large fascinated eyes. He had been trying to attract her attention for some time.

"Carver," the woman said suddenly. "Come heah!"

When he saw that the spotlight was on him at last, Carver drew his feet up and turned himself toward Julian's mother and giggled.

"Carver!" the woman said. "You heah me? Come heah!"

Carver slid down from the seat but remained squatting with his back against the base of it, his head turned slowly around toward Julian's mother, who was smiling at him. The woman reached a hand across the aisle and snatched him to her. He righted himself and hung backwards on her knees, grinning at Julian's mother. "Isn't he cute?" Julian's mother said to the woman with the protruding teeth.

"I reckon he is," the woman said without conviction.

The Negress yanked him upright but he eased out of her grip and shot across the aisle and scrambled, giggling wildly, onto the seat beside his love.

"I think he likes me," Julian's mother said, and smiled at the woman. It was the smile she used when she was being particularly gracious to an inferior. Julian saw everything lost. The lesson had rolled off her like rain on a roof.

The woman stood up and yanked the little boy off the seat as if she were snatching him from contagion. Julian could feel the rage in her at having no weapon like his mother's smile. She gave the child a sharp slap across his leg. He howled once and then thrust his head into her stomach and kicked his feet against her shins. "Behave," she said vehemently.

The bus stopped and the Negro who had been reading the newspaper got off. The woman moved over and set the little boy down with a thump between herself and Julian. She held him firmly by the knee. In a moment he put his hands in front of his face and peeped at Julian's mother through his fingers.

"I see yoooooooo!" she said and put her hand in front of her face and peeped at him.

The woman slapped his hand down. "Quit yo' foolishness," she said, "before I knock the living Jesus out of you!"

Julian was thankful that the next stop was theirs. He reached up and pulled the cord. The woman reached up and pulled it at the same time. Oh my God, he thought. He had the terrible intuition that when they got off the bus together, his mother would open her purse and give the little boy a nickel. The gesture would be as natural to her as breathing. The bus stopped and the woman got up and lunged to the front, dragging the child, who wished to stay on, after her. Julian and his mother got up and followed. As they neared the door, Julian tried to relieve her of her pocketbook.

"No," she murmured, "I want to give the little boy a nickel."

"No!" Julian hissed. "No!"

She smiled down at the child and opened her bag. The bus door opened and the woman picked him up by the arm and descended with him, hanging at her hip. Once in the street she set him down and shook him.

Julian's mother had to close her purse while she got down the bus step but as soon as her feet were on the ground, she opened it again and began to rummage inside. "I can't find but a penny," she whispered, "but it looks like a new one."

"Don't do it!" Julian said fiercely between his teeth. There was a streetlight on the corner and she hurried to get under it so that she could better see into her pocketbook. The woman was heading off rapidly down the street with the child still hanging backward on her hand.

"Oh little boy!" Julian's mother called and took a few quick steps and caught up with them just beyond the lamppost. "Here's a bright new penny for you," and she held out the coin, which shone bronze in the dim light.

The huge woman turned and for a moment stood, her shoulder's lifted and her face frozen with frustrated rage, and stared at Julian's mother. Then all at once she seemed to explode like a piece of machinery that had been given one ounce of pressure too much. Julian saw the black fist swing out with the red pocketbook. He shut his eyes and cringed as he heard the woman shout, "He don't take nobody's pennies!" When he opened his eyes, the woman was disappearing down the street with the little boy staring wide-eyed over her shoulder. Julian's mother was sitting on the sidewalk.

"I told you not to do that," Julian said angrily. "I told you not to do that!"

He stood over her for a minute, gritting his teeth. Her legs were stretched out in front of her and her hat was on her lap. He squatted down and looked her in the face. It was totally expressionless. "You got exactly what you deserved," he said. "Now get up."

He picked up her pocketbook and put what had fallen out back in it.

He picked the hat up off her lap. The penny caught his eye on the sidewalk and he picked that up and let it drop before her eyes into the purse. Then he stood up and leaned over and held his hands out to pull her up. She remained immobile. He sighed. Rising above them on either side were black apartment buildings, marked with irregular rectangles of light. At the end of the block a man came out of a door and walked off in the opposite direction. "All right," he said, "suppose somebody happens by and wants to know why you're sitting on the sidewalk?"

She took the hand and, breathing hard, pulled heavily up on it and then stood for a moment, swaying slightly as if the spots of light in the darkness were circling around her. Her eyes, shadowed and confused, finally settled on his face. He did not try to conceal his irritation. "I hope this teaches you a lesson," he said. She leaned forward and her eyes raked his face. She seemed trying to determine his identity. Then, as if she found nothing familiar about him, she started off with a headlong movement in the wrong direction.

"Aren't you going on to the Y?" he asked.

"Home," she muttered.

"Well, are we walking?"

For answer she kept going. Julian followed along, his hands behind him. He saw no reason to let the lesson she had had go without backing it up with an explanation of its meaning. She might as well be made to understand what had happened to her. "Don't think that was just an uppity Negro woman," he said. "That was the whole colored race which will no longer take your condescending pennies. That was your black double. She can wear the same hat as you, and to be sure," he added gratuitously (because he thought it was funny), "it looked better on her than it did on you. What all this means," he said, "is that the old world is gone. The old manners are obsolete and your graciousness is not worth a damn." He thought bitterly of the house that had been lost for him. "You aren't who you think you are," he said.

She continued to plow ahead, paying no attention to him. Her hair had come undone on one side. She dropped her pocketbook and took no notice. He stooped and picked it up and handed it to her but she did not take it.

"You needn't act as if the world had come to an end," he said, "because it hasn't. From now on you've got to live in a new world and face a few realities for a change. Buck up," he said, "it won't kill you."

She was breathing fast.

"Let's wait on the bus," he said.

"Home," she said thickly.

"I hate to see you behave like this," he said. "Just like a child. I should be able to expect more of you." He decided to stop where he was and make her stop and wait for a bus. "I'm not going any farther," he said, stopping. "We're going on the bus."

She continued to go on as if she had not heard him. He took a few steps and caught her arm and stopped her. He looked into her face and caught his breath. He was looking into a face he had never seen before. "Tell Grandpa to come get me," she said.

He stared, stricken.

"Tell Caroline to come get me," she said.

Stunned, he let her go and she lurched forward again, walking as if one leg were shorter than the other. A tide of darkness seemed to be sweeping her from him. "Mother!" he cried. "Darling, sweetheart, wait!" Crumpling, she fell to the pavement. He dashed forward and fell at her side, crying, "Mamma, Mamma!" He turned her over. Her face was fiercely distorted. One eye, large and staring, moved slightly to the left as if it had become unmoored. The other remained fixed on him, raked his face again, found nothing, and closed.

"Wait here, wait here!" he cried and jumped up and began to run for help toward a cluster of lights he saw in the distance ahead of him. "Help, help!" he shouted, but his voice was thin, scarcely a thread of sound. The lights drifted farther away the faster he ran and his feet moved numbly as if they carried him nowhere. The tide of darkness seemed to sweep him back to her, postponing from moment to moment his entry into the world of guilt and sorrow.

[1965]

ALICE ADAMS (b. 1926) was born in Fredericksburg, Virginia. Her parents were interested in literature, although she remembers she never saw her father "read a book for pleasure." As a young girl Adams wrote poetry and had her work published in school magazines. Then she went to Radcliffe College, where she took a short story class and "fell totally and permanently in love" with James Joyce, Katherine Mansfield, Katherine Anne Porter, John Cheever, and many other writers. She graduated from Radcliffe in 1945, married, had children, and then was divorced, all the time continuing to write fiction. Her first novel, Careless Love (1966), was published when she was forty.

Living in San Francisco, Adams now publishes regularly and no longer works the succession of office jobs she used to support herself and her family until she earned enough money from her writing. She is a frequent contributor of short stories to The Atlantic Monthly, The New Yorker, and Paris Review. To date she has published three more novels: Families and Survivors (1975), Listening to Billie (1978) — referring to the blues singer Billie Holiday — and Rich Rewards (1980). She has published two collections of short stories, Beautiful Girl (1979) and To See You Again (1982). In 1982 she also won the O. Henry Award for Continuing Achievement as a short story writer.

In her essay "Why I Write," Adams revealed that "The Swastika on Our Door" was the first story she ever wrote that pleased her. Now, twenty years later, she says that she writes "mainly because it is what I most enjoy doing." Her most recent publication is Superior Women (1984). (See Adams's Commentary on page 1326.)

Alice Adams

‰

THE SWASTIKA ON OUR DOOR

Normally, Karen Washington took a warmly nostalgic interest in stories about and especially pictures of her husband's former girls. They had all been pretty, some beautiful. And they reminded her that her very successful and preoccupied lawyer husband had once been a lively bachelor, vigorously engaged in the pursuit of women. But the large glossy picture of Roger and his brother Richard, who was now dead, and a girl, that she found on the top shelf of her husband's shirt closet disturbed her considerably. Why had Roger put it there? She was not jealous; she did not suspect that he perpetuated an old liaison, but she felt left out. Why had he chosen not to tell her about this particular beautiful girl, in her high-collared coat?

To the left was fat Roger, grinning and blinking into the flashbulb, having raised his glass of wine to the nightclub camera: a man out on the town, celebrating, having a good time. "The jolly Roger": with his peculiar private irony Richard had sometimes called his brother that. On the right was skinny tortured Richard, who was staring at his brother with a gaze that was at the same time stern and full of an immoderate love. Between them, recessed into half shadow, was the long-necked beautiful dark girl, who was looking at Richard as though she thought he was either marvelous or crazy. Or perhaps she herself looked crazy. In the bright flat light her collar made an odd shadow on her cheek, and her eyes were a strange shape — very narrow and long, like fish.

Karen sighed heavily, and then sneezed from the dust. Although of German extraction she was a poor housekeeper, and did not like to be reminded of that fact, of which both the dust and the presence of that picture on an untouched shelf did remind her. Retreating from the closet, she put the picture on her husband's dressing table, meaning to ask him about it that night. She was a big dark handsome girl, descended from successful generations of Berlin bankers; her father, the last of the line, had come to San Francisco in the Twenties, well before Hitler, and had been prominent in the founding of a local bank. Karen had already, in ten years of marriage to Roger, produced five sons, five stalwart big Washingtons who did not remember their difficult doomed Southern uncle, Uncle Richard, cartons of whose books were still unpacked in the basement.

Karen remembered Richard very well, and she thought of him for a great deal of that day as she moved about the enormous, unwieldy, and expensive house on Pacific Street, bought when Richard died and they inherited his money. The house from its northern windows had mammoth views of the Bay, and the bridge, Sausalito, the hills of Marin County. That day, that March, there were threatening rain clouds, a shifting kaleidoscope of them, an infinite variety of grays.

Karen had felt and still did feel an uncomfortable mixture of emotions in regard to Richard, one of which was certainly the guilty impatience of the healthy with the sick. Richard had been born with a defective heart, ten months after Roger's healthy and very normal birth, and had suffered greatly during his lifetime. But beyond his irremediable physical pain he had seemed, somehow, to choose to be lonely and miserable. He lived in a strange hotel even after he got his money; he was given to isolated, hopeless love affairs, generally with crazy girls ("Affairs with psychopaths are a marvelous substitute for intimacy," he had been heard to say.) He only bought books and records; his clothes were impossible.

Like many very secure and contented people, Karen tended to be somewhat unimaginative about the needs, emotional and otherwise, of those who were not content, of those who were in fact miserable. To her credit she knew this, and so she sighed as she moved incompetently about her house with the vacuum cleaner; she sighed for Richard and for her own failure to have understood or in any way to have helped him.

Karen's deficiencies as a housekeeper were more than made up for by her abilities as a cook, or so her greedy husband and most of their greedy friends thought. That afternoon, as heavy dark rains enshrouded the city and the Bay, Karen made a superior moussaka, which was one of Roger's favorites. It had also been a favorite of Richard's, and she was pleased to remember that she had at least done that for him.

Then, just as she had finished, from upstairs she heard the youngest child begin to whimper, waking up from his nap, and she went up to get him, to bathe and dress him before the older boys all tumbled home from school.

The maid would come at three and stay until after dinner, since Roger liked a formal evening meal.

Karen was dressing, and lost in a long skirt that she tried to pull down over big breasts, down over her increasing thighs, when Roger came in and asked her about the picture.

"What's that doing out here?" "Here" was "heah"; Roger had kept his Southern voice, though less strongly than Richard had.

Her head came out of the dress, and she bridled at the annoyance in his tone. "Why not? It was up on your top shirt shelf." At worst, in some atavistic Germanic way, Karen became coy. "Some old girl friend you haven't told me about?" she said.

Roger was holding the picture, blinking at it in the harsh light from Karen's makeup lamp, holding it closer and closer to the bulb as though he would burn it if the picture did not reveal all that he wanted to know. He was not thinking about Karen.

"She's beautiful," said Karen. She came to look over his shoulder, and pressed her cheek against his arm. She knew that he loved her.

"She was Richard's girl. Ellen. After that." He pointed unnecessarily at the picture. "We were celebrating his money, after he finally sold his land. That was the night he met her."

Karen was quiet, looking at the peculiar girl, and at Richard, whom no large sums of money had cheered, and at jolly Roger.

"What a creepy girl," Roger said. "Richard's worst. She finally had to be locked up. Probably still is."

"Oh." Karen shuddered.

Roger put the picture down with a heavy sigh. He was fatter now than when it was taken; his neck was deeply creased with fat, and his big cheeks drooped.

Then abruptly he turned around and embraced Karen with unaccustomed vigor. "What's for dinner?" he asked. "Did I smell what I think I did?"

Because Richard had been sick so much and had been tutored, he and Roger ended by finishing high school in the same June of 1943, and that July they entered Harvard together, two Southern 4-F's in giddy wartime

Cambridge, fat Roger, who also had a punctured eardrum, and thin sick Richard. They both reacted to that scene with an immediate and violent loneliness. Together they were completely isolated from all those uniforms, from the desperately gay urgency of that war, that bright New England climate.

Roger's fat and Richard's illnesses had also isolated them in childhood; they were unpopular boys who spent most of their afternoons at home, reading or devising private games. But to be isolated and unpopular in a small town where everyone knows you is also to be surrounded — if not with warmth at least with the knowledge of your history. There is always the old lady approaching on the sidewalk who says, "Aren't you Sophie Washington's boys? I declare, the fat one is the living spit of your grandfather." Or the mean little girl in the corner grocery store who chants softly, "Skinny and fat, skinny and fat, I never saw two brothers like that."

They had too an enormous retreat from the world: that huge house full of books everywhere. And the aging pale parents, Josiah and Sophie Washington, who had been and continued to be surprised at finding themselves parents, who retreated from parenthood to long conversations about the histories of other Southern families. "It was a perfect background for eccentrics of the future," Richard later told Ellen.

Both Roger and Richard had chosen history as their field of concentration at Harvard. During those summer afternoons, and into the gaudy fall, while R.O.T.C. units drilled in the Yard and pretty Radcliffe girls — in sloppy sweaters and skirts, white athletic socks and loafers — lounged on the steps of Widener Library, Richard and Roger studied furiously in their ground-floor rooms in Adams House, and at night they went to movies. Every night a movie, in suburbs as far-lying as the subway system would carry them, until one night when the only movie they had not seen twice was *I Wanted Wings*, in Arlington. So they stayed home and for a joke read chapters of *Lee's Lieutenants* aloud to each other, which was not one of the texts for History I but which was the only book in the room they had not already read. It had been an off-to-college present from their not very imaginative mother. In stage Southern accents they read to each other about Fredericksburg and Chickamauga, Appomattox and Antietam.

Roger had a photographic memory, of which Richard was wildly proud. His own memory was erratic; he easily memorized poetry but he had a lot of trouble with names and dates, with facts. As they walked across the Yard in the brilliant September air, Roger recited several pages from that book, still in that wildly exaggerated accent: ". . . and before the Northern armies could marshal their forces . . ." while Richard gamboled beside him, laughing like a monkey.

They were taking a course called Philosophic Problems of the Postwar World. With everyone else they stood around outside Emerson Hall, waiting for the hour to sound. Richard was overheard to say to Roger, in that crazy Southern voice, "As I see it, the chief postwar problem is what to do with the black people."

At the end of the summer Roger had four A's and Richard had two A's, a C, and a D, the D being in Biology. They had no friends. Richard regarded their friendlessness as a sign of their superiority; no one else was as brilliant, as amusing, as his brother, and thus they were unappreciated. Roger didn't think much about that sort of thing then. He was solely concentrated on getting top grades.

Those Harvard years were, or perhaps became in memory, the happiest of Richard's life. Completely isolated from their classmates and from the war that for most people dominated the scene, he and Roger went about their scholarly pursuits; he had Roger's almost undivided attention, and it was a time when Roger laughed at all his jokes.

Aside from the Southern joke, which was their mainstay, they developed a kind of wild irony of their own, an irony that later would have been called sick, or black. Roger's obesity came into this. "You must have another hot dog, you won't last the afternoon," Richard would say as Roger wolfed down his seventh hot dog at lunch at the corner stand. And when Roger did order and eat another hot dog they both thought that wildly funny. Richard's heart was funny too. At the foot of the steps of Widener Roger would say, "Come on, I'll race you up to the top," and they would stand there, helplessly laughing.

That was how Richard remembered those years: big fat Roger, tilted to one side chuckling hugely, and himself, dark and wiry and bent double laughing, in the Cambridge sun. And he remembered that he could even be careless about his health in those years; he almost never hurt. They went for long walks in all the variously beautiful weathers of Cambridge. Years later, in seasonless California, Richard would sigh for some past Cambridge spring, or summer or fall. Roger remembered much less: for one thing he was in later life so extremely busy.

They were reacted to at Harvard for the most part with indifference; other people were also preoccupied, and also that is how, in general, Harvard is — it lets you alone. However, they did manage to be irritating: to the then current remark, "Don't you know there's a war on?" both Roger and Richard Washington had been heard to respond, "Sir, the War has been over for almost a hundred years." Also, those were very "liberal" years; racism, or what sounded like it, was very unpopular. No one made jokes about black people, no one but Roger and Richard.

Therefore, it is not too surprising that one night Roger and Richard came back from the movies (a revival of a *Broadway Melody* in Dorchester: Roger loved musicals) to find that someone had put a swastika in black chalk on the door to their room. Richard was absolutely enchanted; in a way it was the highest moment of his life. All his sense of the monstrosity of the outside world was justified, as well as his fondness for drama; he was persecuted and isolated with his brother. "Roger," he said very loudly and very Southernly, "do you reckon that's some kind of Indian sign they've gone and put on our door?"

Roger laughed too, or later Richard remembered Roger as laughing, but he recalled mainly his own delight in that climatic illuminated moment. They went into their room and shut the door, and after them someone yelled from down the stairwell, "Southern Fascists!" Richard went on chortling with pleasure, lying across the studio couch, while Roger walked thoughtfully about the room, that big bare room made personal only by their books and some dark curtains now drawn against the heady Cambridge spring night. Then Roger put a Lotte Lenya record on the player.

That was more or less that. The next day the janitor washed the chalk off, and Roger and Richard did not speculate as to who had put it there. Anyone could have.

But a week or so later Roger told Richard that he was tired of history; he was switching his field of concentration to economics. And then he would go to law school. "Fat makes you already eccentric," he said. "And eccentrics have to be rich."

"In that case I'll switch to Greek," Richard countered furiously, "and remain land poor."

And that shorthand conversation made perfect sense to both of them.

They both did what they said they would, except that soon after their graduation (Roger *summa cum laude* and Phi Beta) Richard had a heart attack that kept him in the hospital at home in Virginia, off and on for a couple of years, fending off his anxious mother and writing long funny letters to Roger, who seemed to be enjoying law school.

So it worked out that by the time Richard went back to Harvard for his master's in Greek literature, Roger had got out of law school and gone out to San Francisco, where he began to succeed as a management consultant to increasingly important firms. He was too busy even to come home for the funerals of his parents, who died within a month of each other during his first winter in San Francisco — Josiah and Sophie Washington, who had, they thought, divided their land equally between their two sons. Roger sold his immediately for thirty thousand, and thought he had done very well. He urged Richard to do the same, but Richard lazily or perversely held on to his, until the advent of a freeway forced him to sell, for a hundred thousand.

Richard did not enjoy his second time at Harvard, except in the sense that one does enjoy a season of mourning. He was terribly lonely, he missed Roger vividly, everywhere in Cambridge, and his heart hurt most of the time.

Thus it was not until the early Fifties that Richard got his teaching job in the boys' school in San Francisco, and came out to see his brother again. And then came into his money, and met Ellen.

In those days, even after getting his money, Richard lived in a downtown hotel — his eccentricity. He had a large room that the maid was not allowed to enter. ("In that case why live in a hotel?" practical Roger had asked.) The room was stacked everywhere with books, with records and papers. Richard took most of his meals in the hotel dining room; after he came home from a day of teaching he rarely went out. He was not well; much of the time he felt dizzy, and he ached, but again it was hard to gauge the degree to which his loneliness was chosen. If Roger, for example, had had a bad heart he would undoubtedly have had it continually in the midst of a crowd.

Indeed, in the years since his Harvard isolation Roger had become extremely gregarious. Professionally he was hyperactive; his entire intelligence and energy were occupied. And a vivid social life grew out of professional contacts. People whose adviser he was in a legal economic sense also asked him to dinner, and he became known as a very courtly, if somewhat ponderous bachelor, as well as an astute businessman. Roger was greedy for company; he reveled in all his invitations, his cocktails and dinners and his girls.

Girls who fell in love with Richard were always girls with whom Roger had not been successful; that was how Richard met girls. In one of their rare conversations about relationships with women, Roger remarked on Richard's perfect score with women; Richard had never been turned down.

"But with how many ladies have I — uh — attempted to prove my valor?" Richard asked, in the parody Southern manner that he sometimes tried to continue with Roger. "Four, or is it three? I sometimes lose track of these — uh — astronomicals."

Ellen made five.

One March afternoon, a few months after they had met, Richard lay across some tufts of new grass on the bank of a duck pond in Golden Gate Park, watching Ellen, who was out wading among the ducks. Like a child, she held her skirt bunched up in front of her, at the top of her long thin childish legs. Water still had spattered the shabby gray flannel; Ellen visibly didn't care. She splashed out toward some brown ducks who were peacefully squatted on the surface of the pond. They fled, scuttering across the water, submarining under, as Ellen screamed out, "See! They know I'm here!"

Her long fish eyes that day were almost blue with excitement. When she was unhappy or simply remote they were gray. After she finally went mad they were gray all the time.

At the farther edge of the pond were willows, now thickly green with spring; they grew out into the water in heavy clusters. And all about the pond were tall eucalyptus, scenting the air with lemon, shedding their bark in long strips, as the breeze fluttered their sad green scimitar leaves above Richard's heavy head.

Out of the water, out of her element, Ellen became a detached and languorous girl who sat on the grass not far from Richard, clutching her arms about her knees and watching him curiously, listening to that tormented and violent Southern talk.

"Interest! *Interest!*" was what Richard was saying. "My own brother, my *heir*, and he offers me interest on a loan. My God, I told him, 'You're my brother, take all the money, but for God's sake don't offer me interest.'"

Above the trees pale-gray clouds drifted ceremoniously across the sky. Half closing her eyes, Ellen turned them into doves, flocks and flocks of pale soft gray doves.

"God, if I'd only sold the bloody land when Roger sold his," said Richard for the tenth or perhaps the hundredth time that day. "And got only thirty thousand like him instead of this bloody hundred."

Richard's wildness and the intensity of his pain had oddly a calming effect on Ellen. Unlike most people, who were frightened or impatient or even — like Roger — bored, Ellen experienced with Richard a reduction of the panic in which she normally lived. Rather reasonably she asked him what she had often been told but had forgotten: "Why didn't you sell it then?"

"I preferred to be land poor." This was in the old stage Southern voice. "Ah pruhfuhd." Then, "Christ, I didn't want the money. I still don't. If I could only just give it to him. Without dying, that is." And he laughed wildly.

By this time pain had deeply lined Richard's face. There were heavy lines across his forehead, lines down the sides of his nose and beside his wide, intensely compressed mouth. Many people, especially recent friends of Roger's, considered Richard to be crazy, but even they were aware that what sounded like madness could have been an outcry against sheer physical suffering.

"I may not even go to New York," Ellen said. "It takes so much nerve."

Ellen was a mathematician — "of all things," as most people said. Especially her Oakland-Baptist-John Birch Society mother said that, and often. Ellen was talented and had been offered a fellowship at Columbia.

"Stay here," Richard said. "Let me keep you. God, won't anybody take my money?"

The melodramatic note in that last told Ellen that Richard was going to talk about Roger again, and she sighed. She liked it better when he was reading poetry to her, or when he didn't talk at all and played records, Telemann and Boccherini, Haydn and Schubert, in his cluttered and most personal room.

But Richard said, "Roger wants to invest in some resort land at Squaw Valley, with some of his rich new German friends. Do you know the altitude at Squaw Valley? Six thousand feet. I wouldn't last a minute there. How to explain why his brother is never invited for weekends or summer vacations. I am socially unacceptable to my brother — isn't that marvelous?"

Richard's eyes were beautiful; they were large and clear and gray, in that agonized face. Those eyes exposed all his pain and anger and despair, his eyes and his passionate deep Southern voice. He was really too much for anyone, and certainly for himself. And there were times, especially when he ranted endlessly and obsessively about Roger, when even Ellen wanted to be away from him, to be with some dull and ordinary person.

Ellen had met Roger, who always retained a few intellectual friends, at a Berkeley cocktail party, and she had had dinner with him a couple of times before the night they celebrated Richard's money at the silly expensive restaurant, where the picture was taken. Ellen had not liked Roger very much. He was exceptionally bright; she recognized and responded to that, but she was used to very bright people, and all the money-power-society talk that Roger tried to impress her with alarmed her. "You could marry extremely well if you wanted to," Roger told her. "With your skin and those eyes and those long legs. And no one should marry on less than thirty thousand a year. It can't be done." Then he had laughed. "But you'd probably rather marry a starving poet, wouldn't you? Come and meet my crazy brother, though, even if he has just come into money."

And so Richard and Ellen met, and in their fashions fell in love.

Now, feeling dizzy, Richard lay back on the bright-green grass and stared up through the lowering maze of silvered leaves to the gray procession of clouds. Sickness sometimes made him maudlin; now he closed his eyes and imagined that instead of the pond there was a river near his feet, the Virginia James of his childhood, or the Charles at Harvard, with Roger.

Not opening his eyes but grinning wildly to himself, he asked Ellen, "Did I ever tell you about the night they put the swastika on our door?"

Of course Richard lent Roger the money, with no interest, and their dwindling relationship continued.

Sometimes even in the midst of his burgeoning social life Roger was lonely; he hated to be alone. Sometimes late at night he would telephone to Richard, who always stayed up late reading and playing records. These conversations, though never long, were how they kept in touch.

At some point, a couple of years after Richard had met Ellen, Roger began to talk about a girl named Karen Erdman, and Richard knew that she was the one he would marry. But Roger took a long time deciding — Karen was a patient girl. Richard did not meet Karen until the engagement party, but he was so intuitively attuned to his brother that he could see her and feel the quality of her presence: that big generous and intelligent girl who adored his brother. After all, Richard also loved Roger.

"The question seems to me," advised Richard, "as to whether you want to marry at all. If you do, obviously Karen is the girl you should marry."

"I have a very good time as a bachelor," Roger mused. "But it takes too much of my time. You break off with one girl and then you have to go looking for another, and at first you have to spend all that time talking to them."

"God, what a romantic view. In that case perhaps you should marry."

"But she wants children. I find it impossible to imagine children."

"Sir, what kind of a man would deplore the possibility of progeny?" Richard asked, in their old voice.

"I can't decide what to do," said Roger. Then, as an afterthought: "How is Ellen?"

"Marvelous. She has managed to turn down four fellowships in one year."

"She's crazy."

"You're right there."

"Well. Good night."

"Good night."

A heavy engraved invitation invited Richard to the Erdmans' engagement party for their daughter. "Oddly enough," Richard said to Ellen. "Since they're being married at Tahoe I'm surprised they didn't do the whole thing up there. Or simply not mention it till later. God knows I don't read the society pages."

Richard was not asked to bring Ellen.

The Erdman house, in Seacliff, was manorial. Broad halls led into broader, longer rooms; immense windows showed an enormous view of the Bay. And the décor was appropriately sumptuous: satins and velvets and silks, walnut and mahogany and gilt. Aubusson and Louis XV. For that family those were the proper surroundings. They were big dark rich people who dressed and ate and entertained extremely well.

In those crowded, scented, overheated rooms Richard's pale lined face was wet. He went out so infrequently; the profusion and brilliance of expensive clothes, in all possible fabrics, of jewels — all made him dizzily stare. The acres of tables of incredibly elaborate food made him further perspire. He stood about in corners, trying to cope with his dizziness and wildly wondering what he could find to say to anyone there. Lunatic phrases of gallantry came to him. Could he say to the beautiful blonde across the room, "I just love the way you do your hair, it goes so well with your shoes"? Or, to the tall distinguished European, who was actually wearing his decorations, "I understand you're in money, sir. I'm in Greek myself. Up to my ass in Greek." No, he could not say anything. He had nothing to say.

Roger's new circle included quite a few Europeans, refugees like his father-in-law to be, and Mr. Erdman's friends, and transients: visiting representatives of banks, commercial attachés and consuls. The rest were mainly San Francisco's very solid merchant upper class: German Jewish families who had had a great deal of money for a long time. They were very knowledgeable about music and they bought good paintings on frequent trips to Europe. Among those people Roger looked completely at home; even his heavy Southern courtliness took on a European flavor.

Mrs. Erdman was still a remarkably pretty woman, with smooth dark hair in wings and round loving eyes as she regarded both her husband and her daughter. Richard found this especially remarkable; he had never known a girl with a nice mother and he imagined that such girls were a breed apart. Ellen's mother had jumped under a train when Ellen was thirteen and miraculously survived with an amputated foot.

Mrs. Erdman was a very nice woman and she wanted to be nice to Richard, once it was clear to her who he was. The two boys were so unlike that it was hard to believe. "I'm so sorry that you won't be able to come up to the lake for the wedding," she said sympathetically.

"But who'd want a corpse at a wedding?" Richard cackled. "Where on earth would you hide it?" Then, seeing her stricken face and knowing how rude he had been, and how well she had meant, he tried again: "I just love the way you do your hair — " But that was no good either, and he stopped, midsentence.

Mrs. Erdman smiled in a vague and puzzled way. It was sad, and obvious that poor Richard was insane. And how difficult for poor Roger that must be.

Roger was beaming. His creased fat face literally shone with pleasure, which, for the sake of dignity, he struggled to contain. Having decided to marry, he found the idea of marriage very moving, and he was impressed by the rightness of his choice. People fall in love in very divergent ways; in Roger's way he was now in love with Karen, and he would love her more in years to come. He was even excited by the idea of children, big handsome Californian children, who were not eccentric. He stood near the middle of the enormous entrance hall, with Karen near his side, and beamed. He was prepared for nothing but good.

Then suddenly, from the midst of all that rich good will, from that air that was heavy with favorable omens, he heard the wild loud voice of his brother, close at hand. "Say, Roger, remember the night they put the swastika on our door?"

There was a lull in the surrounding conversations as that terrible word reverberated in the room. Then an expectant hum began to fill the vacuum. Feeling himself everywhere stared at, and hearing one nervous giggle, Roger attempted a jolly laugh. "You're crazy," he said. "You've been reading too many books. Karen, darling, isn't it time we went into the other room?"

It is perhaps to the credit of everyone's tact that Richard was then able to leave unobtrusively, as the front door opened to admit new guests.

And a month later, two months before the June wedding at Lake Tahoe, Richard had a severe heart attack and died at Mount Zion Hospital, with Ellen and Roger at his bedside.

They had been watching there at close intervals for almost the entire past week, and they were both miserably exhausted. Even their customary wariness in regard to each other had died, along with Richard.

"Come on, let me buy you some coffee," said Roger, fat and paternal. "You look bad."

"So do you," she said. "Exhausted.. Thanks, I'd like some coffee."

He took her to a quiet bar in North Beach, near where she was then living, and they sat in a big recessed booth, in the dim late-afternoon light, and ordered espresso. "Or would you like a cappuccino?" Roger asked. "Something sweet?"

"No. Thanks. Espresso is fine."

The waiter went away.

"Well," said Roger.

"Well," echoed Ellen. "Of course it's not as though we hadn't known all along. What was going to happen."

The flat reasonableness of her tone surprised Roger. Ellen was never reasonable. So he looked at her with a little suspicion, but there was nothing visible on her white face but fatigue and sadness. The strain of her effort at reasonableness, at control, was not visible.

Roger said, "Yes. But I wonder if we really believed it. I mean Richard talked so much about dying that it was hard to believe he would."

The coffee came.

Stirring in sugar, regarding her cup, Ellen said, "People who talk about jumping under trains still sometimes do it. But I know what you mean. We somehow didn't behave as though he would die. Isn't that it?" She lifted her very gray eyes to his blinking pale blue.

He took the sugar, poured and stirred. "Yes, but I wonder what different we would have done."

In her same flat sensible tone Ellen said, "I sometimes wouldn't see him when he wanted to. I would be tired or just not up to it, or sometimes seeing someone else. Even if the other person was a boring nothing." She looked curiously at Roger.

But he had only heard the literal surface of what she had said, to which he responded with a little flicker of excitement. "Exactly!" he said. "He was hurt and complained when I went to boring dinners or saw business friends instead of him, but I had to do that. Sometimes for my own protection."

"Yes," said Ellen, still very calm but again with an oblique, upward look at Roger, which he missed.

"People grow up and they change." Roger sighed. "I could hardly remember all that time at Harvard and he always wanted to talk about it."

"Of course not," she said, staring at him and holding her hands tightly together in her lap, as though they contained her mind.

Roger was aware that he was acting out of character; normally he loathed these intimate, self-revelatory conversations. But he was extremely tired and, as he afterward told himself, he was understandably upset; it is not every day that one's only brother dies. Also, as he was vaguely aware, some quality in Ellen, some quality of her listening, drove him on. Her flat silence made a vacuum that he was compelled to fill.

"And remember that time a couple of years ago when I wanted to borrow the money?" Roger said. "He was so upset that I offered him interest. Of course I'd offer him interest. Otherwise it wouldn't have been fair."

"Of course not," said Ellen, looking deeply into his eyes. "Everyone has to pay interest," she reasonably said.

"It was the least I could do," Roger said. "To be fair to him. And I couldn't spend the rest of my life thinking and talking about how things were almost twenty years ago."

"Of course not," Ellen said again, and soon after that he took her home and they parted — friends.

But in the middle of that night Roger's phone rang, beside his wide bachelor bed, and it was Ellen.

"Pig pig pig pig pig pig pig pig pig!" she screamed. "Horrible fat ugly murdering pig, you killed him with your never time to see him and your wall of fat German business friends always around you and your everything for a purpose and your filthy pig-minded greed and your all-American pig success and your so socially acceptable ambitions. Richard was all Greek to you and you never tried to learn him, how lovely he was and suffering and you found him not socially acceptable to your new society and your new pig friends and I would even rather be thin and miserable and ugly me than fat you with your blubber neck and your compound interest and you couldn't believe his heart and now you can get filthy blubber fatter on his money — "

She seemed to have run down, and into the pause Roger asked, "Ellen, do you need money? I'd be more than happy — "

She screamed, but it was less a scream than a sound of total despair, from an absolute aloneness.

Then she hung up, and a few weeks later Roger heard that she had had a complete breakdown and was hospitalized, perhaps for good.

After the excellent dinner of moussaka, salad and strawberries in cream, Karen and Roger settled in the living room with strong coffee and snifters of brandy. It was an attractive, comfortable, if somewhat disheveled room, very much a family room. Karen's tastes were simpler than those of her parents. Her furnishings were contemporary; the fabrics were sturdy wools or linen; the broad sofa was done in dark-brown leather.

Roger leaned back; he blinked and then sighed, looking up to the ceiling. Karen could tell that he was going to say something about Richard.

"I sometimes wish," said Roger, "that I'd taken the time somewhere along the line to have learned a little Greek. It seemed to give Richard so much pleasure."

"But, darling, when would you ever have had the time?"

"That's just it, I never had the time." Roger's tone when talking about or in any way alluding to his brother was one of a softly sentimental regret; Karen gathered that he regretted both his brother's death and their lack of rapport in those final years.

Roger also sounded sentimentally regretful when he referred to anything cultural — those soft pleasures which he valued but for which he had never had time.

"I wonder what's ever happened to that girl, Ellen," said Karen.

"I'm not sure I'd even want to know," said Roger. "Did I ever tell you that she called me the night he died?"

"Really? No."

"Yes, she was quite hysterical. I think she was angry because she knew I was Richard's heir." By now Roger had come to believe that this was indeed the case. He was convinced that other people's motives were basically identical to his own. "Yes," he said. "She probably thought I should give her some of his money."

In the large safe room, beneath the other large rooms where her sons were all sleeping, Karen shuddered, and together she and Roger sighed, for Richard's pain and death and for poor lost Ellen's madness.

"Here," said Karen, "have more coffee. Poor darling, you look as though you need it."

"You're right. I do." And Roger reached out to stroke his big wife's smooth dark cheek.   [1967]

GABRIEL GARCÍA MÁRQUEZ (b. 1928) was born in the remote small town of Aracataca in Magdalena province, near the Caribbean seacoast of Colombia. As the oldest of twelve children of a poverty-stricken telegraph operator and his wife, he was raised in the home of his maternal grandparents. When he was eight years old he was sent away to school near Bogotá, and after his graduation in 1946 he studied law until civil war in Colombia closed the university. A writer from childhood, García Márquez published his first stories in 1947. After he began to earn his living as a reporter and film critic, he worked on a novel and short fiction. His first book was Leaf Storm and Other Stories (1955), which included "A Very Old Man with Enormous Wings," originally published in English translation in The New American Review. García Márquez spent the next few years in Paris, where he wrote two short novels, No One Writes to the Colonel (1958) and In Evil Hour (1961). After the Cuban Revolution, he returned to Central America and worked as a journalist and screenwriter. His great comic masterpiece, the novel One Hundred Years of Solitude (1967), was written while he lived in Mexico City; it received several major international literary prizes. In 1972 he published a new collection of stories, The Incredible and Sad Tale of Innocent Erendira and Her Heartless Grandmother. The Autumn of the Patriarch (1975), a novel about the life of a Latin American dictator, was acclaimed as a work at least as important as the earlier One Hundred Years of Solitude. In 1982 García Márquez received the Nobel Prize for Literature.

García Márquez's fiction has been compared by the London Times Literary Supplement to Cervantes's Don Quixote, because, like Cervantes, García Márquez writes allegories in which his characters are placed "in a hybrid world in which the imaginary and the marvelous are weighted down by drab and sordid reality." He mingles realistic and fantastic details in all of his fiction, including "A Very Old Man with Enormous Wings," to suggest a sense of the world's mystery. As the author Paul Theroux has recognized, "Religion is often seen as barren and stultifying, a stubborn and constricting preoccupation, but there are minds which find release in it and then soar to tremendous heights of imagination. Gabriel García Márquez may not be pious in the traditional sense; however, there is in his stories . . . a pervasive tone of imaginative religiosity, a mystical lyricism in even the simplest exchange."

The book Leaf Storm and Other Stories was written after García Márquez returned from a visit to the house in Aracataca where he had spent his early childhood. As he later explained to an interviewer from The Paris Review:

I'm not sure whether I had already read Faulkner or not, but I know now that only a technique like Faulkner's could have enabled me to write down what I was seeing. The atmosphere, the decadence, the heat in the village were roughly the same as what I had felt in Faulkner. It was a banana plantation region inhabited by a lot of Americans from the fruit companies which gave it the same sort of atmosphere I had found in the writers of the Deep South. Critics have spoken of the literary influence of Faulkner but I see it as a coincidence: I had simply found material that had to be dealt with in the same way that Faulkner had treated similar material. . . .

What really happened to me in that trip to Aracataca was that I realized that everything that had occurred in my childhood had a literary value that I was only now appreciating. From the moment I wrote Leaf Storm *I realized I wanted to be a writer and that nobody could stop me and that the only thing left for me to do was to be the best writer in the world.*

Gabriel García Márquez

෧෧

A Very Old Man with Enormous Wings

– translated by Gabriel García Márquez

On the third day of rain they had killed so many crabs inside the house that Pelayo had to cross his drenched courtyard and throw them into the sea, because the newborn child had a temperature all night and they thought it was due to the stench. The world had been sad since Tuesday. Sea and sky were a single ash-gray thing and the sands of the beach, which on March nights glimmered like powdered light, had become a stew of mud and rotten shellfish. The light was so weak at noon that when Pelayo was coming back to the house after throwing away the crabs, it was hard for him to see what it was that was moving and groaning in the rear of the courtyard. He had to go very close to see that it was an old man, a very old man, lying face down in the mud, who, in spite of his tremendous efforts, couldn't get up, impeded by his enormous wings.

Frightened by that nightmare, Pelayo ran to get Elisenda, his wife, who was putting compresses on the sick child, and he took her to the rear of the courtyard. They both looked at the fallen body with mute stupor. He was dressed like a ragpicker. There were only a few faded hairs left on his bald skull and very few teeth in his mouth, and his pitiful condition of a drenched great-grandfather had taken away any sense of grandeur he might have had. His huge buzzard wings, dirty and half-plucked, were forever entangled in the mud. They looked at him so long and so closely that Pelayo and Elisenda very soon overcame their surprise and in the end found him familiar. Then they dared speak to him, and he answered in an incomprehensible dialect with a strong sailor's voice. That was how they skipped over the inconvenience of the wings and quite intelligently concluded that he was a lonely castaway from some foreign ship wrecked by the storm. And yet, they called in a neighbor woman who knew everything about life and death to see him, and all she needed was one look to show them their mistake.

"He's an angel," she told them. "He must have been coming for the child, but the poor fellow is so old that the rain knocked him down."

On the following day everyone knew that a flesh-and-blood angel was held captive in Pelayo's house. Against the judgment of the wise neighbor woman, for whom angels in those times were the fugitive survivors of a celestial conspiracy, they did not have the heart to club him to death. Pelayo watched over him all afternoon from the kitchen, armed with his bailiff's club, and before going to bed he dragged him out of the mud and locked him up with the hens in the wire chicken coop. In the middle of the night, when the rain stopped, Pelayo and Elisenda were still killing crabs. A short time afterward the child woke up without a fever and with a desire to eat. Then they felt magnanimous and decided to put the angel on a raft with fresh water and provisions for three days and leave him to his fate on the high seas. But when they went out into the courtyard with the first light of dawn, they found the whole neighborhood in front of the chicken coop having fun with the angel, without the slightest reverence, tossing him things to eat through the openings in the wire as if he weren't a supernatural creature but a circus animal.

Father Gonzaga arrived before seven o'clock, alarmed at the strange news. By that time onlookers less frivolous than those at dawn had already arrived and they were making all kinds of conjectures concerning the captive's future. The simplest among them thought that he should be named mayor of the world. Others of sterner mind felt that he should be promoted to the rank of five-star general in order to win all wars. Some visionaries hoped that he could be put to stud in order to implant on earth a race of winged wise men who could take charge of the universe. But Father Gonzaga, before becoming a priest, had been a robust woodcutter. Standing by the wire, he reviewed his catechism in an instant and asked them to open the door so that he could take a close look at that pitiful man who looked more like a huge decrepit hen among the fascinated chickens. He was lying in a corner drying his open wings in the sunlight among the fruit peels and breakfast leftovers that the early risers had thrown him. Alien to the impertinences of the world, he only lifted his antiquarian eyes and murmured something in his dialect when Father Gonzaga went into the chicken coop and said good morning to him in Latin. The parish priest had his first suspicion of an impostor when he saw that he did not understand the language of God or know how to greet His ministers. Then he noticed that seen close up he was much too human: he had an unbearable smell of the outdoors, the back side of his wings was strewn with parasites and his main feathers had been mistreated by terrestrial winds, and nothing about him measured up to the proud dignity of angels. Then he came out of the chicken coop and in a brief sermon warned the curious against the risks of being ingenuous. He reminded them that the devil had the bad habit of making use of carnival tricks in order to confuse the unwary. He argued that if wings were not the essential element in determining the difference between a hawk and an airplane, they were even less so in the recognition of angels. Nevertheless, he promised to write a letter to his bishop so that the latter would write to his primate so that the latter would write to the Supreme Pontiff in order to get the final verdict from the highest courts.

His prudence fell on sterile hearts. The news of the captive angel spread with such rapidity that after a few hours the courtyard had the bustle of a marketplace and they had to call in troops with fixed bayonets to disperse the mob that was about to knock the house down. Elisenda, her spine all twisted from sweeping up so much marketplace trash, then got the idea of fencing in the yard and charging five cents admission to see the angel.

The curious came from far away. A traveling carnival arrived with a flying acrobat who buzzed over the crowd several times, but no one paid any attention to him because his wings were not those of an angel but, rather, those of a sidereal[1] bat. The most unfortunate invalids on earth came in search of health: a poor woman who since childhood had been counting her heartbeats and had run out of numbers; a Portuguese man who couldn't sleep because the noise of the stars disturbed him; a sleep-walker who got up at night to undo the things he had done while awake; and many others with less serious ailments. In the midst of that shipwreck disorder that made the earth tremble, Pelayo and Elisenda were happy with fatigue, for in less than a week they had crammed their rooms with money and the line of pilgrims waiting their turn to enter still reached beyond the horizon.

The angel was the only one who took no part in his own act. He spent his time trying to get comfortable in his borrowed nest, befuddled by the hellish heat of the oil lamps and sacramental candles that had been placed along the wire. At first they tried to make him eat some mothballs, which, according to the wisdom of the wise neighbor woman, were the food prescribed for angels. But he turned them down, just as he turned down the papal lunches that the penitents brought him, and they never found out whether it was because he was an angel or because he was an old man that in the end he ate nothing but eggplant mush. His only supernatural virtue

---

[1] coming from the stars.

seemed to be patience. Especially during the first days, when the hens pecked at him, searching for the stellar parasites that proliferated in his wings, and the cripples pulled out feathers to touch their defective parts with, and even the most merciful threw stones at him, trying to get him to rise so they could see him standing. The only time they succeeded in arousing him was when they burned his side with an iron for branding steers, for he had been motionless for so many hours that they thought he was dead. He awoke with a start, ranting in his hermetic language and with tears in his eyes, and he flapped his wings a couple of times, which brought on a whirlwind of chicken dung and lunar dust and a gale of panic that did not seem to be of this world. Although many thought that his reaction had been one not of rage but of pain, from then on they were careful not to annoy him, because the majority understood that his passivity was not that of a hero taking his ease but that of a cataclysm in repose.

Father Gonzaga held back the crowd's frivolity with formulas of maidservant inspiration while awaiting the arrival of a final judgment on the nature of the captive. But the mail from Rome showed no sense of urgency. They spent their time finding out if the prisoner had a navel, if his dialect had any connection with Aramaic, how many times he could fit on the head of a pin, or whether he wasn't just a Norwegian with wings. Those meager letters might have come and gone until the end of time if a providential event had not put an end to the priest's tribulations.

It so happened that during those days, among so many other carnival attractions, there arrived in town the traveling show of the woman who had been changed into a spider for having disobeyed her parents. The admission to see her was not only less than the admission to see the angel, but people were permitted to ask her all manner of questions about her absurd state and to examine her up and down so that no one would ever doubt the truth of her horror. She was a frightful tarantula the size of a ram and with the head of a sad maiden. What was most heart-rending, however, was not her outlandish shape but the sincere affliction with which she recounted the details of her misfortune. While still practically a child she had sneaked out of her parents' house to go to a dance, and while she was coming back through the woods after having danced all night without permission, a fearful thunderclap rent the sky in two and through the crack came the lightning bolt of brimstone that changed her into a spider. Her only nourishment came from the meatballs that charitable souls chose to toss into her mouth. A spectacle like that, full of so much human truth and with such a fearful lesson, was bound to defeat without even trying that of a haughty angel who scarcely deigned to look at mortals. Besides, the few miracles attributed to the angel showed a certain mental disorder, like the blind man who didn't recover his sight but grew three new teeth, or the paralytic who didn't get to walk but almost won the lottery, and the leper whose sores sprouted sunflowers. Those consolation miracles, which were more like mocking fun, had already ruined the angel's reputation when the woman who had been changed into a spider finally crushed him completely. That was how Father Gonzaga was cured forever of his insomnia and Pelayo's courtyard went back to being as empty as during the time it had rained for three days and crabs walked through the bedrooms.

The owners of the house had no reason to lament. With the money they saved they built a two-story mansion with balconies and gardens and high netting so that crabs wouldn't get in during the winter, and with iron bars on the windows so that angels wouldn't get in. Pelayo also set up a rabbit warren close to town and gave up his job as bailiff for good, and Elisenda bought some satin pumps with high heels and many dresses of iridescent silk, the kind worn on Sunday by the most desirable women in those times. The chicken coop was the only thing that didn't receive any attention. If they washed it down with creolin and burned tears of myrrh inside it every so often, it was not in homage to the angel but to drive away the dungheap stench that still hung everywhere like a ghost and was turning the new house into an old one. At first, when the child learned to walk, they were careful that he not get too close to the chicken coop. But then they began to lose their fears and got used to the smell, and before the child got his second teeth he'd gone inside the chicken coop to play, where the wires were falling apart. The angel was no less standoffish with him than with other mortals, but he tolerated the most ingenious infamies with the patience of a dog who had no illusions. They both came down with chicken pox at the same time. The doctor who took care of the child couldn't resist the temptation to listen to the angel's heart, and he found so much whistling in the heart and so many sounds in his kidneys that it seemed impossible for him to be alive. What surprised him most, however, was the logic of his wings. They seemed so natural on that completely human organism that he couldn't understand why other men didn't have them too.

When the child began school it had been some time since the sun and rain had caused the collapse of the chicken coop. The angel went dragging himself about here and there like a stray dying man. They would drive him out of the bedroom with a broom and a moment later find him in the kitchen. He seemed to be in so many places at the same time that they grew to think that he'd been duplicated, that he was reproducing himself all through the house, and the exasperated and unhinged Elisenda shouted that it was awful living in that hell full of angels. He could scarcely eat and his antiquarian eyes had also become so foggy that he went about bumping into posts. All he had left were the bare cannulae[2] of his last feathers. Pelayo threw a blanket over him and extended him the charity of letting him sleep in the shed, and only then did they notice that he had a temperature at night, and was delirious with the tongue twisters of an old Norwegian. That was one of the few times they became alarmed, for they thought he

[2] the tubular pieces by which feathers are attached to a body.

was going to die and not even the wise neighbor woman had been able to tell them what to do with dead angels.

And yet he not only survived his worst winter, but seemed improved with the first sunny days. He remained motionless for several days in the farthest corner of the courtyard, where no one would see him, and at the beginning of December some large, stiff feathers began to grow on his wings, the feathers of a scarecrow, which looked more like another misfortune of decrepitude. But he must have known the reason for those changes, for he was quite careful that no one should notice them, that no one should hear the sea chanteys that he sometimes sang under the stars. One morning Elisenda was cutting some bunches of onions for lunch when a wind that seemed to come from the high seas blew into the kitchen. Then she went to the window and caught the angel in his first attempts at flight. They were so clumsy that his fingernails opened a furrow in the vegetable patch and he was on the point of knocking the shed down with the ungainly flapping that slipped on the light and couldn't get a grip on the air. But he did manage to gain altitude. Elisenda let out a sigh of relief, for herself and for him, when she saw him pass over the last houses, holding himself up in some way with the risky flapping of a senile vulture. She kept watching him even when she was through cutting the onions and she kept on watching until it was no longer possible for her to see him, because then he was no longer an annoyance in her life but an imaginary dot on the horizon of the sea.

[1955]

CYNTHIA OZICK (b. 1928) sees a clear distinction between art and life: "As for life, I don't like it. I notice no 'interplay of life and art.' Life is that which — pressingly, persistently, unfailingly, imperially — interrupts." In Ozick's life there has been a long time between what Grace Paley would call "knowing and telling." Ozick received a B.A. from New York University in 1949 and an M.A. from Ohio State University in 1950 with a thesis titled "Parable in Henry James." She didn't publish her first work, the novel Trust, until 1966. Three collections of short fiction followed: The Pagan Rabbi and Other Stories (1971), Bloodshed and Three Novellas (1976), and Levitation (1981). Her latest books are a novel, The Cannibal Galaxy, and a group of essays, Art and Ardor, both published in 1983. Recently Ozick received the first $25,000 Rea Award, given annually to a living American writer whose short stories have made a significant contribution to this literary form.

In her essay "The Lesson of the Master" in Art and Ardor, Ozick described how as a young writer she was betrayed by Henry James. After college she worshiped literature, seeing herself "a priest at that altar, and that altar was all of my life." She felt that James was trying to teach her a lesson through his fiction, that an aspiring writer ought "to live immaculately, unspoiled by what we mean when we say 'life' — relationship, family mess, distraction, exhaustion, anxiety, above all disappointment." At the age of twenty-two, Ozick remembers herself as a nearsighted young woman "infected with the commonplace intention of writing a novel" and trying to live "like the elderly bald-headed Henry James." Years later, she realized her mistake. To be a writer, "one must keep one's psychological distance from the supreme artists. . . . The true Lesson of the Master, then, is, simply, never to venerate what is complete, burnished, whole. . . . never to worship ripe Art or the ripened artist; but instead to seek to be young while young, primitive while primitive, ungainly when ungainly — to look for crudeness and rudeness, to husband one's own stupidity or ungenius."

Yet Ozick also understands that life "interrupts," and the journey to art is beset with difficulties. In her best short fiction, like the Holocaust story "The Shawl," she accepts the challenge of her craft, writing in a swiftly imagistic style. She admits that "in beginning a story I know nothing at all: surely not where I am going, and hardly at all how to get there."

Cynthia Ozick

ᔥ

THE SHAWL

Stella, cold, cold, the coldness of hell. How they walked on the roads together, Rosa with Magda curled up between sore breasts, Magda wound up in the shawl. Sometimes Stella carried Magda. But she was jealous of Magda. A thin girl of fourteen, too small, with thin breasts of her own, Stella wanted to be wrapped in a shawl, hidden away, asleep, rocked by the march, a baby, a round infant in arms. Magda took Rosa's nipple, and Rosa never stopped walking, a walking cradle. There was not enough milk; sometimes Magda sucked air; then she screamed. Stella was ravenous. Her knees were tumors on sticks, her elbows chicken bones.

Rosa did not feel hunger; she felt light, not like someone walking but like someone in a faint, in trance, arrested in a fit, someone who is already a floating angel, alert and seeing everything, but in the air, not there, not touching the road. As if teetering on the tips of her fingernails. She looked into Magda's face through a gap in the shawl: a squirrel in a nest, safe, no one could reach her inside the little house of the shawl's windings. The face, very round, a pocket mirror of a face: but it was not Rosa's bleak complexion, dark like cholera, it was another kind of face altogether, eyes blue as air, smooth feathers of hair nearly as yellow as the Star sewn into Rosa's coat. You could think she was one of *their* babies.

Rosa, floating, dreamed of giving Magda away in one of the villages. She could leave the line for a minute and push Magda into the hands of any woman on the side of the road. But if she moved out of line they might shoot. And even if she fled the line for half a second and pushed the shawl-bundle at a stranger, would the woman take it? She might be surprised, or afraid; she might drop the shawl, and Magda would fall out and strike her head and die. The little round head. Such a good child, she gave up screaming, and sucked now only for the taste of the drying nipple itself. The neat grip of the tiny gums. One mite of a tooth tip sticking up in the bottom gum, how shining, an elfin tombstone of white marble, gleaming there. Without complaining, Magda relinquished Rosa's teats, first the left, then the right; both were cracked, not a sniff of milk. The duct crevice extinct, a dead volcano, blind eye, chill hole, so Magda took the corner of the shawl and milked it instead. She sucked and sucked, flooding the threads with wetness. The shawl's good flavor, milk of linen.

It was a magic shawl, it could nourish an infant for three days and three nights. Magda did not die, she stayed alive, although very quiet. A peculiar smell, of cinnamon and almonds, lifted out of her mouth. She held her eyes open every moment, forgetting how to blink or nap, and Rosa and sometimes Stella studied their blueness. On the road they raised one burden of a leg after another and studied Magda's face. "Aryan," Stella said, in a voice grown as thin as a string; and Rosa thought how Stella gazed at Magda like a young cannibal. And the time that Stella said "Aryan," it sounded to Rosa as if Stella had really said, "Let us devour her."

But Magda lived to walk. She lived that long, but she did not walk very well, partly because she was only fifteen months old, and partly because the spindles of her legs could not hold up her fat belly. It was fat with air, full and round. Rosa gave almost all her food to Magda, Stella gave nothing; Stella was ravenous, a growing child herself, but not growing much. Stella did not menstruate. Rosa did not menstruate. Rosa was ravenous, but also not; she learned from Magda how to drink the taste of a finger in one's mouth. They were in a place without pity, all pity was annihilated in Rosa, she looked at Stella's bones without pity. She was sure that Stella was waiting for Magda to die so she could put her teeth into the little thighs.

Rosa knew Magda was going to die very soon; she should have been dead already, but she had been buried away deep inside the magic shawl, mistaken there for the shivering mound of Rosa's breasts; Rosa clung to the shawl as if it covered only herself. No one took it away from her. Magda was mute. She never cried. Rosa hid her in the barracks, under the shawl, but she knew that one day someone would inform; or one day someone, not even Stella, would steal Magda to eat her. When Magda began to walk Rosa knew that Magda was going to die very soon, something would happen. She was afraid to fall asleep; she slept with the weight of her thigh on Magda's body; she was afraid she would smother Magda under her thigh. The weight of Rosa was becoming less and less; Rosa and Stella were slowly turning into air.

Magda was quiet, but her eyes were horribly alive, like blue tigers. She watched. Sometimes she laughed — it seemed a laugh, but how could it be? Magda had never seen anyone laugh. Still, Magda laughed at her shawl when the wind blew its corners, the bad wind with pieces of black in it, that made Stella's and Rosa's eyes tear. Magda's eyes were always clear and tearless. She watched like a tiger. She guarded her shawl. No one could touch it; only Rosa could touch it. Stella was not allowed. The shawl was Magda's own baby, her pet, her little sister. She tangled herself up in it and sucked on one of the corners when she wanted to be very still.

Then Stella took the shawl away and made Magda die.

Afterward Stella said: "I was cold."

And afterward she was always cold, always. The cold went into her heart: Rosa saw that Stella's heart was cold. Magda flopped onward with her little pencil legs scribbling this way and that, in search of the shawl; the pencils faltered at the barracks opening, where the light began. Rosa saw and pursued. But already Magda was in the square outside the barracks, in the jolly light. It was the roll-call arena. Every morning Rosa had to conceal Magda under the shawl against a wall of the barracks and go out and stand in the arena with Stella and hundreds of others, sometimes for hours, and Magda, deserted, was quiet under the shawl, sucking on her corner. Every day Magda was silent, and so she did not die. Rosa saw that today Magda was going to die, and at the same time a fearful joy ran in Rosa's two palms, her fingers were on fire, she was astonished, febrile: Magda, in the sunlight, swaying on her pencil legs, was howling. Ever since the drying up of Rosa's nipples, ever since Magda's last scream on the road, Magda had been devoid of any syllable; Magda was a mute. Rosa believed that something had gone wrong with her vocal cords, with her windpipe, with the cave of her larynx; Magda was defective, without a voice; perhaps she was deaf; there might be something amiss with her intelligence; Magda was dumb. Even the laugh that came when the ash-stippled wind made a clown out of Magda's shawl was only the air-blown showing of her teeth. Even when the lice, head lice and body lice, crazed her so that she became as wild as one of the big rats that plundered the barracks at daybreak looking for carrion, she rubbed and scratched and kicked and bit and rolled without a whimper. But now Magda's mouth was spilling a long viscous rope of clamor.

"Maaaa —"

It was the first noise Magda had ever sent out from her throat since the drying up of Rosa's nipples.

"Maaaa . . . aaa!"

Again! Magda was wavering in the perilous sunlight of the arena, scribbling on such pitiful little bent shins. Rosa saw. She saw that Magda was grieving the loss of her shawl, she saw that Magda was going to die. A tide of commands hammered in Rosa's nipples: Fetch, get, bring! But she did not know which to go after first, Magda or the shawl. If she jumped out into the arena to snatch Magda up, the howling would not stop, because Magda would still not have the shawl; but if she ran back into the barracks to find the shawl, and if she found it, and if she came after Magda holding it and shaking it, then she would get Magda back, Magda would put the shawl in her mouth and turn dumb again.

Rosa entered the dark. It was easy to discover the shawl. Stella was heaped under it, asleep in her thin bones. Rosa tore the shawl free and flew — she could fly, she was only air — into the arena. The sunheat murmured of another life, of butterflies in summer. The light was placid, mellow. On the other side of the steel fence, far away, there were green meadows speckled with dandelions and deep-colored violets; beyond them, even farther, innocent tiger lilies, tall, lifting their orange bonnets. In the barracks they spoke of "flowers," of "rain": excrement, thick turd-braids, and the slow stinking maroon waterfall that slunk down from the upper bunks, the stink mixed with a bitter fatty floating smoke that greased Rosa's skin. She stood for an instant at the margin of the arena. Sometimes the electricity inside the fence would seem to hum; even Stella said it was only an imagining, but Rosa heard real sounds in the wire: grainy sad voices. The farther she was from the fence, the more clearly the voices crowded at her. The lamenting voices strummed so convincingly, so passionately, it was impossible to suspect them of being phantoms. The voices told her to hold up the shawl, high; the voices told her to shake it, to whip with it, to unfurl it like a flag. Rosa lifted, shook, whipped, unfurled. Far off, very far, Magda leaned across her air-fed belly, reaching out with the rods of her arms. She was high up, elevated, riding someone's shoulder. But the shoulder that carried Magda was not coming toward Rosa and the shawl, it was drifting away, the speck of Magda was moving more and more into the smoky distance. Above the shoulder a helmet glinted. The light tapped the helmet and sparkled it into a goblet. Below the helmet a black body like a domino and a pair of black boots hurled themselves in the direction of the electrified fence. The electric voices began to chatter wildly. "Maamaa, maaamaaa," they all hummed together. How far Magda was from Rosa now, across the whole square, past a dozen barracks, all the way on the other side! She was no bigger than a moth.

All at once Magda was swimming through the air. The whole of Magda traveled through loftiness. She looked like a butterfly touching a silver vine. And the moment Magda's feathered round head and her pencil legs and balloonish belly and zigzag arms splashed against the fence, the steel voices went mad in their growling, urging Rosa to run and run to the spot where Magda had fallen from her flight against the electrified fence; but of course Rosa did not obey them. She only stood, because if she ran they would shoot, and if she tried to pick up the sticks of Magda's body they would shoot, and if she let the wolf's screech ascending now through the ladder of her skeleton break out, they would shoot; so she took Magda's shawl and filled her own mouth with it, stuffed it in and stuffed it in, until she was swallowing up the wolf's screech and tasting the cinnamon and almond depth of Magda's saliva; and Rosa drank Magda's shawl until it dried.

[1984]

MILAN KUNDERA *(b. 1929) was born in Brno, Czechoslovakia. As a child he intended to become a musician, following the example of his father, Ludvík Kundera, a pianist and pupil of the great Czech composer Leoš Janaček, but in 1948 Kundera decided this was not his true vocation. Instead he studied scriptwriting and directing at the Prague Academy of Music and Dramatic Arts. Four years later he joined the film faculty there. Having written poetry since the age of fourteen, Kundera published his first book in 1953, a volume of verse entitled* Man a Broad Garden. *Two more poetry collections followed, and a play in 1961, but he felt he discovered his voice as a writer when, at nearly thirty, he wrote the first short stories of the cycle* Laughable Loves. *"The Hitchhiking Game" is from the second of the three volumes of that cycle, published in 1969.*

Like other Czech students of his generation, Kundera had joined the Communist Party — when he was eighteen — but he was expelled from it in 1950, reinstated in 1956, and expelled yet again, after he made a speech in front of the congress of Czech writers in 1967 advocating greater artistic freedom. This act caused him trouble when the Soviets invaded the country in 1968. He was charged with being a "counterrevolutionary" and forced to leave his teaching job. In 1975 he was given an extended travel visa by the Czech government so he could accept a position as professor at the University of Rennes, France. Now he lives in Paris while retaining his Czech citizenship. (As one of his first official acts, France's Socialist President François Mitterand — himself a writer — granted Kundera and several other exiled writers honorary French citizenship in 1981.) Kundera's novels include The Joke *(1969),* Life Is Elsewhere *(1974), and* The Farewell Party *(1976) — the last two published only in Europe and America, because after he left his native country publication of his works was forbidden there.* The Book of Laughter and Forgetting *(1980), generally considered his best work, is a collection of interrelated stories, mixing fantasy and nostalgia with brutal realism to create a picture of modern humanity in a world of alienation and political oppression which victimizes for no apparent reason. In 1985 he published another novel,* The Unbearable Lightness of Being.

Kundera has also completed a study of Franz Kafka. He feels that although the drama of politics is often present in his books, his fictional characters are not taking part in any particular politics, but acting in more general realms of humor, irony, and imagination. "It's in this sense that I don't much like the idea of committed literature. For me the only commitment of the novelist ought to be to oppose the ironic wisdom of the novel to ideological simplifications of every sort." Unlike Aleksandr Solzhenitsyn, another dissident writer who lives in the West, Kundera believes that "ideology is a school of intolerance. . . . Today, when politics have become a religion, I see the novel as one of the last forms of atheism."

Philip Roth's introduction to the English edition of Laughable Loves *discusses Kundera as a writer so attuned to the harsh role that contemporary politics has played in his life that he has become intrigued "by the startling consequences that can flow from playing around." Erotic play and power are at the center of Kundera's stories, dramatizing the way in which, as in "The Hitchhiking Game," the most cunningly woven net of sexual intrigue is likely to descend around the plotter. "Simply by fooling around and indulging their curiosity," Roth noted, "the lovers find they have managed to deepen responsibility as well as passion. . . . What is so often laughable, in the stories of Kundera's Czechoslovakia, is how grimly serious just about everything turns out to be, jokes and games and pleasure included; what's laughable is how terribly little there is to laugh at with any joy."*

Milan Kundera

ର୍ଷ୍ୟ

THE HITCHHIKING GAME

– translated by Suzanne Rappaport

I

The needle on the gas gauge suddenly dipped toward empty and the young driver of the sports car declared that it was maddening how much gas the car ate up. "See that we don't run out of gas again," protested the girl (about twenty-two), and reminded the driver of several places where this had already happened to them. The young man replied that he wasn't worried, because whatever he went through with her had the charm of adventure for him. The girl objected; whenever they had run out of gas on the highway it had, she said, always been an adventure only for her. The young man had hidden and she had had to make ill use of her charms by thumbing a ride and letting herself be driven to the nearest gas station, then thumbing a ride back with a can of gas. The young man asked the girl whether the drivers who had given her a ride had been unpleasant, since she spoke as if her task had been a hardship. She replied (with awkward flirtatiousness) that sometimes they had been *very* pleasant but that it hadn't done her any good as she had been burdened with the can and had had to leave them before she could get anything going. "Pig," said the young man. The girl protested that she wasn't a pig, but that he really was. God knows how many girls stopped him on the highway, when he was driving the car alone! Still driving, the young man put his arm around the girl's shoulders and kissed her gently on the forehead. He knew that she loved him and that she was jealous. Jealousy isn't a pleasant quality, but if it isn't overdone (and if it's combined with modesty), apart from its inconvenience there's even something touching about it. At least that's what the young man thought. Because he was only twenty-eight, it seemed to him that he was old and knew everything that a man could know about women. In the girl sitting beside him he valued precisely what, until now, he had met with least in women: purity.

The needle was already on empty, when to the right the young man caught sight of a sign, announcing that the station was a quarter of a mile ahead. The girl hardly had time to say how relieved she was before the young man was signaling left and driving into a space in front of the pumps. However, he had to stop a little way off, because beside the pumps was a huge gasoline truck with a large metal tank and a bulky hose, which was refilling the pumps. "We'll have to wait," said the young man to the girl and got out of the car. "How long will it take?" he shouted to the man in overalls. "Only a moment," replied the attendant, and the young man said: "I've heard that one before." He wanted to go back and sit in the car, but he saw that the girl had gotten out the other side. "I'll take a little walk in the meantime," she said. "Where to?" the young man asked on purpose, wanting to see the girl's embarrassment. He had known her for a year now but she would still get shy in front of him. He enjoyed her moments of shyness, partly because they distinguished her from the women he'd met before, partly because he was aware of the law of universal transience, which made even his girl's shyness a precious thing to him.

II

The girl really didn't like it when during the trip (the young man would drive for several hours without stopping) she had to ask him to stop for a moment somewhere near a clump of trees. She always got angry when, with feigned surprise, he asked her why he should stop. She knew that her shyness was ridiculous and old-fashioned. Many times at work she had noticed that they laughed at her on account of it and deliberately provoked her. She always got shy in advance at the thought of how she was going to get shy. She often longed to feel free and easy about her body, the way most of the women around her did. She had even invented a special course in self-persuasion: she would repeat to herself that at birth every human being received one out of the millions of available bodies, as one would receive an allotted room out of the millions of rooms in an enormous hotel. Consequently, the body was fortuitous and impersonal, it was only a ready-made, borrowed thing. She would repeat this to herself in different ways, but she could never manage to feel it. This mind-body dualism was alien to her. She was too much one with her body; that is why she always felt such anxiety about it.

She experienced this same anxiety even in her relations with the young man, whom she had known for a year and with whom she was happy, perhaps because he never separated her body from her soul and she could live with him *wholly*. In this unity there was happiness, but right behind the happiness lurked suspicion, and the girl was full of that. For instance, it often occurred to her that the other women (those who weren't anxious) were more attractive and more seductive and that the young man, who did not conceal the fact that he knew this kind of woman well, would someday leave her for a woman like that. (True, the young man declared that he'd had enough of them to last his whole life, but she knew that he was still much younger than he thought.) She wanted him to be completely hers and she to be completely his, but it often seemed to her that the more she tried to give him everything, the more she denied him something: the very thing that a light and superficial love or a flirtation gives to a person. It worried her that she was not able to combine seriousness with lightheartedness.

But now she wasn't worrying and any such thoughts were far from her mind. She felt good. It was the first day of their vacation (of their two-week vacation, about which she had been dreaming for a whole year), the sky was blue (the whole year she had been worrying about whether the sky would really be blue), and he was beside her. At his, "Where to?" she blushed, and left the car without a word. She walked around the gas station, which was situated beside the highway in total isolation, surrounded by fields. About a hundred yards away (in the direction in which they were traveling), a wood began. She set off for it, vanished behind a little bush, and gave herself up to her good mood. (In solitude it was possible for her to get the greatest enjoyment from the presence of the man she loved. If his presence had been continuous, it would have kept on disappearing. Only when alone was she able to *hold on* to it.)

When she came out of the wood onto the highway, the gas station was visible. The large gasoline truck was already pulling out and the sports car moved forward toward the red turret of the pump. The girl walked on along the highway and only at times looked back to see if the sports car was coming. At last she caught sight of it. She stopped and began to wave at it like a hitchhiker waving at a stranger's car. The sports car slowed down and stopped close to the girl. The young man leaned toward the window, rolled it down, smiled, and asked, "Where are you headed, miss?" "Are you going to Bystritsa?" asked the girl, smiling flirtatiously at him. "Yes, please get in," said the young man, opening the door. The girl got in and the car took off.

III

The young man was always glad when his girl friend was gay. This didn't happen too often; she had a quite tiresome job in an unpleasant environment, many hours of overtime without compensatory leisure and, at home, a sick mother. So she often felt tired. She didn't have either particularly good nerves or self-confidence and easily fell into a state of anxiety and fear. For this reason he welcomed every manifestation of her gaiety with the tender solicitude of a foster parent. He smiled at her and said: "I'm lucky today. I've been driving for five years, but I've never given a ride to such a pretty hitchhiker."

The girl was grateful to the young man for every bit of flattery; she wanted to linger for a moment in its warmth and so she said, "You're very good at lying."

"Do I look like a liar?"

"You look like you enjoy lying to women," said the girl, and into her words there crept unawares a touch of the old anxiety, because she really did believe that her young man enjoyed lying to women.

The girl's jealousy often irritated the young man, but this time he could easily overlook it for, after all, her words didn't apply to him but to the unknown driver. And so he just casually inquired, "Does it bother you?"

"If I were going with you, then it would bother me," said the girl and her words contained a subtle, instructive message for the young man; but the end of her sentence applied only to the unknown driver, "but I don't know you, so it doesn't bother me."

"Things about her own man always bother a woman more than things about a stranger" (this was now the young man's subtle, instructive message to the girl), "so seeing that we are strangers, we could get on well together."

The girl purposely didn't want to understand the implied meaning of his message, so she now addressed the unknown driver exclusively:

"What does it matter, since we'll part company in a little while?"

"Why?" asked the young man.

"Well, I'm getting out at Bystritsa."

"And what if I get out with you?"

At those words the girl looked up at him and found that he looked exactly as she imagined him in her most agonizing hours of jealousy. She was alarmed at how he was flattering her and flirting with her (an unknown hitchhiker), and *how becoming it was to him.* Therefore she responded with defiant provocativeness, "What would *you* do with me, I wonder?"

"I wouldn't have to think too hard about what to do with such a beautiful woman," said the young man gallantly and at this moment he was once again speaking far more to his own girl than to the figure of the hitchhiker.

But this flattering sentence made the girl feel as if she had caught him at something, as if she had wheedled a confession out of him with a fraudulent trick. She felt toward him a brief flash of intense hatred and said, "Aren't you rather too sure of yourself?"

The young man looked at the girl. Her defiant face appeared to him to be completely convulsed. He felt sorry for her and longed for her usual, familiar expression (which he used to call childish and simple). He leaned toward her, put his arm around her shoulders, and softly spoke the name with which he usually addressed her and with which he now wanted to stop the game.

But the girl released herself and said: "You're going a bit too fast!"

At this rebuff the young man said: "Excuse me, miss," and looked silently in front of him at the highway.

IV

The girl's pitiful jealousy, however, left her as quickly as it had come over her. After all, she was sensible and knew perfectly well that all this was merely a game. Now it even struck her as a little ridiculous that she had repulsed her man out of a jealous rage. It wouldn't be pleasant for her if he found out why she had done it. Fortunately women have the miraculous ability to change the meaning of their actions after the event. Using this ability, she decided that she had repulsed him not out of anger but so that she could go on with the game, which, with its whimsicality, so well suited the first day of their vacation.

So again she was the hitchhiker, who had just repulsed the overenterprising driver, but only so as to slow down his conquest and make it more exciting. She half turned toward the young man and said caressingly:

"I didn't mean to offend you, mister!"

"Excuse me, I won't touch you again," said the young man.

He was furious with the girl for not listening to him and refusing to be herself when that was what he wanted. And since the girl insisted on continuing in her role, he transferred his anger to the unknown hitchhiker whom she was portraying. And all at once he discovered the character of his own part: he stopped making the gallant remarks with which he had wanted to flatter his girl in a roundabout way, and began to play the tough guy who treats women to the coarser aspects of his masculinity: willfulness, sarcasm, self-assurance.

This role was a complete contradiction of the young man's habitually solicitous approach to the girl. True, before he had met her, he had in fact behaved roughly rather than gently toward women. But he had never resembled a heartless tough guy, because he had never demonstrated either a particularly strong will or ruthlessness. However, if he did not resemble such a man, nonetheless he had *longed* to at one time. Of course it was a quite naive desire, but there it was. Childish desires withstand all the snares of the adult mind and often survive into ripe old age. And this childish desire quickly took advantage of the opportunity to embody itself in the proffered role.

The young man's sarcastic reserve suited the girl very well — it freed her from herself. For she herself was, above all, the epitome of jealousy. The moment she stopped seeing the gallantly seductive young man beside her and saw only his inaccessible face, her jealousy subsided. The girl could forget herself and give herself up to her role.

Her role? What was her role? It was a role out of trashy literature. The hitchhiker stopped the car not to get a ride, but to seduce the man who was driving the car. She was an artful seductress, cleverly knowing how to use her charms. The girl slipped into this silly, romantic part with an ease that astonished her and held her spellbound.

V

There was nothing the young man missed in his life more than light-heartedness. The main road of his life was drawn with implacable precision. His job didn't use up merely eight hours a day, it also infiltrated the remaining time with the compulsory boredom of meetings and home study, and, by means of the attentiveness of his countless male and female colleagues, it infiltrated the wretchedly little time he had left for his private life as well. This private life never remained secret and sometimes even became the subject of gossip and public discussion. Even two weeks' vacation didn't give him a feeling of liberation and adventure; the gray shadow of precise planning lay even here. The scarcity of summer accommodations in our country compelled him to book a room in the Tatras six months in advance, and since for that he needed a recommendation from his office, its omnipresent brain thus did not cease knowing about him even for an instant.

He had become reconciled to all this, yet all the same from time to time the terrible thought of the straight road would overcome him — a road along which he was being pursued, where he was visible to everyone, and from which he could not turn aside. At this moment that thought returned to him. Through an odd and brief conjunction of ideas the figurative road became identified with the real highway along which he was driving — and this led him suddenly to do a crazy thing.

"Where did you say you wanted to go?" he asked the girl.

"To Banska Bystritsa," she replied.

"And what are you going to do there?"

"I have a date there."

"Who with?"

"With a certain gentleman."

The car was just coming to a large crossroads. The driver slowed down so he could read the road signs, then turned off to the right.

"What will happen if you don't arrive for that date?"

"It would be your fault and you would have to take care of me."

"You obviously didn't notice that I turned off in the direction of Nove Zamky."

"Is that true? You've gone crazy!"

"Don't be afraid, I'll take care of you," said the young man.

So they drove and chatted thus — the driver and the hitchhiker who did not know each other.

The game all at once went into a higher gear. The sports car was moving away not only from the imaginary goal of Banska Bystritsa, but also from the real goal, toward which it had been heading in the morning: the Tatras and the room that had been booked. Fiction was suddenly making an assault upon real life. The young man was moving away from himself and from the implacable straight road, from which he had never strayed until now.

"But you said you were going to the Low Tatras!" The girl was surprised.

"I am going, miss, wherever I feel like going. I'm a free man and I do what I want and what it pleases me to do."

VI

When they drove into Nove Zamky it was already getting dark.

The young man had never been here before and it took him a while to orient himself. Several times he stopped the car and asked the passersby directions to the hotel. Several streets had been dug up, so that the drive to the hotel, even though it was quite close by (as all those who had been asked asserted), necessitated so many detours and roundabout routes that it was almost a quarter of an hour before they finally stopped in front of it. The hotel looked unprepossessing, but it was the only one in town and the young man didn't feel like driving on. So he said to the girl, "Wait here," and got out of the car.

Out of the car he was, of course, himself again. And it was upsetting for him to find himself in the evening somewhere completely different from his intended destination — the more so because no one had forced him to do it and as a matter of fact he hadn't even really wanted to. He blamed himself for this piece of folly, but then became reconciled to it. The room in the Tatras could wait until tomorrow and it wouldn't do any harm if they celebrated the first day of their vacation with something unexpected.

He walked through the restaurant — smoky, noisy, and crowded — and asked for the reception desk. They sent him to the back of the lobby near the staircase, where behind a glass panel a superannuated blonde was sitting beneath a board full of keys. With difficulty, he obtained the key to the only room left.

The girl, when she found herself alone, also threw off her role. She didn't feel ill-humored, though, at finding herself in an unexpected town. She was so devoted to the young man that she never had doubts about anything he did, and confidently entrusted every moment of her life to him. On the other hand the idea once again popped into her mind that perhaps — just as she was now doing — other women had waited for her man in his car, those women whom he met on business trips. But surprisingly enough this idea didn't upset her at all now. In fact, she smiled at the thought of how nice it was that today she was this other woman, this irresponsible, indecent other woman, one of those women of whom she was so jealous. It seemed to her that she was cutting them all out, that she had learned how to use their weapons; how to give the young man what until now she had not known how to give him: lightheartedness, shamelessness, and dissoluteness. A curious feeling of satisfaction filled her, because she alone had the ability to be all women and in this way (she alone) could completely captivate her lover and hold his interest.

The young man opened the car door and led the girl into the restaurant. Amid the din, the dirt, and the smoke he found a single, unoccupied table in a corner.

VII

"So how are you going to take care of me now?" asked the girl provocatively.

"What would you like for an aperitif?"

The girl wasn't too fond of alcohol, still she drank a little wine and liked vermouth fairly well. Now, however, she purposely said: "Vodka."

"Fine," said the young man. "I hope you won't get drunk on me."

"And if I do?" said the girl.

The young man did not reply but called over a waiter and ordered two vodkas and two steak dinners. In a moment the waiter brought a tray with two small glasses and placed it in front of them.

The man raised his glass, "To you!"

"Can't you think of a wittier toast?"

Something was beginning to irritate him about the girl's game. Now sitting face to face with her, he realized that it wasn't just the *words* which were turning her into a stranger, but that her *whole persona* had changed, the movements of her body and her facial expression, and that she unpalatably and faithfully resembled that type of woman whom he knew so well and for whom he felt some aversion.

And so (holding his glass in his raised hand), he corrected his toast: "O.K., then I won't drink to you, but to your kind, in which are combined so successfully the better qualities of the animal and the worse aspects of the human being."

"By 'kind' do you mean all women?" asked the girl.

"No, I mean only those who are like you."

"Anyway it doesn't seem very witty to me to compare a woman with an animal."

"O.K.," the young man was still holding his glass aloft, "then I won't drink to your kind, but to your soul. Agreed? To your soul, which lights up when it descends from your head into your belly, and which goes out when it rises back up to your head."

The girl raised her glass. "O.K., to my soul, which descends into my belly."

"I'll correct myself once more," said the young man. "To your belly, into which your soul descends."

"To my belly," said the girl, and her belly (now that they had named it specifically), as it were, responded to the call; she felt every inch of it.

Then the waiter brought their steaks and the young man ordered them another vodka and some water (this time they drank to the girl's breasts), and the conversation continued in this peculiar, frivolous tone. It irritated the young man more and more how *well able* the girl was to become the lascivious miss. If she was able to do it so well, he thought, it meant that she really *was* like that. After all, no alien soul had entered into her from somewhere in space. What she was acting now was she herself; perhaps it was the part of her being which had formerly been locked up and which the pretext of the game had let out of its cage. Perhaps the girl supposed that by means of the game she was *disowning* herself, but wasn't it the other way around? Wasn't she becoming herself only through the game? Wasn't she freeing herself through the game? No, opposite him was not sitting a strange woman in his girl's body; it was his girl, herself, no one else. He looked at her and felt growing aversion toward her.

However, it was not only aversion. The more the girl withdrew from him *psychically*, the more he longed for her *physically*. The alien quality of her soul drew attention to her body, yes, as a matter of fact it turned her body into a body for *him* as if until now it had existed for the young man hidden within clouds of compassion, tenderness, concern, love, and emotion, as if it had been lost in these clouds (yes, as if this body had been lost!). It seemed to the young man that today he was seeing his girl's body for the first time.

After her third vodka and soda the girl got up and said flirtatiously, "Excuse me."

The young man said, "May I ask you where you are going, miss?"

"To piss, if you'll permit me," said the girl and walked off between the tables back toward the plush screen.

VIII

She was pleased with the way she had astounded the young man with this word, which — in spite of all its innocence — he had never heard from her. Nothing seemed to her truer to the character of the woman she was playing than this flirtatious emphasis placed on the word in question. Yes, she was pleased, she was in the best of moods. The game captivated her. It allowed her to feel what she had not felt till now: a *feeling* of *happy-go-lucky irresponsibility*.

She, who was always uneasy in advance about her every next step, suddenly felt completely relaxed. The alien life in which she had become involved was a life without shame, without biographical specifications, without past or future, without obligations. It was a life that was extraordinarily free. The girl, as a hitchhiker, could do anything, *everything was permitted her*. She could say, do, and feel whatever she liked.

She walked through the room and was aware that people were watching her from all the tables. It was a new sensation, one she didn't recognize: *indecent joy caused by her body*. Until now she had never been able to get rid of the fourteen-year-old girl within herself who was ashamed of her breasts and had the disagreeable feeling that she was indecent, because they stuck out from her body and were visible. Even though she was proud of being pretty and having a good figure, this feeling of pride was always immediately curtailed by shame. She rightly suspected that feminine beauty functioned above all as sexual provocation and she found this distasteful. She longed for her body to relate only to the man she loved. When men stared at her breasts in the street it seemed to her that they were invading a piece of her most secret privacy which should belong only to herself and her lover. But now she was the hitchhiker, the woman without a destiny. In this role she was relieved of the tender bonds of her love and began to be intensely aware of her body. And her body became more aroused the more alien the eyes watching it.

She was walking past the last table when an intoxicated man, wanting to show off his worldliness, addressed her in French: "*Combien, mademoiselle?*"

The girl understood. She thrust out her breasts and fully experienced every movement of her hips, then disappeared behind the screen.

IX

It was a curious game. This curiousness was evidenced, for example, in the fact that the young man, even though he himself was playing the unknown driver remarkably well, did not for a moment stop seeing his girl in the hitchhiker. And it was precisely this that was tormenting. He saw his girl seducing a strange man, and had the bitter privilege of being present, of seeing at close quarters how she looked and of hearing what she said when she was cheating on him (when she had cheated on him, when she would cheat on him). He had the paradoxical honor of being himself the pretext for her unfaithfulness.

This was all the worse because he worshipped rather than loved her. It had always seemed to him that her inward nature was *real* only within the bounds of fidelity and purity, and that beyond these bounds it simply didn't exist. Beyond these bounds she would cease to be herself, as water ceases to be water beyond the boiling point. When he now saw her crossing this horrifying boundary with nonchalant elegance, he was filled with anger.

The girl came back from the rest room and complained: "A guy over there asked me: *Combien, mademoiselle?*"

"You shouldn't be surprised," said the young man, "after all, you look like a whore."

"Do you know that it doesn't bother me in the least?"

"Then you should go with the gentleman!"

"But I have you."

"You can go with him after me. Go and work out something with him."

"I don't find him attractive."

"But in principle you have nothing against it, having several men in one night."

"Why not, if they're good-looking."

"Do you prefer them one after the other or at the same time?"

"Either way," said the girl.

The conversation was proceeding to still greater extremes of rudeness; it shocked the girl slightly but she couldn't protest. Even in a game there lurks a lack of freedom; even a game is a trap for the players. If this had not been a game and they had really been two strangers, the hitchhiker could long ago have taken offense and left. But there's no escape from a game. A team cannot flee from the playing field before the end of the match, chess pieces cannot desert the chessboard: the boundaries of the playing field are fixed. The girl knew that she had to accept whatever form the game might take, just because it was a game. She knew that the more extreme the game became, the more it would be a game and the more obediently she would have to play it. And it was futile to evoke good sense and warn her dazed soul that she must keep her distance from the game and not take it seriously. Just because it was only a game her soul was not afraid, did not oppose the game, and narcotically sank deeper into it.

The young man called the waiter and paid. Then he got up and said to the girl, "We're going."

"Where to?" The girl feigned surprise.

"Don't ask, just come on," said the young man.

"What sort of way is that to talk to me?"

"The way I talk to whores," said the young man.

X

They went up the badly lit staircase. On the landing below the second floor a group of intoxicated men was standing near the rest room. The young man caught hold of the girl from behind so that he was holding her breast with his hand. The men by the rest room saw this and began to call out. The girl wanted to break away, but the young man yelled at her: "Keep still!" The men greeted this with general ribaldry and addressed several dirty remarks to the girl. The young man and the girl reached the second floor. He opened the door of their room and switched on the light.

It was a narrow room with two beds, a small table, a chair, and a washbasin. The young man locked the door and turned to the girl. She was standing facing him in a defiant pose with insolent sensuality in her eyes. He looked at her and tried to discover behind her lascivious expression the familiar features which he loved tenderly. It was as if he were looking at two images through the same lens, at two images superimposed one upon the other with the one showing through the other. These two images showing through each other were telling him that *everything* was in the girl, that her soul was terrifyingly amorphous, that it held faithfulness and unfaithfulness, treachery and innocence, flirtatiousness and chastity. This disorderly jumble seemed disgusting to him, like the variety to be found in a pile of garbage. Both images continued to show through each other and the young man understood that the girl differed only on the surface from other women, but deep down was the same as they: full of all possible thoughts, feelings, and vices, which justified all his secret misgivings and fits of jealousy. The impression that certain outlines delineated her as an individual was only a delusion to which the other person, the one who was looking, was subject — namely himself. It seemed to him that the girl he loved was a creation of his desire, his thoughts, and his faith and that the *real* girl now standing in front of him was hopelessly alien, hopelessly *ambiguous*. He hated her.

"What are you waiting for? Strip," he said.

The girl flirtatiously bent her head and said, "Is it necessary?"

The tone in which she said this seemed to him very familiar; it seemed to him that once long ago some other woman had said this to him, only he no longer knew which one. He longed to humiliate her. Not the hitchhiker, but his own girl. The game merged with life. The game of humiliating the hitchhiker became only a pretext for humiliating his girl. The young man had forgotten that he was playing a game. He simply hated the woman standing in front of him. He stared at her and took a fifty-crown bill from his wallet. He offered it to the girl. "Is that enough?"

The girl took the fifty crowns and said: "You don't think I'm worth much."

The young man said: "You aren't worth more."

The girl nestled up against the young man. "You can't get around me like that! You must try a different approach, you must work a little!"

She put her arms around him and moved her mouth toward his. He put his fingers on her mouth and gently pushed her away. He said: "I only kiss women I love."

"And you don't love me?"

"No."

"Whom do you love?"

"What's that got to do with you? Strip!"

XI

She had never undressed like this before. The shyness, the feeling of inner panic, the dizziness, all that she had always felt when undressing in front of the young man (and she couldn't hide in the darkness), all this was gone. She was standing in front of him self-confident, insolent, bathed in light, and astonished at where she had all of a sudden discovered the gestures, heretofore unknown to her, of a slow, provocative striptease. She took in his glances, slipping off each piece of clothing with a caressing movement and enjoying each individual stage of this exposure.

But then suddenly she was standing in front of him completely naked and at this moment it flashed through her head that now the whole game would end, that, since she had stripped off her clothes, she had also stripped away her dissimulation, and that being naked meant that she was now herself and the young man ought to come up to her now and make a gesture with which he would wipe out everything and after which would follow only their most intimate love-making. So she stood naked in front of the young man and at this moment stopped playing the game. She felt embarrassed and on her face appeared the smile, which really belonged to her — a shy and confused smile.

But the young man didn't come to her and didn't end the game. He didn't notice the familiar smile. He saw before him only the beautiful, alien body of his own girl, whom he hated. Hatred cleansed his sensuality of any sentimental coating. She wanted to come to him, but he said: "Stay where you are, I want to have a good look at you." Now he longed only to treat her like a whore. But the young man had never had a whore and the ideas he had about them came from literature and hearsay. So he turned to these ideas and the first thing he recalled was the image of a woman in black underwear (and black stockings) dancing on the shiny top of a piano. In the little hotel room there was no piano, there was only a small table covered with a linen cloth leaning against the wall. He ordered the girl to climb up on it. The girl made a pleading gesture, but the young man said, "You've been paid."

When she saw the look of unshakable obsession in the young man's eyes, she tried to go on with the game, even though she no longer could and no longer knew how. With tears in her eyes she climbed onto the table. The top was scarcely three feet square and one leg was a little bit shorter than the others so that standing on it the girl felt unsteady.

But the young man was pleased with the naked figure, now towering above him, and the girl's shy insecurity merely inflamed his imperiousness. He wanted to see her body in all positions and from all sides, as he imagined other men had seen it and would see it. He was vulgar and lascivious. He used words that she had never heard from him in her life. She wanted to refuse, she wanted to be released from the game. She called him by his first name, but he immediately yelled at her that she had no right to address him so intimately. And so eventually in confusion and on the verge of tears, she obeyed, she bent forward and squatted according to the young man's wishes, saluted, and then wiggled her hips as she did the Twist for him. During a slightly more violent movement, when the cloth slipped beneath her feet and she nearly fell, the young man caught her and dragged her to the bed.

He had intercourse with her. She was glad that at least now finally the unfortunate game would end and they would again be the two people they had been before and would love each other. She wanted to press her mouth against his. But the young man pushed her head away and repeated that he only kissed women he loved. She burst into loud sobs. But she wasn't even allowed to cry, because the young man's furious passion gradually won over her body, which then silenced the complaint of her soul. On the bed there were soon two bodies in perfect harmony, two sensual bodies, alien to each other. This was exactly what the girl had most dreaded all her life and had scrupulously avoided till now: love-making without emotion or love. She knew that she had crossed the forbidden boundary, but she proceeded across it without objections and as a full participant — only somewhere, far off in a corner of her consciousness, did she feel horror at the thought that she had never known such pleasure, never so much pleasure as at this moment — beyond that boundary.

XII

Then it was all over. The young man got up off the girl and, reaching out for the long cord hanging over the bed, switched off the light. He didn't want to see the girl's face. He knew that the game was over, but didn't feel like returning to their customary relationship. He feared this return. He lay beside the girl in the dark in such a way that their bodies would not touch.

After a moment he heard her sobbing quietly. The girl's hand diffidently, childishly touched his. It touched, withdrew, then touched again, and then a pleading, sobbing voice broke the silence, calling him by his name and saying, "I am me, I am me. . . ."

The young man was silent, he didn't move, and he was aware of the sad emptiness of the girl's assertion, in which the unknown was defined in terms of the same unknown quantity.

And the girl soon passed from sobbing to loud crying and went on endlessly repeating this pitiful tautology: "I am me, I am me, I am me. . . ."

The young man began to call compassion to his aid (he had to call it from afar, because it was nowhere near at hand), so as to be able to calm the girl. There were still thirteen days' vacation before them.

[1969]

URSULA LE GUIN (b. 1929) *is the daughter of Theodora Kroeber, a writer, and Alfred Louis Kroeber, a pioneering anthropologist at the University of California at Berkeley. From her family background Le Guin acquired a double orientation, humanistic and scientific, that shows in all her writing. She was educated at Radcliffe College and Columbia University, where she completed a master's thesis in medieval romance literature. In 1953 she married the historian Charles Le Guin, with whom she has had three children. Although she wrote her first science-fiction story at the age of twelve, she didn't begin publishing until twenty years later. One of her stories, "Semley's Necklace," grew into her first published novel,* Rocannon's World *(1966). Another story, "Winter's King," introduced the setting which she developed for her first major success, the novel* The Left Hand of Darkness *(1969). These stories and novels, along with* Planet of Exile *(1966),* City of Illusions *(1967),* The Dispossessed *(1974), the novella* The Word for World is Forest *(1976), and stories in* The Wind's Twelve Quarters *(1976), form the Hainish cycle, a series of independent works sharing a common imaginary historic background. Le Guin has also published several other fantasy novels and three more story collections.*

Although Le Guin's earliest work primarily attracted a devoted audience of science-fiction readers, her later work — especially The Left Hand of Darkness *— has wider appeal. In that novel she explored the theme of androgyny on the planet Winter (Gethen), where inhabitants may adopt alternately male and female roles. Le Guin insists on Aristotle's definition of Homo sapiens as social animals, and she shows how difficult it is to think of our fellow humans as people, rather than as men and women.*

Le Guin brings to the writing of fantasy fiction a wealth of literary scholarship, crediting Leo Tolstoy, Anton Chekhov, and Virginia Woolf (among others) as her primary influences. Most of her stories, like "The Ones Who Walk Away from Omelas," are about reciprocal relationships, illustrating the sort of golden rule that whatever you touch, touches you. This maxim has scientific backings in ecology and philosophical echoes in Taoism and in Zen. Le Guin doesn't claim to be a brilliant stylist or an original thinker. She has said modestly that she works best with what she calls "fortune cookie ideas" suggested by someone else. Through her stories she shows how simple concepts hide a mass of complexity and contradiction that can create anarchy when human beings try to act on them. In 1979 Le Guin published a book developing her ideas about writing, The Language of Night: Essays on Fantasy and Science Fiction. *(See Le Guin's Commentary about "The Ones Who Walk Away from Omelas" on page 1331.)*

Ursula Le Guin

ཙ

THE ONES WHO WALK AWAY FROM OMELAS

With a clamor of bells that set the swallows soaring, the Festival of Summer came to the city. Omelas, bright-towered by the sea. The rigging of the boats in harbor sparkled with flags. In the streets between houses with red roofs and painted walls, between old moss-grown gardens and under avenues of trees, past great parks and public buildings, processions moved. Some were decorous: old people in long stiff robes of mauve and grey, grave master workmen, quiet, merry women carrying their babies and chatting as they walked. In other streets the music beat faster, a shimmering of gong and tambourine, and the people went dancing, the procession was a dance. Children dodged in and out, their high calls rising like the swallows' crossing flights over the music and the singing. All the processions wound towards the north side of the city, where on the great water-meadow called the Green Fields boys and girls, naked in the bright air, with mud-stained feet and ankles and long, lithe arms, exercised their restive horses before the race. The horses wore no gear at all but a halter without bit. Their manes were braided with streamers of silver, gold, and green. They flared their nostrils and pranced and boasted to one another; they were vastly excited, the horse being the only animal who has adopted our ceremonies as his own. Far off to the north and west the mountains stood up half encircling Omelas on her bay. The air of morning was so clear that the snow still crowning the Eighteen Peaks burned with white-gold fire across the miles of sunlit air, under the dark blue of the sky. There was just enough wind to make the banners that marked the racecourse snap and flutter now and then. In the silence of the broad green meadows one could hear the music winding through the city streets, farther and nearer and ever approaching, a cheerful faint sweetness of the air that from time to time trembled and gathered together and broke out into the great joyous clanging of the bells.

Joyous! How is one to tell about joy? How describe the citizens of Omelas?

They were not simple folk, you see, though they were happy. But we do not say the words of cheer much any more. All smiles have become archaic. Given a description such as this one tends to make certain assumptions. Given a description such as this one tends to look next for the King, mounted on a splendid stallion and surrounded by his noble knights, or perhaps in a golden litter borne by great-muscled slaves. But there was no king. They did not use swords, or keep slaves. They were not barbarians. I do not know the rules and laws of their society, but I suspect that they were singularly few. As they did without monarchy and slavery, so they also got on without the stock exchange, the advertisement, the secret police, and the bomb. Yet I repeat that these were not simple folk, not dulcet shepherds, noble savages, bland utopians. They were not less complex than us. The trouble is that we have a bad habit, encouraged by pedants and sophisti- cates, of considering happiness as something rather stupid. Only pain is in- tellectual, only evil interesting. This is the treason of the artist: a refusal to admit the banality of evil and the terrible boredom of pain. If you can't lick 'em, join 'em. If it hurts, repeat it. But to praise despair is to condemn de- light, to embrace violence is to lose hold of everything else. We have almost lost hold; we can no longer describe a happy man, nor make any celebration of joy. How can I tell you about the people of Omelas? They were not naïve and happy children — though their children were, in fact, happy. They were mature, intelligent, passionate adults whose lives were not wretched. O miracle! but I wish I could describe it better. I wish I could convince you. Omelas sounds in my words like a city in a fairy tale, long ago and far away, once upon a time. Perhaps it would be best if you imagined it as your own fancy bids, assuming it will rise to the occasion, for certainly I cannot suit you all. For instance, how about technology? I think that there would be no cars or helicopters in and above the streets; this follows from the fact that the people of Omelas are happy people. Happiness is based on a just dis- crimination of what is necessary, what is neither necessary nor destructive, and what is destructive. In the middle category, however — that of the un- necessary but undestructive, that of comfort, luxury, exuberance, etc. — they could perfectly well have central heating, subway trains, washing ma- chines, and all kinds of marvelous devices not yet invented here, floating light-sources, fuelless power, a cure for the common cold. Or they could have none of that: it doesn't matter. As you like it. I incline to think that people from towns up and down the coast have been coming in to Omelas during the last days before the Festival on very fast little trains and double- decked trams and that the train station of Omelas is actually the hand- somest building in town, though plainer than the magnificent Farmers' Market. But even granted trains, I fear that Omelas so far strikes some of you as goody-goody. Smiles, bells, parades, horses, bleh. If so, please add an orgy. If an orgy would help, don't hesitate. Let us not, however, have tem- ples from which issue beautiful nude priests and priestesses already half in ecstasy and ready to copulate with any man or woman, lover or stranger, who desires union with the deep godhead of the blood, although that was my first idea. But really it would be better not to have any temples in Omelas — at least, not manned temples. Religion yes, clergy no. Surely the beautiful nudes can just wander about, offering themselves like divine souf- flés to the hunger of the needy and the rapture of the flesh. Let them join the processions. Let tambourines be struck above the copulations, and the glory of desire be proclaimed upon the gongs, and (a not unimportant point) let the offspring of these delightful rituals be beloved and looked after by all. One thing I know there is none of in Omelas is guilt. But what else should there be? I thought at first there were no drugs, but that is puritanical. For those who like it, the faint insistent sweetness of *drooz* may perfume the ways of the city, *drooz* which first brings a great lightness and brilliance to the mind and limbs, and then after some hours a dreamy languor, and wonderful visions at last of the very arcana and inmost secrets of the Universe, as well as exciting the pleasure of sex beyond all belief; and it is not habit-forming. For more modest tastes I think there ought to be beer. What else, what else belongs in the joyous city? The sense of victory, surely, the celebration of courage. But as we did without clergy, let us do without soldiers. The joy built upon successful slaughter is not the right kind of joy; it will not do; it is fearful and it is trivial. A boundless and generous contentment, a magnanimous triumph felt not against some outer enemy but in communion with the finest and fairest in the souls of all men everywhere and the splendor of the world's summer: this is what swells the hearts of the people of Omelas, and the victory they celebrate is that of life. I really don't think many of them need to take *drooz*.

Most of the processions have reached the Green Fields by now. A marvelous smell of cooking goes forth from the red and blue tents of the provisioners. The faces of small children are amiably sticky; in the benign grey beard of a man a couple of crumbs of rich pastry are entangled. The youths and girls have mounted their horses and are beginning to group around the starting line of the course. An old woman, small, fat, and laughing, is passing out flowers from a basket, and tall young men wear her flowers in their shining hair. A child of nine or ten sits at the edge of the crowd, alone, playing on a wooden flute. People pause to listen, and they smile, but they do not speak to him, for he never ceases playing and never sees them, his dark eyes wholly rapt in the sweet, thin magic of the tune.

He finishes, and slowly lowers his hands holding the wooden flute.

As if that little private silence were the signal, all at once a trumpet sounds from the pavillion near the starting line: imperious, melancholy, piercing. The horses rear on their slender legs, and some of them neigh in answer. Sober-faced, the young riders stroke the horses' necks and soothe them, whispering, "Quiet, quiet, there my beauty, my hope. . . ." They begin to form in rank along the starting line. The crowds along the racecourse are like a field of grass and flowers in the wind. The Festival of Summer has begun.

Do you believe? Do you accept the festival, the city, the joy? No? Then let me describe one more thing.

In a basement under one of the beautiful public buildings of Omelas, or perhaps in the cellar of one of its spacious private homes, there is a room. It has one locked door, and no window. A little light seeps in dustily between cracks in the boards, secondhand from a cobwebbed window somewhere across the cellar. In one corner of the little room a couple of mops, with stiff, clotted, foul-smelling heads, stand near a rusty bucket. The floor is dirt, a little damp to the touch, as cellar dirt usually is. The room is about three paces long and two wide: a mere broom closet or disused tool room. In the room a child is sitting. It could be a boy or a girl. It looks about six, but actually is nearly ten. It is feeble-minded. Perhaps it was born defective, or perhaps it has become imbecile through fear, malnutrition, and neglect. It picks its nose and occasionally fumbles vaguely with its toes or genitals, as it sits hunched in the corner farthest from the bucket and the two mops. It is afraid of the mops. It finds them horrible. It shuts its eyes, but it knows the mops are still standing there; and the door is locked; and nobody will come. The door is always locked; and nobody ever comes, except that some- times — the child has no understanding of time or interval — sometimes the door rattles terribly and opens, and a person, or several people, are there. One of them may come in and kick the child to make it stand up. The others never come close, but peer in at it with frightened, disgusted eyes. The food bowl and the water jug are hastily filled, the door is locked, the eyes disappear. The people at the door never say anything, but the child, who has not always lived in the tool room, and can remember sun- light and its mother's voice, sometimes speaks. "I will be good," it says. "Please let me out. I will be good!" They never answer. The child used to scream for help at night, and cry a good deal, but now it only makes a kind of whining, "eh-haa, eh-haa," and it speaks less and less often. It is so thin there are no calves to its legs; its belly protrudes; it lives on a half-bowl of corn meal and grease a day. It is naked. Its buttocks and thighs are a mass of festered sores, as it sits in its own excrement continually.

They all know it is there, all the people of Omelas. Some of them have come to see it, others are content merely to know it is there. They all know that it has to be there. Some of them understand why, and some do not, but they all understand that their happiness, the beauty of their city, the tender- ness of their friendships, the health of their children, the wisdom of their scholars, the skill of their makers, even the abundance of their harvest and the kindly weathers of their skies, depend wholly on this child's abominable misery.

This is usually explained to children when they are between eight and twelve, whenever they seem capable of understanding; and most of those who come to see the child are young people, though often enough an adult comes, or comes back, to see the child. No matter how well the matter has been explained to them, these young spectators are always shocked and sickened at the sight. They feel disgust, which they had thought themselves superior to. They feel anger, outrage, impotence, despite all the explana- tions. They would like to do something for the child. But there is nothing they can do. If the child were brought up into the sunlight out of that vile place, if it were cleaned and fed and comforted, that would be a good thing, indeed; but if it were done, in that day and hour all the prosperity and beauty and delight of Omelas would wither and be destroyed. Those are the terms. To exchange all the goodness and grace of every life in Omelas for that single, small improvement: to throw away the happiness of thousands for the chance of the happiness of one: that would be to let guilt within the walls indeed.

The terms are strict and absolute; there may not even be a kind word spoken to the child.

Often the young people go home in tears, or in a tearless rage, when they have seen the child and faced this terrible paradox. They may brood over it for weeks or years. But as time goes on they begin to realize that even if the child could be released, it would not get much good of its freedom: a little vague pleasure of warmth and food, no doubt, but little more. It is too degraded and imbecile to know any real joy. It has been afraid too long ever to be free of fear. Its habits are too uncouth for it to respond to humane treatment. Indeed, after so long it would probably be wretched without walls about it to protect it, and darkness for its eyes, and its own excrement to sit in. Their tears at the bitter injustice dry when they begin to perceive the terrible justice of reality and to accept it. Yet it is their tears and anger, the trying of their generosity and the acceptance of their helplessness, which are perhaps the true source of the splendor of their lives. Theirs is no vapid, irresponsible happiness. They know that they, like the child, are not free. They know compassion. It is the existence of the child, and their knowledge of its existence, that makes possible the nobility of their architecture, the poignancy of their music, the profundity of their science. It is because of the child that they are so gentle with children. They know that if the wretched one were not there snivelling in the dark, the other one, the flute-player, could make no joyful music as the young riders line up in their beauty for the race in the sunlight of the first morning of summer.

Now do you believe in them? Are they not more credible? But there is one more thing to tell, and this is quite incredible.

At times one of the adolescent girls or boys who go to see the child does not go home to weep or rage, does not, in fact, go home at all. Sometimes also a man or woman much older falls silent for a day or two, and then leaves home. These people go out into the street, and walk down the street alone. They keep walking, and walk straight out of the city of Omelas, through the beautiful gates. They keep walking across the farmlands of Omelas. Each one goes alone, youth or girl, man or woman. Night falls; the traveler must pass down village streets, between the houses with yellow-lit windows, and on out into the darkness of the fields. Each alone, they go west or north, towards the mountains. They go on. They leave Omelas, they walk ahead into the darkness, and they do not come back. The place they go towards is a place even less imaginable to most of us than the city of happiness. I cannot describe it at all. It is possible that it does not exist. But they seem to know where they are going, the ones who walk away from Omelas.

[1976]

JOHN BARTH (b. 1930) was born in Cambridge, Maryland, on the Eastern Shore of the Chesapeake Bay. He has an older brother and a twin sister. He regards being born a twin as influential in his development as a writer. Having an "established sidekick" from birth, he says that "one might reasonably therefore expect a twin who becomes a storyteller never to take language for granted; to be ever at it, tinkering, foregrounding it, perhaps unnaturally conscious of it. Language is for relating to the Others." Music was Barth's first vocation. He was a student of orchestration for a year at the Juilliard School in New York City before he enrolled as a journalism major on a scholarship at Johns Hopkins University, earning his B.A. in 1951 and his M.A. in 1952. Barth's job as a book filer in the university library stacks developed his taste for fiction: "I was permanently impressed with the size of literature and its wild variety; likewise, as I explored the larger geography of the stacks, with the variety of temperaments, histories, and circumstances from which came the literature I came to love." In his writing class as an undergraduate he began but did not finish a cycle of 100 stories about Dorchester County, Maryland. He has said that his "affair with Scheherazade is an old and continuing one." Scheherazade — the storyteller in Tales of an Arabian Night, and a character Barth himself called on in the three long stories that make up his book Chimera (1972) — can be taken as a figure for "the estate of the fictioner in general and the particular endeavors and aspirations of this one, at least, who can wish for nothing better than to spin like the vizier's excellent daughter, through what nights remain to him tales within tales within tales."

In 1953 Barth joined the faculty of Pennsylvania State University as an instructor in English. He began to publish his novels a few years later. The Floating Opera (1956) and The End of the Road (1958) are conventional in form and language, but The Sot-Weed Factor (1960) and Giles Goat-Boy (1966) are very long, experimental comic novels, indebted to the fiction of Jorge Luis Borges and Vladimir Nabokov. Reviewers praised both of these novels for their display of erudition and bawdy wit. His later novels include Letters (1979) and Sabbatical: A Romance (1982). Barth's talent for parody is evident in all his works. "At heart I'm an arranger still, whose chiefest literary pleasure is to take a received melody — an old narrative poem, a classical myth, a shopworn literary convention, a shard of my experience . . . and, improvising like a jazzman within its constraints, reorchestrate it to present purpose."

Barth has published only one book of short stories so far, Lost in the Funhouse (1968), subtitled Fiction for Print, Tape, Live Voice. It was influenced by his friendships with the philosopher Marshall McLuhan and the scholar and critic Leslie Fiedler, formed after he began to teach at the State University of New York at Buffalo in 1965. The title story, "Lost in *the Funhouse," like his other short experimental pieces in the collection, suggests that Barth has lost faith in fiction and instead is self-consciously concerned with what happens when a writer writes, and what happens when a reader reads — "the metaphysical plight of imagination engaging with imagination." As John Updike has observed, Barth "hit the floor of nihilism hard and returns to us covered with coal dust. . . . [He] seems to me a very strongminded and inventive and powerful voice from another planet."*

John Barth

ဢ

LOST IN THE FUNHOUSE

For whom is the funhouse fun? Perhaps for lovers. For Ambrose it is *a place of fear and confusion.* He has come to the seashore with his family for the holiday, *the occasion of their visit is Independence Day, the most important secular holiday of the United States of America.* A single straight underline is the manuscript mark for italic type, *which in turn* is the printed equivalent to oral emphasis of words and phrases as well as the customary type for titles of complete works, not to mention. Italics are also employed, in fiction stories especially, for "outside," intrusive, or artificial voices, such as radio announcements, the texts of telegrams and newspaper articles, et cetera. They should be used *sparingly.* If passages originally in roman type are italicized by someone repeating them, it's customary to acknowledge the fact. *Italics mine.*

Ambrose was "at that awkward age." His voice came out high-pitched as a child's if he let himself get carried away; to be on the safe side, therefore, he moved and spoke with *deliberate calm* and *adult gravity.* Talking soberly of unimportant or irrelevant matters and listening consciously to the sound of your own voice are useful habits for maintaining control in this difficult interval. *En route* to Ocean City he sat in the back seat of the family car with his brother Peter, age fifteen, and Magda G ——— , age fourteen, a pretty girl and exquisite young lady, who lived not far from them on B——— Street in the town of D——— , Maryland. Initials, blanks, or both were often substituted for proper names in nineteenth-century fiction to enhance the illusion of reality. It is as if the author felt it necessary to delete the names for reasons of tact or legal liability. Interestingly, as with other aspects of realism, it is an *illusion* that is being enhanced, by purely artificial means. Is it likely, does it violate the principle of verisimilitude, that a thirteen-year-old boy could make such a sophisticated observation? A girl of fourteen is *the psychological coeval* of a boy of fifteen or sixteen; a thirteen-year-old boy, therefore, even one precocious in some other respects, might be three years *her emotional junior.*

Thrice a year — on Memorial, Independence, and Labor Days — the family visits Ocean City for the afternoon and evening. When Ambrose and Peter's father was their age, the excursion was made by train, as mentioned in the novel *The 42nd Parallel* by John Dos Passos. Many families from the same neighborhood used to travel together, with dependent relatives and often with Negro servants; schoolfuls of children swarmed through the railway cars; everyone shared everyone else's Maryland fried chicken, Virginia ham, deviled eggs, potato salad, beaten biscuits, iced tea. Nowadays (that is, in 19— , the year of our story) the journey is made by automobile — more comfortably and quickly though without the extra fun though without the *camaraderie* of a general excursion. It's all part of the deterioration of American life, their father declares; Uncle Karl supposes that when the boys take *their* families to Ocean City for the holidays they'll fly in Autogiros. Their mother, sitting in the middle of the front seat like Magda in the second, only with her arms on the seat-back behind the men's shoulders, wouldn't want the good old days back again, the steaming trains and stuffy long dresses; on the other hand she can do without Autogiros, too, if she has to become a grandmother to fly in them.

Description of physical appearance and mannerisms is one of several standard methods of characterization used by writers of fiction. It is also important to "keep the senses operating"; when a detail from one of the five senses, say visual, is "crossed" with a detail from another, say auditory, the reader's imagination is oriented to the scene, perhaps unconsciously. This procedure may be compared to the way surveyors and navigators determine their positions by two or more compass bearings, a process known as triangulation. The brown hair on Ambrose's mother's forearms gleamed in the sun like. Though right-handed, she took her left arm from the seat-back to press the dashboard cigar lighter for Uncle Karl. When the glass bead in its handle glowed red, the lighter was ready for use. The smell of Uncle Karl's cigar smoke reminded one of. The fragrance of the ocean came strong to the picnic ground where they always stopped for lunch, two miles inland from Ocean City. Having to pause for a full hour almost within sound of the breakers was difficult for Peter and Ambrose when they were younger; even at their present age it was not easy to keep their anticipation, *stimulated by the briny spume*, from turning into short temper. The Irish author James Joyce, in his unusual novel entitled *Ulysses*, now available in this country, uses the adjectives *snot-green* and *scrotum-tightening* to describe the sea. Visual, auditory, tactile, olfactory, gustatory. Peter and Ambrose's father, while steering their black 1936 LaSalle sedan with one hand, could with the other remove the first cigarette from a white pack of Lucky Strikes and, more remarkably, light it with a match forefingered from its book and thumbed against the flint paper without being detached. The matchbook cover merely advertised U.S. War Bonds and Stamps. A fine metaphor, simile, or other figure of speech, in addition to its obvious "first-order" relevance to the thing it describes, will be seen upon reflection to have a second order of significance: it may be drawn from the *milieu* of the action, for example, or be particularly appropriate to the sensibility of the narrator, even hinting to the reader things of which the narrator is unaware; or it may cast further and subtler lights upon the things it describes, sometimes ironically qualifying the more evident sense of the comparison.

To say that Ambrose's and Peter's mother was *pretty* is to accomplish nothing; the reader may acknowledge the proposition, but his imagination is not engaged. Besides, Magda was also pretty, yet in an altogether different way. Although she lived on B—— Street she had very good manners and did better than average in school. Her figure was very well developed for her age. Her right hand lay casually on the plush upholstery of the seat, very near Ambrose's left leg, on which his own hand rested. The space between their legs, between her right and his left leg, was out of the line of sight of anyone sitting on the other side of Magda, as well as anyone glancing into the rear-view mirror. Uncle Karl's face resembled Peter's — rather, vice versa. Both had dark hair and eyes, short husky statures, deep voices. Magda's left hand was probably in a similar position on her left side. The boys' father is difficult to describe; no particular feature of his appearance or manner stood out. He wore glasses and was principal of a T—— County grade school. Uncle Karl was a masonry contractor.

Although Peter must have known as well as Ambrose that the latter, because of his position in the car, would be first to see the electrical towers of the power plant at V——, the halfway point of their trip, he leaned forward and slightly toward the center of the car and pretended to be looking for them through the flat pinewoods and tuckahoe creeks along the highway. For as long as the boys could remember, "looking for the Towers" had been a feature of the first half of their excursions to Ocean City, "looking for the standpipe" of the second. Though the game was childish, their mother preserved the tradition of rewarding the first to see the Towers with a candy-bar or piece of fruit. She insisted now that Magda play the game; the prize, she said, was "something hard to get nowadays." Ambrose decided not to join in; he sat far back in his seat. Magda, like Peter, leaned forward. Two sets of straps were discernible through the shoulders of her sun dress; the inside right one, a brassiere-strap, was fastened or shortened with a small safety pin. The right armpit of her dress, presumably the left as well, was damp with perspiration. The simple strategy for being first to espy the Towers, which Ambrose had understood by the age of four, was to sit on the right-hand side of the car. Whoever sat there, however, had also to put up with the worst of the sun, and so Ambrose, without mentioning the matter, chose sometimes the one and sometimes the other. Not impossibly Peter had never caught on to the trick, or thought that his brother hadn't simply because Ambrose on occasion preferred shade to a Baby Ruth or tangerine.

The shade-sun situation didn't apply to the front seat, owning to the windshield; if anything the driver got more sun, since the person on the passenger side not only was shadowed below by the door and dashboard but might swing down his sunvisor all the way too.

"Is that them?" Magda asked. Ambrose's mother teased the boys for letting Magda win, insinuating that "somebody [had] a girlfriend." Peter and Ambrose's father reached a long thin arm across their mother to butt his cigarette in the dashboard ashtray, under the lighter. The prize this time for seeing the Towers first was a banana. Their mother bestowed it after chiding their father for wasting a half-smoked cigarette when everything was so scarce. Magda, to take the prize, moved her hand from so near Ambrose's that he could have touched it as though accidentally. She offered to share the prize, things like that were so hard to find; but everyone insisted it was hers alone. Ambrose's mother sang an iambic trimeter couplet from a popular song, femininely rhymed:

> *"What's good is in the Army;*
> *What's left will never harm me."*

Uncle Karl tapped his cigar ash out the ventilator window; some particles were sucked by the slipstream back into the car through the rear window on the passenger side. Magda demonstrated her ability to hold a banana in one hand and peel it with her teeth. She still sat forward; Ambrose pushed his glasses back onto the bridge of his nose with his left hand, which he then negligently let fall to the seat cushion immediately behind her. He even permitted the single hair, gold, on the second joint of his thumb to brush the fabric of her skirt. Should she have sat back at that instant, his hand would have been caught under her.

Plush upholstery prickles uncomfortably through gabardine slacks in the July sun. The function of the *beginning* of a story is to introduce the principal characters, establish their initial relationships, set the scene for the main action, expose the background of the situation if necessary, plant motifs and foreshadowings where appropriate, and initiate the first complication or whatever of the "rising action." Actually, if one imagines a story called "The Funhouse," or "Lost in the Funhouse," the details of the drive to Ocean City don't seem especially relevant. The *beginning* should recount the events between Ambrose's first sight of the funhouse early in the afternoon and his entering it with Magda and Peter in the evening. The *middle* would narrate all relevant events from the time he goes in to the time he loses his way; middles have the double and contradictory function of delaying the climax while at the same time preparing the reader for it and fetching him to it. Then the *ending* would tell what Ambrose does while he's lost, how he finally finds his way out, and what everybody makes of the experience. So far there's been no real dialogue, very little sensory detail, and nothing in the way of a *theme*. And a long time has gone by already without anything happening; it makes a person wonder. We haven't even reached Ocean City yet: we will never get out of the funhouse.

The more closely an author identifies with the narrator, literally or metaphorically, the less advisable it is, as a rule, to use the first-person narrative viewpoint. Once three years previously the young people *aforementioned* played Niggers and Masters in the backyard; when it was Ambrose's turn to be Master and theirs to be Niggers Peter had to go serve his evening papers; Ambrose was afraid to punish Magda alone, but she led him to the whitewashed Torture Chamber between the woodshed and the privy in the Slaves Quarters; there she knelt sweating among bamboo rakes and dusty Mason jars, pleadingly embraced his knees, and while bees droned in the lattice as if on an ordinary summer afternoon, purchased clemency at a surprising price set by herself. Doubtless she remembered nothing of this event; Ambrose on the other hand seemed unable to forget the least detail of his life. He even recalled how, standing beside himself with awed impersonality in the reeky heat, he'd stared the while at an empty cigar box in which Uncle Karl kept stone-cutting chisels: beneath the words *El Producto*, a laureled, loose-toga'd lady regarded the sea from a marble bench; beside her, forgotten or not yet turned to, was a five-stringed lyre. Her chin reposed on the back of her right hand; her left depended negligently from the bench-arm. The lower half of scene and lady was peeled away; the words EXAMINED BY —— were inked there into the wood. Nowadays cigar boxes are made of pasteboard. Ambrose wondered what Magda would have done, Ambrose wondered what Magda would do when she sat back on his hand as he resolved she should. Be angry. Make a teasing joke of it. Give no sign at all. For a long time she leaned forward, playing cow-poker with Peter against Uncle Karl and Mother and watching for the first sign of Ocean City. At nearly the same instant, picnic ground and Ocean City standpipe hove into view; an Amoco filling station on their side of the road cost Mother and Uncle Karl fifty cows and the game; Magda bounced back, clapping her right hand on Mother's right arm; Ambrose moved clear "in the nick of time."

At this rate our hero, at this rate our protagonist will remain in the funhouse forever. Narrative ordinarily consists of alternating dramatization and summarization. One symptom of nervous tension, paradoxically, is repeated and violent yawning; neither Peter nor Magda nor Uncle Karl nor Mother reacted in this manner. Although they were no longer small children, Peter and Ambrose were each given a dollar to spend on boardwalk amusements in addition to what money of their own they'd brought along. Magda too, though she protested she had ample spending money. The boys' mother made a little scene out of distributing the bills; she pretended that her sons and Magda were small children and cautioned them not to spend the sum too quickly or in one place. Magda promised with a merry laugh and, having both hands free, took the bill with her left. Peter laughed also and pledged in a falsetto to be a good boy. His imitation of a child was not clever. The boys' father was tall and thin, balding, fair-complexioned. Assertions of that sort are not effective; the reader may acknowledge the proposition, but. We should be much farther along than we are; something has gone wrong; not much of the preliminary rambling seems relevant. Yet everyone begins in the same place; how is it that most go along without difficulty but a few lose their way?

"Stay out from under the boardwalk," Uncle Karl growled from the side of his mouth. The boys' mother pushed his shoulder *in mock annoyance.* They were all standing before Fat May the Laughing Lady who advertised the funhouse. Larger than life, Fat May mechanically shook, rocked on her heels, slapped her thighs while recorded laughter — uproarious, female — came amplified from a hidden loudspeaker. It chuckled, wheezed, wept; tried in vain to catch its breath; tittered, groaned, exploded raucous and anew. You couldn't hear it without laughing yourself, no matter how you felt. Father came back from talking to a Coast-Guardsman on duty and reported that the surf was spoiled with crude oil from tankers recently torpedoed offshore. Lumps of it, difficult to remove, made tarry tidelines on the beach and stuck on swimmers. Many bathed in the surf nevertheless and came out speckled; others paid to use a municipal pool and only sunbathed on the beach. We would do the latter. We would do the latter. We would do the latter.

Under the boardwalk, matchbook covers, grainy other things. What is the story's theme? Ambrose is ill. He perspires in the dark passages, candied apples-on-a-stick, delicious-looking, disappointing to eat. Funhouses need men's and ladies' rooms at intervals. Others perhaps have also vomited in corners and corridors; may even have had bowel movements liable to be stepped in in the dark. The word *fuck* suggests suction and/or and/or flatulence. Mother and Father; grandmothers and grandfathers on both sides; great-grandmothers and great-grandfathers on four sides, et cetera. Count a generation as thirty years: in approximately the year when Lord Baltimore was granted charter to the province of Maryland by Charles I, five hundred twelve women — English, Welsh, Bavarian, Swiss — of every class and character, received into themselves the penises the intromittent organs of five hundred twelve men, ditto, in every circumstance and posture, to conceive the five hundred twelve ancestors of the two hundred fifty-six ancestors of the et cetera et cetera et cetera et cetera et cetera et cetera et cetera et cetera of the author, of the narrator, of this story, *Lost in the Funhouse.* In alleyways, ditches, canopy beds, pinewoods, bridal suites, ship's cabins, coach-and-fours, coaches-and-four, sultry toolsheds; on the cold sand under boardwalks, littered with *El Producto* cigar butts, treasured with Lucky Strike cigarette stubs, Coca-Cola caps, gritty turds, cardboard lollipop sticks, matchbook covers warning that A Slip of the Lip Can Sink a Ship. The shluppish whisper, continuous as seawash round the globe, tidelike falls and rises with the circuit of dawn and dusk.

Magda's teeth. She *was* left-handed. Perspiration. They've gone all the way, through, Magda and Peter, they've been waiting for hours with Mother and Uncle Karl while Father searches for his lost son; they draw french-fried potatoes from a paper cup and shake their heads. They've named the children they'll one day have and bring to Ocean City on holidays. Can spermatozoa properly be thought of as male animalcules when there are no female spermatozoa? They grope through hot, dark windings, past Love's Tunnel's fearsome obstacles. Some perhaps lose their way.

Peter suggested then and there that they do the funhouse; he had been through it before, so had Magda, Ambrose hadn't and suggested, his voice cracking on account of Fat May's laughter, that they swim first. All were chuckling, couldn't help it; Ambrose's father, Ambrose's and Peter's father came up grinning like a lunatic with two boxes of syrup-coated popcorn, one for Mother, one for Magda; the men were to help themselves. Ambrose walked on Magda's right; being by nature left-handed, she carried the box in her left hand. Up front the situation was reversed.

"What are you limping for?" Magda inquired of Ambrose. He supposed in a husky tone that his foot had gone to sleep in the car. Her teeth flashed. "Pins and needles?" It was the honeysuckle on the lattice of the former privy that drew the bees. Imagine being stung there. How long is this going to take?

The adults decided to forgo the pool; but Uncle Karl insisted they change into swimsuits and do the beach. "He wants to watch the pretty girls," Peter teased, and ducked behind Magda from Uncle Karl's pretended wrath. "You've got all the pretty girls you need right here," Magda declared, and Mother said: "Now that's the gospel truth." Magda scolded Peter, who reached over her shoulder to sneak some popcorn. "Your brother and father aren't getting any." Uncle Karl wondered if they were going to have fireworks that night, what with the shortages. It wasn't the shortages, Mr. M—— replied; Ocean City had fireworks from pre-war. But it was too risky on account of the enemy submarines, some people thought.

"Don't seem like Fourth of July without fireworks," said Uncle Karl. The inverted tag in dialogue writing is still considered permissible with proper names or epithets, but sounds old-fashioned with personal pronouns. "We'll have 'em again soon enough," predicted the boys' father. Their mother declared she could do without fireworks: they reminded her too much of the real thing. Their father said all the more reason to shoot off a few now and again. Uncle Karl asked *rhetorically* who needed reminding, just look at people's hair and skin.

"The oil, yes," said Mrs. M——.

Ambrose had a pain in his stomach and so didn't swim but enjoyed watching the others. He and his father burned red easily. Magda's figure was exceedingly well developed for her age. She too declined to swim, and got mad, and became angry when Peter attempted to drag her into the pool.

She always swam, he insisted; whát did she mean not swim? Why did a person come to Ocean City?

"Maybe I want to lay here with Ambrose," Magda teased.

Nobody likes a pedant.

"Aha," said Mother. Peter grabbed Magda by one ankle and ordered Ambrose to grab the other. She squealed and rolled over on the beach blanket. Ambrose pretended to help hold her back. Her tan was darker than even Mother's and Peter's. "Help out, Uncle Karl!" Peter cried. Uncle Karl went to seize the other ankle. Inside the top of her swimsuit, however, you could see the line where the sunburn ended and, when she hunched her shoulders and squealed again, one nipple's auburn edge. Mother made them behave themselves. "*You* should certainly know," she said to Uncle Karl. Archly. "That when a lady says she doesn't feel like swimming, a gentleman doesn't ask questions." Uncle Karl said excuse *him*; Mother winked at Magda; Ambrose blushed; stupid Peter kept saying "Phooey on *feel like!*" and tugging at Magda's ankle; then even he got the point, and cannonballed with a holler into the pool.

"I swear," Magda said, in mock *in feigned* exasperation.

The diving would make a suitable literary symbol. To go off the high board you had to wait in a line along the poolside and up the ladder. Fellows tickled girls and goosed one another and shouted to the ones at the top to hurry up, or razzed them for bellyfloppers. Once on the springboard some took a great while posing or clowning or deciding on a dive or getting up their nerve; others ran right off. Especially among the younger fellows the idea was to strike the funniest pose or do the craziest stunt as you fell, a thing that got harder to do as you kept on and kept on. But whether you hollered *Geronimo!* or *Sieg heil!*, held your nose or "rode a bicycle," pretended to be shot or did a perfect jackknife or changed your mind halfway down and ended up with nothing, it was over in two seconds, after all that wait. Spring, pose, splash. Spring, neat-o, splash. Spring, aw fooey, splash.

The grown-ups had gone on; Ambrose wanted to converse with Magda; she was remarkably well developed for her age; it was said that that came from rubbing with a turkish towel, and there were other theories. Ambrose could think of nothing to say except how good a diver Peter was, who was showing off for her benefit. You could pretty well tell by looking at their bathing suits and arm muscles how far along the different fellows were. Ambrose was glad he hadn't gone in swimming, the cold water shrank you up so. Magda pretended to be uninterested in the diving; she probably weighed as much as he did. If you knew your way around in the funhouse like your own bedroom, you could wait until a girl came along and then slip away without ever getting caught, even if her boyfriend was right with her. She'd think *he* did it! It would be better to be the boyfriend, and act outraged, and tear the funhouse apart.

Not act; *be*.

"He's a master diver," Ambrose said. In feigned admiration. "You really have to slave away at it to get that good." What would it matter anyhow if he asked her right out whether she remembered, even teased her with it as Peter would have?

There's no point in going farther; this isn't getting anybody anywhere; they haven't even come to the funhouse yet. Ambrose is off the track, in some new or old part of the place that's not supposed to be used; he strayed into it by some one-in-a-million chance, like the time the roller-coaster car left the tracks in the nineteen-teens against all the laws of physics and sailed over the boardwalk in the dark. And they can't locate him because they don't know where to look. Even the designer and operator have forgotten this other part, that winds around on itself like a whelk shell. That winds around the right part like the snakes on Mercury's caduceus. Some people, perhaps, don't "hit their stride" until their twenties, when the growing-up business is over and women appreciate other things besides wisecracks and teasing and strutting. Peter didn't have one-tenth the imagination *he* had, not one-tenth. Peter did this naming-their-children thing as a joke, making up names like Aloysius and Murgatroyd, but Ambrose knew *exactly* how it would feel to be married and have children of your own, and be a loving husband and father, and go comfortably to work in the mornings and to bed with your wife at night, and wake up with her there. With a breeze coming through the sash and birds and mockingbirds singing in the Chinese-cigar trees. His eyes watered, there aren't enough ways to say that. He would be quite famous in his line of work. Whether Magda was his wife or not, one evening when he was wise-lined and gray at the temples he'd smile gravely, at a fashionable dinner party and remind her of his youthful passion. The time they went with his family to Ocean City; the *erotic fantasies* he used to have about her. How long ago it seemed, and childish! Yet tender, too, *n'est-ce pas?* Would she have imagined that the world-famous whatever remembered how many strings were on the lyre on the bench beside the girl on the label of the cigar box he'd stared at in the toolshed at age ten while, she, age eleven. Even then he had felt *wise beyond his years;* he'd stroked her hair and said in his deepest voice and correctest English, as to a dear child: "I shall never forget this moment."

But though he had breathed heavily, groaned as if ecstatic, what he'd really felt throughout was an odd detachment, as though someone else were Master. Strive as he might to be transported, he heard his mind take notes upon the scene: *This is what they call* passion. *I am experiencing it.* Many of the digger machines were out of order in the penny arcades and could not be repaired or replaced for the duration. Moreover the prizes, made now in USA, were less interesting than formerly, pasteboard items for the most part, and some of the machines wouldn't work on white pennies. The gypsy fortune-teller machine might have provided a foreshadowing of the climax of this story if Ambrose had operated it. It was even dilapidateder than most: the silver coating was worn off the brown metal handles, the glass windows around the dummy were cracked and taped, her kerchiefs and silks long-faded. If a man lived by himself, he could take a department-store mannequin with flexible joints and modify her in certain ways. *However:* by the time he was that old he'd have a real woman. There was a machine that stamped your name around a white-metal coin with a star in the middle: A ———. His son would be the second, and when the lad reached thirteen or so he would put a strong arm around his shoulder and tell him calmly: "It is perfectly normal. We have all been through it. It will not last forever." Nobody knew how to be what they were right. He'd smoke a pipe, teach his son how to fish and softcrab, assure him he needn't worry about himself. Magda would certainly give, Magda would certainly yield a great deal of milk, although guilty of occasional solecisms. It don't taste so bad. Suppose the lights came on now!

The day wore on. You think you're yourself, but there are other persons in you. Ambrose gets hard when Ambrose doesn't want to, *and obversely.* Ambrose watches them disagree; Ambrose watches him watch. In the funhouse mirror room you can't see yourself go on forever, because no matter how you stand, your head gets in the way. Even if you had a glass periscope, the image of your eye would cover up the thing you really wanted to see. The police will come; there'll be a story in the papers. That must be where it happened. Unless he can find a surprise exit, an unofficial backdoor or escape hatch opening on an alley, say, and then stroll up to the family in front of the funhouse and ask where everybody's been; *he's* been out of the place for ages. That's just where it happened, in that last lighted room: Peter and Magda found the right exit; he found one that you weren't supposed to find and strayed off into the works somewhere. In a perfect funhouse you'd be able to go only one way, like the divers off the highboard; getting lost would be impossible; the doors and halls would work like minnow traps or the valves in veins.

On account of German U-boats, Ocean City was "browned out": streetlights were shaded on the seaward side; shop-windows and boardwalk amusement places were kept dim, not to silhouette tankers and Liberty-ships for torpedoing. In a short story about Ocean City, Maryland, during World War II, the author could make use of the image of sailors on leave in the penny arcades and shooting galleries, sighting through the crosshairs of toy machine guns at swastika'd subs, while out in the black Atlantic a U-boat skipper squints through his periscope at real ships outlined by the glow of penny arcades. After dinner the family strolled back to the amusement end of the boardwalk. The boys' father had burnt red as always and was masked with Noxzema, a minstrel in reverse. The grownups stood at the end of the boardwalk where the Hurricane of '33 had cut an inlet from the ocean to Assawoman Bay.

"Pronounced with a long o," Uncle Karl reminded Magda with a wink. His shirt sleeves were rolled up; Mother punched his brown biceps with the arrowed heart on it and said his mind was naughty. Fat May's laugh came suddenly from the funhouse, as if she'd just got the joke; the family laughed too at the coincidence. Ambrose went under the boardwalk to search for out-of-town matchbook covers with the aid of his pocket flashlight; he looked out from the edge of the North American continent and wondered how far their laughter carried over the water. Spies in rubber rafts; survivors in lifeboats. If the joke had been beyond his understanding, he could have said: "*The laughter was over his head.*" And let the reader see the serious wordplay on second reading.

He turned the flashlight on and then off at once even before the woman whooped. He sprang away, heart athud, dropping the light. What had the man grunted? Perspiration drenched and chilled him by the time he scrambled up to the family. "See anything?" his father asked. His voice wouldn't come; he shrugged and violently brushed sand from his pants legs.

"Let's ride the old flying horses!" Magda cried. I'll never be an author. It's been forever already, everybody's gone home, Ocean City's deserted, the ghost-crabs are tickling across the beach and down the littered cold streets. And the empty halls of clapboard hotels and abandoned funhouses. A tidal wave; an enemy air raid; a monster-crab swelling like an island from the sea. *The inhabitants fled in terror.* Magda clung to his trouser leg; he alone knew the maze's secret. "He gave his life that we might live," said Uncle Karl with a scowl of pain, as he. The fellow's hands had been tattooed; the woman's legs, the woman's fat white legs had. *An astonishing coincidence.* He yearned to tell Peter. He wanted to throw up for excitement. They hadn't even chased him. He wished he were dead.

One possible ending would be to have Ambrose come across another lost person in the dark. They'd match their wits together against the funhouse, struggle like Ulysses past obstacle after obstacle, help and encourage each other. Or a girl. By the time they found the exit they'd be closest friends, sweethearts if it were a girl; they'd know each other's inmost souls, be bound together *by the cement of shared adventure*; then they'd emerge into the light and it would turn out that his friend was a Negro. A blind girl. President Roosevelt's son. Ambrose's former archenemy.

Shortly after the mirror room he'd groped along a musty corridor, his heart already misgiving him at the absence of phosphorescent arrows and other signs. He'd found a crack of light — not a door, it turned out, but a seam between the plyboard wall panels — and squinting up to it, espied a small old man, *in appearance not unlike* the photographs at home of Ambrose's late grandfather, nodding upon a stool beneath a bare, speckled bulb. A crude panel of toggle- and knife-switches hung beside the open fuse box near his head; elsewhere in the little room were wooden levers and ropes belayed to boat cleats. At the time, Ambrose wasn't lost enough to rap or call; later he couldn't find that crack. Now it seemed to him that he'd possibly dozed off for a few minutes somewhere along the way; certainly he was exhausted from the afternoon's sunshine and the evening's problems; he couldn't be sure he hadn't dreamed part or all of the sight.

Had an old black wall fan droned like bees and shimmied two flypaper streamers? Had the funhouse operator — gentle, somewhat sad and tired-appearing, in expression not unlike the photographs at home of Ambrose's late Uncle Konrad — murmured in his sleep? Is there really such a person as Ambrose, or is he a figment of the author's imagination? Was it Assawoman Bay or Sinepuxent? Are there other errors of fact in this fiction? Was there another sound besides the little slap slap of thigh on ham, like water sucking at the chine-boards of a skiff?

When you're lost, the smartest thing to do is stay put till you're found, hollering if necessary. But to holler guarantees humiliation as well as rescue; keeping silent permits some saving of face — you can act surprised at the fuss when your rescuers find you and swear you weren't lost, if they do. What's more you might find your own way yet, *however belatedly.*

"Don't tell me your foot's still asleep!" Magda exclaimed as the three young people walked from the inlet to the area set aside for ferris wheels, carrousels, and other carnival rides, they having decided in favor of the vast and ancient merry-go-round instead of the funhouse. What a sentence, everything was wrong from the outset. People don't know what to make of him, he doesn't know what to make of himself, he's only thirteen, *athletically and socially inept,* not astonishingly bright, but there are antennae; he has . . . some sort of receivers in his head; things speak to him, he understands more than he should, the world winks at him through its objects, grabs grinning at his coat. Everybody else is in on some secret he doesn't know; they've forgotten to tell him. Through simple *procrastination* his mother put off his baptism until this year. Everyone else had it done as a baby; he'd assumed the same of himself, as had his mother, so she claimed, until it was time for him to join Grace Methodist-Protestant and the oversight came out. He was mortified, but pitched sleepless through his private catechizing, intimidated by the ancient mysteries, a thirteen year old would never say that, resolved to experience conversion like St. Augustine. When the water touched his brow and Adam's sin left him, he contrived by a strain like defecation to bring tears into his eyes — but felt nothing. There was some simple, radical difference about him; he hoped it was genius, feared it was madness, devoted himself to amiability and inconspicuousness. Alone on the seawall near his house he was seized by the terrifying transports he'd thought to find in toolshed, in Communion-cup. The grass was alive! The town, the river, himself, were not imaginary; time roared in his ears like wind; the world was *going on!* This part ought to be dramatized. The Irish author James Joyce once wrote. Ambrose M—— is going to scream.

There is no *texture of rendered sensory detail,* for one thing. The faded distorting mirrors beside Fat May; the impossibility of choosing a mount when one had but a single ride on the great carrousel; the *vertigo attendant on his recognition* that Ocean City was worn out, the place of fathers and grandfathers, straw-boatered men and parasoled ladies survived by their amusements. Money spent, the three paused at Peter's insistence beside Fat May to watch the girls get their skirts blown up. The object was to tease Magda, who said: "I swear, Peter M —— , you've got a one-track mind! Amby and me aren't *interested* in such things." In the tumbling-barrel, too, just inside the Devil's-mouth entrance to the funhouse, the girls were upended and their boyfriends and others could see up their dresses if they cared to. Which was the whole point, Ambrose realized. Of the entire funhouse! If you looked around, you noticed that almost all the people on the boardwalk were paired off into couples except the small children; in a way, that was the whole point of Ocean City! If you had X-ray eyes and could see everything going on at that instant under the boardwalk and in all the hotel rooms and cars and alleyways, you'd realize that all that normally *showed*, like restaurants and dance halls and clothing and test-your-strength machines, was merely preparation and intermission. Fat May screamed.

Because he watched the going-ons from the corner of his eye, it was Ambrose who spied the half-dollar on the boardwalk near the tumbling-barrel. Losers weepers. The first time he'd heard some people moving through a corridor not far away, just after he'd lost sight of the crack of light, he'd decided not to call to them, for fear they'd guess he was scared and poke fun; it sounded like roughnecks; he'd hoped they'd come by and he could follow in the dark without their knowing. Another time he'd heard just one person, unless he imagined it, bumping along as if on the other side of the plywood; perhaps Peter coming back for him, or Father, or Magda lost too. Or the owner and operator of the funhouse. He'd called out once, as though merrily: "Anybody know where the heck we are?" But the query was too stiff, his voice cracked, when the sounds stopped he was terrified: maybe it was a queer who waited for fellows to get lost, or a longhaired filthy monster that lived in some cranny of the funhouse. He stood rigid for hours it seemed like, scarcely respiring. His future was shockingly clear, in outline. He tried holding his breath to the point of unconsciousness. There ought to be a button you could push to end your life absolutely without pain; disappear in a flick, like turning out a light. He would push it instantly! He despised Uncle Karl. But he despised his father too, for not being what he was supposed to be. Perhaps his father hated *his* father, and so on, and his son would hate him, and so on. Instantly!

Naturally he didn't have nerve enough to ask Magda to go through the funhouse with him. With incredible nerve and to everyone's surprise he invited Magda, quietly and politely, to go through the funhouse with him. "I warn you, I've never been through it before," he added, *laughing easily;* "but I reckon we can manage somehow. The important thing to remember, after all, is that it's meant to be a *fun*house; that is, a place of amusement. If people really got lost or injured or too badly frightened in it, the owner'd go out of business. There'd even be lawsuits. No character in a work of fiction can make a speech this long without interruption or acknowledgment from the other characters."

Mother teased Uncle Karl: "Three's a crowd, I always heard." But actually Ambrose was relieved that Peter now had a quarter too. Nothing was what it looked like. Every instant, under the surface of the Atlantic Ocean, millions of living animals devoured one another. Pilots were falling in flames over Europe; women were being forcibly raped in the South Pacific. His father should have taken him aside and said: "There is a simple secret to getting through the funhouse, as simple as being first to see the Towers. Here it is. Peter does not know it; neither does your Uncle Karl. You and I are different. Not surprisingly, you've often wished you weren't. Don't think I haven't noticed how unhappy your childhood has been! But you'll understand, when I tell you, why it had to be kept secret until now. And you won't regret not being like your brother and your uncle. *On the contrary!*" If you knew all the stories behind all the people on the boardwalk, you'd see that *nothing* was what it looked like. Husbands and wives often hated each other; parents didn't necessarily love their children; et cetera. A child took things for granted because he had nothing to compare his life to and everybody acted as if things were as they should be. Therefore each saw himself as the hero of the story, when the truth might turn out to be that he's the villain, or the coward. And there wasn't one thing you could do about it!

Hunchbacks, fat ladies, fools — that no one chose what he was was unbearable. In the movies he'd meet a beautiful young girl in the funhouse; they'd have hairs-breadth escapes from real dangers; he'd do and say the right things; she also; in the end they'd be lovers; their dialogue lines would match up; he'd be perfectly at ease; she'd not only like him well enough, she'd think he was *marvelous*; she'd lie awake thinking about *him*, instead of vice versa — the way *his* face looked in different lights and how he stood and exactly what he'd said — and yet that would be only one small episode in his wonderful life, among many many others. Not a *turning point* at all. What had happened in the toolshed was nothing. He hated, he loathed his parents! One reason for not writing a lost-in-the-funhouse story is that either everybody's felt what Ambrose feels, in which case it goes without saying, or else no normal person feels such things, in which case Ambrose is a freak. "Is anything more tiresome, in fiction, than the problems of sensitive adolescents?" And it's all too long and rambling, as if the author. For all a person knows the first time through, the end could be just around any corner; perhaps, *not impossibly* it's been within reach any number of times. On the other hand he may be scarcely past the start, with everything yet to get through, an intolerable idea.

Fill in: His father's raised eyebrows when he announced his decision to do the funhouse with Magda. Ambrose understands now, but didn't then, that his father was wondering whether he knew what the funhouse was *for* — especially since he didn't object, as he should have, when Peter decided to come along too. The ticket-woman, witchlike, mortifying him when inadvertently he gave her his name-coin instead of the half-dollar, then unkindly calling Magda's attention to the birthmark on his temple: "Watch out for him, girlie, he's a marked man!" She wasn't even cruel, he understood, only vulgar and insensitive. Somewhere in the world there was a young woman with such splendid understanding that she'd see him entire, like a poem or story, and find his words so valuable after all that when he confessed his apprehensions she would explain why they were in fact the very things that made him precious to her . . . and to Western Civilization! There was no such girl, the simple truth being. Violent yawns as they approached the mouth. Whispered advice from an old-timer on a bench near the barrel: "Go crabwise and ye'll get an eyeful without upsetting!" Composure vanished at the first pitch: Peter hollered joyously, Magda tumbled, shrieked, clutched her skirt; Ambrose scrambled crabwise, tight-lipped with terror, was soon out, watched his dropped name-coin slide among the couples. Shame-faced he saw that to get through expeditiously was not the point; Peter feigned assistance in order to trip Magda up, shouted "I see Christmas!" when her legs went flying. The old man, his latest betrayer, cackled approval. A dim hall then of black-thread cobwebs and recorded gibber: he took Magda's elbow to steady her against revolving discs set in the slanted floor to throw your feet out from under, and explained to her in a calm, deep voice his theory that each phase of the funhouse was triggered either automatically, by a series of photoelectric devices, or else manually by operators stationed at peepholes. But he lost his voice thrice as the discs unbalanced him; Magda was anyhow squealing; but at one point she clutched him about the waist to keep from falling, and her right cheek pressed for a moment against his belt-buckle. Heroically he drew her up, it was his chance to clutch her close as if for support and say: "I love you." He even put an arm lightly about the small of her back before a sailor-and-girl pitched into them from behind, sorely treading his left big toe and knocking Magda asprawl with them. The sailor's girl was a string-haired hussy with a loud laugh and light blue drawers; Ambrose realized that he wouldn't have said "I love you" anyhow, and was smitten with self-contempt. How much better it would be to be that common sailor! A wiry little Seaman 3rd, the fellow squeezed a girl to each side and stumbled hilarious into the mirror room, closer to Magda in thirty seconds than Ambrose had got in thirteen years. She giggled at something the fellow said to Peter; she drew her hair from her eyes with a movement so womanly it struck Ambrose's heart; Peter's smacking her backside then seemed particularly coarse. But Magda made a pleased indignant face and cried, "All right for *you*, mister!" and pursued Peter into the maze without a backward glance. The sailor followed after, leisurely, drawing his girl against his hip; Ambrose understood not only that they were all so relieved to be rid of his burdensome company that they didn't even notice his absence, but that he himself shared their relief. Stepping from the treacherous passage at last into the mirror-maze, he saw once again, more clearly than ever, how readily he deceived himself into supposing he was a person. He even foresaw, wincing at his dreadful self-knowledge, that he would repeat the deception, at ever-rarer intervals, all his wretched life, so fearful were the alternatives. Fame, madness, suicide; perhaps all three. It's not believable that so young a boy could articulate that reflection, and in fiction the merely true must always yield to the plausible. Moreover, the symbolism is in places heavy-footed. Yet Ambrose M—— understood, as few adults do, that the famous loneliness of the great was no popular myth but a general truth — furthermore, that it was as much cause as effect.

All the preceding except the last few sentences is exposition that should've been done earlier or interspersed with the present action instead of lumped together. No reader would put up with so much with such *prolixity*. It's interesting that Ambrose's father, though presumably an intelligent man (as indicated by his role as grade-school principal), neither encouraged nor discouraged his sons at all in any way — as if he either didn't care about them or cared all right but didn't know how to act. If this fact should contribute to one of them's becoming a celebrated but wretchedly unhappy scientist, was it a good thing or not? He too might someday face the question; it would be useful to know whether it had tortured his father for years, for example, or never once crossed his mind.

In the maze two important things happened. First, our hero found a name-coin someone else had lost or discarded: *AMBROSE*, suggestive of the famous lightship and of his late grandfather's favorite dessert, which his mother used to prepare on special occasions out of coconut, oranges, grapes, and what else. Second, as he wondered at the endless replication of his image in the mirrors, second, as he *lost himself in the reflection* that the necessity for an observer makes perfect observation impossible, better make him eighteen at least, yet that would render other things unlikely, he heard Peter and Magda chuckling somewhere together in the maze. "Here!" "No, here!" they shouted to each other; Peter said, "Where's Amby?" Magda murmured. "Amb?" Peter called. In a pleased, friendly voice. He didn't reply. The truth was, his brother was a *happy-go-lucky youngster* who'd've been better off with a regular brother of his own, but who seldom complained of his lot and was generally cordial. Ambrose's throat ached; there aren't enough different ways to say that. He stood quietly while the two young people giggled and thumped through the glittering maze, hurrah'd their discovery of its exit, cried out in joyful alarm at what next beset them. Then he set his mouth and followed after, as he supposed, took a wrong turn, strayed into the pass *wherein he lingers yet*.

The action of conventional dramatic narrative may be represented by a diagram called Freitag's Triangle:

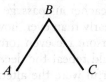

or more accurately by a variant of that diagram:

in which *AB* represents the exposition, *B* the introduction of conflict, *BC* the "rising action," complication, or development of the conflict, *C* the climax, or turn of the action, *CD* the dénouement, or resolution of the conflict. While there is no reason to regard this pattern as an absolute necessity, like many other conventions it became conventional because great numbers of people over many years learned by trial and error that it was effective; one ought not to forsake it, therefore, unless one wishes to forsake as well the effect of drama or has clear cause to feel that deliberate violation of the "normal" pattern can better can better effect that effect. This can't go on much longer; it can go on forever. He died telling stories to himself in the dark; years later, when that vast unsuspected area of the funhouse came to light, the first expedition found his skeleton in one of its labyrinthine corridors and mistook it for part of the entertainment. He died of starvation telling himself stories in the dark; but unbeknownst unbeknownst to him, an assistant operator of the funhouse, happening to overhear him, crouched just behind the plyboard partition and wrote down his every word. The operator's daughter, an exquisite young woman with a figure unusually well developed for her age, crouched just behind the partition and transcribed his every word. Though she had never laid eyes on him, she recognized that here was one of Western Culture's truly great imaginations, the eloquence of whose suffering would be an inspiration to unnumbered. And her heart was torn between her love for the misfortunate young man (yes, she loved him, though she had never laid though she knew him only — but how well! — through his words, and the deep, calm voice in which he spoke them) between her love et cetera and her womanly intuition that only in suffering and isolation could he give voice et cetera. Lone dark dying. Quietly she kissed the rough plyboard, and a tear fell upon the page. Where she had written in shorthand *Where she had written in shorthand* Where she had written in shorthand *Where she* et cetera. A long time ago we should have passed the apex of Freitag's Triangle and made brief work of the *dénouement*; the plot doesn't rise by meaningful steps but winds upon itself, digresses, retreats, hesitates, sighs, collapses, expires. The climax of the story must be its protagonist's discovery of a way to get through the funhouse. But he had found none, may have ceased to search.

What relevance does the war have to the story? Should there be fireworks outside or not?

Ambrose wandered, languished, dozed. Now and then he fell into his habit of rehearsing to himself the unadventurous story of his life, narrated from the third-person point of view, from his earliest memory parenthesis of maple leaves stirring in the summer breath of tidewater Maryland end of parenthesis to the present moment. Its principal events, on this telling, would appear to have been A, B, C, and D.

He imagined himself years hence, successful, married, at ease in the world, the trials of his adolescence far behind him. He has come to the seashore with his family for the holiday: how Ocean City has changed! But at one seldom at one ill-frequented end of the boardwalk a few derelict amusements survive from times gone by: the great carrousel from the turn of the century, with its monstrous griffins and mechanical concert band; the roller coaster rumored since 1916 to have been condemned; the mechanical shooting gallery in which only the image of our enemies changed. His own son laughs with Fat May and wants to know what a funhouse is; Ambrose hugs the sturdy lad close and smiles around his pipestem at his wife.

The family's going home. Mother sits between Father and Uncle Karl, who teases him good-naturedly who chuckles over the fact that the comrade with whom he'd fought his way shoulder to shoulder through the funhouse had turned out to be a blind Negro girl — to their mutual discomfort, as they'd opened their souls. But such are the walls of custom, which even. Whose arm is where? How must it feel. He dreams of a funhouse vaster by far than any yet constructed; but by then they may be out of fashion, like steamboats and excursion trains. Already quaint and seedy: the draperied ladies on the frieze of the carrousel are his father's father's mooncheeked dreams; if he thinks of it more he will vomit his apple-on-a-stick.

He wonders: will he become a regular person? Something has gone wrong; his vaccination didn't take; at the Boy-Scout initiation campfire he only pretended to be deeply moved, as he pretends to this hour that it is not so bad after all in the funhouse, and that he has a little limp. How long will it last? He envisions a truly astonishing funhouse, incredibly complex yet utterly controlled from a great central switchboard like the console of a pipe organ. Nobody had enough imagination. He could design such a place himself, wiring and all, and he's only thirteen years old. He would be its operator: panel lights would show what was up in every cranny of its cunning of its multivarious vastness; a switch-flick would ease this fellow's way, complicate that's, to balance things out; if anyone seemed lost or frightened, all the operator had to do was.

He wishes he had never entered the funhouse. But he has. Then he wishes he were dead. But he's not. Therefore he will construct funhouses for others and be their secret operator — though he would rather be among the lovers for whom funhouses are designed.

[1968]

DONALD BARTHELME (b. 1931) was raised in Texas, where his father was a prominent architect. While a high school student, he won awards for his stories and poetry, and at the University of Houston he edited the campus newspaper and wrote film criticism for the Houston Post. At age thirty he became director of the Contemporary Arts Museum in Houston. In 1962 he moved to New York City, where he continues to live when he is not teaching at the University of Houston as Cullen Distinguished Professor of English.

For the past twenty years Barthelme has been contributing short fiction to The New Yorker, and his literary style has often been imitated. His stories amuse readers who turn to the magazine for light browsing, but they also intrigue readers who want to give them more serious attention, since they often explore the fragmented nature of human relationships and the anxiety attendant upon many contemporary experiences. The language of the best of his stories, like "The President," suggests an eerie element of social criticism.

Barthelme's style depends on our awareness of how language has been corrupted by politics and advertising. As the critic Jerome Klinkowitz has recognized, Barthelme's fiction is "pure artifice. . . . [His] genius is to take the form in which we are used to hearing something — having heard it so often that we have become anaesthetized to it — and then insert a patent absurdity to shake us back to our senses and make us realize how our supposedly 'realistic' lives have been conducted on the brink of pure silliness." Barthelme has published two novels, Snow White (1967) and The Dead Father (1975), and eight volumes of short stories. Sixty Stories (1981) is the most representative collection of his work.

Donald Barthelme

⟶⟵

THE PRESIDENT

I am not altogether sympathetic to the new President. He is, certainly, a strange fellow (only forty-eight inches high at the shoulder). But is strangeness alone enough? I spoke to Sylvia: "Is strangeness alone enough?" "I love you," Sylvia said. I regarded her with my warm kind eyes. "Your thumb?" I said. One thumb was a fiasco of tiny crusted slashes. "Pop-top beer cans," she said. "He is a *strange fellow*, all right. He has some magic charisma which makes people — " She stopped and began again. "When the band begins to launch into his campaign song, 'Struttin' with Some Barbecue,' I just . . . I can't . . ."

The darkness, strangeness, and complexity of the new President have touched everyone. There has been a great deal of fainting lately. Is the President at fault? I was sitting, I remember, in Row EE at City Center, the opera was *The Gypsy Baron*,, Sylvia was singing in her green-and-blue gypsy costume in the gypsy encampment. I was thinking about the President. Is he, I wondered, right for this period? He is a *strange fellow*, I thought — not like the other Presidents we've had. Not like Garfield. Not like Taft. Not like Harding, Hoover, either of the Roosevelts, or Woodrow Wilson. Then I noticed a lady sitting in front of me, holding a baby. I tapped her on the shoulder. "Madam," I said, "your child has I believe fainted." "Giscard!" she cried, rotating the baby's head like a doll's. "Giscard, what has happened to you?" The President was smiling in his box.

"The President!" I said to Sylvia in the Italian restaurant. She raised her glass of warm red wine. "Do you think he liked me? My singing?" "He looked pleased," I said. "He was smiling." "A brilliant whirlwind campaign, I thought," Sylvia stated. "Winning was brilliant," I said. "He is the first President we've had from City College," Sylvia said. A waiter fainted behind us. "But is he right for the period?" I asked. "Our period is perhaps not so choice as the previous period, still — "

"He thinks a great deal about death, like all people from City," Sylvia said. "The death theme looms large in his consciousness. I've known a great many people from City, and these people, with no significant exceptions, are hung up on the death theme. It's an obsession, as it were." Other waiters carried the waiter who had fainted out into the kitchen.

"Our period will be characterized in future histories as a period of tentativeness and uncertainty, I feel," I said. "A kind of parenthesis. When he rides in his black limousine with the plastic top I see a little boy who has blown an enormous soap bubble which has trapped him. The look on his face — " "The other candidate was dazzled by his strangeness, newness, smallness, and philosophical grasp of the death theme," Sylvia said. "The other candidate didn't have a prayer," I said. Sylvia adjusted her green-and-blue veils in the Italian restaurant. "Not having gone to City College and sat around the cafeterias there discussing death," she said.

I am, as I say, not entirely sympathetic. Certain things about the new President are not clear. I can't make out what he is thinking. When he has finished speaking I can never remember what he has said. There remains only an impression of strangeness, darkness . . . On television, his face clouds when his name is mentioned. It is as if hearing his name frightens him. Then he stares directly into the camera (an actor's preempting gaze) and begins to speak. One hears only cadences. Newspaper accounts of his speeches always say only that he "touched on a number of matters in the realm of . . ." When he has finished speaking he appears nervous and unhappy. The camera credits fade in over an image of the President standing stiffly, with his arms rigid at his sides, looking to the right and to the left, as if awaiting instructions. On the other hand, the handsome meliorist who ran against him, all zest and programs, was defeated by a fantastic margin.

People are fainting. On Fifty-seventh Street, a young girl dropped in her tracks in front of Henri Bendel. I was shocked to discover that she wore only a garter belt under her dress. I picked her up and carried her into the store with the help of a Salvation Army major — a very tall man with an orange hairpiece. "She fainted," I said to the floorwalker. We talked about the new President, the Salvation Army major and I. "I'll tell you what *I* think," he said. "I think he's got something up his sleeve nobody knows about. I think he's keeping it under wraps. One of these days . . ." The Salvation Army major shook my hand. "I'm not saying that the problems he faces aren't tremendous, staggering. The awesome burden of the Presidency. But if anybody — any *one man* . . ."

What is going to happen? What is the President planning? No one knows. But everyone is convinced that he will bring it off. Our exhausted age wishes above everything to plunge into the heart of the problem, to be able to say, *Here is the difficulty*. And the new President, that tiny, strange, and brilliant man, seems cankered and difficult enough to take us there. In the meantime, people are fainting. My secretary fell in the middle of a sentence. "Miss Kagle," I said. "Are you all right?" She was wearing an anklet of tiny silver circles. Each tiny silver circle held an initial: @@@@@@@@@@@@@@@@. Who is this person "A"? What is he in your life, Miss Kagle?

I gave her water with a little brandy in it. I speculated about the President's mother. Little is known about her. She presents herself in various guises:

A little lady, 5' 2", with a cane.
A big lady, 7' 1", with a dog.
A wonderful old lady, 4' 3", with an indomitable spirit.
A noxious old sack, 6' 8", excaudate, because of an operation.

Little is known about her. We are assured, however, that the same damnable involvements that obsess us obsess her too. Copulation. Strangeness. Applause. She must be pleased that her son is what he is — loved and looked up to, a mode of hope for millions. "Miss Kagle. Drink it down. It will put you on your feet again, Miss Kagle." I regarded her with my warm kind eyes.

At Town Hall I sat reading the program notes to *The Gypsy Baron*. Outside the building, eight mounted policemen collapsed en bloc. The well-trained horses planted their feet delicately among the bodies. Sylvia was singing. They said a small man could never be President (only forty-eight inches high at the shoulder). Our period is not the one I would have chosen, but it has chosen me. The new President must have certain intuitions. I am convinced that he has these intuitions (although I am certain of very little else about him; I have reservations, I am not sure). I could tell you about his mother's summer journey, in 1919, to western Tibet — about the dandymen and the red bear, and how she told off the Pathan headman, instructing him furiously to rub up his English or get out of her service — but what order of knowledge is this? Let me instead simply note his small-ness, his strangeness, his brilliance, and say that we expect great things of him. "I love you," Sylvia said. The President stepped through the roaring curtain. We applauded until our arms hurt. We shouted until the ushers set off flares enforcing silence. The orchestra tuned itself. Sylvia sang the second lead. The President was smiling in his box. As the finale, the entire cast slipped into the orchestra pit in a great, swooning mass. We cheered until the ushers tore up our tickets.

                                                                        [1968]

ALICE MUNRO (b. 1931) grew up on a farm in a rural community near Lake Huron in Ontario, Canada, where her father raised silver foxes. After attending the University of Western Ontario for two years, she married and moved to British Columbia. Munro remembers that she began writing things down when she was about twelve, and at age fifteen she decided she would soon write a great novel. "But I thought perhaps I wasn't ready so I would write a short story in the meantime." She began publishing her stories when she was a university student, but her writing progressed very slowly during the next several years after she married and raised a family. Then her career blossomed. In 1968 she published her first collection of stories, Dance of the Happy Shades, which won the Governor General's Award in Canada. Three years later she published her second book, a novel titled Lives of Girls and Women. Another collection of stories, Something I've Been Meaning to Tell You, appeared in 1974, and a series of connected stories titled Who Do You Think You Are? was published in 1978, giving Munro her second Governor General's Award.

Almost all Munro's stories are set in the landscape of southern Ontario, where she grew up and where she now lives with her second husband. She sees herself as an anachronism, "because I write about places where your roots are and most people don't live that kind of life any more at all. Most writers, probably, the writers who are most in tune with our time, write about places that have no texture because this is where most of us live."

Munro has said that she does not find long narrative structures congenial to her talent. She is primarily a short story writer. Although Lives of Girls and Women was published as a novel, she first wrote it as a series of stories, which she later revised in a loosely patterned autobiographical structure. Frequently her narrator is a young girl who notes in great detail the attitudes and standards of conduct in the small town life around her, but does not make judgments on what she sees. Munro's themes are often familiar ones of initiation and romantic love, as in the story "How I Met My Husband." Literary critics have observed that her stories about small town life are reminiscent of the fiction of earlier American writers like William Faulkner, Eudora Welty, and Flannery O'Connor.

Alice Munro

∾

How I Met My Husband

We heard the plane come over at noon, roaring through the radio news, and we were sure it was going to hit the house, so we all ran out into the yard. We saw it come in over the treetops, all red and silver, the first close-up plane I ever saw. Mrs. Peebles screamed.

"Crash landing," their little boy said. Joey was his name.

"It's okay," said Dr. Peebles. "He knows what he's doing." Dr. Peebles was only an animal doctor, but had a calming way of talking, like any doctor.

This was my first job — working for Dr. and Mrs. Peebles, who had bought an old house out on the Fifth Line, about five miles out of town. It was just when the trend was starting of town people buying up old farms, not to work them but to live on them.

We watched the plane land across the road, where the fairgrounds used to be. It did make a good landing field, nice and level for the old race track, and the barns and display sheds torn down now for scrap lumber so there was nothing in the way. Even the old grandstand bays had burned.

"All right," said Mrs. Peebles, snappy as she always was when she got over her nerves. "Let's go back in the house. Let's not stand here gawking like a set of farmers."

She didn't say that to hurt my feelings. It never occurred to her.

I was just setting the dessert down when Loretta Bird arrived, out of breath, at the screen door.

"I thought it was going to crash into the house and kill youse all!"

She lived on the next place and the Peebleses thought she was a countrywoman, they didn't know the difference. She and her husband didn't farm, he worked on the roads and had a bad name for drinking. They had seven children and couldn't get credit at the HiWay Grocery. The Peebleses made her welcome, not knowing any better, as I say, and offered her dessert.

Dessert was never anything to write home about, at their place. A dish of Jello-O or sliced bananas or fruit out of a tin. "Have a house without a pie, be ashamed until you die," my mother used to say, but Mrs. Peebles operated differently.

1042

Loretta Bird saw me getting the can of peaches.

"Oh, never mind," she said. "I haven't got the right kind of a stomach to trust what comes out of those tins, I can only eat home canning."

I could have slapped her. I bet she never put down fruit in her life.

"I know what he's landed here for," she said. "He's got permission to use the fairgrounds and take people up for rides. It costs a dollar. It's the same fellow who was over at Palmerston last week and was up the lakeshore before that. I wouldn't go up, if you paid me."

"I'd jump at the chance," Dr. Peebles said. "I'd like to see this neighborhood from the air."

Mrs. Peebles said she would just as soon see it from the ground. Joey said he wanted to go and Heather did, too. Joey was nine and Heather was seven.

"Would you, Edie?" Heather said.

I said I didn't know. I was scared, but I never admitted that, especially in front of children I was taking care of.

"People are going to be coming out here in their cars raising dust and trampling your property, if I was you I would complain." Loretta said. She hooked her legs around the chair rung and I knew we were in for a lengthy visit. After Dr. Peebles went back to his office or out on his next call and Mrs. Peebles went for her nap, she would hang around me while I was trying to do the dishes. She would pass remarks about the Peebleses in their own house.

"She wouldn't find time to lay down in the middle of the day, if she had seven kids like I got."

She asked me did they fight and did they keep things in the dresser drawer not to have babies with. She said it was a sin if they did. I pretended I didn't know whaat she was talking about.

I was fifteen and away from home for the first time. My parents had made the effort and sent me to high school for a year, but I didn't like it. I was shy of strangers and the work was hard, they didn't make it nice for you or explain the way they do now. At the end of the year the averages were published in the paper, and mine came out at the very bottom, 37 percent. My father said that's enough and I didn't blame him. The last thing I wanted, anyway, was to go on and end up teaching school. It happened the very day the paper came out with my disgrace in it, Dr. Peebles was staying at our place for dinner, having just helped one of our cows have twins, and he said I looked smart to him and his wife was looking for a girl to help. He said she felt tied down, with the two children, out in the country. I guess she would, my mother said, being polite, though I could tell from her face she was wondering what on earth it would be like to have only two children and no barn work, and then to be complaining.

When I went home I would describe to them the work I had to do, and it made everybody laugh. Mrs. Peebles had an automatic washer and dryer, the first I ever saw. I have had those in my own home for such a long time now it's hard to remember how much of a miracle it was to me, not having to struggle with the wringer and hang up and haul down. Let alone not having to heat water. Then there was practically no baking. Mrs. Peebles said she couldn't make pie crust, the most amazing thing I ever heard a woman admit. I could, of course, and I could make light biscuits and a white cake and dark cake, but they didn't want it, she said they watched their figures. The only thing I didn't like about working there, in fact, was feeling half hungry a lot of the time. I used to bring back a box of doughnuts made out at home, and hide them under my bed. The children found out, and I didn't mind sharing, but I thought I better bind them to secrecy.

The day after the plane landed Mrs. Peebles put both children in the car and drove over to Chesley, to get their hair cut. There was a good woman then at Chesley for doing hair. She got hers done at the same place, Mrs. Peebles did, and that meant they would be gone a good while. She had to pick a day Dr. Peebles wasn't going out into the country, she didn't have her own car. Cars were still in short supply then, after the war.

I loved being left in the house alone, to do my work at leisure. The kitchen was all white and bright yellow, with fluorescent lights. That was before they ever thought of making the appliances all different colors and doing the cupboards like dark old wood and hiding the lighting. I loved light. I loved the double sink. So would anybody new-come from washing dishes in a dishpan with a rag-plugged hole on an oilcloth-covered table by light of a coal-oil lamp. I kept everything shining.

The bathroom too. I had a bath in there once a week. They wouldn't have minded if I took one oftener, but to me it seemed like asking too much, or maybe risking making it less wonderful. The basin and the tub and the toilet were all pink, and there were glass doors with flamingoes painted on them, to shut off the tub. The light had a rosy cast and the mat sank under your feet like snow, except that it was warm. The mirror was three-way. With the mirror all steamed up and the air like a perfume cloud, from things I was allowed to use, I stood up on the side of the tub and admired myself naked, from three directions. Sometimes I thought about the way we lived out at home and the way we lived here and how one way was so hard to imagine when you were living the other way. But I thought it was still a lot easier, living the way we lived at home, to picture something like this, the painted flamingoes and the warmth and the soft mat, than it was anybody knowing only things like this to picture how it was the other way. And why was that?

I was through my jobs in no time, and had the vegetables peeled for supper and sitting in cold water besides. Then I went into Mrs. Peebles' bedroom. I had been in there plenty of times, cleaning, and I always took a good look in her closet, at the clothes she had hanging there. I wouldn't have looked in her drawers, but a closet is open to anybody. That's a lie. I would have looked in drawers, but I would have felt worse doing it and been more scared she could tell.

Some clothes in her closet she wore all the time, I was quite familiar with them. Others she never put on, they were pushed to the back. I was disappointed to see no wedding dress. But there was one long dress I could just see the skirt of, and I was hungering to see the rest. Now I took note of where it hung and lifted it out. It was satin, a lovely weight on my arm, light bluish-green in color, almost silvery. It had a fitted, pointed waist and a full skirt and an off-the-shoulder fold hiding the little sleeves.

Next thing was easy. I got out of my own things and slipped it on. I was slimmer at fifteen than anybody would believe who knows me now and the fit was beautiful. I didn't, of course, have a strapless bra on, which was what it needed, I just had to slide my straps down my arms under the material. Then I tried pinning up my hair, to get the effect. One thing led to another. I put on rouge and lipstick and eyebrow pencil from her dresser. The heat of the day and the weight of the satin and all the excitement made me thirsty, and I went out to the kitchen, got-up as I was, to get a glass of ginger ale with ice cubes from the refrigerator. The Peebleses drank ginger ale, or fruit drinks, all day, like water, and I was getting so I did too. Also there was no limit on ice cubes, which I was so fond of I would even put them in a glass of milk.

I turned from putting the ice tray back and saw a man watching me through the screen. It was the luckiest thing in the world I didn't spill the ginger ale down the front of me then and there.

"I never meant to scare you. I knocked but you were getting the ice out, you didn't hear me."

I couldn't see what he looked like, he was dark the way somebody is pressed up against a screen door with the bright daylight behind them. I only knew he wasn't from around here.

"I'm from the plane over there. My name is Chris Watters and what I was wondering was if I could use that pump."

There was a pump in the yard. That was the way the people used to get their water. Now I noticed he was carrying a pail.

"You're welcome," I said. "I can get it from the tap and save you pumping." I guess I wanted him to know we had piped water, didn't pump ourselves.

"I don't mind the exercise." He didn't move, though, and finally he said, "Were you going to a dance?"

Seeing a stranger there had made me entirely forget how I was dressed.

"Or is that the way ladies around here generally get dressed up in the afternoon?"

I didn't know how to joke back then. I was too embarrassed.

"You live here? Are you the lady of the house?"

"I'm the hired girl."

Some people change when they find that out, their whole way of looking at you and speaking to you changes, but his didn't.

"Well, I just wanted to tell you you look very nice. I was so surprised when I looked in the door and saw you. Just because you looked so nice and beautiful."

I wasn't even old enough then to realize how out of the common it is, for a man to say something like that to a woman, or somebody he is treating like a woman. For a man to say a word like *beautiful.* I wasn't old enough to realize or to say anything back, or in fact to do anything but wish he would go away. Not that I didn't like him, but just that it upset me so, having him look at me, and me trying to think of something to say.

He must have understood. He said good-bye, and thanked me, and went and started filling his pail from the pump. I stood behind the Venetian blinds in the dining room, watching him. When he had gone, I went into the bedroom and took the dress off and put it back in the same place. I dressed in my own clothes and took my hair down and washed my face, wiping it on Kleenex, which I threw in the wastebasket.

The Peebleses asked me what kind of man he was. Young, middle-aged, short, tall? I couldn't say.

"Good-looking?" Dr. Peebles teased me.

I couldn't think a thing but that he would be coming to get his water again, he would be talking to Dr. or Mrs. Peebles, making friends with them, and he would mention seeing me that first afternoon, dressed up. Why not mention it? He would think it was funny. And no idea of the trouble it would get me into.

After supper the Peebleses drove into town to go to a movie. She wanted to go somewhere with her hair fresh done. I sat in my bright kitchen wondering what to do, knowing I would never sleep. Mrs. Peebles might not fire me, when she found out, but it would give her a different feeling about me altogether. This was the first place I ever worked but I already had picked up things about the way people feel when you are working for them. They like to think you aren't curious. Not just that you aren't dishonest, that isn't enough. They like to feel you don't notice things, that you don't think or wonder about anything but what they liked to eat and how they liked things ironed, and so on. I don't mean they weren't kind to me, because they were. They had me eat my meals with them (to tell the truth I expected to, I didn't know there were families who don't) and sometimes they took me along in the car. But all the same.

I went up and checked on the children being asleep and then I went out. I had to do it. I crossed the road and went in the old fairgrounds gate. The plane looked unnatural sitting there, and shining with the moon. Off at the far side of the fairgrounds, where the bush was taking over, I saw his tent.

He was sitting outside it smoking a cigarette. He saw me coming.

"Hello, were you looking for a plane ride? I don't start taking people up till tomorrow." Then he looked again and said, "Oh, it's you. I didn't know you without your long dress on."

My heart was knocking away, my tongue was dried up. I had to say something. But I couldn't. My throat was closed and I was like a deaf-and-dumb.

"Did you want a ride? Sit down. Have a cigarette."

I couldn't even shake my head to say no, so he gave me one.

"Put it in your mouth or I can't light it. It's a good thing I'm used to shy ladies."

I did. It wasn't the first time I had smoked a cigarette, actually. My girlfriend out home Muriel Lowe, used to steal them from her brother.

"Look at your hand shaking. Did you just want to have a chat, or what?"

In one burst I said, "I wisht you wouldn't say anything about that dress."

"What dress? Oh, the long dress."

"It's Mrs. Peebles'."

"Whose? Oh, the lady you work for? Is that it? She wasn't home so you got dressed up in her dress, eh? You got dressed up and played queen. I don't blame you. You're not smoking the cigarette right. Don't just puff. Draw it in. Did anybody ever show you how to inhale? Are you scared I'll tell on you? Is that it?"

I was so ashamed at having to ask him to connive this way I couldn't nod. I just looked at him and he saw *yes*.

"Well I won't. I won't in the slightest way mention it or embarrass you. I give you my word of honor."

Then he changed the subject, to help me out, seeing I couldn't even thank him.

"What do you think of this sign?"

It was a board sign lying practically at my feet.

SEE THE WORLD FROM THE SKY. ADULTS $1.00, CHILDREN 50¢. QUALIFIED PILOT.

"My old sign was getting pretty beat up, I thought I'd make a new one. That's what I've been doing with my time today."

The lettering wasn't all that handsome, I thought. I could have done a better one in half an hour.

"I'm not an expert at sign making."

"It's very good," I said.

"I don't need it for publicity, word of mouth is usually enough. I turned away two carloads tonight. I felt like taking it easy. I didn't tell them ladies were dropping in to visit me."

Now I remembered the children and I was scared again, in case one of them had waked up and called me and I wasn't there.

"Do you have to go so soon?"

I remembered some manners. "Thank you for the cigarette."

"Don't forget. You have my word of honor."

I tore off across the fairgrounds, scared I'd see the car heading home from town. My sense of time was mixed up, I didn't know how long I'd been out of the house. But it was all right, it wasn't late, the children were asleep. I got in bed myself and lay thinking what a lucky end to the day, after all, and among things to be grateful for I could be grateful Loretta Bird hadn't been the one who caught me.

The yard and borders didn't get trampled, it wasn't as bad as that. All the same it seemed very public, around the house. The sign was on the fairgrounds gate. People came mostly after supper but a good many in the afternoon, too. The Bird children all came without fifty cents between them and hung on the gate. We got used to the excitement of the plane coming in and taking off, it wasn't excitement anymore. I never went over, after that one time, but would see him when he came to get his water. I would be out on the steps doing sitting-down work, like preparing vegetables, if I could.

"Why don't you come over? I'll take you up in my plane."

"I'm saving my money," I said, because I couldn't think of anything else.

"For what? For getting married?"

I shook my head.

"I'll take you up for free if you come sometime when it's slack. I thought you would come, and have another cigarette."

I made a face to hush him, because you never could tell when the children would be sneaking around the porch, or Mrs. Peebles herself listening in the house. Sometimes she came out and had a conversation with him. He told her things he hadn't bothered to tell me. But then I hadn't thought to ask. He told her he had been in the war, that was where he learned to fly a plane, and now he couldn't settle down to ordinary life, this was what he liked. She said she couldn't imagine anybody liking such a thing. Though sometimes, she said, she was almost bored enough to try anything herself, she wasn't brought up to living in the country. It's all my husband's idea, she said. This was news to me.

"Maybe you ought to give flying lessons," she said.

"Would you take them?"

She just laughed.

Sunday was a busy flying day in spite of it being preached against from two pulpits. We were all sitting out watching. Joey and Heather were over on the fence with the Bird kids. Their father had said they could go, after their mother saying all week they couldn't.

A car came down the road past the parked cars and pulled up right in the drive. It was Loretta Bird who got out, all importance, and on the driver's side another woman got out, more sedately. She was wearing sunglasses.

"This is a lady looking for the man that flies the plane," Loretta Bird said. "I heard her inquire in the hotel coffee shop where I was having a Coke and I brought her out."

"I'm sorry to bother you," the lady said. "I'm Alice Kelling, Mr. Watters' fiancée."

This Alice Kelling had on a pair of brown and white checked slacks and a yellow top. Her bust looked to me rather low and bumpy. She had a worried face. Her hair had had a permanent, but had grown out, and she wore a yellow band to keep it off her face. Nothing in the least pretty or even young-looking about her. But you could tell from how she talked she was from the city, or educated, or both.

Dr. Peebles stood up and introduced himself and his wife and me and asked her to be seated.

"He's up in the air right now, but you're welcome to sit and wait. He gets his water here and he hasn't been yet. He'll probably take his break about five."

"That is him, then?" said Alice Kelling, wrinkling and straining at the sky.

"He's not in the habit of running out on you, taking a different name?" Dr. Peebles laughed. He was the one, not his wife, to offer iced tea. Then she sent me into the kitchen to fix it. She smiled. She was wearing sunglasses too.

"He never mentioned his fiancée," she said.

I loved fixing iced tea with lots of ice and slices of lemon in tall glasses. I ought to have mentioned before, Dr. Peebles was an abstainer, at least around the house, or I wouldn't have been allowed to take the place. I had to fix a glass for Loretta Bird too, though it galled me, and when I went out she had settled in my lawn chair, leaving me the steps.

"I knew you was a nurse when I first heard you in that coffee shop."

"How would you know a thing like that?"

"I get my hunches about people. Was that how you met him, nursing?"

"Chris? Well yes. Yes, it was."

"Oh, were you overseas?" said Mrs. Peebles.

"No, it was before he went overseas. I nursed him when he was stationed at Centralia and had a ruptured appendix. We got engaged and then he went overseas. My, this is refreshing, after a long drive."

"He'll be glad to see you," Dr. Peebles said. "It's a rackety kind of life, isn't it, not staying one place long enough to really make friends."

"Youse've had a long engagement," Loretta Bird said.

Alice Kelling passed that over. "I was going to get a room at the hotel, but when I was offered directions I came on out. Do you think I could phone them?"

"No need," Dr. Peebles said. "You're five miles away from him if you stay at the hotel. Here, you're right across the road. Stay with us. We've got rooms on rooms, look at this big house."

Asking people to stay, just like that, is certainly a country thing, and maybe seemed natural to him now, but not to Mrs. Peebles, from the way she said, oh yes, we have plenty of room. Or to Alice Kelling, who kept protesting, but let herself be worn down. I got the feeling it was a temptation to her, to be that close. I was trying for a look at her ring. Her nails were painted red, her fingers were freckled and wrinkled. It was a tiny stone. Muriel Lowe's cousin had one twice as big.

Chris came to get his water, late in the afternoon just as Dr. Peebles had predicted. He must have recognized the car from a way off. He came smiling.

"Here I am chasing after you to see what you're up to," called Alice Kelling. She got up and went to meet him and they kissed, just touched, in front of us.

"You're going to spend a lot on gas that way," Chris said.

Dr. Peebles invited Chris to stay for supper, since he had already put up the sign that said: NO MORE RIDES TILL 7 P.M. Mrs. Peebles wanted it served in the yard, in spite of the bugs. One thing strange to anybody from the country is this eating outside. I had made a potato salad earlier and she had made a jellied salad, that was one thing she could do, so it was just a matter of getting those out, and some sliced meat and cucumbers and fresh leaf lettuce. Loretta Bird hung around for some time saying, "Oh, well, I guess I better get home to those yappers," and, "It's so nice just sitting here, I sure hate to get up," but nobody invited her, I was relieved to see, and finally she had to go.

That night after rides were finished Alice Kelling and Chris went off somewhere in her car. I lay awake till they got back. When I saw the car lights sweep my ceiling I got up to look down on them through the slats of my blind. I don't know what I thought I was going to see. Muriel Lowe and I used to sleep on her front veranda and watch her sister and her sister's boy friend saying good night. Afterward we couldn't get to sleep, for longing for somebody to kiss us and rub up against us and we would talk about suppose you were out in a boat with a boy and he wouldn't bring you in to shore unless you did it, or what if somebody got you trapped in a barn, you would have to, wouldn't you, it wouldn't be your fault. Muriel said her two girl cousins used to try with a toilet paper roll that one of them was a boy. We wouldn't do anything like that; just lay and wondered.

All that happened was that Chris got out of the car on one side and she got out on the other and they walked off separately — him toward the fairgrounds and her toward the house. I got back in bed and imagined about me coming home with him, not like that.

Next morning Alice Kelling got up late and I fixed a grapefruit for her the way I had learned and Mrs. Peebles sat down with her to visit and have another cup of coffee. Mrs. Peebles seemed pleased enough now, having company. Alice Kelling said she guessed she better get used to putting in a day just watching Chris take off and come down, and Mrs. Peebles said she didn't know if she should suggest it because Alice Kelling was the one with the car, but the lake was only twenty-five miles away and what a good day for a picnic.

Alice Kelling took her up on the idea and by eleven o'clock they were in the car, with Joey and Heather and a sandwich lunch I had made. The only thing was that Chris hadn't come down, and she wanted to tell him where they were going.

"Edie'll go over and tell him," Mrs. Peebles said. "There's no problem."

Alice Kelling wrinkled her face and agreed.

"Be sure and tell him we'll be back by five!"

I didn't see that he would be concerned about knowing this right away, and I thought of him eating whatever he ate over there, alone, cooking on his camp stove, so I got to work and mixed up a crumb cake and baked it, in between the other work I had to do; then, when it was a bit cooled, wrapped it in a tea towel. I didn't do anything to myself but take off my apron and comb my hair. I would like to have put some makeup on, but I was too afraid it would remind him of the way he first saw me, and that would humiliate me all over again.

He had come and put another sign on the gate: NO RIDES THIS P.M. APOLOGIES. I worried that he wasn't feeling well. No sign of him outside and the tent flap was down. I knocked on the pole.

"Come in," he said, in a voice that would just as soon have said *Stay out*.

I lifted the flap.

"Oh, it's you. I'm sorry. I didn't know it was you."

He had been just sitting on the side of the bed, smoking. Why not at least sit and smoke in the fresh air?

"I brought a cake and hope you're not sick," I said.

"Why would I be sick? Oh — that sign. That's all right. I'm just tired of talking to people. I don't mean you. Have a seat." He pinned back the tent flap. "Get some fresh air in here."

I sat on the edge of the bed, there was no place else. It was one of those fold-up cots, really: I remembered and gave him his fiancée's message.

He ate some of the cake. "Good."

"Put the rest away for when you're hungry later."

"I'll tell you a secret. I won't be around here much longer."

"Are you getting married?"

"Ha ha. What time did you say they'd be back?"

"Five o'clock."

"Well, by that time this place will have seen the last of me. A plane can get further than a car." He unwrapped the cake and ate another piece of it, absent-mindedly.

"Now you'll be thirsty."

"There's some water in the pail."

"It won't be very cold. I could bring some fresh. I could bring some ice from the refrigerator."

"No," he said. "I don't want you to go. I want a nice long time of saying good-bye to you."

He put the cake away carefully and sat beside me and started those little kisses, so soft, I can't ever let myself think about them, such kindness in his face and lovely kisses, all over my eyelids and neck and ears, all over, then me kissing back as well as I could (I had only kissed a boy on a dare before, and kissed my own arms for practice) and we lay back on the cot and pressed together, just gently, and he did some other things, not bad things or not in a bad way. It was lovely in the tent, that smell of grass and hot tent cloth with the sun beating down on it, and he said, "I wouldn't do you any harm for the world." Once, when he had rolled on top of me and we were sort of rocking together on the cot, he said softly, "Oh, no," and freed himself and jumped up and got the water pail. He splashed some of it on his neck and face, and the little bit left, on me lying there.

"That's to cool us off, miss."

When we said good-bye I wasn't at all sad, because he held my face and said "I'm going to write you a letter. I'll tell you where I am and maybe you can come and see me. Would you like that? Okay then. You wait." I was really glad I think to get away from him, it was like he was piling presents on me I couldn't get the pleasure of till I considered them alone.

No consternation at first about the plane being gone. They thought he had taken somebody up, and I didn't enlighten them. Dr. Peebles had phoned he had to go to the country, so there was just us having supper, and then Loretta Bird thrusting her head in the door and saying, "I see he's took off."

"What?" said Alice Kelling, and pushed back her chair.

"The kids come and told me this afternoon he was taking down his tent. Did he think he'd run through all the business there was around here? He didn't take off without letting you know, did he?"

"He'll send me word," Alice Kelling said. "He'll probably phone tonight. He's terribly restless, since the war."

"Edie, he didn't mention to you, did he?" Mrs. Peebles said. "When you took over the message?"

"Yes," I said. So far so true.

"Well why didn't you say?" All of them were looking at me. "Did he say where he was going?"

"He said he might try Bayfield," I said. What made me tell such a lie? I didn't intend it.

"Bayfield, how far is that?" said Alice Kelling.

Mrs. Peebles said, "Thirty, thirty-five miles."

"That's not far. Oh, well, that's really not far at all. It's on the lake, isn't it?"

You'd think I'd be ashamed of myself, setting her on the wrong track. I did it to give him more time, whatever time he needed. I lied for him, and also, I have to admit, for me. Women should stick together and not do things like that. I see that now, but didn't then. I never thought of myself as being in any way like her, or coming to the same troubles, ever.

She hadn't taken her eyes off me. I thought she suspected my lie.

"When did he mention this to you?"

"Earlier."

"When you were over at the plane?"

"Yes."

"You must've stayed and had a chat." She smiled at me, not a nice smile. "You must've stayed and had a little visit with him."

"I took a cake," I said, thinking that telling some truth would spare me telling the rest.

"We didn't have a cake," said Mrs. Peebles rather sharply.

"I baked one."

Alice Kelling said, "That was very friendly of you."

"Did you get permission," said Loretta Bird. "You never know what these girls'll do next," she said. "It's not they mean harm so much, as they're ignorant."

"The cake is neither here nor there," Mrs. Peebles broke in. "Edie, I wasn't aware you knew Chris that well."

I didn't know what to say.

"I'm not surprised," Alice Kelling said in a high voice. "I knew by the look of her as soon as I saw her. We get them at the hospital all the time." She looked hard at me with her stretched smile. "Having their babies. We have to put them in a special ward because of their diseases. Little country tramps. Fourteen and fifteen years old. You should see the babies they have, too."

"There was a bad woman here in town had a baby that pus was running out of its eyes," Loretta Bird put in.

"Wait a minute," said Mrs. Peebles. "What is this talk? Edie. What about you and Mr. Watters? Were you intimate with him?"

"Yes," I said. I was thinkng of us lying on the cot and kissing, wasn't that intimate? And I would never deny it.

They were all one minute quiet, even Loretta Bird.

"Well," said Mrs. Peebles. "I am surprised. I think I need a cigarette. This is the first of any such tendencies I've seen in her," she said, speaking to Alice Kelling, but Alice Kelling was looking at me.

"Loose little bitch." Tears ran down her face. "Loose little bitch, aren't you? I knew as soon as I saw you. Men despise girls like you. He just made use of you and went off, you know that, don't you? Girls like you are just nothing, they're just public conveniences, just filthy little rags!"

"Oh, now," said Mrs. Peebles.

"Filthy," Alice Kelling sobbed. "Filthy little rags!"

"Don't get yourself upset," Loretta Bird said. She was swollen up with pleasure at being in on this scene. "Men are all the same."

"Edie, I'm very surprised," Mrs. Peebles said. "I thought your parents were so strict. You don't want to have a baby, do you?"

I'm still ashamed of what happened next. I lost control, just like a six-year-old, I started howling. "You don't get a baby from just doing that!"

"You see. Some of them are that ignorant," Loretta Bird said.

But Mrs. Peebles jumped up and caught my arms and shook me.

"Calm down. Don't get hysterical. Calm down. Stop crying. Listen to me. Listen. I'm wondering, if you know what being intimate means. Now tell me. What did you think it meant?"

"Kissing," I howled.

She let go. "Oh, Edie. Stop it. Don't be silly. It's all right. It's all a misunderstanding. Being intimate means a lot more than that. Oh, I *wondered.*"

"She's trying to cover up, now," said Alice Kelling. "Yes. She's not so stupid. She sees she got herself in trouble."

"I believe her," Mrs. Peebles said. "This is an awful scene."

"Well there is one way to find out," said Alice Kelling, getting up. "After all, I am a nurse."

Mrs. Peebles drew a breath and said, "No. No. Go to your room, Edie. And stop that noise. This is too disgusting."

I heard the car start in a little while. I tried to stop crying, pulling back each wave as it started over me. Finally I succeeded, and lay heaving on the bed.

Mrs. Peebles came and stood in the doorway.

"She's gone," she said. "That Bird woman too. Of course, you know you should never have gone near that man and that is the cause of all this trouble. I have a headache. As soon as you can, go and wash your face in cold water and get at the dishes and we will not say any more about this."

Nor we didn't. I didn't figure out till years later the extent of what I had been saved from. Mrs. Peebles was not very friendly to me afterward, but she was fair. Not very friendly is the wrong way of describing what she was. She had never been very friendly. It was just that now she had to see me all the time and it got on her nerves, a little.

As for me, I put it all out of my mind like a bad dream and concentrated on waiting for my letter. The mail came every day except Sunday, between one-thirty and two in the afternoon, a good time for me because Mrs. Peebles was always having her nap. I would get the kitchen all cleaned and then go up to the mailbox and sit in the grass, waiting. I was perfectly happy, waiting, I forgot all about Alice Kelling and her misery and awful talk and Mrs. Peebles and her chilliness and the embarrassment of whether she told Dr. Peebles and the face of Loretta Bird, getting her fill of other people's troubles. I was always smiling when the mailman got there, and continued smiling even after he gave me the mail and I saw today wasn't the day. The mailman was a Carmichael. I knew by his face because there are a lot of Carmichaels living out by us and so many of them have a sort of sticking-out top lip. So I asked his name (he was a young man, shy, but good-humored, anybody could ask him anything) and then I said, "I knew by your face!" He was pleased by that and always glad to see me and got a little less shy. "You've got the smile I've been waiting on all day!" he used to holler out the car window.

It never crossed my mind for a long time a letter might not come. I believed in it coming just like I believed the sun would rise in the morning. I just put off my hope from day to day, and there was the goldenrod out around the mailbox and the children gone back to school, and the leaves turning, and I was wearing a sweater when I went to wait. One day walking back with the hydro bill stuck in my hand, that was all, looking across at the fairgrounds with the full-blown milkweed and dark teasels, so much like fall, it just struck me: *No letter was ever going to come.* It was an impossible idea to get used to. No, not impossible. If I thought about Chris's face when he said he was going to write to me, it was impossible, but if I forgot that and thought about the actual tin mailbox, empty, it was plain and true. I kept on going to meet the mail, but my heart was heavy now like a lump of lead. I only smiled because I thought of the mailman counting on it, and he didn't have an easy life, with the winter driving ahead.

Till it came to me one day there were women doing this with their lives, all over. There were women just waiting and waiting by mailboxes for one letter or another. I imagined me making this journey day after day and year after year, and my hair starting to go gray, and I thought, I was never made to go on like that. So I stopped meeting the mail. If there were women all through life waiting, and women busy and not waiting, I knew which I had to be. Even though there might be things the second kind of women have to pass up and never know about, it still is better.

I was surprised when the mailman phoned the Peebleses' place in the evening and asked for me. He said he missed me. He asked if I would like to go to Goderich, where some well-known movie was on, I forget now what. So I said yes, and I went out with him for two years and he asked me to marry him, and we were engaged a year more while I got my things together, and then we did marry. He always tells the children the story of how I went after him by sitting by the mailbox every day, and naturally I laugh and let him, because I like for people to think what pleases them and makes them happy.

[1974]

JOHN UPDIKE (b. 1932) was born in Shillington, Pennsylvania, an only child. His father taught algebra in a local high school, and his mother wrote short stories and novels, none of them ever published. From her Updike says he gathered that "either drawing or writing would be a noble and gay way of making a living; and I think I was very young when image-making dawned on me as a way of defying mortality." His mother's consciousness of a special destiny, combined with his family's meager income — they lived with his mother's parents for the first thirteen years of Updike's life — made him both arrogant and shy as a teenager, writing stories, drawing cartoons, and clowning for the approval of his peers. After getting straight As in high school, he went to Harvard on a full scholarship, studying English and graduating summa cum laude in 1954. He spent a year at Oxford on a fellowship, then joined the staff of The New Yorker. *In 1959 Updike published both his first book of short fiction,* The Same Door, *and his first novel,* The Poorhouse Fair. *That year he also decided to move from New York City to a coastal town in Massachusetts where he has lived most of the time since.*

In the 1960s, 1970s, and early 1980s, Updike continued to alternate novels and collections of stories, also adding occasional volumes of verse, two collections of essays, and one play. His novels include Rabbit, Run *(1960),* The Centaur *(1963),* Of the Farm *(1965),* Couples *(1968),* Rabbit Redux *(1971),* A Month of Sundays *(1975), and* Marry Me *(1976). In* The Coup *(1978), an account of an American-educated revolutionary leader in a fictitious African country, Updike turned his attention beyond the contemporary American urban and suburban people who had been his subjects until then, and won great critical acclaim.* Rabbit Is Rich *(1981), continuing the story of Harry "Rabbit" Angstrom, a suburban Pennsylvanian whom Updike has traced through adolescence, marriage, fatherhood, and middle age, won virtually every major American literary award for that year. Updike's collections of stories include* Pigeon Feathers *(1962),* The Music School *(1966),* Museums and Women *(1972), and* Problems and Other Stories *(1981). In 1983 Updike won the National Book Critics Circle Award for his collection of essays and criticism* Hugging the Shore.

The majority of Updike's early stories, like "Flight," refer to his youth in Pennsylvania, and he says he is indebted to J. D. Salinger's stories for the literary form he adopted to describe the painful experience of adolescence. "I learned a lot from Salinger's short stories; he did remove the short narrative from the wise-guy, slice-of-life stories of the thirties and forties. Like most innovative artists, he made new room for shapelessness, for life as it is lived." Updike writes realistic narrative, believing that "fiction is a tissue of lies that refreshes and informs our sense of actuality. Reality is — chemically, atomically, biologically — a fabric of microscopic accuracies." His

1056

fiction concentrates on these "microscopic accuracies," tiny details of characterization and setting brilliantly described. "Son" is a virtuosic display of Updike's facility in shifting the narrative point of view in different time sequences. (See Updike's Commentary about Kafka on page 1270 and his Interview about "Flight" on page 1333.)

John Updike

ཙཙ

FLIGHT

At the age of seventeen I was poorly dressed and funny-looking, and went around thinking about myself in the third person. "Allen Dow strode down the street and home." "Allen Dow smiled a thin sardonic smile." Consciousness of a special destiny made me both arrogant and shy. Years before, when I was eleven or twelve, just on the brink of ceasing to be a little boy, my mother and I, one Sunday afternoon — my father was busy, or asleep — hiked up to the top of Shale Hill, a child's mountain that formed one side of the valley that held our town. There the town lay under us, Olinger, perhaps a thousand homes, the best and biggest of them climbing Shale Hill toward us, and beyond them the blocks of brick houses, one- and two-family, the homes of my friends, sloping down to the pale thread of the Alton Pike, which strung together the high school, the tennis courts, the movie theatre, the town's few stores and gasoline stations, the elementary school, the Lutheran church. On the other side lay more homes, including our own, a tiny white patch placed just where the land began to rise toward the opposite mountain, Cedar Top. There were rims and rims of hills beyond Cedar Top, and looking south we could see the pike dissolving in other towns and turning out of sight amid the patches of green and brown farmland, and it seemed the entire country was lying exposed under a thin veil of haze. I was old enough to feel embarrassment at standing there alone with my mother, beside a wind-stunted spruce tree, on a long spine of shale. Suddenly she dug her fingers into the hair on my head and announced, "There we all are, and there we'll all be forever." She hesitated before the word "forever," and hesitated again before adding, "Except you, Allen. You're going to fly." A few birds were hung far out over the valley, at the level of our eyes, and in her impulsive way she had just plucked the image from them, but it felt like the clue I had been waiting all my childhood for. My most secret self had been made to respond, and I was intensely embarrassed, and irritably ducked my head out from under her melodramatic hand.

She was impulsive and romantic and inconsistent. I was never able to develop this spurt of reassurance into a steady theme between us. That she continued to treat me like an ordinary child seemed a betrayal of the vision she had made me share. I was captive to a hope she had tossed off and forgotten. My shy attempts to justify irregularities in my conduct — reading late at night or not coming back from school on time — by appealing to the image of flight were received with a startled blank look, as if I were talking nonsense. It seemed outrageously unjust. Yes, but, I wanted to say, yes, but it's *your* nonsense. And of course it was just this that made my appeal ineffective: her knowing that I had not made it mine, that I cynically intended to exploit both the privileges of being extraordinary and the pleasures of being ordinary. She feared my wish to be ordinary; once she did respond to my protest that I was learning to fly, by crying with red-faced ferocity, "You'll never learn, you'll stick and die in the dirt just like I'm doing. Why should you be better than your mother?"

She had been born ten miles to the south, on a farm she and her mother had loved. Her mother, a small fierce woman who looked more like an Arab than a German, worked in the fields with the men, and drove the wagon to market ten miles away every Friday. When still a tiny girl, my mother rode with her, and my impression of those rides is of fear — the little girl's fear of the gross and beery men who grabbed and hugged her, her fear of the wagon breaking, of the produce not selling, fear of her mother's possible humiliation and of her father's condition when at nightfall they returned. Friday was his holiday, and he drank. His drinking is impossible for me to picture; for I never knew him except as an enduring, didactic, almost Biblical old man, whose one passion was reading the newspapers and whose one hatred was of the Republican Party. There was something public about him; now that he is dead I keep seeing bits of him attached to famous politicians — his watch chain and his plump square stomach in old films of Theodore Roosevelt, his high-top shoes and the tilt of his head in a photograph of Alfalfa Bill Murray. Alfalfa Bill is turning his head to talk, and holds his hat by the crown, pinching it between two fingers and a thumb, a gentle and courtly grip that reminded me so keenly of my grandfather that I tore the picture out of *Life* and put it in a drawer.

Laboring in the soil had never been congenial to my grandfather, though with his wife's help he prospered by it. Then, in an era when success was hard to avoid, he began to invest in stocks. In 1922 he bought our large white home in the town — its fashionable section had not yet shifted to the Shale Hill side of the valley — and settled in to reap his dividends. He believed to his death that women were foolish, and the broken hearts of his two must have seemed specially so. The dignity of finance for the indignity of farming must have struck him as an eminently advantageous exchange. It strikes me that way, too, and how to reconcile my idea of those fear-ridden wagon rides with the grief that my mother insists she and her mother felt at being taken from the farm? Perhaps prolonged fear is a ground of love. Or perhaps, and likelier, the equation is long and complex, and the few factors I know — the middle-aged woman's mannish pride of land, the adolescent girl's pleasure in riding horses across the fields, their common feeling of rejection in Olinger — are enclosed in brackets and heightened by coefficients that I cannot see. Or perhaps it is not love of land but its absence that needs explaining, in my grandfather's fastidiousness and pride. He believed that as a boy he had been abused, and bore his father a grudge that my mother could never understand. Her grandfather to her was a saintly slender giant, over six feet tall when this was a prodigy, who knew the names of everything, like Adam in Eden. In his old age he was blind. When he came out of the house, the dogs rushed forward to lick his hands. When he lay dying, he requested a Gravenstein apple from the tree on the far edge of the meadow, and his son brought him a Krauser from the orchard near the house. The old man refused it, and my grandfather made a second trip, but in my mother's eyes the outrage had been committed, a savage insult insanely without provocation. What had his father done to him? The only specific complaint I ever heard my grandfather make was that when he was a boy and had to fetch water for the men in the fields, his father would tell him sarcastically, "Pick up your feet; they'll come down themselves." How incongruous! As if each generation of parents commits atrocities against their children which by God's decree remain invisible to the rest of the world.

I remember my grandmother as a little dark-eyed woman who talked seldom and who tried to feed me too much, and then as a hook-nosed profile pink against the lemon cushions of the casket. She died when I was seven. All the rest I know about her is that she was the baby of thirteen children, that while she was alive she made our yard one of the most beautiful in town, and that I am supposed to resemble her brother Pete.

My mother was precocious; she was fourteen when they moved, and for three years had been attending the county normal school. She graduated from Lake College, near Philadelphia, when she was only twenty, a tall handsome girl with a deprecatory smile, to judge from one of the curling photographs kept in a shoebox that I was always opening as a child, as if it might contain the clue to the quarrels in my house. My mother stands at the end of our brick walk, beside the elaborately trimmed end of our privet hedge — in shape a thick square column mounted by a rough ball of leaf. The ragged arc of a lilac bush in flower cuts into the right edge of the photograph, and behind my mother I can see a vacant lot where there has been a house ever since I can remember. She poses with a kind of country grace in a long fur-trimmed coat, unbuttoned to expose her beads and a short yet somehow demure flapper dress. Her hands are in her coat pockets, a beret sits on one side of her bangs, and there is a swank about her that seemed incongruous to me, examining this picture on the stained carpet of an ill-lit old house in the evening years of the thirties and in the dark of the warring forties. The costume and the girl in it look so up-to-date, so formidable. It was my grandfather's pleasure, in his prosperity, to give her a generous clothes allowance. My father, the penniless younger son of a Presbyterian minister in Passaic, had worked his way through Lake College by waiting on tables, and still speaks with mild resentment of the beautiful clothes that Lillian Baer wore. This aspect of my mother caused me some pain in high school; she was a fabric snob, and insisted on buying my slacks and sports shirts at the best store in Alton, and since we had little money, she bought me few, when of course what I needed was what my classmates had — a wide variety of cheap clothes.

At the time the photograph was taken, my mother wanted to go to New York. What she would have done there, or exactly what she wanted to do, I don't know; but her father forbade her. "Forbid" is a husk of a word today, but at that time, in that quaint province, in the mouth of an "indulgent father," it apparently was still viable, for the great moist weight of that forbidding continued to be felt in the house for years, and when I was a child, as one of my mother's endless harangues to my grandfather screamed toward its weeping peak, I could feel it around and above me, like a huge root encountered by an earthworm.

Perhaps in a reaction of anger my mother married my father, Victor Dow, who at least took her as far away as Wilmington, where he had made a beginning with an engineering firm. But the depression hit, my father was laid off, and the couple came to the white house in Olinger, where my grandfather sat reading the newspapers that traced his stocks' cautious decline into worthlessness. I was born. My grandmother went around as a cleaning lady, and grew things in our quarter-acre yard to sell. We kept chickens, and there was a large plot of asparagus. After she had died, in a frightened way I used to seek her in the asparagus patch. By midsummer it would be a forest of dainty green trees, some as tall as I was, and in their frothy touch a spirit seemed to speak, and in the soft thick net of their intermingling branches a promise seemed to be caught, as well as a menace. The asparagus trees were frightening; in the center of the patch, far from the house and the alley, I would fall under a spell, and become tiny, and wander among the great smooth green trunks expecting to find a little house with a smoking chimney, and in it my grandmother. She herself had believed in ghosts, which made her own ghost potent. Even now, sitting alone in my own house, a board creaks in the kitchen and I look up fearing she will come through the doorway. And at night, just before I fall asleep, her voice calls my name in a penetrating whisper, or calls, "*Pete.*"

My mother went to work in an Alton department store, selling inferior fabric for $14 a week. During the daytime of my first year of life it was my father who took care of me. He has said since, flattering me as he always does, that it was having me on his hands that kept him from going insane. It may have been this that made my affection for him so inarticulate, as if I were still a wordless infant looking up into the mothering blur of his man's face. And that same shared year helps account, perhaps, for his gentleness with me, for his willingness to praise, as if everything I do has something sad and crippled in it. He feels sorry for me; my birth coincided with the birth of a great misery, a national misery — only recently has he stopped calling me by the nickname "Young America." Around my first birthday he acquired a position teaching arithmetic and algebra in the Olinger high school, and though he was so kind and humorous he couldn't enter a classroom without creating uproarious problems of discipline, he endured it day by day and year by year, and eventually came to occupy a place in this alien town, so that I believe there are now one or two dozen ex-students, men and women nearing middle age, who carry around with them some piece of encouragement my father gave them, or remember some sentence of his that helped shape them. Certainly there are many who remember the antics with which he burlesqued his discomfort in the classroom. He kept a confiscated cap pistol in his desk, and upon getting an especially stupid answer, he would take it out and, wearing a preoccupied, regretful expression, shoot himself in the head.

My grandfather was the last to go to work, and the most degraded by it. He was hired by the borough crew, men who went around the streets shoveling stones and spreading tar. Bulky and ominous in their overalls, wreathed in steam, and associated with dramatic and portentous equipment, these men had grandeur in the eyes of a child, and it puzzled me, as I walked to and from elementary school, that my grandfather refused to wave to me or confess his presence in any way. Curiously strong for a fastidious man, he kept at it well into his seventies, when his sight failed. It was my task then to read his beloved newspapers to him as he sat in his chair by the bay window, twiddling his high-top shoes in the sunshine. I teased him, reading too fast, then maddeningly slow, skipping from column to column to create one long chaotic story; I read him the sports page, which did not interest him, and mumbled the editorials. Only the speed of his feet's twiddling betrayed vexation. When I'd stop, he would plead mildly in his rather beautiful, old-fashioned, elocutionary voice, "Now just the obituaries, Allen. Just the names to see if anyone I know is there." I imagined, as I viciously barked at him the list of names that might contain the name of a friend, that I was avenging my mother; I believed that she hated him, and for her sake I tried to hate him also. From her incessant resurrection of mysterious grievances buried far back in the confused sunless earth of the time before I was born, I had been able to deduce only that he was an evil man, who had ruined her life, that fair creature in the beret. I did not understand. She fought with him not because she wanted to fight but because *she could not bear to leave him alone.*

Sometimes, glancing up from the sheet of print where our armies swarmed in retreat like harried insects, I could catch the old man's head in the act of lifting slightly to receive the warm sunshine on his face, a dry frail face ennobled by its thick crown of combed cornsilk hair. It would dawn on me then that his sins as a father were likely no worse than any father's. But my mother's genius was to give the people closest to her mythic immensity. I was the phoenix. My father and grandmother were legendary invader-saints, she springing out of some narrow vein of Arab blood in the German race and he crossing over from the Protestant wastes of New Jersey, both of them serving and enslaving their mates with their prodigious powers of endurance and labor. For my mother felt that she and her father alike had been destroyed by marriage, been made captive by people better yet less than they. It was true, my father had loved Mom Baer, and her death made him seem more of an alien than ever. He, and her ghost, stood to one side, in the shadows but separate from the house's dark core, the inheritance of frustration and folly that had descended from my grandfather to my mother to me, and that I, with a few beats of my grown wings, was destined to reverse and redeem.

At the age of seventeen, in the fall of my senior year, I went with three girls to debate at a high school over a hundred miles away. They were, all three, bright girls, A students; they were disfigured by A's as if by acne. Yet even so it excited me to be mounting a train with them early on a Friday morning, at an hour when our schoolmates miles away were slumping into the seats of their first class. Sunshine spread broad bars of dust down the length of the half-empty car, and through the windows Pennsylvania unravelled in a long brown scroll scribbled with industry. Black pipes raced beside the tracks for miles. At rhythmic intervals one of them looped upward, like the Greek letter Ω. "Why does it do that?" I asked. "Is it sick?"

"Condensation?" Judith Potteiger suggested in her shy, transparent voice. She loved science.

"No," I said. "It's in pain. It's withering! It's going to grab the train! Look out!" I ducked, honestly a little scared. All the girls laughed.

Judith and Catharine Miller were in my class, and expected me to be amusing; the third girl, a plump small junior named Molly Bingaman, had not known what to expect. It was her fresh audience I was playing to. She was the best dressed of us four, and the most poised; this made me suspect that she was the least bright. She had been substituted at the last moment for a sick member of the debating team; I knew her just by seeing her in the halls and in assembly. From a distance she seemed dumpy and prematurely adult. But up close she was gently fragrant, and against the weary purple cloth of the train seats her skin seemed luminous. She had beautiful skin, heartbreaking skin a pencil dot would have marred, and large blue eyes equally clear. Except for a double chin, and a mouth too large and thick, she would have been perfectly pretty, in a little woman's compact and cocky way. She and I sat side by side, facing the two senior girls, who more and more took on the wan slyness of matchmakers. It was they who had forced the seating arrangements.

We debated in the afternoon, and won. Yes, the German Federal Republic *should* be freed of all Allied control. The school, a posh castle on the edge of a miserable coal city, was the site of a statewide cycle of debates that was to continue into Saturday. There was a dance Friday night in the gym. I danced with Molly mostly, though to my annoyance she got in with a set of Harrisburg boys while I conscientiously pushed Judith and Catharine around the floor. We were stiff dancers, the three of us; only Molly made me seem good, floating backward from my feet fearlessly as her cheek rumpled my moist shirt. The gym was hung with orange and black crepe paper in honor of Hallowe'en, and the pennants of all the competing schools were fastened to the walls, and a twelve-piece band pumped away blissfully on the year's sad tunes — "Heartaches," "Near You," "That's My Desire." A great cloud of balloons gathered in the steel girders was released. There was pink punch, and a local girl sang.

Judith and Catharine decided to leave before the dance was over, and I made Molly come too, though she was in a literal sweat of pleasure; her perfect skin in the oval above her neckline was flushed and glazed. I realized, with a little shock of possessiveness and pity, that she was unused to attention back home, in competition with the gorgeous Olinger ignorant.

We walked together to the house where the four of us had been boarded, a large white frame owned by an old couple and standing with lonely decency in a semi-slum. Judith and Catharine turned up the walk, but Molly and I, with a diffident decision that I believe came from her initiative, continued, "to walk around the block." We walked miles, stopping off after midnight at a trolley-car-shaped diner. I got a hamburger, and she impressed me by ordering coffee. We walked back to the house and let ourselves in with the key we had been given; but instead of going upstairs to our rooms we sat downstairs in the dark living room and talked softly for more hours.

What did we say? I talked about myself. It is hard to hear, much less remember, what we ourselves say, just as it might be hard for a movie projector, given life, to see the shadows its eye of light is casting. A transcript, could I produce it, of my monologue through the wide turning point of that night, with all its word-by-word conceit, would distort the picture: this living room miles from home, the street light piercing the chinks in the curtains and erecting on the wallpaper rods of light the size of yardsticks, our hosts and companions asleep upstairs, the incessant sigh of my voice, coffee-primed Molly on the floor beside my chair, her stockinged legs stretched out on the rug; and this odd sense in the room, a tasteless and odorless aura unfamiliar to me, as of a pool of water widening.

I remember one exchange. I must have been describing the steep waves of fearing death that had come over me ever since early childhood, about one every three years, and I ended by supposing that it would take great courage to be an atheist. "But I bet you'll become one," Molly said. "Just to show yourself that you're brave enough." I felt she overestimated me, and was flattered. Within a few years, while I still remembered many of her words, I realized how touchingly gauche our assumption was that an atheist is a lonely rebel; for mobs of men are united in atheism, and oblivion — the dense lead-like sea that would occasionally sweep over me — is to them a weight as negligible as the faint pressure of their wallets in their hip pockets. This grotesque and tender misestimate of the world flares in my memory of our conversation like one of the innumerable matches we struck.

The room filled with smoke. Too weary to sit, I lay down on the floor beside her, and stroked her silver arm in silence, yet still was too timid to act on the wide and negative aura that I did not understand was of compliance. On the upstairs landing, as I went to turn into my room, Molly came forward with a prim look and kissed me. With clumsy force I entered the negative space that had been waiting. Her lipstick smeared in little unflattering flecks into the skin around her mouth; it was as if I had been given a face to eat, and the presence of bone — skull under skin, teeth behind lips — impeded me. We stood for a long time under the burning hall light, until my neck began to ache from bowing. My legs were trembling when we finally parted and sneaked into our rooms. In bed I thought, "Allen Dow tossed restlessly," and realized it was the first time that day I had thought of myself in the third person.

On Saturday morning, we lost our debate. I was sleepy and verbose and haughty, and some of the students in the audience began to boo whenever I opened my mouth. The principal came up on the stage and made a scolding speech, which finished me and my cause, untrammeled Germany. On the train back, Catharine and Judith arranged the seating so that they sat behind Molly and me, and spied on only the tops of our heads. For the first time, on the ride home, I felt what it was to bury a humiliation in the body of a woman. Nothing but the friction of my face against hers drowned out the echo of those boos. When we kissed, a red shadow would well under my lips and eclipse the hostile hooting faces of the debate audience, and when our lips parted, the bright inner sea would ebb, and there the faces would be again, more intense than ever. With a shudder of shame I'd hide my face on her shoulder and in the warm darkness there, while a frill of her prissy collar gently scratched my nose, I felt united with Hitler and all the villains, traitors, madmen, and failures who had managed to keep, up to the moment of capture or death, a woman with them. This had puzzled me. In high school, females were proud and remote; in the newspapers they were fantastic monsters of submission. And now Molly administered reassurance to me with small motions and bodily adjustments that had about them a strange flavor of the practical.

Our parents met us at the station. I was startled at how tired my mother looked. There were deep blue dents on either side of her nose, and her hair seemed somehow dissociated from her head, as if it were a ragged, half-gray wig she had put on carelessly. She was a heavy woman, and her weight, which she usually carried upright, like a kind of wealth, had slumped away from her ownership and seemed, in the sullen light of the railway platform, to weigh on the world. I asked, "How's Grandpa?" He had taken to bed several months before with pains in his chest.

"He still sings," she said rather sharply. For entertainment in his increasing blindness my grandfather had long ago begun to sing, and his shapely old voice would pour forth hymns, forgotten comic ballads, and camp-meeting songs at any hour. His memory seemed to improve the longer he lived.

My mother's irritability was more manifest in the private cavity of the car; her heavy silence oppressed me. "You look so tired, Mother," I said, trying to take the offensive.

"That's nothing to how you look," she answered. "What happened up there? You stoop like an old married man."

"Nothing happened," I lied. My cheeks were parched, as if her high steady anger had the power of giving sunburn.

"I remember that Bingaman girl's mother when we first moved to town. She was the smuggest little snip south of the pike. They're real old Olinger stock, you know. They have no use for hillbillies."

My father tried to change the subject. "Well, you won one debate, Allen, and that's more than I would have done. I don't see how you do it."

"Why, he gets it from you, Victor. I've never won a debate with you."

"He gets it from Pop Baer. If that man had gone into politics, Lillian, all the misery of his life would have been avoided."

"Dad was never a debater. He was a bully. Don't go with little women, Allen. It puts you too close to the ground."

"I'm not *going* with *any*body, Mother. Really, you're so fanciful."

"Why, when she stepped off the train from the way her chins bounced I thought she had eaten a canary. And then making my poor son, all skin and bones, carry her bag. When she walked by me I honestly was afraid she'd spit in my eye."

"I had to carry somebody's bag. I'm sure she doesn't know who you are." Though it was true I had talked a good deal about my family the night before.

My mother turned away from me. "You see, Victor — he defends her. When I was his age that girl's mother gave me a cut I'm still bleeding from, and my own son attacks me on behalf of her fat little daughter. I wonder if her mother put her up to catching him."

"Molly's a nice girl," my father interceded. "She never gave me any trouble in class like some of those smug bastards." But he was curiously listless, for so Christian a man, in pronouncing this endorsement.

I discovered that nobody wanted me to go with Molly Bingaman. My friends — for on the strength of being funny I did have some friends, class-mates whose love affairs went on over my head but whom I could accom-pany, as clown, on communal outings — never talked with me about Molly, and when I brought her to their parties gave the impression of ig-noring her, so that I stopped taking her. Teachers at school would smile an odd tight smile when they saw us leaning by her locker or hanging around in the stairways. The eleventh-grade English instructor — one of my "boosters" on the faculty, a man who was always trying to "challenge" me, to "exploit" my "potential" — took me aside and told me how stupid she was. She just couldn't grasp the principles of syntax. He confided her pars-ing mistakes to me as if they betrayed — as indeed in a way they did — an obtuseness her social manner cleverly concealed. Even the Fabers, an ultra-Republican couple who ran a luncheonette near the high school, showed malicious delight whenever Molly and I broke up, and persistently treated my attachment as being a witty piece of play, like my pretense with Mr. Faber of being a Communist. The entire town seemed ensnarled in my mother's myth, that escape was my proper fate. It was as if I were a sport that the ghostly elders of Olinger had segregated from the rest of the live-stock and agreed to donate in time to the air; this fitted with the ambiguous sensation I had always had in the town, of being simultaneously flattered and rejected.

Molly's parents disapproved because in their eyes my family was vir-tually white trash. It was so persistently hammered into me that I was too good for Molly that I scarcely considered the proposition that, by another scale, she was too good for me. Further, Molly herself shielded me. Only once, exasperated by some tedious, condescending confession of mine, did she state that her mother didn't like me. "Why not?" I asked, genuinely surprised. I admired Mrs. Bingaman — she was beautifully preserved — and I always felt gay in her house, with its white woodwork and matching furniture and vases of iris posing before polished mirrors.

"Oh, I don't know. She thinks you're flippant."

"But that's not true. Nobody takes himself more seriously than I do."

While Molly protected me from the Bingaman side of the ugliness, I conveyed the Dow side more or less directly to her. It infuriated me that nobody allowed me to be proud of her. I kept, in effect, asking her, Why was she stupid in English? Why didn't she get along with my friends? Why did she look so dumpy and smug? — this last despite the fact that she often, especially in intimate moments, looked beautiful to me. I was especially angry with her because this affair had brought out an ignoble, hysterical, brutal aspect of my mother that I might never have had to see otherwise. I had hoped to keep things secret from her, but even if her intuition had not been relentless, my father, at school, knew everything. Sometimes, indeed, my mother said that she didn't care if I went with Molly; it was my father who was upset. Like a frantic dog tied by one leg, she snapped in any direction, mouthing ridiculous fancies — such as that Mrs. Bingaman had sicked Molly on me just to keep me from going to college and giving the Dows something to be proud of — that would make us both suddenly start laughing. Laughter in that house that winter had a guilty sound. My grandfather was dying, and lay upstairs singing and coughing and weeping as the mood came to him, and we were too poor to hire a nurse, and too kind and cowardly to send him to a "home." It was still his house, after all. Any noise he made seemed to slash my mother's heart, and she was unable to sleep upstairs near him, and waited the nights out on the sofa downstairs. In her desperate state she would say unforgivable things to me even while the tears streamed down her face. I've never seen so many tears as I saw that winter.

Every time I saw my mother cry, it seemed I had to make Molly cry. I developed a skill at it; it came naturally to an only child who had been surrounded all his life by adults ransacking each other for the truth. Even in the heart of intimacy, half-naked each of us, I would say something to humiliate her. We never made love in the final, coital sense. My reason was a mixture of idealism and superstition; I felt that if I took her virginity she would be mine forever. I depended overmuch on a technicality; she gave herself to me anyway, and I had her anyway, and have her still, for the longer I travel in a direction I could not have taken with her, the more clearly she seems the one person who loved me without advantage. I was a homely, comically ambitious hillbilly, and I even refused to tell her I loved her, to pronounce the word "love" — an icy piece of pedantry that shocks me now that I have almost forgotten the context of confusion in which it seemed wise.

In addition to my grandfather's illness, and my mother's grief, and my waiting to hear if I had won a scholarship to the one college that seemed good enough for me, I was burdened with managing too many petty affairs of my graduating class. I was in charge of yearbook writeups, art editor of the school paper, chairman of the Class Gift Committee, director of the Senior Assembly, and teachers' workhorse. Frightened by my father's tales of nervous breakdowns he had seen, I kept listening for the sounds of my brain snapping, and the image of that gray, infinitely interconnected mass seemed to extend outward, to become my whole world, one dense organic dungeon, and I felt I had to get out; if I could just get out of this, into June, it would be blue sky, and I would be all right for life.

One Friday night in spring, after trying for over an hour to write thirty-five affectionate words for the yearbook about a dull girl in the Secretarial Course I had never spoken a word to, I heard my grandfather begin coughing upstairs with a sound like dry membrane tearing, and I panicked. I called up the stairs, "Mother! I must go out."

"It's nine-thirty."

"I know, but I have to. I'm going insane."

Without waiting to hear her answer or to find a coat, I left the house and got our old car out of the garage. The weekend before, I had broken up with Molly again. All week I hadn't spoken to her, though I had seen her once in Faber's, with a boy in her class, averting her face while I, hanging by the side of the pinball machine, made wisecracks in her direction. I didn't dare go up to her door and knock so late at night; I just parked across the street and watched the lit windows of her house. Through their living-room window I could see one of Mrs. Bingaman's vases of hothouse iris standing on a white mantel, and my open car window admitted the spring air, which delicately smelled of wet ashes. Molly was probably out on a date with that moron in her class. But then the Bingamans' door opened, and her figure appeared in the rectangle of light. Her back was toward me, a coat was on her arm, and her mother seemed to be screaming. Molly closed the door and ran down off the porch and across the street and quickly got into the car, her eyes downcast in their sockets of shadow. *She came.* When I have finally forgotten everything else, her powdery fragrance, her lucid cool skin, the way her lower lip was like a curved pillow of two cloths, the dusty red outer and wet pink inner, I'll still be grieved by this about Molly, that she came to me.

After I returned her to her house — she told me not to worry, her mother enjoyed shouting — I went to the all-night diner just beyond the Olinger town line and ate three hamburgers, ordering them one at a time, and drank two glasses of milk. It was close to two o'clock when I got home, but my mother was still awake. She lay on the sofa in the dark, with the radio sitting on the floor murmuring Dixieland piped up from New Orleans by way of Philadelphia. Radio music was a steady feature of her insomniac life; not only did it help drown out the noise of her father upstairs but she seemed to enjoy it in itself. She would resist my father's pleas to come to bed by saying that the New Orleans program was not over yet. The radio was an old Philco we had always had; I had once drawn a fish on the orange disc of its celluloid dial, which looked to my child's eyes like a fishbowl.

Her loneliness caught at me; I went into the living room and sat on a chair with my back to the window. For a long time she looked at me tensely out of the darkness. "Well," she said at last, "how was little hot-pants?" The vulgarity this affair had brought out in her language appalled me.

"I made her cry," I told her.

"Why do you torment the girl?"

"To please you."

"It doesn't please me."

"Well, then, stop nagging me."

"I'll stop nagging you if you'll solemnly tell me you're willing to marry her."

I said nothing to this, and after waiting she went on in a different voice, "Isn't it funny, that you should show this weakness?"

"Weakness is a funny way to put it when it's the only thing that gives me strength."

"Does it really, Allen? Well. It may be. I forget, you were born here."

Upstairs, close to our heads, my grandfather, in a voice frail but still melodious, began to sing, "There is a happy land, far, far away, where saints in glory stand, bright, bright as day." We listened; and his voice broke into coughing, a terrible rending cough growing in fury, struggling to escape, and loud with fear he called my mother's name. She didn't stir. His voice grew enormous, a bully's voice, as he repeated, "Lillian! Lillian!" and I saw my mother's shape quiver with the force coming down the stairs into her; she was like a dam; and then the power, as my grandfather fell momentarily silent, flowed toward me in the darkness, and I felt intensely angry, and hated that black mass of suffering, even while I realized, with a rapid light calculation, that I was too weak to withstand it.

In a dry tone of certainty and dislike — how hard my heart had become! — I told her. "All right. You'll win this one, Mother; but it'll be the last one you'll win."

My pang of fright following this unprecedentedly cold insolence seemed to blot my senses; the chair ceased to be felt under me, and the walls and furniture of the room fell away — there was only the dim orange glow of the radio dial down below. In a husky voice that seemed to come across a great distance my mother said, with typical melodrama, "Goodbye, Allen."

[1962]

John Updike

ॐ

Son

He is often upstairs, when he has to be home. He prefers to be else-where. He is almost sixteen, though beardless still, a man's mind indignantly captive in the frame of a child. I love touching him, but don't often dare. The other day, he had the flu, and a fever, and I gave him a back rub, marveling at the symmetrical knit of muscle, the organic tension. He is high-strung. Yet his sleep is so solid he sweats like a stone in the wall of a well. He wishes for perfection. He would like to destroy us, for we are, variously, too fat, too jocular, too sloppy, too affectionate, too grotesque and heedless in our ways. His mother smokes too much. His younger brother chews with his mouth open. His older sister leaves unbuttoned the top button of her blouses. His younger sister tussles with the dogs, getting them overexcited, avoiding doing her homework. Everyone in the house talks nonsense. He would be a better father than his father. But time has tricked him, has made him a son. After a quarrel, if he cannot go outside and kick a ball, he retreats to a corner of the house and reclines on the beanbag chair in an attitude of strange, infantile or leonine, torpor. We exhaust him, without meaning to. He takes an interest in the newspaper now, the front page as well as the sports, in this tiring year of 1973.

He is upstairs, writing a musical comedy. It is a Sunday in 1949. Somehow, he has volunteered to prepare a high-school assembly program; people will sing. Songs of the time go through his head, as he scribbles new words. *Up in de mornin', down at de school, work like a debil for my grades.* Below him, irksome voices grind on, like machines working their way through tunnels. His parents each want something from the other. "Marion, you don't understand that man like I do; he has a heart of gold." This father's charade is very complex: the world, which he fears, is used as a flail on his wife. But from his cringing attitude he would seem to an outsider the one being flailed. With burning red face, the woman accepts the role of aggressor as penance for the fact, the incessant shameful fact, that *he* has to wrestle with the world while she hides here, in solitude, on this farm. This is normal, but does not seem to them to be so. Only by convolution have they arrived at the dominant submissive relationship society has assigned them. For the man is maternally kind and with a smile hugs to himself his jewel, his certainty of being victimized; it is the mother whose tongue is sharp, who sometimes strikes. "Well, he gets you out of the house, and I guess that's gold to you." His answer is "Duty calls," pronounced mincingly. "The social contract is a balance of compromises." This will infuriate her, the son knows; as his heart thickens, the downstairs overflows with her hot voice. "*Don't* wear that smile at me! And *take* your hands off your hips; you look like a sissy!" Their son tries not to listen. When he does, visual details of the downstairs flood his mind: the two antagonists, circling with their coffee cups; the shabby mismatched furniture; the hopeful books; the docile framed photographs of the dead, docile and still as cowed students. This matrix of pain that bore him — he feels he is floating above it, sprawled on the bed as on a cloud, stealing songs as they come into his head (*Across the hallway from the guidance room/Lives a French instructor called Mrs. Blum*), contemplating the brown meadow from the upstairs window (last summer's burdock stalks like the beginnings of an alphabet, an apple tree holding three rotten apples as if pondering why they failed to fall) yearning for Monday, for the ride to school with his father, for the bell that calls him to homeroom, for the excitements of class, for Broadway, for fame, for the cloud that will carry him away, out of this, out.

He returns from his paper-delivery route and finds a few Christmas presents for him on the kitchen table. I must guess at the year. 1913? Without opening them, he knocks them to the floor, puts his head on the table, and falls asleep. He must have been consciously dramatizing his plight: his father was sick, money was scarce, he had to work, to win food for the family when he was still a child. In his dismissal of Christmas, he touched a nerve: his love of anarchy, his distrust of the social contract. He treasured this moment of proclamation; else why remember it, hoard a memory so bitter, and confide it to his son many Christmases later? He had a teaching instinct, though he claimed that life miscast him as a school-teacher. I suffered in his classes, feeling the confusion as a persecution of him, but now wonder if his rebellious heart did not court confusion, not as Communists do, to intrude their own order, but, more radical still, as an end pleasurable in itself, as truth's very body. Yet his handwriting (an old pink permission slip recently fluttered from a book where it had been mark-ing a page for twenty years) was always considerately legible, and he was sitting up doing arithmetic the morning of the day he died.

And letters survive from that yet prior son, written in brown ink, in a tidy tame hand, home to his mother from the Missouri seminary where he was preparing for his vocation. The dates are 1887, 1888, 1889. Nothing much happened: he missed New Jersey, and was teased at a church social for escorting a widow. He wanted to do the right thing, but the little sheets of faded penscript exhale a dispirited calm, as if his heart already knew he would not make a successful minister, or live to be old. His son, my father, when old, drove hundreds of miles out of his way to visit the Missouri town from which those letters had been sent. Strangely, the town had not changed; it looked just as he had imagined, from his father's descriptions: tall wooden houses, rain-soaked, stacked in a bluff. The town was a sepia postcard mailed homesick home and preserved in an attic. My father cursed: his father's old sorrow bore him down into depression, into hatred of life. My mother claims his decline in health began at that moment.

He is wonderful to watch, playing soccer. Smaller than the others, my son leaps, heads, dribbles, feints, passes. When a big boy knocks him down, he tumbles on the mud, in his green and black school uniform, in an ecstasy of falling. I am envious. Never for me the jaunty pride of the school uni-form, the solemn ritual of the coach's pep talk, the camaraderie of shook hands and slapped backsides, the shadow-striped hush of late afternoon and last quarter, the solemn vaulted universe of official combat, with its cheer-ing mothers and referees exotic as zebras and the bespectacled timekeeper alert with his claxon. When the boy scores a goal, he runs into the arms of his teammates with upraised arms and his face alight as if blinded by tri-umph. They lift him from the earth in a union of muddy hugs. What spirit! What valor! What skill! His father, watching from the sidelines, inwardly registers only one complaint: he feels the boy, with his talent, should be more aggressive.

They drove across the state of Pennsylvania to hear their son read in Pittsburgh. But when their presence was announced to the audience, they did not stand; the applause groped for them and died. My mother said afterward she was afraid she might fall into the next row if she tried to stand in the dark. Next morning was sunny, and the three of us searched for the house where once they had lived. They had been happy there; I imagined, indeed, that I had been conceived there, just before the slope of the Depression steepened and fear gripped my family. We found the library where she used to read Turgenev, and the little park where the bums slept close as paving stones in the summer night; but their street kept eluding us, though we circled in the car. On foot, my mother found the tree. She claimed she recognized it, the sooty linden she would gaze into from their apartment windows. The branches, though thicker, had held their pattern. But the house itself, and the entire block, were gone. Stray bricks and rods of iron in the grass suggested that the demolition had been recent. We stood on the empty spot and laughed. They knew it was right, because the railroad tracks were the right distance away. In confirmation, a long freight train pulled itself east around the curve, its great weight gliding as if on a river current; then a silver passenger train came gliding as effortlessly in the other direction. The curve of the tracks tipped the cars slightly toward us. The Golden Triangle, gray and hazed, was off to our left, beyond a forest of bridges. We stood on the grassy rubble that morning, where something once had been, beside the tree still there, and were intensely happy. Why? We knew.

" 'No,' Dad said to me, 'the Christian ministry isn't a job you choose, it's a vocation for which you got to receive a call.' I could tell he wanted me to ask him. We never talked much, but we understood each other, we were both scared devils, not like you and the kid. I asked him, Had he ever received the call? He said No. He said No, he never had. Received the call. That was a terrible thing, for him to admit. And I was the one he told. As far as I knew he never admitted it to anybody, but he admitted it to me. He felt like hell about it, I could tell. That was all we ever said about it. That was enough."

He has made his younger brother cry, and justice must be done. A father enforces justice. I corner the rat in our bedroom; he is holding a cardboard mailing tube like a sword. The challenge flares white-hot; I roll my weight toward him like a rock down a mountain, and knock the weapon from his hand. He smiles. Smiles! Because my facial expression is silly? Because he is glad that he can still be overpowered, and hence is still protected? Why? I do not hit him. We stand a second, father and son, and then as nimbly as on the soccer field he steps around me and out the door. He slams the door. He shouts obscenities in the hall, slams all the doors he can find on the way to his room. Our moment of smilingly shared silence was the moment of compression; now the explosion. The whole house rocks with it. Downstairs, his siblings and mother come to me and offer advice and psychological analysis. I was too aggressive. He is spoiled. What they can never know, my grief alone to treasure, was that lucid many-sided second of his smiling and my relenting, before the world's wrathful pantomime of power resumed.

As we huddle whispering about him, my son takes his revenge. In his room, he plays his guitar. He has greatly improved this winter; his hands getting bigger is the least of it. He has found in the guitar an escape. He plays the Romanza wherein repeated notes, with a sliding like the heart's valves, let themselves fall along the scale:

The notes fall, so gently he bombs us, drops feathery notes down upon us, our visitor, our prisoner.

[1973]

WOODY ALLEN *was born Allen Stewart Konigsberg in 1935 and grew up in what he calls "a typical, noisy ethnic family" in Brooklyn, New York. "Probably if my parents had pushed me along more cultural lines, I might have started out being a serious writer, because that's what has always interested me. But I had no cultural background whatsoever. . . . I didn't go to a play until I was about eighteen years old, almost never went to a museum, listened only to popular music, and never read at all." After graduating from high school, Allen attended and dropped out of both New York University and the City College of New York. While still a student he sold original jokes to newspaper columnists, and at the age of seventeen, in 1952, he joined the National Broadcasting Corporation as a staff writer.*

In 1964 Allen wrote his first screen play, What's New Pussycat? *Since then he has written, directed, and often starred in more than fifteen films. He is one of the few major American filmmakers to insist on total control over his productions, which he equates with artistic freedom. "I'm only making films because I'm as free there as if I were writing novels. You can't create unless you're completely free." Writing was important to Allen even as a child. "From the first grade, I was always the class writer. I remember very distinctly, I'd buy those little black and white notebooks and say, 'Today I'll write a mystery story.' I'd go home and write, and invariably they'd come out funny. I certainly couldn't care less if I ever performed again, and don't care much if I ever direct another film, but I would not like to be in a position not to write."*

Allen has published three books of comic stories and sketches: Getting Even *(1971),* Without Feathers *(1975), and* Side Effects *(1980). Like his films his short fiction reveals a humorously skeptical, yet romantic, mind at work. He is also an astute analyzer of his own work. "If it's successful, the laughs don't come from jokes, they come from characters in emotionally desperate circumstances." "The Kugelmass Episode", which first appeared in* The New Yorker, *won the annual O.Henry Award as one of the best stories of 1978. As the critic Sanford Pinsker noted, in this story Allen "has written a comic fantasy that is a worthy successor to James Thurber's 'The Secret Life of Walter Mitty' . . . [Allen's] story reveals as much about our cultural moment as Thurber's tale did about his."*

Woody Allen

ന്ദ

THE KUGELMASS EPISODE

Kugelmass, a professor of humanities at City College, was unhappily married for the second time. Daphne Kugelmass was an oaf. He also had two dull sons by his first wife, Flo, and was up to his neck in alimony and child support.

"Did I know it would turn out so badly?" Kugelmass whined to his analyst one day. "Daphne had promise. Who suspected she'd let herself go and swell up like a beach ball? Plus she had a few bucks, which is not in itself a healthy reason to marry a person, but it doesn't hurt, with the kind of operating nut I have. You see my point?"

Kugelmass was bald and as hairy as a bear, but he had soul.

"I need to meet a new woman," he went on. "I need to have an affair. I may not look the part, but I'm a man who needs romance. I need softness, I need flirtation. I'm not getting younger, so before it's too late I want to make love in Venice, trade quips at '21,'[1] and exchange coy glances over red wine and candlelight. You see what I'm saying?"

Dr. Mandel shifted in his chair and said, "An affair will solve nothing. You're so unrealistic. Your problems run much deeper."

"And also this affair must be discreet," Kugelmass continued. "I can't afford a second divorce. Daphne would really sock it to me."

"Mr. Kugelmass —"

"But it can't be anyone at City College, because Daphne also works there. Not that anyone on the faculty at C.C.N.Y. is any great shakes, but some of those coeds . . ."

"Mr. Kugelmass — "

"Help me. I had a dream last night. I was skipping through a meadow holding a picnic basket and the basket was marked 'Options.' And then I saw there was a hole in the basket."

"Mr. Kugelmass, the worst thing you could do is act out. You must simply express your feelings here, and together we'll analyze them. You have been in treatment long enough to know there is no overnight cure. After all, I'm an analyst, not a magician."

[1] a famous restaurant in New York City.

"Then perhaps what I need is a magician," Kugelmass said, rising from his chair. And with that he terminated his therapy.

A couple of weeks later, while Kugelmass and Daphne were moping around in their apartment one night like two pieces of old furniture, the phone rang.

"I'll get it," Kugelmass said. "Hello."

"Kugelmass?" a voice said. "Kugelmass, this is Persky."

"Who?"

"Persky. Or should I say The Great Persky?"

"Pardon me?"

"I hear you're looking all over town for a magician to bring a little exotica into your life? Yes or no?"

"Sh-h-h," Kugelmass whispered. "Don't hang up. Where are you calling from, Persky?"

Early the following afternoon, Kugelmass climbed three flights of stairs in a broken-down apartment house in the Bushwick section of Brooklyn. Peering through the darkness of the hall, he found the door he was looking for and pressed the bell. I'm going to regret this, he thought to himself.

Seconds later, he was greeted by a short, thin, waxy-looking man.

"*You're* Persky the Great?" Kugelmass said.

"The Great Persky. You want a tea?"

"No, I want romance. I want music. I want love and beauty."

"But not tea, eh? Amazing. O.K., sit down."

Persky went to the back room, and Kugelmass heard the sounds of boxes and furniture being moved around. Persky reappeared, pushing before him a large object on squeaky roller-skate wheels. He removed some old silk handkerchiefs that were lying on its top and blew away a bit of dust. It was a cheap-looking Chinese cabinet, badly lacquered.

"Persky," Kugelmass said, "what's your scam?"

"Pay attention," Persky said. "This is some beautiful effect. I developed it for a Knights of Pythias date last year, but the booking fell through. Get into the cabinet."

"Why, so you can stick it full of swords or something?"

"You see any swords?"

Kugelmass made a face and, grunting, climbed into the cabinet. He couldn't help noticing a couple of ugly rhinestones glued onto the raw plywood just in front of his face. "If this is a joke," he said.

"Some joke. Now, here's the point. If I throw any novel into this cabinet with you, shut the doors, and tap it three times, you will find yourself projected into that book."

Kugelmass made a grimace of disbelief.

"It's the emess,"[2] Persky said. "My hand to God. Not just a novel, either. A short story, a play, a poem. You can meet any of the women

---

[2] the truth.

created by the world's best writers. Whoever you dreamed of. You could carry on all you like with a real winner. Then when you've had enough you give a yell, and I'll see you're back here in a split second."

"Persky, are you some kind of outpatient?"

"I'm telling you it's on the level," Persky said.

Kugelmass remained skeptical. "What are you telling me — that this cheesy homemade box can take me on a ride like you're describing?"

"For a double sawbuck."[3]

Kugelmass reached for his wallet. "I'll believe this when I see it," he said.

Persky tucked the bills in his pants pocket and turned toward his bookcase. "So who do you want to meet? Sister Carrie? Hester Prynne? Ophelia? Maybe someone by Saul Bellow? Hey, what about Temple Drake?[4] Although for a man your age she'd be a workout."

"French, I want to have an affair with a French lover."

"Nana?"[5]

"I don't want to have to pay for it."

"What about Natasha in 'War and Peace'?"

"I said French. I know! What about Emma Bovary?[6] That sounds to me perfect."

"You got it, Kugelmass. Give me a holler when you've had enough." Persky tossed in a paperback copy of Flaubert's novel.

"You sure this is safe?" Kugelmass asked as Persky began shutting the cabinet doors.

"Safe. Is anything safe in this crazy world?" Persky rapped three times on the cabinet and then flung open the doors.

Kugelmass was gone. At the same moment, he appeared in the bedroom of Charles and Emma Bovary's house at Yonville. Before him was a beautiful woman standing alone with her back turned to him as she folded some linen. I can't believe this, thought Kugelmass, staring at the doctor's ravishing wife. This is uncanny. I'm here. It's her.

Emma turned in surprise. "Goodness, you startled me," she said. "Who are you?" She spoke in the same fine English translation as the paperback.

It's simply devastating, he thought,. Then, realizing that it was he whom she had addressed, he said, "Excuse me, I'm Sidney Kugelmass. I'm from City College. A professor of humanities. C.C.N.Y.? Uptown. I — oh, boy!"

Emma Bovary smiled flirtatiously and said, "Would you like a drink? A glass of wine, perhaps?"

---

[3] $20.

[4] Carrie Meeber is the heroine of Theodore Dreiser's novel *Sister Carrie* (1900); Hester Prynne is in Nathaniel Hawthorne's *The Scarlet Letter* (1850); Ophelia is in *Hamlet* (c. 1600); and Temple Drake is a character is William Faulkner's novel *Sanctuary* (1931).

[5] Nana is in Emile Zola's *Nana* (1880).

[6] Emma Bovary is the heroine of Gustave Flaubert's novel *Madame Bovary* (1865).

She is beautiful, Kugelmass thought. What a contrast with the troglodyte who shared his bed! He felt a sudden impulse to take this vision into his arms and tell her she was the kind of woman he had dreamed of all his life.

"Yes, some wine," he said hoarsely. "White. No, red. No, white. Make it white."

"Charles is out for the day," Emma said, her voice full of playful implication.

After the wine, they went for a stroll in the lovely French countryside. "I've always dreamed that some mysterious stranger would appear and rescue me from the monotony of this crass rural existence," Emma said, clasping his hand. They passed a small church. "I love what you have on," she murmured. "I've never seen anything like it around here. It's so . . . so modern."

"It's called a leisure suit," he said romantically. "It was marked down." Suddenly he kissed her. For the next hour they reclined under a tree and whispered together and told each other deeply meaningful things with their eyes. Then Kugelmass sat up. He had just remembered he had to meet Daphne at Bloomingdale's. "I must go," he told her. "But don't worry. I'll be back."

"I hope so." Emma said.

He embraced her passionately, and the two walked back to the house. He held Emma's face cupped in his palms, kissed her again, and yelled, "O.K., Persky! I got to be at Bloomingdale's by three-thirty."

There was an audible pop, and Kugelmass was back in Brooklyn.

"So? Did I lie?" Persky asked triumphantly.

"Look, Persky, I'm right now late to meet the ball and chain at Lexington Avenue, but when can I go again? Tomorrow?"

"My pleasure. Just bring a twenty. And don't mention this to anybody."

"Yeah. I'm going to call Rupert Murdoch."[7]

Kugelmass hailed a cab and sped off to the city. His heart danced on point. I am in love, he thought, I am the possessor of a wonderful secret. What he didn't realize was that at this very moment students in various classrooms across the country were saying to their teachers, "Who is this character on page 100? A bald Jew is kissing Madame Bovary?" A teacher in Sioux Falls, South Dakota, sighed and thought, Jesus, these kids, with their pot and acid. What goes through their minds!

Daphne Kugelmass was in the bathroom-accessories department at Bloomingdale's when Kugelmass arrived breathlessly. "Where've you been?" she snapped. "It's four-thirty."

"I got held up in traffic," Kugelmass said.

Kugelmass visited Persky the next day, and in a few minutes was again passed magically to Yonville. Emma couldn't hide her excitement at seeing

---

[7] Rupert Murdoch (b. 1931) is an Australian newspaper tycoon.

him. The two spent hours together, laughing and talking about their different backgrounds. Before Kugelmass left, they made love. "My God, I'm doing it with Madame Bovary!" Kugelmass whispered to himself. "Me, who failed freshman English."

As the months passed, Kugelmass saw Persky many times and developed a close and passionate relationship with Emma Bovary. "Make sure and always get me into the book before page 120," Kugelmass said to the magician one day. "I always have to meet her before she hooks up with this Rodolphe character."

"Why?" Persky asked. "You can't beat his time?"

"Beat his time. He's landed gentry. Those guys have nothing better to do than flirt and ride horses. To me, he's one of those faces you see in the pages of *Women's Wear Daily*. With the Helmut Berger hairdo. But to her he's hot stuff."

"And her husband suspects nothing?"

"He's out of his depth. He's a lack-lustre little paramedic who's thrown in his lot with a jitterbug. He's ready to go to sleep by ten, and she's putting on her dancing shoes. Oh, well . . . See you later."

And once again Kugelmass entered the cabinet and passed instantly to the Bovary estate at Yonville. "How you doing, cupcake?" he said to Emma.

"Oh, Kugelmass," Emma sighed. "What I have to put up with. Last night at dinner, Mr. Personality dropped off to sleep in the middle of the dessert course. I'm pouring my heart out about Maxim's and the ballet, and out of the blue I hear snoring."

"It's O.K., darling, I'm here now," Kugelmass said, embracing her. I've earned this, he thought, smelling Emma's French perfume and burying his nose in her hair. I've suffered enough. I've paid enough analysts. I've searched till I'm weary. She's young and nubile, and I'm here a few pages after Léon and just before Rodolphe. By showing up during the correct chapters, I've got the situation knocked.

Emma, to be sure, was just as happy as Kugelmass. She had been starved for excitement, and his tales of Broadway night life, of fast cars and Hollywood and TV stars, enthralled the young French beauty.

"Tell me again about O. J. Simpson," she implored that evening, as she and Kugelmass strolled past Abbé Bournisien's church.

"What can I say? The man is great. He sets all kinds of rushing records. Such moves. They can't touch him."

"And the Academy Awards?" Emma said wistfully. "I'd give anything to win one."

"First you've got to be nominated."

"I know. You explained it. But I'm convinced I can act. Of course, I'd want to take a class or two. With Strasberg maybe. Then, if I had the right agent — "

"We'll see, we'll see. I'll speak to Persky."

That night, safely returned to Persky's flat, Kugelmass brought up the idea of having Emma visit him in the big city.

"Let me think about it," Persky said. "Maybe I could work it. Stranger things have happened." Of course, neither of them could think of one.

"Where the hell do you go all the time?" Daphne Kugelmass barked at her husband as he returned home late that evening. "You got a chippie stashed somewhere?"

"Yeah, sure, I'm just the type." Kugelmass said wearily. "I was with Leonard Popkin. We were discussing Socialist agriculture in Poland. You know Popkin. He's a freak on the subject."

"Well, you've been very odd lately," Daphne said. "Distant. Just don't forget about my father's birthday. On Saturday?"

"Oh, sure, sure," Kugelmass said, heading for the bathroom.

"My whole family will be there. We can see the twins. And Cousin Hamish. You should be more polite to Cousin Hamish — he likes you."

"Right, the twins," Kugelmass said, closing the bathroom door and shutting out the sound of his wife's voice. He leaned against it and took a deep breath. In a few hours, he told himself, he would be back in Yonville again, back with his beloved. And this time, if all went well, he would bring Emma back with him.

At three-fifteen the following afternoon, Persky worked his wizardry again. Kugelmass appeared before Emma, smiling and eager. The two spent a few hours at Yonville with Binet and then remounted the Bovary carriage. Following Persky's instructions, they held each other tightly, closed their eyes, and counted to ten. When they opened them, the carriage was just drawing up at the side door of the Plaza Hotel, where Kugelmass had optimistically reserved a suite earlier in the day.

"I love it! It's everything I dreamed it would be," Emma said as she whirled joyously around the bedroom, surveying the city from their window. "There's F. A. O. Schwarz. And there's Central Park, and the Sherry is which one? Oh, there — I see. It's too divine."

On the bed there were boxes from Halston and Saint Laurent. Emma unwrapped a package and held up a pair of black velvet pants against her perfect body.

"The slacks suit is by Ralph Lauren," Kugelmass said. "You'll look like a million bucks in it. Come on, sugar, give us a kiss."

"I've never been so happy!" Emma squealed as she stood before the mirror. "Let's go out on the town. I want to see *Chorus Line* and the Guggenheim and this Jack Nicholson character you always talk about. Are any of his flicks showing?"

"I cannot get my mind around this," a Stanford professor said. "First a strange character named Kugelmass, and now she's gone from the book. Well, I guess the mark of a classic is that you can reread it a thousand times and always find something new."

The lovers passed a blissful weekend. Kugelmass had told Daphne he would be away at a symposium in Boston, and would return Monday. Savoring each moment, he and Emma went to the movies, had dinner in Chinatown, passed two hours at a discothèque, and went to bed with a TV movie. They slept till noon on Sunday, visited SoHo, and ogled celebrities at Elaine's. They had caviar and champagne in their suite on Sunday night and talked until dawn. That morning, in the cab taking them to Persky's apartment, Kugelmass thought, It was hectic, but worth it. I can't bring her here too often, but now and then it will be a charming contrast with Yonville.

At Persky's, Emma climbed into the cabinet, arranged her new boxes of clothes neatly around her, and kissed Kugelmass fondly. "My place next time," she said with a wink. Persky rapped three times on the cabinet. Nothing happened.

"Hmm," Persky said, scratching his head. He rapped again, but still no magic. "Something must be wrong," he mumbled.

"Persky, you're joking!" Kugelmass cried. "How can it not work?"

"Relax, relax. Are you still in the box, Emma?"

"Yes."

Persky rapped again — harder this time.

"I'm still here, Persky."

"I know, darling. Sit tight."

"Persky, we *have* to get her back," Kugelmass whispered. "I'm a married man, and I have a class in three hours. I'm not prepared for anything more than a cautious affair at this point."

"I can't understand it," Persky muttered. "It's such a reliable little trick."

But he could do nothing. "It's going to take a little while," he said to Kugelmass. "I'm going to have to strip it down. I'll call you later."

Kugelmass bundled Emma into a cab and took her back to the Plaza. He barely made it to his class on time. He was on the phone all day, to Persky and to his mistress. The magician told him it might be several days before he got to the bottom of the trouble.

"How was the symposium?" Daphne asked him that night.

"Fine, fine," he said, lighting the filter end of a cigarette.

"What's wrong? You're as tense as a cat."

"Me? Ha, that's a laugh. I'm as calm as a summer night. I'm just going to take a walk." He eased out the door, hailed a cab, and flew to the Plaza.

"This is no good," Emma said. "Charles will miss me."

"Bear with me, sugar," Kugelmass said. He was pale and sweaty. He kissed her again, raced to the elevators, yelled at Persky over a pay phone in the Plaza lobby, and just made it home before midnight.

"According to Popkin, barley prices in Kraków have not been this stable since 1971," he said to Daphne, and smiled wanly as he climbed into bed.

The whole week went by like that. On Friday night, Kugelmass told

Daphne there was another symposium he had to catch, this one in Syracuse. He hurried back to the Plaza, but the second weekend there was nothing like the first. "Get me back into the novel or marry me," Emma told Kugelmass. "Meanwhile, I want to get a job or go to class, because watching TV all day is the pits."

"Fine. We can use the money," Kugelmass said. "You consume twice your weight in room service."

"I met an Off Broadway producer in Central Park yesterday, and he said I might be right for a project he's doing," Emma said.

"Who is this clown?" Kugelmass asked.

"He's not a clown. He's sensitive and kind and cute. His name's Jeff Something-or-Other, and he's up for a Tony."

Later that afternoon, Kugelmass showed up at Persky's drunk.

"Relax." Persky told him. "You'll get a coronary."

"Relax. The man says relax. I've got a fictional character stashed in a hotel room, and I think my wife is having me tailed by a private shamus."[8]

"O.K., O.K. We know there's a problem." Persky crawled under the cabinet and started banging on something with a large wrench.

"I'm like a wild animal," Kugelmass went on. "I'm sneaking around town, and Emma and I have had it up to here with each other. Not to mention a hotel tab that reads like the defense budget."

"So what should I do? This is the world of magic," Persky said, "It's all nuance."

"Nuance, my foot. I'm pouring Dom Pérignon and black eggs into this little mouse, plus her wardrobe, plus she's enrolled at the Neighborhood Playhouse and suddenly needs professional photos. Also, Persky, Professor Fivish Kopkind, who teaches Comp Lit and who has always been jealous of me, has identified me as the sporadically appearing character in the Flaubert book. He's threatened to go to Daphne. I see ruin and alimony; jail. For adultery with Madame Bovary, my wife will reduce me to beggary."

"What do you want me to say? I'm working on it night and day. As far as your personal anxiety goes, that I can't help you with. I'm a magician, not an analyst."

By Sunday afternoon, Emma had locked herself in the bathroom and refused to respond to Kugelmass's entreaties. Kugelmass stared out the window at the Wollman Rink and contemplated suicide. Too bad this is a low floor, he thought, or I'd do it right now. Maybe if I ran away to Europe and started life over . . . Maybe I could sell the *International Herald Tribune*, like those young girls used to.

The phone rang. Kugelmass lifted it to his ear mechanically.

"Bring her over," Persky said. "I think I got the bugs out of it."

Kugelmass's heart leaped. "You're serious?" he said. "You got it licked?"

[8] detective.

"It was something in the transmission. Go figure."

"Persky, you're a genius. We'll be there in a minute. Less than a minute."

Again the lovers hurried to the magician's apartment, and again Emma Bovary climbed into the cabinet with her boxes. This time there was no kiss. Persky shut the doors, took a deep breath, and tapped the box three times. There was the reassuring popping noise, and when Persky peered inside, the box was empty. Madame Bovary was back in her novel. Kugelmass heaved a great sigh of relief and pumped the magician's hand.

"It's over," he said. "I learned my lesson. I'll never cheat again, I swear it." He pumped Persky's hand again and made a mental note to send him a necktie.

Three weeks later, at the end of a beautiful spring afternoon, Persky answered his doorbell. It was Kugelmass, with a sheepish expression on his face.

"O.K., Kugelmass," the magician said. "Where to this time?"

"It's just this once," Kugelmass said. "The weather is so lovely, and I'm not getting any younger. Listen, you've read *Portnoy's Complaint*? Remember The Monkey?"[9]

"The price is now twenty-five dollars, because the cost of living is up, but I'll start you off with one freebie, due to all the trouble I caused you."

"You're good people," Kugelmass said, combing his few remaining hairs as he climbed into the cabinet again. "This'll work all right?"

"I hope. But I haven't tried it much since all that unpleasantness."

"Sex and romance," Kugelmass said from inside the box. "What we go through for a pretty face."

Persky tossed in a copy of *Portnoy's Complaint* and rapped three times on the box. This time, instead of a popping noise there was a dull explosion, followed by a series of crackling noises and a shower of sparks. Persky leaped back, was seized by a heart attack, and dropped dead. The cabinet burst into flames, and eventually the entire house burned down.

Kugelmass, unaware of his catastrophe, had his own problems. He had not been thrust into *Portnoy's Complaint*, or into any other novel, for that matter. He had been projected into an old textbook, *Remedial Spanish*, and was running for his life over a barren, rocky terrain as the word *tener* ("to have") — a large and hairy irregular verb — raced after him on its spindly legs.

[1977]

[9] The Monkey is the sexually liberated heroine of Philip Roth's novel *Portnoy's Complaint* (1969).

GAIL GODWIN (b. 1937) was born in Birmingham, Alabama. After her parents were divorced, she grew up in Asheville, North Carolina, where her mother worked for the local newspaper and wrote love stories for women's magazines to support her daughter while Godwin's grandmother ran the house. Godwin says that by the age of five she had allied herself with the typewriter rather than the stove. Early in life she absorbed the discipline of the working writer from her mother's example. Godwin remembers that her grandmother was the first reader of her mother's stories in rough draft form: " 'It moves a little slowly here,' she'd say, or 'I didn't understand why the girl did this.' And the tempo would be stepped up, the heroine's ambiguous action sharpened in the afternoon draft; for if my grandmother didn't follow tempo and motive, how would all those other women who would buy the magazine?"

After Godwin graduated from the University of North Carolina in 1959, she worked briefly as a reporter for the Miami Herald, got married and divorced, and wrote a novel and some short stories. In 1970 she published her first novel, The Perfectionists. Five other novels followed: Glass People (1972), The Odd Woman (1974), Violet Clay (1978), A Mother and Two Daughters (1982), and The Finishing School (1985). During this time she also published two collections of stories, Dream Children (1976) and Mr. Bedford and the Muses (1983), a book consisting of stories about the relation of artists to their material.

Godwin's novels have received more attention than her short fiction, which has been criticized as slickly ingenious. She is angered by the label woman writer and defends the right of women to write popular fiction in conventional forms. Her best stories, like "Dream Children," are penetrating studies of extreme psychological states. One of the most remarkable stories Godwin ever told is the anecdote about herself that she gave to an interviewer from Contemporary Authors in 1984. Talking about her childhood and how her mother read to her every night, Godwin said, "My favorite book that she read was a little empty address book — it had a picture of some faraway place on the front — and she would read stories out of this blank book. It was just fascinating. That was a real treat: that was the special book, a tiny book with no writing at all in it."

Gail Godwin

ဢၭ

DREAM CHILDREN

*The worst thing. Such a terrible thing to happen to a young woman.
It's a wonder she didn't go mad.*

As she went about her errands, a cheerful, neat young woman, a wife,
wearing pants with permanent creases and safari jackets and high-necked
sweaters that folded chastely just below the line of the small gold hoops she
wore in her ears, she imagined people saying this, or thinking it to themselves. But nobody knew. Nobody knew anything, other than that she and
her husband had moved here a year ago, as so many couples were moving
farther away from the city, the husband commuting, or staying in town
during the week — as hers did. There was nobody here, in this quaint, unspoiled village, nestled in the foothills of the mountains, who could have
looked at her and guessed that anything out of the ordinary, predictable,
auspicious spectrum of things that happen to bright, attractive young
women had happened to her. She always returned her books to the local library on time; she bought liquor at the local liquor store only on Friday,
before she went to meet her husband's bus from the city. He was something
in television, a producer? So many ambitious young couples moving to this
Dutch farming village, founded in 1690, to restore ruined fieldstone houses
and plant herb gardens and keep their own horses and discover the relief of
finding oneself insignificant in Nature for the first time!

*A terrible thing. So freakish. If you read it in a story or saw it on TV,
you'd say no, this sort of thing could never happen in an American hospital.*

DePuy, who owned the old Patroon farm adjacent to her land, frequently glimpsed her racing her horse in the early morning, when the mists
still lay on the fields, sometimes just before the sun came up and there was a
frost on everything. "One woodchuck hole and she and that stallion will
both have to be put out of their misery," he told his wife. "She's too reckless. I'll bet you her old man doesn't know she goes streaking to hell across
the fields like that." Mrs. DePuy nodded, silent, and went about her business. She, too, watched that other woman ride, a woman not much younger
than herself, but with an aura of romance — of tragedy, perhaps. The way
she looked: like those heroines in English novels who ride off their bad tempers and unrequited love affairs, clenching their thighs against the flanks of

1085

spirited horses with murderous red eyes. Mrs. DePuy, who had ridden since the age of three, recognized something beyond recklessness in that elegant young woman, in her crisp checked shirts and her dove-gray jodhpurs. *She has nothing to fear anymore,* thought the farmer's wife, with sure feminine instinct; she both envied and pitied her. "What she needs is children," remarked DePuy.

"A Dry Sack, a Remy Martin, and . . . let's see, a half-gallon of the Chablis, and I think I'd better take a Scotch . . . and the Mouton-Cadet . . . and maybe a dry vermouth." Mrs. Frye, another farmer's wife, who runs the liquor store, asks if her husband is bringing company for the weekend. "He sure is; we couldn't drink all that by ourselves," and the young woman laughs, her lovely teeth exposed, her small gold earrings quivering in the light. "You know, I saw his name — on the television the other night," says Mrs. Frye. "It was at the beginning of that new comedy show, the one with the woman who used to be on another show with her husband and little girl, only they divorced, you know the one?" "Of course I do. It's one of my husband's shows. I'll tell him you watched it." Mrs. Frye puts the bottles in an empty box, carefully inserting wedges of cardboard between them. Through the window of her store she sees her customer's pert bottle-green car, some sort of little foreign car with the engine running, filled with groceries and weekend parcels, and that big silver-blue dog sitting up in the front seat just like a human being. "I think that kind of thing is so sad," says Mrs. Frye; "families breaking up, poor little children having to divide their loyalties." "I couldn't agree more," replies the young woman, nodding gravely. Such a personable, polite girl! "Are you sure you can carry that, dear? I can get Earl from the back. . . ." But the girl has it hoisted on her shoulder in a flash, is airily maneuvering between unopened cartons stacked in the aisle, in her pretty boots. Her perfume lingers in Mrs. Frye's store for a half-hour after she has driven away.

After dinner, her husband and his friends drank brandy. She lay in front of the fire, stroking the dog, and listening to Victoria Darrow, the news commentator, in person. A few minutes ago, they had all watched Victoria on TV. "That's right; thirty-nine!" Victoria now whispered to her. "What? That's kind of you. I'm photogenic, thank God, or I'd have been put out to pasture long before. . . . I look five, maybe seven years younger on the screen . . . but the point I'm getting at is, I went to this doctor and he said, 'If you want to do this thing, you'd better go home today and get started.' He told me — did you know this? Did you know that a woman is born with all the eggs she'll ever have, and when she gets to my age, the ones that are left have been rattling around so long they're a little shop-worn; then every time you fly you get an extra dose of radioactivity, so those poor eggs. He told me when a woman over forty comes into his office pregnant, his heart sinks; that's why he quit practicing obstetrics, he said; he could still remember the screams of a woman whose baby he delivered . . . she was having natural childbirth and she kept saying, 'Why won't you let me see it, I insist on seeing it,' and so he had to, and he says he can still hear her screaming."

"Oh, what was — what was wrong with it?"

But she never got the answer. Her husband, white around the lips, was standing over Victoria ominously, offering the Remy Martin bottle. "Vicky, let me pour you some more," he said. And to his wife, "I think Blue Boy needs to go out."

"Yes, yes, of course. Please excuse me, Victoria. I'll just be . . ."

Her husband followed her to the kitchen, his hand on the back of her neck. "Are you okay? That stupid yammering bitch. She and her twenty-six-year-old lover! I wish I'd never brought them, but she's been hinting around the studio for weeks."

"But I like them, I like having them. I'm fine. Please go back. I'll take the dog out and come back. Please . . ."

"All right. If you're sure you're okay." He backed away, hands dangling at his sides. A handsome man, wearing a pink shirt with Guatemalan embroidery. Thick black hair and a face rather boyish, but cunning. Last weekend she had sat beside him, alone in this house, just the two of them, and watched him on television: a documentary, in several parts, in which TV "examines itself." There was his double, sitting in an armchair in his executive office, coolly replying to the questions of Victoria Darrow. *Do you personally watch all the programs you produce, Mr. McNair?*" She watched the man on the screen, how he moved his lips when he spoke, but kept the rest of his face, his body perfectly still. Funny, she had never noticed this before. He managed to say that he did and did not watch all the programs he produced.

Now, in the kitchen, she looked at him backing away, a little like a renegade in one of his own shows — a desperate man, perhaps, who has just killed somebody and is backing away, hands dangling loosely at his sides, Mr. McNair, her husband. That man on the screen. Once a lover above her in bed. That friend who held her hand in the hospital. One hand in hers, the other holding the stopwatch. For a brief instant, all the images coalesce and she feels something again. But once outside, under the galaxies of autumn-sharp stars, the intelligent dog at her heels like some smart gray ghost, she is glad to be free of all that. She walks quickly over the damp grass to the barn, to look in on her horse. She understands something: her husband, Victoria Darrow lead double lives that seem perfectly normal to them. But if she told her husband that she, too, is in two lives, he would become alarmed; he would sell this house and make her move back to the city where he could keep an eye on her welfare.

She is discovering people like herself, down through the centuries, all over the world. She scours books with titles like *The Timeless Moment,*

The Sleeping Prophet, Between Two Worlds, Silent Union: A Record of Unwilled Communication; collecting evidence, weaving a sort of underworld net of colleagues around her.

A rainy fall day. Too wet to ride. The silver dog asleep beside her in her special alcove, a padded window seat filled with pillows and books. She is looking down on the fields of dried lithrium, and the fir trees beyond, and the mountains gauzy with fog and rain, thinking, in a kind of terror and ecstasy, about all these connections. A book lies face down on her lap. She has just read the following:

> Theodore Dreiser and his friend John Cowper Powys had been dining at Dreiser's place on West Fifty Seventh Street. As Powys made ready to leave and catch his train to the little town up the Hudson, where he was then living, he told Dreiser, "I'll appear before you here, later in the evening."
>
> Dreiser laughed. "Are you going to turn yourself into a ghost, or have you a spare key?" he asked. Powys said he would return "in some form," he didn't know exactly what kind.
>
> After his friend left, Dreiser sat up and read for two hours. Then he looked up and saw Powys standing in the doorway to the living room. It was Powys' features, his tall stature, even the loose tweed garments which he wore. Dreiser rose at once and strode towards the figure, saying, "Well, John, you kept your word. Come on in and tell me how you did it." But the figure vanished when Dreiser came within three feet of it.
>
> Dreiser then went to the telephone and called Powys' house in the country. Powys answered. Dreiser told him what had happened and Powys said, "I told you I'd be there and you oughtn't to be surprised." But he refused to discuss how he had done it, if, indeed, he knew how.

"But don't you get frightened, up here all by yourself, alone with all these creaky sounds?" asked Victoria the next morning.

"No, I guess I'm used to them," she replied, breaking eggs into a bowl. "I know what each one means. The wood expanding and contracting . . . the wind getting caught between the shutter and the latch. . . . Sometimes small animals get lost in the stone walls and scratch around till they find their way out . . . or die."

"Ugh. But don't you imagine things? I would, in a house like this. How old? That's almost three hundred years of lived lives, people suffering and shouting and making love and giving birth, under this roof. . . . You'd think there'd be a few ghosts around."

"I don't know," said her hostess blandly. "I haven't heard any. But of course, I have Blue Boy, so I don't get scared." She whisked the eggs, unable to face Victoria. She and her husband had lain awake last night, embarrassed at the sounds coming from the next room. No ghostly moans, those. "Why can't that bitch control herself, or at least lower her voice," he said angrily. He stroked his wife's arm, both of them pretending not to remember. She had bled for an entire year afterward, until the doctor said they would have to remove everything. "I'm empty," she had said when her husband had tried again, after she was healed. "I'm sorry, I just don't feel anything." Now they lay tenderly together on these weekends, like childhood friends, like effigies on a lovers' tomb, their mutual sorrow like a sword between them. She assumed he had another life, or lives, in town. As she had here. Nobody is just one person, she had learned.

"I'm sure I would imagine things," said Victoria. "I would see things and hear things inside my head much worse than an ordinary murderer or rapist."

The wind caught in the shutter latch . . . a small animal dislodging pieces of fieldstone in its terror, sending them tumbling down the inner walls, from attic to cellar . . . a sound like a child rattling a jar full of marbles, or small stones . . .

"I have so little imagination," she said humbly, warming the butter in the omelet pan. She could feel Victoria Darrow's professional curiosity waning from her dull country life, focusing elsewhere.

Cunning!

As a child of nine, she had gone through a phase of walking in her sleep. One summer night, they found her bed empty, and after an hour's hysterical search they had found her in her nightgown, curled up on the flagstones beside the fishpond. She woke, baffled, in her father's tense clutch, the stars all over the sky, her mother repeating over and over again to the night at large, "Oh, my God, she could have drowned!" They took her to a child psychiatrist, a pretty Austrian woman who spoke to her with the same vocabulary she used on grownups, putting the child instantly at ease. "It is not at all uncommon what you did. I have known so many children who take little night journeys from their beds, and then they awaken and don't know what all the fuss is about! Usually these journeys are quite harmless, because children are surrounded by a magical reality that keeps them safe. Yes, the race of children possesses magically sagacious powers! But the grownups, they tend to forget how it once was for them. They worry, they are afraid of so many things. You do not want your mother and father, who love you so anxiously, to live in fear of you going to live with the fishes." She had giggled at the thought. The woman's steady gray-green eyes were trained on her carefully, suspending her in a kind of bubble. Then she had rejoined her parents, a dutiful "child" again, holding a hand up to each of them. The night journeys had stopped.

A thunderstorm one night last spring. Blue Boy whining in his insulated house below the garage. She had lain there, strangely elated by the nearness of the thunderclaps that tore at the sky, followed by instantaneous flashes of jagged light. Wondering shouldn't she go down and let the dog in; he hated storms. Then dozing off again . . .

She woke. The storm had stopped. The dark air was quiet. Something had changed, some small thing — what? She had to think hard before she found it: the hall light, which she kept burning during the week-nights when she was there alone, had gone out. She reached over and switched the button on her bedside lamp. Nothing. A tree must have fallen and hit a wire, causing the power to go off. This often happened here. No problem. The dog had stopped crying. She felt herself sinking into a delicious, deep reverie, the kind that sometimes came just before morning, as if her being broke slowly into tiny pieces and spread itself over the world. It was a feeling she had not known until she had lived by herself in this house: this weightless though conscious state in which she lay, as if in a warm bath, and yet was able to send her thoughts anywhere, as if her mind contained the entire world.

And as she floated in this silent world, transparent and buoyed upon the dream layers of the mind, she heard a small rattling sound, like pebbles being shaken in a jar. The sound came distinctly from the guest room, a room so chosen by her husband and herself because it was the farthest room from their bedroom on this floor. It lay above what had been the old side of the house, built seventy-five years before the new side, which was completed in 1753. There was a bed in it, and a chair, and some plants in the window. Sometimes on weekends when she could not sleep, she went and read there, or meditated, to keep from waking her husband. It was the room where Victoria Darrow and her young lover would not sleep the following fall, because she would say quietly to her husband, "No . . . not that room. I — I've made up the bed in the other room." "What?" he would want to know. "The one next to ours? Right under our noses?"

She did not lie long listening to this sound before she understood it was one she had never heard in the house before. It had a peculiar regularity to its rhythm; there was nothing accidental about it, nothing influenced by the wind, or the nerves of some lost animal. *K-chunk, k-chunk, k-chunk*, it went. At intervals of exactly a half-minute apart. She still remembered how to time such things, such intervals. She was as good as any stopwatch when it came to timing certain intervals.

K-chunk, k-chunk, k-chunk. That determined regularity. Something willed, something poignantly repeated, as though the repetition was a means of consoling someone in the dark. Her skin began to prickle. Often, lying in such states of weightless reverie, she had practiced the trick of sending herself abroad, into rooms of the house, out into the night to check on Blue Boy, over to the barn to look in on her horse, who slept standing up. Once she had heard a rather frightening noise, as if someone in the basement had turned on a faucet, and so she forced herself to "go down," floating down two sets of stairs into the darkness, only to discover what she had known all the time: the hookup system between the hot-water tank and the pump, which sounded like someone turning on the water.

Now she went through the palpable, prickly darkness, without lights, down the chilly hall in her sleeveless gown, into the guest room. Although there was no light, not even a moon shining through the window, she could make out the shape of the bed and then the chair, the spider plants on the window, and a small dark shape in one corner, on the floor, which she and her husband had painted a light yellow.

K-chunk, k-chunk, k-chunk. The shape moved with the noise.

Now she knew what they meant, that "someone's hair stood on end." It was true. As she forced herself across the borders of a place she had never been, she felt, distinctly, every single hair on her head raise itself a millimeter or so from her scalp.

She knelt down and discovered him. He was kneeling, a little cold and scared, shaking a small jar filled with some kind of pebbles. (She later found out, in a subsequent visit, that they were small colored shells, of a triangular shape, called coquinas: she found them in a picture in a child's nature book at the library.) He was wearing pajamas a little too big for him, obviously hand-me-downs, and he was exactly two years older than the only time she had ever held him in her arms.

The two of them knelt in the corner of the room, taking each other in. His large eyes were the same as before: dark and unblinking. He held the small jar close to him, watching her. He was not afraid, but she knew better than to move too close.

She knelt, the tears streaming down her cheeks, but she made no sound, her eyes fastened on that small form. And then the hall light came on silently, as well as the lamp beside her bed, and with wet cheeks and pounding heart she could not be sure whether or not she had actually been out of the room.

But what did it matter, on the level where they had met? He traveled so much farther than she to reach that room. (*"Yes, the race of children possesses magically sagacious powers!"*)

She and her husband sat together on the flowered chintz sofa, watching the last of the series in which TV purportedly examined itself. She said, "Did you ever think that the whole thing is really a miracle? I mean, here we sit, eighty miles away from your studios, and we turn on a little machine and there is Victoria, speaking to us as clearly as she did last weekend when she was in this very room. Why, it's magic, it's time travel and space travel right in front of our eyes, but because it's been 'discovered,' because the world understands that it's only little dots that transmit Victoria electrically to us, it's *all right.* We can bear it. Don't you sometimes wonder about all the miracles that haven't been officially approved yet? I mean, who knows, maybe in a hundred years everybody will take it for granted that they can send an image of themselves around in space by some perfectly natural means available to us now. I mean, when you think about it, what *is* space? What *is* time? Where do the so-called boundaries of each of us begin and end? Can anyone explain it?"

He was drinking Scotch and thinking how they had decided not to renew Victoria Darrow's contract. Somewhere on the edges of his mind hovered an anxious, growing certainty about his wife. At the local grocery store this morning, when he went to pick up a carton of milk and the paper, he had stopped to chat with DePuy. "I don't mean to interfere, but she doesn't know those fields," said the farmer. "Last year we had to shoot a mare, stumbled into one of those holes. . . . It's madness, the way she rides."

And look at her now, her face so pale and shining, speaking of miracles and space travel, almost on the verge of tears. . . .

And last night, his first night up from the city, he had wandered through the house, trying to drink himself into this slower weekend pace, and he had come across a pile of her books, stacked in the alcove where, it was obvious, she lay for hours, escaping into science fiction, and the occult.

Now his own face appeared on the screen. "I want to be fair," he was telling Victoria Darrow. "I want to be objective. . . . Violence has always been part of the human makeup. I don't like it any more than you do, but there it is. I think it's more a question of whether we want to face things as they are or escape into fantasies of how we would like them to be."

Beside him, his wife uttered a sudden bell-like laugh.

(". . . *It's madness, the way she rides.*")

He did want to be fair, objective. She had told him again and again that she liked her life here. And he — well, he had to admit he liked his own present setup.

"I am a pragmatist," he was telling Victoria Darrow on the screen. He decided to speak to his wife about her riding and leave her alone about the books. She had the right to some escape, if anyone did. But the titles: *Marvelous Manifestations, The Mind Travellers, A Doctor Looks At Spiritualism, The Other Side.* . . . Something revolted in him, he couldn't help it; he felt an actual physical revulsion at this kind of thinking. Still it was better than some other escapes. His friend Barnett, the actor, who said at night he went from room to room, after his wife was asleep, collecting empty glasses. ("Once I found one by the Water Pik, a second on the ledge beside the tub, a third on the back of the john, and a fourth on the floor beside the john. . . .")

He looked sideways at his wife, who was absorbed, it seemed, in watching him on the screen. Her face was tense, alert, animated. She did not look mad. She wore slim gray pants and a loose-knit pullover made of some silvery material, like a knight's chain mail. The lines of her profile were clear and silvery themselves, somehow sexless and pure, like a child's profile. He no longer felt lust when he looked at her, only a sad determination to protect her. He had a mistress in town, whom he loved, but he had explained, right from the beginning, that he considered himself married for the rest of his life. He told this woman the whole story. "And I am implicated in it. I could never leave her." An intelligent, sensitive woman, she had actually wept and said, "Of course not."

He always wore the same pajamas, a shade too big, but always clean. Obviously washed again and again in a machine that went through its cycles frequently. She imagined his "other mother," a harassed woman with several children, short on money, on time, on dreams — all the things she herself had too much of. The family lived, she believed, somewhere in Florida, probably on the west coast. She had worked that out from the little coquina shells: their bright colors, even in moonlight shining through a small window with spider plants in it. His face and arms had been suntanned early in the spring and late into the autumn. They never spoke or touched. She was not sure how much of this he understood. She tried and failed to remember where she herself had gone, in those little night journeys to the fishpond. Perhaps he never remembered afterward, when he woke up, clutching his jar, in a roomful of brothers and sisters. Or with a worried mother or father come to collect him, asleep by the sea. Once she had a very clear dream of the whole family, living in a trailer, with palm trees. But that was a dream; she recognized its difference in quality from those truly magic times when, through his own childish powers, he somehow found a will strong enough, or innocent enough, to project himself upon her still-floating consciousness, as clearly and as believably as her own husband's image on the screen.

There had been six of those times in six months. She dared to look forward to more. So unafraid he was. The last time was the day after Victoria Darrow and her young lover and her own good husband had returned to the city. She had gone farther with the child than ever before. On a starry-clear, cold September Monday, she had coaxed him down the stairs and out of the house with her. He held to the banisters, a child unused to stairs, and yet she knew there was no danger; he floated in his own dream with her. She took him to see Blue Boy. Who disappointed her by whining and backing away in fear. And then to the barn to see the horse. Who perked up his ears and looked interested. There was no touching, of course, no touching or speaking. Later she wondered if horses, then, were more magical than dogs. If dogs were more "realistic." She was glad the family was poor, the mother harassed. They could not afford any expensive child psychiatrist who would hypnotize him out of his night journeys.

He loved her. She knew that. Even if he never remembered her in his other life.

"At last I was beginning to understand what Teilhard de Chardin meant when he said that man's true home is the mind. I understood that when the mystics tell us that the mind is a place, they *don't mean it as a metaphor*. I found these new powers developed with practice. I had to detach myself from my ordinary physical personality. The intelligent part of me had to remain wide awake, and move down into this world of thoughts, dreams, and memories. After several such journeyings I understood something else: dream and reality aren't competitors, but reciprocal sources of consciousness." This she read in a "respectable book," by a "respectable man," a scientist, alive and living in England, only a few years older than herself. She looked down at the dog, sleeping on the rug. His lean silvery body actually ran as he slept! Suddenly his muzzle lifted, the savage teeth snapped. Where was he "really" now? Did the dream rabbit in his jaws know it was a dream? There was much to think about, between her trips to the nursery.

Would the boy grow, would she see his body slowly emerging from its child's shape, the arms and legs lengthening, the face thinning out into a man's — like a certain advertisement for bread she had seen on TV where a child grows up, in less than a half-minute of sponsor time, right before the viewer's eyes. Would he grow into a man, grow a beard . . . outgrow the nursery region of his mind where they had been able to meet?

And yet, some daylight part of his mind must have retained an image of her from that single daylight time they had looked into each other's eyes.

The worst thing, such an awful thing to happen to a young woman. . . . She was having this natural childbirth, you see, her husband in the delivery room with her, and the pains were coming a half-minute apart, and the doctor had just said, "This is going to be a breeze, Mrs. McNair," and they never knew exactly what went wrong, but all of a sudden the pains stopped and they had to go in after the baby without even time to give her a saddle block or any sort of anesthetic. . . . They must have practically had to tear it out of her . . . the husband fainted. The baby was born dead, and they gave her a heavy sedative to put her out all night.

When she woke the next morning, before she had time to remember what had happened, a nurse suddenly entered the room and laid a baby in her arms. "Here's your little boy," she said cheerfully, and the woman thought, with a profound, religious relief, *So that other nightmare was a dream,* and she had the child at her breast feeding him before the nurse realized her mistake and rushed back into the room, but they had to knock the poor woman out with more sedatives before she would let the child go. She was screaming and so was the little baby and they clung to each other till she passed out.

They would have let the nurse go, only it wasn't entirely her fault. The hospital was having a strike at the time; some of the nurses were outside picketing and this nurse had been working straight through for forty-eight hours, and when she was questioned afterward she said she had just mixed up the rooms, and yet, she said, when she had seen the woman and the baby clinging to each other like that, she had undergone a sort of revelation in her almost hallucinatory exhaustion: the nurse said she saw that all children and mothers were interchangeable, that nobody could own anybody or anything, any more than you could own an idea that happened to be passing through the air and caught on your mind, or any more than you owned the rosebush that grew in your back yard. There were only mothers and children, she realized; though, afterward, the realization faded.

It was the kind of freakish thing that happens once in a million times, and it's a wonder the poor woman kept her sanity.

In the intervals, longer than those measured by any stopwatch, she waited for him. In what the world accepted as "time," she shopped for groceries, for clothes; she read; she waved from her bottle-green car to Mrs. Frye, trimming the hedge in front of the liquor store, to Mrs. DePuy, hanging out her children's pajamas in the back yard of the old Patroon farm. She rode her horse through the fields of the waning season, letting him have his head; she rode like the wind, a happy, happy woman. She rode faster than fear because she was a woman in a dream, a woman anxiously awaiting her child's sleep. The stallion's hoofs pounded the earth. Oiling his tractor, DePuy resented the foolish woman and almost wished for a woodchuck hole to break that arrogant ride. Wished deep in a violent level of himself he never knew he had. For he was a kind, distracted father and husband, a practical, hard-working man who would never descend deeply into himself. Her body, skimming through time, felt weightless to the horse.

Was she a woman riding a horse and dreaming she was a mother who anxiously awaited her child's sleep; or was she a mother dreaming of herself as a free spirit who could ride her horse like the wind because she had nothing to fear?

I am a happy woman, that's all I know. Who can explain such things?
[1976]

RAYMOND CARVER (b. 1938) *grew up in a logging town in Ore-gon, where his father worked in a mill and his mother held odd jobs. After graduating from high school, Carver married at the age of eighteen and had two children. Working hard to support his wife and family, he managed to enroll briefly in 1958 as a student at Chico State College in California, where he took a creative writing course from a then-unknown young novel-ist named John Gardner. Carver remembers that he decided to try to be-come a writer because he liked to read pulp novels and magazines about hunting and fishing. He credits Gardner for giving him a strong sense of di-rection as a writer: "A writer's values and craft. This is what the man taught and what he stood for, and this is what I've kept by me in the years since that brief but all-important time."*

In 1963 Carver received his B.A. degree from Humboldt State College in northern California. The following year he studied writing at the Univer-sity of Iowa. But the 1960s were difficult for him and his wife.

> *I learned a long time ago when my kids were little and we had no money, and we were working our hearts out and weren't getting anywhere, even though we were giving it our best, my wife and I, that there were more important things than writing a poem or a story. That was a very hard real-ization for me to come to. But it came to me, and I had to accept it or die. Getting milk and food on the table, getting the rent paid, if a choice had to be made, then I had to forgo writing.*

Carver's desire to be a writer was so strong that he kept on writing long after the "cold facts" of his life told him he ought to quit. His first collec-tion of stories, Will You Please Be Quiet, Please, *was nominated for a Na-tional Book Award in 1976. Four more collections of stories followed in the next decade, along with four books of poetry. The spare, laconic conversa-tional style and bleak atmosphere of Carver's fiction have evoked compari-sons to the stories of Sherwood Anderson; both writers describe what one* New York Times *critic has called "the country of arduous life." Like that of Anderson before him, Carver's skillful, quiet voice is a strong influence on a generation of young writers, making him America's preeminent contempo-rary short story author. Both of the stories included here are from Carver's third collection,* What We Talk about When We Talk about Love (1981). *(See Carver's Commentary on page 1335.)*

Raymond Carver

ನ಄

WHAT WE TALK ABOUT
WHEN WE TALK ABOUT LOVE

My friend Mel McGinnis was talking. Mel McGinnis is a cardiologist, and sometimes that gives him the right.

The four of us were sitting around his kitchen table drinking gin. Sunlight filled the kitchen from the big window behind the sink. There were Mel and me and his second wife, Teresa — Terri, we called her — and my wife, Laura. We lived in Albuquerque then. But we were all from somewhere else.

There was an ice bucket on the table. The gin and the tonic water kept going around, and we somehow got on the subject of love. Mel thought real love was nothing less than spiritual love. He said he'd spent five years in a seminary before quitting to go to medical school. He said he still looked back on those years in the seminary as the most important years in his life.

Terri said the man she lived with before she lived with Mel loved her so much he tried to kill her. Then Terri said, "He beat me up one night. He dragged me around the living room by my ankles. He kept saying, 'I love you, I love you, you bitch.' He went on dragging me around the living room. My head kept knocking on things." Terri looked around the table. "What do you do with love like that?"

She was a bone-thin woman with a pretty face, dark eyes, and brown hair that hung down her back. She liked necklaces made of turquoise, and long pendant earrings.

"My God, don't be silly. That's not love, and you know it," Mel said. "I don't know what you'd call it, but I sure know you wouldn't call it love."

"Say what you want to, but I know it was," Terri said. "It may sound crazy to you, but it's true just the same. People are different, Mel. Sure, sometimes he may have acted crazy. Okay. But he loved me. In his own way maybe, but he loved me. There was love there, Mel. Don't say there wasn't."

Mel let out his breath. He held his glass and turned to Laura and me. "The man threatened to kill me," Mel said. He finished his drink and reached for the gin bottle. "Terri's a romantic. Terri's of the kick-me-so-I'll-know-you-love-me school. Terri, hon, don't look that way." Mel reached across the table and touched Terri's cheek with his fingers. He grinned at her.

"Now he wants to make up," Terri said.

"Make up what?" Mel said. "What is there to make up? I know what I know. That's all."

"How'd we get started on this subject, anyway?" Terri said. She raised her glass and drank from it. "Mel always has love on his mind," she said. "Don't you, honey?" She smiled, and I thought that was the last of it.

"I just wouldn't call Ed's behavior love. That's all I'm saying, honey," Mel said. "What about you guys?" Mel said to Laura and me. "Does that sound like love to you?"

"I'm the wrong person to ask," I said. "I didn't even know the man. I've only heard his name mentioned in passing. I wouldn't know. You'd have to know the particulars. But I think what you're saying is that love is an absolute."

Mel said, "The kind of love I'm talking about is. The kind of love I'm talking about, you don't try to kill people."

Laura said, "I don't know anything about Ed, or anything about the situation. But who can judge anyone else's situation?"

I touched the back of Laura's hand. She gave me a quick smile. I picked up Laura's hand. It was warm, the nails polished, perfectly manicured. I encircled the broad wrist with my fingers, and I held her.

"When I left, he drank rat poison," Terri said. She clasped her arms with her hands. "They took him to the hospital in Sante Fe. That's where we lived then, about ten miles out. They saved his life. But his gums went crazy from it. I mean they pulled away from his teeth. After that, his teeth stood out like fangs. My God," Terri said. She waited a minute, then let go of her arms and picked up her glass.

"What people won't do!" Laura said.

"He's out of the action now," Mel said. "He's dead."

Mel handed me the saucer of limes. I took a section, squeezed it over my drink, and stirred the ice cubes with my finger.

"It gets worse," Terri said. "He shot himself in the mouth. But he bungled that too. Poor Ed," she said. Terri shook her head.

"Poor Ed nothing," Mel said. "He was dangerous."

Mel was forty-five years old. He was tall and rangy with curly soft hair. His face and arms were brown from the tennis he played. When he was sober, his gestures, all his movements, were precise, very careful.

"He did love me though, Mel. Grant me that," Terri said. "That's all I'm asking. He didn't love me the way you love me. I'm not saying that. But he loved me. You can grant me that, can't you?"

"What do you mean, he bungled it?" I said.

Laura leaned forward with her glass. She put her elbows on the table and held her glass in both hands. She glanced from Mel to Terri and waited with a look of bewilderment on her open face, as if amazed that such things happened to people you were friendly with.

"How'd he bungle it when he killed himself?" I said.

"I'll tell you what happened," Mel said. "He took this twenty-two pistol he'd bought to threaten Terri and me with. Oh, I'm serious, the man was always threatening. You should have seen the way we lived in those days. Like fugitives. I even bought a gun myself. Can you believe it? A guy like me? But I did. I bought one for self-defense and carried it in the glove compartment. Sometimes I'd have to leave the apartment in the middle of the night. To go to the hospital, you know? Terri and I weren't married then, and my first wife had the house and kids, the dog, everything, and Terri and I were living in this apartment here. Sometimes, as I say, I'd get a call in the middle of the night and have to go in to the hospital at two or three in the morning. It'd be dark out there in the parking lot, and I'd break into a sweat before I could even get to my car. I never knew if he was going to come up out of the shrubbery or from behind a car and start shooting. I mean, the man was crazy. He was capable of wiring a bomb, anything. He used to call my service at all hours and say he needed to talk to the doctor, and when I'd return the call, he'd say, 'Son of a bitch, your days are numbered.' Little things like that. It was scary, I'm telling you."

"I still feel sorry for him," Terri said.

"It sounds like a nightmare," Laura said. "But what exactly happened after he shot himself?"

Laura is a legal secretary. We'd met in a professional capacity. Before we knew it, it was a courtship. She's thirty-five, three years younger than I am. In addition to being in love, we like each other and enjoy one another's company. She's easy to be with.

"What happened?" Laura said.

Mel said, "He shot himself in the mouth in his room. Someone heard the shot and told the manager. They came in with a passkey, saw what had happened, and called an ambulance. I happened to be there when they brought him in, alive but past recall. The man lived for three days. His head swelled up to twice the size of a normal head. I'd never seen anything like it, and I hope I never do again. Terri wanted to go in and sit with him when she found out about it. We had a fight over it. I didn't think she should see him like that. I didn't think she should see him, and I still don't."

"Who won the fight?" Laura said.

"I was in the room with him when he died," Terri said. "He never came up out of it. But I sat with him. He didn't have anyone else."

"He was dangerous," Mel said. "If you call that love, you can have it."

"It was love," Terri said. "Sure, it's abnormal in most people's eyes. But he was willing to die for it. He did die for it."

"I sure as hell wouldn't call it love," Mel said. "I mean, no one knows what he did it for. I've seen a lot of suicides, and I couldn't say anyone ever knew what they did it for."

Mel put his hands behind his neck and tilted his chair back. "I'm not interested in that kind of love," he said. "If that's love, you can have it."

Terri said, "We were afraid. Mel even made a will out and wrote to his brother in California who used to be a Green Beret. Mel told him who to look for if something happened to him."

Terri drank from her glass. She said, "But Mel's right — we lived like fugitives. We were afraid. Mel was, weren't you, honey? I even called the police at one point, but they were no help. They said they couldn't do anything until Ed actually did something. Isn't that a laugh?" Terri said.

She poured the last of the gin into her glass and waggled the bottle. Mel got up from the table and went to the cupboard. He took down another bottle.

"Well, Nick and I know what love is," Laura said. "For us, I mean," Laura said. She bumped my knee with her knee. "You're supposed to say something now," Laura said, and turned her smile on me.

For an answer, I took Laura's hand and raised it to my lips. I made a big production out of kissing her hand. Everyone was amused.

"We're lucky," I said.

"You guys," Terri said. "Stop that now. You're making me sick. You're still on the honeymoon, for God's sake. You're still gaga, for crying out loud. Just wait. How long have you been together now? How long has it been? A year? Longer than a year?"

"Going on a year and a half," Laura said, flushed and smiling.

"Oh, now," Terri said. "Wait awhile."

She held her drink and gazed at Laura.

"I'm only kidding," Terri said.

Mel opened the gin and went around the table with the bottle.

"Here, you guys," he said. "Let's have a toast. I want to propose a toast. A toast to love. To true love," Mel said.

We touched glasses.

"To love," we said.

Outside in the backyard, one of the dogs began to bark. The leaves of the aspen that leaned past the window ticked against the glass. The afternoon sun was like a presence in this room, the spacious light of ease and generosity. We could have been anywhere, somewhere enchanted. We raised our glasses again and grinned at each other like children who had agreed on something forbidden.

"I'll tell you what real love is," Mel said. "I mean, I'll give you a good example. And then you can draw your own conclusions." He poured more gin into his glass. He added an ice cube and a sliver of lime. We waited and sipped our drinks. Laura and I touched knees again. I put a hand on her warm thigh and left it there.

"What do any of us really know about love?" Mel said. "It seems to me we're just beginners at love. We say we love each other and we do, I don't doubt it. I love Terri and Terri loves me, and you guys love each other too. You know the kind of love I'm talking about now. Physical love, that impulse that drives you to someone special, as well as love of the other person's being, his or her essence, as it were. Carnal love and, well, call it sentimental love, the day-to-day caring about the other person. But sometimes I have a hard time accounting for the fact that I must have loved my first wife too. But I did, I know I did. So I suppose I am like Terri in that regard. Terri and Ed." He thought about it and then he went on. "There was a time when I thought I loved my first wife more than life itself. But now I hate her guts. I do. How do you explain that? What happened to that love? What happened to it, is what I'd like to know. I wish someone could tell me. Then there's Ed. Okay, we're back to Ed. He loves Terri so much he tries to kill her and he winds up killing himself." Mel stopped talking and swallowed from his glass. "You guys have been together eighteen months and you love each other. It shows all over you. You glow with it. But you both loved other people before you met each other. You've both been married before, just like us. And you probably loved other people before that too, even. Terri and I have been together five years, been married for four. And the terrible thing, the terrible thing is, but the good thing too, the saving grace, you might say, is that if something happened to one of us — excuse me for saying this — but if something happened to one of us tomorrow I think the other one, the other person, would grieve for a while, you know, but then the surviving party would go out and love again, have someone else soon enough. All this, all of this love we're talking about, it would just be a memory. Maybe not even a memory. Am I wrong? Am I way off base? Because I want you to set me straight if you think I'm wrong. I want to know. I mean, I don't know anything, and I'm the first one to admit it."

"Mel, for God's sake," Terri said. She reached out and took hold of his wrist. "Are you getting drunk? Honey? Are you drunk?"

"Honey, I'm just talking," Mel said. "All right? I don't have to be drunk to say what I think. I mean, we're all just talking, right?" Mel said. He fixed his eyes on her.

"Sweetie, I'm not criticizing," Terri said.

She picked up her glass.

"I'm not on call today," Mel said. "Let me remind you of that. I am not on call," he said.

"Mel, we love you," Laura said.

Mel looked at Laura. He looked at her as if he could not place her, as if she was not the woman she was.

"Love you too, Laura," Mel said. "And you, Nick, love you too. You know something?" Mel said. "You guys are our pals," Mel said.

He picked up his glass.

Mel said, "I was going to tell you about something. I mean, I was going to prove a point. You see, this happened a few months ago, but it's still going on right now, and it ought to make us feel ashamed when we talk like we know what we're talking about when we talk about love."

"Come on now," Terri said. "Don't talk like you're drunk if you're not drunk."

"Just shut up for once in your life," Mel said very quietly. "Will you do me a favor and do that for a minute? So as I was saying, there's this old couple who had this car wreck out on the interstate. A kid hit them and they were all torn to shit and nobody was giving them much chance to pull through."

Terri looked at us and then back at Mel. She seemed anxious, or maybe that's too strong a word.

Mel was handing the bottle around the table.

"I was on call that night," Mel said. "It was May or maybe it was June. Terri and I had just sat down to dinner when the hospital called. There'd been this thing out on the interstate. Drunk kid, teenager, plowed his dad's pickup into this camper with this old couple in it. They were up in their mid-seventies, that couple. The kid — eighteen, nineteen, something — he was DOA. Taken the steering wheel through his sternum. The old couple, they were alive, you understand. I mean, just barely. But they had everything. Multiple fractures, internal injuries, hemorrhaging, contusions, lacerations, the works, and they each of them had themselves concussions. They were in a bad way, believe me. And, of course, their age was two strikes against them. I'd say she was worse off than he was. Ruptured spleen along with everything else. Both kneecaps broken. But they'd been wearing their seatbelts and, God knows, that's what saved them for the time being."

"Folks, this is an advertisement for the National Safety Council," Terri said. "This is your spokesman, Dr. Melvin R. McGinnis, talking." Terri laughed. "Mel," she said, "sometimes you're just too much. But I love you, hon," she said.

"Honey, I love you," Mel said.

He leaned across the table. Terri met him halfway. They kissed.

"Terri's right," Mel said as he settled himself again. "Get those seatbelts on. But seriously, they were in some shape, those oldsters. By the time I got down there, the kid was dead, as I said. He was off in a corner, laid out on a gurney. I took one look at the old couple and told the ER nurse to get me a neurologist and an orthopedic man and a couple of surgeons down there right away."

He drank from his glass. "I'll try to keep this short," he said. "So we took the two of them up to the OR and worked like fuck on them most of the night. They had these incredible reserves, those two. You see that once in a while. So we did everything that could be done, and toward morning we're giving them a fifty-fifty chance, maybe less than that for her. So here they are, still alive the next morning. So, okay, we move them into the ICU, which is where they both kept plugging away at it for two weeks, hitting it better and better on all the scopes. So we transfer them out to their own room."

Mel stopped talking. "Here," he said, "let's drink this cheapo gin the hell up. Then we're going to dinner, right? Terri and I know a new place. That's where we'll go, to this new place we know about. But we're not going until we finish up this cut-rate, lousy gin."

Terri said, "We haven't actually eaten there yet. But it looks good. From the outside, you know."

"I like food," Mel said. "If I had it to do all over again, I'd be a chef, you know? Right, Terri?" Mel said.

He laughed. He fingered the ice in his glass.

"Terri knows," he said. "Terri can tell you. But let me say this. If I could come back again in a different life, a different time and all, you know what? I'd like to come back as a knight. You were pretty safe wearing all that armor. It was all right being a knight until gunpowder and muskets and pistols came along."

"Mel would like to ride a horse and carry a lance," Terri said.

"Carry a woman's scarf with you everywhere," Laura said.

"Or just a woman," Mel said.

"Shame on you," Laura said.

Terri said, "Suppose you came back as a serf. The serfs didn't have it so good in those days," Terri said.

"The serfs never had it good," Mel said. "But I guess even the knights were vessels to someone. Isn't that the way it worked? But then everyone is always a vessel to someone. Isn't that right? Terri? But what I liked about knights, besides their ladies, was that they had that suit of armor, you know, and they couldn't get hurt very easy. No cars in those days, you know? No drunk teenagers to tear into your ass."

"Vassals." Terri said.

"What?" Mel said.

"Vassals," Terri said. "They were called vassals, not vessels."

"Vassals, vessels," Mel said, "what the fuck's the difference? You knew what I meant anyway. All right," Mel said. "So I'm not educated. I learned my stuff. I'm a heart surgeon, sure, but I'm just a mechanic. I go in and I fuck around and I fix things. Shit," Mel said.

"Modesty doesn't become you," Terri said.

"He's just a humble sawbones," I said. "But sometimes they suffocated in all that armor, Mel. They'd even have heart attacks if it got too hot and they were too tired and worn out. I read somewhere that they'd fall off their horses and not be able to get up because they were too tired to stand with all that armor on them. They got trampled by their own horses sometimes."

"That's terrible," Mel said. "That's a terrible thing, Nicky. I guess they'd just lay there and wait until somebody came along and made a shish kebab out of them."

"Some other vessel," Terri said.

"That's right," Mel said. "Some vassal would come along and spear the bastard in the name of love. Or whatever the fuck it was they fought over in those days."

"Same things we fight over these days," Terri said.

Laura said, "Nothing's changed."

The color was still high in Laura's cheeks. Her eyes were bright. She brought her glass to her lips.

Mel poured himself another drink. He looked at the label closely as if studying a long row of numbers. Then he slowly put the bottle down on the table and slowly reached for the tonic water.

"What about the old couple?" Laura said. "You didn't finish that story you started."

Laura was having a hard time lighting her cigarette. Her matches kept going out.

The sunshine inside the room was different now, changing, getting thinner. But the leaves outside the window were still shimmering, and I stared at the pattern they made on the panes and on the Formica counter. They weren't the same patterns, of course.

"What about the old couple?" I said.

"Older but wiser," Terri said.

Mel stared at her.

Terri said, "Go on with your story, hon. I was only kidding. Then what happened?"

"Terri, sometimes," Mel said.

"Please, Mel," Terri said. "Don't always be so serious, sweetie. Can't you take a joke?"

"Where's the joke?" Mel said.

He held his glass and gazed steadily at his wife.

"What happened?" Laura said.

Mel fastened his eyes on Laura. He said, "Laura, if I didn't have Terri and if I didn't love her so much, and if Nick wasn't my best friend, I'd fall in love with you. I'd carry you off, honey," he said.

"Tell your story," Terri said. "Then we'll go to that new place, okay?"

"Okay," Mel said. "Where was I?" he said. He stared at the table and then he began again.

"I dropped in to see each of them every day, sometimes twice a day if I was up doing other calls anyway. Casts and bandages, head to foot, the both of them. You know, you've seen it in the movies. That's just the way they looked, just like in the movies. Little eye-holes and nose-holes and mouth-holes. And she had to have her legs slung up on top of it. Well, the husband was very depressed for the longest while. Even after he found out that his wife was going to pull through, he was still very depressed. Not about the accident, though. I mean, the accident was one thing, but it wasn't everything. I'd get up to his mouth-hole, you know, and he'd say no, it wasn't the accident exactly but it was because he couldn't see her through his eye-holes. He said that was what was making him feel so bad. Can you imagine? I'm telling you, the man's heart was breaking because he couldn't turn his goddamn head and *see* his goddamn wife."

Mel looked around the table and shook his head at what he was going to say.

"I mean, it was killing the old fart just because he couldn't *look* at the fucking woman."

We all looked at Mel.

"Do you see what I'm saying?" he said.

Maybe we were a little drunk by then. I know it was hard keeping things in focus. The light was draining out of the room, going back through the window where it had come from. Yet nobody made a move to get up from the table to turn on the overhead light.

"Listen," Mel said. "Let's finish this fucking gin. There's about enough left here for one shooter all around. Then let's go eat. Let's go to the new place."

"He's depressed," Terri said.. "Mel, why don't you take a pill?"

Mel shook his head. "I've taken everything there is."

"We all need a pill now and then," I said.

"Some people are born needing them," Terri said.

She was using her finger to rub at something on the table. Then she stopped rubbing.

"I think I want to call my kids," Mel said. "Is that all right with everybody? I'll call my kids," he said.

Terri said, "What if Marjorie answers the phone? You guys, you've heard us on the subject of Marjorie? Honey, you know you don't want to talk to Marjorie. It'll make you feel even worse."

"I don't want to talk to Marjorie," Mel said. "But I want to talk to my kids."

"There isn't a day goes by that Mel doesn't say he wishes she'd get married again. Or else die," Terri said. "For one thing," Terri said, "she's bankrupting us. Mel says it's just to spite him that she won't get married again. She has a boyfriend who lives with her and the kids, so Mel is supporting the boyfriend too."

"She's allergic to bees," Mel said. "If I'm not praying she'll get married again, I'm praying she'll get herself stung to death by a swarm of fucking bees."

"Shame on you," Laura said.

"Bzzzzzzz," Mel said, turning his fingers into bees and buzzing them at Terri's throat. Then he let his hands drop all the way to his sides.

"She's vicious," Mel said. "Sometimes I think I'll go up there dressed like a beekeeper. You know, that hat that's like a helmet with the plate that comes down over your face, the big gloves, and the padded coat? I'll knock on the door and let loose a hive of bees in the house. But first I'd make sure the kids were out, of course."

He crossed one leg over the other. It seemed to take him a lot of time to do it. Then he put both feet on the floor and leaned forward, elbows on the table, his chin cupped in his hands.

"Maybe I won't call the kids, after all. Maybe it isn't such a hot idea. Maybe we'll just go eat. How does that sound?"

"Sounds fine to me," I said. "Eat or not eat. Or keep drinking. I could head right on out into the sunset."

"What does that mean, honey?" Laura said.

"It just means what I said," I said. "It means I could just keep going. That's all it means."

"I could eat something myself," Laura said. "I don't think I've ever been so hungry in my life. Is there something to nibble on?"

"I'll put out some cheese and crackers," Terri said.

But Terri just sat there. She did not get up to get anything.

Mel turned his glass over. He spilled it out on the table.

"Gin's gone," Mel said.

Terri said, "Now what?"

I could hear my heart beating. I could hear everyone's heart. I could hear the human noise we sat there making, not one of us moving, not even when the room went dark.

[1981]

Raymond Carver

ल्ल

WHY DON'T YOU DANCE?

In the kitchen, he poured another drink and looked at the bedroom suite in his front yard. The mattress was stripped and the candy-striped sheets lay beside two pillows on the chiffonier. Except for that, things looked much the way they had in the bedroom — nightstand and reading lamp on his side of the bed, nightstand and reading lamp on her side.

His side, her side.

He considered this as he sipped the whiskey.

The chiffonier stood a few feet from the foot of the bed. He had emptied the drawers into cartons that morning, and the cartons were in the living room. A portable heater was next to the chiffonier. A rattan chair with a decorator pillow stood at the foot of the bed. The buffed aluminum kitchen set took up a part of the driveway. A yellow muslin cloth, much too large, a gift, covered the table and hung down over the sides. A potted fern was on the table, along with a box of silverware and a record player, also gifts. A big console-model television set rested on a coffee table, and a few feet away from this stood a sofa and chair and a floor lamp. The desk was pushed against the garage door. A few utensils were on the desk, along with a wall clock and two framed prints. There was also in the driveway a carton with cups, glasses, and plates, each object wrapped in newspaper. That morning he had cleared out the closets, and except for the three cartons in the living room, all the stuff was out of the house. He had run an extension cord on out there and everything was connected. Things worked, no different from how it was when they were inside.

Now and then a car slowed and people stared. But no one stopped. It occurred to him that he wouldn't, either.

"It must be a yard sale," the girl said to the boy.

This girl and this boy were furnishing a little apartment.

"Let's see what they want for the bed," the girl said.

"And for the TV," the boy said.

The boy pulled into the driveway and stopped in front of the kitchen table.

They got out of the car and began to examine things, the girl touching the muslin cloth, the boy plugging in the blender and turning the dial to MINCE, the girl picking up a chafing dish, the boy turning on the television set and making little adjustments.

He sat down on the sofa to watch. He lit a cigarette, looked around, flipped the match into the grass.

The girl sat on the bed. She pushed off her shoes and lay back. She thought she could see a star.

"Come here, Jack. Try this bed. Bring one of those pillows," she said.

"How is it?" he said.

"Try it," she said.

He looked around. The house was dark.

"I feel funny," he said. "Better see if anybody's home."

She bounced on the bed.

"Try it first," she said.

He lay down on the bed and put the pillow under his head.

"How does it feel?" she said.

"It feels firm," he said.

She turned on her side and put her hand to his face.

"Kiss me," she said.

"Let's get up," he said.

"Kiss me," she said.

She closed her eyes. She held him.

He said, "I'll see if anybody's home."

But he just sat up and stayed where he was, making believe he was watching the television.

Lights came on in houses up and down the street.

"Wouldn't it be funny if," the girl said and grinned and didn't finish.

The boy laughed, but for no good reason. For no good reason, he switched the reading lamp on.

The girl brushed away a mosquito, whereupon the boy stood up and tucked in his shirt.

"I'll see if anybody's home," he said. "I don't think anybody's home. But if anybody is, I'll see what things are going for."

"Whatever they ask, offer ten dollars less. It's always a good idea," she said. "And, besides, they must be desperate or something."

"It's a pretty good TV," the boy said.

"Ask them how much," the girl said.

The man came down the sidewalk with a sack from the market. He had sandwiches, beer, whiskey. He saw the car in the driveway and the girl on the bed. He saw the television set going and the boy on the porch.

"Hello," the man said to the girl. "You found the bed. That's good."

"Hello," the girl said, and got up. "I was just trying it out." She patted the bed. "It's a pretty good bed."

"It's a good bed," the man said, and put down the sack and took out the beer and the whiskey.

"We thought nobody was here," the boy said. "We're interested in the bed and maybe in the TV. Also maybe the desk. How much do you want for the bed?"

"I was thinking fifty dollars for the bed," the man said.

"Would you take forty?" the girl asked.

"I'll take forty," the man said.

He took a glass out of the carton. He took the newspaper off the glass. He broke the seal on the whiskey.

"How about the TV?" the boy said.

"Twenty-five."

"Would you take fifteen?" the girl said.

"Fifteen's okay. I could take fifteen," the man said.

The girl looked at the boy.

"You kids, you'll want a drink," the man said. "Glasses in that box. I'm going to sit down. I'm going to sit down on the sofa."

The man sat on the sofa, leaned back, and stared at the boy and the girl.

The boy found two glasses and poured whiskey.

"That's enough," the girl said. "I think I want water in mine."

She pulled out a chair and sat at the kitchen table.

"There's water in that spigot over there," the man said. "Turn on that spigot."

The boy came back with the watered whiskey. He cleared his throat and sat down at the kitchen table. He grinned. But he didn't drink anything from his glass.

The man gazed at the television. He finished his drink and started another. He reached to turn on the floor lamp. It was then that his cigarette dropped from his fingers and fell between the cushions.

The girl got up to help him find it.

"So what do you want?" the boy said to the girl.

The boy took out the checkbook and held it to his lips as if thinking.

"I want the desk," the girl said. "How much money is the desk?"

The man waved his hand at this preposterous question.

"Name a figure," he said.

He looked at them as they sat at the table. In the lamplight, there was something about their faces. It was nice or it was nasty. There was no telling.

"I'm going to turn off this TV and put on a record," the man said. "This record-player is going, too. Cheap. Make me an offer."

He poured more whiskey and opened a beer.

"Everything goes," said the man.

The girl held out her glass and the man poured.

"Thank you," she said. "You're very nice," she said.

"It goes to your head," the boy said. "I'm getting it in the head." He held up his glass and jiggled it.

The man finished his drink and poured another, and then he found the box with the records.

"Pick something," the man said to the girl, and he held the records out to her.

The boy was writing the check.

"Here," the girl said, picking something, picking anything, for she did not know the names on these labels. She got up from the table and sat down again. She did not want to sit still.

"I'm making it out to cash," the boy said.

"Sure," the man said.

They drank. They listened to the record. And then the man put on another.

Why don't you kids dance? he decided to say, and then he said it. "Why don't you dance?"

"I don't think so," the boy said.

"Go ahead," the man said. "It's my yard. You can dance if you want to."

Arms about each other, their bodies pressed together, the boy and the girl moved up and down the driveway. They were dancing. And when the record was over, they did it again, and when that one ended, the boy said, "I'm drunk."

The girl said, "You're not drunk."

"Well, I'm drunk," the boy said.

The man turned the record over and the boy said, "I am."

"Dance with me," the girl said to the boy and then to the man, and when the man stood up, she came to him with her arms wide open.

"Those people over there, they're watching," she said.

"It's okay," the man said. "It's my place," he said.

"Let them watch," the girl said.

"That's right," the man said. "They thought they'd seen everything over here. But they haven't seen this, have they?" he said.

He felt her breath on his neck.

"I hope you like your bed," he said.

The girl closed and then opened her eyes. She pushed her face into the man's shoulder. She pulled the man closer.

"You must be desperate or something," she said.

Weeks later, she said: "The guy was about middle-aged. All his things right there in his yard. No lie. We got real pissed and danced. In the driveway. Oh, my God. Don't laugh. He played us these records. Look at this record-player. The old guy gave it to us. And all these crappy records. Will you look at this shit?"

She kept talking. She told everyone. There was more to it, and she was trying to get it talked out. After a time, she quit trying.

[1981]

*J*OYCE CAROL OATES (b. 1938) was born in Lockport, New York, one of three children in a Roman Catholic family. She dismisses her childhood as "dull, ordinary, nothing people would be interested in." There was nothing ordinary, however, about her desire to express her imagination. She began to put picture stories down on paper even before she could write, and she remembers that her parents "dutifully" supplied her with lined tablets for her stories and gave her a typewriter at the age of fourteen. She had written thousands of pages of prose by the time she discovered Hemingway's In Our Time in the public library as a high school sophomore. She proceeded to write several novels in imitation of his book, though not of his prose style, "that ironic burnt-out voice being merely monotonous to my adolescent ear." In 1956, after Oates graduated from high school, she went on a scholarship to major in English at Syracuse University, where she resumed writing short stories and graduated Phi Beta Kappa and class valedictorian in 1960. The previous year she had won the annual Mademoiselle college fiction award with her story "In the Old World." Other stories began to be published in Cosmopolitan, Prairie Schooner, and The Literary Review, but she did not devote most of her time to writing until after she received her M.A. at the University of Wisconsin in 1961. Discovering by chance that one of her stories had been cited in the honor roll of Martha Foley's annual Best American Short Stories, Oates assembled the fourteen stories in her first book, By the North Gate (1963). Her first novel, With Shuddering Fall, written during her renunciation of Catholicism, was published the next year. This was followed in 1966 by a second collection of stories, Upon the Sweeping Flood. A "thematic trilogy" of novels came next, the third of which — them — won the National Book Award for fiction in 1970. Later memorable novels include Do with Me What You Will (1973), Childwold (1976), Bellefleur (1980), A Bloodsmoor Romance (1982), and Marya: A Life (1985). Her most recent book is a collection of stories, Raven's Wing (1986).

Oates has published almost forty books, including about 100 stories. She also writes poetry and literary criticism, including the volume New Heaven, New Earth (1974), analyzing the "visionary experience in literature" as exemplified in the work of Henry James, Virginia Woolf, Franz Kafka, D. H. Lawrence, Flannery O'Connor, and others. As a writer, critic, and professor at Princeton University, she dedicates her life to "promoting and exploring literature. . . . I am not conscious of being in any particular literary tradition, though I share with my contemporaries an intense interest in the formal aspects of writing; each of my books is an experiment of a kind, an investigation of the relationship between a certain consciousness and its formal aesthetic expression. My method has always been to combine

the 'naturalistic' world and the 'symbolic' method of expression, so that I
am always — or usually — writing about real people in a real society, but
the means of expression may be naturalistic, realistic, surreal, or parodistic.
In this way I have, to my own satisfaction at least, solved the old problem — should one be faithful to the 'real' world, or to one's imagination?"

   The story "Where Are You Going, Where Have You Been?" was first
published in Epoch in 1966; it was included in Best American Stories of
1967 and Prize Stories: The O. Henry Awards 1968. Oates has said that
this story, based on an article in Life magazine about a Texas murderer, has
been "constantly misunderstood by one generation, and intuitively understood by another." She sees the story as dealing with a human being
"struggling heroically to define personal identity in the face of incredible
opposition, even in the face of death itself." "The Lady with the Pet Dog,"
included in Marriages and Infidelities (1972), is her reworking of the Chekhov story. The same volume includes her version of Kafka's "The Metamorphosis." (See Oates's Commentary on page 1339.)

Joyce Carol Oates

∽

WHERE ARE YOU GOING,
WHERE HAVE YOU BEEN?

For Bob Dylan

   Her name was Connie. She was fifteen and she had a quick nervous
giggling habit of craning her neck to glance into mirrors, or checking other
people's faces to make sure her own was all right. Her mother, who noticed
everything and knew everything and who hadn't much reason any longer to
look at her own face, always scolded Connie about it. "Stop gawking at
yourself, who are you? You think you're so pretty?" she would say. Connie
would raise her eyebrows at these familiar complaints and look right
through her mother, into a shadowy vision of herself as she was right at that
moment: she knew she was pretty and that was everything. Her mother had
been pretty once too, if you could believe those old snapshots in the album,
but now her looks were gone and that was why she was always after Connie.

   "Why don't you keep your room clean like your sister? How've you
got your hair fixed — what the hell stinks? Hair spray? You don't see your
sister using that junk."

   Her sister June was twenty-four and still lived at home. She was a secretary in the high school Connie attended, and if that wasn't bad enough — with her in the same building — she was so plain and chunky and steady that Connie had to hear her praised all the time by her mother and her mother's sisters. June did this, June did that, she saved money and helped clean the house and cooked and Connie couldn't do a thing, her mind was all filled with trashy daydreams. Their father was away at work most of the time and when he came home he wanted supper and he read the newspaper at supper and after supper he went to bed. He didn't bother talking much to them, but around his bent head Connie's mother kept picking at her until Connie wished her mother was dead and she herself was dead and it was all over. "She makes me want to throw up sometimes," she complained to her friends. She had a high, breathless, amused voice which made everything she said a little forced, whether it was sincere or not.

There was one good thing: June went places with girl friends of hers, girls who were just as plain and steady as she, and so when Connie wanted to do that her mother had no objections. The father of Connie's best girl friend drove the girls the three miles to town and left them off at a shopping plaza, so that they could walk through the stores or go to a movie, and when he came to pick them up again at eleven he never bothered to ask what they had done.

They must have been familiar sights, walking around that shopping plaza in their shorts and flat ballerina slippers that always scuffed the sidewalk, with charm bracelets jingling on their thin wrists; they would lean together to whisper and laugh secretly if someone passed by who amused or interested them. Connie had long dark blond hair that drew anyone's eye to it, and she wore part of it pulled up on her head and puffed out and the rest of it she let fall down her back. She wore a pullover jersey blouse that looked one way when she was at home and another way when she was away from home. Everything about her had two sides to it, one for home and one for anywhere that was not home: her walk that could be childlike and bobbing, or languid enough to make anyone think she was hearing music in her head, her mouth which was pale and smirking most of the time, but bright and pink on these evenings out, her laugh which was cynical and drawling at home — "Ha, ha, very funny" — but high-pitched and nervous anywhere else, like the jingling of the charms on her bracelet.

Sometimes they did go shopping or to a movie, but sometimes they went across the highway, ducking fast across the busy road, to a drive-in restaurant where older kids hung out. The restaurant was shaped like a big bottle, though squatter than a real bottle, and on its cap was a revolving figure of a grinning boy who held a hamburger aloft. One night in midsummer they ran across, breathless with daring, and right away someone leaned out a car window and invited them over, but it was just a boy from high school they didn't like. It made them feel good to be able to ignore him. They went up through the maze of parked and cruising cars to the bright-lit, fly-infested restaurant, their faces pleased and expectant as if they were entering a sacred building that loomed out of the night to give them what haven and what blessing they yearned for. They sat at the counter and crossed their legs at the ankles, their thin shoulders rigid with excitement and listened to the music that made everything so good: the music was always in the background like music at a church service, it was something to depend upon.

A boy named Eddie came in to talk with them. He sat backwards on his stool, turning himself jerkily around in semi-circles and then stopping and turning again, and after a while he asked Connie if she would like something to eat. She said she did and so she tapped her friend's arm on her way out — her friend pulled her face up into a brave droll look — and Connie said she would meet her at eleven, across the way. "I just hate to leave her like that," Connie said earnestly, but the boy said that she wouldn't be alone for long. So they went out to his car and on the way Connie couldn't help but let her eyes wander over the windshields and faces all around her, her face gleaming with the joy that had nothing to do with Eddie or even this place; it might have been the music. She drew her shoulders up and sucked in her breath with the pure pleasure of being alive, and just at that moment she happened to glance at a face just a few feet from hers. It was a boy with shaggy black hair, in a convertible jalopy painted gold. He stared at her and then his lips widened into a grin. Connie slit her eyes at him and turned away, but she couldn't help glancing back and there he was still watching her. He wagged a finger and laughed and said, "Gonna get you, baby," and Connie turned away again without Eddie noticing anything.

She spent three hours with him, at the restaurant where they ate hamburgers and drank Cokes in wax cups that were always sweating, and then down an alley a mile or so away, and when he left her off at five to eleven only the movie house was still open at the plaza. Her girl friend was there, talking with a boy. When Connie came up the two girls smiled at each other and Connie said, "How was the movie?" and the girl said, "*You* should know." They rode off with the girl's father, sleepy and pleased, and Connie couldn't help but look at the darkened shopping plaza with its big empty parking lot and its signs that were faded and ghostly now, and over at the drive-in restaurant where cars were still circling tirelessly. She couldn't hear the music at this distance.

Next morning June asked her how the movie was and Connie said, "So-so."

She and that girl and occasionally another girl went out several times a week that way, and the rest of the time Connie spent around the house — it was summer vacation — getting in her mother's way and thinking, dreaming, about the boys she met. But all the boys fell back and dissolved into a single face that was not even a face, but an idea, a feeling, mixed up with the urgent insistent pounding of the music and the humid night air of July. Connie's mother kept dragging her back to the daylight by finding things for her to do or saying suddenly, "What's this about the Pettinger girl?"

And Connie would say nervously, "Oh, her. That dope." She always drew thick clear lines between herself and such girls, and her mother was simple and kindly enough to believe her. Her mother was so simple, Connie thought, that it was maybe cruel to fool her so much. Her mother went scuffling around the house in old bedroom slippers and complained over the telephone to one sister about the other, then the other called up and the two of them complained about the third one. If June's name was mentioned her mother's tone was approving, and if Connie's name was mentioned it was disapproving. This did not really mean she disliked Connie and actually Connie thought that her mother preferred her to June because she was prettier, but the two of them kept up a pretense of exasperation, a sense that they were tugging and struggling over something of little value to either of them. Sometimes, over coffee, they were almost friends, but something would come up — some vexation that was like a fly buzzing suddenly around their heads — and their faces went hard with contempt.

One Sunday Connie got up at eleven — none of them bothered with church — and washed her hair so that it could dry all day long, in the sun. Her parents and sister were going to a barbecue at an aunt's house and Connie said no, she wasn't interested, rolling her eyes, to let mother know just what she thought of it. "Stay home alone then," her mother said sharply. Connie sat out back in a lawn chair and watched them drive away, her father quiet and bald, hunched around so that he could back the car out, her mother with a look that was still angry and not at all softened through the windshield, and in the back seat poor old June all dressed up as if she didn't know what a barbecue was, with all the running yelling kids and the flies. Connie sat with her eyes closed in the sun, dreaming and dazed with the warmth about her as if this were a kind of love, the caresses of love, and her mind slipped over onto thoughts of the boy she had been with the night before and how nice he had been, how sweet it always was, not the way someone like June would suppose but sweet, gentle, the way it was in movies and promised in songs; and when she opened her eyes she hardly knew where she was, the back yard ran off into weeds and a fence-line of trees and behind it the sky was perfectly blue and still. The asbestos "ranch house" that was now three years old startled her — it looked small. She shook her head as if to get awake.

It was too hot. She went inside the house and turned on the radio to drown out the quiet. She sat on the edge of her bed, barefoot, and listened for an hour and a half to a program called XYZ Sunday Jamboree, record after record of hard, fast, shrieking songs she sang along with, interspersed by exclamations from "Bobby King": "An' look here you girls at Napoleon's — Son and Charley want you to pay real close attention to this song coming up!"

And Connie paid close attention herself, bathed in a glow of slow-pulsed joy that seemed to rise mysteriously out of the music itself and lay languidly about the airless little room, breathed in and breathed out with each gentle rise and fall of her chest.

After a while she heard a car coming up the drive. She sat up at once, startled, because it couldn't be her father so soon. The gravel kept crunching all the way in from the road — the driveway was long — and Connie ran to the window. It was a car she didn't know. It was an open jalopy, painted a bright gold that caught the sun opaquely. Her heart began to pound and her fingers snatched at her hair, checking it, and she whispered "Christ. Christ," wondering how bad she looked. The car came to a stop at the side door and the horn sounded four short taps as if this were a signal Connie knew.

She went into the kitchen and approached the door slowly, then hung out the screen door, her bare toes curling down off the step. There were two boys in the car and now she recognized the driver: he had shaggy, shabby black hair that looked crazy as a wig and he was grinning at her.

"I ain't late, am I?" he said.

"Who the hell do you think you are?" Connie said.

"Toldja I'd be out, didn't I?"

"I don't even know who you are."

She spoke sullenly, careful to show no interest or pleasure, and he spoke in a fast bright monotone. Connie looked past him to the other boy, taking her time. He had fair brown hair, with a lock that fell onto his forehead. His sideburns gave him a fierce, embarrassed look, but so far he hadn't even bothered to glance at her. Both boys wore sunglasses. The driver's glasses were metallic and mirrored everything in miniature.

"You wanta come for a ride?" he said.

Connie smirked and let her hair fall loose over one shoulder.

"Don'tcha like my car? New paint job," he said. "Hey."

"What?"

"You're cute."

She pretended to fidget, chasing flies away from the door.

"Don'tcha believe me, or what?" he said.

"Look, I don't even know who you are," Connie said in disgust.

"Hey, Ellie's got a radio, see. Mine's broke down." He lifted his friend's arm and showed her the little transistor the boy was holding, and now Connie began to hear the music. It was the same program that was playing inside the house.

"Bobby King?" she said.

"I listen to him all the time. I think he's great."

"He's kind of great," Connie said reluctantly.

"Listen, that guy's *great*. He knows where the action is."

Connie blushed a little, because the glasses made it impossible for her to see just what this boy was looking at. She couldn't decide if she liked him or if he was just a jerk, and so she dawdled in the doorway and wouldn't come down or go back inside. She said, "What's all that stuff painted on your car?"

"Can'tcha read it?" He opened the door very carefully, as if he was afraid it might fall off. He slid out just as carefully, planting his feet firmly on the ground, the tiny metallic world in his glasses slowing down like gelatine hardening and in the midst of it Connie's bright green blouse. "This here is my name, to begin with," he said. ARNOLD FRIEND was written in tar-like black letters on the side, with a drawing of a round grinning face that reminded Connie of a pumpkin, except it wore sunglasses. "I wanta introduce myself, I'm Arnold Friend and that's my real name and I'm gonna be your friend, honey, and inside the car's Ellie Oscar, he's kinda shy." Ellie brought his transistor up to his shoulder and balanced it there. "Now these numbers are a secret code, honey," Arnold Friend explained. He read off the numbers 33, 19, 17 and raised his eyebrows at her to see what she thought of that, but she didn't think much of it. The left rear fender had been smashed and around it was written, on the gleaming gold background: DONE BY CRAZY WOMAN DRIVER. Connie had to laugh at that. Arnold Friend was pleased at her laughter and looked up at her. "Around the other side's a lot more — you wanta come and see them?"

"No."

"Why not?"

"Why should I?"

"Don'tcha wanta see what's on the car? Don'tcha wanta go for a ride?"

"I don't know."

"Why not?"

"I got things to do."

"Like what?"

"Things."

He laughed as if she had said something funny. He slapped his thighs. He was standing in a strange way, leaning back against the car as if he were balancing himself. He wasn't tall, only an inch or so taller than she would be if she came down to him. Connie liked the way he was dressed, which was the way all of them dressed: tight faded jeans stuffed into black, scuffed boots, a belt that pulled his waist in and showed how lean he was, and a white pull-over shirt that was a little soiled and showed the hard small muscles of his arms and shoulders. He looked as if he probably did hard work, lifting and carrying things. Even his neck looked muscular. And his face was a familiar face, somehow: the jaw and chin and cheeks slightly darkened, because he hadn't shaved for a day or two, and the nose long and hawk-like, sniffing as if she were a treat he was going to gobble up and it was all a joke.

"Connie, you ain't telling the truth. This is your day set aside for a ride with me and you know it," he said, still laughing. The way he straightened and recovered from his fit of laughing showed that it had been all fake.

"How do you know what my name is?" she said suspiciously.

"It's Connie."

"Maybe and maybe not."

"I know my Connie," he said, wagging his finger. Now she remembered him even better, back at the restaurant, and her cheeks warmed at the thought of how she sucked in her breath just at the moment she passed him — how she must have looked to him. And he had remembered her. "Ellie and I come out here especially for you," he said. "Ellie can sit in back. How about it?"

"Where?"

"Where what?"

"Where're we going?"

He looked at her. He took off the sunglasses and she saw how pale the skin around his eyes was, like holes that were not in shadow but instead in light. His eyes were like chips of broken glass that catch the light in an amiable way. He smiled. It was as if the idea of going for a ride somewhere, to some place, was a new idea to him.

"Just for a ride, Connie sweetheart."

"I never said my name was Connie," she said.

"But I know what it is. I know your name and all about you, lots of things," Arnold Friend said. He had not moved yet but stood still leaning back against the side of his jalopy. "I took a special interest in you, such a pretty girl, and found out all about you like I know your parents and sister are gone somewheres and I know where and how long they're going to be gone, and I know who you were with last night, and your best friend's name is Betty. Right?"

He spoke in a simple lilting voice, exactly as if he were reciting the words to a song. His smile assured her that everything was fine. In the car Ellie turned up the volume on his radio and did not bother to look around at them.

"Ellie can sit in the back seat," Arnold Friend said. He indicated his friend with a casual jerk of his chin, as if Ellie did not count and she should not bother with him.

"How'd you find out all that stuff?" Connie said.

"Listen: Betty Schultz and Tony Fitch and Jimmy Pettinger and Nancy Pettinger," he said, in a chant. "Raymond Stanley and Bob Hutter — "

"Do you know all those kids?"

"I know everybody."

"Look, you're kidding. You're not from around here."

"Sure."

"But — how come we never saw you before?"

"Sure you saw me before," he said. He looked down at his boots, as if he were a little offended. "You just don't remember."

"I guess I'd remember you," Connie said.

"Yeah?" He looked up at this, beaming. He was pleased. He began to mark time with the music from Ellie's radio, tapping his fists lightly together. Connie looked away from his smile to the car, which was painted so bright it almost hurt her eyes to look at it. She looked at that name, ARNOLD FRIEND. And up at the front fender was an expression that was familiar — MAN THE FLYING SAUCERS. It was an expression kids had used the year before, but didn't use this year. She looked at it for a while as if the words meant something to her that she did not yet know.

"What're you thinking about? Huh?" Arnold Friend demanded. "Not worried about your hair blowing around in the car, are you?"

"No."

"Think I maybe can't drive good?"

"How do I know?"

"You're a hard girl to handle. How come?" he said. "Don't you know I'm your friend? Didn't you see me put my sign in the air when you walked by?"

"What sign?"

"My sign." And he drew an X in the air, leaning out toward her. They were maybe ten feet apart. After his hand fell back to his side the X was still in the air, almost visible. Connie let the screen door close and stood perfectly still inside it, listening to the music from her radio and the boy's blend together. She stared at Arnold Friend. He stood there so stiffly relaxed, pretending to be relaxed, with one hand idly on the door handle as if he were keeping himself up that way and had no intention of ever moving again. She recognized most things about him, the tight jeans that showed his thighs and buttocks and the greasy leather boots and the tight shirt, and even that slippery friendly smile of his, that sleepy dreamy smile that all the boys used to get across ideas they didn't want to put into words. She recognized all this and also the singsong way he talked, slightly mocking, kidding, but serious and a little melancholy, and she recognized the way he tapped one fist against the other in homage to the perpetual music behind him. But all these things did not come together.

She said suddenly, "Hey, how old are you?"

His smile faded. She could see then that he wasn't a kid, he was much older — thirty, maybe more. At this knowledge her heart began to pound faster.

"That's a crazy thing to ask. Can'tcha see I'm your own age?"

"Like hell you are."

"Or maybe a coupla years older, I'm eighteen."

"Eighteen?" she said doubtfully.

He grinned to reassure her and lines appeared at the corners of his mouth. His teeth were big and white. He grinned so broadly his eyes became slits and she saw how thick the lashes were, thick and black as if painted with a black tar-like material. Then he seemed to become embarrassed, abruptly, and looked over his shoulder at Ellie. "*Him*, he's crazy," he said. "Ain't he a riot, he's a nut, a real character." Ellie was still listening to the music. His sunglasses told nothing about what he was thinking. He wore a bright orange shirt unbuttoned halfway to show his chest, which was a pale, bluish chest and not muscular like Arnold Friend's. His shirt collar was turned up all around and the very tips of the collar pointed out past his chin as if they were protecting him. He was pressing the transistor radio up against his ear and sat there in a kind of daze, right in the sun.

"He's kinda strange," Connie said.

"Hey, she says you're kinda strange! Kinda strange!" Arnold Friend cried. He pounded on the car to get Ellie's attention. Ellie turned for the first time and Connie saw with shock that he wasn't a kid either — he had a fair, hairless face, cheeks reddened slightly as if the veins grew too close to the surface of his skin, the face of a forty-year-old baby. Connie felt a wave of dizziness rise in her at this sight and she stared at him as if waiting for something to change the shock of the moment, make it all right again. Ellie's lips kept shaping words, mumbling along with the words blasting his ear.

"Maybe you two better go away," Connie said faintly.

"What? How come?" Arnold Friend cried. "We come out here to take you for a ride. It's Sunday." He had the voice of the man on the radio now. It was the same voice, Connie thought. "Don'tcha know it's Sunday all day and honey, no matter who you were with last night today you're with Arnold Friend and don't you forget it! — Maybe you better step out here," he said, and this last was in a different voice. It was a little flatter, as if the heat was finally getting to him.

"No. I got things to do."

"Hey."

"You two better leave."

"We ain't leaving until you come with us."

"Like hell I am — "

"Connie, don't fool around with me. I mean, I mean, don't fool *around*," he said, shaking his head. He laughed incredulously. He placed his sunglasses on top of his head, carefully, as if he were indeed wearing a wig, and brought the stems down behind his ears. Connie stared at him, another wave of dizziness and fear rising in her so that for a moment he wasn't even in focus but was just a blur, standing there against his gold car, and she had the idea that he had driven up the driveway all right but had come from nowhere before that and belonged nowhere and that everything about him and even the music that was so familiar to her was only half real.

"If my father comes and sees you — "

"He ain't coming. He's at a barbecue."

"How do you know that?"

"Aunt Tillie's. Right now they're — uh — they're drinking. Sitting around," he said vaguely, squinting as if he were staring all the way to town and over to Aunt Tillie's back yard. Then the vision seemed to clear and he nodded energetically. "Yeah. Sitting around. There's your sister in a blue dress, huh? And high heels, the poor sad bitch — nothing like you, sweetheart! And your mother's helping some fat woman with the corn, they're cleaning the corn — husking the corn —"

"What fat woman?" Connie cried.

"How do I know what fat woman. I don't know every goddam fat woman in the world!" Arnold Friend laughed.

"Oh, that's Mrs. Hornby. . . . Who invited her?" Connie said. She felt a little light-headed. Her breath was coming quickly.

"She's too fat. I don't like them fat. I like them the way you are, honey," he said, smiling sleepily at her. They stared at each other for a while, through the screen door. He said softly, "Now what you're going to do is this: you're going to come out that door. You're going to sit up front with me and Ellie's going to sit in the back, the hell with Ellie, right? This isn't Ellie's date. You're my date. I'm your lover, honey."

"What? You're crazy —"

"Yes, I'm your lover. You don't know what that is but you will," he said. "I know that too. I know all about you. But look: it's real nice and you couldn't ask for nobody better than me, or more polite. I always keep my word. I'll tell you how it is, I'm always nice at first, the first time. I'll hold you so tight you won't think you have to try to get away or pretend anything because you'll know you can't. And I'll come inside you where it's all secret and you'll give in to me and you'll love me —"

"Shut up! You're crazy!" Connie said. She backed away from the door. She put her hands against her ears as if she'd heard something terrible, something not meant for her. "People don't talk like that, you're crazy," she muttered. Her heart was almost too big now for her chest and its pumping made sweat break out all over her. She looked out to see Arnold Friend pause and then take a step toward the porch lurching. He almost fell. But, like a clever drunken man, he managed to catch his balance. He wobbled in his high boots and grabbed hold of one of the porch posts.

"Honey?" he said. "You still listening?"

"Get the hell out of here!"

"Be nice, honey. Listen."

"I'm going to call the police —"

He wobbled again and out of the side of his mouth came a fast spat curse, an aside not meant for her to hear. But even this "Christ!" sounded forced. Then he began to smile again. She watched this smile come, awkward as if he were smiling from inside a mask. His whole face was a mask, she thought wildly, tanned down onto his throat but then running out as if he had plastered make-up on his face but had forgotten about his throat.

"Honey — ? Listen, here's how it is. I always tell the truth and I promise you this: I ain't coming in that house after you."

"You better not! I'm going to call the police if you — if you don't — "

"Honey," he said, talking right through her voice, "honey, I'm not coming in there but you are coming out here. You know why?"

She was panting. The kitchen looked like a place she had never seen before, some room she had run inside but which wasn't good enough, wasn't going to help her. The kitchen window had never had a curtain, after three years, and there were dishes in the sink for her to do — probably — and if you ran your hand across the table you'd probably feel something sticky there.

"You listening, honey? Hey?"

" — going to call the police — "

"Soon as you touch the phone I don't need to keep my promise and can come inside. You won't want that."

She rushed forward and tried to lock the door. Her fingers were shaking. "But why lock it," Arnold Friend said gently, talking right into her face. "It's just a screen door. It's just nothing." One of his boots was at a strange angle, as if his foot wasn't in it. It pointed out to the left, bent at the ankle. "I mean, anybody can break through a screen door and glass and wood and iron or anything else if he needs to, anybody at all and specially Arnold Friend. If the place got lit up with a fire, honey, you'd come running out into my arms, right into my arms and safe at home — like you knew I was your lover and'd stopped fooling around. I don't mind a nice shy girl but I don't like no fooling around." Part of those words were spoken with a slight rhythmic lilt, and Connie somehow recognized them — the echo of a song from last year, about a girl rushing into her boy friend's arms and coming home again —

Connie stood barefoot on the linoleum floor, staring at him. "What do you want?" she whispered.

"I want you," he said.

"What?"

"Seen you that night and thought, that's the one, yes sir. I never needed to look any more."

"But my father's coming back. He's coming to get me. I had to wash my hair first — " She spoke in a dry, rapid voice, hardly raising it for him to hear.

"No, your daddy is not coming and yes, you had to wash your hair and you washed it for me. It's nice and shining and all for me, I thank you, sweetheart," he said, with a mock bow, but again he almost lost his balance. He had to bend and adjust his boots. Evidently his feet did not go all the way down; the boots must have been stuffed with something so that he would seem taller. Connie stared out at him and behind him Ellie in the car, who seemed to be looking off toward Connie's right, into nothing. This Ellie said, pulling the words out of the air one after another as if he were just discovering them, "You want me to pull out the phone?"

"Shut your mouth and keep it shut," Arnold Friend said, his face red from bending over or maybe from embarrassment because Connie had seen his boots. "This ain't none of your business."

"What — what are you doing? What do you want?" Connie said. "If I call the police they'll get you, they'll arrest you — "

"Promise was not to come in unless you touch that phone, and I'll keep that promise," he said. He resumed his erect position and tried to force his shoulders back. He sounded like a hero in a movie, declaring something important. He spoke too loudly and it was as if he were speaking to someone behind Connie. "I ain't made plans for coming in that house where I don't belong but just for you to come out to me, the way you should. Don't you know who I am?"

"You're crazy," she whispered. She backed away from the door but did not want to go into another part of the house, as if this would give him permission to come through the door. "What do you. . . . You're crazy, you. . . . "

"Huh? What're you saying, honey?"

Her eyes darted everywhere in the kitchen. She could not remember what it was, this room.

"This is how it is, honey: you come out and we'll drive away, have a nice ride. But if you don't come out we're gonna wait till your people come home and then they're all going to get it."

"You want that telephone pulled out?" Ellie said. He held the radio away from his ear and grimaced, as if without the radio the air was too much for him.

"I toldja shut up, Ellie." Arnold Friend said, "You're deaf, get a hearing aid, right? Fix yourself up. This little girl's no trouble and's gonna be nice to me, so Ellie keep to yourself, this ain't your date — right? Don't hem in on me. Don't hog. Don't crush. Don't bird dog. Don't trail me," he said in a rapid meaningless voice, as if he were running through all the expressions he'd learned but was no longer sure which one of them was in style, then rushing on to new ones, making them up with his eyes closed, "Don't crawl under my fence, don't squeeze in my chipmunk hole, don't sniff my glue, suck my popsicle, keep your own greasy fingers on yourself!" He shaded his eyes and peered in at Connie, who was backed against the kitchen table. "Don't mind him, honey, he's just a creep. He's a dope. Right? I'm the boy for you and like I said you come out here nice like a lady and give me your hand, and nobody else gets hurt, I mean, your nice old bald-headed daddy and your mummy and your sister in her high heels. Because listen: why bring them in this?"

"Leave me alone," Connie whispered.

"Hey, you know that old woman down the road, the one with the chickens and stuff — you know her?"

"She's dead!"

"Dead? What? You know her?" Arnold Friend said.

"She's dead — "

"Don't you like her?"

"She's dead — she's — she isn't here any more — "

"But don't you like her, I mean, you got something against her? Some grudge or something?" Then his voice dipped as if he were conscious of rudeness. He touched the sunglasses on top of his head as if to make sure they were still there. "Now you be a good girl."

"What are you going to do?"

"Just two things, or maybe three," Arnold Friend said. "But I promise it won't last long and you'll like me that way you get to like people you're close to. You will. It's all over for you here, so come on out. You don't want your people in any trouble, do you?"

She turned and bumped against a chair or something, hurting her leg, but she ran into the back room and picked up the telephone. Something roared in her ear, a tiny roaring, and she was so sick with fear that she could do nothing but listen to it — the telephone was clammy and very heavy and her fingers groped down to the dial but were too weak to touch it. She began to scream into the phone, into the roaring. She cried out, she cried for her mother, she felt her breath start jerking back and forth in her lungs as if it were something Arnold Friend were stabbing her with again and again with no tenderness. A noisy sorrowful wailing rose all about her and she was locked inside it the way she was locked inside this house.

After a while she could hear again. She was sitting on the floor, with her wet back against the wall.

Arnold Friend was saying from the door, "That's a good girl. Put the phone back."

She kicked the phone away from her.

"No, honey. Pick it up. Put it back right."

She picked it up and put it back. The dial tone stopped.

"That's a good girl. Now you come outside."

She was hollow with what had been fear, but what was now just an emptiness. All that screaming had blasted it out of her. She sat, one leg cramped under her, and deep inside her brain was something like a pinpoint of light that kept going and would not let her relax. She thought, I'm not going to see my mother again. She thought, I'm not going to sleep in my bed again. Her bright green blouse was all wet.

Arnold Friend said, in a gentle-loud voice that was like a stage voice, "The place where you came from ain't there any more, and where you had in mind to go is cancelled out. This place you are now — inside your daddy's house — is nothing but a cardboard box I can knock down any time. You know that and always did know it. You hear me?"

She thought, I have got to think. I have to know what to do.

"We'll go out to a nice field, out in the country here where it smells so nice and it's sunny," Arnold Friend said. "I'll have my arms tight around you so you won't need to try to get away and I'll show you what love is like, what it does. The hell with this house! It looks solid all right," he said. He ran a fingernail down the screen and the noise did not make Connie shiver, as it would have the day before. "Now put your hand on your heart, honey. Feel that? That feels solid too but we know better, be nice to me, be sweet like you can because what else is there for a girl like you but to be sweet and pretty and give in? — and get away before her people come back?"

She felt her pounding heart. Her hands seemed to enclose it. She thought for the first time in her life that it was nothing that was hers, that belonged to her, but just a pounding, living thing inside this body that wasn't hers either.

"You don't want them to get hurt," Arnold Friend went on. "Now get up, honey. Get up all by yourself."

She stood.

"Now turn this way. That's right. Come over here to me — Ellie, put that away, didn't I tell you? You dope. You miserable creepy dope," Arnold Friend said. His words were not angry but only part of an incantation. The incantation was kindly. "Now come out through the kitchen to me honey and let's see a smile, try it, you're a brave sweet little girl and now they're eating corn and hotdogs cooked to bursting over an outdoor fire, and they don't know one thing about you and never did and honey you're better than them because not one of them would have done this for you."

Connie felt the linoleum under her feet; it was cool. She brushed her hair back out of her eyes. Arnold Friend let go of the post tentatively and opened his arms for her, his elbows pointing up toward each other and his wrists limp, to show that this was an embarrassed embrace and a little mocking, he didn't want to make her self-conscious.

She put out her hand against the screen. She watched herself push the door slowly open as if she were safe back somewhere in the other doorway, watching this body and this head of long hair moving out into the sunlight where Arnold Friend waited.

"My sweet little blue-eyed girl," he said, in a half-sung sigh that had nothing to do with her brown eyes but was taken up just the same by the vast sunlit reaches of the land behind him and on all sides of him, so much land that Connie had never seen before and did not recognize except to know that she was going to it.

[1970]

Joyce Carol Oates

∽⧜∾

THE LADY WITH THE PET DOG

I

Strangers parted as if to make way for him.

There he stood. He was there in the aisle, a few yards away, watching her.

She leaned forward at once in her seat, her hand jerked up to her face as if to ward off a blow — but then the crowd in the aisle hid him, he was gone. She pressed both hands against her cheeks. He was not there, she had imagined him.

"My God," she whispered.

She was alone. Her husband had gone out to the foyer to make a telephone call; it was intermission at the concert, a Thursday evening.

Now she saw him again, clearly. He was standing there. He was staring at her. Her blood rocked in her body, draining out of her head . . . she was going to faint. . . . They stared at each other. They gave no sign of recognition. Only when he took a step forward did she shake her head *no — no — keep away.* It was not possible.

When her husband returned, she was staring at the place in the aisle where her lover had been standing. Her husband leaned forward to interrupt that stare.

"What's wrong?" he said. "Are you sick?"

Panic rose in her in long shuddering waves. She tried to get to her feet, panicked at the thought of fainting here, and her husband took hold of her. She stood like an aged woman, clutching the seat before her.

At home he helped her up the stairs and she lay down. Her head was like a large piece of crockery that had to be held still, it was so heavy. She was still panicked. She felt it in the shallows of her face, behind her knees, in the pit of her stomach. It sickened her, it made her think of mucus, of something thick and gray congested inside her, stuck to her, that was herself and yet not herself — a poison.

She lay with her knees drawn up toward her chest, her eyes hotly open, while her husband spoke to her. She imagined that other man saying, *Why did you run away from me?* Her husband was saying other words. She tried to listen to them. He was going to call the doctor, he said, and she tried to sit up. "No, I'm all right now," she said quickly. The panic was like lead inside her, so thickly congested. How slow love was to drain out of her, how fluid and sticky it was inside her head!

Her husband believed her. No doctor. No threat. Grateful, she drew her husband down to her. They embraced, not comfortably. For years now they had not been comfortable together, in their intimacy and at a distance, and now they struggled gently as if the paces of this dance were too rigorous for them. It was something they might have known once, but had now outgrown. The panic in her thickened at this double betrayal: she drew her husband to her, she caressed him wildly, she shut her eyes to think about that other man.

A crowd of men and women parting, unexpectedly, and there he stood — there he stood — she kept seeing him, and yet her vision blotched at the memory. It had been finished between them, six months before, but he had come out here . . . and she had escaped him, now she was lying in her husband's arms, in his embrace, her face pressed against his. It was a kind of sleep, this love-making. She felt herself falling asleep, her body falling from her. Her eyes shut.

"I love you," her husband said fiercely, angrily.

She shut her eyes and thought of that other man, as if betraying him would give her life a center.

"Did I hurt you? Are you — ?" her husband whispered.

Always this hot flashing of shame between them, the shame of her husband's near failure, the clumsiness of his love —

"You didn't hurt me," she said.

II

They had said good-by six months before. He drove her from Nantucket, where they had met, to Albany, New York, where she visited her sister. The hours of intimacy in the car had sealed something between them, a vow of silence and impersonality: she recalled the movement of the highways, the passing of other cars, the natural rhythms of the day hypnotizing her toward sleep while he drove. She trusted him, she could sleep in his presence. Yet she could not really fall asleep in spite of her exhaustion, and she kept jerking awake, frightened, to discover that nothing had changed — still the stranger who was driving her to Albany, still the highway, the sky, the antiseptic odor of the rented car, the sense of a rhythm behind the rhythm of the air that might unleash itself at any second. Everywhere on this highway, at this moment, there were men and women driving together, bonded together — what did that mean, to be together? What did it mean to enter into a bond with another person?

No, she did not really trust him; she did not really trust men. He would glance at her with his small cautious smile and she felt a declaration of shame between them.

Shame.

In her head she rehearsed conversations. She said bitterly, "You'll be relieved when we get to Albany. Relieved to get rid of me." They had spent so many days talking, confessing too much, driven to a pitch of childish excitement, laughing together on the beach, breaking into that pose of laughter that seems to eradicate the soul, so many days of this that the silence of the trip was like the silence of a hospital — all these surface noises, these rattles and hums, but an interior silence, a befuddlement. She said to him in her imagination, "One of us should die." Then she leaned over to touch him. She caressed the back of his neck. She said, aloud, "Would you like me to drive for a while?"

They stopped at a picnic area where other cars were stopped — couples, families — and walked together, smiling at their good luck. He put his arm around her shoulders and she sensed how they were in a posture together, a man and a woman forming a posture, a figure, that someone might sketch and show to them. She said slowly, "I don't want to go back. . . ."

Silence. She looked up at him. His face was heavy with her words, as if she had pulled at his skin with her fingers. Children ran nearby and distracted him — yes, he was a father too, his children ran like that, they tugged at his skin with their light, busy fingers.

"Are you so unhappy?" he said.

"I'm not unhappy, back there. I'm nothing. There's nothing to me," she said.

They stared at each other. The sensation between them was intense, exhausting. She thought that this man was her savior, that he had come to her at a time in her life when her life demanded completion, an end, a permanent fixing of all that was troubled and shifting and deadly. And yet it was absurd to think this. No person could save another. So she drew back from him and released him.

A few hours later they stopped at a gas station in a small city. She went to the women's rest room, having to ask the attendant for a key, and when she came back her eye jumped nervously onto the rented car — why? did she think he might have driven off without her? — onto the man, her friend, standing in conversation with the young attendant. Her friend was as old as her husband, over forty, with lanky, sloping shoulders, a full body, his hair thick, a dark, burnished brown, a festive color that made her eye twitch a little — and his hands were always moving, always those rapid conversational circles, going nowhere, gestures that were at once a little aggressive and apologetic.

She put her hand on his arm, a claim. He turned to her and smiled and she felt that she loved him, that everything in her life had forced her to this moment and that she had no choice about it.

They sat in the car for two hours, in Albany, in the parking lot of a

Howard Johnson's restaurant, talking, trying to figure out their past. There was no future. They concentrated on the past, the several days behind them, lit up with a hot, dazzling August sun, like explosions that already belonged to other people, to strangers. Her face was faintly reflected in the green-tinted curve of the windshield, but she could not have recognized that face. She began to cry; she told herself: *I am not here, this will pass, this is nothing.* Still, she could not stop crying. The muscles of her face were springy, like a child's, unpredictable muscles. He stroked her arms, her shoulders, trying to comfort her. "This is so hard . . . this is impossible . . ." he said. She felt panic for the world outside this car, all that was not herself and this man, and at the same time she understood that she was free of him, as people are free of other people, she would leave him soon, safely, and within a few days he would have fallen into the past, the impersonal past. . . .

"I'm so ashamed of myself!" she said finally.

She returned to her husband and saw that another woman, a shadow-woman, had taken her place — noiseless and convincing, like a dancer performing certain difficult steps. Her husband folded her in his arms and talked to her of his own loneliness, his worries about his business, his health, his mother, kept tranquillized and mute in a nursing home, and her spirit detached itself from her and drifted about the rooms of the large house she lived in with her husband, a shadow-woman delicate and imprecise. There was no boundary to her, no edge. Alone, she took hot baths and sat exhausted in the steaming water, wondering at her perpetual exhaustion. All that winter she noticed the limp, languid weight of her arms, her veins bulging slightly with the pressure of her extreme weariness. *This is fate*, she thought, to be here and not there, to be one person and not another, a certain man's wife and not the wife of another man. The long, slow pain of this certainty rose in her, but it never became clear, it was baffling and imprecise. She could not be serious about it; she kept congratulating herself on her own good luck, to have escaped so easily, to have freed herself. So much love had gone into the first several years of her marriage that there wasn't much left, now, for another man. . . . She was certain of that. But the bath water made her dizzy, all that perpetual heat, and one day in January she drew a razor blade lightly across the inside of her arm, near the elbow, to see what would happen.

Afterward she wrapped a small towel around it, to stop the bleeding. The towel soaked through. She wrapped a bath towel around that and walked through the empty rooms of her home, lightheaded, hardly aware of the stubborn seeping of blood. There was no boundary to her in this house, no precise limit. She could flow out like her own blood and come to no end.

She sat for a while on a blue love seat, her mind empty. Her husband telephoned her when he would be staying late at the plant. He talked to her always about his plans, his problems, his business friends, his future. It was obvious that he had a future. As he spoke she nodded to encourage him, and her heartbeat quickened with the memory of her own, personal shame, the shame of this man's particular, private wife. One evening at dinner he leaned forward and put his head in his arms and fell asleep, like a child. She sat at the table with him for a while watching him. His hair had gone gray, almost white, at the temples — no one would guess that he was so quick, so careful a man, still fairly young about the eyes. She put her hand on his head, lightly, as if to prove to herself that he was real. He slept, exhausted.

One evening they went to a concert and she looked up to see her lover there, in the crowded aisle, in this city, watching her. He was standing there, with his overcoat on, watching her. She went cold. That morning the telephone had rung while her husband was still home, and she had heard him answer it, heard him hang up — it must have been a wrong number — and when the telephone rang again, at 9:30, she had been afraid to answer it. She had left home to be out of the range of that ringing, but now, in this public place, in this busy auditorium, she found herself staring at that man, unable to make any sign to him, any gesture of recognition. . . .

He would have come to her but she shook her head. No. *Stay away.*

Her husband helped her out of the row of seats, saying, "Excuse us, please. Excuse us," so that strangers got to their feet, quickly, alarmed, to let them pass. Was that woman about to faint? What was wrong?

At home she felt the blood drain slowly back into her head. Her husband embraced her hips, pressing his face against her, in that silence that belonged to the earliest days of their marriage. She thought, *He will drive it out of me.* He made love to her and she was back in the auditorium again, sitting alone, now that the concert was over. The stage was empty; the heavy velvet curtains had not been drawn; the musicians' chairs were empty, everything was silent and expectant; in the aisle her lover stood and smiled at her — Her husband was impatient. He was apart from her, working on her, operating on her; and then, stricken, he whispered, "Did I hurt you?"

The telephone rang the next morning. Dully, sluggishly, she answered it. She recognized his voice at once — that "Anna?" with its lifting of the second syllable, questioning and apologetic and making its claim — "Yes, what do you want?" she said.

"Just to see you. Please — "

"I can't."

"Anna, I'm sorry, I didn't mean to upset you — "

"I can't see you."

"Just for a few minutes — I have to talk to you — "

"But why, why now? Why now?" she said.

She heard her voice rising, but she could not stop it. He began to talk again, drowning her out. She remembered his rapid conversation. She remembered his gestures, the witty energetic circling of his hands.

"Please don't hang up!" he cried.

"I can't — I don't want to go through it again — "

"I'm not going to hurt you. Just tell me how you are."

"Everything is the same."

"Everything is the same with me."

She looked up at the ceiling, shyly. "Your wife? Your children?"

"The same."

"Your son?"

"He's fine — "

"I'm glad to hear that. I — "

"Is it still the same with you, your marriage? Tell me what you feel. What are you thinking?"

"I don't know. . . ."

She remembered his intense, eager words, the movement of his hands, that impatient precise fixing of the air by his hands, the jabbing of his fingers.

"Do you love me?" he said.

She could not answer.

"I'll come over to see you," he said.

"No," she said.

What will come next, what will happen?

Flesh hardening on his body, aging. Shrinking. He will grow old, but not soft like her husband. They are two different types: he is nervous, lean, energetic, wise. She will grow thinner, as the tension radiates out from her backbone, wearing down her flesh. Her collarbones will jut out of her skin. Her husband, caressing her in their bed, will discover that she is another woman — she is not there with him — instead she is rising in an elevator in a downtown hotel, carrying a book as a prop, or walking quickly away from that hotel, her head bent and filled with secrets. Love, what to do with it? . . . Useless as moths' wings, as moths' fluttering. . . . She feels the flutterings of silky, crazy wings in her chest.

He flew out to visit her every several weeks, staying at a different hotel each time. He telephoned her, and she drove down to park in an underground garage at the very center of the city.

She lay in his arms while her husband talked to her, miles away, one body fading into another. He will grow old, his body will change, she thought, pressing her cheek against the back of one of these men. If it was her lover, they were in a hotel room: always the propped-up little booklet describing the hotel's many services, with color photographs of its cocktail lounge and dining room and coffee shop. Grow old, leave me, die, go back to your neurotic wife and your sad, ordinary children, she thought, but still her eyes closed gratefully against his skin and she felt how complete their silence was, how they had come to rest in each other.

"Tell me about your life here. The people who love you," he said, as he always did.

One afternoon they lay together for four hours. It was her birthday and she was intoxicated with her good fortune, this prize of the afternoon, this man in her arms! She was a little giddy, she talked too much. She told him about her parents, about her husband. . . . "They were all people I believed in, but it turned out wrong. Now, I believe in you. . . ." He laughed as if shocked by her words. She did not understand. Then she understood. "But I believe truly in you. I can't think of myself without you," she said. . . . He spoke of his wife, her ambitions, her intelligence, her use of the children against him, her use of his younger son's blindness, all of his words gentle and hypnotic and convincing in the late afternoon peace of this hotel room . . . and she felt the terror of laughter, threatening laughter. Their words, like their bodies, were aging.

She dressed quickly in the bathroom, drawing her long hair up around the back of her head, fixing it as always, anxious that everything be the same. Her face was slightly raw, from his face. The rubbing of his skin. Her eyes were too bright, wearily bright. Her hair was blond but not so blond as it had been that summer in the white Nantucket air.

She ran water and splashed it on her face. She blinked at the water. Blind. Drowning. She thought with satisfaction that soon, soon, he would be back home, in that house on Long Island she had never seen, with that woman she had never seen, sitting on the edge of another bed, putting on his shoes. She wanted nothing except to be free of him. Why not be free? *Oh,* she thought suddenly, *I will follow you back and kill you. You and her and the little boy. What is there to stop me?*

She left him. Everyone on the street pitied her, that look of absolute zero.

III

A man and a child, approaching her. The sharp acrid smell of fish. The crashing of waves. Anna pretended not to notice the father with his son — there was something strange about them. That frank, silent intimacy, too gentle, the man's bare feet in the water and the boy a few feet away, leaning away from his father. He was about nine years old and still his father held his hand.

A small yipping dog, a golden dog, bounded near them.

Anna turned shyly back to her reading; she did not want to have to speak to these neighbors. She saw the man's shadow falling over her legs, then over the pages of her book, and she had the idea that he wanted to see what she was reading. The dog nuzzled her; the man called him away.

She watched them walk down the beach. She was relieved that the man had not spoken to her.

She saw them in town later that day, the two of them brown-haired and patient, now wearing sandals, walking with that same look of care. The man's white shorts were soiled and a little baggy. His pullover shirt was a faded green. His face was broad, the cheekbones wide, spaced widely apart, the eyes stark in their sockets, as if they fastened onto objects for no reason, ponderous and edgy. The little boy's face was pale and sharp; his lips were perpetually parted.

Anna realized that the child was blind.

The next morning, early, she caught sight of them again. For some reason she went to the back door of her cottage. She faced the sea breeze eagerly. Her heart hammered. . . . She had been here, in her family's old house, for three days, alone, bitterly satisfied at being alone, and now it was a puzzle to her how her soul strained to fly outward, to meet with another person. She watched the man with his son, his cautious, rather stooped shoulders above the child's small shoulders.

The man was carrying something, it looked like a notebook. He sat on the sand, not far from Anna's spot of the day before, and the dog rushed up to them. The child approached the edge of the ocean, timidly. He moved in short jerky steps, his legs stiff. The dog ran around him. Anna heard the child crying out a word that sounded like "Ty" — it must have been the dog's name — and then the man joined in, his voice heavy and firm.

"Ty—"

Anna tied her hair back with a yellow scarf and went down to the beach.

The man glanced around at her. He smiled. She stared past him at the waves. To talk to him or not to talk — she had the freedom of that choice. For a moment she felt that she had made a mistake, that the child and the dog would not protect her, that behind this man's ordinary, friendly face there was a certain arrogant maleness — then she relented, she smiled shyly.

"A nice house you've got there," the man said.

She nodded her thanks.

The man pushed his sunglasses up on his forehead. Yes, she recognized the eyes of the day before — intelligent and nervous, the sockets pale, untanned.

"Is that your telephone ringing?" he said.

She did not bother to listen. "It's a wrong number," she said.

Her husband calling: she had left home for a few days, to be alone.

But the man, settling himself on the sand, seemed to misinterpret this. He smiled in surprise, one corner of his mouth higher than the other. He said nothing. Anna wondered: *What is he thinking?* The dog was leaping about her, panting against her legs, and she laughed in embarrassment. She bent to pet it, grateful for its busyness. "Don't let him jump up on you," the man said. "He's a nuisance."

The dog was a small golden retriever, a young dog. The blind child, standing now in the water, turned to call the dog to him. His voice was shrill and impatient.

"Our house is the third one down — the white one," the man said.

She turned, startled. "Oh, did you buy it from Dr. Patrick? Did he die?"

"Yes, finally. . . ."

Her eyes wandered nervously over the child and the dog. She felt the nervous beat of her heart out to the very tips of her fingers, the fleshy tips of her fingers: little hearts were there, pulsing. *What is he thinking?* The man had opened his notebook. He had a piece of charcoal and he began to sketch something.

Anna looked down at him. She saw the top of his head, his thick brown hair, the freckles on his shoulders, the quick, deft movement of his hand. Upside down, Anna herself being drawn. She smiled in surprise.

"Let me draw you. Sit down," he said.

She knelt awkwardly a few yards away. He turned the page of the sketch pad. The dog ran to her and she sat, straightening out her skirt beneath her, flinching from the dog's tongue. "Ty!" cried the child. Anna sat, and slowly the pleasure of the moment began to glow in her; her skin flushed with gratitude.

She sat there for nearly an hour. The man did not talk much. Back and forth the dog bounded, shaking itself. The child came to sit near them, in silence. Anna felt that she was drifting into a kind of trance while the man sketched her, half a dozen rapid sketches, the surface of her face given up to him. "Where are you from?" the man asked.

"Ohio. My husband lives in Ohio."

She wore no wedding band.

"Your wife —" Anna began.

"Yes?"

"Is she here?"

"Not right now."

She was silent, ashamed. She had asked an improper question. But the man did not seem to notice. He continued drawing her, bent over the sketch pad. When Anna said she had to go, he showed her the drawings — one after another of her, Anna, recognizably Anna, a woman in her early thirties, her hair smooth and flat across the top of her head, tied behind by a scarf. "Take the one you like best," he said, and she picked one of her with the dog in her lap, sitting very straight, her brows and eyes clearly defined, her lips girlishly pursed, the dog and her dress suggested by a few quick irregular lines.

"Lady with pet dog," the man said.

She spent the rest of the day reading, nearer her cottage. It was not really a cottage — it was a two-story house, large and ungainly and weathered. It was mixed up in her mind with her family, her own childhood, and she glanced up from her book, perplexed, as if waiting for one of her parents or her sister to come up to her. Then she thought of the man, the man with the blind child, the man with the dog, and she could not concentrate on her reading. Someone — probably her father — had marked a passage that must be important, but she kept reading and rereading it: *We try to dis-*

*cover in things, endeared to us on that account, the spiritual glamour which
we ourselves have cast upon them; we are disillusioned, and learn that they
are in themselves barren and devoid of the charm that they owed, in our
minds, to the association of certain ideas. . . .*

She thought again of the man on the beach. She lay the book aside
and thought of him: his eyes, his aloneness, his drawings of her.

They began seeing each other after that. He came to her front door in
the evening, without the child; he drove her into town for dinner. She was
shy and extremely pleased. The darkness of the expensive restaurant released her; she heard herself chatter; she leaned forward and seemed to be
offering her face up to him, listening to him. He talked about his work on a
Long Island newspaper and she seemed to be listening to him, as she stared
at his face, arranging her own face into the expression she had seen in that
charcoal drawing. Did he see her like that, then? — girlish and withdrawn
and patrician? She felt the weight of his interest in her, a force that fell
upon her like a blow. A repeated blow. Of course he was married, he had
children — of course she was married, permanently married. This flight
from her husband was not important. She had left him before, to be alone,
it was not important. Everything in her was slender and delicate and not
important.

They walked for hours after dinner, looking at the other strollers, the
weekend visitors, the tourists, the couples like themselves. Surely they were
mistaken for a couple, a married couple. *This is the hour in which everything is decided,* Anna thought. They had both had several drinks and they
talked a great deal. Anna found herself saying too much, stopping and
starting giddily. She put her hand to her forehead, feeling faint.

"It's from the sun — you've had too much sun — " he said.

At the door to her cottage, on the front porch, she heard herself asking
him if he would like to come in. She allowed him to lead her inside, to close
the door. *This is not important,* she thought clearly, *he doesn't mean it, he
doesn't love me, nothing will come of it.* She was frightened, yet it seemed
to her necessary to give in; she had to leave Nantucket with that act completed, an act of adultery, an accomplishment she would take back to Ohio
and to her marriage.

Later, incredibly, she heard herself asking: "Do you . . . do you
love me?"

"You're so beautiful!" he said, amazed.

She felt this beauty, shy and glowing and centered in her eyes. He
stared at her. In this large, drafty house, alone together, they were like accomplices, conspirators. She could not think: how old was she? which year
was this? They had done something unforgivable together, and the knowledge of it was tugging at their faces. A cloud seemed to pass over her. She
felt herself smiling shrilly.

Afterward, a peculiar raspiness, a dryness of breath. He was silent felt a strange, idle fear, a sense of the danger outside this room and this old, comfortable bed — a danger that would not recognize her as the lady in that drawing, the lady with the pet dog. There was nothing to say to this man, this stranger. She felt the beauty draining out of her face, her eyes fading.

"I've got to be alone," she told him.

He left, and she understood that she would not see him again. She stood by the window of the room, watching the ocean. A sense of shame overpowered her: it was smeared everywhere on her body, the smell of it, the richness of it. She tried to recall him, and his face was confused in her memory: she would have to shout to him across a jumbled space, she would have to wave her arms wildly. *You love me! You must love me!* But she knew he did not love her, and she did not love him; he was a man who drew everything up into himself, like all men, walking away, free to walk away, free to have his own thoughts, free to envision her body, all the secrets of her body. . . . And she lay down again in the bed, feeling how heavy this body had become, her insides heavy with shame, the very backs of her eyelids coated with shame.

"This is the end of one part of my life," she thought.

But in the morning the telephone rang. She answered it. It was her lover: they talked brightly and happily. She could hear the eagerness in his voice, the love in his voice, that same still, sad amazement — she understood how simple life was, there were no problems.

They spent most of their time on the beach, with the child and the dog. He joked and was serious at the same time. He said, once, "You have defined my soul for me," and she laughed to hide her alarm. In a few days it was time for her to leave. He got a sitter for the boy and took the ferry with her to the mainland, then rented a car to drive her up to Albany. She kept thinking: *Now something will happen. It will come to an end.* But most of the drive was silent and hypnotic. She wanted him to joke with her, to say again that she had defined his soul for him, but he drove fast, he was serious, she distrusted the hawkish look of his profile — she did not know him at all. At a gas station she splashed her face with cold water. Alone in the grubby little rest room, shaky and very much alone. In such places are women totally alone with their bodies. The body grows heavier, more evil, in such silence. . . . On the beach everything had been noisy with sunlight ⁿd gulls and waves; here, as if run to earth, everything was cramped and ` and dead.

ᵥent outside, squinting. There he was, talking with the station at-
ᶜould not think as she returned to him whether she wanted to

` ᶦbany for a few days, then flew home to her husband.
` near the luggage counter, where her three pieces
were brought to him on a conveyer belt, to be

claimed by him. He kissed her on the cheek. They shook hands, a little embarrassed. She had come home again.

"How will I live out the rest of my life?" she wondered.

In January her lover spied on her: she glanced up and saw him, in a public place, in the DeRoy Symphony Hall. She was paralyzed with fear. She nearly fainted. In this faint she felt her husband's body, loving her, working its love upon her, and she shut her eyes harder to keep out the certainty of his love — sometimes he failed at loving her, sometimes he succeeded, it had nothing to do with her or her pity or her ten years of love for him, it had nothing to do with a woman at all. It was a private act accomplished by a man, a husband or a lover, in communion with his own soul, his manhood.

Her husband was forty-two years old now, growing slowly into middle age, getting heavier, softer. Her lover was about the same age, narrower in the shoulders, with a full, solid chest, yet lean, nervous. She thought, in her paralysis, of men and how they love freely and eagerly so long as their bodies are capable of love, love for a woman; and then, as love fades in their bodies, it fades from their souls and they become immune and immortal and ready to die.

Her husband was a little rough with her, as if impatient with himself. "I love you," he said fiercely, angrily. And then, ashamed, he said, "Did I hurt you? . . ."

"You didn't hurt me," she said.

Her voice was too shrill for their embrace.

While he was in the bathroom she went to her closet and took out that drawing of the summer before. There she was, on the beach at Nantucket, a lady with a pet dog, her eyes large and defined, the dog in her lap hardly more than a few snarls, a few coarse soft lines of charcoal . . . her dress smeared, her arms oddly limp . . . her hands not well drawn at all. . . . She tried to think: did she love the man who had drawn this? did he love her? The fever in her husband's body had touched her and driven her temperature up, and now she stared at the drawing with a kind of lust, fearful of seeing an ugly soul in that woman's face, fearful of seeing the face suddenly through her lover's eyes. She breathed quickly and harshly, staring at the drawing.

And so, the next day, she went to him at his hotel. She wept, pressing against him, demanding of him, "What do you want? Why are you here? Why don't you let me alone?" He told her that he wanted nothing. He expected nothing. He would not cause trouble.

"I want to talk about last August," he said.

"Don't —" she said.

She was hypnotized by his gesturing hands, his nervousness, his obvious agitation. He kept saying, "I understand. I'm making no claims upon you."

They became lovers again.

He called room service for something to drink and they sat side by side on his bed, looking through a copy of *The New Yorker*, laughing at the cartoons. It was so peaceful in this room, so complete. They were on a holiday. It was a secret holiday. Four-thirty in the afternoon, on a Friday, an ordinary Friday: a secret holiday.

"I won't bother you again," he said.

He flew back to see her again in March, and in late April. He telephoned her from his hotel — a different hotel each time — and she came down to him at once. She rose to him in various elevators, she knocked on the doors of various rooms, she stepped into his embrace, breathless and guilty and already angry with him, pleading with him. One morning in May, when he telephoned, she pressed her forehead against the doorframe and could not speak. He kept saying, "What's wrong? Can't you talk? Aren't you alone?" She felt that she was going insane. Her head would burst. Why, why did he love her, why did he pursue her? Why did he want her to die?

She went to him in the hotel room. A familiar room: had they been here before? "Everything is repeating itself. Everything is stuck," she said. He framed her face in his hands and said that she looked thinner — was she sick? — what was wrong? She shook herself free. He, her lover, looked about the same. There was a small, angry pimple on his neck. He stared at her, eagerly and suspiciously. Did she bring bad news?

"So you love me? You love me?" she asked.

"Why are you so angry?"

"I want to be free of you. The two of us free of each other."

"That isn't true — you don't want that — "

He embraced her. She was wild with that old, familiar passion for him, her body clinging to his, her arms not strong enough to hold him. Ah, what despair! — what bitter hatred she felt! — she needed this man for her salvation, he was all she had to live for, and yet she could not believe in him. He embraced her thighs, her hips, kissing her, pressing his warm face against her, and yet she could not believe in him, not really. She needed him in order to live, but he was not worth her love, he was not worth her dying. . . . She promised herself this: when she got back home, when she was alone, she would draw the razor more deeply across her arm.

The telephone rang and he answered it: a wrong number.

"Jesus," he said.

They lay together, still. She imagined their posture like this, the two of them one figure, one substance; and outside this room and this bed there was a universe of disjointed, separate things, blank things, that had nothing to do with them. She would not be Anna out there, the lady in the drawing. He would not be her lover.

"I love you so much. . . ." she whispered.

"Please don't cry! We have only a few hours, please. . . ."

It was absurd, their clinging together like this. She saw them as a single figure in a drawing, their arms and legs entwined, their heads pressing mutely together. Helpless substance, so heavy and warm and doomed. It was absurd that any human being should be so important to another human being. She wanted to laugh: a laugh might free them both.

She could not laugh.

Sometime later he said, as if they had been arguing, "Look. It's you. You're the one who doesn't want to get married. You lie to me — "

"Lie to you?"

"You love me but you won't marry me, because you want something left over — Something not finished — All your life you can attribute your misery to me, to our not being married — you are using me — "

"Stop it! You'll make me hate you!" she cried.

"You can say to yourself that you're miserable because of *me*. We will never be married, you will never be happy, neither one of us will ever be happy — "

"I don't want to hear this!" she said.

She pressed her hands flatly against her face.

She went to the bathroom to get dressed. She washed her face and part of her body, quickly. The fever was in her, in the pit of her belly. She would rush home and strike a razor across the inside of her arm and free that pressure, that fever.

The impatient bulging of the veins: an ordeal over.

The demand of the telephone's ringing: that ordeal over.

The nuisance of getting the car and driving home in all that five o'clock traffic: an ordeal too much for a woman.

The movement of this stranger's body in hers: over, finished.

Now, dressed, a little calmer, they held hands and talked. They had to talk swiftly, to get all their news in: he did not trust the people who worked for him, he had faith in no one, his wife had moved to a textbook publishing company and was doing well, she had inherited a Ben Shahn painting from her father and wanted to "touch it up a little" — she was crazy! — his blind son was at another school, doing fairly well, in fact his children were all doing fairly well in spite of the stupid mistake of their parents' marriage — and what about her? what about her life? She told him in a rush the one thing he wanted to hear: that she lived with her husband lovelessly, the two of them polite strangers, sharing a bed, lying side by side in the night in that bed, bodies out of which souls had fled. There was no longer even any shame between them.

"And what about me? Do you feel shame with me still?" he asked.

She did not answer. She moved away from him and prepared to leave.

Then, a minute later, she happened to catch sight of his reflection in the bureau mirror — he was glancing down at himself, checking himself mechanically, impersonally, preparing also to leave. He too would leave this room: he too was headed somewhere else.

She stared at him. It seemed to her that in this instant he was breaking from her, the image of her lover fell free of her, breaking from her . . . and she realized that he existed in a dimension quite apart from her, a mysterious being. And suddenly, joyfully, she felt a miraculous calm. This man was her husband, truly — they were truly married, here in this room — they had been married haphazardly and accidentally for a long time. In another part of the city she had another husband, a "husband," but she had not betrayed that man, not really. This man, whom she loved above any other person in the world, above even her own self-pitying sorrow and her own life, was her truest lover, her destiny. And she did not hate him, she did not hate herself any longer; she did not wish to die; she was flooded with a strange certainty, a sense of gratitude, of pure selfless energy. It was obvious to her that she had, all along, been behaving correctly; out of instinct.

What triumph, to love like this in any room, anywhere, risking even the craziest of accidents!

"Why are you so happy? What's wrong?" he asked, startled. He stared at her. She felt the abrupt concentration in him, the focusing of his vision on her, almost a bitterness in his face, as if he feared her. What, was it beginning all over again? Their love beginning again, in spite of them? "How can you look so happy?" he asked. "We don't have any right to it. Is it because. . . ?"

"Yes," she said.

[1972]

TONI CADE BAMBARA (b. 1939) was born in New York City and grew up in Harlem and Bedford-Stuyvesant. As a child she began scribbling stories on the margins of her father's copies of the Daily News and the squares of thin white cardboard her mother's stockings came wrapped around. She says

> I was raised by my family and community to be a combatant. Forays to the Apollo [Theater in Harlem] with my daddy and hanging tough on Speakers Corner with my mama taught me the power of the word, the importance of the resistance tradition, and the high standards our [black] community had regarding verbal performance. While my heart is a laughing gland and my favorite thing to be doing is laughing so hard I have to lower myself on the wall to keep from falling down, near that chamber is a blast furnace where a rifle pokes from the ribs.

In high school and at Queens College, Bambara remembers that she "hogged the lit journal." She took writing courses and wrote novels, stories, plays, film scripts, operas, "you-name-its." After her college graduation, she worked various jobs and studied for her M.A. at City College of New York while she wrote fiction in "the predawn in-betweens." In 1960 she began to publish her stories. "The Hammer Man" first appeared in Negro Digest in 1966. Six years later she published her first book, a collection of stories titled Gorilla, My Love. It wasn't until Bambara returned from a trip to Cuba in 1973 that she thought of herself as a writer. "There I learned what Langston Hughes and others, most especially my colleagues in the Neo-Black Arts Movement, had been teaching for years — that writing is a legitimate way, an important way, to participate in the empowerment of the community that names me." Her books include The Black Woman (1970), Tales and Stories for Black Folks (1971), The Sea Birds Are Still Alive: Collected Stories (1977), and a novel, The Salt Eaters (1980).

Like Hughes and Zora Neale Hurston, whom Bambara credits with giving her new ways to consider literary material (folkways as the basis of art) and new categories of perception (women's images), Bambara often uses humor in her fiction. She says that "what I enjoy most in my work is the laughter and the outrage and the attention to language." Her stories, like "The Hammer Man," are often about children, but Bambara tries to avoid sentimentality. She attempts to keep her torrents of language and feeling in control by remembering the premises from which she proceeds as a black writer: "One, we are at war. Two, the natural response to oppression, ignorance, evil, and mystification is wide-awake resistance. Three, the natural response to stress and crisis is not breakdown and capitulation, but transformation and renewal."

Toni Cade Bambara

203

THE HAMMER MAN

I was glad to hear that Manny had fallen off the roof. I had put out the tale that I was down with yellow fever, but nobody paid me no mind, least of all Dirty Red who stomped right in to announce that Manny had fallen off the roof and that I could come out of hiding now. My mother dropped what she was doing, which was the laundry, and got the whole story out of Red. "Bad enough you gots to hang around with boys," she said. "But fight with them too. And you would pick the craziest one at that."

Manny was supposed to be crazy. That was his story. To say you were bad put some people off. But to say you were crazy, well, you were officially not to be messed with. So that was his story. On the other hand, after I called him what I called him and said a few choice things about his mother, his face did go through some piercing changes. And I did kind of wonder if maybe he sure was nuts. I didn't wait to find out. I got in the wind. And then he waited for me on my stoop all day and all night, not hardly speaking to the people going in and out. And he was there all day Saturday, with his sister bringing him peanut-butter sandwiches and cream sodas. He must've gone to the bathroom right there cause every time I looked out the kitchen window, there he was. And Sunday, too. I got to thinking the boy was mad.

"You got no sense of humor, that's your trouble," I told him. He looked up, but he didn't say nothing. All at once I was real sorry about the whole thing. I should've settled for hitting off the little girls in the school yard, or waiting for Frankie to come in so we could raise some kind of hell. This way I had to play sick when my mother was around cause my father had already taken away my BB gun and hid it.

I don't know how they got Manny on the roof finally. Maybe the Wakefield kids, the ones who keep the pigeons, called him up. Manny was a sucker for sick animals and things like that. Or maybe Frankie got some nasty girls to go up on the roof with him and got Manny to join him. I don't know. Anyway, the catwalk had lost all its cement and the roof always did kind of slant downward. So Manny fell off the roof. I got over my yellow fever right quick, needless to say, and ventured outside. But by this time I had already told Miss Rose that Crazy Manny was after me. And Miss Rose, being who she was, quite naturally went over to Manny's house and said a few harsh words to his mother, who, being who she was, chased Miss

1142

Rose out into the street and they commenced to get with it, snatching bottles out of the garbage cans and breaking them on the johnny pumps and stuff like that.

Dirty Red didn't have to tell us about this. Everybody could see and hear all. I never figured the garbage cans for an arsenal, but Miss Rose came up with sticks and table legs and things, and Manny's mother had her share of scissor blades and bicycle chains. They got to rolling in the streets and all you could see was pink drawers and fat legs. It was something else. Miss Rose is nutty but Manny's mother's crazier than Manny. They were at it a couple of times during my sick spell. Everyone would congregate on the window sills or the fire escape, commenting that it was still much too cold for this kind of nonsense. But they watched anyway. And then Manny fell off the roof. And that was that. Miss Rose went back to her dream books and Manny's mother went back to her tumbled-down kitchen of dirty clothes and bundles and bundles of rags and children.

My father got in on it too, cause he happened to ask Manny one night why he was sitting on the stoop like that every night. Manny told him right off that he was going to kill me first chance he got. Quite naturally this made my father a little warm, me being his only daughter and planning to become a doctor and take care of him in his old age. So he had a few words with Manny first, and then he got hold of the older brother, Bernard, who was more his size. Bernard didn't see how any of it was his business or my father's business, so my father got mad and jammed Bernard's head into the mailbox. Then my father started getting messages from Bernard's uncle about where to meet him for a showdown and all. My father didn't say a word to my mother all this time; just sat around mumbling and picking up the phone and putting it down, or grabbing my stickball bat and putting it back. He carried on like this for days till I thought I would scream if the yellow fever didn't have me so weak. And then Manny fell off the roof, and my father went back to his beer-drinking buddies.

I was in the school yard, pitching pennies with the little boys from the elementary school, when my friend Violet hits my brand-new Spaudeen over the wall. She came running back to tell me that Manny was coming down the block. I peeked beyond the fence and there he was all right. He had his head all wound up like a mummy and his arm in a sling and his leg in a cast. It looked phony to me, especially that walking cane. I figured Dirty Red had told me a tale just to get me out there so Manny could stomp me, and Manny was playing it up with costume and all till he could get me.

"What happened to him?" Violet's sisters whispered. But I was too busy trying to figure out how this act was supposed to work. Then Manny passed real close to the fence and gave me a look.

"You had enough, Hammer Head," I yelled. "Just bring your crummy self in this yard and I'll pick up where I left off." Violet was knocked out and the other kids went into a huddle. I didn't have to say anything else. And when they all pressed me later, I just said, "You know that hammer he always carries in his fatigues?" And they'd all nod waiting for the rest of a long story. "Well, I took it away from him." And I walked off nonchalantly.

Manny stayed indoors for a long time. I almost forgot about him. New kids moved into the block and I got all caught up with that. And then Miss Rose finally hit the numbers and started ordering a whole lot of stuff through the mail and we would sit on the curb and watch these weird-looking packages being carried in, trying to figure out what simpleminded thing she had thrown her money away on when she might just as well wait for the warm weather and throw a block party for all her godchildren.

After a while a center opened up and my mother said she'd increase my allowance if I went and joined because I'd have to get out of my pants and stay in skirts, on account of that's the way things were at the center. So I joined and got to thinking about everything else but old Hammer Head. It was a rough place to get along in, the center, but my mother said that I needed to be be'd with and she needed to not be with me, so I went. And that time I sneaked into the office, that's when I really got turned on. I looked into one of those not-quite-white folders and saw that I was from a deviant family in a deviant neighborhood. I showed my mother the word in the dictionary, but she didn't pay me no mind. It was my favorite word after that. I ran it in the ground till one day my father got the strap just to show how deviant he could get. So I gave up trying to improve my vocabulary. And I almost gave up my dungarees.

Then one night I'm walking past the Douglas Street park cause I got thrown out of the center for playing pool when I should've been sewing, even though I had already decided that this was going to be my last fling with boy things, and starting tomorrow I was going to fix my hair right and wear skirts all the time just so my mother would stop talking about her gray hairs, and Miss Rose would stop calling me by my brother's name by mistake. So I'm walking past the park and there's ole Manny on the basketball court, perfecting his lay-ups and talking with himself. Being me, I quite naturally walk right up and ask what the hell he's doing playing in the dark, and he looks up and all around like the dark had crept up on him when he wasn't looking. So I knew right away that he'd been out there for a long time with his eyes just going along with the program.

"There was two seconds to go and we were one point behind," he said, shaking his head and staring at his sneakers like they was somebody. "And I was in the clear. I'd left the man in the backcourt and there I was, smiling, you dig, cause it was in the bag. They passed the ball and I slid the ball up nice and easy cause there was nothing to worry about. And . . ." He shook his head. "I muffed the goddamn shot. Ball bounced off the rim . . ." He stared at his hands. "The game of the season. Last game." And then he ignored me altogether, though he wasn't talking to me in the first place. He went back to the lay-ups, always from the same spot with his arms crooked in the same way, over and over. I must've gotten hypnotized cause I probably stood there for at least an hour watching like a fool till I couldn't even see the damn ball, much less the basket. But I stood there anyway for no

reason I know of. He never missed. But he cursed himself away. It was torture. And then a squad car pulled up and a short cop with hair like one of
the Marx Brothers came out hitching up his pants. He looked real hard at
me and then at Manny.

"What are you two doing?"

"He's doing a lay-up. I'm watching." I said with my smart self.

Then the cop just stood there and finally turned to the other one who
was just getting out of the car.

"Who unlocked the gate?" the big one said.

"It's always unlocked," I said. Then we three just stood there like a
bunch of penguins watching Manny go at it.

"This on the level?" the big guy asked, tilting his hat back with the
thumb the way big guys do in hot weather. "Hey you," he said, walking
over to Manny. "I'm talking to you." He finally grabbed the ball to get
Manny's attention. But that didn't work. Manny just stood there with his
arms out waiting for the pass so he could save the game. He wasn't paying
no mind to the cop. So, quite naturally, when the cop slapped him upside
his head it was a surprise. And when the cop started counting three to go,
Manny had already recovered from the slap and was just ticking off the seconds before the buzzer sounded and all was lost.

"Gimme the ball, man." Manny's face was all tightened up and ready
to pop.

"Did you hear what I said, black boy?"

Now, when somebody says that word like that, I gets warm. And crazy
or no crazy, Manny was my brother at that moment and the cop was the
enemy.

"You better give him back his ball," I said. "Manny don't take no
mess from no cops. He ain't bothering nobody. He's gonna be Mister Basketball when he grows up. Just trying to get a little practice in before the
softball season starts."

"Look here, sister, we'll run you in too," Harpo said.

"I damn sure can't be your sister seeing how I'm a black girl. Boy, I
sure will be glad when you run me in so I can tell everybody about that.
You must think you're in the South, mister."

The big guy screwed his mouth up and let one of them hard-day sighs.
"The park's closed, little girl, so why don't you and your boyfriend go on
home."

That really got me. The "little girl" was bad enough but that "boyfriend" was too much. But I kept cool, mostly because Manny looked so
pitiful waiting there with his hands in a time-out and there being no one to
stop the clock. But I kept my cool mostly cause of that hammer in Manny's
pocket and no telling how frantic things can get what with a big-mouth like
me, a couple of wise cops, and a crazy boy too.

"The gates are open," I said real quiet-like, "and this here's a free
country. So why don't you give him back his ball?"

The big cop did another one of those sighs, his specialty I guess, and then he bounced the ball to Manny who went right into his gliding thing clear up to the backboard, damn near like he was some kind of very beautiful bird. And then he swooshed that ball in, even if there was no net, and you couldn't really hear the swoosh. Something happened to the bones in my chest. It was something.

"Crazy kids anyhow," the one with the wig said and turned to go. But the big guy watched Manny for a while and I guess something must've snapped in his head, cause all of a sudden he was hot for taking Manny to jail or court or somewhere and started yelling at him and everything, which is a bad thing to do to Manny, I can tell you. And I'm standing there thinking that none of my teachers, from kindergarten right on up, none of them knew what they were talking about. I'll be damned if I ever knew one of them rosy-cheeked cops that smiled and helped you get to school without neither you or your little raggedy dog getting hit by a truck that had a smile on its face, too. Not that I ever believed it. I knew Dick and Jane was full of crap from the get-go, especially them cops. Like this dude, for example, pulling on Manny's clothes like that when obviously he had just done about the most beautiful thing a man can do and not be a fag. No cop could swoosh without a net.

"Look out, man," was all Manny said, but it was the way he pushed the cop that started the real yelling and threats. And I thought to myself, Oh God here I am trying to change my ways, and not talk back in school, and do like my mother wants, but just have this last fling, and now this — getting shot in the stomach and bleeding to death in Douglas Street park and poor Manny getting pistol-whipped by those bastards and whatnot. I could see it all, practically crying too. And it just wasn't no kind of thing to happen to a small child like me with my confirmation picture in the paper next to my weeping parents and schoolmates. I could feel the blood sticking to my shirt and my eyeballs slipping away, and then that confirmation picture again; and my mother and her gray hair; and Miss Rose heading for the precinct with a shotgun; and my father getting old and feeble with no one to doctor him up and all.

And I wished Manny had fallen off the damn roof and died right then and there and saved me all this aggravation of being killed with him by these cops who surely didn't come out of no fifth-grade reader. But it didn't happen. They just took the ball and Manny followed them real quiet-like right out of the park into the dark, then into the squad car with his head drooping and his arms in a crook. And I went on home cause what the hell am I going to do on a basketball court, and it getting to be nearly midnight?

I didn't see Manny no more after he got into that squad car. But they didn't kill him after all cause Miss Rose heard he was in some kind of big house for people who lose their marbles. And then it was spring finally, and me and Violet was in this very boss fashion show at the center. And Miss Rose bought me my first corsage — yellow roses to match my shoes.

[1966]

MARGARET ATWOOD (b. 1939) is a Canadian writer of poetry and fiction. Born in Ottawa, Ontario, she spent the first eleven years of her life in the sparsely settled "bush" country of northern Ontario and Quebec, where her father, an entomologist, did research. She remembers that

> I did not spend a full year in school until I was in Grade Eight. I began to write at the age of five — poems, "novels," comic books and plays — but I had no thought of being a professional writer until I was sixteen. I entered Victoria College, University of Toronto, when I was seventeen and graduated in 1961. I won a Woodrow Wilson Fellowship to Harvard, where I studied Victorian Literature, and spent the next ten years in one place after another: Boston, Montreal, Edmonton, Toronto, Vancouver, England and Italy, alternately teaching and writing.

Atwood's first poem was published when she was nineteen. She found it took a while to discover her own literary culture because in Canada "authors were published in small editions and not generally known. This changed during the next decade, when I was becoming active as a poet and prose fiction writer. At the beginning of the 1960s there was only a handful of magazines and indigenous publishing houses; at the end there were many, and writers had become public figures." She felt she was encouraged to write as a young author because among Canadians of her generation, the urge to develop a national literature was very strong.

Today one of the best known contemporary Canadian writers, Atwood published her first important collection of poetry in 1964 and her first novel, The Edible Woman, in 1969. As she has matured, her writing has become increasingly political. In 1972 she published her most widely discussed novel, Surfacing, a powerful attack on the attitude toward nature that Atwood identifies as American — the belief that nature is to be subdued, controlled, and destroyed. That same year she published Survival, a "thematic guide" to Canadian literature. In this work she concluded that Canadian writers have tended to create fictional characters who end as victims of their own society and of American power. "When It Happens," from her 1982 collection Dancing Girls and Other Stories, illustrates Atwood's belief that most works of Canadian literature center on the theme of survival. Her protagonist in the story considers herself a victim since there is no possibility in her situation of exhibiting a frontier spirit of risk and adventure, and no likelihood of experiencing an ultimate triumph. To date Atwood has published six novels, two collections of short stories, and more than a dozen books of poetry.

Margaret Atwood

∽

WHEN IT HAPPENS

Mrs. Burridge is putting up green tomato pickles. There are twelve quarts in each lot with a bit left over, and that is the end of the jars. At the store they tell her there's a strike on at the factory where they get made. She doesn't know anything about that but you can't buy them anywhere, and even before this they were double what they were last year; she considers herself lucky she had those in the cellar. She has a lot of green tomatoes because she heard on the weather last night there was going to be a killer frost, so she put on her parka and her work gloves and took the lantern out to the garden in the pitch-dark and picked off all the ones she could see, over three bushels. She can lift the full baskets herself but she asked Frank to carry them in for her; he grumbles, but he likes it when she asks. In the morning the news said the growers had been hit and that would shoot the price up, not that the growers would get any of it themselves, everyone knows it's the stores that make the money.

She feels richer than she did yesterday, but on the other hand there isn't that much you can do with green tomatoes. The pickles hardly made a dint in them, and Frank has said, as he does every year, that they will never eat twenty-four quarts of green tomato pickle with just the two of them and the children gone. Except when they come to visit and eat me out of house and home, Mrs. Burridge adds silently. The truth is she has always made two batches and the children never liked it anyway, it was Frank ate them all and she knows perfectly well he'll do it again, without even noticing. He likes it on bread and cheese when he's watching the hockey games, during every commercial he goes out to the kitchen and makes himself another slice, even if he's just had a big meal, leaving a trail of crumbs and bits of pickle from the counter across the floor and over the front-room rug to his big chair. It used to annoy Mrs. Burridge, especially the crumbs, but now she watches him with a kind of sadness; she once thought their life together would go on forever but she has come to realize this is not the case.

She doesn't even feel like teasing him about his spare tire any more, though she does it all the same because he would miss it if she stopped. "There you go," she says, in the angular, prodding, metallic voice she cannot change because everyone expects it from her, if she spoke any other way they would think she was ill, "you keep on munching away like that and it'll be easy for me to get you out of bed in the mornings, I'll just give you a push and you'll roll all the way down the stairs like a barrel." And he answers in his methodical voice, pretending to be lazy even though he isn't, "You need a little fun in life," as though his pickles and cheese are slightly disreputable, almost like an orgy. Every year he tells her she's made too much but there would be a fuss all right if he went down to the cellar one day and there wasn't any left.

Mrs. Burridge has made her own pickles since 1952, which was the first year she had the garden. She remembers it especially because her daughter Sarah was on the way and she had trouble bending down to do the weeding. When she herself was growing up everyone did their own pickles, and their own canning and preserving too. But after the war most women gave it up, there was more money then and it was easier to buy things at the store. Mrs. Burridge never gave it up, though most of her friends thought she was wasting her time, and now she is glad she didn't, it kept her in practice while the others were having to learn all over again. Though with the sugar going up the way it is, she can't understand how long anyone is going to be able to afford even the homemade things.

On paper Frank is making more money than he ever has; yet they seem to have less to spend. They could always sell the farm, she supposes, to people from the city who would use it as a weekend place; they could get what seems like a very high price, several of the farms south of them have gone that way. But Mrs. Burridge does not have much faith in money; also it is a waste of the land, and this is her home, she has it arranged the way she wants it.

When the second batch is on and simmering she goes to the back door, opens it, and stands with her arms folded across her stomach, looking out. She catches herself doing this four or five times a day now and she doesn't quite know why. There isn't much to see, just the barn and the back field with the row of dead elms Frank keeps saying he's going to cut down, and the top of Clarke's place sticking over the hill. She isn't sure what she is looking for but she has the odd idea she may see something burning, smoke coming up from the horizon, a column of it or perhaps more than one column, off to the south. This is such a peculiar thought for her to have that she hasn't told it to anyone else. Yesterday Frank saw her standing at the back door and asked her about it at dinner; anything he wants to talk to her about he saves up till dinner, even if he thinks about it in the morning. He wondered why she was at the back door, doing nothing at all for over ten minutes, and Mrs. Burridge told him a lie, which made her very uneasy. She said she heard a strange dog barking, which wasn't a good story because their own dogs were right there and they didn't notice a thing. But Frank let it pass; perhaps he thinks she is getting funny in her old age and doesn't want to call attention to it, which would be like him. He'll track mud all over her nice shiny kitchen floor but he'd hate to hurt anyone's feelings. Mrs. Burridge decides, a little wistfully, that despite his pig-headedness he is a kind and likeable man, and for her this is like renouncing a cherished and unquestionable belief, such as the flatness of the earth. He has made her angry so many times.

When the pickles are cool she labels them as she always does with the name and the date and carries them down the cellar stairs. The cellar is the old kind, with stone walls and a dirt floor. Mrs. Burridge likes to have everything neat — she still irons her sheets — so she had Frank build her some shelves right after they were married. The pickles go on one side, jams and jellies on the other, and the quarts of preserves along the bottom. It used to make her feel safe to have all that food in the cellar; she would think to herself, Well, if there's a snowstorm or anything and we're cut off, it won't be so bad. It doesn't make her feel safe any more. Instead she thinks that if she has to leave suddenly she won't be able to take any of the jars with her, they'd be too heavy to carry.

She comes back up the stairs after the last trip. It's not as easy as it used to be, her knee still bothers her as it has ever since she fell six years ago, she tripped on the second-last step. She's asked Frank a million times to fix the stairs but he hasn't done it, that's what she means by pig-headed. If she asks him more than twice to do something he calls it nagging, and maybe it is, but who's going to do it if he won't? The cold vacant hole at the back of this question is too much for her.

She has to stop herself from going to the back door again. Instead she goes to the back window and looks out, she can see almost the same things anyway. Frank is going towards the barn, carrying something, it looks like a wrench. The way he walks, slower than he used to, bent forward a little — from the back he's like an old man, how many years has he been walking that way? — makes her think, He can't protect me. She doesn't think this on purpose, it simply occurs to her, and it isn't only him, it's all of them, they've lost the power, you can tell by the way they walk. They are all waiting, just as Mrs. Burridge is, for whatever it is to happen. Whether they realize it or not. Lately when she's gone to the Dominion Store in town she has seen a look on the faces of the women there, she knows most of them, she wouldn't be mistaken — an anxious, closed look, as if they are frightened of something but won't talk about it. They're wondering what they will do, perhaps they think there's nothing they can do. This air of helplessness exasperates Mrs. Burridge, who has always been practical.

For weeks she has wanted to go to Frank and ask him to teach her how to use the gun. In fact he has two guns, a shotgun and a twenty-two rifle; he used to like going after a few ducks in the fall, and of course there are the groundhogs, they have to be shot because of the holes they make in the fields. Frank drives over on the tractor five or six times a year. A lot of men get injured by overturning tractors. But she can't ask him because she can't explain to him why she needs to know, and if she doesn't explain he will only tease. "Anyone can shoot a gun," he'll say, "all you have to do is pull the trigger . . . oh, you mean you want to hit something, well now, that's different, who you planning to kill?" Perhaps he won't say that; perhaps this is only the way he talked twenty years ago, before she stopped taking an interest in things outside the house. But Mrs. Burridge will never know because she will never ask. She doesn't have the heart to say to him, *Maybe you'll be dead. Maybe you'll go off somewhere when it happens, maybe there will be a war.* She can remember the last war.

Nothing has changed outside the window, so she turns away and sits down at the kitchen table to make out her shopping list. Tomorrow is their day for going into town. She tries to plan the day so she can sit down at intervals; otherwise her feet start swelling up. That began with Sarah and got worse with the other two children and it's never really gone away. All her life, ever since she got married, she has made lists of things that have to be bought, sewed, planted, cooked, stored; she already has her list made for next Christmas, all the names and the gift she will buy for each, and the list of what she needs for Christmas dinner. But she can't seem to get interested in it, it's too far away. She can't believe in a distant future that is orderly like the past, she no longer seems to have the energy; it's as if she is saving it up for when she will have to use it.

She is even having trouble with the shopping list. Instead of concentrating on the paper — she writes on the backs of the used-up days of the page-a-day calendar Frank gives her every New Year — she is gazing around the kitchen, looking at all the things she will have to leave behind when she goes. That will be the hardest part. Her mother's china, her silver, even though it is an old-fashioned pattern and the silver is wearing off, the egg timer in the shape of a chicken Sarah gave her when she was twelve, the ceramic salt and pepper shakers, green horses with perforated heads, that one of the other children brought back from the Ex. She thinks of walking up the stairs, the sheets folded in the chest, the towels stacked neatly on the shelves, the beds made, the quilt that was her grandmother's, it makes her want to cry. On her bureau, the wedding picture, herself in a shiny satin gown (the satin was a mistake, it emphasized her hips), Frank in the suit he has not worn since except to funerals, his hair cut too short on the sides and a surprising tuft at the top, like a woodpecker's. The children when they were babies. She thinks of her girls now and hopes they will not have babies; it is no longer the right time for it.

Mrs. Burridge wishes someone would be more precise, so she could make better plans. Everyone knows something is going to happen, you can tell by reading the newspapers and watching the television, but nobody is sure what it will be, nobody can be exact. She has her own ideas about it though. At first it will simply become quieter. She will have an odd feeling that something is wrong but it will be a few days before she is able to pin it down. Then she will notice that the planes are no longer flying over on their way to the Malton Airport, and that the noise from the highway two miles away, which is quite distinct when the leaves are off the trees, has almost disappeared. The television will be non-committal about it; in fact, the television, which right now is filled with bad news, of strikes, shortages, famines, layoffs, and price increases, will become sweet-tempered and placating, and long intervals of classical music will appear on the radio. About this time Mrs. Burridge will realize that the news is being censored as it was during the war.

Mrs. Burridge is not positive about what will happen next; that is, she knows what will happen but she is not positive about the order. She expects it will be the gas and oil: the oil delivery man will simply not turn up at his usual time, and one morning the corner filling station will be closed. Just that, no explanations, because of course they — she does not know who "they" are, but she has always believed in their existence — they do not want people to panic. They are trying to keep things looking normal, possibly they have already started on this program and that is in fact why things still do look normal. Luckily she and Frank have the diesel fuel tank in the shed, it is three-quarters full, and they don't use the filling station anyway, they have their own gas pump. She has Frank bring in the old wood stove, the one they stored under the barn when they had the furnace and the electricity put in, and for once she blesses Frank's habit of putting things off. She was after him for years to take that stove to the dump. He cuts down the dead elms, finally, and they burn them in the stove.

The telephone wires are blown down in a storm and no one comes to fix them; or this is what Mrs. Burridge deduces. At any rate, the phone goes dead. Mrs. Burridge doesn't particularly mind, she never liked using the phone much anyway, but it does make her feel cut off.

About now men begin to appear on the back road, the gravel road that goes past the gate, walking usually by themselves, sometimes in pairs. They seem to be heading north. Most of them are young, in their twenties, Mrs. Burridge would guess. They are not dressed like the men around here. It's been so long since she has seen anyone *walking* along this road that she becomes alarmed. She begins leaving the dogs off their chains, she has kept them chained at night ever since one of them bit a Jehovah's Witness early one Sunday morning. Mrs. Burridge doesn't hold with the Witnesses — she is United — but she respects their perseverance, at least they have the courage of their convictions which is more than you can say for some members of her own church, and she always buys a *Watchtower*. Maybe they have been right all along.

It is about this time too that she takes one of the guns, she thinks it will be the shotgun as she will have a better chance of hitting something, and hides it, along with the shells, under a piece of roofing behind the barn. She does not tell Frank; he will have the twenty-two. She has already picked out the spot.

They do not want to waste the little gasoline they still have left in the pump, so they do not make unnecessary trips. They begin to eat the chickens, which Mrs. Burridge does not look forward to. She hates cleaning and plucking them, and the angriest she ever got at Frank was the time he and Henry Clarke decided to go into turkey farming. They did it too, despite all she had to say against it, and she had to cope with the turkeys escaping and scratching in the garden and impossible to catch, in her opinion they were the stupidest birds in God's creation, and she had to clean and pluck a turkey a week until luckily the blackhead wiped out a third of the flock, which was enough to discourage them, they sold off the rest at a loss. It was the only time she was actually glad to see Frank lose money on one of his ventures.

Mrs. Burridge will feel things are getting serious on the day the electricity goes off and does not come back on. She knows, with a kind of fatalism, that this will happen in November, when the freezer is full of the vegetables but before it is cold enough to keep the packages frozen outside. She stands and looks at the Pliofilm bags of beans and corn and spinach and carrots, melting and sodden, and thinks, Why couldn't they have waited till spring? It is the waste, of food and also of her hard work, that aggravates her the most. She salvages what she can. During the Depression, she remembers, they used to say those on farms were better off than those in the city, because at least they had food; if you could keep the farm, that is; but she is no longer sure this is true. She feels beleaguered, isolated, like someone shut up inside a fortress, though no one has bothered them, in fact no one has passed their way for days, not even the solitary walking men.

With the electricity off they can no longer get the television. The radio stations, when they broadcast at all, give out nothing but soothing music, which Mrs. Burridge does not find soothing in the least.

One morning she goes to the back door and looks out and there are the columns of smoke, right where she's been expecting to see them, off to the south. She calls Frank and they stand watching. The smoke is thick and black, oily, as though something has exploded. She does not know what Frank is thinking; she herself is wondering about the children. She has had no news of them in weeks, but how could she? They stopped delivering mail some time now.

Fifteen minutes later, Henry Clarke drives into the yard in his half-ton truck. This is very unusual as no one has been driving anywhere lately. There is another man with him, and Mrs. Burridge identifies him as the man three farms up who moved in four or five years ago. Frank goes out and talks with them, and they drive over to the gas pump and start pumping the rest of the precious gas into the truck. Frank comes back to the house. He tells her there's a little trouble down the road, they are going along to see about it and she isn't to worry. He goes into the back room, comes out with the twenty-two, asks her where the shotgun is. She says she doesn't know. He searches for it, fruitlessly — she can hear him swearing, he does not swear in her presence — until he gives up. He comes out, kisses her goodbye, which is unusual too, and says he'll be back in a couple of hours. She watches the three of them drive off in Henry Clarke's truck, towards the smoke, she knows he will not come back. She supposes she ought to feel more emotional about it, but she is well prepared, she has been saying goodbye to him silently for years.

She re-enters the house and closes the door. She is fifty-one, her feet hurt, and she does not know where she can go, but she realizes she cannot stay here. There will now be a lot of hungry people, those that can make it this far out of the cities will be young and tough, her house is a beacon, signalling warmth and food. It will be fought over, but not by her.

She goes upstairs, searches in the cupboard, and puts on her heavy slacks and her two thickest sweaters. Downstairs she gathers up all the food that will be light enough for her to carry: raisins, cooking chocolate, dried prunes and apricots, half a loaf of bread, some milk powder which she puts into a quart freezer bag, a piece of cheese. Then she unearths the shotgun from behind the barn. She thinks briefly of killing the livestock, the chickens, the heifers, and the pig, so no one will do it who does not know the right way; but she herself does not know the right way, she has never killed anything in her life, Frank always did it, she contents herself with opening the henhouse door and the gate into the back field. She hopes the animals will run away but she knows they probably will not.

She takes one last look around the house. As an afterthought, she adds her toothbrush to the bundle: she does not like the feel of unbrushed teeth. She does not go down into the cellar but she has an image of her carefully sealed bottles and jars, red and yellow and purple, shattered on the floor, in a sticky puddle that looks like blood. Those who come will be wasteful, what they cannot eat themselves they will destroy. She thinks about setting fire to the house herself, before anyone else can do it.

Mrs. Burridge sits at her kitchen table. On the back of her calendar page, it's for a Monday, she has written *Oatmeal*, in her evenly spaced public-school handwriting that always got a star and has not changed very much since then. The dogs are a problem. After some thought she unchains them, but she does not let them past the gate: at a crucial moment they might give her away. She walks north in her heavy boots, carrying her parka because it is not yet cold enough to put it on, and her package of food and the shotgun which she has taken care to load. She passes the cemetery where her father and mother and her grandmother and grandfather are buried; the church used to be there but it burned down sixteen years ago and was rebuilt closer to the highway. Frank's people are in the other cemetery, his go back to the great-grandfather but they are Anglican, not that he kept it up. There is no one else on the road; she feels a little foolish. What if she is wrong and Frank comes back after all, what if nothing, really, is the matter? *Shortening*, she writes. She intends to make a lemon meringue pie for Sunday, when two of the children are coming up from the city for dinner.

It is almost evening and Mrs. Burridge is tired. She is in a part of the country she cannot remember, though she has stayed on the same road and it is a road she knows well; she has driven along it many times with Frank. But walking is not the same as driving. On one side there is a field, no buildings, on the other a woodlot; a stream flows through a culvert under the road. Mrs. Burridge kneels down to drink: the water is ice-cold and tastes of iron. Later there will be a frost, she can feel it. She puts on her parka and her gloves, and turns into the forest where she will not be seen. There she will eat some raisins and cheese and try to rest, waiting for the moon to rise so she can continue walking. It is now quite dark. She smells earth, wood, rotting leaves.

Suddenly her eye is caught by a flicker of red, and before she can turn back — how can this happen so quickly? — it takes shape, it is a small fire, off to the right, and two men are crouching near it. They have seen her, too: one of them rises and comes towards her. His teeth bare, he is smiling; he thinks she will be easy, an old woman. He says something but she cannot imagine what it is, she does not know how people dressed like that would talk.

They have spotted her gun, their eyes have fastened on it, they want it. Mrs. Burridge knows what she must do. She must wait until they are close enough and then she must raise the gun and shoot them, using one barrel for each, aiming at the faces. Otherwise they will kill her, she has no doubt about that. She will have to be fast, which is too bad because her hands feel thick and wooden; she is afraid, she does not want the loud noise or the burst of red that will follow, she has never killed anything in her life. She has no pictures beyond this point. You never know how you will act in a thing like that until it actually happens.

Mrs. Burridge looks at the kitchen clock. On her list she writes *Cheese*, they are eating more cheese now than they used to because of the price of meat. She gets up and goes to the kitchen door.

[1982]

BOBBIE ANN MASON (b. 1942) grew up on a farm outside Mayfield, Kentucky. As a child she loved to read, and her parents always made sure she had books, mostly popular fiction about the Bobbsey Twins and the Nancy Drew mysteries. After she majored in journalism at the University of Kentucky, she took several jobs in New York City with movie magazines, writing articles about Annette Funicello, Troy Donahue, Fabian, and other teen stars. Next she went to graduate school at the University of Connecticut, where she received her Ph.D. in literature with a disseration on Vladimir Nabokov's Ada. This study was later published in paperback as Nabokov's Garden.

After graduate school, Mason wrote a book called The Girl Sleuth about her favorite childhood reading; then, in her late thirties, she started writing short stories. In 1980 The New Yorker published her first story. "It took me a long time to discover my material," she says. "It wasn't a matter of developing writing skills, it was a matter of knowing how to see things. And it took me a very long time to grow up. I'd been writing for a long time, but was never able to see what there was to write about. And I always aspired to things away from home, so it took me a long time to look back at home and realize that that's where the center of my thoughts was."

Mason's first collection, Shiloh and Other Stories, won the 1982 Hemingway Foundation Award. In 1985, reviewers of her novel In Country compared her with Ann Beattie and other "writers of her generation who chronicle aimless lives in prose that tends to be as laconic and stripped down as her characters' emotional range." Mason doesn't regard herself as a feminist writer, despite the heroine in her often reprinted story "Shiloh." Mason feels that she writes about ordinary people "who've got a toe-hold in the middle class. They're people who are from the lower class and who've moved up in the world a little.... The people I write about — it seems they either want to get away from home, get away from town, see the world, or they want to stay home, and they're afraid to leave, so they accommodate — or it wouldn't occur to them to leave. But I'm interested in that tension between longing to stay and longing to go. And I think that world sets up a lot of frustrations and there are a lot of limits set for people." (See Mason's Interview on page 1345.)

Bobbie Ann Mason

∽∾

SHILOH

Leroy Moffitt's wife, Norma Jean, is working on her pectorals. She lifts three-pound dumbbells to warm up, then progresses to a twenty-pound barbell. Standing with her legs apart, she reminds Leroy of Wonder Woman.

"I'd give anything if I could just get these muscles to where they're real hard," says Norma Jean. "Feel this arm. It's not as hard as the other one."

"That's 'cause you're right-handed," says Leroy, dodging as she swings the barbell in an arc.

"Do you think so?"

"Sure."

Leroy is a truckdriver. He injured his leg in a highway accident four months ago, and his physical therapy, which involves weights and a pulley, prompted Norma Jean to try building herself up. Now she is attending a body-building class. Leroy has been collecting temporary disability since his tractor-trailer jackknifed in Missouri, badly twisting his left leg in its socket. He has a steel pin in his hip. He will probably not be able to drive his rig again. It sits in the backyard, like a gigantic bird that has flown home to roost. Leroy has been home in Kentucky for three months, and his leg is almost healed, but the accident frightened him and he does not want to drive any more long hauls. He is not sure what to do next. In the meantime, he makes things from craft kits. He started by building a miniature log cabin from notched Popsicle sticks. He varnished it and placed it on the TV set, where it remains. It reminds him of a rustic Nativity scene. Then he tried string art (sailing ships on black velvet), a macramé owl kit, a snap-together B–17 Flying Fortress, and a lamp made out of a model truck, with a light fixture screwed on the top of the cab. At first the kits were diversions, something to kill time, but now he is thinking about building a full-scale log house from a kit. It would be considerably cheaper than building a regular house, and besides, Leroy has grown to appreciate how things are put together. He has begun to realize that in all the years he was on the road he never took time to examine anything. He was always flying past scenery.

"They won't let you build a log cabin in any of the new subdivisions," Norma Jean tells him.

"They will if I tell them it's for you," he says, teasing her. Ever since they were married, he has promised Norma Jean he would build her a new home one day. They have always rented, and the house they live in is small and nondescript. It does not even feel like a home, Leroy realizes now.

Norma Jean works at the Rexall drugstore, and she has acquired an amazing amount of information about cosmetics. When she explains to Leroy the three stages of complexion care, involving creams, toners, and moisturizers, he thinks happily of other petroleum products — axle grease, diesel fuel. This is a connection between him and Norma Jean. Since he has been home, he has felt unusually tender about his wife and guilty over his long absences. But he can't tell what she feels about him. Norma Jean has never complained about his traveling; she has never made hurt remarks, like calling his truck a "widow-maker." He is reasonably certain she has been faithful to him, but he wishes she would celebrate his permanent homecoming more happily. Norma Jean is often startled to find Leroy at home, and he thinks she seems a little disappointed about it. Perhaps he reminds her too much of the early days of their marriage, before he went on the road. They had a child who died as an infant, years ago. They never speak about their memories of Randy, which have almost faded, but now that Leroy is home all the time, they sometimes feel awkward around each other, and Leroy wonders if one of them should mention the child. He has the feeling that they are waking up out of a dream together — that they must create a new marriage, start afresh. They are lucky they are still married. Leroy has read that for most people losing a child destroys the marriage — or else he heard this on *Donahue*. He can't always remember where he learns things anymore.

At Christmas, Leroy bought an electric organ for Norma Jean. She used to play the piano when she was in high school. "It don't leave you," she told him once. "It's like riding a bicycle."

The new instrument had so many keys and buttons that she was bewildered by it at first. She touched the keys tentatively, pushed some buttons, then pecked out "Chopsticks." It came out in an amplified fox-trot rhythm, with marimba sounds.

"It's an orchestra!" she cried.

The organ had a pecan-look finish and eighteen preset chords, with optional flute, violin, trumpet, clarinet, and banjo accompaniments. Norma Jean mastered the organ almost immediately. At first she played Christmas songs. Then she bought *The Sixties Songbook* and learned every tune in it, adding variations to each with the rows of brightly colored buttons.

"I didn't like these old songs back then," she said. "But I have this crazy feeling I missed something."

"You didn't miss a thing," said Leroy.

Leroy likes to lie on the couch and smoke a joint and listen to Norma Jean play "Can't Take My Eyes Off You" and "I'll Be Back." He is back again. After fifteen years on the road, he is finally settling down with the woman he loves. She is still pretty. Her skin is flawless. Her frosted curls resemble pencil trimmings.

Now that Leroy has come home to stay, he notices how much the town has changed. Subdivisions are spreading across western Kentucky like an oil slick. The sign at the edge of town says "Pop: 11,500" — only seven hundred more than it said twenty years before. Leroy can't figure out who is living in all the new houses. The farmers who used to gather around the courthouse square on Saturday afternoons to play checkers and spit tobacco juice have gone. It has been years since Leroy has thought about the farmers, and they have disappeared without his noticing.

Leroy meets a kid named Stevie Hamilton in the parking lot at the new shopping center. While they pretend to be strangers meeting over a stalled car, Stevie tosses an ounce of marijuana under the front seat of Leroy's car. Stevie is wearing orange jogging shoes and a T-shirt that says CHATTAHOOCHEE SUPER-RAT. His father is a prominent doctor who lives in one of the expensive subdivisions in a new white-columned brick house that looks like a funeral parlor. In the phone book under his name there is a separate number, with the listing "Teenagers."

"Where do you get this stuff?" asks Leroy. "From your pappy?"

"That's for me to know and you to find out," Stevie says. He is slit-eyed and skinny.

"What else you got?"

"What you interested in?"

"Nothing special. Just wondered."

Leroy used to take speed on the road. Now he has to go slowly. He needs to be mellow. He leans back against the car and says, "I'm aiming to build me a log house, soon as I get time. My wife, though, I don't think she likes the idea."

"Well, let me know when you want me again," Stevie says. He has a cigarette in his cupped palm, as though sheltering it from the wind. He takes a long drag, then stomps it on the asphalt and slouches away.

Stevie's father was two years ahead of Leroy in high school. Leroy is thirty-four. He married Norma Jean when they were both eighteen, and their child Randy was born a few months later, but he died at the age of four months and three days. He would be about Stevie's age now. Norma Jean and Leroy were at the drive-in, watching a double feature (*Dr. Strangelove* and *Lover Come Back*), and the baby was sleeping in the back seat. When the first movie ended, the baby was dead. It was the sudden infant death syndrome. Leroy remembers handing Randy to a nurse at the emergency room, as though he were offering her a large doll as a present. A dead baby feels like a sack of flour. "It just happens sometimes," said the doctor, in what Leroy always recalls as a nonchalant tone. Leroy can hardly remember the child anymore, but he still sees vividly a scene from *Dr. Strangelove* in which the President of the United States was talking in a folksy voice on the hot line to the Soviet premier about the bomber accidentally headed toward Russia. He was in the War Room, and the world map was lit up. Leroy remembers Norma Jean standing catatonically beside him in the hospital and himself thinking: Who is this strange girl? He had forgotten who she was. Now scientists are saying that crib death is caused by a virus. Nobody knows anything, Leroy thinks. The answers are always changing.

When Leroy gets home from the shopping center, Norma Jean's mother, Mabel Beasley, is there. Until this year, Leroy has not realized how much time she spends with Norma Jean. When she visits, she inspects the closets and then the plants, informing Norma Jean when a plant is droopy or yellow. Mabel calls the plants "flowers," although there are never any blooms. She always notices if Norma Jean's laundry is piling up. Mabel is a short, overweight woman whose tight, brown-dyed curls look more like a wig than the actual wig she sometimes wears. Today she has brought Norma Jean an off-white dust ruffle she made for the bed; Mabel works in a custom-upholstery shop.

"This is the tenth one I made this year," Mabel says. "I got started and couldn't stop."

"It's real pretty," says Norma Jean.

"Now we can hide things under the bed," says Leroy, who gets along with his mother-in-law primarily by joking with her. Mabel has never really forgiven him for disgracing her by getting Norma Jean pregnant. When the baby died, she said that fate was mocking her.

"What's that thing?" Mabel says to Leroy in a loud voice, pointing to a tangle of yarn on a piece of canvas.

Leroy holds it up for Mabel to see. "It's my needlepoint," he explains. "This is a *Star Trek* pillow cover."

"That's what a woman would do," says Mabel. "Great day in the morning!"

"All the big football players on TV do it," he says.

"Why, Leroy, you're always trying to fool me. I don't believe you for one minute. You don't know what to do with yourself— that's the whole trouble. Sewing!"

"I'm aiming to build us a log house," says Leroy. "Soon as my plans come."

"Like *heck* you are," says Norma Jean. She takes Leroy's needlepoint and shoves it into a drawer. "You have to find a job first. Nobody can afford to build now anyway."

Mabel straightens her girdle and says. "I still think before you get tied down y'all ought to take a little run to Shiloh."

"One of these days, Mama," Norma Jean says impatiently.

Mabel is talking about Shiloh, Tennessee. For the past few years, she has been urging Leroy and Norma Jean to visit the Civil War battleground there. Mabel went there on her honeymoon — the only real trip she ever took. Her husband died of a perforated ulcer when Norma Jean was ten, but

Mabel, who was accepted into the United Daughters of the Confederacy in 1975, is still preoccupied with going back to Shiloh.

"I've been to kingdom come and back in that truck out yonder," Leroy says to Mabel, "but we never yet set foot in that battleground. Ain't that something? How did I miss it?"

"It's not even that far," Mabel says.

After Mabel leaves, Norma Jean reads to Leroy from a list she has made. "Things you could do," she announces. "You could get a job as a guard at Union Carbide, where they'd let you set on a stool. You could get on at the lumberyard. You could do a little carpenter work, if you want to build so bad. You could — "

"I can't do something where I'd have to stand up all day."

"You ought to try standing up all day behind a cosmetics counter. It's amazing that I have strong feet, coming from two parents that never had strong feet at all." At the moment Norma Jean is holding on to the kitchen counter, raising her knees one at a time as she talks. She is wearing two-pound ankle weights.

"Don't worry," says Leroy. "I'll do something."

"You could truck calves to slaughter for somebody. You wouldn't have to drive any big old truck for that."

"I'm going to build you this house," says Leroy. "I want to make you a real home."

"I don't want to live in any log cabin,."

"It's not a cabin. It's a house."

"I don't care. It looks like a cabin."

"You and me together could lift those logs. It's just like lifting weights."

Norma Jean doesn't answer. Under her breath, she is counting. Now she is marching through the kitchen. She is doing goose steps.

Before his accident, when Leroy came home he used to stay in the house with Norma Jean, watching TV in bed and playing cards. She would cook fried chicken, picnic ham, chocolate pie — all his favorites. Now he is home alone much of the time. In the mornings, Norma Jean disappears, leaving a cooling place in the bed. She eats a cereal called Body Buddies, and she leaves the bowl on the table, with the soggy tan balls floating in a milk puddle. He sees things about Norma Jean that he never realized before. When she chops onions, she stares off into a corner, as if she can't bear to look. She puts on her house slippers almost precisely at nine o'clock every evening and nudges her jogging shoes under the couch. She saves bread heels for the birds. Leroy watches the birds at the feeder. He notices the peculiar way goldfinches fly past the window. They close their wings, then fall, then spread their wings to catch and lift themselves. He wonders if they close their eyes when they fall. Norma Jean closes her eyes when they are in bed. She wants the lights turned out. Even then, he is sure she closes her eyes.

He goes for long drives around town. He tends to drive a car rather carelessly. Power steering and an automatic shift make a car feel so small and inconsequential that his body is hardly involved in the driving process. His injured leg stretches out comfortably. Once or twice he has almost hit something, but even the prospect of an accident seems minor in a car. He cruises the new subdivisions, feeling like a criminal rehearsing for a robbery. Norma Jean is probably right about a log house being inappropriate here in the new subdivisions. All the houses look grand and complicated. They depress him.

One day when Leroy comes home from a drive he finds Norma Jean in tears. She is in the kitchen making a potato and mushroom-soup casserole, with grated-cheese topping. She is crying because her mother caught her smoking.

"I didn't hear her coming. I was standing here puffing away pretty as you please," Norma Jean says, wiping her eyes.

"I knew it would happen sooner or later," says Leroy, putting his arm around her.

"She don't know the meaning of the word 'knock,' " says Norma Jean. "It's a wonder she hadn't caught me years ago."

"Think of it this way," Leroy says. "What if she caught me with a joint?"

"You better not let her!" Norma Jean shrieks. "I'm warning you, Leroy Moffitt!"

"I'm just kidding. Here, play me a tune. That'll help you relax."

Norma Jean puts the casserole in the oven and sets the timer. Then she plays a ragtime tune, with horns and banjo, as Leroy lights up a joint and lies on the couch, laughing to himself about Mabel's catching him at it. He thinks of Stevie Hamilton — a doctor's son pushing grass. Everything is funny. The whole town seems crazy and small. He is reminded of Virgil Mathis, a boastful policeman Leroy used to shoot pool with. Virgil recently led a drug bust in a back room at a bowling alley, where he seized ten thousand dollars' worth of marijuana. The newspaper had a picture of him holding up the bags of grass and grinning widely. Right now, Leroy can imagine Virgil breaking down the door and arresting him with a lungful of smoke. Virgil would probably have been alerted to the scene because of all the racket Norma Jean is making. Now she sounds like a hard-rock band. Norma Jean is terrific. When she switches to a Latin-rhythm version of "Sunshine Superman," Leroy hums along. Norma Jean's foot goes up and down, up and down.

"Well, what do you think?" Leroy says, when Norma Jean pauses to search through her music.

"What do I think about what?"

His mind had gone blank. Then he says, "I'll sell my rig and build us a house." That wasn't what he wanted to say. He wanted to know what she thought — what she *really* thought — about them.

"Don't start in on that again," says Norma Jean. She begins playing "Who'll Be the Next in Line?"

Leroy used to tell hitchhikers his whole life story — about his travels, his hometown, the baby. He would end with a question: "Well, what do you think?" It was just a rhetorical question. In time, he had the feeling that he'd been telling the same story over and over to the same hitchhikers. He quit talking to hitchhikers when he realized how his voice sounded — whining and self-pitying, like some teenage-tragedy song. Now Leroy has the sudden impulse to tell Norma Jean about himself, as if he had just met her. They have known each other so long they have forgotten a lot about each other. They could become reacquainted. But when the oven timer goes off and she runs to the kitchen, he forgets why he wants to do this.

The next day, Mabel drops by. It is Saturday and Norma Jean is cleaning. Leroy is studying the plans of his log house, which have finally come in the mail. He has them spread out on the table — big sheets of stiff blue paper, with diagrams and numbers printed in white. While Norma Jean runs the vacuum, Mabel drinks coffee. She sets her coffee cup on a blueprint.

"I'm just waiting for time to pass," she says to Leroy, drumming her fingers on the table.

As soon as Norma Jean switches off the vacuum, Mabel says in a loud voice, "Did you hear about the datsun dog that killed the baby?"

Norma Jean says, "The word is 'dachshund.'"

"They put the dog on trial. It chewed the baby's legs off. The mother was in the next room all the time." She raises her voice. "They thought it was neglect."

Norma Jean is holding her ears. Leroy manages to open the refrigerator and get some Diet Pepsi to offer Mabel. Mabel still has some coffee and she waves away the Pepsi.

"Datsuns are like that," Mabel says. "They're jealous dogs. They'll tear a place to pieces if you don't keep an eye on them."

"You better watch out what you're saying, Mabel," says Leroy.

"Well, facts is facts."

Leroy looks out the window at his rig. It is like a huge piece of furniture gathering dust in the backyard. Pretty soon it will be an antique. He hears the vacuum cleaner. Norma Jean seems to be cleaning the living room rug again.

Later, she says to Leroy, "She just said that about the baby because she caught me smoking. She's trying to pay me back."

"What are you talking about?" Leroy says, nervously shuffling blueprints.

"You know good and well," Norma Jean says. She is sitting in a kitchen chair with her feet up and her arms wrapped around her knees. She looks small and helpless. She says, "The very idea, her bringing up a subject like that! Saying it was neglect."

"She didn't mean that," Leroy says.

"She might not have *thought* she meant it. She always says things like that. You don't know how she goes on."

"But she didn't really mean it. She was just talking."

Leroy opens a king-sized bottle of beer and pours it into two glasses, dividing it carefully. He hands a glass to Norma Jean and she takes it from him mechanically. For a long time, they sit by the kitchen window watching the birds at the feeder.

Something is happening. Norma Jean is going to night school. She has graduated from her six-week body-building course and now she is taking an adult-education course in composition at Paducah Community College. She spends her evenings outlining paragraphs.

"First you have a topic sentence," she explains to Leroy. "Then you divide it up. Your secondary topic has to be connected to your primary topic."

To Leroy, this sounds intimidating. "I never was any good in English," he says.

"It makes a lot of sense."

"What are you doing this for, anyhow?"

She shrugs. "It's something to do." She stands up and lifts her dumbbells a few times.

"Driving a rig, nobody cared about my English."

"I'm not criticizing your English."

Norma Jean used to say, "If I lose ten minutes' sleep, I just drag all day." Now she stays up late, writing compositions. She got a B on her first paper —a how-to theme on soup-based casseroles. Recently Norma Jean has been cooking unusual foods — tacos, lasagna, Bombay chicken. She doesn't play the organ anymore, though her second paper was called "Why Music Is Important to Me." She sits at the kitchen table, concentrating on her outlines, while Leroy plays with his log house plans, practicing with a set of Lincoln Logs. The thought of getting a truckload of notched, numbered logs scares him, and he wants to be prepared. As he and Norma Jean work together at the kitchen table, Leroy has the hopeful thought that they are sharing something, but he knows he is a fool to think this. Norma Jean is miles away. He knows he is going to lose her. Like Mabel, he is just waiting for time to pass.

One day, Mabel is there before Norma Jean gets home from work, and Leroy finds himself confiding in her. Mabel, he realizes, must know Norma Jean better than he does.

"I don't know what's got into that girl," Mabel says. "She used to go to bed with the chickens. Now you say she's up all hours. Plus her a-smoking. I like to died."

"I want to make her this beautiful home," Leroy says, indicating the Lincoln Logs. "I think she even wants it. Maybe she was happier with me gone."

"She don't know what to make of you, coming home like this."

"Is that it?"

Mabel takes the roof off his Lincoln Log cabin. "You couldn't get *me* in a log cabin," she says. "I was raised in one. It's no picnic, let me tell you."

"They're different now," says Leroy.

"I tell you what," Mabel says, smiling oddly at Leroy.

"What?"

"Take her down to Shiloh. Y'all need to get out together, stir a little. Her brain's all balled up over them books."

Leroy can see traces of Norma Jean's features in her mother's face. Mabel's worn face has the texture of crinkled cotton, but suddenly she looks pretty. It occurs to Leroy that Mabel has been hinting all along that she wants them to take her with them to Shiloh.

"Let's all go to Shiloh," he says. "You and me and her. Come Sunday."

Mabel throws up her hand in protest. "Oh, no, not me. Young folks want to be by themselves."

When Norma Jean comes in with groceries, Leroy says excitedly, "Your mama here's been dying to go to Shiloh for thirty-five years. It's about time we went, don't you think?"

"I'm not going to butt in on anybody's second honeymoon," Mabel says.

"Who's going on a honeymoon, for Christ's sake?" Norma Jean says loudly.

"I never raised no daughter of mine to talk that-a-way," Mabel says.

"You ain't seen nothing yet," says Norma Jean. She starts putting away boxes and cans, slamming cabinet doors.

"There's a log cabin at Shiloh," Mabel says. "It was there during the battle. There's bullet holes in it."

"When are you going to *shut up* about Shiloh, Mama?" asks Norma Jean.

"I always thought Shiloh was the prettiest place, so full of history," Mabel goes on. "I just hoped y'all could see it once before I die, so you could tell me about it." Later, she whispers to Leroy, "You do what I said. A little change is what she needs."

"Your name means 'the king,' " Norma Jean says to Leroy that evening. He is trying to get her to go to Shiloh, and she is reading a book about another century.

"Well, I reckon I ought to be right proud."

"I guess so."

"Am I still king around here?"

Norma Jean flexes her biceps and feels them for hardness. "I'm not fooling around with anybody, if that's what you mean," she says.

"Would you tell me if you were?"

"I don't know."

"What does *your* name mean?"

"It was Marilyn Monroe's real name."

"No kidding!"

"Norma comes from the Normans. They were invaders," she says. She closes her book and looks hard at Leroy. "I'll go to Shiloh with you if you'll stop staring at me."

On Sunday, Norma Jean packs a picnic and they go to Shiloh. To Leroy's relief, Mabel says she does not want to come with them. Norma Jean drives, and Leroy, sitting beside her, feels like some boring hitchhiker she has picked up. He tries some conversation, but she answers him in monosyllables. At Shiloh, she drives aimlessly through the park, past bluffs and trails and steep ravines. Shiloh is an immense place, and Leroy cannot see it as a battleground. It is not what he expected. He thought it would look like a golf course. Monuments are everywhere, showing through the thick clusters of trees. Norma Jean passes the log cabin Mabel mentioned. It is surrounded by tourists looking for bullet holes.

"That's not the kind of log house I've got in mind," says Leroy apologetically.

"I know *that*."

"This is a pretty place. Your mama was right."

"It's O.K." says Norma Jean. "Well, we've seen it. I hope she's satisfied."

They burst out laughing together.

At the park museum, a movie on Shiloh is shown every half hour, but they decide that they don't want to see it. They buy a souvenir Confederate flag for Mabel, and then they find a picnic spot near the cemetery. Norma Jean has brought a picnic cooler, with pimiento sandwiches, soft drinks, and Yodels. Leroy eats a sandwich and then smokes a joint, hiding it behind the picnic cooler. Norma Jean has quit smoking altogether. She is picking cake crumbs from the cellophane wrapper, like a fussy bird.

Leroy says, "So the boys in gray ended up in Corinth. The Union soldiers zapped 'em finally. April 7, 1862."

They both know that he doesn't know any history. He is just talking about some of the historical plaques they have read. He feels awkward, like a boy on a date with an older girl. They are still just making conversation.

"Corinth is where Mama eloped to," says Norma Jean.

They sit in silence and stare at the cemetery for the Union dead and, beyond, at a tall cluster of trees. Campers are parked nearby, bumper to bumper, and small children in bright clothing are cavorting and squealing.

Norma Jean wads up the cake wrapper and squeezes it tightly in her hand. Without looking at Leroy, she says, "I want to leave you."

Leroy takes a bottle of Coke out of the cooler and flips off the cap. He holds the bottle poised near his mouth but cannot remember to take a drink. Finally he says, "No, you don't."

"Yes, I do."

"I won't let you."

"You can't stop me."

"Don't do me that way."

Leroy knows Norma Jean will have her own way. "Didn't I promise to be home from now on?" he says.

"In some ways, a woman prefers a man who wanders," says Norma Jean. "That sounds crazy, I know."

"You're not crazy."

Leroy remembers to drink from his Coke. Then he says, "Yes, you *are* crazy. You and me could start all over again. Right back at the beginning."

"We *have* started all over again," says Norma Jean. "And this is how it turned out."

"What did I do wrong?"

"Nothing."

"Is this one of those women's lib things?" Leroy asks.

"Don't be funny."

The cemetery, a green slope dotted with white markers, looks like a subdivision site. Leroy is trying to comprehend that his marriage is breaking up, but for some reason he is wondering about white slabs in a graveyard.

"Everything was fine till Mama caught me smoking," says Norma Jean, standing up. "That set something off."

"What are you talking about?"

"She won't leave me alone — *you* won't leave me alone." Norma Jean seems to be crying, but she is looking away from him. "I feel eighteen again. I can't face that all over again." She starts walking away. "No, it *wasn't* fine. I don't know what I'm saying. Forget it."

Leroy takes a lungful of smoke and closes his eyes as Norma Jean's words sink in. He tries to focus on the fact that thirty-five hundred soldiers died on the grounds around him. He can only think of that war as a board game with plastic soldiers. Leroy almost smiles, as he compares the Confederates' daring attack on the Union camps and Virgil Mathis's raid on the bowling alley. General Grant, drunk and furious, shoved the southerners back to Corinth, where Mabel and Jet Beasley were married years later, when Mabel was still thin and good-looking. The next day, Mabel and Jet visited the battleground, and then Norma Jean was born, and then she married Leroy and they had a baby, which they lost, and now Leroy and Norma Jean are here at the same battleground. Leroy knows he is leaving out a lot. He is leaving out the insides of history. History was always just names and dates to him. It occurs to him that building a house out of logs is similarly empty — too simple. And the real inner workings of a marriage, like most of history, have escaped him. Now he sees that building a log house is the dumbest idea he could have had. It was clumsy of him to think Norma Jean would want a log house. It was a crazy idea. He'll have to think of something else, quickly. He will wad the blueprints into tight balls and fling them into the lake. Then he'll get moving again. He opens his eyes. Norma Jean has moved away and is walking through the cemetery, following a serpentine brick path.

Leroy gets up to follow his wife, but his good leg is asleep and his bad leg still hurts him. Norma Jean is far away, walking rapidly toward the bluff by the river, and he tries to hobble toward her. Some children run past him, screaming noisily. Norma Jean has reached the bluff, and she is looking out over the Tennessee River. Now she turns toward Leroy and waves her arms. Is she beckoning to him? She seems to be doing an exercise for her chest muscles. The sky is unusually pale — the color of the dust ruffle Mabel made for their bed.

[1982]

ALICE WALKER (b. 1944) was the eighth and youngest child of Willie Lee and Minnie Lou Grant Walker, sharecroppers in Eatonton, Georgia. Walker did well in school, encouraged by her teachers and her mother, who gave her the most emotional support in her early life. For two years she attended Spelman College in Atlanta, the oldest college for black women in America. Then she studied at Sarah Lawrence College in New York, where she began her writing career by publishing a book of poetry, Once (1968). Since that time Walker has published three more collections of poetry, three novels, two volumes of short stories, and many essays. Her best-known novel, The Color Purple (1982), won the American Book Award and the Pulitzer Prize and has been made into a motion picture.

Walker's books show her commitment to the idea of radical social change. She was active in the civil rights movement in Mississippi, where she met and married a civil rights lawyer from whom she separated after the birth of their daughter. In confronting the painful struggle of black people's history, Walker asserts that the creativity of black women, the extent to which they are permitted to express themselves, is a measure of the health of the entire American society. She calls herself a "womanist," her term for a black feminist. In her definition, "womanism" is preferable to "feminism" because, as she says,

> Part of our tradition as black women is that we are universalists. Black children, yellow children, red children, brown children, that is the black woman's normal, day-to-day relationship. In my family alone, we are about four different colors. When a black woman looks at the world, it is so different . . . when I look at the people in Iran they look like kinfolk. When I look at the people in Cuba, they look like my uncles and nieces.

Walker credits many writers for influencing her prose style in her two story collections. Virginia Woolf, Zora Neale Hurston, and Gabriel García Márquez seem to Walker to be "like musicians; at one with their cultures and their historical subconscious." Her two books of stories, published eight years apart, show a clear progression of theme. The women of In Love and Trouble (1973), like the title character in "Roselily," struggle against social injustice almost in spite of themselves, while the heroines of You Can't Keep a Good Woman Down (1981) consciously challenge conventions. Walker says that in her opinion, "Writing really helps you heal yourself. I think if you write long enough, you will be a healthy person. That is, if you write what you need to write, as opposed to what will make money, or what will make fame."

Alice Walker

ဢဢ

ROSELILY

Dearly Beloved,

She dreams; dragging herself across the world. A small girl in her mother's white robe and veil, knee raised waist high through a bowl of quicksand soup. The man who stands beside her is against this standing on the front porch of her house, being married to the sound of cars whizzing by on highway 61.

we are gathered here

Like cotton to be weighed. Her fingers at the last minute busily removing dry leaves and twigs. Aware it is a superficial sweep. She knows he blames Mississippi for the respectful way the men turn their heads up in the yard, the women stand waiting and knowledgeable, their children held from mischief by teachings from the wrong God. He glares beyond them to the occupants of the cars, white faces glued to promises beyond a country wedding, noses thrust forward like dogs on a track. For him they usurp the wedding.

in the sight of God

Yes, open house. That is what country black folks like. She dreams she does not already have three children. A squeeze around the flowers in her hands chokes off three and four and five years of breath. Instantly she is ashamed and frightened in her superstition. She looks for the first time at the preacher, forces humility into her eyes, as if she believes he is, in fact, a man of God. She can imagine God, a small black boy, timidly pulling the preacher's coattail.

to join this man and this woman

She thinks of ropes, chains, handcuffs, his religion. His place of worship. Where she will be required to sit apart with covered head. In Chicago, a

1170

word she hears when thinking of smoke, from his description of what a cinder was, which they never had in Panther Burn. She sees hovering over the heads of the clean neighbors in her front yard black specks falling, clinging, from the sky. But in Chicago. Respect, a chance to build. Her children at last from underneath the detrimental wheel. A chance to be on top. What a relief, she thinks. What a vision, a view, from up so high.

in holy matrimony.

Her fourth child she gave away to the child's father who had some money. Certainly a good job. Had gone to Harvard. Was a good man but weak because good language meant so much to him he could not live with Roselily. Could not abide TV in the living room, five beds in three rooms, no Bach except from four to six on Sunday afternoons. No chess at all. She does not forget to worry about her son among his father's people. She wonders if the New England climate will agree with him. If he will ever come down to Mississippi, as his father did, to try to right the country's wrongs. She wonders if he will be stronger than his father. His father cried off and on throughout her pregnancy. Went to skin and bones. Suffered nightmares, retching and falling out of bed. Tried to kill himself. Later told his wife he found the right baby through friends. Vouched for, the sterling qualities that would make up his character.

     It is not her nature to blame. Still, she is not entirely thankful. She supposes New England, the North, to be quite different from what she knows. It seems right somehow to her that people who move there to live return home completely changed. She thinks of the air, the smoke, the cinders. Imagines cinders big as hailstones; heavy, weighing on the people. Wonders how this pressure finds it way into the veins, roping the springs of laughter.

If there's anybody here that knows a reason why

But of course they know no reason why beyond what they daily have come to know. She thinks of the man who will be her husband, feels shut away from him because of the stiff severity of his plain black suit. His religion. A lifetime of black and white. Of veils. Covered head. It is as if her children are already gone from her. Not dead, but exalted on a pedestal, a stalk that has no roots. She wonders how to make new roots. It is beyond her. She wonders what one does with memories in a brand-new life. This had seemed easy, until she thought of it. "The reasons why . . . the people who" . . . she thinks, and does not wonder where the thought is from.

these two should not be joined

She thinks of her mother, who is dead. Dead, but still her mother. Joined. This is confusing. Of her father. A gray old man who sold wild mink, rabbit, fox skins to Sears, Roebuck. He stands in the yard, like a man waiting for a train. Her young sisters stand behind her in smooth green dresses, with flowers in their hands and hair. They giggle, she feels, at the absurdity of the wedding. They are ready for something new. She thinks the man beside her should marry one of them. She feels old. Yoked. An arm seems to reach out from behind her and snatch her backward. She thinks of cemeteries and the long sleep of grandparents mingling in the dirt. She believes that she believes in ghosts. In the soil giving back what it takes.

together,

In the city. He sees her in a new way. This she knows, and is grateful. But is it new enough? She cannot always be a bride and virgin, wearing robes and veil. Even now her body itches to be free of satin and voile, organdy and lily of the valley. Memories crash against her. Memories of being bare to the sun. She wonders what it will be like. Not to have to go to a job. Not to work in a sewing plant. Not to worry about learning to sew straight seams in workingmen's overalls, jeans, and dress pants. Her place will be in the home, he has said, repeatedly, promising her rest she had prayed for. But now she wonders. When she is rested, what will she do? They will make babies — she thinks practically about her fine brown body, his strong black one. They will be inevitable. Her hands will be full. Full of what? Babies. She is not comforted.

let him speak

She wishes she had asked him to explain more of what he meant. But she was impatient. Impatient to be done with sewing. With doing everything for three children, alone. Impatient to leave the girls she had known since childhood, their children growing up, their husbands hanging around her, already old, seedy. Nothing about them that she wanted, or needed. The fathers of her children driving by, waving, not waving; reminders of times she would just as soon forget. Impatient to see the South Side, where they would live and build and be respectable and respected and free. Her husband would free her. A romantic hush. Proposal. Promises. A new life! Respectable, reclaimed, renewed. Free! In robe and veil.

or forever hold

She does not even know if she loves him. She loves his sobriety. His refusal to sing just because he knows the tune. She loves his pride. His blackness and his gray car. She loves his understanding of her *condition*. She thinks she loves the effort he will make to redo her into what he truly wants. His love of her makes her completely conscious of how unloved she was before. This is something; though it makes her unbearably sad. Melancholy. She blinks her eyes. Remembers she is finally being married, like other girls.

Like other girls, women? Something strains upward behind her eyes. She thinks of the something as a rat trapped, concerned, scurrying to and fro in her head, peering through the windows of her eyes. She wants to live for once. But doesn't know quite what that means. Wonders if she has ever done it. If she ever will. The preacher is odious to her. She wants to strike him out of the way, out of her light, with the back of her hand. It seems to her he has always been standing in front of her, barring her way.

his peace.

The rest she does not hear. She feels a kiss, passionate, rousing, within the general pandemonium. Cars drive up blowing their horns. Firecrackers go off. Dogs come from under the house and begin to yelp and bark. Her husband's hand is like the clasp of an iron gate. People congratulate. Her children press against her. They look with awe and distaste mixed with hope at their new father. He stands curiously apart, in spite of the people crowding about to grasp his free hand. He smiles at them all but his eyes are as if turned inward. He knows they cannot understand that he is not a Christian. He will not explain himself. He feels different, he looks it. The old women thought he was like one of their sons except that he had somehow got away from them. Still a son, not a son. Changed.

She thinks how it will be later in the night in the silvery gray car. How they will spin through the darkness of Mississippi and in the morning be in Chicago, Illinois. She thinks of Lincoln, the president. That is all she knows about the place. She feels ignorant, *wrong*, backward. She presses her worried fingers into his palm. He is standing in front of her. In the crush of well-wishing people, he does not look back.

[1973]

MARK HELPRIN (b. 1947) was born and raised in New York City. He took his B.A. and M.A. degrees at Harvard University and served with the Israeli Army and Air Force in 1972–73. Two years later he published his first book, A Dove of the East and Other Stories (1975). In 1976, Helprin did postgraduate work at Magdalen College, Oxford. The following year he published his first novel, Refiner's Fire (1977). A second book of short stories, Ellis Island and Other Stories, (1980), and a best-selling fantasy novel, Winter's Tale (1983), have also appeared to date. Helprin has received many literary awards, among them the Prix de Rome, the National Jewish Book award, and a citation from the American Academy and Institute of Arts and Letters.

Critics praised the virtuosic range and force of Helprin's imagination in his first two books, but his reputation was established with the publication of Ellis Island and Other Stories. As Seymour Krim wrote, Helprin's

> combination of the realistic and fantastic intertwining of experience, guided by compassion and a prose style as clear and shining as a northern star, gave hope on two levels: it opened up possibilities beyond realism for a transportation of life that could no longer be contained by the literal, and it gave almost therapeutic faith to those disillusioned and wearied by much serious fiction. Helprin was that rare thing: a first-rate technician who was also a sincere standard bearer for a new dawn in humankind's endless effort to lift itself out of suffering and injustice.

"North Light" is a story from Ellis Island and Other Stories. Subtitled "A Recollection in the Present Tense," it is based on Helprin's experience with the Israeli Army and Air Force. He has a great regard for the heroism of these men at war, engaged in what he considers justifiable combat against their enemies in the Syrian Army.

Mark Helprin

৯৯

NORTH LIGHT

A Recollection in the Present Tense

We are being held back. We are poised at a curve in the road on the southern ridge of a small valley. The sun shines from behind, illuminating with flawless light the moves and countermoves of several score tanks below us. For a long time, we have been absorbed in the mystery of matching the puffs of white smoke from tank cannon with the sounds that follow. The columns themselves move silently: only the great roar rising from the battle proves it not to be a dream.

A man next to me is deeply absorbed in sniffing his wrist. "What are you doing?" I ask.

"My wife," he says. "I can still smell her perfume on my wrist, and I taste the taste of her mouth. It's sweet."

We were called up this morning. The war is two days old. Now it is afternoon, and we are being held back — even though our forces below are greatly outnumbered. We are being held back until nightfall, when we will have a better chance on the plain; for it is packed with tanks, and we have only two old half-tracks. They are loaded with guns — it is true — but they are lightly armored, they are slow, and they present high targets. We expect to move at dusk or just before. Then we will descend on the road into the valley and fight amid the shadows. No one wants this: we all are terrified.

The young ones are frightened because, for most of them, this is the first battle. But their fear is not as strong as the blood which is rising and fills their chests with anger and strength. They have little to lose, being, as they are, only eighteen. They look no more frightened than members of a sports team before an important match: it is that kind of fear, for they are responsible only to themselves.

Married men, on the other hand, are given away by their eyes and faces. They are saying to themselves, "I must not die; I *must not die.*" They are remembering how they used to feel when they were younger; and they know that they have to fight. They may be killed, but if they don't fight they will surely be killed, because the slow self-made fear which demands constant hesitation is the most efficient of all killers. It is not the cautious who die, but the overcautious. The married men are trying to strike an exact balance between their responsibility as soldiers, their fervent desire to stay alive, and their only hope — which is to go into battle with the smooth, courageous, trancelike movements that will keep them out of trouble. Soldiers who do not know how (like dancers or mountain climbers) to let their bodies think for them are very liable to be killed. There is a flow to hard combat; it is not (as it has often been depicted) entirely chance or entirely skill. A thousand signals and signs speak to you, much as in music. And what a sad moment it is when you must, for one reason or another, ignore them. The married men fear this moment. We should have begun hours ago. Being held back is bad luck.

"What time is it?" asks one of the young soldiers. Someone answers him.

"Fourteen hundred." No one in the Israeli Army except high-ranking officers (colonels, generals — and we have here no colonels or generals) tells time in this fashion.

"What are you, a general?" asks the young soldier. Everyone laughs, as if this were funny, because we are scared. We should not be held back like this.

Another man, a man who is close to fifty and is worrying about his two sons who are in Sinai, keeps on looking at his watch. It is expensive and Japanese, with a black dial. He looks at it every minute to see what time it is, because he has actually forgotten. If he were asked what the time was, he would not be able to respond without checking the watch, even though he has done so fifty times in the last hour. He too is very afraid. The sun glints off the crystal and explodes in our eyes.

As younger men who badly wanted to fight, we thought we knew what courage was. Now we know that courage is the forced step of going into battle when you want anything in the world but that, when there is every reason to stay out, when you have been through all the tests, and passed them, and think that it's all over. Then the war hits like an artillery shell and you are forced to be eighteen again, but you can't be eighteen again; not with the taste of your wife's mouth in your mouth, not with the smell of her perfume on your wrists. The world turns upside down in minutes.

How hard we struggle in trying to remember the easy courage we once had. But we can't. We must either be brave in a different way, or not at all. What is that way? How can we fight like seasoned soldiers when this morning we kissed our children? There is a way, hidden in the history of war. There must be, for we can see them fighting in the valley; and, high in the air, silver specks are dueling in a dream of blue silence.

Why are we merely watching? To be restrained this way is simply not fair. A quick entrance would get the fear over with, and that would help. But, then again, in the Six Day War, we waited for weeks while the Egyptian Army built up against us. And then, after that torture, we burst out and we leapt across the desert, sprinting, full of energy and fury that kept us like dancers — nimble and absorbed — and kept us alive. That is the secret: You have to be angry. When we arrived on the ridge this morning, we were

anything but angry. Now are are beginning to get angry. It is our only salvation. We are angry because we are being held back.

We swear, and kick the sides of the half-tracks. We hate the voice on
our radio which keeps telling us to hold to our position. We hate that man
more than we hate the enemy, for now we want engagement with the
enemy. We are beginning to crave battle, and we are getting angrier, and
angrier, because we know that by five o'clock we will be worn out. They
should let us go now.

A young soldier who has been following the battle, through binoculars, screams. "God!" he says. "Look! Look!"

The Syrians are moving up two columns of armor that will overwhelm
our men on the plain below. The sergeant gets on the radio, but from it we
hear a sudden waterfall of talk. Holding the microphone in his hand, he listens with us as we discover that they know. They are demanding more air
support.

"What air support?" we ask. There is no air-to-ground fighting that we
can see. As we watch the Syrians approach, our hearts are full of fear for
those of us below. How did our soldiers know? There must be spotters or a
patrol somewhere deep in, high on a hill, like us. What air support? There
are planes all over the place, but not here.

Then we feel our lungs shaking like drums. The hair on our arms and
on the back of our necks stands up and we shake as flights of fighters roar
over the hill. They are no more than fifty feet above us. We can feel the
heat from the tailpipes, and the orange flames are blinding. The noise is superb. They come three at a time; one wave, two, three, four, five, and six.
These are our pilots. The mass of the machinery flying through the air is so
great and graceful that we are stunned beyond the noise: We cheer in anger
and in satisfaction. It seems the best thing in the world when, as they pass
the ridge (How they hug the ground; what superb pilots!) they dip their
wings for our sake. They are descending into a thicket of anti-aircraft missiles and radar-directed guns — and they dip their wings for us.

Now we are hot. The married men feel as if rivers are rushing through
them, crossing and crashing, for they are angry and full of energy. The sergeant depresses the lever on the microphone. He identifies himself and says,
"In the name of God, we want to go in *now*. Damn you if you don't let us
go in."

There is hesitation and silence on the other end. "Who is this?" they
ask.

"This is Shimon."

More silence, then, "Okay, Shimon. Move! Move!"

The engines start. Now we have our own thunder. It is not even three
o'clock. It is the right time; they've caught us at the right time. The soldiers
are not slow in mounting the half-tracks. The sound of our roaring engines
has magnetized them and they *jump* in. The young drivers race the engines,
as they always do.

For a magnificent half minute, we stare into the north light, smiling.

The man who tasted the sweet taste of his wife kisses his wrist. The young soldiers are no longer afraid, and the married men are in a perfect sustained fury. Because they love their wives and children, they will not think of them until the battle is over. Now we are soldiers again. The engines are deafening. No longer are we held back. We are shaking; we are crying. Now we stare into the north light, and listen to the explosion below. Now we hear the levers of the gearshifts. Now our drivers exhale and begin to drive. Now we are moving.

[1981]

ANN BEATTIE (b. 1947) was born in Washington, D.C. She grew up in Chevy Chase, Maryland, the only child of parents who sent her to a suburban school that she called "a civilized concentration camp" because of its strict dress code and stern disciplinary system. She rebelled by bleaching her hair, wearing fishnet stockings, smoking cigarettes, and graduating in the bottom tenth of her class: "That took a little effort on my part." In 1969 she received a B.A. from American University, and the following year she went on to the University of Connecticut as a graduate student in English literature. Her short stories attracted the interest of Professor J. D. O'Hara there. "He said that he heard that I wrote, and if I was so good at it, why didn't I let him see what I was doing? So I took one of the few stories I had and put it in his mailbox, and it came back with comments all over it — more comments than I'd ever seen, more words than there were in the story. I would put something in his mailbox every few days and he would return it. He taught me a lot . . . about the technical process of writing." Beattie began to send her stories to magazines, and her first publication, "A Rose for Judy Garland's Casket," appeared in the Western Humanities Review in 1972. The next year another story won an Atlantic Monthly "first" award, and shortly thereafter she began publishing in The New Yorker. Beattie estimates that she sent thirteen stories to that magazine before one was accepted. "You see, I was living in Eastford, Connecticut, at the time and I was bored. You either wrote a story every night or watched television. I wrote a story every night."

Her first book of nineteen stories, Distortions, was published in 1976, the same year as her first novel, Chilly Scenes of Winter, which was later made into a film. In 1978 she published her second collection of stories, Secrets and Surprises. She published a second novel, Falling in Place, in 1980, and a third collection, The Burning House, in 1982. Her most recent book is the novel Love Always (1985). Critics have compared her fiction to the work of John Cheever and John Updike for its exploration of American suburban life and its "weird domesticities." Beattie herself sees little resemblance: "I think they're fine writers, but I don't see any comparison in the world between us. . . . Updike's style, that learned elegance, that intrusion of self into the material and that very careful way he orchestrates everything, and the same thing with Cheever — they're writing traditionally well-made stories." She says she writes about chaos, "and many of the simple flat statements that I bring together are usually non sequiturs or bordering on being non sequiturs — which reinforces the chaos. I write in these flat simple sentences because that's the way I think."

A common theme in Beattie's fiction, including "Waiting," from The

Burning House, *is one of lives wrenched out of shape by bad timing or*
faulty perception; yet her sense of the world is that "you can take the cor-
rect steps and obtain the correct answers and a tree will fall on your head."
Although she admires the stories of Flannery O'Connor, Beattie resists a
religious answer to the "huge questions" of life, preferring the "surprises"
that emerge in the creation of her work and tell her things she did not know
before.

Ann Beattie

ᚕᚕ

WAITING

"It's beautiful," the woman says.

"How did you come by this?"

She wiggles her finger in the mousehole. It's a genuine mousehole:
sometime in the eighteenth century a mouse gnawed its way into the cupboard, through the two inside shelves, and out the bottom.

"We bought it from an antique dealer in Virginia," I say.

"Where in Virginia?"

"Ruckersville. Outside of Charlottesville."

"That's beautiful country," she says. "I know where Ruckersville is. I
had an uncle who lived in Keswick."

"Keswick was nice," I say. "The farms."

"Oh," she says. "The tax writeoffs, you mean? Those mansions with
one sheep grazing out front?"

She is touching the wood, stroking lightly in case there might be a
splinter. Even after so much time, everything might not have been worn
down to smoothness. She lowers her eyes. "Would you take eight hundred?" she says.

"I'd like to sell it for a thousand," I say. "I paid thirteen hundred, ten
years ago."

"It's beautiful," she says. "I suppose I should try to tell you it has
some faults, but I've never seen one like it. Very nice. My husband
wouldn't like my spending more than six hundred to begin with, but I can
see that it's worth eight." She is resting her index finger on the latch.
"Could I bring my husband to see it tonight?"

"All right."

"You're moving?" she says.

"Eventually," I say.

"That would be something to load around." She shakes her head. "Are you going back South?"

"I doubt it," I say.

"You probably think I'm kidding about coming back with my husband," she says suddenly. She lowers her eyes again. "Are other people interested?"

"There's just been one other call. Somebody who wanted to come out Saturday." I smile. "I guess I should pretend there's great interest."

"I'll take it," the woman says. "For a thousand. You probably could sell it for more and I could probably resell it for more. I'll tell my husband that."

She picks up her embroidered shoulder bag from the floor by the corner cabinet. She sits at the oak table by the octagonal window and rummages for her checkbook.

"I was thinking, What if I left it home? But I didn't." She takes out a checkbook in a red plastic cover. "My uncle in Keswick was one of those gentleman farmers," she says. "He lived until he was eighty-six, and enjoyed his life. He did everything in moderation, but the key was that he did *everything*." She looks appraisingly at her signature. "Some movie actress just bought a farm across from the Cobham store," she says. "A girl. I never saw her in the movies. Do you know who I'm talking about?"

"Well, Art Garfunkel used to have a place out there," I say.

"Maybe she bought his place." The woman pushes the check to the center of the table, tilts the vase full of phlox, and puts the corner of the check underneath. "Well," she says. "Thank you. We'll come with my brother's truck to get it on the weekend. What about Saturday?"

"That's fine," I say.

"You're going to have some move," she says, looking around at the other furniture. "I haven't moved in thirty years, and I wouldn't want to."

The dog walks through the room.

"What a well-mannered dog," she says.

"That's Hugo. Hugo's moved quite a few times in thirteen years. Virginia. D.C. Boston. Here."

"Poor old Hugo," she says.

Hugo, in the living room now, thumps down and sighs.

"Thank you," she says, putting out her hand. I reach out to shake it, but our hands don't meet and she clasps her hand around my wrist. "Saturday afternoon. Maybe Saturday evening. Should I be specific?"

"Any time is all right."

"Can I turn around on your grass or no?"

"Sure. Did you see the tire marks? I do it all the time."

"Well," she says. "People who back into traffic. I don't know. I honk at them all the time."

I go to the screen door and wave. She is driving a yellow Mercedes, an old one that's been repainted, with a license that says "RAVE-1." The car stalls. She re-starts it and waves. I wave again.

When she's gone, I go out the back door and walk down the driveway. A single daisy is growing out of the foot-wide crack in the concrete. Somebody has thrown a beer can into the driveway. I pick it up and marvel at how light it is. I get the mail from the box across the street and look at it as cars pass by. One of the stream of cars honks a warning at me, although I am not moving, except for flipping through the mail. There is a C.L.&P. bill, a couple of pieces of junk mail, a postcard from Henry in Los Angeles, and a letter from my husband in — he's made it to California. Berkeley, California, mailed four days ago. Years ago, when I visited a friend in Berkeley we went to a little park and some people wandered in walking two dogs and a goat. An African pygmy goat. The woman said it was housebroken to urinate outside and as for the other she just picked up the pellets.

I go inside and watch the moving red band on the digital clock in the kitchen. Behind the clock is an old coffee tin decorated with a picture of a man and a woman in a romantic embrace; his arms are nearly rusted away, her hair is chipped, but a perfectly painted wreath of coffee beans rises in an arc above them. Probably I should have advertised the coffee tin, too, but I like to hear the metal top creak when I lift it in the morning to take the jar of coffee out. But if not the coffee tin, I should probably have put the tin breadbox up for sale.

John and I liked looking for antiques. He liked the ones almost beyond repair — the kind that you would have to buy twenty dollars' worth of books to understand how to restore. When we used to go looking, antiques were much less expensive than they are now. We bought them at a time when we had the patience to sit all day on folding chairs under a canopy at an auction. We were organized; we would come and inspect the things the day before. Then we would get there early the next day and wait. Most of the auctioneers in that part of Virginia were very good. One, named Wicked Richard, used to lace his fingers together and crack his knuckles as he called the lots. His real name was Wisted. When he did classier auctions and there was a pamphlet, his name was listed as Wisted. At most of the regular auctions, though, he introduced himself as Wicked Richard.

I cut a section of cheese and take some crackers out of a container. I put them on a plate and carry them into the dining room, feeling a little sad about parting with the big corner cupboard. Suddenly it seems older and bigger — a very large thing to be giving up.

The phone rings. A woman wants to know the size of the refrigerator that I have advertised. I tell her.

"Is it white?" she says.

The ad said it was white.

"Yes," I tell her.

"This is your refrigerator?" she says.

"One of them," I say. "I'm moving."

"Oh," she says. "You shouldn't tell people that. People read these ads to figure out who's moving and might not be around, so they can rob them. There were a lot of robberies in your neighborhood last summer."

The refrigerator is too small for her. We hang up.

The phone rings again, and I let it ring. I sit down and look at the corner cupboard. I put a piece of cheese on top of a cracker and eat it. I get up and go into the living room and offer a piece of cheese to Hugo. He sniffs and takes it lightly from my fingers. Earlier today, in the morning, I ran him in Putnam Park. I could hardly keep up with him, as usual. Thirteen isn't so old, for a dog. He scared the ducks and sent them running into the water. He growled at a beagle a man was walking, and tugged on his leash until he choked. He pulled almost as hard as he could a few summers ago. The air made his fur fluffy. Now he is happy, slowly licking his mouth, getting ready to take his afternoon nap.

John wanted to take Hugo across country, but in the end we decided that, as much as Hugo would enjoy terrorizing so many dogs along the way, it was going to be a hot July and it was better if he stayed home. We discussed this reasonably. No frenzy — nothing like the way we had been swept in at some auctions to bid on things that we didn't want, just because so many other people were mad for them. A reasonable discussion about Hugo, even if it was at the last minute: Hugo, in the car, already sticking his head out the window to bark goodbye. "It's too hot for him," I said. I was standing outside in my nightgown. "It's almost July. He'll be a hassle for you if campgrounds won't take him or if you have to park in the sun." So Hugo stood beside me, barking his high-pitched goodbye, as John backed out of the driveway. He forgot: his big battery lantern and his can opener. He remembered: his tent, the cooler filled with ice (he couldn't decide when he left whether he was going to stock up on beer or Coke), a camera, a suitcase, a fiddle, and a banjo. He forgot his driver's license, too. I never understood why he didn't keep it in his wallet, but it always seemed to get taken out for some reason and then be lost. Yesterday I found it leaning up against the Excedrin in the medicine cabinet.

Bobby calls. He fools me with his imitation of a man with an English accent who wants to know if I also have an avocado-colored refrigerator for sale. When I say I don't, he asks if I know somebody who paints refrigerators.

"Of course not," I tell him.

"That's the most decisive thing I've heard you say in five years," Bobby says in his real voice. "How's it going, Sally?"

"Jesus," I say. "If you'd answered this phone all morning, you wouldn't think that was funny. Where are you?"

"New York. Where do you think I am? It's my lunch hour. Going to

Le Relais to get tanked up. A little *le pain et le beurre*,[1] put down a few
Scotches."

"Le Relais," I say. "Hmm."

"Don't make a bad eye on me," he says, going into his Muhammad
Ali imitation. "Step on my foot and I kick you to the moon. Glad-hand me
and I shake you like a loon." Bobby clears his throat. "I got the company
twenty big ones today," he says. "Twenty Gs."

"Congratulations. Have a good lunch. Come out for dinner, if you feel
like the drive."

"I don't have any gas and I can't face the train." He coughs again. "I
gave up cigarettes," he says. "Why am I coughing?" He moves away from
the phone to cough loudly.

"Are you smoking grass in the office?" I say.

"Not this time," he gasps. "I'm goddam dying of something." A
pause. "What did you do yesterday?"

"I was in town. You'd laugh at what I did."

"You went to the fireworks."

"Yeah, that's right. I wouldn't hesitate to tell you that part."

"What'd you do?" he says.

"I met Andy and Tom at the Plaza and drank champagne. They
didn't. I did. Then we went to the fireworks."

"Sally at the *Plaza?*" He laughs. "What were they doing in town?"

"Tom was there on business. Andy came to see the fireworks."

"It rained, didn't it?"

"Only a little. It was O.K. They were pretty."

"The fireworks," Bobby says. "I didn't make the fireworks."

"You're going to miss lunch, Bobby," I say.

"God," he says. "I am. Bye."

I pull a record out from under the big library table, where they're kept
on the wide mahogany board that connects the legs. By coincidence, the
record I pull out is the Miles Davis Sextet's "Jazz at the Plaza." At the
Palm Court on the Fourth of July, a violinist played "Play Gypsies, Dance
Gypsies" and "Oklahoma!" I try to remember what else and can't.

"What do you say, Hugo?" I say to the dog. "Another piece of cheese,
or would you rather go on with your siesta?"

He knows the word "cheese." He knows it as well as his name. I love
the way his eyes light up and he perks his ears for certain words. Bobby tells
me that you can speak gibberish to people, ninety percent of the people, as
long as you throw in a little catchword now and then, and it's the same
when I talk to Hugo: "Cheese." "Tag." "Out."

No reaction. Hugo is lying where he always does, on his right side,
near the stereo. His nose is only a fraction of an inch away from a plant in a

---

[1] bread and butter.

basket beneath the window. The branches of the plant sweep the floor. He seems very still.

"Cheese?" I whisper. "Hugo?" It is as loud as I can speak.

No reaction. I start to take a step closer, but stop myself. I put down the record and stare at him. Nothing changes. I walk out into the back yard. The sun is shining directly down from overhead, striking the dark-blue doors of the garage, washing out the color to the palest tint of blue. The peach tree by the garage, with one dead branch. The wind chimes tinkling in the peach tree. A bird hopping by the iris underneath the tree. Mosquitoes or gnats, a puff of them in the air, clustered in front of me. I sink down into the grass. I pick a blade, split it slowly with my fingernail. I count the times I breathe in and out. When I open my eyes, the sun is shining hard on the blue doors.

After a while — maybe ten minutes, maybe twenty — a truck pulls into the driveway. The man who usually delivers packages to the house hops out of the United Parcel truck. He is a nice man, about twenty-five, with long hair tucked behind his ears, and kind eyes.

Hugo did not bark when the truck pulled into the drive.

"Hi," he says. "What a beautiful day. Here you go."

He holds out a clipboard and a pen.

"Forty-two," he says, pointing to the tiny numbered block in which I am to sign my name. A mailing envelope is under his arm.

"Another book," he says. He hands me the package.

I reach up for it. There is a blue label with my name and address typed on it.

He locks his hands behind his back and raises his arms, bowing. "Did you notice that?" he says, straightening out of the yoga stretch, pointing to the envelope. "What's the joke?" he says.

The return address says "John F. Kennedy."

"Oh," I say. "A friend in publishing." I look up at him. I realize that that hasn't explained it. "We were talking on the phone last week. He was — People are still talking about where they were when he was shot, and I've known my friend for almost ten years and we'd never talked about it before."

The U.P.S. man is wiping sweat off his forehead with a handkerchief. He stuffs the handkerchief into his pocket.

"He wasn't making fun," I say. "He admired Kennedy."

The U.P.S. man crouches, runs his fingers across the grass. He looks in the direction of the garage. He looks at me. "Are you all right?" he says.

"Well — " I say.

He is still watching me.

"Well," I say, trying to catch my breath. "Let's see what this is."

I pull up the flap, being careful not to get cut by the staples. A large paperback called "If Mountains Die." Color photographs. The sky above the Pueblo River gorge in the book is very blue. I show the U.P.S. man.

"Were you all right when I pulled in?" he says. "You were sitting sort of funny."

I still am. I realize that my arms are crossed over my chest and I am leaning forward. I uncross my arms and lean back on my elbows. "Fine," I say. "Thank you."

Another car pulls into the driveway, comes around the truck, and stops on the lawn. Ray's car. Ray gets out, smiles, leans back in through the open window to turn off the tape that's still playing. Ray is my best friend. Also my husband's best friend.

"What are you doing here?" I say to Ray.

"Hi," the U.P.S. man says to Ray. "I've got to get going. Well." He looks at me. "See you," he says.

"See you," I say. "Thanks."

"What am I doing here?" Ray says. He taps his watch. "Lunchtime. I'm on a business lunch. Big deal. Important negotiations. Want to drive down to the Redding Market and buy a couple of sandwiches, or have you already eaten?"

"You drove all the way out here for lunch?"

"Big business lunch. Difficult client. Takes time to bring some clients around. Coaxing. Takes hours." Ray shrugs.

"Don't they care?"

Ray sticks out his tongue and makes a noise, sits beside me and puts his arm around my shoulder and shakes me lightly toward him and away from him a couple of times. "Look at that sunshine," he says. "Finally. I thought the rain would never stop." He hugs my shoulder and takes his arm away. "It depresses me, too," he says. "I don't like what I sound like when I keep saying that nobody cares." Ray sighs. He reaches for a cigarette. "Nobody cares," he says. "Two-hour lunch. Four. Five."

We sit silently. He picks up the book, leafs through. "Pretty," he says. "You eat already?"

I look behind me at the screen door. Hugo is not there. No sound, either, when the car came up the driveway and the truck left.

"Yes," I say. "But there's some cheese in the house. All the usual things. Or you could go to the market."

"Maybe I will," he says. "Want anything?"

"Ray," I say, reaching my hand up. "Don't go to the market."

"What?" he says. He sits on his heels and takes my hand. He looks into my face.

"Why don't you — There's cheese in the house," I say.

He looks puzzled. Then he sees the stack of mail on the grass underneath our hands. "Oh," he says. "Letter from John." He picks it up, sees that it hasn't been opened. "O.K.," he says. "Then I'm perplexed again. Just that he wrote you? That he's already in Berkeley? Well, he had a bad winter. We all had a bad winter. It's going to be all right. He hasn't called? You don't know if he hooked up with that band?"

I shake my head no.

"I tried to call you yesterday," he says. "You weren't home."

"I went into New York."

"And?"

"I went out for drinks with some friends. We went to the fireworks."

"So did I," Ray says. "Where were you?"

"Seventy-sixth Street."

"I was at Ninety-eighth. I knew it was crazy to think I might run into you at the fireworks."

A cardinal flies into the peach tree.

"I did run into Bobby last week," he says. "Of course, it's not really running into him at one o'clock at Le Relais."

"How was Bobby?"

"You haven't heard from him, either?"

"He called today, but he didn't say how he was. I guess I didn't ask."

"He was O.K. He looked good. You can hardly see the scar above his eyebrow where they took the stitches. I imagine in a few weeks when it fades you won't notice it at all."

"You think he's done with dining in Harlem?"

"Doubt it. It could have happened anywhere, you know. People get mugged all over the place."

I hear the phone ringing and don't get up. Ray squeezes my shoulder again. "Well," he says. "I'm going to bring some food out here."

"If there's anything in there that isn't the way it ought to be, just take care of it, will you?"

"What?" he says.

"I mean — If there's anything wrong, just fix it."

He smiles. "Don't tell me. You painted a room what you thought was a nice pastel color and it came out electric pink. Or the chairs — you didn't have them reupholstered again, did you?" Ray comes back to where I'm sitting. "Oh, God," he says. "I was thinking the other night about how you'd had that horrible chintz you bought on Madison Avenue put onto the chairs and when John and I got back here you were afraid to let him into the house. God — that awful striped material. Remember John standing in back of the chair and putting his chin over the back and screaming, 'I'm innocent!' Remember him doing that?" Ray's eyes are about to water, the way they watered because he laughed so hard the day John did that. "That was about a year ago this month," he says.

I nod yes.

"Well," Ray says. "Everything's going to be all right, and I don't say that just because I want to believe in one nice thing. Bobby thinks the same thing. We agree about this. I keep talking about this, don't I? I keep coming out to the house, like you've cracked up or something. You don't want to keep hearing my sermons." Ray opens the screen door. "Anybody can take a trip," he says.

I stare over at him.

"I'm getting lunch," he says. He is holding the door open with his foot. He moves his foot and goes into the house. The door slams behind him.

"Hey!" he calls out. "Want iced tea or something?"

The phone begins to ring.

"Want me to get it?" he says.

"No. Let it ring."

"Let it ring?" he hollers.

The cardinal flies out of the peach tree and onto the sweeping branch of a tall fir tree that borders the lawn — so many trees so close together that you can't see the house on the other side. The bird becomes a speck of red and disappears.

"Hey, pretty lady!" Ray calls. "Where's your mutt?"

Over the noise of the telephone, I can hear him knocking around in the kitchen. The stuck drawer opening.

"You *honestly* want me not to answer the phone?" he calls.

I look back at the house. Ray, balancing a tray, opens the door with one hand, and Hugo is beside him — not rushing out, the way he usually does to get through the door, but padding slowly, shaking himself out of sleep. He comes over and lies down next to me, blinking because his eyes are not yet accustomed to the sunlight.

Ray sits down with his plate of crackers and cheese and a beer. He looks at the tears streaming down my cheeks and shoves over close to me. He takes a big drink and puts the beer on the grass. He pushes the tray next to the beer can.

"Hey," Ray says. "Everything's cool, O.K.? No right and no wrong. People do what they do. A neutral observer, and friend to all. Same easy advice from Ray all around. Our discretion assured." He pushes my hair gently off my wet cheeks. "It's O.K.," he says softly, turning and cupping his hands over my forehead. "Just tell me what you've done."

[1982]

JAMAICA KINCAID (b. 1949) was born and educated in St. Johns, Antigua, in the West Indies. Her father was a carpenter, and her family doted upon her, the only child. Kincaid remembers:

> My mother did keep everything I ever wore, and basically until I was quite grown up my past was sort of a museum to me. Clearly, the way I became a writer was that my mother wrote my life for me and told it to me. I can't help but think that it made me interested in the idea of myself as an object. I can't account for the reason I became a writer any other way, because I certainly didn't know writers. And not only that. I thought writing was something that people just didn't do anymore, that went out of fashion, like the bustle. I really didn't read a book that was written in the twentieth century until I was about seventeen and away from home.

Kincaid left Antigua to study in the United States, but she found college "a dismal failure," so she educated herself. She began writing and published her stories in Rolling Stone, The Paris Review, *and* The New Yorker, *where she became a staff writer in 1978. Six years later she published her first book,* At the Bottom of the River, *a collection of stories, which won the Morton Dauwen Zabel Award of the American Academy and Institute of Arts and Letters. In 1985 her book of interrelated stories,* Annie John, *about a girl's coming of age in the West Indies, was also much praised. In her autobiographical writing, Kincaid often explores the idea that her deep affection for her family and her native country developed into a conflicting need for independence and separation as she grew into adolescence.*

Typically Kincaid writes in a deliberately precise rhythmic style about states of intense emotions, as in her story "Girl." Her fiction is free of conventional plots, characters, and dialogue. The critic Suzanne Freeman has recognized that "what Kincaid has to tell me, she tells, with her singsong style, in a series of images that are as sweet and mysterious as the secrets that children whisper in your ear." Although Kincaid is married to an American and lives in New York City, she feels that the West Indies will continue to be the source for her fiction. "What I really feel about America is that it's given me a place to be myself — but myself as I was formed somewhere else."

Jamaica Kincaid

∽∾

GIRL

Wash the white clothes on Monday and put them on the stone heap; wash the color clothes on Tuesday and put them on the clothesline to dry; don't walk barehead in the hot sun; cook pumpkin fritters in very hot sweet oil; soak your little clothes right after you take them off; when buying cotton to make yourself a nice blouse, be sure that it doesn't have gum on it, because that way it won't hold up well after a wash; soak salt fish overnight before you cook it; is it true that you sing benna in Sunday School?; always eat your food in such a way that it won't turn someone else's stomach; on Sundays try to walk like a lady and not like the slut you are so bent on becoming; don't sing benna in Sunday School; you mustn't speak to wharf-rat boys, not even to give directions; don't eat fruits on the street — flies will follow you; *but I don't sing benna on Sundays at all and never in Sunday school*; this is how to sew on a button; this is how to make a buttonhole for the button you have just sewed on; this is how to hem a dress when you see the hem coming down and so to prevent yourself from looking like the slut I know you are so bent on becoming; this is how you iron your father's khaki shirt so that it doesn't have a crease; this is how you iron your father's khaki pants so that they don't have a crease; this is how you grow okra — far from the house, because okra tree harbors red ants; when you are growing dasheen, make sure it gets plenty of water or else it makes your throat itch when you are eating it; this is how you sweep a corner; this is how you sweep a whole house; this is how you sweep a yard; this is how you smile to someone you don't like too much; this is how you smile to someone you don't like at all; this is how you smile to someone you like completely; this is how you set a table for tea; this is how you set a table for dinner; this is how you set a table for dinner with an important guest; this is how you set a table for lunch; this is how you set a table for breakfast; this is how to behave in the presence of men who don't know you very well, and this way they won't recognize immediately the slut I have warned you against becoming; be sure to wash every day, even if it is with your own spit; don't squat down to play marbles — you are not a boy, you know; don't pick people's flowers — you might catch something; don't throw stones at blackbirds, because it might not be a blackbird at all; this is how to make a bread pudding; this is how to make doukona; this is how to make pepper pot; this is how to make a good medicine for a cold; this is how to make a good medicine to throw away a child before it even becomes a child; this is how to catch a fish; this is how to throw back a fish you don't like, and that way something bad won't fall on you; this is how to bully a man; this is how a man bullies you; this is how to love a man, and if this doesn't work there are other ways, and if they don't work don't feel too bad about giving up; this is how to spit up in the air if you feel like it, and this is how to move quick so that it doesn't fall on you; this is how to make ends meet; always squeeze bread to make sure it's fresh; *but what if the baker won't let me feel the bread?*; you mean to say that after all you are really going to be the kind of woman who the baker won't let near the bread?

[1984]

JAYNE ANNE PHILLIPS (b. 1952) *was born in Buckhannon, West Virginia. Her father was in the road construction business and her mother was a schoolteacher. As a child, Phillips was encouraged by her mother to be independent, and later she helped put herself through the University of West Virginia by working for a home improvements company. She also began publishing poetry at that time. After graduating in 1974, she traveled across the country and supported herself by waitressing. She feels herself a member of a generation that survived a difficult decade:*

> *Unlike the people of the '60s, we didn't have a strong sense of goals, nor the illusion we could make a difference. They were very organized and considered themselves a community. Their enemy was an obvious one. By the '70s, people began to experience a kind of massive ennui. People felt on their own. Kids dropping acid did it to obliterate themselves, not to have a religious experience. Only people with a strong sense of self came through.*

In 1976 Phillips submitted some poetry and two short stories to the University of Iowa writing program, which accepted her. That summer she published her first book with a small press, 24 one-page prose pieces in a collection titled Sweethearts. *Phillips then thought of herself as a prose writer: "I became more challenged by the difficulty of writing fiction; I was really attracted by the subversive look of the paragraph," she recalls. "In a poem you're always having to confront the identity of the writer. In fiction the reader becomes less defended against that identity and more open to the text."*

A collection of Phillips's long and short stories, Black Tickets, *appeared in 1979. "Cheers" is from that book; it features a local character in a small West Virginia town like the one Phillips grew up in. She writes about ordinary people in order to make a political statement about the value of everyday life, like the writers she says have influenced her choice of subject matter — Katherine Anne Porter, William Faulkner, and Eudora Welty. Phillips's next book, the novel* Machine Dreams *(1984) develops incidents and themes from some of the stories in* Black Tickets. *She says she writes for her own "psychic survival," not following any kind of plan, "because the whole point is to follow the story to its center, not to impose some point of view. I believe that you are led to discover what things mean and how things are related to each other through the process of doing the work."*

Jayne Anne Phillips

∽∾

CHEERS

The sewing woman lived across the tracks, down past Arey's Feed Store. Row of skinny houses on a mud alley. Her rooms smelled of salted grease and old newspaper. Behind the ironing board she was thin, scooping up papers that shuffled open in her hands. Her eyebrows were arched sharp and painted on.

She made cheerleading suits for ten-year-olds. Threading the machine, she clicked her red nails on the needle and pulled my shirt over my head. In the other room the kids watched *Queen for a Day*. She bent over me. I saw each eyelash painted black and hard and separate. Honey, she said. Turn around this way. And on the wall there was a postcard of orange trees in Florida. A man in a straw hat reached up with his hand all curled. Beautiful Bounty said the card in wavy red letters.

I got part of it made up, she said, fitting the red vest. You girls are bout the same size as mine. All you girls are bout the same. She pursed her red lips and pinched the cloth together. Tell me somethin Honey. How'd I manage all these kids an no man. On television there was loud applause for the queen, whose roses were sharp and real. Her machine buzzed like an animal beside the round clock. She frowned as she pressed the button with her foot, then furled the red cloth out and pulled me to her. Her pointed white face was smudged around the eyes. I watched the pale strand of scalp in her hair. There, she said.

When I left she tucked the money in her sweater. She had pins between her teeth and lipstick gone grainy in the cracks of her mouth. I had a red swing skirt and a bumpy A on my chest. Lord, she said. You do look pretty.

[1979]

LOUISE ERDRICH (b. 1954) is of German and Chippewa Indian descent. She grew up in Wahpeton, North Dakota, as a member of the Turtle Mountain Band of Chippewa. For many years her grandfather was tribal chair of the reservation. At Dartmouth College, Erdrich won several prizes for her fiction and poetry, including the American Academy of Poets Prize. After graduating in 1976, she returned to North Dakota, where she taught in the Poetry in the Schools Program. In 1979 she received her M.A. in creative writing from Johns Hopkins University. Erdrich is married to a professor of Native American studies at Dartmouth College and has four children.

Erdrich has been an editor of the Boston Indian Council newspaper, The Circle. Her stories have appeared in Redbook, The New England Review, and Mississippi Valley Review and have been included in Earth Power Coming, an anthology of Native American literature, as well as in That's What She Said: Contemporary Poetry and Fiction by Native American Women. In 1984, a collection of her poetry, Jacklight, was published; and her first work of fiction, Love Medicine, won the National Book Critics Circle Award. Her most recent book is Beet Queen (1986).

"The Red Convertible" is a chapter from Love Medicine. Each chapter is a self-enclosed narrative that also functions as a separate short story about the lives of two families, the Kashpaws and the Lamartines, on a North Dakota reservation between 1934 and 1984. The fictional characters know one another and figure in one another's stories. Erdrich's book has won praise for its psychological depth and its literary excellence; it is a landmark work in its depiction of the lives of the contemporary Native Americans. As the novelist Peter Matthiessen has recognized, Love Medicine is "quick with agile prose, taut speech, poetry, and power, conveying unflinchingly the funkiness, humor, and great unspoken sadness of the Indian reservations, and a people exiled to a no-man's-land between two worlds."

Louise Erdrich

ᖇᐋ

THE RED CONVERTIBLE

Lyman Lamartine

I was the first one to drive a convertible on my reservation. And of course it was red, a red Olds. I owned that car along with my brother Henry Junior. We owned it together until his boots filled with water on a windy night and he bought out my share. Now Henry owns the whole car, and his youngest brother Lyman (that's myself), Lyman walks everywhere he goes.

How did I earn enough money to buy my share in the first place? My own talent was I could always make money. I had a touch for it, unusual in a Chippewa. From the first I was different that way, and everyone recognized it. I was the only kid they let in the American Legion Hall to shine shoes, for example, and one Christmas I sold spiritual bouquets for the mission door to door. The nuns let me keep a percentage. Once I started, it seemed the more money I made the easier the money came. Everyone encouraged it. When I was fifteen I got a job washing dishes at the Joliet Café, and that was where my first big break happened.

It wasn't long before I was promoted to bussing tables, and then the short-order cook quit and I was hired to take her place. No sooner than you know it I was managing the Joliet. The rest is history. I went on managing. I soon became part owner, and of course there was no stopping me then. It wasn't long before the whole thing was mine.

After I'd owned the Joliet for one year, it blew over in the worst tornado ever seen around here. The whole operation was smashed to bits. A total loss. The fryalator was up in a tree, the grill torn in half like it was paper. I was only sixteen. I had it all in my mother's name, and I lost it quick, but before I lost it I had every one of my relatives, and their relatives, to dinner, and I also bought that red Olds I mentioned, along with Henry.

The first time we saw it! I'll tell you when we first saw it. We had gotten a ride up to Winnipeg, and both of us had money. Don't ask me why, because we never mentioned a car or anything, we just had all our money. Mine was cash, a big bankroll from the Joliet's insurance. Henry had two checks — a week's extra pay for being laid off, and his regular check from the Jewel Bearing Plant.

We were walking down Portage anyway, seeing the sights, when we saw it. There it was, parked, large as life. Really as *if* it was alive. I thought of the word *repose*, because the car wasn't simply stopped, parked, or whatever. That car reposed, calm and gleaming, a FOR SALE sign in its left front window. Then, before we had thought it over at all, the car belonged to us and our pockets were empty. We had just enough money for gas back home.

We went places in that car, me and Henry. We took off driving all one whole summer. We started off toward the Little Knife River and Mandaree in Fort Berthold and then we found ourselves down in Wakpala somehow, and then suddenly we were over in Montana on the Rocky Boys, and yet the summer was not even half over. Some people hang on to details when they travel, but we didn't let them bother us and just lived our everyday lives here to there.

I do remember this one place with willows. I remember I laid under those trees and it was comfortable. So comfortable. The branches bent down all around me like a tent or a stable. And quiet, it was quiet, even though there was a powwow close enough so I could see it going on. The air was not too still, not too windy either. When the dust rises up and hangs in the air around the dancers like that, I feel good. Henry was asleep with his arms thrown wide. Later on, he woke up and we started driving again. We were somewhere in Montana, or maybe on the Blood Reserve — it could have been anywhere. Anyway it was where we met the girl.

All her hair was in buns around her ears, that's the first thing I noticed about her. She was posed alongside the road with her arm out, so we stopped. That girl was short, so short her lumber shirt looked comical on her, like a nightgown. She had jeans on and fancy moccasins and she carried a little suitcase.

"Hop on in," says Henry. So she climbs in between us.

"We'll take you home," I says. "Where do you live?"

"Chicken," she says.

"Where the hell's that?" I ask her.

"Alaska."

"Okay," says Henry, and we drive.

We got up there and never wanted to leave. The sun doesn't truly set there in summer, and the night is more a soft dusk. You might doze off, sometimes, but before you know it you're up again, like an animal in nature. You never feel like you have to sleep hard or put away the world. And things would grow up there. One day just dirt or moss, the next day flowers and long grass. The girl's name was Susy. Her family really took to us. They fed us and put us up. We had our own tent to live in by their house, and the kids would be in and out of there all day and night. They couldn't get over me and Henry being brothers, we looked so different. We told them we knew we had the same mother, anyway.

One night Susy came in to visit us. We sat around in the tent talking of this thing and that. The season was changing. It was getting darker by that time, and the cold was even getting just a little mean. I told her it was time for us to go. She stood up on a chair.

"You never seen my hair," Susy said.

That was true. She was standing on a chair, but still, when she unclipped her buns the hair reached all the way to the ground. Our eyes opened. You couldn't tell how much hair she had when it was rolled up so neatly. Then my brother Henry did something funny. He went up to the chair and said, "Jump on my shoulders." So she did that, and her hair reached down past his waist, and he started twirling, this way and that, so her hair was flung out from side to side.

"I always wondered what it was like to have long pretty hair," Henry says. Well we laughed. It was a funny sight, the way he did it. The next morning we got up and took leave of those people.

On to greener pastures, as they say. It was down through Spokane and across Idaho then Montana and very soon we were racing the weather right along under the Canadian border through Columbus, Des Lacs, and then we were in Bottineau County and soon home. We'd made most of the trip, that summer, without putting up the car hood at all. We got home just in time, it turned out, for the army to remember Henry had signed up to join it.

I don't wonder that the army was so glad to get my brother that they turned him into a Marine. He was built like a brick outhouse anyway. We liked to tease him that they really wanted him for his Indian nose. He had a nose big and sharp as a hatchet, like the nose on Red Tomahawk, the Indian who killed Sitting Bull, whose profile is on signs all along the North Dakota highways. Henry went off to training camp, came home once during Christmas, then the next thing you know we got an overseas letter from him. It was 1970, and he said he was stationed up in the northern hill country. Whereabouts I did not know. He wasn't such a hot letter writer, and only got off two before the enemy caught him. I could never keep it straight, which direction those good Vietnam soldiers were from.

I wrote him back several times, even though I didn't know if those letters would get through. I kept him informed all about the car. Most of the time I had it up on blocks in the yard or half taken apart, because that long trip did a hard job on it under the hood.

I always had good luck with numbers, and never worried about the draft myself. I never even had to think about what my number was. But Henry was never lucky in the same way as me. It was at least three years before Henry came home. By then I guess the whole war was solved in the government's mind, but for him it would keep on going. In those years I'd put his car into almost perfect shape. I always thought of it as his car while he was gone, even though when he left he said, "Now it's yours," and threw me his key.

"Thanks for the extra key," I'd say. "I'll put it up in your drawer just in case I need it." He laughed.

When he came home, though, Henry was very different, and I'll say this: the change was no good. You could hardly expect him to change for the better, I know. But he was quiet, so quiet, and never comfortable sitting still anywhere but always up and moving around. I thought back to times we'd sat still for whole afternoons, never moving a muscle, just shifting our weight along the ground, talking to whoever sat with us, watching things. He'd always had a joke, then, too, and now you couldn't get him to laugh, or when he did it was more the sound of a man choking, a sound that stopped up the throats of other people around him. They got to leaving him alone most of the time, and I didn't blame them. It was a fact: Henry was jumpy and mean.

I'd bought a color TV set for my mom and the rest of us while Henry was away. Money still came very easy. I was sorry I'd ever bought it though, because of Henry. I was also sorry I'd bought color, because with black-and-white the pictures seem older and farther away. But what are you going to do? He sat in front of it, watching it, and that was the only time he was completely still. But it was the kind of stillness that you see in a rabbit when it freezes and before it will bolt. He was not easy. He sat in his chair gripping the armrests with all his might, as if the chair itself was moving at a high speed and if he let go at all he would rocket forward and maybe crash right through the set.

Once I was in the room watching TV with Henry and I heard his teeth click at something. I looked over, and he'd bitten through his lip. Blood was going down his chin. I tell you right then I wanted to smash that tube to pieces. I went over to it but Henry must have known what I was up to. He rushed from his chair and shoved me out of the way, against the wall. I told myself he didn't know what he was doing.

My mom came in, turned the set off real quiet, and told us she had made something for supper. So we went and sat down. There was still blood going down Henry's chin, but he didn't notice it and no one said anything, even though every time he took a bite of his bread his blood fell onto it until he was eating his own blood mixed in with the food.

While Henry was not around we talked about what was going to happen to him. There were no Indian doctors on the reservation, and my mom was afraid of trusting Old Man Pillager because he courted her long ago and was jealous of her husbands. He might take revenge through her son. We were afraid that if we brought Henry to a regular hospital they would keep him.

"They don't fix them in those places," Mom said; "they just give them drugs."

"We wouldn't get him there in the first place," I agreed, "so let's just forget about it."

Then I thought about the car.

Henry had not even looked at the car since he'd gotten home, though like I said, it was in tip-top condition and ready to drive. I thought the car might bring the old Henry back somehow. So I bided my time and waited for my chance to interest him in the vehicle.

One night Henry was off somewhere. I took myself a hammer. I went out to that car and I did a number on its underside. Whacked it up. Bent the tail pipe double. Ripped the muffler loose. By the time I was done with the car it looked worse than any typical Indian car that has been driven all its life on reservation roads, which they always say are like government promises — full of holes. It just about hurt me, I'll tell you that! I threw dirt in the carburetor and I ripped all the electric tape off the seats. I made it look just as beat up as I could. Then I sat back and waited for Henry to find it.

Still, it took him over a month. That was all right, because it was just getting warm enough, not melting, but warm enough to work outside.

"Lyman," he says, walking in one day, "that red car looks like shit."

"Well it's old," I says. "You got to expect that."

"No way!" says Henry. "That car's a classic! But you went and ran the piss right out of it, Lyman, and you know it don't deserve that. I kept that car in A-one shape. You don't remember. You're too young. But when I left, that car was running like a watch. Now I don't even know if I can get it to start again, let alone get it anywhere near its old condition."

"Well you try," I said, like I was getting mad, "but I say it's a piece of junk."

Then I walked out before he could realize I knew he'd strung together more than six words at once.

After that I thought he'd freeze himself to death working on that car. He was out there all day, and at night he rigged up a little lamp, ran a cord out the window, and had himself some light to see by while he worked. He was better than he had been before, but that's still not saying much. It was easier for him to do the things the rest of us did. He ate more slowly and didn't jump up and down during the meal to get this or that or look out the window. I put my hand in the back of the TV set, I admit, and fiddled around with it good, so that it was almost impossible now to get a clear picture. He didn't look at it very often anyway. He was always out with that car or going off to get parts for it. By the time it was really melting outside, he had it fixed.

I had been feeling down in the dumps about Henry around this time. We had always been together before. Henry and Lyman. But he was such a loner now that I didn't know how to take it. So I jumped at the chance one day when Henry seemed friendly. It's not that he smiled or anything. He just said, "Let's take that old shitbox for a spin." Just the way he said it made me think he could be coming around.

We went out to the car. It was spring. The sun was shining very bright. My only sister, Bonita, who was just eleven years old, came out and made us stand together for a picture. Henry leaned his elbow on the red car's windshield, and he took his other arm and put it over my shoulder, very carefully, as though it was heavy for him to lift and he didn't want to bring the weight down all at once.

"Smile," Bonita said, and he did.

That picture, I never look at it anymore. A few months ago, I don't know why, I got his picture out and tacked it on the wall. I felt good about Henry at the time, close to him. I felt good having his picture on the wall, until one night when I was looking at television. I was a little drunk and stoned. I looked up at the wall and Henry was staring at me. I don't know what it was, but his smile had changed, or maybe it was gone. All I know is I couldn't stay in the same room with that picture. I was shaking. I got up, closed the door, and went into the kitchen. A little later my friend Ray came over and we both went back into that room. We put the picture in a brown bag, folded the bag over and over tightly, then put it way back in a closet.

I still see that picture now, as if it tugs at me, whenever I pass that closet door. The picture is very clear in my mind. It was so sunny that day Henry had to squint against the glare. Or maybe the camera Bonita held flashed like a mirror, blinding him, before she snapped the picture. My face is right out in the sun, big and round. But he might have drawn back, because the shadows on his face are deep as holes. There are two shadows curved like little hooks around the ends of his smile, as if to frame it and try to keep it there — that one, first smile that looked like it might have hurt his face. He has his field jacket on and the worn-in clothes he'd come back in and kept wearing ever since. After Bonita took the picture, she went into the house and we got into the car. There was a full cooler in the trunk. We started off, east, toward Pembina and the Red River because Henry said he wanted to see the high water.

The trip over there was beautiful. When everything starts changing, drying up, clearing off, you feel like your whole life is starting. Henry felt it, too. The top was down and the car hummed like a top. He'd really put it back in shape, even the tape on the seats was very carefully put down and glued back in layers. It's not that he smiled again or even joked, but his face looked to me as if it was clear, more peaceful. It looked as though he wasn't thinking of anything in particular except the bare fields and windbreaks and houses we were passing.

The river was high and full of winter trash when we got there. The sun was still out, but it was colder by the river. There were still little clumps of dirty snow here and there on the banks. The water hadn't gone over the banks yet, but it would, you could tell. It was just at its limit, hard swollen glossy like an old gray scar. We made ourselves a fire, and we sat down and watched the current go. As I watched it I felt something squeezing inside me and tightening and trying to let go all at the same time. I knew I was not just feeling it myself; I knew I was feeling what Henry was going through at that moment. Except that I couldn't stand it, the closing and opening. I jumped to my feet. I took Henry by the shoulders and I started shaking him. "Wake up," I says, "wake up, wake up, wake up!" I didn't know what had come over me. I sat down beside him again.

His face was totally white and hard. Then it broke, like stones break all of a sudden when water boils up inside them.

"I know it," he says. "I know it. I can't help it. It's no use."

We start talking. He said he knew what I'd done with the car. It was obvious it had been whacked out of shape and not just neglected. He said he wanted to give the car to me for good now, it was no use. He said he'd fixed it just to give it back and I should take it.

"No way," I says, "I don't want it."

"That's okay," he says, "you take it."

"I don't want it, though," I says back to him, and then to emphasize, just to emphasize, you understand, I touch his shoulder. He slaps my hand off.

"Take that car," he says.

"No," I say, "make me," I say, and then he grabs my jacket and rips the arm loose. That jacket is a class act, suede with tags and zippers. I push Henry backwards, off the log. He jumps up and bowls me over. We go down in a clinch and come up swinging hard, for all we're worth, with our fists. He socks my jaw so hard I feel like it swings loose. Then I'm at his ribcage and land a good one under his chin so his head snaps back. He's dazzled. He looks at me and I look at him and then his eyes are full of tears and blood and at first I think he's crying. But no, he's laughing. "Ha! Ha!" he says. "Ha! Ha! Take good care of it."

"Okay," I says, "okay, no problem. Ha! Ha!"

I can't help it, and I start laughing, too. My face feels fat and strange, and after a while I get a beer from the cooler in the trunk, and when I hand it to Henry he takes his shirt and wipes my germs off. "Hoof-and-mouth disease," he says. For some reason this cracks me up, and so we're really laughing for a while, and then we drink all the rest of the beers one by one and throw them in the river and see how far, how fast, the current takes them before they fill up and sink.

"You want to go on back?" I ask after a while. "Maybe we could snag a couple nice Kashpaw girls."

He says nothing. But I can tell his mood is turning again.

"They're all crazy, the girls up here, every damn one of them."

"You're crazy too," I say, to jolly him up. "Crazy Lamartine boys!"

He looks as though he will take this wrong at first. His face twists, then clears, and he jumps up on his feet. "That's right!" he says. "Crazier 'n hell. Crazy Indians!"

I think it's the old Henry again. He throws off his jacket and starts swinging his legs out from the knees like a fancy dancer. He's down doing something between a grouse dance and a bunny hop, no kind of dance I ever saw before, but neither has anyone else on all this green growing earth. He's wild. He wants to pitch whoopee! He's up and at me and all over. All this time I'm laughing so hard, so hard my belly is getting tied up in a knot.

"Got to cool me off!" he shouts all of a sudden. Then he runs over to the river and jumps in.

There's boards and other things in the current. It's so high. No sound comes from the river after the splash he makes, so I run right over. I look around. It's getting dark. I see he's halfway across the water already, and I know he didn't swim there but the current took him. It's far. I hear his voice, though, very clearly across it.

"My boots are filling," he says.

He says this in a normal voice, like he just noticed and he doesn't know what to think of it. Then he's gone. A branch comes by. Another branch. And I go in.

By the time I get out of the river, off the snag I pulled myself onto, the sun is down. I walk back to the car, turn on the high beams, and drive it up the bank. I put it in first gear and then I take my foot off the clutch. I get out, close the door, and watch it plow softly into the water. The headlights reach in as they go down, searching, still lighted even after the water swirls over the back end. I wait. The wires short out. It is all finally dark. And then there is only the water, the sound of it going and running and going and running and running.

[1984]

DAVID LEAVITT (b. 1961) grew up as a "facbrat" in Palo Alto, California, where his father taught at Stanford University. At an early age Leavitt was a sensitive observer of the instability of family life around him:

> In a community where the divorce rate had reached a record high, and every family seemed to have at least one child in prison, or in a hospital, or dead of an overdose, my parents had never even separated. Still, there were sharp words, often, and a sense of desperate effort and hard, unrewarded labor through it all. . . . Sometimes it seemed to me that we walked around the house opened up and bleeding; yet talking, laughing, smiling, like actors in a horror movie who, during a break in the shooting, simply forget to remove the prop knives from their backs or mop up the imitation blood. In this case the blood was real, though we pretended it wasn't.

After Leavitt's graduation from Yale University in 1983, he began, as he says, "to lead the sort of life that makes a good biographical note in the back of a literary magazine." He worked an office job in Manhattan and started to publish his stories and articles in The New Yorker, Harper's, and Esquire. In 1984 he won an O. Henry Prize for his short fiction. That same year his first collection of stories, Family Dancing, was nominated for the National Book Critics Circle Award.

Leavitt says he feels himself a member of a new generation of young people "determined to find in their adulthood the stability that eluded them in childhood. Homes, families, marriages claim them, and they know they must make peace with those claims, but they also take as a given the constant possibility that everything will blow up in their faces." Like Grace Paley, a writer whom he admires, Leavitt feels that a nuclear disaster is something to prepare for. Stories like "Territory" dramatize his sense of the futility of planning for the future in what he calls "an age of ironic hopelessness [the 1980s]. . . . It came to me very early, that ironic and distanced view on things, and it's stayed."

David Leavitt

ᕫᕬ

TERRITORY

Neil's mother, Mrs. Campbell, sits on her lawn chair behind a card table outside the food co-op. Every few minutes, as the sun shifts, she moves the chair and table several inches back so as to remain in the shade. It is a hundred degrees outside, and bright white. Each time someone goes in or out of the co-op a gust of air-conditioning flies out of the automatic doors, raising dust from the cement.

Neil stands just inside, poised over a water fountain, and watches her. She has on a sun hat, and a sweatshirt over her tennis dress; her legs are bare, and shiny with cocoa butter. In front of her, propped against the table, a sign proclaims: MOTHERS, FIGHT FOR YOUR CHILDREN'S RIGHTS — SUPPORT A NONNUCLEAR FUTURE. Women dressed exactly like her pass by, notice the sign, listen to her brief spiel, finger pamphlets, sign petitions or don't sign petitions, never give money. Her weary eyes are masked by dark glasses. In the age of Reagan, she has declared, keeping up the causes of peace and justice is a futile, tiresome, and unrewarding effort; it is therefore an effort fit only for mothers to keep up. The sun bounces off the window glass through which Neil watches her. His own reflection lines up with her profile.

Later that afternoon, Neil spreads himself out alongside the pool and imagines he is being watched by the shirtless Chicano gardener. But the gardener, concentrating on his pruning, is neither seductive nor seducible. On the lawn, his mother's large Airedales — Abigail, Lucille, Fern — amble, sniff, urinate. Occasionally, they accost the gardener, who yells at them in Spanish.

After two years' absence, Neil reasons, he should feel nostalgia, regret, gladness upon returning home. He closes his eyes and tries to muster the proper background music for the cinematic scene of return. His rhapsody, however, is interrupted by the noises of his mother's trio — the scratchy cello, whining violin, stumbling piano — as she and Lillian Havalard and Charlotte Feder plunge through Mozart. The tune is cheery, in a Germanic sort of way, and utterly inappropriate to what Neil is trying to feel. Yet it *is* the music of his adolescence; they have played it for years, bent over the notes, their heads bobbing in silent time to the metronome.

It is getting darker. Every few minutes, he must move his towel so as to remain within the narrowing patch of sunlight. In four hours, Wayne, his lover of ten months and the only person he has ever imagined he could spend his life with, will be in this house, where no lover of his has ever set foot. The thought fills him with a sense of grand terror and curiosity. He stretches, tries to feel seductive, desirable. The gardener's shears whack at the ferns; the music above him rushes to a loud, premature conclusion. The women laugh and applaud themselves as they give up for the day. He hears Charlotte Feder's full nasal twang, the voice of a fat woman in a pink pants suit — odd, since she is a scrawny, arthritic old bird, rarely clad in anything other than tennis shorts and a blouse. Lillian is the fat woman in the pink pants suit; her voice is thin and warped by too much crying. Drink in hand, she calls out from the porch, "Hot enough!" and waves. He lifts himself up and nods to her.

The women sit on the porch and chatter; their voices blend with the clink of ice in glasses. They belong to a small circle of ladies all of whom, with the exception of Neil's mother, are widows and divorcées. Lillian's husband left her twenty-two years ago, and sends her a check every month to live on; Charlotte has been divorced twice as long as she was married, and has a daughter serving a long sentence for terrorist acts committed when she was nineteen. Only Neil's mother has a husband, a distant sort of husband, away often on business. He is away on business now. All of them feel betrayed — by husbands, by children, by history.

Neil closes his eyes, tries to hear the words only as sounds. Soon, a new noise accosts him: his mother arguing with the gardener in Spanish. He leans on his elbows and watches them; the syllables are loud, heated, and compressed, and seem on the verge of explosion. But the argument ends happily; they shake hands. The gardener collects his check and walks out the gate without so much as looking at Neil.

He does not know the gardener's name; as his mother has reminded him, he does not know most of what has gone on since he moved away. Her life has gone on, unaffected by his absence. He flinches at his own egoism, the egoism of sons.

"Neil! Did you call the airport to make sure the plane's coming in on time?"

"Yes," he shouts to her. "It is."

"Good. Well, I'll have dinner ready when you get back."

"Mom —"

"What?" The word comes out in a weary wail that is more of an answer than a question.

"What's wrong?" he says, forgetting his original question.

"Nothing's wrong," she declares in a tone that indicates that everything is wrong. "The dogs have to be fed, dinner has to be made, and I've got people here. Nothing's wrong."

"I hope things will be as comfortable as possible when Wayne gets here."

"Is that a request or a threat?"

"Mom —"

Behind her sunglasses, her eyes are inscrutable. "I'm tired," she says. "It's been a long day. I . . . I'm anxious to meet Wayne. I'm sure he'll be wonderful, and we'll all have a wonderful, wonderful time. I'm sorry. I'm just tired."

She heads up the stairs. He suddenly feels an urge to cover himself; his body embarrasses him, as it has in her presence since the day she saw him shirtless and said with delight, "Neil! You're growing hair under your arms!"

Before he can get up, the dogs gather round him and begin to sniff and lick at him. He wriggles to get away from them, but Abigail, the largest and stupidest, straddles his stomach and nuzzles his mouth. He splutters and, laughing, throws her off. "Get away from me, you goddamn dogs," he shouts, and swats at them. They are new dogs, not the dog of his childhood, not dogs he trusts.

He stands, and the dogs circle him, looking up at his face expectantly. He feels renewed terror at the thought that Wayne will be here so soon: Will they sleep in the same room? Will they make love? He has never had sex in his parents' house. How can he be expected to be a lover here, in this place of his childhood, of his earliest shame, in this household of mothers and dogs?

"Dinnertime! Abbylucyferny, Abbylucyferny, dinnertime!" His mother's litany disperses the dogs, and they run for the door.

"Do you realize," he shouts to her, "that no matter how much those dogs love you they'd probably kill you for the leg of lamb in the freezer?"

Neil was twelve the first time he recognized in himself something like sexuality. He was lying outside, on the grass, when Rasputin — the dog, long dead, of his childhood — began licking his face. He felt a tingle he did not recognize, pulled off his shirt to give the dog access to more of him. Rasputin's tongue tickled coolly. A wet nose started to sniff down his body, toward his bathing suit. What he felt frightened him, but he couldn't bring himself to push the dog away. Then his mother called out, "Dinner," and Rasputin was gone, more interested in food than in him.

It was the day after Rasputin was put to sleep, years later, that Neil finally stood in the kitchen, his back turned to his parents, and said, with unexpected ease, "I'm a homosexual." The words seemed insufficient, reductive. For years, he had believed his sexuality to be detachable from the essential him, but now he realized that it was part of him. He had the sudden, despairing sensation that though the words had been easy to say, the fact of their having been aired was incurably damning. Only then, for the first time, did he admit that they were true, and he shook and wept in regret for what he would not be for his mother, for having failed her. His father hung back, silent; he was absent for that moment as he was mostly absent — a strong absence. Neil always thought of him sitting on the edge of the bed in his underwear, captivated by something on television. He said, "It's O.K., Neil." But his mother was resolute; her lower lip didn't quaver.

She had enormous reserves of strength to which she only gained access at moments like this one. She hugged him from behind, wrapped him in the childhood smells of perfume and brownies, and whispered, "It's O.K., honey." For once, her words seemed as inadequate as his. Neil felt himself shrunk to an embarrassed adolescent, hating her sympathy, not wanting her to touch him. It was the way he would feel from then on whenever he was in her presence — even now, at twenty-three, bringing home his lover to meet her.

All through his childhood, she had packed only the most nutritious lunches, had served on the PTA, had volunteered at the children's library and at his school, had organized a successful campaign to ban a racist history textbook. The day after he told her, she located and got in touch with an organization called the Coalition of Parents of Lesbians and Gays. Within a year, she was president of it. On weekends, she and the other mothers drove their station wagons to San Francisco, set up their card tables in front of the Bulldog Baths, the Liberty Baths, passed out literature to men in leather and denim who were loathe to admit they even had mothers. These men, who would habitually do violence to each other, were strangely cowed by the suburban ladies with their informational booklets, and bent their heads. Neil was a sophomore in college then, and lived in San Francisco. She brought him pamphlets detailing the dangers of bathhouses and back rooms, enemas and poppers, wordless sex in alleyways. His excursion into that world had been brief and lamentable, and was over. He winced at the thought that she knew all his sexual secrets, and vowed to move to the East Coast to escape her. It was not very different from the days when she had campaigned for a better playground, or tutored the Hispanic children in the audiovisual room. Those days, as well, he had run away from her concern. Even today, perched in front of the co-op, collecting signatures for nuclear disarmament, she was quintessentially a mother. And if the lot of mothers was to expect nothing in return, was the lot of sons to return nothing?

Driving across the Dumbarton Bridge on his way to the airport, Neil thinks, I have returned nothing; I have simply returned. He wonders if she would have given birth to him had she known what he would grow up to be.

Then he berates himself: Why should he assume himself to be the cause of her sorrow? She has told him that her life is full of secrets. She has changed since he left home — grown thinner, more rigid, harder to hug. She has given up baking, taken up tennis; her skin has browned and tightened. She is no longer the woman who hugged him and kissed him, who said, "As long as you're happy, that's all that's important to us."

The flats spread out around him; the bridge floats on purple and green silt, and spongy bay fill, not water at all. Only ten miles north, a whole city has been built on gunk dredged up from the bay.

He arrives at the airport ten minutes early, to discover that the plane had landed twenty minutes early. His first view of Wayne is from behind, by the baggage belt. Wayne looks as he always looks — slightly wind-blown — and is wearing the ratty leather jacket he was wearing the night they met. Neil sneaks up on him and puts his hands on his shoulders; when Wayne turns around, he looks relieved to see him.

They hug like brothers, only in the safety of Neil's mother's car do they dare to kiss. They recognize each other's smells, and grow comfortable again. "I never imagined I'd actually see you out here," Neil says, "but you're exactly the same here as there."

"It's only been a week."

They kiss again. Neil wants to go to a motel, but Wayne insists on being pragmatic. "We'll be there soon. Don't worry."

"We could go to one of the bathhouses in the city and take a room for a couple of aeons," Neil says. "Christ, I'm hard up. I don't even know if we're going to be in the same bedroom."

"Well, if we're not," Wayne says, "we'll sneak around. It'll be romantic."

They cling to each other for a few more minutes, until they realize that people are looking in the car window. Reluctantly, they pull apart. Neil reminds himself that he loves this man, that there is a reason for him to bring this man home.

He takes the scenic route on the way back. The car careers over foot-hills, through forests, along white four-lane highways high in the moun-tains. Wayne tells Neil that he sat next to a woman on the plane who was once Marilyn Monroe's psychiatrist's nurse. He slips his foot out of his shoe and nudges Neil's ankle, pulling Neil's sock down with his toe.

"I have to drive," Neil says. "I'm very glad you're here."

There is a comfort in the privacy of the car. They have a common fear of walking hand in hand, of publicly showing physical affection, even in the permissive West Seventies of New York — a fear that they have admitted only to one another. They slip through a pass between two hills, and are suddenly in residential Northern California, the land of expensive ranch-style houses.

As they pull into Neil's mother's driveway, the dogs run barking to-ward the car. When Wayne opens the door, they jump and lap at him, and he tries to close it again. "Don't worry. Abbylucyferny! Get in the house, damn it!"

His mother descends from the porch. She has changed into a blue flower-print dress, which Neil doesn't recognize. He gets out of the car and halfheartedly chastises the dogs. Crickets chirp in the trees. His mother looks radiant, even beautiful, illuminated by the headlights, surrounded by the now quiet dogs, like a Circe with her slaves. When she walks over to Wayne, offering her hand, and says, "Wayne, I'm Barbara," Neil forgets that she is his mother.

"Good to meet you, Barbara," Wayne says, and reaches out his hand. Craftier than she, he whirls her around to kiss her cheek.

Barbara! He is calling his mother Barbara! Then he remembers that Wayne is five years older than he is. They chat by the open car door, and

Neil shrinks back — the embarrassed adolescent, uncomfortable, unwanted.

So the dreaded moment passes and he might as well not have been there. At dinner, Wayne keeps the conversation smooth, like a captivated courtier seeking Neil's mother's hand. A faggot son's sodomist — such words spit into Neil's head. She has prepared tiny meatballs with fresh coriander, fettucine with pesto. Wayne talks about the street people in New York; El Salvador is a tragedy; if only Sadat had lived; Phyllis Schlafly — what can you do?

"It's a losing battle," she tells him. "Every day I'm out there with my card table, me and the other mothers, but I tell you, Wayne, it's a losing battle. Sometimes I think us old ladies are the only ones with enough patience to fight."

Occasionally, Neil says something, but his comments seem stupid and clumsy. Wayne continues to call her Barbara. No one under forty has ever called her Barbara as long as Neil can remember. They drink wine; he does not.

Now is the time for drastic action. He contemplates taking Wayne's hand, then checks himself. He has never done anything in her presence to indicate that the sexuality he confessed to five years ago was a reality and not an invention. Even now, he and Wayne might as well be friends, college roommates. Then Wayne, his savior, with a single, sweeping gesture, reaches for his hand, and clasps it, in the midst of a joke he is telling about Saudi Arabians. By the time he is laughing, their hands are joined. Neil's throat contracts; his heart begins to beat violently. He notices his mother's eyes flicker, glance downward; she never breaks the stride of her sentence. The dinner goes on, and every taboo nurtured since childhood falls quietly away.

She removes the dishes. Their hands grow sticky; he cannot tell which fingers are his and which Wayne's. She clears the rest of the table and rounds up the dogs.

"Well, boys, I'm very tired, and I've got a long day ahead of me tomorrow, so I think I'll hit the sack. There are extra towels for you in Neil's bathroom, Wayne. Sleep well."

"Good night, Barbara," Wayne calls out. "It's been wonderful meeting you."

They are alone. Now they can disentangle their hands.

"No problem about where we sleep, is there?"

"No," Neil says. "I just can't imagine sleeping with someone in this house."

His leg shakes violently. Wayne takes Neil's hand in a firm grasp and hauls him up.

Later that night, they lie outside, under redwood trees, listening to the hysteria of the crickets, the hum of the pool cleaning itself. Redwood leaves prick their skin. They fell in love in bars and apartments, and this is the first time that they have made love outdoors. Neil is not sure he has enjoyed the experience. He kept sensing eyes, imagined that the neighborhood cats were staring at them from behind a fence of brambles. He remembers he once hid in this spot when he and some of the children from the neighborhood were playing sardines, remembers the intoxication of small bodies packed together, the warm breath of suppressed laughter on his neck. "The loser had to go through the spanking machine," he tells Wayne.

"Did you lose often?"

"Most of the time. The spanking machine never really hurt — just a whirl of hands. If you moved fast enough, no one could actually get you. Sometimes, though, late in the afternoon, we'd get naughty. We'd chase each other and pull each other's pants down. That was all. Boys and girls together!"

"Listen to the insects," Wayne says, and closes his eyes.

Neil turns to examine Wayne's face, notices a single, small pimple. Their lovemaking usually begins in a wrestle, a struggle for dominance, and ends with a somewhat confusing loss of identity — as now, when Neil sees a foot on the grass, resting against his leg, and tries to determine if it is his own or Wayne's.

From inside the house, the dogs begin to bark. Their yelps grow into alarmed falsettos. Neil lifts himself up. "I wonder if they smell something," he says.

"Probably just us," says Wayne.

"My mother will wake up. She hates getting waked up."

Lights go on in the house; the door to the porch opens.

"What's wrong, Abby? What's wrong?" his mother's voice calls softly.

Wayne clamps his hand over Neil's mouth. "Don't say anything," he whispers.

"I can't just — " Neil begins to say, but Wayne's hand closes over his mouth again. He bites it, and Wayne starts laughing.

"What was that?" Her voice projects into the garden. "Hello?" she says.

The dogs yelp louder. "Abbylucyferny, it's O.K., it's O.K." Her voice is soft and panicked. "Is anyone there?" she asks loudly.

The brambles shake. She takes a flashlight, shines it around the garden. Wayne and Neil duck down; the light lands on them and hovers for a few seconds. Then it clicks off and they are in the dark — a new dark, a darker dark, which their eyes must readjust to.

"Let's go to bed, Abbylucyferny," she says gently. Neil and Wayne hear her pad into the house. The dogs whimper as they follow her, and the lights go off.

Once before, Neil and his mother had stared at each other in the glare of bright lights. Four years ago, they stood in the arena created by the headlights of her car, waiting for the train. He was on his way back to San Francisco, where he was marching in a Gay Pride Parade the next day. The train station was next door to the food co-op and shared its parking lot. The co-op, familiar and boring by day, took on a certain mystery in the night. Neil recognized the spot where he had skidded on his bicycle and broken his leg. Through the glass doors, the brightly lit interior of the store glowed, its rows and rows of cans and boxes forming their own horizon, each can illuminated so that even from outside Neil could read the labels. All that was missing was the ladies in tennis dresses and sweatshirts, pushing their carts past bins of nuts and dried fruits.

"Your train is late," his mother said. Her hair fell loosely on her shoulders, and her legs were tanned. Neil looked at her and tried to imagine her in labor with him — bucking and struggling with his birth. He felt then the strange, sexless love for women which through his whole adolescence he had mistaken for heterosexual desire.

A single bright light approached them; it preceded the low, haunting sound of the whistle. Neil kissed his mother, and waved goodbye as he ran to meet the train. It was an old train, with windows tinted a sort of horrible lemon-lime. It stopped only long enough for him to hoist himself on board, and then it was moving again. He hurried to a window, hoping to see her drive off, but the tint of the window made it possible for him to make out only vague patches of light — street lamps, cars, the co-op.

He sank into the hard, green seat. The train was almost entirely empty; the only other passenger was a dark-skinned man wearing bluejeans and a leather jacket. He sat directly across the aisle from Neil, next to the window. He had rough skin and a thick mustache. Neil discovered that by pretending to look out the window he could study the man's reflection in the lemon-lime glass. It was only slightly hazy — the quality of a bad photograph. Neil felt his mouth open, felt sleep closing in on him. Hazy red and gold flashes through the glass pulsed in the face of the man in the window, giving the curious impression of muscle spasms. It took Neil a few minutes to realize that the man was staring at him, or, rather, staring at the back of his head — staring at his staring. The man smiled as though to say, I know exactly what you're staring at, and Neil felt the sickening sensation of desire rise in his throat.

Right before they reached the city, the man stood up and sat down in the seat next to Neil's. The man's thigh brushed deliberately against his own. Neil's eyes were watering; he felt sick to his stomach. Taking Neil's hand, the man said, "Why so nervous, honey? Relax."

Neil woke up the next morning with the taste of ashes in his mouth. He was lying on the floor, without blankets or sheets or pillows. Instinctively, he reached for his pants and as he pulled them on came face to face with the man from the train. His name was Luis; he turned out to be a dog groomer. His apartment smelled of dog.

"Why such a hurry?" Luis said.

"The parade. The Gay Pride Parade. I'm meeting some friends to march."

"I'll come with you," Luis said. "I think I'm too old for these things, but why not?"

Neil did not want Luis to come with him, but he found it impossible to say so. Luis looked older by day, more likely to carry diseases. He dressed again in a torn T-shirt, leather jacket, bluejeans. "It's my everyday apparel," he said, and laughed. Neil buttoned his pants, aware that they had been washed by his mother the day before. Luis possessed the peculiar combination of hypermasculinity and effeminacy which exemplifies faggotry. Neil wanted to be rid of him, but Luis's mark was on him, he could see that much. They would become lovers whether Neil liked it or not.

They joined the parade midway. Neil hoped he wouldn't meet anyone he knew; he did not want to have to explain Luis, who clung to him. The parade was full of shirtless men with oiled, muscular shoulders. Neil's back ached. There were floats carrying garishly dressed prom queens and cheerleaders, some with beards, some actually looking like women. Luis said, "It makes me proud, makes me glad to be what I am." Neil supposed that by darting into the crowd ahead of him he might be able to lose Luis forever, but he found it difficult to let him go; the prospect of being alone seemed unbearable.

Neil was startled to see his mother watching the parade, holding up a sign. She was with the Coalition of Parents of Lesbians and Gays; they had posted a huge banner on the wall behind them proclaiming: OUR SONS AND DAUGHTERS, WE ARE PROUD OF YOU. She spotted him; she waved, and jumped up and down.

"Who's that woman?" Luis asked.

"My mother. I should go say hello to her."

"O.K.," Luis said. He followed Neil to the side of the parade. Neil kissed his mother. Luis took off his shirt, wiped his face with it, smiled.

"I'm glad you came," Neil said.

"I wouldn't have missed it, Neil. I wanted to show you I cared."

He smiled, and kissed her again. He showed no intention of introducing Luis, so Luis introduced himself.

"Hello, Luis," Mrs. Campbell said. Neil looked away. Luis shook her hand, and Neil wanted to warn his mother to wash it, warned himself to check with a V.D. clinic first thing Monday.

"Neil, this is Carmen Bologna, another one of the mothers," Mrs. Campbell said. She introduced him to a fat Italian woman with flushed cheeks, and hair arranged in the shape of a clamshell.

"Good to meet you, Neil, good to meet you," said Carmen Bologna. "You know my son, Michael? I'm so proud of Michael! He's doing so well now. I'm proud of him, proud to be his mother I am, and your mother's proud, too!"

The woman smiled at him, and Neil could think of nothing to say but "Thank you." He looked uncomfortably toward his mother, who stood listening to Luis. It occurred to him that the worst period of his life was probably about to begin and he had no way to stop it.

A group of drag queens ambled over to where the mothers were standing. "Michael! Michael!" shouted Carmen Bologna, and embraced a stick-like man wrapped in green satin. Michael's eyes were heavily dosed with green eyeshadow, and his lips were painted pink.

Neil turned and saw his mother staring, her mouth open. He marched over to where Luis was standing, and they moved back into the parade. He turned and waved to her. She waved back; he saw pain in her face, and then, briefly, regret. That day, he felt she would have traded him for any other son. Later, she said to him, "Carmen Bologna really was proud, and, speaking as a mother, let me tell you, you have to be brave to feel such pride."

Neil was never proud. It took him a year to dump Luis, another year to leave California. The sick taste of ashes was still in his mouth. On the plane, he envisioned his mother sitting alone in the dark, smoking. She did not leave his mind until he was circling New York, staring down at the dawn rising over Queens. The song playing in his earphones would remain hovering on the edges of his memory, always associated with her absence. After collecting his baggage, he took a bus into the city. Boys were selling newspapers in the middle of highways, through the windows of stopped cars. It was seven in the morning when he reached Manhattan. He stood for ten minutes on East Thirty-fourth Street, breathed the cold air, and felt bubbles rising in his blood.

Neil got a job as a paralegal — a temporary job, he told himself. When he met Wayne a year later, the sensations of that first morning returned to him. They'd been up all night, and at six they walked across the park to Wayne's apartment with the nervous, deliberate gait of people aching to make love for the first time. Joggers ran by with their dogs. None of them knew what Wayne and he were about to do, and the secrecy excited him. His mother came to mind, and the song, and the whirling vision of Queens coming alive below him. His breath solidified into clouds, and he felt happier than he had ever felt before in his life.

The second day of Wayne's visit, he and Neil go with Mrs. Campbell to pick up the dogs at the dog parlor. The grooming establishment is decorated with pink ribbons and photographs of the owner's champion pit bulls. A fat, middle-aged woman appears from the back, leading the newly trimmed and fluffed Abigail, Lucille, and Fern by three leashes. The dogs struggle frantically when they see Neil's mother, tangling the woman up in their leashes. "Ladies, behave!" Mrs. Campbell commands, and collects the dogs. She gives Fern to Neil and Abigail to Wayne. In the car on the way back, Abigail begins pawing to get on Wayne's lap.

"Just push her off," Mrs. Campbell says. "She knows she's not supposed to do that."

"You never groomed Rasputin," Neil complains.

"Rasputin was a mutt."

"Rasputin was a beautiful dog, even if he did smell."

"Do you remember when you were a little kid, Neil, you used to make Rasputin dance with you? Once you tried to dress him up in one of my blouses."

"I don't remember that," Neil says.

"Yes. I remember," says Mrs. Campbell. "Then you tried to organize a dog beauty contest in the neighborhood. You wanted to have runners-up — everything."

"A dog beauty contest?" Wayne says.

"Mother, do we have to — "

"I think it's a mother's privilege to embarrass her son," Mrs. Campbell says, and smiles.

When they are about to pull into the driveway, Wayne starts screaming, and pushes Abigail off his lap. "Oh, my God!" he says. "The dog just pissed all over me."

Neil turns around and sees a puddle seeping into Wayne's slacks. He suppresses his laughter, and Mrs. Campbell hands him a rag.

"I'm sorry, Wayne," she says. "It goes with the territory."

"This is really disgusting," Wayne says, swatting at himself with the rag.

Neil keeps his eyes on his own reflection in the rearview mirror and smiles.

At home, while Wayne cleans himself in the bathroom, Neil watches his mother cook lunch — Japanese noodles in soup. "When you went off to college," she says, "I went to the grocery store. I was going to buy you ramen noodles, and I suddenly realized you weren't going to be around to eat them. I started crying right then, blubbering like an idiot."

Neil clenches his fists inside his pockets. She has a way of telling him little sad stories when he doesn't want to hear them — stories of dolls broken by her brothers, lunches stolen by neighborhood boys on the way to school. Now he has joined the ranks of male children who have made her cry.

"Mama, I'm sorry," he says.

She is bent over the noodles, which steam in her face. "I didn't want to say anything in front of Wayne, but I wish you had answered me last night. I was very frightened — and worried."

"I'm sorry," he says, but it's not convincing. His fingers prickle. He senses a great sorrow about to be born.

"I lead a quiet life," she says. "I don't want to be a disciplinarian. I just don't have the energy for these — shenanigans. Please don't frighten me that way again."

"If you were so upset, why didn't you say something?"

"I'd rather not discuss it. I lead a quiet life. I'm not used to getting woken up late at night. I'm not used — "

"To my having a lover?"

"No, I'm not used to having other people around, that's all. Wayne is charming. A wonderful young man."

"He likes you, too."

"I'm sure we'll get along fine."

She scoops the steaming noodles into ceramic bowls. Wayne returns, wearing shorts. His white, hairy legs are a shocking contrast to hers, which are brown and sleek.

"I'll wash those pants, Wayne," Mrs. Campbell says. "I have a special detergent that'll take out the stain."

She gives Neil a look to indicate that the subject should be dropped. He looks at Wayne, looks at his mother; his initial embarrassment gives way to a fierce pride — the arrogance of mastery. He is glad his mother knows that he is desired, glad it makes her flinch.

Later, he steps into the back yard; the gardener is back, whacking at the bushes with his shears. Neil walks by him in his bathing suit, imagining he is on parade.

That afternoon, he finds his mother's daily list on the kitchen table:

TUESDAY
7:00 — breakfast
Take dogs to groomer
Groceries (?)

Campaign against Draft — 4–7

Buy underwear
Trios — 2:00
Spaghetti
Fruit
Asparagus if sale
Peanuts
Milk

Doctor's Appointment(make)
Write Cranston/Hayakawa
re disarmament

Handi-Wraps
Mozart
Abigail
Top Ramen
Pedro

Her desk and trash can are full of such lists; he remembers them from the earliest days of his childhood. He had learned to read from them. In his own life, too, there have been endless lists — covered with check marks and arrows, at least one item always spilling over onto the next day's agenda. From September to November, "Buy plane ticket for Christmas" floated from list to list to list.

The last item puzzles him: Pedro. Pedro must be the gardener. He observes the accretion of names, the arbitrary specifics that give a sense of his mother's life. He could make a list of his own selves: the child, the adolescent, the promiscuous faggot son, and finally the good son, settled, relatively successful. But the divisions wouldn't work; he is today and will always be the child being licked by the dog, the boy on the floor with Luis; he will still be everything he is ashamed of. The other lists — the lists of things done and undone — tell their own truth: that his life is measured more properly in objects than in stages. He knows himself as "jump rope," "book," "sunglasses," "underwear."

"Tell me about your family, Wayne," Mrs. Campbell says that night, as they drive toward town. They are going to see an Esther Williams movie at the local revival house: an underwater musical, populated by mermaids, underwater Rockettes.

"My father was a lawyer," Wayne says. "He had an office in Queens, with a neon sign. I think he's probably the only lawyer in the world who had a neon sign. Anyway, he died when I was ten. My mother never remarried. She lives in Queens. Her great claim to fame is that when she was twenty-two she went on 'The $64,000 Question.' Her category was mystery novels. She made it to sixteen thousand before she got tripped up."

"When I was about ten, I wanted you to go on 'Jeopardy,' " Neil says to his mother. "You really should have, you know. You would have won."

"You certainly loved 'Jeopardy,' " Mrs. Campbell says. "You used to watch it during dinner. Wayne, does your mother work?"

"No," he says. "She lives off investments."

"You're both only children," Mrs. Campbell says. Neil wonders if she is ruminating on the possible connection between that coincidence and their "alternative life style."

The movie theater is nearly empty. Neil sits between Wayne and his mother. There are pillows on the floor at the front of the theater, and a cat is prowling over them. It casts a monstrous shadow every now and then on the screen, disturbing the sedative effect of water ballet. Like a teen-ager, Neil cautiously reaches his arm around Wayne's shoulder. Wayne takes his hand immediately. Next to them, Neil's mother breathes in, out, in, out. Neil timorously moves his other arm and lifts it behind his mother's neck. He does not look at her, but he can tell from her breathing that she senses what he is doing. Slowly, carefully, he lets his hand drop on her shoulder; it twitches spasmodically, and he jumps, as if he had received an electric shock. His mother's quiet breathing is broken by a gasp; even Wayne notices. A sudden brightness on the screen illuminates the panic in her eyes, Neil's arm frozen above her, about to fall again. Slowly, he lowers his arm until his fingertips touch her skin, the fabric of her dress. He has gone too far to go back now; they are all too far.

Wayne and Mrs. Campbell sink into their seats, but Neil remains stiff, holding up his arms, which rest on nothing. The movie ends, and they go on sitting just like that.

"I'm old," Mrs. Campbell says later, as they drive back home. "I remember when those films were new. Your father and I went to one on our first date. I loved them, because I could pretend that those women underwater were flying — they were so graceful. They really took advantage of Technicolor in those days. Color was something to appreciate. You can't know what it was like to see a color movie for the first time, after years of black-and-white. It's like trying to explain the surprise of snow to an East Coaster. Very little is new anymore, I fear."

Neil would like to tell her about his own nostalgia, but how can he explain that all of it revolves around her? The idea of her life before he was born pleases him. "Tell Wayne how you used to look like Esther Williams," he asks her.

She blushes. "I was told I looked like Esther Williams, but really more like Gene Tierney," she says. "Not beautiful, but interesting. I like to think I had a certain magnetism."

"You still do," Wayne says, and instantly recognizes the wrongness of his comment. Silence and a nervous laugh indicate that he has not yet mastered the family vocabulary.

When they get home, the night is once again full of the sound of crickets. Mrs. Campbell picks up a flashlight and calls the dogs. "Abbylucyferny, Abbylucyferny," she shouts, and the dogs amble from their various corners. She pushes them out the door to the back yard and follows them. Neil follows her. Wayne follows Neil, but hovers on the porch. Neil walks behind her as she tramps through the garden. She holds out her flashlight, and snails slide from behind bushes, from under rocks, to where she stands. When the snails become visible, she crushes them underfoot. They make a wet, cracking noise, like eggs being broken.

"Nights like this," she says, "I think of children without pants on, in hot South American countries. I have nightmares about tanks rolling down our street."

"The weather's never like this in New York," Neil says. "When it's hot, it's humid and sticky. You don't want to go outdoors."

"I could never live anywhere else but here. I think I'd die. I'm too used to the climate."

"Don't be silly."

"No, I mean it," she says. "I have adjusted too well to the weather."

The dogs bark and howl by the fence. "A cat, I suspect," she says. She aims her flashlight at a rock, and more snails emerge — uncountable numbers, too stupid to have learned not to trust light.

"I know what you were doing at the movie," she says.

"What?"

"I know what you were doing."

"What? I put my arm around you."

"I'm sorry, Neil," she says. "I can only take so much. Just so much."

"What do you mean?" he says. "I was only trying to show affection."

"Oh, affection — I know about affection."

He looks up at the porch, sees Wayne moving toward the door, trying not to listen.

"What do you mean?" Neil says to her.

She puts down the flashlight and wraps her arms around herself. "I remember when you were a little boy," she says. "I remember, and I have to stop remembering. I wanted you to grow up happy. And I'm very tolerant, very understanding. But I can only take so much."

His heart seems to have risen into his throat. "Mother," he says, "I think you know my life isn't your fault. But for God's sake, don't say that your life is my fault."

"It's not a question of fault," she says. She extracts a Kleenex from her pocket and blows her nose. "I'm sorry, Neil. I guess I'm just an old woman with too much on her mind and not enough to do." She laughs half-heartedly. "Don't worry. Don't say anything," she says. "Abbylucyferny, Abbylucyferny, time for bed!"

He watches her as she walks toward the porch, silent and regal. There is the pad of feet, the clinking of dog tags as the dogs run for the house.

He was twelve the first time she saw him march in a parade. He played the tuba, and as his elementary-school band lumbered down the streets of their then small town she stood on the sidelines and waved. Afterward, she had taken him out for ice cream. He spilled some on his red uniform, and she swiped at it with a napkin. She had been there for him that day, as well as years later, at that more memorable parade; she had been there for him every day.

Somewhere over Iowa, a week later, Neil remembers this scene, remembers other days, when he would find her sitting in the dark, crying. She had to take time out of her own private sorrow to appease his anxiety. "It was part of it," she told him later. "Part of being a mother."

"The scariest thing in the world is the thought that you could unknowingly ruin someone's life," Neil tells Wayne. "Or even change someone's life. I hate the thought of having such control. I'd make a rotten mother."

"You're crazy," Wayne says. "You have this great mother, and all you do is complain. I know people whose mothers have disowned them."

"Guilt goes with the territory," Neil says.

"Why?" Wayne asks, perfectly seriously.

Neil doesn't answer. He lies back in his seat, closes his eyes, imagines he grew up in a house in the mountains of Colorado, surrounded by snow — endless white snow on hills. No flat places, and no trees; just white hills. Every time he has flown away, she has come into his mind, usually sitting alone in the dark, smoking. Today she is outside at dusk, skimming leaves from the pool.

"I want to get a dog," Neil says.

Wayne laughs. "In the city? I'd suffocate."

The hum of the airplane is druglike, dazing. "I want to stay with you a long time," Neil says.

"I know." Imperceptibly, Wayne takes his hand.

"It's very hot there in the summer, too. You know, I'm not thinking about my mother now."

"It's O.K."

For a moment, Neil wonders what the stewardess or the old woman on the way to the bathroom will think, but then he laughs and relaxes.

Later, the plane makes a slow circle over New York City, and on it two men hold hands, eyes closed, and breathe in unison.

[1984]

PART TWO

THE COMMENTARIES

The next part of this book consists of critical comments on the short story form and on various individual stories. In the preface to his story collection *Twice-told Tales*, Nathaniel Hawthorne wrote that a writer "would have reason to be ashamed if he could not criticize his own work as fairly as another man's, and — though it is little his business, and perhaps still less his interest — he can hardly resist a temptation to achieve something of the sort. If writers were allowed to do so, and would perform the task with perfect sincerity and unreserve, their opinions of their own productions would often be more valuable and instructive than the works themselves." While Hawthorne was not entirely serious in this last statement, there is some truth in what he said. Writers' attitudes about creating short fiction can often clarify their work, place their stories in a larger context of literary history, and shed light on the creative process.

The commentaries in this section are arranged chronologically to follow the order of the stories in the anthology.

NATHANIEL HAWTHORNE *began to keep a journal in 1835, after having graduated from college, when he was living in Salem and beginning to write magazine fiction. In the journal he often made brief notes about his thoughts and observations, which he would later work up into tales. As his biographer Newton Arvin has stated, Hawthorne "had a predilection . . . for men and women on the edge of things, outcasts, 'wrecks,' people who had somehow failed to swing into the general march of life, or had somehow fallen out of it." About his actual process of composition or his theory of short fiction, Hawthorne wrote very little. After his marriage to Sophia Peabody in July 1842, the couple went to live in Concord, where they settled into the "Old Manse," near the homes of Ralph Waldo Emerson and Henry David Thoreau. In March 1843 Hawthorne went back to Salem for a short visit. Separated from his beloved wife, he found himself in an introspective mood. In his journal he mocked the "agonies of inspiration" he had gone through in his Salem bedroom years before, when he had been struggling to establish his career as a writer.*

`⇥ 1 ⇤`

Nathaniel Hawthorne

Passage from

THE AMERICAN NOTEBOOKS

Salem. — . . . Here I am, in my old chamber, where I produced those stupendous works of fiction which have since impressed the universe with wonderment and awe! To this chamber, doubtless, in all succeeding ages, pilgrims will come to pay their tribute of reverence; they will put off their shoes at the threshold for fear of desecrating the tattered old carpets! "There," they will exclaim, "is the very bed in which he slumbered, and where he was visited by those ethereal visions which he afterwards fixed forever in glowing words! There is the wash-stand at which this exalted personage cleansed himself from the stains of earth, and rendered his outward man a fitting exponent of the pure soul within. There, in its mahogany frame, is the dressing-glass, which often reflected that noble brow, those hyacinthine locks, that mouth bright with smiles or tremulous with feeling, that flashing or melting eye, that — in short, every item of the magnanimous face of this unexampled man. There is the pine table, — there the old flag-bottomed chair on which he sat, and at which he scribbled, during his agonies of inspiration! There is the old chest of drawers in which he kept what shirts a poor author may be supposed to have possessed! There is the closet in which was reposited his threadbare suit of black! There is the worn-out shoe-brush with which this polished writer polished his boots. There is" — but I believe this will be pretty much all, so here I close the catalogue. . . .

A cloudy veil stretches over the abyss of my nature. I have, however, no love of secrecy and darkness. I am glad to think that God sees through my heart, and, if any angel has power to penetrate into it, he is welcome to know everything that is there. Yes, and so may any mortal who is capable of full sympathy, and therefore worthy to come into my depths. But he must find his own way there. I can neither guide nor enlighten him. It is this involuntary reserve, I suppose, that has given the objectivity to my writings; and when people think that I am pouring myself out in a tale or an essay, I am merely telling what is common to human nature, not what is peculiar to myself. I sympathize with them, not they with me. . . .

[1843]

*H*ERMAN MELVILLE *wrote an eloquent essay on Hawthorne's volume of short stories,* Mosses from an Old Manse, *for the New York periodical* The Literary World *in August 1850. Unlike Poe in his review of Hawthorne's short fiction, Melville did not use the opportunity to theorize about the form of the short story. Instead, he conveyed his enthusiasm for Hawthorne's "blackness," the aspect of Hawthorne's work that seemed most congenial to his own genius while he continued work that summer on his novel-in-progress,* Moby Dick.

✎ 2 ✎

Herman Melville

on Blackness in Hawthorne's

YOUNG GOODMAN BROWN

It is curious, how a man may travel along a country road, and yet miss the grandest or sweetest of prospects, by reason of an intervening hedge so like all other hedges as in no way to hint of the wide landscape beyond. So has it been with me concerning the enchanting landscape in the soul of this Hawthorne, this most excellent Man of Mosses. His *Old Manse* has been written now four years, but I never read it till a day or two since. I had seen it in the bookstores — heard of it often — even had it recommended to me by a tasteful friend, as a rare, quiet book, perhaps too deserving of popularity to be popular. But there are so many books called "excellent" and so much unpopular merit, that amid the thick stir of other things, the hint of my tasteful friend was disregarded; and for four years the Mosses on the Old Manse never refreshed me with their perennial green. It may be, however, that all this while, the book, like wine, was only improving in flavor and body. . . .

But it is the least part of genius that attracts admiration. Where Hawthorne is known, he seems to be deemed a pleasant writer, with a pleasant style — a sequestered, harmless man, from whom any deep and weighty thing would hardly be anticipated: a man who means no meanings. But there is no man, in whom humor and love, like mountain peaks, soar to such a rapt height, as to receive the irradiations of the upper skies; there is no man in whom humor and love are developed in that high form called genius — no such man can exist without also possessing, as the indispensable complement of these, a great, deep intellect, which drops down into the universe like a plummet. Or, love and humor are only the eyes, through which such an intellect views this world. The great beauty in such a mind is but the product of its strength. . . .

For spite of all the Indian-summer sunlight on the hither side of Hawthorne's soul, the other side — like the dark half of the physical sphere — is shrouded in a blackness, ten times black. But this darkness but gives more effect to the ever-moving dawn, that forever advances through it, and circumnavigates his world. Whether Hawthorne has simply availed himself of this mystical blackness as a means to the wondrous effects he makes it to produce in his lights and shades; or whether there really lurks in him, perhaps unknown to himself, a touch of Puritanic gloom — this I cannot altogether tell. Certain it is, however, that this great power of blackness in him derives its force from its appeals to that Calvinistic sense of Innate Depravity and Original Sin, from whose visitations, in some shape or other, no deeply thinking mind is always and wholly free. For, in certain moods, no man can weigh this world, without throwing in something, somehow like Original Sin, to strike the uneven balance. . . .

But with whatever motive, playful or profound, Nathaniel Hawthorne has chosen to entitle his pieces in the manner he has, it is certain that some of them are directly calculated to deceive — egregiously deceive — the superficial skimmer of pages. To be downright and candid once more, let me cheerfully say that two of these titles did dolefully dupe no less an eagle-eyed reader than myself; and that, too, after I had been impressed with a sense of the great depth and breadth of this American man. "Who in the name of thunder" (as the country people say in this neighborhood), "who in the name of thunder," would anticipate any marvel in a piece entitled "Young Goodman Brown"? You would of course suppose that it was a simple little tale, intended as a supplement to "Goody Two-Shoes." Whereas it is deep as Dante; nor can you finish it, without addressing the author in his own words: "It is yours to penetrate, in every bosom, the deep mystery of sin." And with Young Goodman, too, in allegorical pursuit of his Puritan wife, you cry out in your anguish,

> "Faith!" shouted Goodman Brown, in a voice of agony and desperation; and the echoes of the forest mocked him, crying — "Faith! Faith!" as if bewildered wretches were seeking her, all through the wilderness.

Now this same piece, entitled "Young Goodman Brown," is one of the two that I had not at all read yesterday; and I allude to it now, because it is, in itself, such a strong positive illustration of that blackness in Hawthorne which I had assumed from the mere occasional shadows of it, as revealed in several of the other sketches. But had I previously perused "Young Goodman Brown," I should have been at no pains to draw the conclusion which I came to at a time when I was ignorant that the book contained one such direct and unqualified manifestation of it. . . .

[1850]

*E*DGAR ALLAN POE *was one of the earliest writers to discuss the aesthetic qualities of the short story as a distinct prose narrative form. In his day literary criticism was still a new field of thought, lacking a terminology and developed concepts. His two long reviews praising the tales of Nathaniel Hawthorne were published in* Graham's Magazine *in 1842 and* Godey's Lady's Book *in 1847; they are pioneering examples of the analytic literary essay. The following excerpt is taken from the 1847 piece, where Poe amplified his theory of the short story and his views on the nature of originality in literature.*

❧ 3 ❧

Edgar Allan Poe

on the Importance of the Single Effect

in a Prose Tale

But it is of [Hawthorne's] tales that I desire principally to speak. The tale proper, in my opinion, affords unquestionably the fairest field for the exercise of the loftiest talent, which can be afforded by the wide domains of mere prose. Were I bidden to say how the highest genius could be most advantageously employed for the best display of its own powers, I should answer, without hesitation — in the composition of a rhymed poem, not to exceed in length what might be perused in an hour. Within this limit alone can the highest order of true poetry exist. I need only here say, upon this topic, that, in almost all classes of composition, the unity of effect or impression is a point of the greatest importance. It is clear, moreover, that this unity cannot be thoroughly preserved in productions whose perusal cannot be completed at one sitting. We may continue the reading of a prose composition, from the very nature of prose itself, much longer than we can persevere, to any good purpose, in the perusal of a poem. This latter, if truly fulfilling the demands of the poetic sentiment, induces an exaltation of the soul which cannot be long sustained. All high excitements are necessarily transient. Thus a long poem is a paradox. And, without unity of impression, the deepest effects cannot be brought about. Epics were the offspring of an imperfect sense of Art, and their reign is no more. A poem *too* brief may produce a vivid, but never an intense or enduring impression. Without a certain continuity of effort — without a certain duration or repetition of purpose — the soul is never deeply moved. There must be the dropping of the water upon the rock. . . .

Were I called upon, however, to designate that class of composition which, next to such a poem as I have suggested, should best fulfill the demands of high genius — should offer it the most advantageous field of exertion — I should unhesitatingly speak of the prose tale, as Mr. Hawthorne has here exemplified it. I allude to the short prose narrative, requiring from a half-hour to one or two hours in its perusal. The ordinary novel is objectionable, from its length, for reasons already stated in substance. As it cannot be read at one sitting, it deprives itself, of course, of the immense force derivable from *totality*. Worldly interests intervening during the pauses of perusal, modify, annul, or counteract, in a greater or less degree, the impressions of the book. But simple cessation in reading would, of itself, be sufficient to destroy the true unity. In the brief tale, however, the author is enabled to carry out the fulness of his intention, be it what it may. During the hour of perusal the soul of the reader is at the writer's control. There are no external or extrinsic influences — resulting from weariness or interruption.

A skillful literary artist has constructed a tale. If wise, he has not fashioned his thoughts to accommodate his incidents; but having conceived, with deliberate care, a certain unique or single *effect* to be wrought out, he then invents such incidents — he then combines such events as may best aid him in establishing this preconceived effect. If his very initial sentence tend not to the outbringing of this effect, then he has failed in his first step. In the whole composition there should be no word written, of which the tendency, direct or indirect, is not to the one pre-established design. And by such means, with such care and skill, a picture is at length painted which leaves in the mind of him who contemplates it with a kindred art, a sense of the fullest satisfaction. The idea of the tale has been presented unblemished, because undisturbed; and this is an end unattainable by the novel. Undue brevity is just as exceptionable here as in the poem; but undue length is yet more to be avoided.

We have said that the tale has a point of superiority even over the poem. In fact, while the *rhythm* of this latter is an essential aid in the development of the poem's highest idea — the idea of the Beautiful — the artificialities of this rhythm are an inseparable bar to the development of all points of thought or expression which have their basis in *Truth*. But Truth is often, and in very great degree, the aim of the tale. Some of the finest tales are tales of ratiocination. Thus the field of this species of composition, if not in so elevated a region on the mountain of Mind, is a table-land of far vaster extent than the domain of the mere poem. Its products are never so rich, but infinitely more numerous, and more appreciable by the mass of mankind. The writer of the prose tale, in short, may bring to his theme a vast variety of modes or reflections of thought and expression — (the ratiocinative, for example, the sarcastic, or the humorous) which are not only antagonistical to the nature of the poem, but absolutely forbidden by one of its most peculiar and indispensable adjuncts; we allude, of course, to rhythm. It may be added, here, *par parenthèse*, that the author who aims at the purely beautiful in a prose tale is laboring at a great disadvantage. For

Beauty can be better treated in the poem. Not so with terror, or passion, or horror, or a multitude of such other points. . . .

Of Mr. Hawthorne's "Tales" we would say, emphatically, that they belong to the highest region of Art — an Art subservient to genius of a very lofty order. We have supposed, with good reason for so supposing, that he had been thrust into his present position by one of the impudent cliques which beset our literature, and whose pretensions it is our full purpose to expose at the earliest opportunity; but we have been most agreeably mistaken. We know of few compositions which the critic can more honestly commend than these "Twice-Told Tales." As Americans, we feel proud of the book.

Mr. Hawthorne's distinctive trait is invention, creation, imagination, originality — a trait which, in the literature of fiction, is positively worth all the rest. But the nature of the originality, so far as regards its manifestation in letters, is but imperfectly understood. The inventive or original mind as frequently displays itself in novelty of *tone* as in novelty of matter. Mr. Hawthorne is original in *all* points.

It would be a matter of some difficulty to designate the best of these tales; we repeat that, without exception, they are beautiful. "Wakefield" is remarkable for the skill with which an old idea, — a well-known incident, — is worked up or discussed. A man of whims conceives the purpose of quitting his wife and residing *incognito*, for twenty years, in her immediate neighborhood. Something of this kind actually happened in London. The force of Mr. Hawthorne's tale lies in the analysis of the motives which must or might have impelled the husband to such folly, in the first instance, with the possible causes of his perseverance. Upon this thesis a sketch of singular power has been constructed.

[1847]

DAVID HERBERT LAWRENCE *published* Studies in Classic American Literature *in 1923. It includes his responses to the writings of Poe, Hawthorne, Melville, and the poet Walt Whitman, among others. As an Englishman, Lawrence read American authors for their contribution to the cultural life of the Western world, and not merely as writers of children's books, which he said was how most European readers viewed American authors at the time. Lawrence's judgments are often startling, sometimes extreme, but never dull. They reflect the same moral passion exhibited in the rest of his work, especially his abhorrence of possessive love.*

❧ 4 ☙

D. H. Lawrence
on the Lust of Hate in Poe's
THE CASK OF AMONTILLADO

The best [of Poe's] tales all have the same burden. Hate is as inordinate as love, and as slowly consuming, as secret, as underground, as subtle. All this underground vault business in Poe only symbolizes that which takes place *beneath* the consciousness. On top, all is fair-spoken. Beneath, there is the awful murderous extremity of burying alive. Fortunato, in "The Cask of Amontillado," is buried alive out of perfect hatred, as the lady Madeline of Usher[1] is buried alive out of love. The lust of hate is the inordinate desire to consume and unspeakably possess the soul of the hated one, just as the lust of love is the desire to possess, or to be possessed by, the beloved, utterly. But in either case the result is the dissolution of both souls, each losing itself in transgressing its own bounds.

The lust of Montresor is to devour utterly the soul of Fortunato. It would be no use killing him outright. If a man is killed outright his soul remains integral, free to return into the bosom of some beloved, where it can enact itself. In walling-up his enemy in the vault, Montresor seeks to bring about the indescribable capitulation of the man's soul, so that he, the victor, can possess himself of the very being of the vanquished. Perhaps this can actually be done. Perhaps, in the attempt, the victor breaks the bonds of his own identity, and collapses into nothingness, or into the infinite. Becomes a monster.

[1923]

---

[1] in Poe's story "The Fall of the House of Usher."

VLADIMIR NABOKOV delivered lectures on Russian literature to his classes at Cornell University from 1948 to 1958. Forced to leave his native country at the age of twenty to escape what he called "the bloated octopus of the state" after the Russian Revolution, he took with him a passionate love for his homeland and for the "fiery, fanciful, free" literature of pre-revolutionary Russia. For Nabokov, the great Russian writers of the nineteenth century (he began his lecture series with Gogol) were more than artists: They were the last free voices in Russia for whom the government did not dictate absolute limits of imagination.

~✷5✷~

Vladimir Nabokov

on Gogol's Genius in

THE OVERCOAT

Gogol was a strange creature, but genius is always strange; it is only your healthy second-rater who seems to the grateful reader to be a wise old friend, nicely developing the reader's own notions of life. Great literature skirts the irrational. *Hamlet* is the wild dream of a neurotic scholar. Gogol's *The Overcoat* is a grotesque and grim nightmare making black holes in the dim pattern of life. The superficial reader of that story will merely see in it the heavy frolics of an extravagant buffoon; the solemn reader will take for granted that Gogol's prime intention was to denounce the horrors of Russian bureaucracy. But neither the person who wants a good laugh, nor the person who craves for books "that make one think" will understand what *The Overcoat* is really about. Give me the creative reader; this is a tale for him.

Steady Pushkin,[1] matter-of-fact Tolstoy, restrained Chekhov have all had their moments of irrational insight which simultaneously blurred the sentence and disclosed a secret meaning worth the sudden focal shift. But with Gogol this shifting is the very basis of his art, so that whenever he tried to write in the round hand of literary tradition and to treat rational ideas in a logical way, he lost all trace of talent. When, as in his immortal *The*

---

[1] Aleksandr Pushkin (1799–1837), considered by many (including Nabokov) the greatest Russian poet. Nabokov translated his novel in verse, *Eugene Onegin*, into English. For introductions to Leo Tolstoy and Anton Chekhov, see pages 125 and 330.

Overcoat, he really let himself go and pottered happily on the brink of his private abyss, he became the greatest artist that Russia has yet produced.

The sudden slanting of the rational plane of life may be accomplished of course in many ways, and every great writer has his own method. With Gogol it was a combination of two movements: a jerk and a glide. Imagine a trap-door that opens under your feet with absurd suddenness, and a lyrical gust that sweeps you up and then lets you fall with a bump into the next traphole. The absurd was Gogol's favorite muse — but when I say "the absurd," I do not mean the quaint or the comic. The absurd has as many shades and degrees as the tragic has, and moreover, in Gogol's case, it borders upon the latter. It would be wrong to assert that Gogol placed his characters in absurd situations. You cannot place a man in an absurd situation if the whole world he lives in is absurd; you cannot do this if you mean by "absurd" something provoking a chuckle or a shrug. But if you mean the pathetic, the human condition, if you mean all such things that in less weird worlds are linked up with the loftiest aspirations, the deepest sufferings, the strongest passions — then of course the necessary breach is there, and a pathetic human, lost in the midst of Gogol's nightmarish, irresponsible world would be "absurd," by a kind of secondary contrast.

On the lid of the tailor's snuff-box there was "the portrait of a General; I do not know what general because the tailor's thumb has made a hole in the general's face and a square of paper had been gummed over the hole." Thus with the absurdity of Akaky Akakievich Bashmachkin. We did not expect that, amid the whirling masks, one mask would turn out to be a real face, or at least the place where that face ought to be. The essence of mankind is irrationally derived from the chaos of fakes which form Gogol's world. Akaky Akakievich, the hero of *The Overcoat*, is absurd *because* he is pathetic, *because* he is human, and *because* he has been engendered by those very forces which seem to be in such contrast to him.

He is not merely human and pathetic. He is something more, just as the background is not mere burlesque. Somewhere behind the obvious contrast there is a subtle genetic link. His being discloses the same quiver and shimmer as does the dream world to which he belongs. The allusions to something else behind the crudely painted screens, are so artistically combined with the superficial texture of the narration that civic-minded Russians have missed them completely. But a creative reading of Gogol's story reveals that here and there in the most innocent descriptive passage, this or that word, sometimes a mere adverb or a preposition, for instance the word "even" or "almost," is inserted in such a way as to make the harmless sentence explode in a wild display of nightmare fireworks; or else the passage that had started in a rambling colloquial manner all of a sudden leaves the tracks and swerves into the irrational where it really belongs; or again, quite as suddenly, a door bursts open and a mighty wave of foaming poetry rushes in only to dissolve in bathos,[2] or to turn into its own parody, or to be checked by the sentence breaking and reverting to a conjuror's patter, that patter which is such a feature of Gogol's style. It gives one the sensation of something ludicrous and at the same time stellar, lurking constantly around the corner — and one likes to recall that the difference between the comic side of things, and their cosmic side, depends upon one sibilant.

So what is that queer world, glimpses of which we keep catching through the gaps of the harmless looking sentences? It is in a way the *real* one but it looks wildly absurd to us, accustomed as we are to the stage setting that screens it. It is from these glimpses that the main character of *The Overcoat*, the meek little clerk, is formed, so that he embodies the spirit of that secret but real world which breaks through Gogol's style. He is, that meek little clerk, a ghost, a visitor from some tragic depths who by chance happened to assume the disguise of a petty official. Russian progressive critics sensed in him the image of the underdog and the whole story impressed them as a social protest. But it is something much more than that. The gaps and black holes in the texture of Gogol's style imply flaws in the texture of life itself. Something is very wrong and all men are mild lunatics engaged in pursuits that seem to them very important while an absurdly logical force keeps them at their futile jobs — this is the real "message" of the story. In this world of utter futility, of futile humility and futile domination, the highest degree that passion, desire, creative urge can attain is a new cloak which both tailors and customers adore on their knees. I am not speaking of the moral point or the moral lesson. There can be no moral lesson in such a world because there are no pupils and no teachers: this world *is* and it excludes everything that might destroy it, so that any improvement, any struggle, any moral purpose or endeavor, are as utterly impossible as changing the course of a star. It is Gogol's world and as such wholly different from Tolstoy's world, or Pushkin's, or Chekhov's, or my own. But after reading Gogol one's eyes may become gogolized and one is apt to see bits of his world in the most unexpected places. I have visited many countries, and something like Akaky Akakievich's overcoat has been the passionate dream of this or that chance acquaintance who never had heard about Gogol.

[1981]

---

[2] One source has defined *bathos* as "pathos [the evoking of sympathy, sorrow, or pity] so overdone that it evokes laughter rather than pity."

*H*ENRY JAMES *described the origin of his story "The Real Thing" in his notebook entry for February 22, 1891. He kept a record of his works-in-progress for more than thirty years; his notes, often written hastily, were simply for his own eyes. In 1947 the scholars F. O. Matthiessen and Kenneth Murdock published* The Notebooks of Henry James, *a carefully edited volume that is invaluable for any study of James's fiction. It is also of interest to the aspiring writer, because it is full of James's insights into the process of literary creation.*

~6~

Henry James

on the Genesis of

THE REAL THING*

In pursuance of my plan of writing some very short tales — things of from 7,000 to 10,000 words, the easiest length to "place," I began yesterday the little story that was suggested to me some time ago by an incident related to me by George du Maurier — the lady and gentleman who called upon him with a word from Frith, an oldish, faded, ruined pair — he an officer in the army — who unable to turn a penny in any other way, were trying to find employment as models. I was struck with the pathos, the oddity, and typicalness of the situation — the little tragedy of good-looking gentlefolk, who had been all their life stupid and well-dressed, living, on a fixed income, at country-houses, watering places, and clubs, like so many others of their class in England, and were now utterly unable to *do* anything, had no cleverness, no art nor craft to make use of as a *gagne-pain*[1] — could only *show* themselves, clumsily, for the fine, clean, well-groomed animals that they were, only hope to make a little money by — in this manner — just simply *being.* I thought I saw a subject for very brief treatment in this *donnée*[2] — and I think I do still; but to do anything worth while with it I must (as always, great Heavens!) be very clear as to what is in it and what I

* "Henry James on the Genesis of 'The Real Thing' " (editor's title) is from *The Notebooks of Henry James* by F. O. Matthiessen and Kenneth Murdock, published by Oxford University Press, Inc.
[1] a way to earn their bread.
[2] literally, "given"; the situation or assumption with which one begins an argument.

wish to get out of it. I tried a beginning yesterday, but I instantly became conscious that I must straighten out the little idea. It must be an idea — it can't be a "story" in the vulgar sense of the word. It must be a picture; it must illustrate something. God knows that's enough — if the thing *does* illustrate. To make little anecdotes of this kind real *morceaux de vie*[3] is a plan quite inspiring enough. *Voyons un peu,*[4] therefore, what one can put into this one — I mean how much of life. One must put a little action — not a stupid, mechanical, arbitrary action, but something that is of the real essence of the subject. I thought of representing the husband as jealous of the wife — that is, jealous of the artist employing her, from the moment that, in point of fact, she begins to sit. But this is vulgar and obvious — worth nothing. What I wish to represent is the baffled, ineffectual, incompetent character of their attempt, and how it illustrates once again the everlasting English amateurishness — the way superficial, untrained, unprofessional effort goes to the wall when confronted with trained, competitive, intelligent, *qualified* art — in whatever line it may be a question of. It is out of *that* element that my little action and movement must come; and now I begin to see just how — as one always *does* — Glory be to the Highest — when one begins to look at a thing hard and straight and seriously — to fix it — as I am so sadly lax and desultory about doing. What subjects I should find — for *everything* — if I could only achieve this more as a habit! Let my contrast and complication here come from the opposition — to my melancholy Major and his wife — of a couple of little vulgar professional people *who know*, with the consequent bewilderment, vagueness, depression of the former — their failure to understand how such people can be better than *they* — their failure, disappointment, disappearance — going forth into the vague again. *Il y a bien quelque chose d tirer de ça.*[5] They have no pictorial sense. They are only clean and stiff and stupid. The others are dirty, even — the melancholy Major and his wife remark on it, wondering. The artist is beginning a big illustrated book, a new edition of a famous novel — say *Tom Jones:*[6] and he is willing to try to work them in — for he takes an interest in their predicament, and feels — skeptically, but, with his flexible artistic sympathy — the appeal of their type. He is willing to give them a trial. Make it out that *he* himself is on trial — he is young and "rising," but he has still his golden spurs to win. He can't afford, *en somme,*[7] to make many mistakes. He has regular work in drawing every week for a serial novel in an illustrated paper; but the great project — that of a big house — of issuing an illustrated Fielding promises him a big lift. He has been intrusted with (say) *Joseph Andrews,*[8] experimentally; he will have to do this brilliantly in order to have the engagement for the rest con-

---

[3] slice of life.
[4] "Let us examine for a bit. . . ."
[5] "There is indeed something to draw from that."
[6] novel by Henry Fielding (1707–1754).
[7] in sum.
[8] another, earlier novel by Fielding.

firmed. He has already two models in his service — the "complication" must come from *them*. One is a common, clever, London girl, of the smallest origin and without conventional beauty, but of aptitude, of perceptions — knowing thoroughly *how*. She says "lydy" and "plice" but she has the pictorial sense; and can look like anything he wants her to look like. She poses, in short, in perfection. So does her colleague, a professional Italian, a little fellow — ill dressed, smelling of garlic, but admirably serviceable, quite universal. They must be contrasted, confronted, *juxtaposed* with the others; whom they take for people who *pay*, themselves, till they learn the truth when they are overwhelmed with derisive amazement. The denouncement simply that the melancholy Major and his wife won't do — they're not "in it." Their surprise — their helpless, proud assent — without other prospects: yet at the same time *their* degree of more silent amazement at the success of the two inferior people — who are so much less nice-looking than themselves. Frankly, however, is this contrast enough of a *story*, by itself? It seems to me Yes — for it's an IDEA — and how the deuce should I get *more* into 7,000 words? It must be simply fifty pp. of my manuscript. The little tale of *The Servant* (*Brooksmith*) which I did the other day for *Black and White* and which I thought of at the same time as this, proved a very tight squeeze into the same tiny number of words, and I probably shall find that there is much more to be done with this than the compass will admit of. Make it tremendously succinct — with a very short pulse or rhythm — and the closest selection of detail — in other words *summarize* intensely and keep down the lateral development. It *should* be a little gem of bright, quick, vivid form. I shall get every grain of "action" that the space admits of if I make something, for the artist, hang in the balance — depend on the way he does this particular work. It's when he finds that he shall lose his great opportunity if he keeps on with them, that he has to tell the gentlemanly couple, that, frankly, they won't serve his turn — and make them wander forth into the cold world again. I must keep them the age I've made them — fifty and forty — because it's more touching; but I must bring up the age of the two real models to almost the same thing. That increases the incomprehensibility (to the amateurs) of their usefulness. Picture the immanence, in the latter, of the idle, provided-for, country-house habit — the blankness of their *manière d'être*.[9] But in how tremendously few words I must do it. This is a lesson — a *magnificent* lesson — if I'm to do a good many. Something as admirably compact and *selected* as Maupassant.

[1891]

---

[9] manner of being.

Guy de Maupassant wrote an analysis of how he created fiction in the lengthy preface to his novel Pierre and Jean in 1888. In this excerpt he analyzes his intent as a writer and presents his view of realism. Maupassant wanted to clarify the point that no fiction could be called "realistic," if that term meant a mirror image of life. Henry James later wrote that Maupassant's preface contains many insights into the nature of literature, including an important distinction between different kinds of fiction. James realized that Maupassant's "readers must be grateful to him for such a passage as that in which he remarks that whereas the public at large very legitimately says to a writer, 'Console me, amuse me, terrify me, make me cry, make me dream, or make me think,' what the sincere critic says is, 'Make me something fine in the form that shall suit you best, according to your temperament.' This seems to me to put into a nutshell the whole question of the different classes of fiction. . . . There are simply as many different kinds as there are persons practising the art, for if a picture, a tale, or a novel be a direct impression of life (and that surely constitutes its interest and value), the impression will vary according to the plate [temperament] that takes it, the particular structure and mixture of the recipient."

⌇7⌇

Guy de Maupassant
on the Writer's Goal from His Preface to
PIERRE AND JEAN

—translated by Mallay Charters

[The serious writer's] goal is not to tell us a story, to entertain or to move us, but to make us think and to make us understand the deep and hidden meaning of events. By virtue of having seen and meditated, he views the universe, objects, facts, and human beings in a certain way which is personal, the result of combining his observations and reflections. It is this personal view of the world that he tries to communicate to us by reproducing it in fiction. To move us, as he has been moved himself by the spectacle of life, he must reproduce it before our eyes with a scrupulous accuracy. He should compose his work so adroitly, and with such dissimulation and apparent simplicity, that it is impossible to uncover its plan or to perceive his intentions.

Instead of fabricating an adventure and spinning it out in a way that keeps it interesting until the end, the writer will pick up his characters at a certain point of their existence and carry them, by natural transitions, to the following period. He will show how minds are modified under the influence of environmental circumstances, and how sentiments and passions are developed. In this fashion, he will show our loves, our hates, our struggles in all kinds of social conditions; and how social interests, financial interests, political interests, and personal interests all compete with each other.

The writer's cleverness with his plot will thus consist not in the use of sentiment or charm, in an engaging beginning or an emotional catastrophe, but in the adroit grouping of small constant facts from which the reader will grasp a definitive sense of the work. . . . [The author] should know how to eliminate, among the minute and innumerable daily occurrences, all those which are useless to him. He must emphasize those which would have escaped the notice of less clear-sighted observers, which give the story its effect and value as fiction. . . .

A writer would find it impossible to describe everything in life, because he would need at least a volume a day to list the multitude of unimportant incidents filling up our hours.

Some selectivity is required — which is the first blow to the "entire truth" theory [of realistic literature].

Life, moreover, is composed of the most unpredictable, disparate, and contradictory elements. It is brutal, inconsequential, and disconnected, full of inexplicable, illogical, catastrophes.

This is why the writer, having selected a theme, will take from this chaotic life, encumbered with hazards and trivialities, only the details useful to his subject and omit all the others.

One example out of a thousand: The number of people in the world who die every day in accidents is considerable. But can we drop a roof tile on a main character's head, or throw him under the wheels of a car, in the middle of a narrative, under the pretext that it is necessary to have an accident?

Life can leave everything the same as it was. Or it can speed up some events and drag out others. Literature, on the other hand, presents cleverly orchestrated events and concealed transitions, essential incidents highlighted by the writer's skill alone. In giving every detail its exact degree of shading in accordance with its importance, the author produces the profound impression of the particular truth he wishes to point out.

To make things seem real on the page consists in giving the complete *illusion* of reality, following the logical order of facts, and not servilely transcribing the pell-mell succession of chronological events in life.

I conclude from this analysis that writers who call themselves realists should more accurately call themselves illusionists.

How childish, moreover, to believe in an absolute reality, since we each carry a personal one in our thoughts and in our senses. Our eyes, our ears, our sense of smell and taste create as many truths as there are individuals. Our minds, diversely impressed by the reception of the senses' information, comprehend, analyze, and judge as if each of us belonged to a separate race.

Thus each of us makes, individually, a personal illusion of the world. It may be a poetic, sentimental, joyful, melancholy, sordid, or dismal one, according to our nature. The writer's goal is to reproduce this illusion of life faithfully, using all the literary techniques at his disposal.

[1888]

KATE CHOPIN *made a number of translations, mostly of stories by Guy de Maupassant, and she published several essays on literature in St. Louis periodicals. She wrote about the influence of Maupassant on her fiction in response to an invitation from the editor of* The Atlantic Monthly *in 1896. He returned her first version of the essay, however, advising her to "set forth the matter directly." Her revised version was later included in the magazine with the title "In the Confidence of a Story-Teller," but the section describing how she first encountered Maupassant's tales and the impression they made on her was dropped, perhaps because she spoke so enthusiastically about the French writer's escape "from tradition and authority." This portion of the essay is reprinted from the manuscript included in volume 2 of* The Complete Works of Kate Chopin *(1969).*

～❦8❦～

Kate Chopin
on How She Stumbled upon
Maupassant

About eight years ago there fell accidentally into my hands a volume of Maupassant's tales. These were new to me. I had been in the woods, in the fields, groping around; looking for something big, satisfying, convincing, and finding nothing but — myself; a something neither big nor satisfying but wholly convincing. It was at this period of my emerging from the vast solitude in which I had been making my own acquaintance, that I stumbled upon Maupassant. I read his stories and marvelled at them. Here was life, not fiction; for where were the plots, the old fashioned mechanism and stage trapping that in a vague, unthinking way I had fancied were essential to the art of story making? Here was a man who had escaped from tradition and authority, who had entered into himself and looked out upon life through his own being and with his own eyes; and who, in a direct and simple way, told us what he saw. When a man does this, he gives us the best that he can; something valuable for it is genuine and spontaneous. He gives us his impressions. Someone told me the other day that Maupassant had gone out of fashion. I was not grieved to hear it. He has never seemed to me to belong to the multitude, but rather to the individual. He is not one whom we gather in crowds to listen to — whom we follow in procession —

with beating of brass instruments. He does not move us to throw ourselves into the throng — having the integral of an unthinking whole to shout his praise. I even like to think that he appeals to me alone. You probably like to think that he reaches you exclusively. A whole multitude may be secretly nourishing the belief in regard to him for all I know. Someway I like to cherish the delusion that he has spoken to no one else so directly, so intimately as he does to me. He did not say, as another might have done, "do you see these are charming stories of mine? take them into your closet — study them closely — mark their combination — observe the method, the manner of their putting together — and if ever you are moved to write stories you can do no better than to imitate. . . ."

[1896]

*Sean o'faolain defined the qualities of the successful short story as
"punch" and "poetry," in the sense of a combination of realistic plausibility
and personal voltage which "does something to the material . . . it makes it
fume in the memory as an aroma or essence which clings to us even when
we have forgotten the details of the yarn." In his literary study* The Short
Story *(1951) he analyzes the fiction of Guy de Maupassant, "the relentless
realist," as opposed to Anton Chekhov, "the persistent moralist." O'Faolain also quotes Maupassant saying, "The short story is but scantily relished
in England, where readers take their fiction rather by the volume than by
the page, and the novelist's idea is apt to resemble one of those old fashioned carriages which require a wide court to turn around. In America . . .
the short tale has had a better fortune."*

❧9❧

Sean O'Faolain

on Maupassant's Interest in Elemental Passion in

Miss Harriet

As to our specific point — Maupassant's refusal to indulge in elaborate psychology: somebody has called this picture of Miss Harriet "a bizarre
silhouette" and the adjective seems fair, but "silhouette" is less just. The
woman is persuasive; her emotions are sufficiently elaborate; her conflict
sufficiently disturbing. What prompted the word was, probably, Maupassant's interest in elemental passion and his almost savage insistence on
keeping to that plane. This is where he pursues his path to the cliff's edge,
as he does consistently throughout his work. . . . This is where, at the end,
we are in a position to appraise his power and measure his weakness — his
price that he willingly pays, believing it to be not a weakness but a final and
irrefragable[1] strength.

The truth is that Maupassant saw life as a puritan moralist: he saw it,
as he believed, without sentiment, and saw it therefore as evil; he saw what
a Christian would call the seven deadly sins, and he saw little else. He saw
men and women ridden by pride, covetousness, lust, anger, gluttony, envy,
and sloth: Norman farmers, Parisian civil-servants, small-town bourgeoisie.
What he denied was the slightest trace of soul in any one of them, the least

[1] impossible to deny or refute.

speck of godliness, all hope of redemption here or hereafter. That was *his* reality, and it was in pursuit of it that he reduced human nature to its most elemental passions. Miss Harriet might be a Pantheist; she would die as a dog dies; the most that even an artist could strew on her grave was pity and flowers, and the thought that she would persist as a flower or as grass and as the flesh of an ox and the flesh of those after her who would eat her body and drink her blood. He reduced life to the senses and he revelled in them as a man and as a writer. . . .

The mass of his work is clean and classical in its raillery, its optimism, its stoical acceptance of a most ascetic and uncompromising view of life.

One's quarrel with such a writer, and one's admiration of him, will never be purely literary: They will be colored by what, for short, one may call our philosophies, our own personal view of life, and we will approve or disapprove of Maupassant not as a writer but as a man with a similar, or with another (and unacceptable) view of life. It would not have troubled him, but the fact remains that he challenges such approvals and disapprovals more than any other writer of short stories. There is room in the house of Chekhov, Stevenson,[2] or Henry James for men of many philosophies. Maupassant invites a select company, or else a very tolerant one. That was his choice. He chose his way; he never diverged from it; he succeeded in it. He defined his own notion of reality early in his career — in *"Boule de Suif,"* his first published story; which is to say he defined his own temperament and its needs. When he had finished he looked into the abyss and it received him.

[1951]

---

[2] Robert Louis Stevenson (1850–1894), whose stories include "The Strange Case of Dr. Jekyll and Mr. Hyde" and "The Bottle Imp."

ANTON CHEKHOV *described his theories of literature and his practice as a storyteller in countless letters to his family and friends. He was not a systematic critic, and he did not necessarily follow his own advice to other writers. Brevity and concentration on a few essentials of scene and character were the essence of his technique, but he was not always as drastically laconic in his stories as his letters suggest. What is consistently clear in his advice to other writers is his own unwearying compassion and his desire to speak honestly in his efforts to help them. He wrote in his notebook, "Man will only become better when you make him see what he is like."*

These letters are to his older brother, his publisher, and a younger author whose work he admired.

⁓ 10 ⁓

Anton Chekhov

on Technique in Writing

a Short Story

From a Letter to Alexander P. Chekhov

In my opinion a true description of Nature should be very brief and have a character of relevance. Commonplaces such as, "the setting sun bathing in the waves of the darkening sea, poured its purple gold, etc." — "the swallows flying over the surface of the water twittered merrily" — such commonplaces one ought to abandon. In descriptions of Nature one ought to seize upon the little particulars, grouping them in such a way that, in reading, when you shut your eyes, you get a picture.

For instance, you will get the full effect of a moonlight night if you write that on the mill-dam a little glowing star-point flashed from the neck of a broken bottle, and the round, black shadow of a dog, or a wolf, emerged and ran, etc. Nature becomes animated if you are not squeamish about employing comparisons of her phenomena with ordinary human activities, etc.

In the sphere of psychology, details are also the thing. God preserve us from commonplaces. Best of all is it to avoid depicting the hero's state of mind; you ought to try to make it clear from the hero's actions. It is not necessary to portray many characters. The center of gravity should be in two persons: him and her.

[1886]

From a Letter to Aleksey S. Suvorin

You abuse me for objectivity, calling it indifference to good and evil, lack of ideals and ideas, and so on. You would have me, when I describe horse-thieves, say: "Stealing horses is an evil." But that has been known for ages without my saying so. Let the jury judge them; it's my job simply to show what sort of people they are. I write: You are dealing with horse-thieves, so let me tell you that they are not beggars but well-fed people, that they are people of a special cult, and that horse-stealing is not simply theft but a passion. Of course it would be pleasant to combine art with a sermon, but for me personally it is extremely difficult and almost impossible, owing to the conditions of technique. You see, to depict horse-thieves in seven hundred lines I must all the time speak and think in their tone and feel in their spirit, otherwise, if I introduce subjectivity, the image becomes blurred and the story will not be as compact as all short stories ought to be. When I write, I reckon entirely upon the reader to add for himself the subjective elements that are lacking in the story.

[1890]

From a Letter to Maxim Gorky

More advice: when reading the proofs, cross out a host of terms qualifying nouns and verbs. You have so many such terms that the reader's mind finds it a task to concentrate on them, and he soon grows tired. You understand it at once when I say, "The man sat on the grass"; you understand it because it is clear and makes no demands on the attention. On the other hand, it is not easily understood, and it is difficult for the mind, if I write, "A tall, narrow-chested, middle-sized man, with a red beard, sat on the green grass, already trampled by pedestrians, sat silently, shyly, and timidly looked about him." That is not immediately grasped by the mind, whereas good writing should be grasped at once — in a second.

[1899]

VLADIMIR NABOKOV *was a skillful guide to fiction in his* Lectures on Russian Literature. *As this excerpt from his analysis of Chekhov's stories shows, he blended wit, irreverence, and critical insight in his summary of the intricacies of plot and character, illuminating the artistic achievements of the author. Nabokov felt that Chekhov's books were "sad books for humorous people" — that is, only a reader with a sense of humor could really appreciate their sadness. Chekhov's subtle humor pervades the grayness of the lives he created, flickering through his prose style: "He did it," said Nabokov, "by keeping all his words in the same dim light and of the same exact tint of gray, a tint between the color of an old fence and that of a low cloud."*

~❧ 11 ❧~

Vladimir Nabokov

on Anton Chekhov's

THE LADY WITH THE LITTLE DOG

Chekhov comes into the story "The Lady with the Little Dog" without knocking. There is no dilly-dallying. The very first paragraph reveals the main character, the young fair-haired lady followed by her white Spitz dog on the waterfront of a Crimean resort, Yalta, on the Black Sea. And immediately after, the male character Gurov appears. His wife, whom he has left with the children in Moscow, is vividly depicted: her solid frame, her thick black eyebrows, and the way she has of calling herself "a woman who thinks." One notes the magic of the trifles the author collects — the wife's manner of dropping a certain mute letter in spelling and her calling her husband by the longest and fullest form of his name, both traits in combination with the impressive dignity of her beetle-browed face and rigid poise forming exactly the necessary impression. A hard woman with the strong feminist and social ideas of her time, but one whom her husband finds in his heart of hearts to be narrow, dull-minded, and devoid of grace. The natural transition is to Gurov's constant unfaithfulness to her, to his general attitude toward women — "that inferior race" is what he calls them, but without that inferior race he could not exist. It is hinted that these Russian romances were not altogether as light-winged as in the Paris of Maupassant. Complications and problems are unavoidable with those decent hesitating people of Moscow who are slow heavy starters but plunge into tedious difficulties when once they start going.

Then with the same neat and direct method of attack, with the bridging formula "and so . . ." (or perhaps still better rendered in English by that "Now" which begins a new paragraph in straightforward fairy tales), we slide back to the lady with the dog. Everything about her, even the way her hair was done, told him that she was bored. The spirit of adventure — though he realized perfectly well that his attitude toward a lone woman in a fashionable sea town was based on vulgar stories, generally false — this spirit of adventure prompts him to call the little dog, which thus becomes a link between her and him. They are both in a public restaurant.

> He beckoned invitingly to the Spitz, and when the dog approached him, shook his finger at it. The Spitz growled; Gurov threatened it again.
> The lady glanced at him and at once dropped her eyes.
> "He doesn't bite," she said and blushed.
> "May I give him a bone?" he asked; and when she nodded he inquired affably, "Have you been in Yalta long?"
> "About five days."

They talk. The author has hinted already that Gurov was witty in the company of women; and instead of having the reader take it for granted (you know the old method of describing the talk as "brilliant" but giving no samples of the conversation), Chekhov makes him joke in a really attractive, winning way. "Bored, are you? An average citizen lives in . . . (here Chekhov lists the names of beautifully chosen, super-provincial towns) and is not bored, but when he arrives here on his vacation it is all boredom and dust. One could think he came from Granada" (a name particularly appealing to the Russian imagination). The rest of their talk, for which this sidelight is richly sufficient, is conveyed indirectly. Now comes a first glimpse of Chekhov's own system of suggesting atmosphere by the most concise details of nature, "the sea was of a warm lilac hue with a golden path for the moon"; whoever has lived in Yalta knows how exactly this conveys the impression of a summer evening there. This first movement of the story ends with Gurov alone in his hotel room thinking of her as he goes to sleep and imagining her delicate weak-looking neck and her pretty gray eyes. It is to be noted that only now, through the medium of the hero's imagination, does Chekhov give a visible and definite form to the lady, features that fit perfectly with her listless manner and expression of boredom already known to us.

> Getting into bed he recalled that she had been a schoolgirl only recently, doing lessons like his own daughter; he thought how much timidity and angularity there was still in her laugh and her manner of talking with a stranger. It must have been the first time in her life that she was alone in a setting in which she was followed, looked at, and spoken to for

one secret purpose alone, which she could hardly fail to guess. He thought of her slim, delicate throat, her lovely gray eyes.

"There's something pathetic about her, though," he thought, and dropped off.

The next movement (each of the four diminutive chapters or movements of which the story is composed is not more than four or five pages long), the next movement starts a week later with Gurov going to the pavilion and bringing the lady iced lemonade on a hot windy day, with the dust flying; and then in the evening when the sirocco subsides, they go on the pier to watch the incoming steamer. "The lady lost her lorgnette in the crowd," Chekhov notes shortly, and this being so casually worded, without any direct influence on the story — just a passing statement — somehow fits in with that helpless pathos already alluded to.

Then in her hotel room her awkwardness and tender angularity are delicately conveyed. They have become lovers. She was now sitting with her long hair hanging down on both sides of her face in the dejected pose of a sinner in some old picture. There was a watermelon on the table. Gurov cut himself a piece and began to eat unhurriedly. This realistic touch is again a typical Chekhov device.

She tells him about her existence in the remote town she comes from and Gurov is slightly bored by her naiveté, confusion, and tears. It is only now that we learn her husband's name: von Dideritz — probably of German descent.

They roam about Yalta in the early morning mist.

> At Oreanda they sat on a bench not far from the church, looked down at the sea, and were silent. Yalta was barely visible through the morning mist; white clouds rested motionlessly on the mountaintops. The leaves did not stir on the trees, the crickets chirped, and the monotonous muffled sound of the sea that rose from below spoke of the peace, the eternal sleep awaiting us. So it rumbled below when there was no Yalta, no Oreanda here; so it rumbles now, and it will rumble as indifferently and hollowly when we are no more. . . . Sitting beside a young woman who in the dawn seemed so lovely, Gurov, soothed and spellbound by these magical surroundings — the sea, the mountains, the clouds, the wide sky — thought how everything is really beautiful in this world when one reflects: everything except what we think or do ourselves when we forget the higher aims of life and our own human dignity.
>
> A man strolled up to them — probably a watchman — looked at them and walked away. And this detail, too, seemed so mysterious and beautiful. They saw a steamer arrive from Feodosia, its lights extinguished in the glow of dawn.
>
> "There is dew on the grass," said Anna Sergeievna, after a silence.
>
> "Yes, it's time to go home."

Then several days pass and then she has to go back to her home town.

" 'Time for me, too, to go North,' thought Gurov as he returned after seeing her off." And there the chapter ends.

The third movement plunges us straight into Gurov's life in Moscow. The richness of a gay Russian winter, his family affairs, the dinners at clubs and restaurants, all this is swiftly and vividly suggested. Then a page is devoted to a queer thing that has happened to him: he cannot forget the lady with the little dog. He has many friends, but the curious longing he has for talking about his adventure finds no outlet. When he happens to speak in a very general way of love and women, nobody guesses what he means, and only his wife moves her dark eyebrows and says: "Stop that fatuous posing; it does not suit you."

And now comes what in Chekhov's quiet stories may be called the climax. There is something that your average citizen calls romance and something he calls prose — though both are the meat of poetry for the artist. Such a contrast has already been hinted at by the slice of watermelon which Gurov crunched in a Yalta hotel room at a most romantic moment, sitting heavily and munching away. This contrast is beautifully followed up when at last Gurov blurts out to a friend late at night as they come out of the club: If you knew what a delightful woman I met in Yalta! His friend, a bureaucratic civil servant, got into his sleigh, the horses moved, but suddenly he turned and called back to Gurov. Yes? asked Gurov, evidently expecting some reaction to what he had just mentioned. By the way, said the man, you were quite right. That fish at the club was decidedly smelly.

This is a natural transition to the description of Gurov's new mood, his feeling that he lives among savages where cards and food are life. His family, his bank, the whole trend of his existence, everything seems futile, dull, and senseless. About Christmas he tells his wife he is going on a business trip to St. Petersburg, instead of which he travels to the remote Volga town where the lady lives.

Critics of Chekhov in the good old days when the mania for the civic problem flourished in Russia were incensed with his way of describing what they considered to be trivial unnecessary matters instead of thoroughly examining and solving the problems of bourgeois marriage. For as soon as Gurov arrives in the early hours to that town and takes the best room at the local hotel, Chekhov, instead of describing his mood or intensifying his difficult moral position, gives what is artistic in the highest sense of the word: he notes the gray carpet, made of military cloth, and the inkstand, also gray with dust, with a horseman whose hand waves a hat and whose head is gone. That is all: it is nothing but it is everything in authentic literature. A feature in the same line is the phonetic transformation which the hotel porter imposes on the German name von Dideritz. Having learned the address Gurov goes there and looks at the house. Opposite was a long gray fence with nails sticking out. An unescapable fence, Gurov says to himself, and here we get the concluding note in the rhythm of drabness and grayness already suggested by the carpet, the inkstand, the illiterate accent of the porter. The unexpected little turns and the lightness of the touches are what places Chekhov, above all Russian writers of fiction, on the level of Gogol and Tolstoy.

Presently he saw an old servant coming out with the familiar little white dog. He wanted to call it (by a kind of conditional reflex), but suddenly his heart began beating fast and in his excitement he could not remember the dog's name — another delightful touch. Later on he decides to go to the local theatre, where for the first time the operetta *The Geisha* is being given. In sixty words Chekhov paints a complete picture of a provincial theatre, not forgetting the town-governor who modestly hid in his box behind a plush curtain so that only his hands were visible. Then the lady appeared. And he realized quite clearly that now in the whole world there was none nearer and dearer and more important to him than this slight woman, lost in a small-town crowd, a woman perfectly unremarkable, with a vulgar lorgnette in her hand. He saw her husband and remembered her qualifying him as a flunkey — he distinctly resembled one.

A remarkably fine scene follows when Gurov manages to talk to her, and then their mad swift walk up all kinds of staircases and corridors, and down again, and up again, amid people in the various uniforms of provincial officials. Neither does Chekhov forget "two schoolboys who smoked on the stairs and looked down at him and her."

> "You must leave," Anna Sergeievna went on in a whisper. "Do you hear, Dmitri Dmitrich? I will come and see you in Moscow. I have never been happy; I am unhappy now, and I never, never shall be happy, never! So don't make me suffer still more! I swear I'll come to Moscow. But now let us part. My dear, good, precious one, let us part!"
>
> She pressed his hand and walked rapidly downstairs, turning to look round at him, and from her eyes he could see that she really was unhappy. Gurov stood for a while, listening, then when all grew quiet, he found his coat and left the theatre.

The fourth and last little chapter gives the atmosphere of their secret meetings in Moscow. As soon as she would arrive she used to send a red-capped messenger to Gurov. One day he was on his way to her and his daughter was with him. She was going to school, in the same direction as he. Big damp snowflakes were slowly coming down.

The thermometer, Gurov was saying to his daughter, shows a few degrees above freezing point (actually 37° above, Fahrenheit), but nevertheless snow is falling. The explanation is that this warmth applies only to the surface of the earth, while in the higher layers of the atmosphere the temperature is quite different.

And as he spoke and walked, he kept thinking that not a soul knew or would ever know about these secret meetings.

What puzzled him was that all the false part of his life, his bank, his club, his conversations, his social obligations — all this happened openly, while the real and interesting part was hidden.

> He had two lives: an open one, seen and known by all who needed to know of it, full of conventional truth and conventional falsehood, ex-

actly like the lives of his friends and acquaintances; and another life that went on in secret. And through some strange, perhaps accidental, combination of circumstances, everything that was of interest and importance to him, everything that was essential to him, everything about which he felt sincerely and did not deceive himself, everything that constituted the core of his life, was going on concealed from others; while all that was false, the shell in which he hid to cover the truth — his work at the bank for instance, his discussions at the club, his references to the "inferior race," his appearances at anniversary celebrations with his wife — all that went on in the open. Judging others by himself, he did not believe what he saw, and always fancied that every man led his real, most interesting life under cover of secrecy as under cover of night. The personal life of every individual is based on secrecy, and perhaps it is partly for that reason that civilized man is so nervously anxious that personal privacy should be respected.

The final scene is full of that pathos which has been suggested in the very beginning. They meet, she sobs, they feel that they are the closest of couples, the tenderest of friends, and he sees that his hair is getting a little gray and knows that only death will end their love.

> The shoulders on which his hands rested were warm and quivering. He felt compassion for this life, still so warm and lovely, but probably already about to begin to fade and wither like his own. Why did she love him so much? He always seemed to women different from what he was, and they loved in him not himself, but the man whom their imagination had created and whom they had been eagerly seeking all their lives; and afterwards, when they saw their mistake, they loved him nevertheless. And not one of them had been happy with him. In the past he had met women, come together with them, parted from them, but he had never once loved; it was anything you please, but not love. And only now when his head was gray he had fallen in love, really, truly — for the first time in his life.

They talk, they discuss their position, how to get rid of the necessity of this sordid secrecy, how to be together always. They find no solution and in the typical Chekhov way the tale fades out with no definite full-stop but with the natural motion of life.

> And it seemed as though in a little while the solution would be found, and then a new and glorious life would begin; and it was clear to both of them that the end was still far off, and that what was to be most complicated and difficult for them was only just beginning.

All the traditional rules of story telling have been broken in this wonderful short story of twenty pages or so. There is no problem, no regular climax, no point at the end. And it is one of the greatest stories ever written.

[1981]

HAMLIN GARLAND wrote his preface to Main-Travelled Roads *in 1922, after the book had enjoyed considerable success. Since its first appearance in 1891, the collection had gone through several reprintings. For the new edition, Garland decided to describe how he came to write the book. The life of the midwestern farmer had improved so much since Garland had written the stories that he considered them "historical fiction." In part the improvement had come about because* Main-Travelled Roads *had stirred up so much controversy that it had helped provoke much-needed agrarian reform.*

⌇12⌇

Hamlin Garland

from the Preface to

MAIN-TRAVELLED ROADS

In the summer of 1887, after having been three years in Boston and six years absent from my old home in northern Iowa, I found myself with money enough to pay my railway fare to Ordway, South Dakota, where my father and mother were living, and as it cost very little extra to go by way of Dubuque and Charles City, I planned to visit Osage, Iowa, and the farm we had opened on Dry Run prairie in 1871.

Up to this time I had written only a few poems and some articles descriptive of boy life on the prairie, although I was doing a good deal of thinking and lecturing on land reform, and was regarded as a very intense disciple of Herbert Spencer[1] and Henry George[2] — a singular combination, as I see it now. On my way westward, that summer day in 1887, rural life presented itself from an entirely new angle. The ugliness, the endless drudgery, and the loneliness of the farmer's lot smote me with stern insistence. I was the militant reformer.

The farther I got from Chicago the more depressing the landscape became. It was bad enough in our former home in Mitchell County, but my pity grew more intense as I passed from northwest Iowa into southern Dakota. The houses, bare as boxes, dropped on the treeless plains, the barbed-wire fences running at right angles, and the towns mere assemblages of flimsy wooden sheds with painted-pine battlement, produced on me the effect of an almost helpless and sterile poverty.

[1] Herbert Spencer (1820–1903), English philosopher.
[2] Henry George (1839–1897), American economist.

My dark mood was deepened into bitterness by my father's farm, where I found my mother imprisoned in a small cabin on the enormous sunburned, treeless plain, with no expectation of ever living anywhere else. Deserted by her sons and failing in health, she endured the discomforts of her life uncomplainingly — but my resentment of "things as they are" deepened during my talks with her neighbors, who were all housed in the same unshaded cabins in equal poverty and loneliness. The fact that at twenty-seven I was without power to aid my mother in any substantial way added to my despairing mood.

My savings for the two years of my teaching in Boston were not sufficient to enable me to purchase my return ticket, and when my father offered me a stacker's wages in the harvest field I accepted and for two weeks or more proved my worth with the fork, which was still mightier — with me — than the pen.

However, I did not entirely neglect the pen. In spite of the dust and heat of the wheat ricks I dreamed of poems and stories. My mind teemed with subjects for fiction, and one Sunday morning I set to work on a story which had been suggested to me by a talk with my mother, and a few hours later I read to her (seated on the low sill of that treeless cottage) the first two thousand words of "Mrs. Ripley's Trip," the first of the series of sketches which became *Main-Travelled Roads*.

I did not succeed in finishing it, however, till after my return to Boston in September. During the fall and winter of '87 and the winter and spring of '88, I wrote the most of the stories in *Main-Travelled Roads*. . . .

The mood of bitterness in which [this book was] written was renewed and augmented by a second visit to my parents in 1889, for during my stay my mother suffered a stroke of paralysis due to overwork and the dreadful heat of the summer. She grew better before the time came for me to return to my teaching in Boston, but I felt like a sneak as I took my way to the train, leaving my mother and sister on that bleak and sun-baked plain. . . .

Life on the farms of Iowa and Wisconsin — even on the farms of Dakota — has gained in beauty and security, I will admit, but there are still wide stretches of territory in Kansas and Nebraska where the farmhouse is a lonely shelter. Groves and lawns, better roads, the rural free delivery, the telephone, and the motorcar have done much to bring the farmer into a frame of mind where he is contented with his lot, but much remains to be done before the stream of young life from the country to the city can be checked.

The two volumes of *Main-Travelled Roads* can now be taken to be what William Dean Howells[3] called them, "historical fiction," for they form a record of the farmer's life as I lived it and studied it. In these two books is a record of the privations and hardships of the men and women who subdued the midland wilderness and prepared the way for the present golden age of agriculture.

[1922]

---

[3] William Dean Howells (1837–1920), American novelist and literary critic.

*E*DITH WHARTON *wrote about "Telling a Short Story" in her book* The Writing of Fiction *(1925), from which this excerpt is taken. Her disciplined attempt to state a theory of narrative form was modeled on the example of her mentor, Henry James. She took as the epigraph of her book a quotation from the early English poet Thomas Traherne: "Order the beauty even of Beauty is." Concerned with defining the difference between the short story and longer forms of prose narrative, Wharton was herself an accomplished writer of both.*

～ゝ 13 ゝ～

Edith Wharton

Every Subject Must Contain within Itself

Its Own Dimensions

It is sometimes said that a "good subject" for a short story should always be capable of being expanded into a novel.

The principle may be defendable in special cases; but it is certainly a misleading one on which to build any general theory. Every "subject" (in the novelist's sense of the term) must necessarily contain within itself its own dimensions; and one of the fiction-writer's essential gifts is that of discerning whether the subject which presents itself to him, asking for incarnation, is suited to the proportions of a short story or of a novel. If it appears to be adapted to both the chances are that it is inadequate to either.

It would be as great a mistake, however, to try to base a hard-and-fast theory on the denial of the rule as on its assertion. Instances of short stories made out of subjects that could have been expanded into a novel, and that are yet typical short stories and not mere stunted novels, will occur to everyone. General rules in art are useful chiefly as a lamp in a mine, or a handrail down a black stairway; they are necessary for the sake of the guidance they give, but it is a mistake, once they are formulated, to be too much in awe of them.

There are at least two reasons why a subject should find expression in novel-form rather than as a tale; but neither is based on the number of what may be conveniently called incidents, or external happenings, which the narrative contains. There are novels of action which might be condensed into short stories without the loss of their distinguishing qualities. The marks of the subject requiring a longer development are, first, the gradual unfolding of the inner life of its characters, and secondly the need of producing in the reader's mind the sense of the lapse of time. Outward events of the most varied and exciting nature may without loss of probability be crowded into a few hours, but moral dramas usually have their roots deep in the soul, their rise far back in time; and the suddenest-seeming clash in which they culminate should be led up to step by step if it is to explain and justify itself.

There are cases, indeed, when the short story may make use of the moral drama at its culmination. If the incident dealt with be one which a single retrospective flash sufficiently lights up, it is qualified for use as a short story; but if the subject be so complex, and its successive phases so interesting, as to justify elaboration, the lapse of time must necessarily be suggested, and the novel-form becomes appropriate.

The effect of compactness and instantaneity sought in the short story is attained mainly by the observance of two "unities" — the old traditional one of time, and that other, more modern and complex, which requires that any rapidly enacted episode shall be seen through only one pair of eyes. . . .

One thing more is needful for the ultimate effect of probability; and that is, never to let the character who serves as reflector record anything not naturally within his register. It should be the story-teller's first care to choose this reflecting mind deliberately, as one would choose a building-site, or decide upon the orientation of one's house, and when this is done, to live inside the mind chosen, trying to feel, see and react exactly as the latter would, no more, no less, and, above all, no otherwise. Only thus can the writer avoid attributing incongruities of thought and metaphor to his chosen interpreter.

[1925]

*S*HERWOOD ANDERSON *commented on his practice of writing short stories in his autobiography,* A Story Teller's Story, *published in 1924. This book was his first attempt to write his memoirs and authenticate his "legend"— an impoverished childhood, a revolt against business life, and an entrance into the avant-garde literary circles of Chicago, New Orleans, and New York. He was more concerned with the meaning than with the facts of his life. In his rejection of the "plot" story (a story emphasizing plot over character, setting, or theme), which he considered contrived fiction, he became a strong influence on many subsequent American writers of short stories.*

~14~

Sherwood Anderson

on Form, Not Plot, in

the Short Story

For such men as myself you must understand there is always a great difficulty about telling the tale after the scent has been picked up. . . . Having, from a conversation overheard or in some other way, got the tone of a tale, I was like a woman who has just become impregnated. Something was growing inside me. At night when I lay in my bed I could feel the heels of the tale kicking against the walls of my body. Often as I lay thus every word of the tale came to me quite clearly but when I got out of bed to write it down the words would not come.

I had constantly to seek in roads new to me. Other men had felt what I had felt, had seen what I had seen — how had they met the difficulties I faced? My father when he told his tales walked up and down the room before his audience. He pushed out little experimental sentences and watched his audience narrowly. There was a dull-eyed old farmer sitting in a corner of the room. Father had his eyes on the fellow. "I'll get him," he said to himself. He watched the farmer's eyes. When the experimental sentence he had tried did not get anywhere he tried another and kept trying. Beside words he had — to help the telling of his tales — the advantage of being able to act out those parts for which he could find no words. He could frown, shake his fists, smile, let a look of pain or annoyance drift over his face.

These were his advantages that I had to give up if I was to write my tales rather than tell them and how often I had cursed my fate.

How significant words had become to me! At about this time an American woman living in Paris, Miss Gertrude Stein, had published a book called *Tender Buttons* and it had come into my hands. How it had excited me! Here was something purely experimental and dealing in words separated from sense — in the ordinary meaning of the word sense — an approach I was sure the poets must often be compelled to make. Was it an approach that would help me? I decided to try it.

A year or two before the time of which I am now writing an American painter, Mr. Felix Russman, had taken me one day into his workshop to show me his colors. He laid them out on a table before me and then his wife called him out of the room and he stayed for half an hour. It had been one of the most exciting moments of my life. I shifted the little pans of color about, laid one color against another. I walked away and came near. Suddenly there had flashed into my consciousness, for perhaps the first time in my life, the secret inner world of the painters. Before that time I had wondered often enough why certain paintings, done by the old masters, and hung in our Chicago Art Institute, had so strange an effect upon me. Now I thought I knew. The true painter revealed all of himself in every stroke of his brush. Titian made one feel so utterly the splendor of himself; from Fra Angelico and Sandro Botticelli there came such a deep human tenderness that on some days it fairly brought tears to the eyes; in a most dreadful way and in spite of all his skill Bouguereau gave away his own inner nastiness while Leonardo made one feel all of the grandeur of his mind just as Balzac[1] had made his readers feel the universality and wonder of his mind.

Very well then, the words used by the tale-teller were as the colors used by the painter. Form was another matter. It grew out of the materials of the tale and the teller's reaction to them. It was the tale trying to take form that kicked about inside the tale-teller at night when he wanted to sleep.

And words were something else. Words were the surfaces, the clothes of the tale. I thought I had begun to get something a little clearer now. I had smiled to myself a little at the sudden realization of how little native American words had been used by American story-writers. When most American writers wanted to be very American they went in for slang. Surely we American scribblers had paid long and hard for the English blood in our veins. The English had got their books into our schools, their ideas of correct forms of expression were firmly fixed in our minds. Words as commonly used in our writing were in reality an army that marched in a certain array and the generals in command of the army were still English. One saw the words as marching, always just so — in books — and came to think of them so — in books.

---

[1] Honoré de Balzac (1799–1850), French novelist, one of the earliest realists.

But when one told a tale to a group of advertising men sitting in a barroom in Chicago or to a group of laborers by a factory door in Indiana one instinctively disbanded the army. There were moments then for what have always been called by our correct writers "unprintable words." One got now and then a certain effect by a bit of profanity. One dropped instinctively into the vocabulary of the men about, was compelled to do so to get the full effect sought for the tale. Was the tale he was telling not just the tale of a man named Smoky Pete and how he caught his foot in the trap set for himself? — or perhaps one was giving them the Mama Geigans story. The devil. What had the words of such a tale to do with Thackeray[2] or Fielding?[3] Did the men to whom one told the tale not know a dozen Smoky Petes and Mama Geigans? Had one ventured into the classic English models for tale-telling at that moment there would have been a roar. "What the devil! Don't you go high-toning us!"

And it was sure one did not always seek a laugh from his audience. Sometimes one wanted to move the audience, make them squirm with sympathy. Perhaps one wanted to throw an altogether new light on a tale the audience already knew.

Would the common words of our daily speech in shops and offices do the trick? Surely the Americans among whom one sat talking had felt everything the Greeks had felt, everything the English felt? Deaths came to them, the tricks of fate assailed their lives. I was certain none of them lived felt or talked as the average American novel made them live feel and talk and as for the plot short stories of the magazines — those bastard children of de Maupassant, Poe, and O. Henry[4] — it was certain there were no plot short stories ever lived in any life I had known anything about.

[1924]

---

[2] William Makepeace Thackeray (1811–1863), English novelist.
[3] Henry Fielding (1707–1754), one of the first English novelists.
[4] O. Henry, pseudonym of William Sydney Porter (1862–1910), famous American author of short stories with elaborate plots and often "trick" endings.

*J*AMES *JOYCE kept no rough draft of any* Dubliners *story. Scholars think it very probable that he composed his stories fairly completely in his head before writing them down. This draft of "The Sisters" was printed for the first time in Robert Scholes and A. Walton Litz's text of* Dubliners *in 1961. A similar version appeared in the Dublin agricultural journal* The Irish Homestead *for the week of August 13, 1904. Joyce made extensive alterations and additions to "The Sisters" when he revised it to become the introduction to the whole collection of* Dubliners *stories in 1916. Scholes and Litz state that "the revisions can be seen as improvements to this one story or as adjustments made so that the story could better serve its function as an introduction to the others — or as both of these things."*

❧ 15 ❧

James Joyce

An Early Version of

THE SISTERS

Three nights in succession I had found
myself in Great Britain Street at
that hour, as if by providence. Three
nights I had raised my eyes to that
lighted square of window and speculated.
I seemed to understand that it would
occur at night. But in spite of the
providence which had led my feet
and in spite of the reverent curiosity
of my eyes I had discovered nothing.
Each night the square was lighted
in the same way, faintly and evenly.
It was not the light of candles so
far as I could see. Therefore it had
not ~~yet~~ occurred yet.
    On the fourth night at that
hour I was in another part of the
city. It may have been the same
providence that led me there — a
whimsical kind of providence — to
take me at a disadvantage. As I ·

went home I wondered was that
square of window lighted as before
or did it reveal the ceremonious
candles in the light of which the
Christian must take his last sleep.
I was not surprised, then, when at
supper I found myself a prophet.
Old Cotter and my uncle were talking
at the fire, smoking. Old Cotter was
a retired distiller who owned a batch
of prize setters. He used to be very
interesting when I knew him first,
talking about *faints* and *worms*, but[1]

afterwards he became tedious.
    While I was eating my stirabout
I heard him say to my uncle:
— Without a doubt. The upper storey
(he tapped an unnecessary hand
at his forehead) was gone —
— So they said. I never could see
much of it. I thought he was
sane enough —
— So he was, at times, said old
Cotter —
    I sniffed the *was* apprehensively
and gulped down some stirabout.

Jack — Is he any better, Uncle ~~John~~? —
— He's dead —
— O. . . . . —
— Died a few hours ago —
— Who told you? —
— Mr Cotter here brought us the
news. He was passing. . . . —
— Yes, I just happened to be passing
and I noticed the windows. . . . You
know. So I just knocked softly —
— Do you think they will bring him
to the chapel? asked my aunt —
— O, no, ma'am. I wouldn't say so —
— Very unlikely, my uncle agreed —
    So old Cotter had got the better
of me for all my vigilance of
three nights. It is often annoying

[1] In the original manuscript, pages ended at the space breaks.

the way people will blunder on
what you have elaborately planned
for. I was sure he would die
at night.

The following morning after breakfast
I went down to look at the little
house in Great Britain Street.
It was an unassuming shop
registered under the vague name
of *Drapery*. The drapery consisted
chiefly of children's boots and
umbrellas and on ordinary days
there used to be a notice hanging
in the window which said *Umbrellas
Recovered*. There was no notice
visible now for the shop-blinds
were drawn down and a crape
bouquet was tied to the knocker
of the door with white ribbons.
Three women of the people and
a telegram boy were reading
the card pinned on the crape. I
also went over and read:
　　　　July 2nd, 1890
　　The Rev. James Flynn
　　(formerly of S. Catherine's
　　Church, Meath Street) aged
　　Sixty-five Years.
　　　　R.I.P.
Only sixty-five! He looked
much older than that. I often saw
him sitting at the fire in the close
dark room behind the shop, nearly
smothered in his great coat. He
seemed to have almost stupefied
himself with heat and the gesture
of his large trembling hand to
his nostrils had grown automatic.
My aunt, who is what they call
good-hearted, never went into
the shop without bringing him

some High Toast; and he used to
take the packet of snuff from
her hands, gravely inclining his

head for sign of thanks. He used
to sit in that stuffy room for
the greater part of the day from
early morning while Nannie
(who was almost stone deaf)
read out the newspaper to him.
His other sister, Eliza, used to
mind the shop. These two old
women used to look after him,
feed him and clothe him. The
task of clothing him was not
difficult for his ancient priestly
clothes were quite green with
age and his dogskin slippers
were everlasting. When he was
tired of hearing the news he used
to rattle his snuff-box on the
arm of his chair to avoid
shouting at her and then he
used to make believe to read
his prayerbook. Make believe
because whenever Eliza brought
him a cup of soup from the
kitchen she had always to
waken him.

    As I stood looking up at the
crape and the card which bore
his name I could not convince
myself that he was dead. He
seemed like one who could have
gone on living for ever if only
he had wanted to; his life was

so methodical and uneventful.
I think he said more to me than
to anyone else. He had an
egoistic contempt for all
women-folk and suffered all
their services to him in polite
silence. Of course neither of
his sisters was very intelligent.
Nannie, for instance, had been
reading out the newspaper
to him every day for years and
could read tolerably well and
yet she always spoke of it

as the *Freeman's General*.
Perhaps he found me more
intelligent and honoured me
with words for that reason.
Nothing, practically nothing,
ever happened to remind him
of his former life (I mean friends
or visitors) but still he could
remember every detail of it
in his own fashion. He had
studied at the college in Rome

pronounce and he taught me to ~~speak~~
Latin in the Italian way. He
often put me through the
responses of the Mass, smiling
often and pushing huge pinches
of snuff up each nostril
alternately. When he smiled
he used to uncover his big
discoloured teeth and let his
tongue lie on his lower lip.
At first this habit of his used

to make me feel uneasy. Then
I grew used to it.
    That evening my aunt
visited the house of mourning
and took me with her. It was
an oppressive summer evening
of faded gold. Nannie received
us in the hall and, as it was
no use saying anything to
her, my aunt shook hands
with her for all. We followed
the old woman upstairs and
into the dead-room. The room
through the lace end of the
blind was suffused with
dusky golden light amid
which the candles seemed
like pale thin flames. He
had been coffined. Nannie
gave the lead and we three
knelt down at the foot of
the bed. There was no sound
in the room for some minutes

except the sound of Nannie's
mutterings, for she prayed
noisily. The fancy came
to me that the old priest
was smiling as he lay there
in his coffin.

But no. When we rose
and went up to the head
of the bed I saw that he was
not smiling. There he lay

solemn and copious, vested
as for the altar, his large
hands loosely retaining a
cross. His face was very grey
and massive with distended
nostrils and circled with a
scanty white fur. There was
a heavy odour in the room, the
flowers.

We sat downstairs in the
little room behind the shop,
my aunt and I and the two
sisters. We, as visitors, were
given a glass of sherry each.
Nannie sat in a corner and
said nothing but her lips
moved from speaker to
speaker with a painfully
intelligent movement. I
said nothing either, being
too young, but my aunt said
a great deal for she was a
gossip, a harmless one.

— Ah, well, he's gone! —

— To enjoy his eternal reward,
Miss Flynn, I'm sure. He was
a good and holy man —

— He was a good man but . . . . .
you see . . . . he was a disappointed
man. You see . . . . his life was,
you might say, crossed —

— Ah, yes. I know what you mean —

— Not that he was anyway mad,
   as you know yourself: but he
   was always a little queer. Even

when we were all growing up
together he was queer. One
time he didn't speak hardly
for a month. You know, he
was that kind always —
— Perhaps he read too much,
Miss Flynn —
— O, he read a good deal but
not latterly. It was his
scrupulousness, you see, that
affected his mind. The duties
of the priesthood were too
much for him —
— Did he . . . . peacefully? —
— O, quite peacefully, ma'am. You
couldn't tell when the breath
went out of him. He had a
beautiful death, God be
praised —
— And everything . . . . . . ? —
— Father O'Rourke was in with
him yesterday and gave him
the Last Sacrament —
— He knew then? —
— Yes. He was quite resigned —
     Nannie gave a sleepy nod
and looked ashamed.
— Poor Nannie, said her sister,

she's worn out. All the work
we had getting in a woman
and laying him out! And
then the coffin and arranging
about the mass in the chapel.
God knows we did all we could,
as poor as we are. We wouldn't
see him want anything at
the last —
— Indeed you were both very
kind to him while he lived —
— Ah, poor James! He was no
great trouble to us. You wouldn't
hear him in the house any
more than now. Still I know
he's gone and all that I
won't be bringing him in
his soup any more nor Nannie

reading him out the paper
nor you, ma'am, bringing
him his snuff! Poor James! —
— O, yes, you'll miss him in a
day or two more than you
do now —
    Silence invaded the room
until memory reawakened
it, Eliza speaking slowly:
— It was that chalice he broke.
Of course, it was all right.
I mean it contained nothing.
But still . . . . . They say it was
the boy's fault. But poor

James was so nervous. God be
merciful to him! —
— Yes, Miss Flynn, I heard that
about the chalice. He . . . . his
mind was a bit affected by
that —
— He began to mope by himself,
talking to no-one and wandering
about. Often he couldn't be
found. One night he was wanted
and they looked high up and
low down and couldn't find
him. Then the clerk suggested
the chapel. So they opened the
chapel (it was late at night)
and brought in a light to look
for him . . . . . And there, sure
enough, he was sitting in his
confession-box in the dark, wide
awake, and laughing like —
softly to himself. Then they knew
something was wrong —
— God rest his soul! —

[1904]

*F*RANK O'CONNOR *analyzed the stories in James Joyce's* Dubliners *in a chapter entitled "Work in Progress" in his 1963 study of the short story,* The Lonely Voice. *O'Connor addressed himself to the question of why Joyce gave up writing stories after* Dubliners; *he understood that "it is as difficult to think of a real storyteller, like Chekhov, who had experienced the thrill of the completed masterpiece, giving up short stories forever as it is to think of Keats giving up lyric poetry." The answer, for O'Connor, can be found by comparing the formal differences between the stories at the beginning of the book and "The Dead" at the end. That is where his analysis begins.*

~ 16 ~

Frank O'Connor

on the Elaboration of Style and Form in Joyce's

THE DEAD

"The Dead," Joyce's last story, is entirely different from all the others. It is also immensely more complicated, and it is not always easy to see what any particular episode represents, though it is only too easy to see that it represents something. The scene is the annual dance of the Misses Morkan, old music teachers on Usher's Island, and ostensibly it is no more than a report of what happened at it, except at the end, when Gabriel Conroy and his wife Gretta return to their hotel room. There she breaks down and tells him of a youthful and innocent love affair between herself and a boy of seventeen in Galway, who had caught his death of cold from standing under her bedroom window. But this final scene is irrelevant only in appearance, for in effect it is the real story, and everything that has led up to it has been simply an enormously expanded introduction, a series of themes all of which find their climax in the hotel bedroom.

The setting of the story in a warm, vivacious lighted house in the midst of night and snow is an image of life itself, but every incident, almost every speech, has a crack in it through which we perceive the presence of death all about us, as when Gabriel says that Gretta "takes three *mortal* hours to dress herself," and the aunts say that she must be "perished alive" — an Irishism that ingeniously suggests both life and death. Several times the warmth and gaiety give rise to the idea of love and marriage, but each time it is knocked dead by phrase or incident. At the very opening of the story Gabriel suggests to the servant girl, Lily, that they will soon be attending her wedding, but she retorts savagely that "the men that is now is only all palaver and what they can get out of you," the major theme of the story, for all grace is with the dead: The younger generation have not the generosity of the two old sisters, the younger singers (Caruso, for instance!) cannot sing as well as some long dead English tenor. Gabriel's aunt actually sings "Arrayed for the Bridal," but she is only an old woman who has been dismissed from her position in the local church choir.

Gabriel himself is fired by passion for his wife, but when they return to their hotel bedroom the electric light has failed, and his passion is also extinguished when she tells him the story of her love for a dead boy. Whether it is Gabriel's quarrel with Miss Ivors, who wants him to spend his summer holiday patriotically in the West of Ireland (where his wife and the young man had met), the discussion of Cistercian monks who are supposed to sleep in their coffins, "to remind them of their last end," or the reminiscences of old singers and old relatives, everything pushes Gabriel toward that ultimate dissolution of identity in which real things disappear from about us, and we are as alone as we shall be on our deathbeds.

But it is easy enough to see from "The Dead" why Joyce gave up storytelling. One of his main passions — the elaboration of style and form — had taken control, and the short story is too tightly knit to permit expansion like this. And — what is much more important — it is quite clear from "The Dead" that he had already begun to lose sight of the submerged population that was his original subject. There are little touches of it here and there, as in the sketches of Freddy Malins and his mother — the old lady who finds everything "beautiful" — "beautiful crossing," "beautiful house," "beautiful scenery," "beautiful fish" — but Gabriel does not belong to it, nor does Gretta nor Miss Ivors. They are not characters but personalities, and Joyce would never again be able to deal with characters, people whose identity is determined by their circumstances. His own escape to Trieste, with its enlargement of his own sense of identity, had caused them to fade from his mind or — to put it more precisely — had caused them to reappear in entirely different guises. This is something that is always liable to happen to the provincial storyteller when you put him into a cosmopolitan atmosphere.

[1963]

GUSTAV JANOUCH *published his recollections of Kafka in* Conversations with Kafka *(1953). Janouch's father worked in the Workers' Accident Insurance Institute with Kafka, and he introduced his son to Kafka in 1920 because they were both "scribblers." Janouch was only seventeen at the time, and very impressionable. Having read* The Metamorphosis, *he was disappointed by his first sight of Kafka: " 'So this is the creator of the mysterious bug, Samsa,' I said to myself, disillusioned to see before me a simple, well-mannered man." But when their conversation was over that day — after Kafka had told Janouch that he wrote at night because daytime was a "great enchantment . . . it distracts from the darkness within" — Janouch asked himself, "Is he not himself the unfortunate bug in* The Metamorphosis?" *Their acquaintance ripened into a friendship, which lasted until Kafka's death in 1924.*

➤ 17 ✍

Gustav Janouch

on Franz Kafka's View of

THE METAMORPHOSIS

–translated by Goronwy Rees

I spent my first week's wages on having Kafka's three stories — *The Metamorphosis, The Judgement,* and *The Stoker* — bound in a dark brown leather volume, with the name *Franz Kafka* elegantly tooled in gold lettering.

The book lay in the brief-case on my knee as I told Kafka about the warehouse-cinema. Then I proudly took the volume out of the case and gave it across the desk to Kafka.

"What is this?" he asked in astonishment.

"It's my first week's wages."

"Isn't that a waste?"

Kafka's eyelids fluttered. His lips were sharply drawn in. For a few seconds he contemplated the name in the gold lettering, hastily thumbed through the pages of the book and — with obvious embarrassment — placed it before me on the desk. I was about to ask why the book offended him, when he began to cough. He took a handkerchief from his pocket, held it to his mouth, replaced it when the attack was over, stood up and went to the small washstand behind his desk and washed his hands, then said as he dried them: "You overrate me. Your trust oppresses me."

He sat himself at his desk and said, with his hands to his temples: "I am no burning bush. I am not a flame."

I interrupted him. "You shouldn't say that. It's not just. To me, for example, you are fire, warmth, and light."

"No, no!" he contradicted me, shaking his head. "You are wrong. My scribbling does not deserve a leather binding. It's only my own personal spectre of horror. It oughtn't to be printed at all. It should be burned and destroyed. It is without meaning."

I became furious. "Who told you that?" I was forced to contradict him — "How can you say such a thing? Can you see into the future? What you are saying to me is entirely your subjective feeling. Perhaps your scribbling, as you call it, will tomorrow represent a significant voice in the world. Who can tell today?"

I drew a deep breath.

Kafka stared at the desk. At the corners of his mouth were two short, sharp lines of shadow.

I was ashamed of my outburst, so I said quietly, in a low, explanatory tone: "Do you remember what you said to me about the Picasso exhibition?"

Kafka looked at me without understanding.

I continued: "You said that art is a mirror which — like a clock running fast — foretells the future. Perhaps your writing is, in today's *Cinema of the Blind*, only a mirror of tomorrow."

"Please, don't go on," said Kafka fretfully, and covered his eyes with both hands.

I apologized. "Please forgive me, I didn't mean to upset you. I'm stupid."

"No, no — you're not that!" Without removing his hands, he rocked his whole body to and fro. "You are right. You are certainly right. Probably that's why I can't finish anything. I am afraid of the truth. But can one do otherwise?" He took his hands away from his eyes, placed his clenched fists on the table, and said in a low, suppressed voice: "One must be silent, if one can't give any help. No one, through his own lack of hope, should make the condition of the patient worse. For that reason, all my scribbling is to be destroyed. I am no light. I have merely lost my way among my own thorns. I'm a dead end."

Kafka leaned backwards. His hands slipped lifelessly from the table. He closed his eyes.

"I don't believe it," I said with utter conviction, yet added appeasingly: "And even if it were true, it would be worthwhile to display the dead end to people."

Kafka merely shook his head slowly. "No, no ... I am weak and tired."

"You should give up your work here," I said gently, to relax the tension which I felt between us.

Kafka nodded. "Yes, I should. I wanted to creep away behind this office desk, but it only increased my weakness. It's become — ," Kafka looked at me with an indescribably painful smile, " — a cinema of the blind."

Then he closed his eyes again.

I was glad at this moment there was a knock on the door behind me.

[1953]

JOHN UPDIKE wrote a foreword to The Complete Stories of Franz
Kafka *in 1983. Updike began his essay by quoting "He," one of Kafka's
aphorisms: "All that he does seems to him, it is true, extraordinarily new,
but also, because of the incredible spate of new things, extraordinarily ama-
teurish, indeed scarcely tolerable, incapable of becoming history, breaking
short the chain of the generations, cutting off for the first time at its most
profound source the music of the world, which before him could at least be
divined. Sometimes in his arrogance he has more anxiety for the world than
for himself." Updike has great sympathy for Kafka and wrote about him
with considerable perception.*

⚜ 18 ⚜

John Updike

on Franz Kafka and

THE METAMORPHOSIS

The century since Franz Kafka was born has been marked by the idea
of "modernism" — a self-consciousness new among centuries, a consciousness of being new. Sixty years after his death, Kafka epitomizes one aspect
of this modern mind-set: a sensation of anxiety and shame whose center
cannot be located and therefore cannot be placated; a sense of an infinite
difficulty within things, impeding every step; a sensitivity acute beyond usefulness, as if the nervous system, flayed of its old hide of social usage and
religious belief, must record every touch as pain. In Kafka's peculiar and
highly original case this dreadful quality is mixed with immense tenderness,
oddly good humor, and a certain severe and reassuring formality. The combination makes him an artist; but rarely can an artist have struggled against
greater inner resistance and more sincere diffidence as to the worth of his
art. . . .

Kafka dated his own maturity as a writer from the long night of September 22nd–23rd, 1912, in which he wrote "The Judgment" at a single
eight-hour sitting. He confided to his diary that morning, "Only *in this way*
can writing be done, only with such coherence, with such a complete opening out of the body and the soul." Yet the story is not quite free of the un-
declared neurotic elements that twist the earlier work; the connection between the engagement and the father seems obscure, and the old man's fury

illogical. But in staring at, with his hero Georg, "the bogey conjured up by his father," Kafka broke through to a great cavern of stored emotion. He loved this story, and among friends praised — he who deprecated almost everything from his own pen — its *Zweifellosigkeit*, its "indubitableness." Soon after its composition, he wrote, in a few weeks, "The Metamorphosis," an indubitable masterpiece. It begins with a fantastic premise, whereas in "The Judgment" events become fantastic. This premise — the gigantic insect — established in the first sentence, "The Metamorphosis" unfolds with a beautiful naturalness and a classic economy. It takes place in three acts: three times the metamorphosed Gregor Samsa ventures out of his room, with tumultuous results. The members of his family — rather simpler than Kafka's own, which had three sisters — dispose themselves around the central horror with a touching, as well as an amusing, plausibility. The father's fury, roused in defense of the fragile mother, stems directly from the action and inflicts a psychic wound gruesomely objectified in the rotting apple Gregor carries in his back; the evolutions of the sister, Grete, from shock to distasteful ministration to a certain sulky possessiveness and finally to exasperated indifference are beautifully sketched, with not a stroke too much. The terrible but terribly human tale ends with Grete's own metamorphosis, into a comely young woman. This great story resembles a great story of the nineteenth century, Tolstoy's "The Death of Ivan Ilyich"; in both, a hitherto normal man lies hideously, suddenly stricken in the midst of a family whose irritated, banal daily existence flows around him. The abyss within life is revealed, but also life itself.

What kind of insect is Gregor? Popular belief has him a cockroach, which would be appropriate for a city apartment; and the creature's retiring nature and sleazy dietary preferences would seem to conform. But, as Vladimir Nabokov, who knew his entomology, pointed out in his lectures upon "The Metamorphosis" at Cornell University, Gregor is too broad and convex to be a cockroach. The charwoman calls him a "dung beetle" (*Mistkäfer*) but, Nabokov said, "it is obvious that the good woman is adding the epithet only to be friendly." Kafka's Eduard Raban of "Wedding Preparations" daydreams, walking along, "As I lie in bed I assume the shape of a big beetle, a stag beetle or a cockchafer, I think." Gregor Samsa, awaking, sees "numerous legs, which were pitifully thin compared to the rest of his bulk." If "numerous" is more than six, he must be a centipede — not an insect at all. From evidence in the story he is brown in color and about as long as the distance between a doorknob and the floor; he is broader than half a door. He has a voice at first, "but with a persistent horrible twittering squeak behind it like an undertone," which disappears as the story progresses. His jaws don't work as ours do but he has eyelids, nostrils, and a neck. He is, in short, impossible to picture except when the author wants to evoke his appearance, to bump the reader up against some astounding, poignant new aspect of Gregor's embodiment. The strange physical discomfort noted in the earlier work is here given its perfect allegorical envelope. A wonderful moment comes when Gregor, having been painfully striving to achieve human postures, drops to his feet:

> Hardly was he down when he experienced for the first time this morning a sense of physical comfort; his legs had firm ground under them; they were completely obedient, as he noted with joy; they even strove to carry him forward in whatever direction he chose; and he was inclined to believe that a final relief from all his sufferings was at hand.

When "The Metamorphosis" was to be published as a book in 1915, Kafka, fearful that the cover illustrator "might want to draw the insect itself," wrote the publisher, "Not that, please not that! . . . The insect itself cannot be depicted. It cannot even be shown from a distance." He suggested instead a scene of the family in the apartment with a locked door, or a door open and giving on darkness. Any theatrical or cinematic version of the story must founder on this point of external representation: a concrete image of the insect would be too distracting and shut off sympathy; such a version would lack the very heart of comedy and pathos which beats in the unsteady area between objective and subjective, where Gregor's insect and human selves swayingly struggle. Still half-asleep, he notes his extraordinary condition yet persists in remembering and trying to fulfill his duties as a travelling salesman and the mainstay of this household. Later, relegated by the family to the shadows of a room turned storage closet, he responds to violin music and creeps forward, covered with dust and trailing remnants of food, to claim his sister's love. Such scenes could not be done except with words. In this age that lives and dies by the visual, "The Metamorphosis" stands as a narrative absolutely literary, able to exist only where language and the mind's hazy wealth of imagery interect.

"The Metamorphosis" stands also as a gateway to the world Kafka created after it. His themes and manner were now all in place. His mastery of official pomposity — the dialect of documents and men talking business — shows itself here for the first time, in the speeches of the chief clerk. Music will again be felt, by mice and dogs, as an overwhelming emanation in Kafka's later fables — a theme whose other side is the extreme sensitivity to noise, and the longing for unblemished silence, that Kafka shared with his hero in "The Burrow." Gregor's death scene, and Kafka's death wish, return in "A Hunger Artist" — the saddest, I think, of Kafka's stories, written by a dying man who was increasingly less sanguine (his correspondence reveals) about dying. The sweeping nature of the hunger artist's abstention is made plain by the opposing symbol of the panther who replaces him in his cage: "the joy of life streamed with such ardent passion from his throat that for the onlookers it was not easy to stand the shock of it." In 1920 Milena Jesenská wrote to Brod: "Frank cannot live. Frank does not have the capacity for living. . . . He is absolutely incapable of living, just as he is incapable of getting drunk. He possesses not the slightest refuge. For that reason he is exposed to all those things against which we are protected. He is like a naked man among a multitude who are dressed." After Gregor

Samsa's incarnation, Kafka showed a fondness for naked heroes — animals who have complicated and even pedantic confessions to make but who also are distinguished by some keenly observed bestial traits — the ape of "A Report to an Academy" befouls himself and his fur jumps with fleas; the dog of "Investigations" recalls his young days when, very puppylike, "I believed that great things were going on around me of which I was the leader and to which I must lend my voice, things which must be wretchedly thrown aside if I did not run for them and wag my tail for them"; the mouse folk of "Josephine the Singer" pipe and multiply and are pervaded by an "unexpended, ineradicable childishness"; and the untaxonomic inhabitant of "The Burrow" represents the animal in all of us, his cheerful consumption of "small fry" existentially yoked to a terror of being consumed himself. An uncanny empathy broods above these zoömorphs, and invests them with more of their creator's soul than all but a few human characters receive. So a child, cowed and bored by the world of human adults, makes companions of pets and toy animals.

[1983]

*W*ILLIAM CARLOS WILLIAMS *wrote "A Beginning on the Short Story" as a series of notes in 1949. As an experimental writer, he felt that the principal feature of the story is that it is short, "and so must pack in what it has to say, unless it be snipped off a large piece as prose-for-quality writing which might be justifiable." Another aspect of the story that Williams investigated was using it as "a practice sheet for the novel one might discover in it." Basically he considered it "a good medium for nailing down a single conviction. Emotionally." Williams felt that you can't study the work of a writer in order to "learn" to write a story. All you can learn is what the other writer did.*

⧫ 19 ⧫

William Carlos Williams

Notes on

A BEGINNING ON THE SHORT STORY

The short story isn't a snippet from the newspaper. It isn't realism. It is, as in all forms of art, taking the materials of every day (or otherwise) and using them to raise the consciousness of our lives to higher levels by the use of the art: to get something said.

As in the poem, it must be stressed that the short story uses the same materials as rewrite, the same dregs — the same in fact as Shakespeare and Greek tragedy: the elevation of spirit that occurs when a consciousness of form, art in short, is imposed upon materials debased by dispirited and crassly cynical handling. What the newspaper uses on the lowest (sentimental) level, the short story had best elevate to the level of other interests.

This should make apparent that a mere "thrilling" account of an occurrence from daily life, a transcription of a fact, is not of itself and for that reason a short story. You get the fact, it interests you for whatever reason; of the fact you *make*, using words, a story. A thing. A piece of writing, as in the case of de Maup't, A Piece of String[1]. . . .

In other words when you begin to write a short story you should really know what you're writing about — because, if you write skilfully enough, sooner or later someone is going to find it out and judge you as a man for it.

Oh, but am I making a mistake? Perhaps all you want is to write a

---

[1] A reference to Maupassant's story "The String."

story and not be judged a liar because you lie. I'm really afraid I'm in the wrong bin. I'm taking the art of the short story seriously.

What will it do?

For instance — what was my problem or urge or opportunity for realization of my insights in 1932?

What was going on? A depression. Cheatery.

How did I resolve it? Why did I choose the short story and how much must it have been modified from stereotype to be serviceable to me?

I do not mean to imply that the choice was a conscious one altogether. I mean, looking back upon it, what were the elements involved in my coming upon the short story as a means? — that is during The Depression?

Answer: The character of the evidence: to accommodate itself to the heterogeneous character of the people, the elements involved, the situation in hand. In other words, the materials and the temporal situation dictated the terms.

I lived among these people. I knew them and saw the essential qualities, (not stereotype) the courage, the humor (an accident), the deformity, the basic tragedy of their lives — and the *importance* of it. You can't write about something unimportant to yourself. I, was involved.

That wasn't all. I saw how they were maligned by their institutions of church and state — and "betters." I saw how all that was acceptable to the ear about them maligned them. I saw how stereotype falsified them.

Nobody was writing about them, anywhere, as they ought to be written about. There was no chance of writing anything acceptable, certainly not saleable, about them.

It was my duty to raise the level of consciousness, not to say discussion, of them to a higher level, a higher plane. Really to tell.

Why the short story? Not for a sales article but as I had conceived them. The briefness of their chronicles, its brokenness and heterogeneity — isolation, color. A novel was unthinkable.

And so to the very style of the stories themselves.

This wasn't the "acceptable," the unshocking stuff, the slippery, in the sense that it can be slipped into them while they are semiconscious of a Saturday evening. Not acceptable to a mag and didn't get into them. But one [that] was made for them by a guy who was broke. . . .

We speak of a man's "mettle" — it might better be metal. It is as with other metals, when it is heated it melts. It is when the metal is fluid the imagination can be said to become active; it is the melting, the rendering fluid of the imagination that describes the mind as entering upon creative work.

It must be melted to recreate itself, fluid, unfettered by anything. Maybe shock treatment may some day be part of the curriculum.

The characteristic of being melted is, for the object, to have lost the form it was in. It can be played with, made into a new form as we desire.

With the short story as with any sort of creation, I am trying to say, the imagination (that is the mind in a fluid state, is a melted state) has to be given play.

Now, we know by knowledge of the physiology of the brain that it acts only when it has been supplied oxygen in abundance. So it glows and sweats when it is active — as with anything else.

What is the origin of that heat? Something has stirred us, some perception linked with emotion. We are angry, we are committed to something in our lives, as with the poem. It doesn't matter what it has been — anything. We heat up, grow incandescent. This incentive is usually secret, it is guided by our fears perhaps. But we are heated and (if we can get quiet enough, as in jail, or running away — finally) we melt and the imagination is set to flow into its new mold.

The short story, since flights of the imagination, rocketlike, will be short, though they may penetrate far if we let them go — UP! I should say that the short story consists of one single flight of the imagination, complete: up and down.

What shall the story be written *about*. That's the final step. Obviously not, if it is serious, the mere sentimental characters. . . .

What then? Something that interests the writer seriously, as a writer (not necessarily a man, for in that case the interest would be moral and perhaps best NOT represented as a short story). He writes about the way his interests, as a writer, strike upon the materials, of some event, graphically presented.

The result is life, not morals. It is THE LIFE which comes alive in the telling. It is the life under specified conditions — so that it is relived in the telling — as it strikes off flashes from the materials. The material is the metal against which a flint of action makes sparks.

Thus anything can be used without fear of sentimentality. The THING we are writing, directing all our wit, our intelligence to discover and set down — is revealed as it hits against whatever may be in its path. That's the modern understanding — and I guess it's pretty hard to comprehend, whatever it may be for each man who writes. What good are you? Prove it. Or what do you see, young as you are? Do you think a prostitute is "bad" becuse she's a prostitute? And yet how shall you show her "good" except by speaking of her in the conditions of her prostitution. By using that material, graphically, specifically you must learn to tell all you want to tell — whatever YOU want to say. That is the art.

[1949]

*W*ILLA CATHER *read the fiction of other writers with a shrewd and discriminating eye. In the volume* On Writing *(1949), a collection of her critical essays on literature as art, she analyzed the stories of Sarah Orne Jewett and Katherine Mansfield, among other authors. Cather essentially wrote in praise of the simplest spirit in human beings. There was no theory about the art of fiction in her discussion, but instead "a vision as level and wide as the landscapes and skyscapes of the West," where she grew up.*

⌇ 20 ⌇

Willa Cather
on Katherine Mansfield

Every writer and critic of discernment who looked into Katherine Mansfield's first volume of short stories must have felt that here was a very individual talent. At this particular time few writers care much about their medium except as a means for expressing ideas. But in Katherine Mansfield one recognized virtuosity, a love for the medium she had chosen.

The qualities of a second-rate writer can easily be defined, but a first-rate writer can only be experienced. It is just the thing in him which escapes analysis that makes him first-rate. One can catalogue all the qualities that he shares with other writers, but the thing that is his very own, his timbre, this cannot be defined or explained any more than the quality of a beautiful speaking voice can be.

It was usually Miss Mansfield's way to approach the major forces of life through comparatively trivial incidents. She chose a small reflector to throw a luminous streak out into the shadowy realm of personal relationships. I feel that personal relationships, especially the uncatalogued ones, the seemingly unimportant ones, interested her most. To my thinking, she never measured herself up so fully as in the two remarkable stories about an English family in New Zealand, "Prelude" and "At the Bay."

I doubt whether any contemporary writer has made one feel more keenly the many kinds of personal relationships which exist in an everyday "happy family" who are merely going on living their daily lives, with no crises or shocks or bewildering complications to try them. Yet every individual in that household (even the children) is clinging passionately to his individual soul, is in terror of losing it in the general family flavour. As in most families, the mere struggle to have anything of one's own, to be one's self at all, creates an element of strain which keeps everybody almost at the breaking-point.

One realizes that even in harmonious families there is this double life: the group life, which is the one we can observe in our neighbour's household, and, underneath, another — secret and passionate and intense — which is the real life that stamps the faces and gives character to the voices of our friends. Always in his mind each member of these social units is escaping, running away, trying to break the net which circumstances and his own affections have woven about him. One realizes that human relationships are the tragic necessity of human life; that they can never be wholly satisfactory, that every ego is half the time greedily seeking them, and half the time pulling away from them. In those simple relationships of loving husband and wife, affectionate sisters, children and grandmother, there are innumerable shades of sweetness and anguish which make up the pattern of our lives day by day, though they are not down in the list of subjects from which the conventional novelist works.

Katherine Mansfield's peculiar gift lay in her interpretation of these secret accords and antipathies which lie hidden under our everyday behavior, and which more than any outward events make our lives happy or unhappy. Had she lived, her development would have gone on in this direction more than in any other. When she touches this New Zealand family and those faraway memories ever so lightly, as in "The Doll's House," there is a magic one does not find in the other stories, fine as some of them are. With this theme the very letters on the page become alive. She communicates vastly more than she actually writes. One goes back and runs through the pages to find the text which made one know certain things about Linda or Burnell or Beryl, and the text is not there — but something was there, all the same — is there, though no typesetter will ever set it. It is this overtone, which is too fine for the printing press and comes through without it, that makes one know that this writer had something of the gift which is one of the rarest things in writing, and quite the most precious. That she had not the happiness of developing her powers to the full is sad enough. She wrote the truth from Fontainebleau a few weeks before she died: *"The old mechanism isn't mine any longer, and I can't control the new."* She had lived through the first stage, had outgrown her young art, so that it seemed false to her in comparison with the new light that was breaking within. The "new mechanism," big enough to convey the new knowledge, she had not the bodily strength to set in motion.

Katherine Mansfield's published *Journal* begins in 1914 and ends in 1922, some months before her death. It is the record of a long struggle with illness, made more cruel by lack of money and by the physical hardships that war conditions brought about in England and France. At the age of twenty-two (when most young people have a secret conviction that they are immortal), she was already ill in a Bavarian *pension*. From the time when she left New Zealand and came back to England to make her own way, there was never an interval in which she did not have to drive herself beyond her strength. She never reached the stage when she could work with a relaxed elbow. In her story "Prelude," when the family are moving, and the storeman lifts the little girl into the dray and tucks her up, he says: "Easy does it." She knew this, long afterward, but she never had a chance to put that method into practice. In all her earlier stories there is something fierce about her attack, as if she took up a new tale in the spirit of overcoming it. "Do or die" is the mood, — indeed, she must have faced that alternative more than once: a girl come back to make her living in London, without health or money or influential friends, — with no assets but talent and pride.

In her volume of stories entitled *Bliss*, published in 1920 (most of them had been written some years before and had appeared in periodicals), she throws down her glove, utters her little challenge in the high language which she knew better than did most of her readers:

> But I tell you, my lord fool, out of this nettle, danger, we pluck this flower, safety.

A fine attitude, youthful and fiery: out of all the difficulties of life and art we will snatch *something*. No one was ever less afraid of the nettle; she was defrauded unfairly of the physical vigour which seems the natural accompaniment of a high and daring spirit.

At thirteen Katherine Mansfield made the long voyage to England with her grandmother, to go to school in London. At eighteen she returned to her own family in Wellington, New Zealand. It was then the struggle against circumstances began. She afterward burned all her early diaries, but it is those I should have liked to read. Exile may be easy to bear for those who have lived their lives. But at eighteen, after four years of London, to be thrown back into a prosperous commercial colony at the end of the world was starvation. There is no homesickness and no hunger so unbearable. Many a young artist would sell his future, all his chances, simply to get back to the world where other people are doing the only things that, to his inexperience, seem worth doing at all.

Years afterward, when Katherine Mansfield had begun to do her best work but was rapidly sinking in vitality, her homesickness stretched all the other way — backwards, for New Zealand and that same crude Wellington. Unpromising as it was for her purpose, she felt that it was the only territory she could claim, in the deepest sense, as her own. The *Journal* tells us how often she went back to it in her sleep. She recounts these dreams at some length: but the entry which makes one realize that homesickness most keenly is a short one, made in Cornwall in 1918:

> *June 20th.* The twentieth of June 1918.
> C'est de la misère.

> Non, pas ça exactement. Il y a quelque chose — une profonde mal-
> aise me suive comme un ombre.
>   Oh, why write bad French? Why write at all? 11,500 miles are so
> many — too many by 11,499¾ for me.

Eleven thousand five hundred miles is the distance from England to New
Zealand.

By this, 1918, she had served her apprenticeship. She had gone
through a succession of enthusiasms for this master and that, formed
friendships with some of the young writers of her own time. But the person
who had freed her from the self-consciousness and affectations of the experimenting young writer, and had brought her to her realest self, was not
one of her literary friends but, quite simply, her own brother.

He came over in 1915 to serve as an officer. He was younger than she,
and she had not seen him for six years. After a short visit with her in London he went to the front, and a few weeks later was killed in action. But he
had brought to his sister the New Zealand of their childhood, and out of
those memories her best stories were to grow. For the remaining seven years
of her life (she died just under thirty-five) her brother seems to have been
almost constantly in her mind. A great change comes over her feelings
about art; what it is, and why it is. When she prays to become "humble," it
is probably the slightly showy quality in the early stories that she begs to be
delivered from — and forgiven for. The *Journal* from 1918 on is a record of
a readjustment to life, a changing sense of its deepest realities. One of the
entries in 1919 recounts a dream in which her brother, "Chummie," came
back to her:

> I hear his hat and stick thrown on to the hall-table. He runs up the stairs,
> three at a time. 'Hullo, darling!' But I can't move — I can't move. He
> puts his arm round me, holding me tightly, and we kiss — a long, firm,
> family kiss. And the kiss means: We are of the same blood; we have abso-
> lute confidence in each other; we love; all is well; nothing can ever come
> between us.

In the same year she writes:

> Now it is May 1919. Six o'clock. I am sitting in my own room thinking of
> Mother: I want to cry. But my thoughts are beautiful and full of gaiety. I
> think of *our* house, *our* garden, *us* children — the lawn, the gate and
> Mother coming in. "Children! Children!" I really only ask for time to
> write it all.

But she did not find too late the things she cared for most. She could
not have written that group of New Zealand stories when she first came to
London. There had to be a long period of writing for writing's sake. The
spontaneous untutored outpouring of personal feeling does not go very far
in art. It is only the practiced hand that can make the natural gesture, —

and the practiced hand has often to grope its way. She tells us that she made four false starts on "At the Bay," and when she finished the story it took her nearly a month to recover.

The *Journal*, painful though it is to read, is not the story of utter defeat. She had not, as she said, the physical strength to write what she now knew were, to her, the most important things in life. But she had found them, she possessed them, her mind fed on them. On them, and on the language of her greatest poet. (She read Shakespeare continually, when she was too ill to leave her bed.) The inexhaustible richness of that language seems to have been like a powerful cordial, warmed her when bodily nourishment failed her.

Among the stories she left unfinished there is one of singular beauty, written in the autumn of 1922, a few months before her death, the last piece of work she did. She called it "Six Years After": Linda and Burnell grown old, and the boy six years dead. It has the same powerful slightness which distinguishes the other New Zealand stories, and an even deeper tenderness.

Of the first of the New Zealand stories, "Prelude," Miss Mansfield wrote an answer to the inquiries of an intimate friend:

> This is about as much as I can say about it. You know, if the truth were known, I have a perfect passion for the island where I was born. Well, in the early morning there I always remember feeling that this little island has dipped back into the dark blue sea during the night only to rise again at gleam of day, all hung with bright spangles and glittering drops. (When you ran over the dewy grass you positively felt that your feet tasted salt.) I tried to catch that moment — with something of its sparkle and its flavour. And just as on those mornings white milky mists rise and uncover some beauty, then smother it again and then again disclose it, I tried to lift that mist from my people and let them be seen and then to hide them again. . . . It's so difficult to describe all this and it sounds perhaps over-ambitious and vain.

An unpretentious but very suggestive statement of how an artist sets to work, and of the hazy sort of thing that almost surely lies behind and directs interesting or beautiful design. And not with the slighter talents only. Tolstoy himself, one knows from the different lives and letters, went to work in very much the same way. The long novels, as well as the short tales, grew out of little family dramas, personal intolerances and predilections, — promptings not apparent to the casual reader and incomprehensible to the commercial novel-maker.

[1949]

KATHERINE ANNE PORTER gave an interview to the Paris Review *that was published in the second volume of* Writers at Work *in 1963. She spoke at great length of her beginnings as a writer and of the difficulty of learning her craft during her long apprenticeship. Her comments on "Flowering Judas" give the background of the story, and suggest her commitment as a writer who had taken up her vocation with the highest seriousness: "Practice an art for love and the happiness of your life — you will find it outlasts almost everything but breath!"*

⁓⋟ 21 ⋞⁓

Katherine Anne Porter

on the Origins of

FLOWERING JUDAS

Interviewer: Has a story never surprised you in the writing? A character suddenly taken a different turn?

Porter: Well, in the vision of death at the end of "Flowering Judas" I knew the real ending — that she was not going to be able to face her life, what she'd done. And I knew that the vengeful spirit was going to come in a dream to tow her away into death, but I didn't know until I'd written it that she was going to wake up saying, "No!" and be afraid to go to sleep again.

Interviewer: That was, in a fairly literal sense, a "true" story, wasn't it?

Porter: The truth is, I have never written a story in my life that didn't have a very firm foundation in actual human experience — somebody else's experience quite often, but an experience that became my own by hearing the story, by witnessing the thing, by hearing just a word perhaps. It doesn't matter, it just takes a little — a tiny seed. Then it takes root, and it grows. It's an organic thing. That story had been on my mind for years, growing out of this one little thing that happened in Mexico. It was forming and forming in my mind, until one night I was quite desperate. People are always so sociable, and I'm sociable too, and if I live around friends. . . . Well, they were insisting that I come and play bridge. But I was very firm, because I knew the time had come to write that story, and I had to write it.

Interviewer: What was that "little thing" from which the story grew?

Porter: Something I saw as I passed a window one evening. A girl I knew had asked me to come and sit with her, because a man was coming to see her, and she was a little afraid of him. And as I went through the court-yard, past the flowering judas tree, I glanced in the window and there she was sitting with an open book on her lap, and there was this great big fat man sitting beside her. Now Mary and I were friends, both American girls living in this revolutionary situation. She was teaching at an Indian school, and I was teaching dancing at a girls' technical school in Mexico City. And we were having a very strange time of it. I was more skeptical, and so I had already begun to look with a skeptical eye on a great many of the revolutionary leaders. Oh, the idea was all right, but a lot of men were misapplying it.

And when I looked through the window that evening, I saw something in Mary's face, something in her pose, something in the whole situation, that set up a commotion in my mind. Because until that moment I hadn't really understood that she was not able to take care of herself, because she was not able to face her own nature and was afraid of everything. I don't know why I saw it. I don't believe in intuition. When you get sudden flashes of perception, it is just the brain working faster than usual. But you've been getting ready to know it for a long time, and when it comes, you feel you've known it always.

Interviewer: You speak of a story "forming" in your mind. Does it begin as a visual impression, growing to a narrative? Or how?

Porter: All my senses were very keen; things came to me through my eyes, through all my pores. Everything hit me at once, you know. That makes it very difficult to describe just exactly what is happening. And then, I think the mind works in such a variety of ways. Sometimes an idea starts completely inarticulately. You're not thinking in images or words or — well, it's exactly like a dark cloud moving in your head. You keep wondering what will come out of this, and then it will dissolve itself into a set of — well, not images exactly, but really thoughts. You begin to think directly in words. Abstractly. Then the words transform themselves into images. By the time I write the story my people are up and alive and walking around and taking things into their own hands. They exist as independently inside my head as you do before me now. I have been criticized for not enough detail in describing my characters, and not enough furniture in the house. And the odd thing is that I see it all so clearly.

Interviewer: What about the technical problems a story presents — its formal structure? How deliberate are you in matters of technique? For example, the use of the historical present in "Flowering Judas"?

Porter: The first time someone said to me, "Why did you write 'Flowering Judas' in the historical present?" I thought for a moment and said, "Did I?" I'd never noticed it. Because I didn't *plan* to write it any way. A story forms in my mind and forms and forms, and when it's ready to go, I strike it down — it takes just the time I sit at the typewriter. I never think about form at all. In fact, I would say that I've never been interested in anything about writing after having learned, I hope, to write. That is, I mastered my craft as well as I could. There is a technique, there is a craft, and you have to learn it. Well, I did as well as I could with that, but now all in the world I am interested in is telling a story. I have something to tell you that I, for some reason, think is worth telling, and so I want to tell it as clearly and purely and simply as I can. But I had spent fifteen years at least learning to write. I practiced writing in every possible way that I could. I wrote a pastiche of other people, imitating Dr. Johnson and Laurence Sterne, and Petrarch and Shakespeare's sonnets, and then I tried writing my own way. I spent fifteen years learning to trust myself: that's what it comes to. Just as a pianist runs his scales for ten years before he gives his concert: because when he gives that concert, he can't be thinking of his fingering or of his hands; he has to be thinking of his interpretation, of the music he's playing. He's thinking of what he's trying to communicate. And if he hasn't got his technique perfected by then, he needn't give the concert at all.

[1963]

WILLIAM FAULKNER *was writer-in-residence at the University of Virginia in 1957 and 1958. During that time he encouraged students to ask questions about his writing. He answered more than 2,000 queries on everything from spelling to the nature of man, including a series of questions about "A Rose for Emily" addressed to him at different interviews by students of Frederick Gwynn and Joseph Blotner. These professors later edited the book* Faulkner in the University (1959), *in which the following excerpt first appeared.*

❧22❧

William Faulkner

on the Meaning of

A ROSE FOR EMILY

Q. What is the meaning of the title "A Rose for Emily"?

A. Oh, it's simply the poor woman had had no life at all. Her father had kept her more or less locked up and then she had a lover who was about to quit her, she had to murder him. It was just "A Rose for Emily" — that's all.

Q. I was wondering, one of your short stories, "A Rose for Emily," what ever inspired you to write this story . . . ?"

A. That to me was another sad and tragic manifestation of man's condition in which he dreams and hopes, in which he is in conflict with himself or with his environment or with others. In this case there was the young girl with a young girl's normal aspirations to find love and then a husband and a family, who was brow-beaten and kept down by her father, a selfish man who didn't want her to leave home because he wanted a housekeeper, and it was a natural instinct of — repressed which — you can't repress it — you can mash it down but it comes up somewhere else and very likely in a tragic form, and that was simply another manifestation of man's injustice to man, of the poor tragic human being struggling with its own heart, with others, with its environment, for the simple things which all human beings want. In that case it was a young girl that just wanted to be loved and to love and to have a husband and a family.

Q. And that purely came from your imagination?

A. Well, the story did but the condition is there. It exists. I didn't in-

vent that condition, I didn't invent the fact that young girls dream of someone to love and children and a home, but the story of what her own particular tragedy was was invented, yes. . . .

Q. Sir, it has been argued that "A Rose for Emily" is a criticism of the
North, and others have argued saying that it is a criticism of the South.
Now, could this story, shall we say, be more properly classified as a criticism
of the times?

A. Now that I don't know, because I was simply trying to write about
people. The writer uses environment — what he knows — and if there's a
symbolism in which the lover represented the North and the woman who
murdered him represents the South, I don't say that's not valid and not
there, but it was no intention of the writer to say, Now let's see, I'm going
to write a piece in which I will use a symbolism for the North and another
symbol for the South, that he was simply writing about people, a story
which he thought was tragic and true, because it came out of the human
heart, the human aspiration, the human — the conflict of conscience with
glands, with the Old Adam. It was a conflict not between the North and the
South so much as between, well you might say, God and Satan.

Q. Sir, just a little more on that thing. You say it's a conflict between
God and Satan. Well, I don't quite understand what you mean. Who is —
did one represent the ——

A. The conflict was in Miss Emily, that she knew that you do not murder people. She had been trained that you do not take a lover. You marry,
you don't take a lover. She had broken all the laws of her tradition, her
background, and she had finally broken the law of God too, which says you
do not take human life. And she knew she was doing wrong, and that's why
her own life was wrecked. Instead of murdering one lover, and then to go
and take another and when she used him up to murder him, she was ex-
piating her crime.

Q. Was the "Rose for Emily" an idea or a character? Just how did you
go about it?

A. That came from a picture of the strand of hair on the pillow. It was
a ghost story. Simply a picture of a strand of hair on the pillow in the abandoned house.

[1959]

*E*LIZABETH BOWEN *wrote a special preface to the American edition of* The Demon Lover and Other Stories (1945). *She described the chaos around her in wartime London and the difficulty of writing during that time. Though she was trying to finish a novel, she agreed to write occasional short stories for magazines. "The Demon Lover" is one of these stories. Bowen regarded the material she used for this fiction as "impressions that stored themselves up and acquired force without being analyzed or considered." These stories are the only record of experience she kept from the war.*

✎ 23 ✎

Elizabeth Bowen

Preface to the American Edition of

THE DEMON LOVER

The stories in this collection, *The Demon Lover,* were written in wartime London — between the spring of 1941 and the late autumn of 1944. They were written for the magazines or papers in which they originally appeared. During these last years, I did not always write a story when I was asked for one; but I did not write any story that I was not asked for. For, at the same time, I have been writing a novel; and sometimes I did not want to imperil its continuity.

Does this suggest that these stories have been in any way forced or unwilling work? If so, that is not the case. Actually, the stimulus of being asked for a story, and the compulsion created by having promised to write one were both good — I mean, they acted as releases. Each time I sat down to write a story I opened a door; and the pressure against the other side of that door must, I found, have been very great, for things — ideas, images, emotions — came through with force and rapidity, sometimes violence. I do not say that these stories wrote themselves — aesthetically or intellectually speaking, I found the writing of some of them very difficult — but I was never in a moment's doubt as to *what* I was to write. The stories had their own momentum, which I had to control. The acts in them had an authority which I could not question. Odd enough in their way — and now some seem very odd — they were flying particles of something enormous and inchoate that had been going on. They were sparks from experience — an experience not necessarily my own.

During the war I lived, both as a civilian and as a writer, with every pore open; I lived so many lives, and, still more, lived among the packed repercussions of so many thousands of other lives, all under stress, that I see now it would have been impossible to have been writing only one book. I want my novel, which deals with this same time, to be comprehensive. But a novel must have form; and, for the form's sake, one is always having to make relentless exclusions. Had it not been for my from-time-to-time promises to write stories, much that had been pressing against the door might have remained pressing against the door in vain.

I do not feel I "invented" anything written here. It seems to me that during the war in England the overcharged subconsciousnesses of everybody overflowed and merged. It is because the general subconsciousness saturates these stories that they have an authority nothing to do with me.

These are all wartime, none of them *war*, stories. There are no accounts of war action even as I knew it — for instance, air raids. Only one character (in "Mysterious Kôr") is a soldier; and he only appears as a homeless wanderer round a city. These are, more, studies of climate, war-climate, and of the strange growths it raised. I see war (or should I say feel war?) more as a territory than as a page of history: of its impersonal active historic side I have, I find, not written. Arguably, writers are always slightly abnormal people: certainly, in so-called "normal" times my sense of the abnormal has been very acute. In war, this feeling of slight differentiation was suspended: I felt one with, and just like, everyone else. Sometimes I hardly knew where I stopped and everyone else began. The violent destruction of solid things, the explosion of the illusion that prestige, power, and permanence attach to bulk and weight, left all of us, equally, heady and disembodied. Walls went down; and we felt, if not knew, each other. We all lived in a state of lucid abnormality.

Till the proofs of *The Demon Lover* came, I had not re-read these stories since they were, singly, written. Reading the stories straight through as a collection, I am most struck by what they have in common. This integrates them and gives them a cumulative and collective meaning that no one of them, taken singly, has by itself. *The Demon Lover* is an organic whole: not merely a collection but somehow — for better or worse — a book. Also, the order in which the stories stand — an order come at, I may say, casually — seems itself to have a meaning, or to add a meaning, I did not foresee. We begin with a hostess who has not learned how with grace to open her own front door; we end with a pair of lovers with no place in which to sleep in each other's arms. In the first story, a well-to-do house in a polite square gives the impression of having been organically dislocated by shock; in the last, a pure abstract empty timeless city rises out of a little girl's troubled mind. Through the stories — in the order in which they are here placed — I find a rising tide of hallucination.

The stories are not placed in the time-order in which they were first written — though, by chance, "In the Square," placed first here, *is* the first in the book I wrote, in a hot, raid-less patch of 1941 summer, just after Germany had invaded Russia.

The hallucinations in the stories are not a peril; nor are the stories studies of mental peril. The hallucinations are an unconscious, instinctive, saving resort on the part of the characters: life, mechanized by the controls of wartime, and emotionally torn and impoverished by changes, had to complete itself in some other way. It is a fact that in Britain, and especially in London, in wartime many people had strange deep intense dreams. "Whatever else I forget about the war," a friend said to me, "I hope I may never forget my own dreams, or some of the other dreams I have been told. We have never dreamed like this before; and I suppose we shall never dream like this again."

Dreams by night, and the fantasies — these often childishly innocent — with which formerly matter-of-fact people consoled themselves by day were compensations. Apart from them, I do not think that the desiccation, by war, of our day-to-day lives can be enough stressed. The outside world war news was stupefying: headlines and broadcasts came down and down on us in hammerlike chops, with great impact but oddly little reverberation. The simple way to put it was: "One cannot take things in." What was happening was out of all proportion to our faculties for knowing, thinking, and checking up. The circumstances under which ordinary British people lived were preposterous — so preposterous that, in a dull way, they simplified themselves. And all the time we knew that compared to those on the Continent we in Britain could not be said to suffer. Foreign faces about the London streets had personal pain and impersonal history sealed up behind the eyes. All this pressure drove egotism underground, or made it whiten like grass under a stone. And self-expression in small ways stopped — the small ways had been so very small that we had not realized how much they amounted to. Planning pleasures, choosing and buying things, wondering and wandering, dressing yourself up, and so on. All that stopped. You used to know what you were like from the things you liked, and chose. Now there was not what you liked, and you did not choose. Any remaining choices and pleasures shot into new proportion and new value: people paid big money for little bunches of flowers.

Literature of the Resistance is now steadily coming in from France. I wonder whether in a sense all wartime writing is not resistance writing? In no way dare we who were in Britain compare ourselves with the French. But personal life here put up its own resistance to the annihilation that was threatening it — war. Everyone here, as is known, read more: and what was sought in books — old books, new books — was the communicative touch of personal life. To survive, not only physically but spiritually, was essential. People whose homes had been blown up went to infinite lengths to assemble bits of themselves — broken ornaments, odd shoes, torn scraps of the curtains that had hung in a room — from the wreckage. In the same way, they assembled and checked themselves from stories and poems, from their memories, from one another's talk. Outwardly, we accepted that at this time individual destiny had to count for nothing; inwardly, individual destiny became an obsession in every heart. You cannot depersonalize persons. Every writer during this time was aware of the passionate attachment of men and women to every object or image or place or love or fragment of memory with which his or her destiny seemed to be identified, and by which the destiny seemed to be assured.

The search for indestructible landmarks in a destructible world led many down strange paths. The attachment to these when they had been found produced small worlds-within-worlds of hallucination — in most cases, saving hallucination. Writers followed the paths they saw or felt people treading, and depicted those little dear saving illusory worlds. I have done both in the *The Demon Lover* stories.

You may say that these resistance-fantasies are in themselves frightening. I can only say that one counteracts fear by fear, stress by stress. In "The Happy Autumn Fields," a woman is projected from flying-bombed London, with its day-and-night eeriness, into the key emotional crisis of a Victorian girlhood. In "Ivy Gripped the Steps," a man in his early forties peers though the rusted fortifications and down the dusty empty perspectives of a seaside town at the Edwardian episode that long ago crippled his faculty for love. In "The Inherited Clock," a girl is led to find the key to her own neurosis inside a timepiece. The past, in all these cases, discharges its load of feeling into the anæsthetized and bewildered present. It is the "I" that is sought — and retrieved, at the cost of no little pain. And, the ghosts — definite in "Green Holly," questionable (for are they subjective purely?) in "Pink May," "The Cheery Soul," and "The Demon Lover": what part do they play? They are the certainties. The bodiless foolish wanton, the puritan "other" presence, the tipsy cook with her religion of English fare, the ruthless young soldier lover unheard of since 1916: hostile or not, they rally, they fill the vacuum for the uncertain "I."

I am sorry that the stories in *The Demon Lover*, now going to readers on the other side of the Atlantic, do not contain more "straight" pictures of the British wartime scene. Such pictures could have been interesting: they *are* interesting in much of the brilliant reportage that exists. I know, in these stories the backgrounds, and sometimes the circumstances, are only present by inference. Allow for the intensely subjective mood into which most of the characters have been cast! Remember that these impulsive movements of fantasy are by-products of the non-impulsive major routine of war. These are between-time stories — mostly reactions from, or intermissions between, major events. They show a levelled-down time, when a bomb on your house was as inexpedient, but not more abnormal, than a cold in your head. There was an element of chanciness and savageness about everything — even, the arrival at a country house for Christmas. The claustrophobia of not being able to move about freely and without having to give account of yourself — not, for instance, being able to visit a popular seaside resort, within seventy miles of London, between 1940 and 1944 — appears in many: notably, in "Ivy Gripped the Steps." The ghostly social pattern of London life — or, say, the conventional pattern one does not easily break, and is loth to break because it is "I" saving — appears in the vacant politeness of "In the Square" and in the inebriate night-club conversation, and in "Careless Talk." These are ways in which some of us did go on — after all, we have to go on *some* way. And the worthless little speaker in "Pink May" found the war made moratorium for her married conscience. Yes, only a few were heroic purely: and see how I have not drawn the heroic ones! But everyone was pathetic — more than they knew. Owing, though, to the thunder of those inordinate years, we were shaken out of the grip of our own pathos.

In wartime, even in Britain, much has been germinating. *What*, I do not know — who does, yet, know? — but I felt the germination; and feel it, here and there, in these stories now that I read them through. These are received impressions of happening things; impressions that stored themselves up and acquired force without being analyzed or considered. These, as wartime stories, are at least contemporary — twenty, forty, sixty years hence they may be found interesting as documents, even if they are found negligible as art. This discontinuous writing, nominally "inventive," is the only diary I have kept. Transformed into images in the stories, there *may* be important psychological facts: if so, I did not realize their importance. Walking in the darkness of the nights of six years (darkness which transformed a capital city into a network of inscrutable canyons) one developed new bare alert senses, with their own savage warnings and notations. And by day one was always making one's own new maps of a landscape always convulsed by some new change. Through it all, one probably picked up more than can be answered for. I cannot answer for much that is in these stories, except to say that I know they are all true — true to the general life that was in me at the time. Taken singly, they are disjected shapshots — snapshots taken from close up, too close up, in the middle of the *mêlée* of a battle. You cannot *render*, you can only embrace — if it means embracing to suffocation point — something vast that is happening right on top of you. Painters have painted, and photographers who were artists have photographed, the tottering lacelike architecture of ruins, dark mass-movements of people, and the untimely brilliance of flaming skies. I cannot paint or photograph like this — I have isolated; I have made for the particular, spot-lighting faces or cutting out gestures that are not even the faces or gestures of great sufferers. This is how I am, how I feel, whether in war or peace time; and only as I am and feel can I write. As I said at the start, though I criticize these stories now afterwards, intellectually, I cannot criticize their content. They are the particular. But through the particular, in wartime, I felt the high-voltage current of the general pass.

[1945]

JORGE LUIS BORGES was invited to talk several times to the students in the graduate writing program at Columbia University in the spring of 1971. At one of these meetings, those present were provided with the text of "The End of the Duel." Translator Norman Thomas di Giovanni read the story line by line, with Borges interrupting when he wished to comment. Then there was a general conversation in which Borges explained how he gradually transformed his material into a story. A transcript of the entire meeting was included in the book Borges on Writing (1973), edited by Norman Thomas di Giovanni, Daniel Halpern, and Frank MacShane.

❧ 24 ❧

Jorge Luis Borges
on the Meaning and Form of
THE END OF THE DUEL

di Giovanni: *Spurts of blood gushed from the men's throats. They dashed forward a number of steps before tumbling face down. Cardoso, as he fell, stretched out his arms. Perhaps never aware of it, he had won.*

Borges: This is what always happens: We never know whether we are victors or whether we are defeated.

di Giovanni: Borges, how long did you carry this story around in your head before you set it down?

Borges: I must have carried it some twenty-five or thirty years. When I first heard it, I thought it was striking. The man who told it to me published it in *La Nación* under the title "*Crepusculo rojo*" — "Reddish Twilight" — but as he wrote it in a style full of purple patches, I felt I could hardly compete with him. After his death I wrote it down in as straightforward a way as possible. In between times, I carried it around in my memory for years, boring my friends with it. . . .

di Giovanni: But can you say something about how you sift the material and take only what you want? For instance, can you remember any facts that you didn't use from the anecdote you were told?

Borges: No, because I was told it in a very bare way, and then Reyles wrote it down in a way full of purple patches and fine writing — the kind of thing I do my best to avoid. I can't write like that; I only went in for what might be called circumstantial invention. For example, I had to make them play *truco*, and I invented the episode about the sheep dog, and I gave him the right name — Treinta y Tres — because that's the kind of name a dog might have, although they are generally called Jazmín.

MacShane: Do you sometimes take one factual episode and combine it with another to make something new — a new story from two completely disconnected and different sources?

Borges: Yes. In this story, for example, I witnessed the *truco* game not in Uruguay, but in the old Northside of Buenos Aires. . . .

Question: I believe that in one of your essays you wrote that a short story can be centered either on the characters or on the situation. In this story, characterization is at a minimum . . .

Borges: It had to be minimal because the two characters are more or less the same character. They are two gauchos, but they could be two hundred or two thousand. They are not Hamlets or Raskolnikovs or Lord Jims.[1] They are just gauchos.

Question: Then the situation is what counts?

Borges: Yes, in this case. And generally speaking, what I think is most important in a short story is the plot or situation, while in a novel what's important are the characters. You may think of *Don Quixote* as being written with incidents, but what is really important are the two characters, Don Quixote and Sancho Panza. In the Sherlock Holmes saga, also, what is really important is the friendship between a very intelligent man and a rather dumb fellow like Dr. Watson. Therefore — if I may be allowed a sweeping statement — in writing a novel, you should know all about the characters, and any plot will do, while in a short story it is the situation that counts. That would be true for Henry James, for example, or for Chesterton.[2]

Question: Do you find some special vision of life in the anecdotes you use?

Borges: I find that most of my stories come from anecdotes, although I distort or change them. Some, of course, come from characters, from people I know. In the short story, I think an anecdote may serve as a beginning point.

Question: Do you think the changes you make are inherent in the anecdote?

Borges: Well, that's a hard nut to crack. I don't know if they're inherent in the anecdote or not, but I know that I need them. If I told a story swiftly and curtly, it wouldn't be effective at all. I have tried to make this

---

[1] Raskolnikov is the main character in the novel *Crime and Punishment* by Russian writer Fyodor Dostoevsky (1821–1881). Lord Jim is the title character in a novel by Joseph Conrad; for information on Conrad, see the introduction to his stories on page 262.

[2] G. K. Chesterton (1874–1936), English critic, theologian, and short story writer. Like Borges, Chesterton experimented with the detective story.

one effective by slowing it down. I couldn't begin by saying, "Two gauchos hated each other," because nobody would believe it. I had to make the hatred seem real. . . .

MacShane: Do you think [political and social issues] should be dealt with in fiction?

Borges: In this story, there was nothing of the kind.

di Giovanni: But there is.

Borges: There may have been, for all I know, but I wasn't concerned about that. I was concerned with the idea of the two men running a race with their throats cut and of the whole thing's being thought of as a joke or prank. Naturally, this story is wound up with the history of Argentina and of Uruguay and of the gauchos. It has associations with the whole of South American history, the wars of liberation, and so on. But I wasn't concerned about that. I was merely trying to tell my story in a convincing way. That was all I was concerned about, although you can link it to anything you like.

di Giovanni: And in spite of your aims, it's a hell of a statement about politics at that time and in that place. It should satisfy anybody.

Borges: And perhaps it's about the politics of any time or any place, I don't know. Of course, these politics are a bit picturesque.

Question: How do you think the artist should relate to his own time?

Borges: Oscar Wilde said that modernity of treatment and subject should be carefully avoided by the modern artist. Of course, he was being witty, but what he was saying was based on an obvious truth. Homer, for example, wrote several centuries after the Trojan war. The idea that a writer should be contemporaneous is itself modern, but I should say it belongs more to journalism than to literature. No real writer ever tried to be contemporary.

[1973]

*L*ANGSTON HUGHES *wrote an introduction entitled "Who Is Simple?" for the 1961 collection* The Best of Simple. *There he said, "I cannot truthfully state, as some novelists do at the beginning of their books, that these stories are about 'nobody living or dead.' The facts are that these tales are about a great many people — although they are stories about no specific persons as such. But it is impossible to live in Harlem and not know at least a hundred Simples. . . ."*

❧ 25 ❧

Langston Hughes

Who Is Simple?

Simple Speaks His Mind had hardly been published when I walked into a Harlem cafe one night and the proprietor said, "Listen, I don't know where you got that character, Jesse B. Semple, but I want you to meet one of my customers who is *just* like him." He called to a fellow at the end of the bar. "Watch how he walks," he said, "exactly like Simple. And I'll bet he won't be talking to you two minutes before he'll tell you how long he's been standing on his feet, and how much his bunions hurt — just like your book begins."

The barman was right. Even as the customer approached, he cried, "Man, my feet hurt! If you want to see me, why don't you come over here where I am? I stands on my feet all day."

"And I stand on mine all night," said the barman. Without me saying a word, a conversation began so much like the opening chapter in my book that even I was a bit amazed to see how nearly life can be like fiction — or vice versa.

Simple, as a character, originated during the war. His first words came directly out of the mouth of a young man who lived just down the block from me. One night I ran into him in a neighborhood bar and he said, "Come on back to the booth and meet my girl friend." I did and he treated me to a beer. Not knowing much about the young man, I asked where he worked. He said, "In a war plant."

I said, "What do you make?"

He said, "Cranks."

I said, "What kind of cranks?"

He said, "Oh, man, I don't know what kind of cranks."

I said, "Well, do they crank cars, tanks, buses, planes, or what?"

He said, "I don't know what them cranks crank."

Whereupon, his girl friend, a little put out at this ignorance of his job, said, "You've been working there long enough. Looks like by now you ought to know what them cranks crank."

"Aw, woman," he said, "you know white folks don't tell colored folks what cranks crank."

That was the beginning of Simple. I have long since lost track of the fellow who uttered those words. But out of the mystery as to what the cranks of this world crank, to whom they belong and why, there evolved the character in this book, wondering and laughing at the numerous problems of white folks, colored folks, and just folks — including himself. He talks about the wife he used to have, the woman he loves today, and his one-time play-girl, Zarita. Usually over a glass of beer, he tells me his tales, mostly in high humor, but sometimes with a pain in his soul as sharp as the occasional hurt of that bunion on his right foot. Sometimes, as the old blues says, Simple might be "laughing to keep from crying." But even then, he keeps you laughing, too. If there were not a lot of genial souls in Harlem as talkative as Simple, I would never have these tales to write down there that are "just like him." He is my ace-boy, Simple. I hope you like him, too.

[1961]

*F*RANK O'CONNOR *was a skilled teacher of the short story, and his comments on the literary form can be as irreverent as they are profound. In this interview in the* Paris Review, *reprinted from the first volume of* Writers at Work, *collections of interviews from that journal, in 1958, O'Connor compared himself to Guy de Maupassant and then went on to discuss his own practice as a writer. His analysis of the history of the short story appeared in more extended form in his book* The Lonely Voice, *published in 1963.*

~26~

Frank O'Connor

The Nearest Thing to Lyric Poetry

Is the Short Story

Interviewer: Why do you prefer the short story for your medium?

O'Connor: Because it's the nearest thing I know to lyric poetry — I wrote lyric poetry for a long time, then discovered that God had not intended me to be a lyric poet, and the nearest thing to that is the short story. A novel actually requires far more logic and far more knowledge of circumstances, whereas a short story can have the sort of detachment from circumstances that lyric poetry has. . . .

Interviewer: What about working habits? How do you start a story?

O'Connor: "Get black on white" used to be Maupassant's advice — that's what I always do. I don't give a hoot what the writing's like, I write any sort of rubbish which will cover the main outlines of the story, then I can begin to see it. When I write, when I draft a story, I never think of writing nice sentences about, "It was a nice August evening when Elizabeth Jane Moriarty was coming down the road." I just write roughly what happened, and then I'm able to see what the construction looks like. It's the design of the story which to me is most important, the thing that tells you there's a bad gap in the narrative here and you really ought to fill that up in some way or another. I'm always looking at the design of the story, not the treatment. Yesterday I was finishing off a piece about my friend A. E. Coppard, the greatest of all the English storytellers, who died about a fortnight ago. I was describing the way Coppard must have written these stories, going around with a notebook, recording what the lighting looked like, what that house looked like, and all the time using metaphor to suggest it to himself, "The road looked like a mad serpent going up the hill," or something of the kind, and "She said so-and-so, and the man in the pub said something else." After he had written them all out, he must have got the outline of his story, and he'd start working in all the details. Now, I could never do that at all. I've got to see what these people did, first of all, and *then* I start thinking of whether it was a nice August evening or a spring evening. I have to wait for the theme before I can do anything.

Interviewer: Do you rewrite?

O'Connor: Endlessly, endlessly, endlessly. And keep on rewriting, and after it's published, and then after it's published in book form, I usually rewrite it again. I've rewritten versions of most of my early stories and one of these days, God help, I'll publish these as well.

Interviewer: Do you keep notes as a source of supply for future stories?

O'Connor: Just notes of themes. If somebody tells me a good story, I'll write it down in my four lines; that is the secret of the theme. If you make the subject of a story twelve or fourteen lines, that's a treatment. You've already committed yourself to the sort of character, the sort of surroundings, and the moment you've committed yourself, the story is already written. It has ceased to be fluid, you can't design it any longer, you can't model it. So I always confine myself to my four lines. If it won't go into four, that means you haven't reduced it to its ultimate simplicity, reduced it to the fable.

[1958]

*I*SAAC BASHEVIS SINGER *was invited to the University of Connecticut to receive an honorary degree in May 1985. While in Storrs, he kindly consented to discuss the background of his story "A Crown of Feathers" for* The Story and Its Writer.

❧ 27 ❧

Isaac Bashevis Singer

on A CROWN OF FEATHERS

I must have written "A Crown of Feathers" ten or twelve years ago. As a rule my stories are first published in magazines, but not this one. It came out in a collection of stories under the same title.

I don't remember the origin of the story. Either I had read about a crown of feathers in an occult magazine, or I had heard an anecdote about it. Whatever the source, I thought it was a good idea for a story, the belief that feathers in a pillow come together to create a crown. I don't know if they ever actually did, or if someone had the illusion they saw a crown. The legend had nothing to do with Poland — in fact, I read or heard about it long after I had come to America.

When I began to write this story, I had a feeling about halfway through that I was going nowhere. I didn't know how to finish it. I put it away in my desk, and as usual in my drawers things got mixed up. Sometimes pages even get lost altogether. About two years later I found the story in fragments, but when I began to read it again I knew immediately what to do. The plot came in a moment, the idea that a person who has doubts about religion — an agnostic — finds in the crown of feathers two things which contradict one another. As far as religion is concerned for me, it could only be two things: Judaism or Christianity. And so the same story I considered a failure because I didn't know how to finish it suddenly became one of my better stories.

I rewrote the story after I had found it in the drawer. Now everything in it looks as if planned from the beginning, but this is what always happens if a story succeeds. As a rule I always rewrite my stories until I am satisfied with them. The fact that I have written a story means nothing to me. I am a reader as well as a writer, and a critical reader, so it has to please me.

I also revised the story again when I worked with Laurie Colwin on the translation from Yiddish to English. I've been collaborating this way with different translators for fifty years. When a writer makes a translation of his own work, he finds many mistakes in the style he wouldn't have seen in the original version, because when you translate there's nothing to cover up your mistakes. I think your native language hypnotizes you, so when you translate it's like getting undressed: you see the prose naked, what is good and what is bad. You fight against repetition, which is a very dangerous thing in short fiction. Every sentence, every line of a story should matter. Once you begin to elaborate, to add anything nonessential, you kill the story. You can elaborate in a novel, but a story is made to be precise, short, and to the point. If one sentence is pointless, it does damage to the entire story.

The ambiguity in the theme of "A Crown of Feathers" is most important. Here is Akhsa, a person who sees two crowns of feathers, a Christian version and a Jewish one. The ambiguity in the story shows that anyone seeking religious truth, like Akhsa, finds out that although religions appear to be different, they are all based on the same belief. The world is not an accident; it was planned by a higher power, the Almighty. This belief is the opposite of the scientific Big Bang theory, that creation was the result of the haphazard explosion of a Cosmic Bomb.

Another ambiguity explored in the story is that the human mind can never see beyond good and evil. Perhaps in reality God and the Devil merge in some higher sphere, but they cannot merge in our minds. We mortals cannot say that the Supreme Being who creates a child out of love and the Supreme Being who kills a child in a tragic accident are one and the same.

I based the characters in "A Crown of Feathers" on the old Jewish tradition that worldliness was more a feminine attribute than a masculine one. "After her grandmother's death, Akhsa refused to rely on anyone else's judgment in the choice of a husband — not even her grandfather's. Just as her grandmother saw only bad, Reb Naftali saw only good." In my background seventy-five and more years ago in Central Europe, men studied the Torah (the Jewish law) and women minded the store. Women had to have a more practical, worldly view for the family to survive.

Near the end of the story Akhsa, sick as she is, goes out on a hot summer day to the meadow to gather sorrel so she can cook soup for her husband as women were traditionally supposed to do in the village. I imagined the setting and the events in "A Crown of Feathers" from what I had seen when I was a child in Poland. I didn't have to close my eyes to see them; I could see them with my eyes open as I wrote the story. When Akhsa comes home, Zemach berates her for being late: "Why were you so long? Because of you I couldn't say my evening prayers in peace. You confused my thoughts." Zemach was not only a scholar, he was also an ascetic. This didn't automatically make him a good man. The ascetic who tortures himself searching for religious truth can be understood and forgiven, but the ascetic who tortures other people is a madman.

The story ends where it does because there's no telling where Akhsa went after she died. The ending has to be left ambiguous. This is quite the right kind of ending. If I said she went to Heaven, then the question would be what kind of heaven, Jewish or Christian? Maybe she didn't go anyplace. Remember, "if there is such a thing as truth it is as intricate and hidden as a crown of feathers."

[1985]

*E*UDORA WELTY *included this discussion of her story "The Worn Path" in her book* The Eye of the Story *(1977). It appeared in the section called "On Writing," along with her most extensive essays on the art of short fiction — essays that take up such general topics as place and time in fiction, and the art of reading and writing stories. Her reviews of the work of Isak Dinesen, Virginia Woolf, Ralph Ellison, and William Faulkner from the* New York Times *are also included in this collection.*

⤙ 28 ⤚

Eudora Welty

Is Phoenix Jackson's Grandson

Really Dead?

A story writer is more than happy to be read by students; the fact that these serious readers think and feel something in response to his work he finds life-giving. At the same time he may not always be able to reply to their specific questions in kind. I wondered if it might clarify something, for both the questioners and myself, if I set down a general reply to the question that comes to me most often in the mail, from both students and their teachers, after some classroom discussion. The unrivaled favorite is this: "Is Phoenix Jackson's grandson really *dead*?"

It refers to a short story I wrote years ago called "A Worn Path," which tells of a day's journey an old woman makes on foot from deep in the country into town and into a doctor's office on behalf of her little grandson; he is at home, periodically ill, and periodically she comes for his medicine; they give it to her as usual, she receives it and starts the journey back.

I had not meant to mystify readers by withholding any fact; it is not a writer's business to tease. The story is told through Phoenix's mind as she undertakes her errand. As the author at one with the character as I tell it, I must assume that the boy is alive. As the reader, you are free to think as you like, of course: The story invites you to believe that no matter what happens, Phoenix for as long as she is able to walk and can hold to her purpose will make her journey. The *possibility* that she would keep on even if he were dead is there in her devotion and its single-minded, single-track errand. Certainly the *artistic* truth, which should be good enough for the fact, lies in Phoenix's own answer to that question. When the nurse asks, "He isn't dead, is he?" she speaks for herself: "He still the same. He going to last."

The grandchild is the incentive. But it is the journey, the going of the errand, that is the story, and the question is not whether the grandchild is in reality alive or dead. It doesn't affect the outcome of the story or its meaning from start to finish. But it is not the question itself that has struck me as much as the idea, almost without exception implied in the asking, that for Phoenix's grandson to be dead would somehow make the story "better."

It's *all right*, I want to say to the students who write to me, for things to be what they appear to be, and for words to mean what they say. It's all right, too, for words and appearances to mean more than one thing — ambiguity is a fact of life. A fiction writer's responsibility covers not only what he presents as the facts of a given story but what he chooses to stir up as their implications; in the end, these implications, too, become facts, in the larger, fictional sense. But it is not all right, not in good faith, for things *not* to mean what they say.

The grandson's plight was real and it made the truth of the story, which is the story of an errand of love carried out. If the child no longer lived, the truth would persist in the "wornness" of the path. But his being dead can't increase the truth of the story, can't affect it one way or the other. I think I signal this, because the end of the story has been reached before old Phoenix gets home again: she simply starts back. To the question "Is the grandson really dead?" I could reply that it doesn't make any difference. I could also say that I did not make him up in order to let him play a trick on Phoenix. But my best answer would be: "*Phoenix* is alive."

The origin of a story is sometimes a trustworthy clue to the author — or can provide him with the clue — to its key image; maybe in this case it will do the same for the reader. One day I saw a solitary old woman like Phoenix. She was walking; I saw her, at middle distance, in a winter country landscape, and watched her slowly make her way across my line of vision. That sight of her made me write the story. I invented an errand for her, but that only seemed a living part of the figure she was herself: What errand other than for someone else could be making her go? And her going was the first thing, her persisting in her landscape was the real thing, and the first and the real were what I wanted and worked to keep. I brought her up close enough, by imagination, to describe her face, make her present to the eyes, but the full-length figure moving across the winter fields was the indelible one and the image to keep, and the perspective extending into the vanishing distance the true one to hold in mind.

I invented for my character, as I wrote, some passing adventures — some dreams and harassments and a small triumph or two, some jolts to her pride, some flights of fancy to console her, one or two encounters to scare her, a moment that gave her cause to feel ashamed, a moment to dance and preen — for it had to be a *journey*, and all these things belonged to that, parts of life's uncertainty.

A narrative line is in its deeper sense, of course, the tracing out of a meaning, and the real continuity of a story lies in this probing forward. The real dramatic force of a story depends on the strength of the emotion that has set it going. The emotional value is the measure of the reach of the story. What gives any such content to "A Worn Path" is not its circumstances but its *subject*: the deep-grained habit of love.

What I hoped would come clear was that in the whole surround of this story, the world it threads through, the only certain thing at all is the worn path. The habit of love cuts through confusion and stumbles or contrives its way out of difficulty, it remembers the way even when it forgets, for a dumfounded moment, its reason for being. The path is the thing that matters.

Her victory — old Phoenix's — is when she sees the diploma in the doctor's office, when she finds "nailed up on the wall the document that had been stamped with the gold seal and framed in the gold frame, which matched the dream that was hung up in her head." The return with the medicine is just a matter of retracing her own footsteps. It is the part of the journey, and of the story, that can now go without saying.

In the matter of function, old Phoenix's way might even do as a sort of parallel to your way of work if you are a writer of stories. The way to get there is the all-important, all-absorbing problem, and this problem is your reason for undertaking the story. Your only guide, too, is your sureness about your subject, about what this subject is. Like Phoenix, you work all your life to find your way, through all the obstructions and the false appearances and the upsets you may have brought on yourself, to reach a meaning — using inventions of your imagination, perhaps helped out by your dreams and bits of good luck. And finally too, like Phoenix, you have to assume that what you are working in aid of is life, not death.

But you would make the trip anyway — wouldn't you? — just on hope.

[1977]

*J*OHN CHEEVER *wrote this article for the October 30, 1978, issue of* Newsweek. *He was newsworthy at that time because he had just published a collection of short fiction,* The Stories of John Cheever, *which had become a best-seller. Cheever humorously referred to his early financial struggles in the article, but in Susan Cheever's book about her father, she remembered that he was often deeply frustrated by how little he earned from* The New Yorker: *"The money they paid him just wasn't enough to live on — even in the years when we children were in public schools and the family in a rented house." The second part of the* Newsweek *article almost becomes a story about Cheever's suburban neighborhood. Evidently there was nothing in the contemporary scene that he couldn't scoop up and turn into a narrative.*

❦ 29 ❦

John Cheever

Why I Write Short Stories

To publish a definitive collection of short stories in one's late 60s seems to me, as an American writer, a traditional and a dignified occasion, eclipsed in no way by the fact that a great many of the stories in my current collection were written in my underwear.

This is not to say that I was ever a Bohemian. Hardly a man is now alive who can remember when Harold Ross edited *The New Yorker* magazine, but I am one of these. The Ross editorial queries were genuinely eccentric. In one short story of mine, I invented a character who returned home from work and changed his clothes before dinner. Ross wrote on the galley margin, "Eh? What's this? Cheever looks to me like a one-suiter." He was so right. At the space rates he paid, I could afford exactly one suit. In the mornings, I dressed in this and took the elevator to a windowless room in the basement where I worked. Here I hung my suit on a hanger, wrote until nightfall when I dressed and returned to our apartment. A great many of my stories were written in boxer shorts.

A collection of short stories appears like a lemon in the current fiction list, which is indeed a garden of love, erotic horseplay, and lewd and ancient family history; but so long as we are possessed by experience that is distinguished by its intensity and its episodic nature, we will have the short story in our literature, and without a literature we will, of course, perish. It was F. R. Leavis who said that literature is the first distinction of a civilized man.

Who reads short stories? one is asked, and I like to think that they are read by men and women in the dentist's office, waiting to be called to the chair; they are read on transcontinental plane trips instead of watching a banal and vulgar film spin out the time between our coasts; they are read by discerning and well-informed men and women who seem to feel that narrative fiction can contribute to our understanding of one another and the sometimes bewildering world around us.

The novel, in all its greatness, demands at least some passing notice of the classical unities, preserving that mysterious link between esthetics and moral fitness; but to have this unyielding antiquity exclude the newness in our ways of life would be regrettable. This newness is known to some of us through "Star Wars," to some of us through the melancholy that follows a fielder's error in the late innings of a ball game. In the pursuit of this newness, contemporary painting seems to have lost the language of the landscape, the still-life, and — most important — the nude. Modern music has been separated from those rhythms and tonalities that are most deeply ingrained in our memories, but literature still possesses the narrative — the story — and one would defend this with one's life.

In the short stories of my esteemed colleagues — and in a few of my own — I find those rented summer houses, those one-night love affairs, and those lost key rings that confound traditional esthetics. We are not a nomadic people, but there is more than a hint of this in the spirit of our great country — and the short story is the literature of the nomad.

I like to think that the view of a suburban street that I imagine from my window would appeal to a wanderer or to someone familiar with loneliness. Here is a profoundly moving display of nostalgia, vision, and love, none of it more than 30 years old, including most of the trees. Here are white columns from the manorial South, brick and timber walls from Elizabethan England, saltbox houses from our great maritime past, and flat-roofed echoes of Frank Lloyd Wright and his vision of a day when we would all enjoy solar heating, serene and commodious interiors, and peace on earth.

The lots are 1½ acres, flowers and vegetables grow in the yards, and here and there one finds, instead of tomatoes, robust stands of cannabis with its feathery leaf. Here, in this victorious domesticity, the principle crop is a hazardous drug. And what do I see hanging in the Hartshores' clothesyard but enough seasoning marijuana to stone a regiment.

Is forgetfulness some part of the mysteriousness of life? If I speak to Mr. Hartshore about his cannabis crop, will he tell me that the greatness of Chinese civilization stood foursquare on the fantasies of opium? But it is not I who will speak to Mr. Hartshore. I will be Charlie Dilworth, a very abstemious man who lives in the house next door. He has a No Smoking sign on his front lawn, and his passionate feelings about marijuana have been intelligently channeled into a sort of reverse blackmail.

I hear them litigating late one Saturday afternoon when I have come back from playing touch football with my sons. The light is going. It is autumn. Charlie's voice is loud and clear and can be heard by anyone interested. "You keep your dogs off my lawn, you cook your steaks in the house, you keep your record player down, you keep your swimming-pool filter off in the evenings, and you keep your window shades drawn. Otherwise, I'll report your drug crop to the police and with my wife's uncle sitting as judge this month you'll get at least six months in the can for criminal possession."

They part. Night falls. Here and there a housewife, apprehending the first frost, takes in her house plants while from an Elizabethan, a Nantucket, and a Frank Lloyd Wright chimney comes the marvelous fragrance of wood smoke. You can't put this scene in a novel.

[1978]

RALPH ELLISON *gave an interview for the "Art of Fiction" series of the* Paris Review *that was reprinted in his volume of essays,* Shadow and Act *(1964). In the introduction to that book he said that what is basic to the fiction writer's confrontation with the world is "converting experience into symbolic action. Good fiction is made of that which is real, and reality is difficult to come by. So much of it depends upon the individual's willingness to discover his true self, upon his defining himself — for the time being at least — against his background."*

❦ 30 ❧

Ralph Ellison

on the Influence of Folklore on

BATTLE ROYAL

Interviewers: Can you give us an example of the use of folklore in your own novel?

Ellison: Well, there are certain themes, symbols, and images which are based on folk material. For example, there is the old saying amongst Negroes: If you're black, stay back; if you're brown, stick around; if you're white, you're right. And there is the joke Negroes tell on themselves about their being so black they can't be seen in the dark. In my book this sort of thing was merged with the meanings which blackness and light have long had in Western mythology: evil and goodness, ignorance and knowledge, and so on. In my novel the narrator's development is one through blackness to light; that is, from ignorance to enlightenment: invisibility to visibility. He leaves the South and goes North; this, as you will notice in reading Negro folktales, is always the road to freedom — the movement upward. You have the same thing again when he leaves his underground cave for the open.

It took me a long time to learn how to adapt such examples of myth into my work — also ritual. The use of ritual is equally a vital part of the creative process. I learned a few things from Eliot, Joyce, and Hemingway, but not how to adapt them. When I started writing, I knew that in both *The Waste Land*[1] and *Ulysses*[2] ancient myth and ritual were used to give form and significance to the material; but it took me a few years to realize

---

[1] long, extremely influential poem (1922) by T. S. Eliot (1888–1965).
[2] experimental novel (1922) by James Joyce (1882–1941).

that the myths and rites which we find functioning in our everyday lives could be used in the same way. In my first attempt at a novel — which I was unable to complete — I began by trying to manipulate the simple structural unities of *beginning, middle,* and *end,* but when I attempted to deal with the psychological strata — the images, symbols, and emotional configurations — of the experience at hand, I discovered that the unities were simply cool points of stability on which one could suspend the narrative line — but beneath the surface of apparently rational human relationships there seethed a chaos before which I was helpless. People rationalize what they shun or are incapable of dealing with; these superstitions and their rationalizations become ritual as they govern behavior. The rituals become social forms, and it is one of the functions of the artist to recognize them and raise them to the level of art.

I don't know whether I'm getting this over or not. Let's put it this way: Take the "Battle Royal" passage in my novel, where the boys are blindfolded and forced to fight each other for the amusement of the white observers. This is a vital part of behavior pattern in the South, which both Negroes and whites thoughtlessly accept. It is a ritual in preservation of caste lines, a keeping of taboo to appease the gods and ward off bad luck. It is also the initiation ritual to which all greenhorns are subjected. This passage which states what Negroes will see I did not have to invent; the patterns were already there in society, so that all I had to do was present them in a broader context of meaning. In any society there are many rituals of situation which, for the most part, go unquestioned. They can be simple or elaborate, but they are the connective tissue between the work of art and the audience.

Interviewers: Do you think a reader unacquainted with this folklore can properly understand your work?

Ellison: Yes, I think so. It's like jazz; there's no inherent problem which prohibits understanding but the assumptions brought to it. We don't all dig Shakespeare uniformly, or even *Little Red Riding Hood.* The understanding of art depends finally upon one's willingness to extend one's humanity and one's knowledge of human life. I noticed, incidentally, that the Germans, having no special caste assumptions concerning American Negroes, dealt with my work simply as a novel. I think the Americans will come to view it that way in twenty years — if it's around that long.

Interviewers: Don't you think it will be?

Ellison: I doubt it. It's not an important novel. I failed of eloquence, and many of the immediate issues are rapidly fading away. If it does last, it will be simply because there are things going on in its depth that are of more permanent interest than on its surface. I hope so, anyway.

[1964]

SHIRLEY JACKSON wrote this "biography of a story" in 1960 as a lecture to be delivered before reading "The Lottery" to college audiences. After her death it was included in Come Along with Me *(1968), edited by her husband, Stanley Edgar Hyman. The lecture also contained extensive quotations from letters she had received from readers who took the story literally. These so disgusted Jackson that she promised her listeners at the conclusion of her talk, "I am out of the lottery business for good."*

❧ 31 ❧

Shirley Jackson

on the Morning of June 28, 1948, and

THE LOTTERY

On the morning of June 28, 1948, I walked down to the post office in our little Vermont town to pick up the mail. I was quite casual about it, as I recall — I opened the box, took out a couple of bills and a letter or two, talked to the postmaster for a few minutes, and left, never supposing that it was the last time for months that I was to pick up the mail without an active feeling of panic. By the next week I had had to change my mailbox to the largest one in the post office, and casual conversation with the postmaster was out of the question, because he wasn't speaking to me. June 28, 1948, was the day *The New Yorker* came out with a story of mine in it. It was not my first published story, nor my last, but I have been assured over and over that if it had been the only story I ever wrote or published, there would be people who would not forget my name.

I had written the story three weeks before, on a bright June morning when summer seemed to have come at last, with blue skies and warm sun and no heavenly signs to warn me that my morning's work was anything but just another story. The idea had come to me while I was pushing my daughter up the hill in her stroller — it was, as I say, a warm morning, and the hill was steep, and beside my daughter the stroller held the day's groceries — and perhaps the effort of that last fifty yards up the hill put an edge to the story; at any rate, I had the idea fairly clearly in my mind when I put my daughter in her playpen and the frozen vegetables in the refrigerator, and, writing the story, I found that it went quickly and easily, moving from beginning to end without pause. As a matter of fact, when I read it over later I decided that except for one or two minor corrections, it needed no changes, and the story I finally typed up and sent off to my agent the next day was almost word for word the original draft. This, as any writer of stories can tell you, is not a usual thing. All I know is that when I came to read the story over I felt strongly that I didn't want to fuss with it. I didn't think it was perfect, but I didn't want to fuss with it. It was, I thought, a serious, straightforward story, and I was pleased and a little surprised at the ease with which it had been written; I was reasonably proud of it, and hoped that my agent would sell it to some magazine and I would have the gratification of seeing it in print.

My agent did not care for the story, but — as she said in her note at the time — her job was to sell it, not to like it. She sent it at once to *The New Yorker*, and about a week after the story had been written I received a telephone call from the fiction editor of *The New Yorker*; it was quite clear that he did not really care for the story, either, but *The New Yorker* was going to buy it. He asked for one change — that the date mentioned in the story be changed to coincide with the date of the issue of the magazine in which the story would appear, and I said of course. He then asked, hesitantly, if I had any particular interpretation of my own for the story; Mr. Harold Ross, then the editor of *The New Yorker*, was not altogether sure that he understood the story, and wondered if I cared to enlarge upon its meaning. I said no. Mr. Ross, he said, thought that the story might be puzzling to some people, and in case anyone telephoned the magazine, as sometimes happened, or wrote in asking about the story, was there anything in particular I wanted them to say? No, I said, nothing in particular; it was just a story I wrote.

I had no more preparation than that. I went on picking up the mail every morning, pushing my daughter up and down the hill in her stroller, anticipating pleasurably the check from *The New Yorker*, and shopping for groceries. The weather stayed nice and it looked as though it was going to be a good summer. Then, on June 28, *The New Yorker* came out with my story.

Things began mildly enough with a note from a friend at *The New Yorker*: "Your story has kicked up quite a fuss around the office," he wrote. I was flattered; it's nice to think that your friends notice what you write. Later that day there was a call from one of the magazine's editors; they had had a couple of people phone in about my story, he said, and was there anything I particularly wanted him to say if there were any more calls? No, I said, nothing particular; anything he chose to say was perfectly all right with me; it was just a story.

I was further puzzled by a cryptic note from another friend: "Heard a man talking about a story of yours on the bus this morning," she wrote. "Very exciting. I wanted to tell him I knew the author, but after I heard what he was saying I decided I'd better not."

One of the most terrifying aspects of publishing stories and books is the realization that they are going to be read, and read by strangers. I had never fully realized this before, although I had of course in my imagination dwelt lovingly upon the thought of the millions and millions of people who were going to be uplifted and enriched and delighted by the stories I wrote. It had simply never occurred to me that these millions and millions of people might be so far from being uplifted that they would sit down and write me letters I was downright scared to open; of the three-hundred-odd letters that I received that summer I can count only thirteen that spoke kindly to me, and they were mostly from friends. Even my mother scolded me: "Dad and I did not care at all for your story in *The New Yorker*," she wrote sternly; "it does seem, dear, that this gloomy kind of story is what all you young people think about these days. Why don't you write something to cheer people up?"

By mid-July I had begun to perceive that I was very lucky indeed to be safely in Vermont, where no one in our small town had ever heard of *The New Yorker*, much less read my story. Millions of people, and my mother, had taken a pronounced dislike to me.

The magazine kept no track of telephone calls, but all letters addressed to me care of the magazine were forwarded directly to me for answering, and all letters addressed to the magazine — some of them addressed to Harold Ross personally; these were the most vehement — were answered at the magazine and then the letters were sent me in great batches, along with carbons of the answers written at the magazine. I have all the letters still, and if they could be considered to give any accurate cross section of the reading public, or the reading public of *The New Yorker*, or even the reading public of one issue of *The New Yorker*, I would stop writing now.

Judging from these letters, people who read stories are gullible, rude, frequently illiterate, and horribly afraid of being laughed at. Many of the writers were positive that *The New Yorker* was going to ridicule them in print, and the most cautious letters were headed, in capital letters: NOT FOR PUBLICATION or PLEASE DO NOT PRINT THIS LETTER, or, at best, THIS LETTER MAY BE PUBLISHED AT YOUR USUAL RATES OF PAYMENT. Anonymous letters, of which there were a few, were destroyed. *The New Yorker* never published any comment of any kind about the story in the magazine, but did issue one publicity release saying that the story had received more mail than any piece of fiction they had ever published; this was after the newspapers had gotten into the act, in midsummer, with a front-page story in the San Francisco *Chronicle* begging to know what the story meant, and a series of columns in New York and Chicago papers pointing out that *New Yorker* subscriptions were being canceled right and left.

Curiously, there are three main themes which dominate the letters of that first summer — three themes which might be identified as bewilderment, speculation, and plain old-fashioned abuse. In the years since then, during which the story has been anthologized, dramatized, televised, and even — in one completely mystifying transformation — made into a ballet, the tenor of letters I receive has changed. I am addressed more politely, as a rule, and the letters largely confine themselves to questions like what does this story mean? The general tone of the early letters, however, was a kind of wide-eyed, shocked innocence. People at first were not so much concerned with what the story meant; what they wanted to know was where these lotteries were held, and whether they could go there and watch.

[1968]

GRACE PALEY talked with Ann Charters about her experiences as a short story writer during lunch in her Greenwich Village apartment on a snowy day in February 1986. On the wall above the kitchen table hung an oil painting, a still life of vegetables painted by her father after his retirement from the practice of medicine. Paley mentioned her father's interest in art in her story "A Conversation with My Father."

⤳ 32 ⤶

Grace Paley

A Conversation with Ann Charters

AC: Some literary critics think that short stories are more closely related to poetry than to the novel. Would you agree?

GP: I would say that stories are closer to poetry than they are to the novel because first they are shorter, and second they are more concentrated, more economical, and that kind of economy, the pulling together of all the information and making leaps across the information, is really close to poetry. By leaps I mean thought leaps and feeling leaps. Also, when short stories are working right, you pay more attention to language than most novelists do.

AC: Poe said unity was an essential factor of short stories. Do you have any ideas about this in your own work?

GP: I suppose there has to be some kind of unity, but that's true in a novel too. It seems to me that unity is form. Form is really the vessel in which the story or poem or novel exists. The reason I don't have an answer for you is that there's really no telling — sometimes I like to start a story with one thing and end it with another. I don't know where the unity is in that case. I see the word *unity* meaning that something has to be whole, even if it ends in an open way.

AC: You mean, as you wrote in "A Conversation with My Father," that "everyone, real or invented, deserves the open destiny of life."

GP: Yes.

AC: You started writing poetry before short stories, and the language of your fiction is often as compressed and metaphorical as the language of poetry. Can you describe the process of how you learned to write?

GP: Let me put it this way: I went to school to poetry — that was where I learned how to write. People learn to write by doing various things. I suppose I also wrote a lot of letters, since it was the time of the Second

World War. But apart from that I wrote poems, that's what I wrote. I thought about language a lot. That was important to me. That was my teacher. My fiction teacher was poetry.

AC: What poets did you read when you were learning how to write?

GP: I just read all the poets. If there was an anthology of poets, I read every single one. I knew all the Victorians. I read the Imagists. At a certain point I fell in love with the Englishmen who came to America — Christopher Isherwood, Stephen Spender, and W. H. Auden. I thought Auden was the greatest. And I loved the poetry of Dylan Thomas. Yeats meant a lot to me. I paid attention to all of them and listened to all of them. Some of them must have gotten into my ear. That's not up to me to say. That's for the reader to say. The reader of my stories will tell me, "This is whom you're influenced by," but I can't say that. I feel I was influenced by everybody.

AC: Why did you stop writing poetry and start writing stories? What did the form of the short story offer you that the poem didn't?

GP: First of all, I began to think of certain subject matter, women's lives specifically, and what was happening around me. I was in my thirties, which I guess is the time people start to notice these things, women's and men's lives and what their relationship is. I knew lots of women with small kids, and I was developing very close relationships with a variety of women. All sorts of things began to worry me, and I began to think about them a lot. I couldn't deal with any of this subject matter in poetry; I just didn't know how. I didn't have the technique. Other people can, but I didn't want to write poems saying "I feel this" and "I feel that." That was the last thing I wanted to do.

I can give you a definition that can be proven wrong in many ways, but for me it was that in writing poetry I wanted to talk to the world, I wanted to address the world, so to speak. But writing stories, I wanted to get the world to explain itself to me, to speak to me. And for me that was the essential difference between writing poetry and stories, and it still is, in many ways. So I had to get that world to talk to me. I had to reach out to it, a very different thing than writing poems. I had to reach out to the world and get it to tell me what it was all about, because I didn't understand it. I just didn't understand. Also, I'd always been very interested in people and told funny stories, and I didn't have any room for doing that in poems, again because of my own self. My poems were too literary, that's the real reason.

AC: What do you mean, you had to get the world to tell you what it was all about?

GP: In the first story I ever wrote, "The Contest," I did exactly what I just told you — I got this guy to talk. That's what I did. I had a certain guy in mind. In fact, I stuck pretty close to my notion of what he was, and the story was about a contest he had told me about. The second story I wrote was about Aunt Rose in "Goodbye and Good Luck." That began with my husband's aunt visiting us, and saying exactly the sentence I used to start the story: "I was popular in certain circles." But the rest has nothing to do with her life at all. She looked at us, this aunt of his, and she felt we didn't appreciate her, so she looked at us and she said to us, "Listen," she said. "I was popular in certain circles." That statement really began that particular story. That story was about lot of older women I knew who didn't get married, and I was thinking about them. These are two examples of how I began, how I got to my own voice by hearing and using all these other voices.

AC: I suppose "A Conversation with My Father" isn't typical of your work, because the story you make up for him isn't what he wants, the old-fashioned Chekhov or Maupassant story, and it's not really one of your "voice" stories either, is it?

GP: No. I'm just trying to oblige him.

AC: So that may be one of the jokes of the story?

GP: It could be, but I never thought of it that way. I think it's a good story. People have found it useful in literature classes, which I think is funny, but nice.

AC: Did you make up the plot of "A Conversation with My Father," or did it actually happen when you were visiting him before he died?

GP: My father was eighty-six years old and in bed. I spent a lot of time with him. He was an artist, and he painted pictures after he retired from being a doctor. I visited him at least once a week, and we were very close. We would have discussions. I never wrote a story for him about this neighbor, but he did say to me once, "Why can't you write a regular story, for God's sake?" something like that. So that particular story is both about literature and about that particular discussion, but it's also about generational differences, about different ways of looking at life. What my father thought could be done in the world was due to his own history. What I thought could be done in the world was different, not because I was a more open person, because he was also a very open person, but because I lived in a particularly open time, the late 1960s. The story I wrote for him was about all these druggies. It was made up, but it was certainly true. I could point out people on my block whose kids became junkies. Many of them have recovered from being junkies and are in good shape now.

AC: Did you know any mothers in Greenwich Village who became junkies to keep their kids company?

GP: Sure. It was a very open neighborhood then, with lots of freedom. But my father was born into a very different time. He was born in Czarist Russia and came over to America when he was twenty and worked hard and studied medicine and had a profession.

AC: When you were growing up did you read the writers your father admired — Maupassant and Chekhov?

GP: Actually, he had never mentioned Maupassant to me before. He did mention him in that conversation. He did read a lot, he loved Chekhov. And when he came to this country, he taught himself English by reading Dickens.

AC: So the idea for the story came to you when he mentioned Maupassant?

GP: Well, not really. He had just read my story "Faith in a Tree," and there are a lot of voices coming from all over in that story. And so he asked me, "What is this? All those voices? Voices from who knows where?" He wasn't actually that heavy. But when I wrote about our conversation it became a fiction, and it's different from what really happened.

AC: It must have been fun for you to make up the two versions of the story about your neighbor in "A Conversation with My Father."

GP: I enjoyed writing that story. Some stories you don't enjoy, because they're very hard. I didn't write it right off, but I enjoyed it.

AC: How many days did it take you to write?

GP: There's no such thing as days with me when I write a story. More like months. I write it and I write slow, and then I rewrite, and then I put it away, and then I take it out again. It's tedious in some respects. But that's the way it works.

AC: When do you decide it's finished?

GP: When I've gone over it and I can't think of another thing to change.

AC: I was looking over your book *Enormous Changes at the Last Minute*, which is where "A Conversation with My Father" appears, and I noticed you've placed it between two very dark stories, "The Little Girl," about a runaway in the village who commits suicide after she's raped, and "The Immigrant Story," about the starvation of the young children in a Jewish family in Poland before the mother emigrates to America. I assume you did this for a reason. When you put a collection of short fiction together, how do you order the stories?

GP: I always have something in mind. I like to put one or two at the beginning that will be readable immediately, and then I just work it out. I like to mix the long and the short, and the serious and the funny ones. But I did put those two dark stories around "A Conversation with My Father" to show him I could look tragedy in the face. Remember he asks me at the end of the story, "When will you look it in the face?"

AC: Was that one of the things he actually said to you when you visited him?

GP: Well, he did tend to say that I wouldn't look things in the face. That things were hard, and I wasn't looking at it. I didn't see certain problems with my kids when they were small, and he was in some degree right. In "The Immigrant Story" a man tells me, "You have a rotten rosy temperament." But then she says, "Rosiness is not a worse windowpane than gloomy gray when viewing the world." They're both just prisms to look through.

AC: Is that what you still believe?

GP: Well, I do believe it, but I also believe that things are bad.

AC: A theme that some students find when reading "A Conversation with My Father" is that one of the things you don't want to look in the face that your father is trying to prepare you for is his own death. Were you conscious of that when you wrote the story?

GP: No.

AC: Can you see that theme in it now?

GP: No. But maybe you're right. As I said, that's not up to me to say. Maybe the reader of a particular story knows better than the writer what it means. But I know I wasn't thinking about that when I wrote it. I wasn't thinking of his death at all. I was thinking of him being sick and trying not to get him excited.

[1986]

*N*ADINE GORDIMER *wrote "The Flash of Fireflies" as a representative from South Africa in the International Short Story Symposium conducted by the* Kenyon Review *in its fourth issue in 1968. The essay analyzes the connection between the social and aesthetic implications of this literary form, sharing insights Gordimer had gained over twenty years of storytelling. It is reprinted here in its entirety.*

⛬ 33 ⛬

Nadine Gordimer

The Flash of Fireflies

Why is it that while the death of the novel is good for post-mortem at least once a year, the short story lives on unmolested? It cannot be because — to borrow their own jargon — literary critics regard it as merely a minor art form. Most of them, if pressed, would express the view that it is a highly specialized and skilful form, closer to poetry, etc. But they would have to be pressed; otherwise they wouldn't bother to discuss it at all. When Chekhov crops up, it is as a playwright, and Katherine Mansfield is a period personality from the Lady Chatterley set. Yet no one suggests that we are practicing a dead art form. And, like a child suffering from healthy neglect, the short story survives.

"To say that no one now much likes novels is to exaggerate very little. The large public which used to find pleasure in prose fictions prefer movies, television, journalism, and books of 'fact,' " Gore Vidal wrote recently (*Encounter*, December 1967). If the cinema and television have taken over so much of the novel's territory, just as photography forced painting into wastelands which may or may not be made to bloom, hasn't the short story been overrun, too? This symposium is shoptalk and it would seem unnecessary for us to go over the old definitions of where and how the short story differs from the novel, but the answer to the question must lie somewhere here. Both novel and story use the same material: human experience. Both have the same aim: to communicate it. Both use the same medium: the written word. There is a general and recurrent dissatisfaction with the novel as a means of netting ultimate reality — another term for the quality of human life — and inevitably there is even a tendency to blame the tools: words have become hopelessly blunted by overuse, dinned to death by admen, and, above all, debased by political creeds that have twisted and changed their meaning. Various ways out have been sought. In England, a return to classicism in technique and a turning to the exoticism of sexual aberration and physical and mental abnormality as an extension of human experience and therefore of subject matter; in Germany and America, a splendid abandon in making a virtue of the vice of the novel's inherent clumsiness by stuffing it not with nineteenth-century horsehair narrative but twentieth-century anecdotal-analytical plastic foam; in France, the "laboratory novel" struggling to get away from the anthropocentric curse of the form and the illusion of depth of the psychological novel, and landing up very much where Virginia Woolf was, years ago, staring at the mark on the wall. Burroughs[1] has invented the reader-participation novel. For the diseased word, George Steiner has even suggested silence.

If the short story is alive while the novel is dead, the reason must lie in approach and method. The short story, as a form and as a *kind of creative vision*, must be better equipped to attempt the capture of ultimate reality at a time when (whichever way you choose to see it) we are drawing nearer to the mystery of life or are losing ourselves in a bellowing wilderness of mirrors, as the nature of that reality becomes more fully understood or more bewilderingly concealed by the discoveries of science and the proliferation of communication media outside the printed word.

Certainly the short story always has been more flexible and open to experiment than the novel. Short-story writers always have been subject at the same time to both a stricter technical discipline and a wider freedom than the novelist. Short-story writers have known — and solved by nature of their choice of form — what novelists seem to have discovered in despair only now: the strongest convention of the novel, prolonged coherence of tone, to which even the most experimental of novels must conform unless it is to fall apart, is false to the nature of whatever can be grasped of human reality. How shall I put it? Each of us has a thousand lives and a novel gives a character only one. *For the sake of the form.* The novelist may juggle about with chronology and throw narrative overboard; all the time his characters have the reader by the hand, there is a consistency of relationship throughout the experience that cannot and does not convey the quality of human life, where contact is more like the flash of fireflies, in and out, now here, now there, in darkness. Short-story writers see by the light of the flash; theirs is the art of the only thing one can be sure of — the present moment. Ideally, they have learned to do without explanation of what went before, and what happens beyond this point. How the characters will appear, think, behave, comprehend, tomorow or at any other time in their lives, is irrelevant. A discrete moment of truth is aimed at — not *the* moment of truth, because the short story doesn't deal in cumulatives.

The problem of how best to take hold of ultimate reality, from the technical and stylistic point of view, is one that the short-story writer is accustomed to solving specifically in relation to an area — event, mental

---

[1] William Burroughs (b. 1910), author of *Naked Lunch* and other experimental novels.

state, mood, appearance — which is heightenedly manifest in a single situation. Take fantasy for an example. Writers are becoming more and more aware of the waviness of the line that separates fantasy from the so-called rational in human perception. It is recognized that fantasy is no more than a shift in angle; to put it another way, the rational is simply another, the most obvious, kind of fantasy. Writers turn to the less obvious fantasy as a wider lens on ultimate reality. But this fantasy is something that changes, merges, emerges, disappears as a pattern does viewed through the bottom of a glass. It is true for the moment when one looks down through the glass; but the same vision does not transform everything one sees, consistently throughout one's whole consciousness. Fantasy in the hands of short-story writers is so much more successful than when in the hands of novelists because it is necessary for it to hold good only for the brief illumination of the situation it dominates. In the series of developing situations of the novel the sustainment of the tone of fantasy becomes a high-pitched ringing in the reader's ears. How many fantasy novels achieve what they set out to do: convey the shift and change, to and fro, beneath, above, and around the world of appearances? The short story recognizes that full comprehension of a particular kind in the reader, like full apprehension of a particular kind in the writer, is something of limited duration. The short story is a fragmented and restless form, a matter of hit or miss, and it is perhaps for this reason that it suits modern consciousness — which seems best expressed as flashes of fearful insight alternating with near-hypnotic states of indifference.

These are technical and stylistic considerations. Marxist criticism sees the survival of an art form in relation to social change. What about the socio-political implications of the short story's survival? George Lukács has said that the novel is a bourgeois art form whose enjoyment presupposes leisure and privacy. It implies the living room, the armchair, the table lamp; just as epic implies the illiterates round the tribal story-teller, and Shakespeare implies the two audiences — that of the people and that of the court — of a feudal age. From this point of view the novel marks the apogee of an exclusive, individualist culture; the nearest it ever got to a popular art form (in the sense of bringing people together in direct participation in an intellectually stimulating experience) was the nineteenth-century custom of reading novels aloud to the family. Here again it would seem that the short story shares the same disadvantages as the novel. It is an art form solitary in communication; yet another sign of the increasing loneliness and isolation of the individual in a competitive society. You cannot enjoy the experience of a short story unless you have certain minimum conditions of privacy in which to read it; and these conditions are those of middle-class life. But of course a short story, by reason of its length and its *completeness*, totally contained in the brief time you give to it, depends less than the novel upon the classic conditions of middle-class life, and perhaps corresponds to the breakup of that life which is taking place. In that case, although the story may outlive the novel, it may become obsolete when the period of disintegration is replaced by new social forms and the art forms that express them. One doesn't have to embrace the dreariness of conventional "social realism" in literature to grant this. That our age is threshing about desperately for a way out of individual human isolation, and that our present art forms are not adequate to it, it is obvious to see in all the tatty dressing-up games, from McLuhan's theories to pop art, in which we seek a substitute for them.

[1968]

*F*LANNERY O'CONNOR *first made the following remarks at Hollins College, Virginia, to introduce a reading of her story in October 1963. They were later included in* Mystery and Manners *(1969), a collection of her essays and lectures. The style of this talk is informal, and O'Connor experimented with it, changing the organization and delivery of the material when she appeared before different audiences. Her own interpretation of the themes in her fiction is essential to understanding her stories. As she said, "There are perhaps other ways than my own in which this story could be read, but none other by which it could have been written."*

❧ 34 ❧

Flannery O'Connor

on the Element of Suspense in

A GOOD MAN IS HARD TO FIND

A story really isn't any good unless it successfully resists paraphrase, unless it hangs on and expands in the mind. Properly, you analyze to enjoy, but it's equally true that to analyze with any discrimination, you have to have enjoyed already, and I think that the best reason to hear a story read is that it should stimulate that primary enjoyment.

I don't have any pretensions to being an Aeschylus or Sophocles and providing you in this story with a cathartic experience out of your mythic background, though this story I'm going to read certainly calls up a good deal of the South's mythic background, and it should elicit from you a degree of pity and terror, even though its way of being serious is a comic one. I do think, though, that like the Greeks you should know what is going to happen in this story so that any element of suspense in it will be transferred from its surface to its interior.

I would be most happy if you had already read it, happier still if you knew it well, but since experience has taught me to keep my expectations along these lines modest, I'll tell you that this is the story of a family of six which, on its way driving to Florida, gets wiped out by an escaped convict who calls himself the Misfit. The family is made up of the Grandmother and her son, Bailey, and his children, John Wesley and June Star and the baby, and there is also the cat and the children's mother. The cat is named Pitty Sing, and the Grandmother is taking him with them, hidden in a basket.

Now I think it behooves me to try to establish with you the basis on which reason operates in this story. Much of my fiction takes its character from a reasonable use of the unreasonable, though the reasonableness of my use of it may not always be apparent. The assumptions that underlie this use of it, however, are those of the central Christian mysteries. These are assumptions to which a large part of the modern audience takes exception. About this I can only say that there are perhaps other ways than my own in which this story could be read, but none other by which it could have been written. Belief, in my own case anyway, is the engine that makes perception operate.

The heroine of this story, the Grandmother, is in the most significant position life offers the Christian. She is facing death. And to all appearances she, like the rest of us, is not too well prepared for it. She would like to see the event postponed. Indefinitely.

I've talked to a number of teachers who use this story in class and who tell their students that the Grandmother is evil, that in fact, she's a witch, even down to the cat. One of these teachers told me that his students, and particularly his southern students, resisted this interpretation with a certain bemused vigor, and he didn't understand why. I had to tell him that they resisted it because they all had grandmothers or great-aunts just like her at home, and they knew, from personal experience, that the old lady lacked comprehension, but that she had a good heart. The southerner is usually tolerant of those weaknesses that proceed from innocence, and he knows that a taste for self-preservation can be readily combined with the missionary spirit.

This same teacher was telling his students that morally the Misfit was several cuts above the Grandmother. He had a really sentimental attachment to the Misfit. But then a prophet gone wrong is almost always more interesting than your grandmother, and you have to let people take their pleasures where they find them.

It is true that the old lady is a hypocritical old soul; her wits are no match for the Misfit's, nor is her capacity for grace equal to his; yet I think the unprejudiced reader will feel that the Grandmother has a special kind of triumph in this story which instinctively we do not allow to someone altogether bad.

I often ask myself what makes a story work, and what makes it hold up as a story, and I have decided that it is probably some action, some gesture of a character that is unlike any other in the story, one which indicates where the real heart of the story lies. This would have to be an action or a gesture which was both totally right and totally unexpected; it would have to be one that was both in character and beyond character; it would have to suggest both the world and eternity. The action or gesture I'm talking about would have to be on the anagogical level, that is, the level which has to do with the Divine life and our participation in it. It would be a gesture that transcended any neat allegory that might have been intended or any pat moral categories a reader could make. It would be a gesture which somehow made contact with mystery.

There is a point in this story where such a gesture occurs. The Grandmother is at last alone, facing the Misfit. Her head clears for an instant and she realizes, even in her limited way, that she is responsible for the man before her and joined to him by ties of kinship which have their roots deep in the mystery she has been merely prattling about so far. And at this point, she does the right thing, she makes the right gesture.

I find that students are often puzzled by what she says and does here, but I think myself that if I took out this gesture and what she says with it, I would have no story. What was left would not be worth your attention. Our age not only does not have a very sharp eye for the almost imperceptible intrusions of grace, it no longer has much feeling for the nature of the violences which precede and follow them. The devil's greatest wile, Baudelaire has said, is to convince us that he does not exist.

I suppose the reasons for the use of so much violence in modern fiction will differ with each writer who uses it, but in my own stories I have found that violence is strangely capable of returning my characters to reality and preparing them to accept their moment of grace. Their heads are so hard that almost nothing else will do the work. This idea, that reality is something to which we must be returned at considerable cost, is one which is seldom understood by the casual reader, but it is one which is implicit in the Christian view of the world.

I don't want to equate the Misfit with the devil. I prefer to think that, however unlikely this may seem, the old lady's gesture, like the mustard-seed, will grow to be a great crow-filled tree in the Misfit's heart, and will be enough of a pain to him there to turn him into the prophet he was meant to become. But that's another story.

This story has been called grotesque, but I prefer to call it literal. A good story is literal in the same sense that a child's drawing is literal. When a child draws, he doesn't intend to distort but to set down exactly what he sees, and as his gaze is direct, he sees the lines that create motion. Now the lines of motion that interest the writer are usually invisible. They are lines of spiritual motion. And in this story you should be on the lookout for such things as the action of grace in the Grandmother's soul, and not for the dead bodies.

We hear many complaints about the prevalence of violence in modern fiction, and it is always assumed that this violence is a bad thing and meant to be an end in itself. With the serious writer, violence is never an end in itself. It is the extreme situation that best reveals what we are essentially, and I believe these are times when writers are more interested in what we are essentially than in the tenor of our daily lives. Violence is a force which can be used for good or evil, and among other things taken by it is the kingdom of heaven. But regardless of what can be taken by it, the man in the violent situation reveals those qualities least dispensable in his personality, those qualities which are all he will have to take into eternity with him; and since the characters in this story are all on the verge of eternity, it is appropriate to think of what they take with them. In any case, I hope that if you consider these points in connection with the story, you will come to see it as something more than an account of a family murdered on the way to Florida.

[1969]

ALICE ADAMS *wrote this essay for the anthology compiled by Joyce Carol Oates,* First Person Singular: Writers on Their Craft *(1983). In it Adams described her early background and the gradual process by which she became a writer and produced what she considers her first successful short story, "The Swastika on Our Door." Her personal account, Oates felt, is "confessional in the best sense of the word."*

ᴧ 35 ᴧ

Alice Adams

Why I Write

A year or so ago my son went back to Chapel Hill, which is where I am from, on a somewhat problematical errand for me, to be combined with projects of his own, in New York (he is a painter, and wanted to take slides around). On his return to San Francisco, among other pithy remarks — he had been gratifyingly observant — he said, "Well, now I can really see why you're a writer."

His errand had involved the sale of the house in which I grew up, but which I did not inherit. I had been invited to choose certain things that I might want from the house, but although there were indeed a couple of things that I would have liked, I was withheld from making the trip myself both by reasons of sentiment, not wanting to revisit those scenes of disorderly family history — and by an experienced instinct which instructed me that the things I wanted would be mysteriously unavailable. Thus I readily accepted Peter's offer; he went to Chapel Hill, he stayed with a friend of mine, Max Steele, who teaches at the university there, and he spent time with various people who had been extremely important to me, including my childhood best friend, Josephine; and he met a woman whom I had known as the wife of another distinguished writer-teacher of many years back, Phillips Russell (I took a short story course from him, one significant summer, over thirty years ago). Thus, when Peter returned from his travels and said that he now knew why I am a writer I took him up very eagerly — he could have meant anything at all, perhaps some unravelling of dark familial mysteries. I asked, "Oh, why?"

"Well, writing books is all anyone ever talks about down there. Everyone is going to write a book, if they haven't already," Peter said.

Well, that was not quite the answer I expected, but as an observation it is absolutely true. Certainly during the thirties, the time of my childhood

1326

there, the town was rife with writers — past, permanent, and just passing through. Gertrude Stein even came from Paris, in 1932, with Alice Toklas, a visit arranged for by my mother, I believe. (I did not meet them because, humiliatingly, I had chickenpox at the time.) Thomas Wolfe had been around almost the day before, as a student; his brooding, contradictory legend haunted the place. Paul Green, the playwright, was still there, and Prof. Koch, of Playmaker fame. And handsome Phillips Russell. And most local people knew at least a few writers from other places; my parents knew Allen Tate, who visited from Southern Pines; and Ralph Bates, the English novelist, who came to raise money for Loyalist Spain, in 1938. Everyone talked a great deal about all those writers, as well as distant William Faulkner and poor almost-discarded James Branch Cabell; they were our local folk heros, and heroines. Their drinking habits were endlessly fascinating, their lives were charmed — or so I interpreted what I was listening to, as a child.

The situation in my particular family with regard to writers and writing was slightly puzzling (as what was not). My mother had a considerable reputation as a literary woman, and was known to write poetry, which no one ever saw. But she was not a writer. I concluded that she wanted to be one and somehow had failed in that effort, which served to further exalt the calling, in my view; anything that my formidably intelligent mother could not do must be remarkable indeed, and it took a lot of nerve to resolve to exceed her, as I must secretly, unconsciously have done. My father was another sort of puzzle; he seemed to like writers, and he told a lot of writer stories, along with everyone else, but I never saw him read a book for pleasure.

Most people admired and were interested in writers, then, it seemed safe to assume, but the languge in which this came through was highly ambiguous, as was much of the language that I heard, early on. In fact I was very slow to understand what could be called Polite Southern Conversation; it was years before I understood that the words, "Oh, if you're not just the smartest thing!" did not connote praise. To be smart, in P.S.C., meant to be out of line, somehow; if you were a woman, it meant that you were being most unwomanly.

Last summer in Alaska I heard Robert Stone speak movingly about early efforts to understand a schizophrenic mother. And I think that perhaps many of us began to write for somewhat similar reasons: to make sense of what seemed and sounded senseless, all around us.

Strongly motivated, then, I began to write small poems at what was considered to be a very early age. I found this an exceptionally pleasant pastime, all those nice words tidily arranged, and I was happily surprised by the attention and praise thus so easily acquired. A friend of mine has a theory that men who cook are often overpraised by women; for a man to cook at all still seems, in many circles, something remarkable. "Honestly, Andrew made the whole dinner by himself, I only cut up a few vegetables, and did the risotto." And so it often is, I believe, with child poets. "Oh, what a darling poem, and Alice is only six. Isn't she just the smartest little thing?" (I took this remark at face value, of course, and was awed by my own precocity).

This process of poems and praise, with a very young person, can continue for quite a while. I went on writing poems, literally hundreds of them, for at least a dozen years, roughly between the ages of five and seventeen. School magazines published them, I won prizes, and the notion of myself as a poet filled me with a sense of virtue that other areas of my life did not (I was known by my parents and teachers to be "difficult," "rebellious"; and they were quite right, I was). I was dimly, distantly aware that what I wrote myself did not quite come up to the poems I read and most admired; my sonnets, written at eleven and twelve, had no sound of Shakespeare or Shelley, or even Edna Millay, but for a twelve-year-old to be writing sonnets at all was considered both virtuous and unusual, by everyone, including myself. I suppose, if I wondered at all about this gap in literary distinction, I assumed that by the time I was twice as old, was twenty-four, at least, my poems would be at least twice as remarkable, and I would be a Poet. In the meantime I continued to write enthusiastically about Nature, and in a more melancholy vein, of Love.

I went to a boarding school in Virginia where Polite Southern Conversation was elevated to an almost religious principle. There were no Jews in the school, which was Episcopalian, because, "Of course," in P.S.C., "they would not be comfortable here." The headmistress of that school, a most distracted lady who at sixty had married a handsome gentleman of eighty-two (was she or was she not a virgin? this was a popular topic for girlish speculation), was fond of reading to us from *The Prophet* (her idea of poetry, I guess) and she had a network of spies who reported to her on girls who did not always speak in P.S.C., who were in fact overheard to use words like "damn" or "hell."

I hated everything about the school, the ugly uniforms and terrible food, the lack of boys; I was often reported as using bad words, but I did have some good friends, similarly rebellious. They were mostly girls from Boston or New York who had somehow strayed down to Virginia, and who seemed to speak a new and vigorous language.

Partly for that reason, my attraction to un-Southern and especially to New England talk, I chose to go to Radcliffe, and there, almost at once, everything in my life changed radically, for the better. My new friends all spoke a language that I could at last understand. And the courses that I took at Harvard were overwhelmingly exciting. I remember coming out of Harvard Hall, from a course with F. O. Matthiessen in the criticism of poetry, and being almost unable to breathe, in that heady Cambridge spring air; I was so bedazzled by the brilliance of his lecture, and by sudden contact with poets I had not read before: Donne, Yeats, Eliot, and Auden — to name only a few.

Reasonably enough, at about this time I began to recognize that my own poetry was pretty bad. The relative painlessness of this recognition now seems surprising, and I can only attribute it to my generally radiant mood of that time.

I still wrote an occasional poem, though, and I tried to enroll in a poetry writing workshop, to be given by Theodore Spencer; however the dean emphatically told me that my science requirement came first. And so I signed up for astronomy, and also for a short-story class. I began to read and to write short stories, and I fell totally and permanently in love with that form. I read stories by Elizabeth Bowen and Katherine Mansfield and Katherine Anne Porter, James Joyce and Henry James. Hemingway, Fitzgerald, and John O'Hara. Mark Schorer and John Cheever. And I spent many happy afternoons in and around my writing classes in those distant lovely falls and springs.

Whenever one of us got an A or even a strong B+ we would instantly, with a wild and nutty gambler's optimism, whip that story off to *The New Yorker*. We could have papered our rooms with those politely printed form rejection slips.

I even took a writing course one summer vacation, at home in Chapel Hill, from Phillips Russell. He said that most short stories could be divided into three, or sometimes five sections, or acts; and he wrote outlines for both methods on the blackboard. I was impressed by his beautifully flaring eyebrows, but since he was so old (about forty, then, I think) and a friend of my parents *and* a most polite Southerner, I dismissed and forgot almost everything he said, or so I thought.

After college I went on writing stories, along with quite a few other much less rewarding occupations. The quality of the stories improved, over the years, although in a disconcertingly uneven way; I would write what I believed to be a fairly good story, and that story would be succeeded by others which were clearly much less good. Some of the stories were published, along with a novel that I wrote somewhere along the way. But it was many years, in fact almost twenty years after Radcliffe and those early writing courses, before I at last wrote a story that really pleased me, that I knew to be good. And that story, curiously, involved a return to Polite Southern.

The story began in my mind when two men whom I knew during the early sixties had a serious quarrel over money. They were both European, and had been intensely close friends since their own college days, at International House, in Berkeley. I was fond of them both, and I was strongly moved and disturbed by the nature of their quarrel. I first wanted and then had to write about it. In brief, what happened was that one friend, who had recently married, wanted to borrow some money from the other friend, who had just come into an inheritance. The would-be borrower offered a reasonable interest rate on the loan, and it was this that so deeply offended his friend, the offer of interest. "I would so gladly have given it to him," the wounded friend cried out, "and he offers me interest!"

For the purposes of my story I made the two men Southern, rather than European (and brothers rather than friends), both because a Southern background would come more naturally to me, and also because that particular, violently pained indignation seemed Southern: "You offer me interest!" — I could hear it in Southern voices. In my story, in fact, the two men often burlesqued Polite Southern. It was as though I could not learn to write until I had learned to master what was, after all, my earliest language.

Also, to cope with the long time span of their friendship, I used the Phillips Russell five-act outline, which fortuitously arrived at my mind, as I began to think about writing that story.

In any case, I thought it worked out, my story, and with some difficulty I persuaded my agent — at that time a most unimaginative young man — to send it to *The New Yorker* (he had me pegged as a "woman's writer," in those days a condescending term that precluded writing for good magazines like *The New Yorker*). *The New Yorker* bought the story, it won an O. Henry prize — and it was quite a while before I wrote another as good.

[1983]

*U*RSULA LE GUIN *published* The Wind's Twelve Quarters, *the collection of short fiction in which "Those Who Walk Away from Omelas" appeared, in 1975. The stories in this book form a disturbing group, posing unforgettable questions that stay with the reader long after each story is finished. In her commentary Le Guin described the source for the idea of her story.*

⤙ 36 ⤚

Ursula Le Guin

on The Ones Who

Walk Away from Omelas

The central idea of this psychomyth, the scapegoat, turns up in Dostoyevsky's *Brothers Karamazov,* and several people have asked me, rather suspiciously, why I gave the credit to William James. The fact is, I haven't been able to re-read Dostoyevsky, much as I loved him, since I was twenty-five, and I'd simply forgotten he used the idea. But when I met it in James's "The Moral Philosopher and the Moral Life," it was with a shock of recognition. Here is how James puts it:

> Or if the hypothesis were offered us of a world in which Messrs. Fourier's and Bellamy's and Morris's utopias should all be outdone, and millions kept permanently happy on the one simple condition that a certain lost soul on the far-off edge of things should lead a life of lonely torment, what except a specific and independent sort of emotion can it be which would make us immediately feel, even though an impulse arose within us to clutch at the happiness so offered, how hideous a thing would be its enjoyment when deliberately accepted as the fruit of such a bargain?

The dilemma of the American conscience can hardly be better stated. Dostoyevsky was a great artist, and a radical one, but his early social radicalism reversed iself, leaving him a violent reactionary. Whereas the American James, who seems so mild, so naïvely gentlemanly — look how he says "us," assuming all his readers are as decent as himself — was, and remained, and remains, a genuinely radical thinker. Directly after the "lost soul" passage he goes on,

> All the higher, more penetrating ideals are revolutionary. They present themselves far less in the guise of effects of past experience than in that of

probable causes of future experience, factors to which the environment and the lessons it has so far taught us must learn to bend.

The application of those two sentences to this story, and to science fiction, and to all thinking about the future, is quite direct. Ideals as "the probable causes of future experience" — that is a subtle and an exhilarating remark!

Of course I didn't read James and sit down and say, Now I'll write a story about that "lost soul." It seldom works that simply. I sat down and started a story, just because I felt like it, with nothing but the word "Omelas" in mind. It came from a road sign: Salem (Oregon) backwards. Don't you read road signs backwards? POTS, WOLS nerdlihc. Ocsicnarf Nas . . . Salem equals schelomo equals salaam equals Peace. Melas. O melas. Omelas. Homme hélas. "Where *do* you get your ideas from, Ms. Le Guin?" From forgetting Dostoyevsky and reading road signs backwards, naturally. Where else?

[1975]

JOHN UPDIKE gave an interview to the Paris Review *that was later reprinted in the fourth volume of* Writers at Work *(1976). His meticulous craftsmanship as a writer was evident in his handling of the interview. On his guard when first approached, he initially refused to be interviewed, saying, "Perhaps I have written fiction because everything unambiguously expressed seems somehow crass to me; and when the subject is myself, I want to jeer and weep. Also, I really don't have a great deal to tell interviewers; the little I learned about life and the art of fiction I try to express in my work." When he consented to the interview the following year, he insisted that written questions be submitted to him in advance. Finally, Updike revised the transcript of his spoken comments before agreeing to publication. In the interview he disavowed any important connection between the facts of his life and the fiction he created on paper, although he acknowledged a "submerged thread" of autobiography in stories like "Flight."*

❧ 37 ❧

John Updike

on Writing about Adolescence in

FLIGHT

Interviewer: What I meant to ask is . . . why you write so much about what most people take to be your own adolescence and family. . . .

Updike: I suppose there's no avoiding it — my adolescence seemed interesting to me. In a sense my mother and father, considerable actors both, were dramatizing my youth as I was having it so that I arrived as an adult with some burden of material already half formed. There is, true, a submerged thread connecting certain of the fictions, and I guess the submerged thread is the autobiography. . . .

When I was little, I used to draw disparate objects on a piece of paper — toasters, baseballs, flowers, whatnot — and connect them with lines. But every story, really, is a fresh start for me, and these little connections — recurrences of names, or the way, say, that Piet Hanema's insomnia takes him back into the same high school that John Nordholm, and David Kern, and Allen Dow[1] sat in — are in there as a kind of running, oblique coherence. Once I've coined a name, by the way, I feel utterly hid-

---

[1] The names are all of characters in Updike's fiction.

den behind that mask, and what I remember and what I imagine become indistinguishable. I feel no obligation to the remembered past; what I create on paper must, and for me does, soar free of whatever the facts were. Do I make any sense?

Interviewer: Some.

Updike: In other words, I disavow any essential connection between my life and whatever I write. I think it's a morbid and inappropriate area of concern, though natural enough — a lot of morbid concerns are natural. But the work, the words on the paper, must stand apart from our living presences; we sit down at the desk and become nothing but the excuse for these husks we cast off. But apart from the somewhat teasing little connections, there is in these three novels and the short stories of *Pigeon Feathers* a central image of flight or escape or loss, the way we flee from the past, a sense of guilt. . . .

The sense that in time as well as space we leave people as if by volition and thereby incur guilt and thereby owe them, the dead, the forsaken, at least the homage of rendering them. The trauma or message that I acquired in Olinger had to do with suppressed pain, with the amount of sacrifice I suppose that middle-class life demands, and by that I guess I mean civilized life. The father, whatever his name, is sacrificing freedom of motion, and the mother is sacrificing in a way — oh, sexual richness, I guess; they're all stuck, and when I think back over these stories (and you know, they *are* dear to me and if I had to give anybody one book of me it would be the Vintage *Olinger Stories*), I think especially of that moment in "Flight" when the boy, chafing to escape, fresh from his encounter with Molly Bingaman and a bit more of a man but not enough quite, finds the mother lying there buried in her own peculiar messages from far away, the New Orleans jazz, and then the grandfather's voice comes tumbling down the stairs singing, "There is a happy land far far away." This is the way it was, is. There has never been anything in my life quite as compressed, simultaneously as communicative to me of my own power and worth and of the irremediable grief in just living, in just going on.

I really don't think I'm alone among writers in caring about what they experienced in the first eighteen years of life. Hemingway cherished the Michigan stories out of proportion, I would think, to their merit. Look at Twain. Look at Joyce. Nothing that happens to us after twenty is as free from self-consciousness because by then we have the vocation to write. Writers' lives break into two halves. At the point where you get your writerly vocation you diminish your receptivity to experience. Being able to write becomes a kind of shield, a way of hiding, a way of too instantly transforming pain into honey — whereas when you're young, you're so impotent you cannot help but strive and observe and feel.

[1976]

*R*AYMOND CARVER *was inspired by the example of the novelist John Gardner when Carver was just beginning to think of himself as a writer. In this essay Carver reminisced about what he learned from Gardner both in and outside the creative writing classroom. Carver wrote the essay as the foreword to Gardner's book* On Becoming a Novelist *(1983), in which Gardner distilled his personal experience as an accomplished novelist and a committed teacher of fiction writing.*

❧ 38 ☙

Raymond Carver

Creative Writing 101

A long time ago — it was the summer of 1958 — my wife and I and our two baby children moved from Yakima, Washington, to a little town outside of Chico, California. There we found an old house and paid twenty-five dollars a month rent. In order to finance this move, I'd had to borrow a hundred and twenty-five dollars from a druggist I'd delivered prescriptions for, a man named Bill Barton.

This is by way of saying that in those days my wife and I were stone broke. We had to eke out a living, but the plan was that I would take classes at what was then called Chico State College. But for as far back as I can remember, long before we moved to California in search of a different life and our slice of the American pie, I'd wanted to be a writer. I wanted to write, and I wanted to write anything — fiction, of course, but also poetry, plays, scripts, articles for *Sports Afield, True, Argosy,* and *Rogue* (some of the magazines I was then reading), pieces for the local newspaper — anything that involved putting words together to make something coherent and of interest to someone besides myself. But at the time of our move, I felt in my bones I had to get some education in order to go along with being a writer. I put a very high premium on education then — much higher in those days than now, I'm sure, but that's because I'm older and have an education. Understand that nobody in my family had ever gone to college or for that matter had got beyond the mandatory eighth grade in high school. I didn't *know anything,* but I knew I didn't know anything.

So along with this desire to get an education, I had this very strong desire to write; it was a desire so strong that, with the encouragement I was given in college, and the insight acquired, I kept on writing long after "good sense" and the "cold facts" — the "realities" of my life told me, time and again, that I ought to quit, stop the dreaming, quietly go ahead and do something else.

That fall at Chico State I enrolled in classes that most freshman students have to take, but I enrolled as well for something called Creative Writing 101. This course was going to be taught by a new faculty member named John Gardner, who was already surrounded by a bit of mystery and romance. It was said that he'd taught previously at Oberlin College but had left there for some reason that wasn't made clear. One student said Gardner had been fired — students, like everyone else, thrive on rumor and intrigue — and another student said Gardner had simply quit after some kind of flap. Someone else said his teaching load at Oberlin, four or five classes of freshman English each semester, had been too heavy and that he couldn't find time to write. For it was said that Gardner was a real, that is to say a practicing, writer — someone who had written novels and short stories. In any case, he was going to teach CW 101 at Chico State, and I signed up.

I was excited about taking a course from a real writer. I'd never laid eyes on a writer before, and I was in awe. But where were these novels and short stories, I wanted to know. Well, nothing had been published yet. It was said that he couldn't get his work published and that he carried it around with him in boxes. (After I became his student, I was to see those boxes of manuscript. Gardner had become aware of my difficulty in finding a place to work. He knew I had a young family and cramped quarters at home. He offered me the key to his office. I see that gift now as a turning point. It was a gift not made casually, and I took it, I think, as a kind of mandate — for that's what it was. I spent part of every Saturday and Sunday in his office, which is where he kept the boxes of manuscript. The boxes were stacked up on the floor beside the desk. *Nickel Mountain*, grease-pencilled on one of the boxes, is the only title I recall. But it was in his office, within sight of his unpublished books, that I undertook my first serious attempts at writing.) . . .

For short story writers in his class, the requirement was one story, ten to fifteen pages in length. For people who wanted to write a novel — I think there must have been one or two of these souls — a chapter of around twenty pages, along with an outline of the rest. The kicker was that this one short story, or the chapter of the novel, might have to be revised ten times in the course of the semester for Gardner to be satisfied with it. It was a basic tenet of his that a writer found what he wanted to say in the ongoing process of *seeing* what he'd said. And this seeing, or seeing more clearly, came about through revision. He *believed* in revision, endless revision; it was something very close to his heart and something he felt was vital for writers, at whatever stage of their development. And he never seemed to lose patience rereading a student story, even though he might have seen it in five previous incarnations.

I think his idea of a short story in 1958 was still pretty much his idea of a short story in 1982; it was something that had a recognizable beginning, middle, and an end to it. Once in a while he'd go to the blackboard and draw a diagram to illustrate a point he wanted to make about rising or falling emotion in a story — peaks, valleys, plateaus, resolution, *denouement,* things like that. Try as I might, I couldn't muster a great deal of interest or really understand this side of things, the stuff he put on the blackboard. But what I did understand was the way he would comment on a student story that was undergoing class discussion. Gardner might wonder aloud about the author's reasons for writing a story about a crippled person, say, and leaving out the fact of the character's crippledness until the very end of the story. "So you think it's a good idea not to let the reader know this man is crippled until the last sentence?" His tone of voice conveyed his disapproval, and it didn't take more than an instant for everyone in class, including the author of the story, to see that it wasn't a good strategy to use. Any stragegy that kept important and necessary information away from the reader in the hope of overcoming him by surprise at the end of the story was cheating.

In class he was always referring to writers whose names I was not familiar with. Or if I knew their names, I'd never read the work. . . . He talked about James Joyce and Flaubert and Isak Dinesen as if they lived just down the road, in Yuba City. He said, "I'm here to tell you who to read as well as teach you how to write." I'd leave class in a daze and make straight for the library to find books by these writers he was talking about.

Hemingway and Faulkner were the reigning authors in those days. But altogether I'd probably read at the most two or three books by these fellows. Anyway, they were so well-known and so much talked about, they couldn't be all that good, could they? I remember Gardner telling me, "Read all the Faulkner you can get your hands on, and then read all of Hemingway to clean the Faulkner out of your system."

He introduced us to the "little" or literary periodicals by bringing a box of these magazines to class one day and passing them around so that we could acquaint ourselves with their names, see what they looked like and what they felt like to hold in the hand. He told us that this was where most of the best fiction in the country and just about all of the poetry was appearing. Fiction, poetry, literary essays, book reviews of recent books, criticism of *living* authors *by* living authors. I felt wild with discovery in those days.

For the seven or eight of us who were in his class, he ordered heavy black binders and told us we should keep our written work in these. He kept his own work in such binders, he said, and of course that settled it for us. We carried our stories in those binders and felt we were special, exclusive, singled out from others. And so we were.

I don't know how Gardner might have been with other students when it came time to have conferences with them about their work. I suspect he gave everybody a good amount of attention. But it was and still is my impression that during that period he took my stories more seriously, read them closer and more carefully, than I had any right to expect. I was completely unprepared for the kind of criticism I received from him. Before our conference he would have marked up my story, crossing out unacceptable sentences, phrases, individual words, even some of the punctuation; and he gave me to understand that these deletions were not negotiable. In other cases he would bracket sentences, phrases, or individual words, and these were items we'd talk about, these cases were negotiable. And he wouldn't hesitate to add something to what I'd written — a word here and there, or else a few words, maybe a sentence that would make clear what I was trying to say. We'd discuss commas in my story as if nothing else in the world mattered more at that moment — and, indeed, it did not. He was always looking to find something to praise. When there was a sentence, a line of dialogue, or a narrative passage that he liked, something that he thought "worked" and moved the story along in some pleasant or unexpected way, he'd write "Nice" in the margin, or else "Good!" And seeing these comments, my heart would lift.

It was close, line-by-line criticism he was giving me, and the reasons behind the criticism, why something ought to be this way instead of that; and it was invaluable to me in my development as a writer. After this kind of detailed talk about the text, we'd talk about the larger concerns of the story, the "problem" it was trying to throw light on, the conflict it was trying to grapple with, and how the story might or might not fit into the grand scheme of story writing. It was his conviction that if the words in the story were blurred because of the author's insensitivity, carelessness, or sentimentality, then the story suffered from a tremendous handicap. But there was something even worse and something that must be avoided at all costs: if the words and the sentiments were dishonest, the author was faking it, writing about things he didn't care about or believe in, then nobody could ever care anything about it.

A writer's values and craft. This is what the man taught and what he stood for, and this is what I've kept by me in the years since that brief but all-important time.

[1983]

*J*OYCE CAROL OATES *composed this essay about how she began to write fiction as a response to an invitation from* The New York Times Book Review, *which published contributions by eminent contemporary authors in a series entitled "The Making of a Writer." Oates's article appeared in July 1982. Since she is such a prolific writer, her description of her entry into a "fictional world" is an illuminating statement about her practice as a storyteller.*

⤳ 39 ⤶

Joyce Carol Oates
on the Making of a Writer

Telling stories, I discovered at the age of three or four, is a way of being told stories. One picture yields another; one set of words, another set of words. Like our dreams, the stories we tell are also the stories we are told. If I say that I write with the enormous hope of altering the world — and why write without that hope? — I should first say that I write to discover what it is *I will have written.* A love of reading stimulates the wish to write — so that one can read, as a reader, the words one has written. Storytellers may be finite in number but stories appear to be inexhaustible.

For many days — in fact for weeks — I have been tormented by the proposition that if I could set down, in reasonably lucid prose, the story of "the making of the writer Joyce Carol Oates," I might in some rudimentary way be defined, at least to myself. Stretched upon a grammatical framework, who among us does not appear to make sense? But the story will not cohere. The necessary words will not arrange themselves. Of the forty-odd pages I have written (each, I should confess, with the rapt, naïve certainty, *At last I have it*) very little strikes me as useful. The miniature stories I have told myself, by way of analyzing "myself," are not precisely lies; but, since each contains so small a fraction of the truth, it is untrue. Each angle of vision, each voice, yields (by way of that process of fictional abiogenesis[1] all storytellers know) a separate writer-self, an alternative Joyce Carol Oates. Each miniature story exerts so powerful an appeal (to the author, that is) that it could, in time, evolve into a novel — for me the divine form, the ultimate artwork, toward which all the arts aspire. Consequently this "story" you are reading is an admission of failure, or, at the very most, a record of

[1] creation of life from lifeless material.

failed attempts. If knowing oneself is an alphabet, I seem to be stuck at A, and take solace from the elderly Yeats's remark in a letter: "Man can embody truth but he cannot know it."

One of the stories I tell myself has to do with the dream of a "sacred text."

Perhaps it is a dream, an actual dream: to set down words with such talismanic[2] precision, such painstaking love, that they cannot be altered — that they constitute a reality of their own, and are not merely referential. It is one of the enigmas of our craft (so my writer friends agree) that, with the passage of time, *how* becomes an obsession, rather than *what:* It becomes increasingly more difficult to say the simplest things. Content yields to form, theme to "voice." But we don't know what voice is.

The story of the elusive sacred text has something to do with a childlike notion of omnipotent thoughts, a wish for immortality through language, a command that time stand still. What is curious is that writing, the act of writing, often satisfies these demands. We throw ourselves into it with such absorption, writing eight or ten hours at a time, writing in our daydreams, composing in our sleep; we enter that fictional world so deeply that time seems to warp or to fold back in upon itself. Where do you find the time, people ask, to write so much? But the time I inhabit is protracted; my interior clock moves with frustrating slowness.

The melancholy secret at the heart of all creative activity (we are not talking here of quality, that ambiguous term) has something to do with our desire to complete a work and to perfect it — this very desire bringing with it our exclusion from that phase of our lives. Though a novel must be begun, often with extraordinary effort, it eventually acquires its own rhythm, its own voice, and begins to write itself; and when it is completed, the writer is expelled — the door closes slowly upon him or her, but it does close. A work of prose may be many things to many people, but to the author it is a monument to a certain chunk of time: so many pulsebeats, so much effort.

[1982]

---

[2] like an object that magically produces good fortune and wards off evil.

*T*ONI CADE BAMBARA *was interviewed by Claudia Tate for the book* Black Women Writers at Work *(1985). A quotation from Bambara's book* The Black Woman *(1970) served as epigraph for the interview, summing up her revolutionary stance toward life:* "Revolution begins with the self, in the self. The individual, the basic revolutionary unit, must be purged of poison and lies that assault the ego and threaten the heart, that hazard the next larger unit — the couple or pair, that jeopardize the still larger unit — the family or cell, that put the entire movement in peril."

❧ 40 ❧

Toni Cade Bambara

A Conversation with Claudia Tate

C.T.: How do you fit writing into your life?

Bambara: Up until recently, I had never fully appreciated the sheer anguish of that issue. I never knew what the hell people were talking about when they asked, "How do you manage to juggle the demands of motherhood, teaching, community work, writing, and the rest?" Writing had never been a central activity in my life. It was one of the things I did when I got around to it or when the compulsion seized me and sat me down. The short story, the article, the book review, after all, are short-term pieces. I would simply commandeer time, space, paper and pen, close the door, unplug the phone, get ugly with would-be intruders, and get to work for a few days. Recently, however, working on a novel and a few movie scripts — phew! I now know what that question means and I despair. I had to renegotiate a great many relationships that fell apart around me; the novel took me out of action for nearly a year. I was unfit to work — couldn't draft a simple office memo, couldn't keep track of time, blew meetings, refused to answer the door, wasn't interested in hanging out in any way, shape, or form. My daughter hung in there, screened calls, learned to iron her own clothes, and generally kept out of my sight. My mama would look at me funny every now and then, finding that days had gone by and I hadn't gotten around to combing my hair or calling her to check in and just chat. Short stories are a piece of time. The novel is a way of life. . . .

I have no shrewd advice to offer developing writers about this business of snatching time and space to work. I do not have anything profound to offer mother-writers or worker-writers except to say that it will cost you something. Anything of value is going to cost you something. I'm not much of a caretaker, for example, in relationships. I am not consistent about giving vibrancy and other kinds of input to a relationship. I don't always remember the birthdays, the anniversaries. There are periods when I am the most attentive and thoughtful lover in the world, and periods, too, when I am just unavailable. I have never learned, not yet anyway, to apologize for or continually give reassurance about what I'm doing. I'm not terribly accountable or very sensitive to other people's sense of being beat back, cut out, blocked, shunted off. I will have to learn because the experience of *The Salt Eaters*[1] tells me that I will be getting into that long-haul writing again, soon and often.

I've had occasion, as you can well imagine, to talk about just this thing with sister writers. How do the children handle your "absence" — standing at the stove flipping them buckwheats but being totally elsewhere? How does your man deal with the fact that you are just not there and it's nothing personal? Atrocity tales, honey, and sad. I've known playwrights, artists, filmmakers — brothers I'm talking about — who just do not understand, or maybe pretend not to understand, that mad fit that gets hold of me and makes me prefer working all night and morning at the typewriter to playing poker or going dancing. It's a trip. But some years ago, I promised myself a period of five years to tackle this writing business in a serious manner. It's a priority item now — to master the craft, to produce, to stick to it no matter how many committee meetings get missed.

My situation isn't nearly as chary as others I know. I'm not a wife, and my daughter couldn't care less what the house looks like so long as the hamper isn't overflowing. I'm not a husband; I do not have the responsibility of trying to live up to "provider." I'm not committed to any notion of "career." Also, I'm not addicted to anything — furniture, cars, wardrobe, etc. — so there's no sense of sacrifice or foolishness about how I spend my time in non-money-making pursuits. Furthermore, I don't feel obliged to structure my life in respectably routine ways; that is to say, I do not mind being perceived as a "weirdo" or whatever. My situation is, perhaps, not very characteristic; I don't know. But to answer the question — I just flat out announce I'm working, leave me alone and get out of my face. When I "surface" again, I try to apply the poultices and patch up the holes I've left in relationships around me. That's as much as I know how to do . . . so far.

C.T.: What determines your responsibility to yourself and to your audience?

Bambara: I start with the recognition that we are at war, and that war is not simply a hot debate between the capitalist camp and the socialist camp over which economic/political/social arrangement will have hegemony in the world. It's not just the battle over turf and who has the right to utilize resources for whomsoever's benefit. The war is also being fought over the truth: what is the truth about human nature, about the human potential? My responsibility to myself, my neighbors, my family, and the human

[1] a novel by Toni Cade Bambara.

family is to try to tell the truth. That ain't easy. There are so few truth-speaking traditions in this society in which the myth of "Western civilization" has claimed the allegiance of so many. We have rarely been encouraged and equipped to appreciate the fact that the truth works, that it releases the Spirit, and that it is a joyous thing. We live in a part of the world, for example, that equates criticism with assault, that equates social responsibility with naive idealism, that defines the unrelenting pursuit of knowledge and wisdom as fanaticism.

I do not think that literature is *the* primary instrument for social transformation, but I do think it has potency. So I work to tell the truth about people's lives; I work to celebrate struggle, to applaud the tradition of struggle in our community, to bring to center stage all those characters, just ordinary folks on the block, who've been waiting in the wings, characters we thought we had to ignore because they weren't pimp-flashy or hustler-slick or because they didn't fit easily into previously acceptable modes or stock types. I want to lift up some usable truths — like the fact that the simple act of cornrowing one's hair is radical in a society that defines beauty as blonde tresses blowing in the wind; that staying centered in the best of one's own cultural tradition is hip, is sane, is perfectly fine despite all claims to universality-through-Anglo-Saxonizing and other madnesses.

It would be dishonest, though, to end my comments there. First and foremost I write for myself. Writing has been for a long time my major tool for self-instruction and self-development. I try to stay honest through pencil and paper. I run off at the mouth a lot. I've a penchant for flamboyant performance. I exaggerate to the point of hysteria. I cannot always be trusted with my mouth open. But when I sit down with the notebooks, I am absolutely serious about what I see, sense, know. I write for the same reason I keep track of my dreams, for the same reason I meditate and practice being still — to stay in touch with me and not let too much slip by me. We're about building a nation; the inner nation needs building, too. I would be writing whether there were a publishing industry or not, whether there were presses or not, whether there were markets or not.

I began writing in a serious way — though I can't recall a time when I wasn't jotting stuff down and trying to dramatize lessons learned — when I got into teaching. It was a way to keep track of myself, to monitor myself. I'm a very seductive teacher, persuasive, infectious, overwhelming, irresistible. I worked hard in the classroom to teach students to critique me constantly, to protect themselves from my nonsense; but let's face it, the teacher-student relationship we've been trained in is very colonial in nature. It's fraught with dangers. The power given teachers over students' minds, students' spirits, students' development — my God! To rise above that, to insist of myself and of them that we refashion that relationship along progressive lines demanded a great deal of courage, imagination, energy, and will. Writing was a way to "hear" myself, check myself. Writing was/is an act of discovery. I frequently discovered that I was dangerous, a menace, virtually unfit to move the students and myself into certain waters. I would have to go into the classroom and beat them up for not taking me to the wall, for succumbing to mere charm and flash, when they should have been challenging me, "kicking my ass." I will be eternally grateful to all those students at City College and Livingston/Rutgers for the caring and courageous way they helped to develop me as a teacher, a person, a writer . . . and a mother, too. Fortunately, for all concerned, my daughter, a ninety-nine-year-old wise woman who travels under the guise of a young thumb-sucking kid, knows when to walk away from me, close her ears, turn my rantings into a joke, call me on a contradiction. But even after she is grown, and even if I never teach again, I will still use writing as a way to stay on center, for I'll still be somebody's neighbor, somebody's friend, and I'll still be a member of our community under siege or in power. I'll still need to have the discipline writing affords, demands. I do not wish to be useless or dangerous, so I'll write. And too, hell, I'm a writer. I am compelled to write.

[1985]

*B*OBBIE ANN MASON *gave an interview about how she writes fiction to Lila Havens at the University of Houston in February 1984, published the following year in the literary magazine* Crazy Horse. *Mason said that she started writing because she was preoccupied with her past: "I think I'm wondering how the people I left behind turned out. I left because I felt trapped in a conventional small-town culture, so I try to imagine what that world is like for people who don't leave."*

❧41❧

Bobbie Ann Mason

A Conversation with Lila Havens

LH: What writers have influenced you?

BAM: In general I absorbed influences back in college like Hemingway and Fitzgerald and Salinger; then later on, I think I picked up a lot from the New Journalists and also Lillian Ross, a *New Yorker* writer who has written extensively for "Talk of the Town." And then there was E. B. White. He was very important to me. Most of all, I admire his clean style.

LH: In 1975, you published a book entitled *The Girl Sleuth: A Feminist Guide to the Bobbsey Twins, Nancy Drew, and Their Sisters.* This might lead one to expect an anti-masculine slant in your stories, but in fact you portray your male characters with great compassion. I am thinking naturally of Leroy, the bewildered out-of-work truck driver in "Shiloh," and Emmett, the uncle of the main character of [the novel] *In Country* who cannot bring himself to lead what others would consider a normal life after he has been through the trauma of Vietnam. If you had written "Shiloh" or *In Country* in the '70s, would your male characters have been the same, or is this compassion new?

BAM: I doubt if they would have been very different. I went through the compulsory stage of feminism, but I don't think I ever was demonstrative about it, possibly because I bypassed a lot of the typical problems women have. I had always felt I was competing in a man's world. So "sisterhood" was, as for all of us, a radical discovery. I think I internalized feminism and figured out where my experience fit into the whole thing, and then, as far as I was concerned, it was time to move on.

Right now I'm generally more interested in the cultural effects on men than I am the women characters in my stories because women are in an incredible position right now. It isn't true for every woman, and certainly the goals of equality have not been reached, but the women are on their way. I'm not worried about women. I'm interested in these *men* who are immersed in a culture where they had a certain role, and now all of a sudden these women are going off and going to school, getting strange jobs. They're walking out on the men and the men don't know what to do. I feel there's a lot of pathos in that.

LH: You've said you're interested in the culture shock one can experience because of geographical or economic isolation. What do you see as other concerns in your work?

BAM: There are certain themes that come through, like the idea of residents and transients, the title of one of my stories. Some people stay home and others are born to run. But my larger concerns are tending, I think, toward a strong curiosity about the sympathy for the lower classes. I don't mean to sound political and I have no political statement to make, but I'm constantly preoccupied with the class struggle and I'm exploring various kinds of culture shock — people moving from one class to another, people being intimidated by the class above them, people being status conscious, people being threatened by other people's ways and values — and the way those attitudes come into play with each other, especially when people do leave home or when the outside world comes prancing in via the television. My characters are anxious to get in on the prosperity this country has known, and they're very afraid of losing what they've already attained. So in a way they're very materialistic . . .

LH: Often in strange ways.

BAM: In *very* strange ways. My characters are members of the shopping mall generation. And there's a whole other, larger thing that's going on in terms of the classes, and it's reflected in many short stories being written now. John Barth calls them "blue-collar minimalist hyper-realist"! An editor in England calls it "dirty realism." I love those terms! Throughout American literature, the hero was the alienated superior sensibility, the artist, the sensitive young man. . . . I read so much of that in school that by the time I was ready to write, I was sick of reading about that guy, and I thought, "At least he could be a woman," or maybe someone who was *not* sensitive and was *not* superior. I think that's how I finally arrived at knowing who I was going to write about, and I think probably many other writers have had a similar reaction against the artist-hero so now you find all these stories about truck drivers and waitresses. I think our interest in these people reflects something bigger that is going on throughout the world.

LH: So you see this as a cultural shift of some sort?

BAM: Yeah. The masses want their share of the good life. This country is incredibly rich, but not everybody gets to have a color TV and a house with a two-car garage. The middle class and the upper class are very threatened, I think, by the whole world's demand to be in on this. And the people in charge of what is called "high culture" are especially threatened because for them it's a matter of taste as well as a matter of what's proper. I guess I find a certain amount of hypocrisy in this, wealth being distributed as it is, and so I tend to identify with the popular culture. And it's no longer embarrassing.

LH: Isn't this shift an effect, at least in part, of the increased availability of education? Now people from farm families have Ph.D.s and are writing stories and finding themselves able to embrace their pasts and admit where they came from.

BAM: Yes. Suddenly we're discovering that store clerks and cowboys also have valid lives, complicated lives, and are as sensitive as the artist-hero. A student in a class I visited made a remark about how I wrote about K-Mart clerks, and he said, "You know, I never really noticed those people. I go in there to buy something and I never really thought of them as individual human beings." Not that he was being condescending, he just hadn't taken the time to think about them.

Basically, I'm trying to portray a world of some people who are aspiring to a better life for themselves, and I think I'm trying to understand them on their own terms and not judge them.

LH: You have published, I believe, thirty stories in the past five years and now a novel, which makes you a very prolific writer. I was wondering how long it usually takes you to work through a story.

BAM: It depends. There was one year when I was really working hard and turned out about twenty stories, or an average of about one every three weeks. Not that I did them consecutively. Sometimes I'll spend weeks and weeks and then maybe put the story aside and come back to it six months later; other times I may just dash it out. I wrote "Shiloh" in exactly eleven days. I wrote "Offerings" in about an hour. That was the first draft, and then I spent about two days polishing. I consider those accidents. And I had no sense that "Shiloh" was any different or better than any other I'd written up to that point.

LH: What is the process of writing like for you? How do you work through a story?

BAM: Oh, it varies, but the best way is when I just start from the beginning and work through to the end and get the gist of the story in one draft. It doesn't always work that easily — sometimes it comes in bits and pieces — but the initial inspiration very often is a first line or detail. It's not a strong conception of a character. Sometimes it's a situation.

LH: You don't necessarily conceive of your characters first?

BAM: No, I usually just start with a physical detail or a line of dialogue or just something that triggers my imagination, that gets me going to explore a character or a situation. It's a way of finding out what I've got inside.

It amazes me, the way the creative process works. When I was studying literature, I was studying it in terms of its meaning and learning how to analyze image patterns and symbols and themes; and I had the notion that the authors must have had all that in mind from the beginning. It wasn't until I started writing that I discovered how different that could be. First of all, I had to learn how to write from scratch: no amount of studying literature prepared me for knowing how a story is coaxed out of the imagination. I knew how to analyze and read the finished product but not how to create it. So I started out, really at an elementary level, and began to discover things about plot and character and unity. It was amazing to discover something as simple as the principle of unity at the creative level. And then what was even more astounding was the discovery of how much order can come out of the unconscious. Often I would come up with elements that fit together but quite without my knowing it. It's still one of the greatest pleasures in writing, to find those things out, especially when readers discover things in the stories that I didn't know were there. I'm awed by that, because I feel like I wrote the stories so innocently! I heard about a student who wrote a paper on "Shiloh." He did his paper on the ending image of the story, a dust ruffle the same color as the sky. He wrote a term paper about this ruffle and what it meant in the story. That just blows me away! Probably he came up with a very meaningful argument about it, but I'm sure when I wrote the story, the dust ruffle just appeared spontaneously.

LH: Once you've written a story, is there someone you give it to for comments? I know your husband is an editor — does he read your stories?

BAM: No. Sometimes I get some feedback on the stories from Ted Solotaroff at Harper and Row, my book editor; and then I send them to *The New Yorker.*

LH: How did your relationship with *The New Yorker* begin?

BAM: I very boldly and arrogantly sent my second finished story to *The New Yorker.* It seems like such a silly thing to have done. It was very naive. But lo and behold, I got a response about it, and I sent another story . . .

LH: That was from Roger Angell?

BAM: Yes. I think it was just a note. The next time I sent a story, I got a letter from him, so I kept sending stories and he kept sending me encouraging comments when he sent the stories back. We developed a correspondence and he really encouraged me a great deal, and I got very excited about what I was doing and worked very hard. Usually what he told me were not bits of advice on revising but just sort of subjective responses about the central reasons he didn't think they could publish the story, and he would offer a general criticism. He might say, "The dialogue is good and the details are strong, but there's not enough feeling" — something like that. It was fairly general, but usually he would make one or two comments that would hit right at the problem with the story, and it would give me something to think about.

I was very excited about this attention from *The New Yorker.* Roger was the first person in the world who ever said to me, "You're a writer, you have talent." And I flipped out at that! That was just so marvelous. He didn't have to say very much: that was enough to get me going. By contrast, in the past, whenever I got negative responses to writing I had attempted, I would just quit. So I was really very vulnerable and hadn't a strong sense of myself, my direction.

That went on with *The New Yorker* for about a year and a half, and I sent in twenty stories before they bought one. After I had two or three stories taken by them, they gave me what they call a first-reading agreement, which means that they see all of my stories first.

LH: How did you go about getting an agent?

BAM: When "Shiloh" came out in the *The New Yorker*, it got a fair amount of attention; this was in late 1980 — and Amanda Urban, an agent at International Creative Management, read the story and liked it and called me up and asked if she could be my agent.

LH: On the basis of one story?

BAM: Yes. And I said, "Why?" (Laughter) I didn't know why I needed an agent. She said that it would be helpful when I started thinking about collecting my stories as a book. And she was right. Also, within two weeks of my initial conversation with her, several things happened: a movie studio wanted a film option on "Shiloh," and a number of publishers were writing to me. So it became apparent that an agent would be a good idea. It has turned out to be a very good relationship.

LH: What are your writing habits like?

BAM: I generally just set aside the whole day and try not to let other things interfere. I'm not very disciplined, but I have it worked out so that I *seem* to be disciplined. I do a lot of busy work — re-reading, editing; the actual writing I don't spend a lot of time on.

LH: Do you have dry spells when you feel that you can't work?

BAM: No. I think I always have that writer's block, but I wouldn't call it a dry spell. I think writer's block means inhibitions, and I'm *always* working against inhibitions of various sorts. I don't know how to describe it, but it's a matter of having access to your imagination, to your unconsciousness, and I find it very difficult to get at it. I think it's a whole lifetime full of barriers I've set up, and it's hard to move them out of the way. That lack of self-confidence that I mentioned: I think that's probably dominant. Just to have free access to your resources can be very difficult.

[1985]

A Brief History
of the Short Story

The history of storytelling extends far back to a time long before the invention of the printing press. Stories have such a long history, and their forms are so diverse, that anyone attempting to investigate their earliest development in close detail would be taking on a herculean task. For thousands of years this genre could hardly be described as an entity cohesive enough to "evolve." A brief chronological survey, however, may help readers gain a perspective on the human miracle that is the modern literary form.

In their broadest categories, stories can be intended and accepted as *factual* — examples include histories or narratives of real battles, victories, happenings, and so forth — or *fictional*, stories made up to entertain or instruct the listener. Early fictional narratives are what interest us here. The first tales we know of are those of the oral tradition, the creation myths of primitive tribal peoples who were trying to explain how things got started.

Literary scholars believe that the next important stage in the evolution of storytelling was the period of the beast fables, stories in which animals are shown acting like humans in order to teach a moral lesson. The fables of the Greek slave Aesop (620?–560? B.C.) are still well known, and the beast fable form is even used occasionally by modern writers, as in Paul Bowles's story "The Hyena."

Another very early form of the story is the religious parable, a short and pithy story with a moral twist, such as the parable of the wise and foolish virgins in the New Testament. These stories, as well as passages of narrative in the Old Testament like the description of the creation of the universe in Genesis or the story of Samson in Judges, were not intended as fiction. Early religious parables were meant as explicit didactic lessons justifying the ways of God. Nearly two thousand years later, the great Russian writer Leo Tolstoy wrote memorable religious parables like "The Three Hermits."

In the classical and postclassical literature of Greece and Rome, brief tales were often included in larger narrative collections, like the *Satyricon* of Petronius in the first century A.D. and the *Metamorphoses* of Apuleius in the second century. These stories, along with fiction from Oriental cultures, which was brought to Europe from the East by various means, became part of the reservoir of traditional material for later storytellers. An example of the torturous path taken by such works is the *Panchatantra*. Its original Sanskrit form dates back at least to the early sixth century. In a variety of translations it spread through Europe in the Middle Ages. Finally, according to the editor Frank Edgerton, it was translated by Thomas North into English in 1570 from "an Italian version of a Latin version of a Hebrew version of an Arabic version of a [lost] Pahlavi [middle Iranian] version of some [lost] Sanskrit version of the original *Panchatantra*."

In the medieval period in Europe, short narratives were most commonly written in verse, whether they were heroic episodes such as the *Battle of Maldon* or low-life comic tales of French origin called *fabliaux*. Prose was usually reserved for devotional and instructive pieces until the fourteenth century. Around that time a great variety of secular tales in both prose and verse became popular, most notably the short prose tales of the Italian writer Giovanni Boccaccio (1313–1375). His best-known book is the *Decameron*, a series of one hundred tales told by seven ladies and three gentlemen who fled the plague that devastated Florence in 1348. In the same century, the Englishman Geoffrey Chaucer (d. 1400) wrote the *Canterbury Tales*, a collection of religious and secular tales, some derived from Boccaccio. Most of Chaucer's stories were narrated in verse.

The *Canterbury Tales* include several different short fictional genres like the religious parable, the romance, and the fabliau. While Chaucer's collection exhibits remarkable stylistic polish and variety, a common theme is the unresolved relation between art and morality. The Chaucerian scholar David Benson has investigated the widely held medieval distrust of purely imaginative literature. This distrust extends far back in European culture, appearing in Plato's philosophy as well as in many other sources.

Boccaccio and Chaucer took great care to assure their readers that their stories would give both pleasure and moral instruction. The "moral behind the story" was a guarantee that the tales were more than mere entertainment. In the thirteenth century, the Christian theologian St. Thomas Aquinas cautioned against what he called "secular eloquence." Aquinas said, "He who strives principally after eloquence does not intend that men should admire what he says, but strives rather to gain their admiration for himself. Eloquence, however, is commendable when the speaker has no desire to display himself but wishes only to benefit his listeners." Imaginative stories were distrusted because they could be too entertaining. Five hundred years ago the first book ever printed was a collection of *exempla*, short prose narratives meant to serve as the basis for instruction by clergy, illustrating what an early writer called "excellent Lessons of Morality."

The medieval distrust of stories as entertainment took hundreds of years to overcome. Most of the Renaissance storytellers in Italy, England, France, and Spain are part of the Boccaccian tradition and include a structure of moral and religious values in their narratives. Through the centuries writers in different countries drew from the tales of preceding collections, so that by 1795, according to the scholar Roger Paulin, "the claim of a given story to be unusual or extraordinary, original or authentic, often did not stand up to very close scrutiny."

It wasn't until the eighteenth century, after secularization had gathered force in Europe, that fictional narratives were given the opportunity to evolve into forms we recognize as closer relations of modern stories and novels. These prose forms developed in periodicals popular with European readers from the emerging middle class, who had the education and the leisure time to enjoy them. The new periodicals printed a variety of prose — character sketches, satires, gothic tales, rogue stories, simple adventure stories, and sentimental sketches with predictable moral outcomes in which the hero or heroine is rewarded and the villain is punished. In France, Voltaire also composed his philosophical tales in the mid-eighteenth century, and his contemporaries Diderot and the Marquis de Sade wrote stories to illustrate their theories of morality and psychology. These authors used satire to convey their views of the debasement of morality in conventional fiction, and the falsification of reality in many traditional tales. The older tradition had played itself out, and a new era of storytelling was about to begin.

The periodicals, with a rapidly growing number of readers, became a market for professional writers of stories. This literary form was also shaped and given vitality by the spirit of its age, the romantic period in European literature. At that time originality and imagination were valued above all other qualities in writing. This was in contrast to the emphasis on tradition and reason that shaped the attitude of eighteenth-century, neoclassical writers. In short fiction from the early years of the new periodicals, there is also a fascination with psychology and with unusual or eccentric behavior. Horror stories and criminal stories became popular, and gradually narratives opened up, as Paulin has stated, "to take in more moral and social awareness, satire, and the realm of the fancy and romantic imagination."

But the mostly anonymous early writers for periodicals are not credited with inventing what is known today as the short story, even if their writing prepared the way for it. Most historians of this genre agree that the short story did not appear until the nineteenth century, almost a hundred years after the novel began to flourish as a literary form. Then a different kind of short fictional narrative emerged, an original prose work in which every word chosen in the structure of the plot, and every detail of description and characterization, contributes to a unified impression.

German writers were the first to experiment and develop this new form into original, imaginative narratives that resemble what we call short stories. Johann Wolfgang von Goethe (1749–1832) wrote some short prose fiction, but he composed his stories in collections or included them in his novels. His contemporary Ludwig Tieck (1773–1853), a reader of English gothic tales and the fantastic novels of Laurence Sterne (1713–1768) was more of an innovator. Tieck was a slick popular writer for magazines, and he experimented with stories he called "novelle," which blend fantasy and reality in ways that influenced his contemporaries, especially the German writers E. T. A. Hoffmann (1776–1822) and Heinrich von Kleist (1777–1811).

Kleist presented events as more logically connected than in Tieck's and Hoffmann's stories, but even Kleist's fiction plays with the notion that a tale doesn't always have to follow a rational pattern or allow for a moral explanation. Probably the most famous German writers from the early nineteenth century are the brothers Grimm. They assembled a collection of

"Childhood and Household Tales" from folk material; it was soon translated throughout the world. In our century the Danish writer Isak Dinesen revitalized some of these early Germanic forms of short fiction containing supernatural elements, as in her fairy story "The Blue Stones."

More than a hundred and fifty years ago, the writer Washington Irving (1783–1859) read these German authors and was inspired to create Americanized versions of European folktales. Irving's *Sketch Book* (1819–1820) contains "Rip Van Winkle" and "The Legend of Sleepy Hollow," two of the earliest short stories in the United States. (In 1827 Irving's contemporary Walter Scott [1771–1832] published the first modern short story in England, "The Two Drovers.") Irving's tales had an enormous influence on the next generation of writers in America. He handled fictional narrative in a relaxed, predominantly descriptive and discursive manner, saying, "I consider a story merely as a frame on which to sketch my materials."

Shortly afterward, the young writers Nathaniel Hawthorne and Edgar Allan Poe began contributing fiction to magazines. They chose similar romantic subjects, writing about colorful or extraordinary individuals living in remote times and places, but they structured their narratives differently than Irving did. They used more dramatic compression in developing their plots and revealing their characters. Most literary historians credit them as the first American writers to create a considerable number of successful short stories.

Hawthorne never explained fully how he wrote his stories, but Poe published his theories about short fiction in his book reviews. He did not insist that a short story be written any certain way. Instead, he stressed the concept that power and unity could be achieved in works of short fiction. This idea was a novelty in Poe's time, when the short story was not a highly regarded literary form. This anthology begins with the stories of Hawthorne and Poe to illustrate the development of the genre in English and includes short fiction by European writers who brought important innovations to the form and influenced authors after them.

Most critics regard Edgar Allan Poe and Nikolai Gogol as the two greatest and most influential writers of short fiction during the romantic era. Their stories, together with the moral fiction of Hawthorne, are more properly called "tales," the label the writers themselves gave to their magazine work. The tale, according to the scholar Northrop Frye's definition, is closer to the prose romance than to the novel. In the tale the author makes no attempt to delineate the characters as real people. Instead, they are stylized figures who "expand into psychological archetypes."

Herman Melville's "Bartleby, the Scrivener," on the other hand, is more of a story. Melville subtitled it "A Story of Wall Street." He was acutely aware of the fickle literary tastes of his readers, and in "Bartleby, the Scrivener," his first published story, which appeared in 1853, he consciously created a humorous surface that he hoped would have popular appeal while concealing the serious meanings. The attorney who narrates the story of Bartleby is not a psychological abstraction like Hawthorne's Goodman

Brown or Poe's Montresor. Melville gave us so many realistic details about the lawyer's life that we feel the tug of his perplexity in the face of his mysterious scrivener's stubborn will.

Bartleby is also one of the "little men" who Frank O'Connor theorized is the true subject of the short story, a character originating in a "submerged population group." O'Connor argued that Melville's scrivener, and Gogol's even earlier Russian clerk in "The Overcoat," were the progenitors of fictional offspring who would later emerge in scores of stories by important writers of short fiction, including Guy de Maupassant, Anton Chekhov, Sherwood Anderson, and James Joyce. They would also create, in O'Connor's words, "outlawed figures wandering about the fringes of society, superimposed sometimes on symbolic figures whom they caricature and echo — Christ, Socrates, Moses."

But we jump ahead of ourselves. The mid-nineteenth century was a time of great transition in literature; the earlier mode of romanticism slowly gave way to realism. If the tale is a close relation of the early prose romance, then the short story is akin to the later realist novel. Instead of being, as Frye says, "idealized by revery," in a romance, characters in a novel (and in short stories) wear recognizable social masks and reflect an everyday reality.

Gustave Flaubert's and Leo Tolstoy's fiction illustrates this realist mode. In their stories the characters are products of a highly developed society, and their fictive world is a mirror of the actual world of men and women at the time. Realist authors usually refrain from commenting at great length on their characters' psychology. Instead, their psychology is manifested in things said and done by the characters themselves. While romantic writers are interested in subjective states of awareness per se, realist writers are likely to be more concerned with the social causes and consequences of those states. They put greater emphasis on the particular physical circumstances in which they place their characters.

In America around the time of the Civil War, the popular magazine tale slowly gave way to the more realistic story. This is when local-color stories, set in particular regions (for example, New England, the Midwest, the South), emerged. Mark Twain, Sarah Orne Jewett, Kate Chopin, Mary E. Wilkins Freeman, and Hamlin Garland are a few of the important writers in this idiom.

In the 1890s Ambrose Bierce developed the macabre world of Poe's fantasy vision, writing short stories with a realistic surface that explore the workings of the protagonist's mind. Sometimes — as in "An Occurrence at Owl Creek Bridge" — Bierce ventured close to the steam-of-consciousness technique developed by later modernist writers. Bierce's fiction combines elements of romanticism, realism, and modernism. Trying to fit his stories into a neat historical category illustrates the impossibility of presenting the history of the short story as a smooth, linear evolution. The literary form developed spectacularly in the nineteenth century. As the critic William Sheidley has remarked, it was "like a package of firecrackers going off."

The realists Henry James, Edith Wharton, Stephen Crane, Willa Cather, and Jack London were America's most distinguished short story authors at the end of the century. But European influences were also strong. In 1893, in his introduction to Hamlin Garland's story collection *Main-Travelled Roads*, William Dean Howells wrote that magazine fiction was so popular in America that finally "the hour of the short story in book form has struck." To account for what he called the "material prosperity" of short fiction, Howells credited — among other factors — "the vogue that Maupassant's tales in the original or in versions have enjoyed."

Two Europeans, the Frenchman Guy de Maupassant and the Russian Anton Chekhov, were the most influential writers of short fiction at the end of the nineteenth century. They brought remarkable innovations to the content and form of the short story. Both wrote realistic fiction, and both are considered modern writers because of the content of their stories. They insisted on focusing on the particular here-and-now quality of ordinary human existence rather than proselytizing for any particular religious, philosophical, or political system of belief.

As Kate Chopin realized, Maupassant was a writer "who had escaped from tradition and authority, who had entered into himself and looked out upon life through his own being and with his own eyes; and who, in a direct and simple way, told us what he saw." This is reminiscent of Chekhov's statement about his own difficult process of squeezing "the slave out of himself" in order to become a decent human being and a writer.

In Maupassant's short stories plots are tightly organized and usually conclude with a decisive action. Details of the characters' appearance and behavior are sharply etched into the narrative, as if their physicality were especially important to the skeptical materialist Maupassant. In Chekhov's stories, on the other hand, plots include less decisive action. They are subordinate to sympathetic dramatization of the characters' psychology and mood. The writer Sean O'Faolain has labeled Maupassant "the relentless realist" and Chekhov "the persistent moralist" to distinguish further between them.

Experimental writers of the next generation were primarily influenced by Chekhov, developing his less sharply detailed, more subtly impressionistic atmosphere in their work. These were the modernist writers in the early years of the twentieth century, who challenged the conventions of the dominant literature and culture. In Europe this group included Joseph Conrad, Virginia Woolf, James Joyce, Franz Kafka, D. H. Lawrence, Katherine Mansfield, and Isaac Babel. Influenced profoundly by both Chekhov and Maupassant were the American modernists, including Sherwood Anderson, Katherine Anne Porter, William Faulkner, Ernest Hemingway, and Richard Wright.

The modernist writers explored the concept of an interiorized plot. As Mansfield said, "If we are not to look for [external] facts and events . . . we must be sure of finding these central points of significance transferred to the endeavors and emotions of the characters portrayed." Joyce's *Dubliners,* fifteen stories begun in 1904 and published in 1916, was one of the land-marks of this period.

Rather than constructing his stories around a dramatic climax in the action, Joyce heightened the climactic moment of self-realization that he found in Chekhov's stories. He coined a special literary term, *epiphany* (a "showing forth"), for this inner revelation. Such often painful flashes of recognition illuminate Joyce's fluid narratives, for instance, the boy's realization at the end of "Araby": "Gazing up into the darkness I saw myself as a creature driven and derided by vanity; and my eyes burned with anguish and anger."

The critic Ian Reid has pointed out that the significant revelation in modernist stories may sometimes be only for perceptive readers, not for the fictional character. Gregor Samsa's consciousness is but a dimly flickering spark at the conclusion of Kafka's "The Metamorphosis," and he expires still trapped inside his suffocating transformation. Else in Mansfield's "The Doll's House" sees the little lamp at the end of the story. But she may not recognize any meaning beyond her simple pleasure at getting to see this object in her wealthy classmate's dollhouse, whereas the sympathetic reader may be able to see in Else's personal triumph a larger truth about the society Mansfield portrayed. Similarly, Hemingway's protagonist, Harry, in "The Snows of Kilimanjaro" dies before the next-to-last section of the story, dramatizing his epiphany flying to the top of the mountain. He spiritually experiences the event (or so we imagine), whereas the reader is free to understand the section as a final integration — or mocking — of Harry's previously fragmented, unhappy existence.

Since the end of the modernist period, authors have explored a variety of patterns of short narrative fiction. Most writers of popular magazine fiction favor old-fashioned closed plots, dramatizing a single, unified incident with a decisive conclusion. But we now enjoy a great diversity of periodicals — mass-circulation specialty magazines, little magazines, highbrow magazines, and regional magazines. Authors of "quality fiction" for these periodicals, like Ann Beattie and Donald Barthelme in *The New Yorker*, for example, or Alice Walker and Louise Erdrich in *Ms. Magazine*, often favor short stories dramatizing less conclusive action, which does not rise to any momentous peak. These writers invite close thematic scrutiny. Their stories seem to lack both the certain meaning of earlier realist stories and the consistent subjective point of view of the nineteenth-century romantic tales. Thus, they force us to recognize that traditional meanings and attitudes are in human beings, not in the world.

Literary critics distinguish between two types of stories being written today: "traditional stories," descending from Poe and Maupassant, which are plotted and closed (like the work of Eudora Welty, Aleksandr Solzhenitsyn, and Doris Lessing, among many others in this anthology), and "modern stories," descending from Chekhov and Joyce, which are less plotted and more open (like the work of Grace Paley, John Barth, and Jamaica Kincaid, among others). The same writer may use either traditional or modern storytelling in different works, depending on the material. The short story is so flexible that it may well be ideally suited, as Nadine Gordimer has said, to "convey the quality of human life, where contact is more like the flash of fireflies, in and out, now here, now there, in darkness. Short-story writers see by the light of the flash; theirs is the art of the only thing one can be sure of — the present moment."

Fiction by contemporary writers is so close to us that it is better examined on a thematic or aesthetic spectrum, as the critic Susan Lohafer has suggested in her book *Coming to Terms with the Short Story*. She even poked fun at the conventional historical survey of the short story in introductory literature courses at American colleges and universities:

> As the result of undergraduate survey courses, there are many people who can tell you how the form developed; how it emerged from the sleepy hollows of Washington Irving; took on the moral and arabesque shapes of Hawthorne and Poe; how it stretched socially and regionally to James and Jewett; how it spoke the vernacular in Calaveras County, turned naturalistic in an open boat, reached deep into the psyche in Winesburg, in Babylon, and, of course, In Our Time; how it branched out southern and suburban and ethnic and far. . . .

In one great sweep, Lohafer first surveyed the contribution of our earliest writers. Then she alluded to particular stories by Mark Twain ("Calaveras County"), Stephen Crane ("open boat"), Sherwood Anderson ("Winesburg"), F. Scott Fitzgerald ("Babylon"), and Ernest Hemingway (his earliest story collection, *In Our Time*). She went on to refer to the stories of William Faulkner, Eudora Welty, and Flannery O'Connor ("southern"); John Cheever, John Updike, and Joyce Carol Oates ("suburban"); Zora Neale Hurston, Langston Hughes, Richard Wright, Ralph Ellison, and Bernard Malamud ("ethnic"); and John Barth, Donald Barthelme, Woody Allen, Ann Beattie, and other practitioners of "far" stories that some readers find too fanciful or freaky. However facetious Lohafer's summary, her conclusion is helpful: Once readers have a solid context for the evolution of the short story form, the guideline of its historical development may be less important than the quality of the individual voices of contemporary authors.

Today the short story is alive and well in the hands of writers in every country of the world. The flood of new magazine fiction often carries with it stories of real literary distinction. The significant differences among contemporary short stories are not historical or geographical, but are in the attitudes toward life which govern an author's sense of reality, and the literary techniques of expression that these attitudes call forth.

As John Cheever realized, "so long as we are possessed by experience that is distinguished by its intensity and its episodic nature, we will have the short story in our literature." The history of the short story is open-ended, as befits a mature and vigorous literary form. The ideal reader is also open to new writing, ready to be enchanted by the magic of each writer's imagination, revealed in his or her engagement with the short story.

For reference and further reading, see Walter Allen, *The Short Story in English* (1981); Peter Brooks, *Reading for the Plot* (1984); Frank Edgerton, *The Panchatantra* (1965); Norman Friedman, *Form and Meaning in Fiction* (1975); Susan Lohafer, *Coming to Terms with the Short Story* (1985); Charles E. May (ed.), *Short Story Theories* (1976); Frank O'Connor, *The Lonely Voice* (1963); Sean O'Faolain, *The Short Story* (1951); Roger Paulin, *The Brief Compass: The Nineteenth-Century German Novelle* (1985); Ian Reid, *The Short Story* (1977); and Danforth Ross, *The American Short Story* (1961).

THE ELEMENTS
OF FICTION

Plot

SINCE THE SHORT STORY is defined as a prose narrative usually involving one connected episode or a sequence of related events, the element of plot is basic to this literary form. *Plot* is the sequence of events in a story and their relation to one another. Usually they are related by causation, and their meaning lies in this relation.

Many readers who enjoy short stories have pondered the question, Why is a short story short? There seem to be various reasons, but two are fundamental. Often the material that the writer takes for his or her story is in itself restricted, consisting of one incident or a closely related sequence of events. Or, if the material is broader, the story may be short because the writer has compressed it.

Literary critics have made an important distinction between the object of representation in a narrative (the events or action of the story that the writer is referring to) and the written story itself (the way the author uses words to present the action). The critic Norman Friedman has suggested that "a short story may be short not because its action is inherently small, but rather because the author has chosen — in working with an episode or plot — to omit certain of its parts. In other words, an action may be large in size and still be short in the telling because not all of it is there."

A short story can cover the events of a brief episode, like Grace Paley's "A Conversation with My Father," or encompass action that takes years to conclude, like Isaac Bashevis Singer's "A Crown of Feathers." Usually stories that are static, where little change occurs, are relatively short (as Paley's), while more dynamic actions, covering a longer time and involving the characters' changes from one state to another, are longer (as Singer's). Yet the narrative possibilities are endless. The writer may omit or condense complex episodes to intensify their dramatic effect (Isaac Babel's "My First Goose") or expand a single incident to make a relatively long story (John Barth's "Lost in the Funhouse").

Regardless, the short story usually has an end orientation — the outcome of the action or the conclusion of the plot — inherent in its opening paragraphs, what Poe called the "single effect." The storyteller must stay within the limits of this "single effect" established early on in the narrative. The novelist may conclude a single episode long before the end of a novel and then pick up the thread of another narrative, or interpret an event from another angle in a different character's point of view, chaining episode to episode and character to character so that each casts light on the others. But a story stops earlier. Its narrative dramatizes a single effect complete unto itself, even if a writer may conceive of it in the larger framework of a story cycle, like Sherwood Anderson's *Winesburg, Ohio,* James Joyce's *Dubliners,* or Louise Erdrich's *Love Medicine.*

The plot of a short story usually involves a conflict or struggle between opposing forces. The discerning reader can see it develop in a pattern during the course of the narration, whether its events proceed chronologically or are rearranged with flashbacks and dream sequences, as in Ernest Hemingway's "Snows of Kilimanjaro." Usually authors arrange their plots to dramatize a strategy of exposition. Whatever the strategy, a plot always includes the basic pattern of a beginning, a middle, and an end, even if it lacks a momentous peak in the action.

In most stories the beginning sets up the problem or conflict; the middle is where the author introduces various complications that prolong suspense and make the struggle more meaningful; and the end resolves the conflict to a greater or lesser degree. In successful stories the writer shapes these stages into a complex structure that impresses the reader with its balance and proportion.

The first part of the plot, called the *exposition,* introduces characters, scene, time, and situation. The particular pattern varies from story to story, of course, and from author to author. Hawthorne began "Young Goodman Brown," for example, with only a few short paragraphs of exposition, the leave-taking between Goodman Brown and his young wife, Faith. Herman Melville devoted pages to exposition in his much longer story "Bartleby, the Scrivener," describing the lawyer, his two eccentric copyists, and his office boy before introducing the title character.

The second part of the plot is called the *rising action,* the dramatization of events that complicate the situation and gradually intensify the conflict. In "Young Goodman Brown" the rising action is twofold. Goodman Brown's walk through the forest with the devil, when he meets Goody Cloyse and then hides to spy on the minister and the deacon, is the beginning of the rising action. It leads to the scene when Goodman Brown looks to heaven, hears a young woman's lamentations, and sees a pink ribbon flutter through the air and catch on the branch of a tree. After this, he shouts "My Faith is gone," and the reader is told that he has become "the chief horror of the scene."

Then the narration proceeds to a further development of the rising action, which takes the reader to the *climax* of the plot or *turning point* of the story, its emotional high point. Goodman Brown speeds through the forest and joins the devil's congregation inside the ring of fire formed by the four burning pines. He stands beside his wife and prepares to participate in an unholy communion, the scene "beneath the canopy of fire" that Hawthorne illuminated with brilliant descriptive power. There Goodman Brown summons the courage to beseech his wife to "resist the wicked one"; this is the climax of the plot. The pace of the narration breaks off dramatically at this point. In a single sentence Hawthorne then shows us Goodman Brown alone "amid calm night and solitude."

Now begins the fourth stage of the narration, called the *falling action,* where the problem or conflict presented in the earlier sections proceeds toward resolution. This last section of the plot, and the *conclusion* which follows in the final paragraph, is comparatively brief in this story, balancing the short exposition at the beginning. Nevertheless, in these last parts of the story, Hawthorne was careful to bring the sequence of related events to an end.

A story's ending often contains an element of surprise, just as the other stages of narration engage the reader's curiosity, heighten suspense, and prolong the expectation of a satisfying conclusion. There is little surprise in finding Goodman Brown "a distrustful, if not a desperate man" after his fearful night in the forest, but Hawthorne gave the story a final unexpected twist in the last sentence describing the funeral. Goodman Brown's survivors "carved no hopeful verse upon his tombstone, for his dying hour was gloom." Hawthorne's continuation of the narrative to a point in time beyond his main character's death places the individual conflict dramatized in the story in a larger moral context and reveals to the reader a deeper perception of the situation, a more subtle reflection of what life is like.

Plot can work in several ways. It can be an outgrowth of a character's personality or will, as in Young Goodman Brown's insistence on his meeting with the devil or in Montresor's insane scheme of revenge against Fortunato in Edgar Allan Poe's "The Cask of Amontillado." It can be propelled by an apparent accident of fate, as when two mustachioed thieves appear out of nowhere on a winter night in Nikolai Gogol's "The Overcoat" and steal Akaky Akakievich's new overcoat right off his back. It can be controlled by the setting, as in Stephen Crane's "The Open Boat" or Jack London's "To Build a Fire." Most often the plots of stories can be understood as the interaction of character with circumstances: for example, in Gustave Flaubert's "A Simple Heart," F. Scott Fitzgerald's "Babylon Revisited," or Grace Paley's "A Conversation with My Father."

Plot does not emerge just through the description of events in the story. It can also be carried forward in dialogue, as when Hawthorne introduced the characters, the time, and the situation through the conversation between Goodman Brown and his wife in the beginning of the story. Readers also respond to *foreshadowing* and *dramatic irony* as the plot moves along, anticipating a turn of events which may or may not go along with our expectations. In the opening of Flannery O'Connor's "A Good Man Is Hard to Find," we can visualize the grandmother beginning the car trip dressed in navy blue trimmed with white organdy and lace and a sachet of cloth violets so that "in case of an accident, anyone seeing her dead on the highway would know at once that she was a lady." Later in the story we learn that although she survives the car accident, being dressed so neatly doesn't save her from being killed by the Misfit after she pleads with him, "I know you wouldn't shoot a lady!"

Regardless of the author's method of narration, the goal is the same: The writer of short stories must *show* the reader what is important through the dramatic action of the plot and the other elements of the story, and not just explicitly *tell* the reader what to think. Invention, not preaching, enchants the reader. Hawthorne dramatized his own final judgment of Goodman Brown by inventing the detail of his tombstone, not by concluding with an explicit, solemn pronouncement about the necessity of keeping faith in human nature alive. The illusion of reality must always be sustained by the plot. Until the end of the story, events should continue to unfold with the easy forward movement of an apparently endless silk handkerchief drawn from a skillful magician's coat sleeve.

Character

The action of the plot is performed by the *characters* in the story, the people who make something happen or produce an effect. (And not always just people. Various authors have experimented with other animals, such as cows, cats, and bugs, and with trees, chairs, and shoes as characters — even as narrators — with varying degrees of success. But when we say *character*, we usually mean a person.) With a plot we do not just ask, What next? We also ask, Why?

The answer is usually found in the characters, who are plausible if we can understand their actions. The characters themselves don't always have a conscious awareness of why they act the way they do, or — if they have an awareness — it isn't always accurate. Yet there always *are* reasons, and the reader may discover them before the characters do. The reader instinctively wants to connect the events of a story by more than their simple chronological sequence. Assuming a relation between the events and the characters makes the story seem coherent.

How are the characters in a short story to be understood? Any discussion of character tends to drift sooner or later into a value judgment, since our principles of definition and evaluation for fictional characters are based on the ones we use for real people, controversial and confused as they may be for most of us. The important distinction to remember is that we are reading about *fictional* characters in a short story, not real ones.

We are on firmer ground in literary discussions when we analyze the writer's method of characterization as well as the character's personality. We know that Montresor is a murderer in Poe's "The Cask of Amontillado," but pigeonholing his character does not bring us very close to understanding the miracle of horror that Poe accomplished in the story. We can approach it more readily by relishing the language Poe used in dialogue and description to show us the specific mental processes of his main character as he proceeds with his plan to avenge his honor.

In all successful fiction characters come alive as individuals. They must materialize on the page through the accumulation of details about their appearance, actions, and responses, as seen, heard, and felt physical realities. Hawthorne told us little about the physical appearance of Goodman Brown except that he is young and newly married. We do not even know his first name — "Goodman" was used by the Puritans as a title of respect for those below the rank of gentleman. We know more about his wife — her name is Faith, she is pretty and affectionate, and she wears pink ribbons on her cap.

The lack of physical details about him makes Goodman Brown less than flesh and blood to most readers. He remains an abstraction in a moral allegory. Thus Hawthorne was able to reveal more clearly the figure of a man on trial for his belief in good and evil. As we are caught up in reading the story, Goodman Brown's actions as a fictional "person" provoke our curiosity and his responses arouse our alarm. If he continues to interest us after we have finished reading the story, it is because we are fascinated, as Hawthorne was, with the moral dilemma that the narrative dramatizes.

Characters are sometimes called *round* or *flat*. For characters in a story to emerge as round, the reader must feel the play and pull of their actions and responses to situations. If the reader sees the characters as capable of alternatives, then the characters become more real, or round. Characters can also be called *dynamic* or *static*. Ivan Ilych in Leo Tolstoy's story "The Death of Ivan Ilych" is both round (he has a multifaceted personality as presented in the story) and dynamic (he changes). His wife is both flat and static, or so we think from her brief appearances.

Each writer of short fiction puts his or her own emphasis on character. An attentive reader can perceive that Anton Chekhov and Jorge Luis Borges, for example, did not develop characters in the same way. Chekhov, a great nineteenth-century realist, placed highest emphasis on character, believing that it determines our fate. Borges, a contemporary teller of philosophical tales, believes that our subjective nature makes it impossible for us to understand the essential riddle of human action, so he makes plot more important than character.

Different fictional worlds make different demands on the reader, who realizes that the importance given to characterization by various storytellers is an indication of their vision of life. Regardless of the emphasis on character, what is most important is the truth of the fictional character, flat or round, dynamic or static. Avoiding *sentimentality* (emotional overindulgence) and *stereotyping* (generalized, oversimplified judgment) in the creation of characters, the writer must be able to suggest enough complexity to engage the reader's emotions or the story will not be a success.

Setting

Setting is the place and time of the story. To set the scene, the writer attempts to create in the reader's visual imagination the illusion of a solid world in which the story takes place. With a few deft strokes in the opening paragraph of "Young Goodman Brown," Hawthorne sketched a street in Salem village during Puritan times, but the mass of details about the physical landscape are not given to us until Goodman Brown enters the forest. Then Hawthorne painted a gloomy growth of "innumerable trunks and . . . thick boughs overhead" that serves as the main scene for his character's troubled journey. Sometimes the setting is merely the backdrop for the action, as while Goodman Brown talks with Faith in the first scene; at other times it is central to the action, as it becomes when Goodman Brown enters the forest.

When the writer locates the narrative in a physical setting, the reader is moved along step by step toward acceptance of the fiction. The *external* reality of the setting is always an appearance, an illusion, a mirage of language as insubstantial as a shimmering oasis in a desert or a Puritan wilderness evoked in 1835 on the page of a young author's manuscript. Yet this invented setting is essential if the reader is to be given the opportunity to glimpse a truth about *internal* life from the characters and the plot. When Goodman Brown enters the dark, tangled world of the seventeenth-century forest surrounding Salem village, the reader may perceive that he really enters the dreary, dark world of his own mind, which has brought him to exchange the companionship of his young wife for the dubious attractions of the devil.

The setting of a story furnishes the location for its world of feeling, the different emotional associations awakened in the reader's mind by a Puritan forest in a Hawthorne story or by the stifling depotism of the Russian council office suggested in Gogol's "The Overcoat." A sense of place is essential if readers are to begin to engage themselves in the fictional characters' situations. Place helps make the characters seem real, but, to be most effective, the setting must also have a dramatic use. It must be shown, or at least felt, to affect character or plot. The gloom of the Puritan forest increases the doubt in Goodman Brown's mind that he has taken the right path. The miserly wages paid to clerks in the council office make it a struggle and a sacrifice for Akaky Akakievich to afford a decent, warm overcoat.

In the most basic sense, place is where writers have their roots. It provides the experience of life out of which they write. Hawthorne was rooted in the Puritan setting of many of his stories through his ancestral connections in Salem. Gogol knew at first hand about the arrogance of bureaucratic officials and the corruption of legal process in Russia. Selecting, combining, superimposing, and altering the details of the outside world in the creation of a story, the writer must exert his or her talent to make the reader see only the fictional world that emerges on the printed page, under the illusion that while the story unfolds, it is the real world itself.

Point of View

As a specific literary term, *point of view* refers to the way the story is told. In giving an account of the events in a story, the author must decide whether to employ a *first-person narrator*, using the pronoun "I", or a *third-person narrator*, using the pronouns "he," "she," and "they." (The second-person narrator, "you," is rarely used, since a forced identification of the reader with the fictional world is usually difficult to maintain successfully.) If the chosen point of view is not right for the complete dramatic ordering of the subject, the narrative will not reveal all its possibilities to the writer, and the pattern of the story will be incomplete. If Hawthorne had chosen to tell his story from the point of view of Goodman Brown, for example, using the first-person narrator to describe how an evening in the forest with the devil ruined his life forever, it is likely that the story would have struck the reader as the gloomy ruminations of a religious fanatic. It would also necessarily have ended with Goodman Brown's death, and its larger meaning would not have emerged so explicitly.

The most frequently used ways of telling stories fall into two major categories:

First-person narrator (narrator a participant in the story)
    a. A major character
    b. A minor character

Third-person narrator (narrator a nonparticipant in the story)
    a. Omniscient — seeing into all characters
    b. Limited Omniscient — seeing into one or, infrequently, two characters.

FIRST-PERSON NARRATOR

When the narrator is one of the characters in the story, he or she can be either a major or a minor character in the action. Poe's "The Cask of Amontillado" presents the narrator as the central character. On the other hand, both Guy de Maupassant's "Miss Harriet" and Joseph Conrad's "Heart of Darkness" are frame stories that begin with first-person narration by a character so minor that he exists mostly to introduce the person who will proceed to narrate the story.

The first-person narrator can move freely within the fictional world, and he or she can approach other fictional characters as closely as one human being can approach another, but the narrator has no way of understanding these characters except by observation of what they say and do. By making his narrator a major character in the action, Poe intensified the impact of Montresor's insane behavior, showing us his apparent imperviousness to the horror of what he is doing.

The authority of a first-person narrator is limited, though it is immediate and compelling as far as it goes. He or she is an eyewitness. The first-person narrator can also summarize less important events or back off from the immediate scene and meditate on its significance, since he or she is usually telling a story that happened in the past. But his or her meditations, like Montresor's, are not always trustworthy. The biased report of the first-person narrator must have a dramatic significance in the story, since there is often a discrepancy between the way he or she sees characters and events and the reader's sense of what really happened. At the end of "The Cask of Amontillado," Montresor says that his heart "grew sick — on account of the dampness of the catacombs." The reader may perceive the truth differently, and feel that Montresor has at least subconsciously realized the horror of what he has just done to Fortunato.

THIRD-PERSON NARRATOR

The third-person narrator is not a participant in the story. There are two general kinds of third-person narration. The *omniscient* point of view is most clearly apparent in fairy tales beginning "Once upon a time," when the teller knows everything there is to know about all the characters, both inside and out — what they think and feel as well as what they do. In the hands of a master like Hawthorne, a feeling for the complexity of human life emerges through the controlling authority of the omniscient narrator. This is achieved by a continual shifting of focus from the close view to a larger perspective. When this type of narration is used by a writer who is also a genius at the realistic rendering of experience, like Tolstoy in "The Death of Ivan Ilych," the powerful combination of the author's great imaginative ability and moral genius invests the various characters and scenes with such reality that we accept them without question.

Limited omniscient narration is usually confined to revealing the thoughts of one character. This method was first developed in fiction by Flaubert, who exchanged the distancing of "once upon a time" (with its implied moral view) for an interior, more subjective view of characters and events. Flaubert's story "A Simple Heart" is an example of limited omniscient narration. Its narrator also sticks to *impartial* (not judgmental) *omniscience*; he tells the story without really evaluating or commenting on the actions, which speak for themselves.

Henry James formulated another theory about limited omniscient narration. He referred to certain characters in his stories as the *central intelligence*. Stories told by this method of narration are not always about a single central character. They do, however, involve a character, placed at the center of the story's action, through whose "intelligence" the author registers and evaluates everything that happens, including what happens to and within that character. In this kind of story, like James Joyce's "The Dead," this character's psyche is the stage for the drama. Having established this single evaluating intelligence, the writer may range over the whole cast of characters and dramatize their views of the action. These will, however, always be perceived through or measured against the thoughts and feelings of the central intelligence, who may not understand what is going on at the time, but will finally perceive the truth. In "The Dead" the central character, Gabriel Conroy, sees himself as a very different man at the end of the story from the fellow he fancied himself at the beginning. The actual drama of the story is not the events described, but rather Gabriel's growth in moral awareness.

The stories of Stephen Crane are another variant of the limited omniscient point of view. The narration may at any given moment in a Crane story reveal a different character's perceptions and feelings. In "The Open Boat" Crane rendered the sensations of the various participants in the shipwreck, constantly changing point of view to borrow the eyes, ears, and tactile senses of all four men in the boat. If the war correspondent has the last word, it is because the author found him the best person to say what the pattern of the story required at that point.

Narration can be classified into further subcategories — for example, stream-of-consciousness first- or third-person narrator, and the effaced third-person narrator — but the different ways of telling stories available to writers are always more flexible than rigid categories imply. Franz Kafka, who used Gregor Samsa as his central intelligence through most of "The Metamorphosis," continued the story well beyond Gregor's death. Awareness of the pattern of narration helps the reader become sensitive to the construct of language that is the story. The way the story is written is an essential part of what it is saying. Adherence to the conventions of narration helps authors achieve their intended effects as they impress the reality of the story upon the reader's imagination.

Style

Style is the language the author uses in narration. It is made up of various elements, including *tone*, the way the writer uses words to convey unstated attitudes toward the subject. The dry restraint in Hawthorne's comment about Goodman Brown's "excellent resolve" as he turns the corner by the meetinghouse and enters the forest is an example the way tone contributes to the dignified, lofty prose style. A subtle *irony*, drawing attention to the differences between what is said and what Hawthorne really thought, helped him keep an emotional distance from his characters suitable to the level of abstraction he created in the narrative. Hawthorne's tone is completely unlike that of a writer like Sherwood Anderson, who used everyday speech and more understated irony to set up a feeling of intimacy with the reader. This suggests a sympathy for the characters in his realistic stories about frustrated, small-town lives, like "Death in the Woods."

The way authors use language to tell a story conveys the quality of their mind to the reader. Through the magic of their literary style, we seem to hear their tone of voice as well as understand their attitude toward the story they are telling — humorous or serious, excited or compassionate. Style conveys part of the story's meaning. For example, D. H. Lawrence's fairy-tale tone at the beginning of "The Rocking Horse Winner" prepares the reader for the strange, otherworldly events as the story progresses. (Be careful in judging the tone of stories that have been translated from foreign languages. It is nearly impossible for a translation to capture the exact tone of the original language, even if it renders most other details of the story accurately.)

Another aspect of style is the use of *symbols*. A symbol is usually defined as something that stands for something else. The words that create symbols may be figurative or literal — usually they are both. But the symbol is the *thing described*, not the words used to describe it. Consider the stiff dolls, too big for their house, in Katherine Mansfield's "The Doll House." They are symbolic of the society Mansfield was portraying in the story, but they are quite literally stiff and too big as well.

After closing the book and thinking about a story, the reader will often recall most vividly the author's use of symbols — the way language can suggest deeper meaning by bringing together different images to elicit emotional responses. Charlotte Perkins Gilman uses "The Yellow Wallpaper" in this way. Sometimes the entire story will seem to exist in the reader's imagination more on an abstract, symbolic level than on a realistic level. Shirley Jackson's "The Lottery" is such a story. Most readers take Kafka's "The Metamorphosis" both literally and symbolically; they are not precisely sure what the monstrous insect symbolizes.

Symbols are not always understood the same way by different readers. Faith's pink ribbons in "Young Goodman Brown," an apparently realistic detail in an otherwise clearly allegorical story (the devil has a walking stick that turns into a snake before Goodman Brown's eyes), may symbolize her youth and innocence to one reader, and her femininity and coquettishness to another. Faith is such an abstract character that either interpretation is possible. We can never know for sure whether she was actually at the witches' coven in the forest or whether her presence there was part of her husband's hallucination while she spent the night quietly in her own snug bed in her house in Salem.

Regardless of how the symbol of Faith's ribbons is interpreted, they are experienced as a dominant image in the somber landscape of Hawthorne's fiction. Some readers may even see them as an example of Hawthorne's exploration of the ambiguous nature of signs, similar to the ambiguous nature of Young Goodman Brown's night in the forest. Symbols are more eloquent as specific images — visual ideas — than any paraphrase. This is the source of their appeal to storytellers.

Theme

Theme is a generalization about the meaning of a story. While the plot of a story can be summarized by saying what happened in the action (a young Puritan husband loses his faith in God and humankind after attending a witches' coven), the theme is an even more general statement of the meaning of the story (losing faith destroys a person's life). It is often difficult for readers to find words to describe what a story means. Sometimes, after many futile minutes of trying to "boil down" a story to a one-sentence essence, the words that come irresistibly to mind are the ones written in another context by the American poet Archibald MacLeish: "A poem should not mean/But be."

What makes the statement of a theme so difficult is that the theme must be true to any and all of the specific details in the narrative. This is the test to apply to a theme, once it has been stated. Finding a summary of the plot or a statement of the theme does not mean that you understand a story and so can skip reading it, however. The theme or meaning of any good story is inseparable from the language of the complete narrative. In fact, the way the writer fleshes out a dramatic structure to embody the theme is, in the final sense, the most important achievement of the story, infinitely more significant than the bare theme standing alone in its unconvincing nakedness on a sheet of notebook paper. A reader who does not know this should try to recreate a story from memory after writing a one-sentence summary of its theme.

Some readers tend to look for moral judgments about life when they think about the meaning of a story, but literature does not demand that they do. It is possible that an interesting, well-constructed story will also contain a meaning with moral implications, as Hawthorne's "Young Goodman Brown" does. It is equally possible that an interesting, well-constructed story will be without a moral, existing as a complete and satisfactory aesthetic pattern in itself, like Poe's "The Cask of Amontillado." Ultimately, all great literature makes a statement beyond morality. The innate impulse to tell a story does not necessarily originate in a moral sense or a conscience. It probably arises from the mysterious and inexplicable human urge to communicate and to create, to provide a personal expression of what life is like.

The storyteller says, "Let me tell you how it is," and our interest as readers is always in what the story can show us about human experience. Theme is an abstract formulation of that truth, the author's vision of the meaning of life. Chekhov's theme in "The Lady with the Pet Dog," for instance, is better rendered not as a moral injunction (do not commit adultery), but as a statement of a deep truth (love is a serious business). That same theme emerges from Maupassant's "Miss Harriet" and scores of other stories. We can understand the limitations of theme as a substitute for the work of art, but our attempt to state the theme is not necessarily foolish or misleading. Often it can help us understand the story better.

Most writers do not like to tell what their stories are "about." Even when they do, as Flannery O'Connor did in her explanation of the theme of her story "A Good Man Is Hard to Find," or Isaac Bashevis Singer did in his commentary on "The Crown of Feathers," some readers agree intellectually but not emotionally with the writer's interpretation. O'Connor said that she understood her story might be read in different ways by different people, but she could only have written it with the one meaning she had in mind.

Theme comes last in a discussion of the elements of fiction because all the other elements must be accounted for in determining it. The structure and theme of a story are fused like the body and soul of a reader; their interaction creates a living pattern. While the various actions of the plot must strike the reader as realistic and inevitable, the complete truth that it reveals is in essence indefinable and untranslatable outside the story. Trying to arrive at the theme of a story teaches us that no statement of it can be final, except that magical entity, the story itself. As Leo Tolstoy once told a friend:

The most important thing in a work of art is that it should have a kind of focus, i.e., there should be some place where all the rays meet or from which they issue. *And this focus must not be able to be completely explained in words.* This indeed is one of the significant facts about a true work of art — that its content in its entirety can be expressed only by itself.

WRITING
ABOUT SHORT STORIES

IN WRITING an essay about literature, you clarify your relationship to what you have read. This relationship goes beyond a basic emotional response to the story, whether you enjoyed it or not. You write to reveal what Ernest Hemingway referred to as "the measure of what you brought to the reading." As soon as you ask the smallest question about the meaning or structure of a story and try to answer it, you are beginning a critical inquiry that involves your intellect as well as your emotions. This activity is called the interpretation of the text. What makes it valuable is that it reveals to you and to others how you respond to the stories after they have entertained, instructed, and perhaps enchanted you. Now it is your turn to explain their effect on you, and to analyze how they did it. Once you have asked yourself what there is about a story that gives you pleasure — the style, the form, the meaning — you have begun discovering "the measure of what you brought to the reading." The next stage is to communicate your ideas to someone else. Turning yourself from a reader into a writer takes time, but if you understand the various steps involved, the process becomes much easier.

Writing the Paper

An essay about literature can take various forms and be various lengths, depending on the nature of the assignment. But whether you are writing an essay of only a few paragraphs or a research paper of several thousand words, the basic requirement is always the same. You must keep in mind that an essay on short stories (or on any subject, for that matter) is a type of expository writing, and *expository* means "serving to clarify, set forth, or explain in detail" an idea about the subject. Writing about literature helps you clarify your ideas. If you want your essay to communicate these ideas clearly to a reader, you must understand that it always requires two things to be effective: a strong thesis sentence or central idea about your topic, and an adequate development of your thesis sentence. How you organize your paper will depend on the way you choose to develop your central idea. The three principal ways of organizing essays about short stories — explication, analysis, and comparison and contrast — will be taken up after a discussion of ways to find a thesis sentence.

GETTING IDEAS FOR YOUR TOPIC AND THESIS SENTENCE

Most effective short papers (about 500 words) usually treat one aspect of the story: its theme, characterization, setting, point of view, or literary style. These are some of the possible *topics* for your paper, the general subject you are going to write about. Usually your first response to a story is a jumble of impressions that do not separate themselves into neat categories of *topics* and *thesis sentences*. You must sort through these impressions to select a topic on which to concentrate in order to get ideas for your thesis sentence.

Before you can start your essay, you should feel that you understand the story thoroughly as a whole. Read it again to remind yourself of the passages that strike you with particular force. Underline the words and sentences you consider significant — or, even better, make a list of what seems important while you are reading the story. These can be outstanding descriptions of the characters or settings, passages of meaningful dialogue, details showing the way the author builds toward the story's climax, or hints that foreshadow the conclusion. To stimulate ideas about topics, you may want to jot down answers to the following questions about the elements of the story as you reread it.

Plot. Does the plot depend on chance or coincidence, or does it grow out of the personalities of the characters? Are any later incidents foreshadowed early in the story? Are the episodes presented in chronological order? If not, why not? Does the climax indicate a change in a situation or a change in a character? How dramatic is this change? Or is there no change at all?

Character. Are the characters believable? Are they stereotypes? Do they suggest real people, or abstract qualities? Is there one protagonist or are there several? Does the story have an antagonist? How does the author tell you about the main character — through description of physical appearance, actions, thoughts, and emotions, or through contrast with a minor character? Does the main character change in the course of the story? How? Why?

Setting. How does the setting influence the plot and the characters? Does it help to suggest or develop the meaning of the story?

Point of View. How does the point of view shape the theme? Would the story change if told from a different viewpoint? In first-person narration, can you trust the narrator?

Style. Is the author's prose style primarily literal or figurative? Can you find examples of irony in dialogue or narrative passages? If dialect or colloquial speech is used, what is its effect? Does the author call attention to the way he or she uses words, or is the literary style inconspicuous?

Theme. Does the story's title help explain its meaning? Can you find a suggestion of the theme in specific passages of dialogue or description? Are certain symbols or repetitions of images important in revealing the author's intent in the story?

Now put the text aside and look over your notes. Can you see any pattern in them? You may find that you have been most impressed by the way the author developed characterizations, for example. Then you will have a possible topic for your paper. Certainly if you have a choice, you should pick whatever appeals to you most in the story and concentrate on it.

If you still cannot come up with a topic, ask for help in your next class. Perhaps your instructor will suggest something: "Why don't you discuss the way Hawthorne used irony in 'Young Goodman Brown'?" Often the class will be assigned one topic to write about. Some students think assigned topics make writing more difficult; others find they make it easier to begin to write.

A topic, however, is not the same as a thesis sentence. A topic is a general subject (for example, the character of Goodman Brown). A thesis sentence, on the other hand, makes a statement about a topic; it is usually the result of thinking about the topic and narrowing it down to focus on some relationship of the topic to the story as a whole. A good thesis sentence has two important functions. First, it suggests a way for you to write about the story. Second, it makes clear to your reader the approach you have taken toward the topic. To *write* critically about short fiction, you must *think* critically about it. You start with an interpretation of the entire story and then show how some particular aspect of it contributes to what you think is its overall pattern and meaning.

Narrowing Ideas to a Thesis

A thesis sentence states the central idea you will develop in your paper. It should be easy for the reader of your essay to recognize — even if it's sometimes hard for you to formulate. A thesis sentence is a complete sentence that points the way you will take to clarify your interpretation of the story. In Hawthorne's story, for example, you might decide to write about the character of Goodman Brown (*topic*). You interpret the story to be a warning about the danger of losing religious faith (*theme*). If you think about the way your topic relates to the theme, your analysis might lead you to the idea that Goodman Brown lost his religious faith through the sin of pride. This thought process narrows the topic into a thesis, which you can state as the sentence "The story 'Young Goodman Brown' shows how a man can lose his religious faith through the sin of pride."

The test of a good thesis sentence is whether your *subject* ("The story 'Young Goodman Brown'") is followed by a clearly focused *predicate* ("shows how a man can lose his religious faith through the sin of pride"). What you want is a statement of an idea that you can then develop in your essay.

Finding a thesis sentence is often the biggest stumbling block for writers of expository prose. How do you know if your idea is worth developing in a paper? Generally speaking, a thesis will work if it expresses a specific idea about the story that you want to develop. If you are not interested to begin with, or do not like the story you are writing about, you probably will not write effectively. You almost always write better about a story you have enjoyed reading. Certainly you will feel more sympathetic to the intent of the author if you are not hostile to the assignment in the first place. Remember also that as a literary critic you must always keep an open mind when interpreting a story. Your ideas about it are as valid as anyone else's, so long as you can support them with examples from the text. There are many possible ways to read a story, although the author may have felt the original impulse to write it because of a particular idea or feeling about the subject.

Sometimes the thesis sentence occurs to you while you are thinking about the story; then you can jot it down as a fully formed idea right away. Other times you may find that you are unable to formulate any definite idea about the story until you start to write. No single procedure works for all writers at all times. You might begin writing with a trial thesis in mind, putting down rough ideas or a string of sentences as you think about the general topic you have chosen. Or you might decide to go back to the notes you took while reading the story and try to organize them into a simple outline about your topic, looking for connections between things that might suggest a direction to take in a trial essay and then hoping a thesis sentence will emerge while you free-associate with paper and pencil in hand. You might also get an idea for a thesis sentence by talking about the story with a friend. Whatever way you start, do not settle for anything quick and easy. "Hawthorne's use of irony in 'Young Goodman Brown' is interesting" is much too general to be helpful to you in writing a good essay. Keep thinking or scribbling away at your first rough draft until you find an idea that gives you a specific direction to take in your paper. "Hawthorne's use of irony in 'Young Goodman Brown' suggests his judgment of the Puritan moral code" is a thesis sentence that has a clearly focused predicate. It states a definite relationship of the topic to the meaning of the thesis you want to explore. Then you know you are on your way to writing a good essay.

WRITING AND REVISING

If you begin the first paragraph of your essay with a strong thesis sentence, your ideas will usually flow in writing and revising the paper. You will often discover further possibilities for refining your thesis while using it to interpret the text. That is one reason you should allow plenty of time to complete a writing assignment. It's an unusual first draft in which the central idea is developed coherently and fully enough to be turned in as a finished paper. Revision often stimulates further thought, sharpening and strengthening the development of your thesis. In the process of writing, you will come to understand the story more fully as your thesis takes you closer to its meaning.

Try not to become discouraged about writing by visualizing some distant final product — a well-organized essay, neatly typed on clean, white paper, shimmering on the page in what looks like pristine perfection. Remember that it took time to get that way. Your essay originated in half-formed, often confused thoughts that had to be coaxed to arrange themselves into coherent paragraphs linked by what only much later appear to be inevitable transitions. More often than not, the 500 words you might think are a perfect essay when you turn in your final paper will be the end result — if you took enough time in writing — of winnowing down 1,000 or more words from your rough drafts. You must amplify and clarify your thesis, editing your sentences and paragraphs so that each one relates coherently to your central idea. Then your essay will express your insights about the story so clearly that they can be understood as you intended.

At the beginning, it is best to forget about the end result and give all your thought and effort to the *process* of writing. If you find it useful, make an outline and try to follow it, but this practice varies with different writers. Some find it valuable to organize their notes about the story into a formal outline, while others prefer to make a rough sketch of the steps they plan to follow in developing their central idea. You may find that you do not want to use an outline at all, although in general it can help to keep you from straying too far from the point you are trying to make. Remember, too, that there is no fixed rule about the number of drafts or the amount of revision necessary before you have a finished essay. Every essay changes from the first rough draft through various revisions; an essay is often gone over several times in the days or weeks between getting the assignment and bringing the finished paper to class. In the various stages of writing, different aspects of the central idea often reveal themselves and are integrated into the paper, depending on your degree of concentration and involvement in the assignment. Even if you scrap sentences or whole paragraphs that do not relate to your final discussion, you have not wasted your time, because your early efforts to put your thoughts down on paper bring you to the point where you have better insights.

You will probably have to rewrite your opening paragraph many times to tailor your thesis sentence to the final shape your ideas have taken. Some writers just sketch in the first paragraph and go back to polish it when the rest of the essay is finished. Often you will want to amplify and refine your thesis sentence, dividing it into several sentences in your introductory remarks. Then it becomes a *thesis statement*, rather than a single sentence.

DEVELOPING THE THESIS

While it is possible to write many different kinds of papers about short fiction, most college instructors assign students the task of interpreting the text. The literary terms used in the headnotes on each writer in this anthology and defined in the glossary (pages 1403–1410) can help you find a vocabulary to express your ideas. You cannot write intelligently about any subject without using the special terminology of that subject, whether it is English, economics, psychology, or engineering. At the same time, dropping the terms in your paper the way a person might drop names at a party will not impress your readers. Understand what the terms mean so you can use them to think and write critically about the elements of a story when you begin to interpret the text in the light of your central idea.

You will usually develop your thesis statement in the body of your essay by following one or more of the three common methods of writing about literature: *explication, analysis,* and *comparison and contrast.*

Types of Literary Papers

EXPLICATION

The word *explication* is derived from a Latin word that means "unfolding." When you explicate a text, you unfold its meaning in an essay, proceeding carefully to interpret it passage by passage, sometimes even line by line or word by word. A good explication concentrates on details, quoting the text of the story to bring them to the attention of a reader who might have missed them approaching the story from a different perspective. An entire story is usually too long to explicate completely — the explication would be far longer than the story — so you will usually select a short passage or section that relates to the idea you are developing. Often this short section is a key scene, a crucial conversation, or an opening or closing paragraph where the implications of the text can be revealed to develop the central idea of your essay.

Although explication does not concern itself with the author's life or times, his or her historical period may determine the definitions of words or the meaning of concepts that appear in the passage being interpreted. If the story is a century or more old, the meanings of some words may have changed. The explication is supposed to reveal what the author might have meant when he or she wrote the story, not assuming conscious intentions, but aware of possibilities. For older stories, you will have to do a little research if the passage chosen for explication contains words whose meanings have changed. The *Oxford English Dictionary,* available in the reference section of your college library, will give you the meaning of a word in a particular era. The philosophical, religious, scientific, or political beliefs of the author, or of the author's age, may also enter into your interpretation of the text. The main emphasis in explication, however, is on the meaning of the words — both *denotative* and *connotative* — and the way those words affect the reader.

The following student paper is an example of how explication is used to develop a central idea in an essay.

The Devil's Tricks in "Young Goodman Brown"

Use quotes for
titles of stories.

Hawthorne's "Young Goodman Brown" is the story of a man whose
life is ruined because of the sin of pride, which makes him lose his
faith in God. Goodman Brown agrees to meet the devil in the forest,
and his faith is destroyed when he sees a pink ribbon fluttering to
earth. He believes this ribbon could only have fallen from his
beloved wife's cap. It is this scene in the story that reveals his
weakness. His pride makes him trust the evidence of his own senses
more than his faith in God.

Start with general
thesis sentence.

Narrow the thesis
to show specific
direction your
paper will take.

Hawthorne begins the scene in which Goodman Brown loses his
faith by leaving him without other characters around him for the
first time in the story. Alone with his soul, he has only himself
to depend on. The devil has abandoned him in the middle of the
dark woods with the maple staff that became a witch's broomstick
when it was borrowed by Goody Cloyse earlier in the evening. Thus
the reader has already seen the devil's tricks.

Transition:
Repeat key words
of thesis.

Suggest
background of
scene before you
begin explication.

Other black magic is in store for Goodman Brown. Gazing upward
"into the deep arch of the firmament," he lifts his hands to pray.
The word "firmament," with its biblical connotations, suggests that
Goodman Brown has set his mind on God. He has scarcely begun his
prayer, however, when his concentration is broken: "a cloud, though
no wind was stirring, hurried across the zenith and hid the brightening stars." The devil's magic show has begun, although Goodman Brown
is not aware of it.

Start to quote
from the story.
Do not set off
short quote.

He accepts the appearance of the "black mass" of the cloud overhead and forgets his prayer, listening instead to a "confused and
doubtful sound of voices. . . . The next moment, so indistinct were
the sounds, he doubted whether he had heard aught. . . ." The
adjectives and verbs I have underlined in Hawthorne's description
suggest the lack of substance in what Goodman Brown hears and sees;
he is, after all, standing under a dark cloud. The next moment he
believes he hears the voice "of a young woman, uttering lamentations,
yet with an uncertain sorrow, and entreating for some favor, which,
perhaps, it would grieve her to obtain; and all the unseen multitude,
both saints and sinners, seemed to encourage her onward."

Main section of
the explication:
Text quoted in
the order it
appears.

OK to use I;
italics are not in
original.

At this point Goodman Brown believes not only that he hears the
voice of a young woman, but also that the woman is his wife, Faith.
By now he is completely deluded. When he shouts his wife's name he
is mocked by the ghosts he senses around him: "The echoes of the
forest mocked him, crying, 'Faith! Faith!' as if bewildered wretches
were seeking her all through the wilderness." Here Hawthorne has

Good active
verbs.

built his description out of thin air. The echoes of Goodman Brown's voice sound as if bewildered, which is certainly ironic, since he himself is truly bewildered here.

Paragraph concludes with a strong idea about Hawthorne's use of irony in the scene.

Goodman Brown's temptation leads to his fall in the next paragraph, when "the dark cloud swept away, leaving the clear and silent sky above Goodman Brown. But something fluttered lightly down through the air and caught on the branch of a tree. The young man seized it, and beheld a pink ribbon." Hawthorne's language has changed, becoming simple and stark. It suggests the physicality of what it describes. Goodman Brown might have doubted the evidence of his eyes and ears if he stopped to reflect on what he had been shown in the "clear and silent sky" above his head, but before he could reflect, the devil gave him what he took to be something tangible to hold onto, something that looks like a pink ribbon.

Good insight into change in language.

Thoughtful analysis of character's motivation.

On the evidence of what he sees as a ribbon, Goodman Brown jumps to the conclusion that Faith has joined in the worship of the devil. He surrenders his trust in God forever. He becomes a victim of his own pride, believing in the evidence of his own senses more than in God. As a Puritan, Goodman Brown believes in the devil as much as he believes in God. Hawthorne might be suggesting that this belief contributed to his downfall. The story shows that it is but a short step from believing in the devil to being taken in by him.

End explication; start conclusion, tying back to thesis.

Conclusion goes one step further, to a wider implication of the thesis (logically connected).

Whether you accept the student's interpretation of the scene with the pink ribbon or not, it is a good example of the use of explication to show a way to read the text that develops the central idea of an essay. The thesis statement is clearly presented in the opening paragraph, so the reader knows what the essay will be about. At first the student approached the explication with the idea that Goodman Brown's essential weakness was his pride in trusting his senses more than his faith in God. He felt from the start that the entire scene with the ribbon was a trick played on the protagonist. Rereading the story, he found evidence in Hawthorne's words to support this interpretation. Then, in writing the essay, he developed this thesis a step further, concluding the paper with two sentences about the "short step from believing in the devil to being taken in by him." This is an example of how the writing process itself can clarify and develop ideas. Just be sure the ideas are closely related, so your reader can follow you. Do not get sidetracked or introduce a new topic.

Quotation of passages from the story is always more effective than a simple summary of events. Giving a plot summary is a common error of inexperienced essay writers. Most stories are so short that the reader remembers them without a summary. Some instructors assign plot summaries as writing exercises, but they should not be confused with interpretive essays. An essay is organized according to logic, not simply the sequence of the plot.

Give evidence that develops your thesis statement logically by quoting from the text. Explication — at its simplest, a quotation followed by your interpretation of the words — should develop an *idea* about the story, which is the reason you were asked to write your interpretation in the first place.

ANALYSIS

An *analysis* of a story is the result of the process of separating it into its parts in order to study the whole. Analysis is commonly applied in thinking about almost any complex subject. When you are asked to analyze a story, you must break it down into various parts and then usually select a single aspect for close study. If you are writing a short essay, try to keep the topic small enough to handle in a few paragraphs. Often what you are analyzing is one of the elements of fiction, an aspect of style, characterization, setting, or symbolism, for example.

While explication deals with a specific section of the text, analysis can range further, discussing details throughout the narrative that are related to your thesis. It is not possible to analyze every word of an entire story, any more than you would attempt to explicate an entire work. You may begin with a general idea, or arrive at one by thinking about some smaller detail in the story that catches your attention.

Perhaps you begin by noticing the path through the forest as you read "Young Goodman Brown." When you stop to think about it later, you realize that Hawthorne's various descriptions of this path contribute to the pattern of the story. You sense a connection of the path with the effect of "blackness" you feel building up in the narrative. This single detail of the setting can suggest a central idea that you might want to investigate. You could write, for example, about the path the protagonist takes on his walk through the forest and analyze the way its use in the different sections of the narrative develops what Melville called Hawthorne's "power of blackness."

Regardless of where you start to think analytically — with the whole or with one of its parts — you will usually begin to write an essay that is developed by analysis by moving from a general thesis statement to the particular part of the story being analyzed. Here is an example of a student essay that analyzes "Young Goodman Brown" by following Hawthorne's references to the path through the forest.

```
                    The Path toward Evil

    The path's purpose in "Young Goodman Brown" is to show that "evil
is the nature of mankind," which is the dominent theme of Hawthorne's
story.  It is a very black theme, as Herman Melville realized in his
1850 review of Hawthorne's Mosses from an Old Manse.  Satan has been
with the Puritans since they came to America.  The "dreary . . . narrow"
path Goodman Brown follows through the gloomy forest is proof that
```

Thesis sentence, supported by evidence from supplementary reading.

human beings have frequently walked with the devil in the new land.
Goodman Brown's journey on the path makes him realize there are two
kinds of evil: social and personal. He meets social evil first, and is
confused by it. Then he meets the "blackness" that is the evil within
himself, and he is totally destroyed.

Analysis narrows thesis and points to direction of paper's development.

When he begins to walk on the path with the devil, Goodman Brown
is too innocent to understand what he hears. He does not realize that
the religious intolerance of the early Puritan settlers is wrong. So
his companion, the devil, enlightens him further, telling him about
present-day corruption in the community. The church deacons have drunk
the communion wine, and the lawyers "are firm supporters of my interest." Now Goodman Brown is horrified because he understands the
meaning of the devil's remarks. He takes the first step along the
path from innocence to disillusionment when he recognizes hypocrisy in
the respected village elders.

Analysis is coherent — organized from beginning of story to end.

Quote from story to illustrate idea.

He proceeds a step further when he sees his own catechism teacher,
the deacon, and the minister on the forest path, too. He does not
understand what they are doing there. He asks himself, "Whither, then,
could these holy men be journeying so deep into the heathen wilderness?" While Goodman Brown now recognizes social evil, he does not
understand it. He must go further along the path to discover his own
evil nature.

Good transition: One step leads to another.

Quote evidence for assertion.

End of first part (social evil).

Goodman Brown finds the answer to his question in the story's
climax. The path takes him and the "holy men" to the same destination.
After he has come to believe that his wife is about to become one of
the devil's accomplices, he runs desperately down the path, which
"grew wilder and more faintly traced, and vanished at length, leaving
him in the heart of the dark wilderness, still rushing onward with
the instinct that guides mortal man to evil." Although the trail is
a path toward evil, it is, paradoxically, his last connection with the
familiar Puritan life that has sustained him. When it stops, he is
lost.

Begin second part (personal evil).

Good comment on the quote — relates it to central idea.

The path terminates in the forest clearing, with its altar dedi-
cated to the worship of Satan. Here he learns "to behold the whole
earth one stain of guilt, one mighty blood spot." There are no paths
out of the wilderness now for Goodman Brown. The whole earth is bathed
in blood, with no firm ground upon which to fix a path that will lead
him safely home. Overwhelmed by his visions in the forest, he is a
lost soul. He has realized his own evil nature.

Evidence to support the analysis of the personal evil in Goodman Brown.

As Hawthorne knew, the Puritan settlers of Salem felt the forest
was evil. They had to make paths in order to live in it. They would

have died of exposure if left alone in the woods, and they needed
paths to other nearby settlements. To journey alone in the forest
was, as Goodman Brown learned, to leave the clearly defined, if
hypocritical, moral path of the established religious community and
so to invite damnation. Hawthorne dramatized his dark theme of man's
essentially evil nature by showing Goodman Brown's fate. He leaves
the apparently straight and narrow path of the religious settlement
for the twisting, crooked path of the forest. It is a dark journey
of his soul to meet "the deep mystery" of original sin.

*Begin conclusion:
Historical
background
relates to
particular details
of the story.*

*Restatement of
thesis.*

Here the thesis sentence opens the essay, and the analysis follows from it. The student separated the story into various parts, analyzing the way the path figured in it at each stage of narration. You will notice that explication also plays a role in this essay. Even when analysis is your chosen method of developing your central idea, you should quote examples from the story to support your main points. Each time you use a quotation, comment on it to integrate it smoothly into your discussion.

COMPARISON AND CONTRAST

If you were to write about two of the Hawthorne stories in this anthology, or to develop an idea about any two stories, you would probably use comparison and contrast. When using the technique of comparison, you place the two stories side by side and comment on their similarities. In contrasting two stories, you point out their differences. Most of the time you will use both methods, since no two stories are exactly the same. It is always more meaningful to compare and contrast two stories that have something in common than two that are unrelated. As you work on your essay you will find that if there are no important similarities in the stories, your discussion will be as strained and pointless as an attempt to link closely any two dissimilar objects, whether mismatched stories or apples and oranges.

You can also compare and contrast two or more elements within a single story. For example, in Poe's "The Cask of Amontillado," you could discuss the character of Montresor as he sees himself and as he is viewed by the reader, or the differences between the two characters, Fortunato and Montresor. If your topic calls for you to use the method of comparison and contrast to elucidate your central idea, it is usually smoother to mingle your treatment of the two stories or elements as you go along than to write the first half of your paper about one and the second half about the other. The result of such a fifty-fifty split is rarely a unified essay; rather, it tends to give the impression of two separate commentaries flimsily linked together.

Here is an example of a paper whose thesis is developed by the method of comparison and contrast.

The Single Effect in

Hawthorne's "Young Goodman Brown"

and Poe's "The Cask of Amontillado"

In addition to writing short fiction, Edgar Allan Poe published literary criticism, in which he explained his own standards for prose tales. Poe stated that the primary goal in creating works in this literary genre should be the development of a "certain single effect." According to Poe, an author invents such incidents in the story as will establish this "preconceived effect." Poe introduced this theory in one of his reviews of a collection of Nathaniel Hawthorne's tales. The theory was conceived by Poe and based on the work of Hawthorne; so the stories of both men emphasize the creation of such a "single effect."

General background information on topic.

Summary of most important facts about topic.

Topic narrowed to thesis sentence.

Hawthorne's "Young Goodman Brown" and Poe's "The Cask of Amontillado" show each author's use of the method of "single effect." Poe's story examines the psychological processes in a madman's plot for revenge, and Hawthorne's story describes a man's fall from innocence, but both tales are constructed similarly. The action of both stories features a single character. Both stories are unified by a central theme. Every word, phrase, and image used by the author moves the theme closer to complete development. Neither story is realistic--that is, the events described are not plausible as real-life experiences. When Goodman Brown walks with a flesh-and-blood devil, for example, it is immediately clear that the story is a fantasy, because flesh-and-blood devils did not exist in Puritan Salem. A similar world of fantasy operates in "The Cask of Amontillado." The ease with which the narrator is able to lead Fortunato to his death is not true to life as we know it.

Important similarities.

Single protagonist.
Central theme.

Not realistic.

Specific examples.

Both stories feature a single character, and both emphasize a unity of single effect in developing their themes, but there are some fundamental differences between the stories. The first is created by the nature of the two literary forms the authors use. Hawthorne was writing a moral allegory. Every aspect of the story symbolizes some-thing else. Goodman Brown's wife, for example, is the embodiment of morality and simple faith; even her name, "Faith," contributes to this symbolic meaning. The story would have a different effect if she were named "Gertrude." Poe was writing a psychological fantasy. Fortunato is shown dressed in a cap similar to one that would be worn by a court jester. By calling attention to this outfit, the narrator, Montresor, adds to the degradation of Fortunato, which is part of the aim of his plan for revenge. Poe's fantasy is based on human emotions, while Hawthorne's allegory is based on intellect.

Begin analyzing differences.

Hawthorne's form.

Good example.

Contrast with Poe's form.

Summarize differences.

There is another major difference in the style of the two stories. Poe said that the first sentence of any tale should bring out the effect on which the rest depends. Although Poe set up the rules, Hawthorne did not keep to them. The opening sentence of "Young Goodman Brown" is in no hurry: "Young Goodman Brown came forth at sunset into the street at Salem village; but put his head back, after crossing the threshold, to exchange a parting kiss with his young wife." Goodman Brown is going on a journey, but the nature of the journey—which is central to the theme—is not clear. The concise opening of Poe's tale, however, reveals the theme: "The thousand injuries of Fortunato I had borne as I best could; but when he ventured upon insult, I vowed revenge." This sentence leaves no doubt in the reader's mind about the meaning of the story. The narrator declares that revenge is foremost in his mind, and the action that follows develops the idea of a character obsessed by the desire for revenge.

Another feature of Poe's theory related to another difference in the stories.

Quote to give evidence of difference.

Contrast with Hawthorne.

Both Poe and Hawthorne were artists deeply interested in creating works of fiction. Despite their differences of form and literary style, both created unified stories based on a "single effect," as shown in the two classic tales "Young Goodman Brown" and "The Cask of Amontillado."

Concluding summary clear, but a little brief.

In this essay the student shaped the first paragraph to conclude with the central idea, serving as an introduction to the comparison and contrast of the two stories. The stories' similarities were discussed in the next paragraph, and their differences analyzed in the rest of the paper. Throughout, elements of both stories were compared and contrasted side by side, sometimes with general analytic comments, at other times with explication and interpretation of the text. The technique of comparison and contrast is also a way to analyze stories. Specific quotations from the texts always help the reader get a clearer idea of the general points you are making in your analysis.

WRITING ABOUT THE CONTEXT OF THE STORIES

In addition to developing an idea about short fiction by explication, analysis, or comparison and contrast — all methods primarily involving a close reading of the text — there are other ways to write about short stories. The *context* of short fiction is important as well as the text, as the headnotes to each author's work in this anthology have stressed. The context of literature is usually defined as the biographical and historical background of the work. Literature does not exist in a vacuum. Created by a human being at some particular time in history, it is intended to speak to other human beings about ideas that have human relevance. Any critical method that clarifies the meaning and the pattern of a short story is valuable, and often literary critics use more than one method in their approach to a text.

A paper on the context of a story is also an expository essay based on the development of a central idea or thesis statement. Usually this kind of critical essay develops the thesis of the paper by suggesting the connection of *cause and effect*. That is to say, you maintain that the story has characteristics that originate from causes or sources in the author's background — personal life, historical period, or literary influences. For example, you can use Kate Chopin's statement on her discovery of Maupassant's stories (on page 1238) to show something about her own method of writing short fiction. To establish this connection between the life and work of a writer, you could also analyze or explicate a Chopin story, or compare one of her stories with one of Maupassant's. The amount of time you spend on the context or the text of the story will depend on the emphasis you wish to make in your paper. You have already read two student essays that briefly mention the context of the stories, referring in one case to Melville's recognition of the power of blackness in Hawthorne's short fiction, and in the other to Poe's theory of the single effect (pages 1387 and 1390).

You have probably written papers about literature in a biographical context. A favorite high school term paper project is to assign the student an author to write about, requiring library research into his or her life or historical period. If you wrote this kind of a paper, you may have organized your material chronologically, tracing the life of your author and briefly describing his or her most important literary works, often with no clearly defined thesis in mind. In writing an essay based on a unified central idea, on the other hand, you must ask yourself how knowing the facts of an author's life can help you understand that author's story. You should never assume a connection between a writer's life and the literary work. A story can reflect the life of the man or woman who wrote it, but there are often disparities between the work of fiction and the realities of the life that are as important as the connections you can draw between them. If you plan to give a biographical analysis of Melville's "Bartleby, the Scrivener," for example, showing how it illustrates Melville's own decision to stop earning his living as a writer, you must remember that he wrote the story in 1853, several years before he decided to give up writing fiction for a popular audience. In 1853, Bartleby's "I would prefer not to" was not yet Melville's conscious choice. This particular biographical reading of the story will not take you very far in your interpretation of its psychological, sociological, or philosophical complexities.

Remember that D. H. Lawrence advised us to trust the tale, not the teller. A biographical approach to literature requires at least as much care as textual criticism of the story, care in discovering and presenting the facts of an author's life and in using a sensitive interpretation of them to show relevant connections between a writer and a story. Writers often employ their own experience as the basis for their fiction, as Fitzgerald did in "Babylon Revisited" and Hemingway in "The Snows of Kilimanjaro." Your task as a critic is to show how an awareness of Fitzgerald's experiences in Paris or Hemingway's safari in Africa helps you to understand the stories.

You will usually be proceeding on firmer ground when you combine biographical facts with a discussion of an author's thematic or aesthetic intentions in writing fiction, and then relate this material to specific stories. Here again, be cautious. Statements by writers about how and why they created short stories are not necessarily the same as what a given story may show. Use your judgment carefully. Poe wrote model stories based on his theory of the "single effect," but Anton Chekhov did not always follow his own advice about how to write fiction. In "The Lady with the Pet Dog" (page 336) he wrote beautifully about the physical setting of Yalta, instead of restricting himself to the barest description, as he advised another writer to do in his letters (page 1242).

The contexts supplied by the writers themselves in the commentaries on the short story form and on particular stories included in this anthology are meant to stimulate ideas for your essays. They give the historical and biographical backgrounds of some of the stories. These excerpts can furnish a perspective from which you may view the individual stories, as did the students who used the quotations of Melville and Poe in two of the sample essays here. Or you can write about the commentaries as a subject in themselves, part of the wider context of short story literature. You can report on the entire books they came from (Frank O'Connor's study of the short story form, for example, or Eudora Welty's *The Eye of the Story*), if they are available in your college library.

OTHER PERSPECTIVES

Material from other classes can also be used in papers about short stories. If you major in history or psychology, for example, you can investigate the way stories are sometimes read to give valuable historical or psychological information about the world they describe. You are not limited to writing about remote times when considering essays that take this approach. Joyce Carol Oates's story "Where Are You Going, Where Have You Been" is about modern teenage life. A paper about it could investigate the connection between Oates's fantasy and psychological theories about adolescence in contemporary America. Characters in literature are often used in psychological and sociological textbooks to illustrate pathological symptoms or complexes. Sociology textbooks, for example, cite Oates's fictional characters as representing current tendencies toward *anomie*, a condition in which normative standards of conduct have weakened or disappeared. It is possible in writing about literature to illustrate philosophical, historical, sociological, or psychological material you are familiar with through your work in other college courses.

Finally, you can argue a particular ideological point of view in writing about literature. You can read a story, for example, from a feminist, Marxist, or Freudian point of view (though not usually from all three in the same paper). A reader committed to a particular ideology may feel that literature contributes insights into conditioned cultural patterns of thought, whether they are consciously or unconsciously held by the writer. Needless to say, you must take no less care in using this critical approach than you would in reading the text closely as an aesthetic statement in itself. At times the background of the author can suggest an ideological approach: Jack London was a Socialist, Flannery O'Connor was a Catholic, Tillie Olsen is a feminist, and so forth. At other times an ideology held by the student but not necessarily by the author can lead to a fresh reading of a story. Proceed with great care, realizing that you might become insensitive to nuances of meaning other than those you are predisposed to find in a doctrinaire interpretation of the text. At the same time, an ideological approach can illuminate aspects of a story that are valid and relevant for contemporary readers. A feminist interpretation of "Young Goodman Brown," for example, must not take the story literally, since Hawthorne wrote it as a moral allegory; but a feminist could use the story to argue provocatively about implied sexual stereotyping in Hawthorne's characterization of women.

Woman as Victim in "Young Goodman Brown"

In these feminist times, Hawthorne can be accused of portraying his female characters not as powerful individuals but rather as innocent victims. In "Young Goodman Brown," the women characters are clearly powerless to prevent the eventual destruction of the protagonist, Goodman Brown.

Introduction to thesis statement.

While Hawthorne never intended any of the characters in his moral allegory to be read realistically (their names clearly indicate that they function on an abstract, symbolic level of meaning in the story), his attitude toward women as weak and pitiful creatures is apparent in every scene in which they appear. In the exposition of the story, Goodman Brown is kissing his Faith good-bye. It is no coincidence that he then begins his journey to the forest, where he loses his faith in humankind. Faith is described as sweet and pretty. The pinkness of her cap ribbons blatantly advertises her youth and innocence. When she pleads with her husband to remain home with her, he speaks to her as if she were a small child and bids her say her bedtime prayers. Then, to add insult to injury, Hawthorne describes her as "peeping" (not looking) after him with a dependent, "melancholy air," as if she were incapable of spending a night alone.

Narrow thesis.

Begin analysis.

This marriage is plainly not one of equals. Goodman Brown seems more
like a father than like a newlywed husband in this scene. "Poor
little Faith!" he thinks, the diminutive "little" emphasizing his
attitude that a wife is someone to be looked after, not listened to.

Even when "sweet" Faith is surrounded by the unholy coven later
in the story, she is not portrayed as being evil. She utters lamentations "with an uncertain sorrow." Has this married woman no mind
of her own? Doesn't she, like her husband, have to agree to come
to this meeting on her own? Instead, she is portrayed as an innocent
victim, which makes sense on an allegorical level, but hardly does
credit to women in general.

Repetition of central idea.

Finally, at the end of the story, when Goodman Brown is busy
living out his life in gloomy thought, Faith's happy nature has
absolutely no power to combat his cynicism. How could she be happy
to live the rest of her life with such a man? Hawthorne never
explained how Faith reacted to her husband's changed outlook after
his night in the forest. Are we to believe that she merely accepted
his change, docile as ever?

More evidence.

Analysis of minor characters.

Two other women appear in the story--Goody Cloyse and Goodman
Brown's mother--but neither is portrayed as powerful or worthy of
more than brief consideration. Goody Cloyse was shown to be so frail
that she has to enlist the help of a male (the devil) to get to the
meeting. Goodman Brown's mother, who "threw out her hand to warn him
back" at the witches' coven, has no more power over him than poor
little Faith. These three women nourish the brief portion of this
earthly life that Goodman Brown enjoyed, but are unable to save his
blind masculine soul in the end. Taking the longer view, who was the
true victim--the women in the story or Goodman Brown?

Conclusion.

As this student essay shows, arguments based on independent judgments about literature are acceptable as long as they are supported by evidence from the text of the story. Contemporary feminist criticism can produce insights into a Hawthorne text. Writers do not intend their readers to
worship literature like priests at an altar, never questioning it. As Vladimir
Nabokov once advised, the ideal reader should keep a psychological distance from the story. Try to express your own ideas *through* the text. You
misread stories if you think of them as absolute, perfect, final statements far
removed from the commonplaces of life. Through their aesthetic patterns,
stories show us what life is like. What they are ultimately saying, in their
affirmation of life and human creativity, is — in the words of Henry
James — "Live! Live!"

Some Common Problems in Writing about Stories

Interpret, don't summarize. Summarizing the plot in an essay is not the same as giving insights into a story's pattern and meaning. Occasionally you can summarize the plot in a sentence if you are making a transition from one part of your paper to another, but keep in mind that the reader of your paper is usually your teacher, who has already read the story and will get the impression that you do not know much about what you are doing if you ramble on about the plot.

Write about how you read the story. If you find yourself summarizing the story in more than a couple of sentences, it is probably because you did not organize your essay around a strong thesis. Your impressions and ideas are the measure of your encounter with literature. Writing about stories encourages your clarification of these ideas. Be sure to state your central idea in a sentence in your paper. It does not matter where it appears, although if you include it in your opening paragraph it will help you keep to the point in your discussion.

Avoid long personal anecdotes. Writing on the basis of your personal experience can result in a fine memoir, but such an essay is usually not about the literature you were asked to discuss. You may want to introduce an analysis of D. H. Lawrence's "The Rocking Horse Winner" with a short anecdote about a relevant experience you had as a child with a rocking horse, but make sure your anecdote goes on for only a few sentences before you connect it explicitly with your central idea about Lawrence's story.

Use the text to check your interpretation. Opinions about literature can be wrong. Do not insist on ideas that will not fit the details of the story. You may stumble on a central idea for your paper with an intuitive leap or a hunch about the story's meaning, but be sure the specific details of the story support your interpretation. The student who had an intuition that Goodman Brown was being tricked by the devil in the scene with the pink ribbon went back to Hawthorne's words for evidence to support his theory (see page 1385). You may decide that Hawthorne's story is a heavily veiled nineteenth-century treatment of a wife's infidelity and her husband's resulting nervous breakdown, but can you prove it by quoting from the text? "Whatever I discover in the story is right for me," you may say, but that will not take you very far when writing a paper for an English class. Stories are tough, tangible constructions of language, not shifting tea leaves in the bottom of an empty cup into which you can project whatever meaning you like.

Make good use of quotations. You must quote from the story to give evidence for your interpretation. Usually a sentence should introduce and follow each quotation, linking it to the idea being developed in your paper. In the comparison and contrast essay on page 1390, for example, the student discussed the opening sentences of the Hawthorne and Poe tales to make a point about their differences. Each time she quoted, she introduced the quotation and followed it by a comment of her own to explain how the quotation related to her main idea. Never drop quotations into the body of your essay without a comment.

Be careful not to quote too much. Use only those passages that are relevant to your discussion. Overquoting can weaken an essay, easily turning it into a string of short quotations choppily connected by a few insufficient words from you. Be sure to make it clear to the reader why the passage you are quoting is important.

When the quotation is short (four lines or less), it should be enclosed in quotation marks and included within the regular text, as you have seen in the sample essays. When typing a quotation longer than four lines, separate it from the preceding typewritten line with a double space. Then indent ten spaces, *omit quotation marks*, and type with double spacing (unless your instructor tells you differently). If you had a reason to include the opening paragraph of "Young Goodman Brown" in your essay, for example, you would type it like this:

```
Young Goodman Brown came forth at sunset into the street at Salem
village; but put his head back, after crossing the threshold, to
exchange a parting kiss with his young wife.  And Faith, as the wife
was aptly named, thrust her own pretty head into the street, letting
the wind play with the pink ribbons of her cap while she called to
Goodman Brown.
```

In a shorter passage in which you use a quotation within a quotation, such as a line of dialogue inside an excerpt from a story, use double and single quotation marks: "The echoes of the forest mocked him, crying, 'Faith! Faith!' as if bewildered wretches were seeking her all through the wilderness."

If you wish to leave out words in a quoted passage, use ellipsis points, that is, three periods (or four periods if the omitted material includes the end of a sentence): "And Faith . . . thrust her own pretty head into the street. . . ."

Always quote the exact wording, punctuation, and capitalization of the original text. If you underline words in a quotation for emphasis, say that you have done so, as the writer of the first student paper did in his explication of Hawthorne's text (see page 1385).

If you find an error, for example a misspelled word in a quotation, indicate that the error is in the original by inserting *sic*, a Latin word meaning "thus," in brackets after the error itself.

Last but not least, punctuate sentences that appear in quotation marks correctly. Commas and periods always belong *inside* the quotation marks, whether or not they appeared in the original text. Semicolons, question marks, colons, and exclamation points, however, belong *outside* the quotation marks, unless they are part of the quoted material.

Avoid plagiarism. Any material you borrow from other sources and include in your paper must be documented. If you present someone else's material (other than factual information) as if it were your own, you may be open to the charge of plagiarism. Even with factual information, if you use the exact wording of a source, you must indicate that it is a quotation. To be on the safe side, it is always better to footnote your original source, or give credit by working into your essay the name of the author and the title of the work in which you found the material you borrowed.

The one exception to this principle is information that is considered *common knowledge.* Common knowledge is material that is repeated in a number of sources, so that it is difficult to tell what the original source might have been. Such items as the basic biographical facts about an author or information about the publication of specific stories do not need footnoting, unless you quote someone's exact words at length in your essay.

Know when and how to document your sources. Include the name of the author and the page number in a parenthetical citation or in the text itself:

In Richard J. Jacobson's study, we learn that Hawthorne feared the artist might become "insulated from the common business of life" (27).

If you cite from more than one book by an author, mention the title in the text, or include a shortened form of the title in the citation:

We learn that Hawthorne feared the artist might become "insulated from the common business of life" (Jacobson, Hawthorne's Conception 27).

If your instructor asks you to use footnotes or endnotes, instead of parenthetical citation, you may place notes at the bottom of the page on which the reference appears, or they may be gathered together on a separate *notes* page at the end of your essay. When you footnote a source, indent the first line of each footnote five spaces before listing the author's first and last name; the title of the book; the city of publication, publisher, and date in parentheses; and the page number cited:

[1] Richard J. Jacobson, Hawthorne's Conception of the Creative Process (Cambridge, MA: Harvard UP, 1965) 27.

Instructions for basic documentation form for different sources — books, magazines, encyclopedias, and so on — appear in every handbook and guide to writing college papers. They may also be found in various manuals of style and style sheets that should be available in the reference section of your college library.

Guidelines: How to Write an Essay about Short Stories

1. Do not wait until the last minute to start. Allow plenty of time to write and revise.

2. Be sure you have a clear idea of what you want to say about the story. Can you state this idea as a sharply focused thesis sentence? Remember that all expository writing serves to clarify, set forth, or explain in detail an idea about a topic.

3. Read the story over again, taking notes that will help you amplify your central idea. It might help at this point to assemble a short outline, to stake out the ground you intend your essay to cover. Look for an approach that is distinctive enough to be worth your time and effort, yet manageable enough to be handled in a paper of the length you are assigned.

4. Decide how you want to proceed to develop your thesis. Will you use explication, analysis, or comparison and contrast? Is it appropriate to show a cause in an author's life or times and its effect on the work? If you have notes from your reading or research, assemble and number them in the order you intend to use them to develop your central idea.

5. Write a rough draft of your essay. Be sure to state your central idea as a thesis sentence somewhere — depending on how you organize your discussion of the story. If you are using an outline, try to follow it, but allow yourself the possibility of discovering something new that you did not know you had to say about the story while you are writing. If you have taken notes or jotted down quotations from your reading, try to introduce such material smoothly into your discussion. Remember that the heart of literary criticism is good quotation. Brief, accurate examples from the text that illustrate the points you are trying to make about your thesis are essential in writing about stories.

6. Allow some time to pass before you look over your rough draft — at least a day. Then make at least one thorough revision before you copy or type a finished draft of your paper. Some students find they need several revisions before they are satisfied with what they have written. When you review your rough draft, concentrate and read critically. Remember that Isaac Babel would sometimes write 100 drafts of a story before he was satisfied. Let your words stimulate a flow of ideas about your topic; this will lead you to find more ways to illustrate your thesis or develop your train of thought. Fill out paragraphs that seem thin. Be sure transitions between paragraphs are smooth and quotations are integrated into the discussion. If you sense that your sentences are wordy, try to be more concise. Eliminate repetition. Be sure your general organization is coherent and your discussion proceeds in a clear, logical order.

7. Check over your rough draft one last time to make sure you have always used complete sentences and correct spelling and punctuation.

Avoid sentence fragments and exclamation points, unless they are part of a quotation.

8. Type the paper or write it neatly in its final form. If your instructor requires some particular style for class papers, such as extra-wide margins or triple-spacing, follow those instructions. Use 8½-by-11-inch paper. Type if you can, double spacing between lines. If you write by hand, use ink and write on only one side of each piece of paper. Leave generous margins at the top, bottom, and sides. Number the pages, beginning with the number 2 (not the word *two*) in the upper-right-hand corner of the second page. (Your title on the first page will indicate that it is the first page.) Clip or staple your pages together in the upper-left-hand corner. Be sure your name, your instructor's name, your class and section number, and the date appear on your paper.

9. Read your essay over one last time for typographical errors. Make legible corrections in ink. Have you put quotation marks around titles of short stories ("The Snows of Kilimanjaro") and underlined the titles of books (The Snows of Kilimanjaro and Other Stories)? Have you placed commas and periods *within* quotation marks in the titles and quotations that appear in your essay? Have you inadvertently left out any words or sentences when you went from the rough draft to the final version of your essay?

10. Finally, make a copy of your paper — a carbon or a photocopy — before you hand it in, and keep it. It is a good idea to save your notes and rough drafts as well, in case the accuracy of a quotation or the originality of your work is called into question.

What do you do after you hand in your paper? You have probably spent so much time on it, thinking, organizing, writing, and rewriting, that you feel you may never want to read it again. The act of writing the essay will have clarified your thinking about the story, so you carry with you the intangible benefit of something learned in the writing process. Returning to your essay in the future might have one final benefit: Your paper will refresh your memory, reminding you of what you did not know you knew, about both yourself and the short story.

GLOSSARY
OF LITERARY TERMS

ABSTRACT LANGUAGE Language that describes ideas or qualities rather than specific, observable people, places, and things, which are described in CONCRETE LANGUAGE.

ACTION At its simplest, the thing or things that happen in a story's PLOT — what the CHARACTERS do and what is done to them. A story may have more than one action (a plot and one or more SUBPLOTS), but a successful short story usually has one identifiable central action.

ALLEGORY A narrative in which CHARACTERS, places, things, and events represent general qualities, and their interactions are meant to reveal a general or abstract truth. Such characters, places, things, and events thus often function as SYMBOLS of the concepts or ideas referred to.

ALLUSION An implied or indirect reference to something with which the reader is supposed to be familiar.

AMBIGUITY A situation expressed in such a way as to admit more than one possible interpretation; also, the way of expressing such a situation. Many short story writers intend some element of their work to be ambiguous, but careless or sloppy writing often creates unintentional ambiguity, or *vagueness*.

ANECDOTE A brief, unified NARRATION of one incident or EPISODE, often humorous and often based on an actual event. Some very good short stories may consist of nothing more than an anecdote; others may be made up of several anecdotes strung together, or may use one or more anecdotes as a way of advancing the PLOT or developing a CHARACTER.

ANTAGONIST A CHARACTER in some stories who is in real or imagined opposition to the PROTAGONIST or HERO. The CONFLICT between these characters makes up the ACTION, or PLOT, of the story. It is usually resolved in some way, but it need not be.

ANTICLIMAX An unexpected, insignificant RESOLUTION to a narrative, sometimes appearing in the place of a CLIMAX, sometimes after a true climax. Many anticlimaxes are the unintended result of inept writing, but often — especially in modern works — they are used intentionally to indicate the randomness, futility, or boredom of human life and action.

ANTI-STORY An experimental short story that attempts to convey objective reality by avoiding what its authors consider the false CONVENTIONS of PLOT, CHARACTER, and THEME, relying instead on seemingly uninterpreted and unarranged fragments of direct experience and language.

ATMOSPHERE The MOOD, feeling, or quality of life in a story as conveyed by the author's choices of language and organization in describing the SETTING in which the speech and activity of the CHARACTERS takes place. The atmosphere in which an author makes characters appear and events occur is often important in determining the TONE of the particular work.

CENTRAL INTELLIGENCE A CHARACTER (often but not always the NARRATOR) through whose perception the author observes the ACTION of a story, and whose perspective thus shapes the reader's view of that action. The term was coined by Henry James, who felt, essentially, that the true subject matter of FICTION is the effect of the action on the understanding of this central intelligence.

CHARACTER Any person who plays a part in a narrative. Characters may be FLAT — simple, one-dimensional, unsurprising, and usually unchanging or *static* — or ROUND — complex, full, described in detail, often contradictory, and usually *dynamic*, i.e., changing in some way during the story. The main character in the story can usually be labeled the PROTAGONIST or HERO; he or she is often in CONFLICT with some other character, an ANTAGONIST. Other characters who affect the ACTION slightly or only indirectly may be called *minor* characters; but, depending on the intention or the skill of the author, the main characters need not be round, nor the minor characters flat. Minor characters are often as full and complex as major characters, or fuller.

CLIMAX The turning point or point of highest interest in a narrative; the point at which the most important part of the ACTION takes place and the final outcome or RESOLUTION of the PLOT becomes inevitable. Leading up to the climax is the RISING ACTION of the story; after the climax, the FALLING ACTION takes the reader to the DENOUEMENT or conclusion, in which the results of the climactic action are presented.

COINCIDENCE An event or situation that arises for no apparent reason and with little or no preparation, and then has a significant effect on the working out of the PLOT or the lives of one or more of the CHARACTERS in a work; a chance happening that has an important consequence or result; an accident of fate.

COMPLICATION The introduction and development of a CONFLICT between CHARACTERS or between a character and his or her situation. A complication moves the PLOT forward by exciting the reader's expectation that the conflict so introduced must lead to a CLIMAX and reach some ultimate RESOLUTION as a result.

COMPRESSION The use of few or short words, sentences, or paragraphs, or of very brief descriptions of CHARACTERS and SETTINGS and narrations of incidents, to tell a story as clearly and simply as possible; in general, an economical use of language.

CONCRETE LANGUAGE Language that describes or portrays specific, observable persons, places, and things rather than general ideas or qualities, which are described in ABSTRACT LANGUAGE.

CONFLICT The opposition presented to the main CHARACTER (or PROTAGONIST) of a narrative by another character (an ANTAGONIST), by events or situations, by fate, or by some aspect of the protagonist's own personality or nature. The conflict is introduced by means of a COMPLICATION that sets in motion the RISING ACTION, usually toward a CLIMAX and eventual RESOLUTION.

CONNOTATION The meaning of a word (or words) that is implied or suggested by the specific associations the word calls to mind and by the TONE in which it is used, as opposed to its literal meaning or denotation.

CONVENTION A traditional or commonly accepted technique of writing or device used in writing, often an unbelievable device that the reader agrees to believe — such as, for example, the fact that a FIRST-PERSON NARRATOR is addressing the reader in a friendly and intimate manner.

CONVENTIONAL Following or observing CONVENTIONS; often used in a derogatory manner to indicate a certain overreliance on such conventions and thus a lack of originality or failure of imagination on the part of the writer.

CRISIS The turning point in a narrative; the point at which the ACTION reaches its CLIMAX and its RESOLUTION becomes inevitable.

DENOUEMENT The conclusion of an ACTION or PLOT, in which the FALLING ACTION is brought to a close and the outcome or outcomes of the CLIMAX are presented to the reader; from a French word meaning "the untying of a knot."

DESCRIPTION The use of language to present the features of a person, place, or thing.

DIALOGUE The written presentation of words spoken by CHARACTERS in a narrative; used to introduce the CONFLICT, give some impressions of the lives and personalities of the characters who are speaking, and advance the action to its CLIMAX and RESOLUTION.

DICTION The choice and arrangement of specific words and types of words to tell a story. A writer's diction is an important element of STYLE, and has a significant effect on the meaning of a story: The same ACTION will leave a different impression on the reader when it is narrated in street slang, in the simple, precise language of an old schoolteacher, or in the professional jargon of a lawyer or a social scientist.

DIDACTIC A term used to describe a narrative or other work of art that is presented in order to teach a specific lesson, convey a MORAL, or inspire and provide a model for proper behavior.

DISTANCE An author's or a NARRATOR's spatial or temporal — and hence emotional — removal or aloofness from the ACTION of a narrative, and hence from its CHARACTERS.

DRAMATIC IRONY The reader's awareness of a discrepancy between a CHARACTER's perception of his or her own situation or activities, or of their consequences, and the true nature of that situation or those consequences.

EPIGRAPH A quotation an author places at the beginning of a literary work that often suggests its THEME.

EPIPHANY A "showing forth" or sudden revelation of the true nature of a CHARACTER or situation through a specific event — a word, gesture, or other action — that causes the reader to see the significance of that character or situation in a new light. The term was first popularized in modern literature by James Joyce.

EPISODE A specific, usually very brief incident, often complete in itself and usually narrated at once and as a whole (as in an ANECDOTE). A story may consist of the NARRATION of one episode, or of several episodes strung together and united by a common SETTING or common CHARACTERS or proceeding toward a single CLIMAX and RESOLUTION; the latter kind of story is referred to as an *episodic* narrative.

EXPLICATION The act of explaining or interpreting the meaning of a text.

EXPOSITION The presentation of background information that a reader must be aware of, especially of situations that exist and events that have occurred before the ACTION of a story begins.

FABLE A very short, often humorous narrative told to present a MORAL. A fable's CHARACTERS are often animals, and particular animals have CONVENTIONAL associations with specific abstract qualities or values — the fox represents wiliness, the ant industry, and the lion nobility, for example. Leo Tolstoy said that "the bad fable has a moral, while the good fable is a moral."

FAIRY TALE A story or FANTASY that appeals to our sense of the marvelous, in which we suspend disbelief and let our subconscious patterns of wish fulfillment express themselves through magical occurrences, characters, or objects.

FALLING ACTION The events of a narrative that follow the CLIMAX and resolve the CONFLICT that reached its highest point in that climax before bringing the story to its conclusion or DENOUEMENT.

FANTASY A narrative or events in a narrative that have no possible existence in reality and could not have occurred in the real world; used sometimes to amuse or delight readers, sometimes to comment on or illustrate by contrast some aspect of reality, and sometimes, as in a FABLE, to present a clear MORAL that will not be complicated or diminished by the untidiness or inconsistency of reality, or as in a FAIRY TALE, to express patterns of wish-fulfillment.

FICTION A narrative drawn from an author's imagination, made up of an ACTION or PLOT of imagined events involving imagined CHARACTERS in imagined or imaginatively reconstructed SETTINGS; lies told with the tolerance, consent, and even complicity of the listener or reader.

FIGURATIVE LANGUAGE The use of a word or a group of words that is literally inaccurate to describe or define a person, event, or thing vividly by calling forth the sensations or responses that person, event, or thing evokes. Such language often takes the form of METAPHORS, in which one thing is equated with another, or of SIMILES, in which one thing is compared to another by using *like*, *as*, or some other such connecting word.

FIRST-PERSON NARRATION The telling of a story by a person who was involved in or directly observed the ACTION narrated. Such a NARRATOR refers to himself or herself as *I* and becomes a CHARACTER in the story, with his or her understanding shaping the reader's perception of the events and characters.

FLASHBACK A technique of EXPOSITION in which the flow of events in a narrative is interrupted to present to the reader an earlier incident or situation that has a bearing on the story or its CHARACTERS.

FLAT CHARACTER A simple, one-dimensional, usually unchanging CHARACTER who shows none of the human depth, complexity, and contrariness of a ROUND CHARACTER or of most real people.

FOLKTALE A narrative that comes out of the tradition — usually the oral tradition — of a specific culture, and is used to communicate that culture's beliefs, values, history, and MYTHS from generation to generation.

FORESHADOWING The introduction of specific words, IMAGES, or events into a narrative to suggest or anticipate later events that are central to the ACTION and its RESOLUTION.

FRAME STORY A story within a story; a narrative told within the framework of another fictional setting and situation.

GENRE A type of literary work, like the SHORT STORY, NOVEL, essay, play, or poem. The term may also be used to classify literature within a type, like science-fiction stories or detective novels.

HERO/HEROINE The PROTAGONIST of a story or other narrative; the main CHARACTER, whose CONFLICT is presented and resolved in the ACTION or PLOT. Traditionally, *heroine* has been used to refer to a female hero, but *hero* may be, and is more and more being, used to refer to a protagonist of either sex.

IMAGE A word or group of words used to give a CONCRETE representation, either literal or FIGURATIVE, of a sensory experience or an object that is perceived by the senses.

IMAGERY The use of IMAGES, especially of a consistent pattern of related images — often FIGURATIVE ones — to convey an overall sensory impression.

IMPARTIAL OMNISCIENCE The telling of a story by a THIRD-PERSON NARRATOR whose OMNISCIENCE does not allow for any evaluation or judgment of the CHARACTERS and their activities.

IMPRESSIONISM A way of writing in which an author presents CHARACTERS and events in a highly subjective and personal light, freely admitting an authorial POINT OF VIEW and effectively denying any claim to OBJECTIVITY or disinterestedness; after the style of the French impressionist painters of the late years of the nineteenth century, who sought to free painting from the REALISTIC, representational CONVENTIONS of the day.

IRONY The reader's or audience's awareness of a reality that differs from the reality the CHARACTERS perceive (DRAMATIC IRONY) or the literal meaning of the author's words (VERBAL IRONY).

LIMITED OMNISCIENCE The ability of a THIRD-PERSON NARRATOR to tell the reader directly about any events that have occurred, are occurring, or will occur in the PLOT of a story, and about the thoughts and feelings of one particular CHARACTER, or a few characters; distinguished from simple OMNISCIENCE, whereby such a NARRATOR can tell the reader directly about the thoughts and feelings of any character.

METAPHOR An implied comparison of two different things that is achieved by a FIGURATIVE verbal equation of those things. "Love is a rose," "War is hell," and "The exam was a killer" are all metaphors, intended not to define the first terms mentioned but to attribute certain qualities to the things being discussed.

MODERNISM A label loosely applied to the work of certain writers of the late nineteenth and early twentieth centuries who investigated the structure and texture of literature and challenged its CONVENTIONS.

MOOD The ATMOSPHERE that is created by the author's choice of details and the words with which to present them.

MORAL The lesson to be drawn from a story, especially from a FABLE or (in this sense the word is often used disparagingly) from a heavily DIDACTIC story.

MOTIVATION The external forces (SETTING, circumstance) and internal forces (personality, temperament, morality, intelligence) that compel a CHARACTER to act as he or she does in a narrative.

MYTH A traditional story, often a FOLKTALE arising out of a culture's oral tradition and involving gods or superhumanly heroic figures, that is used to explain the way things are and the way things happen, and to transmit the culture's values and beliefs from generation to generation.

NARRATION The dramatic telling of the events that make up the ACTION or PLOT of a story. FIRST-PERSON NARRATION is the telling of a story by a NARRATOR who participated in or directly observed the events being recounted, and who is thus a CHARACTER in the story, identifying himself or herself as *I*. THIRD-PERSON NARRATION is the telling of a story by a detached, almost always anonymous voice who refers to the characters as *he, she,* and *they*. A third-person narrator may or may not be OMNISCIENT.

NARRATIVE A sequence of events, often (but not always) unified and connected in storytelling.

NARRATOR The teller of a story; usually either a CHARACTER who participates in the story's ACTION (see FIRST-PERSON NARRATION) or a detached, anonymous observer who may or may not present himself or herself as OMNISCIENT of the story's action from the beginning (see THIRD-PERSON NARRATION).

NATURALISM An extreme form of REALISM in which authors present their work as a scientific observation of a world in which people's acts are strictly determined by their nature and the nature of their surroundings.

NOVEL A long fictional prose narrative.

NOVELLA A short novel; a work of prose FICTION whose length falls somewhere between that of a SHORT STORY and that of a NOVEL; sometimes (though infrequently today) referred to as a *novelette*. Different critics have attempted to specify different standards of length for a novella or short novel — some saying 15,000 to 50,000 words, others 50 to 125 ordinary book pages — but there is no universal agreement on such a standard.

OBJECTIVITY An attempt by an author to remove himself or herself from any personal involvement with the CHARACTERS and ACTIONS of a story, to tell the story without bias and without expressing any personal opinions or making any personal judgments of the characters.

OMNISCIENCE Literally, "all-knowingness"; the ability of an author or a NARRATOR (usually a THIRD-PERSON NARRATOR) to tell the reader directly about any events that have occurred, are occurring, or will occur in the PLOT of a story, and about the thoughts and feelings of any CHARACTER.

PACE The rate at which the ACTION of a story progresses. Pace may be affected by varying the lengths of words, sentences, and paragraphs, by COMPRESSING or expanding the NARRATION of certain incidents or EPISODES, or by introducing and repeating certain key words and formulaic phrases.

PARABLE A narrative, usually short, that is told to answer a difficult moral question or teach a moral truth; often a form of ALLEGORY, because each person, event, or thing in the parable represents a literally unrelated person, event, thing, or quality that is involved in the moral dilemma being examined.

PARODY A humorous imitation of another, usually serious, work or type of work, in which the parodist adopts the quirks of STYLE or the CONVENTIONS of the work or works being imitated and uses them in extreme and ridiculous ways, or applies them to a comically inappropriate subject matter.

PATHOS The quality in a work that evokes sorrow or pity. Inappropriate pathos, or a too-frequent resorting to pathetic effects, can reduce a work to SENTIMENTALITY or *bathos*.

PERSONA The fictional mask or voice an author may adopt to tell a story.

PLOT The series of events in a narrative that form the ACTION of the story, in which a CHARACTER or characters face an internal or external CONFLICT that propels the story to a CLIMAX and an ultimate RESOLUTION.

POINT OF VIEW The perspective from which an author lets the reader view the ACTION of a narrative; thus, the choice of who tells the story. In FIRST-PERSON NARRATION the NARRATOR tells a story he or she took part in or observed directly; such a narrator usually knows only what has been explicitly revealed, or what he or she has been able to deduce from that. In THIRD-PERSON NARRATION the narrator is not directly involved in the story, and so views it from a certain DISTANCE. Such a narrator may be OMNISCIENT about the CHARACTERS and their actions and MOTIVATIONS, or his or her knowledge may be LIMITED to what one or a few characters know, or even to the plainly observable speeches and acts of the characters.

PROTAGONIST The main CHARACTER of a narrative; its HERO. The ACTION of the story is usually the presentation and RESOLUTION of some internal or external CONFLICT of the protagonist; if the conflict is with another major character, that character may be called the ANTAGONIST.

REALISM The telling of a story in a manner that is faithful to the reader's experience of real life, limiting events in the PLOT to things that might actually happen and CHARACTERS to people who might actually exist.

RESOLUTION The FALLING ACTION of a narrative, in which the CONFLICT, set in motion during the RISING ACTION and reaching its high point in the CLIMAX, is settled, or at least significantly altered, and the story moves swiftly toward its conclusion or DENOUEMENT.

REVERSAL Any turnabout in the fortunes of a CHARACTER, especially of the PROTAGONIST.

RISING ACTION The event or events that present and develop the CONFLICT whose dramatization is the story's ACTION; the COMPLICATION (or set of complications) that leads up to the CLIMAX.

ROMANTICISM A literary movement that flourished in the nineteenth century, valuing individuality, imagination, and the truth revealed in nature.

ROUND CHARACTER A full, complex, multidimensional CHARACTER whose personality reveals some of the richness and contradictoriness we are accustomed to observing in actual people, rather than the transparent obviousness of a FLAT CHARACTER.

SARCASM An extreme form of VERBAL IRONY intended to ridicule or belittle its subject.

SATIRE A work that ridicules some aspect of human behavior by portraying it at its most extreme; distinguished from PARODY, which burlesques the STYLE or content of another *work* or type of work.

SENTIMENTALITY An overreliance on emotional effect or PATHOS so great as to strain the reader's willingness to believe; also referred to as *bathos.*

SETTING The place and time in which a story's ACTION takes place; also, in a broader sense, the culture and the ways of life of the CHARACTERS, and the shared beliefs and assumptions that guide their lives.

SHORT STORY A short fictional prose narrative. The term is often applied to any work of narrative prose fiction shorter than a NOVEL. Poe said its distinguishing factors were that it possesses aesthetic unity and can be read in one sitting. The trouble with that definition, as the writer William Saroyan once pointed out, is that some people can sit longer than others. See the discussion of this term in the Introduction and in The Elements of Fiction.

SIMILE A FIGURATIVE comparison of one thing to another, especially to one that is not usually thought of as similar. The comparison is achieved by using such connecting words as *like* or *as.* An old country song says, "Life is like a mountain railway," and then goes on to describe the narrow, tortuous paths people must follow in dealing with life's moral dilemmas, and the steep fall that awaits those who are not careful. The simile makes possible this figurative comparison of two such dissimilar things as *life,* a very large abstraction, and *mountain railway,* a very specific and seemingly unrelated object.

SKETCH A relaxed, static, predominantly descriptive literary composition often close to an essay in form.

STEREOTYPE A generalized, oversimplified CHARACTER (often a STOCK CHARACTER) whose thoughts and actions are excessively predictable because they are used so frequently that they have become CONVENTIONAL.

STOCK CHARACTERS CONVENTIONAL CHARACTERS who appear in numerous works, especially in works of the same type, and behave in predictable ways. Examples include the cruel stepmother in FAIRY TALES, or the hard-boiled detective in certain mystery stories.

STREAM OF CONSCIOUSNESS The narrative technique by which an author attempts to capture the flow of a CHARACTER's thoughts, often in a series of separate and apparently unrelated passages that unite to give an IMPRESSIONISTIC view of reality as seen by that character.

STYLE The habitual manner of expression of an author. An author's style is the product of choices, made consciously or unconsciously, about such things as vocabulary, organization, DICTION, IMAGERY, PACE, and even certain recurring THEMES or subjects.

SUBPLOT A minor PLOT, often involving one or more secondary CHARACTERS, that may add a COMPLICATION to the ACTION of a narrative, or may reinforce that action or provide an enlightening contrast to it or a welcome relief from its tension.

SURREALISM A way of writing that involves the presentation of a superreal, dreamlike world where CONVENTIONS are upended and rationality is dispensed with. The spontaneous creations of the unconscious are depicted in a surrealistic work through the use of FANTASTY and incongruous IMAGERY.

SUSPENSE The anxious uncertainty an author creates in a reader about the outcome of a story's ACTION. Suspense is often resolved when the action reaches a CLIMAX, after which the RESOLUTION is more or less inevitable.

SYMBOL A person, event, or thing that stands for or represents by association some other, usually broader, idea or range of ideas, in addition to maintaining its own literal meaning.

TALE An early form of the SHORT STORY, usually involving remote places and times, and events leading to a dramatic, conclusive ending.

TALL TALE A TALE or SHORT STORY based on a consciously ludicrous distortion.

THEME The central, unifying point or idea that is made concrete, developed, and explored in the ACTION and the IMAGERY of a work of FICTION.

THIRD-PERSON NARRATION The telling of a story by a detached, usually anonymous NARRATOR, a voice who refers to all the characters as *he, she,* and *they.* Such a narrator may view the story with full OMNISCIENCE, which may or may not be IMPARTIAL OMNISCIENCE; or he or she may have only LIMITED OMNISCIENCE, seeing through the eyes of only one or a few CHARACTERS.

TONE The expression of the author's attitude toward his or her subject matter — the CHARACTERS, their SETTING, and the ACTION they undertake or undergo. Tone is revealed in the author's DICTION, IMAGERY, organization, vocabulary, and various other choices that contribute to the making of a STYLE.

UNITY The relation of all parts of a work to one central or organizing principle that forms them into a complete and coherent whole.

UNRELIABLE NARRATOR A fictional CHARACTER telling the story whose knowledge or judgment about events and other characters is so flawed as to make him or her a misleading guide to the author's intentions.

VERBAL IRONY The reader's awareness of a discrepancy between the real meaning of the situation being presented and the literal meaning of the author's words in presenting it.

VERISIMILITUDE The use of certain lifelike details to give an imaginative narrative work the semblance of reality or actuality.

YARN An elaborated ANECDOTE or series of ancedotes narrated in colloquial language.

Acknowledgments (*continued from page iv*)

Jorge Luis Borges. "The End of the Duel" copyright © 1967 by Grove Press, Inc. Reprinted by permission of Grove Press, Inc. "On the Meaning and Form of 'The End of the Duel' " from *Borges on Writing* by Jorge Luis Borges, edited by Norman Thomas diGiovanni, Daniel Halpern, and Frank MacShane. Copyright © 1972, 1973 by Jorge Luis Borges, Norman Thomas diGiovanni, Daniel Halpern, and Frank MacShane. Reprinted by permission of the publisher, E. P. Dutton, a division of New American Library.

Elizabeth Bowen. "The Demon Lover." Copyright 1946 and renewed 1974 by Elizabeth Bowen. Reprinted from *The Collected Stories of Elizabeth Bowen*, by permission of Alfred A. Knopf, Inc. Preface to the American edition of "The Demon Lover" from *The Mulberry Tree: The Writings of Elizabeth Bowen*, edited by Hermoine Lee, published by Virago Press Ltd 1986. Copyright © 1986 Curtis Brown Ltd, London, the Literary Executors of Elizabeth Bowen.

Paul Bowles. "The Hyena" copyright © 1967 by Paul Bowles. Reprinted from *The Collected Stories of Paul Bowles* with the permission of Black Sparrow Press.

Ray Bradbury. "August 2026: There Will Come Soft Rains" copyright 1950 by Crowell Collier Publishing Company. Renewed 1977 by Ray Bradbury. Reprinted by permission of Don Congdon Associates, Inc.

Raymond Carver. "What We Talk About When We Talk About Love," and "Why Don't You Dance" copyright © 1981 by Raymond Carver. Reprinted from *What We Talk About When We Talk About Love*, by Raymond Carver, by permission of Alfred A. Knopf, Inc. "Foreword" (abridged) by Raymond Carver from *On Becoming a Novelist* by John Gardner. Foreword copyright © 1983 by Raymond Carver. Reprinted by permission of Harper & Row, Publishers, Inc.

Willa Cather. "On Katherine Mansfield" copyright 1936 by Willa Cather. Reprinted from *Willa Cather on Writing: Critical Studies on Writing as an Art*, by Willa Cather, by permission of Alfred A. Knopf, Inc.

John Cheever. "The Enormous Radio" and "The Swimmer" copyright 1947, © 1964 by John Cheever. Reprinted from *The Stories of John Cheever*, by John Cheever, by permission of Alfred A. Knopf, Inc. "Why I Write Short Stories" by John Cheever copyright 1978 by Newsweek, Inc. all rights reserved. Reprinted by permission.

Anton Chekhov. "A Trifle from Real Life" from *Russian Silhouettes* by Anton Chekhov, translated by Marian Fell. Copyright 1915 Charles Scribner's Sons; copyright renewed 1943 Olivia Fell Vans Agnew. Reprinted with the permission of Charles Scribner's Sons. "The Lady with the Pet Dog" from *The Portable Chekhov*, edited and translated by Avrahm Yarmolinsky. Copyright 1947, 1968 by The Viking Press, Inc. Copyright © 1975 by Avrahm Yarmolinsky. Reprinted by permission of Viking Penguin Inc. "On Technique in Writing a Short Story" excerpted from *Letters on the Short Story, the Drama, and Other Literary Topics* (1924), by Anton Chekhov, trans. Constance Garnett. Reprinted by permission of the Estate of the late Constance Garnett.

Isak Dinesen. "The Blue Stones" excerpted from "Peter and Rosa" and "The Blue Jar" excerpted from "The Young Man with the Carnation" from *Winter's Tales*, by Isak Dinesen. Copyright 1942 by Random House, Inc. and renewed 1970 by Johan Philip Thomas Ingerslev, c/o The Rungstedlund Foundation. Reprinted by permission of Random House, Inc. and the Rungstedlund Foundation of Denmark.

Ralph Ellison. "Chapter 1, Battle Royal." Copyright 1947 by Ralph Ellison. Reprinted from *Invisible Man*, by Ralph Ellison, by permission of Random House, Inc. "On the Influence of Folklore on 'Battle Royal' " from *Writers at Work: The Paris Review Interviews*, Second Series, edited by George Plimpton. Copyright © 1963 by The Paris Review, Inc. Reprinted by permission of the William Morris Agency.

Louise Erdrich. "The Red Convertible" from *Love Medicine* by Louise Erdrich. Copyright © 1984 by Louise Erdrich. Reprinted by permission of Henry Holt and Company.

William Faulkner. "A Rose for Emily" and "Dry September." Copyright 1930 and renewed 1958 by William Faulkner. Rreprinted from *Collected Stories of William Faulkner*, by permission of Random House, Inc. "On the Meaning of 'A Rose for Emily' " from *Faulkner in the University*, ed. Gwynn and Blotner. Reprinted by permission of the University Press of Virginia.

F. Scott Fitzgerald. "Babylon Revisited" from *Taps at Reveille*. Copyright 1931 Curtis Publishing Company; copyright renewed © 1959 Frances Scott Fitzgerald Lanahan. Reprinted with the permission of Charles Scribner's Sons.

Gustave Flaubert. "A Simple Heart" from *Flaubert: Three Tales*, trans. Robert Baldick (Penguin Classics, 1961). Copyright © Robert Baldick, 1961. Reprinted by permission of Penguin Books Ltd.

E. M. Forster. "Mr. Andrews" from *The Eternal Moment* by E. M. Forster. Copyright 1928 by Harcourt Brace Jovanovich, Inc.; renewed 1956 by E. M. Forster. Reprinted by permission of the publisher.

Gabriel García Márquez. "A Very Old Man with Enormous Wings" from *Leaf Storm and Other Stories* by Gabriel García Márquez, translated by Gregory Rabassa. English translation copyright © 1971 by Gabriel García Márquez. Reprinted by permission of Harper & Row, Publishers, Inc.

Gail Godwin. "Dream Children." Copyright © 1976 by Gail Godwin. Reprinted from *Dream Children*, by Gail Godwin, by permission of Alfred A. Knopf, Inc.

Nikolai Gogol. "The Overcoat." Translation by Constance Garnett, in *The Overcoat and Other Stories.* Translation revised by Leonard J. Kent in *The Complete Tales of Nikolai Gogol,* Vol. 2, edited by Leonard J. Kent (The University of Chicago Press). Reprinted by permission of A. P. Watt on behalf of the Executors of the Estate of Constance Garnett, Chatto & Windus, and Leonard J. Kent.

Nadine Gordimer. "Town and Country Lovers" from *A Soldier's Embrace* by Nadine Gordimer. Copyright © 1975 by Nadine Gordimer. Originally published in *The New Yorker.* Reprinted by permission of Viking Penguin Inc. "The Flash of Fireflies" from *The Kenyon Review,* Fall 1968 (under the heading "South Africa: Nadine Gordimer"). Reprinted by permission of the author and *The Kenyon Review.*

Lila Havens. "Residents and Transients: An Interview with Bobbie Ann Mason" from *Crazyhorse,* 29 (Fall 1985). Reprinted by permission of *Crazyhorse,* Department of English, University of Arkansas at Little Rock.

Mark Helprin. "North Light" excerpted from the book *Ellis Island and Other Stories* by Mark Helprin. Copyright © 1981 by Mark Helprin. Reprinted by permission of Delacorte Press/Seymour Lawrence.

Ernest Hemingway. "The Snows of Kilimanjaro" from *The Short Stories of Ernest Hemingway.* Copyright © 1936 Ernest Hemingway; copyright renewed © 1964 Mary Hemingway. Reprinted with the permission of Charles Scribner's Sons.

Langston Hughes. "Radioactive Red Caps" and "Who Is Simple?" from *The Best of Simple* by Langston Hughes. Copyright © 1961 by Langston Hughes. Reprinted by permission of Hill and Wang, a division of Farrar, Straus and Giroux, Inc.

Zora Neale Hurston. "Spunk" from *The Selected Short Stories of Zora Neale Hurston.* Copyright 1985 by Turtle Island Foundation.

Shirley Jackson. "The Lottery." Reprinted by permission of Farrar, Straus, and Giroux, Inc. "The Lottery" from *The Lottery* by Shirley Jackson. Copyright 1948, 1949 by Shirley Jackson. Copyright renewed © 1976, 1977 by Laurence Hyman, Barry Hyman, Mrs. Sarah Webster, and Mrs. Joanne Schnurer. "The Lottery" originally appeared in *The New Yorker.* "On the Morning of June 28, 1948, and 'The Lottery,' " from "Biography of a Story" from *Come Along With Me* by Shirley Jackson. Copyright © 1968 by Stanley Edgar Hyman. Reprinted by permission of Viking Penguin Inc.

Henry James. "On the Genesis of 'The Real Thing' " (editor's title) from *The Notebooks of Henry James* by F. O. Matthiessen and Kenneth Murdock. Copyright © 1947, 1974 by Oxford University Press, Inc. Reprinted by permission.

Gustave Janouch. "On Franz Kafka's View of 'The Metamorphosis' " from Gustave Janouch, *Conversations with Kafka.* Copyright © 1968 by Fischer Verlag GmbH, Frankfurt-am-Main. Reprinted by permission of New Directions Publishing Corporation and Joan Daves.

James Joyce. "The Sisters," "Araby," and "The Dead" from *Dubliners* by James Joyce. Copyright 1916 by B. W. Huebsch. Definitive text Copyright © 1967 by the Estate of James Joyce. "An Early Version of 'The Sisters' " from *James Joyce: Dubliners, The Viking Critical Library Edition,* edited by Robert Scholes and A. Walton Litz. Copyright 1916 by B. W. Huebsch. Definitive text Copyright © 1967 by the Estate of James Joyce. Copyright © 1969 by The Viking Press, Inc. Reprinted by permission of Viking Penguin Inc.

Franz Kafka. "The Metamorphosis" from *The Penal Colony* by Franz Kafka, translated by Willa and Edwin Muir. Copyright © 1948, 1976 by Schocken Books Inc. Reprinted by permission of Schocken Books Inc.

Jamaica Kincaid. "Girl" from *At the Bottom of the River* by Jamaica Kincaid. Copyright © 1978, 1979, 1981, 1982, 1983 by Jamaica Kincaid. "Girl" originally appeared in *The New Yorker.* Reprinted by permission of Farrar, Straus and Giroux, Inc.

Milan Kundera. "The Hitchhiking Game" from *Laughable Loves,* by Milan Kundera, translated by Suzanne Rappaport. Copyright © 1974 by Alfred A. Knopf, Inc. Reprinted by permission of the publisher.

D. H. Lawrence. "Odour of Chrysanthemums" from *The Complete Short Stories of D. H. Lawrence,* Vol. Two. Copyright 1922 by Thomas Seltzer, Inc., renewed 1950 by Frieda Lawrence. "The Rocking-Horse Winner" from *The Complete Short Stories of D. H. Lawrence,* Vol. Three. Copyright 1933 by the Estate of D. H. Lawrence. Copyright renewed © 1961 by Angelo Ravagli and C. M. Weekley, Executors of the Estate of Frieda Lawrence Ravagli. "On the Lust of Hate in Poe's 'The Cask of Amontillado' " from *Studies in Classic American Literature* by D. H. Lawrence. Copyright 1923 by Thomas Seltzer, Inc.; renewed 1950 by Frieda Lawrence. Copyright © 1961 by The Estate of the late Mrs. Frieda Lawrence. Reprinted by permission of Viking Penguin Inc.

David Leavitt. "Territory" from *Family Dancing,* by David Leavitt. Copyright © 1983, 1984 by David Leavitt. Reprinted by permission of Alfred A. Knopf, Inc.

Ursula K. LeGuin. "The Ones Who Walk Away From Omelas" copyright © 1973, 1975 by Ursula K. LeGuin; reprinted by permission of the author and her agent Virginia Kidd. Introductory note, © 1975 by Ursula K. LeGuin, also reprinted by permission.

Doris Lessing. "To Room 19" from *A Man and Two Women.* Copyright © 1958, 1962, 1963 by Doris Lessing. Reprinted by permission of Simon & Schuster, Inc. and Jonathan Clowes Ltd., London, on behalf of Doris Lessing.

Bernard Malamud. "The Jewbird" from *Idiots First* by Bernard Malamud. Copyright © 1963 by Bernard Malamud. Reprinted by permission of Farrar, Straus and Giroux, Inc.

Katherine Mansfield. "Bliss" copyright 1920 by Alfred A. Knopf, Inc. and renewed 1948 by John Middleton Murry. "The Doll's House" copyright 1920, 1923 by Alfred A. Knopf, Inc. and renewed 1948, 1951 by John Middleton Murry. Both reprinted from *The Short Stories of Katherine Mansfield,* by permission of the publisher.

Bobbie Ann Mason. "Shiloh" from *Shiloh and Other Stories* by Bobbie Ann Mason. Copyright © 1982 by Bobbie Ann Mason. Reprinted by permission of Harper & Row, Publishers, Inc.

Guy de Maupassant. "The String" and "Miss Harriet" copyright 1923 and renewed 1951 by Alfred A. Knopf, Inc. Reprinted from *The Collected Novels and Stories of Guy de Maupassant,* translated by Ernest Boyd and others, by permission of the publisher.

Yukio Mishima. "Three Million Yen" from *Death in Midsummer.* Copyright © 1966 by New Directions Publishing Corporation. Reprinted by permission of New Directions Publishing Corporation.

Alice Munro. "How I Met My Husband" copyright © 1974 by Alice Munro. Originally from *Something I've Been Meaning to Tell You.* Published in the United States by New American Library and in Canada by McGraw-Hill Ryerson. All rights reserved. Reprinted by permission of Virginia Barber Literary Agency.

Vladimir Nabokov. "On Anton Chekhov's 'The Lady with the Little Dog' " from *Lectures on Russian Literature* by Vladimir Nabokov, copyright © 1981 by the Estate of Vladimir Nabokov. Reprinted by permission of Harcourt Brace Jovanovich, Inc. "On Gogol's Genius in 'The Overcoat' " from *Nikolai Gogol* by Vladimir Nabokov. Copyright © 1944 by New Directions. Reprinted by permission of Mrs. Vladimir Nabokov.

R. K. Narayan. "Under the Banyan Tree" from *Under the Banyan Tree and Other Stories* by R. K. Narayan. Copyright © 1985 by R. K. Narayan. Reprinted by permission of Viking Penguin Inc.

Joyce Carol Oates. "Where Are You Going, Where Have You Been?" reprinted from *The Wheel of Love* by Joyce Carol Oates by permission of the publisher, Vanguard Press, Inc. Copyright © 1970, 1969, 1968, 1967, 1966, 1965 by Joyce Carol Oates. "The Lady with the Pet Dog" reprinted from *Marriages and Infidelities* by Joyce Carol Oates by permission of the publisher, Vanguard Press, Inc. Copyright © 1968, 1969, 1970, 1971, 1972 by Joyce Carol Oates. "On the Making of A Writer" (editor's title) from "Stories That Define Me" by Joyce Carol Oates. *The New York Times Book Review,* July 11, 1982. Copyright © 1982 by the New York Times Company. Reprinted by permission.

Flannery O'Connor. "A Good Man Is Hard to Find" copyright 1953 by Flannery O'Connor; copyright renewed 1981 by Mrs. Regina O'Connor. "A Temple of the Holy Ghost" copyright 1954 by Flannery O'Connor; renewed 1982 by Mrs. Regina O'Connor. Both stories from *A Good Man Is Hard to Find and Other Stories,* reprinted by permission of Harcourt Brace Jovanovich, Inc. "Everything That Rises Must Converge" from *Everything That Rises Must Converge* by Flannery O'Connor. Copyright © 1961, 1965 by the Estate of Mary Flannery O'Connor. Selection from "On Her Own Fiction," retitled "On the Element of Suspense in 'A Good Man Is Hard to Find' " from *Mystery and Manners* by Flannery O'Connor, selected and edited by Sally and Robert Fitzgerald. Copyright © 1957, 1961, 1963, 1964, 1966, 1967, 1969 by the Estate of Mary Flannery O'Connor. The latter two selections reprinted by permission of Farrar, Straus and Giroux, Inc.

Frank O'Connor. "Guests of the Nation" from *Collected Stories,* by Frank O'Connor. Copyright © 1981 by Harriet O'Donovan Sheehy, Executrix of the Estate of Frank O'Connor. Reprinted by permission of Alfred A. Knopf, Inc. and Joan Daves. "On the Elaboration of Style and Form in Joyce's 'The Dead' " from *The Lonely Voice* by Frank O'Connor. Copyright © 1963 by Frank O'Connor. Reprinted by permission of Joan Daves. "The Nearest Thing to Lyric Poetry Is the Short Story" from *Writers at Work: The Paris Review Interviews,* First Series, edited by Malcolm Cowley. Copyright © 1957, 1958 by The Paris Review, Inc. Reprinted by permission of Viking Penguin, Inc.

Sean O'Faolain. "On Maupassant's Interest in Elemental Passion in 'Miss Harriet' " from *The Short Story* by Sean O'Faolain. Copyright © 1951 by the Devin Adair Co. Reprinted by permission of the Devin Adair Co.

Tillie Olsen. "I Stand Here Ironing" excerpted from the book *Tell Me a Riddle* by Tillie Olsen. Copyright © 1956 by Tillie Olsen. Reprinted by permission of Delacorte Press/Seymour Lawrence.

Cynthia Ozick. "The Shawl" copyright © 1980 by Cynthia Ozick. Reprinted by permission of Cynthia Ozick and her agents Raines & Raines. This story first appeared in *The New Yorker.*

Grace Paley. "A Conversation with My Father" from *Enormous Changes at the Last Minute* by Grace Paley. Copyright © 1972, 1974 by Grace Paley. Reprinted by permission of Farrar, Straus and Giroux, Inc.

Jayne Anne Phillips. "Cheers" excerpted from the book *Black Tickets* by Jayne Anne Phillips. Copyright © 1975, 1976, 1978, 1979 by Jayne Anne Phillips. Reprinted by permission of Delacorte Press/Seymour Lawrence.

Katherine Anne Porter. "Flowering Judas" copyright 1930, 1958 by Katherine Anne Porter. Reprinted from her volume *Flowering Judas and Other Stories* by permission of Harcourt Brace Jovanovich, Inc. "On the Origins of 'Flowering Judas' " from *Writers at Work: The Paris Review Interviews*, Second Series, edited by George Plimpton. Copyright © 1963 by The Paris Review, Inc. Reprinted by permission of Viking Penguin Inc.

Isaac Bashevis Singer. "A Crown of Feathers" from *A Crown of Feathers* by Isaac Bashevis Singer. Copyright © 1972, 1973 by Isaac Bashevis Singer. "A Crown of Feathers" originally appeared in *The New Yorker*. Reprinted by permission of Farrar, Straus and Giroux, Inc.

Aleksandr Solzhenitsyn. "The Right Hand" from *Stories and Prose Poems* by Aleksandr Solzhenitsyn, translated by Michael Glenny. English translation copyright © 1970, 1971 by Michael Glenny. Reprinted by permission of Farrar, Straus and Giroux, Inc. and The Bodley Head.

John Steinbeck. "The Chrysanthemums" from *The Long Valley* by John Steinbeck. Copyright 1937, renewed © 1965 by John Steinbeck. Reprinted by permission of Viking Penguin Inc.

Peter Taylor. "First Heat" from *The Collected Stories of Peter Taylor*. Copyright © 1968 by Peter Taylor. Reprinted by permission of Farrar, Straus and Giroux, Inc.

James Thurber. "The Secret Life of Walter Mitty." Copyright © 1942 by James Thurber. Copyright © 1970 Helen W. Thurber and Rosemary T. Sauers. From *My World — and Welcome to It*, published by Harcourt Brace Jovanovich, Inc.

Leo Tolstoy. "The Death of Ivan Ilych" from *The Death of Ivan Ilych and Other Stories* by Leo Tolstoy, translated by Louise and Aylmer Maude (1935). "The Three Hermits" from *Twenty-Three Tales* by Leo Tolstoy, translated by Louise and Aylmer Maude (1906). Reprinted by permission of Oxford University Press, Oxford.

John Updike. "Flight" copyright © 1962 by John Updike. "Son" copyright © 1973 by John Updike. Reprinted from *Problems and Other Stories*, by John Updike. Reprinted from *Pigeon Feathers and Other Stories*, by John Updike. Both reprinted by permission of Alfred A. Knopf, Inc. "On Writing about Adolescence in 'Flight' " from *Writers at Work: The Paris Review Interviews*, Fourth Series, edited by George Plimpton. Copyright © 1974, 1976 by The Paris Review, Inc. Reprinted by permission of Viking Penguin, Inc. "John Updike on Kafka" (editor's title) from "Reflections," *The New Yorker*, May 9, 1983. Reprinted by permission; copyright © 1983 by John Updike. Originally appeared in *The New Yorker*.

Alice Walker. "Roselily." Copyright © 1972 by Alice Walker. Reprinted from her volume *In Love & Trouble* by permission of Harcourt Brace Jovanovich, Inc.

Eudora Welty. "Lily Daw and the Three Ladies" copyright 1937 by University of Nebraska; renewed 1965 by Eudora Welty. "A Worn Path" copyright 1941, 1969 by Eudora Welty. Both stories from *A Curtain of Green and Other Stories* by Eudora Welty reprinted by permission of Harcourt Brace Jovanovich, Inc. "Is Phoenix Jackson's Grandson Really Dead?" copyright © 1974 by Eudora Welty. Reprinted from *The Eye of the Story: Selected Essays and Reviews*, by Eudora Welty, by permission of Random House, Inc.

Edith Wharton. "Roman Fever" from *Roman Fever and Other Stories*. Copyright 1934 Liberty Magazine; copyright renewed © 1962 William R. Tyler. Excerpt here entitled "Every Subject Must Contain Within Itself Its Own Dimensions" from *The Writing of Fiction* by Edith Wharton. Copyright 1925 Charles Scribner's Sons; copyright renewed 1953 Frederick R. King. Both reprinted with the permission of Charles Scribner's Sons.

William Carlos Williams. "A Night In June" from William Carlos Williams, *The Doctor Stories*. Copyright 1938 by William Carlos Williams. "A Beginning on the Short Story (Notes)" from William Carlos Williams, *Selected Essays*. Copyright 1949 by William Carlos Williams. Both reprinted by permission of New Directions Publishing Corporation.

Virginia Woolf. "Moments of Being" from *A Haunted House and Other Stories* by Virginia Woolf, copyright 1944, 1972 by Harcourt Brace Jovanovich, Inc. Reprinted by permission of Harcourt Brace Jovanovich, Inc., the Virginia Woolf estate, and the Hogarth Press.

Richard Wright. "The Man Who Was Almost a Man." Copyright © 1961 by Richard Wright from *Eight Men* by Richard Wright © 1940 by T. Y. Crowell Co. Reprinted by permission of John Hawkins & Associates, Inc.

5/96

ML

ALPHABETICAL LISTING OF WRITERS